FROM HERE
TO ETERNITY

"The Sphinx must solve her own riddle. If the whole of history is in one man, it is all to be explained from individual experience."

—Emerson, Essays: First Series, *History*

FROM HERE TO ETERNITY

by JAMES JONES

INTERNATIONAL COLLECTORS LIBRARY

GARDEN CITY, NEW YORK

TO THE
UNITED STATES ARMY

"I have eaten your bread and salt.
I have drunk your water and wine.
The deaths ye died I have watched beside,
And the lives ye led were mine."

. . . . RUDYARD KIPLING

Gentlemen-rankers out on a spree,
Damned from here to Eternity,
God ha' mercy on such as we,
　　Ba! Yah! Bah!

—From *Gentlemen-Rankers, in Barrack-room Ballads,*
　　　　by RUDYARD KIPLING

Contents

SPECIAL NOTE

This book is a work of fiction. The characters are imaginary, and any resemblance to actual persons is accidental. However, certain of the Stockade scenes did happen. They did not happen at the Schofield Barracks Post Stockade but at a post within the United States at which the author served, and they are true scenes of which the author had first-hand knowledge and personal experience.

Robinson, Illinois
February 27, 1950

Book One

THE TRANSFER

Chapter 1

When he finished packing, he walked out on to the third-floor porch of the barracks brushing the dust from his hands, a very neat and deceptively slim young man in the summer khakis that were still early morning fresh.

He leaned his elbows on the porch ledge and stood looking down through the screens at the familiar scene of the barracks square laid out below with the tiers of porches dark in the faces of the three-story concrete barracks fronting on the square. He was feeling a half-sheepish affection for this vantage point that he was leaving.

Below him under the blows of the February Hawaiian sun the quadrangle gasped defenselessly, like an exhausted fighter. Through the heat haze and the thin mid-morning film of the parched red dust came up a muted orchestra of sounds: the clankings of steel-wheeled carts bouncing over brick, the slappings of oiled leather slingstraps, the shuffling beat of scorched shoesoles, the hoarse expletives of irritated noncoms.

Somewhere along the line, he thought, these things have become your heritage. You are multiplied by each sound that you hear. And you cannot deny them, without denying with them the purpose of your own existence. Yet now, he told himself, you are denying them, by renouncing the place that they have given you.

In the earthen square in the center of the quad a machine gun company went listlessly through the motions of its Loading Drill.

Behind him in the high-ceiling squadroom was the muffled curtain of sound that comes from men just waking and beginning to move around, testing cautiously the flooring of this world they had last night forsaken. He listened to it, hearing also the footsteps coming up behind him, but thinking of how good a thing it had been to sleep late every morning as a member of this Bugle Corps and wake up to the sounds of the line companies already outside at drill.

"You didnt pack my garrison shoes?" he asked the footsteps. "I meant to tell you. They scuff so easy."

"They're on the bed, both pair," the voice behind him said. "With the clean uniforms from your wall locker you didnt want to get mussed up. I pack your diddy box and extra hangers and your field shoes in the extra barricks bag."

"Then I guess thats everything," the young man said. He stood up then, sighing, not a sigh of emotion but the sigh that is the relaxing of a tension. "Lets eat," he said. "I got an hour yet before I have to report to G Compny."

"I still think you're makin a bad mistake," the man behind him said.

"Yeah I know; you told me. Every day for two weeks now. You just dont understand it, Red."

"Maybe not," the other said. "I aint no tempermental genius. But I understand somethin else. I'm a good bugler and I know it. But I cant touch you on a bugle. You're the best bugler in this Regiment, bar none. Probly the best in Schofield Barricks."

The young man thoughtfully agreed. "Thats true."

"Well. Then why you want to quit and transfer?"

"I dont want to, Red."

"But you are."

"Oh no I'm not. You forget. I'm being transferred. Theres a difference."

"Now listen," Red said hotly.

"You listen, Red. Lets go over to Choy's and get some breakfast. Before this crowd gets over there and eats up all his stock." He jerked his head back at the awakening squadroom.

"You're actin like a kid," Red said. "You're not bein transferred, any more than I am. If you hadnt of gone and shot your mouth off to Houston none of this would ever happened."

"Thats right."

"Maybe Houston did make his young punk First Bugler over you. So what? Its only a formality. You still got your rating. All the brunser gets out of it is to play the Taps for funerals and sound Retreat for the shorttimer parades."

"Thats all."

"It aint as if Houston had had you busted, and give the kid your rating. Then I wouldnt blame you. But you still got your rating."

"No I aint. Not since Houston asked the Old Man to have me transferred."

"If you'd go see the Old Man like I tell you and say one word only, you'd have it back. Chief Bugler Houston or no Chief Bugler Houston."

"Thats right. And Houston's punk would still be First Bugler. Besides, the papers've gone through already. Signed; sealed; and delivered."

"Aw hell," Red said disgustedly. "Signed papers you can stick up you know where, for all they mean. You're on the inside, Prew, or at least you could be."

"Do you want to eat with me?" the young man said, "or dont you?"

"I'm broke," Red said.

"Did I ask you to pay? This is on me. I'm the one thats transferrin."

"You better save your money. They can feed us in the kitchen."

"I dont feel like eating that crap, not this morning."

"They had fried eggs this morning," Red corrected. "We can still get them hot. You'll need your money where you're goin."

"All right, for Chrisake," the young man admitted wearily. "Then this is just for the hell of it. Because I want to spend it. Because I'm leavin and I want to spend it. Now do you want to go? or dont you?"

"I'll go," Red said disgustedly.

They walked down the flights of steps and out the walk in front of A Company, where the Bugle Corps was quartered, crossed the street and walked along Headquarters building to the sallyport. The sun heat hit them, bearing down, as they left the porch and left them just as sharply as they stepped inside the tunnel through Hq building that was called the sallyport now, in honor of the old days of the forts. It was painted emphatically with the Regimental colors and housed the biggest of the Regiment's athletic trophies in their lacquered case.

"Its a bad thing," Red said tentatively. "You're gettin yourself a reputation as a bolshevik. You're settin yourself up for all kinds of trouble, Prew." Prew did not answer.

The restaurant was empty. Young Choy and his father, Old Choy, were chattering behind the counter. The white beard and black skull cap disappeared at once back into the kitchen and Young Choy, Young Sam Choy, waited on them.

"Herro, Prew," Young Choy said. "Me hear you move 'closs stleet some time soon I think so maybe, eh?"

"Thats right," Prew said. "Today."

"Today!" Young Choy grinned. "You no snowem? Tlansfe' today?"

"Thats her," he said grudgingly. "Today."

Young Choy, grinning, shook his head with sorrow. He looked at Red. "Clazy dogface. Do stlaight duty, 'stead of Bugle Corpse."

"Listen," Prew said. "How about bringin our goddam food?"

"Aw light," Young Choy grinned. "Bling light now."

5

He went behind the counter to the swinging kitchen door and Prew watched him. "Goddam gook," he said.

"Young Choy's all right," Red said.

"Sure. So's Old Choy all right."

"He only wants to help."

"Sure. Like everybody else."

Red shrugged, sheepishly, and they sat silent in the dim comparative coolness, listening to the laziness of the electric fan high up on one wall, until Young Choy brought out the eggs and ham and coffee. Through the sallyport screen door a weak breeze carried the sleepily regular belltones of the monotonously jerked bolt handles, Dog Company's Loading Drill, a ghostly prophecy that haunted Prew's enjoyment of that sense of loafing while the morning's work moves on around you.

"You one number one boy," Young Choy said, returning, grinning, as he shook his head in sorrow. "You le-enlistment matelial."

Prew laughed. "You said it, Sam. I'm a Thirty—Year—Man."

Red was cutting up an egg. "Whats your wahine goin to say? when she finds out you took a bust to transfer?"

Prew shook his head and began to chew.

"Everything's against you," Red said, reasonably. "Even your wahine is against you."

"I wish she was against me, right up against me, right now," Prew grinned.

Red would not laugh. "Private pussies dont grow on no trees," he said. "Whores are all right; for the first year; for kids. But a good shack-job is hard to find. Too hard to take a chance on losin. You wont be able to make that trip to Haleiwa every night when you're pullin straight duty in a rifle compny."

Prew stared down at his round ham bone before he picked it up and sucked the marrow out. "I reckon she'll have to make up her own mind, Red. Like every man has got to do, in the end. You know this thing's been comin for a long, long time. It aint just because Houston made his angelina First Bugler over me."

Red studied him; Chief Bugler Houston's tastes in young men were common knowledge and Red wondered if he could have made a pass at Prew. But it could not be that; Prewitt would have half-killed him, Chief Warrant Officer or no.

"Thats good," Red said bitterly, "made up her own mind. Where is her mind? In her head, or down between her legs?"

"Watch your goddam mouth. Since when is my private life your business anyway? For your information, its between her legs and thats the way I like it, see?" You liar, he thought.

"Okay," Red said. "Dont blow your top. Whats it to me if you transfer? Its nothing in my young life." He took a piece of bread and washed his hands of all of it by wiping the yellow from his plate and swilling it down with coffee.

Prew lit a tailormade and turned to watch a group of company clerks who had just come in, sitting over coffee in the far corner when they were supposed to be upstairs in Personnel working. They all looked alike, tall thin boys with the fragile faces that gravitated naturally toward the mental superiority of paper work. He caught the words "Van Gogh" and "Gauguin." One tall boy talked a little while and the others waiting to get in their say, then in a pause for breath another tall boy took over and the first frowned and the others waiting impatiently again. Prew grinned.

It was queer, he thought, how a man was always being forced to decide these things. You decided one thing right, with much effort, and then you thought you'd coast a while. But tomorrow you had to decide another thing. And as long as you decided the way you knew was right you had to go right on deciding. Every day a Millennium, he thought. And on the other hand was Red, and those kids over there, who because they decided wrong just once were free from any more deciding. Red placed his bet on Comfort out of Security by Conformity. As usual, Comfort won. Red could retire and enjoy his winnings. Red would not quit a soft deal like the Bugle Corps because his pride was hurt. Sometimes he got confused and could not quite remember what the reason was, the necessity that had been at the beginning of this endless chain of new decidings.

Red was trying logic on him. "You got a Pfc and a Fourth Class Specialist. You practice two hours a day and the rest of your time's your own. You got a good life.

"Every Regiment's got a Drum and Bugle Corps. Thats S. O. P. Its just like a craft on the Outside. We get the gravy because we got special ability."

"The crafts on the Outside aint been gettin gravy. They been lucky if they had jobs at all."

"That aint the point," Red said disgustedly. "Thats the Depression— why you think I'm in the goddam army?"

"I dont know. Why are you?"

"Because." Red paused triumphantly. "Same reason as you: Because I could live better on the Inside than I could on the Outside. I wasnt ready to starve yet."

"Thats logical," Prew grinned.

"Goddam right. I'm a logical guy. Its ony common sense. Why you think I'm in this Bugle Corps?"

"Because its logical," Prew said. "Only, that aint the reason I'm in the army. And it aint the reason I'm in, *was* in, this Bugle Corps."

"I know," Red said disgustedly. "Now he's going to start that crap about the thirty year men."

"All right," Prew said. "But what else would I be? Where else would I go? Me! A man has got to have some place."

"Okay," Red said. "But if you're a thirty year man, and you love to bugle so, why are you quitting? That aint like no thirty year man."

"All right," Prew said. "Lets look at you: Since the Depression's gettin over, since they started makin stuff to send to England for this war, since they started this peacetime draft—you're on the Inside behind your common sense, like a man behind the bars. Your old job's waitin for you, and you cant even buy out now since the peacetime draft came in."

"I'm markin time," Red explained to him. "I dint starve while Prosperity was behind that stack of howitzers, and before *we* get in this goddam war my hitch will be up, and I'll be back home with a good safe job makin periscopes for tanks, while you thirty year men are gettin your ass shot off."

As Prew listened the mobile face before him melted to a battle-blackened skull as though a flamethrower had passed over it, kissed it lightly, and moved on. The skull talked on to him about its health. And he remembered now the reason for this urgency of deciding right. It was like with a virgin, one wrong decision was enough to do it; after one you were not ever the same again. A man who ate too much got fat, and the only way to keep from getting fat was not to eat too much. There was no short cut in elastic trusses for ex-athletes, or in the patented rowing machines, or in synthetic diet; not if you ate too much. When you cut with life you had to use the house deck, not your own.

The reason was, he wanted to be a bugler. Red could play a bugle well because Red was not a bugler. It was really very simple, so simple that he was surprised he had not seen it standing there before. He had to leave the Bugle Corps because he was a bugler. Red did not have to leave it. But he had to leave, because he wanted most of all to stay.

Prew stood up, looking at his watch. "Its nine-fifteen," he said. "I got to be at G Company at nine-thirty for my interview." He grinned as he pulled the last word with his mouth, twisting it the way a badly silvered mirror subtly changes faces.

"Sit down a minute more," Red said. "I wasnt going to mention this, unless I had to."

Prew looked down at him and then sat down, knowing what it was that he would say. "Make it quick," he said. "I got to go."

"You know who the Compny Commander of G Compny is, dont you, Prew?"

"Yeah," Prew said. "I know."

Red could not let it ride. "Captain Dana E. Holmes," he said. " 'Dynamite' Holmes. The Regimental boxing coach."

"Okay," Prew said.

"I know all about why you transferred into this outfit last year," Red said. "I know all about Dixie Wells. You never told me, Prew, but I know it. Everybody knows it."

"All right," Prew said. "I dont care who knows it. I dint expect it could be hid," he said.

"You had to leave the 27th," Red told him. "When you quit the boxing squad and refused to fight any more, you had to transfer out. Because they wouldnt let you alone, wouldnt let you just quit in peace. They followed you around and put the pressure on. Until you had to transfer out."

"I did what I wanted to do," Prew said.

"Did you?" Red said. "Dont you see?" he said. "They'll always follow you around. You cant go your own way in peace, not in our time. Unless you're willing to play ball.

"Maybe back in the old days, back in the time of the pioneers, a man could do what he wanted to do, in peace. But he had the woods then, he could go off in the woods and live alone. He could live well off the woods. And if they followed him there for this or that, he could just move on. There was always more woods on up ahead. But a man cant do that now. He's got to play ball with them. He has to divide it all by two.

"I never mentioned it to you," Red sued. "I saw you fight in the Bowl last year. Me and several thousand other guys. Holmes saw you, too. I've been sweatin him out to put the pressure on you, any time."

"So have I," Prew said. "I just guess he never found out I was here."

"He wont miss it on your Form 20 when you're in his compny. He'll *want* you for his boxing squad."

"Theres nothin in the ARs says a man has got to jockstrap when he doesnt want to."

"Come on," Red taunted. "You think the ARs'll bother him? when the Great White Father wants to keep that championship? You think he'll let a fighter who's got the rep you have just hibernate? in his own company? without fightin for the Regment? just because you decided once you wouldnt fight no more? Even a genius like you cant be that simple."

"I dont know," Prew said. "Chief Choate's in his compny. Chief Choate use to be the heavyweight champ of Panama."

"Yes," Red said. "But Chief Choate's the Great White Father's fairhaired boy because he's the best first baseman in the Hawaiian Department. Holmes cant pressure him. But even so, Chief Choate's been in G Compny four years now, and he's still a corporal."

"Well," Prew said. "If the Chief would transfer out, he could make Staff in any other compny. I guess if it gets too rough I can always transfer out myself."

"Yeah?" Red said. "You think so? You know who the top kicker of George Co is?"

"Sure," Prew said. "I know. Warden."

"Thats right, man," Red said. "Milton Anthony Warden. Who use to be our Staff in A Compny. The meanest son of a bitch in Schofield Barricks. And who hates you worse than poison."

"Thats funny," Prew said slowly. "I never felt that Warden hated me. I dont hate him."

Red smiled bitterly. "After all the run-ins you've had with him? Even you cant be that green."

"It wasnt him," Prew said. "It was just that that was what his job was."

"A man is his job," Red said. "And now he's not a Staff; he's got two rockers and a diamond now. Listen, Prew. Everything's against you. You're movin into a game where every card is in the other hand."

Prew nodded. "I know that," he said.

"Go up and see the Old Man," Red pleaded. "Theres still time this morning. I wouldnt steer you wrong. I've had to play politics all my life for what I wanted. I can sense the way a thing is going. All you got to do is see The Man, and he will tear them papers up."

Prew stood up then, and standing, looking down into the anxious face of him who was his friend, he could feel the energy of sincerity that was pouring from Red's eyes, pouring over him with a firehose concentration whose name was sincerity. And somehow it was a thing that startled him, that it should be there, and that he could see it, pleading with him.

"I cant do it, Red," he said.

As if for the first time he was really giving up, was actually believing it, Red slumped back in his chair, the concentrated pouring dispersed and dissipated against this wall he did not understand.

"I hate to see you go," he said.

"I just cant help it, Red," Prew said.

"Okay," Red said. "Have it your way, kid. Its your funeral."

"Thats whats the matter," Prewitt said.

Red ran his tongue over his teeth slowly, probing. "What do you aim to do about the git-tar, Prew?"

"You keep it. Its half yours anyway. I wont have no use for it," Prew said.

The other coughed. "I ought at least to pay you for your half. Ony I'm broke right now," he added, hastily.

Prewitt grinned; this was the Red he knew again. "I'm giving you my half, Red. No strings attached. Whats a matter? Dont you want it?"

"Sure. But?"

"Then keep it. If your conscience hurts you, you can say its payment for helping me to pack."

"I hate to do that," Red said.

"Figure it this way," Prew said. "I'll come back over now and then. I'm not going Stateside. I'll come over and use it, every now and then."

"No, you wont," Red said. "We both know you wont. When a guy moves, he moves it all. The distance doesnt matter."

Before this sudden honesty Prew had to look away. Red was right and Prew knew it, and Red knew he knew it. Transferring in the army was comparable to a civilian moving from one city to another. His friends either moved with him or they lost him. Even when he moved from, perhaps, a city that he loved to a city where he was the stranger. The chances for adventure in such moves were vastly overrated by the movies, and both knew it. It was not adventure Prewitt wanted; Red knew that he had no more illusions of adventure.

"The best bugler in the Regiment," Red said helplessly. "He just dont quit and go back to straight duty. They just dont do it."

"The git-tar's yours," Prew said. "I'll come back and play it now and then though," he lied. He turned away quickly so he would not have to meet Red's eyes. "I got to go."

Red watched him toward the door and humanely did not contradict him. Prew never had been able to lie convincingly.

"Luck to you," Red called after him. He watched until the screendoor slammed. Then he took his coffeecup over to where Young Choy was sweating industriously at the steamy nickel urn with its spouts and glass tube gauges, wishing it was five o'clock and he could have a beer instead.

Outside in the sallyport Prew donned his campaign hat, adjusting it meticulously, low on the forehead, high in back, cocked just a little bit. Around the band was the robin's-egg-blue cord and acorns of the Infantry. Stiff as a board with sugar and the hatter's iron it rode his head, a fresh blocked crown, the proud badge of his profession.

For a moment he stood looking at the lacquered trophycase, feeling the scant breeze the shadowed sallyport collected like a funnel collects rain. Among the other cups and statues in it, holding the place of honor, was the Hawaiian Division traveling trophy that Holmes's boys had won last year, two golden fighters in a roped ring of gold.

He shrugged, and then he turned and paused, seeing the scene that never failed to touch him, a painting done in solid single tones, the timbre diminishing with the deepening perspective, framed by the entryway of the sallyport. The pale red-dusted green of the earthen square and on it the blue fatigues of Dog Company, and the olive halos. Behind them the screaming whiteness of the Second Battalion barracks; and behind the barracks, rising slowly, the red-and-green striping that was the mathematical fields of pineapple, immaculate as a well-kept tomato patch, a few bent figures indistinct in the distance toiling over them. And then the foothills, rolling higher, in that juicy green that has never starved for water. And then, fulfilling all the rising promise, the black peaks of the Waianae Range, biting a sky that echoed the fatigues, and cut only by the deep V of Kolekole Pass that was like a whore's evening dress, promising things on the other side. More like a whore's evening dress because he had been to Waianae and looked with disappointment on the other side.

Along the flanks of the hills his eye picked out the thin tracery of a line that faded out to the South. That was the Honouliuli Trail, the officers went riding there, with their women. You could always find innumerable condoms along the trail, and trees where the idle horses had chewed off bark. Your eyes always hunted for them, hiking, with a vicarious breathlessness that, if it had not been visible in each man's face, would have shamed you.

Did a pineapple enjoy its life? or did it maybe get sick of being trimmed like seven thousand other pineapples? fed the same fertilizer as seven thousand other pineapples? standing till death did them part in the same rank and file like seven thousand other pineapples? You never knew. But you never saw a pineapple turn itself into a grapefruit, did you?

He stepped down on the sidewalk treading catlike on the balls of his feet the way a fighter treads, hat tilted, clean, immaculate, decisive, the picture of a soldier.

Chapter 2

Robert E. Lee Prewitt had learned to play a guitar long before he ever learned to bugle or to box. He learned it as a boy, and with it he learned a lot of blues songs and laments. In the Kentucky Mountains along the West Virginia Line life led him swiftly to that type of music. And this was long before he ever seriously considered becoming a member of The Profession.

In the Kentucky Mountains along the West Virginia Line guitar playing is not considered the accomplishment it is most places. Every wellbred boy learns to chord a guitar when he is still small enough to hold it like a string bass. The boy Prewitt loved the songs because they gave him something, an understanding, a first hint that pain might not be pointless if you could only turn it into something. The songs stayed with him, but the guitar playing did not give him anything. It left him cold. He had no call for it at all.

He had no call for boxing either. But he was very fast and had an incredible punch, developed by necessity on the bum, before he entered The Profession. People always find those things out. They tend to become manifest. Especially in The Profession where sports are the nourishment of life and boxing is the most manly sport. Beer, in The Profession, is the wine of life.

To tell the truth, he had no call for The Profession. At least not then. As a dissatisfied son of a Harlan County miner he just naturally gravitated toward it, the only profession open to him.

He really had no call for anything until the first time he handled a bugle.

It started as a joke on a battalion beer convention and he only held it and blew a couple of bleats, but he knew at once that this was something different. It was somehow something sacred, the way you sit out at night and watch the stars and your eye consciously spans that distance and you wonder if you're sitting on an electron that revolves around a proton in a series of infinite universes, and you suddenly see how strange a tree would look to one who had never lived upon the earth.

He had wild visions, for a moment, of having once played a herald's trumpet for the coronations and of having called the legions to bed down around the smoking campfires in the long blue evenings of old Palestine. It was then he remembered that hint about pointlessness that the blues songs and laments had given him; he knew then that if he could play a bugle the way he thought a bugle he would have found his justification. He even realized, all at once, holding the bugle, the reason why he had ever got into The Profession at all, a problem that had stumped him up till then. That was actually how much it meant to him. He recognized he had a call.

He had heard a lot about The Profession as a boy. He would sit on the railless porch with the men when the long tired, dirty-faced evening rolled down the narrow valley, thankfully blotting out the streets of shacks, and listen to them talk. His Uncle John Turner, tall, rawboned and spare, had run away as a boy and joined The Profession, to find Adventure. He had been a corporal in the Philippine Insurrection.

The boy Prewitt's father and the others had never been beyond the hills, and in the boy's mind, already even then bludgeoning instinctively against the propaganda of the walls of slag as the fœtus kicks frantically against the propaganda of the womb, this fact of The Profession gave to Uncle John Turner a distinction no one else could claim.

The tall man would squat on his hams in the little yard—the coal dirt was too thick on all the ground to sit—and in an abortive effort to dispel the taste of what the Encyclopedias call "Black Gold" he would tell them stories that proved conclusively there was a world beyond the slag heaps and these trees whose leaves were always coated black.

Uncle John would tell about the Moro juramentados, how their native Moslem datu would call the single volunteer up before the tribe and anoint him and consecrate him to the heaven he was getting ready to attend and then, practically, bind his balls and pecker with wet rawhide before he ran amok, so that the pain of the contraction of the drying leather would keep him going. That was why, said Uncle John, the Army first adopted the .45. Because six slugs from a .38 Special would not knock a juramentado down. And, in his condition, obviously, you had to knock him down to stop him. The .45 was guaranteed to knock any man off his feet, if it only hit the tip of his little finger, or your money back. And the Army, said Uncle John, had been using it effectively ever since.

The boy Prewitt doubted that about the little finger, but he liked the story. It impressed him with a sense of seeing history made, as did the stories of young Hugh Drum and young John Pershing and the expedition on Mindanao and the trek around the edge of Lake Lanao. They proved the Moros were good men, worthy opponents of his Uncle John. Sometimes when his Uncle John had swilled enough white lightning he would sing the song about the "monkeys have no tails in Zamboanga" that had been his Regimental song. And he would alternate the Philippines with Mexico and stories of an older, much less informal Blackjack and of young Sandy Patch, not yet too great a man to be informal.

But Uncle John always made it plain, especially to the boy, the reason why he had come home in 1916 and stayed in Harlan mining coal all during the World War. Uncle John wanted to be a farmer, and it was probably this that kept him from acquiring that Great, American, Retrospective Spirit of Romance.

It would be nice to think of a grubby miner's son with a dirt-rimmed mouth possessed of so burning a dream to see the world and help make history, via The Profession, that he refused to have it thwarted. But Uncle John Turner was not the kind of man who'd let his nephew dream of a life of adventure, via The Profession, and have it on his conscience.

It happened quite, quite differently.

When the boy Prewitt was in the seventh grade his mother died of the consumption. There was a big strike on that winter and she died in the middle of it. If she had had her choice, she could have picked a better time. Her husband, who was a striker, was in the county jail with two stab wounds in his chest and a fractured skull. And her brother, Uncle John, was dead, having been shot by several deputies. Years later there was a lament written and sung about that day. They said blood actually ran like rainwater in the gutters of Harlan that day. They gave Uncle John Turner the top billing, a thing he doubtless would have decried with vigor.

The boy Prewitt saw that battle, at least as near as any man can ever come to seeing any battle. The only thing he saw and could remember was his Uncle John. He and two other boys stood in a yard to watch until one of the other boys got hit with a stray bullet, then they ran home and did not watch the rest.

Uncle John had had his .45 and he shot three deputies, two of them as he was going down. He only got to fire three times. The boy was interested in proving the guarantee of the .45, but since all the deputies were hit in the head they would have gone down anyway. Uncle John did not hit any of them on the tip of the little finger.

So when his mother died there was nobody to stop him except his father in the jail, and since his father had beaten him again just two days before the battle he did not figure his father counted either. Having made up his mind, he took the two dollars that was in the grocery jar, telling himself his mother would not need it and it would be good enough for his father and would help to put them square, and he left. The neighbors took up a collection for his mother's funeral but he did not want to see it.

The disintegration of a family, where the family still has meaning, emotes tragedy in every one. Its consolatory picture is of the surviving member freed to follow his lifelong ambition, a sort of Dick Whittington with a bandanna tied to a stick but no cat. But it was not this with him either, any more than it was the burning dream to see the world and help make history. He had never heard of a Lord Mayor and he had no ambition. The Profession, and the bugle, came much later.

As she was dying his mother made him promise her one thing. "Promise me one thing, Robert," she wheezed at him. "From your father you got pride and endurance and I knowed that you would need it. But one of you would have kilt the other if it hatnt of been for me. And now, I wont be standin atween you no more."

"I'll promise anything you want, ma, whatever you say for me to promise, whatever it is you say," the boy, watching her die in front of him, looking at her above his haze of disbelief for signs of immortality, said woodenly.

"A deathbed promise is the most sacred one there is," she hawked at him from the lungs that were almost, but not quite, filled up yet, "and

I want you to make me this promise on my deathbed: Promise me you wont never hurt nobody unless its absolute a must, unless you jist have to do it."

"I promise you," he vowed to her, still waiting for the angels to appear. "Are you afraid?" he said.

"Give me your hand on it, boy. It is a deathbed promise, and you'll never break it."

"Yes maam," he said, giving her his hand, drawing it back quickly, afraid to touch the death he saw in her, unable to find anything beautiful or edifying or spiritually uplifting in this return to God. He watched a while longer for signs of immortality. No angels came, however, there was no earthquake, no cataclysm, and it was not until he had thought over often this first death that he had had a part in that he discovered the single uplifting thing about it, that being the fact that in this last great period of fear her thought had been upon his future, rather than her own. He wondered often after that about his own death, how it would come, how it would feel, what it would be like to know that this breath, now, was the last one. It was hard to accept that he, who was the hub of this known universe, would cease to exist, but it was an inevitability and he did not shun it. He only hoped that he would meet it with the same magnificent indifference with which she who had been his mother met it. Because it was there, he felt, that the immortality he had not seen was hidden.

She was a woman of an older time set down in a later world and walled off from knowing it by mountains. If she had known the effect of the promise she exacted from her son, upon his life, she would not have asked it of him. Such promises belong in an older, simpler, less complex and more naïve, forgotten time.

Three days after he was seventeen he got accepted for enlistment. Having been used to certain elemental comforts back in Harlan, he had already been turned down a number of times all over the country because he was too young. Then he would go back on the bum awhile and try some other city. He was on the East Coast at the time he was accepted and they sent him to Fort Myer. That was in 1936. There were lots of other men enlisting then.

It was at Myer he learned to box, as distinguished from fight. He was really very fast, even for a bantamweight, and with that punch, all out of proportion to his size, he found he might have a future in The Profession. It got him a Pfc in the first year of his hitch, a thing that, in 1936, when getting any rating at all in your first hitch was considered a sin that made for laxity of character by every soldier who had begun his second three-year term, bespoke his talent.

It was also at Myer where he first handled the bugle. It made a change in him right away and he dropped out of the boxing squad to get himself apprenticed to the Bugle Corps. When he truly found a thing he never wasted time, and since he was still a long ways from being a Class I fighter then the coach did not think it worth his while to hold him. The whole squad watched him go without any sense of loss, figuring that he did not have the staying power, that the going was too rough, that he would never be a champion like Lew Jenkins from Fort Bliss, as they would be, and marked him off the list.

He was too busy then to care much what they thought. With the call driving him he worked hard for a year and a half and earned himself another, totally different reputation. At the end of that year and a half he had earned himself a rating of First and Third and he was good, good enough to play the Armistice Day Taps at Arlington, the Mecca of all Army buglers. He really had a call.

Arlington was the high point and it was a great experience. He had finally found his place and he was satisfied to settle into it. His enlistment was almost up by then and he planned to re-enlist at Myer. He planned to stay there in that Bugle Corps for his full thirty years. He could see ahead down the line, obviously, and quite clearly, how smoothly it would go and the fullness it would be. That was before the other people began to come into it.

Up until then it had only been himself. Up to then it had been a private wrestle between him and himself. Nobody else much entered into it. After the people came into it he was, of course, a different man. Everything changed then and he was no longer the virgin, with the virgin's right to insist upon platonic love. Life, in time, takes every maidenhead, even if it has to dry it up; it does not matter how the owner wants to keep it. Up to then he had been the young idealist. But he could not stay there. Not after the other people entered into it.

At Myer all the boys hung out in Washington on their passes and he hung out there too. That was where he met the society girl. He picked her up at a bar, or she picked him up. It was his first introduction into the haute monde, outside of the movies, and she was good looking and definitely high class, was going to college there, to be a journalist. It was not a great love or anything like that; half of it, for him, for both of them, was that the miner's son was dining at the Ritz, just like the movies said. She was a nice kid but very bitter and they had a satisfying affair. They had no poor little rich girl trouble because he did not mind spending her money and they did not worry and stew about an unladylike marriage. They had good fun for six months, up until she gave him the clap.

When he got out of the GU Clinic his job was gone and his rating with it. The army did not have sulfa then, it could not make up its mind to adopt the doubtful stuff until the war, and it was a long and painful process, getting cured, with lots of long-handled barbs and cutters. One boy he met there was on his fourth trip through the Clinic.

Unofficially, nobody really minded the clap. It was a joke to those who had never had it and to those who had been over it for a little while. No worse than a bad cold, they said. Apparently the only time it was not a joke was when you had it. And instead of hurting your unofficial reputation it boosted you a notch, it was like getting a wound stripe. They said that in Nicaragua they used to give out Purple Hearts.

But officially it hurt your Service Record, and it automatically lost you your rating. On your papers it put a stigma on you. When he put in to get back in the Bugle Corps, he found that while he was away they had suddenly gone overstrength. He went back on straight duty for the rest of his enlistment.

Already the other people were beginning to come into it. It seemed that any man could drive a car, but the only man who never had a wreck was the guy who drove not only for himself but for the other driver too.

When his time was up they tried to re-enlist him for the same outfit, there at Myer. He wanted that hundred and fifty dollar bonus, but he wanted to get as far away from there as he could go. That was why he picked Hawaii.

He went up once, to see his society girl before he left. He had heard guys say they would kill any woman who gave them the clap; or they would go out and give it to every woman they could lay; or they would beat her up until she wished she had of died. But having the clap did not make him bitter against all women or anything like that. It was a chance you took with every woman, white, black or yellow. What disillusioned him, what he did not understand, was that this of the clap should have cost him his bugle when he still could play it just as well as ever, and also that a society girl had given it to him. And what made him mad was that she did not tell him first and leave it up to him to choose, then it would not have been her fault. He found out, that last time he went to see her, after he had convinced her he was not going to beat her up, that she had not known she had it. After she saw he wouldnt hit her, she cried and she was very sorry. It was a society boy she had known since she was a kid. She was disillusioned, too. And she was having a hell of a time getting herself cured, and on the sly, so her parents would not know. And she was truly very sorry.

When he arrived in Schofield Barracks he was still very bitter about the bugle. It was this that made him go back to fighting, here in the Pineapple Army where fighting was even more prolific than it was at Myer. That was his error, but it did not seem so then. The bitterness about the bugle, added to all the other bitternesses, gave him something. Also he had put on more weight and filled out more until he was a welterweight. He won the Company Smoker championship of the 27th and for that he got a corporalcy. Then he went on, when the Division season opened, to make Schofield Class I and become the runner-up in the welterweight division. For that, and because they expected him to win it the next year, he got a sergeantcy. Also, the bitternesses in some subtle way seemed to make him more likeable to every one, although he never did quite figure that one out.

Everything would probably have gone on like that indefinitely, since he had convinced himself that bugling was nothing, had it not been for that deathbed promise to his mother and for Dixie Wells. And actually it happened after the season was over. Perhaps it was his temperament, but he seemed to have a very close working alliance with irony.

Dixie Wells was a middleweight who loved boxing and lived for boxing. He had enlisted because business was not so good for fighters during the Depression, and because he wanted time to mature his style and season it without being overmatched in some ham and egger, and without having to live on the beans a ham and egger has to eat while he is trying to work up to the big time. He planned to come out of the Army and go right into the upper brackets. A lot of people on the Outside had their eye on him and he was already having fights downtown in Honolulu at the Civic Auditorium.

Dixie liked to work with Prewitt because of the other's speed and Prewitt learned a lot from Dixie. They worked together often. Dixie was a heavy middle, but then Prewitt was a heavy welter. They are very professional about those things in the Army; they keep every pound that they can squeeze; they always figure a man for ten pounds more than what he weighs in at when they match him; they dry him out and then after he has weighed in they feed him steak and lots of water.

It was Dixie who asked him to work this time, because he had a fight coming up downtown. Also, it was Dixie who wanted to use the six ounce gloves, and they never wore headgear anyway.

Things like that happen more often than any one suspects. Prew knew that, and there was no reason why he should feel guilty. He had known a wizard lightweight at Myer who also had a future. Until he went into a civilian gym half-tight one night and wanted to put them on. They used new gloves, and the man who tied them on forgot to cut the metal tips off the laces. Gloves often come untied. This was like the old kid game of crack the whip, a wrist flick drove the metal into the wizard lightweight's eye like an arrow into a target. The fluid of his eye ran down over his cheek and he had to buy a glass one, and as a wizard lightweight he was through. Things like that just happen, every now and then.

Prew was set, flat on his feet when he caught Dixie wide with this no more than ordinarily solid cross. Dixie just happened to be standing solid too. Maybe he had heard something. From the way he fell, dead weight, a falling ingot or a sack of meal dropped from the haymow that shudders the barn and bursts its own seams, Prew knew. Dixie lit square on his face and did not roll over. Fighters do not light on their faces any more than judo men. Prew jerked back his hand and stared at it, like a kid who touched the stove. Then he went downstairs to get the Doc.

Dixie Wells was in a coma for a week but he finally came out of it. The only thing was that he was blind. The doctor at the Station Hospital said something about concussion and a fracture, a pressure on or injury to a nerve. Prew went up to see him twice but after the second time he could not go back. The second time they got to talking about fighting and Dixie cried. It was seeing the tears coming out of those eyes that could not see that made him stay away.

Dixie did not hate him, nor was he bitter, he was just unhappy. As soon as he was able, he told Prew that last time, they would ship him back to the States, to an old soldier's home, or to one of Hines's VA hospitals which was even worse.

Prew had seen a lot of those things happen. If you hang around any profession long enough you will learn about the things the brethren never talk about to the public. But just seeing them had been like it is with getting wounded, this man's handless arms have no relation to yourself, it happens to the other guy, but never you.

He felt a great deal like an amnesia case must feel, upon waking in some foreign land where he had never been and hears the language that he cannot understand, having only a vague, dream-haunted picture of how he ever got there. How came you here? he asks himself, among these strange outlandish people? but is afraid to listen to the answer himself gives him back.

My god! he wondered. Are you a misfit? What happened to you does not bother any of these others. Why should you be so different? But fighting had never been his calling, bugling was his calling. For what reason then was he here, posing as a fighter?

It would probably, after Dixie Wells, have been the same whether or not he had been haunted by his promise to his mother. But the old, ingenuous, Baptist-like promise was the clincher. Because the uninitiated boy had taken it, not like a Baptist, but literally.

One way, he thought, the whole thing of ring fighting was hurting somebody else, deliberately, and particularly when it was not necessary. Two men who have nothing against each other get in a ring and try to hurt each other, to provide vicarious fear for people with less guts than themselves. And to cover it up they called it sport and gambled on it.

He had never looked at it that way before, and if there was any single thing he could not endure it was to be a dupe.

Since the boxing season was already over he could have waited until next December before he told them his decision. He could have kept his mouth shut and rested on his hard-earned laurels, until the time came round again to prove his right to them. But he was not honest enough to do a thing like that. He was not honest enough to dupe them, when he himself refused to be their dupe. He had not the makings of that honest man to whom success comes naturally.

At first when he told them why he was quitting they would not believe him. Then, later when they saw that it was true, they decided he had only been in the sport for what he could get out of it and did not love it like they did, and with righteous indignation had him busted. Then, still later, when he did not come around, they really did not understand it. They began to build him up then, they began to heckle him, they called him in and talked to him man to man, told him how good he was, explained what hope we have in you and are you going to let us down, enumerated what he owed the regiment, showed him how he ought to be ashamed. It was then they really began not to let him alone. And it was then he transferred.

He transferred to this other regiment because it had the best Bugle Corps in the Lower Post. He did not have any trouble. As soon as they heard him play they got him transferred quick. They had really, truly, wanted a good bugler there.

Chapter 3

At eight o'clock that same morning, when Prewitt was still packing, First Sergeant Milton Anthony Warden came out from the Orderly Room of G Company. The Orderly Room opened onto a well-waxed corridor that ran from the porch inside the quad to the Dayroom that was on the outside street. Warden stopped in the corridor doorway and leaned against the jamb, smoking, his hands jammed deep in his pockets, watching the Company lining up for drill with rifles and web belts in the dustless early morning. He stood a moment in the sun rays slanting in on him from the east, and feeling the coolness that was already seeping away from what would be a hot day again. The spring rainy season would be breaking soon now, but until it did it would be hot and parched in February, just as it was hot and parched in December, and then when the rainy season broke it would be very damp, and chill in the night, and the saddlesoap would be out and fighting desperately against the mould on all the leather. He had just finished the Sickbook and the Morning Report, and sent them out and now he was smoking a cigaret in laziness, watching the Company go out because he was glad he did not go out, before he went into the Supply Room to work hard again, this time at work that was not his.

He threw the cigaret in the flat iron pot painted red and black, the Regimental colors, and watched the tail end of the Company move out the truck entrance and out of sight, then stepped down onto the slick concrete of the porch and walked along it to the Supply Room's open door.

Milton Anthony Warden was thirty-four years old. In the eight months he had been topkicker of G Company he had wrapped that outfit around his waist like a money belt and buttoned his shirt over it. At intervals he liked to remind himself of this proud fact. He was a veritable demon for work; he liked to remind himself of that, too. He had also pulled this slovenly organization out of the pitfalls of lax administration. In fact, when he thought about it, and he often did, he had never met a man who was as amazingly adept at anything he put his hand to as was Milton Anthony Warden.

"The monk in his cell," he taunted, entering the open one of the double doors. After the brilliant sunlight he had to pause and let his eyes adjust to the windowless Supply Room where two electric bulbs like burning tears dangling from the ends of chains increased the gloom. Ceiling-high cupboards, shelves and stacks of crates closed in heavily on the homemade desk where First-Fourth Leva, wry and bloodless as if the perpetual gloom of his castle had been transfused into his veins, sat, his thin nose greasy in a pool of light from the desk lamp, laboriously typing with two fingers.

"With a suit of sackcloth and a tub of ashes," said Warden, whom a fond mother had named for St. Anthony, "and you could get yourself canonized tomorrow, Niccolo."

"Go to hell," said Leva, not looking up or stopping. "Has that new transfer showed up yet?"

"Saint Niccolo of Wahiawa," Warden plagued him. "Dont you ever get tired of this life? I bet you got leather mould all over your balls."

"Has he showed? or not," Leva said. "I got his papers ready."

"Not yet," Warden leaned his elbows on the counter, "and for my dough I hope he never does."

"Why not?" Leva asked, innocently. "I hear he's a damn good soldier."

"He's a hardhead," Warden said, amiably. "I know him. A goddam hardhead. Have you been over to Wahiawa to Big Sue's lately? Her girls will fix that mould up for you. They got good saddlesoap, home-made."

"How can I?" Leva said. "On what you people pay me? I hear that this Prewitt is quite a fighter," he teased, "that he will be a fine addition to Dynamite's menagerie."

"That he will be another worthless mouth for me to feed," Warden said. "Did you hear that too? Why not? I'm used to it. Its too bad he had to wait till February, till the ending of the boxing season. Now he'll have to wait till next December for his sergeantcy."

"You poor, poor, unhappy man," Leva said, "that everybody takes advantage of." He leaned back and waved his hand at the piles of equipment stacked everywhere and that he had been working on for three days now. "I'm glad I got a nice soft easy well-paid job."

"A goddam hardhead," Warden lamented, grinning, "a worthless Kentuckian, but who will be a corporal in six weeks, but who will still be a worthless goddam hardhead."

"But a good bugler though," Leva said. "I've heard him. A damn good bugler. The best bugler on the Post," he said, grinning.

Warden banged his fist down on the counter. "Then he should of stayed in the Bugle Corps," he shouted, "instead of fouling up my outfit." He flung back the folding countertop, kicked open the plywood door and went inside the counter, threading through the piles of shirts and pants and leggins on the floor.

Leva ducked his head back down to his typewriter and began to poke it, snuffling softly through his long thin nose.

"Have you got this goddam clothing issue stuff closed out yet?" Warden raged at him.

"What the hell you think I am?" Leva asked, still laughing silently.

"A goddam supply clerk, whose job is to get this stuff done instead of gossiping about transfers all the time. You should have had this done two days ago."

"Tell it to Supply Sergeant O'Hayer," Leva said, "I'm only the clerk here."

Warden stopped his raging as suddenly as he had started it and looking at Leva with a speculative shrewdness scratched his chin and grinned. "Has your illustrious mentor, Mister O'Hayer, been in this morning yet?"

"What do you think?" Leva said. He unwound his jerked-leather frame from around the desk and lit a cigaret.

"Well," Warden said. "I would be inclined to say no. Just as a guess."

"Well," Leva said. "You would be entirely right."

Warden grinned at him. "Well, after all, its only eight. You cant expect a man of his station, and with his cares, to get up at eight o'clock with clerks like you."

"Its a joke to you," Leva said, peevishly. "You can laugh about it. Its no joke to me."

"Maybe he was counting the take," Warden grinned, "from his game in the sheds last night. I bet you wish you had a nice easy life like that."

"I wish I had ten percent of the dough he takes in every payday in that shed," Leva said, thinking of the maintenance sheds across the street from the dayroom where every month, when they had moved out the 37 millimeters and the machine gun carts and all the rest of it, most of the money in the Lower Post finally wound up and where, of the four sheds, O'Hayer's always had the biggest take.

"I understood," said Warden, "that he give you almost that much to do his work here for him."

Leva gave him a withering look and Warden chuckled.

"I believe you," Leva said. "Next thing, you'll be askin me for a cut on what he give me, or else have me busted."

"Now thats an idea," Warden grinned. "Thanks. I'd of never thought of that."

"It wont be so goddam funny," Leva said grimly, "some day. Some day when I transfer the hell out and leave you with this supplyroom in your lap with nobody to do the work but O'Hayer who dont know a Form 32 from a 33."

"You'll never transfer out of this Compny," Warden scoffed. "If you was to go outdoors before sundown you'd be blind as a bat. This supplyroom's in your blood. You couldnt leave it if you had to."

"Oh," Leva said. "Is that the way it is? I'm gettin tard of doin the supply sergeant's work while Jim O'Hayer gets the credit and the money because he's Dynamite's number one lightheavy and pays off in Regiment to run that shed. He aint even a good fighter."

"He's a good gambler, though," Warden said indifferently. "Thats what counts."

"He's a good gambler, all right. The mother sucker. I wonder how much, in addition to Regiment, he gives Dynamite every month."

"Why, Niccolo," Warden chortled. "You know such a thing is illegal. It says so in the ARs."

"Fuck the ARs," Leva said, his face congested. "I'm telling you, some day he's gonna make me mad. I could transfer out tomorrow and get a supplyroom of my own. I've been inquiring around some lately. M Company lookin for a supply man, Milt." He stopped suddenly, aware he had let loose a secret he had not intended to divulge, aware that Warden had needled him into it. His face a mixture of start and sullenness he swung back to his desk in silence.

Warden, catching the fleeting look on Leva's face, making a careful mental note of this new thing he had discovered and must find some way to combat if he wanted to keep his supplyroom running, stepped over to the desk and said, "Dont worry, Niccolo. Things wont be this way forever. I got some irons in that fire myself," he hinted broadly. "You ought to have that rating, and you'll get it. You're doin all the work. I aim to see you get it," he said, soothingly.

"But you wont," Leva said grudgingly. "Not while Dynamite is the CC. Not as long as O'Hayer is on his boxing squad and pays his rent to Regiment. You're hooked through the bag and you cant get off."

"You mean you dont trust me?" Warden said, indignantly. "Dint I tell you I got an angle?"

"I aint no ree-croot," Leva said. "I dont trust nobody. I been in this man's army thirteen years."

"How you comin with this stuff?" Warden said, pointing to one of several stacks of forms. "You need some help?"

"Hell, no," Leva said. "I dont need no help." He thumbed a pile of forms four fingers deep. "I hardly get enough work to keep me busy. Thats why my morale is low. You know: like the Personnel boys say: No work for idle hands hurts the morale."

"Gimme half them," Warden said, with mock weariness. "Along with everything else I got to suffer, I got to be supply clerk." He took the forms that Leva handed him and grinned and winked down at the cadaverous Italian. "Two good men like us can get this done today," he said, noting Leva was not swallowing the flattery. "I dont know where the hell I'd be if I didnt have you in this outfit, Niccolo."

He didnt believe that about the angle, either, Warden thought, any more than you did. You cant snow an old bull like him with promises, you have to put it on the personal basis, you have to work on his friendship, on his pride.

"We get this done," he said, "and you'll have a rest for a month or two. You're as bad as the kitchen force, Niccolo. Always threatening to quit because Preem is the mess sergeant. But they never do. A rifle scares them to death." He laid the pile of forms out on the counter, separating them into neat piles he could work from. From the corner he pulled a high stool and sat down at the counter and pulled out his old pen.

"I wouldnt blame them none," Leva said, "if they did quit."

"Well, they wont. I wish to hell they would. And you wont either, but not for the same reason. You couldnt quit me, Niccolo, and leave me in the lurch. You're as big a fool as I am."

"Yeah? You watch me, Milt. You just watch me," but the timbre of his voice had changed; it was no longer serious but taunting.

Warden snorted at him. "Lets work. Or I'll make you re-enlist."

"In a pig's asshole," Leva said, completing the chant.

Oh, Milton, Warden thought, what a son of a bitch you are, what a fine lyin son of a bitch. You'd sell your own mother to Lucky Luciano if it would secure the hatches on this outfit. You'll lie and cajole poor old Niccolo into staying, just to make your supply efficient. You've lied so much now, he told himself, you dont know whats true and what aint. And all because you want to make your company *Superior*. You mean Holmes's company, he thought. "Dynamite" Holmes, boxing coach, horseman, and number one brownnoser with our Great White Father Colonel Delbert. Its his company, not yours. Why dont you let him do it? Why dont you let him sacrifice his soul upon the altar of efficiency? Yes, he thought, why dont you? Why dont you get out of it? When *are* you going to get out of it and save your self-respect? Never, he told himself. Because its been so long now you're afraid to find out if you've still got the self-respect to save. Have you got it? he asked himself. No, Milton, no, I dont think you have. Thats why you dont get out of it. You're hooked through the bag, like Leva said.

He turned to the forms before him and went to work with that wild swift energy that is one hundred percent efficient, that makes no errors, and gets the work done so fast and sure that you are not even there, you are some place else and when you come back you see the work is done but you did not do it; the same energy with which Niccolo Leva behind him was working.

They were still working an hour later when O'Hayer came in. He stood momentarily in the bright doorway, a wide shouldered shadow adjusting his eyes, and an aura of chill seemed to come in with him that killed the warm gush of energy for work that had been in the others.

O'Hayer looked at the paper and equipment scattered around distastefully. "This place looks like hell," he said. "We've got to clean this place up, Leva."

He moved to come in through the counter and Warden had to move all his papers and get up so O'Hayer could pass through. He watched the tall dapper Irishman step with the lithe delicacy of a fighter over the piles of equipment and lean down to peer over Leva's shoulder. O'Hayer was wearing one of his hand tailored uniforms that were made for him in Honolulu and upon which the three stripes of sergeant had been hand embroidered. Warden put his stuff back on the counter and went back to work.

"How you coming, Leva?" O'Hayer said.

Leva looked up wryly. "So-so, Sergeant. So-so."

"Thats good. We're late, you know." O'Hayer's smile was easy, his dark eyes unchanged before the irony. Leva looked at him a moment and went back to work.

26

O'Hayer took a turn around the small space, looking at the piles of equipment, turning some things over, straightening a pile or two.

"These things are going to have to be separated for size," he said.

"They already been separated," Warden said, without looking up. "Where were you when the shit hit the fan?"

"They have?" O'Hayer said easily. "Well, we'll have to find a place for them. Cant leave them lying here. They'll be getting in everybody's way."

"They may get in your way," Warden said, pleasantly. "They dont get in mine." This was a delicate situation, and he felt he had to restrain himself. Every time he talked to Jim O'Hayer it was a delicate situation, he thought. Delicate situations always irritated him. If they insisted on him being a *supply* sergeant, why didnt they send him to a goddamned school?

"I want you to get this stuff up off the floor," O'Hayer said to Leva. "The Old Man wont like it, messy like this. This place is crummy."

Leva leaned back from his desk and sighed. "Okay, Sergeant," he said. "You want me to do it now?"

"Sometime today," O'Hayer said. He turned back to the room and began to look in all the big square pigeon holes.

Warden put his mind back on the work with difficulty, feeling he should have spoken up just now, irritated because he didnt. A moment later he rose swiftly to check a size number and bumped into O'Hayer. He dropped his arms disgustedly and bent his head over to one side.

"For Christ's sake!" he bellowed. "Get the hell out and go some place. Go any place. Go take a ride in your Dusenberg. Go over to the sheds and count last night's take. We're doin your work. Just go away and dont worry about it." It was a long bellow for one breath and the last of it tapered off.

O'Hayer smiled at him slowly, his arms hanging half-loosely with readiness at his sides, and staring back out of his cool gambler's eyes that the smile did not ever reach.

"Okay, Top," he said. "You know I never argue with the First Sergeant."

"First Sergeant, hell," Warden said. He stared back into the flat eyes, curious as to just how far you had to push this smiling gambler to make him show some emotion. There must be some feeling some place among the tumblers of this adding machine. Dispassionately, he considered knocking him down, just to see what he would do. From the desk Leva was watching them. "I wasnt talking as the goddamned First Sergeant. I was talking as Milt Warden. And I still say get the hell out and go away."

O'Hayer smiled again. "Okay, Top. No matter who you're speaking as, you're still the top. I'll see you later," he said offhandedly to Leva and stepped around the other, deliberately offering his back, and left without a word.

"Some day he's gonna make me mad," Warden said, staring at the door. "Some day I'd like to make *him* mad. I wonder if he *can* get mad."

"You ever see him fight?" Leva asked, casually.

"Yes-I-seen-him-fight. I seen him win that decision over Taylor. I figured I might as well get something out of all this work of his I'm doin."

"He fouled Taylor six times," Leva said. "I counted them. Each time a different foul, so the referee could only warn him. It made Taylor mad. But when Taylor fouled him back he didnt get mad. He's a smart boy."

"I wonder just how smart he is," Warden said speculatively.

"He makes a lot of money," Leva said. "I wish I was smart enough to make that much money. He made enough money from his shed to bring his whole family over from the States, buy his dad a restaurant on the Wahiawa Midway, buy his sister a millinery shop downtown where all the ritzies go, and also build them a ten room house in Wahiawa. Thats fairly smart. . . .

"I hear he's running around with the society downtown now. Got him a society dame."

"For when his Chinese shackjob's got the monthly, 'ey?" Warden said. "Christ!" he said hopefully. "You suppose he'll marry her and retire?"

"We aint that lucky," Leva said.

"He's more trouble to me than Preem. Preem's only a drunk."

"Maybe we can work now," Leva said.

They had not been working very long when a car drove up in the company street outside.

"What the hell?" Warden said. "Since when is this place the goddam Royal Hawaiian?"

"Who is it now?" Leva said disgustedly.

Warden watched the tall lean blonde woman get out of the car. A nine-year-old boy clambered out after her and began to hang on the kneehigh guardrails along the walk. The woman moved on up the walk, the faces of her breasts always falling slightly, under the purple sweater. Warden looked at them closely and decided she was not wearing a brassiere, they moved too much and were too pointed.

"Who is it?" Leva said.

"Holmes's wife," he said contemptuously.

Leva straightened his back and lit another cigaret. "Goddam her," he said. "Her and them sweaters. She'll come in here if there aint nobody in the Orderly Room. And every time she comes in here it costs me three bucks with Mrs Kipfer at the New Congress and a buck round-trip taxifare to town. Big Sue's girls aint good enough to take that picture off my mind."

"She's a good lookin woman," Warden admitted grudgingly. He watched the tight skirt under which, over her hip, passed a thin bulge that was the hem of her panties, fading out of sight. Framing the volute power of her life that no woman ever will acknowledge, he thought. Warden had a theory about women: For years he had been asking them to sleep with him, the ones that interested him. "Will you go to bed with me?" and they were always shocked, even the rummy barflies. Of course, they always did, but that was only later, after he had fulfilled the proper requirements of approach. No woman ever said, "Why, yes, I'd like to go to bed with you." They couldn't do it. It wasnt in them to be that honest.

"Sure," Leva said. "She is good lookin. And she knows what its for."

"Is that right?" Warden said. "And I suppose you've made her."

"Hell, no, not me. I aint got enough stripes. But I've seen her in here talkin to O'Hayer. Just last week he drove her over to Wahiawa in that Chrysler, to *shop*," he mimicked.

"Looks like I'll have to buy a car myself," Warden said. But secretly he did not believe it. It always went by some other name with women. They never called it by the right, the only proper name, unless they were professional whores.

"Now dont tell me she's never made a pass at you," Leva said.

"Hell, no," he said. "I'd of given her this."

"Well you're the only one," Leva said. "If I had that rating you been promisin me I could get some of it myself. But you got to be at least a corporal to make time with that one, she dont take to us privates," he said bitterly. He held up five fingers and ticked off the names he mentioned. "O'Hayer, a sergeant. Sgt Henderson, from Dynamite's old outfit at Bliss, who now takes care of Holmes's horses up at the Pack Train and goes riding with her three times a week. Cpl Kling, who is Holmes's dogrobber. She's laid them all. Everybody in the Compny knows it. She must have some kind of a *per*verse yen for all her husband's noncoms because he cant take care of her."

"What've you been doin? Studyin psychology?"

They listened for a moment to her knocking on the Orderly Room door and when there was no answer, heard the door squeak open.

"I dont need to know psychology to know that much," Leva said. "I guess you didnt see her kiss Champ Wilson when he won the lightweight championship last year?"

"Sure I seen it. So what? Wilson is Dynamite's prize punchie and he won the crown. Natural enough."

"Thats what she knew you'd think, and everybody else," Leva said. "But there was more to it than that. She kissed him right on the lips, blood, collodion and all, and flung her bare arms around his back and rubbed them on the sweat. When she let him go her dress was dark with it and blood all over her face, dont tell me."

"I aint tellin you," Warden said, "you're tellin me."

"The only reason she aint picked you yet is because you're new here."

"I been here eight months now," he said. "That ought to be long enough."

Leva shook his head. "She cant take no chances. Them others, all but O'Hayer, was at Bliss with Holmes. Wilson, Henderson, and Kling. About the only one of them from Bliss she hasnt picked is old Ike Galovitch, who is *too* old. She . . ." He stopped, hearing the Orderly Room door slam again. "Now she'll goddam well be in here," he said. "Four bucks it costs me. Every time she comes here. If you dont get me that rating so I can get some of it, I'll be in debt to the twenty percent men."

"To hell with her," Warden said. "We got work to do," listening to her footsteps in the corridor and then on the porch and then before him at the door.

"Where is the First Sergeant," Mrs Holmes demanded, coming in.

"I'm the First Sergeant, Maam," Warden bawled, putting in his voice that sudden vehemence that always was so startling, like a thunderclap in a cloudless sky, and that he had developed purposely, ever since he'd been a noncom.

"Oh," the woman said. "Yes, of course. How are you, Sergeant?"

"What can I do for you, Mrs Holmes?" Warden said, not getting up from his stool.

"Oh, you know who I am then?"

"Why shouldnt I, Maam, I've seen you often enough." Warden looked her slowly up and down, making his light blue eyes wide under the bushy brows and black hair, putting into them the secret, unsayable challenge.

"I'm looking for my husband," Mrs Holmes said, emphasizing it a little. She smiled thinly at him and waited.

Warden stared at her unsmiling and waited too.

"Do you know where he is?" she asked, finally.

"No, Maam. I dont," Warden said, and waited again.

"Has he been in this morning?" Mrs Holmes stared back at him now, with the coldest eyes he had ever met in any woman.

"You mean before now, Maam?" Warden raised his heavy brows. "Before eight-thirty?" Leva, working at his desk, was grinning. When Warden said them, the Army's rigidly enforced titles of respect had quite a different meaning from the one the ARs intended them to have.

"He said he was coming over here," Mrs Holmes said.

"Well now, Maam." He changed his tactics now and stood up, effusively polite. "He usually does come here, sooner or later. There is some work here for him to do, now and then. He'll probably be in this morning, some time. I'll tell him you want him, if I can catch him. Or I can leave a message if you want."

Smiling, he opened the countertop and stepped out suddenly into the tiny counterspace with her. Involuntarily Mrs Holmes backed out onto the porch. Warden followed her, ignoring the grinning Leva.

"He was to pick up some things for me," Mrs Holmes said. This was the first time, to her, the first sergeant had ever been more than a lifeless stageprop in the melodrama of her husband's life. It disconcerted her.

The little boy was still trying to chin himself on the pipe no higher than his waist.

"Junior!" Mrs Holmes shrilled. "Stop that! Get back in the car! And I thought," she said to Warden in a normal tone, "that he might have purchased them and left them for me."

Warden grinned, broadly. She would never have used that word purchased unless he had got beneath her skin. He watched her eyes go slightly out of focus as she understood the grin. But she brought them right back in again and tried to stare him down. He decided she had guts.

Karen Holmes was suddenly aware of the impish twist of the eyebrows on his wide face, like a small boy who has pulled a fast one. She saw his sleeves, turned back, exposing black silky hairs on the thick wrists and muscled forearms. In the tight shirt the round bunches of muscle bulged at the tips of his shoulders, and they rippled tautly as he moved. These things, too, she had never seen in him before.

"Well, Maam," he said politely, simultaneously aware of her awareness and his grin widening and squeezing up against his eyes to give his face a slyness, "we can sure take a look in the Orderly Room, seef your things is there. He just might of come in and gone out while I was in the Supply Room working."

She followed him inside, although she had just come from there herself.

"Well," he said, surprised. "They aint here."

"I wonder *where* he could be," she said irritably, half to herself. At the mention of her husband a tight unpleasant little frown cut her forehead with twin lines above her nose.

Warden waited deliberately, timing it exactly. Then he slipped it to her. "Well, Maam, if I know the Capn, him and Colonel Delbert is already up at the Club, having a few snorts, discussing the servant problem."

Mrs Holmes turned her cold eyes on him slowly, as if he were a slide beneath a microscope. Her scrutiny knew nothing at all about Col Delbert's stags he held up at the Club, or about his partiality to Kanaka maids.

But Warden, watching her, thought he could detect a fine faint gleam, almost of amusement behind her eyes.

"Thank you very much for your trouble, Sergeant," she said coolly, from a very great distance. She turned and left.

"Thats quite all right, Maam," he called cheerily. "Any time that I can help. Any time at all."

He strolled out onto the porch to watch her climb in and drive off. In spite of her efforts a long smooth flash of thigh winked at him and he grinned.

Leva was still sitting at his desk when he went back in the Supply Room. "You been down to Mrs Kipfer's lately, Milt?" he grinned.

"No," Warden said. "I aint. How's the dear lady gettin along?"

"Got two new girls in fresh from the States. One redhead and one brunette. Interested?"

"No," he said. "I aint."

"You aint?" Leva grinned. "I kind of thought you might want to go along with me tonight. I thought you might feel like it."

"Go to hell, Niccolo. When I have to pay for it I'll quit."

Leva laughed, high up in his nose, making a sound like the spluttering of Diesel exhaust. "Well," he said, "I just thought. Man, but that Holmes woman is one, aint she?"

"One what?"

"One woman."

"I've seen better," Warden said indifferently.

"Wonder why a man wants to go lookin for Kanaky maids when he got that at home, and with a bed too."

"She's cold," Warden said. "Thats why. Cold as hell."

"Yes?" Leva taunted. "I guess thats right. I guess thats why all these guys get tired of her. Anyway, I never seen a piece of ass yet was worth twenty years in Leavenworth."

"Me neither," Warden said.

"A man that fools with that stuff's a sucker to take a chance of gettin his fingers burnt, an officer's woman."

"Thats right," Warden said. "All she'd have to do, if she got caught with you, would be to holler rape and it would be Dear John, thats all she wrote." He was looking out the door across the quad where Dog Company was toiling through its drill for stoppages. Through the truck entrance at the southeast corner showed the front half of Holmes's house with two windows in its sidewall. That back window was the bedroom window, he had been in it once when Holmes had been changing uniforms and he had had to have him sign some papers. As he watched now he saw the car stop out in front of it and Karen Holmes climb out and walk, long-leggedly smooth and clean below the skirt, up to the porch and he remembered, now, how the other of the twin beds had looked with the woman's shoes beneath it.

"Lets fall to on this work," he reproved Leva. "I got that transfer comin in at nine-thirty. Also, I got a conference with Holmes and one of them goddamned complaining cooks that was scheduled for eight-thirty, but which, since Holmes aint showed up yet, will probly start at nine-thirty and last till eleven. I wont got that transfer out till noon. So if you want help, we better get on the ball."

"Okay, Chief," Leva grinned at him. "Anything you say, Chief."

"And remember," Warden said, "Mon-sewer O'Hayer says you got to straighten up this mess sometime today."

"Your face," Leva said.

"Your mother's box," Milt said. "Get to work."

Chapter 4

Milt Warden, in the Orderly Room, heard Prewitt come in on the concrete of the ground-level porch. The conference with the complaining cook that had begun late was still in progress, but over and above it he heard the new man's footsteps and recognized them with that wide angle range tuning of his mind that was never a part of what he happened to be doing. How would it be, he asked himself listening to Holmes's voice, how would it just be that if some day, just once, you could do a thing without having to listen for new angles that you might use? He did not need to answer. It would be fine. The complaining conference, which had begun with the complainings of this cook and had now progressed to the counter complainings of Capt Holmes, and would wind up with usual pep talk, was a long way from finished yet. This cook, whose name was Willard and who was the most complaining cook of all of them and who was bucking hard to get the rating of Mess/Sgt Preem, had complained excellently about Preem's drunkenness and inefficiency and of the fact that he, Willard, was doing the work of a Mess/Sgt on the pay of a First Cook. He had complained superlatively, even outdoing all of his own former complaints, but Holmes, to whom Preem was still one of those who had served with him at Bliss, had also surpassed himself, weathering all of it very well and finally coming out in the lead with his own complaints of Willard who was, Holmes felt, not doing a good enough job as

Mess/Sgt to earn his First Cook's pay. Warden was indifferent to the outcome but since now and then he found an opportunity to stick in complaints about both Preem, whom he wanted busted, and Willard, whom he did not want to replace him, he had remained attentive, hoping always for some chance to break it up and end it so he could get on to this transfer and then be free to go back to helping Leva, who was just about the only good man in the outfit and whose loss would be a blow from which the Company Administration never would recover.

The monotonic buzzing of the voices carried outside to Prewitt on the porch and he sat down in one of the backless chairs and leaned against the wall, prepared to wait, fingering the mouthpiece in his pocket that was his own and that he always carried with him. He had bought it back in Myer with a crapgame winnings and it was the mouthpiece he had used to play the Taps at Arlington. Pulling it out now and looking into the ruby bell as if it were a crystal ball brought that day back to him. The President himself had been there, with all his aides and guards, leaning on the arm of one of them. There had been a colored bugler who played the echo to his own Taps from the stand. The Negro was a better bugler, but because he was not white he had been stationed in the hills to play the echo. It should have been himself who played the echo. Thinking about it all, he put the beauty back in his pocket and folded his arms across his chest, still waiting.

From the G Company supplyroom came the sound of a spasmodically clicking typewriter, and before the kitchen screen-door, sitting in the sun, was a KP peeling spuds, stopping now and then to slap at the flies buzzing around his head. Prew watching him, feeling all around him that sunny buzzing inarticulateness that is nine-thirty in the morning on a duty day.

"Wonderful day, aint it?" the KP, a tiny curly-headed Italian with narrow bony shoulders jutting from his undershirt, said to him. Scowling, he speared another spud ferociously and raised it, triumphantly, like a caught fish from the dirty water of the number 18 kettle.

"Yeah," Prew said.

"Fine way to pass the time," the KP said, motioning with the speared spud before he went to peeling it. "Good for the mind. You the new transfer?"

"Thats whats the matter," Prew, who had never liked Italians, said.

"Ha," the KP said. "You picked a helluva outfit to get into, friend, thats all." Peeling automatically, he scratched his hairless chin on one naked shoulder.

"I didnt pick it."

"Unless," the KP said, ignoring the answer, "you happen to be a jockstrap. Any kind of a jockstrap, just any kind, but preferably a

34

punchie. If you're a punchie you picked the right place and I'll be salutin you for a corporal in six days."

"I aint no jockstrap," Prew said.

"Then I pity you, friend," said the KP fervently. "Thats all. I pity you. My name's Maggio and as you can see I aint no jockstrap neither. But I'm a spudpeeler though. I'm one helluva hotshot spudpeeler. I'm the best spudpeeler in Schofield Barricks, T.H. I got a medal."

"What part of Brooklyn you come from?" Prew grinned.

The dark intent eyes under the hairy brows flared up as if Prew had lighted candles in a dim cathedral. "Atlantic Avenue. You know Brooklyn?"

"No. I was never there. But I had a buddy at Myer was from Brooklyn."

The candles were snuffed out. "Oh," Maggio said. Then with the air of a man who has nothing more to lose he asked cautiously, "Whats his name?"

"Smith," Prew said. "Jimmy Smith."

"Jesus Christ!" Maggio said and crossed himself with the patented potato scraper. "Smith, no less. I'll kiss your ass in Macy's window at high noon on Sataday if I ever heard of a Smith in Brooklyn."

Prew laughed. "That was his name."

"Yeah?" Maggio said, scowling at a new spud. "Thats fine. Now I knew a Jew named Hodenpyl onct. I thought you knew Brooklyn." He subsided into silence, muttering, "Jimmy Smith. From Brooklyn. My bleeding back."

Prew, grinning, lit a cigaret, listening to the buzzing from the Orderly Room suddenly raise itself an octave.

"Hear that?" Maggio said. He stabbed his scraper at the window. "Thats what you're lettin yourself into, friend. You better, if you're smart, turn right around and let yourself back out."

"I cant," Prew said. "I was transferred by request."

"Oh," Maggio said sagely. "Another fuckup. Like me. Well, friend, I feel for you," he said bitterly, "but from my position I cant quite reach you."

"Whats going on in there?"

"Oh, nothin unusual. Happens all a time. 'The Warden' and 'Dynamite' is just givin Willard a ass eatin, thats all. Not a thing unusual. Willard just happens to be on shift today. After they get through with him he'll take it out on me.

"Willard is a schmuck amingia, he wouldnt make a good KP in any other outfit. Here it's a First Cook because they cant get any other cooks to transfer in. This is because Preem is passed out on his fartsack full a vanilla extrack all a time."

"Sounds like a wonderful outfit to transfer into," Prew said to him.

"Ah," Maggio scowled, "it is. You'll love it, friend, just simply love it. Specially if you was a jockstrap. I been out of ree-croot drill six weeks and already I wish I'm back in Gimbel's basement as a shipping clerk." Dolefully he shook his head. "If somebody had of told me that six months ago I'd of told him to take it and stick it."

He put his arm down in the kettle and fished around and brought up one last spud. "Dont mind me, friend. I'm just bitter. What I need is a trip to Mrs Kipfer's. Then I be all right for a nuther week." He sighed.

"You play cards?" he said suddenly. "Like to diddle up the cubes? Poker? blackjack? cut high card? roll high dice or low dice? anything you like?"

"You sound like a spotter for O'Hayer's shed," Prew grinned. "Sure, I like them all."

"I was for a while, but their hours is too long," Maggio said. "You got any money?"

"Some," Prew said.

"Then I'll be around tonight," Maggio said, his dark eyes glowing. "We'll have a little private game. That is, if I can find this joe in F Compny who owes me three."

"There aint enough money in two-handed games," Prew said.

"Oh, yes, there is," Maggio said, "if you happen to be broke and need a piece of ass." He inspected the fresh, dark spots on Prew's sleeves where his stripes had been. "Wait'll you begin to draw your twenty-one a month, brother."

He stood up and stretched and scratched his tangled mop. "Leave me give you a tip, friend. Theys a war goin on here. And I can tell you who will win the friggin thing. If you're smart you'll learn to jockstrap, and learn quick, and get on the gravytrain, if you want to be a successful soljer. I was smart, I'd of joined the CYO when I was young and learned to be a good jockstrap myself, instead of playing pee pool. Then I would of been on Dynamite's good list instead of on his shitlist. If only I'd of listened to my dear sainted mother," he said. "Balls to spuds. This is the Army, they can give it back to Custer." Mumbling something about more spuds he disappeared into the kitchen, a gnarled disillusioned gnome who had been cheated of Valhalla.

Prew flipped his cigaret at the red and black painted pot and went inside, down the corridor past the Orderly Room to the Dayroom. The dayroom orderly, fugitive from straight duty, sat on one of the moth-eaten upholstered chairs, boredly scanning a comic book, his mop between his knees. He did not even bother to look up.

Prew stepped back out of the dayroom, feeling very much a stranger, and stood looking at the pooltable in the half light of the alcove, feeling tangibly the new forces here that had begun already to work on him. Thinking about little Maggio and Gimbel's basement, he grinned and switched on the light, selected a cue and chalked it and broke the rack of balls.

The solid crack of the break in the heavy silence of mid-morning when the company was gone brought a man to the corridor door who stuck in his head. Recognizing Prewitt, he fingered his narrow bristling mustache and the hooked satanic eyebrows quivered like a dog's nose with a new scent. He tiptoed gracefully, and silently, up to Prewitt's elbow and his voice boomed out startlingly in the stillness broken only by the clack of pool balls.

"What the hell're you doin?" he bawled indignantly. "Why aint you out with the Compny? Whats your name?"

The bellow had not made Prew jump and now he turned his bent head slowly above the cue. "Prewitt. Transfer from A Compny," he said. "You know me, Warden."

The big man was silent, his sudden disconcerting indignation as suddenly and as disconcertingly gone, and ran his fingers through his wildly rumpled hair.

"Oh," he said, grinning slyly, then dropping the grin as suddenly as it had come. "To see The Man."

"Thats whats the matter," Prew said, shooting another ball.

"I remember you," Warden said darkly. "Little boy bugle. . . . I'll call you." Before Prew could answer he was gone.

Prew went on shooting pool, thinking how typical it was of Warden not to order him to stop, any other topkick would have, but Warden did not work that way. He went on shooting, methodically, first one ball and then another, missing only once. The table clean, he racked the balls and hung up his cue, feeling how the thing had gone flat now. He stood looking at the table for a minute and then switched off the light and went out to the porch.

They were still going strong in the Orderly Room. Maggio was still concentratedly peeling spuds. From the kitchen came the moist sounds of someone banging pots and pans around. The irregular clacking of the typewriter in the supplyroom had ceased. He seemed suspended in a void of bodyless activity, while G Company's morning moved on ponderously and implacably all around him, indifferent to this transfer that was so monumental in his life, and of which he was not a part. He was, it seemed like, standing on a high place where all the highways met and there were signposts to all places, and where the variegated colors of the license plates whizzed by and did not see him standing there and none would stop and pick him up.

The cook, in whites, came out, his face still red. He went into the kitchen slamming the door after first telling Maggio to get the goddam hell out of the road with his goddam can of spuds and things began to move again for Prew.

"What'd I tell you?" Maggio leered at him.

He grinned and flipped his cigaret and exhaled, watching the smoke float into the sun where it suddenly became full-bodied, visible in all its unending swirls. That was G Company, he thought, deceptively simple yet in the light full of hidden complex designs, unending meanings, in which he was entangled now.

Before the cigaret hit the ground Warden bellowed, "All right, Prewitt!" out the window at him. With a grudging admiration Prew felt he had been subtly scored on. How could Warden know that he had left the dayroom? There was an uncanny sardonic insight in The Warden that approached the supernatural.

Prew slung his hat up on his shoulder with his arm shoved through the strap, so nobody could steal it while he was inside, and entered.

"Private Prewitt reporting to the Compny Commander as ordered, Sir," he mouthed the formula, whatever humanness there was inside him falling out, leaving only a juiceless meatless shell.

Capt Dynamite Holmes, who was a favorite with the Islands sport fans, directed his long, high-foreheaded face with its high cheekbones and eagle's nose and the hair combed sideways across the just beginning bald spot, sternly at the man before him and picked up the Special Orders that announced the transfer without looking at them.

"At ease," he said.

His desk was right before the door, and at right angles on the left was the First Sergeant's desk, where Milt Warden sat with folded elbows leaning on it. As he moved his left foot and crossed his hands behind his back, Prew spared him one swift glance. Warden stared back at him, half-gleefully, half-foreboding; he seemed to be poised and waiting for his chance.

Capt Holmes swung his swivel chair to the right and stared sternly out the window for a moment, offering Prew a profile of the jutting jaw, grim mouth, and sharp commanding nose. Then suddenly he swung back around, the swivel creaking, and began to speak.

"I always make it a policy to talk to my new men, Prewitt," he said sternly. "I dont know what you've been used to in the Bugle Corps, but in my outfit we run it by the book. Any man who fucksup gets broken—quick and hard. The Stockade is the place for fuckups until they learn to soldier."

He paused and stared at Prewitt sternly, and crossed his booted legs whose spurs jangled punctuation to the warning. Capt Holmes was warming to his subject. Here, said the long boned, eagle's face to Prew, is a soldier who is not afraid to talk to his men in their own language, who does not mince the words, and who understands his men.

"I have," he said, "a damned fine smoothrunning outfit. I do not allow anything to bitch it up. But—if a man does his work, and keeps his nose clean, does as I say, he'll get along. Plenty of room for advancement here, because in this organization there is no favoritism. I make it my business to see that each man gets just what he earns. No more, no less.

"You start with a clean slate, Prewitt. What you do with it is up to you.

"Understood?"

"Yes, Sir," Prew said.

"Good," said Capt Holmes, and nodded sternly.

Milt Warden, at his own desk, was watching the progress of this conference that was not new to him with acumen. Crap! cried the king, he thought, and twenty thousand royal subjects squatted and strained, for in those days the king's word was law! His face straight, he grinned at Prew with his eyebrows, and a devilish pixy peered out from behind his face with unholy glee.

"To get a rating in my Company," Capt Holmes was saying sternly, "a man has got to know his stuff. He has to soldier. He has to show me he's got it on the ball." He looked up sharply.

"Understood?"

"Yes, Sir," Prew said.

"Good," said Capt Holmes. "Understood. Its always important for an officer and his men to understand each other." Then he pushed his chair back and smiled at Prewitt, handsomely. "Glad to have you aboard, Prewitt," he smiled, "as our colleagues in the navy say. I can always use a good man in my outfit and I'm glad to have you."

"Thank you, Sir," Prew said.

"How would you like to be my Company bugler, temporarily?" Holmes paused to light himself a cigaret. "I saw your fight with Connors of the 8th Field in the Bowl last year," he said. "A damned fine show. Damned fine. With any luck you should have won it. I thought for a while in there, in the second round, you were going to knock him out."

"Thank you, Sir," Prew said. Capt Holmes was talking almost joyously now. Here it comes, Prew told himself; well, bud, you asked for it, now figure it out. Figure it out yourself, he thought. Better yet, just let him figure it out.

"If I'd known you were in the Regiment last December when the season started I'd have looked you up," Holmes smiled.

Prew said nothing. On his left he could feel, not hear, The Warden snorting softly with disgust as he began to study a sheaf of papers with the elaborate I'm-not-with-him air of a sober man whose friend is drunk.

"I can use a good bugler, Prewitt," Holmes smiled. "My regular Company bugler hasnt the experience. And his apprentice only has his job because he's such a fuckup I was afraid he'd shoot somebody on a problem." He laughed and looked at Prew, inviting him to join in.

Milt Warden, who was the one who had suggested Salvatore Clark for the apprentice bugler, after Clark almost shot himself on guard, went on studying his papers, but his eyebrows quivered.

"A Pfc rating goes with the job," Holmes said to Prew. "I'll have Sergeant Warden post the order, first thing tomorrow."

He waited then, but Prew said nothing, watching the dry ironic sunlight coming through the open window, wondering how long now it would take him to catch on, unable to believe that they had not heard it all before, and feeling how his uniform that had been fresh at eight o'clock was damp and musty now with sweat, beginning to be soaked.

"I realize," Holmes smiled indulgently, "a Pfc isnt very much, but our TO quota of noncoms is all filled up. We have two noncoms who are shorttimers though," he said. "They'll be leaving on next month's boat.

"Its too bad the season's almost over or you could start training this afternoon, but the schedule ends the last of February. But then," he smiled, "if you dont fight Regimental this year, you'll be eligible for Company Smokers in the fall.

"Have you seen any of our boys in the Bowl this year?" he asked. "We've got some good ones, I'm confident we'll keep the trophy. I'd like to get your opinion on a couple of them."

"I havent been to any of the fights this year, Sir," Prew said.

"What?" Holmes said, not believing it. "You havent?" He stared at Prew a moment curiously, then looked at Warden knowingly. He picked up a freshly sharpened pencil from his desk and studied it. "Why is it," Capt Holmes said softly, "that you've been in the Regiment a whole year, Prewitt, and nobody knew a thing about it? I should have thought you would have come around to see me, since I am the boxing coach and since we're the Division champions."

Prew moved his weight from one foot to the other and took one deep breath. "I was afraid you'd want me to go out for the squad, Sir," he said. There it is, he thought, its out now, you've got it now. Now he can carry the ball. He felt relieved.

"Of course," Holmes said. "Why not? We can use a man as good as you are. Especially since you're a welterweight. We're poor in that division. If we lose the championship this year, it will be because we lost the welterweight division."

"Because I left the 27th because I had quit fighting, Sir," Prew said.

Again Holmes looked at Warden knowingly, this time apologetically, as if now he could believe it since he'd heard it from the man himself, before he spoke. "Quit fighting?" he said. "What for?"

"Maybe you heard about what happened with Dixie Wells, Sir," Prew said, hearing Warden lay his papers down, feeling Warden grinning.

Holmes stared at him innocently, eyes wide with it. "Why, no," he said. "What was that?"

Prew went through the story for him, for both of them, standing there with his feet one foot apart and his hands clasped behind his back, and feeling all the time he spoke it was superfluous, that both of them already knew all about the deal already, yet forced to play the role that Holmes had set for him.

"Thats too bad," Holmes said, when he had finished. "I can understand why you might feel that way. But those things happen, in this game. A man has got to accept that possibility when he fights."

"Thats one reason why I decided I would quit, Sir," Prew said.

"But on the other hand," Holmes said, much less warmly now, "look at it this way. What if all fighters felt like that?"

"They dont, Sir," Prew said.

"I know," Holmes said, much less warmly still. "What would you have us do? Disband our fighting program because one man got hurt?"

"No, Sir," Prew said. "I didnt say . . ."

"You might as well," Holmes said, "say stop war because one man got killed. Our fighting season is the best morale builder that we have off here away from home."

"I dont want it disbanded, Sir," Prew said, and then felt the absurdity to which he had been forced. "But I dont see," he went on doggedly, "why any man should fight unless he wanted to."

Holmes studied him with eyes that had grown curiously flat, and were growing flatter. "And that was why you left the 27th?"

"Yes, Sir. Because they tried to make me go on fighting."

"I see." Capt Holmes seemed all at once to have lost interest in this interview. He looked down at his watch, remembering suddenly he had a riding date with Major Thompson's wife at 12:30. He stood up and picked up his hat from the IN file on his desk.

It was a fine hat, a soft expensive unblocked Stetson, with its brim bent up fore and aft, its four dents creased to a sharp point at the peak, and it bore the wide chinstrap of the Cavalry, instead of the thin strap authorized for the Infantry that went behind the head. Beside it lay his riding crop he always carried. He picked that up, too. He had not always been an Infantryman.

"Well," he said, with very little interest, "theres nothing in the ARs that says a man must be a boxer if he doesnt want to. You'll find that we wont put any pressure on you here, like they did in the 27th. I dont believe in that sort of thing. If you dont want to fight we dont want you on our squad." He walked to the door and then turned back sharply.

"Why did you leave the Bugle Corps?"

"It was a personal matter, Sir," Prew said, taking refuge in the taboo that says a man's, even a private's, personal matters are his own affair.

"But you were transferred at the Chief Bugler's request," Holmes told him. "What kind of trouble was it you were in, over there?"

"No, Sir," Prew said. "No trouble. It was a personal matter," he repeated.

"Oh," Holmes said, "I see." That it might be a personal matter he had not considered and he looked uneasily at Warden, not sure of how to approach this angle, but Warden, who had been following everything with interest, was suddenly staring unconcernedly at the wall. Holmes cleared his throat, but Warden did not get it.

"Have you anything you wish to add, Sergeant?" he had to ask him, finally.

"Who? me? Why, yes, Sir," exploded Warden with that sudden violence. He was, quite suddenly, in a state of indignation. His brows hooked upward, two harriers ready to pounce upon the rabbit.

"What kind of rating you have in the Bugle Corps, Prewitt?"

"First and Fourth," Prew said, looking at him steadily.

Warden looked at Holmes and raised his eyebrows eloquently.

"You mean," he said, astounded, "you took a bust from First-Fourth to transfer to a rifle company as a buckass private, just because you like to hike?"

"I didnt have no trouble," Prew said stolidly, "if thats what you mean."

"Or," Warden grinned, "was it just because you couldnt stand to bugle?"

"It was a personal matter," Prew said.

"Thats up to the Compny Commander's discretion to decide," Warden corrected instantly. Holmes nodded. And Warden grinned at Prewitt velvetly. "Then you didnt transfer because Mr Houston made young MacIntosh First Bugler? Over you?"

"I was transferred," Prew said, staring at the other. "It was a personal matter."

Warden leaned back in his chair and snorted softly. "What a helluva thing to transfer over. Kids in the Army we got now. Someday you punks will learn that good jobs dont grow on trees."

In the electric antagonism that flashed between the two of them and hung heavy like ozone in the air Capt Holmes had been forgotten. He broke in now, as was his right.

"It looks to me," he said indifferently, "as if you were fast acquiring a reputation as a bolshevik, Prewitt. Bolsheviks never get anywhere in the Army. You'll find that straight duty in this outfit is considerably tougher than SD in the Bugle Corps."

"I've done straight duty before, Sir," Prew said. "In the Infantry. I dont mind doing it again." You liar, he told himself, like hell you do not mind it. How is it that people make you lie so easily?

"Well," Holmes said, pausing for the effect, "it looks as though you'll get a chance to do it." But he was no longer jocular. "You're not a recruit and you should know that in the Army its not the individual that counts. Every man has certain responsibilities to fulfill. Moral responsibilities that go beyond the ARs' regulations. It might look as thought I were a free agent, but I'm not. No matter how high you get there is always somebody over you, and who knows more about it all than you do.

"Sergeant Warden will take care of you and get you assigned to a squad." Nothing more was said about the Company bugler's job. He turned to Warden. "Is there anything else for me to take care of today, Sergeant?"

"Yes, Sir," Warden, who had been listening to this abstract conversation, said violently. "The Compny Fund Report has got to be checked and made out. Its due tomorrow morning."

"You make it out," Holmes said, undisturbed by the regulation that says no one but an officer may touch the Company Fund. "Fix it up and I'll be in early tomorrow to sign it. I havent time to bother with details. Is that all?"

"*No*, Sir," Warden said vehemently.

"Well, whatever it is, you fix it. If theres anything that has to go in this afternoon, sign my name. I wont be back." He looked at Warden angrily and turned back to the door, ignoring Prewitt.

"Yes, *Sir*," Warden raged. "Ten-nsh-HUT!" he bawled, bellowing it at the top of his lungs in the smallness of the room.

"Carry on," Holmes said. He touched his crop to hat brim and disappeared. A moment later his voice came in the open window.

"Sergeant Warden!"

"*Yes*, Sir!" Warden bellowed, jumping to the window.

"Whats the matter with this outfit? This place needs policing. Look there. And there. And over by the garbage rack. Is this a barracks or a pigpen? I want it policed up! Immediately!"

"Yes, *Sir!*" bellowed Warden, "Maggio!"

Maggio's gnomelike body bobbed up in its undershirt before the window. "Yesser."

"Maggio," said Capt Holmes. "Wheres your goddam fatigue blouse? Get your blouse and put it on. This is no goddamned bathing beach."

"Yessir," Maggio said. "I'll get it, Sir."

"Maggio," Warden bellowed. "Get the other KPs and police the goddam area. Dint you hear what the Compny Commander said?"

"Okay, Sarge," said Maggio resignedly.

Warden leaned his elbows on the sill and watched Holmes's broad back move through the midst of Dog Company, called to attention by their duty sergeant. "Carry on," Holmes thundered. After Holmes had passed, the blue-dressed figures sat back down to go on with their stoppage drill.

"The hell for leather Cavalryman," Warden muttered. "Errol Flynn with fifty extra pounds." He walked deliberately over to his desk and smashed his fist into his own rigidly blocked, flat-peaked issue hat hanging on the wall. "The son of a bitch'd try to ship me down if I bent up my hat like his." Then he went back to the window.

Holmes was climbing the outside stair to Regimental Hq, going up to Col Delbert's office. Warden had a theory about officers: Being an officer would make a son of a bitch out of Christ himself. And they had you by the nuts. You couldnt do a thing. That was why they were such ones.

But beyond the Hq stairs the bedroom window of Holmes's house peered at him coyly through the truck entrance. And maybe right now, behind that unrevealing window, she was languorously undressing the long flowing milk of that blonde body, garment by garment like a stripper in a honkytonk, to take a bath or something. Maybe she had a man in there with her now.

Warden felt his chest swelling potently with maleness, as if a great balloon were being blown up inside him. He turned from the window and sat back down.

Prew was waiting for him, standing quietly before the desk, feeling worn out now and very tired, feeling the sweat still dripping slowly from his armpits with the strain of subduing his own fear and disagreeing with authority. The collar of the shirt that had been fresh at eight o'clock was wilted and the sweat had soaked clear through the back. Only a little more of this and you are through, he told himself. Then you can relax.

Warden picked up a paper from his desk and began to read it, as if he were alone. When he finally looked up there was hurt surprise and indignation on his face, as if wondering how this man had got into his office uninvited and without his knowing it.

"Well?" Milt Warden said. "What the hell do you want?"

Prew stared at him levelly, not answering, not disconcerted. And for a time both were silent, studying each other, like two opposing checker players taking each other's measure before the game began. There was no open dislike in the face of either, only a sort of cold inherent antagonism. They were like two philosophers starting from the same initial premise of life and each, by irrefutable argument, arriving at a diametrically opposite conclusion. Yet these two conclusions were like twin brothers of the same flesh and heritage and blood.

Warden broke the spell. "You havent changed a bit, have you, Prewitt?" he said sarcastically. "Havent learned a thing. Fools rush in where angels fear to re-enlist, as some great wit once said. All a man has to do is to leave it up to you and you'll put your own head in the noose for him."

"A man like you, you mean," Prew said.

"No, not me. I like you."

"I love you too," Prew said. "And you aint changed none either."

"Put his own head in the noose," Warden shook his head sorrowfully. "Thats what you did just now; you know that, dont you? When you turned down Dynamite's Boxing Squad?"

"I thought you didnt like jockstraps and SD men," Prew said.

"I dont," Warden said. "But did it ever occur to you that in a way I'm an SD man myself? I dont do straight duty."

"Yeah," Prew said. "I've thought of that. Thats why I couldnt see why you hated us guys in the Bugle Corps so much."

"Because," Warden grinned, "SD men and jockstraps are all the same, fugitives from straight duty. They aint got what it takes so they ride the gravytrain."

"And make life a hellhole for every one they can, like you."

"No," Warden said. "Guess again. I dont make hell for nobody. I'm only the instrument of a laughing Providence. Sometimes I dont like it myself, but I couldnt help it if I was born smart."

"We cant all be smart," Prew said.

"Thats right," Warden nodded. "We cant. Its a shame too. You been in the army what now? Five years? Fivenahalf? Its about time for you to get over bein a punk ree-croot and begin to get smart, aint it? That is, if you're ever goin to."

"Maybe I'd rather not be smart."

Warden unfolded his arms and proceeded to light a cigaret, lazily, taking his time. "You had a soft deal as a bugler," he said, "but you toss it up because Queer Houston hurt your feelins. And then you turn Holmes down when he wants you for his boxing squad," he said, mincing the words. "You should of took him up, Prewitt. You wont like straight duty in my compny."

"I can soljer with any man," Prew said. "I'll take my chances."

"Okay," Warden said. "So what? Since when has bein a good soljer had anything to do with the Army? Do you think bein a good soljer will get you a sergeant's rating in this outfit? after what you just pulled? It wont even get you Pfc.

"You're the kind of soljer ought to be jockstrappin, Prewitt. Then you could get your name in all the Honolulu papers and be a hero. Because you'll never make a real soljer. Never in God's world.

"When you change your mind and decide you might as well jockstrap for Dynamite after all, remember this: the jockstraps dont run this compny—in spite of Holmes.

"This aint A Compny now, Prewitt. This is G Compny, of which I am First Sergeant. I run this compny. Holmes is the CO, but he is like the rest of the officer class: a dumb bastard that signs papers an rides horses an wears spurs an gets stinking drunk up at the stinking Officers' Club. I'm the guy that runs this compny."

"Yeah?" Prew grinned. "Well, you aint doin a very goddam good job of it, buddy. If you run this outfit, how come Preem's the mess sergeant? And how come O'Hayer's the supply sergeant, when Leva does the work? And how come most every noncom in 'your compny' is one of Holmes's punchies? Dont give me that crap."

The whites of Warden's eyes turned slowly red. "You dont know the half of it yet, kid," he grinned. "Wait till you been here for a while. Theres a lot more yet. You dont know Galovitch, and Henderson, and Dhom, the duty sergeant."

He removed the cigaret from the corner of his mouth and knocked it with deliberate slowness on the ashtray. "But the point is, Holmes would strangle on his own spit if I wasnt here to swab out his throat for him." He stuffed the burning coal out savagely and then rose languidly like a stretching cat. "So at least we know where we stand," he said, "dont we, kid?"

"I know where I stand," Prew said. "I aint never been able to figure out where you stand. I think . . ." The sound of someone coming in the corridor made him cut it off, because this was a private argument, a thing between himself and Warden that rank, whether high or low, would not appreciate. Warden grinned at him.

"Rest, rest, rest," a voice said through the door. "Dont get up for me, men," though both of them were standing. The voice was followed by a little man, shorter yet than Prewitt, who came walking quick-stepping with a ramrod back behind it through the door, dressed in dapper, tailored CKCs and sporting 2nd Lieutenant's bars. He stopped when he saw Prewitt.

"I dont know you, do I, soldier?" said the little man. "Whats your name?"

"Prewitt, Sir," Prew said, looking around at Warden who was grinning wryly.

"Prewitt, Prewitt, Prewitt," said the little man. "You must be a new man, a transfer. Because I dont know that name."

"Transferred from A Compny, this morning, Sir," Prew said.

"Ah," said the little man. "I knew it. If I didnt know that name, I knew it wasnt in the Company. I spent three bloody weeks sweating out a roster of this Company just so I could call each man by his name. My father always told me a good officer knows every man in his outfit by name, preferably by his nickname. Whats your nickname, soldier?"

"They call me Prew, Sir," Prew said, still not acute, awake or cognizant before this swiftly talking blob of energy.

"Of course," said the little man. "I should have known that. I'm Lt Culpepper, recently of West-Point-on-the-Hudson, now of this Company. You're the new fighter, arent you, the welterweight? Too bad you didnt get here before the close of the season. Glad to have you aboard, Prewitt, glad to have you aboard, as the Old Man and his colleagues in the navy would say."

Lt Culpepper sprinted around the little room laying papers here and there in their different boxes. "You probably know of me," he said, "if you have read the Regimental Chronicles. My father and his grandfather before him both began their careers in this Company as 2nd Looies, both rose to command of this Company, then to command of this Regiment before they became general officers. I am following in their illustrious footsteps. Hear hear.

"Hey, hey," he said. "Wheres my golf bag, Sergeant Warden? I have a golf date with Colonel Prescott's daughter in fifteen minutes, then lunch, then more golf."

"Its in the closet there," Warden said aloofly, "behind the filing cabinet."

"Ah, yes," said Lt Culpepper, son of Brigadier Culpepper, grandson of Lt General Culpepper, great grandson of Lt Col Culpepper, C.S.A. "I'll get it, Sergeant, dont bother," he said to Warden who had not moved. "I've got to do my eighteen holes today. Big party at the Club tonight and I've got to be in shape."

He pulled the golf bag out from behind the green art metal filing cabinet, knocking a sheaf of files off the corner of the table which he did not pick up, and breezed out as swiftly as he had come, saying nothing more to Prewitt.

Disgustedly Warden picked the files up and put them back where they had been. "Come on," he said to Prewitt. "I'll fix you up. I got work to do."

He walked over behind Holmes's desk and stood looking at the chart of the Company's personnel organization that hung there with little cardboard tabs containing each man's name and separated into platoons and squads and hanging from screw hooks.

"Wheres your stuff?" he said.

"Still at A Compny. I dint want to pack my clean uniforms."

Warden grinned his sly pixy grin. "Still the dude, hunh? Havent changed a bit. Takes more than clothes to make a soljer, Prewitt. A whole helluva lot more."

He took a blank tab from one of Holmes's desk drawers and printed Prewitt's name on it. "Theres a machine-gun cart leaning up against the wall outside the supplyroom. Take that over for your stuff. Save you makin four five trips."

"Okay," Prew said, surprised at the beneficence and unable to keep it off his face.

Warden grinned at him, relishing the surprise. "I'd hate to see you muss them uniforms, kid. I hate to see any kind of energy wasted, even if its been wasted once already.

"We ought to be able to fix you up in a good squad," he grinned. "Now how would you like to be in Chief Choate's squad?"

"What're you tryin to do?" Prew said, "kid me? I dont see you puttin me in Big Chief's squad. I more likely see you puttin me in a squad that one of Holmes's punchies runs."

"You do?" Warden's eyebrows hooked and quivered delicately. He hung the tab up on the chart under Cpl Choate's name.

"There. You see? I'm probably the best friend you ever had, kid, and you dont even know it. Lets go the supplyroom and draw your stuff."

In the supplyroom rawboned bald and wryfaced Leva stopped his scribbling long enough to dole out sheets and mattress covers, shelter-half and blankets, pack and all the rest of it and get Prew's initials on the Form.

"Hello, Prew," he grinned.

"Hello, Niccolo," Prew said. "You still in this outfit?"

"You come to stay a spell with us?" Leva said, "or is this just temporary?"

"He'll probly," Warden said, "stay quite a while."

He led him upstairs to the row of bunks that Choate's squad inhabited and pointed out the one for him to take.

"You got till one o'clock to get straightened out," The Warden said. "You fall out for Fatigue at one P.M. Just like us common people."

Prew set himself to stowing all his stuff. The big squadroom was very still with nobody in it. His heels clacked very loudly. The squadroom was too big for one man alone, and the banging of his wall locker was too loud, echoing deeply back and forth across the room.

Chapter 5

Capt Holmes, when he left the Orderly Room, was feeling good. He felt he had given a pretty good account of himself with the cook Willard, but particularly with the new man, Prewitt, the welter from the 27th. He had already heard the story about his quitting fighting and now, after the interview, he was confident Prewitt would come around and change his mind, before summer and the Company Smoker season.

Capt Holmes liked to climb the stairs to Hq Building. They did not look like concrete, they looked like old marble streaked gray and black. Age had polished down the once porous concrete and rounded the raw edges with rain and feet, and given it a smooth slick gloss. When the stairs were wet they always caught and perpetuated the rainbow, like a promise. There will always be an Army, they said to him.

Heavy concrete and mortared brick had been molded around a concept Capt Holmes believed and given it reality. His orderly faithfully saddlesoaped and polished his riding boots once a day, it was the same thing. As he raised first one foot then the other to the step above the soft pliant leather bent in long smooth wrinkles, with none of those crowsfeet that show poor care. Once a day, regular as the monthly pay voucher.

His sense of accomplishment was though, just now, dimmed by a slight uneasiness at the prospect of meeting Col Delbert. Not that he disliked the Old Man. But when a man had the rank on you and held your majority in the palm of his hand you naturally had to watch every word.

In the middle of the upper porch a dumpy private in fatigues was expertly swinging a mop over the glazed floor, never lifting it, each stroke sweeping from wall to wall. Capt Holmes paused automatically for him to stop to let him pass, but the private was too intent upon his job to see him. When he did not stop Capt Holmes, still thinking about the Colonel, stepped across from dry to wet between the strokes. The beard of the mop slapped his heel, and the private looked up startled, then popped to a guilty wide-eyed Attention, the mop dangling from his hand. He looked down at it a moment indecisively, then jerked the stick up along his right side like a guidon and looked at Holmes. Capt Holmes gave him one disdainful look, disgusted at such chaotic and unreasonable fear of officers which always irritated him, and went on silently.

Col Delbert was in his office. Behind the big desk and across the long expanse of gleaming floor, between the two tall flags, one the country's the other the Regiment's, he looked deceptively small. But he was a big man, big enough that the tiny irongray mustache he wore always embarrassed Capt Holmes, no matter how hard he tried not to judge. Outside of the black cocker that slept on the floor and two straight chairs the office was properly and soldierly bare.

Everything went off as Holmes saluted coldly and impersonally. Even the cocker seemed no longer to be breathing. The Old Man returned it with the same precision, then everything came on again and the Colonel smiled. When he smiled he was really, truly almost fatherly.

"Well," the Col said, pushing back his chair and slapping his hands down on his knees. "Whats on your mind, eh, 'Dynamite'?"

Capt Holmes smiled back and got one of the chairs from against the wall, wishing he could get rid of that ridiculous uneasiness.

"Well, Sir. One of my old men . . ."

"We certainly looked bad last Sunday in baseball." The Col clipped the words. "You see the game? A rout. A veritable rout. The 21st ran over us roughshod, I say. It'd 've been much worse if 't had n't been for Big Chief Choate. Best firstbaseman ever saw. Really ought to transfer him to Hq Company and give him a Staff Sergeancy." Col Delbert beamed and the short mustache bent sharply in the middle like a distant bird in flight. "Fact, I would if we had a team at all in baseball, but he's the only thing we've got."

Capt Holmes debated in the pause whether the Col intended to go on, or whether he could go ahead with what he wanted. He decided it would be better to wait than interrupt him if he did go on.

"We wont do anything in baseball this year," the Col went on. Holmes chalked up a hit. "Your boxing squad was only athletic championship we won all year last year. Looks like the only one we'll have a chance of winning this year. I've taken some mighty strong ribbing about our athletic prowess lately."

"Yes, Sir," Capt Holmes said in the next pause. "Thank you, Sir."

"Every soldier knows," the Col said, "that good athletics make for good soldiering. Our Regiment's athletic reputation has suffered badly this last year. Even the downtown newspapers were lampooning us. A thing like that is never good. You, my boy, are about the only bright spot on our horizon."

"Thank you, Sir," Capt Holmes said, trying to figure what it was leading up to.

Col Delbert paused, sagely screwing up his eyes. "Do you think we'll win that championship again this year, Captain?"

"Well, Sir," Capt Holmes said. "We've got a fifty-fifty chance so far. We're ahead of the 27th on points; but not with enough margin to have a cinch," he added.

"Then you dont think we'll win it?" Col Delbert said.

"I didnt say that, Sir," said Capt Holmes.

"Well," the Col said, "either you think we'll win it, or you dont think we'll win it. Dont you?"

"Yes, Sir," Holmes said.

"Then which?"

"What?" Holmes said. "Oh, we'll win it, Sir."

"Good. Good," the Col said. "There hasnt been enough work put on athletics here the last two years."

Capt Holmes considered carefully. "Yes, Sir," he said. "But I think all we coaches did our best."

The Col nodded, emphatically. "Think so too. But we 've got to get results. Our S-3 training is all very fine, soldiers need to drill to keep them busy. But in peacetime we both know its our athletic programs that keep us before the public's eye. Particularly here in the Islands where there are no big time sports. Have talked to the rest of our athletic heads, except for you; your season isnt over yet. Am relieving Major Simmons from football."

The Col smiled significantly and the little mustache became a chicken hawk. "Results. Results what counts. He has requested reassignment to the Mainland, of course," he added.

Capt Holmes nodded, thinking fast. This was recent. Today. Or he would have heard about it. That left a majority open—unless they imported somebody. Of course, the rating wasnt open, but the job was, and if a man got appointed to the job it would probably mean his own promotion would be recommended.

The Col placed his big hands flat upon the serenity of his desk. "Well," he said. "What was it you wanted, 'Dynamite'?"

Holmes had almost forgotten what he came for. "Oh," he said. "One of my old men, Sir. Came to see me a week ago. Wants to transfer up here with me. He's at Fort Kamehameha, Coast Artillery. Served with me at Bliss. I wanted to see you about him so I could be sure it went through all right."

The little mustache flapped its wings slyly. "Another fighter, eh. We 're little over strength, but it can be arranged. I 'll even write letter to Department on 't."

Capt Holmes bent down to pat the Colonel's dog. "Why, no, Sir. He's not a fighter. He's a cook. A good man, though. Best cook I ever had."

"Oh," the Col said.

"He served with me at Bliss, Sir. I'll vouch for him personally."

"I 'll have it attended to," Col Delbert said. "Tell me, how 's that outfit of yours getting along? Still balling the jack? Your company interests me. It proves my theory: good athletes make good noncoms and good leaders; good leaders make a good organization. Simple logic. Plenty of cattle in this world, that have to be driven. But without good leaders nothing 's ever accomplished."

Capt Holmes's eyes went opaque and out of focus with his shyness. "I flatter myself, Sir," he smiled, "that I have the most efficient outfit in the Regiment."

"Yes. Now First Sergeant Warden is an example of my logic. An all around athlete before he—ah—took up the grail, as I call it."

Capt Holmes laughed.

"I imagine he bitches a lot," the Col said, "but a *good* soldier always bitches. Good for him. Good soldiers are born—born wild and wooly, like Sergeant Warden. Only time to worry about a good soldier is when he stops bitching. My grandfather taught me that."

Capt Holmes nodded vigorously. "Yes, Sir," he said, although this philosophy had not originated with the Colonel's grandfather. It was widespread and he had heard it all before. But it was good. That about Warden, particularly, was so true. He was feeling better.

Col Delbert suddenly brought his swivel chair back up level and scooted it up to the desk. He spoke sharply.

"Now tell me, Captain: Just what are your prospects for next year? You say you'll win this year, so we'll dismiss that. You're as good as your word with me, sir. But if we are to win we must begin to plan early. That 's a maxim, my grandfather. Winning this year is not enough. We must plan on winning next year. In this world it is the winner who gets spoils. I dont know about the next world but I imagine it 's the same thing there, in spite of what our skypilots tell us. Would you say we 've a good chance of winning?"

Capt Holmes felt suddenly hedged in. There was a condition attached to the majority, provided of course he won this year, and he was being pinned down for it.

"Well, yes, Sir," he said.

"As good a chance as we have now? of winning this year?"

"Well, Sir. No. I wouldnt say exactly that." Capt Holmes racked his brain. "We're due to lose three Class I boys, Sir, you know, as short timers."

"Ah," the Col said. "I know. But you still have Sgt Wilson and Sgt O'Hayer. Do we have nothing else by way of replacement?"

"I have one new man who did fairly well this year in the Bowl. Pvt

Bloom. I'm thinking of grooming him for a shot at the middleweight next year."

The Col kept staring at him and his eyes kept slipping out of focus off the Colonel's face, hard as he tried to keep them there. His left cheek itched and he wished he had a stick of gum. But then he could not chew it. He wished he'd never come up here in the first place.

"Bloom?" the Col said. "Bloom. Great big Jewish boy with a flat head and kinky hair? And that 's all?"

"Well, Sir, no, Sir. I wanted to ask you about that, I have no heavyweight worth a damn. Corporal Choate was Heavyweight Champion of Panama not so long ago. I've been trying to get him to go out ever since I came here."

"Ah," the Col said. "He wont go out."

"No, Sir."

"Corporal Choate is probably the best firstbaseman in the Islands. We dont want to lose our firstbaseman, do we?"

"No, Sir."

"I 'm afraid you could n't count on Choate."

Capt Holmes nodded. The baseball team would lose out anyway, but they wanted you to win. They always wanted you to win. The winner gets the gravy. The Colonel's goddamned dog was still boredly asleep, hind legs spread flat and belly to the floor, front legs crossed as nonchalantly as a male lead in morning trousers. Every officer in the Regiment had to coddle the little bastard.

Why dont you chuck it, Holmes? he thought. And do what? Go where?

"I have one new man, Sir," he said, though he had meant to save this one back. "Name is Prewitt. Fought for the 27th. Runnerup in the welterweight division. He was transferred to my Company from the Bugle Corps."

The fatherly smile appeared. "Well now, fine. That 's fine. You say he was *in* the Regiment? in the *Bugle Corps?*"

Holmes was tired. "Yes, Sir." That damned smug dog. "Been here a year." Sleeping and eating and allowing himself to be coddled. "Ever since last boxing season." Son of a bitching little fat dog with such a goddamned easy life.

"Remarkable!" the Col said. "In the Bugle Corps. Too bad we didnt know about it this year. Could have used him. But then no one ever knows who 's in the Bugle Corps. You've talked to him?"

"Yes, Sir," Holmes said. Might as well give him all of it, now. "He refuses to go out." If you had an ounce of guts, Holmes, you would have added, "too."

Col Delbert turned his head on stiff shoulders. "He cant refuse to go out."

"He did, Sir." Capt Holmes realized he had made an error. He didnt give a damn, to hell with it. Still, where would you go? He refrained from mentioning the Company Bugler job.

"No, he did n't," the Col said precisely. His eyes were curiously flat. "You just think he did. It 's your job to see th't he does go out.

"If he knew it was for the Regiment's sake he would want to go out. All you have to do is convince him. Let him know how much the Regiment needs him."

The Regiment, Capt Holmes thought. Thats all. The honor and reputation of the Regiment. Col Delbert's Regiment. And he doesnt even want to know why he wont go out. At least I asked him that, he told himself. You already knew it, himself said.

The fatherly smile lubricated the flatted eyes, creating a peculiarly imperfect picture. "If you 're going to need the man, you must convince him.

"And from what you 've told me I gather you will need him?"

"I could certainly use him, Sir."

"Then convince him. I might as well be frank. We have *got* to win that next year. Because that is all we *can* win. Keep that in mind. I want you to keep your hand in. A few workouts now and then. You can have the gym afternoons now and then. Start building now. That 's important: Plan Now."

"Yes, Sir," Capt Holmes said. "I'll start in soon."

But his voice was overwhelmed by the screek of an opening drawer, the traditional indication that the interview was ended. Col Delbert raised his eyes from the drawer and looked at Holmes inquiringly, but Capt Holmes was already on his feet replacing the chair against the wall. Anyway, he had gotten a green light on Stark's transfer and that was what he came for.

The wood noises woke the cocker and he rose and stretched himself, one leg at a time, unrolling his pink tongue in an insolent yawn. He licked his chops and stared at Holmes accusingly. Holmes stared back, lost in sudden thought, his hand still on the chair, enviously watching the sleek black wellfed arrogance stretch itself back out on the polished floor and resume its interrupted meditation. He remembered his hand on the chair then, removed it, turned around for the impersonal ritual of saluting. With all its time-stopping associations of the Point, and God, it seemed to draw him in again to the Old Man, by its very deliberateness. But he knew it did not change anything.

"Oh," the Col said, as Holmes reached the door. "How is Miss Karen getting along? She feeling better?"

"She's feeling a little better lately," Capt Holmes said, turning back. The Colonel's eyes had lost their flatness and become deep, very deep with a little red light at the bottom.

"A fine lady," Col Delbert said. "Last time I saw her was at General Hendricks' party at the Club. My wife is giving a bridge party this week. She would like to have her come."

Capt Holmes forced himself to shake his head. "I know she'd be delighted," he said, "but I doubt very much if she'll be feeling up to it, Sir. She's none too strong, you know. Things like that excite her so."

"Ah," the Col said. "Too bad. Told my wife I was afraid of that. Ah, will she be feeling well enough by the time the Brigadier's party comes up?"

"I hope so, Sir," Capt Holmes said. "I know how badly she would hate to miss it."

"Ah," the Col said. "Certainly hope'll be able to come. We all enjoy her company so much. Charmin' lady, really, Captain."

"Thank you, Sir," Capt Holmes said, not looking back at that red light at the bottom of the deepness.

"By the way, Captain, I 'm giving another little stag next week. I 've secured the same apartment upstairs at the Club. You 're invited, of course."

Holmes's eyes went opaque again as he grinned, shamefacedly. "I'll be there, Sir."

"Ah," the Col said, opening his mouth and tilting back his head and looking at the other down his nose. "Fine. Good. Thats good." He opened another of his desk drawers.

Capt Holmes left.

The stag made him feel a little better, in spite of the pinning down. How could anyone say positively who would win? But at least he wasnt on the shitlist yet, those stags were exclusive, nothing but rank there.

But down deep it did not change a thing and the porch and stairs, as he went down going home now to lunch, had lost their sense of permanence. Some day he would be reassigned, back to the States he hoped, anyway some place where there was Cavalry again. What a wild idea this had been, this going in the Infantry just to do a tour in the Islands, the goddamned Paradise of the Pacific.

Still, he told himself, it isnt as if you're going to spend the rest of your life in Schofield Barracks. What can he do?

He would have to speak to Karen, though. The Colonel would want her at the Brigadier's party. He would have to talk her into going, some way. If she would only consent to be nice to the old duffer, it might mean the majority even if the squad lost, this year or next. He didnt want her to sleep with him or anything like that. Just be nice to him.

Walking out the truck entrance he returned the salutes of several privates coming from the PX without seeing them, and crossed the street to the house.

Chapter 6

Karen Holmes was absorbed in the brushing of her long blonde hair when she heard the back door slam and the heavy tread of Holmes across the kitchen floor.

She had been brushing it now almost an hour, rapt in the purely sensual pleasure of it that required no thought, free for once in this that did not make her think of freedom, alive to these long golden hairs that singly and in masses curved themselves about the stiff long bristles of the brush, until it had, as she desired, entranced her, away from all of it. Away where nothing else existed but this mirror in which she saw the rhythm of this moving arm that was herself.

That was why she loved to brush her hair so. She loved to cook, too; for the same reason. She was an excellent cook, when she felt like it. She also read voraciously. She could even enjoy the poor books, when she had to. She was not, accurately, of the stuff from which an Army wife is made.

The slamming door broke the rapture, and she found that she was staring into the eyes of her own deathmask, pale and wan with all the blood sucked out by a modern vampire called Embalmer, leaving only the gashed bloody wound that was her lipsticked mouth. It was urging her to hurry up and find the thing.

Leave me, Mask, she said at it.

If, replied the Mask, you shrink from evil when its cloak is flung upon your shoulders, the more closely will it wrap its suffocating folds around you.

She laid aside the brush and covered with her hands the face that haunted her most of all with its futility of emptiness, hearing the footsteps of Military Doom coming swift across the dining room.

Holmes barged into the room, his hat still on his head.

"Oh," he said, guiltily. "Hello. I didnt know you were home. I just came in to change my uniform."

Karen picked up the brush and went back to her hair. "The car is parked outside," she said.

"It is?" Holmes said. "I didnt see it."

"I went over to the Company this morning," Karen said, "looking for you."

"What for?" Holmes said. "You know I dont like to have you over there, around the men."

"I wanted you to get some things for me," she lied. "I thought you'd be there."

"I had some business to attend to before I went in," Holmes lied. He undid his tie and threw it on the bed and sat down with the boot jack. Karen did not answer. "That *was* all right, wasnt it?" he protested.

"But of course," she said. "I have no right to inquire into your actions. That was the agreement."

"Then why bring it up?"

"Because I wanted you to know I'm not as stupid as you maintain all women are."

Holmes stood the boots up by the bed and stripped off sweatdamp shirt and breeches. "Now what does that mean? What are you accusing me of now?"

"Of nothing," Karen smiled. "Its no longer any of my business how many you go out with, is it? But I wish for God's sake you could just be honest about it once."

"Now," he cried disgustedly, seeing the excitement of the riding date fading rapidly before him. "Now! All I did was come home to change my uniform and get some lunch. Thats all."

"I thought," she said, "you didnt know I was here."

"I didnt, goddam it. I just thought, you might be here," he finished lamely, flustered at being caught up in the lie. "God damn," he blustered. "Other women. What brings that on this time? How many times do I have to tell you I havent any other women before you'll believe me?"

"Dana," Karen said. "Give me credit for a little brains." She laughed, and looking in the mirror, broke off suddenly, shocked at the hatred that was on her face.

"If I had them," he said, self pity in his voice, putting on fresh socks, "dont you think I'd admit it to you? Theres no reason I should try to hide it, is there? the way things are between us now?" he asked her bitterly. "What right have you to always be accusing me of that?"

"What right?" Karen said, looking at him in the mirror.

Under the indictment of her eyes Holmes cringed. "All right," he said dejectedly. "*That* again. How long will it be, I wonder, before I am allowed to live *that* down? How many times do I have to tell you, It Was An Accident?"

"That makes it all all right, I suppose," she said. "That takes all the scars away, and we can just pretend it didnt happen."

"I didnt say that," Holmes cried. "I know what its done to you. But how was I to know? I didnt know it myself until too late. What more is there for me to say, except I'm sorry?" Looking back at her in the mirror he tried to be indignant, but had to drop his eyes. The uniform on the floor shamed him with the existence of the wet spots of his body water on its cloth.

"Please, Dana," Karen said shrilly, franticness in her voice. "You know how much I hate to talk about it. I'm trying to forget it."

"All right," Holmes said. "You brought it up. I dont like to think about it either, but neither one of us will ever be allowed to forget it. I've lived with it for eight years now." He stood up wearily, walking to the closet for another uniform, temporarily defeated. All the anticipation of this afternoon's adventure was gone now, hardly seeming worth the trouble.

"So have I lived with it," Karen called after him. "You got off easy. At least it didnt scar you any."

Furtively, on the side away from him, privately, she slipped her hand down to her belly, feeling with her fingers the thick ridge of the scar. There lies the evil, she thought hysterically, the grape torn open and the seed plucked out and left withering on the vine. All the foulness of all the soppy secret dampness, the sliding slippery airless dark came back on her now and overwhelmed her as the gaseous bubble burst in her mind, scenting it with the memory of foulness that she must escape.

In the closet Holmes made up his mind to go riding anyway, whether he wanted to or not, because to hell with it and he'd take a bottle. Under the unpleasantness he dreaded he grinned back at himself.

When he stepped out in fresh underwear the change in him was already apparent. The dejection and the guilt were gone and in their place was sureness. He had assumed the hangdog air of a synthetic plaintiveness that was his last defense that always wrested victory from the acceptance of defeat.

Karen recognized the attitude. In the mirror she could see him in his underwear, massive, hairy, legs bowed grotesquely by so many hours on a horse—at Bliss he had been the captain of the polo team—and the thick black hair on his chest padding out the T shirt like excelsior a cushion. His face, heavy bearded, had that gross blue sensuality of a fecund priest, and the same proud-suffering air. He had only shaved below his collarline, and the black curls reached up to the shaved neck like living flames sucked up a flue. Her stomach flopped in her sickeningly, like a big fish slimy on the hook, at the sight of him who was her husband. She moved along the seat before the dressing table until she could no longer see his reflection.

"I saw Colonel Delbert this morning," Holmes said. "He asked me if we were coming to General Hendricks' party." His big jaw set, watching her levelly, he moved over to where his image was before her in the mirror again, casually, as he was putting on the breeches.

Karen watched him do it, knowing what he was doing now, yet still unable to keep her nerves from jangling like a plucked guitar string.

"We'll have to go," he said. "Theres no way out of it. Also, his wife is having another tea; I got you out of that."

"You can get me out of the other, too," Karen said, but her tone had lost its commanding air and was half-hearted. "If you want to go, go by yourself."

"I cant keep on going by myself forever," Holmes said plaintively.

"You can if you tell them I'm sick, which will be the truth. Let them think I'm an invalid, I'm near enough one to make it ethical."

"Simmons has been shipped down from football," he said. "That leaves a majority open. The Old Man told me about it, then asked if you werent coming to the party."

"The last time I went to a party where he was, you remember, I came home with my gown torn nearly off."

"He was a little tight," Holmes said. "He didnt really mean anything by it."

"I hope not," Karen said thinly. "If I wanted a man to sleep with I'd *pick* a man, not that beery tub of guts."

"I'm serious," Holmes said, transferring the insignia from the dirty shirt to the clean one. "Your being nice to him might mean all the difference now, since this Simmons thing has opened up."

"I've helped you with your work all I can," she said. "You know I have. I've gone to parties I've hated. Its been my part of the bargain, to play the loving wife. But the one thing I wont do is sleep with Colonel Delbert for you."

"Nobody wants you to. All I'm asking is that you be decent to him."

"You cant be decent with a lecherous old roué. It makes me physically sick." Unconsciously, she picked up the brush and began to brush her hair again, distractedly.

"A majority is worth getting physically sick over," Holmes said, pleadingly. "A man with a majority now, if he graduated from the Point, will be a General officer when this war thats coming ends. All you have to do is smile and listen to him talk about his grandfather."

"A smile, to him, is only an invitation to put his hands between your legs. He's got a wife. Why doesnt he take it out on her?"

"Yes," Holmes said tautly. "Why doesnt he?"

Karen winced before the accusation, even knowing it was purely theoretical. Before this melancholy suffering-lover role the nerve ends of her body vibrated shatteringly.

"It was your part of our agreement," Holmes said sadly.

"All right," she said. "All right. I'll go. There I said it, now lets talk about something else."

"What are we having for lunch?" Holmes said. "I'm hungry, hungry as hell. I've had one hell of a day, listening to Delbert. He can talk your leg off. Then having to argue half the morning with the kitchen force, and this new transfer Prewitt." He looked at her closely. "It completely exhausts me nervously."

She waited until he finished. "You know this is the maid's day off."

Holmes's eyes crinkled painfully. "Is it? By god! What is today? Thursday? I thought today was Wednesday." He looked hopefully at his watch, then shrugged. "Well, its too late to go up to the Club now. Wouldnt I do it though?"

Karen, feeling him watching her closely, tried to go on brushing to escape the sense of guilt because she was not offering to fix a lunch for him. He never ate lunch at home and it was not in her part of the bargain they had made, yet still he was making her feel like a heartless criminal.

"I guess I'll just have to catch one of those lousy sandwiches at the PX," Holmes said resignedly. He fidgeted around a minute and sat down on the bed. "What do you eat for lunch?" he said with the air of one who shamefacedly makes a great imposition.

"I usually just fix soup for myself," Karen said, breathing deeply.

"Oh," he said. "You know I dont eat soup."

"You asked me, didnt you?" she said, trying to keep her voice from going higher. "I fix myself soup. Why should I lie?"

Holmes got up hastily. "Now, darling," he said. "Now take it easy. I'll just go on over to the PX. I dont mind. You know what it does to you to get upset. You just cant stand it. You'll have yourself sick in bed."

"Theres nothing wrong with me," she protested. "I'm no bedfast invalid," thinking how he had no right to use that word with her, to call her darling. He always did it, in these spells, and the word was like a skewer pinning her to the beaverboard among the other butterflies of his collection. In her imagination she saw herself rising up, telling him what she thought of him, packing a bag and leaving, to live her own life and earn her own way. She would get a job and an apartment someplace. What kind of a job? she asked herself. In your physical condition what can you do? what training have you? Besides to be a wife.

"You know your nerves arent strong, darling," Holmes was saying. "Just quiet down now and take it easy. Just relax." He walked over and put his hands soothingly on her shoulders, gripping them affectionately and lightly, and looking solicitously into her eyes in the mirror.

Karen felt them on her, holding her down, tying her down, as her life was tied down, and she had the same sensation she remembered having as a child when out in the woods she had caught her dress on the barbs of a wire fence, and she had lunged and plunged and pulled until she got loose leaving half her dress behind, even though her mother was coming all the time to help her.

"Thats it, relax," Holmes smiled. "Now you just fix yourself lunch the way you would if I wasnt here and I'll eat whatever you have for yourself. Now. Hows that?"

"I can fix you a toasted cheese sandwich," Karen said weakly.

"Okay," he smiled. "Cheese will be fine."

He followed her out to the kitchen and while she got the lunch ready, sat at the kitchen table following her with his eyes. When she measured out the coffee, his eyes watched her solicitously. When she greased the skillet and set it on the burner, his eyes watched her, carefully protecting. Karen prided herself on her cooking, it was her only art and she had learned to do it well and with the least amount of wasted time and motion. But now, for some reason, she forgot about the coffee, and it boiled over. When she grabbed up the pot she burnt her hand.

Holmes jumped up with magnificent speed and grabbed a dishtowel to wipe up the stove. "Now, now," he said. "Just forget it. I'll clean it up. You sit down. You're worn out."

Karen put her hands up to her face. "No, I'm not," she said. "Just let me fix it. I'm sorry I boiled it. I can fix it all right. Please. Let me fix it."

It was then she smelled the smoke. She caught the cheese sandwich just in time to keep it from burning. It was black on one side.

"Thats all right," Holmes smiled bravely. "Now just forget it, darling. I dont want you to get upset. This is perfectly all right."

"Let me scrape it for you," Karen said.

"No, no. Its perfectly all right like this. This is good. It really is."

He chomped on the sandwich to show how fine it was. He ate it with gusto. He did not drink any coffee.

"I'll catch a cup at the PX," he smiled. "I have to go back over to the Company to sign some papers anyway. You go in and lie down and get some rest. It was really a fine lunch, truly it was."

Karen stood in the screendoor watching him go down the alley. After he was gone she went back in the bedroom. She put her hands down at her sides and forced herself to relax them. She coughed once or twice, rackingly, but she did not cry. She made herself breathe deeply. She relaxed her muscles, but the nerves inside them went on fluttering frantically.

Furtively, as if it had an intelligence of its own, her hand moved up to her stomach and touched the ridge of scar tissue, and the horror she held of her own body, of the pusiness, of the cheesy degenerations, began to rise up queasily. The grape torn open and the seed plucked out, withering before it ever came to fruition.

That isnt so, she told herself, you know it isnt so. You've borne his heir for him, who can say your life is fruitless? How can you be fruitless? You've been a mother, havent you?

There must be more, there must be, something told her, someplace, somewhere, there must be another reason, above, beyond, somewhere another Equation beside this virgin+marriage+motherhood+grand-motherhood = honor, justification, death. There must be another language, forgotten unheard unspoken, than the owning of an American's Homey Kitchen complete with dinette, breakfast nook, and fluorescent lighting.

Among the broken bathroom fixtures and the sticky brightly colored rainwashed labels on the emptied cans, Karen Holmes was searching through the city dump of civilization, desperately hunting for her life, and the muck she got upon her fingers didnt matter.

There was so much of it already, Karen felt, upon her.

Chapter 7

Prewitt was sitting on his bunk waiting for chow, playing solitaire to forget the sense of strangeness, when Anderson and Clark, the G Company buglers, came in the big unsympathetic squadroom. He had carted his stuff over from A Company and stowed it, made up the bare mattress into a precisely square-cornered bunk, arranged his uniforms in the wall locker, rolled a neat combat pack and old timer's envelope roll, set his shoes and foot locker on the stand, and he was home. He had put on a clean suit of tailormade blue fatigues and sat down with the cards. In less than half an hour he had accomplished what it would have taken a recruit like Maggio doubtful hours to accomplish, but it had been unpleasant and he did not feel satisfied. It was always unpleasant, moving like this; it always brought home to you the essential rootlessness of yourself and all men like you, always on the move, never really stopping anywhere, never really home. But you could forget anything with solitaire, for a while at least; solitaire was the game of exiles.

Prewitt knew the G Company buglers by sight. He put down his cards and watched them cross the squadroom. He had seen and listened to them playing their guitars evenings around the quad; they were much better on the guitars than they were on the bugle. . . .

The instinctive judgment swept him with the air and atmosphere of the Corps and he felt a sudden wave of unbearable homesickness. The smell of the ball diamond bleachers during the morning drill period with the sun shining brightly on the weathered wood. The heavy bleats from the different-pitched bugles, drifting up to the golf course on the wind, rolling metallically into the edge of the woods. The many bugles conflicting, the calls begun in confidence and then left hanging doubtfully unfinished. And now and then the rare well-executed phrase, rising over all, sharp, insistent, catching the moment and the mood and carrying them to distant unseen ears. He felt a hunger for the acrid smell of metal polish that hung about his bugle as he played.

Almost enviously he watched the two men pass between the rows of bunks. It was eleven and the Corps had been dismissed. They were through for the day. It was a standing joke in the Corps about the way these two watched the clock. They were always the first to leave the bleachers and sprinted back to the barracks so they could have an hour alone to practice before the Company came in from drill.

But bugling meant nothing to them, except as a means to escape straight duty and to get more time to practice on guitars. They wanted to play guitars, but there were no chairs for guitars in the Regimental Band. These two possessed the things that Prewitt valued, but they wanted something else instead. It seemed the very fact they did not want what they had led life to conspire to help them keep it; and he who loved to bugle had to give it up because he loved it. It was not right.

Anderson stopped when he saw Prewitt. He seemed to be debating whether to go on or to go back out. He made up his mind, and passed by without speaking, his deepset eyes sullenly on the floor. Clark stopped when Anderson stopped and looked at his mentor to see what he would do. When Anderson went on he followed, but he could not disregard Prewitt's eyes. He nodded embarrassedly, his long Italian nose almost hiding his shy smile.

They dragged out their guitars and began to play furiously, as if by putting their souls into it they could dispel the alien presence. After a while their playing tapered off and finally stopped and they looked in Prewitt's direction. Then they went into a huddle.

Listening to them play Prewitt realized for the first time how good they really were. He had never paid much attention to them before but being in their Company suddenly made him aware of them as individuals. Even their faces were subtly changed, were the faces of different men, no longer indistinct. It was a thing he had noted before: how you could live beside a man for years and have no positive picture of him, until you were suddenly thrown into his company to find that he was not just a vague personality but an individual with an individual's life.

Anderson and Clark came out of their huddle and put their guitars away. They passed by Prewitt again, without speaking, and went on into the latrine at the end of the porch. They were deliberately avoiding him. Prewitt lit a tailormade cigaret and stared at it impassively, acutely aware of being the stranger.

He was sorry they had stopped playing. They played his kind of songs—blues songs, and hillbilly music—the kind of music the ex-bums and field laborers and factory workers who had tried to escape their barren lives by enlisting in the Army understood and always played. Prewitt picked up his cards and started to deal himself a new game when he heard the two guitar players walking back down the porch toward the stairs.

"What the hell you think?" part of Anderson's indignant protest came through the open door. "The best goddam bugler in the Regiment for Chrisake!"

"Yeah, but he wouldnt . . ." Clark said perplexedly; the rest was only a mumble as they passed beyond the door.

Prewitt dropped his cards and threw the cigaret to the floor. He moved swiftly and caught them on the stairs.

"Come back here," he said.

Anderson's head, amputated by the floor level, turned to face him with consternation, a balloon in suspension. The ominous insistence made his legs carry him back up the stairs before his mind had decided what to do. Clark tagged reluctantly along after his mental guide, without choice.

Prewitt wasted no time on preliminaries. "I dont want your goddamned job," he said in a low white voice. "If I'd wanted to bugle, I'd of stayed right where I was. Its a cinch I wouldnt come here and cut you out of your stinkin little job."

Anderson shifted his feet evasively. "Well," he said uneasily, without meeting Prewitt's eyes, "you're good enough you could get my job any time you wanted."

"I know it," Prewitt said. A white wall of anger descended over his eyes like the polar icecap descending over the globe. "But I never check a cinch into nobody—outside of a game. I dont play that way, see? If I wanted the goddam job, I wouldnt sneak in here and cutthroat you out of it."

"Okay," Anderson said placatingly. "Okay, Prew. Take it easy."

"Dont call me Prew."

Clark stood silently by, grinning embarrassedly, his soft eyes wide, looking from one to the other like the spectator at a wreck who watches a man bleed to death because he doesnt know what he should do and fears making a fool of himself.

Prewitt had meant to say that Holmes had offered him the job and he had turned it down, but some look in Anderson's eyes touched his mind and made him hold it back.

"Nobody likes to do straight duty," Anderson said lamely; you never

64

could tell about a fireball like Prewitt. "I know I aint as good as you are when you played a Taps at Arlington. You could get my job easy, and it wouldnt be a square thing." It ended up in the air as if unfinished.

"I dont want you to get down sick," Prewitt said. "You can quit worrying about it now."

"Well . . . thanks, Prew," Anderson said painfully. "I dont want you to think I . . . I mean I didnt . . ."

"Go to hell," Prewitt said. "And dont call me Prew. I'm Prewitt to you." He turned on his heel and went back inside. He picked up his cigaret that was still burning on the cement floor and took a deep drag, listening to their slow steps on the stairs. With a sudden movement of bitterness he picked up some of the scattered cards and ripped them across. Then he threw them down on the bed. Unsatisfied, he picked up the rest of the deck and methodically tore each card in two. Might as well; they were no good now anyway. A hell of a fine start; as if he would try to rob them out of a stinking twobit job.

He pulled his mouthpiece out of his pocket and sat, hefting it in his hand, running his thumb over the cup. It was a fine mouthpiece; it was undoubtedly the best investment he ever made for thirty bucks of crap money.

He wished the weekend would hurry up and come, so he could get out of this screwedup rathole and go up to Haleiwa and see Violet. A lot of guys went around bragging about a shackjob here and a shackjob there. Very few of them were ever lucky enough to have one. They all talked about it, trying to convince each other and themselves of the wonderful women they had—and then they went down to the Service Rooms or the New Congress and had their ashes hauled at three dollars a throw. Prewitt knew how lucky he was to have Violet to shack up with him.

He sat on his bunk, angry and disgusted, waiting for chow, waiting for the weekend.

On the way to the PX Clark kept looking at Anderson sideways. Several times he started to speak.

"You dint have no call to think that, Andy," he blurted out finally. "He's a good joe. You can see he's a good joe."

"I know it, goddam it," Andy burst out. "For Chrisake, shut up about it. I know he's a good joe."

"Okay," Clark said. "Okay. We'll be late for chow."

"To hell with it," Andy said.

When the chow whistle blew Prew went down in the thronging crowd that stampeded for the messhall. They swarmed down the stairs and clustered on the porch before the door that would not admit them fast enough, looking like good material for a recruiting poster with their shining laughing faces and clean hands and fatigue blouses splashed with water, for unless you knew them or looked closely you did not see the black high-water mark around their wrists or the line of dust that ran down from their temples past their ears and on their necks. There was much goosing, grabbing of crotches and accusations of "You eat it!" with the hooting laughter. But Prew was outside of all of it.

Two or three men whose names he knew spoke to him soberly with great reserve and then turned back to share their laughter with the others. G Company was a single personality formed by many men, but he was not a part of it. Amid the gnash and clash of cutlery on china and the humming conversation he ate in silence, feeling from time to time the many curious eyes inspecting him.

After chow they wandered back upstairs by twos and threes, subdued now and with full bellies, the boisterousness caused by the prospect of an hour's recess replaced now by the unpleasant prospect of Fatigue Call and working on full bellies. The scattered horseplay that broke out now died in infancy, bayoneted by the cynical glances of the others.

Prew took his plate and got in the line to the kitchen, scraped his slops off in the muggy bucket, dropped his plate and cup into the hectic scrabbling KP's sink where Maggio paused long enough to wink at him, and went back up to his bunk. He lit a cigaret and dropped the match into the coffee can he had hunted up to serve as ashtray and stretched out on the bunk with all the sounds around him. His arm behind his head, and smoking, he saw Chief Choate coming toward him.

The huge Indian of full Choctaw blood, slow-spoken, slow-moving, level-eyed, dead-faced—except when in the midst of some athletic battle and then as swift as any panther—sat down on the bunk beside him, with a shy brief grin. They would have shaken hands, under these new circumstances, if it had not been a conventionalism that embarrassed both of them.

The sight of Chief's great slow bulk that exuded confidence and calm for a radius of twenty yards about him, wherever he might be, brought back to Prew all the mornings they had sat in Choy's with Red and argued over breakfast. He looked at Chief wishing there was some way to communicate all the memories, to tell him how glad he was to be in his squad, without embarrassing both of them.

All last fall, during the football season when Chief Choate was excused from drill, almost every morning, they had, with Red, had their breakfasts together in Choy's restaurant, the two buglers on Special Duty and the big Indian who was excused from drill because it was football season. After he had got to know the bulky moon-faced Choctaw, he had gone religiously to every game and every meet the Indian participated in, which was almost every one, because Wayne Choate jockstrapped the whole year round. Football in the fall where Chief played guard and was the only player on the team who could stand a full sixty minutes of the Army's brand of football; in the winter it was basketball and Chief playing guard again, the third highest scorer in the Regiment; and in the summer baseball, Chief playing, some said, the best first base in the whole of the Army; and track in the spring, where Chief was always good for a 1st or 2nd in the shotput and the javelin and worth a few more points in the dashes. In his youth before he had acquired a GI beer paunch Chief had set a record for the 100 yards in the Philippine Department that still stood unbroken, but that had been some years ago.

He had never pulled a single day's fatigue in his four years in the Company, and if he had consented to fight for Holmes he would have been a Staff Sergeant in two weeks. No one knew why he did not transfer to some other company where he could better himself or why he did not fight for Holmes, because he did not talk about his reasons. Instead of bettering himself, he stayed in G Company, a perennial Corporal, and drank himself into a stupor every night in Choy's on beer so that on an average of three times a week he had to have a five-man detail come and get him and cart him home in one of the steel-wheeled machinegun carts.

He had a foot locker full of gold medals from PI, Panama, and Puerto Rico upon which he drew for beer money when he was broke, selling them or pawning them to various wouldbe athletes on the Post, and every time he moved on to a new post left a wastebasket full of athletic citations behind him. His fans and admirers all over Honolulu would have been shocked to see him bleary-eyed every night in Choy's with his enormous gut drum-tight full of unbelievable amounts of beer.

Prew watched him now, thinking wonderingly of all these things, and since he could not say the things he wanted to say, waiting for him to speak.

"The Top says you're put in my squad," Chief said, in his solemn bearlike way. "So I figured I come over and give you the Story on the outfit."

"Okay," Prew said. "Shoot 'em."

"Ike Galovitch is the platoon guide."

"I've heard a little about him," Prew said, "already."

"You'll hear more about him," Chief said with slow solemnity. "He's quite a character. He's acting platoon sergeant now. Wilson is the regular platoon sergeant but he's excused from drill durin fightin season. You wont see much of him till March."

"What kind of a guy is this Champ Wilson?" Prew said.

"He's all right," Chief said slowly, "if you understand him. He never talks much, nor runs around with anybody. You ever see him fight?"

"Yeah," Prew said. "He's tough."

"If you seen him fight, you know as much about him as anybody does. He buddies around with Sgt Henderson who takes care of Holmes's horses. They served together in Holmes's company in Bliss."

"Way he fights," Prew said, "looks like he's got a mean streak in him."

Chief looked at him levelly. "Maybe he does," he said. "If a man leaves him alone though, he aint no trouble. He dont bother much with anybody, unless they argue with him, then he's just as liable to pull his rank and turn them in as not. I've seen him ride a couple guys right into the Stockade."

"Okay," Prew said. "Thanks."

"You won't see much of me around here," Chief said. "Galovitch takes all the responsibilities in this platoon. Even when Wilson's here, Old Ike does all the work. The only thing you're responsible to me for is I have to check your stuff for Sataday morning inspection, but Old Ike checks everybody himself anyway, after the corporals turn in their report, so its the same thing."

"What do you do around here then?" Prew grinned.

"Nothin much. Old Ike does it all. There really aint no need for corporals in this Compny, because there really aint no squads. Everything is by platoons, instead of squads. We fall out for drill by platoons, not squads."

"You mean we dont have any squad roster at all? No BAR men or rifle grenadiers? We just fall out any way?"

"Thats right," Chief said slowly. "Oh, we got them, on the books. But when we fall out the corporals git at the head of the column and everybody else just falls in any way."

"Hell," Prew said. "What kind of soldierin is that? Back at Myer we'd line up everybody in his proper position in each squad."

"This heres the Pineapple Army," Chief said.

"I dont know whether I like that or not," Prew said.

"I dint figure you would," Chief said. "But thats the way she is. Old Ike ought to be around pretty soon, to inspect you, and tell you what your duties is. The only time a corporal really has charge of his men here is in the morning when his squad is on latrine police, but Old Ike is always there to check it anyway."

"This Galovitch must be quite a guy."

Chief pulled a sack of Durham from the pocket of his shirt and dropped his eyes to it. "He is," he said. He rolled a cigaret very delicately with his sausage fingers. "He was at Bliss with Holmes too. Use to be the boiler orderly. Took care of the boilers in the winter. I think

68

maybe he had a Pfc." He lit the brown thin lumpy cigaret and dropped the match in Prew's can, took several drags. But he did not look at Prew, instead he watched the exhaled smoke blandly. "Old Ike is our Close Order expert. On the Drill Schedule we got an hour's Close Order every morning. Galovitch always gives it." The rolled cigaret burned down quickly and Chief dropped it in the can, still not looking up.

"Okay," Prew said. "What is it? Whats eatin on you?"

"Who? me?" Chief said. "Why, nothin. I was just wonderin if you aimed to start trainin now, this late in the season, or if you meant to wait till summer and be eligible for Company Smokers."

"Neither one," Prew said. "I aint doin any fightin."

"Oh," Chief said noncommittally. "I see."

"You think I'm crazy, hunh?" Prew said.

"No," the other said. "I guess not. It kind of surprised me though, when I heard you'd quit the Bugle Corps, a man who plays a bugle the way you do."

"Well," Prew said savagely, "I quit it. And I aint sorry. And I aint doin no fightin. And I aint sorry about that either."

"Then I guess you aint got nothin to worry about, have you?" Chief said.

"Not a goddam thing."

Chief stood up and moved over to the bunk next to Prewitt's. "I think thats Galovitch comin now. I figured he'd be along."

Prew raised his head to look. "Say, Chief. Is this guy Maggio in whose squad, anyway? The little Wop."

"Mine," Chief said. "Why?"

"I just like him. Met him this morning. I'm glad he's in your squad."

"He's a good boy. He's only out of recruit drill a month, and he messes up and catches all the extra details, but he's a good boy. He's got a plenty big sense of humor for such a little guy, keeps everybody laughin all the time."

Galovitch was walking toward them down the aisle. Prew watched him and was astounded. He came on between the bunks, bigfooted, bentkneed, bobbing his trunk and head with every step as if he carried a safe upon his back. His long arms reached awkwardly almost to his knees so that he resembled an ape balancing on his knuckles as he walked, and his small head covered with a cropped brush whose widow's peak came almost to his eyebrows, the tiny closeset ears and long lippy jaw carried out the similarity. He would have been truly apelike, Prew thought, had not the insignificance of his deepset eyes and his scrawny neck made him ineffectual as a monkey.

"Is that Galovitch!" he said.

"Thats him," Chief said, a twinkle gleaming faintly from the depth of his slow solemnity. "Wait'll you hear him talk."

The apparition stopped before them, at the foot of Prewitt's bed. Old Ike stood looking at them, the red eyes set in a well of wrinkles, and worked his loose-hung lips in and out ruminatingly, like a toothless man.

"Prewitt?" Galovitch said.

"Thats me."

"Sargint Galovitch, platoon guide am I of dis platoon," he said, proudly. "When assigned to dis platoon you are, you become under me. Consequental one a my men. Am coming to give for you the lowdown setup." He paused and rested his knobby hams of hands on the bed end and pulled his chin in and worked his lips in inexpressively and stared at Prew.

Prew turned to look at Chief to show his wonderment, but the Indian had lain down on the bunk, his big legs dangling over the side, and his head back on the olive blanket square-cornered over the pillow. He was suddenly outside of all of this, disclaiming all participation.

"Don' look to him," Galovitch commanded. "To you talking it is me not him. He is only corporal. Sargint Vilsahn is platoon sargint and it is for him say to you anything I do not say if for you to do.

"When in the morning you get up the first thing is the bunk to make. With no wrinkles and the extra blanket on the pillow tucked in. I inspect in the platoon every bunks and ones not made up right tear up and the man make up again.

"I am not expecting to be any goldbricks, see? This squad detail every day to clean over the Dayroom the outside porch. After you clean up under you own bunk you get the mops help the porch.

"No man this platoon from fatigue or drill be taking off without I find him gets plenty extra duty." The little red eyes glared at Prew challenging, almost hoping for some disagreement that would force Old Ike to prove his loyalty to Holmes, Wilson, the Company, and the Cause, which might be Better Soldiering; Peacetime Preparedness; or the Perpetuation of An Aristocracy. Nobody could have named the Cause, but then its name was unimportant, as long as the Cause itself remained to levy loyalty.

"And don' think," Old Ike went on, "can come over here a fighter everybody beating up on just because are tough guy. Quickest way to Stockade is who tough guy pulls.

"And now is Fatigue Call five minute you fall out for him," Old Ike concluded, glaring at Prew shortly, looking accusingly at Choate lying back relaxing. Then he clumped back to his own bunk where he took up again his interrupted litany to his unknown god by picking up the shoes he had been shining.

After he was gone, Chief Choate heaved his bulk upright, making the chain springs on the bunk squeak in protest.

"You kin gather what his Close Order Drill sounds like," he said.

"Yes," Prew said. "I can. Is the rest of the outfit as bad as that?"

"Well," Chief said solemnly, "not in the same way as that." He rolled himself another cigaret slowly and with great care.

"I guess he's found out that you aint goin to fight for Holmes," Chief said with slow solemnity.

"How could he have found it out? So soon."

Chief Choate shrugged. "Its hard to say," he said unmoved to exaggeration. "But I think he has. If he hant, knowing you was a fighter come to this outfit, he would have offered you the Compny on a silver platter and sucked your ass from here to Wheeler Field."

Prew laughed but Chief's round solemn face betrayed no hint of humor, or of any other feeling. He only looked a little surprised to find there was cause for laughter, which made Prew laugh the harder.

"Well," he said to the big man, "now we got that figured out, you got any more instructions for me before I take the oath and begin me consecrated life?"

"Not much else," Chief said solemnly. "No bottles in the bottoms of the footlockers. The Old Man doesnt like his men to drink and inspects for them every Sataday, and unless I take them first he takes them."

Prew grinned. "Maybe I'd better get a notebook and make a note of that."

"Also," Chief said slowly, "no women in the barricks after ten o'clock. Unless they're white. All the others, yellow black and brown, I got to turn in to the Orderly Room, where Holmes gives me a receipt and turns them over to the Great White Father." He looked at Prew solemnly as the other pretended to write a note down on his cuff.

"What else?" he said.

"Thats all," Chief said.

Grinning at the Chief, Prew thought about his shackjob at Haleiwa at the mention of the dark-skinned women; it was the third time he'd thought about her since this morning, but strangely, this time the thought did not hurt, and he could think about her freely, believing almost for a minute that there were lovely women standing on each corner, waiting for him to pick them up and be their lover, give them what they wanted, even though he knew it was not so. The warmth of Chief Choate's slow deadpan friendship had filled an empty spot inside him.

Downstairs the whistle blew, and simultaneously the guard bugler began to blow Fatigue Call in the quad, and he could even listen to the call objectively. It was, he decided, very badly played, not near as good as he could have played it for them.

"Its time for you to fall out," Chief said solemnly, heaving his great bulk up from the bunk. "I think I'll go take a nap and get a little sack-time."

"What a prick!" Prew told him, picking up his hat.

"Then, at four," Chief said, "I'll hit Choy's a lick and find out how the beer holds out. This is my training season."

Prew started, laughing, down the aisle, then turned back toward the Indian. "I sure guess them breakfast conversations are all through," he said, and was suddenly embarrassed at what he should not have said.

"What?" Chief said, inexpressively. "Oh, them. Yeah, I guess they are." He turned quickly, went on toward his bunk.

Chapter 8

There is, in the Army, a little known but very important activity appropriately called Fatigue. Fatigue, in the Army, is the very necessary cleaning and repairing of the aftermath of living. Any man who ever owned a gun has known Fatigue, when, after fifteen minutes in the woods and perhaps three shots at an elusive squirrel, he has gone home to spend three-quarters of an hour cleaning up his piece so it will be ready next time he goes to the woods. Any woman who has ever cooked a luscious meal and ladled it out in plates upon the table has known Fatigue, when, after the glorious meal is eaten, she repairs to the kitchen to wash the congealed gravy from the plates and the slick grease from the cooking pots so they will be ready to be used this evening, dirtied, and so washed again. It is the knowledge of the unendingness and of the repetitious uselessness, the do it up so it can be done again, that makes Fatigue fatigue.

And any man who shoots his gun at squirrels and then gives it to his young son with orders to clean, any woman who cooks the succulent meal and gives the dishes to her non-cooking daughter to be washed—those grownups know the way an officer feels about Fatigue. The son and daughter can understand the way an enlisted man feels about Fatigue.

Fatigue, in the Army, occupies fifty percent of the duty time; in the morning there is drill, in the afternoon Fatigue; but it is a fifty percent unmentioned in the enlistment campaigns and the pretty posters outside every Post Office in the nation that are constantly extolling the romance of a soldier's life, the chance for adventurous foreign travel (take the wife), the exceedingly high pay all unattached (if you get the rating), the chance to be a leader (if you get the commission), and the golden merits of learning a trade that will support you all your life. A recruit never finds out about Fatigue until some time after he has held up his right hand and then it is too late.

Most of the details are not too bad, they are only fatiguing. For there is the justification that they are necessary. If there is to be baseball, some one must spread the horse manure on the diamond so the infield will be grassy, and no one could expect that the players do it, since they do the playing.

But in addition to the necessary details that are only fatiguing there are other details, in a Regiment of Infantry, that are not only fatiguing but degrading. It is hard to be Romantic about the cavalry when you have to curry your own horse, and it is hard to be Adventurous about the uniform when you have to polish your own boots. And this explains why officers, who are above such menial tasks, are capable of such exciting memoirs of war. A man may be bored with scrubbing his own cartridge belt after every sashay in the field but he is not disillusioned; but when he goes every afternoon to the Married Officers' Quarters to manicure the lawns, wash the windows, sweep the yards, and clean the streets, he is not only disillusioned but degraded; he has really known Fatigue.

After every party at the Club there must be some loyal and patriotic soul who empties out the ashtrays and wipes up the liquor. But these were not all. There was an even greater test of patriotism. There was the trash collecting detail.

Once every twelve days in its rounds of the battalions this chance for heroism fell to every Company, and the three-man picked detail sortied out in their truck to collect the trash, as distinguished from garbage which the Kanaka garbage truck collected, from the Married Officers' Quarters.

In itself this would not seem very patriotic; but the officers' wives, having no incinerators, fearing to clog the soil pipes, and not wanting to use the garbage truck whose collector was a civilian and could quit, deposited their used menstruation pads in their trash cans. Emptying a single can so used can be very patriotic, but by the end of an afternoon when the truck was full the patriotism required of the detail was immense. They deserved at least a D.S.C. as, walking the two miles to the dump instead of riding in the back, knowing what their best friend would not tell them, they trudged doggedly through the aura of bad fish that clung to them all.

Even the insensitive stomachs of the most patriotic and most common soldiers were inclined to rebel. And the most rebellious of those stomachs, since Warden ran the details for G Company, was invariably Prewitt's.

It became increasingly clear, from day to day, that whenever Prew happened to be at the head of the double line of the Fatigue formation, Warden would happen to call out one of the more patriotic details.

One of these was the butcher shop detail. The butcher shop in addition to its market for the wives supplied the meat for all the individual companies. The butchers, enlisted men on Special Duty, did not mind the more delicate work of cutting steaks and chops, but they applied for Fatigue details to do the heavier slimier work of unloading and moving the sides around. Prew's neat tailormade blue fatigues would be stiff with blood and muck after an afternoon of this. It would be on his face and in his ears and in his hair, and the rancid smell of the butcher shop would waft about him as he walked. Warden would be standing in the corridor doorway as he came in, his sleeves rolled up two turns, smoothly cool and clean after a refreshing shower, and grinning fondly.

"Better hurry up and wash," he'd say. "Chow's almost over. The Company's been in for fifteen minutes. Or maybe," he would grin, "you'd rather go in like you are and wash up later."

"No," Prew would tell him seriously. "I think I'll wash first."

"Still the dude, 'ey?" Warden would grin at him. "Suit yourself."

One day Warden asked him if he shouldnt maybe go out for fighting, or maybe baseball. "You look awful tard, kid," he grinned. "If you was a jockstrap you wouldnt have to pull Fatigue."

"What makes you think I mind it?"

"I didnt say you didnt like it, kid," Warden said complacently. "All I said was you looked tard. Drawn to a fine edge."

"If you think you can push me into fightin, Warden," Prew told him grimly, "you are wrong. I can take everything you hand out. You and Dynamite together. I'm twice the man you are. If you didnt have them stripes, I'd take your big hulk out on the green and beat it to a pulp. And if I couldnt do it with my fists, I'd git me a knife and look you up downtown some night in River Street."

"Dont let the stripes worry you, kid," Warden grinned. "I can always take my shirt off. Take it off right now."

"You'd like that, wouldnt you?" Prew grinned back. "You could get me a year in the Stockade for that one, couldnt you?" He turned to go upstairs.

"What makes you think Holmes has got anything to do with this, kid?" Warden called after him.

And there were other minor inconveniences. He had meant to use his first weekend in G Company to go to Haleiwa for the showdown with his shackjob, but all the first week he had been a victim of The

Warden's Duty Roster, as a new man, his name heading every list for extra details. And The Warden utilized his advantage relentlessly.

As the week went by and he did not see his name on any KP list, his soldier's intuition began to whisper warnings. On Friday when the details for the weekend were posted on the bulletin board the suspicion became fact. Warden had saved his KP back to give him on the weekend. But Warden was even cleverer than he had suspected. Prew was on KP Sunday, and on Saturday he was Room Orderly. There would not even be one day off to go to Haleiwa.

There was a diabolical finesse in this arrangement, too. A Saturday KP got out of standing Saturday Inspection, but the RO had to stand Inspection like everybody else, in addition to his extra work. Warden was a smart man, no doubt of that; when he held the cards nobody could beat him at the way he played the hand.

Early Saturday morning Warden came out of the Orderly Room, all spruced up for inspection, to watch Prewitt manicure the porch. He leaned against the doorjamb grinning lovingly, but Prew worked on grudgingly and ignored him. He occupied himself with wondering whether Holmes had engineered this deal because he would not fight, to force him into going out, or whether it was Warden's own idea for some ungodly reason just because he did not like him.

Sunday Warden came into the kitchen for breakfast around eleven. He was the topkicker and he did not have to eat on schedule like the rest of them. Warden had hotcakes and eggs and sausage; the Company had had hotcakes and bacon, such as it was with Preem sleeping off a hard night in his sack. Warden leaned against the aluminum pastry table with its big utensil rack above it and ate his food with relish, in full view of the sweating KPs. Then he strolled over to the KP room past the huge built-in icebox.

"Well, well," he said straight-faced, leaning leisurely against the jamb. "If it aint my young friend, Prewitt. How do you like straight duty, Prewitt. Life in a rifle company, 'ey."

The cooks and other KPs all were watching, because The Warden almost never spent a weekend on the Post. They were expecting something big.

"I like it, Top," Prew grinned, trying to make the grin convincing, looking up from the steaming sink he was bent over, naked to the waist, his dungarees and shoes soaked with sweat and soapy water. "Thats why I transferred," he said seriously. "Its a great life, this. I find a pearl, I'll cut you in. Fifty-fifty. If it hadnt of been for you, I wouldnt of had no chance to find it."

"Well, well," The Warden said, laughing pleasantly. "Well, well. Thats a friend for you. Thats an honest man. Dynamite had his Preem and Galovitch in Bliss; I had my Prewitt in A Compny. When men have served together, they'll do anything for each other. I'll see if I can fix you up with a lot more, since you like it so much, Prewitt."

He grinned down at the other, his brows hooked up his forehead. Prew always remembered it, later, as having been a look of secret understanding, a glance that swept the cooks, KPs, and kitchen, everything aside, leaving only the two pairs of eyes that recognized each other.

He put his hand comfortably around a mug, heavy, handleless, at the bottom of the sink and waited for Warden to go on. But it was almost as if The Warden saw his hand around the mug beneath the water, for he grinned lovingly again and walked away, leaving Prew standing there absurdly with his daredevilish romantic picture of himself rising with the cup in murderous triumph.

But, in spite of Warden's threat, his name did not come up on the Daily Details sheet again. His second weekend he was free to go to Haleiwa. It was the same curious fact he had noted so many times before, in A Company; Warden was scrupulously fair, in his own eccentric way, he never overstepped his own private, self-constructed line of equity.

He should, he knew, have written Violet a letter, once during the middle of the second week he even thought about it for a minute. But he did not do it. Letters, like long-distance phone calls, could never convince him of the existence of another human far away existing in this same present he existed in. In reality, Violet did not exist until he saw her, then she began again where she had left off before. In-between she existed only in his mind, and how can you write a letter to your own imagination?

He could remember, as a small boy, watching his mother write frequent long letters to different relatives and friends, some of whom he had never seen. It was his mother's hobby, but even then it had seemed strange to him, in the town of Harlan, Kentucky, to write letters to other towns, to people she had not seen for years and probably would never see again. While at any time his father might be caught in a cave-in in the mine and be dead before the answers came. After his mother died that winter of the strike, six letters had come addressed to her. He looked at her name on all the envelopes, the name of her who was already dead still existing on the paper, and then he opened them and read them curiously, and not a one of them had mentioned the fact that she had died. He had thrown them in the stove and burned them. There was a time lag there that seemed to exist in space instead of time, and he could never, after that, account for it.

So he did not write to Violet, because the writing of letters did not have a true connection with the realities of death, and moving on, and eating. He waited till he could get free and went to see her.

She was waiting for him at the door, leaning against the jamb and looking out through the screen, one hand propped against the other jamb as if barring the door to a salesman. It seemed to him that no matter what time of day or night he walked up the macadam road from the highway intersection, she was always waiting in that same position, as if he had just phoned and she was watching for him. It was uncanny, as if she always knew when he was coming. But it was no more strange than anything else connected with her.

He had never pretended to understand her since the first time he met her at Kahuku and took her to the carnival and, knowing carnivals which are the same in any portion of the earth, found that Violet was still a virgin. That in itself surprised him, and he did not get a chance to recover from it from then on.

Violet Ogure. Oh-ǵoo-rdee. You pronounced the r like a drunken d. Even the name was strange and unpredictable. The strangeness of a foreign land is understandable, because you expect it when you go among foreigners, you're even looking for it. But the equation of the simple first name and the alien-tongued surname was unreadable. Violet was like all the other second and third generation Japanese, Chinese, Hawaiian, Portagee, Filipino girls with their first names after English flowers and their last names coming across alien centuries, girls whose parents had been shipped in like cattle to work the cane and pineapple for the Big Five, girls whose sons were often among the numberless hordes of little boys shining your shoes on the sidewalk outside a bar, repeating the antique legend: "Me half Japanee, half Schofield," or, grinning obliquely, "Me half Chinee, half Schofield." A crop fathered by soldiers who had served their hitch and mysteriously vanished into that mythical "Mainland" that was the United States.

Violet was an ambivalent mingling of the intensely familiar and the inscrutably alien; she was like the city of Honolulu with its high-powered, missionary-owned bank buildings and its shanty Japanee-language movie just off Aala Park, a polygenetic blend nobody, least of all Violet, could encompass. He had learned to pronounce her name correctly, and that was all he learned about her.

He walked into the unkempt chicken-defiled front yard and she came out on the homemade leanto porch. He took her hand and helped her down the three rotting steps and they went around to the back, a ritual they repeated every time he came, because in the time he had been coming there he had never been invited or allowed in their front room.

The back porch was three times as large as the leanto on the front, unscreened, and with a network of vines from floor to roof that made it a secluded cave, almost another room, that was the living room of the Ogure family.

And behind the house was the chicken coop, a miniature of its shanty self, where conceited hens stalked complacently about peering beadily this way and that, crooning their smug song of the Sacred Vessel, and squirting their droppings in the grass with the righteousness of saints. The sour odor of their house and clan pervaded the whole place. And forever after the smell of chickens brought to Prew's mind a vivid picture of Violet and of her life.

Her bedroom alongside the kitchen was perpetually cluttered. The covers on the peeling gilt iron bed were always rumpled, and clothes were always draped across the bedfoot and the single chair. There was spilled powder on the homemade dresser, but in one corner there was a closet, made of two by fours for frame and hung with a lushly green and riotously flowered material made especially for Hawaii. Violet had fixed it up herself, to carry all the heavy hope of someday something better.

Prew stripped off his gook shirt and slacks and, naked, hunted through the clutter for his trunks, moving with the ease of long association. The clutter did not bother him; kicking shoes aside and tossing clothes from chair to bed, he was more at home in this flimsy shack than Violet was.

The cluster of shacks, growing up the hills on both sides of the road, might have been his home in Harlan, except for the absence of the soot and coaldust. The back porch with its rusty pump, the chipped sink with its zinc pail and granite dipper, it all was of the fabric of his life, and he moved through the thick air of this poverty with the ease that only a man who has been intimate with it can have.

And as he hunted for the trunks he told her all about the transfer, why he had been so long in coming.

"Why did you transfer, though, Bobbie?" Violet asked him in the clipped twittering voice that always made him chuckle. She sat on the bed and watched him exchange his shoes and socks for the old canvas fishing sneaks.

The bright air slipped in from the outside through the single window that was like an afterthought, and it washed against the dimness and the funky smell of stale bedclothes. It touched his body coolly and he looked at Violet in her shorts and halter, feeling the old wild surge harden his belly and bring sweat to his palms.

"What?" he said vacantly. "Oh. I didnt transfer. I *was* transferred. It was Houston did it, because I spoke my piece.

"Listen," he said. "Theres nobody home, lets you and me take one?" Three weeks, feeling the blood behind his eyes, almost a month, it was too long to wait.

"Wait," she said. "Couldnt you have gone to the officer and asked to stay?"

"Thats right." Prew jerked his head in a nervous nod, thinking the Army made you need it more, made you hungrier. "I could have. But I couldnt. I couldnt be a brown noser."

"Well," Violet said. "Yes. But I would think an argument could be patched up," she said. "I mean when you had a good job you wanted to keep."

"It could of been," he said. "But I dont want any job that bad. Dont you see? There wasnt nothin else to do. Listen," he said. "Come here. Come over here."

"Not now," she told him. She kept on watching him, almost curiously, looking in his face. "It seems a shame to lose such a good job, and lose your rating."

"It is a shame," he said. To hell with it, he thought. "Is there any liquor left around this place?"

"Theres still part of that quart you brought last time," she said. "I havent touched it; it was yours," she got up proudly. "Its in the kitchen. And I think theres another one, unbroken, you brought a long time ago. You want a drink?"

"Yes," he said and followed her into the kitchen. "You see," he explained carefully, "I wont get to come up to see you near as often as I use to now. Also, I'll only be makin twenty-one a month, so I cant give the dough I did, either."

Violet nodded. Inscrutably, she did not seem impressed one way or the other. He decided to let it ride a while, there was no use to spoil it now.

"Lets go up to the place on the hill," he said. "To our place," he added intimately, and was ashamed because he felt now that he was pleading. Being without any for so long could eat into a man, and the blood was pumping through him richer now, and thicker.

"All right," she said. The door to the cupboard had no glass in it, but she opened it anyway, to reach for the bottle inside, the absence of the glass embarrassing her. While her arms were up Prew cupped his hands over her breasts from behind her. Violet jerked her arms down irritably and then he spun her, pinning her arms to her sides, and kissed her, she holding the bottle in one hand. In her bare feet she was not quite as tall as he was.

They climbed up through the matted dry grass, Prew carrying the bottle, the sun pleasantly hot on their bare backs. At the top in the little clump of trees they lay down in the matted green and brown of the dead and living grass. They looked almost straight down at the house.

"Its pretty, isn't it," Prew said.

"No," disagreed Violet. "Its ugly. Horrible ugly."

The cluster of shacks lay spread out below them, a nameless community not on the tourists' maps, looking as if the first strong wind would blow them over. They were, on top of the hill, at the top of a great U where they could look down at the houses curved across the bottom or look straight across at the field of green cane on the other side.

"I lived in a place just like this when I was a kid," Prew said. "Except it was lots bigger. But it was the same," thinking of all the lost forgotten memories that came back now, carrying so much life and emotion, crowding in your mind, and that you never could express to anyone, because they never were connected. A sadness at the loss of them, and at their lack of meaning, came over him.

"Did *you* like it?" Violet asked.

"No," he said. "I dint. But I've lived in a hell of a lot worse places since." He rolled over on his back and watched the sun flickering down through the leaves of the trees. He felt the Saturday afternoon on-pass feeling come down and sweep over him, like leaves do in the fall, back home. Life does not begin again till Monday morning, it whispered. If only all of life could be like this, he whispered. If only all of life could be a three-day pass.

That was a pipedream, Prewitt. He took a drink from the bottle and handed it to Violet. She drank, propped on her elbows, staring down at the houses. She drank the straight whiskey the same way he did, as if it were only water.

"Its terrible," she said, still staring down. "No one should ever have to live in place like this. My Poppa and Momma come here from Hokkaido. Not even this house is theirs." She handed back the bottle to him and he caught her arm and pulled her over. He kissed her, and for the first time she returned it, putting her hand on his cheek.

"Bobbie," she said. "Bobbie."

"Come on," he said, turning. "Come here."

But Violet held back, looking at her cheap wrist watch. "Momma and Poppa will be home any time."

Prew sat up in the grass. "What difference does it make?" he said irritably. "They wont come up here."

"Its not that, Bobbie. Wait till tonight. At night is the time for that."

"No," he said. "Any times the time for that. If you feel like it."

"Thats just it," she said. "I dont feel like it. They'll be coming home."

"But they know we sleep in the same bed at night."

"You know how I feel about Momma and Poppa," Violet said.

"Yes, but they know it," he said. Then he wondered suddenly if they did. "They must know it?"

"Its different in the afternoon. They're not home from work yet. And you're a soldier." She stopped and reached for the bottle on the grass. "I graduated from Leilehua High School," she stated.

You never completed the seventh grade, he told himself. He had seen Leilehua High School in Wahiawa. It was only another high school.

"So what if I am a soljer?" he said. "Whats wrong with a goddam soljer? Theres nothin wrong with a soljer, that isnt wrong with anybody else."

"I know it," Violet said.

"Soljers are only people, just like everybody else," he insisted.

"I know it," Violet said. "But you dont understand. So many Nisei girls go out with the soldiers."

"So what?" he said, remembering the song. *Manuelo Boy, my dear boy, no more hila-hila, sister go with a soldier boy, come home any old time.*

"All the soldiers want to screw them," Violet said.

"Well, they go out with civilians, too. Thats what they want. Whats wrong with that?"

"Nothings wrong with it," she said. "But a wahine girl must be careful. A respectable Nisei girl doesnt go with soldiers."

"Neither does a respectable white girl," Prew said, "or any other kind of girl. But they're no different than the goddam Pfcs. They all want the same goddam thing."

"I know it," Violet said. "Dont get mad. Its just the way the people look at the soldiers."

"Then whynt your folks run me off? or do something? or say something? If they dont like it."

Violet was surprised. "But they would never do that."

"But, hell. All the neighbors see me comin here all the time."

"Yes, but they would never mention it either."

Prewitt looked over at her lying on her back in the dappled sunlight, and the short tight legs of her shorts.

"How would you like to move out of here?" he asked carefully.

"I'd love it."

"Well," he probed, "you may get a chance to soon."

"Except," Violet said, "that I wont shack up with you. You know I cant do that."

"We're shacked up now," he said. "The only thing different from all the other shackjobs is that you're livin with your folks."

"It makes all the difference," Violet said. "Theres no use to talk about it. You know I cant do that."

"Thats right," Prew said. Life did not begin till Monday morning. It could wait till tomorrow. He rolled over on his back and lay staring up into the incredible blue of the Hawaiian sky. "Look off to the west," he said. "Theres a storm blowing up in the west. Look at the cloud bank."

"The clouds are beautiful," Violet said. "So black. And piling higher and higher one on top of the other, like a cliff wall."

"Thats a line squall," Prewitt said. "Thats the first beginning of the rainy season."

"Our roof leaks," Violet said. She reached for the bottle.

Prew was watching the racking mass of clouds. "But whynt your folks kick you out. If its like that. Bringing me here," he asked.

Violet looked surprised. "But I'm their daughter," she said to him.

"Oh," he said. "Come on. We mights well go on back down. It'll rain pretty soon."

The rainstorm came up quickly after it had hurdled the mountains. By suppertime it was raining hard. Prew sat out on the back porch alone while Violet helped her mother fix the meal. Her father sat in the front room, by himself.

The old folks, that was the way he always thought of them, had come home before the rain, chattering Japanese back at the crowded Model T that let them off and then clattered on down the road to the next house. Five families owned the Ford together, just as the whole community had built and owned the miles of water sluices of weathered wood that stuck up all along the little valley like scaffolding that had been used to make the mountains before the dawn of history.

They had rushed through the house to the back porch where Prew and Violet were sitting, and on out to hoe their tidy truck patch that the water sluices emptied into, before the rainstorm came. Prew watched them, stooped and bent, with faces that looked to have been carved from dried and withered apples and he felt a self-righteous indignation at the entire human race for the life these people lived, these who looked to be Violet's grandparents or great-grandparents, and yet were not yet forty years of age.

Their garden, laid out in immaculate little squares and triangles, utilizing every inch of ground, of radishes and cabbages and lettuce and taro and a little underwater rice patch, plus a half a dozen foreign vegetables, was their life; and it showed the industry that was in them. They worked on in it until the rain began to fall before they stopped and put their hoes away. When they came up on the porch, they neither one spoke to Prew or seemed to know that he was there.

Sitting on the porch alone, listening to them fixing supper, he felt again the indignation he had felt before, the sense of loss and the aloneness, the utter defenselessness that was each man's lot, sealed up in his bee cell from all the others in the world. But the smell of boiling vegetables and pork reached him from the inside, the aloneness left him for a while. The warm moist smell promised other people lived and were preparing supper.

He listened to the pouring and the thunder rumblings that sounded hollow like they were in a rainbarrel, shared the excitement and the coziness of the buzzing insects that had sought refuge on the porch, and now and then he slapped detachedly at the mosquitoes, making a sharp crack in the pouring buzzing silence. The porch sheltered him from all but the splashes of the drops that hit the floor and their spray touched him with a pleasant chill. And he was secure, because somewhere out beyond the wall of water humanity still existed, and was preparing supper.

Violet called him and he went in, feeling the Army and the strange wild eyes of Warden were very far away, that Monday morning was a bad dream, an age-old racial memory, as cold as the moon and as far away, and sat before the steaming plate of flat-tasting foreign vegetables and chunks of pork, and ate with relish.

After they finished eating, the old man and woman stacked their plates in the sink and padded silently, without a word, into the front room where the garish little altars were, where Prew had never been invited. They had not said a word all through the meal, but he had learned long ago not to try to talk to them. He and Violet sat silently on in the kitchen drinking the aromatic tea, listening to the wind buffet the shack and the rain drumming its nails deafeningly upon the tin corrugated roof. Then he, like Violet, stacked his dishes in the old chipped sink, feeling completely at home here and content. The one thing he lacked was a cup of coffee.

When they went into her bedroom, Violet unconcernedly left the door wide open although they could see directly into the lighted front room. He could see the flickering light reflecting from her gold body as she turned matter-of-factly to him. The matter-of-factness gave him pleasure, a sense of long-lifedness and continuance that a soldier seldom had; but the irritation of the indifferently open door made him afraid he would be seen, shamed him with his own desire.

He woke once in the middle of the night. The storm was gone and the moon shone in brightly through the open window. Violet lay with her back to him, head pillowed on bent elbow. From the stiffness of her body he knew she was not sleeping, and he put his hand on her naked hip and turned her toward him. In the deep curve of her hip and the indented juncture of ball and socket underneath there was an infinite workmanship of jewel-like precision that awed him, and called up in him an understanding that was like a purge and awakened liquid golden flecks within his eyes.

She rolled willingly, unsleepily, and he wondered what she had been thinking of, lying there awake. As he moved over her, he realized again that he did not know her face or name, that here in this act that brings two human fantasies as close as they can ever come, so close that one moves inside the other, he still did not know her, nor she him, nor could they touch each other. To a man who lives his life among the flat hairy angularities of other men, all women are round and soft, and all are inscrutable and strange. The thought passed quickly.

He awoke in the morning on his back, uncovered. The door was still open, and Violet and her mother were moving around in the kitchen. He smothered an impulse to grab up the covers over his nakedness and rose and donned his trunks, feeling deeply shamed, embarrassed by his own pendulous existence which all women hated. The old woman took no notice of him when he entered the kitchen.

After the morning cleaning was done and the old people had padded silently away to visit neighbors, Prew thought the whole thing over and finally, characteristically, just came out with it.

"I want you to move to Wahiawa and shack up with me," he said bluntly.

Violet sat in her chair on the porch, half-turned toward him, her elbow on the arm, cheek resting on a half closed fist. "Why, Bobbie?" She continued to stare at him curiously, the same curiosity with which she always watched him, as if seeing for the first time the subtle mechanism from which she got her pleasure, and that she had always thought was simple. "You know I cant do that. Why make a showdown of it?"

"Because I wont be able to come up here any more," he said, "like I used to. Before I transferred. If we lived in Wahiawa, I'd come home every night."

"What is wrong with living this way?" she asked him, in the same odd tone. "I dont mind if you only come up on weekends. You dont have to come every night like you used to do, before you transferred."

"Weekends aint enough," he said. "At least not for me."

"If you break off with me," Violet said, "you wont get it even that often, will you? You wont find any woman who will shack up with a private who makes twenty-one dollars."

"I dont like being around your folks," Prew said, "they bother me; they dont like me. If we're goin to be shacked up, we might as well be shacked up. Instead of this half way stuff. Thats the way it is." He said it flatly, like a man enumerating the faults and values of a new spring coat.

"I'd have to quit my job. I'd have to get another job in Wahiawa. That might be hard, unless I took a job as waitress in a bar, and I cant do that.

"I quit my job in Kahuku," she said indifferently, "and left a nice home where I was one of the family—to come back here to this rotten place—against my parents wishes that I not leave my higher position. I did it so I could be near enough for you to come up every night. I did it because you asked me to."

"I know you did," he said, "I know you did. But I didnt know it would be like this."

"What did you expect?" she said. "You dont make enough to pay for shacking up, Bobbie."

"I did. I've got almost a full month's pay as a First-Fourth coming," he said carefully. "It'll be enough to get us set up for a month, until you get a job and I get some more dough. With your job and my twenty-one bucks we can live better than you're livin here. And you dont like it here. Theres no reason for you not to go." He stopped talking, long enough to get his breath, surprised at how fast he had been talking.

"You didnt believe me, did you?" Violet said, "when I said I couldnt go, when I said why make a showdown. You cant force me, Bobbie. Momma and Poppa would not like it, they wouldnt let me go."

"Why wouldnt they like it?" he said, trying to keep his voice from going faster. "Because I'm a soljer. Do you care whether I'm a soljer or not? If you do, why the hell did you go with me in the first place? why did you let me come here? They cant keep you by not wanting you to go. How can they keep you?"

"They would be disgraced," Violet said.

"Oh, balls!" Prew said, letting loose the rein. "If I was a gook beach-boy instead of a soljer it'd be all right though." This was what he knew it would come down to. They'd live like cattle, worse than Harlan miners, but they'd be disgraced if their daughter shacked up with a sol-dier. They'd let the Big Five shove a cane stalk up their keister, but that was not disgraceful. That wasnt soldiers. The poor, he thought, they are always their own worst enemy.

"Its not as if we were married," she said softly.

"Married!" Prew was dumbfounded. The picture of Dhom, the G Company duty sergeant, bald and massive and harassed, crossed his eyes, trailed by his fat sloppy Filipino wife and seven half-caste brats; no wonder Dhom was a bully, condemned to spend his life in foreign service like an exile because he had a Filipino wife.

Violet smiled at his consternation. "You see? You dont want to marry me. Look at my side. Some day you will go back to the Mainland. Will you take me with you? You want me to leave my people, and then be left without them or you either? And maybe with a baby?"

"Would your folks like it if you married me?"

"No, but they would like it better than the other. Or this."

"You mean they'd still be disgraced," Prew said wryly. "Would you go if I married you?"

"Of course. It would be different then. When you went to the Main-land I would go with you. I would be your wife."

My wife, he thought. Well, why dont you do it? There was a rising desire in him to do it. Wait a minute, kid. Thats the way they all feel, all the men who finally get married. Like Dhom felt. On one side they see their freedom, and on the other they see a piece of ass right there where they can always get it, without all the bushwhacking buildup, always there handy to be reached, without the months of preparation, or the sluts that are the other alternative. What do you want?

"If I married you and took you with me," he said cautiously, "there would be no difference. We would both be outcasts. Nobody in the States would associate with us. Anyway, just because I was married to you wouldnt mean I'd have to take you with me. Being married means nothing, to most people it means less than nothing. I know." Like Dhom, he thought, who married for his piece of ass and after he was hooked she suddenly didnt want to give it to him any more.

"But you still dont want to marry me," Violet said.

"You goddam right I dont," he said, his voice rising under the sting and guilt of the truth of what she said. "If I was gonna spend my life in Wahoo it would be different. I'll be movin all over, goin all the time. I'm a thirty year man. And I aint no officer to have the govmint pay for transportin my lovin wife all over the goddam world. As a private, I wouldnt even get subsistence for you. A guy like me aint got no business bein married. I'm a soljer."

"Well, you see?" she said. "Why not go on like we are?"

"Because," he said. "Because once a week just aint enough.

"Theres a war comin in this country. I want to be in on it. I dont want to be held down by nothin that will keep me out of it. Because I am a soljer."

Violet had lain back in her chair and rested her head against the back, her hands dangling, dangling over the ends of the arms of it. She kept on looking at him, curiously, across the chair back. "Well," she said. "You see?"

Prew stood up and stepped toward her. "Why in hell would I marry you?" he shot down at her. "Have a raft of snot-nosed nigger brats? Be a goddam squawman and work in the goddam pineapple fields the rest of my life? or drive a Schofield taxi? Why the hell do you think I got in the Army? Because I didnt want to sweat my heart and pride out in a goddam coalmine all my life and have a raft of snot-nosed brats who look like niggers in the coaldirt, like my father, and his father, and all the rest of them. What the hell do you dames want? to take the heart out of a man and tie it up in barbed wire and give it to your mother for Mother's Day? What the hell do you . . ."

There was no hood of ice over his eyes now, like there was when he had been facing Warden, like there was when he had been trying to talk her into it, they were blazing now, with the fire of a strip mine that smoulders and smoulders and finally breaks out in the open for a

86

little while. He took a deep shuddering breath and got hold of himself.

The girl could almost see the white icecap of anger rolling down across his eyes, like the glaciers of the ice age rolled across the earth. She lay back in her chair letting it sweep over her, helpless as convicts being washed down with the firehose, letting the force hit her, yielding instead of fighting it, with a patience born of centuries of stooped backs and dried apple faces.

"I'm sorry, Violet," Prew said, from behind the ice.

"Its all right," the girl said.

"I didnt mean to hurt you."

"Its all right," she said.

"Its up to you," he said. "This transfer changes my whole routine of living. It works with a different rhythm, like a new song. They aint at all alike, the old song and the new.

"This is the last time I'm comin up. You can either move or not, its okay. When a man changes his life, he has to change it all. He cant keep nothin that reminds him of the old life, or it doesnt work. If I kept comin up here, I'd get dissatisfied with this transfer and I'd try to change it. I dont aim to do that, or let anybody know I want to do it.

"So its up to you," he said.

"I cant go, Bobbie," the girl said, not moving, no change in her voice, still from the chair as she had been before.

"Okay," he said. "Then I'll be leavin. I've seen lots of guys shacked up in Wahiawa. They have a good time. Them and their wahines have parties together and go out together, movies and bars. All like that. The girls aint alone. Not any more," he said, "than any human being is always alone."

"What happens to them when the soldiers leave?" she said. Her eyes were looking off at the hilltop trees.

"I dont know. And I dont give a good goddam. They probly git other soljers. I'll be leavin."

When he came back out he carried the sneaks and the whiskey, the nearly full one and the nearly empty one, rolled up in the trunks, all the things he had owned here, all that he was taking with him. The little that they were, they had been deposited here as security for a pass of entrance, collateral for the loan of a life that existed off the Post, and in taking them away he had revoked his claim.

Violet was still sitting in the same unchanged position, and he made himself grin at her, drawing his lips back tautly across his teeth. But the girl did not see it, or notice him. He walked down the steps and around the corner of the house.

Her voice followed him around the corner. "Goodby, Bobbie."

Prew grinned again. "Aloha nui oe," he called back, playing the role out to the end, with a strong sense of the dramatic.

As he crested the little hill he did not look back, but he could feel through the back of his neck that she was standing in the door, leaning against the jamb, one hand propped against the other side as if barring the door to a salesman. He walked on toward the intersection, never looking back, seeing in his mind the fine tragic picture his figure disappearing down the hill must make, as if it were himself standing back there in the door. And the strange thing was he had never loved her more than at this moment, because at that moment she had become himself.

But thats not love, he thought, thats not what she wants, nor what any of them want, they do not want you to find yourself in them, they want instead that you should lose yourself in them. And yet, he thought, they are always trying to find themselves in you. What a wonderful actor you would have made, Prewitt, he told himself.

It was only when he was below the hill that he could end the role and stop, turning to look back, allowing himself to feel the loss.

And it seemed to him then that every human was always looking for himself, in bars, in railway trains, in offices, in mirrors, in love, especially in love, for the self of him that is there, someplace, in every other human. Love was not to give oneself, but find oneself, describe oneself. And that the whole conception had been written wrong. Because the only part of any man that he can ever touch or understand is that part of himself he recognizes in him. And that he is always looking for the way in which he can escape his sealed bee cell and reach the other airtight cells with which he is connected in the waxy comb.

And the only way that he had ever found, the only code, the only language, by which he could speak and be heard by other men, could communicate himself, was with a bugle. If you had a bugle here, he told himself, you could speak to her and be understood, you could play Fatigue Call for her, with its tiredness, its heavy belly going out to sweep somebody else's streets when it would rather stay at home and sleep, she would understand it then.

But you havent got a bugle, himself said, not here nor any other place. Your tongue has been ripped out. All you got is two bottles, one nearly full, one nearly empty.

And that we cant take through the gate, friend, he told himself, because the MPs will drink it up themself, and that we cant cache along the fence because there are guys who get their whiskey that way, look for it every night. Shall we drink it, friend? I think we'd better. We are much closer, sometimes we can almost see each other, when we're drunk. Lets go to the tree.

The tree, below the hill, halfway to the intersection, was a gnarled old kiawe tree filling up its little field, where on his trips up here he had gone before to sit, and where the brown bottles of his past trips lay in the grass. He walked to it through the kneehigh matted grass, having to lift his legs high until he got under it where there was the flattened smooth place that he always sat with his back against the roughness of the bark and no one could see him from the road because there are times every man must be alone and in the squadroom there is no aloneness, only loneliness.

The ancient thorny-fingered guardian that all day protected its little patch of virgin grass from the philandering sun's greedy demanding of that last maidenhead in the field, spread its warped washerwoman's arms above him now as it had the grass all day, protecting the philandering prodigal now as it had its daughter's greenness, until he drank his whiskey, thinking some about The Warden and the Company, the jockstrap Company, but mostly about Violet and the fact that a man could never move without finding boxes to pack the curtains and the canned goods. It was all one to the tree, him or the grass, since being female all it needed was a thing it could protect.

He added the two bottles to the others on the grass and caught a ride home, to the crowded loneliness of the barracks—home, to the separateness of the squadroom where there is no solitude—home, with a 13th Field Artillery truck taking swimmers back from Haleiwa, and went, drunk, to bed.

And when the end of the month and Payday came, he took his last pay as a First and Fourth, the money that was to have set Violet up in Wahiawa, and with a fitting sense of irony, blew it in the gambling sheds, determined to start even. He lost it all across the crap table at O'Hayer's in fifteen minutes, and he did not even keep out enough to buy a bottle or to buy a piece of ass. It made a lovely gesture, and the large bets he faded created quite a furor.

Book Two

THE COMPANY

Chapter 9

The rainy season was the nearest thing to winter in Hawaii. Perhaps, in the winter months, the sky would be a little duller, more hazy and less blue, and the sun not quite so dazzling. But winter in Hawaii was never more different from summer than was our late September. The temperature remained the same, and the lack of water in the great red plateau of pineapples where Schofield Barracks lay was the same in winter as in summer.

There was never any cold to suffer in the winter in Hawaii. But neither was there any persimmon-flavored air of fall's October, nor any sudden awakening to the warmth and quickened thighs of spring's young April. The only time there was ever any cosmic change, in Hawaii, was in the rainy season and so its change was always welcomed by the ones who could remember winter. All, that is, except the tourists.

It did not come all at once, the rainy season. There was the usual feeble storm or two in waning February, like a man who feebly kicks and struggles just before he dies, but bringing promise and a breath of chill, saying there was water near, hold on a while. Then the early storms gave up, after the thirsty earth had taken all the moisture in them, and they ran away before the onslaught of the sun which dried the mud to dust again, leaving only a caked cracked memory that crumbled underneath the round-toed bluntness of the GI shoes.

But in early March the times between the rains got shorter and the rains themselves got longer, until finally there were no times between, but only rain, of which the earth would avidly drink its fill and then, like a man dehydrated in the desert who cant keep from drinking too much, vomit all the rest it could not assimilate, down the streets and down the hills, along the flumes and irrigation ditches that webbed the carmine earth of the plateau and now were torrential rivers. Until at last the whole earth and everybody on it, like a honeymooning bride, begged for thirst again.

It was then that Schofield moved indoors. Field problems were replaced by lectures on the various armament nomenclatures in the Dayrooms, Close Order and Extended Order were made to step down for dry-run target exercises on the porches and for the hoary venerated triggersqueeze. All, in their monotony, having to compete with the exciting luxury of being under shelter while the rain beat down outside.

Raincoats, of two kinds—the rubberized kind that absorbed the water like a blotter, and the slicker kind that shed both air and water until the wearer was so bathed in sweat he might as well have worn the other kind, appeared from out of hiding in the combat packs hung on each bed foot. And on those evenings when the rain would cease long enough for men to go back to their restless midnight walks the newly issued gadgets called "field jackets" would appear upon the streets and roads.

And now, in the rainy season, when the groups of men moved in on the roofed over Boxing Bowl behind the old Post Chapel, coming from all over, radial spokes about a hub, they carried blankets, both to spread out on the cold concrete that brings down the piles and to wrap around them. And perhaps a hidden pint for extra warmth, if they had been able to sneak it in without the MPs getting wise. And here in Hawaii's autumnal March, under the roof of Schofield's Boxing Bowl where two nameless ciphers fought each other in the ring, football, apples, and October and all the thousand little towns across the nation with their little highschool football teams hovered low above the Bowl, brought momentarily alive again by an illusion.

With three Smokers still to be run off in the Bowl in the second week in March the Hawaiian Division Championship had already been decided. Dynamite Holmes's "Bearcat Cubs" had lost, by thirty points to the 27th Infantry, twice as much as they could hope to pick up in the last three Smokers, and the great gold ring with its golden fighters in it had been removed from its case of honor in the sallyport to be ready for its presentation to the winner when the season ended.

Dynamite could be seen moving around the Post with sagging shoulders and an irritated brow and it was rumored that he would be shipped down, relieved from boxing, and for the first time in several years G Company had two court martials in a single month and sent two men to the Stockade.

But in the big octagonal hole in the ground with its serrated scalloped concrete sides it was not important, to the spectators, who was fighting, or who would win. It was only important that the winy air and excitement of anticipated conflict be enjoyed, bringing back the distant continent of home where all the grave young highschool athletes who, despite their coaches with their turned-up topcoat collars and conflicting visions of Knute Rockne movies and jobs they feared to risk, fought frantically with the magnificent foolishness of youth as if the whole of life depended on this game, and who were still young enough to cry over a defeat, an illusion that their coaches never shared, a thing that like Santa Claus they themselves would lose all too soon before the widening range of vision and the knowledge that their loyalty was a commodity and could be shifted easily, and a thing that the men who perched on the concrete of the Boxing Bowl remembered fondly in their own hunger for a return to innocence.

The Regiment did not suffer over its defeat near as much as Dynamite, or as much as Dynamite thought it did. Its loyalties had been shifted from one outfit to another too many times, and its depression lasted exactly the time it took to walk home from the Bowl and get a small change crapgame started in the latrine. The bright light of the boxing squad faded rapidly. Payday was much nearer than next year's season, and there were rumors that half the houses between River Street and Nuuana Avenue had got in shipments of new girls.

But if the honor of the Regiment had no other exponent except Dynamite, it had a great one there. After his interview with Col Delbert and the securing of his borderline reprieve, he collected his charts and maps and began the planning of next year's campaign which was to be the greatest yet, and would bring the trophy back where it belonged. "It shall return," he said, and even before the last Smoker had been played out he had begun to make his overlays and gather up his forces.

Milt Warden was standing in the corridor doorway when Holmes loosed the thunderbolt of the transfer of the cook, Stark, from Ft. Kamehameha. It was raining hard that day and from the doorway he watched his commander come striding through the silver curtain, oblivious of the muddy quad, his tailored belted topcoat with its collar up around his ears flapping soddenly, but still smartly, around his booted legs, and shamefully there was none of the traditional cheerful adoration in The Warden's heart. Something about the striding figure told him this was not a routine trip to see that everything was running right and he was afflicted with a sense of foreboding ill.

"Boots and saddles," he sneered out loud defiantly, but not loud enough for Holmes to hear, and turned his back upon the coming Captain and went inside, to prove his independence to himself.

"I want these fixed up right away," Holmes said, coming dripping into the Orderly Room and pulling papers from inside his coat. "Wheres Mazzioli?"

"Over at Personnel," Warden said, without enthusiasm. "Sgt/Maj O'Bannon called for all the clerks this morning."

"Then you'll have to fix them," Holmes said, handing him the

95

papers. "I want an endorsement, you know; and a *good* letter of recommendation.

"This man Stark served with me at Bliss and I've already talked to Col Delbert about him. He wrote Department Hq to get his request through channels safely." Holmes took off his Cavalryman's hat and swung it vigorously, scattering the water on the floor.

"My God," he said, "its wet. He's a damned fine man. I always like to do everything I can for my old men."

"Yes, Sir," Warden said, and went on studying the papers.

"I want it sent out today," Holmes said happily. "I'll wait and mail it myself. Theres some other things I want to talk to you about anyway. We've got a Pfc rating open, havent we?"

"Yes, Sir," Warden said, and went on studying the papers.

"Are you listening to me?" Holmes said.

"Yes, Sir," Warden said. He raised the papers up, as if displaying them. "We got a full staff of cooks, Capn," he made it casual. "You'll have to bust somebody to make room for this guy. Have you talked to Sgt Preem about it yet? He aint kicked about his present cooks as far as I know of." But he didnt make it casual enough.

Holmes's face lost its roundness of happiness and became severe, all planes and angles. "I dont think Sgt Preem will contest my decision, Sergeant."

"Not," Warden said, "if you give him a bottle of lemon extrack."

"What?" Holmes said.

"I said," Warden said, "not if he wants to keep on the right track."

Holmes stared at him disbelievingly. "Preem and Stark cooked together in Bliss. And I have never yet found it necessary to bolster my judgment with the advice of subordinates."

"Yes, Sir," Warden said, staring back at him.

"I know what I'm doing, Sergeant. Just let me handle it. When I want advice I'll ask for it."

"Yes, Sir," Warden said, still staring at him. Holmes would never get a better first sergeant, and Holmes knew it, and Warden knew he could get by with it.

Holmes stared back long enough to let himself feel he had not been intimidated, and then he dropped his eyes to his sharp-peaked hat and shook it again to get the water off, unable to face the thing in Warden that just did not give a fuck.

"My God," he mumbled. "Its wet."

"Yes, Sir," Warden said. Watching Holmes sit down at his desk and begin to doodle, feeling he had triumphed momentarily, he decided to beard the destiny once more, while he had the advantage.

"Can this thing wait a couple days, Captain? Leva is way behind in his supply reports and I've been helping him out. I've got work to do thats imperative; and this thing can be fixed up any time." In a couple of days he might cool off and forget his altruism. He had done it before.

Holmes laid his pencil down emphatically. "Whats the matter with Sgt O'Hayer?" he said. "He's the supply sergeant isnt he?"

"Yes, Sir!" Warden said.

"Well then. Let him do it. Thats his job."

"O'Hayer *cant* do it, Sir. He's too goddam busy running his goddam gambling shed."

"What do you mean he *cant* do it? He's the supply sergeant. He *has* to do it. Are you questioning my judgment, Sergeant?"

"No, *Sir!*"

"All right then. Let O'Hayer do his own job. Thats what he's paid for. As long as I'm Company Commander of this outfit every man will do his *own* job, and it will be run as I say. And I want those papers made out now."

"Yes, Sir," Warden said violently. "I'll make them out right now, Sir." And the supply and all the rest of it can go to hell, he thought. Now there would be *five* boys from Bliss to hamstring the outfit. He sat down at his desk and went to work, ignoring Holmes, and in the work belittling him.

"By the way, Sergeant," Holmes interrupted coolly. "About that open Pfc. I want you to have Mazzioli make out a Company Order giving it to Bloom."

Warden looked up from his typewriter, his eyebrows quivering. "Bloom!"

"Yes," Holmes said tranquilly, "Bloom. Bloom's a good man, he's got the makings of a good noncom in him. Sgt Galovitch tells me he works harder and has more initiative than any private in the Company."

"Not *Bloom*," Warden said.

"Why, yes," Holmes said, satisfaction in his voice. "I've had my eye on him for quite a while. I keep my finger on the pulse of this Company much more than you think. Good athletes, I've found, always make the best soldiers," he said maliciously. "Bloom won four of his fights in the Bowl this year. Its not impossible that we'll make a Division Champion out of Bloom next year. Sgt Wilson is going to work with him."

Holmes waited, looking at him, demanding an answer with his eyes. "You have Mazzioli do that tomorrow, will you?" he insisted gently, but firmly.

"Yes, Sir," Warden said without looking up. "Yes-sir, I'll do that."

"Thanks," Holmes said. He picked his pencil up triumphantly.

Warden finished up the papers, wondering if Holmes really believed the things he said or just said them for the effect; aware, as he handed the papers to Holmes, that he had just witnessed the beginning of the complicated mental process that had elevated over half the noncoms in the Company to their present rank.

Holmes looked the papers over with an air of profound well-being. "I suppose these are in good order?"

"Sir?" exploded Warden. "I make them out they're always in good order."

"Now, now, Sergeant," Holmes said, raising his hand as if he were a bishop. "I know you're a good first sergeant. I just want to be sure theres no slip on this transfer."

"I made it out," Warden told him.

"Yes," Holmes smiled, "but your mind was too much on Leva and the supplyroom. If you'd quit worrying about Mess and Supply and trying to do their work in addition to your own, we'd have a lot more efficiency, and a much better outfit."

"Somebody has to worry about it, Sir," Warden said.

"Now, now," Holmes laughed. "It cant be that bad, Sergeant. You look for things to worry about.

"Oh by the way, how is this new man Prewitt making out with straight duty now?"

"Doing fine. That boy is a good soldier."

"I know he is," Holmes said. "Thats what I'm counting on. I never saw a good soldier who liked to do straight duty as a private. I'm expecting to see him out for Company Smokers this summer. Theres an old saying that they tame lions in the Army."

"I think you're wrong," Warden said bluntly. "I dont think you'll ever see him out for boxing."

"Wait until the rainy season's over, Sergeant, before you be so sure. We've got a lot of field work coming up this summer." He winked at Warden knowingly and picked up his rain-dark hat; at the moment he was sure, because Prewitt had been included in the plans of his campaign, and how could he not be on the squad if he was in the plans?

Warden watched him plowing his way back across the rainswept deserted quad, realizing suddenly why he hated Holmes. It was because he had always feared him, not him personally, not his physique or mind, but what he stood for. Dynamite would make a good general someday, if he got the breaks. Good generals ran to a certain type, and Dynamite was it. Good generals had to have the type of mind that saw all men as masses, as numerical groups of Infantry, Artillery, and mortars that could be added and subtracted and understood on paper. They had to be able to see men as abstractions that they worked on paper with. They had to be like Blackjack Pershing who could be worried about the morality of his troops in France so much he tried to outlaw whorehouses to save their mothers heartache, but who was proud of them when they died in battle.

Through the obscuring mist of anger in him, the stark nakedness of the raindrenched earth and muddy grass and the lonely moving figure of Holmes huddled in his topcoat made a picture in his mind of a ghost town street and a strong wind rolling along a tattered scrap of paper in the gutter to some unforeseen and unimportant destination, moaning with the sadness of its duty. From upstairs he could hear the shouts and splashings of the Company washing up for chow, and the chillness that swept in through the open window made him shudder and put on his field jacket that hung on his chair.

He stared out the window, his rage disintegrated, replaced by an unutterable melancholy that had no reason he could find.

Leva's bald head floated leisurely by the open window, heading for the kitchen where he and Warden ate, instead of with the Company in the messhall.

"Whats for chow?" Warden called.

"BS and C," stated the wryfaced Leva laconically, and strolled on.

Roast beef hash and gravy! Again! Preem was getting worse and worse. It kept the Company Fund broke buying GI lemon extract for him.

Warden sat down at his desk and reached into a drawer and brought out the regulation .45 pistol he always kept there, hefting the heavy weighted balance in his hand. Just like the pistol his father had brought home from the War. Same weight, same shape, same heavy blueness. He and Frankie Lindsay up the street had swiped it from his father's bureau, every now and then, and shot caps in it sticking them in the slot before the pinless hammer; they would drop pebbles down the muzzle too and shoot them out a foot or so, playing they were bullets.

The Company was trooping down the stairs for chow.

Warden leveled the pistol at the small doorless closet where the filing cabinets were and cocked it. The raising of the hammer made a dull metallic click that was an ominous expectant sound, and Milt Warden banged his other palm down flat on the desk.

"Ha! you son of a bitch," he said out loud. "Thought I didnt see you."

He stood up, staring at the inoffensive closet, eyes narrowed, brows arched and quivering.

"Re-enlist, will you? I'm Wolf Larsen, see? and nobody re-enlists. Not without answering to old Shark. . . . No you dont!"

He stepped around the desk and strode at the closet, chin thrust forward murderously, stopping in the doorway, pulling the trigger slowly, inexorably.

The hammer fell, inevitable as a clock stroke. The dull click was flatly disappointing after the expectancy of the cocking.

He tossed the heavy pistol on the closet table clatteringly. "Continued next week," he said, looking down at it. In its simple lines and solid gunmetal color it was an entity, beautiful and complete within itself as a woman's calf. But then, he thought, a woman's calf is only a symbol of the rest of it; what man would be satisfied with a woman's calf alone?

Angrily he picked it up and jerked the slide back, letting it slam forward viciously, carrying a cartridge from the clip into the chamber, pointing the now loaded, cocked pistol at his own head and putting his finger lightly on the trigger.

Just where is, he thought, the line that separates insanity? Any man who would pull this trigger now would be insane. Am I insane? because I put it loaded to my head? or because I touch the trigger?

He gazed raptly at the heavy death a moment, then he took it down. He released the magazine expertly and ejected the shell upon his desk. He slipped shell back into clip, clip back into piece, piece back into drawer; and leaned back in his chair listening to the sounds of eating in the messhall.

After a while he rose and took a fifth of whiskey from the second drawer of his file cabinet and had a long, adam's-apple-bobbling drink. Then he went out onto the porch and into the kitchen where Leva was leaning against the castiron sink, eating from a plate in his hand.

Warden's chance came sooner than he had expected. The next afternoon it cleared a little, the rain stopped a while at noon and drew back to reform its ranks before the next assault. It was hanging low and heavy-bellied, ominously, as Holmes came around the quad, staying on the street this time, wearing civvies, a soft brown tweed suit, and carrying his topcoat, to tell him that he was going down to town with Col Delbert and that he would not be back today.

And suddenly Warden knew that he would have to do it. He didnt know why exactly, because this was more than just a woman, there were women enough downtown that he could have. This went much deeper.

Up until now, while he had thought about it, he had only played with the idea. Always before it had been a point with him to steer clear of Army women, they were cold, with no more warmth in them than in a brilliant diamond, and there was no pleasure in them. They did their fornication out of boredom rather than desire. And from what Leva had told him and from what he had seen himself, he suspected Karen Holmes was one of them.

Yet above all that he still knew that he would do it, not as vengeance, or even retribution, but as an expression of himself, to regain the individuality that Holmes and all the rest of them, unknowing, had taken from him. And he understood suddenly why a man who has lived his whole life working for a corporation might commit suicide simply to express himself, would foolishly destroy himself because it was the only way to prove his own existence.

"Will you be back in time to take Retreat?" he said to Holmes casually, not looking up from the papers in his hand he had been reading.

"Hell no," Holmes said happily. "Or Reveille either, probably. I told Culpepper to take them both for me if I dont show up. If he doesnt show up, you take them."

"Yes, Sir," Warden said.

Holmes was walking back and forth across the office, displaying an uninhibited joy and anticipation Warden had seldom seen in him. Under the burning lights that flickered out the window oilily upon the gloomy rainy day, Holmes's normally florid face was flushed a deeper hue of happiness.

"All work and no play," Holmes said, and winked. It was a male wink, implying the turgid weighted pendulum that must be relieved, and it flung a momentary bridge across the gulf of caste that always separated them. "You ought to take a day off yourself," Holmes said. "All you do is sit around this gloom sweating over this paper and that. There are other, happier things in this world besides administration."

"I've been considering it," Warden said thinly, exchanging the papers in his hand for some on his desk and picking up a pencil. This was Thursday, the maid's day off, it was just as good a time as any. He watched the beefy happiness on Holmes's face narrowly, surprised that now at this time he should like him better than he ever had.

"Well," Holmes said. "I'm going. I'm leaving it in your care, Sergeant." There was great trust and feeling in his voice, and in his suddenly powerful emotion he clapped his hand on Warden's shoulder.

"It'll be here when you get back," Warden said. But he was only playing out the role, and his voice was dead.

You've got nothing to go on but your woman's intuition, Milton, Warden told himself, you better play it safe, you better really have it figured out. He watched Holmes leave and sat down at his desk to wait for Mazzioli to come back, because even now, in this big moment, he would not leave the Orderly Room with nobody but the CQ to run it.

It began to rain again before the clerk came back, and Warden occupied himself with cleaning up some odd jobs that had been accumulating. There were a number of letters he had to write out for Mazzioli to copy up for Holmes to sign, and then he made out in the rough the next week's drill schedule, looking up the Field Manuals for the authorization.

Alone in the damp air, he worked savagely, taking out his hatred on the paper, forgetting everything else but this before him, throwing himself headlong at it like a hopped-up Jap attacking a machinegun, and the power of his energy filled the room to bursting.

Mazzioli, the company clerk, was dripping wet when he came in and trying to protect a half a dozen manila envelopes from the water.

"Jesus Christ," he said, looking at Warden with his sleeves turned back. "Its cold enough outside. Shut that window before we both freeze to death."

Warden grinned at him slyly, his eyes squinted up. "Is the poor little delicate baby cold?" he said. "Is him freezin?"

"Aw," the clerk said. "Can it, will you?" He put his folders down and stepped to push it shut himself.

"Leave it open!" Warden roared.

"But its cold," the clerk protested.

"Then freeze," Warden grinned. "I like it open." Suddenly his face hardened. "Where the hella yah been all goddam day?" he snarled.

"You know where I've been," the clerk said primly. "I've been over at the personnel section in Regiment." Having attended a business college on the outside, he exercised his right to intellectual superiority; to this end he prided himself on his good grammar and always sat in on the discussions held by the clerks in Choy's. Now and then he even held a discussion with Pop Karelsen, the sergeant of the weapons platoon, who rumor had it once had been a rich man's son. "I've been working with Sgt/Maj O'Bannon," Mazzioli added bitterly, with a prissy mimic. "If I ever saw an old maid . . ."

"Grant went to the hospital today," Warden interrupted bluntly. He picked the Sickbook up and opened it and held it under Mazzioli's nose. "Did you know Grant was interned? He's got the clap. Know what that is?"

The clerk stepped back, his armor pierced, looking guilty.

Warden grinned sourly. "Yeh. Thats time lost under AW 107," he said, bludgeoning him with it. "Did you make up his individual sick record? did you make a note for the Morning Report? did you make a remark for your pay cards? did you fix my card index roster? The goddam Sickbook is your job. You're the clerk. I cant do your work, too."

"I didnt have time when the Sickbook came back this morning," Mazzioli started. "Those medics never get it back before eleven. They . . ."

"Dont gimme any excuse, collegeboy," Warden sneered. He split the plea apart and dealt with both halves deftly. "The Sickbook was back at nine-thirty. O'Bannon didnt send the orderly around till ten. You sit around here all morning on your dead ass working a crossword. How many times do I hafta tell you? *Keep you work up to date.* Do everything the minute it comes in. Once you get behind you never get caught up."

"Okay, Top," Mazzioli said, crestfallen, all his blandness gone. "I'll do it now. Let me have the book." He reached out to take it, but Warden did not relax his grip. Tall, deepchested, and disgusted he stared down at the clerk, a malignant expression in the ends of his eyebrows.

Mazzioli looked at him. "Oh," he said, guiltily, and let go. "Soon as I finish filin these. I'll do it soon as I finish these." He turned from the silent sarcasm to his folders.

Warden tossed the Sickbook on his desk. "I already done it," he said in a normal tone, disgustedly. "Its all fixed up already."

Mazzioli shot him an admiring glance from the file cabinet. "Thanks, Top," he said.

"Go to hell," Warden said, violent again. "If you dont watch yer step, you're gonna find your ass busted back to private and do a little straight duty. Which would probably kill a college angelina like you. A classic example of the American educational system, thats what you are."

Mazzioli did not believe the threat, but he put a sad expression on his face, just in case. Warden saw completely through it.

"You think I'm kiddin ya?" Warden said, with his overpowering violence. "Keep on like you're goin and watch. You'll find yourself divin for pearls in the kitchen. I'm the first sergeant here, not you, and if theres any leisure around here I get it, see? If there aint enough for two, then you work. And if you dont quit hangin around with them two-bit philosophers over at Regmint you'll be scrubbin this Orderly Room floor for me.

"What was the discussion on today?" he said.

"Van Gogh," Mazzioli said. "He's a painter."

"Well, well," Warden said. "Do tell. A painter. Did you ever read *Lust For Life?*"

"Yes," Mazzioli said, surprised. "Did you?"

"No," Warden said. "I never read."

"You ought to read it, Top. Its a good book."

"Did you ever read *The Moon and Sixpence?*" Warden said.

"Sure," Mazzioli said, surprised again. "Have you?"

"No," Warden said. "I never read."

Mazzioli turned to look at him. "Aw now," he said. "What are you doing, kidding me?"

"Who, me?" Warden said. "Dont flatter yourself, kid."

"I bet you read them," Mazzioli said. He laid down his filing and sat down and lit a cigaret. "You know, I've got a theory on Gauguin."

"To hell with your theories," Warden said. "Lets get them files fixed up. I got some business to attend to myself."

"Okay," Mazzioli said. He got up angrily and went back to work.

Looking at the anger on Mazzioli's face, Warden laughed outright. "So Grant's got the clap, hey?" he said, conversationally.

"I told him he should have taken a pro," Mazzioli said distastefully, but still angrily. "Or at least used a rubber."

Warden snorted contemptuously. "Do you wash your feet with your socks on, kid?"

"I've already heard that one," the clerk said aloofly.

Warden snorted again. "Where'd Grant say he got it?"

"At the Ritz Rooms," Mazzioli said distastefully.

"Serves the son of a bitch right. He should of known better'n to go to that crummy joint. He'll be a goddam private in the rear rank when he gets out of the hospital. So he's payin for it." Warden stood up and banged his fist down on his desk so hard that Mazzioli jumped in spite of himself.

"Let that be a goddam lesson to you, Corporal," Warden said violently, "if you dont want to lose those goddam stripes you love so much."

"Who?" Mazzioli said, astonished. "Me?"

"Yes, you. Stick to your goddamned rubber glove and become a queer, like the sex hygiene lectures advise you."

"Now listen," Mazzioli said indignantly.

"You listen," Warden said. "I got some very, very important business to attend to, see? And I wont be back till probly four o'clock. You stay here in this Orderly Room till I get back, see? and if I hear of you even goin to the latrine, I'll bust you down tomorrow, see?"

"Aw, for Christ's sake, Top," Mazzioli protested. "I got some things I have to do this afternoon."

"This business of mine," Warden said, grinning to himself, "is strictly official. You had the whole goddam morning off to discuss art. You got a soft job; if you dont like it, you can quit any time. How many cupsacoffee you have in Choy's this morning, hah?"

"I only went down for coffee once," Mazzioli protested.

"Four o'clock. And you better be here when I get back. Theres about six letters there to be typed up and next week's drill schedule to type up. Not counting all the filin that you've let get behind."

"Okay, Top," Mazzioli said dejectedly as Warden shouldered himself into his raincoat and picked up a sheaf of papers, seeing his afternoon sacktime departing on the black wings of tyranny. The Warden, and his prisoners. Anything to keep somebody from doing what they wanted. He was a manic-depressive, Mazzioli decided suddenly, happily, or a paranoiac.

He stepped to the window to watch through the dim gloom of the rainy afternoon where The Warden might be going. Official business, my old fanny.

But Warden had anticipated that, and he walked along the street around the quad, resolutely through the rain, it drumming boomingly on his sugar-stiff campaign hat and rustling in his raincoat that was already beginning to wet his back, and climbed the stairs to Regimental Hq above the sallyport.

From the porch he looked back across the quad and saw Mazzioli's head and shoulders dark against the light from the Orderly Room window, almost as if he had his nose pushed against the glass. What a kid, he thought, no more conception of a soldier than a rabbit and taking it out in talking about art.

He laughed out loud, throwing it out defiantly against the sound-blanketing curtain of the rain, feeling in him the smoking sparking pinwheel of the coming profanation of the sacred mark of caste. Maybe she wont even be home, he told himself. Yes she will, she'll be there.

He took the papers out from inside his raincoat to see if they were wet. They were authentic letters, ones Holmes really should have signed before he left. Always be prepared, boy scout, he grinned.

He stopped a moment, grinning more, before the bulletin board just inside the doorway. On the side that had been stencilled PERMANENT was a copy of McCrae's *In Flanders Fields* printed in red old English type on vellum and with the margins adorned with tortured figures in the pancake British helmet of the War. Next to it was a poem called *The Warhorse* by an unknown general, Retired, of the World War, the first World War, comparing an old soldier to the old firehorse who came running every time the bell rang. Then there was Col Delbert's latest memorandum right beside it, complimenting the troops on their spirit and athletic prowess and *esprit de corps,* all tangible results, the memo said, of their high moral character, as propounded by the Chaplain and the Sex Hygiene Lectures, although this was more or less implied.

Warden crossed the hall and started down the other stairs and then he saw the two colonels from Brigade standing in the dusky corridor with its varnished glassfront trophycases talking, the rest of the hall now at two o'clock deserted and the office doors, except for Sgt/Maj O'Bannon's who practically lived in his, closed. He had hoped there would be nobody around and he looked closely at the colonels to make sure they didnt know him. He looked just a little bit too long.

"Oh, Sergeant," one of them called. "Come here, Sergeant."

He came back up the three or four steps and walked over to them and saluted, restraining a powerful urge to look at his watch.

"Where is Colonel Delbert, Sergeant?" the other one asked, the tall one.

"I dont know, Sir. I havent seen him."

"Has he been in today?" the fat one asked, his voice wheezing a little. He wiped his forehead with a handkerchief and unbuttoned the rainwet shiny gabardine of his topcoat that was identical to that of the tall one except in shade of color.

"I'm sure I couldnt say, Sir," Warden said.

"Dont you *work* here, Sergeant?" the tall one asked narrowly.

"No, Sir," Warden said, thinking fast. "I dont work in Hq. I have a company, Sir."

"What company?" the short one wheezed.

"A Company, Sir," he lied. "Sergeant Dedrick of A Company."

"Oh of course," the short one wheezed. "I thought I knew you. I make a point to know our noncoms in Brigade. You just slipped me."

"Dont you know enough to report when you come up to an officer, Sergeant?" the tall one rasped.

"Yes, Sir, but I have some business to attend to and I guess I had it on my mind."

"Thats no excuse," the tall one rasped, militarily. "How long have you been a noncom, Sergeant?"

"Nine years, Sir," Warden said.

"Well," the tall one said. Then he said, "You should know enough to watch things like that then. I'm certainly glad none of your men were here to see the example you just set."

"Yes, Sir," Warden said, wanting to look at his watch. If he would just only brace me now, he thought. Thats all we need. We could play like back at the Point, upperclassmen hazing the Dumbjohns.

"Carry on, Sergeant," the tall one said. "And in the future be more careful."

"Yes, Sir, I will, Sir." He saluted quickly and made for the stairs, before the other changed his mind. Holmes's wife might be going out this afternoon; if she was, and they made him miss her . . . He laughed, inside, to think what those two would think if they had known what he was thinking.

"He sure was in a hurry," he heard the fat one wheeze.

"My god," the tall one said. "They dont care who they give rockers to any more. It didnt use to be like that."

"Dedrick always was a dumb bastard," the short one said. "Thats how I remembered him, his dumbness."

"Its a damned disgrace, what the service's coming to," the tall one said. "In the old days, a noncom would have been busted flat, to do a thing like that. It isnt like it used to be."

"I wonder where the hell Delbert is," the short one wheezed.

Warden, laughing silently, went on down the inside stairs and out into the sallyport past the folding iron gate that would be open until Retreat, in too big a hurry to be mad.

Somebody called to him from Choy's but he only waved and went on, out the front of the sallyport, crossing Waianae Avenue to the officers' quarters, walking along it through the rain till he came to the alley behind Holmes's corner house. He stopped under the shelter of a big old elm, grinning to himself because he was breathing so heavy, feeling the autumnal chill creep up to him under his raincoat when he stopped, thinking this was a fine day for it and that if she had taken all the others there was no reason why she shouldnt take him too, before he went up finally and knocked on the door.

Inside a longlegged black shadow moved across the dimness of the livingroom doorway cutting off the light, and he caught the scissor-flash of naked legs cutting the light and opening again in another step and his breath seemed to go very deep in his chest.

"Mrs Holmes," he called, knocking, his head pulled down between his shoulders in the rain.

The shadow moved again inside without sound and stepped through the door into the kitchen to become Karen Holmes in shorts and halter.

"What is it?" she said. "Oh. If it isnt Sergeant Warden. Hello, Sergeant. You better step inside or you'll get wet. If you're looking for my husband, he isnt here."

"Oh," Warden said, opening the screendoor and jumping in past the water that ran off the eave. "And if I'm not looking for him?" he said.

"He still isnt here," Karen Holmes said. "If that does you any good."

"Well, I'm looking for him. You know where he is?"

"I havent the slightest idea. Perhaps at the Club, having a drink or two," she smiled thinly. "Or was it snort? I guess it was snort you said, wasnt it?"

"Ah," Warden said. "The Club. Why didnt I think of that? I got some papers its important for him to sign today."

He eyed her openly, traveling up the length of leg in the very short homemade-looking trunks, to the hollow of the hidden navel, to the breasts tight against the halter, to the woman's eyes that were watching his progress and his open admiration indifferently, without interest.

"Kind of chilly for trunks, aint it?" he said.

"Yes." Karen Holmes looked at him unsmiling. "Its cool today. Sometimes its very hard to keep warm, isnt it?" she said. "What is it you want, Sergeant?"

Warden felt his breath come in very slowly, and go very deep, clear down into his scrotum.

"I want to go to bed with you," he said, conversationally. That was how he had planned it, how he had wanted to say it, but now hearing it it sounded very foolish to him. He watched the eyes, in the unchanged face, widen only a little, so little that he almost missed it. A cool cool customer, Milton, he said to himself.

"All right," Karen Holmes said disinterestedly.

With Warden, standing dripping on the porch, it was as if he was listening to her but he did not hear her.

"What are the papers?" she said then, reaching for them. "Let me see them. Maybe I can help you."

Warden pulled them back, grinning, feeling the grin stiff on his face, masklike. "You wouldnt know anything about them. These are business."

"I always take an interest in my husband's business," Karen Holmes said.

"Yes," Warden grinned. "Yes, I sure bet you do. Does he take as big an interest in your business?"

"Do you want me to help you with them?"

"Can you sign his name?"

"Yes."

"So it looks like his own signature?"

"I dont know about that," she said, still not smiling. "I never tried."

"Well I can," Warden said. "I can do everything for him but wear his goddamned bars. At that I draw the line. But these papers go to Division and he's got to sign them himself."

"Then I'd better call the Club," she said, "hadnt I? That is where he is."

"Having a drink or two," Warden said.

"But I'll be glad to call him for you, Sergeant."

"To hell with that. I never like to disturb a man drinking. I could use a drink myself right now. Bad."

"But if its business," Karen Holmes said.

"Anyway, I dont think you'll find him at the Club. I got a faint suspicion he went to town with Colonel Delbert," Warden grinned at her.

Karen Holmes did not answer. She stared at him unsmiling from a cold reflective face that did not know he still was there.

"Well," he said. "Aint you going to ask me in?"

"Why, yes, Sergeant," Karen Holmes said. "Come right in."

She moved then, slowly, as if her joints had got rusty from standing still so long, and stepped back up the single step into the kitchen to let him in.

"What kind of drink do you want, Sergeant?"

"I don't care," he said. "Any drink'll do."

"You dont want a drink," Karen Holmes said. "You dont really want a drink. What you really want is this," she said, looking down at her own body and moving her hands out sideways like a sinner at the altar.

"Thats what you really want. Isnt it? Thats what you all want. All all of you ever want."

Warden felt a shiver of fear run down his spine. What the hell is this, Milton? "Yes," he said. "Thats what I really want. But I'll take a drink too," he said.

"All right. But I wont mix it for you. You can mix it yourself or you can drink it straight." She sat down in a chair beside the enameled kitchen table and looked at him.

"Straight's all right," he said.

"The bottle's there," she pointed to a cupboard. "Get it yourself. I wont get it for you." She laid her hand flat on the cool smoothness of the table. "You can have it, Sergeant, but you'll have to do the work yourself."

Warden laid the papers on the table and got the bottle from the cupboard, thinking I can match that, baby. "You want one too?" he said. "You just wait," he said. "You'll help me."

"I dont think I want a drink," Karen Holmes said. Then, "Yes, perhaps I'd better. I'll probably need it, dont you think?"

"Yes," he said. "You probly will." There were glasses on the sink and he took two and poured them both half full, wondering what kind of a woman this one was anyway.

"Here," he said. "To the end of virginity."

"I'll drink to that," she raised her glass. She made a face from the liquor as she set it down. "You're taking an awful chance, you know," she said. "Do you really think its worth it? What if Dana should come home? I'm safe you know: my word is always better than an EM's word. I'd holler rape and you'd get twenty years, at Leavenworth."

"He wont," Warden grinned, repouring in her glass. "I know where he is. He probly wont be home at all tonight. Besides," he said, looking up from filling his own glass, "I got two buddies from PI at Leavenworth, I'd be among friends."

"What happened to them?" she asked, drinking what was in her glass, making another face at it.

"They got caught in a buggy with a colonel's wife by one of MacArthur's gook boy scouts."

"Both of them?"

He nodded. "And with the same dame. She picked them up, they said, but they still got twenty years. The gook was the colonel's orderly. But I've heard it said he did it out of jealousy."

Karen Holmes smiled tolerantly, but she did not laugh. "I think you're bitter, Sergeant." She set down her empty glass and lay back in the chair, sprawled. "My maid is liable to be home any time you know."

Warden shook his head, seeing in his mind a picture of her lying on a bed inviting him, now that his first insecurity was gone. "No she wont," he said. "Thursday's her day off. Today is Thursday."

"You think of everything, dont you, Sergeant?"

"I try," he said. "In my position you have to."

Karen Holmes picked up the papers from the table. "I guess we can dispense with these now, cant we? They're nothing, are they?"

"Yes, they are," he said. "They're letters. You dont think I'd bring something worthless, do you? so Holmes might see them? so you might use them as evidence when you turned me in? And you can call me Milt, now we're intimate."

"Thats what I like about you, Sergeant: You have confidence. Its also what I dislike about you." Slowly she tore the papers into little bits and dropped them in the wastebasket behind her. "Men and their confidence. You can consider these as the payment you had to make. You always pay, dont you?"

"Not if I can help it," Warden said, wondering again what all this amounted to anyway, not expecting anything like this. "I got carbons of those back at the office," he grinned, "so it wont be much work to fix them up."

"At least your confidence is real," she said. "Not false confidence, or bravado—many men have that. Pour me another drink. Tell me, how did you acquire it?"

"My brother is a priest," he said, reaching for the bottle.

"Well?"

"Thats all she wrote," he said.

"What has that to do with it?"

"Everything, baby. In the first place it isnt confidence, its honesty. Being a priest, he believes in celibacy. He has a very heavy beard shaved very close and he believes in mortal sin and he is worshipped by his adoring flock. Makes a very good living at it."

"Well?" she said.

"Whata ya mean, well? After watching him a while, I decided to believe in honesty, which means the opposite of celibacy. Because I did not want to hate myself and everybody else, like him. That was my first mistake, from then on it was easy.

"I decided to not believe in mortal sin, since obviously no Creator who was Just would condemn His creations to eternal hellfire and brimstone for possessing hungers He created in them. He might penalize them fifteen yards for clipping, but He wouldnt stop the ball game. Now would He?"

"You wouldnt think so," Karen said. "But where does that leave you? if there is no such a thing as punishment for sins?"

"Ah," Warden grinned. "You went right to the heart. I dont like this word 'sin.' But since there is obviously punishment, I was forced by irrefutable logic to accept the weird outlandish idea of reincarnation. That was when my brother and I parted. I had to beat him up, to prove my theory; it was the only way. And, to date, the reincarnation is as far as my philosophy has gotten. What do you say we have another drink?"

"Then I take it you dont believe in sin at all?" Karen Holmes said, a kind of interest flickering for the first time in her eyes.

Warden sighed. "I believe the only sin is a conscious waste of energy. I believe all conscious dishonesty, such as religion, politics and the real estate business, are a conscious waste of energy. I believe that at a remarkable cost in energy people agree to pretend to believe each other's lies so they can prove to themselves their own lies are the truth, like my brother. Since I cannot forget what the truth is, I gravitated, naturally, along with the rest of the social misfits who are honest into the Army as an EM. Now what do you say we have another drink? Since we've settled the problems of God, Society, and the Individual I really think we rate another drink."

"Well," the woman smiled, and the momentary flick of interest had gone out, replaced by the old flip and coldness. "He's smart as well as virile. Lucky little female, to be allowed to enclose the erect pride of such virility. But since you believe the conscious waste of energy is a sin, dont you believe the loss of semen is a sin? unless accompanied by impregnation?"

Warden grinned and dipped the bottle in salute, bowing over it. "Madam, you have touched the weak spot in my philosophy. Far be it from me to snow you. All I can say is—not as long as it is not cast out on the ground, or paid for, and sometimes even then. (Have you ever served in the field?) All I can say is—not as long as it is useful."

Karen Holmes emptied her glass and set it on the table, with finality. "Useful. Now we're getting into dialectic."

"Dont such talk always?"

"And I do not believe in dialectic. I dont want to listen to your definition of what useful means."

She put one hand behind her and flipped the snap of her halter and tossed it to the floor. Staring at him with eyes of liquid smoke in which there was a curious and great disinterest she unzipped her shorts and shucked out of them without moving from the chair and dropped them with the halter.

"There," she said. "That is what you want. Thats what all the talk's about. Thats what all you virile men, you intellectual men, always want. Isnt it? You big strong male men who are virile and intelligent, but who are helpless as babies without a fragile female body to root around on."

Warden found himself staring at the twisted navel and the ridge of scar-tissue that ran down from it, disappearing in the hairy mattress, and that was so old now as to almost be a shadow.

"Pretty, isnt it?" she said. "And its a symbol, too. A symbol of the waste of energy."

Warden set his glass down carefully. He moved toward her on the chair, seeing the nipples wrinkled tightly like flowers closed for night, seeing the feminine grossness that he loved, that was always there, that he always knew was there, hidden maybe behind perfume, unmentioned, unacknowledged, even denied, but still always there, existing, the beautiful lovely grossness of the lioness and the honest bitch dog, that no matter how much, shrinking, they tried to say it wasnt so, in the end always had to be admitted.

"Wait," she said. "Not here, you greedy little boy. Come in the bedroom."

He followed, angry at the "greedy little boy" but knowing it was true, and wondering wonderingly what kind of creature this one was with all the buried darknesses.

He wasnt wearing anything under his CKCs and she shut the door, turning to him blindly, her arms out, raising the roundnesses of her breasts and making hollows beside her arms.

"Now," she said. "Here. Now. Here and now and now."

"Which bed is Holmes's?" he said.

"The other one."

"Then you just move over there."

"All right," she said. She laughed, the first time, richly. "You take your cuckoldry seriously dont you, Milt?"

"Where Holmes is concerned I take everything seriously."

"And so do I."

As he moved nearer and nearer to the center of the redness which contained himself, and which he never reached, feeling it blinding him with the light he hungered after and bringing the purring deep down in his throat, the screendoor in the back slammed loudly.

"Listen," Karen said. "Theres someone. Listen." They could hear the footsteps coming phlegmatically, not slowing, not turning, sounding heavy through the walls. "Quick. Take your clothes and get in the closet there and shut the door. Quick. Hurry up. For God's sake, hurry, man."

Warden vaulted the other bed, scooping up the uniform and stepped inside and shut the door. Karen was wrapping on a Chinese silk kimono and sitting before her dressing table by the window that looked through the truckway to the barracks. By the time the bedroom door was knocked on she was brushing calmly at her hair, but her face was very white.

"Who is it?" Karen called, wondering if the trembling in her voice was noticeable.

"Its me," a boy's voice said. "Its Junior." He knocked again, demandingly. "Let me in."

"All right," she said. "Come in. It isnt locked."

Her son, a nine-year-old miniature of Dana Holmes in his long pants and Aloha shirt, came in, wearing the unholy sullenness that is in the faces of so many holy offspring of duly sanctioned misalliances.

"They let us out of school early," he said sullenly. "Your face is white. Whats the matter, you sick again?" he asked, studying his mother's face with the unconscious distaste healthy children have for chronic invalids, and with a measure of the disdainful male superiority that in the last year or two he had picked up from his father.

"I've not been feeling well the last few days," Karen told him, truthfully, trying hard not to be defensive, and looking at this boy who in one short year had become his father, thinking with a kind of sickness that this long-jawed beefy face, once round and merry, had grown inside her flesh, feeling again the old revulsion. Looking at the boy, there was suddenly no guilt inside her for the man hiding in the closet, there was only a dull anger at the furtiveness like the slipping around corners of youths in school going to their first whorehouse.

"I'm going over to the Company this afternoon," the boy said, looking at her from across the battlements of the besieged city that is childhood. "I want my uniform."

"Did you ask your father if it was all right?" Karen said, feeling tears rising behind her eyes at the prospect of what was before him, wanting suddenly to put her arms around him and explain so many things to him. "He isnt there today, you know."

"Who said he was?" the boy said. "He's never there in the afternoon. He don't care if I go over to the Company. Long as I dont get familiar with the men, he said. You got no right to keep me home just because you hate the Company."

"Good God, child," Karen said. "I dont want to keep you home. I dont hate the Company. I just wanted . . ."

"I dont care what you say anyway," the boy said, cramming his fists down in his pockets. "I'm going anyway. Dad said I could go and I'm going."

"I wanted to be sure it was all right with your father," Karen said. "You always ask him first."

"He went to town this noon," the boy said. "If I had to ask him, I'd have to wait till tomorrow morning, probly. You talk like we had company."

"All right," Karen said, wondering if she was being bitchy, so many of them took their bitchiness and anger at their husbands out on the defenseless children; it was one thing she had promised herself that she would never do. "If you were going anyway, why did you even bother to come home and tell me?"

"I didnt come home to tell you," the boy said. "I came home to get my uniform to wear and you have to help me put it on."

"Go get it out then," she said. At least there was one thing she could still do; anyway she could do it when Dana wasnt home. In the last two years his education in both school and life had been taken from her hands, along with all the other things. She felt herself slipping back into the old habit of indifference, and thinking pleasantly about Milt there in the closet. At least there was one way left for a woman to express herself, she thought distastefully, now that the chastity belts were outlawed, now that the stocks and ducking chairs were gone, although the condemnation still was just as bad.

"Well come on," the boy said impatiently. "I'm in a hurry. I'm going to help Sergeant Preem cook supper tonight and eat with them."

"Is that all right with Sergeant Preem?" she said, getting up to follow him.

"It has to be, dont it? If he's my Dad's mess sergeant. Come on, I'm in a hurry."

In the little room he had for himself Karen helped him shuck off his clothes, staring wonderingly at the small naked agility, surprised again that this foreigner and stranger was her child to love and cherish the way all the books on child-care said. Here were bones and nerves and ligaments from her body, a photographic replica his father had made of himself, using the sensitized plate that had been Karen Jennings of Baltimore, Md., as a man might use an old box camera, for the pictures it would take, not caring about the technique of the using.

Now I've borne the heir, she thought. The film is taken out, the negative made, the picture in the process of development. And the crumbling shredding rotting leathered box is put back on the shelf. Useless now. The mechanism of its dark interior having been accidentally broken by a bad exposure. Thats pretty good, my girl. You ought to write yourself. You've got some good material. And I dont think you'd romanticize love so very much. The unspeakable loneliness of self-pity that is blind and tongueless rose up hot in her, trying to bring tears.

She helped the boy to struggle into the one-piece suit some of whose buttons he could not reach, cocked the cap right on his head, and tied the issue tie that was too big for him. Making of him suddenly what he would inevitably become, a fresh young second lieutenant complete with gold bars and Regimental insignias on his shoulders and US and crossed rifles on his collar tabs and all the painful illusions that went with them. God help you, she thought, God truly help you, and the woman you marry in order to reproduce a replica of yourself. The second generation of an Army line, begun by a farm boy from Nebraska who wanted more than farming and whose father knew a Senator.

Karen put her arms around her son. "My boy."

"Hey," he said, distastefully. "Dont do that. Leave me alone." He shrugged out from under the arms and looked at her accusingly.

"You've mussed your cap," Karen said and set it straight.

Junior looked at her again and then inspected himself in the mirror and finally nodded. He picked up his allowance money off the dresser and slipped it in his pocket.

"I may go to the show," he informed her. "Dad said it was all right. Its Andy Hardy. Dad said it was good and I would like it. And for gosh sake," he said, "dont wait up for me, like I was a kid."

He gave her another look to make sure she understood and then he left, wearing his responsibility heavily.

"Watch out for cars," Karen called, and then bit her lip because she said it.

When the backdoor slammed she went back to the bedroom and sat down quickly on the bed and put her face in her hands, waiting for the nausea to leave, afraid she was going to cry. Crying was the last ditch where she always made her stand. She looked down at her hands and saw that they were shaking. After a while she made herself get up and go to open the closet door, sick with the humiliation of this unjust degradation of herself and Warden whom she could hardly face.

"I think you'd better go," she said, pulling back the door. "It was the boy. He's gone now and . . ." She stopped, amazed, the words trailing off forgotten.

Warden sat crosslegged on the pile of his uniform in the cramped space, the skirts of several dresses draped over his head like a crazy turban, and his big square shoulders were shaking helplessly with laughter.

"Whats the matter?" she said. "What are you laughing at? What are you laughing at, you fool?"

Warden shook his head and a dress fell down over his face. He blew his breath weakly, floating it aside, and looked at her, his body still shaking with the laughing and his eyebrows hooked up high.

"Stop it," Karen said. "Stop it, stop it," her voice going off up high. "It isnt funny. Theres nothing funny about it. It would have been twenty years for you, you fool. What are you *laughing* at?"

"I use to be a traveling salesman," Warden gasped.

Staring unbelievingly at the obvious sincerity of his laughter, she sat down on the bed. "A what?" she said.

"A traveling salesman," he laughed, still sitting there. "For two years I was a traveling salesman, and this heres the first time I ever had to hide in anybody's closet."

Karen stared at the laughing face and hooked quivering brows and pointed ears that were like a satyr's. The Traveling Salesman, and The Farmer's Daughter. The Classic Love Story, the Romeo and Juliet, of the American continent. The symbol of the Great American Brand of Humor, and of all the shameful sniggerings and wishful-thinking winks of all the poolroom eunuchs. And suddenly she began to laugh. If the whim had struck this madman he would just as soon have marched right out of the closet naked up behind the boy and hollered boo. In her mind she saw a picture of him doing it and it sent her far off into laughter.

She sat there on the bed, the sense of shame at nearly being exposed in the act of copulation gone, trying to breathe through all the laughing, trying hard to stop the laughing that was making her begin to cry.

It was Warden's turn to stare uncomprehendingly. He uncrossed his legs and took the dresses off his head and got up and went over to her, thinking that somewhere he had judged this whole thing wrong, that Leva had been wrong, that this was something that had never come within his realm of knowledge.

"There," he said helplessly. "There. There," feeling the absurdity, the oppressive impossibility of any human being trying to communicate with and understand another's mind in a life where nothing was ever what it seemed to be. "Please dont cry," he said, searching vainly for a word, "I cant stand to see somebody cry."

"You dont know what its like," Karen said, shivering and whimpering like a puppy in the rain. "The two of them. Its more than anyone was made to stand."

"Ah," Warden said, wondering how in hell he had gotten mixed up in this deal in the first place. He put his arm around her. "Its all right. He's gone. There," he said. "There." Her breast, lying in his cupped palm, was warm and soft like a young bird quivering with fearful trustfulness.

"Dont do that," she said, pulling irritably away from him. "You dont know. You dont even care. Its nothing to you. A piece of ass. What is it to you? Leave me alone."

"Okay," he said. He stood up and went to get his shirt, feeling almost relieved.

"What are you doing?" she cried at him frantically.

"I'm leaving," Warden said. "Wasnt that what you wanted?"

"Dont you want me either?"

Now what the hell, he thought. "Sure," he said. "Hell yes. I thought you wanted me to leave."

"I do," she said, "if you want to. Go ahead. I dont want to force you into anything. I dont blame you, I dont blame you a bit. Why would you want to stay? Since I'm not even a woman any more."

"You're a woman," Warden said, looking at her in the thin kimono. "All woman. Take it from me."

"Not to anyone but you," she said. "I'm nothing. I cant even work. Theres nowhere in the world I'm needed."

"You're needed," Warden said, coming back and sitting down by her. "In this world beautiful women are needed more than any other thing."

"Thats what men always say. Needed to be some man's beautiful whore. But I'm not even that."

"You've got a nice suntan," he said, running his hand across her back, hearing the rain outside. "This is the kind of day to be laying on the beach at Kaneohe. It wont be raining there."

"I dont like Kaneohe," Karen said. "Its damn near as public and as crowded as that goddam Waikiki."

"Ah," he said, "but I know a little beach near Blowhole that is private. Nobody knows about it. Nobody ever goes there. You climb down the cliff wall and there is a little inlet with a sand beach, suddenly, firm and smooth and the rock wall towering above you so the cars on the highway pass just above and they never know its there. You feel like you use to feel when you were a kid and hid by yourself in a cave of bushes and watched the others hunting you. You dont even need to wear a bathing suit at this place, and you can get tanned all over."

"Will you take me there?" she said.

"What?" he said. "Sure. Sure, I'll take you there."

"And can we go at night? and swim there in the moonlight and then lie on the little beach? and you love me there where nobody can see us or know that we are there?"

"Sure. Sure," he said. "We'll do all that."

"Oh, I'd love to do that," Karen said, looking at him worshipfully. "Nobody's ever done anything like that with me. Do you really want to take me?"

"Sure," Warden said. "When you want to go?"

"Next week. Lets go next weekend. I'll take Dana's car and meet you someplace in town. We'll get some sandwiches and take some beer." She smiled at him radiantly and put her arms around his neck and kissed him.

"Okay," Warden said. He returned the kiss, feeling hungrily under his hands the long twin muscles along her spine running from the tiny waist up to the wideness of the shoulders, feeling the searching softness of her lips against him, feeling the twin pressures of her breasts against him, and thinking of the childlike radiance that had been in her face that was so different from the sophisticated hardness that she had worn on it in the kitchen, and wondering what is this anyway? what the hell have you gotten into, Milton, you and your woman's intuition?

"Come here," he said, hoarsely, gently. "Come here, little baby. Come here to me."

The great gentleness that was in him, that he was always wanting to bring forward but never could, rose up in him now like a flood, blindingly.

"Oh," Karen said. "I never knew it could be like this."

Outside the rain thrummed ceaselessly and cascaded ceaselessly from the roof, and in the street the sound of the stiff brooms of afternoon Fatigue grated soothingly, above the rain.

Chapter 10

The appointment of Pvt Bloom to Pfc did not come as a surprise to G Company. It had been expected since late December that the first vacant rating would go to Bloom, who, until he suddenly went out for Company Smokers last year and then followed it up with Regimental and four wins in the Bowl, had only been one of the many other doughy faces peering with forlorn grins out of the Company's yearly photograph. From a less than mediocre soldier Bloom had vaulted, using the sturdy pole of boxing politics, into the position of being the only private, Pfc or otherwise, whom Old Ike ever called out of the ranks to give Close Order and who was being groomed for Corporal. And the non-jockstrap faction in the perpetual feud was very bitter in its denouncement of the obvious favoritism. Capt Holmes would have been shocked, then hurt, then probably indignant, if he could have known the reaction Bloom's Pfc had on the majority of the privates in his Company, but only a little of their muttered comments ever reached him, and that only after it had been watered down until it was considered suitable for his ears by those of his men who told him.

The jockstraps, although none of them had particularly been Bloom's friends, welcomed him into their fold with much brotherliness and defended him violently. They had to do this in order to perpetuate their doctrine that jockstraps made better leaders, and which had always been their justification against the bitter mutterings of the straight duty privates who could not make a rating.

Little Maggio, the gambler and ex-shipping clerk for Gimbel's Basement, was particularly bitter and incensed.

"If I had knew," he said to Prewitt, whose bunk was two beds from his own in Chief Choate's squad, "if I had only knew what this man's

Army had been like. Of all the people in this outfit, they give that vacant Pfc to Bloom. Because he is a punchie."

"What did you expect, Angelo?" Prew grinned.

"He aint even a good soljer, mind you," Maggio said bitterly. "He's ony just a punchie. I'm only out of ree-croot drill a month and I'm a better soljer than Bloom is."

"Soljerin aint what does it."

"But it ought a be. You wait, man. If I ever get out of this Army, you just wait. Draft or no draft, they'll never get me back."

"Balls," Prew grinned. "You got all the makins of a thirty year man. I can see it on you a block away."

"Dont say that," Maggio said, violently. "I mean it. I like you, but I dont like even you that much. Thirty year man! Not me, buddy. If I'm goin to be a valet, yard man, and general handyman for some fuckin officer, I'm goin to get paid for it, see?"

"You'll re-enlist," Prew said.

"I'll re-enlist," Maggio said chanting the old bugle call parody, "in a pig's ass hole. If anybody should of had that rating, man, you should of had it. You're the best soljer in this outfit for my dough. By a hunert million miles."

The rainy season's course of indoor lectures had given Maggio an admiration for Prew as a soldier. His feverish quick-moving eyes had not missed Prew's competence with the rifle, pistol, BAR and MG and with all their nomenclatures, all old stuff from his previous enlistment. But his admiration for Prew as a soldier had jumped a hundred percent when he found out Prew had been a fighter in the 27th and refused to fight for Holmes. He could not understand it, but with his ingrained championing of the underdog, learned at Gimbel's and not lessened by the Army, he admired it. He had watched Prew's soldiering from a distance admiringly, but it was not until he found out about the other thing that he offered open friendship.

"If you'd of decided to punch for Dynamite you would of got that rating. You can bet your balls you'd got it. And you want to spend thirty years of your life in a deal like this!"

Prew grinned, and agreed, but he said nothing. There wasnt anything for him to say.

"Come on," Maggio said disgustedly. "Lets get a game goin in the latrine. Maybe I can win enough to go to town."

"Okay," Prew said, still grinning, following him. The rainy season had been good to him. The leisurely lectures in the Dayroom and the practical work of field- and detail-stripping and assembling the various pieces on the chilly porches with the sound of rain outside were things he liked, and since they were conducted by a single officer or noncom for the Company as a whole, they gave him respite from the vengeful eye of Old Ike Galovitch who seemed bent on protecting the honor of the Great God Holmes, ever since he first found out that Prew had refused to fight. Also, the ending of the boxing season had relieved the tension he had brought into the Company, temporarily at least.

The three globed lights in the first floor latrine burned dimly. A GI blanket, Maggio's, was spread out on the concrete floor between the row of commodes in open stalls on one wall and the urinal trough and washbowls on the other, and the six men sat down around it.

Maggio, shuffling the cards, looked over at the topless, seatless, commodes in their stalls where three men were sitting with their pants down, and held his nose. "Hey," he said, "is this a goddam cardroom? or a la-trine? Attensh-HUT! Da-ress Right, DHRESS!"

The men looked up from their magazines, cursed, and went back to business.

"Deal the cards, Angelo," Anderson, the company bugler, said. "Deal the cards."

"Sure," said Salvatore Clark, the apprentice bugler, grinning shyly under his long Italian nose. "Deal them cards, Wop, or I'll put you down and shove them up you, see?" He laughed then, with rich shy humor, unable to keep to his self-appointed role as tough guy.

"You wait," Maggio said. "I'll deal these cards. I'm stackin these cards." He held the deck in his open left hand, index finger crooked professionally around the top.

"You couldnt stack shit with a shovel, Angelo," Prew said.

"Listen," Maggio said. "I learn to deal these cards in Brooklyn, see? on Atlantic Avenue, where anything less than a royal flush never had a chanct." He riffled the cards from right hand to left, as near as he could come to the delicate card ladder of professional gamblers. He began to deal. The game was stud. And each of them was suddenly alone, engrossed.

Prew laid the fifty cents in nickels he had borrowed from Pop Karelsen, Sgt of the Weapons Platoon and intellectual friend of Cpl Mazzioli, and who had taken a liking to him when he found out he knew machineguns, on the blanket and winked at Clark.

"Boy," said Sal Clark fervently. "How I'd like to make a stake in this game and take it over to O'Hayer's and make a killing." It was the hope and dream of all of them. "I'd take that ol' Honolulu over, I mean. I'd rent me the whole friggin New Congress Hotel for one whole night, and the ones I couldnt lay I'd have to watch and give advice." He, who could never get up nerve enough to even go to a whorehouse unless someone was with him, chuckled and grinned shyly at his own deception. "You aint never been to the New Congress, have you Prew? You aint never been to Mrs Kipfer's, have you?"

"I aint had the money yet," Prew said. He looked at Sal, feeling a warmness of protection, and then across at his sidekick Andy who was engrossed sullenly in his cards, and then back at Sal, on whose account it was mainly that he had finally made friends with them.

Sal Clark with his shy trusting eyes and half-embarrassed grin was like the village idiot boy who is utterly without malice, envy, distrust, or the desire to better himself and so incompetent to maintain himself in our society, and who the prosperous business men, joyously robbing each other every chance they got, fed and clothed and protected tenderly, as if in some metaphysical way he with his undistracted mind might make a plea for them with God, or save them from their consciences. In the same way, Sal Clark was taken care of and respected as the talisman of the Company.

Anderson had made overtures of friendship to Prew several times, and on Payday after Prew had blown in his pay, he even offered to loan him money, but every time he came around Prew had cut him off, because Andy's eyes never focused on his face but always on one side or the other, and Prew did not want for friends men who feared him. And it was not until Sal Clark with his wide, deep, uncomprehending doelike eyes had asked him trustingly to be friends that he suddenly saw he could not refuse.

. . . It happened on one of those warm February nights before the rainy season started when the stars seemed near enough to finger. He had come out of the smoky drunkenness of Choy's feeling the beer all through him lightly and stopped in the lighted tunnel of the sallyport that funneled the large sounds of the night. Across the quad the lights in the 2nd Battalion were still on and shadow figures moved across the porches in front of them. The dark quadrangle was sprinkled with the lightning bugs of cigaret butts, clustered around pitchers of beer, glowing as some one dragged and then fading out again.

From over in the far corner near the bugler's megaphone came the ringing chords of a guitar and voices raised in four-part harmony. It was rule of thumb harmony, but it was closely knit and it carried clear and sharp across the quad, sounding good. And in the slowly moving harmony he recognized Sal's twanging nasal, standing out, more hillbilly than any mountain man, although he was a long nosed Wop from Scranton. They were singing *Truckdriver's Blues*.

"Feelin mighty weary, from my head down to my shoes . . . Got to keep a rollin . . . truckdriver's blues . . . Never did have nothin, got nothin much to lose . . . Got a lowdown feelin . . . truckdriver's blues."

And the utter simplicity of the plaintive lament in Sal Clark's voice reached out and touched him. He felt his anger and indignation at Warden and this setup dwindling away into a kind of deep perceptive melancholy for which there were no words. It was all in the words of the song, but the words actually said nothing at all; except that a truckdriver was weary and had the blues.

The music came to him across the now bright, now dull, slowly burning cigaret of each man's life, telling him its ancient secret of all men, intangible, unfathomable, defying longwinded descriptions, belying intricate cataloguings, simple, complete, asking no more, giving no less, words that said nothing yet said all there was to say. The song of the one-eyed man who had driven the ox sled through the summer hills in the Kentucky mountains, the song of the Choctaw on his reservation, the song of the man who had laid the rollers for the stones heavy as death to build the glorious monument to the king. In the simple meaningless words he saw himself, and Chief Choate, and Pop Karelsen, and Clark, and Anderson, and Warden, each struggling with a different medium, each man's path running by its own secret route from the same source to the same inevitable end. And each man knowing as the long line moved as skirmishers through the night woodsy jungle down the hill that all the others were there with him, each hearing the faint rustlings and straining to communicate, each wanting to reach out and share, each wanting to be known, but each unable, as Clark's whining nasal was unable, to make it known that he was there, and so each forced to face alone whatever it was up ahead, in the unmapped alien enemy's land, in the darkness.

Mazzioli and the other clerks who congregated mornings at Choy's to discuss Art and Life were blind. He knew them, so involved in intricate conversation, so secure in pointless argument, they could not see the thing they sought to grasp lay right before them, all around them, and could be touched only momentarily, but never grasped and held by any sharp dissection. It spoke now from the bottomless shallows of a hillbilly song that in its artless simplicity said everything their four-dollar words could never say, went back to a basic simplicity that gave a sudden flashing picture of all life that could never be explained and an understanding of it that could never be expressed.

The clerks, the kings, the thinkers; they talked, and with their talking ran the world. The truckdrivers, the pyramid builders, the straight duty men; the ones who could not talk, they built the world out of their very tonguelessness—so the talkers could talk about how to run it, and the ones who built it. And when they had destroyed it with their talking the truckdriver and the straight duty man would build it up again, simply because they were hunting for some way to speak. He could feel it all there in the song, and in Sal Clark's howling painful nasal voice. "Feelin mighty weary . . . never did have nothin . . . got a lowdown feelin . . . truckdriver's blues."

He had walked a zigzag trail through the parties of beer drinkers over to the corner and stood on the outskirts of the little crowd that always congregates around a guitar player. There was a small group of five actors who were the center. The others, lumped deferentially as onlookers, stood around and sang or listened, beneath the superiority of the creative circle. Andy and Clark had swung into *San Antonio Rose,* and Prew circled around the outer edge, listening but making no attempt to enter, and Andy had caught sight of him.

"Hey, Prew!" he called, a fawning in his voice. "We need a guitarman. Come on over and sit in."

"No, thanks," he said shortly, as ashamed of the flattery in Andy as if it had been in himself, and turned to go.

"Aw, come on," Andy urged, looking at him through the opening that the crowd had made, his eyes moving all around his face but never resting on it.

"Sure, Prew, come on," Sal seconded eagerly his wide eyes shining blackly with enthusiasm. "Boy, we're havin a lot of fun. We even got beer tonight. Say," he added, rushing the new thought out, "I'm gettin pooped out. How about you takin this one for a while?" It was the greatest offering he could make, but it was the obviousness of it that hit Prew.

"Okay," he said curtly. He walked over and took the proffered guitar and sat down in the middle of the group. "What'll we play?"

"How about *Red River Valley?*" Sal said artlessly, knowing it was Prew's favorite.

Prew nodded and hit a tentative chord, and they swung into it. As they played Clark pressed the beer pitcher upon him.

"It aint as good as Andy's new one," Sal said, nodding at his guitar. "He sold it to me cheap when he bought the new one. Its beat up, but its good enough for me, to learn on."

"Sure," Prew said.

Sal squatted in front of them holding the beer pitcher. He was grinning with great joy and he sang the song in that whining nasal, his eyes half shut, his head back and on one side, almost drowning out the rest. When it ended, he took Prew's empty beercan that had its top cut off to serve as a glass and filled it.

"Here, Prew," he said anxiously. "You gonna play, you'll want to wet your whistle. Singin makes a guy get dry."

"Thanks," Prew said. He drained the can and wiped his mouth with the back of his hand and looked at Andy.

"How about my *Talkin Blues?*" Andy offered. It was his specialty, that he never liked to do when there was a crowd, but now he was offering it to Prew.

"Okay," Prew said, and hit a chord to start it off.

"I been lookin for you to come around," Sal Clark said, above the music. "I been hopin you'd come around, Prew boy."

"I been busy," Prew said, not looking up.

Sal nodded quickly. "Yeah," he said, with grotesque sympathy. "I know you have. Say, any time you want to play this old box, you just get it out a my locker. Dont bother to ever ask me, I never lock it."

Prew had looked up then, at the candid happiness that was on the long thin olive face because he'd lost an enemy and made a friend. "Okay," he'd said, "and thanks, Sal, thanks a lot." He had bent his face back to the strings, feeling warm himself, because he too had made two friends today. . . .

"Two whores," Maggio said, flipping over with its mate the queen he had for hole card.

"Two bullets," Prew grinned, turning up his own. He reached out and scooped in the small handful of change from the blanket. There was a chorus of groans and curses as he added it to the four dollars he had won in the past two hours. "A little more of this," he said, "and I'll have enough to hit O'Hayer's shed for a big lick."

While they had played the guard bugler had sounded a watery Tattoo from the corner of the rainy muddy quad, and there had been a sudden influx of last minute pissers before they went to bed, and the CQ had come around and thrown the light switches in the squadrooms, and now in the darkened squadroom beyond the swinging saloon-doors of the latrine there were the heavy silences and soft stirrings of a great deal of sleep. But the game had gone on concentratedly through it all with that passionate singularity generally attributed to love, but which few men ever feel, for women.

"I might of knew it," Maggio said dejectedly. He pulled down the strap of his undershirt and scratched his bony shoulder tragically. "Old-ace-in-the-hole-Prewitt. Any man catches an ace paired on the last card should have to throw in his hand or be outlawed from our club, thats all."

"You're as cold as a well digger's ass in the Klondike, Angelo," Prew grinned.

"Yeah?" Maggio glowered. "You believe it: its so. Gimme them goddam cards, men. Its my deal." He turned to Clark.

"Hear that, Nose? Prewitt says it: Its so." Maggio fingered his own big nose as he slapped the deck down for Prew to cut. "Was my father ever in Scranton, Pa? If I dint know my father was never out of Brooklyn in his life, I'd lay you money you was my kid brother. If I had money, that is."

Sal Clark grinned shyly. "My nose aint big enough to be your brother."

Maggio rubbed his hands together briskly and then ran each finger and his thumbs across his nose. "Now," he said, "now. Here we go. I've changed my luck. Better'n a nigger any time," he said, patting his big nose. He began to deal. "Who ever pinned you with the monicker of Clark, Ciolli? You're a traitor to the Italian people, Ciolli. You snob."

"Hell," Sal grinned, unable to keep his face straight like Maggio's. "I can help it? if the immigration people couldnt spell Ciolli?"

"Comeon, Angelo," Prew said. "Deal the cards. You cant make money you dont deal the cards."

"I cant win for losin, thats what I cant win for," Maggio said briskly. "You're a Wop, Ciolli. A greasy, hooknosed Wop. I dont know you. First jack bets."

"Bet five." Andy threw in a nickel.

Clark glowered comically, trying to narrow his fawn's eyes. "I'm a hard man, Angelo. Dont mess with me. I'll pull you apart. Ask Prewitt will I pull you apart."

"You'll never get rich on five," Maggio said to Andy. "Lets make it ten." He threw in a dime. "Is that right, Prew? Is this Ciolli boy really tough?"

"I call," Prew said. "Sure he's tough. He's hard. *I'm* teachin him the manly art of self-defense." He looked at his hole card. Sal grinned delightedly under his huge nose.

"Then he's hard," Maggio said. "I quit," he said to Clark. "All right, all right," he said, "its up to you, Jew-boy. Ten to you, you character."

"I call," said Pvt Julius Sussman, who had been losing steadily, "but I dont know why. Where'd you learn to deal such stinking hands?"

"I learn to deal these cards in Brooklyn, as you would know if you had of ever got out of The Bronx for air. I'm a Card Dealer. Queen is high."

"Bets five," Sussman said disgustedly. "You're nutward material, Angelo, thats what you are. The original Ward Eleven Kid. You better re-enlist."

"I'll re-enlist," Maggio said. "Right in your eye, with all six inches of it." He looked at his hole card. "Two more weeks till payday. I'm ona hit Honolulu like a fifty caliber. Look out, Service Rooms!" He picked up the deck. "Last time around," he said.

"Ha!" Sussman said. "A good piece of ass and a ride on my motor would kill you, Angelo."

"Listen to him," Maggio said, looking around. "The Waikiki Beach Kid. Him and his motorcycle and his one string git-tar. Last time around," he said. "Last time around. Any cuts, burns, or bruises."

"Dealem," Prew said.

"The man says dealem." Angelo passed the cards, his thin hand flickering nervously, pouring out the energy, as he deftly made the round. "I aim to win this, friends. Oh, oh. Two Jacks to Andy. Jesus Christ! I closed my eyes. Two Jacks bets."

"Its a ukelele," Sussman explained. "Originally Hawaiian instermint.

And besides, it gets the wahines. Thats all I care. My motor gets more pussy than all the dough in this compny."

"Then why dont you put the other three strings on it?" Maggio said. "You cant even play it anyway."

"I dont have to play it," Sussman said. "Its ony atmosphere."

Maggio peeked tentatively at his holecard. "When I have to start playin a one string fiddle and buy me a motorcycle on time to get wahines, I'll start payin my three bucks at the window."

"You pay your three bucks at the window now, Angelo," Sussman, whose motor was the dearest thing in his life, said testily.

"Thats what I said, dint I?" Maggio said disgustedly. "I call that two bits, Andy, and hump it two. Four bits to Reedy."

"Horse frocky," said Pvt Readall Treadwell, the sixth man, who had not won a single hand and who came from southern Pennsylvania. He heaved the fat-lined barrel that was his chest and belly in a lazy sigh and turned over his cards and tossed them in. His round face grinned lazily, belying the tremendous strength that was underneath the fat. Beside the nervous swiftness of little Maggio he was like a fat cross-legged Buddha. "You guys done broke me. I aint got no business playin cards with sharpers no ways."

"Hell," Maggio said. "You still got twenty cents. Stick around. I'm just beginning to win."

"Gotohell," Treadwell said, getting up. "I got enough for two beers left is all. An I aim to drink em, not you. Ah cant play poker no ways."

"Hell no," Maggio agreed. "All you're good for is a BAR man, to lug that 27 pounds around so some noncom can take it away from you when its time to shoot it."

"Man, you know it," Reedy Treadwell said. But having stood up, he was no longer a part of the circle. He stood behind them looking down a minute, then ambled out, no unhappier than if he had won ten dollars.

"What a character!" Maggio said, shaking his head. "I almost hated to take his money. But I convinced myself. Everybody in this compny is characters except me and Prewitt. And sometimes I'm gettin so I wonder about Prewitt. All right, all right," he said to Andy, "what you gonna do?"

"What you got there?" Andy stalled, sullenly studying Maggio's cards.

"You can see em," Maggio said. "Four clubs up, one club in the hole. That makes a flush."

"Maybe you aint got it," Andy said.

"Call and find out," Maggio said. "Thats my advice to you."

"You checked the bet on the last card," Andy said sullenly. "You checked a cinch into me."

"I dint have that last club on the last card," Maggio said. "Quit stallin. You gonna call?"

Andy looked sulkily at his pair of Jacks, then at the third Jack he had for holecard. "I got to call," he said. "There aint no choice. But you screwed me on that last card, Angelo," he accused.

"Balls!" Maggio said. "You seen them four clubs up before you bet. Put the blame on Mame."

"I call," Andy said.

"Money talks," Maggio said.

Andy threw in a quarter, reluctantly.

"How about you, Prewitt?" Maggio grinned.

"I got to call," Prew said, studying Andy's face. "I'm low man on this totem pole, but if he's ony got a pair I got him beat." He threw in his money.

"Read em and weep," Angelo chortled, triumphantly turning up the fifth club. He reached out and scooped in the money, letting it trickle through his fingers and making a high chuckle like a miser. "You better quit now," he said to Prew, "if you want to keep them winnings. Cause I rubbed the old nose, see? and I'm hot as Big Virginia's double shunt."

"It wont last," Prew said, taking a last drag on his tailormade and flipping it at one of the commodes.

"Hey," Maggio said. "The butt. The butt. Dont throw it away, you capitalist." He scrambled up and picked it up from under the commode, inhaling the smoke luxuriantly. "Lets go," he said, "lets go. Reedy's out: its your deal, Andy.

"Sick a Bull Durham," he said, coming back. "I worked in Gimbel's Basement, I least had tailormade cigarets. You niggerlip them, Prewitt. You're sloppy. You aint a soljer."

"A drag," Clark said. "Gimme a drag."

"My god!" Maggio said. "At the end of the month and two weeks till payday? I just got it. Leave me have a drag myself." He handed over the tiny end, while Andy dealt the second round, face up. Clark took it gingerly and sucked, burning his fingers, and then flipped it into a commode.

"So," Maggio said. "You dont believe it, Prewitt. You dont think I'll take your money. My ace is high, bet two bits."

"Jesus Christ!" Prew said.

"Its your own fault," Maggio said. "I warned you."

Andy dealt the next round and Maggio's ace was still high. It stayed high through the whole hand and won it for him. He won the next hand, and the next one, and the one after that. The sparking energy radiating from his knobby bony frame seemed almost to call to him the cards he wanted and repel the good cards from the others.

127

"Man," Maggio said, "I'm hot. I can feel it in my belly. A nail, Prewitt," he said bitterly, "a stinking nail. I'm thirsty for a nail."

Grinning, Prew reluctantly pulled out his almost empty pack. "First you take my money, then you want me to provide you with tobacco. I had to borrow money to buy this pack."

"Buy another pack," Maggio said. "You got money now, you hebe."

"Buy your own pack. If I furnish butts to the players, then I cut the game. I'll split it," he grinned, "but thats all I'll do, see?" He handed out two of his small stock, one to Maggio and Sussman, the other to Andy and Sal, and took one for himself. The others passed their paired cigarets back and forth between them as they played, and as Angelo went on winning.

Andy was dealing when the saloondoors opened and Pfc Bloom came in, pushing the door back so hard it banged against the wall and then swung back and forth squeaking loudly. Pfc Bloom advanced on the men around the blanket with a heavy, meaty confidence grinning and shaking his flat kinky head, so big the tremendous shoulders seemed to fill the door.

"Quiet, jerk," Maggio said. "You want the CQ up here and break up the game?"

"To hell with the CQ," Bloom said, in his customary loud voice. "And you too, you little Wop."

A transformation went over Maggio. He stood up and walked around the blanket, up to the huge Bloom who towered over him.

"Listen," he said in a contorted voice. "I'm particular who calls me Wop. I aint big and tough, and I aint one of Dynamite's third rate punchies. But I'm still Maggio to you. I wont mess with you. I work you over, I'll do it with a chair or a knife." He stared up at Bloom, his thin face twisted, his eyes blazing.

"Oh yeah?" Bloom said.

"Yeah, yeah," Maggio said sarcastically. Bloom took a step toward him and he leaned his head forward pugnaciously on the thin bony shoulders, and there was the sudden attentive silence that always precedes a fight.

"Lay off, Bloom," Prew said, surprised at the clear loudness of his voice in the silence. "Come on and sit down, Angelo. Five up to you."

"I call," Maggio said without looking around. "Take off, you bum," he said over his shoulder as he walked away. Bloom laughed after him self-confidently and nastily.

"Deal me in," Bloom said, elbowing in between Sussman and Sal Clark.

"We got five players," Maggio said.

"Yeah?" Bloom said. "So what? You can take seven players in draw poker."

"This is stud," Maggio said.

"You can take ten then," Bloom said, missing the point.

"Maybe we dont want no more," Prew said, squinting at his holecard through the smoke of his cigaret.

"Yeah?" Bloom said. "What'sa matter? Aint my money no good?"

"Not if its in *your* pocket," Maggio said. "Its probably counterfeit."

Bloom laughed loudly. "You're a character, Angelo."

"To you I'm Maggio. *Private* Maggio."

"Cheer up," Bloom laughed. "You may make Pfc yourself someday, kid." He looked down and brushed the new stripes on his shirt caressingly.

"I hope not," Maggio said. "I sincerely, truly hope not. I might turn out to be a son of a bitch, too."

"Hey," Bloom said. "You mean me? Are you callin me a son of a bitch?"

"If the shoe fits, friend, you wear it," Maggio said.

Bloom looked at him a minute, puzzled, not sure if he had been insulted or not, not able to understand why the antagonism, then he decided to laugh. "You're a character, Angelo. For a minute I thought you was serious. Who's got all the cigarets?" he asked. Nobody answered. Bloom looked around, and spotted the bulge in Prew's shirt pocket. "Gimme a butt, Prewitt."

"I aint got any," Prew said.

"Yeah? What's that in your pocket? Come on, give us a butt."

Prew raised his face impassively. "An empty pack," he lied, staring in Bloom's eyes without embarrassment. "I just killed it."

"Yeah?" Bloom laughed sarcastically. "All believes that stand on their head. Give us the butt on that one then."

"Sure, friend." Prew flipped the butt of his cigaret contemptuously. It lit on the floor near Bloom, under a commode.

"Hey!" Bloom protested. "You think I'll smoke that? after its rolled in all that piss? Thats a hell of a way for a guy to act, for Christ's sake."

"I smoked one just a while ago," Maggio said. "Tasted good to me."

"Yeah?" Bloom said. "Well maybe I aint sunk that low yet. When I do, I'll pick me up some horseturds and roll my own."

"Suit yourself," Maggio said. He crawled over and picked up the butt in question and smoked it himself. "Just watch out," he said, crawling back, "you dont pick the wrong one up and smoke your self."

Sal Clark had been collecting the cards for the new hand, keeping his face averted embarrassedly from all the antagonism that had come in with Bloom, as if he did not want to see it. "Shall I deal him in?" he asked Prew gently.

"I guess so," Prew said.

"What're you?" Bloom sneered. "His man Friday? Do you ask him when its time to crap?"

Sal hung his head and did not answer, blushing.

"Sure he's my man Friday," Prew shot back, seeing Sal's face. "You dont like it?"

Bloom shrugged indifferently. "Its no skin off my ass."

Sal looked at Prewitt gratefully as he began to deal. But Bloom did not even see it.

With Bloom's entrance the centrality of the game disintegrated and the close comradeship was gone. Everybody played silently. There were no more wisecracks. It might have been the big game in O'Hayer's shed. Maggio won several more hands and every time Bloom cursed loudly.

"For Christ's sake, shut up!" Julius Sussman said finally. "You make me wish I'm not a Jew."

"Yeah?" Bloom snarled elaborately. "What're you? ashamed of being Jewish? Maybe you aint a Jew; maybe you're a stinking greaser."

"Maybe I am."

"Sure, maybe he is," Maggio said. "He aint no frigging kike, thats sure. Deal me out," he said. "I got enough of this. I'm going over to O'Hayer's shed and run this pocketful of change into some real dough."

"Hey, wait a minute," Bloom said, jumping to his feet. "You aint quittin winners, are you?"

"Sure I'm quittin winners," Maggio said. "You think I'm gonna quit losers? Where'd you learn to gamble? your mother's sewing circle?"

"You cant quit winners," Bloom said. "And take the money over to the sheds out of the game."

"Yeah?" Maggio said. "You watch me."

Bloom turned to the seated circle. "You guys gonna let him get by with that? He's got your dough too."

"What do you think we started this game for?" Prew said. "You think we're playin for recreation? and gonna give everybody's money back as soon as we quit? Who the hell wants this chickenfeed except to win some real dough in the sheds? For Christ's sake, act your age."

"Yeah?" Bloom said, accusingly. "What're you doing? workin partners with the Wop? I lost two bucks in this goddam game. A right guy dont quit winners on his friends. I thought you was a straight joe, Prewitt; even when all the boys told me you wouldnt go out for fightin. I told em no, you was a straight joe when they all said you was yellow. Looks like I was wrong."

Prew put the few dimes and nickels he had left in his pocket and stood up, his hands hanging loosely in readiness at his sides, his lips tightened into bloodlessness, his eyes flat as eyes painted on a board.

"Listen, you son of a bitch," he said, feeling an icy calm that was a flaming rapture of abandon. "Keep your big yap away from me, or I'll sew it shut for you. And I wont get in any ring to do it. And I wont need no chair."

"Yeah?" Bloom said, stepping back. "I'm right here. Any time you say." He began to unbutton his shirt and pull it out of his pants.

"When I do," Prew grinned tautly, "you wont have no time to take your shirt off."

"Talk is big," Bloom said, still pulling out his shirt.

Prew started for him, would have hit him while his arms were still tangled in the shirtsleeves, but Maggio stepped in front of him.

"Wait a minute. You'll only get yourself in trouble." He opened his arms in front of Prew. "This is over me, not you. Just take it easy now." He talked soothingly, doing for Prew now what Prew had done for him a while ago, still holding his arms outspread.

Prew stood passively, his arms hanging straight against his sides now, relaxed. "All right," he said, feeling ashamed now for the cold murderousness that had been in him, for the wild ecstasy, wondering what it was in Bloom that made men want to smash him. "Take your arms down," he said to Maggio, "for Christ's sake. There aint nothing going to happen."

"Thats what I figured," Bloom said, sticking his shirt back in and buttoning it, grinning triumphantly as if the stopping of the fight had been his personal victory.

"Take off," Maggio said disgustedly.

"Sure," Bloom grinned. "You dont think I'm goin to donate you guys any more dough, do you? I dint know you was a bunch of sharpers," he said, leaving, having the last word. He slammed the door back loudly, to show his contempt for cheaters.

"Straight shooters always win," Maggio said. "Nobody ask you to play," he called after him. "Someday I'm goin to bust that guy wide open. Someday he's gonna make me mad."

"I aint got anything against him," Prew said. "But for some reason or other he always gets my goat."

"I'll get his goat," Maggio said. "He's a nogood son of a bitch. And I dont like him."

"I guess we didnt treat him very friendly," Prew said.

"You dont treat a guy like that friendly," Maggio said. "Wait'll he makes that corporalcy, he'll treat you and me friendly. He'll make us sweat, buddy."

"I guess," Prew said thoughtfully, wondering what it was, what trait, what quality, what difference of character that made one man likeable and another so dislikeable. He would take things off of Maggio he would never take from Bloom, even when he knew they were meant in joke. You couldnt talk to Bloom without him twisting it around to look like you had insulted him; he always seemed to need to put the other guy in the wrong. Thinking about it, he was suddenly angry again. He wished he had gone ahead and punched him, at least it would have broken the monotony. He wished he had gone on winning. He wished a lot of things. He hadnt had a woman now since before last payday, since the last time he was at Violet's. He wished he had a woman.

"Well," Maggio said, looking at Prew's face, "I'm goin over to the sheds and win me a fortune with this change."

"You better take what you got and go to town," Prew said, "while you got it." He turned and walked back by himself.

Julius Sussman stood up, counting the little money he had left. "Well, it was fine while it lasted. Sure busted up a nice friendly little game, all right. I aint even got enough left for a tank of gas. You dont want to play some more, I guess?" he said to Maggio.

"Not me," Maggio said. "I'm goin to the sheds."

"Thats what I figured," Sussman said. He walked over to a window and stood looking out, his hands jammed in his pockets. "Son of a bitch," he said. "This creepjoint gets me. If this rain would let up a little, I could go for a ride and maybe find some ass, if I had a tank of gas." He stood back and sighed. "I guess I'll see can I scour up some dough for me for a tank of gas."

"Want me to go with you, Angelo?" Sal Clark said, getting up from the game of solitaire he had started on the bench. "I'll sweat them out for you," he offered.

"Naw," Maggio said, defensively. "Sweat them out myself. Get my money's worth."

"I sweat them out for you, you'll win," Sal offered. "I cant never win myself, but I can sweat winners out for everybody else."

Maggio turned to look at him and grinned. "You stay here and sweat them out, Friday. I win I'll bring you all back a five buck loan. Hey, Prew," he called. "Tell your man Friday to stay here and sweat them for me. He wont listen to me."

Prew looked up but he did not grin, and he did not speak.

"If you let me go with you and sweat them," Sal said, "I'll go for nothin. Save you money."

"For Christ's sake, shut up," Andy said sullenly. "Cant you see he dont want you to go? You aint got no goddam pride a tall."

"There wont be hardly nobody over there," Maggio said. "Thats why. This late in the month there'll only be the big winner's poker table goin, and maybe one blackjack game for small fry."

"We're goin to the second show anyway," Andy said. He walked back to Prew. "Loan me twenty cents, Prew, will you? So we can go to the show? I got twenty left, but Sal needs twenty."

"Here," Prew said bitterly, handing him the sixty cents he had. "Take it all. It wont do me no good."

"Aw, I hate to do that," Andy said, but he did not draw back his hand.

"Yeah, you hate it," Prew said. "I know you hate it."

"I do," Andy said. "All I ask you for was twenty cents." He looked at Prew, his eyes going out of focus because he knew he was lying, and he did not want to lie, but still wanted the money.

"Well you got it all, so shut up," Prew said. "And for god sake when you talk to a man look him in the goddam eyes, will you? You give me the goddam willies."

"Okay, Prew," Andy said. "You want me to take it all?"

"You got it, aint you? Go spend it and shut up."

"Okay," Andy said. "Come on, Sal," he said, walking over to the bench. "Lets play couple hands of casino, till its show time."

Prew looked at him disgustedly and went back to the sink, feeling the need of a woman writhing in his belly.

"Hey, Prew," Maggio called cautiously, jerking his head back at the door. "Come on out on the porch a minute."

"What for?" Prew said, knowing he was being bastardly, but unable to stop it. "You got the money, go blow it."

"Come on out here a minute, goddam it," Maggio said.

"Okay," he said, and left the sink. Andy did not look up as he passed, but Sal Clark looked up and grinned with his bashful fawn's eyes at him.

"Take it easy, Friday," Prew said gently.

Chapter 11

Maggio was standing on the porch, waiting for him, his bony shoulders in the undershirt hunched up against the chill, staring at the streams of water falling just outside the screen. The sound of water spattering on the walk below filled the whole porch, drowning the sounds of sleep from in the squadroom.

"You want to go to town with me? if I win?" he asked, turning as Prew came out.

Prew grunted irritably. "What're you doin? invitin me because you feel sorry for me?"

"Ha," Maggio said. "Dont flatter yourself. I just dont like to go to town by myself. I dont know anybody in town."

"Well neither do I," Prew said.

"A guy's more lonesome in town by himself than he is right here," Maggio said.

"Not if he's got money. You better take what you got and go by yourself, while you still got it," Prew said. "You go over to O'Hayer's, you wont have it long," he said bluntly.

"Listen," Angelo said. "You dont want to let that Bloom character get your goat. Everybody knows he's a prize prick."

"You listen. He dont bother me; he fucks with me I'll bust his goddam flat head for him. And that goes for all the rest of them. See?"

"It wouldnt do you any good," Angelo said reasonably.

"Maybe not, but it would make me feel a hell of a lot better."

"He was needling you with all that crap about being yellow," Maggio said. "Nobody believes that."

Prew had started back to the latrine, but now he stopped. "Listen, Angelo," he said, turning back. "Lets drop this. I dont care whether they, or anybody, believe it or not," he said seriously. "They can all of them go screw themselves, and I'll be the first guy to walk across the street and watch it."

"Okay," Maggio said briefly. "I'm sorry I mentioned it. Wait'll I get my shirt. I'm freezin to death. I thought them travel posters said they dint have no winter in Hawaii."

He disappeared into the slowly, rhythmically breathing squadroom, tiptoeing grotesquely, and Prew had to grin. Angelo came back putting on his shirt and carrying his raincoat, wearing the stiffly blocked hat he was so proud of, that he had religiously had blocked once every week since he got out of recruit drill.

"Where'll you be?" he asked, unbuttoning his pants and stuffing in his shirt, as they walked down to the stairs and down them to the ground floor porch where the endlessly falling water made an endless sound that was no longer heard because it had been going on so long.

"I'll be in the Dayroom," Prew said, "or else up in the latrine."

Maggio was putting on his raincoat, as if it was a suit of armor and he was going forth to joust. "Okay," he said. "You better be prepared to bring a footlocker to help bring home the ghelt."

"*You* better *win*," Prew said, "goddam you. I aint had a piece of ass in almost a month."

"No wonder you're pissed off," Angelo grinned. "I aint had one since last payday." He pulled his hat down on his forehead and peered up at Prew from under the knife edge of the brim. "Gimme a butt before I go."

"Jesus Christ!" Prew said, pained, but he reached in his pocket and brought out one, a single tube, from the unseen pack. "Since when did I take you to raise?"

"Whats a matter? You scared I'll steal your lousy tailormades? After I win I'll buy you a whole carton. Now match me and I'm gone."

"Is your mouth dry?" Prew said. "You want me to spit for you?"

"Not on the floor," Angelo said, raising his eyebrows in mock horror. "Not on the floor. Wheres your manners?"

"Aint there something else I can do for you? Use my mouth as an ashtray? cut off my balls and have a game of marbles? You oughta be able think of somethin."

"No," Maggio said. "But thanks. You're a good boy. You ever get to Brooklyn, look me up. I'll treat you right." He opened the book Prew handed him, tore off one, struck it, and handed back the book, the bronze glow lighting up his thin child's face. "I'll see you, kid," he said, puffing luxuriantly, like a rich man on a fifty cent cigar. He swaggered off out into the rain, ducked through the falling sheets of water, swaggered on, his bony shoulders hunched up belligerently, his thin arms swinging widely, his torso swaying from side to side, agitating the formless raincoat that enveloped him.

Prew watched him go, half grinning ruefully, no longer feeling mean, hoping he would win some money. He stood for a while looking out across the rainswept quad to the lighted sallyport, listening to the snatches of song and shouts from Choy's as the door was opened, hearing the rattling of empty cases. He was back in the old familiar round again, hunting and twisting and pinching for the nickels that looked as big as dollars, trying to scour up enough for a few drinks and a piece of ass.

Even if he wins, he thought, you wont find the thing you want, not in any whorehouse, you who talk about a piece of ass so glibly, as if it held the answer. You were a goddamned stupid fool to ever let Violet get away from you, he thought bitterly, wishing now he had not forced the issue, had had some sense, wondering what she was doing tonight, right now. Maybe you didnt have the thing you're always looking for, but at least you could have gone up there once a week; or once a month even. Way it is now you aint got even that. All you got now is the old round, the whorehouses where you never find it either, plus the absence of the money that it costs you to look there and that you have to scrounge for and then never get, except on Payday when they're all so crowded that if you dont get your gun off in three minutes you have to take a raincheck. At least with Violet you had a woman. Maybe you could go back and see her and explain it, but even as he thought it he knew it would be useless, that it was past, that she had already found another soldier, or maybe even one of her own race. That was what she really wanted. Maybe you should have married her. Sure, maybe you should have stayed in the Bugle Corps, too, I guess? Maybe you'll never find the thing it is you're looking for? he thought and turned to go back up.

Andy and Sal Clark were still in the latrine, playing casino on the worn wood bench thats grain was raised and weathered by the shower water that was always getting splashed on it.

"Bloom was back while you was gone," Andy said, looking up from his hand.

"Yeah?" Prew said, feeling very indifferent now. "What'd *he* want?"

"Lookin for somebody to borrow fifty cents from for taxifare to town," Andy said sullenly, looking back down.

"Well? Did you loan it to him?"

"Why would I loan it to him?" Andy said indignantly. "You think I'd run out on you?" Then he looked up and saw Prew was kidding him, and his voice dropped back down. "We ony got eighty cents between us," he muttered. "I loan him four bits, we wouldnt have enough to go to the show."

"I thought maybe you loaned it to him," Prew teased. "You're the richest joe around here now, outside of Angelo."

"Well I dint," Andy said. "If thats what you think. And anytime you want your money back, just ask for it and I'll give it to you."

"Hell no," Prew said happily. "Wont do me any good."

"I s'pose you're goin to town with Angelo," Andy asked him, sulkily.

Prew turned to look at the hurt tone in his voice. "If he wins," he said.

Andy looked at Sal significantly. "Thats what we figured."

"*You* figured what?" Prew said, and walked down to them and stood in front of Andy. "If anybody did some figurin, it was *you*, I'll bet, not Sal. Anything wrong with me goin with Angelo?"

"I guess not," Andy shrugged elaborately. "Except a guy dont usually take off on his pals who's broke."

"You mean you think I ought to stay here and go to the show with you? because you cant go to town?"

"I dint say that," Andy said defensively. "Bloom wanted me to go to town with him tonight."

"Well go ahead," Prew said serenely. "If thats whats eatin you. That wont hurt my feelins any. I dont care who you go to town with. Whats Friday goin to do?"

"He can go to the show by himself," Andy said. "I'm ony takin four bits taxifare."

"Man," Prew said. "You're a hot one."

"I aint goin to the show," Friday said happily. "I'm ona save at thirty cents and stay right here and teach myself how to deal these cards, by god."

"Well," Andy said, "thats up to you. You got the money. You can go if you want to."

"What're you guys goin to do in town?" Prew said. "If I may ask?"

"Just fool around."

"You wont fool very far, takin only four bits taxifare. What'll you do after you get there? How'll you get back?"

"Well," Andy said. "Bloom's got a queer lined up out in Waikiki he thinks we can roll, a guy with quite a bit of dough."

"I wouldnt go," Prew said, "if I was you."

Andy looked up indignantly. "Why not? Its easy for you to say. You're goin down with Angelo."

"Because Bloom's lyin to you, thats why. How long you been in Wahoo? You oughta know by now that Honolulu queers dont get rolled. They never carry money with them. Its too small a place, and theres too many soljers. They'd get rolled every night."

Andy would not look at him. "Bloom said if it didnt work out to roll him, we could get drinks off him anyway, and carfare home. Whats the difference?"

"He lied to you. Thats the difference. Why would he lie to you? He knows nobody can roll a Honolulu queer. Whynt he tell you the truth? I wouldnt trust no guy that lied to me. Maybe he's pimpin for this queer. You're liable to end up gettin made. Theres somethin about Bloom I dont like."

"So I should leave him alone, I guess?" Andy said, angrily, not meeting Prew's eyes. "There aint no queer goin to make me. Who the hell are you to tell me how to run my life? You're goin to town with Maggio, aint you?"

"Okay," Prew said. "Suit yourself, buddy."

"He ast me to go," Andy said. "I dint ask him. And I'm goin. A guy can rot sittin around this goddam barracks. Cant even play the git-tars with the rain on. Be mad at me if you want to, I'm goin anyway."

"Hell," Prew said. "I aint mad at you. I just think you're dumb, thats all. If you want to pick up a queer, go by yourself." He sat down on the end of the bench and picked up the deck that Andy had collected up and stacked, and began practicing the old one-handed cut, remembering the time he'd learned it, in a boxcar, on the bum.

It was also on the bum, at the tender age of twelve, that he'd had his first experience with queers, when a fifty-year-old jocker had seduced him in a rolling boxcar. It was more a rape than a seduction, since another man had had to hold him.

He looked up at Andy, his lips drawn back very tight in a grin that was more a snarl, his eyes very flat and far away and glinty. It was also on the bum, at the not so tender age of fifteen, that he'd knocked another jocker off a steep downgrade in Georgia and later read about them finding the dead body and the resulting roundup of free labor for the State that he had escaped.

"You do whatever you want," he said to Andy thinly. "If the guy turns out to be a jocker and you get pogued, go see the Chaplain. I'll loan you my card; it aint punched out yet."

"You tryin to scare me?" Andy scoffed. "Are you goin now?" he said to Friday. "I got to put my civvies on. I'm meetin Bloom in the Dayroom in fifteen minutes."

"You better listen to him," Sal Clark said. "You better not go with Bloom."

"For Chris' sakes, lay off of me," Andy said. "A man cant sit on his can in these barracks all his life. Are you goin to the show or aint you?"

"I guess I will go to the show," Sal Clark said. "I can practice dealin them cards tomorrow. Whynt you borrow a dime, Prew, and come on with me? You only need a dime. I got thirty cents."

"No thanks, Friday," Prew said, looking at the seriousness of the long thin olive face and feeling the sense of warmth again. "I promised Angelo I'd wait."

"Whatever you say," Sal Clark said. "You have a good time in town."

"Okay," Prew said. "Listen, dont you let Bloom talk *you* into goin queer huntin with him, hear me?"

"Not me," Sal Clark said solemnly. "I dont like queers. They make me feel funny, they make me scared."

"If you want to go queer huntin, go by yourself," Prew said. He watched them leave, then laid out a hand of Sol and began to wait. He didnt have to wait long. The other two had not been gone ten minutes before little Angelo came bursting into the latrine, slamming back the doors so hard they banged.

"Well," Prew said, looking up. "How much did you win?"

"Win?" Maggio said violently. "Win! I won about forty bucks, in one hand. You think that'll be enough to go goddam town?"

"Fair," Prew said dryly. "How much did you lose?"

"Lose? Oh," Maggio said vehemently. "Lose. I lost forty-seven dollars. Also in one hand, the second hand. God," he said, looking around for something he could throw and finding nothing, took his new-blocked hat and slammed it down on the floor. He kicked it viciously, putting a big muddy dent in the papier-mâché-stiff crown, scooting it across the mucky floor.

"Now look what I did," he said sorrowfully and went over to the wall to pick it up. "Well," he said, "whynt you ask me why I didnt quit after I won the forty? Go ahead. Ask me."

"I dont need to ask you," Prew said. "I already know why."

"I thought I could win some *more*," Angelo said, insisting on castigating himself since Prew wouldnt do it. "I thought I could win enough for a *real* trip to town. Maybe *two* real trips to town. Balls," he said. "Tes-tickles." He slammed the muddy, dusty, dented hat back on his head cockeyed and put his knuckles on his hips and looked at Prew. "Oh, balls, balls, balls," he said.

"Well," Prew said. "Thats that." He looked down at the deck in his hands and ripped it suddenly across the middle, tearing the first few top and bottom cards clear in two, bending and ripping the next ones only a little bit, then tossed the scrambled mess up in the air and watched them drift, sideslipping, like autumn leaves, down to the floor. "No ass. Let the goddam latrine detail clean them up in the morning. To hell with it."

"Andy and your boy Friday go to the show?" Angelo asked hopefully.

"Yeah."

"He dint give the money to you back?"

"Nope."

"Damn," Angelo said. "I save out four bits. If I had a buck I know a game in C Compny I could get in where the takeout's a buck only."

"I aint got a cent," Prew said. "Not a red cent. To hell with it. It'd take you all goddam night to win enough to have a stake to hit the sheds."

"Thats right," Angelo said. "You're right." He stripped off his raincoat and began taking off his shirt. "To hell with it. I'll take me fifty cents and go to town and pick me up a queer. I aint never picked me up a goddam queer, but I guess I can do it if other people can. It hadnt ought to be too goddam hard. I'm sick of it," he said, "sick of all of it. Sometimes I get so sick of it I want to puke my goddam guts right out on the floor and lay down in it and die."

Prew was looking at his hands, dangling between his knees. "Sometimes I cant honestly say I blame you a whole hell of a lot," he said.

"Come on and go with me," Maggio said. "You can borrow four bits someplace. If we dont make a strike, we'll hitchhike back."

"No thanks," Prew said. "It beats me. I aint in no mood to go to town and whatever fun there was I'd kill it. And anyway, I dont like queers."

"I got to change my clothes," Angelo said. "So long. I'll see you in the goddam morning, if I get back. If I dont, come around to the Stockade and visit me."

Prew laughed, but it was not a laugh that very many men would recognize. "Okay," he said. "I'll bring you up a carton of butts."

"I'll take one now," Maggio said, "on account?" He looked at Prew apologetically. "I forgot all about buying any, Prew, when I had the dough."

"Sure," Prew said. "Sure. Here." He pulled out the crumpled pack and gave him one, took the last one himself, and threw the crumpled pack in a commode.

"Not if these is your last ones," Maggio said.

"To hell with it," Prew said. "I got plenty rollings."

Maggio nodded, and Prew watched him go; the dwarfed, narrow shouldered, warp-boned heir to a race of city dwellers whose destiny it was to never place their feet upon their earth except for the bottled-in-bond, canned grass of Central Park, whose very lives came out of cans, even to the movies that they tried to pattern their lives after and the beer they drank to forget them; go out toward the squadroom to fumble around in the breathing dark to find his undress uniform for town, the gook shirt and cheap slacks and two-buck shoes.

Prew pushed the twisted cards with his foot and listened to the neverending rain outside and decided he would go down to the Dayroom for a while, since he did not feel like sleeping.

The Dayroom was almost deserted. A couple of men lolled on the cigaret burns and ruptured excelsior of the imitation leather chairs that lined both walls of the narrow room that had been built below the out-side porches. The Dayroom was screened-in from about waist high to the ceiling, and the Dayroom orderly had pulled the chairs along the outside wall out to the middle of the floor to keep the rain from wetting them, narrowing the already narrow space between. The men did not look up at him. They went on flipping the pages of the battered comic books they had been scanning.

He stood in the doorway of the pool alcove that was also deserted now at ten o'clock, an hour before Taps, wondering why in hell he had come down here, looking at the deserted pingpong table at the far end which as far as he knew had never had a net and would not be bothered now until next Payday for a blackjack game, looking at the deserted radio at the near end that had been on the blink now since a week before last Payday, looking out through the screens at the rainy street and the railroad beyond and at the tin roofed sheds beyond the railroad, the places where all the money was and that had been going full blast since Payday and now were tapering off in the middle of the month to one game among the few who had been the heavy winners. Life on the Inside was not measured by hours but by Paydays: Last Payday, Next Payday, and then there was the inbetween that lasted very long but never was remembered.

The plywood magazine rack had been pulled in from the outside wall too, and he went over to it and scanned the heavy cardboard covers made to look like leather but which never did, reading the Company's and Regiment's designation embossed on the blank rectangle in the center. He took out a stack of them and sat down with them in a chair as far from the dripping water as he could get, and started thumbing through them.

They were all there: *Life,* with its cross-section pictures of the world and "The March of Time Marches On" air about it; *Look,* that was so obviously a second-rate imitation that had got on the gravytrain; *Argosy* and *Bluebook,* with their adventure stories about lovely ladies lost in jungles with aviators; *Field & Stream,* with its comfortable hunters in sharp looking coats and breeches carrying fine shotguns and smoking pipes; *Colliers, Redbook, Cosmopolitan, American, The Ladies' Home Journal,* and *The Saturday Evening Post,* and all their starving young actresses and producers, all of them bound together with a running theme of High-, Middle-, and Low-Class Americana on their cover pictures and that overflowed occasionally into a number of the advertisements.

They were all there, subscribed to by the Company, paid for by the Company Fund, provided for the recreation of the men.

And he thumbed through them all, not bothering to read the stories, but looking at the pictures, and the ads.

"There's a *Ford* in your future," they told him. " 'What this country needs . . .' . . . is a good money-saving motor oil for 25¢." "Let me tell you why Jimmy is doing better in school—he eats *Kellogg's Corn Flakes.*" "I like my sleep, says Al Smith—go *Pullman.*" "Rubber does it better." (He got a grin from that one.) "*NOW!* You can own a Cadillac. Only $1345.00." "Give her the *American* kitchen of her dreams."

There was one old issue of the *Post,* battered and rolled and curled and torn and dated back to November 30, 1940, that was a gold mine, a fine opium, with much food for thought.

Its cover, one of those Norman Rockwell paintings of Americana, Prew studied for a long, long time. It showed a young man lying on his topcoat on the ground, strumming on a uke and smoking on a pipe, with his shoeless feet propped on a suitcase that had a thumbing fist and MIAMI painted on it, and the shoes beside it on the ground. It was obvious he was bumming. Maybe, he decided finally, maybe he was a college boy. That must be what it was.

There was a *Pall Mall* ad in it that he liked. It was painted in bright color and showed some happy soldiers on the range. (There were lots of things about the Army now, in all the magazines, since the peacetime draft.) Three of these were in the prone position firing, and the other two were back on the ready line sitting on green grass, and one of these was holding up two cigarets, a *Pall Mall* and a short one. He was a very happy looking soldier.

He studied this one quite a while, too, professionally admiring the artist's observation. The board stiff campaign hats that were definitely

Regular Army, pre-draft, were there. The Infantry's robin's-egg-blue cord and acorns were on the hats. The old style chrome bayonet and white web sheath with its brown leather tip, the shooting jackets made out of the obsolete CKC blouses and ripped up the back for shoulder room, the sheepskin elbow and shoulder pads with the fleece turned in, the new M_1 rifle that had not got to Wahoo yet and that he had only seen in diagrams—they all were there; and the range season with the deep smell of burnt powder and the clinking brassy tubes of cartridges heavy in the hand came back to him as he looked at it. The only thing he could professionally find wrong with it was that none of them had leggins on. Well, maybe they didnt issue leggins now, back in the States. He tore it out, thinking it would look good tacked to the inside of his footlocker top.

The gleaming white tubes of the tailormade cigarets in the picture made him thirsty for a smoke, and he had his hand in his shirt pocket before he remembered he and Angelo had smoked his last two tailor-mades in the latrine. He folded the picture up and put it in the empty pocket and took the sack of Duke's Mixture out of the other pocket and rolled one, before he went on reading.

He went through several magazines from front to back, not bothering with the idiotic stories, looking for the ads. Most of them had women in them and these were what he looked for. The colored photographs were the best for reality in picturing the women, but on the other hand they usually put a few more clothes on these than they did the drawings. The small drawn ads in the back, down the outsides of the pages, the ones with the slightly oversized breasts and the collection of fanning wrinkles around the crotch, with the moulded, deep, fleshy look; these were the best.

Then there was a *Treeburn's Facial Soap* ad, of a long-lined blonde lying on a beach robe being kissed by a handsome head and shoulder of a man, a painting with a kind of unreal fuzzy outline, she lying there full length, stretched out, turned on one hip, her arms above her head, wearing a bathing suit that looked like leopard skin. There was the heavy-lidded, full-pouting-lipped look on her face that women get when they really want it bad. This one was a fine one, better than the others, in fact, the best one yet.

And last, of the three best, there was this small one, a shaded drawing of a dame in a sort of T shirt and soft shorts. *Duchessa Lazidays*, Sleep in 'em Play in 'em Laze in 'em, Duchessa Underwear Corp. and the T shirt fell lightly, swelling under the pressure of the perfect breasts. Shaded half circles and points of light hinted at the rubbery red nipples underneath. The clothes really made no difference; if the artist had left out two dozen lines it would have been a nude. Yet Prew found himself staring and staring, trying vainly to penetrate beneath the plane of the attire to the plane of the figure under it, as if it were three-dimensional. Funny how just a few pencil lines adroitly arranged could suggest the swelling, deep-blooded, pulsating life of a lovely woman.

He could feel his hands beginning to sweat and the muscles along the insides of his thighs begin to tremble.

You better lay off, he told himself, this is no time to be inspecting shunt pictures, not in the middle of the month, and you broke. When it's too late to even borrow three bucks from the twenty percent men to make a flying trip to Big Sue's in Wahiawa. You better go back to *The Saturday Evening Post,* buddy.

But the first thing in the *Post* he saw was another ad, a full page *Greyhound Bus Lines* spread telling about the Glory of Southern Sun, and in the middle a full length figure of a woman, the round lean lines of her hips staring at you from behind the tiny loosely skirted pants of the two piece bathing suit.

All right, he thought, okay; if thats the way it is; a savagery of anger in him now at the pictures. They call them "pin-up girls" and think its cute how "our boys," now that they're drafted, love to hang them in their wall lockers. And then close up all the whorehouses, every place they can, so our young men will not be contaminated.

He ripped the page out of the *Post* and wadded it up, crumpling it in his hands until it was only pulpy paper, and threw it across the narrow room into one of the puddles on the floor. He got up and stepped on it hard, grinding it into a sodden mess under his shoe and then stepped back and looked down at it, ashamed because he had destroyed beauty, had taken a living volute woman's hip and turned it into spitballs.

Climbing the darkened stairs, feeling the maleness in him, the maleness that was denied, hushed, denounced, hedged in, scourged, damned, condemned, and used, feeling the excess that overflowed rancidly, burning acidly all through his blood and settling finally in his throat, a thick acidulous phlegm, feeling all that, he did not wonder that so many men woke up suddenly to find that they were married. But if you weren't, there was only one thing left to do.

Chapter 12

It was barely the middle of March, hardly ten days since Holmes had first brought him the papers, that the transfer of the Fort Kamehameha cook came back, approved, to Warden. For a transfer like that one was, from one branch of service to another, it was an unbelievably short time.

That afternoon that Mazzioli brought the transfer letter over from Regiment, Milt Warden had been sitting at his desk, puzzling over a snapshot Karen Holmes had given him of herself that was before him lying on the papers he had been working on, his cheek sunk on the knuckles of one big fist like a small boy watching a grownup's movie he could not figure out.

She had given it to him the night of the moonlight swim, as he liked to call it now, grinningly. She had given it to him, without him even asking for it, almost as soon as he had climbed into the car. It was, he thought, almost as if she felt it was expected of her.

She had picked him out a good one, showing her as it did in a white bathing suit that was startling against the black-tanned flesh, reclining on a GI blanket in the sun before one of those pineappley palmtrees in her front yard, he recognized the tree, and wearing sun glasses and reading, and with one leg up a little showing perfectly the long full lines of thigh and calf converging delicately at the narrowness of knee. All the womanness of her shown in it, reached out demanding male attention, as a crowded street of long legged, tanned, high breasted women will catch your eye and pull your head around without your having even thought about it. If that was all there was, he thought again, for the fifteenth time today, just that womanness of this picture done in breathing flesh, it would be all right. But the picture didnt show it all. And he was not, he realized, a boy who is so rapt by the solemn religious joy of his first female flesh that he is blinded to the existence of the woman wearing it, does not even know or need to know that she exists. It would be fine if you were that, he thought, but you are not, and have not been for some time now, nor will you ever be again. You cant ignore the woman and keep all the rest, even for the first two weeks, though perhaps that would have been the best, if you could have done it.

She had picked him up, he remembered, going over it once again, downtown in Honolulu at the Kau Kau Korner drive-in where the tourists hung out in their rented cars, and where they had decided there was the least chance of being seen by anyone they knew. He had wanted to drive them out, since he knew the way, to the secret little beach out near the Blowhole that he had seen so often riding past in trucks and had thought how it would be such a wonderful place for a man to take a woman, that he had finally climbed down to it once. But she had been afraid to let him drive this car belonging to her husband. He had given her the directions and she had driven, taking wrong turnings twice and getting very nervous, before she got from Kau Kau

Korner to Kaimuki and Waialae Avenue that became the Kalanianaole Highway to the Blowhole. Maybe that was what had started it, begun the killing of it, and the way he'd pictured it would be. She'd been two totally different women that day at the house and now this time she seemed to be a third one, unrelated to the other two. They had parked the car up near the Blowhole at the little parkway where there was a concrete marker that said you could see Molokai from here on a clear day, and walked back down. She was, she said, with a kind of frantic effort, "very pleased and happy." It was all there, the full moon, the small mild surf showing white, the pale sands of the tiny beach set down among the rocks and glowing weirdly in the moonlight, the low wind surfing through the kiawe trees across the highway, and he had brought a bottle and there was a thermos full of coffee and the sandwiches she had brought, and even blankets. It was really all there and very fine, he'd thought, just like he pictured it. She had slipped climbing down the rocks and skinned her arm, and after they had got down she tore her dress, one of her best ones she said, on a snag. They had waded, nude, out into the water, hand in hand, making, he remembered, a fine picture in the moonlight with the water that seemed to run uphill from the beach breathing heavily around their knees. She had gotten chilled and had to go back and wrap up in a blanket. It was then he had given it up altogether, deciding it had been a damn fool thing, *his* mistake, in the first place. And he had gone back with her, even in the painfulness of feeling so damned foolish, still eager, burning, not feeling any cold at all, and wanting it badly, needing it badly, but how could you have it, as you ought to have it, when you were struggling to keep a blanket over you to keep from chilling her again. That was when he wanted her to take the drink, up to then he had not made an issue of it, though it puzzled him. But she would not drink now at all, any. She had smiled sadly with the great sadness of a Christian martyr who forgives the Romans, and accused herself of how she always messed things up and ruined everything she touched, and how she guessed she just wasnt an outdoor girl, although it had seemed fine when they had talked about it, in the bedroom, back at Schofield, and she really truly thought it would be better if he would get some other woman for it, she wouldnt mind. Driving back to town she said she wanted to be fair and asked him if he wanted to give the picture back now, that she didnt mind, really she wouldnt mind. He had felt guilty then, because he had not asked her for the picture, and because he saw now the whole idea had been stupid in the first place, and had said he wanted to keep the picture very badly, which, he suddenly had realized, he did. It was then, somehow or other, without meaning to, that he had made this other date, for after payday, because, she said, she didnt get much money out of Holmes, and that only after petty squabbling. He had tried then, half heartedly, to get her to take only one small drink, hoping guiltily that if maybe he could get her drunk it would be better, hoping maybe they could go somewhere and get a room, or something, and salvage something. But she would not drink, and she had not fixed an alibi, not figuring to stay away all night, and she would not do it in a car, ever, because, she felt, it was degrading.

He had gone down to Wu Fat's then, on Hotel Street, in the heart of the whorehouse district, after she had let him out, timidly reminding him of the coming date, and gotten very drunk and then made a stud-bull roaring raid on Mrs Kipfer's Hotel New Congress that was intensely satisfying, determined there would be no more dates as far as he was concerned, no matter what he'd told her, and he was still puzzling on it now, with Mazzioli coming in the corridor, wondering what it was had happened and why it had happened anyway and most of all why he could not seem to put his finger on it at all, still completely stumped as he put the snapshot back in his wallet where he kept it hidden behind his SP pass card and could feel smugly conspiratorial every time he flashed his wallet at the MPs at the gate, or took it out in the Orderly Room in front of Dynamite. At least he could understand that much, anyway.

Mazzioli was looking smug and obviously chortling to himself as he handed over the stack of papers that he had hidden the transfer letter in the middle of. He stood around grinning and waiting for the explosion, while Warden leafed impatiently through the four fingers of Memorandums, General and Special Orders, and War Department Circulars he had brought, looking for something that might accidentally turn out to be important.

It was quite a letter. It had gone out through channels, and come back through channels, and picked up another endorsement every place it stopped. Warden, who had been praying fervently some office or other would find some outfit or other overstrength or understrength, looked up at Mazzioli sagely when he found it.

"Well?" he snarled. "What the hell're you standin around for? Aint you got no work to do?"

"Why I aint doing nothing," the clerk objected. "Cant a man just stand still? without you jumping on him? for God's sake?"

"What man?" Warden said. "No. He cant. I cant stand to see people standin still. I'm eccentric. If there aint no work," he threatened, "maybe I can scare you up some."

"But I got to go back to Personnel," protested Mazzioli. "Right away. O'Bannon wants me right back there."

"Then move. Dont stand there with your finger up your ass," Warden said, making it sound ominous, but glad momentarily, even in this catastrophe of the transfer, to get out of the almost frightening bottomlessness of Karen Holmes and the abortive swimming party and onto solid ground he knew, even if only in its barrenness. "Why dont you just move in over there, Mazzioli?"

"I wish to hell I could," the clerk said bitterly, very disappointed because the blowup he expected had not come. "Oh how I wish. What do you think about that transfer, Top?" he needled hopefully. Warden did not answer. "Aint that something?" he asked sympathetically, changing tactics, still hoping. "That letter of the Colonel's sure got quick action, didnt it?"

But Warden only stared at him silently, and kept on staring, until, completely defeated, he left in confusion, still disappointed. And Milt Warden went bitterly back to work, chewing what few germless grains of comfort he could glean from having seen through Mazzioli's plot. I wish I could see through Karen Holmes that easy, he thought, I wish I could even see through what will come out of this transfer that easy.

There were times, he felt, Milt Warden never should of made this rating. This rating wasnt worth it. In a profession where fouling up was SOP, this rating had a reputation that stunk, in every noncoms' club on the Post. To get this rating Milt Warden had taken over a notoriously bogged down outfit no other noncom in the Regiment would touch, and from a notoriously case-hardened old 1st/Sgt who had finally made that thirty-year-long pull up onto the retirement list and didnt have to worry about this any more. You really wanted this rating awful bad, didnt you, you jerk?

He took the letter to his desk to make the necessary notes, feeling the old rage, the rage that always saved him, mounting in him happily, and contemptuously tossed the rest of the pregnant mass of paper stillborn in Mazzioli's filing basket.

Maybe he was a good man once, this old one, my predecessor, but they had worn him down, in thirty years, like a big knife made thin and fragile, needlelike, from constant honings. All that good steel just rubbed away no one knew where. And him, who had been a riproarer in the old days back in China, hanging on by his fingernails the last five years to get that pension, praying the Inspector General's men would not find him out, and covering up his fear with this Victor McLaglen doing one of his movie soldiers act. That was no way to end. When my time comes they can stick their pension up their ass before I'll fawn to get it.

But maybe it was all part of the process of getting old, he thought. All the old ones, the tough ones, ended up that way it seemed, Jones imitating Jones, Smith imitating Smith, playing a role they once had lived. And it wasnt only in the Army.

I think you need a drink, he thought, walking to the filing cabinet for the hidden whiskey, a good stiff drink, to make you madder, you who are in danger of becoming Warden imitating Warden, a really good one, you.

Everything, eventually, got old. There are gray hairs in this head too, already. But part of the process of getting old was not this gradual wearing down of a man by the seas of organization, this eating away of the rock a man could have been except for these lapping waves of affectionate regard driven by the wind of fear against the rock that always crumbled, finally—that was not part of getting old, or if it was, then getting old was wrong and there was no point to any of it and he did not like it at all, and by god I'm not having any.

I think its time we took a break and trimmed up our mustache a little, we want to look pretty for the women, dont we, character? he told himself, and got the paper shears off of Holmes's desk and went in the closet to the mirror, hearing the fatigue details that were beginning to come in now and Pop Karelsen's soft very cultured voice going up the stairs.

Looking at the big face staring angrily at him from the glass, the great shears in the thick-veined hand, feeling the inability to go back to work now after this of the transfer, he wondered if that was what it really was? just getting old? Gimme a place to stand, the old man said, and I will move the world. And all they needed then was a place for him to stand. They were still looking for it.

Looks like you need another drink, he thought, you arent getting mad enough yet apparently. This one this time apparently is going to be more than a one drink job. Personally, I think its more than a two drink job, even. Personally, I think this job is going to be one of those that calls for a workout punching on the heavy bag. Yes, I think thats what it is, he decided, running his tongue over his mustache to see if it was short enough to keep from tickling him and, satisfied, stepped back and raised his arm and tossed the scissors over his shoulder like a rich man giving a bum a dollar, listening happily to the clashing clatter of their fall. There was plenty money in the Company Fund, let them buy some new ones. Let Dynamite take care of it, that was about his speed. He picked them up and laid them, with a full inch of one point broken off, on Holmes's desk on top the transfer letter, in the box marked Urgent, and went upstairs to corner Karelsen, his punching bag, in the room they shared together off the first floor porch. Pop Karelsen, being one of Mazzioli's intellectual confreres, but smarter, made the best heavy bag anywheres around. Mazzioli would serve for a light bag, speed workout, but there wasnt enough weight to him to make a heavy bag that developed power.

"Pete," he bawled, charging in and blowing apart the quiet rainy-day privacy that had been in the little room, "I'm sick of it. I'm turning in my stripes. This is the goddamnedest fuckedup outfit I was ever in.

148

Man like Dynamite's a goddam disgrace to the goddam uniform he sports around. Him and that punk Culpepper."

Pop Karelsen was undressing, sitting on his bunk to ease the aching joints of his arthritis that was so familiar to him now it had become almost a friend, had just taken off his hat and denim blouse, and was disengaging his false teeth, both plates. He looked up noncommittally, irritated that his privacy was invaded, afraid Mad Milton was off on another of his rampages though hoping he was not, but still not wanting to involve himself in anything, until he knew just where he stood.

"In the Old Army," he said profoundly, but discreetly, "an officer was an officer, not a clothes horse," and dropped the teeth into their glass of water on the table, hoping for the best.

"Old Army, my bleeding ass," raged Warden joyously, pouncing on the platitude. "You bums and your Old Army make me want to puke. There never was any Old Army. The boys from the Civil War told it to the Indian War Recruits, just like the oldtimers from the Revolution told it to the boys of 1812. And all of them only tryin to excuse themself, for being bums and taking the shit they've always taken."

"You know all about it, I guess," Karelsen said stiffly, in spite of himself, because he knew now for sure that Milt was off again, and that the only way to handle him when he was a madman like this was to keep your equanimity. "You served with Braddock, didn't you?" The only trouble was, he could never do it.

"I served long enough to know enough not to be snowed with this Old Army shit," Warden bawled at him. "I re-enlisted once myself."

Karelsen only grunted, bending down over his belly to untie his muddy field shoes, trying to keep his equanimity, but Warden plumped down on his own bunk and banged his fist down on the castiron bedrail.

"Pete," he bellowed at the other man accusingly, "I dont have to tell you about this Compny. You're no punk. I'm too good a man to waste my talents in this outfit. They're killin me off, slow but sure. Jockstraps! Boys from Bliss! And now a new one."

Old Pete's face opened up vainly into a smug grin, as it always did when he conceived a mot. "This man's Army," he said distinctly, his equanimity recovered, "has always been a jockstrap Army, ever since Tunney first started fighting for the Marines in France. And it'll probably stay that way." The kid, he thought, Mazzioli, would really have enjoyed that one.

"What do you mean, new one?" Pete said, equanimously slipping it on the end, like a senator sticking his rider on a sure-thing bill. "Did the transfer of this Fort Kam cook go through?"

"Who else?" Warden cried impatiently. "A cook. I got more would be cooks than I know what to do with now. And now he's bringin in this Stark."

"Yeah? Say, thats too bad," Pete comforted comfortably. "By the way," he said, with all the gossip's subtlety, "whats the story on this guy? The Old Man mean to make him Mess Sergeant? What'll he do with Preem?"

"I could transfer out of here tomorrow," Warden raged on happily, "In Grade—get that? In Grade—to any one of ten compnys in this Regmint. Why the hell should I work my ass off here with no cooperation or appreciation?"

"Oh, sure," Pete managed to stick in, the equanimity fading. "Sure you could. I could be Chief of Staff too, except I cant stand leaving all my old buddies. But whats the story?"

"I don't have to take it," Warden bawled. "I'm the best man in their goddam Regmint, and whats more they know it. I'm turning in my stripes, Pete, I mean it. I rather be a buckass private who just does what he's told. If I had knew what was good for me, I'd of stayed in A Compny as a Staff."

"We all know you're indispensable," Pete said bitterly.

"I'm too damn good to waste my talents in this outfit, thats a cinch," Warden bellowed at him, going on unabashed, lashing himself into the cathartic tirade, battering at the other like the stream from a firehose. Why, he said, was Apey Galovitch running the First Platoon? Why did every noncom just happen to be a jockstrap? Why was Gentleman Jim O'Hayer the supply sergeant of this outfit? and where was Dynamite getting his gambling money that he lost like water at poker at the Club? "Officers," he snorted. "West Point socialites. Learn to play polo, poker and bridge and which fork to use, so they can mingle with society and marry a goddam wife with money who can entertain and teach the gook maids how to serve English style and copy the colonial Britisher and be goddam professional soldiers with a private income, just like Lord-Kiss-My-Ass.

"Where do you think Holmes got his wife? Right out of a bargain basement in Washington that specializes in young ingenues, right out of Baltimore, political family with a private fortune. Only Dynamite miscalculated, and this family went broke. Before Holmes could get anything but his four polo ponies and that goddamned pair of sterling silver spurs."

In the midst of his harangue, like a man in the calm center of a hurricane, seeing the curiosity brightening Pete's eyes, he coolly warned himself away from Holmes's wife and calmly steered it back to where he wanted it, on the things Pete already knew, and began on Sgt Henderson who had not pulled one day's drill in almost two years because he was the nursemaid to Holmes's polo ponies up at the Packtrain.

"Oh Jesus Christ!" Pete yelled back finally, putting his fingers in his ears, the equanimity beaten to death now by this wordy stream of energy that was battering him groggy. "Shut up. Leave me alone. Shut up. If you hate this place so much and can transfer out In Grade, why the hell dont you do it? And leave me alone?"

"Why!" Warden bawled indignantly. "You ask me why. Because I'm too goddamned kind-hearted for my own good, thats why. This outfit would collapse like a bamboo hut in a typhoon if I was to leave it."

"I wonder why the General Staff aint never discovered you?" Pete yelled, feeling that what made it all so goddam bad was that damn near all of what he said was true; if it wasnt true, and he was just blowing, it wouldnt be so hard to take.

"Because they're all too goddamned stupid, Pete, thats why," Warden said, suddenly, easily, in a normal voice. "Gimme a butt."

"You'll wear them goddam stripes out," Pete yelled at him. "Taking them off and sewing them back on so much. Sometimes I wonder how any single man so wonderful ever managed to get born."

"Dont get excited," Warden said. "Sometimes I wonder that myself. Gimme a goddam butt, I said."

"I'm not excited. You'll never change the Army," Pete yelled, realizing that Warden wasnt yelling any more and managing to pull his own voice back down to normalcy in the middle of it, "so you might as well relax," he said. He tossed a crumpled raindamp pack over to the grinning Warden. The silence in the little room, with the rain heard dripping down past the open window, deafened him.

"Is these rags all you got?" Warden said distastefully. "They wont even burn, for God sake."

"What do you want?" Pete yelled. "Gold tips?"

"Sure," Warden grinned. "At least that much." He lay back on his bunk, the enema completed, and put his arms contentedly behind his head and crossed his feet.

"You'll never change the Army," Pete said again. He paused and stood up in his socks and turned around to get his towel, exposing buttocks pocked with the syphilis hip shots he had been taking every two weeks for the past year, looking with his narrow shoulders and pussy hips like a child's roundbottomed doll that cant be knocked over. In the pause, Warden could feel the epigram that was coming.

"This outfit's no worse than any other. The Army's been that way," Pete said distinctly, the equanimity miraculously recovered, "ever since Benedict Arnold first put the slippery dong to the Point—and got reamed for his pains."

"Who was Benedict Arnold, Pete?"

"Go to hell," Pete said. "God Damn You."

"Now, Pete," Warden said. "Now, Pete. Now dont get excited now. Keep your equanimity."

"You think I dont know what it is you're doing?" Pete yelled. "When you come up here and ride me like you do? You think nobody's smart but you? You think I'll go on taking it off you forever, just because you're the Topkick. But I wont. Someday I'll move out of here, by god, even if I have to move out in the squadroom with the privates."

Warden looked over at him, almost startled, without moving, a look of actual real hurt coming on his face.

"If you're such a hotshot," Pete yelled, "why didnt you transfer Prewitt into my platoon, like I asked you the other day? Why dont you do it now."

"I want him where he is, Peter, in Galovitch's platoon, thats why."

"He'd be an asset, in my Weapons Platoon."

"He's an asset where he is."

"An asset to the Post Stockade, you mean. With what that boy knows about the MGs he'd make a squad leader right off, and as soon as I had an opening I'd make him section leader."

"Maybe I dont want him to have a rating yet. Maybe I'm tryin to educate him first."

"And maybe you couldnt get Dynamite to sign an order giving him a rating," Pete suggested. "Maybe you couldnt even get him to okay putting the kid in my platoon."

"Maybe I'm training him for bigger things."

"Like what, for instance?"

"Like taking a correspondence course, and recommending him for a reserve commission," Warden sneered.

"Why dont you send him to the Army War College while you're at it?"

"Thats an idea. Maybe I'll do just that. How do you know how a good mind works?"

"Big-Hearted-Harry. You want to know what I think? I think you're *nuts*. Pure plain crazy. Goofy as a loon. Thats what I think. I dont think you know what you mean to do yourself, with anything, least of all Prewitt, or this new transfer."

Maybe he's right, Warden thought. Is he right? He's right all right. Because who does know what they mean to do themself, with anything, anymore, in the world this one's becoming, when no man can do anything without creating some strange result he never had foreseen—like me just now.

"Thats what I think," Pete said again.

Warden only stared at him affectionately, grinning slyly, and he went to his footlocker to get his soapbox and his razor, trying to maintain the dignity he had just had but that was fast slipping away from him in the face of Warden's silent grinning, his body oozing the stale mushy smell of an old man who drinks too much and cannot assimilate the alcohol that in his youth he had thrown off so easily.

But he's a sharp old bastard. But is that the way Milt Warden will grow old? end up pimping for the Old Army? for a whore that never was? to save his face? His face, Milt thought, aint even savable, without the teeth, caved in and crumpled like a crying monkey, like a good sound apple forgotten and left for twenty-two years' service on the shelf, until its crisp moisture was evaporated and it remained, a mushy-smelling echo of itself, shrunken and brown, still whole because unmoved, but ready to crumble at the slightest pressure to move it from the shelf.

There was a legend about old Pete in the Company, one Pete worked hard to foster with his intellectualisms, about how he came of a rich family in Minnesota, and had enlisted to Save the World in the last war, caught the clap from an army nurse in France, and stayed in to get free treatment, so rare and expensive then, and because his family kicked him out. Pete loved the story, so it probably wasnt true. There were so many who prided themselves on being misfits, rebellion for rebellion's sake, a sort of inverse sentimentality, romance in reverse. You do it some yourself. But on the other hand, what? The officers. How to choose between a false success and a fake failure? between a fake God and a false Devil? If the story had been true, it wouldnt have been romantic, to Pete or anybody else. But part of it was true anyway, he thought, the part about the clap was true, whether he got it from an army nurse in France, or from a Paris whore, or from a pickup in Chicago. You could prove that much was true, with the arthritis; on some men it went down into the bones and stayed there.

And yet there remained, when the choppers filled out the watery indistinctness of the crumbled face, a firm intelligent line along the jaw, an echo of forgotten promise; and when the toothless pucker did not obscure the eyes, you could see the clearness in them of a man who knew machineguns and knew he knew them, the only satisfaction left an old man whose hobby now was collecting pornography in pictures.

"Where you going, Little Sir Echo?" Milt asked him as he clumped past to the door in the Japanese style wooden clogs.

"To take my goddam shower, if the First Sergeant's got no objections. Where'd you think? to the movies in this towel?"

Warden sat up and rubbed his face, as if he was trying to rub all of it, Karen, the transfer, Prewitt, Pete, himself, away.

"Thats too bad," he said. "I was just thinkin about goin over to Choy's and lappin up some brew. And I was goin to invite you along."

"I'm broke," Pete said. "I aint got no money."

"I'm buying. Its my party."

"No thanks. You think you can buy me off with beer? Come up here and needle me all afternoon and then buy me a couple of brews and make it all all right. No thanks. I wouldnt drink your beer if it was the last beer in the world."

Warden slapped him on the butt and grinned. "You mean if it was the very *last* beer? and you wouldnt *touch* it?"

Pete was trying hard to keep his craving off his face. "Well," he said. "If it was the *very* last beer. But I hope to God it never gets that low."

Milt Warden smiled, charmingly, all the deep warmth rising from his eyes, striking from the record all the rest of it, in spite of Pete's severity.

"Lets you and me go over to Choy's and get drunkern hell and tear up all the chairs and tables."

Pete had to grin, a little, but he would not renege all the way. "It'll have to be on you," he said.

"Its on me," Warden said. "Everythings on me. The whole fucking world's on me. Go take your bath. I'll wait. Couple days we'll see what this new man Stark is like."

They did not have to wait that long, because the new man Stark arrived the next day, barracks bag and baggage.

It was one of those first clear days that prophesied the ending of the rainy season. It had rained all morning and then suddenly cleared at noon, and the air, freshly washed today, was soft and free of dust, like dark crystal in the sharp clarity and sombre focus it gave to every image. Everything looked clean, smelled clean, and there was that holiday sense that always comes with an impending weather change. To work, on such a day, was sacrilege, but Warden had to be on hand for the arrival, to look him over.

It was, Warden felt, very appropriate that on this day there had been the usual Preem dinner menu of canned franks and canned baked beans, sometimes called "Stars and Stripes," but more often called now, since Preem served them almost every day, "Ratturds and Dogturds."

Sighing inwardly at the helplessness of a man in the hands of Fate when he saw the Hickam Field taxi creeping around the quad like a stranger looking for an address, he waited till it stopped in front of here to unload a man and his equipment on the still-wet grass in this dark clean air that was as tangible as water and then went outside to meet the adversary. At least he could shake his fist at Fate that much, by refusing to fight it as a Defensive Action in the Orderly Room, he thought, prepared for anything.

"I dont care if he is a ex-dogface," the new man said, staring after the departing taxi. "Thats still too much to pay."

"Probly got a gook wife," Warden said, "and half a dozen hapahaole brats to feed."

"Aint my fault," Stark said. "The govmint ought to pay for movin transfers."

"They do. All except the ones that transfer at their own request."

"They ought to pay for all of them," Stark said doggedly, not missing Warden's little dig.

"They will. After they get their Citizen's Army built up to strength and we get in this war."

"When that comes, they wont be no more transfers by request," Stark said, and they exchanged a sudden glance of knowledge that Pete Karelsen could not have shared and that, prepared as he was, surprised Warden with its understanding. That other part of his mind that never entered into anything and always stood outside himself observing, made a mental note.

"They pay it for the officers," Stark said in the same slow dogged drawl. "Everybody sticks the dogface. Even the ex-dogface." He pulled a sack of Golden Grain out of his shirt pocket by its dangling tab and got a paper out. "Where I put my stuff?"

"In the cooks' room," Warden said.

"Do I see the Old Man now? or after?"

"Dynamite aint here now," Warden grinned. "He may be back some time today, and he may not be back at all. But he wants to see you though."

Making the cigaret, the sack dangling from the string held in his teeth, Stark looked up at Warden levelly. "Dint he know I was comin in?"

"Sure," Warden grinned, picking up the biggest bag and the little canvas furlough satchel, "he knew it. But he had important business. At the Club."

"He aint changed much," Stark said. He took the other two blue barracks bags and followed, bending under the double weight balanced delicately on his back, across the porch and through the deserted messhall, dim and ghostlike now with the lights off. Warden led him into the tiny cooks' room that opened off at the back, across the corner from the doors into the Dayroom.

"You can start stowing this. And I'll call you if The Man comes in."

Stark let the bags fall heavily and straightened up and looked around the little room that, shared with all the other cooks, would be home.

"Well," he said, "I reckon I be here. I had to borrow money from the twenty percent men at Kam to git moved up here." He hitched his pants up with one thumb, a dispassionate gesture. "It was rainin like a tall cow pissin on a flat rock, when I left there."

"It'll be rainin here tomorrow," Warden said, going to the door.

"You ought to doubledeck these bunks in here, First," Stark said. "Theyd be more room."

"This is Preem's territory," Warden said from the door. "I never touch it."

"Old Preem," Stark said. "I aint seen him since Bliss. How is he?"

"He's fine," Warden said. "Just fine. Thats why I never touch his territory."

"He aint changed much either," Stark said, untying the drawropes of a bag and reaching in. "Heres my papers, First."

Back in the Orderly Room Warden looked them over closely. Maylon Stark was twenty-four, they told him, had served two hitches and was on his third, had never done any time in a Stockade. That was all, not much to go on.

It was odd, he thought, leaning back and cocking his feet up on his desk, relaxing the big shoulders and thick arms smugly and with satisfaction in the chair, it was odd how there were no ages in the Army. Back in his hometown Stark, who was twenty-four, would have been of a different generation, a newer crop, than himself who was thirty-four; but here they both were contemporaries of Niccolo Leva, who was forty, and of Prewitt, who was only twenty-one. Here they were all the same, of a certain similarity, of a certain common knowledge, of a certain deep unshakeable very flexible something that was in the bony structure of their faces and in the shaded halftones of their voices. But they were not contemporaries of Maggio or Mazzioli or Sal Clark, who were still punk kids. And they were not, either, the contemporaries of guys like Wilson, Henderson, or Turp Thornhill, or O'Hayer. Lets not be romantic now, he thought. But still, with all the romance put aside, there really was this similarity, this difference, this contemporariness, that was not in the others. You could feel it. Chief Choate had it too. Sometimes even Pete Karelsen had it, but not very often. Usually he only had it when he got real mad. Or drunk. Pete had it drunk. It was a thing you felt, even though you could not name it and no word ever said it. He was still mulling this illumination over, trying vainly to find a name for it, when Capt Holmes came in.

By the time the customary interview and peptalk for new men was ended, that other part of Warden's mind knew quite definitely what he meant to do about the kitchen situation.

Maylon Stark stood in the Orderly Room during the whole of Capt Holmes's lecture, after he and Holmes had shaken hands and Holmes had beamed his pleasure at him, with his hands easily behind his back, his campaign hat dangling from them, staring at Holmes reflectively. He expressed his gratitude perfunctorily and said nothing else. At the end of the lecture, still staring reflectively at his new commander, he saluted precisely and withdrew immediately.

Maylon Stark was medium-built and husky. That was the only word to fit him, husky. He had a husky face, and the nose on it was badly bent and flattened huskily. His voice was husky. His head sat huskily on his neck, the way a fighter carries his chin pulled in from habit. It was the huskiness of a man who hunches up his shoulders and hangs on hard with both hands. And with it Maylon Stark had a peculiar perpetual expression, like that of a man who is hanging hard onto the earth to keep it from moving away, out from under him. The line from the right side of his flattened nose to the corner of his mouth was three times as deep as the same line on the left side; his mouth did not curl, but the deepness of this line made him look like he was about to smile sardonically, or cry wearily, or sneer belligerently. You never knew which. And you never found out. Because Maylon Stark never did any of them.

"He's a good man, Sergeant Warden," Holmes insisted, after Stark had left. There was a puzzled, not quite satisfied look on his face. "I can always tell a good man when I see one. Stark'll make me one damn fine cook."

"Yes, Sir," Warden said. "I think he will."

"You do?" Holmes said, surprised. "Well. Well, its like I say, real soldiers dont grow on trees, and you have to look hard before you find one."

Warden did not bother to answer this one. Dynamite had said the same thing about Ike Galovitch, when he made him sergeant, except that he had not looked puzzled.

Capt Holmes cleared his throat and reset his face and began to dictate next week's Drill Schedule to Mazzioli, who had come in while the lecture had been on. Mazzioli stopped his filing to type the Drill Schedule for the Captain. The Captain walked back and forth, his hands behind his back, his head thrown back thoughtfully, dictating slowly so Mazzioli could get it with the typewriter.

Mazzioli typed disgustedly, knowing that later The Warden would haul out his FMs and change the schedule all around and then he would have to type it up again. And Dynamite would sign it without noticing the difference.

As soon as Holmes was gone, Warden beat it out to the cooks' room, almost unhinged by Dynamite's eternal piddling rumination of the Schedule, feeling he had suddenly escaped from an airtight bottle, breathing joyously, and wondering what Holmes would do if he ever realized his own uselessness and the finicking he hid it with; dont worry, he thought, he never will; it would kill him; but mostly hoping Holmes's dawdling had not given any of the cook force time to get back before he got to see Stark alone.

"Come on upstairs," he said, finding Stark was still alone, doubtfully holding up a pair of the old outmoded suntan breeches that he hated to throw away but had no use for any more. "To my room. I got talkin to do thats private. And I dont want none of them cooks around to see me with you."

"Okay, First," Stark said, answering the urgency in his voice, and got up still holding out the breeches. "I had these breeches ever since the year my sis got married."

"Throw them out," Warden decided for him. "When this war comes and we move out you wont have room for half of what you got thats useful."

"Thats right," Stark said. He tossed them on the growing pile of refuse by the door implacably and looked around the tiny room, and at the three barracks bags that held seven years' accumulation of a way of life.

"Aint much, is it?" Warden said.

"Enough, I guess."

"Footlockers aint got room for memories," Warden said. "And barracks bags even less. Hell, I even use to keep a diary. Still dont know what happened to it."

Stark took a leather framed picture of a young woman and three boys from the satchel and set it open on his wall locker shelf. "Well," he said, "I'm home."

"This is important," Warden said. "Lets go."

"I'm with you, First," Stark said, and picked up the pile of castoffs and the breeches. "Ony time I ever got around to clearin out is when I move," he said apologetically.

On the porch he dropped it all into a GI trash can without breaking stride, following Warden up the stairs, but at the landing he looked back at it, once, at the breeches leg with its thin round GI laces whose metal tips had been lost long ago, dangling outside the can.

"Sit down," Warden said, indicating old Pete's bunk. Stark sat down without speaking. Warden sat on his own bunk facing him, and lit a cigaret. Stark rolled one.

"You want a tailormade?"

"I like these better. I awys smoke Golden Grain," Stark said, eyeing him reflectively, but waiting coolly, "if I can get it. If I cant get Golden Grain, I rather smoke Country Gentleman than tailormades."

Warden set the battered ashtray on the floor between them. "I play them straight, Stark. Five cards face up."

"Thats the way I like them."

"You had two strikes on you when you got here, as far as I'm concerned. Because you served with Holmes at Bliss."

"I figured that," Stark said.

"You from Texas, aint you?"

"Thats right. Borned in Sweetwater."

"How come you to leave Fort Kam?"

"Didnt like it."

"Didnt like it," Warden said, almost caressingly. He went to his wall locker and fished around down behind his diddy box till he brought up a fifth of Lord Calvert. "They never inspect my room on Saturday," he said. "Drink?"

"Sure," Stark said. "A breath." He took the bottle and looked at the label, inspecting the longhaired dandy the way a man sweats out his hole card in a big game too rich for his blood, then upended it and drank.

"You ever handled a Mess, Stark?"

Stark's adam's apple paused. "Sure," he said around the bottle and went on with his drink. "I was runnin one in Kam."

"I mean really run one."

"Sure. Thats what I mean. I was acting bellyrobber on one stripe. Only I was never acting."

"How about menus and marketing?"

"Sure," Stark said. "All that." He handed the bottle back reluctantly. "Good," he said.

"What kind of rating did you say?" Warden said, not bothering to drink now.

"Pfc. I was up for a Sixth Class, ony I never got it. I was Second Cook on the TO, but without the money. I ran the mess without even being acting. I did everything but wear the stripes and draw the money."

"And you didnt like it," Warden grinned, repeating back, saying it almost chortlingly.

Stark stared at him reflectively, that peculiar about to laugh, about to cry, about to sneer expression on his face. "The setup? no," he said. "The work? yes. Thats my job," he said.

"Good," Warden said happily and took a drink now. "I need a good man in my Mess, one I can depend on, one *with* the rating. How about First and Fourth, to start with?"

Stark looked at him reflectively. "Sounds reasonable," he said. "If I get it. What then?"

"The Rating," Warden said. "Preem's Rating."

Stark talked it over with his cigaret. "I dont know you," he said, "but I'll call you, First."

"Heres the deal. Theres four men from your old outfit at Bliss in this Compny. They're all four sergeants. You got no trouble there."

Stark nodded. "I can see that far."

"The rest is simple. All you got to do is keep your nose clean and show you're a better man than Preem. You're a First Cook with a First and Fourth, as of today. All you got to do is step in and take over whenever Preem dont show, which is just about every day."

"I'm a new man here. Kitchen crews is clannish people. And Preem's got The Rating."

"Dont worry about The Rating. You dont need The Rating. I'll take care of that end. When you have trouble in the kitchen, come to me. The cooks'll give you lip for a while, especially this fat guy Willard. He's a First Cook and he's bucking for Preem's job. But Dynamite dont like Willard.

"You'll get lots of lip, but dont argue. Be chickenshit. Bring it to me. It'll be all your way."

"Its goin to sure be tough on poor old Preem," Stark said, accepting the bottle Warden was offering him again.

"Have you seen him yet?"

"Not since Bliss." Stark handed the bottle back reluctantly. "Good," he said.

"I like it some myself," Warden said, wiping his mouth with the back of his hand. "Preem likes it too. Preem married it. Preem looks like a man who either seen a miracle, or was hit at the base of the skull with a rubber hammer."

"He was an awful quiet guy when I knew him. Kind of guy to go off and get drunk all by himself."

"He's still that way. Except now he has to go off and get sober by himself."

"Quiet guys like that are bad. The ones that get drunk by theirselves. They awys flip their lid."

"You think so?" Warden said, suddenly narrowly, that other part of his mind tuning in and clocking up the platitude, and reminding him that where theres smoke theres fire and where theres platitude theres liar. "Some of them dont."

Stark shrugged. "Theres just one thing, First. If I take your kitchen, I run it my way. Nobody sings and nobody squares. There'll be no backseat drivin from the Orderly Room if I take your kitchen. Otherwise no soap."

"Forget it," Warden said. "You run it right and its your baby."

"That aint what I said," Stark said doggedly. "I said its all my baby. Right *or* wrong. And the Office keeps its nose out. Or else I dont want any part of it."

Warden grinned at him slyly, the pixy's eyebrows quivering, thinking that he couldnt be *too* dumb. "Fine," he said. Why cant you just be honest once? he thought, just make one promise without keeping your fingers crossed, you bastard.

"Okay," Stark said, with finality. "How about a nuther drink?"

Warden handed him the bottle. The hand was over now, the cards were being collected by the dealer. The spontaneous conversation of relaxed tension broke out bubbling.

"What I dont see," Stark said conversationally, "is what you make on this deal."

"I make nothing," Warden grinned. "You ever hear of the man with the whip? Well, I'm the guy. Holmes only thinks this is his Compny."

The bottle worked back and forth now like a shuttle, weaving brilliant colors, over and under, around the strings of words.

"How many guys from Bliss in the Compny now?"

"Five, counting you. 'Champ' Wilson has the First Platoon," Warden said, skewering the word. "Preem the Mess. Two platoon guides, Henderson and Old Ike Galovitch."

"Ike Galovitch! Jesus Christ! He was our boiler orderly at Bliss, couldnt even speak plain English."

"Thats the boy. He still cant speak it. And he's Dynamite's Close Order expert."

"My God!" Stark said. He was sincerely shocked.

"You see what I'm up against?" Warden grinned happily, watching the lovely beautiful brilliant shuttling of the bottle as it wove and wound and spun the web of unreality, of talk about them both, relaxing into it.

". . . But you're all right. You were at Bliss and that puts you on the inside track." . . .

"These cooks wont like it though." . . .

"To hell with them. Long as I like it, you got no worry." . . .

"Okay, First. You lead the band." . . .

"You goddam right I do. . . .

". . . the setup in the Regiment. Holmes and Colonel Delbert are just like that, see? They . . ."

". . . what I got to work with." . . .

"They's two men you can depend on. . . ."

". . . and heres the setup in the Compny. Strickly a jockstrap outfit, see? Dhom is the Staff because he's trainer for Dynamite's squad, but he's as far as he will ever get and . . ."

The soldier's greatest hobby, he thought as he listened to his own voice talking, the bull session, add a bottle and you have his greatest joy, also his greatest escape, he thought. The unofficial institution that is the first-string substitute for women and the ageold conversation where the man explains his ideals and his hopes for his life and the woman listens and agrees and tells him how wonderful he is. But soldiers are men without women, he thought, and they cannot hold each other's heads upon their breasts and pat each other's hair. But they escape just as well, the other part reminded him.

Ah, if you could only lose this other part of your mind too, like Stark is doing, not lose but forget it for a little while, without thinking about the women, or the men, or all the other angles.

"Gimme a drink," Stark said. "Is that tall blonde wife of his still around?"

"Who?" Warden said.

"His wife," Stark said. "Whats her name. Karen. Is he still married to her?"

"Oh her," Warden said.

Maybe its better for you you cant deliberately distract that other part, he thought. More painful, surely. But maybe in the long run better. Provided, of course, that you can stand it. There is courage, he thought, and then theres courage.

"Yeah," he said, "he's still married to her. She comes over here every once in a while. Why?"

"I just wondered," Stark said, mellow now and feeling philosophical. "I dunno, I aways figure Holmes would of left her before now. She was a regular bitch in heat at Bliss, when I knew her, but mean like, as if she really hated it and all the ones she gave it to. They said she laid half the EM on the Post at Bliss."

"They did?" Warden said.

"Hell yes. I heard she even got the clap down there. Ony thing kept her from bein out and out a whore was she was married."

"You mean she kept her amateur standing," Warden said.

Stark threw back his head and laughed. "Thats it."

"I dont put much stock in stories like that though," Warden said, carefully casual. "You hear them about every woman that lives on a Army Post. Mostly wishful thinking, you ask me."

"Oh yeah?" Stark said indignantly. "Well this aint no story. I fucked her myself, at Bliss. So I know it aint no story."

"Come to think of it," Warden said. "I been hearin some pretty rough stories about her around here." What was it she had said, that afternoon, in the house, with the rain dripping sounding softly at the open window, what was it? Now he had it. She said, *Don't you want me either?*

"You can probly," Stark said, whiskily innocent, "believe them all. Because she's rough. I can see a single woman sleepin around some," he said; "I can even see a married woman steppin out on her old man. But I dont like to see any woman, specially if she's married, just layin for any guy comes along. A whore's a whore, thats how she makes her livin. But theys somethin wrong with a woman who does it for fun, and then dont like it."

"You think thats what she does?" Warden said. "Holmes's wife, I mean?"

"Hell yes. Why should she of laid me down there at Bliss? a buckass private in the rear rank, who didnt even have no dough to spend on her?"

Warden shrugged. "What the hell?" he said. "Its nothing to me. Maybe I can get some of it myself, sometime."

"If you're smart," Stark said, "you'll leave it alone. She's nothin but a topflight bitch. She's coldern hardern any whore I ever saw." His face was adamant, convincing.

"Here," Warden said. "Have another drink. Dont let it get you down, for Christ sake."

Stark took the bottle without looking at it. "I done seen too many of these rich women. They worse than queers. And I dont like them."

"Neither do I," Warden said. If she had as many . . . , Leva had said, she'd be a porcupine, he thought, listening to Stark's voice going on to something else and his own voice answering. And they're both smart boys, he thought, they know their way around, they aint punk kids.

But Leva's only giving you hearsay, he's had no personal experience with her. And Stark was five years younger then, a mere nineteen, a kid, when he had his experience with her. That must have been an experience, he thought, that must really have been quite an experience, to make him talk the way he does now, five years later. Remember he was a juicy green young kid serving his first hitch.

But would the woman who went on the moonlight swimming party have done that? would she have laid for half the EM at Bliss? What do you say? I dont know. Yes, you dont know; and here are two men who do know. But can you trust their judgment? No, you cant. You cant accept what they know, and you dont know. Where does that leave you?

He wanted to take the bottle and rise up and smash it down on this talking, jawbone wagging skull, flatten it out on the floor until the jawbone jutted out of the pancaked matter and ceased wagging. Not because of what Stark had told him, and not because he'd laid this woman he himself had laid (you shy away from the Word, dont you?), no not because of that; he felt almost a curious friendliness and comradeship for him because of that, like two men who use the same toothbrush. Did two men ever use the same toothbrush? No, he wanted to flatten out this wagging skull with this bottle simply because it happened to be here, and he, absurdly, for no reason, felt the need of smashing something. Because what right have you to be mad at Stark because she laid for him? or for all the EM on the Post at Bliss, for that matter?

". . . I think we can make it work," Stark was saying. "We got all the cards."

"Right." Warden caught the shuttle in midpassage and returned it to his footlocker. "You wont see me around after this, Maylon," he said. Might as well call him by his first name, he's practically your brother, it looks as though you've got a lot of brothers. "Bring your troubles to the

Orderly Room," he said, listening to the tones of his own voice carefully. "You'll have plenty of them. But after Retreat you dont know me any better than you do any other noncom in this outfit."

Stark nodded at this wisdom. "Okay, First," he said.

"You better get back down and get that stuff cleaned up now," Warden said, astounded, maybe even proud, at how cool he could make his own voice sound.

"Christ," Stark said, getting up. "I forgotten all about it."

Warden grinned, it felt as if his face was cracking, and waited till he left. Then he lay down on his bunk and put his arms behind his head. And with the other part, that came forward now, that always came forward when he was alone, thinking about it, consciously, like a man who cant quit biting on a sore tooth but wont go to the dentist.

He could see it all in his mind, just the way it must have happened, with Stark holding her, her lying on the bed as he himself had seen her, every secret open and unveiled, the heavy breathing like a distance runner, the eyelids shuddering closed at that moment when you went clear out of your own body and you knew nothing and knew everything, you a long ways off with only a slim silver cord attaching you to yourself back there. Maybe Stark gave her more pleasure than you gave her, he thought, biting on the tooth that was unbearable, maybe all of them gave her more pleasure than you gave her, maybe even Holmes gave her more pleasure than you gave her. He had never thought about Holmes sleeping with her before. But now he thought about it. Now he wondered if she might not be sleeping with Holmes all along, all this time.

Whats the matter with you? he thought, what is it to you? You're not in love with her. Its nothing to you who she sleeps with. You're not even going to see her anymore anyway. You made your mind up to that the night of the swimming party, didnt you?

He would, he decided after a while, just keep that next date, after all. Theres no sense in turning down a piece of free stuff, when it costs three bucks at Mrs Kipfer's. Besides, he would like to find out the true answer to this puzzle, just to satisfy his curiosity, his intellectual curiosity.

I think, piped up the other part of his mind suddenly, I think you wanted to keep it all along, meant to keep it all along.

Maybe, he admitted. But anyway I didnt blow this transfer deal, did I? I could have, but I didnt. This deal should pan out all right now, if we have any luck, dont you think?

Dont change the subject on me, the other part insisted. I think you meant to keep that date even then, that same night, when you went down to Wu Fat's and got drunk, looking for sympathy.

All right, he said to it, but go away. Do you always have to be checking up on me too? like you do with everybody else? Cant you even trust your own flesh and blood?

How much do you know about families? it said to him disgusted, and you ask me that? You're the one I should trust the least.

Listen, he said, I got work to do. This kitchen deal is going to be touch and go for a while, and we'll need all our luck, but I think we can swing it, if we have the luck. So dont bother me with theory. This is practical. And he got up quickly off the bed and went downstairs to make out Stark's promotion, before it had a chance to answer.

They had the luck. Capt Holmes found the order on his desk that night, when he stopped in a minute on his way up to the Club for dinner, and he signed it. It made Stark a First Cook with a First and Fourth, dropped Willard back to Second Cook and First and Sixth, and sent Pfc Sims back to straight duty shorn of his Sixth Class. It was just the way Holmes had planned it, except he had not meant to let Sims keep his Pfc, and he was surprised to find it there like that because he had expected to have trouble out of Warden when he put it through. Nothing serious, just some of Warden's childish balking, and he was glad now, as he signed it, that there would be no argument because he always hated to have to pull his rank, even when it was for the good of his Company.

The rest of it was just as easy as that. It was so ridiculously easy that it seemed incredible. Stark had the anticipated trouble with the cooks. They balked at the assumed authority of the newcomer. Fat Willard, watching the wind change and seeing his own star set, was the ringleader. He agitated brilliantly and complained superlatively until Stark took him out on the green and beat him up so bad he was afraid to speak at all. When the rest of them impeded progress Stark took it to the Orderly Room. Warden gave his decision and Stark departed. By the end of a week Capt Holmes was so sure he had discovered a kitchen genius that he pointed out to Warden the vast importance of proper early training for recruits.

Stark loved his kitchen, it was already "his," with the single-mindedness women have been taught to dream of and expect, demand, and decry when attached to anything but love. Stark drove himself as hard or harder than he drove the cooks and the KPs. The dormant Company Fund was brought into the light, and Stark bought new silverware, he recommended the purchase of newer better equipment. There were even fresh flowers on the tables now and then, a unique experience in G Company. Sloppiness in eating was no longer allowed, and Stark enforced this new rule like a tyrant. A man who slopped catsup over his plate onto the oilcloth would suddenly find himself outside the door in the middle of a meal. The KPs lived a life of hell on earth, yet the reflective eyes in Stark's sad sneering laughing face were always soft and no KP could force himself to hate him. They saw him working just as hard as they did, and they chortled at the way he rode the cooks. Even fat Willard was forced to work.

In less than two weeks, before the end of March, the tall cadaverous Sergeant Preem was broken to a private. Capt Holmes could be as hard as the next man, when it was necessary. He called Preem in and told him bluntly and militarily. Because after all, it was Preem's own fault, nobody could have given him more of a chance than Capt Holmes. If another man was the better man, then by rights he should have the job. He gave Preem a choice between transferring to another company in the Regiment, or transferring to another regiment, because you cant let a former high-ranking noncom stay in his outfit as a private, its bad for discipline.

Preem, who had been rising every day at noon, oozing that stale mushy smell of a middle-aged drunk, and wandering out dazedly through his now bustling sparkling kitchen where there was no room for him, chose the other regiment because he was ashamed. He said nothing. There was nothing he could say. He was through and he knew it. His gravytrain days were over. He heard his fate with a face that was as much dazed as it was impassive. He was a broken man.

"Captain," Warden said, after he had left, "how you want me to make this order out? Busted for 'Inefficiency'?"

"Why, yes," Holmes said. "How else would one make it?"

"Well, I thought maybe we might make it 'Insubordination.' Everybody gets busted for insubordination sometime or other. A man who aint been busted for insubordination aint a soldier yet. But 'Inefficiency,' a man who's got that on his record's done."

"Why, yes, Sergeant," Holmes said. "Make it 'Insubordination.' I dont guess anybody'll know, will they? Preem ought to have a break, as long as it doesnt interfere with the efficiency of my Company. After all, he served with me in Bliss."

"Yes, Sir," Warden said.

The order was made out that way, but he knew it was a futile gesture. The minute Preem appeared at his new outfit with his rubber hammer look they would know the story.

That night Stark bought the traditional boxes of cigars and passed them out at chow. Everybody was happy with the new food, new management, and new rating. Pvt Preem ate in obscurity at a back table, already completely forgotten, displaying that most touching mark in soldiering: the dark spots on his sleeves from which the stripes had been removed.

Stark, Warden, Leva, Choate, and Pop Karelsen celebrated the occasion and christened Stark's three stripes with beer at a private table in the shouting befogged interior of Choy's. There were four fights that night, and Big Chief had to be transported home in the usual manner. Leva went over for the big two-wheeled machinegun cart and with much straining and grunting the huge limp Choctaw was dumped in and carted home by the other four.

In the midst of the festivity Stark sat at the table silently, the perpetual dark rings under his eyes making them look like burning oil at the bottom of two deep wells. He bought all the beer the others could manage to drink between seven and eleven, and he drank a lot of it himself, even though he had had to borrow the money from the twenty percent men to pay for it. But he watched it all reflectively, and the old peculiar almost laughing, almost crying, almost sneering expression did not leave his face.

Prewitt was one of the G Company men who happened in during the evening. Stark bought each one of them the traditional free beer a new noncom always buys. It was the custom to drop in and collect it. But when Prewitt came Warden waxed drunkenly sarcastic.

"Whats a matter, kid?" he wanted to know, swimmingly, his hair down in his eyes. "You broke, kid? Poor kid, he broke. No beer, no money, no nothin. Poor kid. I'll buy you a whole case, kid. I hate to see you come around for the handout, its as hard on a man's pride as a breadline. Hey, Choy! Bring my friend here a case of Pabst, and put it on my account." He laughed uproariously.

Stark watched Warden with reflective eyes and then looked Prewitt over thoughtfully. His eyes crinkled up contemplatively as he studied both of them. Then he offered to buy Prewitt another beer, besides the free one. But Prew refused and left, and Stark nodded thoughtfully.

That night Warden lay in his narrow bunk, his big arms crossed behind his head and listened to Pete's drunken snore. It had been like drawing a flush at stud, when trips was the best possible hand against you. In the dark the pixy look of relish swept over his face, raising the quivering ends of his eyebrows. He looked at Pete's dim form pityingly and then rolled over triumphantly toward sleep.

Dont pity Pete, it told him in the silence.

What, he thought, you again? I thought you went on a trip.

Nope, I'm still here. Did you think you could put me off forever? You've had a good time, the past two weeks, evading me. But the thing with Stark is over now.

Socrates had nothing on me, he thought. You mean you think I've been deliberately avoiding you?

Well? Havent you?

My god, he thought, whats gotten into you anyway? I can remember back when you trusted everybody; not just me, but everybody. And it wasn't so many years ago either, not more than ten. And now you wont even take *my* word of honor.

Thats right, it told him cheerfully. Can you remember all the scrapes we got into back then, too? We trusted this one, and we trusted that one. Man, it really cost us, didnt it? I can even remember a few times when I trusted you, and nearly laid us both right out to cool.

You're exaggerating, he thought, you're just cynical, god damn you.

Is that any way to talk to me? After all I've done for you?

Great God, he thought, I didnt marry you. You're getting so you sound just like my Mother.

Dont blaspheme me, it told him coldly. You pulled a fast one, Milton, it went on relentlessly, on this deal with Stark. It looked good. But it didnt change the Company any. Its still the same. O'Hayer and the jockstraps havent lost an inch. And besides, its no credit to you. Anybody could have won a made to order hand like that one was, with Stark as the old ace in the hole.

All right, he thought, you bastard. I give up. What do you want?

Are you going to keep that date with Karen?

I said I was.

But you didn't admit you'd meant to keep it all along.

I did too admit it.

But you didnt *believe* it.

All right then, he thought, then I *believe* it. Does that suit you, you moralistic bastard? What else do you want me to admit?

Nothing now, it grinned. I'll see you later.

"Oh Jesus," he said aloud, "but you're a distrustful son of a bitch. I wouldnt be like you for anything."

"What?" Pete mumbled, sitting straight up in his bed. "I didnt do it, Sir. Honestly I didnt, Sir. I'm innocent as a new born lamb, Sir, I really am."

"For Christ's sake shut up and go to sleep," Warden bellowed, plumping up his pillow. "You drunken bum."

Chapter 13

Stark was in the stockroom the next morning working on his ordering lists when Preem came through the kitchen.

Preem was leaving shortly and he was making his farewells. Everybody, including the KPs, was ill at ease with him the way a man will fumble awkwardly with his hat and look embarrassed when he passes by the casket of a former friend to view the corpse. This has nothing to do with me, he wants everyone to know. And when Preem came near a man the work suddenly demanded great attention. But Preem didnt seem to notice. He was not so much saying goodby to the men as he was saying goodby to the kitchen itself.

Through the open doors Stark could see him working his way up toward the stockroom. He went on working, but when Preem finally got up to the stockroom, he put aside his list and watched the tall gaunt former mess sergeant with that curious sad, laughing, sneering expression. Because he felt he could not let himself just slide over this meeting, as the others had.

"I just come to say so long," Preem said awkwardly. "You dont mind?"

"Me? Hell no," Stark said. "Help yourself."

Preem walked around the walls. He looked up at the high shelves and down at the low, all of them crowded with cans and sacks. He put his hand on a No. 10 can of pineapple. He punched a 100 lb sack of sugar.

"You'll need to restock on flour," Preem said. "Dont forget it."

"I wont," Stark said. "In fact, it was me pointed it out to you."

Stark did not go back to his work. He sat motionless, watching Preem intently, waiting. Preem closed the doors into the KP room and then came back to the homemade desk.

"Well, Stark, its all yours," Preem said. "And you can have it."

"Thanks," Stark said dryly, the deep crease down the right side of his mouth fixed and unrelenting.

"I'm gettin what I deserve," Preem said, "and I know it. I got no complaints."

"Well now thats fine," Stark said.

Preem ignored him. "I'm through," he went on. "You think you got a good break, Stark. And maybe you have. You just moved in, and this heres your first permanent berth. You makin a lot of changes and you snappin these people up, just like they ought. Its new and you like it. It looks like rosy."

Preem paused, and with what seemed a great effort put his foot up on a crate and leaned on his knee.

Stark said nothing.

"I was the same way when I got my first mess," Preem said. "You cant see nothin bad ahead. But when the new wears off is when you'll see it. In six months Holmes'll find himself a new fair haired boy; Warden'll have a new iron to burn. Then you'll have to fight for ever spud you get. They'll be too many people puttin their oar in and tellin you how to run your mess. They cramp you ever way you turn.

"It wears you down after a while. After one hitch there aint no hotshot mess sergeant. And its the same ever place you go.

"I'm sober, Stark. I'll be drunked up tonight, but I'm sober as a judge right now.

"I dont hold no grudge because I'm gettin what I deserve. I aint makin excuses neither, but a man can only take so much and then he gets tired. It wears you down. Its hard to see somethin you love patchworked by politicians. After twenty years service, I'm goin back to bein a buckass private in the rear rank."

"You werent no hotshot mess sergeant down at Bliss," Stark said. "You was just a cook, like me. And you got this rating the same way I got it: you come up here and pushed some other guy out of it, because you been at Bliss with Holmes."

"Thats right," Preem said, "a guy who never done me no harm in his life. A man thats smart will get out before its too late. Its too late for me. Its better to be a buckass private in the rear rank all a time, rather than go back to it after twenty years. Drill at eight and Fatigue at one. Be smart, Stark, and get out. Thats my advice to you."

"I aint never been smart," Stark said.

"I know," Preem said. "And I aint expectin you to be. But I told you. Theys some men is smart and theys others that aint. Them thats smart gets on in life, and them that aint buys out."

"Buy out," Stark said. "And then what?"

"I don't know," Preem said. "They got you comin and goin. But a young man's at least got a chance. But I never bought out, and you wont neither."

"I said I wasnt smart," Stark said. "Anyways, you cant buy out no more, with this war comin on."

"Thats right," Preem said. "But whenever a man likes somethin, he caint take cover. You got a cut on your eye, thats what the other man tries to hit. If you love the kitchen like I loved the kitchen, then you ought to get out of it and do straight duty. If you liked straight duty, then you ought to get in the kitchen. If clerkin's what you hate, then thats what you ought to do. That way you're safe, you'll be a success then, you'll get the ratings and you'll keep them, because you wont have no weak spot where they can hurt you."

Stark grinned. "That sounds like good advice. But like I said, I aint that smart."

But Preem didnt grin. "One thing, Stark; watch out for Warden. He's on your side now, because you do him some good. But dont ever trust Warden too much."

"I never trust anybody too much," Stark said.

"Okay," Preem said. "You're the hotshot. You dont need no advice. . . . You want to shake hands with me?"

Stark looked down at his list. "Sure," he said.

"How old you think I am?" Preem said as they shook hands.

Stark shook his head. "I dont know."

"I'm thirty-eight," Preem's grin was bitter. "Look fifty-eight, dont I?"

"Look oldern that," Stark said, trying to make a joke of it.

Preem opened the doors and the steamy air from the sinks filled the stockroom.

"I wont be over to Choy's no more," Preem said, "but I ever see you over to the Post Beergarden, I'll buy you a brew."

"Okay, Preem," Stark said. "So long."

He watched the tall gaunt figure walk on through the KP room. It stopped once to look at the big built-in icebox. Stark sat down at his homemade desk and picked up the order list. Then he put it down and picked up his pencil. An order list was an important thing. You had to make one out for every day of the year. Three hundred and sixty-five order lists. Three hundred and sixty-six on leap year. Stark tore up his order list and threw it on the floor. Then he got up and looked at the sweating, water-soaked KPs bending over their sinks. He leaned on the door and studied them with reflective eyes set in a face that seemed about to laugh sardonically, or cry wearily, or sneer belligerently.

After a while he went back to his desk and took out a fresh blank. An order list was important, just as important as your menus.

Chapter 14

It had all of it, Prew questioned, begun with the quitting of the Bugle Corps. Everything else had followed naturally from that. It was like a staircase, with each step logically above the last, and that once you were committed to the very bottom step you had obviously to follow, each foot above the other simply, to get to the place where you were going. Because it was plainly the only way to get upstairs; or in this case, get downstairs. This was, he reflected, a staircase going down, each step *below* the other, the whole parallel column of them stretching down and down, to the point where the parallel lines of the banisters you could not jump over without being injured came together, the point shrouded in the mists of beyond-sight so you could not see it, and which mathematically was not a point at all but only an optical illusion that you never reached. This was the staircase he had entered upon when he had committed himself to the first step and quit the Corps, so he could forget all the subsequent steps (the step of being busted, the step of Violet, the step of not being a punchy, and all the other similar steps) which led down to this present step of no money, of rear rank privacy, of being unable to procure even momentarily (a moment, right now, would be all he needed) a woman when your bowels slid in you suddenly and greasily at the thought of one; led down to this, finally and worstly, present step of suffered scorn. He could forget all these, in looking back and taking stock, and concentrate on the very first step. He had taken that step of his own free will; he knew that then, and now, in ruminating back, he knew it now. But it was, he also knew, an own free will that while it allowed him choice had presented only one alternative for him to choose from. If this was so, and he was quite sure that it was so, then that had not really been the first step at all, that quitting of the Corps, and there was no first step anywhere but only another mythical banister-meeting point shading off above him into god knew how long before he was ever born. Yet these steps were not haphazard. They were well built, well proportioned, all of a piece, and solid. They would never fall out from under you. They had been *put* there, each step a decision that was not a decision, part of a plan that was not a plan, each with its subsequent steps that were not subsequent steps. He saw all this quite clearly, knew it all quite positively, and realized quite surely that he could not have chosen other than he did. It was only that, after a while, not after a dozen steps, not after a hundred steps, not after five hundred steps, but after an infinitely infinite number of steps, the legs that took each single step so easily began to tire.

He pulled his first KP under the new Mess Sergeant two days after Preem's shamefaced capitulation, three days before the end of March and the Payday he had been sweating out so hard. He had expected, knowing that his turn was coming inexorably up, that The Warden would have taken advantage of the fact and arranged it so his KP would fall on Payday, since he had done things like that before. So he was not only surprised, but almost pleased, to pull KP this time. He was certainly not expecting trouble.

Like the rest of the Company, he had watched the battle for the Mess dispassionately, not caring much who won, but knowing beforehand how it would obviously end. It was like watching the intricate, unhumanized move and countermove of pieces in a chess game from a master's textbook, where you knew each move before it came and still must gasp in admiration at the beauty of the logic, but which did not touch the movement of your life. He had not cared at the time that Stark had won.

But after the night of the big celebration, when Stark had offered to buy him a second beer in spite of The Warden's sarcasm, he had been glad that Stark had won. He had felt drawn to Stark and very grateful, even when the pride in him made him refuse because Stark had made a sudden rise to power in the Company, even when he wanted very badly to accept. He had felt there would be understanding there. And

Prewitt needed understanding, male understanding. Almost as bad, or worse than he needed a woman. He saw in Stark an admirable man, and he needed that too. So he was almost looking forward to this KP, as bad as he disliked KP. And he truly did dislike KP; it was amazing how unpleasant good food could become once the meal was over and a subtle chemistry changed it into garbage. He was hoping for a good KP.

But everything went wrong at the start. In the first place, he was on KP with Bloom and Readall Treadwell. Which meant that he would either have to work with Bloom, on dishes, or else take the rotten mucky job of pots and pans and let Reedy work with Bloom. Because there was no hope at all that Readall Treadwell, who never beat anybody anyplace, would beat Bloom down and get the second choice of jobs so Prew could work with him on dishes and leave Bloom the pots and pans. Bloom, who was a Pfc, who was a fighter, who was obviously soon to be a corporal, who had bravely stuck up for Pvt Prewitt when the boys had called him yellow, and whom he would not work with, ever.

Angelo Maggio was on Dining Room Orderly for that day, and he wished repeatedly that Bloom had got the DRO, and Angelo the KP, even though that was tough on Maggio.

He woke early; having kept the thought strong in his mind the night before, dropping off to sleep, that he must be the first down and get first choice of jobs, just in case Reedy did happen to beat Bloom down; and lay a while, watching the sky greying in the east and the night collecting in a pool between the mountains, feeling sleep like a great predatory cat perched heavily on his chest. He forced himself to push it off him and got up and dressed in fatigues and went down to the kitchen through the cool early greyness that was the best time to sleep. It was deserted when he got there, unhuman with its man-made dead machines squatting in the very early morning, and he sat smoking, feeling as he used to feel crawling out of some boxcar in some strange sleeping town at dawn with no lights anywhere to show him life was not extinct, but glad as he smoked that he was first down.

The fat cook Willard, who got his First Cook's rating back when Stark made Sergeant, and who was in charge of the shift that would be on duty, was the first one to roll out, and the real trouble started then. Prew heard his alarm, quickly muffled, go off in the cooks' room; then he came out, soft and fat, still buttoning his pants, and irritably sleepily obnoxious, to light the oil spray stoves and get a pot of coffee on, which was his duty as First Cook.

"Well, look who's here already," he ridiculed obscenely, squinch-eyed with sleepy malice. "You must want that easy job plenty bad, to throw away two hours' sleep to get it."

"No," Prew said. "You just think that, because you like to sleep so goddam much." He did not like the fat cook any better than the rest did, but he did not mind him.

"You sure dint meant to lose that easy job though, did you?" Willard grinned obscenely. "I guess you'd of got up just as early anyway, wouldnt you?"

"Thats right, Fatstuff," Prew said, sneering the hated nickname, suddenly inflamed by this needling cook who hated to get up and was trying to take it out on him. "What do you want? me to say I always pick the hard jobs, like you?"

"I'm sure glad I dont have to pull KP no more," Willard needled, grinning, giving the almost boiling coffee one more stir, and setting it off to settle.

"You pull KP ever day, Fatstuff. Only you're too goddam dumb to know it."

"At least I get paid extra for it."

"Through no fault of yours. If you had to eat the food you cook you'd soon be thin, instead of a fat roasting pig."

"Dont get wise with me, you might find yourself on KP again tomorrow."

"Up yours," Prew said, and helped himself to the coffee, deliberately without asking, pouring in a thin stream of the canned milk.

"Thats cooks' coffee," Willard said. "Wait till you're asked."

"I waited till you asked me I'd be dead. What makes fat men so mean and stingy, Fatstuff? Because they afraid they wont have enough to eat? It must be tough to be a fat man," he grinned and moved up to the stove warmth, the hot dark liquid scalding down him sweetly, burning away the sleep and early morning chill.

"Goddam you," Willard glowered. "You're wise, aint you? I'm telling you, you keep on getting wise with me, you'll find yourself on KP Payday. I still got enough stripes I dont have to take no KP's lip."

"Pullin your rank, 'ey?" Prew grinned, and filled his cup again. "He dishes it out, but when he has to take it he pulls his rank. I always knew you were chicken, Fatstuff."

"You'll think I'm chicken," Willard said. "You dont know what chicken is, wise guy. I only hope you get on pots and pans today, wise guy."

Prew laughed, but not relishing it any more, knowing the fat cook was afraid because he was a fighter, but also knowing Willard would make him pay for this the rest of the day, if he got the chance, simply because he had not kept his mouth shut and taken Willard's gaff.

The rest of them began to come in then, a sudden influx, and Willard let it drop. The kitchen began to fill with pleasant warmth and bustle that soon turned into unpleasant heat and frantic agitation to get the breakfast out on time. Stark was there, in the middle of it from the first, carrying papers in his hand, already doing tomorrow's paperwork, but at the same time overseeing everything.

Prew was frying himself eggs and bacon on the corner of the griddle, a privilege that up until Stark took over Willard had guarded jealously from the KPs, but which Stark had let them have, when Stark called Willard down about the breakfast eggs.

"How many times I have to tell you to measure how much milk you put in scrambled eggs," Stark said. "Throw this mess out."

"But thats wasteful. I'll have to do them over."

"It'd be more wasteful to throw it out after we've served it and the men wont eat it," Stark said. "Throw it out."

"But there wont be time to start another batch, Maylon," Willard said, trying to twist out of it, using Stark's first name as a protection.

"I said throw it out. If we have to hold chow, we'll hold it. But we wont feed these men slop. Will we?"

"My eggs aint slop, Maylon."

"Throw it out, Fatstuff," Stark said, like an umpire calling the play at second base against the crowd. "And when you come back turn your goddam oven down, unless you want to serve them scrambled rubber. You have to do them over twice, you will be late."

"Oh, God," Willard said, looking at the ceiling, "I don't know why it always falls on me. Here," he bawled at Prew, "you. KP. Whatsyername. Throw this stuff out."

"You know my name, Fatstuff," Prew said.

"There," Willard said, squinch-eyed, to Stark. "You hear that? Thats insubordination. He been doin that to me all day."

"Throw it out yourself," Stark grinned. "He's cookin his breakfast. You're the one that ruint it."

"All right," Willard said. "By god all right I will. A Mess Sergeant who wont even stand up for his own cooks."

"Whats that?" Stark said.

"Nothing," Willard, who could not forget the day Stark took him out on the green, said.

After he had gone out, Prew said, "He'll really have it in for me now," and pulled a stool up to the aluminum pastry table and sat down to eat.

"He got it in for you?"

"I dint ask him could I have some coffee before I helped myself."

Stark grinned; his one-sided, off-beat grin. "Always defending his rank. As a pillroller he might be all right. He's fat enough. But as a cook he's lousy. I think he sweats in all the food. Guys like him only talk, they never really bother anybody."

Prew nodded, grinning, believing it when Stark said it because it was so obviously true of all gutless wonders; but it did not work out like Stark said, although Prew did not notice this. It worked out just the opposite. Willard did not let it drop. He shut up about it, but he did not let it drop. And because Pfc Bloom came rushing in shortly after to report, Willard had Prew where he could really bother him, in the kitchen, on pots and pans.

"Well?" Pfc Bloom said energetically, setting his coffee next to Prew, "what job you going to take? We might as well get it figured out. The rinsing sink's the easiest. I dont mind the washing sink, myself. Which one you want?"

"I dont know yet," Prew said, silently cursing Reedy Treadwell's laziness.

"Dont know yet!" Pfc Bloom exclaimed.

"Thats right. I thought maybe you might want pots and pans."

"Are you kidding?" Pfc Bloom asked. "Not me, buddy."

"Some guys like pots and pans," Prew said hopefully. "Some guys claim you get done quicker and get a longer morning break, on pots and pans."

"Thats fine," Pfc Bloom said. "Reedy should be very happy. Just between you and me," Pfc Bloom said confidentially, "I dint want to work with him anyway. He's too slow. You and me now, we can get this stuff done up fast and have time for a good break in the morning and afternoon both."

"We having spuds for dinner," Prew told him.

"Oh, God," said Pfc Bloom.

"You dont want the pots and pans then?"

"Hell no," Pfc Bloom said. "You think I'm crazy?"

"Then I guess I'll take them. You and Reedy can have the dishes."

"You mean you *want* them?"

"Sure," Prew said. "I like them."

"You do? Then whynt you take them in the first place? without asking me what I want?"

"Well," Prew said. "I thought maybe you might like them too. I dint want to cut you out."

"Yeah?" asked Pfc Bloom suspiciously. "Well its okay by me. I wouldnt want to take them from you. I'll take the rinsing sink. Reedy can have the washing sink, since he's last man."

So saying, he charged into the KP room, bull like, not giving the other a chance to change his mind, and hung his fatigue hat on the faucets of this prize that was a windfall. He was very happy to have outwitted Prewitt.

Prew was already washing egg pans at the big double sink in the kitchen when Readall Treadwell finally appeared, having been routed out with the rest of the Company by the CQ at First Call. He saw

Reedy peek in at him, quite surprised, then amble happily into the KP room, so happily that he almost bumped into Dining Room Orderly Maggio who was coming through.

"Comin through!" screamed Maggio, shoving the two empty platters he had in his hands in front of him. "Stand aside! Hot stuff! Comin through! Me and my table waiters," he bawled commandingly, in the protective tone of an officer who looks out for his men, "we workin our ass off. They runnin us to death. Hot Stuff! Comin through hot stuff one side!" He pushed through to the kitchen to refill the platters, joyfully cracking the new whip of his authority that nobody paid any attention to, least of all his eight table waiters.

"Howm I doin?" he asked Prew under his breath. "Man, I'm rough. Puttin in for corporal tomorra."

Prew stopped long enough to grin at him ruefully, before he went back to work, scraping, washing, and rinsing the food-encrusted cooking pans and the mucky mixing basins that were suddenly beginning to pile up on him now, that he had never seen so many of at one time before, and that, work as he would, he could not get caught up with. And he worked fast, listening to Readall Treadwell in the KP room across the entryway asking Bloom what had happened as he hung the soap bucket on his hot faucet and turned it on full force.

"I dont know," future Corporal Bloom said disapprovingly. "Prewitt had first choice and he choosed them. It doesnt matter now, what matters is *you're* late, Treadwell. You make it hard on everybody when you're late. Your sink's half full of plates already."

"You think I'm late?" future and forever Private Readall Treadwell said. "You just dont know. Usually I don' git here till the sink's plumb full. You jist happen to be lucky."

"Personally," future Corporal Bloom said, availing himself of the FMs' morale psychology, "I'd rather work with you than Prewitt, anyway. You and me can really slick them up, Treadwell. But you got to get on the ball, Treadwell. You got to hustle up and show some pride."

"I'm happy," forever Private Treadwell grunted. "You're unhappy. But I'm happy."

The pots and pans kept piling up on Prewitt puzzlingly. Never in his life had he seen a crew of cooks use so many pots and pans so quickly and so often. It took him quite a while to catch on to what Willard was pulling on him. It was so outlandish that for a while he thought it was his imagination, inflamed and offended by the rotten muckiness that covered every pore of him, that it was exaggerating in a wild effort to help him keep his pride. But it was obvious, as the stacks kept getting higher, that no cook ever used that many pans, even for an officers' banquet at the Club, ladies invited.

It was not until the middle of the morning, however—when Maggio had lovingly sent his table waiters off to drill and got his tables all scrubbed, when Bloom and Treadwell had finished up their dishes, the three of them settling down disgustedly with no morning break to peel the spuds for dinner (but working, Prew noticed enviously from his steaming greasy sinks, with the raw spuds crisp and solid in the hands in cool clear water that did not film the arms with grease)—it was not till then that Stark noticed anything was wrong, Willard being far too shrewd to ever complain that Prew was slow.

"Kind of slow with the pots and pans today, aint you, Prewitt?" Stark said, stopping by the sink and looking at the crotch-high stacks of pans stacked all around him. "You should be done by now."

"I guess I'm just slow," Prew said.

"The cook'll need them pans to cook in pretty soon."

"They probly need them now, since I already washed some of them three times already."

"Cooks got to have pans to cook in."

"They dont need them to spit in though, do they? They always taught me a good cook never used more pans than he had to, that a good cook tried to save his KPs work."

"Thats what they supposed to do," Stark said, getting out his sack of Golden Grain and making one, keeping his eyes on it with that self-effacing, almost shamed look good cops and noncoms always have when they have to use their rank.

"Then I guess you better put me on report then. I cant do them any faster than I am."

"I never like to put a man on extra duty less I have to," Stark said noncommittally, with a reluctant but real understanding that made Prew so warm inside he forgot that it was Stark who told him Willard would not bother him.

"You want to hear my side?"

"Sure," Stark said. "I awys want to hear both sides. Whats your side?" he said, looking up, eyes withdrawn into authority but very clearly discerning.

"My side is Willard's using all the pans he can, deliberately, so as to foul me up, because I didnt suck his ass this morning. Thats my side."

"That sort of leaves you suckin hind tit," Stark said, "dont it?"

"It sure as hell does," Prew said. "If you dont believe me, look at him there. Just look at him," he said, "the fat two faced bastard." Willard was watching them from the other end of the kitchen, leaning forward slyly while he pretended to work, his head on one side, listening hard.

"Willard," Stark said. "Come heah! Now! This man's hot as a forty-five shootin downhill," he said when Willard came up. "Claims you deliberately usin pans to make more work and get him in bad. What about it?"

"If I'm goin to cook right I got to use pans."

"Dont stall me, Fatstuff," Stark said.

"Hell," Willard said. "Do I got to count how many pans I use? So a goldbricking KP who's afraid to work?"

"What do you want me to do?" Prew said violently. "Grow couple more arms?"

"All I ask," said Willard dignifiedly, turning on him, "is that you keep the pans washed up, so they're there, clean, when I need them. In order that I am allowed to cook the kind of food I ought to cook, the kind of food required for men who work hard all day and who need good nourishing food to get their nourishment."

"Piss on that noise," Stark said.

"All right," Willard said, "okay. You asked me. Any time, just any old time, you want my job why . . . ?" he left it up in the air.

"Watch out, Fatstuff," Stark said. "I might take you up on it."

"All right," Willard said. "If you think I'm a rat . . . ?"

"I think you're a fat cook," Stark said, "who cant cook. Because he's too busy makin sure the KPs respect his rank. What I want you to do is get your ass back there and cook, and quit using so goddam many pans, because I'll be watching you."

"All right," Willard said. "If thats the way you feel about it." He left them, disdainfully and with great dignity.

"Thats how I feel," Stark said after him. "He wont bother you no more," he said to Prew, "or if he does you come tell me about it. But that dont help you get these ones thats already dirty done," he said, looking at the stacks of pans. "Come on. I'll help you do them up. I'll wash and you rinse and wipe."

He flipped the cigaret end into Prew's garbage pail and grabbed the spatula and began to scrape one of the worst ones with the deftness and economy of a great kitchen stylist, that Prew could only watch admiringly, feeling warmer inside now than he had felt for a long time.

"This'll kill Willard," Stark grinned lopsidedly, "the Mess Sergeant helpin a KP do pots and pans. Back home, when we use to divide our kitchen work up into White and Colored work; pots and pans was Colored work."

"There wasnt any niggers in my home town," Prew said, having to work very hard to keep up with Stark the stylist, but feeling very wonderful and friendly and very high, knowing that all the cooks and even the KPs were secretively watching this because Stark sometimes helped the KPs peel the spuds but pots and pans was something else again. "They dint allow them in the town," he explained, remembering suddenly, for the first time in years, almost angrily, now, fifteen years after, the sign some drunken miners had painted in glaring red and hung up at the station when a nigger stopped to change trains, the sign that then, as a boy, he had only looked at and not minded: "DONT LET THE SUN SET ON YOU IN HARLAN, NIGGER!"

"Well," Stark said, "I can see that, in a town where theres never been any. Its hard to tell a good one from a bad one unless the family lived in the town a while. And all of them wanderin nigras are bad ones, or else they'd of found themself a white man who treated them right and settled down. In my town they'd been there for generations and we knew them."

"No," Prew said. "You dont see what I mean. Once in Richmond, Indiana, on the bum, me and another guy had stole some vegetables and a hunk of meat for a stew. We taken it down to this jungle outside town and there was a bunch already there, one of them a nigger. This guy was going to take it away from us because we were kids and when I wouldnt just give it to him, pulled a knife on me."

"The nigra?" Stark said. "I'd killed the son of a bitch."

"No," Prew said. "Not him. A white guy. The nigger was the one that stopped him. I had got behind a tree and kept circling away from him, still holding on to the food, but I was just a punk kid and he would of caught me if this big buck nigger hadnt stepped out and tripped him up. He got up ragin mad and went for the nigger with the knife, but the nigger blocked it with his arm, just as cool as hell, and hit him with his right hand. Cut his forearm pretty bad, but he took that knife away from the guy and proceeded to beat the piss out of him, literally beat it out of him. Now, he was no bad nigger."

"No," Stark said. "He was a good nigra."

"Sure he was. Out of that whole bunch of guys he was the only one who lifted his finger to keep me from gettin knifed. The rest of them just stood and watched."

"Ordinarily," Stark said, handing him another pan, "I dont hold with a nigra raisin his hand to a white man. I dont like to see that. But, in this case, of course, he was right."

"I hope to Christ he was right! That was me that guy was chasin. I loved that big black nigger. When we cooked our stew we invited him help us eat it."

"Did he wait till he was ask?"

"Sure," Prew said. "He was a gentleman. More gentleman than the rest of those bastards by a long shot. And by god, they didnt any of the rest of them try cut in on our stew either, dont you believe it. They were all scared of him."

"I'm not scared of any nigra that ever lived," Stark said. "Good or bad. But he was a good nigra. But most of them you see on the bum are bad ones, mean ones. This one just happened to be a good one."

"You dont see what I mean," Prew explained. "I think most any nigger on the bum is no badder than any white man on the bum. Or for that matter, off the bum."

"No, I see what you mean," Stark said. "But you dont know them like I do. Most nigras on the bum are runnin away from havin killed some white man or raped some white woman. Though I've met some good ones, too, a lot of them, on the bum. Its just like with town nigras, some are good nigras and some are bad nigras, ony most of the good ones stay home and most of the bad ones end up on the bum. They have to or they'd get lynched. You dont think I'd take anything off any nigra in my home town that I've known all my life, do you?"

"Well I see what *you* mean," Prew said. "I wouldnt take anything off a bad nigger, but I wouldnt take anything off a bad white man either."

"Well with white men its a little different. Theres usually some legitimate reason for them bein bad, if you look into it. But a bad nigra is just borned bad, and the ony way to cure him is to teach him a lesson, thats all. Kill or cure. We had one in our town, just plain pisspoor, mean and shiftless. They finally run him off. Ruther, he took off, to keep from gettin taught his lesson. See what I mean? No guts at all, just bad. He was a young buck and his folks died off in the flu epidemic and he just plain run out. Went on the bum, instead of finding him a good hotassed wench and settlin down, like he should of."

"Thats the same reason I went on the bum," Prew told him. "Except it wasnt flu killed mine. It was the goddam mines."

"Yeah?" Stark said, handing him the last of the pans that they had got through fast, so incredibly fast Prew could not believe that they were done, was almost reluctant they were done, in the warmth of grateful friendliness he felt for the other. "Reason I went on the bum," Stark grinned, "was they was too many mouths to feed at home.

"Well," he said, "that does her."

He straightened his long-bent back and pulled the plug and hung it by the chain on the faucet, looking with his fine natural style like what would have made an example picture for a Good Cook's Handbook, if there had been such a thing.

"When you get these sinks cleaned up go on out and help them to finish peeling the spuds. Willard tries anything else, you let me know."

"I will," Prew said, trying to put in his voice what he could not say without killing, "I sure as hell will."

And thinking happily that sometime, when there was less work and they had leisure, he must explain more fully to his friend Stark what he had meant to say about niggers because he had not quite got it across to him yet apparently, he washed down the sinks and went outside on the entryway porch to where Maggio, Bloom, and Readall

Treadwell were still peeling at the two big No. 18 kettles of spuds, heartily disgusted because they had got no break this morning.

In the afternoon they got a break, a good long one of almost two hours, feeling after the din and frantic work of dinner like rich men with a pocketful of coupons. There were baked beans and franks tonight for supper, not canned franks this time and not even canned baked beans either, and there was no extracurricular KP labor to be done and it was the greatest luxury to them to contemplate almost two hours doing nothing, playing cards, and loafing.

"I'm going up," Dining Room Orderly Maggio, who was done first, called in to him. "When you get through come up and we play some two-hand casino."

"For how much?" Prew said.

"Well," Maggio hedged. "How much you want to play for?"

"I'm broke."

"You are? Then I guess we play for nothin. I'm broke too. Well, what do you know," he said. "Both broke. I thought I could maybe make you for a couple bucks."

"We could play for jawbone," Prew grinned.

"I cant. I owe my payday out already. Unless you want to make it payday after next?"

"Okay."

"I guess I better not," Maggio reflected. "I owe part of that one too. All I want is when that loudmouth Bloom comes up to be doin something. I listened to him tell how he is the middleweight champ next year enough for one day. I be upstairs."

"Okay," Prew said. Willard had not bothered him any more and he finished up the pots and pans from dinner even before Bloom and Readall Treadwell got their dishes done. He wanted to talk to his friend Stark again, not about negroes, not about anything specially, but just to talk, friendlily, about nothing, with another, who was a soldier, of his own category. But Stark was working so he went on upstairs and had a shower, exulting as the steamy scalding water beat the sickening grease off him, and put on a fresh suit of suntans, just to loaf around in and be clean in, until time to report back.

Angelo was stretched out on his bunk in suntans himself, his hair still damp and looking very clean and obviously enjoying it, reading a well rolled, long discarded comic book.

"I get my cards," he said and handed Prew the book. "Man, I feel good. I been readin Tom Mix and the Ralston Straight Shooters. Pow! Pow!" he said, jabbing a forefinger and cocked thumb at the jockstraps and special duty men scattered around on their bunks. "Straight Shooters always win and a nuther thousand yowling redskins bit the dust."

"*The Mystery of the Haunted Ranchhouse, starring Tom Mix,*" Prew read. "This aint the Ralston Straight Shooters. The Ralston Straight Shooters is an ad."

"So whats the difference? I use to be a Junior G Man onct. Its the same difference. Me and J Edgar was like that. Them drawings really look like old Tom, dont they?"

"I wonder what happened to him? You never see him any more."

"His horse died," Maggio said, "and he had to retire."

"Tony," Readall Treadwell said, coming in from the latrine, a towel wrapped around his big, fat, but heavily muscled under the fat, belly with its navel like a dimple and the hair on it thick enough to comb. "His name was Tony."

"Remember Buck Jones's horse Silver?" Prew said. "There was a real horse."

"Yes, man," Maggio said. "Between Buck and his horse they had the two biggest chests in creation."

"He was a deep sea diver," Readall Treadwell said, sitting down, "before he got in the movies. I read it in a movie magazine. *Our Lucky Stars*, it was."

"He was a sailor," Maggio said scornfully. "You dont want to believe the crap in them magazines. Its propaganda. He was a sailor and he bummed around some, like Jack London."

"Well anyway," Readall Treadwell said, "when Buck Jones hit them they stayed hit. Deal me in."

"Dont get my goddam blanket wet," Maggio said, "or I'll hit you so you'll stay hit."

"Remember Bob Steele?" Prew said, as Reedy moved to put a paper under him. "He was the one could hit. He was a natural hooker. He was good to watch when he fought, you could tell he been a fighter."

"I seen him in *Mice and Men*," Maggio said. "He was Curly, the boss's brother-in-law. Boy, he was a mean son of a bitch in that one."

"But he was a good guy in his own pictures though," Readall Treadwell said.

"Sure he was, you jerk," Maggio said disgustedly. "You dont think he'd be the villain when he was the star, do you? I wonder," he said, "what ever happened to old Hoot Gibson? I can just barely remember him. My god, he had grey hair when I was just a kid."

"I think he's dead now," Prew said.

"Jesus," Maggio said. "I wish I had some popcorn."

"Me too," Prew said. "I been wantin some the last ten minutes."

"They got a machine over to the Main PX," Readall Treadwell said hopefully.

"We're broke," Maggio said.

"So'm I," Treadwell said. "If thats what you mean."

"I use to go regular," Maggio said, "ever Sataday afternoon and eat popcorn. Remember Johnny Mack Brown?"

"Had a southern accent?" Prew said. "And a rawhide hatcord? Let his hat hang down his back half the time?"

"Thats the one," Maggio said. "I wonder what ever happened to him? You never see him any more either."

"You said it a while ago," Prew said, laying down his hand. "They die. Or graduate. Or retire. What do you say we talk about something else?"

"We gettin old, men," said Angelo Maggio, aged nineteen and a half. "I never realized it."

"Tom Tyler," Readall Treadwell said. "He was another one."

"I never liked him," Maggio said. "Too handsome. But I remember him. He plays villains now, in the Technicolor ones. The western epics."

"Sagas," Prew said. "They call them sagas."

"All the regular cowboys got to be musicians now," Prew said. "Musicians first and cowboys second. Because they're not Westerns anymore, they're Musicals," he said, suddenly surprisedly realizing sadly that he had watched and been a part of a phase of America that was dying just as surely as the Plains Indians Wars that gave it birth had died, had watched and been a part of it all this time, without ever knowing it for what it was, or that it was dying.

"You mean Gene Autry," Maggio said. "Roy Rogers and his horse-trigger."

"I read Gene Autry was a Eagle Scout when he was a kid," Readall Treadwell said.

"I believe that," Maggio said. "My hometown, the ony ones ever got to be Eagle Scouts was the preachers' sons and the schoolteachers' sons. I was a Second Class onct myself, till they kicked me out of the Troop for gettin in a fight with the Assistant Scout Master."

"Gene Autry cant play *Come to Jesus* in whole notes," Prew said, argumentatively. "Neither one of them can. You cant commercialize that kind of music without killing it."

"Dont look at me," Maggio said. "I dont like them either. You cant commercialize anything without killing it. Look at the radio."

"But those guys," Prew said irritably, because this was a thing of great importance to him, and because he was trying hard to explain it, to find the word for this that always made him angry, "those guys. They're imitation," he said, finally, lamely.

"That Roy Rogers," Maggio grinned. "I was makin a Jewgirl lived on West 84th Street when I work at Gimbel's. Use to go up there and take her to the Schuyler Theater on 84th and Amsterdam."

He stopped dealing and began to laugh to himself. "Well, one night there was a bill of a Roy Rogers show outside, you know? how they put them in the frames on the wall behind the chicken wire? And there was a little bitty Jewboy standin lookin at it. Thats all Jewrish up around in there, see?

"'You like Roy Rogers?' I ask him.

"'Sure, man,' he says. 'Dont you?'

"'Yes, man,' I told him. 'Roy Rogers and his horsetrigger. Ony I aint never found out whats a horsetrigger yet,'

"'A what?' he says.

"'A horsetrigger,' I told him. 'I know whats a hairtrigger, but what is a horsetrigger?'

"'Trigger's the name of his horse, you jerk,' he says, disgusted as hell. 'You know what horses are. They're them animals they ride in the pitcher. Horsetrigger,' he says. 'Where the hell *you* learn about cowboys? I bet you aint even a 'Muricun, but a goddam Wop or immigrunt or sothin.'

"Then he turnt around and stalked off a little ways so nobody would think he was with me," Maggio said, laughing, looking at the others brightly, wanting to be sure they got it. "I never cracked a smile," he explained, "or said a word."

"I bet he still thinks you're a Gestapo spy," Prew, who liked the kind of humor himself, laughed.

"John Wayne was another good one," Readall Treadwell said, almost a hunger in his voice, when they stopped laughing.

"Not any more," Maggio said. "He's graduated into Adventure. Give him five more years he'll move up into Drama."

"Thats the same way Gary Cooper started," Readall Treadwell said. "He really use to be a real cowboy once."

"You cant compare Gary Cooper to John Wayne," Maggio protested.

"I aint comparing them. All I said was they both started out in Westerns. You cant compare none of them to Gary Cooper."

"I guess not," Maggio said. "I hope not. Gary Cooper goes deeper than just plain adventure. If theys anybody shows all the things this country stands for its Gary Cooper."

"Thats what Hedda Hopper says," Readall Treadwell nodded.

"Hedda Hopper, my ass," Maggio said heatedly. "If I like Gary Cooper its my business. And its in spite of Hedda Hopper, not because of Hedda Hopper. Even my old daddy liked Gary Cooper. He go to see him every time he's on, even if its raining, and he cant speak ten words a English."

"All right," Readall Treadwell said, good naturedly with the strong fat man's unrufflability, and with none of the weak fat man's malice that is the worst malice there is except a woman's malice, Prew thought, a world of difference between fat Reedy and fat Willard, "all right. I jist mention it."

"Well dont mention it," Maggio said.

"All right," Readall Treadwell grinned. "You dont care if I read her column, do you, Angelo? You wont beat me up if I read it will you?"

Maggio grinned, then laughed, the fiery Italian anger gone as quick as it had come. "Sure," he said, "I'll beat you up. You think you'd stand a chance with me? I keep a sawed off pool cue in my wall locker just for guys like you."

"All right," Prew said, "beat him up later. Right now, deal the cards."

"I dont feel much like playin any more," Maggio said. "I guess my arm's tired. Theres no fun in gambling without money. I quit. Lets look at my old photograph alabum instead, and I show you a picture of that Jewgirl I was tellin about."

"Okay by me," Prew said. He was bored with the cards too, now that the sudden, memorable conversation had petered out, but the thinking of Willard still making him feel he should utilize this running luxury of time that had been so momentous and now was being spent insignificantly.

He watched Angelo get out the album, a big and nearly completely filled one that he had seen a thousand times before and knew as well as he would have known his own if he had ever had one, but he never had because he did not believe in collecting photographs that were always posed and therefore never truthful, but that now he wished sometimes he had because, even if they were not truthful, they would have shown him himself and all the places he had been and people he had known as they were then, bringing back truthful memories out of their untruthfulness, like this one of Angelo's obviously did for him. The first third of it, that he always showed them first, devoted to a younger Angelo from Atlantic Avenue in Brooklyn and who had a family, believe it or not its true, look and see for yourself, one soldier who really had a family, there they are, the whole fifteen of them; the fat, round faced, obviously too lenient, plainly too undignified, grinning Mr Maggio, trying hard not to grin but to look dignified, and not succeeding; and the even fatter, stern long faced, very hard bargain driving, policy dictating, family dominating, not grinning Mrs Maggio, trying hard to grin and to not look dignified, and not succeeding; both trying very hard to deceive the camera, as everybody tried to deceive the camera, into showing only what they wanted it to show; together with all thirteen of their slicked up grinning offspring, all grinning at the camera with that temporarily donned, fake, denying-anything-but-happiness, happiness that all camera subjects but the most caught-unawares camera subjects (and us artists, he thought grimly remembering how he had to put into a Taps his secrets he could not talk about, us artists who are under a compulsion to be ashamed in public) always grinned at the camera with; each dressed in his own full length snapshot little Angelo could always carry with him; (and the sounds and smells of a grocery store in Atlantic Avenue in Brooklyn with quarters upstairs came back to me who had never been there or seen it and probably never would, but that I knew now just as well as if I had always known them). And then the last two-thirds of it devoted to Hawaii, the Army, and the tourists photographs of Hawaii and the Army, two entirely different things, tourist photographs of Honolulu, the Mormon Temple, Waikiki Beach, the big Hotels (Halekulani, Royal Hawaiian, Moana; that none of us had ever seen the insides of), Diamond Head, a tourist picture of Schofield that looked lovely enough to make you want to enlist for this happy land, pictures of quaint Wahiawa without the smells, all the places the tourists saw from the outside and thought were lovely and whose attitude these photographs reflected, but that we always saw from the inside (excepting of course: Halekulani, Royal Hawaiian, Moana; Lau Yee Chai's, Ala Wai Inn) with an entirely different perspective, a perspective not recorded in any photographs since our photographs of the inside were always jokes; clean jokes: a guy with his helmet on grinning in the Company Street, or a guy in full field grinning at the bayonet on the rifle he was holding in the Long Guard Position, or even two or three guys holding beer bottles and their arms around each other's necks and elaborately crossed legs and grinning in front of a palm tree or the Chapel or the Bowling Bowl; or dirty jokes: like the series of the French-Hawaiian beauty from Big Sue's in Wahiawa, first in her dress, then in her undies, then in her pants, then in nothing, then in an embarrassing position, a strip tease five in all, one buck for the series or two bits apiece; or perhaps the biggest, grandest joke of all: the Company photograph, with the fond smiling Captain and all his grinning men; but always, always jokes, because all of us always grinned reflexively, instinctively, a joke, if a camera (or even a reporter) popped up anywhere within shouting distance, Prewitt thought, which is why nobody ever knows our inside perspective unless they've been there but always see us as Our Simple Boys, and that even if they have they tend to forget because there is nothing anywhere to remind them; and which is why I'm goddamned if I'll collect recorded jokes about things I do not feel like laughing at. But if I had a bugle and could make recordings I'd remind them, he thought. And, but God, how I'd like to be the one.

"You and your goddam tourist photographs," he said to Angelo, bitterly, for perhaps the hundredth time.

"Aw dont start that," Angelo said. "You know thems ony for show-ing to my folks when I get back home. You know they'll want to see what Wahoo's like."

"But Wahoo aint like that."

"Sure it aint. But they wont know it. *This* is what they want to see, not what its like. Here, look at this one," he said, pointing out a new one, a beautiful Chinese girl in a flowered dress and a beret looking lovingly back over her shoulder, obviously at her lover, and with that blankness, absolutely nothingness, of a beautiful Chinese girl simulat-ing lovingness; a picture every soldier on the Post had at least two prints of because they were two-for-a-nickel in every PX on the Island.

"It kills me," Prew said. "It knocks me out."

"But I like it," Readall Treadwell said.

"Its the one," Maggio grinned, "that I'm going to tell them back home is the one I almost married, but shacked up with for a year in-stead, and left behind me."

"The Girl I Left Behind Me," Prew said and began to whistle it sar-castically. But he did not get up and walk away, like he could have.

They were still looking, a little later, when Bloom came in freshly showered from the latrine and leaned down uninvited to look too, standing beside Readall Treadwell across the bed.

The four of them, silently looking, made a momentary still picture that was nowhere apparently dangerous. But Bloom, Prew thought later, was never one to take a backseat for very long, even to a photo-graph album, if he could help it. Probably he only did it to make known the fact that The Great Bloom had arrived on the scene, since no one had acknowledged it. But in doing what he did he made at least two, and maybe three, enemies that would never again be anything else but enemies. It was a thing Bloom was always doing.

It all happened quite swiftly. One moment there was this apparently peaceful still picture of four men looking at an album. Then the pic-ture shuddered, quaked, broke up in the same way dreams shift, and began to move into a series of apparently disjointed actions, one, two, three, right down the line, like a jerky old fashioned movie, too blur-redly swift to be understood, as these things always were, but hanging over it all that utter-complete-bloody-hell-with-it feeling that only comes when a man has an absolutely bellyfull.

Bloom thrust his hand down between their two heads and pointed out a picture of a petite, olive-skinned, sloe-eyed girl of fifteen who was Angelo's youngest sister and who was sitting very Hollywoodishly in a bathing suit in the summer Brooklyn sun upon a tile roof ledge still dusted with last winter's soot, trying to display womanishly the girlish, but very full, young body that she was so proud of because men looked at it, but that obviously was not womanish since obviously she had never tested it out yet and had only the vaguest romantic idea of the womanish uses of it. It was a picture that did not come off very well, but Bloom said delightedly, half teasingly:

"Man, I bet that one's a hotshot piece of ass to lay," and laughed complacently at his own great wit.

Prew, who had not known he was there and who knew the girl was Maggio's sister, and what's more, knew that Bloom knew this because they all had seen the album many times, felt a chill of momentarily time-stopping shock run down through him. Then a red running fire of hatred, half shame for Bloom, half rage for Bloom, who had done this deliberately, whether kiddingly or not certainly stupidly, but probably kiddingly in his bull-like, patronizing, dominating way, but even kiddingly with a deliberate degrading maliciousness, trampling callously over one of the few respected tabus, the things nobody ever said to anybody else, even in the Army, the fire of hatred making him want to beat the living piss out of such stupidity.

But before he could even raise his head he found he was holding the full weight of the album and Maggio was gone, silently to his wall locker, opening it, then turning around silently and calmly and stepping up to Bloom and bringing down the sawed off pool cue on Bloom's head with all his strength.

Prew shut the book carefully, thinking that this was it all right, and tossed it two beds down where it would not get mauled and stood up ready. Readall Treadwell had seen Angelo coming and considerately faded out into the aisle to give him room, to give them both room.

"Why, Jesus Christ!" Bloom said above the reverberating crack of the pool cue on his head. "You hit me, you little Wop!"

"You bet your ass," Maggio said. "With a pool cue. And about to do it again."

"What?" Bloom said, blinking his eyes now, the stun of the blow that should have felled an ox but did not even dent his massive skull enough to knock him down or even make him dizzy enough to sit down just reaching him now, him not understanding it yet, but beginning to, and his indignation mounting as the understanding grew. "With a pool cue?"

"Thats right," Maggio said distinctly, "and I'll do it again, right now, or any other time. Or place, if you come over here around my bunk, or around me, for anything, anything at all."

"But what for? Thats no way to fight. If you want to fight, ask a man out," Bloom said, putting his hand up to his head and bringing away blood. When he saw the blood he understood it, finally and fully, and he went berserker into rage at the sight of his own shed blood.

"I'd stand a big chance with you on the green, wouldnt I?" Maggio said.

"Why, goddam you," Bloom screamed, not hearing him. "You dirty, yellow, sneaking, twofaced, lying, rotten," having to stop because he could find no word to span this breach of sportsmanship, "Wop, you," he said, "yellow little Wop. If thats the way you want to fight," he said. "If thats the way you want to play."

He charged across the squadroom to his own bunk through all the now standing watching men, keeping up a solid, smooth, unbroken stream of screaming cursing, tugging at his pack to pull his bayonet and fumbling with the catch, using every obscenity he could think of, using them again when he ran out of new ones. He charged back with the naked bayonet glinting oilily and evilly in his hand, still screaming cursing, clear across the room where no man tried to stop him, but Maggio moving with his club out into the aisle for clearance and going to meet him, and death suddenly slid into the big room dartingly like a boxer on silent resined feet moving pantherishly in to punch.

But before they could meet in the center stage and put on this show their still-stunned audience did not want to see First Sergeant Warden, with his apparently weird uncanniness of occult knowledge, was suddenly between them brandishing an iron lock bar from the rifle racks and cursing indignantly and vilely for them to come on, he would just as soon kill them both as not anyway. He had come out of his room to stop the racket that had disturbed his nap and then, realizing what was happening, stepped in. But to the dumbstruck audience he seemed like the avenging genii of all Discipline and all Authority risen mystically from the floor, and his mere presence was enough to stop both of them in their tracks.

"If theres any killing in my Compny, I'll do it," The Warden ridiculed, "not a couple unweened punks who the sight of a dead man would make to crap their pants. Well? Come on. Why dont you come on?" he sneered, his mammoth contempt making them look so foolish in their own eyes that it was no longer a hurt to the pride to quit, but was instead the only means of saving it.

"Aint you coming?" The Warden scoffed, "then throw that bayonet down on the bed there if you aint going to use it, Bloom. Like a good little boy now. Thats it."

Bloom did what he was told obediently, silent with the blood running down his forehead, but with an unmistakable look of relief under it.

"Almost scared there wasnt anybody going to stop you for a minute, werent you?" The Warden snorted. "Killers," he said. "Tough guys. Out for blood. Real killers. Give that club to Prewitt, Maggio."

Maggio gave it to him, looking hangdog, and the spell was broken.

"If you guys want to fight," somebody yelled, "fight with fists, and take it outside on the green."

"Shut up," The Warden roared. "There'll be no fight. And there'll be no more goddamned suggestions from any stupid bastards who would stand around and let these two damfools kill each other." He looked around belligerently but no one would meet his eyes.

"And you two men," The Warden said, "neither one of you's grown up enough to be allowed to fight. You have to be a man to fight. If you act like children, you can expect to be treated like children."

Nobody said anything.

"You'll get plenty of fighting," The Warden said. "More fighting than any of you got the stomach for. And it wont be too goddamned long. Wait'll you hear bullets from a sniper you cant even see hitting the tree right above your head, then come around and tell me how you're killers. Then I'll believe you're killers. Killers," he snorted, "real killers. Jee sus Christ!"

Nobody said anything.

"Corporal Miller," The Warden said, "take this baby's bayonet and put it away, he aint old enough to play with it yet. Then take Bloom over and sit him down on his bunk and see he stays there. Have him sit with his face to the wall, thats the way to punish children. The only thing he's allowed to move for is to go to the latrine, and when he does you go with him, and see that he comes back, since he aint to be trusted out by himself. And dont forget to button his pants for him.

"Prewitt, I want you to do the same thing with baby Maggio. They're both to stay there till time to report to the kitchen. And they talk to nobody. Looks like we have to fix up a couple dunces' stools in this Compny.

"If either one of them gives you any back talk I want to know about it. They court-martial men for things like this, although it would be a shame to court-martial babies. Thats the only reason I dont have you both locked up, see?

"Now," he said. "Is there any other little things for me to take care of? If not, maybe you punks'll be quiet enough so I can get my goddam beauty sleep, 'ey?"

He turned and walked off disgustedly, back to his room, not even waiting to see if his orders were carried out. The men moved around stealthily to do as they were told, and the squadroom settled down again with Maggio sitting in one corner and Bloom in the other, and nobody knew that The Warden lay down on his bunk dry mouthed, wiping the sweat of a near thing off his forehead, and made himself lay there for ten minutes before he would pass through the squadroom to get the drink of water that he needed very badly.

"He's right," Maggio whispered to Prewitt. "The Warden. He's a damned good man, you know it?"

"I know it," Prew whispered back. "He could just as easy have had you both in the Stockade. They dont come like him very often."

"I've never even seen a dead man," Maggio whispered. "Except my grandfather in his casket when I was a kid, and that made me sick."

"Well I've seen them, no matter what The Warden says. I've seen a lot of them. They no different than dead dogs, once you get used to the idea."

"Even dead dogs bother me," Maggio whispered. "I made a mistake someplace, I guess, but I dont know where. I dont see how I could of done anything else, after that big stoop said a thing like that."

"I'll tell you where you made your mistake. Your mistake was you didnt hit him hard enough to put him out. He wouldnt of gone off his nut if he'd been unconscious. He might of laid for you after he come to, but I doubt even that."

"My God!" Maggio protested, whispering. "I hit him hard as I could. His head must be solid ivory."

"Personally," Prew whispered, "I think it is. But if he ever messes with me any more it wont be in the head I'll hit him."

"Just the same, I'm sure glad The Warden stopped us."

"So am I," Prew said.

Chapter 15

They sat that way till the cook's whistle shrilled up through the screens, calling them back to work. Then they went down, singly and silently, no one of them talking to any of the others. There was not much conversation and absolutely no horseplay on KP that night. For once even Bloom did not feel like talking. Probably he was still trying to figure out if whether, with the surprise ending the afternoon had taken, his honor had been smirched or not.

Even Stark noticed the gloominess of no talking and he came around to Prew to ask what had happened upstairs to cause such a profound dismalness. Prew told him, although it was obvious he had already heard about it, probably from someone who had run downstairs with the news right after it had happened, as someone always does, and he was only checking stories now and trying to get an inside account, instinctively, as good cops and good noncoms always do. But Prew was glad Stark had picked him to ask and, remembering what Stark had done this morning, he would have told him anyway.

"Maybe it'll teach the big kike a lesson," Stark said.

"Nothing will ever teach that guy a lesson."

"I reckon yore right," Stark said. "Jews never learn. They still think they God's Chosen People. I dont like Jews, you know it? But this one's goin to be a big man around here someday. I heah The Man's sending him to the next NCO School, in April. Wont be long till he makes corprl. He'll make it plenty tough on you and Angelo though, when he gets them stripes."

"Not too tough."

"It never gets too tough," Stark mocked. "For a good man."

"Okay," Prew said. "But theres lots better men than future corporal Bloom ridin my tail in this outfit, tryin to scare me into going out for fighting. And they aint done it."

"Thats right," Stark said. "You dont scare, do you?"

"All right," Prew said. "Okay. But a man cant let himself be pushed around by a bunch of pricks like that."

"No," Stark said, "a man cant do that."

Prew shrugged. "Okay," he said. "But thats still the way I feel. Why not say it? I aint bragging."

"I know yore not. But I never seen any sense in a man goin out of his way to ask them for it."

"I dont go out of my way to ask them for it."

"You dont think so," Stark said. "They think so."

"All I want is to be left alone."

"In this world," Stark said, "today, nobody is left alone."

He sat down on the table beside the sink and got his sack of Golden Grain out, slipped a paper free, opened the sack with his teeth, and poured tobacco delicately and with great absorption into the curl.

"Take a break a while," he said offhand. "Theres no hurry tonight. Listen," he said, "how would you like to come to work for me in the kitchen."

"You mean cooking?" Prew said, laying down the spatula. "Cook for you?"

"What else?" Stark said, without looking up. He offered Prew the sack.

"Thanks," Prew said, taking it. "Well I dont know. I never thought about it."

"I like you," Stark said, absorbedly smoothing the tobacco away from the middle so it would be thick on the ends and not hump in the middle when he rolled it. "I reckon you know you can expect a rough time of it, when the Compny moves back into field training after the rainy season's all done, along with Ike Galovitch, and Wilson and his boy-friend Henderson, together with Baldy Dhom, Dynamite, and all the rest the jockstraps; and with the Compny Smoker season drawin nearer all the time. Unless, of course, you change yore mind and decide to go out for Compny Smokers."

"I suppose you want me to tell you all about why I dont go out?"

"Not me. I heard it all already. Plenty times. Old Ike dont talk about nothing else. If you was in the kitchen, Prewitt, they couldnt none of them get at you."

"I dont need anybody to protect me," Prew said.

"I aint asking you because of charity, buddy," Stark said, suddenly clearly distinctly, no longer hesitantly. "A kitchen dont run on charity. If you couldnt do the work you wouldnt stay. If I dint think you could I wouldnt of ast you."

"I never much liked to work inside," Prew said slowly, seeing he meant it seriously now, and carefully thinking over how good it really would be to work under a man like Stark. Chief Choate was like this too, but in this outfit the corporals didnt run their squads, the platoon guides who couldnt speak English ran them. But Stark really ran the kitchen.

"I been wantin to get rid of Willard quite a while," Stark said. "I could kill two birds. Sims would make First Cook and I'd start you off as Apprentice, so nobody could kick, then move you up to Second Cook and First and Sixth as soons you been there long enough to keep anybody from accusing me of favoritism."

"You think I could do the work?"

"I know damn well," Stark said, "or I wouldnt of ast you."

"Would Dynamite okay a deal like that? When it was me?"

"He would if I promoted it. I'm the fair haired boy right now."

"I like to be outside," Prew said, saying it very, very slowly. "And its messy in a kitchen. Food's all right on the table, but its too sloppy for me in the pan. I lose my appetite."

"Quit stalling me," Stark said. "I aint going to coax you. Either you want it or you dont want it."

"I'd sure like to," Prew said slowly. "But I cant," he said, finally getting it out.

"Okay," Stark said. "Its your funeral."

"Wait a minute," Prew said. "Heres the way I look at it, Stark. I want you to understand it."

"I understand it."

"No you dont. Every man's supposed to have certain rights."

"Certain inalienable rights," Stark said, "to liberty, equality, and the pursuit of happiness. I learnt it in school, as a kid."

"Not that," Prew said. "Thats The Constitution. Nobody believes that any more."

"Sure they do," Stark said. "They all believe it. They just dont do it. But they believe it."

"Sure," Prew said. "Thats what I mean."

"But at least in this country they believe it," Stark said, "even if they dont do it. Other countries they dont even believe it. Look at Spain. Or Germany. Look at Germany."

"Sure," Prew said. "I believe it myself. Thems my ideals, too. But I'm not talking about ideals. I'm talkin about life.

"Every man has certain rights," he said; "in life I mean, not in ideals. And if he dont stand up for his own rights nobody else is going to stand up for them for him.

"Theres nothing in the Law, or in the ARs, that says I have to go out for fighting in this outfit, see? So its my right not to go out, if I dont want. I'm not just doing it to be bastardly, I got a good reason, and if I want to do some thing and I do do it, then I can still go along and live my life, as long as I dont harm nobody, without bein kicked around. Thats my right, as a man. To not be kicked around."

"Persecuted," Stark said.

"Thats it. Well, if I go in the kitchen then I'm giving up one of my rights, see? I'm admitting I'm wrong and dont have that right, and letting them think they're right, and that they've forced me. Whether into fighting or not isnt the point. They still forced me. You see?"

"All right," Stark said. "Yes, I see. But you let me say something now.

"Now in the first place," he said, "you're looking at it all bassackwards, you're going on the idea of the world as people say it is, instead of as it really is. In this world, no man really has any rights at all. Except what rights he can grab holt of and hang on to. And usually the only way he can get *them* is by taking them away from somebody else.

"Now dont ask me why. All I know is its so. And if a man's going to holt onto anything, or gain anything, he's got to take account of that. He got to see how other people get and keep what they got, and then he got to learn to do it that way too.

"The best way, the one most people use the most, is politics. They get friendly with somebody who's got influence they need and then they use that influence. Thats what I did. At Fort Kam I was as bad off as you are here. But I dint walk out on it until I knew where I was goin. It was bad, sam, bad. But I stayed there. I stayed there till I knew for damn sure I was tradin it in on something better, see? I found out old Holmes was up here and come up and used him to get out."

"I dont blame you," Prew said.

"Then compare that to you when you quit the Bugle Corps," Stark said. "If you'd really been smart, sam, you'd stayed there till you found a sure thing to get out into. Instead of runnin off half cocked and blowin your top and transferrin out, like you did, and look where you are now."

"I dint have any good angles," Prew said. "I dint have any angles."

"Thats what I say: You should of stayed till you did. And now, when I'm offering a good angle, one that will get you back onto safe ground, you're turnin it down. It just aint smart, it aint even sensible, because thats the only way anybody can get along in this world."

"I guess I just aint sensible," Prew said. "But I hate to believe that thats the ony way a man can get along. Because if it is, then what a man is dont mean anything at all. A man himself is nothing."

"Well in a way," Stark said, "thats true. Because its who he knows and not the man himself that counts. But in another way its not true either, not true at all. Because listen: What a man is, sam, is always just the same. And nothing in God's world, no kind of philosophy, no Christian Morals, none of that stuff, can change it. What a man is just comes out in a different channel, thats all. Its like a river that finds the old channel dammed up and moves into a new channel where the current's just as strong, only it moves in a different direction."

"Only people lie about it," Prew said. "Thats what confuses you. They say they come up the hard way, by good hard honest labor, but really they married the boss's daughter and inherited it. And what you mean to say is: it takes just as much on the ball for a man to marry the boss's daughter out from under the rest of the competition as it does to beat the competition out the hard way. Which is impossible anyway, any more."

"Always was," Stark corrected.

"Okay, always was. And you mean he's really just as good a man?" Stark frowned. "Well in a way yes, but you put it wrong."

"But if thats true," Prew said, "what becomes of love? I mean, instead of hard work to succeed, its hard work to marry the boss's daughter and succeed. And love is cut out altogether. What happens to love?"

"Did you, personally, ever see any of this love?"

"I dont know. Sometimes I think I did, and then sometimes I think it was imagination."

"It seems to me," Stark said, "that people only love the things they can get something they want out of. And that they dont love anything they cant get what they want out of."

"No," Prew said, remembering Violet, "you're wrong. You cant say that love dont exist except in romance or imagination."

"Hell I dont know," Stark said irritably. "You're gettin in too deep for me now. All I know is what I said.

"Look: We livin in a world thats blowin itself to hell, as fast as five hundred million people can arrange it. In a world like that, theres ony one thing a man can do; and thats to find something thats his, sam, really his and will never let him down, and then work hard at it and for it and it will pay him back. With me its my kitchen . . ."

196

"With me its bugling."

". . . and thats all I can take care of. As long as I do that right I dont have to be ashamed. And if the rest of them dehorn each other, kill each other, blow the whole damned world to hell, its none of my business."

"But they'll blow you up with it," Prew said.

"Fine. Then I wont have to worry."

"But your kitchen will be gone."

"So fine. Because I'll be gone too and it wont make no difference. And thats all I know."

"I'm sorry, Stark," Prew said, slowly because he did not want to say it, harshly because he was having trouble getting it said, wishing there was some way, some argument Stark had said, that would allow him not to say it; really almost angry at Stark because Stark had not convinced him when he wanted so badly to be convinced, "I cant. I just cant, thats all. And dont think I dont appreciate it either."

"I dont," Stark said.

"But if I did, why then everything in my life I've ever done up to now would be no good, thrown away."

"Sometimes its better to throw it away and start from scratch than to hang on to it."

"Not if you got nothing else left, and nothing in sight ahead to take its place. You got your kitchen."

"Okay," Stark said, flipping away his cigaret butt and getting up. "Dont rub it in. I know I'm lucky, but at the same time I took plenty and did a lot of work, to get it."

"I'm not rubbin it in. And I would like to work for you, Stark, really I would like to."

"I see you later," Stark said, "sometime. Almost time for them to be coming in and I got to be out there to see the meal goes off all right."

Prew watched him leave, his face still the face of all good cops or all good noncoms, impassive, consciously a mask of iron legality beyond which now, with Stark, there was no more appeal, and with the human curiosity squeezed out of it altogether except for the blankly interested eyes. They lose a lot, he thought, but then like everybody else they probly gain a lot, things that the rest dont know. At least they get to do the work they like.

Then he dropped the whole thing utterly and went back to work, speeding up his pace to meet the supper stuff that began to come in shortly.

It grows dark quickly on islands, or anywhere near the sea. Sunset is a matter of minutes. One minute it is clear up and still full daylight, the next its down and it is night. Standing on the western beaches you can actually see the sea's deep throat swallowing the golden cracker. Ritz Cracker, he thought, while in the Blue Ridge and the Smokies the sunless mountain twilight lingers bronzely on for hours. You've seen a lot of this world, Prewitt, he told himself, feeling his eyes blinking scratchily trying to adjust to the fading light, thats one thing you've done anyway.

The Company ate its baked beans and franks under the electric lights and laughingly, talkingly took its time to drink its coffee. In garrison the evening is the finest time of day for the soldier because it is his own time and he can waste it. He can spend it prodigally in one great splurge, or he can dole it out like pennies in a candy store, so much for this, so much for that, two jawbreakers, four nigger babies, one licorice stick, and I've still got two cents of my nickel left, to keep.

Anderson and Friday Clark stopped on their way out to ask him if he wanted to sit in when they got the guitars out, later on, Andy who was on guard bugler wearing the web pistol belt and long black holster with the lanyard from the butt up over his shoulder passing under the tucked in tie, and the bugle that he must never let out of sight while on guard hanging down his back.

"I'm tied up at the Guardhouse till nine," he said. "The Corprl wants to go to the show and I got to take his place. But after I blow Tattoo I'm off till Taps. Thats when we figured."

"Okay with me," Prew said, wanting to get done now more than ever. "Me and Angelo fixin to play some pool after we get off here anyway."

"I'll sweat the pool game out?" Friday said. "If you let me, Prew? I cant go over to the Guardhouse since the OD run me off this afternoon."

"You can play if you want."

"Naw, I had rather watch. I aint good enough for you guys."

"Okay, then you can sweat them. But right now take off, will you? And let me get done up."

"Come on," Andy said disgustedly. "Cant you see he's in a hurry? You always fiddlefuck around."

"Lay off of me," Friday said, as they left. "You neednt ack like such a big shot. If you wasnt on guard tonight you'd be downtown with Bloom anyway, chasin queers, and your git-tar locked up in your wall locker." It was the greatest condemnation Friday knew.

With supper over things began to move now all over the Company, the few guys with money calling for a taxi to town, the many guys without money walking out to go to the gate on the highway and hitchhike down, or getting ready to go to the show or to the gym to watch the 35th basketball champs play an exhibition game with the Fort Shafter squad. Prew could hear the groups of voices on the darkened porch discussing all the things to do, and he worked harder listening to them talk.

While he was washing down the sinks Stark came around again.

"I'm going to town tonight, Prew," he said. "You want to go along?"

"I'm broke," Prew said. "Flat."

"I dint ast you you had money. I got the money. I awys save out enough for a big one at the end of the month. I awys make my best one then, when theres nobody much in town, instead of tryin to go down Payday when you cant even get in a bar, let alone a whorehouse."

"Its your money," Prew said. "If you want to spend it on me I should worry. What time?" He was seeing sudden pictures of white, hair shadowed flesh swelling out loud flashy gowns in dim rooms and reflecting jukebox colored lights, the old womanhunger held in check so long rising in him, making his voice thick.

"After Taps is the best time," Stark said. "Its more fun if you got somebody with you," he explained, "and you look like you been hard up for some for quite a spell," he grinned lopsidedly.

"You didnt miss it, brother," Prew said, and that was all either of them would allow himself to say about the unexpected invitation.

"We get down there around midnight," Stark said, "and have time to hit a bar for a while and get prepared. Then around one we go up and hang around till two and take one for all night, maybe take a quickie in the meantime. Thats how I usely work it."

"All night!" Prew said, thinking avidly of the three hours, from two till five, that constituted all night in a Honolulu whorehouse. "Thats fifteen bucks!"

"Sure," Stark said, "but its worth it. When you ony have one big one a month, and save up for it, its more than worth it."

"Buddy," Prew said, "I'm your man. We was plannin to have a session with the git-tars from Tattoo till Taps, so even that will even all work out all right."

"Sure," Stark said. "We wont go till after Taps. Maybe I'll come out and sit in with you myself," he half asked, abruptly.

"Come ahead. You play one?"

"Not enough to count. But I like to listen though. I'll see you then," he growled harshly, almost dislikeably, plainly not wanting any more about it, and walked away, obviously afraid he would be thanked.

Prew grinned after him and went back to scrubbing down, feeling good now, feeling really fine, feeling wonderful, with the ferriswheel sickishness coming in his belly and the heavy, pendulous, full bellying swinging maleness rising, and with Maggio waiting on him in the Dayroom to play pool.

They played straight rotation, no slop and call your shot, the same difference between this game and plain rotation slop as between three cushion billiards and straight billiards, which was a game for amateurs who could not make them any other way, and tonight Prew, feeling very happily the brother of the whole wide world, was hot. It was a pretty even match between them, the Atlantic Avenue champ versus the boy who made his spending money on the bum by taking on the local stars in strange smalltown poolrooms, but Prew had the edge, a very slight one.

Friday leaned on his elbow in one of the windows between the alcove and the Dayroom that had once been a porch and watched, interested but plainly only putting in the time until they got the guitars out. After a while, men even came in from the Dayroom to watch.

Maggio, holding his cue, perched between shots in the other window like an egotistic robin, his stiff blocked hat proudly on his head, pushed back to show curls damp with concentration, happily pointing out the peaks requiring esoteric appreciation, in case the audience had missed them.

"This character is a poolshooter," he announced, with a thumb at Prew. "I know. I can judge. Brooklyn is the home of the original poolshooters, as well as the sharpie pingpong players. Man, what I would not give to have this character in the corner poolroom in my hometown is not worth picking up and put in your pocket. I'd dress him up in overhalls and a straw hat and put a grass in his teeth, and I would make a whole mint of ghelt off him."

"Nine ball off the end rail and side rail in the cross corner pocket," Prew said, and made it.

"See what I mean?" Maggio chortled to the audience.

"Maybe I'll come home with you some day, Angelo," Prew said, chalking up. "For a visit."

"Oh no," Maggio protested. "Not me, friend. My old lady would kick us both out on our can. She is prejudiced against dogfaces. Every since one of them from the Army Base laid my next to biggest sister. She has no use for uniforms."

At nine Andy came in from the Guardhouse, his bugle still down his back, and they broke it up. "Soons I blow Tattoo now I'm off till Taps," he said, going through and out the other door. "Somebody bring the git-tars out."

"I'll get em," Friday said, "I'll get em," coming to life now and starting for the stairs at a run.

"Can I come along and listen?" Angelo said, knowing this was a private session. "I wont say a word. Not a single request."

"I thought you didnt like hillbilly," Prew grinned.

"I dont," Angelo said fervently. "But you guys dont play hillbilly. With Gene Autry its hillbilly, with you guys its music."

"Okay, come on. I wonder what happened to our friend Bloom to-night," Prew said, walking out to the quad. "I aint seen him."

"I aint seen him around," Angelo said. "He probly went to town. To see his queer. I see him all a time down to the Waikiki Tavern when I go down to see mine. He's got himself a steady now, ony his aint got the money mine has got."

"Maybe he dont want the money."

"Maybe not. Maybe he's after a shoulder to cry on. The son of a bitch."

They met the others In the darkness of the quad, Friday eagerly dragging the two guitars, and after Andy finished Lights Out they sat on the back steps of the kitchen, playing the blues, but softly in the darkness so a crowd would not gather now when they did not want a crowd but only the privacy of their own communion. Around the quadrangle the CQs one by one flipped the lights off in the squadrooms. Stark came out from the messhall and sat on the curbing smoking and leaning back against the building, gladly listening but sullenly not speaking, even a solitary word, and staring off across Headquarters building as if he were trying to see Texas. Maggio hunched up on the bottom step like some organgrinder's hairless monkey with his round shoulders, listening as intently as Stark to this music that was foreign to his hometown Brooklyn.

"You know what," he said after a while, "them blues songs sounds like jazz instead of hillbilly, way you play them. Slow jazz, real nigger jazz, like they play in the joints on 52nd Street."

Prew stopped playing and Friday's guitar gradually stopped too. "They are in a way," Prew said. "Theres nobody can tell where hillbilly leaves off and jazz begins. They shade into each other. Me and Andy's got an idea for writing our own blues that will be our private special blues. We been talkin about it, goin to do it someday."

"Sure we are," Friday said. "Gonna call them *The Re-enlistment Blues*. Theres *Truckdriver's Blues* and *Sharecropper's Blues*, but no Army blues, see?"

Stark sat silent, listening to the rising, falling conversation as they went on playing, listening to it all but taking part in none of it, only smoking silently and communing with some bitter silence in himself.

"That was no way to play Tattoo," Prew said to Andy, with the indisputable air of an expert. "Tattoo wants to be staccato. Short, and snappy. You dont waste a second on the long notes. Tattoo is urgent. You're telling them to get them goddam lights out and you dont want argument. So it has to be precise and fast, without slurring the notes. And yet a little sad underneath, because you hate to have to do it."

"We cant all be good," Andy said. "I'm a git-tar player. You stick to the bugle and I'll stick to the git-tar."

"Okay," Prew said. "Here." He handed over the new guitar that was not very new any more but was still Andy's private guitar.

Andy took it and picked up the melody from Friday, still watching Prew's face in the darkness.

"You wanta take my Taps?" he offered. "You can take them tonight if you want."

Prew thought it over. "You sure you dont care?"

"Naw. I aint no bugler, I'm a guitarman, like I said. Go ahead and take them. I never could play them anyway."

"Okay. Gimme the horn. Heres your mouthpiece. I got mine with me. Just happened to have it."

He took the tarnished guard bugle and rubbed at it a little, held it in his lap then, as they sat on in the cool darkness, playing softly and talking a little, but mostly listening, Stark not talking any but only listening, gladly but sullenly. Once a couple of men wandering by stopped to listen for a minute, caught by the haunting hope without hope that sang out in the set blues rhythm. But the silent Stark was alert. He flipped his cigaret viciously out into the street, at them, the falling coal shattering at their feet and showering sparks. It was as if an unseen hand had pushed them away and they went on, but they were strangely lifted.

At five of eleven they stopped and all got up, the four of them walking out to the megaphone in the corner, leaving Stark leaning against the wall still smoking sullenly, tacitly accepting his aloofness, him rolling them and smoking and silently taking it all in, not missing anything.

Prew took his quartz mouthpiece from his pocket and inserted it. He stood before the big tin megaphone, fiddling nervously, testing his lips. He blew two soft tentative tones, then wiped the mouthpiece out angrily and rubbed his lips vigorously.

"My lip's off," he said nervously. "I aint touched a horn in months. I wont be able to play them for nothing. Lip's soft as hell."

He stood there in the moonlight, shifting nervously from one foot to the other, fiddling with the bugle, shaking it angrily, testing it against his lips.

"Christ," he said. "I cant play them like they ought to be played. Taps is special."

"Oh, go ahead, for God sake," Andy said. "You know you can play them."

"All right," he said angrily. "All right. I dint say I wasnt gonna play them, did I? You never get nervous, do you?"

"Never," Andy said.

"Then you aint got no goddam sensitivity," Prew said angrily. "Nor sympathy, nor understanding."

"Not for you," Andy said.

"Well for Christ's sake shut up then," he said angrily nervously.

He looked at his watch and as the second hand touched the top stepped up and raised the bugle to the megaphone, and the nervousness dropped from him like a discarded blouse, and he was suddenly alone, gone away from the rest of them.

The first note was clear and absolutely certain. There was no question or stumbling in this bugle. It swept across the quadrangle positively, held just a fraction longer than most buglers hold it. Held long like the length of time, stretching away from weary day to weary day. Held long like thirty years. The second note was short, almost too short, abrupt. Cut short and too soon gone, like the minutes with a whore. Short like a ten minute break is short. And then the last note of the first phrase rose triumphantly from the slightly broken rhythm, triumphantly high on an untouchable level of pride above the humiliations, the degradations.

He played it all that way, with a paused then hurried rhythm that no metronome could follow. There was no placid regimented tempo to this Taps. The notes rose high in the air and hung above the quadrangle. They vibrated there, caressingly, filled with an infinite sadness, an endless patience, a pointless pride, the requiem and epitaph of the common soldier, who smelled like a common soldier, as a woman once had told him. They hovered like halos over the heads of the sleeping men in the darkened barracks, turning all grossness to the beauty that is the beauty of sympathy and understanding. Here we are, they said, you made us, now see us, dont close your eyes and shudder at it; this beauty, and this sorrow, of things as they are. This is the true song, the song of the ruck, not of battle heroes; the song of the Stockade prisoners itchily stinking sweating under coats of grey rock dust; the song of the mucky KPs, of the men without women who collect the bloody menstrual rags of the officers' wives, who come to scour the Officers' Club—after the parties are over. This is the song of the scum, the Aqua-Velva drinkers, the shameless ones who greedily drain the half filled glasses, some of them lipsticksmeared, that the party-ers can afford to leave unfinished.

This is the song of the men who have no place, played by a man who has never had a place, and can therefore play it. Listen to it. You know this song, remember? This is the song you close your ears to every night, so you can sleep. This is the song you drink five martinis every evening not to hear. This is the song of the Great Loneliness, that creeps in like the desert wind and dehydrates the soul. This is the song you'll listen to on the day you die. When you lay there in the bed and sweat it out, and know that all the doctors and nurses and weeping friends dont mean a thing and cant help you any, cant save you one small bitter taste of it, because you are the one thats dying and not them; when you wait for it to come and know that sleep will not evade it and martinis will not put it off and conversation will not circumvent it and hobbies will not help you to escape it; then you will hear this song and, remembering, recognize it. This song is Reality. Remember? Surely you remember?

"Day   is done . . .
Gone   the sun . . .
From-the-lake
From-the-hill
From-the-sky
Rest in peace
Sol jer brave
God   is   nigh . . ."

And as the last note quivered to prideful silence, and the bugler swung the megaphone for the traditional repeat, figures appeared in the lighted sallyport from inside of Choy's. "I told you it was Prewitt," a voice carried faintly across the quadrangle in the tone of a man who has won a bet. And then the repeat rose to join her quivering tearful sister. The clear proud notes reverberating back and forth across the silent quad. Men had come from the Dayrooms to the porches to listen in the darkness, feeling the sudden choking kinship bred of fear that supersedes all personal tastes. They stood in the darkness of the porches, listening, feeling suddenly very near the man beside them, who also was a soldier, who also must die. Then as silent as they had come, they filed back inside with lowered eyes, suddenly ashamed of their own emotion, and of seeing a man's naked soul.

Maylon Stark, leaning silent against his kitchen wall, looked at his cigaret with a set twisted mouth that looked about to cry, about to laugh, about to sneer. Ashamed. Ashamed of his own good luck that had given him back his purpose and his meaning. Ashamed that this other man had lost his own. He pinched the inoffensive coal between his fingers, relishing the sting, and threw it on the ground with all his strength, throwing with it all the overpowering injustice of the world that he could not stomach nor understand nor explain nor change.

Prewitt lowered the bugle slowly and let the megaphone rest in its swivel. Reluctantly he withdrew his mouthpiece and gave the bugle back to Andy. His lips were pinched and red from the playing.

"Christ," he said huskily. "Jesus Christ. I need a drink a water. I'm tired. Me and Stark goin to town. Wheres Stark?" and fingering his mouthpiece he went vaguely toward the barracks in the darkness, not proud but innocently unaware as yet of what he had created.

"Boy," Maggio said as they watched him go. "That guy kin really play a bugle. Whynt he never play? He should ought to be in the Bugle Corps."

"He was, you jerk," Andy said scornfully. "He quit. He wouldnt play in this old Corps. He played a Taps at Arlington."

"Yeah?" Maggio said. He peered after the retreating figure. "Well," he said. "Well what do you know."

The three of them stood silent, unable to voice it, watching him go, until Stark who had been listening came over to them.

"Wheres he goin?"

"Lookin for you," Andy said, "to go to town. Went up toward the porch."

"Well thanks," Stark mocked, "I never would of guessed it," and went to find him.

"Come on, kid," he said. "Lets go to town. Lets fling a real one."

Book Three

THE WOMEN

Chapter 16

They came up the lightless stairs of the New Congress Hotel, very dark now after the brightly lighted, almost deserted Hotel Street outside, feeling their way half-drunkenly carefully. They had just left the small bar in the downstairs part of Wu Fat's brightly tropically decorated restaurant next door, and now they carried with them, suddenly, all the unmentionable, unspeakable, pride destroying heart shakiness and throat thickness and breath chokiness of men about to mount women, the same attributes displayed so shamelessly by all the male dogs on the Post as they chased down alleys after reluctant bitches, and that they laughed at in the hapless dogs, but that they did not feel like laughing at now, as the disembodied breasts and bellies and long thighs, all of a completely unearthly loveliness, swam through their minds.

All evening (with the foreknowledge of this now goading them into joyness) they had had a fine time, a viciously, pugnaciously, wildly bottle swingingly, fine time; with no fights at all yet, with hardly even any arguments except for the ex-dogface, squawmen taxi drivers who envied them their freedom and so always argued anyway and did not count. Getting out of the Schofield taxi at the big, rambling, palm camouflaged Army-Navy YMCA (with this prospect before them), they had gone immediately at once across the street for the first long drink, the best drink of them all, to the long open-fronted Black Cat Café. The Black Cat was a very successful place, being situated as it was directly across from the Y and the cabstand for all the Pearl Harbor and Schofield cabs. Everybody made for the Black Cat for that first best drink when they got in and stopped there for that last worst drink before going back, so that the Black Cat was always very crowded. And because the Black Cat was very successful and always very crowded both of them disliked it very much and felt it was fattening off their lifeblood and their hunger, and later on just before they went to Wu Fat's they came back to the Black Cat and ordered two toasted limburger cheese sandwiches to go from the stupid Chinese sandwich-man, saying they would be back and pick them up, then walked around the block once and by the time they got back the Black Cat was no longer very crowded, it was not even successful for the moment, it was empty and closed for the night with the iron latticework grill locked across the open front and there was not a soul to be seen in it, or for that matter to be seen in that block on that side of the street, and they shook hands happily (with this prospect still before them) and went for a drink to the nearest bar to celebrate the victory.

Before that, after the first drink there, they had worked their way down angling Hotel Street, stopping for a drink at the bars that appealed to them and watching the cherubfaced Oriental waitresses (able to watch now without anguish, with this prospect before them), the Chinese girls with their thin breastless side view and the startlingly curved front view, the Japanese girls with their stockiness of heavier breasts, shorter legs, and more voluptuous hips, but best of all the hapa-Portagee girls with their hot smoking, cat clawing sexiness, everywhere women, women, women, and them cockily feeling their load (that this prospect would take care of) and the liquor raising the thermometer of the blood higher and higher in the ears. They had not stopped at Wu Fat's then on the first time around but passing it had gone in short bar hops clear down to the river where Hotel angles into King with Aala Park darkly mysterious across the bridge, and from there looking happily up King at the movie houses just letting out the second shows they had cut over to Beretania along the muckiness of River Street and worked their way back up toward the Y, hatching the plot against the smug Black Cat happily while threading their way happily through the groups of sailors rolling along drunkenly arm in arm and the hissing-footed Filipinos padding femininely in twos and threes but never one alone in their padded zoot suits. And (happily, whole-earth-lovingly, now, because this prospect was before them) the one and two storey frame buildings crowding against the sidewalk anxiously offering their charms, the bars, and liquor stores, and restaurants, and shooting galleries, and photo shops; and inbetween each two or three storefronts (this prospect emphasizing their retiringness) the dark stairways leading upstairs to the women and always and eternally everywhere, pervading everything like Fate, the smells of rotting meat and dead wilted vegetables from the open fronted grocery stores with their folding lattice (like an old fashioned wall phone you pulled out to use) drawn across and locked, keeping you out and not keeping in the smells that exquisitely sadly reminded us of the hangover tomorrow and then the next one after that and so on to the last final hangover the biggest most perpetual hangover of rotting meat stashed away on shelves and hairy wilted carrots dissected on the tables, smells that we will forever remember as the attar of Hawaii, that we will never smell again without remembering Hawaii, the Hawaii of our unrepentant unrepented youth, for the rest of our whole lives.

And after the Black Cat's glorious fiasco then down Hotel once more, this time to Wu Fat's to eat won ton soup upstairs and then come back down to the bar downstairs where a thin fine-drawn queer with an English accent had wanted to know with subtle flattery if they were civilian sailors adventuring from home and offered to buy a drink that Stark told him to save for someone who had no money for the whores and would be more appreciative, the queer making a sly womanish crack at him, Stark hitting him happily, the bartender escorting the dazed queer to the door because Stark was spending the more money and then coming back and shaking hands and saying he did not like them either but bartenders have got to live too, and then finally settling down to the serious drinking to get primed, Stark getting really drunk with a wild urgent thirst that Prew had not suspected in that cool, slow talking, levelheadedness, but Stark confiding to him now with the unreserved intimacy of drunkenness that he was not worth a damn in any whorehouse unless he was properly liquored up and he did not know why, but anyway this was the only way to do it, the only way he could do it, but that he sincerely loved it this way, really he did (with the prospect coloring everything with unattainable brilliance, heightening everything with that unattainable ardor that in the end was one pure love of everything that lived, but could be attained no other way), and that by god no matter what anybody said any thing that could make you love the earth as much as this could not be wrong, no matter what they said, or evil, goddam them, or ashamed, screw them, and he would not believe it wrong, the sons of bitches.

Until now, standing at the top of the stairs on the landing with the massive steel door with its square peephole in front of them making a deadend tunnel of the stairway, the great earth love that needed an outlet, the great hunger for love that must be fed, were so great it almost creamed them both.

Stark (very drunk but still able to roll a cigaret deftly in the darkness) struck a match and lit it—the match flare lighting up like echoes of their minds all the pencil drawn naked bodies (male and female) on the walls, the unattached bodyless organs (male and female), the realistic looking vaginas made by holding a burning kitchen matchhead against the wall and then drawing the legs in afterwards, and all the accompanying verses of several generations of artistic soldiers, sailors, marines, and kanaka shoeshine boys—and beat with his fist against the door.

The peephole slid back immediately and a huge, black Hawaiian woman's face peered out at them suspiciously.

"Let us in," Stark said. "We freezin in the cold, cold night," ending with a tragic, from the heart, hiccup.

"You drunk," the great hulk heaved, "go way. We don't want trouble with MP. This a respectable place. Close up. You go home."

"Now dont get tough with me, Minerva," Stark grinned. "Or I have you busted back to the ranks. Go tell Mrs Kipfer her number one boy is here and why aint she on the door where she belongs."

"I see," she said, still suspiciously. "You wait," and slammed the peephole irritably shut.

Prew felt the completely unearthly lovely breasts and bellies and long thighs begin subtlely to fade and grow dim on him. He looked at Stark.

"There," Stark said bitterly. "You see? Woman thinks we drunk."

"Imagine that," Prew said. "Suspicious old bat."

"Any time women see a soljer, think he's drunk. Why? You know why?"

"Because he is."

"Thats *right*. Just plain suspicious. Thats why I dont like to come to these places. No faith in humanity. For two cents I'd go over to the goddam Service Rooms, or Pacific Rooms, or Ritz Rooms, or White Hotel. She thinks this is the ony whorehouse in this town? Theres even a Japanee Electric Massage four doors down the street."

"Lets go there. I never been to one of them."

Stark giggled. "Cant. Close up. Closes at eleven." Then realization dawning, he turned and stared. "You mean you never been to a Japanee Lectric Massage?" he said disbelievingly.

"Never."

"Ones with the little white sign and red letters on it and red streak of lightning under them?"

"Not once."

"Tsk, tsk," Stark said. "Where have you been?"

"I'm a hick," Prew said bitterly. "Plumb green."

"Tsk, tsk. I bet Wahoo's the ony place in whole dam world where a man can get Japanee Lectric Massage. And you refuse to take advantage of your opportunity. You have missed a great experience, Prewitt, you have neglected your education. They lay you on your side," he said, "then one of these hot lookin Japanee girls works you over, all over, with this lectric vibrator. But you cant touch her. They come out naked, and work you over. But they wont let you touch them, not even with a finger. They explain it all beforehand. And just in case someone dont understand instructions they keep a bouncer, a great big judo man. They let you see him when you first go in."

"But I'd want to touch em," Prew said. "I like to touch em."

"So do I. Thats the point, see? You want to but you cant. Very funny feeling. There she is, all of her, but you cant touch it. Practically the same thing as a civilian tryin to make a respectable woman, see? Very peculiar feeling. Really nothing like it. Takes a Japanee to think of a valuble experience like that."

"Takes a Japanee to enjoy it, too, I bet."

"Oh, no," Stark said. "I enjoy it. Makes you hot, so hot you'd almost eat the goddam thing. With me, it invigorates the blood. After a Japanee Lectric Massage I could run any whorehouse out of business, even if I was sober. Makes you realize what a woman's worth, even a whore. Gives you a great understanding of the human race. All of it."

"I still wouldnt like it," Prew said stubbornly.

"You're just stubborn," Stark said stubbornly. "How do you know you wouldnt like it? I liked it. Why wouldnt you like it?"

"Because I like to touch em. I like to more than touch em."

"By Christ," Stark said suddenly, "but that woman's sure been gone a long time." He turned and began to beat his fist against the door again. "An awful long time. Hey! Open up!"

The peephole opened up immediately, almost as if the tall, narrow faced, prettily smiling, white woman who smiled out at them had been standing there all the time listening.

"Why, hello, Maylon," the woman smiled delightedly. "Minerva didnt tell me it was you. How are you?"

"About to bust," Stark said. "Let us in."

"Why, Maylon," she chided, gently but firmly. "Is that any way to talk to me?"

Prew, looking at this ladyhood, this almost maidenhood, felt everything suddenly run down out of him hollowly, like snow suddenly slides off a roof under a February sun exposing the orderly shingles of a former business venture. And, like all the other times, at other places, he was ready to go home now. I wonder what Violet Ogure is doing, he thought, right now, at this minute?

"Jesus Christ!" Stark was storming. "You aint scared we wreck your joint?"

"Not at all," the woman smiled. "I have no fear at all upon that score. And please dont swear at me, Maylon."

"Mrs Kipfer," Stark said, with a sudden subdued sobriety at the seriousness of the situation, "I'm surprised at you, Mrs Kipfer. Did you ever know me to come up here when I was drinking heavily? I ask you honestly, do I look like that kind of a man?"

"Well I had certainly never thought so, Maylon," Mrs Kipfer lied pleasedly. "You have always been a perfect gentleman, around me."

"Thank you, Mam," Stark said. "And now, if there is no further misunderstanding, will you please let us in?"

"Heavy drinking," Mrs Kipfer countered, "just does not mix with the entertainment business. Every respectable decent place must consider its future."

"Mrs Kipfer, Mam," Stark said, "I give you my solemn word your future will be safe with us."

Mrs Kipfer was appeased. "Well," she smiled. "Since you give me your word. I'm sure you will, Maylon."

There was a sound of steel rubbing steel and the door swung inward. Prew saw a sophisticated looking woman with upswept hair and voluptuous figure daintily encased in a lovely doeskin colored evening gown with a corsage of redly purple orchids at her shoulder, looking as if she were the aristocratic lady just stepped out of an International Sterling Silver ad to call her guests to dinner. She smiled at him with forgiving motherly solicitude, and he understood now why everybody who went to whorehouses always talked about Mrs Kipfer and admired her so. It was because Mrs Kipfer was such a lady, and because she was willing to forgive them.

Behind him, Minerva heaved the great door shut and dropped the heavy bar back in its brackets.

"Maylon," Mrs Kipfer said, "I dont think I've met your friend?"

"You never pulled that door routine on me before, Mrs Kipfer," Stark said accusingly. "Almost think this place was illegal, instead of the best whorehouse in Honolulu."

"Lets not be crude," Mrs Kipfer said icily, "just because there was a misunderstanding. You know how I feel about that word. I'd hate to have to ask you to leave, Maylon, but I could, much as I would hate to, if you insist on being nasty."

Stark said nothing stubbornly.

"I think you owe me an apology for that last remark," Mrs Kipfer said. "Dont you?"

"I guess so," Stark said irritably. "I apologize."

"I still havent met your friend," she said.

Stark introduced them politely, and mock-bowed deeply as he did it, looking more like a recalcitrant small boy than an angry man.

"Charmed, I'm sure," Mrs Kipfer smiled at Prew, ignoring the bow as being beneath comment. "I'm always pleased to meet a new member of the Company."

"Pleasetomeetyou," Prew said uneasily, wondering where the hell the women were. He felt awkward before such exquisite manners, and he remembered suddenly bitterly what Uncle John Turner, who had never married, had once told him bitterly. *Women run the world, boy. God dealt them all the cards between their legs*, he said. *They dont have to gamble, like us men, and we mights well admit er.* So bitterly the boy, being a boy, could not understand it then.

"I think," Mrs Kipfer smiled, "that I shall call you Prew. May I?" as she led them from the big wide entryway to the right, on across the narrow hall, and through the doorway to the waiting room.

"Sure," Prew said, seeing women now at last, not the women he had seen in his mind outside, but still at least women. "Nobody calls me by my first name."

There were seven of them in the waiting room, one standing with a soldier at the Wurlitzer, two sitting talking to two sailors. The other four were sitting by themselves, three of them the fat gum-cud-chewing cows wearing the one piece short suits and all looking alike, three that would always sit by themselves, not caring, except when they were thrown into action, still not caring, as reserves during the big Payday attack. But the fourth sitting one was not like them; she was a slight brunette wearing the full length gown of the better grade, and sitting very poised and quiet with her hands clasped serenely in her lap, and he found that he was watching *her*.

He had already seen, with the experienced eye, that the four slim ones, the better grade of which the slight serene brunette was one, all wore full length gowns with the handy full length zippers, separating themselves consciously from the three fat gumchewing ones. He had already deduced, by this, that it was like all the others, this place, no different, pay your three bucks at the window, take your piece and leave, in spite of all he had heard about this one that was the Company hangout being the best. He had seen all that at once, but still he found that he was watching *her*, who was so obviously different even from the other three of the better grade.

"This is Maureen," Mrs Kipfer said, as one of the two of the better grade sitting with the two sailors got up and came over to them at the door, a thin, sharp nosed blonde with the dark triangle of hair showing through the thin material of the long blue gown.

"Prew is new here," Mrs Kipfer told her, "you will introduce him around, wont you, dear?"

"Sure, dear," the blonde said, huskily sarcastic, and put her arm around Prew's neck. "Cmon, Babyface. Hello there, old Stark, old kid," she cried and grabbed for him. "You got a present for me?"

"Watch it," Stark grinned, ducking back. "Or I wont have."

Mrs Kipfer smiled sweetly. "Maureen's our little hustler, arent you, Maureen dear?"

"Thats how I make my livin, dear," Maureen said sweetly. "I hustle. And I admit it."

Mrs Kipfer, still smiling sweetly, turned back to Prew. "You mustnt think we're rushing you, Prew. We want you to look around as long as you like. We want you to be satisfied with your friend. We arent crowded at all tonight, and there is plenty of time, isnt there, Maureen dear?"

"Sure, dear," Maureen said. "All the time in the world. I cant give you romance," she said directly to Prew. "But if a good lay is what you want I've got it, Babyface. Ask Stark, Stark's laid me. Am I a good lay, Stark?" she said, "or not?"

Mrs Kipfer turned on her heel and went back out into the hall.

"Good," Stark said. "But mechanical."

"Why goddam you," Maureen laughed, triumphantly. She grabbed Stark happily by the arm and pulled him to the Wurlitzer. "Just for that, you can play me some music."

Mrs Kipfer came back, then, to Prew still standing in the doorway.

"We have so much trouble getting good help anymore," she said apologetically. "This peacetime draft back home has hurt us terribly over here. You cant know how much. I'm completely helpless, at the mercy of whatever the agency condescends to send me."

"Sure," Prew said. "I can see that."

"Didnt she even introduce you to anyone?" Mrs Kipfer rushed on breathlessly. "Didnt she make you acquainted with anyone?"

"No," Prew said. "Not to a soul."

"Oh, dear," Mrs Kipfer said. "Dear, dear. Well, never you mind. I'll see you are taken care of. You mustnt feel badly."

"All right," Prew said. "I wont."

"Lorene," Mrs Kipfer called. "Are you busy, dear? Would you mind coming here a moment?

"It was really Lorene," she said to him, "that I meant for you to meet. She is really a very nice girl, really. That was really what I had planned," she said apologetically.

"Oh," Prew said. "Sure." He wasnt listening to the rest of it, he was watching the slight brunette, she who had been sitting very poised and quiet by herself, get up and come serenely toward them. He caught something about "almost like a daughter" and "hasnt a mean hair on her head," but he was not really listening. He had found himself watching her before and now he found himself watching her more, while being careful not to stare. Watching her walking he could see the flat triangle of hair under the thinness of the dress, but with her it was not like it had been with Maureen who had been unaware of it completely. This girl was aware of it, aware of him, but she was utterly above it. She was aware of it and she ignored it.

Must be twenty-three or -four, he thought, noticing that she walked very straight and that her hair was done in a circular roll low on her neck and that she had very wide eyes that looked at him serenely openly. She stopped by them and smiled at him and he noticed her mouth was very wide across the thin childishness of her face, he noticed the long lips were very full especially at the corners. She has a beautiful face, he thought.

Mrs Kipfer introduced them formally, and then asked if she wouldnt look after him because he was new here? if she wouldnt show him around?

"Surely," she said, and he noticed how pleasingly low pitched, how poised her voice was. It was the voice that belonged with the rest of her. "Lets sit down, shall we?" she smiled.

She really has a truly beautiful face, he thought again as they sat down, a tragic face, a face thats suffered, a face you'd never expect to find in this place. Suffering doesnt make whores beautiful, it makes them ugly. But thats because they do not understand the suffering. But she understands it. Such poised serenity as this, the poised serenity I've always hunted after for myself and never found, comes only from great wisdom, the wisdom of the understanding of suffering, the wisdom I've never been able to acquire, the wisdom that I need, that maybe all men need, he thought profoundly, and that you never guessed would turn up in a whorehouse. That is probably all it is, he thought, just that I am surprised to see a tragically beautiful face in a whorehouse. That is obviously all it is, he told himself, that and the fact that I am drunk.

"Mrs Kipfer says you are new in Maylon's Company," she said, in that low poised voice, that voice of the profoundest wisdom. "Did you just arrive in the Islands? Or did you transfer in from another outfit?"

"Another outfit," he said, trying to clear the thickness from his throat, sifting his brains to find one thought that was not too stupid to offer up before this wisdom, and failing.

Lorene waited, studying him wide-eyed serenely.

"I been in Wahoo almost two years now," he said.

"And yet," she said, "you've never been up here before. Thats strange. Isnt it?"

"Yeah," he said; it *was* strange, when you thought of it. "You kind of get in the habit of goin places where you already been," he said, trying to explain, feeling foolish at trying to explain. "I seen the sign plenty times. But I dint know anybody who came here. Till I got in G Company, that is."

"I've been here a year," she said.

"You have?" he said. "You dont much like it, do you?"

"Oh," she said, "I dont *like* it, but I dont mind it. I dont expect to stay here, though. I wont be here all my life."

"No. Sure not. I mean, why should you? Theres no reason why you should be here at all."

"Oh, theres a reason. A good reason. I'm not boring you, am I?" she said. "I suppose every whore tells you the same story, dont they?"

"I guess they do," he said, "come to think of it. Now that you mention it. But with them you never pay any attention. With them you always know it isnt serious."

"I have it all figured out. I've been here one year now, by the end of two years I'll be ready to leave. I figured it all out before I ever came here."

"Figured what out?" Prew said, seeing Stark and Maureen coming back toward them from the jukebox.

"How long I meant to stay," Lorene said, and stopped.

"Oh," Prew said. "Oh, I see." He was hoping Stark and Maureen would go right on by, but they didnt.

"Well I be dam," Stark said, "look who's heah. Hello, Princess. I thought you had retired already."

"Hello, Maylon," Lorene said serenely. It was, Prew thought, as if she was looking wide-eyedly clear through Stark and seeing all of him.

"You start out at the top, dont you kid?" Stark said to him. "How'd you manage to meet the Princess? just like that?"

"Mrs Kipfer," Prew told him, feeling suddenly belligerent. "Why?"

"No kiddin?" Stark said, "Mrs Kipfer? She introduced you? Already?"

"Sure," Prew said. "Why not?"

"Hell, kid, you really rate. It took me three trips down here before I even was allowed to meet her. And two more after that before she'd lay me. And even then she was reluctant. Aint that right, Princess?" he grinned.

"I lay anyone who wants what I've got," Lorene said serenely.

Stark stared at her reflectively. "Damn," he said, "aint she a Princess, though? Every inch a Princess, 'ey Princess? every inch."

Maureen laughed raucously and Stark grinned at her and winked.

Prew, looking at Lorene, realized suddenly she did look like a princess, he thought, a serene poised princess, incapable of being ruffled, remote from life and men. Especially men, he thought, the thickness coming back in his throat again.

"She does, dont she?" Stark said. "I ask you. Dont she? Princess Lorene, the Virgin of Waikiki. I think I'll go shake hands with the Mayor," he said suddenly. "Is the latrine still where it use to be?"

"We never change nothing here," Maureen said huskily. She grabbed Prew's arm and pulled him to his feet. "Cmon, Babyface. I'll 'introduce' you around."

Lorene serenely offered no resistance, as Maureen pulled him across the room and sat him in a chair and perched herself heavily on his lap.

"This heres Billy," she said, nodding at the small, dark, Jewish nosed, feverish eyed girl who had been at the jukebox with the soldier when he came in and was now sitting on his lap.

She turned back to Prew. "Stark says you dears goin to stay all night. You got a bottle, Babyface?"

"Nope," Prew said, still looking back across the room at Lorene. "No bottle. I thought they dint allow it anyway."

"They dont," Maureen said. "Anyplace. But most places they let an all night job sneak one in. Here the old bitch even enforces it on *them*. We could still sneak one while she's out in the hall, though. If we had one, that is."

"You dont much like Mrs Kipfer, do you?"

"Like her," Maureen said. "I love her. She kills me. If it wasnt for her I dont know what I'd do for laughs. Her and her stinking highclass ways, acting like she's Mrs Stinking Astor."

"How'd she ever get in this business anyway?"

"Like any of the rest of them. Started at the bottom and worked up to being foreman."

"She's got a damn good figure for it."

"And thats all the good it'll do you," Maureen laughed. "You might as well try to make the Queen of England. Listen, Babyface," she said. "You look artistic, Stark says you a bugler. Imagine something for me. Imagine having your own mother run the whorehouse you work in, can you?"

"No," Prew said. "I cant."

"Then you can see what I mean," Maureen said. "About laughs." She yawned, almost in his face, and stretched her thin arms. "Lets see," she said. "Hows our introductions comin? Thats Sandra," she said, pointing to the other girl who had been sitting with the two sailors when he came in and who was still with them now, a tall brunette who wrinkled her pert nose as she laughed gayly with the sailors, shaking the glistening cascade of long hair whenever she laughed, which was often.

"She's proud of her long hair," Maureen razzed, almost indifferently now, from force of habit. "She also says she's a college grad, some coed school in the Middle West. She's writin a novel now, about her life as a prostitute, suthin like this *Call House Mistress* book."

"Yeah?" Prew grinned.

"Yeah," Maureen said. "And them other three," she said, pointing at the three fat, gum chewing ones, "are Moe, Larry, and Curly."

Prew laughed out loud. "You're a character yourself."

Maureen stared at him quizzically. "I'm goin to buy them a checkerboard after Payday, if they promise to quit chewing gum. Theres four or five more back in the second waiting room, if you want to meet them too. But I wouldn't be surprised they all asleep."

"Dont disturb them."

"Why now, thank you. Dear," Maureen said. "Thats sweet of you."

"Dont mention it."

"Well," she said, "do you see anything you like? or not? I aint got all night."

"I like them all. Especially Moe, Larry, and Curly," he said, looking back across the room now at Lorene.

"The Princess is purty, aint she?" Maureen said.

"Oh," he said. "So-so."

"You mean you think she'll do," Maureen said. "You mean she'd be all right. In a pinch. A good hard pinch."

"Thats it," Prew said.

Maureen stood up suddenly and smoothed her dress.

"I'm afraid you'll have to excuse me, Dear," she minced. "I can plainly see I will be of no use to you much. I seem to lack that virginal quality so profitable in a good whore."

"Nobody seems to like her around here," Prew said. "Why is that?"

"Call it professional jealousy," Maureen said. "For lack of a better name.

"Well," she said, "much as I hate to dash off I am afraid you must allow me to tear myself away. Much as I adore your company, there is still business to attend to. Minerva is opening the door to let someone in, and as Mother Kipfer says, business must come before pleasure."

"Then dont let me detain you," Prew said, "from your duty." He grinned, flatly because all this had stopped being funny, but broadly because he liked this one and did not want to hurt her any more than he had to to get free of her.

She flashed him back a grin that understood his own completely, and he watched her teeter on her meatless hips across the room, walking on her spike heels like a small boy on stilts, humpily with the high thin shoulders swaying precariously; him feeling as he watched her a big, great sadness of inevitability like a bugle's Taps. But underneath this, more urgent and more understandable, the thick chokiness in his throat again as he looked over at Lorene who still sat alone serenely waiting, his blood beating in his eyes because he was free to go back there now.

Then as he got up, from beyond Maureen's head and shoulders in the doorway, he heard the great door thud shut and the bar drop back into its brackets and then, suddenly, the powerful Brooklynese voice of Pvt Angelo Maggio in all its triumphant glory.

"Well what do you know?" it said, booming in a high thin treble that was a very peculiar sound. "Look who's here. If it aint my old friend, compatriot, comrade in arms, and Mess Sergeant, Sgt Stark. Fancy meeting you here, of all places in the world. I bet you never thought you'd see old Angelo here, by god, tonight," the voice accused triumphantly. "Wheres my boy Prewitt?"

"How the hell did you manage to make it into town with money?" Stark's voice wanted to know.

"Ah," Maggio's voice smirked. "It was nothing. It was simple. Anything for a friend, anything for a friend."

The two of them came through the doorway, an arm around each other's neck half drunkenly, past Maureen. Maggio pinched her on the bottom deliciously and said, *"Hello, my love!"* and Maureen laughed and pinched his ear and said *"Angelo my Romeo!"* Maggio loosed his arm and bowed and Prew saw Mrs Kipfer beaming in at Angelo from the entryway. Stark pulled him back erect and they came on, Angelo waving happily at everybody he could see, the conquering hero come home.

"My god," Angelo said drunkenly happily and put his other arm around Prew's neck. "What is this, old home week? Looks like the goddam homecoming game at NYU. Nothin but Jews and Wops and Polacks."

He pulled their heads together in front of him and whispered.

"I'm drunk, friends. Been drinkin champagne cocktails since eleven-thirty and am drunk. And happy. But dont tell Mother Kipfer or she'll throw me out. Also, do not tell her of this fifth of whiskey I got in my belt under this loose flowing gook shirt."

He straightened up and looked around and waved at Sandra sitting with the sailors.

"Wonderful things, gook shirts, aint they, Baby Doll? So loose and cool. Plenty of room to move. I love gook shirts. Do you love gook shirts?"

Sandra wrinkled her pert nose at him and laughed. "I love gook shirts, Angelo." The two sailors stared at Angelo sourly.

Maggio pulled the two heads together in front of him again. "Thats for me," he whispered. "For all-l-l *night*. Unless you men picked her first, you got first choice. Man, I like em tall. I'm the midget who married the fat lady in the circus. Acres and acres," he whispered. "Acres and acres."

"What I want to know," Stark said, "is where the hell all this money come from."

"Simple," Angelo said. "Really nothing. Nothing at all. But its a long story. Shall I tell it?"

"Sure," Prew said. "Lets hear it."

"Shall I really tell it? Well all right then, if you insist. But its a long story. You sure you really want to hear it? Okay then, if you're positive. I will tell it. But lets go back to the latrine first."

"I just been," Stark said.

Maggio slapped himself on the belly. "Yeah, but you dint find there what I'll find there."

"Nuff said," Stark said, and the three of them went arm in arm back to the ammonia strong latrine, foul with the emptied bladders of a thousand men, and while Stark broke the seal on the bottle and they had a drink Maggio told them the triumphant story.

"After you guys left for town I got to wonderin why the hell I should stay home. So I called up my queer, Hal (the one I met that night we went broke in the poker game, remember?), and made him drive up to Wahiawa and pick me up, the bastard.

"He was reluctant, but I blackmailed him with this," he said, holding up a stiffened middle finger. "Ony I was polite about it. He's a intellecshual and very sensitive. I tole him this was a crisis and if he couldnt stand by his friends in a crisis he didnt deserve to have any friends. He seen the light all right.

"He took me back downtown and brought me a big feed of steak and frenchfries at Lau Yee Chai's, get that, Lau Yee Chai's. No tonks for Maggio. When Maggio rides he hits the best. After the feed we went and drunk champagne cocktails at the good old Waikiki Tavern where all the *boys* hang out.

"I explained to old Hal how I'd borrowed twenty bucks off a twenty percent man in the Company and I had to have it back right away to pay him off because he was threatenin to turn me in and if he did I'd go to the Stockade sure and old Hal wouldnt see his little boy for about six months."

He pulled a sheaf of ones out of his pocket and shook it at them happily.

"Thats all there was to it, men. Old Hal came through with a loan of twenty. He wanted to *give* it to me, but I'm too smart for that. I wouldnt take it unless he made it a loan. I know how to handle him. If he could ever prove to himself I'm tryin to take him for a ride I'd never get another dime out of him. So now I owe him twenty bucks," Maggio grinned triumphantly. "But I had rather owe it to him all my life than beat him out of it."

Stark giggled and handed him the bottle. "So you told him you'd go to the Stockade unless you paid off this twenty percent man. What a story, sam. Dont this Hal know loanin money for interest is against the ARs? and that any man who does it cant collect it legal?"

"He dont know nothin about the Army," Maggio grinned. "He tries to ack like he does, but he dont. But he knows the navy though. Just ask him for it how he knows the navy, thats all, friend," he grinned.

He corked the bottle and put it back in his belt, under the hanging shirt. "Say," he said. "Its gettin close on to two o'clock, men. We better be picking our stuff or them sailors out there going to beat our time."

"I got mine picked already," Stark said, suddenly sullenly, not looking at them.

"Yeah?" Maggio said. "Well that Great, Big, Tall, Long Sandra's the one for me. Unless you picked her already. Who'd you pick?" he asked Stark anxiously.

"Billy," Stark said sullenly, still not looking at them. "The little Jewish one. I already ask her and its okay."

"Oh-oh," Maggio grinned. "The little hot eyed job?"

"Sure," Stark said angrily. "Thats right. Whats wrong with that?"

"Not a thing," Maggio grinned. "I been meanin to try that sometime myself."

"All right then," Stark said sullenly. "You pick yours and I'll pick mine. Whats it to you what I pick?"

"Not a dam thing," Maggio said. "Long as I get Big Sandra. I dont care what they are, long as they big and tall."

"Okay," Stark said. "Thats your business. If I like Billy thats my business, aint it? You like Sandra. Well, I just happen to like Billy. So what?"

"So nothing," Maggio said. "All I ask was . . ."

"Well quit asking," Stark said. "Its none of your goddam business. I just like Billy, thats all."

"Maureen is free," Prew said.

"To hell with Maureen," Stark said. "I know what the hell I want. Billy's what I want. You want to argue?"

"Okayokay," Maggio said. "Quit bitching. You got her, aint you? But man," he said, "I love that Sandra. When they that big and tall, man! Man oh man oh *man!* You got yours picked?" he said to Prew.

"Yeah," Prew said. "I got mine picked."

Stark snorted. "He picked the goddam Princess."

"No joke?" Maggio said. "No kidding?"

"No joke," Stark said sourly. "No kidding. Princess Lorene, the Virgin of Waikiki," he taunted.

"She's a snob," Maggio protested.

"All right, so what?" Prew said. "I aint telling you guys what to pick. Dont tell me what to pick."

"I aint telling you what to pick," Stark said. "You can pick Minerva, if you want, for all I give a good goddam. Its nothing to me what you pick."

"We want to be sure now," Maggio said, "that we have them get three rooms right together in a row so we can all use this whiskey. Dont forget that now," he said. "You asked yours yet?" he said to Prew.

"No," Prew said reluctantly. "Not yet."

"Well you better ask her quick, man," Angelo said. "If you want her. Them sailors look to me like they mean to stay all night too."

"You aint ask Sandra yet either, have you?" Prew said.

"God damn no!" Maggio said. "I clean forgot! Lets us get back out there, man. Right now."

Chapter 17

They came back from the latrine down the long hallway past the many doors of tiny bedrooms, past the several short side halls that held only doors of bedrooms, making the right angle turn to the left and past still more doors of bedrooms, before they reached the waitingrooms.

"Big place," Maggio said.

"Got a big business to take care of," Stark said.

Prew said nothing.

He found Lorene still sitting in the same place, looking just as serenely confident, and he felt relieved a little. But now there was a new soldier he had not seen before sitting beside her talking to her, a constant stream of talking to her, that she was listening to serenely, but attentively, and he stopped undecided in the doorway, letting the other two go on in ahead because he felt again the thickness in his throat that all but choked him and now also a new feeling of weak laxness in the backs of his thighs.

He knew he should ask her right away at once before it was too late. But he was very worried suddenly for fear he had already waited too long to ask. And it was suddenly of the greatest importance that he get her instead of another one. It was so important he was afraid to ask and he was very awkward and he could not begin.

Jesus Christ, he raged at himself. Whats wrong with you. She's nothing but a common whore, or at best an uncommon whore, so why should you be awkward. Who cares if this one doesnt like you. Ask Maureen, she likes you. Whats wrong with you, he thought, is you have not had one for so long you are ripe sucker bait for any cunning little cute little snatch that comes along. Thats whats wrong with you, so for god sake quit being awkward. Go and ask Maureen.

"You engaged, Lorene?" he asked her awkwardly.

His voice made the talkative soldier stop talking and look up and grin.

At least something can make him stop talking, Prew thought.

"No, Prew," Lorene smiled serenely. "Just talking." She got up. She smiled down at the talkative soldier and Prew thought he had never seen such a smugly talkative soldier.

"I mean for all night," he said thickly. "Engaged for all night."

"You want to stay all night?" Lorene said. "I thought you meant engaged for right now."

"I meant engaged for all night," he said flatly. "Are you?"

"Not yet, Prew."

"Well you are now," he said, looking at the talkative soldier.

"Its a date," Lorene smiled, "But it is twenty minutes yet. Theres no need for you to hurry. Sit down and relax a while." She patted the seat on the other side of her like a serenely reassuring mother, smiling at him with her long-lipped mouth set into the thin child's face.

"We were talking about surfboarding," she explained, as he dropped into the chair. "Bill is stationed at DeRussey and is quite an expert at it. He describes it thrillingly."

The talkative soldier stopped grinning. He smiled briefly. "You know anything about surfing?" he asked Prew, leaning forward around Lorene.

"No," Prew said, leaning forward around Lorene. "Not a goddam thing."

"Well," the talkative soldier said, smiling at Lorene. "You guys from Schofield, being stationed inland like you are, dont get much chance at it I guess."

"No," Prew said. "But we got mountains. You know anything about mountain climbing?"

"A little bit," the talkative soldier said, smiling at Lorene again. "Are you a mountain climber?"

"No," Prew said. "I dont know anything about mountain climbing. Do you know anything about flying an airplane?"

The talkative soldier smiled briefly. "I've had a few lessons," he said. "Out at John Rodgers."

"Well I cant fly either," Prew said. "What do you know about deep sea diving?"

Lorene, who was sitting facing the talkative soldier, turned clear around to serenely frown at him severely.

The talkative soldier frowned at him too, this time, before he smiled briefly.

"No," the talkative soldier said. "I've never done that. Is it fun?" He leaned back in his chair and returned to his private conversation with Lorene who listened to it with the same serene attentiveness.

Prew leaned back in his own chair, letting him have the floor undisputed, and bit off a hangnail on his thumb, waiting for him to run down, but he did not run down, he took the floor and kept it, with a constant stream of talking that showed no prospects of running down.

"Hey," Prew said finally, leaning forward again around Lorene. "Why dont you take her to bed, Bill? Aint that what you come up here for? Or did you come up here to present her with a charter membership of the Outrigger Club?"

The talkative soldier stopped talking and smiled at Lorene sadly. "Well," he said to her. "An Infantryman who is also a wit."

"At least I'm not a goddamned Coast Artilleryman who is also a surf-boarder," Prew said. "Are you going to screw her or aint you?"

Stiffly Lorene turned clear around to stare at him again, this time not severely but horrifiedly, as if he had just crawled up out of a hole in the mud.

Prew grinned at her. "Well? Are you?" he asked Bill.

"Did you want to go to the room, Bill?" Lorene said, "with me? There is plenty of time if you do, honey."

"Well," Bill said. "Sure. I guess. I think that would be better perhaps, dont you? The air in here seems to have gotten very smelly, hasnt it?"

"Yeah," Prew said deliberately. "I noticed that too. You son of a bitch."

"Listen, fellow . . ." Bill started.

"Shall we go then?" Lorene interrupted him. "I see no point in remaining here, do you? Come on, Bill," she said, taking his hand with virginal shyness. "The sooner we go, the more time we'll have together, Bill."

"All right," Bill said. He let her lead him out. At the door she stopped just long enough to give Prew a very disapproving look and to let him see her smile tremulously shyly at Bill.

Prew grinned at her. "Dont forget to show her the snapshots of your new surfboard, Bill," he called after them.

Then, when they had gone, he let the grin drop off. He leaned back in the chair. He slid down in it until he was sitting on the back of his waist with his chin on his chest. Big Time Operator Prewitt. Who reads off all the other poor unfortunate bastards like himself who are so hungry to talk to a woman they willing to come to a whorehouse and pay three bucks to do it. Really showed him up, dint you? how he would take everything off of you and still not fight. Wanted to fight him bad, didnt you? you who make your brags about never checking a cinch into the next man, you who are so high and mightily humani-tarian you cannot allow yourself to fight for Dynamite's bloody boxing squad. Killer Prewitt, horny fisted veteran of a thousand battles. Blood makes you sick, doesnt it? You really looked good in there, Killer. You were truly championship material, werent you, Caveman? She ought to admire you a lot now. You really made a great impression on her, with your virility and fifteen bucks I bet she'd even go all night with you.

And that was all you wanted, wasnt it, Killer? All you wanted was what she puts out for a living, wasnt it, Caveman? You didnt want her admiration, or friendship, or closeness, or interest, or intimacy, or whatever the hell they call it, the part they keep and dont put out for a living, did you? No, of course you didnt. Who ever wants the interest or admiration of a whore?

Across the room Maggio and the tall long legged Sandra were bidding a fond farewell to two sullen sailors. Did they want the interest of a whore? Sure not, thats why they're sullen, with plenty others in the next room.

Little Billy was sitting on Stark's lap with her mouth to his ear talking feverishly. Did Stark want the admiration of a little hot-eyed whore? Of course not, thats why he's grinning so complacently. Man, you kill me, you really knock me out. Killer Prewitt, the Boy Wonder.

"How you doing, buddy?" Stark grinned at him swimmily. "You got it all fixed up?"

"Yeah," he said. "All fixed up. Fixed up swell."

Maybe you better take up surfboard riding, Killer, he thought.

"Did you tell her about gettin the three rooms together?" Stark asked him.

"No," he said. "I forgot to ask her that."

"We got it fixed up anyway," Stark said. "Its okay. But dont forget to tell her when she comes back, or you'll miss out on the dew." Then little Billy bit him on the ear and he jerked his head and cursed, then laughed, then brought his wide-swinging attention back to her, where she wanted it.

"I wont forget it," Prew said, to nobody. "I wouldnt want to miss out on anything. Anything but that, but missing out on something."

Maggio and Sandra were shaking hands with the sailors in great friendship, like the host and hostess regretfully speeding the departing guests. As soon as the sailors had gone through the connecting doors into the second waitingroom Maggio sat down with a great sigh and pulled Sandra down on his lap, whereupon Maggio completely disappeared from view.

"Hey," Maggio said muffledly. "I dont think this is going to work out so good. How about me sitting on your lap? For a change?"

"Well," Sandra said. "It would be an experience."

She got up, laughing and wrinkling her pert nose and shaking her black cascade of gleaming hair, and they changed places, Maggio looking like a mahout perched on his favorite she elephant, or a circus monkey riding high up in the air on a big breasted Shetland pony.

"Hey," he said, "hey, look at me. *Do You Want One—Of Them Big Fat Mamas—Too*," he sang. It was a perfect mime of Wingy Manone's chortling, whiskey-rusty vocal.

"What do you mean, fat?" Sandra, who except for her breasts was very slender, said indignantly. "I'm not fat, sonny."

"I know it, baby," Maggio said. "Dont call me sonny. I was ony speaking figurtively. Theres no call to get mad on me and insulting.

"Hey, Prew," he said, changing the subject. "Them sailors remind me of what I forgot to tell you. I see our chum Bloom down to the Tavern tonight."

"Yeah?" Prew said listlessly. "Who with?"

"With a great big bastard of a queen he's got on the string named Tommy who's even bigger than Bloom is, if you can picture that."

"Oh," Prew said. "Well, well."

"I cant picture it neither," Maggio said. "Except he's got a lot of shoulder for our boy to cry on. When Bloom seen me and I seen how he looked at me I begun to lookin around for a good big heavy chair."

"You meant he wasnt glad to see you?" Prew said.

Maggio laughed. "He got a patch of tape as big as my mouth on that flat head. My boy Hal knows this Tommy well," he said. "Thats what he said, first time he seen him with Bloom, he said: *'Alas, poor Tommy, I knew him well.'*"

"Thats from Shakespeare," Sandra said. "A corruption. From Shakespeare's *Hamlet: Alas, poor Yorick, I knew him well.*"

"Yeah?" Angelo said. "Well what do you know. My boy Hal is plenty educated, baby. Very poetic, Hal is."

"I bet he is," Sandra grinned. "I bet he's very poetic. They're all poetic. I got a couple odd ones that come up to see me every now and then."

"Well," Maggio mimed. "Whatever for?"

"You guess," Sandra grinned.

"I dont have to guess," Maggio said. "Old Hal," he said to Prew, "says this Tommy borrows his car to take Bloom out with, ever time old Hal will let him have it. He says Tommy hardly makes enough to live on, says he works someplace downtown and writes stories for magazines on the side. Old Hal says he dont make near enough to spend money on our chum Bloom, says he cant hardly buy our chum Bloom drinks even. Frankly, I am getting so I am wondering who is laying whom."

"Sure," Prew said, trying to think of something to say. "I wouldnt doubt it," he added, finally.

"I had dinner down at Lau Yee Chai's tonight," Maggio bragged to Sandra. "Feature that."

"Lau Yee Chai's?" Sandra said indifferently. "Thats my favorite hangout. Its a highclass place. I eat there all the time."

"Will they let you in?"

"Sure," Sandra said. "Why not?"

"I thought The Law said you gals had to live out of town."

"It does," Sandra said. "But at Lau Yee Chai's they think I'm a rich tourist lady."

"You ever eat any of this pa-pa-ya?" Maggio asked her.

"Papaya," Sandra said. "Eat it all the time. I love it."

"Tonight was a first time I ever had some," Angelo said. "Looks like mushmelon, kind of, but it tastes like nothin. They got to put lemon juice on it to make it taste at all."

"Its like olives," Sandra said. "You have to acquire a taste for it."

"Same thing as avocado," Stark said, with authority, "or snails. You got to learn to like it."

"To me," Angelo said, "with lemon on it, it smells just like vomit. I am not acquiring any tastes for vomit." He laughed uproariously half-drunkenly, so hard he almost fell off Sandra's lap. Sandra looked at him inquiringly.

"God damn," Stark said, "if you two dont look like Edgar Bergen and Charlie McCarthy."

"We had a gook waiter tonight," Angelo explained, laughing. "This gook waiter stood around behint me all a time like he was scared I'd pick up the wrong fork and shock the customers. So when he brought this pa-pa-ya with a slice of lemon I whispered to him what this was? and he says, 'Why, thats papaya, Sir.' So I whispered to him, 'Angelo Maggio tries anything once,' and ast him was this how you did it? and squeezed the lemon on it.

" 'Oh, yes, Sir,' he whispers back.

" 'Odd,' I whispered to him back, 'but when you put lemon juice on this pa-pa-ya it smells just like vomit, dont it?' He just stares at me without a word and I whispers, 'Its a good thing I'm crazy about vomit, aint it?' "

All of them, excepting Prew, laughed, even Billy laughed, and Angelo seated on his perch grinned as smugly as the parrot who has just four-letter-worded the old maid out of the room in the cartoon.

"I thought old Hal would bust his gut from laughin," Angelo grinned. "This old waiter dint hover at this elbow no more, after that."

Little Billy got up from Stark's lap suddenly, as if the laughter had released her from a hypnotism. She stretched her small voluptuous body feverishly, the firm small uptilted breasts that many a virtuous woman would have envied and considered a rank malfeasance of her office leaping tautly into prominence, their nipples darkly visible under the thin material, almost in Stark's face.

"Well, how about it, Maylon?" she whispered huskily. "There wont be no more stragglers now, and if there was its too near two o'clock for an all night job like me to take them on." She arched her back toward him thirstily, proudly. "How about a trip around the world, honey?" she said silkily, "to start off with?"

"I thought that was ony for the pay as you go customers?" Stark said thickly.

"It is," Billy said.

"Its five bucks, aint it?"

"Thats right. Five extra. But its worth it, Maylon, it is truly worth it."

Stark sighed deeply. "Okay," he said, "you made a sale." His eyes were blooded and very deep.

"You people comin?" Billy said to Maggio and Sandra. "You got the bottle."

"Shhh," Maggio said.

"Nuts," Billy spat. "To hell with the old bitch."

"We're coming," Sandra grinned at her. "We're coming, kid."

Billy laughed feverishly.

"I don't see how she does it," Sandra said to Maggio. "It would kill me, or any other normal woman."

As she passed Prew, Sandra leaned down and spoke. "When Lorene comes back, tell her we're going across the entryway and back around to the rooms on the hallway above the outside stairs. She'll know where."

"Okay," Prew said indifferently, and watched them all go on across the entryway and disappear around a corner laughing. What the hell, he told himself, it isn't two o'clock yet; Stark is having to pay five bucks extra for that Trip; Angelo aint getting a price reduction for his bottle but them two whores will drink most of it; so what the hell; you got no complaints, he told himself.

He told it to himself repeatedly. But he was alone in the silent wait-ingroom with the darkened Wurlitzer, and there is nothing in the world so lonesome as a silent, darkened Wurlitzer, when the people and the nickels have all gone, and he kept losing count of how many times he said it and having to start over.

When he finally heard Lorene's low, poised voice out in the hallway he got up quickly. Too quickly, he thought angrily, you better sit back down, you want her to think you're anxious?

But he did not sit back down. Lorene said goodby to the Fort DeRussey surfboard rider friendlily out in the hall. It seemed to him that it took her a very long time, more time than necessary, and that she was very friendly, much more friendly than seemed natural, and he wondered if this was to put him in his place again. But even then he didnt care and he was still standing, by the chair, fumbling for a cigaret and lighting it, when Lorene came in smiling. He was very relieved that she was smiling.

"That was a terrible way to have acted," she rebuked him, smiling. "What you did."

"I know it was," he said. "I didnt mean to do it."

"You ought to be ashamed of yourself."

"I am," he said.

"At least you have the money. Poor Bill wanted to stay all night and didnt have the money. I think that this was even his last three dollars, from the way he acted, and now he'll have to walk clear out to Waikiki."

"Poor son of a bitch," he said. "I feel for him, and I'm sorry I was bastardly." He was thinking of himself, broke and on KP, only this afternoon. This afternoon seemed a long way back now, he thought, at least thirty pages back, a thing that happened to another guy. Maybe it happened to poor Bill.

"Before you came over," Lorene smiled sadly, "poor Bill was so desperate he even asked me to loan him the fifteen dollars until Payday. And then you sit there and try to needle him like that."

"I was jealous," he said.

"Jealous?" She smiled serenely. "Over me? A common whore? Don't try to flatter me. You still ought to be ashamed."

"I am," he said. "I said I was. But I'm still jealous."

"You have no right to be."

"I know it. But I am."

"Poor Bill even wanted to give me five dollars interest, and offered to teach me to ride a surfboard, free. I wouldnt even have to rent one, I could use his."

"That takes a lot of guts," Prew said. "Brass guts."

Lorene smiled sadly. "Just the same, I felt bad about it, especially when you came over and started picking on him."

"Why dint you loan it to him then?"

"Well, it wasnt because of you," she said. "How could I loan it to him? I'm in business just like a grocer. I'm here to make money, not because I love the work. You dont run this business on charge accounts. Where would I be? If I let every fellow I liked or felt sorry for open up a charge account with me? I felt like a heel. And you didnt make me feel any better."

"I know it," he said. "But he had to have a brass gut to even ask you a thing like that. These people who have always done everything—surfing, mountain climbing, flying, deep sea diving, anything you mention they've done some of it—that kind always got a pure brass gut. And they've never done anything. I've seen them before."

"Well he knows surfboarding. Because I've seen him on his board at Waikiki, and he's good. He spends all his money on surfing and spear fishing, and to stay in the Outrigger Club. He's always in debt three months ahead. Thats another reason I couldnt loan it to him."

He was getting tired of Bill the surfboard rider.

"Sandra said to tell you they were goin around back, over the outside stairs. She said you'd know. Angelo sneaked in a bottle and we all want to use it."

Lorene looked at him steadily, her eyes very cool, and very serene. "Oh, all right," she said. "I know where. Come on."

"Wait," Prew said. "Are you still mad at me about this other?"

"No," she said. "I'm not mad."

"I think you are. And I had to ask you. Because if you're still mad I'd just rather we called the whole thing off."

She looked at him again, steadily, then she smiled. "You're a funny one. No, I'm not mad. I was, but I got over it."

"I dint want you to be mad at me. I had to ask you."

It was hard to say these things, without feeling foolish, hard to make them seem believable. So many fellows probably said them without meaning them.

"Flatterer," Lorene said coquettishly. It was the first time he had seen her be coquettish and it startled him.

She took his hand and swung their arms together gayly, coquettishly, as they walked across the entryway and around the double corner to the hallway that went back over the stairs, and that had still more doors of tiny bedrooms. She led him gayly, him embarrassed by her sudden gaiety, along the worn carpeting down the narrow dimness that was lighted by a single bare bulb in the ceiling halfway down, to the third door from the end on the street side.

"We never use this part except on Payday," she told him gayly, "when the big rush is on. The rest of the time we keep it for the all night—friends," she said, "those of them who are very special. Nobody walks by here at night and it is quiet and the street is outside where you can hear the buses sometimes through the window. The rooms back there dont have any of that," she said, "and theres no fear of someone barging in on us, like sometimes happens back there."

"Am I one of your specials?" he asked her thickly.

She stopped at the door and laughed back at him over her shoulder. "Well," she said, coquettishly, "you're here, arent you?"

"Sure I'm here. But that could be because of Angelo and Maylon, and the bottle, that they wanted me cut in on," he said, noticing how very feminine she was when she was coquettish. "Billy and Sandra brought them here, not me."

"Is it so important?" Lorene teased.

"Yes, its important," he said urgently. "Important because there are so many of us; thats just faces, to you. So many of you that aint even faces, only just bodies, to us. Do you want to be just a unremembered body? When we come here and then go away we need to know at least that we're remembered. Maybe we seem all alike but none of us is ever

232

all alike. Men are killed by being always all alike, always unremembered. They die inside. Wives earn their money that way just as much as whores do, with this crappy imitation that aint no good but has to work because usually its all there is. But it dries up the well and leaves it nothing but a mudhole, makes it just rich blood poured down a strawy rathole that stinks afterwards, unless you are remembered. We dont ask to be needed, all we ask is to be remembered. Just to be remembered is . . ."

In the dim halflight he could see her looking at him, very surprised, and he shut it off, the little opening that was his mouth from which this torrent he did not know was there had leaped out at her. Flash and fadeout of boy with tongue in dike, he thought. Hans Brinker and the Silver Skates. HERO HOLDS BACK FLOOD THAT THREATENS TO DROWN EARTH!!

In the silence Lorene laughed self-consciously.

"If it is so important to you as all that," she smiled, "then you are one of my specials."

Prew shook his head. "Thats no answer," he said doggedly, and closed it up again with his tongue, the little hole, the little leak, the small Achilles heel.

"Well, what other answer do you want?"

"I dont know," he said, listlessly. "Forget it. Is this our room?"

"Yes," she said. Then she put her fine-boned, woman's hand on his arm and said, "Listen!" half-jokingly, and he could hear the springs squeaking rhythmically in the next room.

"At work already," she joked, trying to erase the page and write it her way, but the uncertainty in her made it fail, fall flat.

"Work, all right," Prew said stonily, listening to the hard, unvarying rhythm. "Hard work." The fine-boned, woman's hand was on his arm, so delicate to hold such power, and he wanted to grab the thinness of her and constrict the breath out of her kissing her, bring her alive to what he knew, make her feel it. But the tabu said you never kissed a whore. They didnt like it. Their kiss was private, like most women's bodies. It was a rooted Law, and she would not feel it, she would only see the broken Law and be angry at the liberty.

"I was joking," Lorene said apologetically.

She turned on the light then, suddenly showing all of it, baring it to the sight: the thin mattressed bed, the stand in the corner that is just as important here as the broom is in the factory because the assembly line must above all always be kept clean or there might be a breakdown in production. He stood looking at it, time honored by tradition like the memorials to dead veterans that are always the same the cannon on the courthouse lawn whether its the Civil War or the World War or this coming war or any future war and you always knew why they were there *By their Cannon Ye shall know Them* on the courthouse lawn, and he almost felt like he was coming home.

"I have to ask you for the money," Lorene said awkwardly.

"Oh. Sure," he said. "I forgotten it." He got his wallet out and gave her Stark's fifteen dollars. Not even your fifteen dollars, he thought, this time.

She tried to hide her awkwardness that surprised her, by getting a couple of cheap quilts out of the high cupboard and tossing them on the bed.

"There. Minerva's Corps only fixes the beds for the transient trade. But we'll need covers," she said gayly, but it was a false attempt that could not be distilled off of her awkwardness and Prew's granite face that could not smile just now, the Great Stone Face, somebody wrote a story about the Great Stone Face.

"All right," she said.

"Oh," he said. "Okay. Sure."

"I wasnt hurrying you. I thought you didnt hear," she said, noticing curiously how he was not awkward at all getting out of his clothes, which was the time when even the hardest of them were always awkward. But he was not awkward. He was not hard. He just did not even seem to be there, and she felt her bowels stir suddenly.

It was, he thought, like water which, when dammed, creates a pressure, a pressure of power that will pour out flooding, from any little channel it can find, from any little opening, flooding forth roaring with a long dammed slowly risen energy of pressure that obliterates the earths and moons and stars and suns, subsiding finally into a ridiculous little trickle that will not even roll a pebble, and you wonder foolishly how this thin trickle ever could have generated power and maybe it was all in your own imagination and your eyelids did not really crumble away the firmament into the one single Sun, the one undying Principle. That, he thought, was what its like.

They lay side by side, not touching, in the bed under the two separate quilts and the window was wide open on the night outside and they heard footsteps sound heavily far off like a cop and a streetcar screeked into action against time and somewhere a bus hissed its air brakes menacingly at them. They did not talk because knowing she did not care one way or the other, to talk or not, he did not want to talk, he did not even want to think, of anything but this that had just gone away and he looked out under the crack below the lowered blind at the roofs across the street and wondered dimly if Angelo was in the middle room and if he had the bottle or Stark had it and whether he should get up and put his pants on and see if he could find it because, very badly, he wanted a drink now.

He did not know exactly how long, it seemed a very short time, it

234

also seemed a very long time, before there was a light knock on the door and without waiting the door opened a little and Angelo Maggio's grinning head (preceded by a naked disembodied arm whose hand had a deathgrip around the neck of a long brown bottle) appeared, and Prew noticed, somewhat absurdly, that Lorene jerked the covers up over her breasts and clutched them daintily about her shoulders.

"I dint hear no sounds of combat," Angelo's head grinned. "So I figured you are taking ten."

"Restin," Prew said.

"I brung you a drink. Or otherwise old Longlegged Sandra would of drank it all by herself clear up. She's a good girl," he said, "a fine girl. But she drinks like a fish. Is it all right I can come in?"

"Sure, come ahead," Prew said. "I been needin a drink."

"Are you sure you decent? You wont embarrass me?"

"Quit clowning and bring the bottle."

Angelo was barefooted, his narrow pigeon breasted shoulders fully exposed, wearing nothing but the civilian slacks that he had bought secondhand from somebody in the Company and that were so much too big for him that his other hand had to clutch them around the scrawny waist to keep them up. He sat down on the bed beside them grinning happily like an amateur conspirator and handed Prew the bottle.

"Thanks," Prew said dryly, finding himself grinning, as he always found himself grinning, whenever little Angelo showed up someplace. "You want a drink?" he asked Lorene.

"No thanks."

"Whats a matter?" Angelo said. "Dont you drink?"

"Not much. And never straight whiskey."

"You dont?" Prew said.

"No," Lorene said. "Oh, I drink a cocktail, or a bottle of beer. But I dont drink. Why? Is there any Law that says every whore must be a drunkard?"

"No," Angelo said. "But most of them are, I guess."

"Well, I'm not. I think it is a weakness."

"I grant you that," Angelo said.

"And I dont like weakness. Do you?" she asked Prew.

"No," Prew said. "I don't like weakness. But I like to drink."

"With you its not a weakness," Lorene said. "With you its more like a virtue, somehow."

"I dont get that," Angelo said. "That beats me."

"I dont get it either," Lorene said. "Still, I feel it somehow." Still holding the quilt tight up around her shoulders she turned her head and smiled at Prew. Then she wiggled her body, it hidden by the quilt, over toward the center of the bed, over toward Prew, to give Angelo more room at the edge, and smiled up at him again, snugly.

235

"There are some people," she said, smiling at him, "whose weaknesses seem to be strength, instead of weakness."

"That is a very profound remark," Angelo said. "Maybe thats why I still dont get it."

"Well its so," Lorene smiled contentedly.

"Hey!" Angelo protested. "What are you gonna do, marry this guy? Way you grinnin at him you look like his wife."

"Do I?" Lorene said. She smiled up at Prew and suddenly, momentarily, it came into both their faces looking at each other that this was just as if she were his wife, his private possession, and as if this bed were their home that an outsider, a much beloved friend but still outsider, had invaded friendlily, the Third Person, another man who did not know her, all of her, as he knew her and whom she did not want to know her as he knew her, and who because of this enhanced this privacy of intimacy.

Prew put his hand out on the shapeless mound of quilt underneath which was the solid, curved, deep-flesh quiveriness of her hip, that he felt suddenly and momentarily truly belonged to him and she seemed to purr silently under his fingers and for the first time he considered with shock the possibility that sleeping with her had not made arise at all, the startling possibility that he was in love with her.

What a possibility, he thought; man, man, what a possibility. But then why not? In this place, on this Rock, who else is it possible for a soldier to fall in love with, except a whore? This Rock, where the white girls, even the middle class white girls, were all little snobs and where there were no white girls below the middle class. This Rock, where even with the gook girls that were the lowest class it was a disgrace to be seen talking to a soldier. So then why not a whore? It was not only possible, it was perfectly logical. Maybe it was even sensible.

And it was a possibility he was to remember all his life and wonder about often, after that. Whether this was just a sudden fleeting appreciation that just happened to hit them both because Angelo came in the room just when he did. Whether it would have happened some other way than this if Angelo had not come in, or maybe not happened at all. Whether it was just that he had not had a woman for so long that this momentary thing had sunk a hook for permanent illusion into him when he was off guard and snared him with an imaginative wishful-thinking of his own creation. Whether maybe, strangest possibility of all, it was that love between a man and a woman happened to them all this way, was born full-grown from the copulation of a chance situation with a meaningless coincidence. It seemed the original possibility opened up a lot of other possibilities, and if during the rest of his life before he died he could have ever resolved that original possibility he felt he could have understood many things.

"You people look happy," Angelo said, sensing it himself. "Are you people happy? I'm happy. Do I look happy?"

"Happy as can be expected," Lorene smiled, answering both at once, and Prew felt her hand under the quilt creep to him and then the fine-boned, woman's fingers resting on the inside of his thigh.

"Watch that!" Angelo grinned. "I seen you. Well for Christ's sake, look at her, Prew. She's blushing."

Lorene, blushing, turned to Prew and winked and he found her fingers with his own hand secretly and pressed them into him hard.

"If you want any more of this whiskey, buddy," Angelo said, "you better get it now. Because it wont be there long, once old Sandra gets aholt of it again."

"Stark had his share yet?"

"Stark aint getting any share," Angelo said. "I went down to his room before I come here. I listened at the door and couldnt hear a sound, and knocked and couldnt raise a soul, and looked through the keyhole and couldnt see a thing. (I think there was a shirt hung on the knob, by God.) I even climbed up on the doorknob to look through the transom to see if he had died and the son of a bitch had hung a towel over it. I call that plain goddam bad manners."

"What you mean is," Prew grinned, "you think he's a suspicious bastard."

"Yeah," Angelo said. "As if anybody would look through his goddam old transom."

He frowned at them so indignantly so long that Lorene giggled and finally had to laugh out loud.

"Well," he said, getting up, "I'm a kind of guy can tell when he's overstayed his welcome. I can tell when I aint wanted. I leave you people to your lovin."

"Aw, stick around," Prew grinned. "Please dont rush off."

"Yas," Angelo said, "I like you too, you bastard. I will just leave you some of this whiskey and then I wont feel so guilty. I put it in a glass and you can drink it at your leisure."

He wandered around, finally finding a tumbler on the stand, one that was full of water that he threw in a solid stream out the window where it hit the screen and sprayed, him saying, *"I hope theres a cop under that,"* and filled the glass full of whiskey from the bottle. Prew watched him grinning, and feeling ridiculously warm inside, almost fatherly, noticing how the whiskey had slowed Angelo's normally high agitation down until he seemed to be moving vaguely slowly like a slow motion film, and how this was the first time he had ever seen the tiny, curly headed Wop relaxed.

"That be enough?" Angelo said.

"Hell, yes. I drink all that I'll be about as much use as a melted candle."

"Okay. I see you then. See you in the morning. We go somewhere," he said, "the three of us, and eat a good expensive breakfast before we go back. Maybe we go to the Alexander Young Hotel, 'ey? They open up early and they serve good breakfasts. Breakfast is important," he said, "after a good night on the town. Okay?"

"Okay," Prew grinned. "I'll see you."

"You like him," Lorene said, after Angelo had closed the door, "don't you? You like him a lot."

"Yes," he said, "I do. He's such a comical little bastard, and yet somehow he makes me always want to cry while I'm laughin at him; and thats why I really like him. I dont know, maybe I'm nuts. Did you ever feel that way about people?"

"Yes," Lorene said. "Often."

"Well, thats *some*thing," he said.

"I feel it about Angelo," she said, "every time I see him. And I think maybe I feel it about you."

"Me!"

"Yes. You know," she said faintly, "you're a funny one, a very funny one."

"One fonny fellow," Prew said. "Am I?"

"Yes you are."

"Arent other fellows funny?"

"Not like you. Not the way you are."

"Well thats good. Maybe you'll remember me then."

"I'll remember you."

"Will you? Will you remember me tomorrow?"

"Yes. Next week, too."

"Will you remember me a month from now?"

"Yes."

"I dont believe it."

"But I will though. Truly I will."

"All right. I believe you. I know I'll remember you."

"Why?"

"Because."

"But why? Why will you remember me?"

"Because," he said, "because of this." And smiling, he took a corner of her quilt and flipped it off her and looked at her lying there.

She did not move and turned her head to smile at him. "Is that the only reason?"

"No. Also because you touched me when Angelo was here."

"Is that all?"

"Maybe not all. But a lot."

"But not because of talking to me?"

"Yes, that too. Definitely that too. But this also," he said looking at her.

"But the talking too?"

"Yes. The talking too. Talking is important."

"To me it is." She smiled contentedly at him and took a corner of his quilt that he was still lying under propped up on one elbow looking down at her and flipped it off of him, like he had done to her.

"Why, look at you," she said.

"I know. Aint it shameful?"

"I wonder what caused that."

"Cant help it. Does it every time."

"We really ought to change that."

He laughed and suddenly they were talking, bed talking, as they had not been at all before. And this time it was different.

Afterwards, grateful, he bent his head down for her lips.

"No," Lorene said. "Dont do that. Please dont."

"But why? Why not?"

"Because I'd rather you wouldnt. Because it would spoil it, and I dont want to spoil it."

"All right," he said. "I'm sorry."

"Dont be sorry. Its all right. But you must remember where we are. You must remember who I am."

"To hell with that. I dont care about that."

"But I care about it. It would make it like all the others, all the drunks, all the brutal ones. All of them, they all try to kiss you, as if in that way they could get something that all the rest dont get."

"Yes," Prew said. "Yes, I guess thats right. I guess thats what they want, isn't it? I'm sorry."

"Theres nothing to be sorry for," Lorene said. "Its just I didnt want it spoiled. Not now. You'd better move now," she said. "Move."

She stood up, finished, and smiled across at him. "Prew," she said, "little Prew boy, who is such a funny one. I'm sorry about when you wanted to kiss me, little Prew boy."

"Its all right."

"No, its not. But I cant help it. Its not you, its because of—this place. And of the others. You dont understand."

"I understand it."

"How could you? never having been a woman?"

She washed her hands, thoroughly and carefully, and came back then and got in the bed and turned off the light. "Sleep a little?" she said.

"Yes," he said in the darkness. "Do you go to the beach often?"

"Beach? What beach?"

"Waikiki Beach. Where Bill The Surfboard Rider struts his stuff."

"Oh, there. Yes, all the time. Every day if I can make it. I love it. Why?"

"I've never seen you out there."

"You wouldnt know me if you saw me."

"Maybe I would."

"No. You wouldnt."

"I think I would now."

"No, you wouldnt. I have to wear a banana leaf hat, and a beach jacket, and wrap my legs with a towel or else wear slacks. To keep from getting tanned. You'd think I was an old, old tourist woman, if you saw me."

"I was wondering how to go about lookin for you, away from here. I'll know what to look for now, when I go out."

"No. Please dont do that. Really."

"Why not?"

"Because. Because its just bad policy, thats all, very bad. Thats why."

"But I dont see why."

"Because I say so," Lorene said sharply, sitting up. "Because if you ever do that, I'll never have another thing to do with you, ever."

"You wouldnt?" he said, hearing the seriousness in her voice now, and not feeling serious nor wanting to argue, turning it aside by making what he had said seriously into a teasing of her. "You really wouldnt?"

"No I would not."

"But why?" he teased. "I could find you easy now, with that description. You'd stick out like a sore thumb, now."

"Well," Lorene said, mollified to see he was only teasing, "you had better never."

"But why not get tanned?" he said. "You would look good tanned." In his mind he could see her on the beach. He wondered where she lived. Sandra's avocation was Lau Yee Chai's, instead of the beach. He wondered where Sandra lived. "You would look fine tanned," he said. "I'd love you tanned."

"Would you want me to get fired?" Her voice was a smile now, in the darkness. "How many times have you been to a Honolulu whorehouse? That you dont know the girls are never tanned?"

"I guess I never noticed it." Where in the city, where on the island, in what unsuspected blank face houses, did they live, the army of them, these women that were the only women on the Rock, for all that we might know?

"If any of them had been tanned," she laughed, "you would have noticed it. They stick out more than sore thumbs, women with tanned arms and legs and stomachs and the rest of them still white. There is a standing house rule against tan, even the face." She paused. "It seems," she said, "that soldiers and sailors seem to like their whores to be pure and virginly white."

"Score!" he said. "You win that round. Just the same, I would like it though. On you." The only women for us anywhere, he thought, and here the only place to find them. If you saw them in the bars, or on the beach, or in the shops, you never recognized them, and if they recognized you they were wonderful at hiding it. Maybe I've even seen her before, in Waikiki, and did not know it. After they left the office, he thought, the business office, and went out to mingle with the city, then they just disappeared. Mingle is a good word, he thought sleepily. Mingle. Mingle. I think I need a drink.

The tumbler was still where Angelo had left it, untouched, and he made himself get up in the dark and hunt around till he found it. Old Doctor Maggio's magic sleeping potion, he thought and drunk half of it and carried it back to the bed and set it on the floor where he could reach it. It did not last him long, but neither did it warm or fill the hollowness that he poured it into.

"I would like to look at the stark white skin," he said to her, "against the deep brown tan. Then I would think about how on the beach the white was all covered up and hidden, so no one could see it, and of how I was going to look at what no one else got to look at."

"You *are* a funny one, little Prew boy."

"You said that before."

"And I say it again. You are a funny one, a very funny one, that I cannot figure out."

"I guess I'm easy to figure out, if you got the key."

"Not to me. I guess I dont have the key."

"No," he said, sleepily. "You aint got it. And that seems to impress you a lot."

"It does. Things I cant figure out make me curious. I like to have things all figured out. One, two, three. In the same way that I had this all figured out before I ever came here."

"Yes," he said, and he noticed that her voice was beginning to come loud, then faint, from across the curtain of the sleepiness. Maybe I'm asleep already, he thought, maybe I'm dreaming. "You said that same thing earlier tonight," he said, "and it struck me. But you aint explained it to me yet. Tell me, how did you ever come to get into this racket?"

"I am a volunteer," Lorene said, and he noticed there was no trace of sleepiness in her voice.

"Maybe you think," she said, "that all whores are virgins who were kidnapped by Lucky Luciano, and raped, and then farmed out. Maybe you think," the voice said, "that all whores are inducted. Well they're not. Lots of them enlist. Some because they just like the life, and dont mind doing what they have to do to get the rest of it. Others because they are bitter against some man who took their cherry and maybe knocked them up and then left them, and now they are getting even in some funny way, or else just dont give a damn, any more.

"Oh," said the voice, "there are lots of us who have enlisted."

"And lots who re-enlist," Prew said. "Lots who end up thirty year men."

"Not necessarily. There are some, but not nearly as many as you think. Lots of them, like me, figure it all out beforehand. Get in for one hitch and clean up and then get out. Lots of them do that."

"Is that what you aim to do?"

"You dont think I mean to do this all my life? For fun? In another year I'll be back home, with a pile of bills big enough to choke a steer. And then I will be all set, for life."

"But what about home?" he asked the voice, sleepily, wonderingly, not sure yet that this was a dream he dreamed and had not really heard at all. "What will the people back home say?"

"They will say nothing. Because they will know nothing. In my hometown, where my mother still lives—on the money that I send her —I am a private secretary to a big, big shot in the Hawaii sugar trade. I am a hometown waitress who went to night school and developed herself and became a private secretary who is saving her money to come home and take care of her poor invalided mother."

"But what if you get caught?" he asked this dream.

"How can I get caught? In the little town in Oregon where I come from nobody but the very rich even venture out as far as Seattle. When I come home wearing all my demure conservative private secretary's clothes and retire, on the modest 'nestegg' I will have, who is to doubt I am and was just what I say I am?"

"Nobody, I guess. But why? How did you ever get hold of the idea?"

"I had a boyfriend," the apparition said. "I was a waitress, working in the local chain drugstore. He was from one of the richest families in town. Old story, with no new twists. I didnt get knocked up, nothing like that. He just married the girl his parents thought was suitable for his position, after two years of sleeping with me."

"Too bad," he murmured to it. Was that the whiskey that was loosening him up so, all through his arms and legs? "Too bad. Rotten."

"It does make a pretty story, doesnt it?" the voice smiled. "Maybe they could make a movie from it."

"They did," he said. "Ten thousand of them."

"But not with the ending this one has. This one does not end with the heroine still devoted, with the heroine going to work for them as maid in their new home, taking care of their children for them, just to be near her beloved, like was in this lovely movie, *The Hollow of Intention.*"

"No," he said. "Life aint like that, not very often. Not at all in the sections of life I've seen."

"Nor in any other sections of it. No it certainly is not. I left town after the marriage and went to Seattle, as a waitress. There was a bigtime pimp use to come in the store, all the girls pointed him out to me. It wasnt very hard to interest him into making a pass, the hard part was in letting him lay me and making him think I liked it. So that I could work him then, when he thought I loved him, into doing what he meant to do all along. Only, I fixed it so I got sent here, instead of Panama or Mexico; because he loved me, you see, and I loved him. He didnt know that every night after he left my place I'd get up and go and puke my guts out."

"Lorene," he said, "Lorene," and he was not sure if he was dreaming this, or saying it out loud. "You've got a lot of guts, Lorene. *I'm* proud of you, Lorene. I understand you now, Lorene, and I am proud of you, no matter what any other bastard says."

"Guts," the voice said. "Guts are nothing. Guts are only good for what you can make them bring you."

"You sound hard, Lorene."

"If prestige, position, money are what the good men need from their wives, why I will get them. The only way they can be got. With money.

"And after I go home with a stocking full of bills, after I build the new home for my mother and myself, after I join the Country Club and take up golf, get in the most acceptable bridge club, read them a book report on *The Hollow of Intention* for the Tuesday Literary Club —then the proper man with the proper position will find me as a proper wife who can keep a proper home and raise the proper children, and I will marry him. And I will be happy."

"Lorene," he dreamed, "I hope you pull it off. By god, I hope you do."

"Theres nothing to pull off. Its all there. One, two, three. In black and white. In my town there are many who have done this, except that they were amateur whores, 'mistresses,' instead of professionals.

"And then," the voice said softly, "with it all arranged and running like a well oiled clock, the other will fade out and die and be only the memory of one of those dreams you dream, and are always afraid will happen to you in real life, but that never do. Because when you are proper, you are safe."

"Lorene," he dreamed, "Lorene. Lorene, I think that I love you, Lorene. You've got guts and beauty and, Lorene, I think thats why I love you, Lorene."

"You're drunk," said the voice. "How could a man love a whore? that he met for the first time in a whorehouse? You're drunk and you had better go to sleep."

"Thats what I thought you'd say," he grinned slyly at the apparition, at the dream. "I knew you'd say that."

"How did you know?" the voice said.

"I just knew," he said. "I know you, Lorene. But will he love you, Lorene, this rich guy? Will he love you like I think I do?"

"You dont love me," the sleepiness around him said. "You're drunk. And he wont be rich."

"But he'll have prestige, position, money, all the things you said, all the things us fucking joes wont never have. But I dont think he'll love you much, Lorene. I just dont think he will, somehow."

"He will never know that I was a whore. There is no way in God's world he could ever find it out."

"It wasnt that I mean, Lorene."

"And for the rest—I'll make him love me. Because by then, I really should know how."

"No. No one ever has it all, Lorene. Some that are lucky are allowed to choose, but even then its not a choice. But no one ever has it all, somehow. Theres not even any use to ask for it, or even fight for it. Dont ever expect it either, Lorene. He will never love you, Lorene, this rich guy. Your mind, Lorene, being what it is, aint goin to let him love you. Thats the part you'll never have, thats the part you'll have to pay. No one ever has it all, and what you get from life at all you pay him dearly for, by giving up what you really wanted more, but never knew it, never realized, until after he high pressured you to sign."

"Its time you went to sleep," the voice said soothingly.

"I know: Because I'm drunk. But its when I'm drunk, Lorene, that I can see the things I cant remember and cant see, when I'm sober. I'm drunk and dreaming, but oh, Lorene, I can see the Truth so plain. I can almost reach out and touch it."

Then, it seemed, the long pale dream gowned in the filmy flowing stuff that did not cover up the nipples or the swelling black triangle that he loved to look at reached down to him the plate with the golden bugle on it and the other plate in the other hand with the two cans of C Ration Meat & Beans, and bent over him and kissed him on the lips because he had chosen the wrong one and the cloudy heavens fell.

"Now go to sleep."

"Why did you kiss me? You think I'm drunk, and that I wont remember. But I'll remember. And I'll come back."

"Shush. Shush. Of course you'll come back."

"You think I wont. But I will. I'll be back. I'll always be back."

"Of course you will, I know you will."

"I'll be back Payday Night."

"And I'll be looking for you."

"And I'll remember everything I saw tonight and explain it to you then. I saw it all so clear, so plain, I know that I'll remember. Dont you think I will remember?"

"Of course you will remember."

"I must remember. Its important. Dont go away, Lorene. Stay here."

"I'll stay right here. You go to sleep now."

"All right," he said, "all right, Lorene."

Chapter 18

He did remember. He had been very drunk and very dreamy, but he remembered. All during the time the three heavily hung-over soldiers, looking very chastened but with their faces newly clean of pressure, meekly ate their breakfast in the rich man's mirror encrusted dining-room of the Alexander Young Hotel in downtown Honolulu and then after the waffles and fried eggs and ham and bacon and much coffee, all of a fortifying excellence, walked across town through the deserted dew-fresh city streets of early morning to the Army-Navy Y to catch a cab back and be late for Reveille—all during this he was remembering. All during the thirty-five mile cab trip back he was remembering.

His head felt very big and very soft to the touch and it was hard to separate the dream of last night from the reality. But he could remember distinctly that she kissed him, on the mouth. Whores do not kiss soldiers on the mouth, neither do they tell them their life story. But he could remember all the details of her story, and how when she was caught up in the telling of it the carefully educated accent and the meticulous serenity, both probably very painfully acquired, had dropped off of her revealing the real Lorene. A hard Lorene, a cold and brilliant, like a diamond; but real, very real, and alive. This was what clinched it for him. He had gotten under her shell, as men very seldom get under women's shells, as soldiers never get under whores' shells, and he was going back payday night, if he had to steal the money, because, he thought, in this world, any more, with things like they are, the hardest of all hard things was to know the real from the illusion, to meet one other human being breath to breath without the prefabricated sound-proofed walls of modern sanitation always in between and know in meeting that this was this human and not this human's momentary role; in this world that was the hardest, because in this world, he thought, each bee out of his own thorax makes the wax for his own cell, to protect his own private stock of honey, but I have broken through, just once, this one time only. Or, at least, he thought, I think I have.

In fact, thinking back about it, the only thing about it all that he could not remember was the old familiar drunken revelation, the moment when he had reached out and grasped the whole of all truth and compressed it into a single sentence that was one single cure-all capsule, easy to swallow, painless to take. Of that all he could remember was that he had done it. He could not remember the sentence. But then, he thought, surely you do not expect to remember that, all your life you have been not remembering that, you should be used to that.

They pulled in home (after taking the precaution to walk the last two blocks, just in case Holmes or The Warden might be watching for them) just as the Company was going upstairs after breakfast. He was a little worried and Angelo was very worried, once they were back inside the half-forgotten confines of the Post, but Stark who did not have to stand Reveille formation was not worried at all, and not above razzing them a little.

But worrying at all was needless, this time they were lucky. Chief Choate, still their Corporal, was waiting for them on the porch. Neither Holmes nor The Warden nor S/Sgt Dhom had taken Reveille this morning, the Chief said, 2nd Lt Culpepper had taken it, and the Chief was able to report his squad all present and get by with it, since Sergeant Platoon Guide Galovitch was as stupid as he was zealous, but goddam them, where had they been.

Feeling very lucky, they both rushed upstairs, like runners who are safe on a steal at second and then get ready to steal third, and changed from their civilians straight into fatigues.

Chief Choate, his deadpan Indian stolidity showing plainly by its walnut blankness that he had not said all there was to say, patiently followed them upstairs, bloodshot-eyed but placid after his customary hard night at Choy's.

"The uniform's been changed," he told them ponderously. "Sidearms and leggins."

"Jesus whynt you tell us?" Maggio, who had thought he was all dressed, said angrily.

"Aint had a chanct," the Chief said. "Up to now."

"We better hurry," Maggio said, and sprinted for his wall locker.

Prew was looking at the Chief's moon face which revealed nothing of the startling implications of the order. "Why, that means we drill outside."

"You guessed it right. They changed the Drill Schedule early this mornin. Looks like the rainy season's over. You better get your leggins on."

Prew nodded and went to his wall locker and Chief Choate lit a cigaret and stared at the knotting string of rising smoke and waited patiently for them to come back.

"Old Ike," he said, "is been snoopin all over hell, since before breakfast, lookin for you. I tole him you run over to the PX for a pack of butts."

"Thanks, Chief," Prew said.

"Thanks nothing," the Chief said. "Thanks hell."

Angelo was feverishly finishing up his first leggin, half hitching the string end. "I always know this guy was chickenshit," he grinned.

The Chief looked at him stolidly. "This is no twobit ass eating, kid. This here is serious. Or maybe you dint hear me? When I said Drill moves outside?"

"No, I dint," Angelo said.

The Chief ignored him. "The word's gone out already," he said to Prew. "From now on its no holts barred. They goin to have practicly a free hand with you, in the field."

Prew slipped his toe in through the leggin strap and worked it back, not saying anything. There was nothing to say. He had known for a long time it was coming, but he had not expected it to come. It was like with dying.

"Another stunt like missin Reveille," the Chief said, "and you gone. I went out on a limb for you this morning. I wont do it again."

"I wouldnt expect you to," Prew said. "Not now."

"I cant afford to," the Chief said, placidly, factually, no guilt in his face or voice. "Maybe you think I let you down, because you and me been friends."

"No."

"I'm lettin you know now where I stand, so you wont think I double-crossed you if I got to turn you in."

"Okay. I got it."

"I got pull with the Colonel," the Chief explained factually, "but I aint got that much pull. I help you out along, what little bit I can, but no more goin out on limbs. I lucky to keep what I got and I aint goin to jeopardize it. I like this outfit."

"So do I," Prew said. "Thats funny aint it?"

"Yes," the Chief said. "Very funny. Ha, ha. Ho, ho."

"Big joke," Prew said. "On me."

"You buckin a big organization, when you buck the fighters in this outfit. They run this outfit. They maybe damn near run the Regmint. And they mean to see you go out for fightin, if they got to wear you down to a flyweight to do it."

"Tell me somethin I dont know."

"Okay. I thought you want the tip. But you tough. You a hard man. They cant touch you." He made as if to get up.

"Wait," Prew said. "Not as long as I keep within the ARs, within the Law, I dont see how they can. As long as I dont break no Laws."

"Maybe not. But they want that Division Championship next winter bad, Dynamite wants it bad."

"I dont see what he can do, long as I break no Laws."

"Dont kid me," the Chief said, "dont snow me. You no ree-croot. You been in quite a while. I guess you aint never seen a bunch get together and give a man The Treatment."

"I've heard about it."

"Whats The Treatment?" Maggio wanted to know.

The Chief ignored him. "Maybe they aint got it developed to a science, like the boys have at The Point, or VMI, or KMI, or Culver," he said to Prew, "but its effective. Theres nothin in this world will bring a man into line quicker. Or else kill him. I seen it just once, in PI. The guy deserted, went back in the hills and married a Moro. When they caught him he got twelve years. He ended up a federal lifer."

"I'm too smart for that," Prew grinned. "And I dont kill easy, Chief," he added, grinning stiffly, feeling the stiffness spreading clear up to his forehead like slow setting plaster, drawing these lips back tight on these teeth and cutting gashes in under these cheekbones, not him doing it, the stiffness doing it, as it always did this stiffness that came over him, over his face, in the ring when a man was trying to hit him, in a drunken brawl when a man drew a knife on him, any time there was fight, any time there was threat, always when there was this word, this kill word, which was the rottenest, foulest stinking word there was, but which some men used so freely and so proudly.

Chief Choate just looked at him stolidly, untouched, but Maggio who was watching him too was touched. Something like Humphrey Bogart, Maggio thought, something like a skull, more like a skull, a lipless cheekless deathshead skull.

"I can take everything they hand out," Prew grinned, "and ask for more."

"Yas," Maggio said, "and me too."

"Do you want a busted head, kid?" Chief Choate asked him seriously.

"No," Maggio said.

"Then keep your big yap shut. This is serious. And if you smart, you keep your big nose out altogether. This is his fight. You ony make it worse on him by gettin in."

"Thats right, Angelo," Prew grinned, feeling the stiffness soften as he looked at the furious narrowshouldered little Wop.

"I hate to see somebody get screwed," Maggio said.

"Then you might as well get use to it," the Chief said. "You probly be seein it often before you die.

"I don't see why you want to do it," he said to Prew. "You ony makin it hard on yourself. But thats your business, its none of my affair. I hate to see you fuck up, is all."

"You refused to fight for Dynamite yourself, once."

"Yas, but with me I knew what was the story. I had enough pull in Regmint I could make it stick. You cant."

"Maybe not. We'll see. I aint never refused a order yet, when its official duty. But I dont think they got the right to order me what to do outside of duty hours."

"It aint a question of right or wrong, its a question of fack. But there is awys been a question if there is any outside duty hours for a soljer, whether the *soljer* has the right to be a man."

"And its gettin more and more that way lately, in this world all over."

"And not ony in the Army," Maggio put in, and Prew could see that Angelo was remembering Gimbel's Basement.

"Thats right," Chief Choate said. "And so what?"

"So this duty stuff is okay, maybe," Maggio said, "for wartime. In wartime a soljer's awys under orders. But not in peacetime."

"Been wartime," Chief Choate said, "ever since I enlisted. And thats thirteen years ago. For an army, its awys wartime."

"Thats right," Prew said. "There aint no peacetime army. But what I dont believe, is that the Regimental Boxing Squad, or fighting for the Regimental Boxing Squad, is essential to the perpetual war effort."

"You ast Dynamite what he thinks," the Chief said, "and see what he says."

"Hell," Angelo Maggio said. "Thats no problem, Mr Anthony. Dynamite's so full of West Point propaganda it runs out of his ears an leaves a yellow stream behind him."

"Maybe," the Chief said, "but he's the Compny Commander."

From out in the quad the guard bugle sounded Drill Call imperatively and Chief Choate got up from the bunk, looking at Prew blankly searchingly.

"Well," he said. "Well, I see you."

"In the Stockade," Prew grinned, and watched the big man dog-trotting lumberingly graceful down the aisle to his end bunk, to get his equipment on. Then he picked up the bayonet scabbard he had forgotten and worked a hook into the wide length of cartridge belt under the old third pocket.

"Nice homecoming gift," he said.

"To hell with them," Angelo Maggio said. "All of them. They cant do nothing. What can they do?"

"Sure," Prew said and hooked in the other hook and shook them down into the belt, watching the Chief buckling into field training harness, the bayonet that became a toothpick when it hung on him, the light pack that looked like a matchbox on his back, the big hefty Springfield '03 like a Woolworth imitation of itself for small boys when the big fist picked it up.

"Him too," Angelo said. "A fine pal."

"No, he's all right." When times changed, you accepted it. The days of Jeb Stuart and the plumed hats and the highwayman came riding riding up to the old inn door; that was the Civil War, that wasnt now. The days when the Emperor was nourished through hardship and the long walk home from Moscow by the full hearted devotion of the Old Guard and the Young Guard who still loved him in defeat, that wasnt now either but even earlier, they didnt have gas warfare then, why, they didnt even kill the enemy, in those days, if they could help it. Times change is all, or maybe those were only stories, maybe only dreamed up afterwards, because they would have liked it to have happened that way. "Just because he use to eat breakfast with me in Choy's, does that make him owe me something? The Chief's a damned good man."

"Sure," Angelo said. "So was Pilate."

"Oh, balls. Can it, will you? You dont understand it. Stick to things you understand."

"Okay," Angelo said and stuffed his cigaret pack and book of matches into a cartridge pocket. "We'll need these. Jesus, my head. And that goddam Stark layin out down in the cooks' room sleepin up a fog. We better be gettin outside?"

The guard bugle in the quad sounding the repeat answered him and from downstairs S/Sgt Dhom's big voice boomed up through the screens, sounding very like a soldier.

"All right, up there, you men. Outside for drill. Everybody outside. Lets jerk that lead. Outside. Drill Call."

"Lets go, my squad," Chief Choate bellowed. "Grab your hats and grab your bats, this war is on." He lumbered gracefully light footed down the stairs singing Drill Call in a natural basso that carried far, *"Fall out for drill, like hell I will, I aint had no chow. I said Fall out for drill, you bet I will, the compny commander's here now."*

"But he can sing," Angelo said grudgingly.

All over the big squadroom men were moving, picking up their rifles and heading for the stairs.

"Well. Lets cut this cake," Prew said, picking up the long wood, clean steel, solidness of his own.

From the third floor porch he could look down out over all of it, the whole ritual of drill call, the first drill call after the rainy season. He stopped to watch it. Angelo stopped too, waiting for him, indifferent to the picture.

It was a good picture though, a soldiering picture, like the *Pall Mall* ad (*they pronounce that Pell Mell, dont they, like the bloody English peerage, I like Pall Mall better though, its American, even if it aint highclass*) that he still had scotch-taped to the inside of his footlocker top, a fine picture, if you were a thirty year man. The quadrangle was alive with men in blue fatigues and the khaki almost faded white of belts and leggins and the sharp-brimmed olive drab campaign hats, pouring out the walks and lining up in their companies, very soldierly, the kind of soldierly that wins a war, he thought proudly, any war, but all those other companies were remote, even the bugle corps was remote he noticed, all faceless figures and remote, a background for our Company, where every face was a face he knew so that the sameness of uniform did not matter, even enhanced the individuality of the faces, each face with its special orbit that revolved around the central sun of Captain Holmes (*dead star,* he thought, *but then maybe The Warden is our sun*), asteroid faces, not big enough for a private orbit, too small to be classed as planets (*like Dhom, or Champ Wilson, or Pop Karelsen, or Turp Thornhill, Jim O'Hayer, Isaac Bloom, Niccolo Leva* –good names, he thought, good old American names—*or like the new man Mallaux who was a coming featherweight, or Old Ike Galovitch—was Ike a planet? Ike was more like a third rate moon*).

Looking down through the screens he could see the asteroid face of Readall Treadwell, that was one of them, Readall Treadwell (christened "Fatstuff" but who was no more fat than Man Mountain Dean was fat) who could hardly read any, let alone read all, but whose solid endurance at carting around the BAR he never got to fire was almost legend. He could see Crandell "Dusty" Rhodes (christened "The Scholar") whose scholarship consisted solely of always turning up with a genuine diamond ring or a real honest-to-God antique Roman coin he was willing to let go to *you* because you were a friend. He could see "Bull" Nair (alias "The Stud").

These were all part of it, he felt, looking down; important parts, as small memories are important parts of the life of a man, parts of your chosen heritage, even of your destiny maybe, small functioning parts of this tiny solar system that is the company that is lost among the galaxies of regiments that make up this universe that is the Army, the parts that give meaning to the only universe you know, he thought, the only universe you want, because it is the only one you ever found a place in yet. And now you are rapidly losing that.

"Come on, Angelo," he said, watching the knot of noncoms clustered around the bald headed, sandhog shouldered Dhom who towered over Chief Choate even, "we better get our asses down there."

"Man, you look sick," Angelo said as they fell in with the 1st Platoon.

"Not sick," Prew said, looking at him sideways under the hat brim low over his eyes. "Just hung over." But it was not the head, he thought, be honest, you've fallen out for drill with bigger heads than this before and always laughed them off. Four hours drill under a hot sun with a head on was as much a part of soldiering as was musketry with a half pint hidden in your belt to help you shoot, or as were forced practice marches with a Listerine mouthwash bottle full of saki on your hip. Soldiering and drinking have always been blood brothers. But what, he thought, is soldiering?

The very, very odd thing was that all this that was costing him, in the Army, had not a thing to do with soldiering. There should be something important, there, he told himself. Reality, he thought. To know the real from the illusion. Man, man, I think you're off your nut, but he could not shake off this new sense of separateness.

The knot of noncoms on the green broke up, the giant Dhom going front and center and the others doubletiming back to their platoons. Standing out in front alone and looking very soldierly Dhom gave them right shoulder sounding very soldierly and the rifles moved and were smartly slapped in unison very satisfyingly soldierly, but even this did not free him from this agonizing separateness that was worse than any loneliness, this feeling that he knew a thing the others did not know.

They marched at attention out the northwest truck entrance and across the intersection where the well-bucked MP was directing the heavy early morning traffic and where they were given route step and somebody in the back began the ancient hallowed dialogue of the Infantry.

"Who won the War?"

"The MPs won it," came the answer.

"How'd they win it?"

"Why, their mothers and sisters laying for Liberty Bonds."

The tall, handsome, statuesque MP flushed deeply, and as they passed Post Theater #1 someone broke into the Regimental Song and the rest took it up, singing the words the regimental yearbook never printed.

> *"Oh, we wont come back to Wahoo any more.*
> *No, we wont come back to Wahoo any more.*
> *We will fuck your black kanaky,*
> *We will drink your goddamned saki,*
> *BUT we wont come back to Wahoo any more."*

And Chief Choate in his deep rich basso took his favorite line of the break alone.

"Kiss me, Charlie, theres some barley,
   Runnin down my leg."

And the voice of authority spoke through the brassy soldierly throat of S/Sgt Dhom.

"Can that, you men, or you can march at attention. Theys liable to be ladies present around here."

And this was soldiering, the column of marching men that was George Company moving on out Kolekole Pass Road toward drill between the rows of tall old elms that lined the road on either side exuding an abiding permanence, but Pvt Robert E Lee Prewitt was untouched, the old shiver was not in his spine, because the soldiering that once was the only real was now obviously the illusion, since the real lay somewhere hidden below its realistic camouflage.

Chapter 19

No officers appeared at drill all morning, even for the usual look-see. It developed into a sort of general Tell-Off-Prewitt field day with first one noncom then another carrying the ball. They gave him a good going over. He had not up to then believed that anything could hurt a man so much, without actually resorting to physical pain. He was, he realized, learning a considerable bit about pain lately.

In the first period Dhom, the calisthenics master (by virtue of being trainer to the boxing squad), read him off over a silent 36-count side straddle hop exercise and had him to do it again alone (as was customary with the awkward squad) while the Company rested. Prew, who had not miscounted a side straddle hop since getting out of recruit drill, did it, perfectly, and was asked to do it once again and this time try to get it right and then warned (as was customary with the awkward squad) to look alive or find himself on extra duty.

Prew knew Dhom, and had never much cared for him. It was Dhom who had once, during a Retreat formation, bulled his way into ranks like a bowling ball making a strike and punched a young recruit in the jaw for talking; he came near getting busted over that one, though never, of course, near enough to worry over. But on the other hand, it was also Dhom who last fall during the annual 30-mile hike had carried four extra rifles and a BAR the last 10 miles to bring G Company in one hundred percent present, the only company in the Regiment to make it. And also, it was Dhom whose perpetual henpecking by his greasy Filipino wife had become a company institution.

Back at the barracks, talking to The Chief, Prew had dismissed being hurt. Being hurt had not entered into it then. Harlan County boys are born with a facility for standing physical pain, if they live at all, and he was proud of his tested capacity, confident in the belief that they could doubletime him forever and work him till he dropped but they could never break that endurance that was the only thing his father had bequeathed him. He saw it as a simple battle of wills on a physical plane—which in a way it was. But it was also more than that, and this he had not seen. He had not seen that these men meant anything to him. Long ago, at Myer, when he first quit fighting to get in the Bugle Corps and saw how they all construed this to be lack of guts, he had had to reluctantly put aside his hope of ever being understood. This caused a certain loneliness but he accepted that because, he told himself, it was probably that in the first place that made him want to bugle. Then later, when they dropped him from the Bugle Corps because he got the clap and nobody of his many friends stepped forward to go to bat for him and try to get him reinstated, this had increased his loneliness, but it also hardened his invulnerability.

And now, being invulnerable since there was nothing left for them to hurt, he had been quite sure that these men meant nothing to him. What he had forgotten, of course, was that these men were men and, being men, could not help but mean something to him, who was also a man. What he had forgotten momentarily was that he was a man, and that these men were, in effect, the same men who had come silently out on the porches last night (only last night, it was) to listen to his Taps. These men were, in effect, the disembodied voice that had come across the quad from Choy's, the abstract spokesman for them all, saying proudly, "I told you it was Prewitt." How this could be, he did not know. He could see this was going to be a hard thing to understand. What he had forgotten entirely was that though he had matched them for his faith in comradeship and understanding and had lost, he still had his faith in men kicking around somewhere, and that this was where they could still reach him. It did not take the hurt long in getting started.

During the second period which was Old Ike's close order he was called down twice, first for missing a pivot on a column movement (during which at least the two men in front of him were also out of step), then second for fouling up on a triple rear march-right flanking movement (during which the entire company except for the first two ranks of four became a shambling mob eating its own dust and cursing). Both times Ike called him out of ranks indignantly and read him off, spraying Prew's shirt with a fine mist of old man's Slavic spit, and after the second reading off sent him with a noncom across the road to the chemical warfare's quarter-mile track to doubletime seven laps with his rifle at high port (as was customary with the awkward squad).

When he came back sweating heavily but silent, all the men of the jockstrap faction glared at him indignantly (as was customary with the awkward squad) while the men of the non-jockstrap faction did not look at him at all but intently studied the modernistic outlines of the new chem warfare barracks. Only Maggio threw him a grin. It was really very interesting.

In a close order drill the caliber of this one (for which Ike Galovitch was famous) being told off for such niceties of execution in the midst of so much fumbling was really laughable. So Prew laughed. The whole thing was quite a triumph of imagination over matter. The men slouched through Ike's close order without snap or smartness, the commands in Ike's perverted English seldom understandable and often given on the wrong foot, at least a third of them always out of step with Ike's uneven cadence. Ike, in commanding, seemed to fluctuate between a chaste uncertain modesty and a grotesque and Mussolini-ish rage of self-assurance. Neither of these was conducive to a snappy drill, and to any man who had ever soldiered it was not only agony, it was unbelievable, it was the ultimate prostitution of soldiering, the greatest sin ever perpetrated by a boiler-orderly.

For the third period they marched up toward the Packtrain to the big sloping field where the bridle path began, just above the golf course where they could watch several religious foursomes of officers (and a couple giggling atheistic threesomes of officers' wives) all playing their morning devotional round.

This field was the customary scene of a traditional lecture on cover and concealment given by Sgt Thornhill, during which lying on their bellies in the shade of the big oaks that lined the field the Company gave themselves over to the enchantments of mumblety-peg and the study of the bottoms of the officers' wives and daughters as they bounced around the field on saddles, and during which this morning Turp Thornhill, a long stringy ferret-headed jawless man from Mississippi with 17 yrs serv, who was not a jockstrap man, or even a non-jockstrap man, gave Prewitt a reading off for inattention. And sent him down with a noncom to the nearest track for seven more laps of the best, at high port.

It was at this time that Maggio's flare for sympathy cost him seven laps himself, when Ike Galovitch saw him make the holy mystic sign to Prew (the one where you close the fist, extend the middle finger, and jab the air) as Prew was leaving, and being incensed at this disrespect for discipline and justice, sent Maggio along this time too.

It went on. And still on. And then further on. First one noncom then another trying his skill, as if they were all bucking to become recruit instructors to the gook draftees that were beginning to come in now from the peacetime draft.

Even Champ Wilson, the lordly ring killer, the cold eyed, the always silent, the perpetually indifferent, condescended to give him a mechanical reading off during a dry-run trigger-squeeze firepower exercise, because, The Champ said, he was not distributing his fire properly.

Prew leaned on his rifle muzzle and listened to this one as he had listened to the other ones, the only thing you can do with a telling off, but now he was only half hearing what The Champ was saying. Because he was not there now. He was standing with The Champ but his mind was thinking of the problem. He could see it all in his mind, unfolding like a film run off the reel between the hands, each picture following the other logically and with a beginning at the one end and an ending at the other, one two three, right down the line.

The only trouble was you could not see the beginning now as it was lost in all the tangled swirls of celluloid on the floor, and you could not see the ending because it was still on the turning reel.

He remembered though that out of all of them the only noncoms who would not take their turn at booting this brand new ball around were Chief Choate and Old Pop Karelsen, both known openly as his friends. But even they had been offered plenty of chances. But like the non-jockstrap Pvts they preferred to stare uncomfortably off into the middle distance. Or watch the dazzling purity of the slow moving glaciers that were the fair weather cumulus cloud formations, white mountains high above dark mountains.

Well, what did you expect them to do, he thought, rise in mutiny and deliver you? You must surely realize you are not being forced into anything, dont you? You are doing all of this of your own free will, you know, he told himself. Yes sir, you are that, he thought, that you are.

Free will, he thought. There is free will. And then there is free love, dont forget free love. And then also there is free—let me see, free what? Free politics! Nope, not free politics. Well, free what then? Why, free beer, of course. Of course, free beer. Free will, free love, free beer.

But this now is free will. Your own free will, thats doing this. Not them thats doing this. They are merely offering your free will a free choice. Kindly but logically, seriously but without malice, a free choice for your free will.

1) You can go out for boxing. 2) You can not go out for boxing and you can blow up and fight back; in that case you go to the Stockade. 3) You can neither go out for boxing nor blow up and fight back; in which case you can continue to suffer indefinitely this unpleasantness that hurts you because you are sensitive and an artistic bugler, instead

of an artistic fighter which would have made it very simple. And, if you continue in this unpleasantness which you are free to choose and which is without malice, but which shows no promise of letting up, the logical sequence will be company punishment for inefficiency plus extra duty plus restrictions plus, eventually inevitably, the Stockade.

Now if we reduce these fractions we have on the one hand, go out for boxing; and, on the other hand, we have go out for the Stockade. Since you are an artistic bugler (instead of an artistic fighter, like The Champ here) we can cancel out the first. So, reducing still further, we have 1) go out for the Stockade; or, 2) go out for the Stockade. The choice is up to you, a rather restricted choice but nevertheless a choice, presented to your free will unemotionally logically without partisanship, and without personal malice or meanness of spirit.

He would, he thought, much have preferred that they hate him, that they band together in the sacred name of Home & Country and oppress him with the mace of Law & Order. As, say, the Nazis do the Jews, for instance. Or as the English do the Indians. Or as the Americans do the Negroes. Then he would have been a hated human, instead of an unhated number (# ASN 6915544, all present and accounted for). But then a man cant have everything.

You did not ever really believe they would do it to you, did you? No, you didnt. Because you know damn well you could never have done it to one of them, having suffered as you have from an overdeveloped sense of justice all your life, not to mention being a hotly fervent espouser of the cause of all underdogs all your life (probably because you have always been one, I imagine).

But he had always believed in fighting for the underdog, against the top dog. He had learned it, not from The Home, or The School, or The Church, but from that fourth and other great moulder of social conscience, The Movies. From all those movies that had begun to come out when Roosevelt went in.

He had been a kid back then, a kid who had not been on the bum yet, but he was raised up on all those movies that they made then, the ones that were between '32 and '37 and had not yet degenerated into commercial imitations of themselves like the Dead End Kid perpetual series that we have now. He had grown up with them, those movies like the very first *Dead End,* like *Winterset,* like *Grapes of Wrath,* like *Dust Be My Destiny,* and those other movies starring John Garfield and the Lane girls, and the on-the-bum and prison pictures starring James Cagney and George Raft and Henry Fonda.

He had only been a green kid but he had learned from all those pictures to believe in fighting for the underdog, against the top dog. He had even made himself a philosophy of life out of it. So that he had gone right on, unable to stop believing that if the Communists were the under dog in Spain then he believed in fighting for the Communists in Spain; but that if the Communists were the top dog back home in Russia and the (what would you call them in Russia? the traitors, I guess) traitors were the bottom dog, then he believed in fighting for the traitors and against the Communists. He believed in fighting for the Jews in Germany, and against the Jews in Wall Street and Hollywood. And if the Capitalists were top dog in America and the proletariat the under dog, then he believed in fighting for the proletariat against the Capitalists. This too-ingrained-to-be-forgotten philosophy of life of his had led him, a Southerner, to believe in fighting for the Negroes against the Whites everywhere, because the Negroes were nowhere the top dog, at least as yet.

It must be a great temptation though, he thought, being top dog. Of course you dont know. You have never been one. But you can imagine how it would be. All you have to do is imagine you are an officer. You can imagine that.

It was, he realized, a very flighty philosophy, a chameleon philosophy always changing its color. You were a Communist one day and the next day you were an anti-Communist. But then this was a very flighty age, a chameleon age in which the chameleon lived perpetually upon a bright Scotch plaid.

So that so what if maybe today you are a Capitalist and tomorrow an anti-Capitalist? And maybe this minute cry over downtrodden Jews and the next minute cry against sadistic Jews? So what? It is a very irrational and emotional philosophy. Well, this is a very irrational and emotional age. I think that your philosophy puts you right in step with life in these United States and life in this disunited world.

But where, you ask, does it put you politically? What are your politics?

I think we can dispense with that question, he told himself. It is a wrong question, one that implies you have to have some kind of politics, and is therefore an unfair question because it restricts your answer to what kind of politics. It is the kind of question a Republican or a Democrat or a Communist would ask you. And anyway, you cant vote, you are in the Army, they wouldnt be interested in you.

Yes, I think we can reject that question. But if we had to answer it, truthfully, under oath (let us suppose that Mr Dies and his Un-American Activities Committee called you up because you refused to go out for boxing), then I would say that politically you are a sort of super arch-revolutionary, the kind that made the Revolution in Russia and that the Communists are killing now, a sort of perfect criminal type, very dangerous, a mad dog that loves under dogs. Thats what I would say you were.

But you better not tell that to anybody unless you have to, Prewitt.

They'll put you in the nut ward. Because here in America, he thought, everybody fights to *become* top dog, and then to *stay* top dog. And maybe, just maybe, that is why the under dogs that get to be top dogs and there is nothing left for them to fight for, wither up and die or else get fat and wheeze and die. Because they no longer got anything to fight for but to stay top dog, to keep what they already got.

All of which, Prewitt, does not do you a whole hell of a lot of good—except to make you feel a little better—since the way things look now it is very unlikely that you will ever get to be top dog and have to worry about getting fat and wheezing. If you were worrying about getting fat and wheezing, all this doubletiming that is sweating you like a nigger at election would ease your mind of that. Maybe they are doing you a favor and do not know it. Well, dont tell them, thats all. Dont ever let them know it.

What a business. You go along trying to mind your business and be yourself and bother nobody and look what happens to you. Yes, look what happens. You get mired in up to your ass in something. Grown men, seriously pushing each other around, over the burning question of whether or not a certain man should or should not go out for a boxing squad. It seemed so silly, suddenly, that it was hard to believe that absolutely serious results for you could ever come out of it.

Yet he knew that those results could and would come out of it for him. You cant disagree with the adopted values of a bunch of people without they get pissed off at you. When people tie their lives to some screwy idea or other and you attempt to point out to them that for you (not for them, mind you, just for you personally) that this idea is screwy, then serious results can always and will always come out of it for you. Because as far as they care you are the same as saying their lives are nothing and this always bothers people, because people prefer anything to being nothing, look at the Nazis, and that is why they tie their lives to things.

Why dont you, he thought, tie your life to something, Prewitt? To a tree, perhaps. It would save us all a lot of trouble and discomfort.

A sort of sullen stubbornness of dull rebellion began to rise up in him. He had plans for Payday, and this very serious foolishness might very easily turn out to have an extra KP in it for him on Payday.

All right. If they want to play, well we will play. Hate they like, hate they will get. We can hate as well as the next one. We were pretty good at it once, in our youth. We can bruise and burn and maim and kill and torture, and call it kindliness and thoughtful discipline, just as subtly and intangibly as the next one. We can play the game of hates and call it free enterprise of competition between individual initiatives too.

That was the only way to handle this. We will hate, and we will be the perfect soldier. We will hate, and we will obey every order perfectly and to the letter. We will hate, and we will not talk back. We will not break a single rule. We will not make a single mistake. We will only hate. Then let them take it and carry it from there. They will have to search hard to find any offense to charge this one with.

He hung on sullen hatefully to that role the rest of the morning. And it worked. They were puzzled. They were perplexed. They were obviously deeply hurt because he hated them, and because he was so perfect as a soldier. Some of them even got angry at him; he had no right to react like that. He was like a damnfool bulldog that has got his teeth into a man simply because the man has beat him, and cannot be swung loose or kicked loose or pulled loose or beaten loose but only made to let go by the cutting of his jaw muscles, which in this case happened to be illegal.

He grinned to himself, tautly and ecstatically, because he knew he had them where it hurt, and because he knew now for sure they could not do him in by Payday, and because for a moment he had wild visions that maybe this might even cure them, next time, and continued to hang on, his only dim hope of any relief at all centered in the coming of the afternoon and fatigue. But as it turned out he got no relief then either. As it turned out, at fatigue, he not only lost the lead he had gained at drill, he went in the hole.

It was his own fault. He was on Ike Galovitch's home labor detail.

He had had for a long time now the habit of hanging around in the barracks until the last minute before falling out for fatigue. This was so that he would be on the very end of the line, in order to circumvent The Warden's little game of *Break It Off In Prewitt*. The last half, or last third, of the Company—depending on the daily demands for fatigue labor that came down from Regiment—was always put to some job of policing in the Company Area and Ike Galovitch, by a standing order to The Warden from Capt Holmes, always had charge of this home use labor section. If Prew was on the end of the line, it was as if he were off limits to The Warden, and he would always get off with this. He would never get the cushy details, like the Officers' Club detail or the golf course detail, but neither would he get the trash truck or the butcher shop. The Warden could easily have simply reversed the order of the Company and started with the other end, or if he wanted, just have held the worse detail back until the very last, after partitioning off Ike's labor for home use. But he had learned that Warden would not do that, that that old private line of equity, drawn with such sharpness and with such close secrecy that it was wholly invisible to everyone but Warden, would not let the big man take advantage of the situation in that way. Every time Prew would forget and fall in with the first half The Warden would be right there waiting savagely joyously with the worst detail the day's crop offered, but as long as Prew was at the other end he was safe. It was, Prew often thought, as if The Warden had applied to his whole life the principle which applied to all other games of sport—that laying down of certain arbitrary rules to make success that much harder for the player to attain, like clipping in football or traveling in basketball, or in the same way, as he had read someplace, that sporting fishermen would use the light six-nine tackle in fishing for sailfish instead of the heavy tackle that makes it easy for the novice, thereby imposing upon themselves voluntarily the harder conditions that made the reward worth more to them. But where the fishermen only did it on their days off or on vacation, to gain some obscure satisfaction that the cut-throat business ethics of their lives no longer gave them, The Warden applied it to his whole life, and stuck by it. Prew knew he stuck by it because, after figuring it out, he had at times, when he felt in the mood, accepted the gambit and played the game by falling in at the head and trying to outwit Warden into giving him an easy detail, and once, the only time he made him miss, Warden had made it a point of giving him the Officers' Club detail for the whole next week, as if penalizing himself, with as great a relish as when he penalized Prewitt. It was fun, and it broke up the monotony of living, and there was a closeness between him and The Warden, an understanding, tacit, never spoken of, but closer and stronger than even what he felt for Maggio. And whenever he did not feel like playing he would fall in at the end and Warden would not touch him. It was like King's X in tag as a kid, except here it was not abused, it was honored. (Maybe that was what it was about The Warden: honor; yet Maggio had honor too, and was with him more often and had done more for him, than Warden, yet there was not as warm a closeness, not as great a love.) He did not understand it, but on this day he did not feel like playing.

After The Warden had read off the details, Old Ike lined his detail up and called them to attention as the other details scattered, marching off across the quad, the feet scuffing reluctantly and the shoulders sagging wearily as they dragged the heavy, food-full, nap-hungry bellies off to work.

"Now tooday," Ike told his boys, his long lippy ape's jaw thrust out commandingly at them, "we are going da inside of dis barricks to clean up. Hupstairs and donstairs all the windows wash and polishing. An of da dayroom an poolroom and CQ's corridor da walls to scrub. Da Gomny Gmandr will inspect tomorrow all of it so you want to do it *right* and none of the goldbricking I want to see. Hokay. Hany queshuns?"

All of them had done this same job at least five times before. There were no questions.

"Dan coun *hoff!*" Ike bawled, raising his chest proudly like a bellows to make room for his close order voice. "Da ones hupstairs and donstairs da windows take. Da twos on da walls will work."

They counted off. Prewitt and Maggio, who had deliberately fallen in one man apart, were both twos. The ones started for the supply room to get their rags and bars of sandsoap in the yellow wrappers labelled *Bon Ami* under the picture of the cuddly little fluffy chick that always outraged all of them with an unspeakable affront because as soldiers their lives had become such a close alliance with the grit of sandsoap. Sgt Lindsay, a fair-to-middling bantamweight, had charge of the ones. The twos started for the kitchen for the GI soap and brushes. Corp Miller, a worse-than-mediocre lightweight and Champ Wilson's running mate, had charge of the twos.

"Hey you," Ike bawled. "You Prewitt Maggio. To me here come, wise guys. How you men both twos are?"

"You counted us off, Ike," Angelo said.

"You think a fast one can over Old Ike pull?" Ike said, glaring at them suspiciously out of the little red eyes behind the hairy brows. "Over my face the wool you can not stretch. I ham separating you two men together. You Maggio go hupstairs the ones wit. Tell Sargint Lindsay to Treadwell send back down the twos wit. Dis a fatigue, not no hold ladies sewing circle or vacation. In charge am I of dis detail and I work want not loafing. See?"

"I'll see you later," Angelo said disgustedly.

"Okay," Prew said, with the unruffled equanimity of the perfect soldier.

"Hokay," Ike bawled. "Move. Not all day. You Prewitt go back the twos wit and dont sometime figur on getting by with from me, see? I be around all time keep eye on you, see? You aint so tough smart guy as maybe think."

Ike was as good as his word. He made his headquarters in the corridor hallway where the twos had set up the one-by-eight on the two stepladders they used for scaffolding, and where Prew was working, first standing on the board, then sitting on it, then kneeling on the floor, washing down swath after swath of the pebbly plaster wall from floor to ceiling.

"Dis a fatigue, not vacation, Prewitt," Ike informed him, grinning wolfishly with the long sallow ape's jaw, from time to time. "I got my eye on you."

And he had. When Prew climbed down to rinse his rag, when he went outside to change the water in his bucket, when he turned around to resoap his GI brush—Old Ike would be there in front of him, watching suspiciously hopefully with the little sharp eyes in the sanguine bullethead like red buttons reflecting firelight on a lumberjack's plaid shirt.

—"Dis a fatigue, not vacation, Prewitt."—

But Ike's hopes were groundless. Prew had been having a lot worse than that all morning, and had weathered it by playing perfect soldier. Ike's efforts were almost pathetic, compared to the imaginative variety that, say, Dhom could give to the riding of a man. This could not get under his skin, not the sharp smell of the dirty soapy water, nor his own white water-wrinkled fingers, nor the stale cracker smell of the wet wall plaster.

It was not, strangely, until Capt Dynamite Holmes came bouncing in from across the quad, freshly showered, shaved, shampooed, and shined, his big boots gleaming—it was not till then that all these things suddenly got under Prewitt's skin.

"Hello there, Sergeant Galovitch," Holmes grinned, stopping in the doorway.

"Atten HUT," Ike bawled, making two distinct words of it, and bracing his bigfooted longarmed missinglink's body into an arch-backed travesty of it proudly. The men went on working.

"Everything under control, Sergeant?" Holmes said fondly. "Are you getting this place slicked up for me tomorrow?"

"Yes, Serr," Ike grunted, uncomfortably because still bracing solidly, his thumbs along the seams of his trousers, somewhere down around his knees. "Slickem up. Everyting I am doing just like the Gomny Gmandr saying."

"Good," Holmes grinned fondly. "Fine." Still grinning fondly, he stepped over to inspect the wall, and nodded. "Looks fine, Sergeant Galovitch, A-1. Keep up the good work."

"Yes, Serr," Ike grunted worshipfully, still bracing. The narrow shouldered barrel ape's chest expanded out until it looked about to burst and Ike saluted, stiffly, grotesquely, looking as if the hand would knock his eye clear out.

"Well," Holmes grinned fondly. "Carry on then, Sergeant." He went on into the orderly room grinning and Old Ike bawled *"Atten HUT"* again, making it two words again, and the men still went on working.

Prew went on rubbing his rag over the pebbly plaster he had just washed and that suddenly sickened him now, feeling his jaws tighten reasonlessly. He felt as if he had just witnessed the sodomitic seduction of a virgin brunser who had liked it.

"All right, you men there," Ike hollered proudly, moving slabfooted up and down behind them. "You men I want on the ball to get, see? Just begause da Gomny Gmandr comes around is to stop working no escuse. Dis a fatigue, not vacation."

The men still went on working, wearily ignoring this new outburst because they had been expecting it, as they wearily ignored the other outbursts, and Prew went with them, suddenly suffocating in the wet plaster smell that enveloped him. He wished he had a pair of bright and shining boots.

"You Prewitt," Ike hollered angrily, not finding anything else to criticize. "Lets looking a life. Dis a fatigue, not vacation for a seminaries of lady. I got to tell you all ready times too many. Now looking a life."

If Ike had not mentioned him by name, with Holmes in there listening taking it all in, he could still have stomached it. But quite suddenly the words were beating against his ears, on and on, so that instinctively he wanted to shake his head to clear it.

"What the hell do you want, me to grow a couple more arms for Chrisake?" he said violently suddenly, hearing his own voice outhollering Ike's astoundedly, yet seeing in his mind the Great God Holmes sitting grinning at his desk listening relishingly to his favorite sergeant. For once maybe The Man might like to hear what his men thought of his favorite sergeant, for a change.

"How?" Ike said flabbergastedly. "What?"

"Yas, what," Prew sneered. "You want this job done so perfect and so fast why dont you grab a brush yourself? Instead of standing around giving orders nobody listens to."

The men stopped mechanically washing and all stared at him, just as mechanically, and he looked at them, the rage filling him, now knowing why. He knew it was senseless, absolutely senseless, even dangerous, but for a moment he was wildly proud.

"Now listen," Ike said, thinking hard. "This back talk are you giving me do I not want. To work get back on the lip shut button."

"Oh blow it out your ass," he said savagely, still mechanically scrubbing with his rag, "I'm working. What do you think, I'm floggin my doggin?"

"What," Ike gasped. "What."

"*AT EASE!*" roared Capt Holmes, appearing in the door. "What the hell is all this racket, Prewitt?"

"Yes, *Serr*," Ike grunted, hopping to attention. "Dis man bolshevik da back talk is giving to a noncom."

"Whats the matter with you, Prewitt?" Capt Holmes said sternly, ignoring the momentarily shattered illusion of his favorite sergeant. "You know better than to talk back to a noncommissioned officer, and in that tone of voice."

"To a noncom, *yes*, Sir," Prew grinned savagely, aware now of the watching eight wide pairs of eyes. "But I have never liked being pissed on, Sir. Even by a noncommissioned officer," he said, twisting the phrase.

264

The Warden appeared in the door behind Holmes and stood looking at all of them, his eyes narrowed thoughtfully, himself aloof from it.

Holmes looked as if someone had dashed a glass of ice water in his face absolutely without reason. His brows were up with disbelief and his eyes were wide with hurt and his mouth was open with surprise. When he spoke his voice quivered openly with both rage and start.

"Private Prewitt, I think you owe both Sergeant Galovitch and myself an apology." He paused and waited.

Prew did not answer. He felt a shrinking in his belly at the thought of what this stupidity would do to his chances Payday, wondering what in hell had possessed him to do a thing like that.

"Well?" Holmes said authoritatively. He was as surprised by it as any of them, as surprised as Prewitt even, and had said the first thing that came into his head but he could not show that. He had to back it up. "Apologize, Prewitt."

"I dont think I owe anybody any apology," Prew said savagely doggedly. "In fact, if apologies are in order, I think they're owed to me," he went on recklessly, wanting suddenly to laugh at the comedy of it, like a mother chastening a child to bring it back in line. But then thats the way they always treat us, isnt it?

"What!" Holmes said. It had not occurred to him that an EM could refuse. He was as much at a loss now as Old Ike had been before and his eyes that had become almost normal size now got wider even than before. He looked at Galovitch, as if for help, then he turned and looked at Warden behind him, then he turned and looked vaguely out the corridor doorway. Corporal Paluso, a second-string Regimental tackle with a big flat murderous face that he tried to make people forget by adopting a heavy-handed bull-laughing sense of humor, and who had not missed a chance to work on Prew at drill all morning, was sitting on one of the backless chairs out on the porch and had turned and looked inside, his hard eyes in the murderous face as wide now as any of the others, as wide as Holmes's.

"Corporal Paluso," Holmes roared, in his battalion close order voice, which was the best in the Regiment.

"Yes, Sir," Paluso said, and jumped up as if stabbed.

"Take this man upstairs and have him roll a full field pack, a complete full field, extra shoes helmet and all, and then take a bicycle and hike him up to Kolekole Pass and back. And see that he hikes all the way. And when he gets back, bring him to me." It was a pretty long speech for his battalion close order voice that had been developed more for short commands.

"Yes, Sir," Paluso said. "Come on, Prewitt."

Prew climbed down meekly off the board without a word. The Warden turned around and disgustedly went back inside. Paluso led him to the stairs and a still-shocked silence reached out after them from the corridor like a cloud.

Prew bit his lips. He got his envelope roll out of the wall locker and the combat pack off the bed foot. He laid them on the floor and opened the light pack. Everyone in the squadroom sat up and watched him silently and speculatively, as they might watch a sick horse upon whose time to die they had gotten up a pool.

"Dont forget the shoes," Paluso said apologetically, in the voice one uses in the presence of a corpse.

He got them off the rack under the footlocker and had to unroll the roll to put them in and then build the whole thing up from scratch in the deadness of the silence.

"Dont forget the helmet," Paluso said apologetically.

He hung it under the snap of the meat can carrier, and picked the whole solid-heavy mess of straps and buckles up and shouldered into it and went to get his rifle from the racks, wanting only to get out of this sad, shocked silence.

"Wait'll I get a bike," Paluso said apologetically, as they came down the stairs.

He stood in the grass and waited. The sixty-five or seventy pounds of pack dragged at his back, already starting to cut in on the circulation of his arms. It was just about five miles to the top of the pass. In the corridor the great silence still reigned.

"Okay," Paluso said, using his clipped official voice because they were downstairs now. "Lets shove."

He slung his rifle and they went out the truck entrance, still followed by the silence. Outside of the quad the rest of the Post moved busily, just as if there had not been a cataclysm. They passed Theater #1, on past the Post gym, past the Regimental drill field, and went on up the road, into the sun, Paluso riding embarrassedly beside him, the front wheel wobbling precariously at the slowness of the pace.

"You want a cigaret?" Paluso offered apologetically.

Prew shook his head.

"Go ahead and have one. Hell," Paluso said, "theres no reason to be mad at me. I dont like this any better than you do."

"I aint mad at you."

"Then have a cigaret."

"Okay." He took a cigaret.

Paluso, looking relieved, started off ahead on the bike. He cut capers on it and looked back grinning with the big murderous face, trying to make him laugh. Prew grinned weakly for him. Paluso gave it up and settled down to the monotony, wobbling along beside him. Then he had another idea. He rode off a hundred yards ahead and then circled back, riding fast, a hundred yards behind, waving as he went by, and then circled back up, pumping as hard as his legs would go, to skid the brakes and slide alongside Prewitt. When this bored him he got off and walked a while.

They passed the golf course, went on past the officers' bridle path, past the Packtrain, past the gas chamber, last outpost of the Reservation, and Prew plodded on concentrating on the hold hiking rhythm, swing up and drop, swing up and drop, using only the thigh muscles on the upswing, not using the calf or ankle or foot muscles at all but letting the feet hit willy-nilly, the body's momentum carrying it forward as the thigh muscles tensed for the next swing up, that he had learned from the old timers at Myer a long time ago. Hell, he could do ten miles standing on his head carrying two packs, he cursed, as the sweat began to run in bigger rivulets down his spine and legs and drip from under his arms and down in his eyes off his face.

When they reached the last steep rise that curved left up to the top of the pass, Paluso stopped and got off his bike.

"We might as well turn back here. Theres no use to go up to the crest. He'll never know it anyway."

"To hell with him," Prew said grimly, plodding on. "He said the pass. The pass it is." He looked over at the Stockade rock quarry cut back into the side of the hill on the right of the curve. Thats where you'll be tomorrow this time. All right. So fine. Fuck em all but six and save them for the pallbearers.

"Whats the matter with you?" Paluso said angrily dumbfoundly. "You're crazy."

"Sure," he called back.

"I aint going to walk this bike up there," Paluso said. "I'll wait on you here."

The prisoners, working in the heavy dust with the big white capital P on the backs of their blue jackets standing out like targets, whooped at the two of them, razzing about the extra duty and the hard life of the Army. Until the big MP guards cursed them down and shut them up and put them back to work.

Paluso waited, smoking disgustedly, at the bottom of the rise and he climbed it doggedly by himself, sweating heavier now on the steeper rise, until at the top the big never-flagging breeze hit him and chilled him and he could look down the steep-dropping snake of road, dropping way down, at least a thousand feet, among the great sharp lava crags, down to Waianae where they had gone last September, where they went every September, for the machinegun training that he liked, fitting the heavy link-curling web belts of identical clinking cartridges every fifth one painted red into the block and touching the trigger lightly between thumb and forefinger and feeling the pistol grip buck against your hand as the belts bobbed through, firing off across the empty western water at the towed targets, the tracers making flat meteor flights of light in the night firing. He breathed some of the stiffness of the breeze. Then he turned around and went back down, the wind dying suddenly, to where Paluso was waiting.

When they got back to the barracks his jacket and his pants down to his knees were soaked clear through. Paluso said, *"Wait here,"* and went in to report and Capt Holmes came back out with him, and he unslung his rifle and came to attention and rendered a smart rifle salute.

"Well," Holmes said deeply, humorously. Sharp lines of lenient humor cut indulgent planes and angles in the handsome aquiline face. "Do you still feel you need to offer advice to the noncoms about how to manage details, Prewitt?"

Prew did not answer. In the first place, he had not expected humor, even indulgent humor, and inside in the corridor they were still scrubbing down the walls, exactly as they had two hours ago, and they looked very safe and secure in their weary bored monotony.

"Then I take it," Holmes said humorously, "that you are ready to apologize to Sergeant Galovitch and myself now, arent you."

"No, Sir, I'm not." Why did he have to say that? why couldnt he just have left it? why did he have to demand it all? couldnt he see what he was doing, how impossible that was.

Paluso made a startled noise behind him that was followed by a very guilty silence. Holmes's eyes only widened imperceptibly, he had better control this time, he knew more what to expect. The indulgent planes and angles of his face shifted, subtly and were neither humorous nor indulgent any more.

Holmes jerked his head at the pass. "Take him back up there again, Paluso. He hasnt had enough yet."

"Yes, Sir," Paluso said, letting go of the handlebars with one hand to salute.

"We'll see how he answers next time," Holmes said narrowly. The red was beginning to mount in his face again. "I dont have a thing planned for all night tonight," he added.

"Yes, Sir," Paluso said. "Come on, Prewitt."

Prew turned and followed him again, feeling bottomlessly sick inside, and feeling tired, feeling very tired.

"Goddam," Paluso protested, as soon as they were out of sight, "you're nuts. Plain crazy. Dont you know you're ony cuttin your own throat? If you dont give a damn about yourself, at least think about me. My legs is gettin tard," he grinned apologetically.

Prew did not even manage a weak grin this time. He knew that, if there had been any chance within the indulgent humor, it was gone now, that this was it, this was how you went to the Stockade. He hiked the ten miles carrying the sixty-five or seventy pounds of pack with that knowledge making an added weight inside of him.

What he did not know was what had happened in the orderly room to put Holmes in the indulgent mood, nor what happened this time, the second time.

The Man's face was congested a brick red when he stomped back inside, the anger he had managed to conceal in front of Prewitt backing up now like a flood behind a bridge.

"You and your bright ideas of leadership," he raged at Warden. "You and your brilliant ideas of how to handle bolsheviks."

Warden was still standing by the window. He had watched all of it. Now he turned around, wishing The Mouth, or would you say The Sword, The Flaming Sword, would step outside to talk to Ike, so The Warden could open up the file cabinet and get a drink.

"Sergeant Warden," The Man said thickly, "I want you to prepare court martial papers for Prewitt. Insubordination and refusing a direct order of an officer. I want them now."

"Yes, Sir," The Warden said.

"I want them to go in to Regiment this afternoon," The Man said.

"Yes, Sir," The Warden said. He went to the blank forms file, where the useless bottle was. He got out four of the long double sheets of the forms and shut the drawer on the bottle and took the papers to the typewriter.

"You cant be decent to a man like that," The Man said thickly. "He has been a troublemaker ever since he hit this outfit. Its time he had a lesson. They tame the lions in the Army, not appease them."

"You want it recommended for a Summary? or a Special," The Warden said indifferently.

"Special," The Man said. His face got redder. "I'd like to make it a goddamned General. I would, if I could. You and your bright ideas."

"Its nothing to me," The Warden shrugged, beginning to type. "All I said was, we've had three court martials in the last six weeks and it might not look so good on the records."

"Then to hell with the records," The Man almost, but not quite, shouted. It was the peak. He sat down in his swivel chair exhausted and leaned back and stared broodingly at the door into the corridor that he had carefully closed.

"Thats all right with me," The Warden said, still typing.

The Man did not appear to hear, but The Warden, typing, still watched him, gauging carefully, making sure it *was* the peak. You could not handle this time like the last time. This was stronger. This was the last time squared, and you would have to square the strength of your approach, and then if you waited till the other's peak was past, then logically you would have it made, but was it worth it? Hell no, it wasnt worth it, not when you might crimp your own concatenation, what was it to you if some damned son of a bitching stupid fool of an antediluvian got himself beheaded by a progressive world by going around in a dream world and trying to live up to a romantic, backward ideal of individual integrity? You could go doing things for a jerk like that forever, and never help him any. It was never worth it, but it would really be a feather in your cap if you could pull it off again now, this time. That would be worth a try, just for the hell of it. If he was doing this, it was not because it was his responsibility to knock himself out taking care of headless chickens who refuse to become modern and grow a head, it was just for the fun of seeing if he could pull it off, not for no stupid ass who still believed in probity.

"Too bad you got to lose a welterweight like that," The Warden said indifferently, after The Man had brooded on the door a while in silence. He took the sheets out of the machine and began to rearrange the carbons for the second page.

"What?" The Man said, looking up. "What do you mean?"

"Well, he'll still be in hock when Compny Smokers comes up, wont he?" The Warden said indifferently.

"To hell with the Company Smokers," The Man said. "All right," he said. "Make it a Summary then."

"But I already got this typed up," The Warden said.

"Then change it, Sergeant," The Man said. "Would you let your laziness make a difference of five months in the Stockade to a man?"

"Jesus Christ," The Warden said. He tore the papers up and went to get some blank ones. "These Kentucky mountain hardheads cause a man more trouble than a regiment of niggers. Might as well leave it as a Special for all the good a break will do a man like that."

"He needs to be taught a lesson," said The Man.

"He sure as hell does," The Warden said fervently. "The only trouble with them guys, they never learn. I've seen too many of them go into the hockshop, and all they make is work. They aint out two weeks before they're right back in again. They had rather let you kill them, than admit they're wrong. No more sense than a goddam GI mule. About the time you get him groomed up for Regimental next December, he'll pull some hair brained deal and get himself right back in hock, just to get even with you. I seen too many of them mountain boys. They're a threat to the freedom of this whole country."

"I dont give a goddam what he does," The Man yelled, sitting up. "Fuck the Regimentals, and fuck the fucking championship. I dont have to stand for insolence like that. I dont have to take it. I'm an officer in this Army, not a boiler orderly." The red outrage of affront was back in his face. He glared at The Warden.

The Warden waited, timing it exactly to the color in the face, before he emphatically told The Man what The Man was thinking.

"You dont mean that, Captain," The Warden said softly, in horror. "You're just mad. You wouldnt say a thing like that, if you werent mad. You dont want to take a chance on losing your championship next winter, just for being mad."

"Mad!" The Man said. "Mad? Mad, he says. Jesus H Christ, Sergeant!" He rubbed his hands over his face, tentatively feeling of the congestion. "All right," he said. "I guess you're right. Theres no sense in losing your head and going off half cocked and cutting off your nose to spite your face. Maybe he didnt even mean any disrespect at all." The Man sighed. "Have you started on those new forms yet?"

"Not yet, Sir," The Warden said.

"Then put them back," said The Man. "I guess."

"Well at least give him a good stiff company punishment," The Warden said.

"Ha," The Man said vehemently. "If I wasnt the boxing coach of this outfit, I'd give him something," he said. "He's getting off damned easy. Okay, you enter it in the Company Punishment Book, will you? Three weeks restriction to quarters. I'm going home now. Home," he said, as if to himself. "Call him in tomorrow and I'll talk to him and initial the book."

"All right, Sir," The Warden said. "If you think thats the way to handle it." He got the stiff leather-bound Company Punishment Book out of his desk and opened it up and got his pen. The Man smiled at him wearily and left, and he closed the book and put it away again and stepped to the window to watch the Captain cross the quad through the lengthening evening shadows, going home. In a way he almost felt sorry for him, any more. But then he asked for everything he got.

The next day when Holmes asked for the book he got it out and opened it. Then he discovered the page was still blank. Shamefacedly he explained how he had had to do some other things. He had forgotten it. The Man was on his way to the Club, he was in a hurry. He told The Warden to have it ready for him tomorrow. "Yes, *Sir*," The Warden told him. "I'll do it right away." He got his pen out. The Man left. He put his pen away.

The next day even Holmes had forgotten all about it, under the stress of more recent things.

It was not, The Warden considered carefully, that he gave a good goddam whether the punk got three weeks' restrictions or not. The fact was, three weeks' restriction would probably do Prewitt some good. Especially since, as Stark had told him, the kid had gone dippy over this snooty whore at Mrs Kipfer's. Three weeks at home for Prewitt would be just about long enough to get him over it. The Warden was sorry now that he had posed this condition on himself that he get Prewitt off scot free or it did not count. He did not feel sorry for him. Prewitt asked for everything he got. Falling for a hard nosed whore at Mrs Kipfer's. That was just about that punk's goddam speed. Prewitt not only asked for everything he got, he begged for it on bended knee. The Warden snorted disagreeably.

Prewitt was relieved to find Holmes was not around when they got back the second time. Paluso was relieved too. He released Prewitt quickly and took off for the PX, to be out of sight. Neither one of them understood that it was over. Prew limped upstairs and unmade the pack and put the stuff away and showered and changed to clean clothes and stretched out on his bunk, and waited for the OD or the Sergeant of the Guard. When they had not come for him by chowtime, he knew then they were not coming. He had been waiting for an hour and a half.

When the chow whistle blew, he knew something had interposed itself between himself and fate. The only possible answer was The Warden, who had seen fit to take a hand for one of those obscure screwy reasons of his own. I dont know what the hell business it is of his, he thought angrily, as he limped downstairs for chow. Why cant he keep his big nose out of things?

After chow, he stretched out on his bunk again, laying the tiredness of his legs out heavily on the blankets. That was when Maggio came over and congratulated him.

"Man, I'm proud of you," said Angelo. "I ony wish I had of been there to see it. Thats all. If it wasnt for that son of a English-butchering bitch Galovitch, I would of been there too. But I'm still proud of you, man. Just the same."

"Yeah," Prew said wearily. He was still trying to grasp where he had got off. He had not only offered them the chance to give him extra duty Payday, which he still might get, he had also given the best opportunity they could have asked for to send him to the Stockade, express. In spite of all the great resolutions about being the perfect soldier and the high plans to make them do all the work. And this, mind you, he told himself, not after a month, not after a week, not even after two days of The Treatment—but on the afternoon of the very first day. It was not, he realized, going to be as easy as it looked. There were apparently hidden subtleties to The Treatment. Apparently it had been devised to gear itself to human nature more cunningly than he had suspected. And he had either woefully underestimated their ability to apply it, or else which was worse, grossly overestimated his own strength of will to fight it. The Treatment, apparently, concentrated all its power on a man's strongest point—his pride in himself as a man. Could it be that that was also his *weakest* point?

Remembering it, a kind of terror at his own utter inadequacy overwhelmed him, overwhelmed even the fear he had of the Stockade when he was not keeping himself pumped full of outrage.

He fell out for drill next day a sadder but a wiser man. He had given up entirely the idea of curing them or teaching them a lesson. He no longer hoped for or expected instantaneous victory. When The Treatment started right where it had left off yesterday, and he went right back into the role of perfect soldier, he was only fighting a holding action, and under the slow smouldering silence of the self-generated hate that was his one defense was only the thought of Lorene and Payday, warming through him like a good stiff drink, a fire at which he could warm himself against this heat of hatred that was slowly freezing him.

Chapter 20

You knock off drill at ten o'clock on Payday. You shower, shave, brush your teeth again, dress carefully in your best inspection uniform, being careful to knot the suntan tie just right. Then, dressed, you work hard on your fingernails before you finally go outside to stand around in the sun in the company yard and wait for them to begin the paying off, being very careful all the time of the knot in the tie and of the fingernails, since all company paying officers have their little idiosyncrasies of personal inspection even if Payday is not a regular inspection day. With some it was the shoes, with others the crease of the pants, with others the haircut. With Capt Holmes it was the knot in the tie and the fingernails and while if these did not satisfy him he did not redline you or anything like that, still you got a rigorous telling off and had to fall out to the end of the line.

You stand around in little groups on Payday and talk about it excitedly and about the half holiday it is, groups that cant stay still and break up and reform with parts of other groups into new groups, continually shifting, not able to stand still, except for the twenty percent men who are already waiting like vultures at the kitchen door where you must emerge. Until then finally you see the guard bugler go up to the megaphone in the quad in the brilliant morning sunshine (more brilliant, oddly, than on any other morning) and sound Pay Call.

"*Pay day,*" the bugle says to you, "*pay day. What you go na do with a drunk en sol jer? Pay day?*"

"*Pay day,*" the bugle answers you, "*pay day. Put him in the guard house till he's so ber. Pay day. P-a-y . . . d-a-y.*"

Then the shifting excitement grows much stronger (oh, the bugler plays a responsible part, a traditional, emotional, important part, a part heavy with the past, with all the past centuries of soldiering) and you see The Warden carrying a GI blanket from the orderly room to the messhall and Mazzioli following him with the Payroll like a lord chamberlain carrying the Great Seal and then the shining-booted Dynamite carrying the black satchel and grinning beneficently. It takes them quite a while to get set up, move the tables, spread the blanket, count the silver out and lay the greenbacks out in sheaves, get the jawbone list of PX checks and show checks ready for The Warden to collect, but already you begin to form the line, by rank, noncoms first, then Pfcs and Pvts in one group together, the men within each group lining up for once without argument or pushing, alphabetically.

Then, finally, they begin to pay and you can see the line moving very slowly up ahead of you, until you stand in the doorway of the dim messhall yourself while the man in front of you gets paid, until they call your last name and you answer with your first name, middle initial and serial number and step up to Dynamite and salute, standing stiffly while he looks you over and you show your fingernails and he, satisfied, pays you off, tossing you one of his pat jokes like, *"Save enough back to go to town on"* or *"Dont drink all this up in one place."* Oh, he is a soldier, Dynamite, a soldier of the old school, Dynamite. And then holding this money (less laundry, less insurance, less allotment if any, less the $1 to the Company Fund) that it took you all month to earn and that they are giving you the rest of this day off to spend, you move down the long blanket covered table to The Warden who collects for PX checks and show checks you have drawn during the month and that you really did not mean to draw at all (promised yourself, last Payday, you would not draw, this month) but drew somehow anyway when they came out on the 10th and the 20th. Then out through the kitchen to the porch where the heavy capital of the financial wizards of twenty percent men like Jim O'Hayer and Turp Thornhill and, to a lesser extent that is really only a hobby, Champ Wilson, takes its toll also from the dwindling pile.

Payday. It is truly an occasion, even the feud between you and the jockstraps is in eclipse when its Payday. In the long, low ceilinged shadiness of the squadroom with the sun very bright outside men are stripping off the suntans feverishly and pulling on the civilians and you know there will not be very many for chow this noon, practically none tonight except for losing gamblers.

Out of his $30.00, after the debts were paid, Prew had exactly $12.00 and two dimes. This, which would not even buy Lorene for one all night session, he blessed and genuflected over and took over to O'Hayer's.

The sheds, across the street from the dayroom and jerrybuilt on the strip of worn near-bald earth between the street and the narrow gauge Post railroad, were already going full blast. The quarter-ton maintenance trucks had been moved to the regimental motor park, the big spools of phone wire were neatly stacked outside, the 37mm anti-tank guns (some the old short-barrelled steel-wheeled that were familiar, some the new long-barrelled rubber-tired looking strange and foreign like the pictures of the German arms in *Life* Magazine) had been rolled out and covered up with tarps, and the spielers hired for a buck an hour called unceasingly like circus barkers from before each shed to "*Come inside, boys. Poker, blackjack, craps, chuckaluck, all inside. Test that luck, boys.*"

In O'Hayer's all five lima-bean-shaped blackjack tables were working full capacity. Under the green shaded lights green visored dealers called the cards in monotonous low voices against the hum. Both dice tables were crowded three deep with players, and the three poker tables that were dealing only stud today to take care of more players had no seats open.

Standing in the door he thought how by the middle of the month all this money would have sifted down into the hands of a few heavy winners who would be at this table where O'Hayer sat playing now, one of his hired help dealing. They would be winners from all over, from as far away as Hickam and Fort Kam and Shafter and Fort Ruger. They would make this the biggest game on the Inland Post, if not on the whole Rock. The thought made his belly flutter, how he might with luck be one of them. He had done it once before, but only once, at Myer. And the resolution to win just enough for town and quit grew dim and wavered and, but for his stiff determination bolstered by the picture of Lorene, would have fled entirely.

He worked methodically with small bets for two hours at a blackjack table (deliberately monotonously, deliberately uninspired) to run his twelve bucks up to the twenty which was the take-out at the poker table. Then he moved over to the one where O'Hayer was to wait for an open seat, which would never be long on Payday when most of the players were just small fry like himself with a table stake wanting to bite into the big boys' capital. They were constantly going broke and dropping out. He waited without excitement, promising himself faithfully that if he won two hands he'd quit, because two wins in this game would give him plenty for tonight with enough left over for a good weekend (today was Thursday) or Saturday night and Sunday night (and maybe Sunday day, if she said okay, maybe at the beach with her) with Lorene. Just two wins. He had it all figured out.

The round green felt with a bite cut out for the dealer's seat was strewn with piles of halfdollars and cartwheels and the red plastic twobit chips for ante-ing. They caught and threw back sardonically the greenglass-shaded light, vividly red and silver against the soft light-absorbing felt. He could see The Warden and Stark among the players. Jim O'Hayer sat relaxed with a rakish, expensive green visor cocked over the coldly rigidly mathematical eyes, constantly rolling two cartwheels one over the other with a click that ate into the nerves.

It was Stark, his hat tipped low over his eyes, who finally pushed back his four legged mess stool and gave himself the coup de grace: "Seat open."

"You aint quittin?" O'Hayer said softly.

"Not for long," Stark said, looking at him reflectively. "Just till I borry some money."

"See you then," O'Hayer grinned. "Good luck with it."

"Well now thank you, Jim," Stark said.

Stark, some kibitzer whispered, had in the last hour dropped the whole $600 he had managed to build up since ten o'clock. Stark stared at him and he subsided, and Stark elbowed slowly out through the press, still looking reflective.

Prew slid onto the empty $600 seat wondering darkly if this was an omen and pushed his little ten and two fives over to the dealer as unobtrusively as possible. The money boys kept the takeout low on Payday, so you could get in, but they stared at your twenty bucks contemptuously, when you did. He got back a stack of 15 cartwheels, 6 halves, and 8 of the plastic chips and fingering them did not any longer mind the contempt because the old familiar alchemy, the best drug of them all against this life, spread over him as he flipped a red chip in there with the others. His heart was beating faster with louder, more emphatic thumps, echoing in his ears. The gambler's flush was spreading across his face, making it feverish. The bottom of his belly dropped away from under him leaving him standing on the edge of which the world stopped moving.

Here, he thought, just here, and only here, held in these pieces of pasteboard being tossed facedown around the table, governed by whatever Laws or fickle Goddess moved them, here lay infinity and the secret of all life and death, what the scientists were seeking, here under your hand if you could only grasp it, penetrate the unreadability. You may shortly win $1000. You may more shortly be completely broke. And any man who could just only learn to understand the reason why would be shaking hands with God. They were playing table stakes and in front of the winners lay thick piles of greenbacks weighted down with silver. The sight of all this crisp green paper that was so important in this life swept him with a greediness to take these crinkly good smelling pieces of paper to himself, not for what they would buy but for their lovely selves. All this was contained in the slow, measured, inexorable dropping of the cards, like time beating slowly but irresistibly in the ears of an old old man.

Around the table twice, twice ten cards, once down, once up. Somebody's watch beat loudly. And the known familiar faces took on new characteristics and became strange. The bright light cast strange shadows down from the impassive brows and noses, making of each man an eyeless hairlip. He did not know these men. That was not Warden there or O'Hayer there, only a pair of bodyless hands moving the top card under the holecard for a secret look, only an armless hand clicking a stack of halves down one on top the other, then lifting all and clicking them down again, and again, perpetually, with measured thoughtfulness. An unreasoning thrill passed down his spine, and all the unpleasantness of his life had become in the last two months fell away from him, dead, forgotten.

The first hand was a big one. He had hoped for a small one, his $20 would not go far in this game. But the cards were high, and the betting heavy. He had jacks backed up and by the third round he was all in, for the side pot his twenty shared, unable because this was table stakes to go into his pocket for more money if he had it which he did not. The pot he could win was shoved to one side and the betting went on in the center, and all he could do was sit and sweat it out. On the fourth card O'Hayer caught the ace to match his holecard that all of them knew he had because Jim O'Hayer never stayed for fun. He raised fifteen. Prew's belly sagged and he looked at his jacks ruefully and was very glad he was all in for the pot. But on the last card he caught another jack, making a pair showing. He felt his heart skip a beat and cursed silently because he was all in for the pot.

There was nearly a hundred and fifty in his pot. O'Hayer won the other, the smaller pot. Warden looked at O'Hayer and then at him and snorted his disgust. Prew grinned, dragging in his pot, and reminded himself that if he won the next one he would quit and check out and Warden could really snort then.

He didnt need to win the next one. What he had from the first was plenty. But he had promised himself two hands, not one, so he stayed in. But he did not win the second hand, Warden won it, and he had dropped $40 which left him only about a hundred and now he felt he needed the second win before he dropped out so he stayed in. But he did not win the third hand either, or the fourth, nor did he win the fifth. He dropped clear down to less than $50, before he finally won another one.

Raking in the money he sighed off the tenseness that had grown in him in ratio to the shrinking of his capital; he had begun to believe he would never win another one. But now though he had a real backlog to work from. The second win put him up to over two hundred. Two hundred was plenty capital. And he began to play careful, weighing each bet. He played shirtfront poker, enjoying it immensely, completely lost in loving it, in matching his brain against the disembodied brains against him. It was true poker, hard monotonous unthrilling, and he truly loved it, and played steadily, losing only a little, dropping out often, winning a small one now and then, playing now against the time when he would win that really big one and check out.

He knew of course all the time that it could not go on indefinitely this way, $200 was no reserve to put up against the capital in this game, but then all he wanted was just one more big win like the first two, one that would be bigger because now he had more money, one he could quit on and check out for good. If he had won the first two like he promised he would have quit then but he hadnt won them he had only won one and now he wanted this last one the one to quit on, before he finally got caught.

But before the big win he was just waiting for to quit on came they caught him, they caught him good.

He had tens backed up, a good hand. On the fourth card he drew another. On the same card Warden paired kings showing. Warden checked to the tens. Prew was cautious, they were not *trying* to play dirty poker in this game but with this much on the table anything went. Warden might have trips and he was not being sucked in, he was not that green. When the bet had checked clear around to him he raised lightly, very lightly, just a touch, a feeler, a protection bet he could afford to abandon and lose. Three men dropped out right away. Only O'Hayer and Warden called, finally. O'Hayer obviously had an ace paired to his holecard and was willing to pay for the chance to catch the third. O'Hayer was a percentage man, twenty percentage man, O'Hayer. And Warden who thought quite a while before he called looked at his holecard twice and then he almost didnt call, so he had no trips.

On the last card O'Hayer missed his ace and dropped out, indifferently. O'Hayer could always afford to drop out indifferently. Warden with his kings still high checked it to Prew, and Prew felt a salve of relief grease over him for sure now Warden had no trips. Warden had two pair and hoped the kings would nose him out since O'Hayer had two bullets. Well, if he wanted to see them he could by god pay for seeing them, like everybody else, and Prew bet twenty-five, figuring to milk the last drop out of him, figuring he had this one cinched, figuring The Warden for his lousy pair to brace his kings. It was a legitimate bet; Warden had checked his kings twice when they were high. Warden raised him sixty dollars.

Looking at Warden's malignant grin he knew then he was caught, really hooked, right through the bag. By three big kings. Outsmarted.

Sucked in like a green kid. The first time somebody checked a cinch into him. His belly flopped over sickeningly with disbelief and he made as if to drop out, but he knew he had to call. There was too much of his money in this pot, which was a big one, to chance a bluff. And The Warden knew just how high to raise without raising too high to get a call.

The hand cost him two hundred even, he had about forty dollars left. He pushed the stool back, way back, and got up then.

"Seat open."

Warden's eyebrows quivered, then hooked up pixishly.

"I hated to do that to you, kid. I really did. If I dint need the money so goddam bad I'd by god give it back."

The table laughed all around.

"Ah, you keep it," Prew said. "You won it, Top, its yours. Check me out," he said to the dealer, thinking why dint you drop out you son of a bitch after that second win like you promised, thinking this is not an original lament.

"Whats wrong, kid?" Warden said. "You look positively unwell."

"Just hungry. Missed noon chow."

Warden winked at Stark who had only just come back. "Too late to catch chow now. You better stick around? Win some of this back? Forty, fifty bucks aint much take home pay."

"Enough," Prew said. "For what I need." Why didnt he let it go? why did he have to rub it in? The son of a bitching bastard whoring bastard.

"Yeah, but you want a bottle too, dont you? Hell, we all friends here, just a friendly game for pastime. Aint that right, Jim?"

Prew could see his eyes clenching into rays of wrinkles as he looked at the gambler.

"Sure," O'Hayer said indifferently. "Long as you got the money to be friendly. Deal the cards."

Warden laughed softly, as if to himself. "You see?" he said to Prew. "No cutthroat. No hardtack. The take out's only twenty."

"Beats me," Prew said. He started to add, "*I've got a widowed mother*," but nobody would have heard it. The cards were already riffling off the deck.

As he moved back Stark goosed him warmly in the ribs and winked, and slipped into the seat.

"Heres fifty," Stark said to the dealer.

Outside the air free of smoke and the moisture of exhaled breath smote Prew like cold water and he inhaled deeply, suddenly awake again, then let it out, trying to let out with it the weary tired unrest that was urging him to go back. He could not escape the belief that he had just lost $200 of his own hard-earned money to that bastard Warden. Come on, cut it out, he told himself, you didnt lose a cent, you're twenty to the good, you got enough for tonight, lets me and you walk from this place.

The air had wakened him and he saw clearly that this was no personal feud, this was a poker game, and you cant break them all, eventually they'll break you. He walked around the sheds and down to the sidewalk. Then he walked across the street. He even got so far his hand was on the doorknob of the dayroom door and the door half open. Before he finally decided to quit kidding himself and slammed the door angrily and turned around and went irritably back to O'Hayer's.

"Well look who's here," Warden grinned. "I thought we'd be seeing you. Is there a seat open? Somebody get up and give this old gambler a seat."

"Aw can it," Prew said savagely and slipped into the seat of another loser who was checking out and grinning unhappily at The Warden with the look of a man who wants to do the right thing and be a good sport but finds it hard.

"Come on, come on," Prew said. "Whats holding things up? Lets get this show on the road."

"Man!" The Warden said. "You sound like you're itchin for a great big lick."

"I am. Look out for yourself. I'm hot. First jack bets."

But he was not hot and knew it, he was only savagely irritated, and there is a difference and it took him just fifteen minutes and three hands to lose the forty dollars, as he had known he would. Where before he had played happily, lost in loving it, savoring every second, now he played with dogged irritation, not giving a damn, angered by even the time it took to deal. You dont win at poker playing that way, and he stood up feeling a welcome sense of release that came with being broke and able to quit now.

"Now I can go home and go to bed. And sleep."

"What!" The Warden said. "At three o'clock in the afternoon?"

"Sure," Prew said. Was it only three o'clock? He had thought they'd played Tattoo already. "Why not?" he said.

The Warden snorted his disgust. "Punks wont never listen to me. I told you you should of quit when you was ahead. But would you listen? A lot you listen."

"Forgot," Prew said. "Forgot all about it. Hows for loanin me a hundred, and I'll remember." It got a laugh around the table.

"Sorry, kid, you know I'm behind myself."

"Hell. And I thought you was winnin." It got another laugh, and he felt better, but he remembered it did not put money back in his pocket. He elbowed his way out.

"What you want to awys be pickin on the kid for, First?" he heard Stark say behind him.

"Pick on him?" Warden said indignantly. "Whatever give you that idea?"

"He dont need you to pick on him," the K Co topkick, a bald fat man with drinker's hollowed eyes, said. "From what I hear."

"Thats right," Stark said. "He doin all right by himself."

Warden snorted then. "He can take it. He's a punchy. He's use to bein hit. Some of them even like it."

"If I was him," the K Co topkick said, "I'd transfer the hell out of there."

"Thats all you know," Warden said. "He cant. Dynamite wont let him."

"Come on," Jim O'Hayer's voice said nasally. "Is this a sewing circle or a card game? King is high, king bets."

"Bet five," Warden said. "You know, thats what I like about you, Jim. Your overwhelming sense of human compassion," he said quizzically. In his mind Prew could see the eyes clenching themselves into those somehow ominous rays of wrinkles.

He let the shaky door swing shut behind him, cutting off the talk, wishing he could find it in him to hate that bitchery Warden but he couldnt, and remembering suddenly he had not even in his passion thought to get a sandwich and coffee from O'Hayer's free lunch for the players. But he would not go back in there now.

He could also remember, suddenly, a lot of other things he had meant to do with part of that money before he risked it. He needed shaving cream and a new bore brush and a new Blizt rag and he had wanted to stock up some tailormades. It was lucky he had a carton of Duke's still stashed away.

Because you are through, Prewitt, he told himself, your wad is shot, your roll is gone, you're through till next month now, and there will be no Lorene for you this month. By next month she may have retired and gone back to the States already.

He jammed his hands in his pockets savagely and found some change, a small pile of dimes and nickels, and brought it out and looked at it, wondering what it was good for. It was enough to get into a small change game in the latrine, but the hopelessness of ever running that little bit back up to two hundred and sixty bucks hit him and he threw it down into the railroad bed viciously and with satisfaction watched it spread like shot but glinting silver, then heard with satisfaction the clink of it hitting the rails. He turned back to the barracks. Lorene, or no Lorene, poker or no poker, you are not borrowing any money at no twenty percent thats for sure. You aint borrowed any twenty percent money since you been on this rock and you aint starting now, school keeps or not.

He found Turp Thornhill in his own shed next to O'Hayer's. Because there was nothing in O'Hayer, even at twenty percent, when he was playing. Turp was neither playing nor dealing. He was moving from dice table to blackjack table to poker table back to dice table, perpetually and nervously, checking up as usual on his dealers to see they were not cheating him.

The tall chinless hawknosed Mississippi peckerwood possessed all the disgusting traits of a backward people with few of the compensating good. But he did loan money, even though he lived an eternal gimlet-eyed suspicion, a grasping pinch-mouthed servile pride in being *"just what he was, by god, and no hifalutin airs, take it or leave it."* He had earned the management of his gambling shed by being in the same company 17 years and ass-kissing his superiors every minute of that time, and now he was in position to compensate for it with a sadistic cruelty toward anyone he calculated he could dominate.

"Haw," Turp hawked, when Prew called him over to one side and hit him up for twenty. He doubled up his long thin frame and prodded the other slyly. "Haw," he hollered, loud enough for everybody in the humming shed to hear, "so Prewitt the Hard's a finally givin in, 'ey? Got his guts all riled over wantin a little, 'ey? So he decide to come around and see ole daddy Turp that aint good enuf for him to talk to 'cept on Payday to borry some money, 'ey? Well, it comes to all on us, boy, it comes to all on us."

He got his wallet out, but did not open it yet, he was not through yet.

"Where you aim to go? The Service? The Ritz? The Pacific? The New Senator? The New Congress Mrs Kipfer runs? I know em all, boy, hell I support em. Listen, now, boy. Let me give you a little tip. Ers a new job over to the Ritz. Not so hot on looks but boys! will she work you over. Hunh? What you say? Kind of gits ye, dont it? Like to have a little bit a that stuff? wunt ye? 'ey? Hows about er, 'ey?"

A number of the players were looking at them now and laughing. Turp grinned back at them smugly, relishing his audience, not wanting to lose it, not just yet.

Prew was still silent but his face was reddening in spite of himself. He cursed silently at his face for reddening.

Turp laughed again, winking at his audience, get this now, this going to be a good one now, just get this. His long bony nose poked into Prewitt's face with each bob of nervous laughter. The grin pulled up the long corners of his chinless mouth making his face into a series of sharp prying Vs. The subdued murky eyes popped into bright intensity like bursting flares, filled with obscene curiosity and insulting laughter. Turp was at his best before an audience, get this now.

"Haw," Turp hawked, winking at his audience. "Why hell, boy, if you'd do it with her her way, you wunt have to borry no money. She'd give it to ye for nuthin, and probly be willin to take you to raise in the bargain. Hows about that, 'ey?"

The audience roared. Old Turp was in form. Even the dice stopped rattling.

"I hear thats what she likes," Turp hawed. "Hows about it, 'ey? Man never knows till he tried it. Maybe he been missin somethin all his life. I hear them boys out in Hollywood make a lot of money that a way. Man awys use a leetle money, caint e? Might even get to like it, who knows?

"Haw, look at im. He blushin. Look at im, boys. Laws, I do declare he blushin. You really want to borry some money now, Prewitt? Or you jist pullin my leg now? Maybe you wont need it now."

Prew stayed silent but he was having trouble with it. He had to keep shut, if he aimed to get the money. And Turp had money. Turp made money. He had been running a shed from G Company when O'Hayer was just an upstart. But O'Hayer's rise had been meteoric and he had topped them all. For this Turp hated and feared the gambler with a sly long-nosed implacability. Yet strangely, he took the small sums he made from his loans and the large sums he made from his shed and lost them all across O'Hayer's poker table along in the middle of the month. After the Payday gambling rush was over and his own shed was closed down, he would sit in on the winners' game, betting wildly, cursing with nervous excitability, losing steadily. It was as if the sterile contamination of his own spavined Mississippi land had gotten like clap into his blood and made even himself an object of his own ingrown suspicious hatred, so that he frantically threw away every cent he could pick up, in order to keep Turp from cheating Thornhill. And in the end the hated O'Hayer, cool and mathematical and impersonal, always collected the profits of Turp's shed in addition to his own.

Turp let him have the twenty, finally, after a pause in his Southern Ku Klux Klan brand of humor, a pause in which white lines of suspicion pinched in upon his mouth and cut down through his laughter while he attempted to divine all the thousand ways this seemingly open man might be trying to crook him, oh, he looked honest enough, but you never can tell, and Turp Thornhill knew a thing or two, Turp Thornhill knew better than to trust a man's looks, Turp Thornhill was like Diogenes, he had never seen an honest man, and he never would. After insulting him, ridiculing him, suspicioning him, torturing him by letting on he could not afford to loan it, Turp generously let him have the whole twenty dollars he had asked for, at twenty percent, and warned him narrowly not to try to pull some wise shenanigan when it come time to pay it back.

Prew, as he dressed for town with the twenty in his pocket, felt the degradation of Turp's foul breath still on him that a shower would not wash off and wondered which was worse, to be poked by Turp's foul breathing Mississippi nose or to be sprayed with Ike Galovitch's foul smelling Slavic spit. This was sure turning out to be some outfit. A fine home, this outfit. He was also wondering, as he dressed, at the humiliations men will suffer for a woman that they will not suffer for any other thing, even for their politics.

Chapter 21

Milt Warden, as he debated checking out of this game himself, was thinking somewhat the same thing, just as wonderingly, but about a different woman.

Perhaps it was because he was meeting Karen Holmes downtown tonight at the Moana, he thought, but every time he looked up from his cards his eyes focused themselves on the battered husky face of Maylon Stark with a kind of shocked disbelief like a man looking at his own arm blown off and lying in his slit trench. It was outrageous, this face, and what was worse it was ruining his game. Because he could not stop looking at it. Two out of the last three hands he'd lost he should have won except that his eyes were staring themselves at this face whose eyes and lips had also caressed the nude self-induced-trance that was like death and that was Karen Holmes when being loved, and that he, Milt Warden, remembered clearly. That undoubtedly Stark remembers clearly too, he thought. Because there was no doubt he had, goddam it. No doubt at all. Any way you turn it. It was not wishful thinking because Stark had not mentioned it again since that first time; Stark was not the artistic type who can imagine things into reality, worse luck. And obviously Stark had not mentioned it to anybody else or it would have got around, clear around, by now; but then Stark was not a bragger either, who needed ego building. No, he thought scrotum-sickeningly, no doubt at all, you cant explain it away, and the worst of that is that it points the finger at the up to now preposterous stories of her and Champ Wilson, and that goddamned perverted Henderson, and even possibly O'Hayer. He looked at O'Hayer. But she said, "I never knew it could be like this"; he remembered distinctly she had said, "I never knew it could be like this."

"Check me out," he said to the dealer, "so's I can get in a goddam game where theres some action. And theres ninety-seven dollars in silver there. I counted it already."

The dealer grinned. "You dont mind if I count it too, do you, Milt?"

"Hell no. I just wanted you to know I counted it."

The dealer laughed, heartily.

"Take this too," Jim O'Hayer yawned. "I'm going to knock off for a little break myself and see how things are going. Just shove this in the drawer with the rest and I'll take it back out later."

"Okay, boss," the dealer, who was a buck sergeant, said. He shoved Warden's bills over to him to keep the piles separate and then shoved O'Hayer's into the drawer that was already full of the red chips and silver he had cut the game for, for O'Hayer.

"It'll be here when you get back, Jim," the dealer promised faithfully proudly, and Warden watched him bland-eyedly neatly palm a ten-spot off the pile as he continued the deal with his left hand, sliding the cards off with his thumb, then bring his right hand back to the deal still palming the folded ten, and then after the round was completed reach his right hand into his shirt pocket for a cigaret.

Warden looked at O'Hayer who was standing stretching after hanging his expensive eyeshade on a nail behind him and lit a cigaret himself and grinning, held the match for the buck sergeant dealer who did not grin back now but looked through him flat-eyedly across the match flame as he lit up.

Warden laughed and flipped the match away and then followed O'Hayer outside and the two of them stood breathing in the fresh air and smoking, O'Hayer silent and somehow sealed mathematically within himself as he stared indifferently at the thinly rusted over railroad rails.

Warden, who had meant to go on to the barracks, stood watching him and smoking, thinking this was as good a time as any to try and get the usual needle in through this thick skin, but wanting to just see if he couldnt make the automatic calculator speak first for once.

"Kitchen must be getting along pretty well now with Preem gone," O'Hayer said finally; it was an indifferent offering to the abstract status of First Sergeant; you got the impression if it was anybody else he would not have even bothered speaking; still, he had spoken.

"Yeah," Warden said, silently congratulating Warden. "I wish the rest of my compny administration was getting along so good."

"Oh?" O'Hayer said coolly. "Mazzioli been giving you some trouble lately?"

Warden grinned. "Who else? And how are you coming? How you making out with the new bayonet issue?"

285

"Oh, that." O'Hayer lifted his head and the cold eyes left their contemplation of the rails to study Warden. "Coming along fine, Top. I've given Leva instructions how to do it. If I remember, he's got about half the chrome bayonets exchanged for the black ones now and the excess chrome ones turned in to ordnance. Its only a question of time," he said.

"How much time?"

"Time," O'Hayer said easily. "Just time. Leva's got a lot of stuff to do, you know. You trying to tell me I'm taking too much time?"

"Oh, no," Warden said. "The rest of the battalion only got their exchange completed and their chrome turned in about two weeks ago. You're about on schedule."

"You know, Top," O'Hayer said, "you get too excited over little things, Top."

"You dont get excited enough, Jim," Warden said. He was feeling again, as he always felt with O'Hayer, that dispassionate itching to step in suddenly and knock him down, not from dislike, just to see if there wasnt some emotion in among the tumblers. Someday I'll do it, he told himself. Someday I'll quit thinking about it and do it, and then they can bust me, and I will go happily back to being a rear rank Rudy with no troubles and nothing to do but get drunk and lug around a rifle and be happy. Someday I will.

"It never pays to get excited," O'Hayer explained. "You're liable to forget little things, Top. Important things. In the excitement."

"You mean like the connections between Regiment and the sheds? Or like the small opinions of Captain Holmes that are always, though, important?"

"Well, I didnt mean that," O'Hayer said. He grinned. It was a tightening of the cheeks that pulled the mouth corners up and showed the teeth. "But since you mention it, I guess that would be a good example."

"If you're tryin to scare me it not only wont work its ridiculous," Warden said. "I pray every night that by next Payday I'll be drawin thirty dollars."

"Sure. All us noncoms got heavy responsibilities," O'Hayer said sympathetically. "Look at me," he waved his hand behind him at the shed.

What was the use? Warden asked himself. You cant talk with him. Only way you can ever talk with him is blow your top and get mad like you did over the clothing issue, and even that dont do you any good. You might as well quit fencing.

"Listen, Jim," he said. "Theres going to be a lot more stuff coming up soon like this change of chrome bayonets for black. We'll be getting the new M1 rifles pretty soon, and they are experimenting with a new style helmet at Benning now. We're getting ready to get into this war and from now on there will be all kinds of changes, not only in equipment but in administration. I'm going to have my hands full with the orderly room and the records, from now on. I wont be able to handle the supply."

"Me and Leva are handling it," O'Hayer said, still untouched. "I aint had any complaints from anybody about how we're handling it. Except from you. I think me and Leva are doing a pretty good job of handling it. Dont you, Top?"

Ah, Warden thought. He held the hypo up to the light then and squirted the needle, just to make sure, just to see that it was working right.

"What would you do," he asked, "if Leva transferred out of this company?"

O'Hayer laughed. It was like with his smile. "Now you're trying to scare me, Top. You know Dynamite would never okay Leva's transfer. I'm ashamed of you, stooping to such tricks."

"But what if the transfer came down from Regiment, from Colonel Delbert?" Warden grinned.

"Why, Dynamite would just take it back to him and explain the facts of life to him, thats all. You know that, Top."

"No I dont," Warden grinned. "And apparently you dont know Dynamite, not if you think he's going to jeopardize his chance of getting that majority he's bucking for by arguing with The Great White Father."

O'Hayer looked at him coolly, Warden could almost see the tumblers moving.

"Leva," Warden grinned complacently, "has been talking it up with M Company, Jim. They want him for supply sergeant. All he has to do is transfer and the rating's his. And M Co's CC wants him so bad he taken it up with the 3rd Battalion Commander, who is *not* a Captain but a Lieutenant Colonel, a Lieutenant Colonel who has taken it up with Delbert, Jim."

"Thanks for the tip," O'Hayer said. "I'll work on it."

"Its no tip," Warden grinned. You're enjoying this, aint you, he thought. What a prick. "If it hadnt already gone too far for you and Dynamite to stop it, I never would of told you, Jim. Leva's a good man. I'm a prick, but I aint that big a one.

"Its only a question of time, Jim," he grinned.

O'Hayer did not say anything.

"So this is no tip. This is a favor I'm asking you. A personal favor. Will you ask Dynamite to relieve you from supply? You can tell him you're bored with it and get him to carry you surplus for straight duty, and let me give Leva that rating? As a personal favor to me. You lose nothing; I get to keep Leva."

O'Hayer was looking at him thoughtfully, the tumblers making little clickings as they moved, still unemotionally, calculating.

"I like it where I am," O'Hayer said, finally. "I see no reason to change my status, not from what you've told me. He might even end up by wanting me to pull drill with the Company, if he carried me surplus for straight duty. I like being the supply."

"You wont when Leva transfers, Jim."

"Maybe he wont transfer."

"He will."

"Maybe not," O'Hayer said again, making a veiled threat of it, as if he knew more than he was telling.

"Okay," Warden said. Well, he thought, it didnt work. He flipped his cigaret down at the rails in the bed below and watched the feeble glow, that was like a lightbulb in the daytime, splash in the gathering dusk.

He turned and walked away, grinning to himself happily. He spoke back over his shoulder just before he rounded the corner of the shed to O'Hayer who was still watching unemotionally.

"You know, Jim," he said, "I really use to believe this stuff that you were one of those rare things, a human being truly without feeling. One of those that things come to naturally because they never mind risking coldbloodedly, or even losing coldbloodedly, what they have. Romantic, hey?"

As he rounded the corner O'Hayer was still looking at him, still unemotionally, all the tumblers apparently still working.

Well, so what if it didnt work. Maybe Dynamite really would have done it for him, Big Jim meant a lot to Dynamite and not just as a punchie, maybe Dynamite really would have carried him as surplus, who knows? You never knew. Dynamite could hardly bust him.

But then Dynamite might also have transferred him. To HQ Company maybe where he would have to work. Or maybe Dynamite would only have clamped down on him in supply and made him work some here, although Christ knows what he could do without going to a supply school first. Well, maybe Dynamite might have sent him to supply school. Dynamite *could* have done any of these, if O'Hayer asked him to be relieved, like you hoped he would. So maybe old tumblers-in-the-head really did figure it out right. Maybe he wasnt scared.

But it was entirely possible Dynamite would have carried him as surplus though, he reminded himself. Entirely possible. And he preferred to believe Dynamite would have, and that old tumblers hadnt figured it out but was only scared to take a chance on losing his soft deal, just like us common mortals. Maybe Dynamite wouldnt have carried him as surplus, but Warden preferred to believe it the other way. It made him happy to believe it the other way.

He went on over to the barracks happily, believing it, to shower and change his clothes and go to town and have some drinks someplace or maybe just wander around happily downtown, not out at Waikiki but downtown, among the bars and shooting galleries and whorehouses, while he waited for time to meet Karen Holmes at the Moana in Waikiki. His T shirt and shirt both were sweated clear through from the gambling and he stopped on the stairs and raised his arm and put his nose to his armpit happily and inhaled the mineral-salts male smell of himself, feeling his chest expanding infinitely with maleness, feeling from inside himself the hard columnar beauty of his thighs and the slim thickly muscled beauty of his waist and loins; he was Milt Warden and he was meeting Karen Holmes in town tonight. But then suddenly, the eyes inside his mind that were not his eyes focused themselves, as his eyes had done, on the husky battered face of Maylon Stark and he straightened up with his nostrils sickened and smashed his fist against the wall, punching stiff-wristed, solid-forearmed as a fighter punches, at the place where Maylon Stark's husky battered face was amorphously hanging and let the numbed hand fall contemptuously at his side and went on upstairs, to shower and change his clothes and go to town to meet Karen Holmes at the Moana.

Pete Karelsen was in their room, sitting on his bunk staring crumplemouthed at the full set of grinning teeth in his open palm. He laid them down on the table quickly.

"What the hell happen to your hand?" he wanted to know eagerly. "You been in a fight again?"

"What the hell happen to your goddam teeth?" Warden said contemptuously. "You been in a goddam messhall again?"

"Okay," Pete said offendedly. "Be wise. I was only interested in your hand."

"Okay," Warden said. "Be hurt. I was only interested in your goddam teeth," and went on looking at his own hated face in the mirror, unbuttoning the thick chenille of his shirt, pulling it up savagely out of his pants.

"All the time making cracks," Pete said. "All the time needling somebody. I merely ask you a simple friendly question. You dont have to go casting aspersions. You dont have to go being snotty."

Warden went on looking in the mirror without answering and finished unbuttoning his shirt and took it off and dropped it on the bed. He unbuckled his belt in silence.

"What are you doing?" Pete said conversationally. "Getting ready to go to town?"

"No. I'm getting ready to go over to Choy's, thats why I'm changing into civilians."

"Okay. Go to hell."

"I'm going over to Choy's and get drunker'n hell."

"I been thinkin of doing that myself," Pete said. "Somehow or other I dont feel much like going to town today. You know," he said, looking stealthily at the teeth on the table, "its really the same old thing, over and over, when you think about it. And what does it get you in the end, going to town? A hangover, is all. I'm getting bored with it," he said. He stole another look at the teeth. "I'm getting any more so I dont much care I go to town or not. Ever. I'd even ruther go to Choy's."

"All right," Warden said, turning away from the mirror. He picked his shirt back up and put it on again and started buttoning it. "Lets go. What the hellar you waitin on?"

"You mean to Choy's? Really?"

"Sure. Why not? Like you say, why go to town?"

"I thought you were snowing me," Pete said. He got up grinning toothlessly and picked the teeth up from the table and leered at them. "Hunh," he said and put them back. "To hell with you. Come on, Milt."

They went out through the deserted squadroom, Warden unbuttoning his pants and stuffing the shirt tail down into them and buttoning them back up again and tying the tie, Pete walking and talking newly animatedly.

"We'll get a case of cans," he said. "Maybe we'll sit out in the kitchen this time. I dont like to sit out front on Payday, with all them young punks yelling around. Or maybe we'll get four or five pitchers instead, take them outside on the green. Maybe that would be better?

"After we get teed up," Pete said as they reached the stairs. "After we're properly soused, maybe we'll go over to Big Sue's in Wahiawa and take one, hey? And come right back. For the hell of it. Wait a minute," he said. "I better go back and get my teeth."

Warden stopped silently. He lit a cigaret and leaned back against the porch banister and crossed his feet and folded his arms, and was suddenly a statue frozen into a perpetual granite immobility, the top half of him a cut black paper silhouette fixed against the deepening dusk outside the screens. He stood so in suspended animation, divorced from life.

When Pete came back he spoke, without moving, the cigaret a bobbling red point that was the only breathing live thing about him.

"The trouble with you, Pete," the voice that did not seem to come from him but from the cigaret said savagely, "is you cant see any further than that douchebag nose of yours. You concern yourself with the petty details of life in order *not* to think, like whether or not to wear them goddam teeth of yours if you think a pussy's gunna see you—just like the goddam housewives in my brother's parish with their makeup when they're going to confession. While the whole damn world is rocketing to hell you got to go back and get your fucking teeth. Whynt you go get in the goddam church and hold hands with the padre and pray for peace, you're at about that age now, and you're suffering from the same disease that afflicts the rest of the human race."

Pete stood stricken motionless in the act of putting in his teeth, transfixed by the sudden sanguinariness of the attack, his mouth open and his thumbs still inside with the teeth, staring at this two dimensional statue cut from tin.

"Its because of you theres Nazis in Germany," the voice that was not Warden sermonized him. "Its because of you there'll be Fascism in this country someday. After we have got in and pulled the chestnuts out again for the rest of the world and won this war for England. And you sit around with Mazzioli and the rest of the commendable clerks and discuss. Any subject, just discuss. Whynt you get up a regular Tuesday Literary Club like the Irish ladies in me brother's parish. Intellectuals!"

The statue moved out of frozen mobility into a dead run for the stairs, his feet flickering down them like a boxer's feet skipping rope.

"Come on, you stupid boob," Warden bawled. "What the hellar you waitin for?"

Pete finished the interrupted teeth insertion and champed his jaws to settle them in and followed silently, shaking his head confoundedly.

"And what the hell do you do?" Pete said indignantly, half running to keep up with the long loping strides as they moved across the quad. His voice was so choked with hurt, after the warm comradely time he had envisioned, that he seemed almost to be crying. "I suppose you dont concern yourself with the petty details of life?"

"Sure," Warden said. "Why not? Dont *bawl,* for Christ sake."

"Then why read me off? I'm not *bawling.* And what do you mean we got to get in and win this war? We're all ready in, except for sending troops."

"Sure," Warden agreed. "Thats it."

"And maybe the Ruskies and the Jerries will get in it with each other and kill each other off and save us the trouble. Anyway, it looks like they will. In spite of this treaty."

"Fine," Warden said. "Fine. The more thats dead the less to feed the more beer for me. What are you arguing about?"

"Why dont you talk sense? I'm not arguing. You're arguing. You started this argument."

"Did I? Well then I'm ending it. As of right now."

He opened the screendoor between the garbage racks and stacks of empty cases on the porch and went into the kitchen of Choy's restaurant irritably, with Pete following cursing chokingly and impotently angrily.

They were among the scant dozen noncoms in the Regiment who had the privilege of sitting and drinking in Choy's kitchen and now they sat down and prepared themselves, unbuttoning their shirts under their loosened ties and rolling up their sleeves two turns and propping their feet up on Choy's freshly scrubbed meatblock, and then called for Old Choy who had been sitting on a high stool in the corner to bring them beer. They were going to make a party.

"Hey, Old Choy, you heathen Chinee," Warden bellowed. "You blingee beer, eh? Blingee two four six beer. Chop-chop!"

He held up ten fingers and the eighty-year-old statue in the corner came to life and shuffled perilously across the kitchen to the ice chest grinning hugely under the thin straggly white beard. Old Choy always grinned at Warden, because since Young Choy, his eldest son, had taken over the business from him the ancient one was not allowed to go out front where the customers were and where Young Choy was now in the shouting Payday hubbub, and the old man, who sat in the kitchen all day every day in his black silk skull cap and long embroidered robe that Young Choy who had given up ancestor worship for American business ethics called bad for blisness, worshipped Warden because Warden liked to come sit in the kitchen and drink beer and kid the old man, whenever he had the blues.

"Huba-huba," Warden bellowed after him with a wink at Pete, "wiki-wiki, chop-chop. You feet, stickee floor, old goat. Me in hully, old man, you bletta snappem shit."

Old Choy tottered to the meatblock with an armload of cans.

"You goat, Old Choy," Warden grinned. "Goat, see? You mother goat. Mama-San she goat, see? She blingee you goat. Goat, see? Goat. Baa-a-a." He put his fingers under his chin and waggled them at the Chinese.

Old Choy set the beer on the block, his almond eyes closed to bright slits, and chuckled with great glee at being called an old goat.

"No goat," he chuckled. "You goat, Walden."

Warden grabbed an empty can off the block, his bright eyes dancing in the broad big face, the energy pouring out of him in dazzling radiations, the lets-make-this-a-party energy.

"See, old goat," he bellowed ferociously, and bent the can double with one movement using his thumbs for fulcrum on the seam. "You do that? You makee can double? You call me goat, I make you double. Like this, see?"

He took another can and bent it. Then he worked his way with a sudden savagery through all the empties standing on the block, bending them viciously easily and tossing them over his shoulder into the trash box. "See? like this. See? like this. You bletta no mess with me, old man goat."

The Chinese stood before him, grinning all over his eroded face, his shoulders shaking with his chuckling, his head doddering with age.

"Blingee beer," Old Choy said. He held out his hand with a delighted grin. "Me blingee beer. Now you play."

"Ha-ha," Warden laughed, "ho-ho. Me no can play. No got cash." He held up his hand in the old, Army gesture, middle finger extended, other fingers closed, thumb and middle finger pinching together repeatedly in the air.

"You blingee woman, me play."

He made the old, Army sign for woman again, under Old Choy's nose.

"You woman, old man goat, me show you how play. My play you then."

"You play," Old Choy said, giggling. "You play, Walden."

Warden got his wallet out and gave him a bill. "You smart like fox, old man goat. You catchee much money, much cash. You son him makee million dollar."

The old Chinese laughed delighted, patting Warden on his big thick shoulder with the thin fine-boned almost transparent hand, and shuffled with the bill to the door out front and called softly in Chinese to his son to come take the money. Then he came back with the change, still grinning, and perched up on his stool to watch the show, his bright old eyes constantly moving.

"Ah," Pete sighed. He wiped the foam from his lip with the back of his hand. Then he pinched off the speck of foam the small hole in the can had left on the end of his nose with his thumb and forefinger and flung it on the cement floor. "Ah," he said. "Ah, man."

Pete had watched the party-ritual sadly, gazing down from the summit of his 22 years service. Now he began his party-ritual.

"You remember the old Bijou Theater in Coconut Grove, Milt?" he said sadly. "I wonder if its still there these many years."

"Sure," Warden grinned, teetering in his chair. "The Red Dog Theater on Balboa Street. They probly closed it up by now since the Zone is gone respectable. If they aint they will, soon as these young virgin draftees start comin in and the Future Gold Star Mothers of America make the whole Army go respectable for the duration. Remember what they done to Storyville in the last war."

"Ah, yes," Pete said sadly. "Nawrlans aint never been the same. They even have tore down the old market and built a new one thats sanitary. Did you know that, Milt?"

"Sure," Warden said indifferently, the party energy beginning to wear thin before this old rehashing. He got himself another can to bolster it.

"Yes, sir," Pete said. He looked off at the ceiling corner with great emotion. "Colon. Balboa. Panama City. Walking post along the locks. Coconut Grove. The old Bijou Theater with nothing but shunt pictures. Newsreel, cartoon, and a feature. I got some of the best and most artistic pictures in my collection down in The Grove. Things aint like they was, Milt. Remember? the MPs had no authority above the ground floor? and if a whore ever got you up on the second floor you might as well kiss the boys goodby? It was a fifty-fifty chance they find you in the river. They were men in those days."

"If you ever get caught with that collection of yours," Warden taunted, "you can kiss the boys goodby. Possessing pornography is five years and a DD, Pete." This that he had heard so often was killing the partiness and the other, the jaw-tightening, the scrotum-sickening, was coming back. "Wouldnt that be a shame," he nagged, "you with only seven years to go for rocking chair money?"

"Once I took a girl down there to the Bijou," Pete reminisced emotionally. "Can you imagine that? But I was a young buck then. I was a fireball."

"How many beers you had, Pete?"

"Only four. As yet. Why? This girl was a planter's daughter, see? Her old man worked about five hundred gooks and she had led a very sheltered life. A very moral young lady, Milt. I took her out to a high class dinner and then to the Bijou. It was a great shock to her to learn about life. But she took it well. She got to like me very much, after that." He took up another can, a fresh one.

"Well," Warden said, "go on. Tell the rest of it."

"Thats all there is," Pete said.

"The last time I heard it you told it different."

"Well," Pete said, his great emotion still secure. "What do you expect? I was in a different mood then."

"Oh," Warden said. "Is that it? Hey, Old Choy. Pappa-San blingee more beer to soljer boys, or Pappa-San gettem beard pulled offem face, eh?"

Old Choy got up and tottered grinning obediently to the ice chest.

"What do you want to make over the old duffer so much for?" Pete asked, still speaking with great emotion. "Whynt you let him die in peace? since he's old and useless?"

"I dont make over him. Him and me got an understanding, aint we, Choy?"

"You play now," Old Choy grinned, setting down the cans. "You play, Walden."

"See?" Warden said.

"Nobody has any use for him any more," Warden said, getting out another bill. "He owns the business but his eldest son runs it and collects the money and gives him his allowance and tells him what to do. Well, I'm the First Sergeant and everybody tells me how they want my compny run. I wear the stripes and draw the money and they tell me who to make and who to bust and how they want it run. Me and Old Choy understands each other."

"Yas," Pete said, "you sure take a beating, dont you?"

"Sure. Even Mazzioli tells me how to run my orderly room. Come on, lets get out of this. What time is it?"

"Eight o'clock. But what for? I'm just beginning to enjoy myself," Pete protested.

"Sure. And we hang around here any more you'll be crying in your goddam beer."

"But you dont understand," Pete said, his great emotion coming back. "The things I've seen, the things I've done. All of them gone. All of them not any more."

"Sure," Warden said, "sure, I know. Come on, for Christ sake. Come on. I cant stand it. You're killing me."

"But you *dont* understand," Pete said. "Where'll we go?"

"Go out front," Warden said. He led the way out of the kitchen and around to the front of the restaurant so no one would see them coming out because it was against regulations.

It was not the same now any more, you could do it all, the same as you use to do it, but it was not the same.

Chief Choate was at his corner table and they sat down with him, ordering more beer. Pretty soon they were joined by the K Company topkick who had just quit a little bit ahead of O'Hayer's game, making the four of them a tight little group of old timers in the smoky room that was crowded with the yelling singing horseplay of the youngsters, amongst whom they sat quietly upon their dignity and talked about the Old Army. Chief retold his story of the time he was on guard duty in PI and caught a black gook with the colonel's wife in a calash parked along the road on his post, in a much-more-than-embarrassing position.

"Did you *see* it?" Warden said. "Did you *see* it? or did you just suspect it?"

"I seen it," the Chief insisted with his ponderous calm. "You think I'd make it up? A thing like that?"

"Hell, I dont know," Warden said, twisting the big shoulders irritably, looking around the room. "How the hell do I know? What do you say we get some pitchers and adjourn to the green? This goddam place gives me the willies."

All of them looked at The Chief for agreement, since this was his table and he rarely left it.

"Its okay by me," The Chief said, "I dont like it much in here myself on Payday."

"I dont believe it," Warden said, as they went out in the sallyport. "You probably heard that story someplace, from some bastard's perverted imagination and just picked it up, thats all."

"I dont give a damn what you believe," The Chief said. "I know what I seen. Whats eating you?"

"Nothings eating me. What makes you think somethings eating me?"

The Chief shrugged. "This is better out here," he said. "A lot nicer."

And it was nicer, as they sat down cross legged on the sparse grass around the pitchers they had brought out. The air was very clear to breathe and good to see through after the deafening confusion and tobacco smoke of Choy's. The quad was dotted with parties of beer drinkers but their conversation made a pleasant insect-like hum out here that was no longer deafening. Now and then a laugh would ring up sharp and clear out of the hum and the stars seemed to be winking at all of them over each other's shoulder. The fights that kept breaking out out here on the green were removed from them and remote, instead of being in their laps. The large warm semi-tropic moon was just coming up, dimming the stars around it, making the clear air golden with a tangible pulsating life, painting new stark shadows on the ground in the perspectiveless planes and angles of a cubist.

Pete and The Chief launched into an argument over the respective merits of PI and the Panama Department, enumerating advantages and disadvantages and weighing them against each other.

"And I served in both of them," The Chief summed up stolidly. "So I ought to know."

Pete was definitely hampered because he had not been in PI.

"China," the K Co top said. "China's the place thats got them all beat. Aint that right, Milt? Your money's worth ten, twelve times as much. In their rate of exchange. A private lives like a general, in China. I'm gunna ship over for China as soon as my time's up in this rotten Pineapple Army. Aint that right, Milt? You served in China, you tell them."

Warden was lying leaning on his elbow watching the moon ascend and looking at the lighted screens along the faces of the barracks; there were few shadows moving along the porches this night. He stirred.

"Ah, whats the difference? They all the ferkin same. Five cents of one, a nickel of the other." He sat up and locked his elbows around his knees. "You bums make me sick. Always wishin you was someplace else then where you are. Always re-enlisting for a new place you aint been in, always changing, always disgusted with it after the first year.

"Anyway," he said, "there wont be no China next year when your time is up. You'll have to re-enlist for Japan."

He lay back down and crossed his arms behind his head. "I knew a White Russian girl in Shanghai, though. Thats the only thing about China. Theres lots of them there. She was some kind of a duchess or princess. A countess, I think she was. Had blonde hair down to her crotch. Boy, she was beautiful. By god. The most beautiful woman I ever seen. And hot. The hottest woman I ever seen too. I should of married the bitch, I guess."

"Oh-oh," Pete winked at the others. "Here we go again."

Warden sat up. "All right, goddam you, I dont give a damn whether you believe it or not. Her old man was a Rusky, got killed with the stinking 27th in Siberia, fighting the Reds. The 27th U.S. infantry Russian Wolfhounds. Ever hear of them, you smug bastard? Your next-door neighbors, is all they are. You dont believe me, I'll take you over there and prove it by Master Sergeant Fisel. He knew her old man."

"I know," Pete grinned. "I know. Have another drink and tell us all about it. Again."

"Go to hell, you son of a bitch."

"Theres the bugler," The Chief said, and they all stopped talking then and turned to look at the corner of the quad where the guard bugler was raising his horn to the big megaphone to sound Tattoo. Sharply, insistently, he blew the complex notes of Lights Out. The four men lay quiet and absorbed until he had finished, blowing the traditional first and repeat, once to one side, then swinging the megaphone and pouring it out to the north against the 3rd Battalion. One by one the lights in the squadrooms around the quad went out.

"Well, thats it," the K Co top said, completely inexpressively, unable to put this solid foundation stone in words. "That boy sure cant touch that Prewitt kid though," he said. "Was you out here the other night he played the Taps? I swear sure as hell I thought I was gonna bawl. Its a shame that boy cant be playin one all the time."

"Yeah, I heard him," The Chief said. "He's had a raw deal, that kid. All the way around."

"He's gettin a worse one now," Pete said. "He's gettin a real beating now."

They all of them watched the guard bugler depart, watching him inexpressively, looking at him inarticulately, seeing in his this fatality of which they were aware but powerless to influence, this that was more than men, an irresistible cosmic force of some kind that defied isolation.

"Well," the K Co top said, getting up, "I think I'll take a quick run over to Big Sue's and back. I got work to do tomorrow."

"I'll go with you," Pete said. "Loan me five, Milt."

"Sure," Warden said. "At twenty percent." All of them laughed. Warden got up holding a full pitcher of beer.

"Fooled you," Pete said. "I got money. Come on and go along?"

"Hell, no," Warden said contemptuously. "When I have to buy it, I quit."

"Well, I'm going," said the K Co top.

"You want to go, Chief?" Pete said.

"Yeah I might as well," Choate said. He heaved his great bulk up. "Come on and go, Milt."

"No. I told you when I have to buy it, I quit."

"Ah, come on," Pete said.

"No!" Warden said. "God damn no!"

He took the full pitcher of beer between his hands and heaved it high into the air over a steel manhole cover in the grass. The beer slopped out in a spray as it fell, and the other three men scattered. Warden stood still, watching the pitcher fall straight like a plummet from star to star, the beer splattering on his uniform and upturned face in tiny drops.

"Whoops!" he yelled as the pitcher smashed on the manhole cover sending a big spray over him.

"You crazy bastard," said the K Co top. "We could of took it in the cab with us."

Warden rubbed his wet palms into his beerwet face. "Leave me alone," he said muffledly from between the vigorously rubbing palms. "Why dont you leave me alone? Get the hell out and leave me alone."

He turned and walked away from them toward the barracks to shower and get dressed in the dark, to go to town and meet Karen Holmes at the Moana.

Chapter 22

Warden wore his comparatively new tan suit of Forstmann tropical worsted with the saddle-stitched lapels that had cost him $120 tourist prices, and that he saved for great occasions. But all the way into town he was furious with himself for coming. His hand hurt him and was swollen fatly and that also was *her* fault. He wished furiously he had stayed with Pete and the guys, forgetting how miserable he had been with them. He wished furiously he had left her and the rest of these middle-class society women to the gigolos who were neurotic enough themselves to be able to understand them. He wished furiously a lot of things. Once he even wished furiously he was dead and in hell. He knew then that he was in love.

When the cab stopped he went straight across to the Black Cat to buy a bottle in the package store and while he was there had several angry drinks at the bar, before he finally walked furiously over to King to catch furiously the Kalakaua Avenue bus that went furiously to Waikiki. Oh he was in love all right. Was in love for sure. And might as well admit it.

By the time he got off the bus in front of the Waikiki Tavern the whiskey on top of all that beer back at the Post had hit him like a hammer and he was not only in love but was also half drunk and spoiling for a fight. But he didnt find any fights. Everybody was too happy. Waikiki was Payday-crowded and even the civilian people's faces showed they were under the spell of the bars-down festivity.

He walked furiously up past the crowded Tavern to where the beach came in almost to the street to form the little triangle of sand they labeled Kuhio Park where the green benches sat amongst the palm trees in the sand, and where he was meeting Karen Holmes. Kuhio Park was also crowded, and soldiers in civilians and sailors in uniform walked back and forth across it and sat on the benches, with or without women, mostly without. He did not expect her to be there.

She was there all right, though. In the midst of all this champing maleness she was sitting reluctantly on one of the most secluded benches trying hard not to see it, any of it. She sat with her ankles crossed primly and her hands folded primly in her lap and with her elbows and shoulders pulled in tensely primly to her sides. She was there all right all right. And she stared perpetually out over the darkling water with her upper lip between her teeth as if trying to be someplace else. He thought he saw the tensed prim shoulders heave up several times as if in heavy sighs. He walked over to her.

"Why hello," she said lightly. "I didnt think you were coming."

"Why not? I aint late." He felt awkward and constrained and sullen and just a little bit tight and very angry. This was not the debonair way a man should act when having an affair with a married woman, he had had other married women, hadnt he? when he first hit this Rock as a p v t he had worked nights as a deckhand on one of the Ala Moana boats that made moonlight cruises to Molokai for the tourists and he had had all the married women he could take care of then, but of course though, he was not in love with them.

"Oh," she said lightly, "I just couldnt see any reason why you should. After all, I did sort of coerce you into making the date. Didnt I?"

"No," he lied.

"Yes I did, you know I did."

"I wouldnt of come if I dint want to, would I?"

"No," she agreed. "You see?" she said lightly. "Thats the same question I've been sitting here asking myself for the last half hour. But then

I came too early, didnt I? I must have been over anxious. You werent over anxious though, were you? You got here right on the dot."

"Whats eating you?" Warden said, looking at and not liking the tensed primness she was still sitting in. "Relax, why dont you? Take it easy."

"Oh," she said, "I'm relaxed. I'm completely relaxed. Its just that I've had five chances to be picked up in the past half hour, before you came."

"Is that whats bothering you? Hell, thats nothing, thats SOP around here."

"One of the offers," Karen said lightly, "was from a woman."

"A big tall wide-shouldered dyed-blonde woman?"

"Why, yes," Karen said. "Do you know her?"

"If you mean is she a personal friend of mine, the answer's no."

"Oh," Karen said. "Well, I only wondered."

"Well dont wonder. I know of her. Every dogface knows of her. She hangs around here all the time and tries to pick them up. The doggies call her The Virgin of Waikiki. Does that satisfy you?"

"You certainly picked a savory spot for our love tryst, darling," Karen said.

"I picked it because there was less chance of being seen by somebody you know. Would you rather of met me in the cocktail lounge of the Royal?"

"I dont think so," Karen smiled lightly. "But you must remember I'm rather new at this sort of thing, darling. All this stealthy secretiveness as if we were doing something sinful. All this having to sneak around corners. All this back alley loving."

"You're beginning to sound like the local president of the PTA," Warden said. "You got any better ideas how to work it?"

"No," Karen said lightly. "No, I havent." She looked back at the softly breathing water and took her lip between her teeth again. "You dont have to be gallant with me, Milt," she said. "If you're bored already, or tired, why just say so. Just come right out and say so, it wont hurt my feelings, really it wont, darling. I understand about men getting tired quickly." She loosed her lip and smiled up at him painfully lightly, obviously waiting for the protest.

"What the hell makes you think I want to back out of anything?"

"Because you probably think I am a whore," she said succinctly, and looked up at him and waited.

He could see he was expected to protest this too and tell her no, but he was looking at the battered husky face of Maylon Stark hanging amorphously on the palm tree, Stark was very masculine she probably cozily enjoyed it a lot with Stark, and he was having all he could do to keep from banging up his other hand.

"What makes you think I'd think you were a whore?" he asked, knowing it was the wrong answer.

Karen laughed, her face curling up suddenly—he thought—with all the sweet prim terrorism of a well-embalmed old maid.

"Why, Milt darling," she smiled, "you mean you cant *see* it on my *face*? Other people see it. My five pickups must have seen it, and the woman surely saw it. The Virgin of Waikiki," she said. "What a person is always shows on their face, you know; as a man thinketh so is he," she quoted. "You dont really believe they'd try to pick up a decent woman?"

"Hell yes. They'd try to pick up any woman, and almost any man. Down here."

"But even the room clerk at the Moana saw it, when I registered as Sgt & Mrs H L Martin. I could see it plainly on his face that he saw it."

"For Christ's sake," Warden said, "he gets them like that all the time. Whats it to him? long as he gets his money? The tourist women who stay at the Halekulani and the Royal all bring their pickups to the Moana, and vice versa. Thats where the hotels get their biggest turnover."

"Well," Karen said, "at least I know with whom I am classed now. I wonder what *their* husbands do, to pass the time?"

"How the hell should I know?" Warden said, gradually being forced back onto the defensive. "Hang around down town and smoke cigars and discuss business prospects for next year, I guess. What would you guess?"

Karen laughed. "I thought perhaps they might go to stags. In a private apartment upstairs in the Officers Club. Thats where mine goes." She stood up primly. "Well, I guess its about time for me to be getting back home, isnt it?" she said.

"Isnt it?" she said lightly.

"Isnt it, Milt?" she said piercingly sweetly. "Isnt it time?"

Warden swallowed his gorge. He saw that if anybody swallowed their gorge it would have to be him, so he swallowed his. "Listen," he said humbly. "What the hell started all this? I didnt start it, or if I did I didnt mean to."

Karen looked at him and then she sat back down. She reached over and took his hand, the nearest one which was the left one. She smiled brimmingly at him through the half dark. "And I would let it all go to pot, wouldn't I? Because of my silly pride.

"I'm not very pleasant to be around, am I?" she said softly. "I wouldn't see why you'd love me. I'm not gay at all. You never see me gay and happy, do you? Sometimes I am gay though, when I'm feeling well, really I am. You'll have to believe I'm gay sometimes. And I'll try and be gay for you."

"Here," Warden said painfully. He handed her the bottle. "I brang you a present, lady."

"Why, darling," Karen said. "A bottle. I love it. Give it to me. I'll drink it all up by myself."

"Hey now," he grinned, "wait a minute. I want a little." He felt, foolishly, very near to crying, and over nothing.

"Give it to me," Karen said again. And she stood up and the prim tenseness had left her completely, leaving her looking suddenly long and loose and free swinging. She took the bottle and held it in her left arm against the confining thinness of the summer print, carrying it that way, cradled lovingly like a baby, and looking at him.

"I'll give it to you, baby," Warden said, watching her. "I'll really give it to you, baby, all of it."

"Will you?" she said, leaning her head back and looking at him. "Really? All of it? You like to give it to me, dont you? I mean because its me?"

"Yes," he said. "Yes."

"Then lets go now," she said emotionally. "Lets go home now, Milt. Little Milt." She took his left hand with her right, still holding the bottle cradled with the other, and swinging them as they walked leaned her head back and looked up at him.

Warden grinned down at her. But inside he felt the irritated anger come back strong, now that he was sure she was not going to run out on him. He was hurt and provoked suddenly because she had made him feel like crying foolishly over nothing, just to satisfy her pride.

"We better walk down the beach," he said, grinning to hide it. "Be hardly nobody on the beach now at night."

"All right," Karen said silkily. "The beach it is. And to hell with them, what do we care for them? A fig for them. Wait a minute," she said and holding onto him with the hand that held the bottle she raised first one long free-moving leg and then the other and slipped her shoes off, wiggling her toes in the sand.

Warden felt his irritated anger fade before a surge of a much stronger emotion.

"Now," she laughed throatily, and leaned her head back and looked at him in that way she had. "Lets go."

They walked down the beach, the narrow, much touted, disappointing, grapefruit rind floating in the daytime but lovely now at night, Waikiki Beach, walking at the water's edge where the sand was firm and damp, Karen in her bare feet and with her head leaned back exposing the long smooth lovely line of throat looking up at him and swinging their two arms childishly still holding the bottle like a baby, and Warden seeing her feet with their painted nails in the now-darker-than-half dark behind the buildings felt a hot flash go over him, must be the change of life, he thought, you having one of those like use to blister poor sister, as they walked through the damp salt air past the backs of the shop buildings with their lean-to arcade to shade daytime swimmers, past the Tavern's outdoor terrace that was not quite crowded now and the wooden bandstand where the beachboys sat under it and played their ukes for atmosphere in the daytime, past the several private homes interspersed with fruitjuice stands, down the long dark deserted beach, to the Moana's three sided patio (this was no patio, this was a lanai) open on the water with its enormous tree (a *ban—yan*, wasn't it?), where Karen put her shoes back on and he felt it again.

"This is it, Sgt Martin," Karen laughed.

"Thats fine, Mrs Martin."

"I asked for, and got, a corner room on the ocean side. More expensive, but worth it, and we can afford it cant we, Sgt Martin?"

"We can afford anything, Mrs Martin."

"Wait till you see it, its big and airy and lovely and we'll have them serve our breakfast in the room tomorrow. Really and truly a fine place, Sgt Martin."

"Fine place for a honeymoon, Mrs Martin?" he said unashamedly.

"Yes," she said, leaning her head back in that way she had and looking at him from under her eyelids, "for a honeymoon, Sgt Martin."

There was nobody around the patio and he kissed her then, standing out on the beach still, the bad of a while ago all gone now, finding it now just as he had thought so long about it being, before they went up to the nice room, the fine room, that was on the second floor and that they walked up to and then down the long corridor that was like every other hotel corridor whether cheap or expensive, clear down to the end, to the last door on the left.

She turned on the lights and then turned around to him smiling and said, "See? *They even closed the venetian blinds for Sgt & Mrs H L Martin. They must know us.*" And Warden saw the familiar face of Capt Holmes's wife that he had seen so often at a distance on the Post before he knew her and he was strangely moved at the strangeness of it all, seeing the loveliness of the big, woman's breasts straining against the summer print, the long legs with their long thighs and the hips that looked thin under the dress but were not thin or even slim but very full without the dress, and he flipped the knob-button-lock and took three steps and had her as she was slipping her arm up out of the tiny sleeve of the dress she had unbuttoned down the back exposing the slip strap on the deep-tanned shoulder, and he did not give a damn for any of it, Stark or Champ Wilson or O'Hayer or any of them or what they said and he did not believe a goddam word of it and he knew it was not true and he didnt give a goddam if it was true it was different now the hell with all of it and all of them because it had never been like this and it would never again be like this and he knew it and he knew he must be wise and deep and brave and great enough to save this to dig it out of the morass of lies and half lies and false truths and hang onto it now that he finally had it and why had he had it when he knew so few ever had it that he was almost ashamed for having so much of it now as he opened his eyes again and saw that it was all still there still really and truly there and looked down at the shining eyes that actually truly seemed to make two great vertical lines of light as if he were looking at one single star through unfocused field glasses such as he had never seen before and he was both proud and humble and he laughed, looking back now at the easy-for-any-Boy-Scout-to-stalk trail of clothes from the doorway to the bed.

"You laugh beautifully, my darling," Karen murmured sleepily, "and you make love beautifully too. When you love me I feel as if I were a goddess being worshipped, a White Goddess to the savages and you the savages, carefully restrained in worship but with filed teeth and a big gold ring in your ear."

He lay on his back in the sweated bed listening to her and staring contentedly at the ceiling half-sleepily like after a full good rich meal, feeling the fine-boned hand that was almost transparent like Old Choy's but smooth and utterly different in kind and texture from Old Choy's fingering lightly on his chest and the high well lighted room gave them the secret and anonymous solitude that only a hotel room can give as outside the locked door he heard rug-muffled footsteps passing along the corridor and whispered voices coming to him faintly and keys rattling and doors slamming shut with secret finality, finality finality finality of finalities saith the Sergeant all is finality what profit hath a man of all his probabilities under the sun one probability passeth away and another probability cometh all things are full of probabilities man cannot utter it but finality abideth forever in a hotel room there is no remembrance of former probabilities neither shall there be anticipation of probabilities that are to come with those that come after thus spakest I the Sergeant who was king over Israel in Jerusalem where I dwelt in the valley of the shadow of a hotel room with my beloved who is the rose of Sharon and the lilies of the valley of the shadow of a hotel room where there is no inconsistency where there is no probabilities where there is finality remain remain O Shulemite remain remain that ye may give me to drink of the spiced wine of the juice of thy pomegranate in a hotel room where nothing is inconstant finality is all is one and is all and abideth for ever and ever and ever amen days without number while all the probabilities run down to the world yet the world is not full.

Then he was awake again back inside himself again where there were probabilities again, where there would always be probabilities again running into the world again yet never filling the world full enough to reach finality. For a minute there you thought you had found a system that would beat the game, didnt you, Warden? Yes you did, yes you did. But without having to get up to look he could feel the old world seeping steadily under the door that he had locked but forgot to calk. The world was up almost to the mattress now. The world was carrying its sheaf of probabilities under its arm like a salesman. The world was selling insurance for the insurance business that was science. Did you know the insurance business is what gives our country its financial stability? Yes, you knew that. Did you know the insurance business which is science developed and propagated the law of probabilities? Yes, you knew. Well, didnt you know that law of probabilities had as its Justinian Code the principle that there is no finality, that there is only probabilities, that constancy is only an illusion composed and perpetuated by an infinite number of inconstancies? Yes, you knew that too, but you did not believe it. Oh, you did not believe it? Just like that. You do not choose to run. Why didnt you believe it? Probably because, he thought, that is in all probability because, you were raised as a Catholic. Oh, I say, come now, really! Well, you asked me. But you are not a Catholic any more, are you? No, you are not. You stopped being a Catholic at fourteen, when you had your first piece of ass and discovered there was nothing to confess. But you surely realize, do you not, that the Song of the Shulemite is really only a metaphor of Christ's love for the Church? The St James version tells you that explicitly; it is not a man's love for a woman or a woman's love for a man; surely you know that? Yes, you know that; but cant you see, you, that it is simply because of that that the law of probabilities which states that there is no constancy and therefore no finality came into being? Unfair! Unfair! Objection overruled! Strike that out! That statement is immaterial, irrelevant, and misleading, and tends to influence the witness. Objection sustained. Time's up. Theres the bell. *Take It Or Leave It* gives that man Sixty-Four Dollars and we have some fine new policies against being drowned in salt water; you knew of course that salt water is much worse to drown in than fresh water? Yes; but is it better to drown in fresh water than in probabilities? We dont know about that but we know it is a hell of a lot harder. Then I'll just take ten thousand against probabilities. Sorry, we cannot insure you against that likelihood without a complete mental examination, that possibility is too great a risk for our company. Ah, then just give me my Sixty-Four Dollars and I'll go. Sorry, time's up, instead of taking it it looks like you leave it, bud.

"Nobody ever loved me like you love me," Karen said snugly cozily.

"Nobody?" he said.

Karen laughed and it was like honey dripping from a spoon back into the jar between you and the sunlight.

"No, nobody," she said.

"Not even one?" he said, jokingly. "Out of all the many men you've been loved by?"

"Well," Karen said still laughingly, "that will take some figuring. Have you got a pencil? How many men do you think I've been loved by, darling?"

"I wouldnt know," he joked. "Cant you even make me a rough estimate?"

"Not without an adding machine," Karen said, a little less laughingly. "Do you have your adding machine with you?"

"No," he joked. "I forgot to bring it."

"Then I guess you wont find out, will you?" Karen said not laughingly at all.

"Maybe I already know."

She sat up in the bed then and looked at him demandingly, suddenly a more positive personality than he had ever seen her, more even than that first time at the house before the kid came home.

"Whats the matter, Milt?" she said still looking at him. It sounded crisp and wifely, as if she had called him Milton.

"Why, nothing," he grinned stiffly. "Why?"

"Yes there is," she said. "What are you hinting at?"

"Hinting at?" he grinned. "I wasnt hinting at anything. I was only kidding you."

"No you werent," she said. "What are you upset about?"

"About nothing," Warden said. "Why? Is there something I should be upset about? Is there something to hint at?"

"I dont know," she said. "Maybe a lot. Or maybe you just think theres a lot.

"Tell me," Capt Holmes's wife said. "What is it? Dont you feel well? Did you eat something?"

"Dont worry about my health, baby."

"Then tell me what it is. Why dont you tell me?"

"Okay," he said. "Did you ever hear of a guy named Maylon Stark?"

"Why, yes," Karen said distinctly. "I know Maylon Stark. He's the company mess sergeant."

"Thats right. He also use to be a cook in Holmes's troop at Bliss. Maybe you knew him then too?"

"Yes," Karen said looking at him. "I knew him then too."

"Maybe you knew him pretty well then?"

"Well enough," Karen said.

"Maybe you know him even better now?"

"No," Karen said looking at him. "I dont know him at all now. In fact, I havent seen him to speak to in eight years." She kept on looking at him, when he did not answer, and then she saw his hand. "You must have hit him very hard," she said.

"I didnt hit him at all," Warden said. "Lets not romanticize anything. I hit the wall. Why should I hit him?"

"Oh, you damn fool," she said angrily. "You crazy damn fool." She picked his hand up tenderly.

"Ouch," he said. "Watch out."

"What did he say to you?" she asked him, still holding his hand tenderly.

Warden looked at her, then at his hand. Then he looked back at her.

"He said he'd fucked you," Warden said.

It spread out across the room like a shell burst and he could have bitten off the tongue that said it. In the sustained suspension of the roar he could see the glaze of shock from the concussion take hold of her. But she recovered quickly. She recovered very quickly, he thought bitterly admiringly. Probably she had known what was coming.

Why are you doing this? What ever made you say a thing like that? Does it make any difference to you if she did? No, it doesnt make any difference to you. Then why are you doing it? But he had known, of course, what he was doing. He knew the first word, once uttered, led inevitably to this. It all seemed remarkably familiar like something he had done before and he was miserable because he was doing it yet he could not stop it. He had to know, when people told you things like that you couldnt just drop them, you couldnt just forget them, not when you had to live with those people every day. God damn people.

"You didnt need to say that," Karen said. She laid his hand down carefully.

"Oh, yes I did. You'll never know how much."

"All right," she said. "Maybe you did. But not like that. You shouldnt have said it like that, Milt. Not without giving me my chance first."

"He also mentioned that Champ Wilson probably had too. Thats the current story. Not to mention Jim O'Hayer. Not to mention Liddell Henderson."

"So I'm the company whore now?" she said. "Well, thats what I get, I guess. I guess I laid myself open for it, didnt I? I asked for it when I first went out with you."

"Nobody knows you been out with me. Nobody," Warden said.

"Only you would really think I would have known, wouldnt you?" she said. "But not me. Oh no, not me. I had to convince myself you were different. I had to go and forget you were a man. And being a man, had the same rotten filthy mind the rest of them have. The same proud rooster masculinity of conquest. Oh, I bet you and Stark had a fine time I bet, talking it over, comparing notes on how good it was. Tell me, how do I stack up, anyway, with the professionals? I'm still an amateur, you know."

She got out of the bed and fumblingly started gathering up her clothes. They were still strewn across the room. She had to sort them out from his. She had trouble with them. Her hair kept falling into her eyes. She had to keep brushing at her eyes with first one hand then the other.

"Leaving?" Warden said.

"I'm considering it. Have you any other suggestions? After all, its over, isnt it? You cant really expect it could ever be the same again, now, do you? It was a nice ride while it lasted. But I think this is where I get off."

"Then I think I'll have a drink," Warden said, feeling sick, feeling castrated. Well, what did you think would happen? How is it people can never talk? Why cant they speak? How come they always say something else than what they mean? He got up and got the bottle from the dresser. "Will you have a drink?" he said.

"No thank you. I'm having all I can do to keep from puking now."

"Oh," he said. "It makes you sick. Dirty little Warden and his nasty little mind. Filthy men whose brains hang between their legs. Did you ever hear the old adage that where theres smoke there must be some fire?" he said viciously.

As he said this viciously, he was looking at those soft tipped breasts that had the sag, the full-bodied necessary little sag of maturity that the virgins and the young stuff never had and always lacked something in not having.

And as he said this viciously, he was feeling the sickness, the eunuch-making sickness, blooming and ballooning through him.

"Yes," Karen said. "I've heard it. Did you ever hear the one about how every living woman dies three times? Once when she is seduced of her virginity, once when she is seduced of her freedom (I believe they call it marriage), and once when she is seduced of her husband. Did you ever hear that one?"

"No," he said. "I never heard it."

"Neither did I," Karen said. "I just thought of it. You might add a fourth one: when she is seduced of her lover. I ought to send it in to the *Readers Digest*, dont you think? Maybe I'd get five bucks for it. But of course they'd have a man for editor."

"You dont like men any better than I like women, do you?" Warden said, leaning on the dresser and not offering to help her.

308

"Why should I? If they're like you and your filthy friends? That was a pretty rotten thing to say to me, you know. Especially since that about all those other men is a lie and isnt true."

"Okay," he said. "But its true about Stark though, isnt it?"

Karen turned on him, her eyes starting and blazing. "You came to my bed a virgin, didnt you?"

"Then it is true," he said. "Well?" he said conversationally, "how was it? Did you like it? Did you really like it? Was he as good as I am? He looks virile enough."

"Well, we've gotten awfully possessive, awfully suddenly, haven't we?" Karen said contemptuously. "What business is that of yours?"

"Oh, I thought maybe I could work up some new ideas, new techniques maybe, if you werent satisfied. G Company prides itself on keeping its customers satisfied."

"That *is* a rotten thing to say," Karen said contortedly. "But if it will ease your mind any, I hated it," she said. "I loathed it."

"How do I know you're not lying?"

"And just who are you? to wonder if I'm lying?"

"Then why did you do it?"

"You want to know why I did it? You really want to know? Maybe I'll tell you sometime. Like hell. You're getting to sound so like a typical husband, why dont you just sweat it out like a typical husband?"

She laughed spitefully, and then her face suddenly seemed to crumple up. Ugly wrinkles gathered around her mouth and eyes and she was crying angrily.

"You son of a bitch," she said. "You son of a bitch you son of a bitch. You dont leave a person anything, do you you son of a bitch?"

"Okay," he said. "Okay. I dont blame you."

She stood staring at him and crying and in her eyes was the greatest hatred he had ever seen, and he had seen some pretty fair hatreds, in his time.

"No," she said. "I think I'll just tell you now. I think now is the time. You can take it back to the barracks with you. It'll make fine conversation in the barracks."

She dropped the clothes that she had had so much trouble gathering, and that she was holding protectively in front of her. She sat down on the bed and pointed at the long scar on her belly, the scar he had noticed every time before but had always been somehow reluctant to mention.

"See that?" she said. "You know what that is? You never noticed that before, did you?

"Well, thats a hysterectomy scar," she said. "A hysterectomy is a uterectomy. A uterectomy is an operation in which they excise the uterus. But they call it hysterectomy. You know what hysterectomy comes from, of course? From hysteria. Hysteria and womb and women are synonymous in the medical profession, you know. Thats where they get their biggest source of income, you see. You know: stupid women who weep and are very nervous and go to pieces and maybe lose their minds as they approach the change of life, but whose husbands always dutifully sorrowfully protect them and lovingly take care of them at home so that they seldom go to institutions. Look in a medical dictionary some time,—if you can ever get hold of one that is, they're very hush-hush and try to pretend they are restricted, so you'll probably have to buy one. I had to buy mine. But look up the prefix hystero- and see the words derived from it. A hysteroscope is an instrument for inspecting the uterus, did you know that? A hysterometer is an instrument for measuring the uterus, did you know that? A hysterograph is an apparatus for measuring the strength of the uterine contractions in labor, did you know that? Two, perhaps three, full pages of small type: hystero-this, hystero-that.

"You go in to them and they look you up and down, appraisingly, then they ask how old you are. You say I'm thirty-five. Oh, they say. They nod. They look knowing. Thirty-five, they say. Change of life coming on, you know. They soothe you. Mustnt be upset. Be calm. Happens to the best of us. They examine you. They're gynecologists and its all professional of course. Then they wash their hands and nod profoundly. Just as I thought, they say, you need a hysterectomy, thats all, just a little old hysterectomy.

"God knows what the medical profession would do if it didnt have its hysterectomies and their hystero-derivities. Probably all go broke and vote for socialized medicine after all, I guess. At the hospital I was in they performed as many as nine hysterectomies in a morning. Surprised? Oh, you dont realize. You dont know how many women there are over thirty in this country. And its really very simple any more. Still a major operation, but they're getting the technique down better every day. Soon it'll be as minor as an appendectomy, then every woman over thirty-five can have one, cheap.

"Its really quite the thing any more, a profession in itself, the excising of the uterus. When they excise the uterus, they take all the rest out with it. Its no good to you any more, with the womb gone. They take it all out, the tubes, the ovaries, all of it. Just in case theres some of the pus producing tissue left. They even take your appendix out too. They throw that in free.

"But after they sew you up, you suddenly discover you're not a woman any more. Oh, the outside's still there, the part the men care about, its not at all like castration. Some doctors even intimate you'll like it better with the fear of getting pregnant gone. You still look and dress the part of woman, your skin and hair dont change, nothing like that, even your breasts dont dry up because they've got some little pills to keep the shell acting just the same as though you werent changed. Hormones, they call them.

"See?" she said; she got a little square green bottle out of the overnight bag she had brought. "You take them every day. The pills you'll never be without. Its really remarkable, isnt it?" She put the bottle back.

"But," she said, "you're still not a woman any more. You still go to bed, the men still get what they want, but the purpose of it all is gone. The meaning of it is gone, too. You're not a woman and you're certainly not a man, you're not even a poor freak of a hermaphrodite. You're not anything. You're a gutted shell. What they need to make next is a pill that will give the meaning back, or at least the illusion of the meaning, then you can take two kinds of pills a day and life will be wonderful. But now—now you're still the rich ripe grape, only the meat has been ripped open and the seed plucked out. You're an empty hulk and the meaning of sex is gone, you cant have children.

"Maybe," she said, "maybe thats why it is you hunt so hungrily for love, why you have to hunt for it, even though you know they all are secretly laughing at you, winking behind your idealistic romantic back —another neurotic woman at the change of life who wants to change the world and give it love, as if the world ever needed love! What would the world do with love?

"But love, if you can find it, you think, might give sex meaning—and give you meaning—might even give life meaning. Love is all you've got then—if you can find it.

"No," she said, "no, dont say anything. Not yet. I'm not finished yet. Let me tell it all, first.

"I've never told it to anybody before, you know. Never talked about it to a living soul—except my doctor, until he wanted to find out what it was like with a woman who had her organs out, after my recuperation.

"So just let me tell it all.

"You know what caused my hysterectomy? I bet you couldnt guess. Gonorrhea caused this one. Gonorrhea causes most of them. Not all of them, of course, but a large majority.

"And where do you think I got my dose of gonorrhea? I bet you couldnt guess that either. I got it from my husband, where most of the wives who get it get it. From Capt Dana E Holmes. Only he was still a 1st/Lt then.

"Dont look so shocked. I'm not being bitter. Wives also give it to their husbands, I've heard. Its not unusual, not nearly as unusual as you think.

"We had been married three years then; when it happened. I had already had the baby then. The heir. The proud bearer of the line. The inheritor of society's blessings. I had already done my duty and had my son. That was lucky, wasnt it?

"Of course, we hadnt been married two months before I knew he was stepping out on me. But then that was no different from the lot of other women. That was all part of being a wife. Your mother tells you that is life. Even your mother-in-law is sympathetic. I finally got used to that, fairly easily; although it wasnt quite the picture of marriage I had been brought up to expect. You see, your mother doesnt tell you all this until *after* it has happened to you.

"Then after the baby was born he gradually stopped sleeping with me. Except on rare occasions. This was a little harder to get used to because I didn't know why. But I got used to that, too, eventually. It was almost a relief, actually, because those rare occasions were so obvious: He would come in late half drunk, all worked up because he obviously hadnt been able to make the woman he'd been out with. It was always the same; I suppose thats why men keep wives at home, isnt it; but somehow I never could get much pleasure out of it.

"Then for a while he stopped all together. It seemed natural enough to me; I supposed he was getting all he wanted elsewhere; how was I to know he was being treated for gonorrhea? Respectable women arent even supposed to know what gonorrhea is, are they? So I didnt think much about it when he came around this one particular night, a little drunker than usual.

"Of course, a little later on I realized. Well, maybe he was just too drunk to remember. Or maybe he just was so worked up that he forgot. You know how those things are."

"Jesus!" Warden said. He had long ago set the bottle down. "Jesus Christ!" he said. "Jesus Jesus Christ!"

Karen smiled at him lividly.

"I'm almost finished now," she said. "Just a little more. I want to tell you about Stark.

"You see, Dana had taken me to his doctor, the one who was treating him. In town, of course. He would have been kicked out of course, if he had gone to the Post Hospital. I dont think the doctor liked him very well over it, but then he was a very scientific little man. Bald and scientific and very objective, like all true scientists, and quite rich, lately. I never knew where Dana got his name, some fellow sufferer on the Post, I imagine. Anyway, the doctor did a thriving business; Texas always was a bad place for gonorrhea. Too near the border, you know."

"Listen," Warden said tensely. "Listen. Please."

"No, no, let me finish. I'm almost through. Stark was after I came back. I had to go away on a trip, you see. Its harder to cure in women than in men. Almost always it entails a hysterectomy. I was gone quite a while. While I was gone Stark came in as a recruit. He was only a kid, I suppose. A regular bragging kid who made a pass at me as a matter of pride. I think he was scared half to death when I took him up on it, me being the Lieutenant's wife. But I had to do something. I had to clean myself out. I was dirty. I had been dirty for so very long and I had been trying so hard to convince myself I wasnt dirty, that it was like what all women had to go through. But quite suddenly I no longer gave a damn what other women went through or didnt go through, I *knew* I was dirty. Maybe they could kid themselves. I couldn't any longer. I *knew*. You can see what I mean, cant you?"

"Listen," Warden said.

"Stark was the instrument I used to clean myself, the first one that came to hand after I got back. Any instrument would have done as well. It only happened once, and it hurt me physically, and I loathed it. But afterwards I was clean. You can see, cant you, how I had to be clean?"

"Yes," Warden said, "I can see how. But listen."

"Thats all," Karen smiled lividly. "I'm through now. Now I'll go."

She sat and looked at him and the livid smile gradually, very gradually, faded off her face and then she was just looking at him, sheer absolute nothingness that was too tired to give a damn on her face. She collapsed kind of sickly down on the bed and lay there sickly, not unconscious, not fainted, not crying, not vomiting, not anything. She was like a recently pregnant woman who has for a long time felt this thing growing and growing in her, this man-made tumor that has to be got out of her but that she is afraid of getting out of her, and then finally does get it out of her, and collapses kind of sickly with relief into sheer nothingness for a while.

Warden got the bottle and took it over to her. "Listen," he said urgently. "Listen to me."

"You want me to go now, dont you?" she said hollowly. "You want to get this rottenness out of your sight, dont you?" She hoisted herself up. "Well, I'll go in a minute. I just want a minute to rest first."

Warden nodded.

She looked at him and took the bottle out of his hand. "I believe I will have a drink, before I go. Why, Milt," she said, "you're crying."

"No I'm not," Warden nodded.

"*You* have a drink," Karen said and gave him back the bottle.

Warden nodded. "I dont *want* you to go, see?" he said. "I'm asking you please not to go."

"I dont want to go," Karen said. "I want to stay. Oh, Milt, I do want to stay, Milt."

"Thats it," he said. "Listen," he said. "Oh, that son of a bitch. That miserable lousy son of a bitch."

"I dont have to be back until tomorrow evening," she said vaguely. "He's going to one of Col Delbert's stags tonight, you see."

"I love you," Warden said. "Oh that son of a bitch."

Chapter 23

Capt Holmes may or may not have been a son of a bitch, it all depended on your point of view, but Capt Holmes was not a stupid man. He knew his wife was having an affair. When you live with another human for twelve years you get so you sense those things. Tonight his wife had refused to cook his dinner for him. His wife never refused to cook his dinner for him. Breakfast, yes; luncheon, always; but not dinner. Cooking dinner was part of the agreement. Agreement? Capt Holmes thought. Treaty. Or perhaps armed truce would be better. This was not a typical marriage. Or was it?

Rather than eat the gook maid's cooking Capt Holmes had dined, and dined well, in the Bachelor Officers' Mess with the other married officers whose wives did not cook dinner for them, and now with a comfortably full bowel he was sitting unhappily at the Payday-deserted bar of the Club Taproom watching the enlisted barman solicitously polishing glasses, while waiting for his Colonel to show up.

Capt Holmes had not been on the best of terms with his Colonel lately, since the loss of the championship. In fact, when he thought about it, he had not been on the best of terms with much of anybody lately. First his Colonel, then his wife; but then, there was always his wife. Neither his 1st/Sgt nor his Mess/Sgt seemed to like him very well. Half the men in his company hated his guts. The other half, whom he *knew* he had done things for, did not even seem to realize it. At times, he suspected they disliked him more than the first half. He did not know why all this was. Apparently, he had not yet located his proper place in life. Logically, he ought to be on the best of terms with everybody because, logically, he had chosen this place in life as the only one he wanted, and he wanted to be on the best of terms with everybody.

Where had it all gone? he wondered, feeling a yawning bottomlessness that always frightened him opening up beneath his feet. Where were the ideals of the leader of men who had marched forth from the Point? Where was the gay and happy marriage, the good liv-

314

ing, the conscientious leadership? Where was the dashing, hell-for-leather young cavalryman? He could not remember having lost them anywhere, and he knew he had not laid them down. What then had happened to it?

It will be a civilian man, he thought. She is too discreet to pick an officer, and she has too much breeding and good taste to take an EM. Ergo, a civilian man, preferably a rich one. Capt Holmes had always been a believer in the efficacy of syllogistic logic.

He ought to be feeling good, he told himself. Now he did not have to go home at all tonight, or any night, unless he felt like it. He was freed of the necessity of keeping up appearances with his wife in name only. Thats good, that: *Wife In Name Only,* I remember a book called that. It was one of those I use to hide from mother in the haymow. Who was it now? Clay. Bertha M Clay. Dear Bertha. Well, it was good to know your wife possessed sexual instincts, just like any other human. Now he had something on *her.* It was a sound basis for a fruitful union. Logically, he really ought to be feeling fine. He had always believed in logic, hadnt he? Deductive reasoning was an absolute necessity in a military man, wasnt it? They inculcated you with that, didnt they? Yes, but just try and apply it. Ah, if you only could apply it.

To rid himself of that frightening bottomlessness Capt Holmes called for another whiskey and soda; he discussed the vagaries of life with the solicitous enlisted barman, who although bored listened solicitously; he allowed himself to wonder cynically where the hell Old Delbert was.

Col Delbert, in fact, arrived a little late bringing with him as his guest a Brigadier. This Brigadier was a sort of exec officer to the Brigade, which was commanded by a Major General. But for once Capt Holmes was not even bothered, although it was a dirty trick to pull on him, without giving him warning. Col Delbert's moustache fluffed its feathers somewhat preeningly as he introduced them—informally. Even this could not cause anxiety in Capt Holmes who still felt his wife should be above such things.

Mentioning that the others (the two Majors from Regiment) would be along later, Col Delbert led them out and along the slab stone dog-trot that ran across the patio that opened on the gulch that separated them from the brightly lighted Station Hospital. He led them through the deserted dining pavilion where they held the mixed dinner parties to the stairs in the deserted main lounge where the ladies usually had their bridge games. The ladies had their club luncheons under the dog-trot. The ladies took their hula lessons in the pavilion. The ladies, if they were around, seldom got upstairs. But this was Payday, and the ladies were not around.

"Flatter m'self," Col Delbert told the Brigadier, "that I pulled off a *tour de force* this time, b' pickin' Payday."

"Oh, indubitably, Colonel," the Brigadier, who was a much younger man than Col Delbert, said thinly. Capt Holmes immediately liked him.

Capt Holmes had met the Brigadier before, of course. He knew who he was. But he had only met him formally. An informal party of this kind was a very different thing, with a general officer. And this Brigadier was a big man on the Post. He was newly from the States and was considered a brilliant tactician and thought to be a comer. The Rumors had it that his present unconventional position in Brigade was only a temporary expedient, until the crotchety old Major General could be eased out and retired to pasture to make room for the younger man. Capt Holmes was glad that he was young enough to see through Col Delbert.

"There'll be five of us," Col Delbert puffed as they climbed the stairs. "Six women. More excitin' that way. Eh? And these, sir, 're all dark. Two Japanese, one Chinese, two Chinese-Hawaiians, and one pure nigger—or damn' near pure: Th' say th' are no pure Hawaiians any more."

"Col Delbert," said Capt Holmes, "believes in taking advantage of the locale in which he's stationed."

The Brigadier laughed and glanced at him slyly. He grinned back happily cynically.

"B' Gad yes," the Col puffed. "Wont be in th' Hawaiian D'pa'tm'nt all m' life. I hope. But this full blood Hawaiian is a rare bird th'ts hard to catch."

Col Delbert had, as usual, hired all three of the apartments and opened the connecting doors between, so that there were six rooms in a shotgun row. The apartments had originally been built on to provide temporary quarters for new officers or visiting officers but they were never used for that any more so that the Club Officer hit upon the idea to rent them out for private parties, in order to make the Club as near self-supporting as possible. After the idea caught on the Club was not only self-supporting but began to show a profit.

"Well, sir," Col Delbert asked proudly. "What do you think of it. Eh?"

There were several Haig & Haig pinchbottles and a few Old Forresters, all with unbroken seals, set artistically about. There were also three trays of syphon bottles and the long thick-bottomed highball glasses with game fowl in color on them.

"Ah." The Brigadier, who was a tall man, stretched himself full out and sniffed the tired air that the open windows had not yet refreshed. "Reminds me of the old secret societies back at the Point."

Col Delbert laughed solicitously. "Already have the steaks arranged for. My orderly, Jeff, takes care of it. Had him bring this stuff from home. Always been a stickler for th' proper equipment, whether in the field or in the bed. Makes all the difference. Eh? Jeff's down in the kitchen arranging for a cook and gettin' some ice."

The Brigadier examined the label on a bottle and did not answer.

Col Delbert spread his arms and said facetiously, "Gen'r'l Slater, we representatives of th' —th Regiment welcome you to th' haven of th' male oppressed."

Capt Holmes was studying his nervous Colonel happily.

The Brigadier collapsed his thin frame into an overstuffed chintz covered chair. "Sam Slater," he corrected. "Sam Slater from Sheboygan. Dont give me that rank crap, Jake. There is nobody who believes in the efficacy of rank and privilege more than me, its my bread and butter. But in the proper time and place, see? Which is not now and here."

"Okay, Sam," Jake Delbert grinned uneasily, "'stand corrected. I . . ."

"And you," Sam Slater shot at Holmes, "might as well call me Sam, too. However, if you ever do such a thing outside on the Post, I'll bust you back to a shavetail, see?"

"Okay," Holmes grinned, liking him still better. "I never been good at blackmail anyway."

Sam Slater looked at him a moment. Then he laughed. "You know, I like your protege, Jake," he said.

"He's a good boy," Jake said apprehensively. "But he's not exactly what you'd call my protege," he started to explain.

Sam Slater was watching both of them speculatively, like a piano virtuoso studying the keys from which he draws his music. "Frankly," he grinned at Holmes, "when old Jake here said he had a young Captain going along on this party I thought oh balls." He looked at Jake. "But I might have known old Jake Delbert knew his onions, mightnt I?" he obviously lied. Even to Jake it was plainly a lie.

"I knew you'd like him though," Jake lied back stoutly. His mustache raised its little wings nervously, like a fledgling that had not quite got used to flying yet.

"I'm sure he gave me quite a build up," Holmes said.

"Oh, he did," Sam Slater said. "Didnt you, Jake? Told me all about you. And about how sorry he was you'd lost that championship, that by rights you really should have had."

"I always try to be as honest as I can," Jake said.

"I would not," Sam Slater said, "have said what I just said, about calling me Sam, to just any junior officer. Even here under these circumstances. Most of them wouldnt understand it, would they, Jake?"

"No, Sam. They sure as hell wouldnt," Jake said, a little dubiously.

He had been watching Holmes. He had never seen him in this irreverent mood before.

Capt Holmes, who had never felt this mood with Col Delbert, felt now some subtle understanding with the Brigadier that not only drew him on but promised safety. He wanted to chuckle. It wasnt often that he got to see the Colonel on the hook and with his back against the wall and frightened.

Jake was obviously relieved when S/Sgt Jefferson came in with the ice. He set him to mixing the first drinks and supervised him relentlessly, then made him bring the field glasses that were within reach on the table and, without thanking him, irritably sent him to Wahiawa for the women.

"And be god damn' careful none of th' civil'ns see you drivin' them around in my official car. Or it 'l be your neck, Jeff. See?"

"Yes, Sir," Jeff said impassively. You felt he should have bowed.

Jake did not even turn around. He was standing carefully back from the window, adjusting the glasses on the lighted windows across the gulch that were the nurses' quarters.

"Not a damn' thin'," he said disconsolately, and flung the glasses on the table. "Not even a bloody nude, b' Gad."

Neither of the others answered him. Sam Slater was still talking to Holmes. He had gone from the particular into the general, concerning junior officers.

"The thing that immediately struck me was you were not afraid. Most junior officers today are just like the EM—insanely afraid of their superiors. Their every thought and action is governed by this perpetual apprehensiveness of official disapproval. In fact, most senior officers are the same way. Its very seldom you can find a man amongst all of them with whom you can talk reasonably, which makes it hard for a man like myself, see?"

"But its always been that way, hasnt it?" Holmes said.

"Ah," Sam Slater smiled. "Thats just where you're wrong. And a little objective thinking will prove you are wrong. It hasnt always been that way. I've got quite a theory about that."

"Well, lets hear it," Dynamite said enthusiastically. "I'm all ears. It isnt often I find a reasonable man to talk to either," he said happily, grinning at Jake.

Jake did not grin back. He had heard this theory before and did not like it. It frightened him somehow and he could not bring himself to believe that life was really like that. Also, he considered it an injury to General Slater's dignity and to his own for the General to discuss it with a Captain, who was not even an aide but only a company commander. He nursed his drink in silence, wondering how such a brilliant man as young Slater, of whom he had always been afraid, could so unbend himself.

"In the past," Sam Slater said carefully, "this fear of authority was only the negative side of a positive moral code of 'Honor, Patriotism, and Service.' In the past, men sought to achieve the positives of the code, rather than simply to avoid its negatives."

He was obviously choosing his words gingerly, as if worried that they would not be understood. And as he talked, he grew still more charming than before as his enthusiasm increased. Sam Slater's enthusiasm, Holmes noticed, affected the man strangely. He did not get excited. Instead of leaning forward and talking faster, he seemed to relax and talk slower and slower, growing calmer and more cold than ever. And yet he was more charming.

"But the advent of materialism and the machine age changed all that, see? We have seen the world change," he said, "in our time. The machine has destroyed the meaning of the old positive code. Obviously, you cannot make a man voluntarily chain himself to a machine because its 'Honorable.' The man knows better."

Holmes nodded his agreement. It was an original idea.

"All that is left, then," Sam Slater went on, "is the standardized negative side of the code as expressed in Law. The fear of authority which was once only a side issue but today is the main issue, because its the only issue left.

"You cant make a man believe it is 'Honorable,' so you have no choice but to make him afraid of *not* chaining himself to his machine. You can do it by making him afraid of his friends' disapproval. You can shame him because he is a social drone. You can make him afraid of starving unless he works for his machine. You can threaten him with imprisonment. Or, in the highest efficiency, you can make him afraid of death by execution.

"But you cant tell him it is 'Honorable' any more. You have to make him afraid."

"By god!" Holmes said. He smacked his fist down into his palm excitedly.

Sam Slater smiled indulgently. "Thats why, today, our junior officers (and our senior officers) have only this fear and nothing else. They are living by the only code their time allows them. In the Civil War they could still believe they fought for 'Honor.' Not any more. In the Civil War the machine won its first inevitable major victory over the individual. 'Honor' died.

"Therefore, it is asinine to attempt to control men with 'Honor' any more. It leads only to inefficiency and ineffective control. And in our present time we must have complete control, because the majority of men must be subservient to the machine, which is society.

319

"Of course, we still pay 'Honor' lip service in the recruiting posters and the industrial editorials, for the sake of appearances, and they eat it up because they are afraid. But do we depend on recruiting for our manpower? It would be absurd, wouldnt it? No, we have a draft, a peacetime draft, the first in our history. Otherwise, we would not have the men. And we must have the men, and have them ready for this war. We have no other choice; its either that, or defeat. Modern armies, like every other brand of modern society, must be governed and controlled by fear. The lot of modern man has become what I call 'perpetual apprehension.' It is his destiny for several centuries to come, until control can become stabilized. If you dont believe me, look at our insane asylums and the increase of their patients. Then look at them again when this war is over."

"I believe you," Holmes said, thinking suddenly of his wife. "But wait a minute. You dont have this fear yourself."

Sam Slater grinned thinly. Rather sadly, Holmes thought.

"Of course not. I understand it. I govern. I am blessed (or cursed) with a logical mind and am capable of perceiving the trend of the time. I, and men like me, are forced to assume the responsibility of governing. If organized society and civilization as we know it is to continue at all, not only must there be a consolidation of power but there must be a complete unquestioned control to head it."

"Yes," Holmes said excitely. "I can see that. I've seen that for a long time."

"Then you are one of the few," Sam Slater smiled at him sadly, "in this country. The Russians, of course, already know it. The Germans are learning it, and learning it remarkably swiftly. The Japanese have always known it, and applied it; but they are unable to adapt to the modern machine techniques, and I doubt if they will—in time. With us here this war will tell the tale. Either we learn it and win the war with it, or else we'll be through. Like England and France and the rest of the decadent Paternalisms are through. And the scepter will pass to other hands. But *if* we learn it, with our productive capacity and industrial machine techniques we will be invincible, even against Russia, when that day comes."

Capt Holmes felt a little chill run down his back. He looked at Sam Slater and the great personal charm of the man swept over him again like the warm light from a revolving beacon, bringing with it a sense of tragedy for this man whom life had forced into such a responsible position.

"Then we'll have to learn it!" Capt Holmes said. He could feel Jake Delbert looking at him sideways with a kind of horror. But Jake Delbert was a long ways off now. This was like something that he had known for a long time, that had lain dusty and misplaced in a back room of his mind and he had suddenly opened the door. "We have no choice but to learn it!"

"Personally," Sam Slater said crisply, "I believe it is our destiny to learn it. But when that day comes, we must have utterly complete control, as they over there already have complete control. Up to now, it has been handled by the great corporations like Ford and General Motors and US Steel and Standard Oil. And mind you, they have done quite well with it, under their banner of 'Paternalism.' They have achieved phenomenal control, and in a rather short time. But now concolidation is the watchword, and the corporations are not powerful enough to bring it off—even if they were willing to consolidate, which they are not. Only the military can consolidate them under one central control."

Capt Holmes saw a sudden picture of a nation with six-lane-highways thrown like a web across it. "The war will take care of that," he said.

"I believe so," Sam Slater said. "Historically, the corporations are already through. They've served their historical purpose. Besides, they have one grievous fault that, unless stopped, can be deadly."

"Whats that?" Holmes asked.

"The fact that they themselves are afraid of authority, even though theres no authority over them," Sam Slater said. "They have put out their paternalism propaganda so long that they believe it themselves, they believe their own Cinderella story, their own Horatio Alger myth of honest poor boy rises to riches. And of course that hamstrings them with a certain amount of sentimental moral obligation; they must play the role of father that they imagined."

"Wait," Holmes said. "I dont quite get that?"

Sam Slater set his empty glass down and smiled at him sadly. "Its the same thing that I was talking about that is wrong with a great many (far too many) of our senior officers. They are all anachronisms of a former generation that grew up in the Victorian era.

"The men who control the corporations and our senior officers are really very much alike, you know: They both utilize this new social fear they have helped develop; and they both are reluctant morally to use it full strength. Its a kind of holdover of Victorian moralism and the dying British school of Paternal Imperialism, the school that would never work the Colonial natives to death unless there was a missionary there to give them their last rites."

Holmes laughed convulsively. "But thats stupid."

Jake Delbert cleared his throat, and set his own glass down.

"Of course its stupid," Sam Slater smiled thinly. "Its a logical absurdity. But all our great industrialists, and most of our present senior officers, still play that role. That same fatherly Britisher role. You can see what it has done to their efficiency of control.

"Social fear is the most tremendous single source of power in existence. The only source, in fact, now that the machine has destroyed the corollary positive code. Yet they waste this power by directing it against such asinine trivialities as the advisability of virginity at marriage, which nobody believes in anyway, and which is like training a firehose on a burning sheet of paper."

Holmes laughed again, so powerfully this time it was almost a seizure. Then he thought of his wife, again, and the laughter dropped out from under him leaving him feeling absolutely nothing, except a startled amazement in the absolute truth in Sam Slater's argument.

"It isnt funny," Sam Slater smiled. "Their absurd false morality causes even greater inefficiency and harm in other ways. When they direct their power on really important problems, problems that need immediate solution, like whether to go to war or not, it is made so diffuse by conflicting sentimentalities of public opinion (such as patriotism versus the love of 'peace') that it does absolutely nothing, it neutralizes itself completely, so that, in the end, we with all our industrial power will sit back and vacillate (when everybody knows war is inevitable) until somebody or other attacks us and makes us fight—and incidentally gets a great big drop on us."

"Thats worse than a logical absurdity," Holmes said angrily. "Thats . . ." he could not say it.

Sam Slater shrugged.

"It makes my blood boil," Holmes said.

Jake Delbert cleared his throat again. "Gentlemen," he said.

"It cant continue to go like that, though," Sam Slater said. "Dont think that in Russia and in Germany the consolidation of power and its control are not being utilized to their fullest. We either have to get rid of our moralists ourselves and replace them with realists, or the Russians and the Germans (not to mention the Japanese) will do it for us, see?" he said, vehement for the first time since he started talking.

"Gentlemen!" Jake Delbert said again. He charged up to his feet. "Ah—" he said. "Your glasses are empty, gentlemen. Dont you think its about time for another drink. Jeff isnt back yet. I'll—ah—do the honors. Eh?"

Nobody laughed.

"This is a party, gentlemen," Jake joked insistently, "not a convention, you know. Eh? Dont you think we ought to perhaps possibly maybe ah . . ." Both of them were looking at him blankly, and gradually he ran down like a phonograph and tapered off into a nervous silence.

"I'm thirsty," Jake said desperately, finally.

Sam Slater smiled at him, openly contemptuously, and Jake felt a spasm of nameless fear.

"Of course, Jake," Sam Slater said soothingly. "Let us have another. Let us all have another."

"But what I dont see," Holmes said suddenly. "What do you suppose makes them all afraid like that? I'm not afraid, not of the *truth*." And he meant it truly. He looked deep inside himself, there was no fear there.

Sam Slater shrugged. "Environmental training, I suppose. Psychologically, its a sort of subjective association of oneself with the external object. Some boys cant shoot birds because they put themselves into the place of the injured bird. Same thing."

Holmes was irritated. "But thats stupid."

"Gentlemen," Jake Delbert said urgently. "Your drinks, gentlemen."

"Thanks, Jake," Sam Slater said soothingly. Somehow, Jake thought, Sam's solace is always ominous. "Of course its stupid," Sam said to Holmes. "Nobody claimed it wasnt stupid. Still, it happens to them."

"Ha," Jake Delbert said aloud, and to hell with them, what are they anyway? "Tell me, Dynamite," Jake said. "How are you makin' out with that new man, whats his name, Prewitt. Have you convinced him he should go out yet?"

"Who?" Holmes said. He looked up startled, jerked from the clarity of the abstract back into the turbid concrete, where the application always has to take place. "Oh," he said. "Prewitt. No, not yet. But my boys are working on him."

"Giving him The Treatment?" Sam Slater interjected.

"Yes," Holmes said reluctantly.

"Thats a good example of my theory. How long do you think we could run an army without noncoms who fear our class so much they will tyrannize their own?"

"Not very long, I guess," Holmes said.

"The secret," Sam Slater said, "is to cause every caste to fear its superiors and be contemptuous of its inferiors. You are wise to have your noncoms do it instead of doing it yourself. That makes even the noncoms more aware of the gulf between EM and officers."

"But has it done any good yet?" Jake insisted, swinging it back again to the concrete, away from that infernal theory of young Slater's. "Your Smoker season is in June this year, instead of August. You havent as much time to pull him into line as you would have had last year, and he hasnt given in yet, has he?"

"I told you no," Holmes said violently, finding he was suddenly just a Captain again. "But I've taken all that other into account. I know what I'm doing. Truly, Sir."

"I'm sure you do, m' boy," Jake said sympathetically. He was back on familiar ground now. He could risk a pointed glance at Slater. "But dont forget, son, that this man is apparently a bolshevik, a true fuckup.

They 're diff'r'nt from the average run, you know. I firmly believe in leading men, myself, but with bolsheviks you have to drive them. Its the only way to handle them. And you cant ever let them best you or you lose prestige with the men and they 'll all be tryin' to take advantage of you."

"Thats true," Sam Slater interjected. "If you've made an open issue of the thing, you must follow it through. Not that the issue itself is important, but because of the over all effect it has on the men."

"I havent made an open issue of it yet," Holmes said, feeling badgered. "The men are doing it practically by themselves, without my help." Immediately he realized he had trapped himself. "What I mean," he said.

"Oh," Jake grinned. He was not missing any tricks now. These young flibertygibets who were always sucking in with the rank; it was all very well to talk theory, but it was the application of it that counted. "But dont you think that 'll look to the men as if you 're tryin' to evade the responsibility?"

"No," Holmes said, seeing what he was doing. "Not at all. I was trying to accomplish it with the noncoms, without coming into it myself, as the General said." He nodded at Sam Slater.

"I wouldnt depend on that completely," Jake said. "If he doesnt come around soon, so that he gets full benefit of the trainin' season, he wont be any good to you anyway, will he?"

"Oh, yes," Holmes said. "What I want him for is the Bowl season next winter, not the Company Smokers." He smiled a little condescendingly, feeling he had won that round.

"Yes," Jake pressed him, "but if he gets out of going out for Smokers, he's still made you back down and lose face. And thats no good. Eh?" he said to Slater. "Am I right?"

Sam Slater looked at him some time before he answered. He had been sitting back, watching both of them, knowing they were playing for his approbation now. It warmed him. Jake of course had all the rank, but Jake was a coward and a member of the old Paternalism school that inevitably someday he and his generation would have to fight. And he liked young Holmes.

"Yes," he said, finally. "Thats right. The important thing," he said to Holmes, "is that you as an officer must not allow even a suspicion that an EM has made you back down. The boxing thing itself is unimportant," he added, looking at Jake.

Jake preferred to ignore that one. He had gained a temporary advantage, and he had changed the subject; that was enough for now. But it was outrageous that he should even have to struggle with Holmes, he a Lieutenant Colonel. "If he doesnt come around soon,'" he told Holmes coldly, "you have to break him. Have no choice. Throw the book at him, so that at least by winter and the Bowl Season he will be ready to talk turkey."

"Yes," Holmes said doubtfully. He had sensed the Brigadier's favor in that last crack about the boxing, but he did not know whether he had enough collateral to plunge. "But I dont think it will work that way," he said, deciding to risk it. "I dont think you can break this man."

"Ha!" Jake said. He looked at the General. "Of course you can break him."

"You can break any man," Sam Slater said coldly. "You are an officer."

"Thats right," Jake said stoutly. "I remember when I served here at Schofield as a Captain and John Dillinger was a private. If there ever was an honest to God maverick that couldnt be broken, there was one. But by God they broke him. They broke him right here in the Post Stockade. I bet you he served most of his enlistment in the Post Stockade, by God," Jake said indignantly. "Thats when he swore he'd get even with the United States if it was the last thing he ever did."

"That doesnt sound like they broke him," Holmes said, unable to back out now. "From the way he went after he got out of here, I would say they never broke him."

"Oh yes they did," Jake said. "J E Hoover and his boys broke him. They broke him right in two, that night in Chicago. Just like they broke Prettyboy Floyd and the rest of them."

"They killed him," Holmes said. "Not broke him."

"Its the same thing," Jake said indignantly. "What the hell 's the difference?"

"I dont know," Holmes said, deciding to give up. "None, I guess." But he knew he did not believe that. It was in his voice.

"No," Sam Slater said. "Jake's wrong. There is a great deal of difference. They never broke Dillinger. You might as well be honest, Jake, and give him his due."

Jake Delbert's face thickened redly.

"You cant understand that," Sam Slater said deliberately. "But I can understand him. And I think Dynamite here can."

Jake sat down in his chair and raised his drink up to his reddened face and sipped it, and Sam Slater stared back at him unmoved. "But the important thing is they did kill him, like they always kill them. The only thing wrong with Dillinger was he was an individualist, and you cant understand that, Jake. But thats why they had to kill him. Crime never pays, see?" he grinned.

Holmes felt vastly relieved, but then as Slater spoke he had a vivid mental picture, suddenly, of how a little difference of opinion in thought, just like this one, say between a private and a noncom, could inextricably lead a man to the Stockade, and from there—unless the opinion in him changed, unless they broke him—lead him on step by irrevocable step to where he sat in a Chevrolet sedan on a sideroad at night holding a snub nosed .38 in an angry frightened hand and waited for the shots to pour out of the darkness into him at any moment, all this occurring in a peaceful nation not at war. It was an overpoweringly weird idea that made him shiver. He just managed to catch himself from thinking that it might even have been himself and then remembered what Slater had said about some boys could not shoot birds. He felt a curiously unreal quality about everything around him. The power of thought, he told himself, all from such an innocent beginning.

"Captain," Jake said to him chokingly, "I'm positively instructing you to give this man Prewitt the goddam book, if he doesnt come around before its too late for him to train for Smokers."

"I've meant to do that all along, Sir," Holmes said, "except that perhaps I've thought that it might not be necessary." He felt a little sorry for the poor old bugger.

"It'll be necessary," Jake said brutally. "You can take my word for that. And that is a direct order, Captain." He sat back in his chair.

Holmes, however, did not feel the least bit anxious. His majority in Regiment that he had had his eye on was nothing compared to a job on the Brigade staff perhaps. And even if the job did not pan out, Delbert could do nothing to him as long as Sam Slater kept an eye on him.

"The important thing," Sam Slater said, moving in like a fencing master who takes advantage of a pause in his pupils' bout to give a little more instruction, "the important thing is to remember the logic behind the thing. You wouldnt let a single cantankerous mule hold up the whole pack train from carrying supplies up the Waianae Range, would you? If you couldnt get him to move, you'd push him off, wouldnt you?"

"No," Holmes said. "Yes."

"Thats all it amounts to."

"That is it, isnt it?" Holmes asked nervously. "You have to think of the majority and the end in view, dont you? You have to be cruel, perhaps, for the good of the whole? That is it, isnt it?"

"Thats it exactly," Sam Slater said, with a curiously feminine satisfaction. "Anyone who governs must be cruel."

"Yes," Holmes said, feeling suddenly for no reason like he had been seduced, the way a woman must feel.

"You're learning swiftly," Sam Slater said to him.

After that Jake did not try to change the subject any more. Sam Slater went right back into his theory, talking almost hurriedly now. The two of them were still talking it when the two Majors from Regiment came in and were duly startled by the presence of a general officer and slunk around to get a reinforcing drink and, finding they were still ignored, slunk off to drink it.

The two of them were still talking when S/Sgt Jefferson came back with the women. And they went on talking, Holmes listening intently because he knew now he was forced by Prewitt into a position where he could no longer evade this thing and so must go on or else go back, Sam Slater elaborating the comforting creed that had evolved from being in a similar position once, his eyes lighting up a little now as he talked.

The two hefty specimens who had attached themselves to their laps drank and listened puzzledly. Jake and the two Majors had already given it up and adjourned to the back rooms to take up the business they had come here for.

But Holmes had almost forgotten that. The talk, for Holmes, was momentarily opening up whole series of new vistas. Things he had not even guessed at before now. And he strained hard concentrating, catching only glimpses before the cloud bank rolled back covering them up, but always opening new ones beyond that he thought he could maybe see completely.

"Reason," Sam Slater said, "is the greatest discovery ever made by man. Yet it is the most disregarded and least used. No wonder reasonable, sensitive men become bitter and disillusioned."

"I've always seen it," Holmes said excitedly. "All my life I've seen it. Always at a distance."

"Its all based on apprehension," Sam Slater smiled. "Apprehension is the key. After you learn to judge the degree of apprehension that is there in each man, you can predict infallibly how far you can trust him, how far you can make him go. The next step, of course, is to induce the apprehension artificially. Its already there, all you got to do is call it forth. The greater the apprehension, the greater the control."

"Whats appre-hension, kiddo?" the Japanese one on Sam Slater's chair arm said.

"Fear," Sam Slater grinned.

"Oh," she said, and frowned puzzledly, over at the other one.

"Lissen," the Chinese one on Holmes's knee said. "What wrong with you guys, any-ways?"

"Not a thing," Sam Slater said.

"You no like us, maybe no?" the Japanese one said.

"Why of course," Sam Slater said. "You're lovely ladies."

"You aint mad at me? are you?" the Chinese one said to Holmes.

"Why should I be mad at you?"

"I no no. Maybe I do something you not like?"

"Come on, Iris," the Japanese one said. "To hell with them. We go find that white-haired old fatty. He with Beulah. Liven it up someways maybe."

Iris got up. "I not do something hurt your feelings?" she coaxed at Holmes.

"Hell, no," Holmes said.

"You see?" Sam Slater grinned, when they had gone. "You see what I mean by apprehension?"

Holmes laughed.

"You know," Sam Slater said. "I've tried to explain this to old Jake a hundred times. I've been explaining it to him ever since I hit this Rock. Jake has a great deal of ability, if he would only learn how to use it."

"He's pretty old," Holmes said cautiously.

"Too old," Sam Slater said. "If I've ever seen a man who's lost and groping in the dark its old Jake Delbert. And you'd think that if anybody had the background and the training to see the trend of our time, Jake Delbert would be one. But no, he's still afraid. Afraid, and so much of a moralist that he would rather spend his life believing the sentimental memos he writes his troops, instead of trying to help humanity. And relieving himself (as with a bowel movement when the moral guts become too full) by throwing these stags.

"Not that I dislike them, mind you. I think they're fine and I enjoy them. In their place. But a man cannot make them his life work. Not without going rotten. A man must have something bigger than himself to believe in."

"Thats it," Holmes said excitedly. "Something bigger than himself. And where in this world today can he find it?"

"Nowhere," Sam Slater said. "Except in reason. You know, you're pretty old for a Captain, Dynamite, but you would still be young for a Major. At your age I was only a Major myself, see? And I hadnt even begun to learn the new logic. If a smart man had not picked me out as a protege I'd still be a Major, and a Jake Delbert, today."

"The thing with you, though," Holmes pointed out. "You were willing to listen to reason, when it was shown you."

"Exactly," Sam Slater said. "And we have great need of proteges who can learn that lesson in our profession, today. And we're going to need them a lot worse, a little later on. There is absolutely no limit to the possibilities open to them."

"I dont care about the rank," Holmes said. He had, he knew, said that before. But this time it was true, this time he really meant it. "All I care about," he said, "is to find a truly firm ground, a foundation a thinking man can stand on, a sound logic that will not let you down. Give me that and the rank can go to hell."

"Thats exactly the way I felt myself," Sam Slater said. He smiled thinly. "You know, I can use a man like you. God knows I've got enough stupid dolts on my staff. I need at least one good man. How would you like to transfer to Brigade and work for me?"

"If you really think I could really do it," Holmes said modestly. He was thinking what would Karen say to this? Ha, if she had her way he would never have gone to any of these stags, at all. And then where would he be? He could just see Jake Delbert's face!

"Do it, hell," Sam Slater said. "Listen, if you want it its yours, see? I'll look into it for you tomorrow.

"You know," he said, "actually the thing with this man Prowitt is important only insofar as it affects you personally. Not for the boxing squad, not even for your prestige. In reality its only a springboard for testing and developing your character."

"I never thought of it that way before."

"I dont think it would be good for you to transfer out until after you handle that thing, just for your own good, see? Then after you handled that and transferred, you could drop the whole damned boxing squad altogether. We'll have better uses for your energy."

"Yes, I could do that," Holmes said, wondering if he wanted to quit coaching.

"Well," Sam Slater grinned, getting up. "I need another drink and I think we've talked damn near enough, dont you? We're wasting valuable time, hey? I'm going to find those goddamned women." He stepped over to the syphon bottle and was very suddenly no longer the philosopher, it was as if part of his mind had been turned off like a spigot.

Capt Holmes was startled, then almost frightened. Because he could not forget it all so easily. He had seen a picture of a new power that would make a brand new world, a world with real meaning based on logic, not just the meaning of the moralists. This was a meaning that would work out in practice, based on a realistic power. A power of great kindness with potentialities to do great good, to raise humanity to new heights despite humanity's own mulishness and inertia. A power that was tragic in its kindness because it would always be misunderstood by the masses who wanted only to fornicate and fill their bellies. A power that only history would vindicate, because the lives of great men and great ideas were always tragic. It had made his belly muscles tighten spasmodically with a sheer desire to just plain yell that he had not felt since he was a boy. How could Slater just shut it off like a faucet?

Then he realized suddenly that he was doubting, here he had just learned it and already he was doubting, and he was frightened worse. Was logic still logic if you could doubt it?

This is old stuff to Slater, he told himself, he's used to it, of course he can turn it off. Its just new to you, thats all. And you've still got that old habit of doubting. Thats all. He wondered if Sam Slater had ever doubted any, when he first learned it? Of course he had, he told himself. But somehow he doubted that. What if Slater had never doubted it? what then? He thought of asking Slater if he ever doubted and his heart suddenly skipped warningly with more than fright, with fear, at the obvious giveaway of his disbelief such a question would confess.

He was not doubting the logic, he realized suddenly, what he was doubting was himself. He was doubting his ability to stop doubting. Perhaps Slater had made a mistake in him?

But if Slater was wrong, then Slater's logic was fallible, wasn't it? Capt Holmes felt the old yawning bottomless feeling coming back on him, felt the earth once again refuse his feet.

What if his wife had not refused to cook his dinner for him, had not gone with her rich civilian?

What if Jake Delbert had warned him beforehand that there would be a General here tonight and given him time beforehand to get apprehensive?

What if Sam Slater had not had the needle out for Jake?

Capt Holmes saw quite clearly very suddenly that he would have been a different man, and that things would have happened very differently, and when Sam Slater handed him his fresh drink his hand was trembling.

"Come on," Sam Slater grinned. "They're all in the next room back here."

"Yeah. Sure," said Capt Holmes, and followed him, hoping only that he had not seen. He wondered if Slater would remember this tomorrow? And he wondered if this world-shaking conversation was in reality only a Holmes-&-Slater-shaking conversation? And he wondered why it was the earth would not ever stand still, would not let you set your feet upon it?

He looked at the people in the room, at the Colonel sprawling drinking on the bed, at the woman drinking with him, at the Majors, at S/Sgt Jefferson handing around another tray of drinks, at Sam Slater grinningly picking out a woman, at the woman he had picked out himself. He did not know them, any of them, and he felt like a man looking out of the window of a skyscraper down the diminishing receding length of wall to where the beautifully miniature cars hum and crawl like beetles in the street, and he had to pull his head back in. Or jump.

Not that, Holmes. You've been that road, that road leads nowhere, thats the road that brought you here. The thing is, to believe. You must believe. You must have faith. Thats the answer. The only answer.

So he looked at Sam Slater and he believed. He looked at the frolicking Sam Slater from Sheboygan, like the woman looks frightenedly but still hopefully at the man beside her whom she has let seduce her, whom she has given it to, and who has turned over and begun to snore.

He knew there must be some logic in all of it someplace. It couldnt all be just so haphazard.

Tomorrow he would buy that new Mixmaster at the PX and have it sitting in the kitchen when she came home. When she walked in the first thing she'd see would be that. Then she'd know.

He stood up swaying only slightly and escorted the hefty Chinese girl back into the back.

Chapter 24

The man whose salvation everybody seemed to be concerned about was not worried at all himself, did not even for the moment realize he was a sinner, as he climbed the stairway to the New Congress Hotel.

Prew had that old on-pass feeling there again, telling him life was postponed until tomorrow morning, that he could think about being a sinner again tomorrow, but that right now he had better not let anything spoil this that was coming. Maybe he could not have the bugling. All right then, he could not have it. But he could have this and this would help to fill the hole and he had better be very careful to hang onto it because he might need it bad someday soon. Right now he much preferred to think about Lorene. There was a name for you. Lorene. That was no whore's name, that was a really truly woman's name, Lorene. It had a special private sound all its own for him, when he said it over, as if no other woman had ever had that name before. Hell, he could transfer out of this jockstrap company, what was to stop him? Get in a real soldiering outfit again and really work hard again. Get a sergeant's rating back again because a rating would mean something again now.

Then he remembered he could not get a transfer out of this outfit.

All right, so he couldnt get a transfer. So what? What did that mean? Not a goddam. All this will have blown over in a year from now. She plans to go on working for another year anyway, dont she? By then you will be due to ship back home, back to the States, in a year from now, by this time next year, in 1942. He knocked on the steel door happily loudly, seeing it all in his mind suddenly, how it would be then, some sturdy little permanent post that drowsed along from day to day, like Jefferson Barracks or Fort Riley, with solid brick barracks and new-cut grass and well kept walks under the long afternoon shadows of big old oak trees that had been standing in the same place since before George Armstrong Custer had his hair cut by the

Sioux, that would be the kind of place to re-enlist for, where the NCO quarters were brick too and not this jerrybuilt ship lathe they have here, and where you can take her right into a community and a little society that the married noncoms made and maintained for themselves alone. Didnt all the old timers like Pete Karelsen always say whores made the best wives? Whores knew how to appreciate the little things, didnt they say, after they've been down and out. Lots of old timers married whores. Look at Baldy Dhom, his wife was a whore in Manila. No, lets not look at Dhom, his wife is a gook, she dont count, thats you if you had married Violet. But you dont want to marry Violet, you want to marry Lorene. And if comfort and security is what she wants, what better place is there to find it than in some little out of the way permanent post that has been the same for sixty-nine years, and will be the same for sixty more?

Why, hell. She could marry him now, today, and still go on working for a year, she planned to do that anyway, what did he care? Respectability had done him a lot of goddam good in his time, hadnt it? Respectability and fifteen cents will get you a beer. Respectability and its matronly advocates who were trying to hide their own youth when they too had been alive, because being alive was always a little obscene, you always made people uncomfortable to be with you when you were alive. Well, up yours, ladies, thats all.

"Why, Prew!"

Mrs Kipfer gracefully admitted him.

"I certainly didnt expect to see you again so soon. This is a surprise."

"Hows business?" he grinned as the thick sawdusty circusday atmosphere broke over him in waves. Mrs Kipfer was looking slightly harassed. Not that it had wilted her corsage, just that the International Sterling lady had been candid-cameraed during a receiving line, or been caught presiding over a difficult dinner for some drunken guest her husband had brought home.

"Isnt it awful though?" she said.

With both waiting rooms full, men moving laughing up and down the hall, the two jukeboxes having a perpetual battle of music, sweating girls slamming doors, spike heels jarring the floor, it looked like a defense plant assembly line in full swing. There was a strong smell of mingled perfumes in the tobacco cloud and a male voice was half drunkenly competing with the jukebox in the second waiting room and from far down the hall a harried voice yelled, "Towels!"

"One might easily," Mrs Kipfer said wearily, "mistake us for the Republican convention in Philadelphia, mightnt they?"

"Or even the American Legion National Convention in Detroit," Prew said.

"Oh, no, not that!"

"Towels!"

Mrs Kipfer winced. "Petunia. Josette needs towels. In number seven."

"Hokay." The great black roll of flowing fat moved off indifferently. Indifferent even to the wisp of cap and tiny apron she had been afflicted with.

"And see if anyone else needs any." Mrs Kipfer brushed at her cheek distractedly. "And *hurry!* Petunia. Her name really is Petunia. Isn't it awful? Just like the movies. But I dont know what I'd do without her though. Minerva is such a goldbrick. She's sick today. She's always sick on Payday. I cant do a thing with her at all." She sucked a breath. "That Minerva! I only have just the two, you know. The Service has at least four maids. But of course they're the biggest place in town."

"Wheres Lorene?" Prew said.

Mrs Kipfer put her hand lightly on his arm and beamed at him sideways knowingly. "Why, Prew! Is that why you came down specially on Payday? What did you do, did you go and borrow money? Just to come down here today and see Lorene?"

"Why would I do that?" Prew said, stiffly. He could feel both his upper lip and his neck get stiff simultaneously. "As a matter of fact," he said stiffly, "I won a little money today and decided to come to town before I lost it back is all."

"Well, I think thats very wise of you." Mrs. Kipfer was smiling at him sideways with her head cocked on one side. "How much did you win, dear?"

Prew felt a hollow fear cut down sharply through his irritation, splitting it into halves that fell away leaving a complete blankness in his mind, and he reached for his wallet quickly as a man will who is used to having to calculate his funds. It was still there. He breathed again.

"Oh," he said. "About a hundred."

"Well. Thats quite good, isnt it?"

"Only fair," he said. He was remembering he had already spent one dollar of the twenty for two drinks to help him drop the trapdoor in his mind (there are times when it is imperative to drop the trapdoor in the mind, but the hinges have a tendency to stick so often) and that left him nineteen. Take a buck out for cab fare both ways (he could not risk hitching back, not this time) and that left eighteen. Fifteen for all night and three for a quickie now, and no bottle at all. It was running him too close for comfort.

Mrs Kipfer was still smiling at him sideways. "You know, I vastly admire your taste, my dear. But there is always such a heavy call for Lorene on Payday, and there are two or three other girls available in the waiting room."

"Listen," he said, wanting now to laugh at her, "I aint in no hurry. Just tell me where to find her."

Mrs Kipfer, smiling, shrugged. "Very well. She's in number nine. Straight down the hall. The best way is to wait and catch her in the hall. Excuse me theres the door."

He grinned after her, still wanting to laugh at how she didnt know near what she thought she knew, and turned away down the hall.

"I'm sorry, boys," Mrs Kipfer was saying through the slot. "We're just completely filled—

"There just isn't a bit of room—

"I'm just awfully sorry—

"Well," she said. "If thats the way you feel, you just go right ahead. I'm sorry.

"Oh, Prew-ew," she called.

"Yes?"

"Drunk as lords," she whispered, coming back. "I wanted to ask you how Sergeant Warden was?"

"Who?"

"Milt Warden. He's still with the company, isn't he?"

"Yes," he said. "Yes, he is."

"He hasnt been in for such a long time now I thought perhaps he had been transferred back to the Mainland. Will you remember me to him?"

"Yes. Well," he said. "Yes, I'll do that." He would do just that, walk up to The Warden after Reveille and tell him exactly that.

"You know," Mrs Kipfer said, "you boys are lucky to have a man like that for your first sergeant."

"You think so?" Prew said. "I think so, too. Oh, in fact, we all think that." Well, well, he thought, well, well. But The Warden! Well, well. Will wonders never cease?

The door of number nine was open and a Marine tech sergeant with the bar under his chevrons instead of the rocker was coming out tying his tie. It was remarkable how every detail of him seemed so very clear and personal to Prew. Prew watched him absorbedly as he went off up the hall.

Lorene came out after him, moving at a swift walk that jarred the spike heels down staccato-ly and he saw her suddenly, heart-jumpingly, as if she had been photographed life size in mid-stride and stuck there and then walked right out of the print into the hall, the unzipped dress held together with one hand that also clutched one white poker chip, a brimming bottle of dark liquid in the other that she swung slightly to keep from spilling the way a waitress swings a cup of coffee. She was moving fast, and she swung her shoulders sideways to pass him in the narrowness of the crowded hall.

"Hey," he said. "Lorene."

"Hello, dear," she said.

"Hey! Wait a minute, will you?"

"I've got to hurry, dear, theres three or four ahead of you." Then she saw him. She stopped. "Oh, its you. Hello. How are you?" She glanced down the hall.

"How am I?" Was that all she had to say? He hunted desperately for an eternity through a mind that was suddenly completely blank. "I'm fine," he said lamely. "How are you?"

"Well thats nice," Lorene said, glancing down the hall. "Listen, dear, I can take care of you in—" she looked at her watch "—say half an hour? Thats the best I can do, honey."

"Yeah?" Prew said, feeling his throat close up as if he had swallowed alum. "Say," he said. He had to work hard to get it said. "Say, do you remember me?"

"Of course I remember you, silly," she said, leaning back and looking down the hall. "Did you think I could forget you? Listen, I just cant talk now, dear. You could come back in an hour, why dont you try that?"

"Ah, forget it. To hell with it." He stepped back, still blankly.

"I guess that wouldnt have worked anyway," Lorene said. "There'll probably be more than four waiting by then anyway."

"Yeah. Mrs Kipfer told me you was popular. Just forget it, I dont want to put you out any."

"I'll tell you what," she said. She looked down the hall. "I dont see any of them around. Maybe I can slip you in ahead, how would that be?"

"Dont do me no goddam favors."

Lorene looked at him then, her eyes coming alive with an anxiety, alive for the first time, as if she was just now seeing something other than a regular customer. "Now dont be like that. What did you expect?"

"I dont know."

"You picked a bad time to come is all. I work here, you know. After all."

"Yeah?" he said. "I'm the guy that was here three days ago and stayed all night with you and promised you faithfully I'd be back tonight. To stay all night with you. Remember? I'm the guy that laid in bed with you and talked for about three hours."

"Of course I remember."

"Hell, you dont even remember my name."

"Of course I do. You're Prew. We talked about why I got into this racket. There. You see? I do remember."

"Yeh," he said.

"Listen, you go on in number nine and wait and I'll be back in just a minute. You can get undressed while you're waiting."

"No thanks. I had rather wait till later, if you dont mind. I never did much go for mass production, somehow."

She had started away again, for the third time, but now she came back and looked at him squarely. But her eyes kept slipping away, off his face. "That wont work either, Prew," she said softly. "I'm already dated up for all night tonight."

"What!" His mouth felt very dry, he noticed, and he worked his lips to moisten it. "You dint tell me that the other night. You told me . . . What is this, the run-around?"

"I didnt know it then," Lorene explained, with great patience. "This is Payday. Remember? I can pick up more credits ahead—" she shook the white chip at him "—on this one day than in the whole last three weeks of the month together. Theres a bunch of the big brass coming down from Shafter for a party and they've engaged the whole place almost. They called Mrs Kipfer up this morning and they asked for me special."

"But you'd already promised me," he protested, "goddam it. Why dint you tell her that?" What're you doing, begging now? he told himself. Dont you know when you're not wanted? You've lost damn near everything else now, do you have to lose that too?

"Listen," Lorene said exasperatedly, "cant you understand? When the brass comes around, Mrs Kipfer closes the whole place up for them. How do you think it would look for the EM to see them here?"

Yes, he thought, that bitch, that lousy bitch, she knew it all along. "I dont give a good goddam how it 'would look.' Not a single good goddam." A big GI in civilians and fat enough to be a first cook pushed through between them elbowing by, and Prew watched him hopefully. "Watch what the hell you're doin, Mack. You son of a bitch," he said, but the big guy did not even turn around. Damn, he thought, cant even insult somebody, oh damn.

"You couldnt have even gotten in," Lorene was saying, "even if I did turn the job down. I just would have lost the commission, thats all, and for nothing. When they come down from Shafter they pay big money. They scatter it around like leaves of lettuce. What is fifteen bucks to them? The girls make more off of one of those nights than they do in a whole ordinary week. I'm sorry, Prew, but what else could I do?"

"You're sorry? How the hell you think I feel? She's sorry," he said. "She's very sorry. I only been counting on this like a goddam kid counts on Christmas." Why dont you shut up, Prewitt? Aint you got any pride left at all?

336

"I am sorry. But you havent got any claims on me, mister. You're not my husband, you know."

"Yeh I know. I sure as hell aint, am I? Jesus Christ, Lorene," he said.

"Listen, every minute we talk here is costing me four bits . . ."

"And thats a lot of money, aint it?"

". . . and theres nothing I can do about the other. Do you want me to slip you in ahead, or dont you? I'm going out of my way to do that as it is."

Thats right, he thought. Women were so *practical*.

"Well," she said, "what do you say?"

He looked at her, at the very wide mouth across the thin child's face that was compressed into a harried impatience, now, wanting to tell her what to do with it, to take it all of it and stick it, and walk out of this ratrace. Instead, he heard himself saying, "*Okay*," and hated himself for saying it.

"All right then," Lorene said. "In number nine. And get undressed. I'll be back soon as I take care of this."

And she was gone then, swiftly, him watching her legging it down the hall twisting and turning through the crowd like a broken field runner. A man reached out an arm and stopped her and she smiled, talked, got irritated and went on.

Another Prewitt, Prewitt thought. He went on into number nine then, after that one, feeling the blankness in him slowly filling up with anger, but the anger kept seeping out the bottom where his stomach no longer was. He sat down on the bed. He could not stop seeing the mental picture he had brought with him, and it made him feel all gone inside.

He heard her coming back. But by the time he could look up the door was already shut, the unzippered gown on the chair. Then she stopped, looking at him stupidly.

"Why you're not even undressed yet!"

"I'm not? By god, I'm not, am I?" he stood up.

Lorene looked like she was going to cry. "I told you to be undressed when I got back, goddam it. I'm slipping you in ahead of them, just as a favor, and you dont even try to help me any."

Prew stood and looked at her. He could not say anything.

"Never mind that now," he said. "Let me look at you."

"Okay," she said.

He handed her the three dollars.

She pushed the damp hair back out of the harried eyes, sweat glistening from the flat place between her chubby little breasts.

"You know there's a time limit on Payday. Petunia will be knocking any time now."

337

He straightened up, looking at her, a tightness of ache deep in his jaws that ran clear down his spine into his buttocks and knotted his belly sourly. She lay naked on the bed, waiting frenetically, her head bent forward irritably to look at him.

"Why don't you come back tomorrow night?" Lorene said. "And stay all night tomorrow?"

He could hear this faintly through the skintight space suit of plexiglass he was encased in, sealed in, a perfect example of the Twentieth Century Man doing his calisthenics to keep healthy and not lose his figure, in his airtight, soundproof, loveproof, hateproof, lifeproof plexiglass space suit that was a marvel of modern industrial accomplishment, a masterpiece of modern industrial engineering design, there should be at least two in every home, and then one each for all the little ones, because a Twentieth Century Man looked so silly naked with his shoes and socks still on, a muscle-knotty squirrel divested of its skin but the footpads not cut off yet. But he was goddamned, stinking slucking goddamned, if he would tell her, now, how he could not come back tomorrow because he had had to borrow twenty from the twenty per cent men, also a marvel of modern industrial accomplishment, to come today at all, and that he would not have the dough to come again tomorrow. Besides, he would have to yell too loud to make it heard outside the plexiglass space suit anyway.

"You'll have to hurry, honey," Lorene said. "If you dont want to take a raincheck."

It was very strange: Robert E Lee Prewitt, the Twentieth Century MAN, who walked upon his mother earth in an up-to-the-minute Twentieth Century PLEXIGLASS SPACE SUIT that industrial techniques produced in such munificent mass abundance that every man woman and child could have one at cost, at less than cost, at nothing actually, because our recent research has so perfected the new process that we can now make the astounding offer of an almost absolute vacuum in our newer models, this modern MAN with so much to be grateful for, with the heritage of the ages in his hands, who could hear his shoes scraping scraping against the gilt-flaking bed frame like one of the higher-priced more accurate metronomes reminding him not to get the clean sheet muddy—this creature was not even HAPPY! Just because he could not get outside his plexiglass space suit, his sanitary all-purpose all-weather space suit, just because he was not *known*, just because he did *know*, just because he could not touch another human soul.

Then, as if to prove it, there was a big broad knock on the door and Petunia hollered, "All right in there, yawl. Y'time's up, Miss Lorene."

"All right," Lorene bawled.

"Try," Lorene panted. "Or I'll have to give you a raincheck."

Try what for?

"To hell with it," he said. He got up and got a handkerchief from his pants and wiped the sweat out of his eyes.

"Whats wrong with you tonight?"

"I guess I had two too many drinks." He put his pants on. Then he put his shirt on. Then he wiped his face again. He did not have to put his shoes on.

"I'm sorry it didnt work, Prew."

"Whats to be sorry for? You done your best, dint you? Your professional best."

As she handed him the printed card and refund, Lorene looked rather like a girl who has failed to pass her finals and been flunked out. She wanted to redeem her reputation.

"Will you be back tomorrow night?"

"I dont think so," Prew said, looking at the buck and a half in his hand that would make the car fare for tomorrow night. "Anyway, dont you hold your breath until you see me, lady."

He tore the card in two and laid it carefully on the bed. "Give that to some other three-minute man. I aint worried about my virility."

"All right, if thats the way you feel."

"Thats exactly how I feel."

"Okay. Well, I've got to go. Maybe I'll see you sometime."

He watched her put the gown on and leave, hoping she would say something else, something more, wanting her to make the overture he could not make. Even in the anger he did not want to destroy it between them. She stopped at the door and looked back at him a second and he knew she was waiting for him to make the overture. But he could not make it. She would have to make it. But she could not make it either. And she left.

He finished dressing in the room alone. The room was muggy like before a storm with evaporated sweat, but when he stepped out in the hall it was no better and his eyes and temples pounded with undischarged, unrelieved, too-rich blood. His face was flushed with it, and already he had sweat through the back of his shirt and the ass of his pants. Well, he thought, thats the first time that ever happened to you. You must be changing somehow. Some way or other. He felt very sick and very angry.

In the hallway he met Maureen standing in the doorway of her room taking a breather. Somebody had sneaked a bottle in to her and she was half drunk.

"Well, look who's here," she bawled. "Hi there, Babyface. Hey, why so glum? Cant you get in to see your own true love?"

"You want to go to the room with me?"

"Who? Me? Whats wrong with the Holy Princess, Babyface?"

"To hell with her. I'm asking you."

"They really keep the Princess on the move, dont they? all the lonesome lovesick joes? God-damn, wish I looked like a virgin. They dont want whores any more, they all want mothers. To protect them. What you need is a wife, Babyface."

"Okay, lets get married."

Maureen stopped guffawing and looked at him. "Hell, you dont need no wife. What you need is a drink, and you need it bad. I know what you got."

"How the hell do you know what I've got? You cant even guess at what I've got."

"You got the same thing I get myself, only I get it about two or three times every week fifty-two weeks a year year in year out. Dont try to snow me, Babyface. This is Maureen."

"Do you want to go to the room?" Prew said. "Or dont you?"

"Goin to the room wont help what you got, Babyface. You take your money to the nearest bar and get yourself drunkern hell. Thats all'll help you, Babyface. I know."

"Who the hell're you? Dorothy Dix? I aint asking you for no advice."

"Well, I'm givin it to you anyway."

"Well, I aint taking it."

"Shut up," Maureen said. "I'm doin the talking."

"Okay, Dorothy Dix. You tell me all about it."

"I am telling you. All you got is a feeling you're locked up in a box thats two sizes too small for you and theres no air in it and you're suffocatin, and all the time outside the box you hear the whole world walkin around laughin and havin a big, big time. Thats all you got." She looked at him.

"Okay," Prew said meekly. "You talk."

"Okay then. Hell, I get what you got all the time, and the ony thing'll fix it is to get drunkern hell. I've experimented, see? What you got to do now is to remember that it aint nobody's fault. Its the system. Nobody's to blame."

"Thats a pretty hard thing to remember."

"Sure. Too hard. Thats why you got to get good and drunk. Because if you dont you'll never remember it, see?"

"Okay. I'm goin to get drunk," he said. "But on my way out I'm going to say hello to Mrs Kipfer. I'm going to tell her what I think of respectable whores' madams. The mealy-mouthed old bitch."

"No you aint. You just leave Mrs Kipfer alone, see? She'll have the goddam MPs on you quickern you can bat your eye. You want to spend a month in the Shafter stockade? You just go get drunk."

"Okay," he said. "Okay. But listen, what the hell can you do? Aint there nothing you can ever do?"

"No," Maureen said. "Not ever. Because nobody's to blame. Its the system. Thats what you got to remember, that nobody's to blame."

"I wont believe that," he said. He put the three back in his wallet. "But its okay. I know what you mean."

"Okay then," Maureen said. "Just take off. I dint take you to raise, did I? I aint got all goddam day."

"Go to hell," he grinned.

"Next!" Maureen bawled, as he closed the door.

He was still grinning when Mrs Kipfer opened the door for him gracefully sweetly, and he managed easily now by just grinning at her and not saying a word.

Thats what you got to remember: its nobody's fault, its the system, he told himself. What did you expect on Payday? A brass band to meet you? A motorcycle escort? She was just busy, thats all. Would you expect to go in a department store and talk to your girlfriend behind her counter while the customers beat each other to death with nylon hose all around you when the big sale was on?

"Thats all it is," he told the stairway. "She's got to earn her living. According to the system. Aint she?"

Thats all it is, he told himself.

But the hard tight sour knot of indigestible outrage in his belly did not dissolve.

I guess she's right then. You got to wash it out with liquor. You got to be drunk enough to be sentimental, before you can believe different. No matter how many times you spiel it. No wonder theres so goddam many alcoholics in this goddam country. In this goddam Twentieth Century.

What a name. Lorene. The perfect whore's name: romantic, very high-toned, and very feminine. Lorene the fair, Lorene the square, Lorene the lily maid of Hotel Street. How could you ever of thought that was a lovely, woman's name? he thought biliously.

Well, he would go up to the corner to Wu Fat's, thats where. He would go in the downstairs bar and he would drink this thirteen-fifty up and then see how we feel. We'll feel like hell, thats how. All right then, after that he would catch a Kalakaua bus out to Waikiki where Maggio said he was going to be with his queer friend Hal, this Payday night, because it had already taken all his money to pay his debts, and we will look them up. We will drink some more off of them. Hell, if he got drunk enough he might even be able to pick himself up one himself. He had tried everything else. He might as well shoot an angle on this azimuth.

Chapter 25

He did not have to go to Waikiki to find Maggio. Maggio was sitting at the bar of the cocktail lounge of Wu Fat's Restaurant, when he walked in, and Prew stood in the doorway of the Payday pandemonium, wanting suddenly to laugh wildly like a condemned man getting a reprieve, feeling the warmth that Maureen's whiskey could not give him beginning to spread through him now, as he watched the little Wop perched high above the press on the withers of a bar stool like a winning jockey in a crowded paddock smiling benignly down from his precarious perch at the screaming mob, and arguing with the barman in Italian.

"Halo, lunsman!" Angelo bawled at him, waving his arm. "Hey, here I am! Over here! This is me!"

Prew worked his way slowly over to the stool, feeling himself begin to grin.

"Can you breathe?" Angelo said.

"No."

"Climb up on my shoulders. You can see everything from up here, and still breathe too. Aint this wonerful?"

"I thought you was headed for Waikiki tonight."

"I am. This here is ony preparation. Would *you* like a little preparation, lunsman?"

"I could do with a little preparation," Prew panted, still elbowing in towards the bar.

"Hey, pizon," Angelo called to the barman. "Bring this other pizon some preparation. This pizon is a personal friend of mine. This pizon badly needs preparation."

The sweatily grinning barman nodded happily and moved away.

"This pizon fought with Garibaldi, too," Angelo howled after him. "He is use to ony the best of service.

"I got him trained," he said to Prew. "Me and that pizon both fought for Garibaldi. I'm tellin him about the beautiful statue of Garibaldi the Americans put up in Washington Square."

"Where'd you get all the goddam money? If I remember, when I hit you up this afternoon you was supposed to be flat broke."

"I was. Honest I was. I happen to run into a guy from Easy Company owed me five from a jawbone latrine game so I settled for two-fifty and call it even. So I could induce a little preparation, before I go out to Waikiki and go to work."

"A likely story."

"You dont believe me? Look at my eyes. Are those the eyes of a liar? *Hey, pizon,*" he yelled down the bar, "*snap up!* You ask the pizon," he said, "are those the eyes of a liar. Me and him fought with Garibaldi."

"That pizon aint even old enough to have fought with Mussolini, let alone Garibaldi. And you're cock-eyed."

"So what? What has them got to do with this? Shut up, here he comes." He nodded at the barman, "This pizon is a pizon," he said loudly to Prew, as the barman set down the drink.

"Hi, pizon," Prew said. "You threwn out any more queers lately?"

"Oh, no. No, no," the barman said. He spread his arms to include the jam at the bar. "No queer today. All queer busy like hell Payday. All queer fodder here, see?"

"Pizon," Angelo said, "it is a beautiful statue. A statue of an incredible loveliness."

The barman shook his sweating head. "Sure like to see him."

"How can I describe it to you?" Angelo said, "the loveliness. When I work in Gimbel's Basement I use to put a wreath on this statue ever payday on Sataday, thats how lovely."

"Garibaldi," the barman grinned. "Fine man. My grandfather fight with Garibaldi."

"There," Angelo said to Prew. "You see?" He turned to the barman and pointed at Prew. "So did this pizon."

"When you put on the wreath," Prew said, "did you wash off the pigeon shit, too?"

"No," Angelo said. "My assistant did that."

"Garibaldi fight for liberty," the barman said.

"Thats right, pizon," Angelo nodded. "Shut up," he said to Prew, as the barman moved away. "You want to spoil it? I'm trying to induce this pizon for some preparation on the house."

"To hell with that pizon. I got thirteen-fifty we can use for preparation. Induce him with that."

"Thats diffrnt," Angelo said. "Why dint you say so?"

"All I got to save out is four bits cab fare home is all. If I miss Reveille any more, now, it'll be my ass."

"Your bloody ass," Angelo corrected. "Man, you are not kidding either. This Army makes me sick, you know it? Look at Garibaldi. Look at George Washington; and Abraham Lincoln. Look at F D R; and Gary Cooper. Then look at this Army."

"Look at General MacArthur," Prew said. "And his son, *General* MacArthur. Look at old Chief of Staff George C."

"Thats right," Angelo said. "Look at the Magna Charta. Look at the Declaration of Independence. Look at the Constitution. Look at the Bill of Rights. Look at the Fourth of July."

"Look at Christmas," Prew suggested.

"Thats right," Angelo said. "Look at Alexander the Great. Then look at this fuckin Army. Dont talk about it any more. I cant stand it."

"Not without inducing some more preparation," Prew said.

"Thats it. Now you got it. Whynt you come out to Waikiki with me later on? This thirteen-fifty will not last forever."

"Maybe I will, after we induce some more. I never did like queers. Every time I get around them I want to punch them in the head."

"Aw, they all right. They just peculiar is all. They maladjusted. Besides, they'll buy you preparation all night long."

"You think you could find me one?" Prew said, hesitating, yet knowing all the time that he would go.

"Sure. Old Hal'll find one for you. Whynt you come on and go?"

Prew was looking around the bar. "I already said I'd go, dint I? Shut up on it. Drop it, for Christ's sake. Matter of fact, I meant to go all along. I was goin out to Waikiki to look you up, after I left here. What is this slop we drinkin anyway?"

"Gin and ginger."

"A goddam woman's drink. Whynt we get whisky? We got money."

"You want whisky, you drink whisky. I'm drinkin this because I got to go to work. I get out to Waikiki I be drinkin champagne cocktails. Hell, thats all I drink out there. Champagne cocktails, buddy."

They left Wu Fat's at ten-thirty. Prew still had two dollars left, besides his cab fare home. They decided to take a taxi out. They dodged catty corner across Hotel to the GI taxi stand in front of the Japanese woman-barber shop and fell in at the end of the mob that was jamming the cab stand almost as badly as the other mob had jammed the bar. Everything was jammed, even the Japanee woman-barber shop had a waiting line.

"Its a lot of crap," Angelo said drunkenly. "Pay fifty cents a head to ride three miles to Waikiki when you pay the same price to ride thirty-five miles to Schofield. But its better than them goddam buses. Especially Payday. But ever fuckin body robs the soljers."

The cab they finally got already had the back seat and the two folding seats filled with Waikiki passengers. They climbed in front with the driver and slammed the door. The driver pulled away expertly quickly to let the cab behind pull in. He eased into the steady traffic, going over to Pauahi Street, moving slowly through the alternating light and dark patches that were bars and whorehouses, on around the block and back to Hotel.

Angelo sighed drunkenly. "I might as well brief you now. Its a good thing you aint in uniform," he added.

"Oh, yeah? How goddam so? Whats wrong with the uniform? I like the uniform."

"But they dont like it," Angelo grinned. "They high-toned friends might get the wrong idea about them and think they was queer, runnin around with uniforms."

"Hell, they never use to mind that in Washington or Baltimore."

"But them are cities. Honolulu is really a small town. Everybody knows everybody else. I dint know you been out with them before?"

"A couple times is all. Me and another guy rolled some rich ones in Washington. They wont go to the law. We carried a GI Irish spud in a GI sock. It worked swell."

"That sounds okay," Angelo said, grudgingly admiringly. "Back home we used a sock full of sand, but trouble with that is the sock's liable to bust first time you sap him."

The cab was moving slowly in the traffic up Hotel Street that was lit up like a carnival. They passed the arcade two doors down from the Army-Navy Y, where a mob was shooting electric eye machineguns at lighted planes or waiting to get their picture taken with their arm drunkenly around the big titted Japanee hula girl against a canvas backdrop of Diamond Head and palms. Something to Send Home, the sign on the photograph booth said.

"But you cant roll them in this town," Angelo said. "They never carry money. Too many dogfaces."

"I know all that," Prew said.

"You got to play them like a fish, see? Hell," Angelo growled, "the cruisers dont even have to buy you drinks, because the market's glutted. I use to play the cruisers, before I got experience. Its like everything else in this world, you got to pay for what you get. You can pay for it by learning, or you can pay for it with experience once you learnt it, or you can pay for it with friendship. But you got to pay. Thats my philosophy. I read it in some book once."

The cab moved at a walking pace past the crowded hotdog stand next door to the Y where a bunch waited to use the dime automatic photograph machine, their mass overflowing onto the already jampacked sidewalk. Then on past the dark palm studded lawn of the Y itself, with the Black Cat across the street and also overflowing. A number of drunks lay passed out on the Y lawn.

"But these tonight aint cruisers," Angelo said. "Tonight is regulars. They carry checkbooks and pay for everything by checks."

Prew was looking out the window at the Y. "Payday at the mines."

"Thats it. And its really a racket, buddy, I mean. Any more. Us honest queer chasers aint got a chance no more. Half the Compny hang out out there at the Tavern any more. You'll see. You'd think the Tavern is a bivouac for George Compny. Harris hangs out out there, and Martuscelli, Knapp goes down, and Dusty Rhodes . . ."

"The Scholar?" Prew grinned fuzzily. "Him too?"

"Sure. And old Readall Treadwell, and Bull Nair, and Johnson. Bloom and Andy's down together most every night. Christ, I dont know who all. It looks like a Compny convention, out there."

"That son of a bitch Andy," Prew said. "I told him to keep away from there, especially if he with Bloom."

Angelo shrugged. "They all there anyway. Hell, there aint enough queens to go around, any more. I'm thinkin of organizin a union, by god. Got to pretect us professionals from the steadily encroaching amatoors and scabs."

The cab turned the corner out of the light into the dark tunnel of Richards Street between the Von Hamm-Young garage and the Palace Square grounds on the left with the light of King Street ahead of them down at the end of the block.

"Thats me," Prew said. "I'm a scab. You and Petrillo."

"Naw. You aint no scab. I'd get you in. Hell, pay your dues myself. You know, they're funny things, queers. This Hal is really a pretty good joe, if he dint hate everything so much. He hates everybody. Everybody but me. I guess he's bitter about being a queen. I spent a lot of time, tryin to figure out what makes them tick. Lots of guy'll tell you if you even talk to them you're queer yourself, that you ought to beat them up all the time. I dont figure like that. I figure those guys just hate them."

"I dont like them," Prew said thoughtfully. "But I dont hate them. I just dont like to be around them." He paused. "Its just that they, well for some reason they make me feel ashamed of something." He paused again. "I dont know what of."

"I know," Angelo said. "Me too. I spent a lot of time trying to figure it. They all say they was born like that. They say they been that way ever since they can remember."

"I wouldnt know," Prew said.

The cab driver turned his head slightly and for the first time spoke. "Thats a lot of bull," he said. "Lissen, let me give you joes a tip. I'm a ex-serviceman myself. You steer clear of them queers. You keep runnin around with them long enough and you'll be queer too. Thats what they want. They like to take young guys like you and make them queer too. They get a charge out of that. I hate the bastards. I'd kill every one I seen."

He swung the cab viciously out of the tunnel into the light of King Street, turning left past the Post Office and the gilded brown-faced statue of Kamehameha in his feather cape and helmet. The street was very wide here with two bus islands in the middle and the traffic was thinner and the driver speeded up a little.

"Yeh, I've heard that," Angelo said to him. "But this guy never tried nothing like that with me."

"I hate them," the driver said.

"Okay," Prew said. "So you hate them. You go right ahead and hate them, Mack. But dont tell us what we ought to do. We aint tellin you what you ought to do."

"Okay," the driver said, "okay. Dont get huffy."

"I wonder if they really are born that way?" Angelo said. He was looking out the window tranquilly, held by the quiet peacefulness of the cab ride that, sitting on the inside and looking out as an observer, divorced them momentarily from the wild bottle-swinging ritual of Payday and helped sober them.

Prew felt it too. The big polyhedral square here that held most of the civic buildings was comparatively serene under the unaugmented street-lights, after the frenzy of Hotel Street and the Y. They passed the darkling dim shapes of the Federal Building and the Judiciary Building, the Palace on the left hidden behind its screen of trees, then the Territorial Office Building and Kawaiahao Church on the right as the street began to narrow again, and the Library and then the City Hall on the left, all of them shut up for the night as they ran on out King, into the gradually deepening dark away from town.

"I dont know," Prew said. "I know that on the bum a lot of good guys went queer, though, because they just wasnt any women. Some of the old timers would take the young kids and train them to be ring tails. Thats what I hate. A kid dont know his own mind. Thats what Chief Bugler Houston was a regular Mister Brown. Thats one reason I got out of the Corps, him and that Angelina of his."

"Yeah," the driver said. "And they'll all do you like that, you give them a chance, dont think they wont, the queer bastards."

"Where'd you learn to play that bugle?" Angelo asked, "like you do? I never heard no guy could play a goddam bugle like that."

"I dont know," Prew said. "I just always could I guess. I always liked it." He was looking out at the sudden deeper darkness that was Thomas Square.

"Thats where all the cruisers hang out," the driver said.

"I sure like to hear you play it," Angelo said. "Its a shame."

"Lets drop it," Prew said. "Lets forget it, what do you say?"

"Okay," Angelo said. "If you say so."

They lapsed into silence then, the cool tranquillity that was the ride, feeling the driver beside them aching to talk, to advise them, but hating to start it again on his own hook, for fear he would seem anxious to talk about it. They did not give him an opening.

They got out in front of the Moana and were suddenly back inside and part of the heated excitement of Payday.

347

"We'll walk down from here," Angelo said. "We dont want to look too well heeled, ridin up to the door in a cab." He stopped on the sidewalk to look back at the driver as he swung out from the curb. "Now thats funny," he said.

"Whats funny, Angelo?"

"If I hadnt of heard that guy talk so, I'd swear that driver was a queer. I can spot them a mile away."

Prew laughed. "Maybe thats why he hates them. Maybe thats what he's afraid of."

"I dont know. But I can sure spot them any more."

The Waikiki Tavern was crowded, too. A little less raucously, a little more refinedly, but crowded just the same.

"I'll wait out here," Prew said. "Till you seef they there."

"Hell. You been here before, aint you? Come on in."

"Sure I been here. But I aint goin in broke."

"You aint broke."

"I aint got enough to buy a drink, have I? To just walk in and walk through and walk right back out, if they aint there. Not me. I'll wait out here."

"Okay. Have it your way. You know what? That cab ride sobered me almost up."

Angelo went on in through the crowded door. Prew stood out on the sidewalk and leaned against a lamp post, his hands in his pockets, watching the people pass. In the lounge next to the bar proper, under colored light and conversation and clinking glass, the lushhead piano player was playing something classical. It was something he had heard before. He had never heard the name. Several well dressed, cool looking white women passed him, talking excitedly to obviously younger men who looked like doggies.

Thats what you ought to have, Prewitt, he told himself. One of them rich tourist dames. Thats better than these tight-fisted queens. All the money in the world they've got. And dont mind spending it. The thought made a small hard excitement in his belly. Then he remembered Lorene down at the New Congress. The small hard excitement turned into a small tight sour knot. I guess that cab ride sobered you up too, he thought, goddam it.

He was considering the question of whether it was legitimate to step out on a woman you loved if she was a whore, provided you only went with tourist women for their money, and if not, whether going out with a queen would be considered the same as going out with a woman— theres one for you, Prewitt, you must look that up in a etiquette book some time—when Angelo came to the door and motioned for him.

"He's here," he said. "And he's already got one for you."

Prew followed him inside, into the subdued atmosphere of richness with the pyramids of glasses doubling themselves in the mirror and the smooth-spoken barmen that always made you feel low class, and on through out onto the terrace.

The two men were sitting in a booth for four with the sea rising dark behind them, beyond the light. One was tall and very slender with a tiny grey moustache and close clipped grey hair and very bright eyes. The other was a big man, over two hundred, with the beginning of a double chin and shoulders almost as wide as the table.

"This is Prewitt," Angelo said, "that I been telling you about. My buddy. And thats Hal," pointing to the thin one, "about whom I've been telling you about. And this is Tommy."

"Hello," Hal said, in a clipped voice that sounded foreign.

"Hello, Prew," Tommy said, in a deep bass voice from down in his barrel chest. "You dont mind if we call you Prew?"

"Thats all right," Prew said. He put his hands in his pockets. Then he took them out. Then he leaned against the booth. Then he stood up straight again.

"Come on, you dears," Hal said in his accented voice. "Sit down."

Here it comes, Prew thought. He sat down beside the big man, Tommy.

"You know Tommy," Angelo said to Prew. "He's the one I told you about was Bloom's girl friend."

"Well," Tommy smiled smugly. "I do declare. I am acquiring a reputation."

"But they've busted up now," Angelo said.

"Yes," Tommy said stiffly. "Everyone makes mistakes. That bitch. He is not only a pig, but he's as queer as a fruit cake."

Hal laughed delightedly. "What will you have to drink?"

"Champagne cocktail," Maggio said.

Hal laughed. "Darling Tony and his champagne cocktails. I had to buy champagne and learn to make them for him. He has an artist's stomach. Saint Anthony Maggio, of the champagne cocktails."

"Nuts," Tommy said. "Horse nuts."

Hal laughed delightedly. "Our friend dislikes the Catholics. He used to be one. Personally, I have no more against the Catholics than any one else."

"I hate them," Tommy said.

"I hate the Americans," Hal smiled. "I used to be one of them."

"Why do you live here then?" Prew asked.

"Because, sadly enough, dear, I have to make a living. Isnt it disgusting? But then I do not consider Hawaii exactly American. Like so many other places, it is not American by choice so much as by necessity.

The necessity of armed force. Like all the pagans they were doomed from the start to be converted to our particularly morbid type of Christianity."

"What do you want to drink, Prew?" Tommy put in.

"Champagne cocktail," Maggio said.

Tommy gave Maggio a withering look and then turned to Prew again.

"Sure," Prew said. "Thats okay, I guess."

"You must excuse me," Hal smiled. "When I get to discussing things I forget everything. Sometimes I even forget to eat."

Hal motioned for the waiter and gave the orders and then turned back to Prew. "You are the type of mentality I like to talk to. It re-affirms my somewhat threadbare faith in the human race. You have an inquiring mind and all it needs is the proper direction."

"I dont need any direction," Prew said. "I make up my own mind. About everything. Including queers."

Across the table Maggio shook his head warningly and scowled. Tommy was looking away at the time.

Hal was sighing heavily. "That is a harsh word to use. But then we are used to that. And of course, you are slightly ill at ease now, your first time meeting us and all."

Prew shifted in his seat and looked up at the blank-faced waiter who was setting the drinks before them. "Yes," he said. "Thats true. I am. But I just wanted to have it straight. I never like to have people tell me how to make up my mind."

"Ah," Hal said. "A man after my own heart."

"Listen," Tommy said abruptly. "Whose date is he, anyway? Yours or mine?"

"Yours of course, dear," Hal smiled. "It is just that I like to talk to new people."

"Okay," Tommy said. "But for Christ's sake quit making a play for him. He's not the intellectual type. Are you, Prew dear?"

"Probably not," Prew said. "Since I never finished the seventh grade."

"Hal's a French teacher," Maggio put in. "He works in a sort of private school, for rich men's kids.

"Tommy's got a job someplace downtown. He never talks about it. Where do you work, Tommy, anyway?" Maggio said. He shook his head again, vigorously, and winked at Prew.

"I'm a writer," Tommy said.

"Sure," Maggio said. "But you work too, dont you?"

Hal laughed delightedly.

"At present," Tommy said stiffly, "I am holding down a job. But its only until I get enough money ahead to devote all my time to my art.

And as far as my job goes, I'd rather not talk about it. I dont like it anyway."

"Even I dont know where he lives," Hal said. "He wont tell me anything. Personally, I dont care who knows about me. In fact, its almost expected of a French teacher. Thats one of the reasons I like being one.

"And incidentally, I am a private tutor. I hold private classes and tutor individuals, but not at any school. Or any 'sort of' school." He smiled at Angelo. "But as I said, as long as I do not mix business with pleasure, these horrible missionaries' descendants dont bother me. In fact, I think they rather like the idea, secretly. Its supposed to be worldly and sophisticated, you see. And of course, I'm not an Oscar Wilde; I dont have a yen for hairless infants; so that they neednt fear for their offspring."

"Lets have another drink," Maggio said. "We walked all the way out here from town."

"Why didnt you call me up?" Hal said. "I would have come after you."

"We wanted to walk," Maggio said. "To get up a thirst."

Hal motioned for the waiter. "Garçon. Another round, please. Sometimes, Tony, I think you are only playing me for what you can get out of me." He turned to Maggio with a sweet almost boyish smile. "Sometimes I think if I didnt buy you things you would drop me like a hot rock. Perhaps that is why I love you so."

"Ah, you know that aint so, Hal," Maggio said. "Hey, look," he said. "Theres Bloom and Andy, Prew. I told you the Compny'd all be down here."

"Not so many today," Hal smiled, "as in the middle of the month."

Prew looked over where Angelo was pointing. Bloom and Andy in slacks and gook shirts had just come in with five other men, none of whom Prew knew. They took a big table in a corner of the terrace, Bloom holding forth loudly, his big arms waving when he talked, him leaning tensely across the table toward another man.

"Dear Bloom," Hal said. "He's dropping down the ladder rung by rung. I shouldnt be surprised if he committed suicide one day."

"He's too much of a pig," Tommy said. "He's not that sensitive. But I love that cute little guitarplayer he drags around with him. He's really sweet, but Bloom wont let any one get near him."

"Bloom's dating Flora now," Hal said sadly. "See that big effeminate blond across the table? That's Flora." He turned to smile at Prew with his bright excited eyes. "I imagine you had some such female conception of us before you met us, did you not?"

Prew watched the blond run his hands carefully over his marcelled hair and then, moving his hands, his big white fluttering hands, elaborately, get up and walk lumpily, swaying big-hippily, to the men's room. "Yes," he said. "I did."

"I suspected as much," Hal smiled. "Well, we are not actors. We do not have to get our kicks out of acting like women. In fact, the less I see and hear of women the better. Of all the things I dislike, I hate women worst."

"But why hate women so much?" Prew said.

Hal made a face. "They're evil. So domineering. And so sickeningly confident. Did you know this country is a true matriarchy? Evil," he said, "evil as sin. And nasty. So wet and soppy and nasty. God," he said.

"If you hate religion, how come you believe in sin?" Prew said. "I'd think it'd be just the opposite."

Hal looked at him and raised his brows. "I did not say I believed in sin. I think you misunderstood me. I only used that as an expression. A simile. As a matter of fact, I do not believe in the conception of sin. It is asinine, and I deny it completely. Do you think I could be what I am, and believe in sin?"

"I dont know. Maybe."

Hal smiled. "I thought you said you werent intellectual?"

"I aint," Prew said. "I told you I never finished the seventh grade. But I can see how that might be possible, about sin."

"Listen," Hal smiled. "I take it you have never studied the rise of the Industrial Revolution and its effect upon humanity, have you?"

"No," Prew said.

"If you had, you would understand the fallacy of sin. In a mechanistic universe, how can there be sin? In this age of the machine human society is also a machine, and if you look at it objectively you will see that Sin, per se, is not a self-evident phenomenon but a thing deliberately constructed for the mechanical control of society. Also, if you can be objective, you will be forced to see that *Sin* differs with the temperaments and opinions of different individuals, so that *Sin* is obviously relative to the man, and not a universal attribute."

"Whew!" Maggio said. He drained his fresh drink.

"But thats just what makes sin," Prew said; "the individual man's idea of it. If each man didnt have his idea of sin, there wouldnt be any sin at all. But as long as you think women are sinful, for you they are. Although that dont affect them any, or affect my idea of women. But if you believe women are evil, then you must believe in sin. Right?"

"I explained to you," Hal smiled, "that I only used that as a simile." He looked away, back at Bloom, and changed the subject. "Tommy was in love with that Bloom character, can you imagine that? They had quite an affair, for a while. I never could see it, myself."

"I was not," Tommy said, "ever in love with Bloom. I didnt even have an 'affair' with him, as you put it. I went out with him a few times. Thats all. He's too crude, too ignorant, and too stupid for anyone of my sensibilities to ever fall in love with."

Hal laughed, delighted. "I was only saying what I heard. And I do know you used to want to bring him up to my apartment." He turned to Prew. "Tommy uses my apartment for his loves, whenever I will let him. With Bloom I wouldnt let him. Otherwise, he takes them out in Kapiolani Park, or else he borrows my car. I think he drives them out to Blowhole. For atmosphere, you understand."

"You bitch," Tommy said heatedly in his deep bass voice.

Prew looked at the big man, suddenly remembering something, some familiar quality in his long thin-nosed face, something he knew well, but he could not get it.

Then he remembered it. When he was at Ft Slocum waiting shipment he had gone on pass to New York and picked up an artistic broad down in Greenwich Village in one of those Third Street bars with queer waiters and queer floor shows, bistros she called them, and next morning this broad had taken him to the Metropolitan Museum of Art where just inside the main door high up on one wall was a marble statue of a nude young Greek boy from the knees up that she had pointed out to him especially and this statue had the same look, no dent in the nose bridge and high cheekbones with softness under them, inbred looking, with over all the face that air of softness, of proud pain, and of conscious aimless beauty. In a word, he thought, decadent. Is America going to go decadent in the next election?

"What a you say we have another drink?" Angelo said. "I would like a champagne cocktail."

"Simply because you happen to have money," Tommy said to Hal. "And I dont. I dont have to take your nasty digs."

"Hey, waiter," Maggio said.

"What I love about you," Hal said to Maggio, ignoring Tommy, "is your wonderful simplicity. You are as clear as glass. Lets break this disgusting party up and go up to my apartment. I have a new case of French champagne that ought to tempt you. Have you ever drunk French champagne?"

"Aint this French champagne?" Maggio said.

"No, this is domestic. Made in America."

"Hell," Maggio said disappointedly. "I thought this was French champagne."

"And," Hal said, "in spite of what Somerset Maugham says, I say domestic champagne cant touch the French. And I ought to know."

"Hal lived in France for a long time," Angelo said to Prew.

"Is that right?" Prew said.

"Yes," Hal said. "Remind me to tell you about it sometime. Come on, lets go. I bought this champagne especially for you, Tony, and its getting harder and harder to get, what with the war. And I want to christen it. Besides, we can be comfortable there. Its so muggy hot in here tonight. I want to get my clothes off."

"Okay," Angelo said. "I dont care. How about you, Prew?"

Prew was watching Bloom's big figure, dominating the table of five thin men and Andy. "What?" he said. "Oh, its okay with me."

"Fine," Hal said. "I suppose if he wouldnt go, you wouldnt either," he said to Angelo.

Maggio winked at Prew. "No, I wouldnt. I cant leave my buddy."

"Such sentiment is very touching," Tommy sniffed.

Hal called the waiter and paid the bill, by check.

"I always pay by check," he said to Prew while they were waiting for the change. "Just in case you get any ideas, dear," he added, smiling that sweet smile that was more in his excited eyes than on his mouth. He tipped the waiter liberally.

"That is all, garçon," he said. "We are leaving."

"What do you always call him garsong for?" Prew said.

"Thats French for waiter," Hal said. "Boy."

"I know it," Prew said. "Thats about all the French I know. But it sounds affected. It sounds like you dont know French at all."

"I dont give a goddam," Hal smiled. "I do it because I like it." He took Prew by the sleeve of his gook shirt and spouted out a stream of French that rose and fell and ran together like distant small arms fire. "There, you see?" he smiled.

They walked out past the same hulking broken-faced bouncer who saluted Hal with one finger, bowing a little, and Prew heard coming from the lounge the same piano music he had listened to outside, as if that same piece had been playing all the time they were inside and was still going, going on forever.

"Whats the name of that piece?" he asked.

"What?" Tommy said. "That? Just a minute. I know it."

"Its Rachmaninoff's *Prelude in C# Minor*," Hal said quickly. "Very common stuff. Its one of that old drunk's specialties. Some pseudo-intellectual is always asking for it. Très chic," he said.

"What is pseudo?" Prewitt asked.

"It means half-assed," Angelo said.

Hal laughed. "Yes. Thats it. Fake would fit it."

"Its a prefix," Tommy said stiffly. "And it means unreal, illusory."

"Pseudo," Prew said. "Half-assed."

Chapter 26

The four of them walked back down Kalakaua past the Moana. At
Kaiulani they crossed over to the other side and walked past the single
string of tourist shops whose display windows displayed water goggles,
spear fishing outfits, the big rubber foot fins for better kicking. One
shop was devoted wholly to beach robes and swimming trunks, all with
a highly floral Hawaiian motif. Another shop was a woman's shop
displaying dresses and coats, also with Hawaiian motif. There was a
jewelry shop with expensive looking little figures carved from Chinese
jade. Beyond the unbroken string of shops was the world famed Waikiki Theater that had living palms growing inside it, but this was
closed now. It was almost midnight and most everything was closed
now, and even the streets were beginning to get their late at night
deserted look. The night air was cooling now and a small sea wind
stirred and only a few clouds high up moved slowly east hiding a
swatch of stars as they went. The palm trees that curved out over the
sidewalk rustled in the small wind softly as they walked.

Beyond the big white bulk of the Waikiki Theater, that was closed
now, Hal turned north away from the beach into one of the little side
streets full of whispering tropical plants that they could not see.

"Isnt this a lovely place to live?" Hal called. "So beautifully simple.
And what a lovely night."

"Oh, isnt it though," Tommy said. "Simply exquisite."

Hal and Maggio were walking ahead, the tall spare Hal bent almost
double as he talked to little Angelo.

"I'm glad you came," Tommy whispered to Prewitt. "I was deathly
afraid for a while that you wouldnt."

"Oh, I've heard a lot about this apartment of Hal's from Angelo. I
want to see it."

"Oh," Tommy said softly. "I had hoped it was because of me."

"Well," Prewitt said. "Partly you." He listened to Hal talking softly
also.

"Where have you been so long, you little savage? You don't know
how I've ached to see you. I never know when to expect you. All I can
do is hope. I'd be afraid to call you, and I dont even know the number
of your regiment anyway. Sometimes I dont think you come to see me
except when you need money."

"I been on extra duty all month," Maggio lied. "I couldnt get away. You can ask Prewitt."

"Is that right, Prew?" Hal called.

"Thats right," Prew called back. "He's on the shitlist."

"You liars," Hal said roguishly. "One lies and the other blandly backs him up. You're all alike, you soldiers. Fickle as fate."

"Hell," Maggio said. "You're just lucky I was broke this Payday, or I would of got drunked up and got on extra duty again."

"It seems," Hal said, "that Tony is always on extra duty around Payday."

"I am," Maggio said stoutly. "Seems I always get drunked up on Payday, and then I got extra duty two or three weeks. I always say I aint going to, but every Payday I do. Except this Payday I was broke. Its not that I dont come down because I got money, its just that when I got money I get drunked up. Then I get on extra duty. You see the difference?"

Hal laughed. "Thats rather a fine point, isnt it?" he said. "My simple child of the primitives," he said. "Thats why I love you. Please dont ever lose your ability to lie so convincingly."

"But its the truth," Maggio protested. "I get drunked up and come to town to get a couple pieces of ass, and the goddam MPs pick me up, and then I'm on extra duty."

"Dont you hate to go to a whorehouse?" Hal asked.

"Well," Angelo said. "I dont say I like it as well as I would a local girl, but I dont hate it. On this Rock a dogface aint got much choice."

Prew wondered if he always tangled himself up like this, wanting to laugh. But Hal did not seem to notice it.

"My god," Tommy said suddenly. "I couldnt stand it. Being a soldier. I'd kill myself. I swear I would."

"So would I," Hal said. "But then we arent primitives. We're abnormally sensitive."

"I guess that is so," Tommy said.

Hal laughed. "But do you see, Tony, how the moral scruples of the local women about soldiers is our gain, Tommy's and mine and the other members of the Third Sex? I think thats very sweetly ironical. It amuses me greatly, because it is indicative of a general turn of affairs that will someday give us the edge entirely."

"I guess it is," Maggio said. "Your gain, I mean."

"Did you hear that, Prew?" Hal called back.

"Yes," Prew said stoically. "I heard it."

"Because all these people hate the soldiers," Hal said, going on and developing the idea like a weaver working for his own amusement, "because they believe soldiers are scum—in fact believe all men are scum, women do, because of that my enemies the women are slowly but inevitably bringing about their own destruction."

"How is that?" Prew said.

"Isnt it obvious?" Hal laughed. "Look at yourself. For you soldiers there are no women, except the whores. The soldiers have to turn to us because we have no sense of sin, like the *respectable* women."

"Oh, I dont know," Prew said, but he could hear the hollowness in his own voice because this was coming too uncomfortably near the truth.

Hal laughed his sweet boyish laugh, but he did not press the advantage. "You see," he said gently, "I have a theory about that. My theory is that homosexuality is the direct result of chastity in women."

"Then how do you explain the lesbians?" Prew countered.

"Touché," Hal laughed. "I believe though, truly, that all homosexuality is the result of frustration and disappointment in life. The more topheavy and abortively respectable a society becomes, the more homosexuals it produces. Decadence, they call it. Did you ever stop to think why is it that it is always in its decadence that a society produces its greatest art?

"Ah, you see? Homosexuality breeds freedom, and it is freedom that makes art. But, alas, with the coming of freedom the topheavy society always collapses. Falls into dust. Is gone. Destroyed. Utterly." Hal laughed merrily.

"What art have you ever produced?" Prew said.

"Who, me? Nothing much. I wrote a novel once, on the life of a bisexual. Nobody would ever publish it. However, everywhere I took it everyone in the office was most anxious to read it. I did not get it back from one publisher for seven months. But I am unimportant. Look at the Greeks, if you dont believe me. Look at the Romans. Look at the Holy Mother Church during the Renaissance."

"Balls," Tommy said.

"I've read a little bit about them things," Prew said. "I'd like to see your novel sometime."

"Someday I'll let you see it," Hal said. "Well, here we are."

He led them around a not old banyan tree, the gnarled above ground roots making them stumble in the darkness, the pencil-thin branch roots not grown into the earth yet and dangling free from the branches slapping them repeatedly in the face.

"Isnt that a truly lovely thing to have in one's yard?" Hal said. "Watch your step now."

They were at the side of a two storey frame house painted white, at the foot of an outside staircase, uncovered and with open stairs supported by white four by fours, all of it painted white.

"We must continue this discussion after we have a drink," Hal whispered to Prew as they all stood on the little landing looking across into the dark bulk of the banyan, while he unlocked the door.

He led them into a little entry hall.

"Just make yourselves at home, you dears. I'm going to get my clothes off. You can take yours off too, if you want," he laughed, and disappeared into a doorway.

"Aint this place somethin?" Maggio said to Prew. "How would you like to have a place like this here? Hunh? How would you? Just imagine it, livin in a place like this. Jesus!"

The two of them stood just inside the little entryway, looking around at the neatness and the order and the niceness of the apartment.

"I cant," Prew said. "I cant imagine it."

"Now you see why I come down here," Maggio said. "Partly. In them goddam concrete barracks a guy forgets there is such places in this world."

Tommy, standing behind them, growing impatient, shoved past and went across and sat in one of the big chrome and real leather modern chairs. It broke the spell.

"I got to piss," Maggio said, "and by god I want a drink. The crapper's in here. I'll be back in a minute."

Prew watched him go through the door where Hal had gone, and then saw beyond into the tiny hall with the bathroom on the left and the bedroom at the end. He turned back to look around the living room.

To the left as you came in the door was a raised place one step up with a wrought iron railing where there was a dinette table and a door that led into the kitchen. Across the room was an enormous bay with small glass panes from floor to ceiling clear around its curve, with drapes half drawn across it, and in the middle set back against the wall a cabinet radio and record-player with two record stands of twelve-inch albums flanking it. On the right wall was a big bookcase that was full, and a well-desk. Prew walked around the room looking at the things, trying hard to think of something to say to Tommy.

"Have you ever had any of your writing published?" he asked finally.

"Of course," Tommy said stiffly. "I had a story in *Collier's* just a few weeks back."

"What kind of a story was it?" Prew was looking at the records, all classical, symphonies and concertos.

"A love story," Tommy said.

Prew looked up at him and Tommy giggled in his deep bass voice.

"Story of an aspiring young actress and a rich young Broadway producer. He married her and made her a star."

"I cant read them kind of stories," Prew said. He looked back at the records.

"I cant either," Tommy giggled.

"Then why write them?"

"Because people want to read them, and will pay for them."

"They aint like real life though," Prew said. "Nothing like that crap ever happens."

"Of course not," Tommy said, stiffly. "Thats why the people read them. You have to give the people what they want."

"I aint so sure that they want that," Prew said.

"What are you?" Tommy giggled bassly. "A sociologist?"

"No. But I figure I'm about like most people. I dont know nothing about great literature, but I cant read them stories."

"Its not the men," Tommy said. "Its the women. The stupid, romantic, filthy, moralistic women. They're the ones that like it. They are the book and magazine buyers. And they eat it up. They have to get their kicks some way, dont they? Their morals wont let them get their kicks in bed."

"Oh, I dont know. I aint convinced of that."

"Women and their moral concepts," Tommy said. "If they dont wake up they'll find themselves without any men at all, someday."

"I can see that," Prew said. "You mean they'll drive all the men into being homos, like Hal said."

"No, I did not say that," Tommy said stiffly. "I did not say that at all. The women have nothing to do with that."

"Maybe they do," Prew said. "I never thought of it before tonight." He was passing by the well-desk.

"What?" Maggio said, coming in. "Do what?"

He walked over to where Prew still stood by the well-desk. Hal came in behind him, wearing a Tahitian pareu wrapped around him that was printed with flaming poincianas smothered in their deep green pinnate leaves. His thin spruce frame looked angular and flat and muscleless now, instead of debonair. The deep burned tan on the thick juiceless skin seemed unnatural, scaly, as if he had been painted with iodine.

"Do have something to do with men becoming homos," Prew said.

"I dont think they do," Angelo said.

"I didnt either," Prew said. "But now, maybe I do."

"Oh?" Hal said. He smiled the sweet boyish smile. "Well, you know some people actually are born that way. Unfortunately, or fortunately, all according to the way you see it. So I wouldnt say the picture was entirely that way."

Prew shook his head, grinning. "I been in too many freak shows, from Times Square to Frisco, to swallow that born stuff."

"You'd be a dear thing," Hal said distastefully, "if you didnt strain so hard to be filthy."

"Filthy?" Prew grinned. "How can anything be filthy, if you dont believe in morals?"

"Its not what you say. Its the manner in which you say it, that is filthy. To me such a tragedy is beautiful."

"Not to me. To me its trick photography."

Hal raised his brows, sweetly, and stared at him. "Sometimes," he said to Angelo, "your buddy almost irritates me."

Prew could feel himself grinning and under the grin his face felt stiff, the way it always felt when he heard somebody use the old kill word. "Way I see it, your idea is just as much wishful thinking as the rich young Broadway producer in Tommy's story."

"I can see I made a mistake about you," Hal smiled. "I can see now that you dont really have imagination at all, that in truth you are rather a dull clod."

"I guess so," Prew grinned. "I guess between the Army and bein on the bum they kicked the imagination all out of me."

"Wheres this champagne, Hal?" Angelo said. "Hunh? Come on, lets break her out, hunh? I'm gettin thirsty."

"In a moment, my pet. Some day," he said to Prew, "as you grow older, you will find imagination sometimes produces a truth that is greater than any fact."

"I can see that," Prew grinned. "But theres something else too, that I dont get. The more I talk to you the more you sound like a priest, for some reason."

Hal smiled. "If you werent Tony's friend, I'd throw you out for that."

Prew turned to grin at him, easily. "I dont think you could. But if you want me out, all you got to do is ask me."

"Well," Hal smiled to Maggio. "Your buddy is a bravo."

"Hell, dont mind him," Maggio said. "He's just hot headed. All's wrong with him is he needs a drink."

"Is that all?" Hal asked Prew.

"Well," Prew said. "I could use one."

Tommy stood up from his chair and walked to Prewitt's side protectively. "Goddam you," he said to Hal. "Cant you leave the poor thing alone a minute? He's my date, not yours, you know. Quit tormenting him."

"Dont do me no favors," Prew said.

"If you dont like the way I treat my guests, Tommy," Hal smiled, "you can always go home. I dont know but what I'd like it better if you did. What time must you boys be back?"

"Six o'clock," Angelo said. "For Reveille." He looked over suddenly at the clock on the desk, as if he had just remembered he would have to die someday. "Son of a bitch," he said. "Come on. For Chrisake lets have a drink."

"Oh, you," Tommy was saying to Hal. "You bitch. You dirty filthy bitch. I've a good notion to walk right out, right now."

Hal laughed merrily. "Suit yourself, Queenie." He turned on his heel and went up the step and into the kitchen.

Tommy stood glaring after him, his great arms straight at his sides, his hams of fists clenched against his thighs.

"You know I wont leave," he said. "You know I have to stay."

Hal stuck his head out the kitchen door. "Of course I know it. Come up here and help me fix these drinks."

"All *right*," Tommy said. He moved his big body stiffly, his hurt feelings on his face.

"Come here, Prew," Maggio nodded, whispering. He led him around the corner and over by the record player in the glassed in bay. "Jesus, take it easy, will you? You want to mess everything up for me? Lay off for a while."

"Okay. I'm sorry. I dont know what got me started. That 'born stuff,' I guess. I dont want to upset your applecart, Angelo. Its just theres something about these guys gets my goat. Always picking at you, just like a goddam chaplain insisting that you come to church and worship God. Why do they have to make you listen to a Salvation Army sermon before you get your sinkers and coffee? Why do they have to convince everybody being a homo is wonderful?"

"Hell, I dont know. Just let them talk. Thats what I do. You think I argue with them? Like hell I argue with them. I just listen and nod my head and let it go and ask them for me a nuther drink."

"I guess I just aint cut out for this kind of life," Prew said.

Angelo shook his head. "Sometime I feel like I'm livin on top a powder keg thats gonna blow any minute. You pay for everything you get in this world, man."

"I've heard a lot of talk about 'great love' between homos, but I aint never seen it. I think its more like hate, probably."

"I dont care what it is. Long as I can keep that income. So take it easy, will you?"

"Sure. I dont want to mess you up."

"Boy," Maggio said, "I'm going to get drunkern a fiddler's bitch. I mean." He looked over at the clock. "Reveille," he said. "Reveille or no Reveille," he said.

Hal came in then from the kitchen, carrying two crystal champagne glasses. Tommy came behind him, carrying two more.

"Sorry we have no tray," Hal smiled. "But at least the glasses are right. You cant drink champagne cocktails from a water glass."

Maggio took a glass and winked secretly at Prew.

"I suggest," Hal said, "that you all get out of those clothes and be comfortable. Since we are all among friends anyway. Arent we?"

"I agree," Tommy said fervently. He handed Prew a glass and set his own down and began to take his clothes off. He took off everything but his shorts and then sat down and picked up his drink. In contrast to Hal's deep tan Tommy was as white as milk except for the rings of tan above his collar and on his forearms. It gave him an unpleasant half-fried look.

"I know you dogfaces never wear shorts," Hal smiled. "I have a pair of trunks I keep for Tony to go swimming, but I havent anything for you."

"Thats okay," Prew said. "I'd just as soon keep my pants on."

Hal laughed merrily, quite good humored again.

They sat around that way, four men baring their bodies to seek what coolness that came through the outside screen door. Someone looking through the glassed in bay would probably have felt a renewing sense of human warmth at seeing four bare-chested men, relaxing, holding glasses, talking in a friendly way.

"This is what I always wear at home," Hal said, flicking a fold of the pareu idly. "Its in keeping with the Hawaiian tradition, dont you think? Of course, the beachboys all wear trunks now, but they used to wear the pareu. That was before the missionaries, of course. In Tahiti they still wear it, but, alas, there is as little use for a French tutor there as there is in France."

"When was you in France?" Prew said.

"I've been in France off and on for fifteen years," Hal smiled. "When I tutored in New York I used to save all my money until I had enough for an extended trip, then I'd go to France and stay, until my money ran out. That was before the war, of course. I came out here after the war started. I decided this would be about the least likely place to run into war. Dont you?"

"I guess so. But I reckon any place in America will be about the same, when we get in the war."

"I'm too old for the draft," Hal smiled.

"I meant restrictions and like that."

Hal shrugged. It was very much a Frenchman's shrug. "At one time I seriously considered becoming a citizen of France. Its the most wonderful country in the world. However," he smiled, "I'm rather glad I didnt, now.

"Its odd. The very traits of freedom that made living there so wonderful are the *very* things that in the end defeated la belle France," Hal smiled, but he looked as if he were about to cry. "That seems to be a law in the very nature of life, I guess," he said.

"It looks like a man's rooked either way, dont it?" Prew said. Finally now, at last, under these last few drinks, he was sitting in the shade of the old on-pass feeling again, finally now he had recovered it again, as he had had it climbing the stairs to the New Congress. He felt very sad. The sun was finally going down now, the heat was moving on, the shade was getting longer now, it was time to rest now. He looked over at Angelo and Angelo was in the deep shade too, mumbling to himself.

"Are you in the deep shade, Angelo?" he said. If they would only let us drink up their shade, he thought, and then leave us alone, not exact their pound of flesh. Why was it you always had to pay for things?

"I dont think the word freedom's got any meaning any more," he said to Hal.

"I think I'm free," Hal said.

Prew laughed in the shade. "How about a nuther drink?"

"All right." Hal took the glass and went out into the kitchen. "Dont you think I'm free?"

"Bring me too one," Angelo said. He got up vaguely and carried out his glass.

"Are you afraid of anything?" Prew called to Hal.

"No," Hal said, coming back with the glasses. "I fear nothing."

"Then you're free," Prew said. He watched Angelo sit down and empty off his glass.

"I'm free," Angelo yelled. He leaned back in the chair and kicked his heels up in the air. "I'm free as a fucking bird. Thats what I am. You aint free," he yelled to Prew. "You goddam thirty year man. You're a goddam thirty year slave. But I'm not. I'm *free*. Till six o'clock in the *morning*."

"Quiet down," Hal said sharply. "You'll wake up my landlady downstairs."

"Gothell," Angelo said. "Up hers. And you gothell."

"I think its time you went to bed, Tony," Hal said sadly. "And slept it off."

"Sure," Angelo said. "Sing for your supper."

"Thats not a very nice thing to say to me," Hal said.

"Sorry, old boy. I cant help it. Its the truth, aint it?"

"Yes," Hal said. "But one doesnt always have to mention the truth, does one?"

"No," Angelo said. "I guess one doesnt."

"Come on," Hal said. "Let me help you up." He went over to Maggio's chair and offered to put his arm around the narrow bony shoulders and help him up. Maggio waved him away.

"Not yet. I'll get up by my goddam self."

"Do you want to stay out here with me?" Tommy asked Prew coyly.

"Sure," Prew said. "Why not? What the hell?"

"Well," Tommy said stiffly. "You dont have to, you know."

"Dont I? Well thats good."

"I'm drunk," Angelo yelled. "Whoopee! If you wasnt a thirty goddam year man, Prewitt, I'd really like you."

Prew grinned. "You said yourself it wasnt much differnt from Gimbel's Basement."

"Thats right," Angelo said. "Thats what I said, didnt I? Listen," he said. "Before my hitch is up we'll be in this fuckinwar. You know that? I hate the Army. Even you hate the Army, Prewitt. You just wont admit it. I hate it. O god how I hate the fucking Army."

He leaned back in his chair and hung his arms over the leather, rolling his head and repeating his passion to himself.

"Do you write under your own name?" Prew asked Tommy.

Hal was standing beside Maggio's chair, looking anxious and wringing his hands a little.

"Of course not," Tommy smiled reasonably. "Do you think I want to put my own name to such stupid stuff?"

"You're sober, aint you?" Prew said. "I bet you never do get drunk. Why dont you get drunk? Why do you want to write it for, then?"

"You dont know my own name anyway," Tommy said. His deepset eyes swung suddenly, wildly at Prew. "You dont, do you? *Do you?*"

Prew was watching Hal trying to get Maggio up on his feet. "No. I dont. You're ashamed of that story, aint you?"

"Of course," Tommy said, relievedly. "Do you think I'd be proud of it?"

"I hate it," Angelo said. "All of it. Everything."

"I wouldnt play a bugle call unless I was proud of it," Prew said. "Thats one thing I got, see? If I did do it, it would never be the same again. I'd never have it any more."

"Oh," Tommy smiled. "A bugler. We've got an artist in our midst, Hal."

"No," Prew said. "Only a bugler. But I dont even bugle any more. And you'll never write no book. You only want to talk about it."

He stood up, feeling the release of the liquor pounding in him, wanting to smash something that would stop the cogs from rotating in tomorrow and Reveille at six o'clock. The self winding springs. He looked around dimly. There was nothing to smash.

"Lissen," he said. He stabbed his finger at the big white bulk of Tommy. "You're queer as a three dollar bill. How did you get to be queer? What made you queer, anyway?"

Tommy's dark eyes that behind the deep purple circles never seemed to focus on anything at all, were on him now and focused, and they became brighter and brighter as he watched them.

"I've always been that way," Tommy said. "I was born that way."

"Like to talk about it, dont you?" Prew grinned. He felt the silence of both Hal and Maggio behind him and knew that they were watching him.

"No," Tommy said. "I hate to talk about it. It was a tragedy, being born that way." He was smiling now and breathing fast, smiling painfully the way a broken dog does when you pat him.

"Balls," Prew said. "Nobody's born that way. When was the first time?"

"When I was ten," Tommy said, talking swiftly now, almost joyously. "I was going to a military school in New York, my parents were divorced and my mother sent me there, a bunch of upperclassmen got,—oh a whole bunch of them, there must have been twelve at least," Tommy's eyes were brighter and his voice was going faster, hardly space between the words to breathe, "—they got me out and tied me up, and beat me, they made me, one right after another, and they beat me till I did it."

Prew watched him talking, his big body jerking nervously in the chair, as if under a whip.

"I dont believe that," Prew snarled. "I bet that wasnt the first time. Because lissen, they could of killed me and I wouldnt of ever done it. If they did it, they did it because you wanted them to do it. No matter how much you tried to fight. You wanted to be beaten, and you wanted to be evil."

Hal moved from beside Maggio and stepped toward the other two. "Thats a lie," he said.

"Its true," Tommy whispered. "It wasnt the first time. But it was the first important time. I did want it. Do you hate me?"

"No," Prew said, contemptuously. "Why should I hate you?"

"But you do. You're contemptuous of me. Arent you? Arent you? You think I'm evil."

"No. You're the one that thinks you're evil. Thats what I think. I dont think you're evil. I think you like to do anything you think is evil, the eviller the better, and the better you will like it. Maybe its because you can show how much you hate the church."

"Thats a lie." Tommy was sitting pushed way back in the chair. "I am evil, and I know it. You dont have to make it easy for me. You dont have to protect me."

"Hell, buddy, I wouldnt make it easy for you. You dont mean nothing to me."

"I know I'm evil," Tommy said. "I know I'm evil."

"Who made you believe that?" Prew said. "Who taught you that? Your mother?"

"No," Tommy said. "No, no, no. My mother was a saint. You dont under*stand*. My mother was a *saint*."

365

"Shut up, Tommy," Hal said narrowly.

Prew swung on him. "If you guys like being queer, why dont you be queer with each other? Instead of all a time trying to cut each other's throat? If you believed that crap about true love you been putting out, why do you get your feelings hurt so easy? Somebody's always hurtin your feelings. Why do you always pick up somebody who aint queer? Because if you're with another queer, you dont feel evil enough, thats why."

"Stop!" Hal said. "This quivering hulk of jelly can say whatever he wants to say. But I am none of these things. I stand as a rebel against society. I hate its falseness and I'll never knuckle down to it. It takes courage to stand by what you believe."

"I dont like it very much myself," Prew grinned. He could feel the warmness and the fumes, rising in his head, the urge, urge, urge, the smash, smash, smash, six o'clock, six o'clock, six o'clock. "Its never done much for me, society. What has it given me? It aint done near as much for me as it has done for you. Look at this place, look at it.

"But I dont hate it like you hate it. You hate it because you hate yourself. You aint rebelling against society, you're rebelling against yourself. You aint rebelling against anything, you're just rebelling."

He stabbed at the tall man with his finger.

"And thats why you're like a priest. You got a gospel to preach. The true gospel. The ony gospel. Thats *all* you got, a gospel. Dont you know life dont fit no gospels? Life makes gospels—afterwards. Gospels dont make life. But you, you and all the rest of the priests, you gunna make life fit *your* gospel. And nobody elses. You wont even admit anything exists but what you say."

He paused. The brightly lighted revelation was surging up now again, in his mind. He could see it. But how to say it? How to express? How to mold it and make it plain? Life was enough, in itself. All men should see life in itself was enough, was all, because it was there. Why did you climb the mountain, Mr Mallory? Because it was there. Life was there, it had been *put* there, for a purpose. That was enough. That was everything.

"If thats courage," he concluded lamely, subduedly, "maybe you got it, buddy. If thats courage."

"Hey, hey," Angelo yelled suddenly. "I got courage. All the courage in the goddam world. I'm free and I got courage. All I want. A dollarn a half at any liquor store."

He struggled up vaguely from the chair and started for the door in desultory tackings.

"Where are you going, Tony?" Hal said. All the rest was forgotten. "Please come back, Tony. Please come back here, I say. You're in no condition to be wandering around."

"Going for a fucking walk," Angelo yelled. "Need some fucking air."

He went out and slammed the screen. They could hear him stumping down the outside stairs in his bare feet. Then they heard a stumbling falling crash and Angelo's hearty cursing of the banyan. Then silence.

"Oh my god," Hal said. "Somebody must stop him. Somebody must do something. He'll get picked up, wandering arouND like that."

"You do it," Prew said. "He's your boyfriend."

"You go after him, Prew," Hal said. "Wont you? You dont want him to get picked up. He's your friend. Isnt he."

"He aint my boyfriend," Prew said. "You go get him." He began to grin a little and sat down heavily on the couch, bouncing a little with drunken resolution.

"But I cant," Hal cried. "Truly I cant. I'd go after him if I could. Why, as drunk as he is, if he got picked up he might bring the police right up here."

"Let him bring em," Prew grinned. His face felt stiff from the liquor and someplace in his head a bell tolled. He was very very drunk and suddenly very happy.

"Oh he cant," Hal said, wringing his hands. "They know us all by report. All they'd need is something like this to make a case against us."

"Thats a shame," Prew said contentedly. "Dont worry about it. You've got courage." He watched Tommy get up from his chair and begin to put his clothes back on.

"Where are you going?" Hal asked sharply.

"I'm going home," Tommy said, with dignity. "Right now."

"Listen, Prew," Hal said. "I'd go get him. Truly I would. You dont know what the little fellow means to me. But if I was picked up, I'd be ruined. And if I'm just seen with him, in his condition, I'd be picked up because they're looking for a chance at me. I'd be thrown out of my tutoring, thrown out of here." He waved his arms around the room. "Thrown out of my home."

"I thought they knew about you," Prew said.

"They do. Oh believe me, they do. But getting picked up by the police and prosecuted in a public scandal is another thing altogether. You couldn't expect them to stand up for me with it in the hands of the police."

"No," Prew said. "I guess not. Life sure is tough, aint it?"

"Please go and get him," Hal begged. "Look. I'll even get down on my knees and ask you. Look. See? Now, please. Please. He is your friend."

Prew began to put his shoes and socks on. He fumbled with one shoelace and Hal, on his knees, tried to tie it for him. Prew slapped the tall man's hand away and tied it for himself.

"You're not too drunk, are you?" Hal said.

"No," he said. "I'm not too drunk. I'm never too drunk."

"You'll get him, wont you, Prew? And if you get picked up you wont bring them back up here, will you?"

"Where I come from its bad manners to even ask that. You take that for granted." He stood up, looking for his gook shirt.

"Goodby, I've had a nice time," Tommy said from the door. "I'll see you later, Hal. And I hope to see you again sometime, Prew," he said. He went out and slammed the door.

Prew sat down on the couch again and began to laugh.

"Polite fella, aint he?" he said to Hal.

"Please go, Prew," Hal said. "Please dont waste any time. Tony's too drunk to know what he's doing. Take him back to the Post and put him to bed."

"His clothes are here."

"Take them with you," Hal said. He began to go around gathering up Maggio's clothes. "If you bring him back here, he may cause trouble, drunk as he is."

"Okay," Prew said. "But I havent got any money for cab fare."

Hal ran into the bedroom for his wallet. "Here," he said, coming back. "Heres a five. That'll be enough for car fare down town and a cab home, wont it?"

"Well, I dont know," Prew grinned. "Its too late for the buses, you know. We'll have to take a cab down town."

"Heres ten then."

"Well," Prew said. He shook his head sorrowfully. "You see, the Schofield cabs stop running at two o'clock I think it is. Its almost two now."

"On Payday?" Hal said.

"Sure," Prew grinned. "Every day."

"All right," Hal said. "Heres twenty then. Please hurry, Prew."

Prew shook his head slowly reluctantly. "Trouble with that Angelo, every time he gets drunked up he wants a piece of ass. If he dont get it, he gets mean and causes trouble. Thats the reason he gets picked up, usually."

"All right," Hal said. "Heres thirty."

"Look," Prew grinned. "I hate to take your money. You just put it away. I'll get him home someway."

"God damn it," Hal said. "Heres forty. Four tens. Thats all the cash I have. But you must hurry. Oh, please hurry, Prew."

"Well, I guess that'd be enough to get us home," Prew said. He took the money and started slowly for the door.

"You're not too drunk, are you?" Hal said anxiously.

"Never too drunk. To do what I got to do. I dont want him picked up any more than you. But for a different reason."

Hal shook his hand at the door. "Come back and see me," he said. "Come back some time when Tony's not along. You dont have to wait for him to bring you. You have a standing invitation."

"Why, thanks, Hal," Prew said. "I may do that. I always like to associate with persons who got the courage of their convictions, you know."

At the corner he looked back. The door was shut and the lights were already out. He grinned hazily. In his pocket, under his hand, the four tens felt very crisp and good.

Chapter 27

The street had that late-at-night deserted look fully developed now. Even the darkened silent houses and the streetlights had that look now.

There was no sign of Angelo, or of Tommy. To hell with Tommy. Angelo was the thing. There was no telling where the drunken little bastard went. He might have gone back up toward Kalakaua. On the other hand, he might just as easily have decided to go the other way, for a quick swim in the Ala Wai Canal. He put the paper sack with Angelo's clothes and shoes in it under his arm; the paper rustle was loud in the clear still night; and reached in his pocket for a coin. There was no coin, only Hal's four tens. He grinned again, and wandered over happily to the gutter to light matches until he found a flat pebble.

There wasnt any hurry now, it was all luck now. No telling where he might have gone. A peaceful drunken fatalism filled him. Somewhere the MPs were hunting in pairs like hawks, but it might take a couple hours yet to find him.

He wiped the pebble off drunkenly carefully, taking his own sweet time in the stillness, feeling happily the stillness, and spit on one side of it and flipped it like you flip a coin. Just like you use to do when you was a kid, he thought.

Hell, the little bastard might even come back to Hal's. Hal would let him in, of course. Then Prewitt would be looking for him when he was back safe at Hal's.

Wet was Kalakaua. Dry was the Canal. He hunted for the pebble in the darkness with a lighted match. The wet side was up.

Okay.

He turned left on the main drag, back toward the Tavern, feeling like a hunter in the forest. Down the long blocks of the wide slightly curving street no thing moved. The street car tracks stretched away. Every other street light was turned off. Not a car, not a bus, no people, no life. His footfalls sounded very loud. He got off the sidewalk and walked on the grass.

He stopped to listen then, once, but he remembered Angelo was bare footed. And wearing trunks, no less!

The MPs were tough babies down here. These were from Shafter and Department Hq. All big boys, like the Schofield bunch, and always in pairs treading heavily in the GI shoes and tight white-washed leggins. At Schofield the MP Company that covered the Post and Wahiawa and the road down under the two columns of tall trees alongside the reservoir, they had men just as big, and just as tough, but Prew knew several of them. So to him they were more human, somehow. He had come over on the boat with several, all good joes then, until they put on the white-washed leggins. Up at Schofield, in a pinch, he had a forty-sixty chance of meeting one of the guys he knew, who could be talked into giving him a break. Down here he knew none of them. And Angelo out drunk bare footed in trunks! He began to laugh out loud tumultuously. The loud sound of his own voice stopped him.

He hunted carefully along Kalakaua, stopping to look in darkened yards and on the benches set on the sidewalk corners, and under them. Man, are you lucky you are not a big man. You might have been a goddam MP yourself. The Provost Marshal didnt take no for an answer when he looked them over as they came down the gangplank off the boat. When The Man picked the biggest for his very very own, they were his and thats all she wrote. He remembered one big guy of six foot four who had been signalled out just ahead of him. The only thing saved that guy was he was in the Air Corps, and was the Provost Marshal pissed off over that one!

He hunted for what seemed an eternity, expecting arms with brassards to grab him any minute from behind. And if they did, well it was dear john, thats all. Those boys knew how to work you over, and they did not have to hide the marks like the civilian cops. He passed Lewers Street, looking on both sides. Then, passing Royal Hawaiian Street he saw, or thought he saw, a shadow move across silent way up in front of him. He crossed Kalakaua and slipped into the edge of the Royal grounds and stalked it. When he got up to Seaside Street, where the Royal Hawaiian Hotel driveway went in off Kalakaua, he could see a figure wearing trunks sitting calmly on a sidewalk bench in front of the Royal grounds.

"Hey, Maggio," he called.

The figure did not move.

He crossed over to the curbing, keeping an eye on the bench as if it were a deer seen through the leaves that he was walking up on, walking down alongside the very tall smooth white royal palms and the vivid green, black now, of a thickness of plants and bushes growing almost to the sidewalk.

There was a streetlight a few feet past the bench. He could tell it was Angelo. He relaxed.

"Goddam you, Maggio," he said.

His own voice sounded eerie. The figure did not move the outstretched arms along the benchtop or the thick curly head that lolled back against it.

"Is that you, Angelo? Wake up, goddam you. Answer me, you bastard."

The figure did not move. He stopped in front of the bench and stood looking down at Maggio, grinning suddenly, feeling the still night around them, feeling suddenly the presence of richness and wealth and ease that seeped through the screen of bushes from the Royal Hawaiian Hotel.

This is where the movie stars stay when they come to Hawaii to rest and play. All the movie stars. Wouldnt it be nice, he thought. He had never been inside the screen but he had walked past the Royal on the beach and seen them on the patio. But wouldnt it be nice, he thought, if a movie star would come out right now and see me here and ask me back inside, up to her room. Maybe she's just been for a midnight swim and the water droplets still on her and just taking the bathing cap off the long falling hair, her arms up to her chin.

He looked up from Maggio suddenly, looking toward the darkened driveway where a faint light showed inside, thinking surely he would see this woman walking out, knowing it positively, her coming looking for a man and finding him available. They said these did it like that all the time. Suddenly there was a very large ache inside his belly, almost like a cramp and he thought about Lorene at the New Congress. He stood looking at the empty driveway. What a way to make a living.

"Hey, come on. Wake up, you dago bastard. Wake up and lets go down town and get a piece of ass."

"I'm sorry, Sir," Angelo said, not opening his eyes or moving. "I wont do it again. Just dont lock me up, Sir. Just dont make me reenlist. Honest I wont."

Prew leaned down and shook him by the naked bony shoulder. "Come on, wake up."

"I'm awake. Its just that I dont feel like moving. I just dont feel like going back."

"We got to go back."

"I know it. But maybe if we was to sit here long enough some movie star will come out from there and pick us up and take us back to the States in her private plane and install us in her private swimming pool.

You suppose? Maybe if we was to just sit here real still and dont move none except to breathe and dont open your eyes, when we open our eyes it wont be here. None of it, no street, no bench, no pass, no Reveille."

"Jesus Christ!" Prew snorted. "Movie stars, no less. My god you are drunk. Come on. Wake up. I got your clothes."

"I dont want clothes," Angelo said.

"I got em anyway."

"Well, give em back to the Indians. The Indians need clothes. All they wear is codpieces. Did I hear you say piece of ass?" Angelo opened his eyes and turned his head to look the question.

"Sure. I made your boyfriend for forty bucks. He was scared you'd get picked up and come back bringin the law with you. Sent me out to find you and take you home."

"Hell," Angelo said. He sat up and rubbed his hands hard against his face. "I aint drunk, friend." He paused. "Hell, man, you dont need no instruction from me, buddy. The very most I ever got out of him was twenty-two-fifty. And then I was suppose to pay it back. I aint though."

Prew laughed. "I couldna got it if he wasn't scared so bad he crapped his pants."

"Did he really?"

"No."

"See, Prew? I aint drunk. I sure had you guys fooled." He stood up and immediately fell back against the lamppost. He grabbed it with both arms to keep from falling. "See?" he said.

"No. You aint drunk."

"I aint. I just stumbled on that crack there." He pushed himself up straight and let go the lamppost cautiously.

"Whoops!" he yelled, throwing his head back and letting it out from the bottom of his lungs.

"Fuck it! I'M GUNNA RE-ENLIST!"

"Shut up, goddam it," Prew said. He stepped in quick and grabbed him by the waistband as he started to fall back flat, clear off balance from the throwing back of his head.

"You want the goddam MPs on us?" Prew said.

"MPs! MPs! MPs!" Angelo yelled. "COME AND GET US. HERE WE IS!"

"You jerk." Prew let go of the trunks suddenly and Angelo fell full length on the sidewalk, without moving a hand to catch himself.

"Look at me, Prew. I'm shot. I'm dead. A poor dead soljer, not a friend in the fuckinworld. Just send the medal home to mother, boys, maybe she can hock it."

"Get up," Prew grinned. "Come on. Lets get out of this."

"Okay." Angelo scrambled to his feet, using the bench to hoist himself up with. "How long you think before we get in the war, Prew?"

"Maybe we wont get in it."

"Oh, yes we will."

"I know it."

"You dont have to protect me," Angelo said, mimicking Tommy's deep bass feminine voice. He started laughing. "I wish I had a decent drink, this slop is filthy," he mimicked Hal's precise speech. "Hell with it. Come on," he said. "Lets go to town."

"We'll have to call a cab, but first we got to get you in your clothes."

"Okay, Prew. Whatever you say, Prew." Angelo grabbed the trunks and jerked them down to his knees and started to step out of them. His foot hung and he fell again.

"Who hit me?" he said. "Who done it? Let me at the bastard."

"God damn," Prew said. He grabbed the little guy by the armpits and hauled him off out of the light into the bushes.

"Hell," Angelo protested. "Take it easy, Prew. You're scrapin my ass on the sandy sidewalk."

"You'll have worse than that scraped, if you dont get into these clothes and get out of here. . . . Listen," he said.

They both held their breath and listened, and Angelo was suddenly very sober. From down the street they heard the heavy footfalls of the GI shoes. They were not running, but they were not walking. There were voices floating with them, and then they heard a single rattle of a billy against a post.

"Goddam it," one voice said. "For Chrisake, be quiet."

"All right, all right," the other voice said. "I want an arrest as bad as you. You and that corporal's rating."

"Shut up, then. Come on."

They came in pairs, at night, dogtrotting heavyfooted, leggins scraping softly, clubs swinging silently, wherever soldiers ever lived. And the air of fear they carried with them went before them always, the Law, holding them inside it, and then they were mean to see the others turn away. They came in pairs, wherever soldiers ever drank to forget or yelled to forget or fought to forget or put their hands in their pockets to remember. Soldiers must not forget, they said, soldiers must not remember; all that is treason.

"Now you did it," Prew said. "Come on, back this way. Lets take off."

"I'm sorry, Prew."

Angelo followed docilely, sober now and ashamed for causing trouble, and they skirted the big wide drive to the movie stars' place of rest, working west through the Royal grounds and passing the Willard Inn that was for officers, and running through the bushes breathlessly till

373

they came to Kalia Road, down near the beach and the rambling swank Halekulani Hotel that was so swank most tourists never heard of it and that was on the beach here where the surf was breathing gently against the sand.

"Now," Prew said. "Take them trunks off and get in these clothes."

"Okay. Gimme the sack. What'll I do with these, old buddy boy?"

"Hell, I dont know. Here, give em to me. Listen, Angelo, are you sure you're sober now? Those guys are going to be waiting back up on Kalakaua. One of them may try to go down Lewers and beat us to Kalia Road there. But our best bet is to walk Kalia down as far as Fort Derussey and walk out from there, without gettin inside the Post. Listen to me, goddam it."

Maggio looked at him, and then Prew could see the tears running down his cheeks.

"Oh, fuck," Angelo said. "Runnin like a goddam criminal. I'm sick of it. All the time scared to fart for fear an MP'll hear you. I'm sick of it. I aint going to take it, see? I aint, I say."

"All right," Prew said. "Take it easy, Angelo. You dont want to get picked up. You're still drunk."

"Sure, I'm drunk. Sure I am. So what? Cant a man get drunk? Cant a man do anything? Cant a man even put his goddam hands in his goddam pockets on the goddam street? Why not get picked up? You might as well be in Leavenworth, anyway, instead of always on the outside looking in and never getting past the glass front, like a kid outside a candy store. Why not get picked up? I aint no coward, to be running from *them*. I aint yellow. I aint no coward. I aint no bum. I aint no scum."

"Okay, okay, okay. Just take it easy. You'll be all right in a minute."

"All right? I'll never be all right again. Its all right for you, if you're a thirty year man. I aint. I dont give a fuck for them, see? Not a single goddam solitary frazzle-assed fuck. I—just—got—my—belly—full."

"Breathe deep, Mack. Take ten, and breathe real deep. I'll be right back, soon as I ditch these trunks."

He stepped down to where the water was still lapping, very softly, an inrush and a froth and then a dripping back. He threw the trunks out into the water and stepped back to where he'd left the boy from Brooklyn. Maggio was gone.

"Hey," Prew said softly. "Hey, Angelo. Hey, buddy. Where are you?"

When there was no answer he turned and started running up the street, up Lewers Street, up towards the light, running hard, very lightly on his toes.

When he got to the edge of the pool of light from the streetlight he stopped and slid back off the sidewalk out of sight.

On the curbing at the corner, in the same pool from the streetlight, little Maggio was fighting the two big MPs from Shafter.

He had one of them on the ground and was hanging crablike on his back, punching with all his wind at the MP's head that was pulled down between his shoulders. While Prewitt watched, the other MP clubbed him on the head and dragged him off the first one's back. He clubbed him again, Maggio holding his hands up over his head, the club hitting skull and fingers, and Maggio went down. He crawled up on his hands and knees and was going for the MP's legs, but slowly now, and the MP clubbed him as he came.

"Go ahead," Maggio said. "Hit me again, you son of a whore."

The first MP was up now and stepped over and began to club him too.

"Sure," Maggio said. "Come on, both of you. Is that the best two great big strong men like you can do? Go ahead and hit me. Come on, hit me. You can do better than that." He tried to get up and was knocked back down.

Prew moved then, back on the sidewalk and into the light and was running up the street at them, running lightly, figuring his footing and the steps before he jumped.

"Get back," Maggio yelled. "I'm handling this. This aint your affair. I dont need no help."

One of the MPs looked around and started down toward Prewitt. On the ground Maggio moved, crablike, and tackled him. As the MP fell, Maggio was on his back, bouncing his head against the street, punctuating his words there was not breath in him to say.

"Sure. You big jokers. And your clubs. Whats the matter. Cant you take it. You can dish it out though. Cant you."

"Go on, take off," he yelled at Prew. "You hear? You keep out of this."

The MP on the ground rose up slowly, Maggio riding his back punching at his head, and arched his back and bucked the demon off, like a horse will toss its rider.

"Go on," Maggio yelled. He lit on his hands and knees and came back up. "Get goin. This aint your affair."

The other MP, standing, was fishing for his pistol. He stepped toward Prewitt, tugging to get it from the holster. Prew turned and faded down the street out of the light and into the bushes. Over his shoulder he saw the first MP's pistol sighted on his back. When he hit the bushes he threw himself down and worked, like a rifleman under fire, crawling further in.

"Put that gun away," the second MP yelled. "Whats the matter with you? You fire in there and kill some moviestar and then we'll both be up shit creek."

"Sure," Maggio said, punching him. "You big ox. Without a paddle."

"Come here and help me with this madman," the MP sobbed.

"The other one'll get away."

"Let him. Come help me hold this one down, or he will too."

"Oh, no," Maggio sobbed. "Not this one. This one wont get away. Sure," he said. "Come on. You better call in another squad while you're at it, too. You think two's enough?"

Prewitt lay in the bushes, breathing hard, not able to see them but hearing all of it.

"Sure," he heard. "Come on. Hit me some more. Come on. Why, you cant even knock me out. Come on and knock me out. Or else let me up. You fucking sons of bitches. Come on. Is that the best you can do? Come on."

Prew lay listening and he could hear the fallings of the clubs, muffled and with a penetrating chunk. There were no sounds of fists now.

"You get on back to the Post," Maggio yelled. "I know what I'm doing. You get on back. You hear?" His voice was muffled.

"Sure. Come on. Why dont you let me up? Come on. I bet you eat Wheaties, dont you?"

The voice stopped after a little while, but the other, the chunking sound, did not. Prewitt lay and listened to it keep on after the voice had stopped. He noticed that his hands were aching and he looked down at them and then unclenched them. He waited till the chunking stopped.

"You want me to go back after the other one, Jack?" he heard one pant.

"Naw, he's gone by now. Lets get this one in."

"You ought to get your sergeancy for this one. I wonder what was wrong with this guy. He's a goddam madman."

"I dont know," the other said. "Come on, lets make the call in."

"This is a lousy job, you know it?"

"I dint ask for it," the other said. "Did you? Come on, lets get that call in for the wagon."

Prew started back down toward the beach and the road, Kalia Road, that led to Derussey, traveling low, keeping in the bushes. When he got to the beach he sat down in the sand a while, listening to the water. That was when he found he was crying.

Then he remembered the forty dollars in his pocket.

Book Four

THE STOCKADE

They held Angelo Maggio three days at the Shafter MP Barracks. Then they shipped him back to Schofield under guard. They sent him straight from Shafter to the Post Stockade. He rode past his Company in a recon, on his way to the Stockade. He was held in confinement at the Stockade as a general prisoner while he waited trial. He worked with a sixteen-pound sledge in the stone quarry up by Kolekole Pass. He waited in the Stockade six weeks for his trial to come up.

First Sergeant Milton A Warden made out the papers on Angelo Maggio. They were throwing the book at Angelo Maggio. The Department Provost Marshal was preferring the charges against him. He was charged with Drunk & Disorderly, with Resisting Arrest, with Insubordination, with Disobeying A Direct Order, and with Striking A Non-Commissioned Officer In The Performance Of His Duty. He was also charged with Conduct Unbecoming To A Soldier. The Department Provost Marshal recommended a Special Court Martial. The maximum penalty for a Special Court Martial was confinement for six months at hard labor and forfeiture of all pay and allowances for like period.

It was rumored in the Regiment that Regimental Sergeant Major Pheneas T O'Bannon had told First Sergeant Warden confidentially that if the Department Provost Marshal could have proved Angelo Maggio had seriously hurt somebody or had been AWOL, the Department Provost Marshal would have recommended a General Court Martial. A General Court Martial is the only military court empowered to try the more serious offenses. The maximum penalty for a General Court Martial is life imprisonment or death. This sentence is not often passed. The maximum penalty for a Summary Court Martial is confinement for one month and forfeiture of two-thirds of all pay and allow-

379

ances. In the case of the United States Army vs Private Angelo Maggio a Summary Court Martial was not considered.

After waiting the six weeks that it required to carry out the manifold paper work necessary for the protection of the accused, Angelo Maggio was conducted under guard to the Regimental Headquarters Building for trial. There was a court of three officers, one of whom had studied law and was the legal member. His defense counsel was there and introduced himself to Angelo Maggio. The Department Provost Marshal who was a full Colonel was not there but his representative, a Major, was present to prosecute. There were three witnesses, Sgt (formerly Corp) John C Archer and Pvt 1cl Thomas D James, patrolmen of the Fort Shafter MP Company, and Pvt 1cl George B Stuart, records clerk of the Fort Shafter MP Company.

Before trial, Angelo Maggio was advised by the court that, in addition to the rights that he would have been assured before a civilian court, he also had the following safeguards:

a. Before trial he had the right to give evidence and to face and cross-examine witnesses in order to show that he was innocent or to minimize his guilt.

b. The type of trial was chosen which would give him the least, not the greatest, punishment consistent with military discipline.

c. That he had been given, at no expense to himself, a defense counsel.

d. At the trial he had the right to make an unsworn statement without subjecting himself to cross-examination.

e. His previous convictions were not allowed to be considered in determining his guilt.

f. He would be given a typewritten record of the trial.

g. He would be given an automatic appeal from the court-martial to the reviewing authority, before the sentence was effective.

h. Three months after confinement to a disciplinary barracks or stockade, his case would be reviewed for clemency by the reviewing authority.

i. At any time during his confinement he could, by showing proper conduct, attitude and ability, be restored to duty as a soldier and become entitled to the advantages and privileges accruing thereto.

The president of the court then advised Angelo Maggio of his right to testify on his own behalf, stating that his failure to do so would not be used against him. He also advised him that if he desired he could make an unsworn statement and not be subjected to cross-examination.

Angelo Maggio said he understood his rights, and he declined to testify.

The witnesses against Angelo Maggio were then called by the prosecution, and the trial began. It lasted fourteen minutes. Angelo Maggio was found guilty on all charges and sentenced to six months confinement at the Post Stockade, Schofield Barracks, T.H. and forfeiture of all pay and allowances for a like period.

Before pronouncing sentence, the president of the court informed Angelo Maggio that because an Army without discipline is a mob, worthless in battle, the rules governing the administration of justice in the Army are contained in the Articles of War, and that they are enacted by Congress, and are based on authority written in the Constitution, and basically they are older than the Constitution itself, that the first Articles of War were prepared by a committee headed by George Washington and were adopted by the Continental Congress in 1775, three days before Washington took command of the Continental Army, and that they have been amended from time to time by Congress to meet changing needs and changing conditions and form a legal code made by civilian authority for the government of the Army. Also that the Articles of War, themselves, provide that soldiers must be given every opportunity to be familiar with the ground rules governing their conduct, and that within six days after a man joins the Army the Articles of War must be read and explained to him and once every six months this must be repeated. Lastly, that this periodic reading and explanation is required by Congress, but the Army takes additional steps to see that soldiers understand military law, and it is the responsibility of the soldier's commanding officer to see that he is fully informed, and it is the soldier's right to be informed.

Angelo Maggio said he understood his rights, and that he had been informed.

The president of the court then pronounced sentence, stating it was not effective until reviewed and approved.

Angelo Maggio was conducted back to the Stockade under guard to wait until the sentence was reviewed. He worked with a sixteen-pound sledge in the stone quarry up by Kolekole Pass. He waited in the Stockade eight days for his sentence to be reviewed.

The sentence was reviewed by Lieutenant Colonel Rutherford B H Delbert, Angelo Maggio's Regimental Commander, and approved in full. The complete record of trial, including the opinion of Colonel Delbert's staff judge advocate and the action of Colonel Delbert, was then sent to Major General Andrew J Smith, Angelo Maggio's Brigade Commander. It was there examined by experienced lawyers in the Brigade Judge Advocate General's Office, who reported to General Smith that the record was legally sufficient to support Colonel Delbert's action. General Smith then issued a special court-martial order finding Angelo Maggio guilty on all counts of all charges brought against him

*and sentencing him to six months confinement at the Post Stockade,
Schofield Barracks, T.H. and forfeiture of all pay and allowances for a
like period. This court-martial order was published throughout the Brigade where Angelo Maggio had served, and posted on the bulletin
board in all orderly rooms of the Brigade.*

*Angelo Maggio in the Stockade was given a typewritten record of
the trial and a copy of the special court-martial order, and began to
serve out his time. He worked with a sixteen-pound sledge in the stone
quarry up by Kolekole Pass. They did not subtract the six weeks waiting for trial or the eight days of waiting for approval of the sentence
from his six months sentence.*

Chapter 28

Something changed in Prewitt after Angelo's one man revolution. It
was something that The Treatment with all its refinements had not
been able to touch. Something went out of him. The Treatment could
never have taken it out of him. It was as if somewhere deep inside himself he could feel bone rubbing somberly against bone, changing gears.
It sounded like a round-edged file on stone.

On April the first, the day after the disastrous payday, Pvt 1cl Bloom
the potential middleweight, Pvt 1cl Malleaux the new man and potential featherweight, and several other Pfcs who were potential went on
Detached Service with the new class at the Regimental NCO School.
The NCO School was encamped in squad tents on one of the old concrete permanent camp sites up near the rifle range where the Regiments lived during their range seasons. It was an eight-weeks course.

Prewitt the potential welterweight watched them pack and go, irrele-
vantly remembering how he had once believed the great American folk-
lore that all Wops were either dead yellow or else killers for the racket-
eers. He also remembered how it was up there, where they were going.
He had been up there last year with the 27th during range season. He
remembered the tents pitched over the concrete foundations, the standing in line for chow with mess kits in the mud, he remembered the
waiting on the ready line in the fleece padded shooting jackets made
from old CKC blouses, the smell of burnt cordite and the ringing ears
and the carbon sight blackeners that smudged up everything and the
two or three privately owned BC scopes of the top notch shooters, he
remembered all of it, the heavy clinking dull glittering unexpended cartridges in the hand, the long deadly streamline disappearing of a car-

tridge slipped into the chamber with the thumb when you were firing singles, the swinging white spot marking off the bulls and the big red flag rising from the pits three hundred yards away. He had made high expert with the '03 last year, and he liked living in the field. Even now, he still liked living in the field.

He still had Hal's forty dollars left. He decided he would use Hal's forty dollars to coldbloodedly seduce Lorene. It looked like that was the only way it could be done, and nobody knew he had it, and he did not have to pay Turp Thornhill till next Payday, and he did not believe Angelo would mind him using it. This time, it would be a planned economy. He laid out a plan for $60, to cover a period of five weeks. He figured he could just about swing it for that, with his plan, without having to count on next Payday which he already owed to Turp.

While waiting for the whorehouse Payday rush to die off he cautiously invested $10, and only $10, of the $40 with O'Hayer's blackjack dealers for a dividend of a little over $20. Blackjack was much less fun than poker, that was why it was a better investment. Forty-five of the $60 would go for three all night jobs at $15 ea. The other $15 would go for three bottles at $3.50 ea. The change would go for cab fare. After he found out where she lived and got her to take him up, he could forget the money part. She had plenty money, and would not mind spending it on him if he played it right. It would be an interesting venture. It would be something to do, while Angelo was waiting trial. He planned it all out. It was absorbing, fascinating mental exercise. He lost himself in it entirely.

He followed the proceedings during the whole seven weeks it took the law to care for Maggio with the same absorption. An absorption that left The Treatment, that was still going on, running a poor second.

Once during the six weeks before the trial, he bought two cartons of tailormades and walked up to the Stockade to visit him. It was almost two miles, up past the tennis courts, then past the golf course, then past the bridle path sun dappled under the big tall trees and the lathery smell of the Packtrain. He sweated walking in the hot sun and he saw many officers, officers' wives, and officers' children. They all looked very tanned and very sportive. The Stockade was a wood building painted white with a green roof and sitting in a cool grove of oaks in the middle of a big flat field on the very edge of the reservation. It looked like a country school house. The tall chain mesh wire fence with the three inleaning strands of barb wire made it look more like a country school house. The chain mesh wire grids over the windows looked like a country school house, too. At the country school house they would not let him in.

It was not a country school. It was a military establishment. They would not let him leave the tailormades for Angelo either. Each internee was issued one sack of Duke's Mixture a day, and there would be no supplementary donations from outsiders. Each internee was a soldier, and would share the same as every other internee soldier. He took the tailormades back home with him. He did not see Angelo.

He felt thankful to them though. They could have easily let him leave the tailormades for Angelo and then the MP guards smoked them up themselves. Later on he smoked the cigarettes himself. He felt guilty about smoking them. He could have thrown them away but they had cost two-fifty, and what good would it have done, it was an empty gesture. So he smoked them. But he felt guilty.

He felt guilty about Angelo too, that was one reason he had wanted to see him. He felt that what had happened Payday was somehow his fault. Angelo had been playing the queers for quite a while now, he had been coming down to Hal's place often, and nothing like this had happened before. Only when Kid Prewitt appeared on the scene, like a catalyst poured into a tranquil beaker, did the mixture begin to boil and then explode. Angelo had not been tainted by the queers; it was only when Kid Galahad Prewitt had stepped in looking for the Holy Grail with his moralistic fears and questionings that Angelo had suddenly felt guilty enough, or tainted enough, to do something drastic. There were times when Prewitt felt a special quality in himself, a strange unpleasant quality that seemed to force everyone he touched into making drastic decisions about their own lives, no wonder people did not like to be around him. The idea frightened him deeply, at such times, because he could not understand what it was and because he did not want to do it. Certainly, he did not try to do it. People went along, living their lives as best they could, not gaining much maybe, but not losing greatly either, and all the time, deeply hidden, the one great personal conflict of fear lay dormant and unhidden. Enter Kid Galahad Prewitt. The action precipitates. The conflict of fear rises flapping from the depths like a giant manta ray, looming big and bigger, looming huge, up out of the deep green depths that you can look down into through a water glass and see the anchor cable dwindling in a long arc down into invisibility, up from far below that even, flapping the two wing fins of choice and the ego caught square in the middle. And they had to choose, had to face it, and whichever way they chose they still got hurt. And all the time he did not want to do it, did not know he did it, until afterwards. It always frightened him, thinking this way, it was one of the things he could most of the time keep down, out of his mind, but sometimes it was too hard to keep the mind going in smooth even waves and he had to let it in and the mind started jumping around yawingly as if there were no bottom under the feet and it always frightened him. Maybe there were things in themselves men should not look at, just as there were things in the very deep bottom of the sea that it was better that men did not know about. He felt that was true, sometimes. Life frightened him, sometimes. But there was nothing to do, anyway. Because this special quality was a thing he could not control in himself, that he could not stop. But then when he was going good he knew it was better to face it, that it was always better to face things no matter what it cost anybody. He knew that. He believed it. Only in the bad spells did life frighten him with its unbelievable cruelty, its inconceivable injustice, its incredible pointlessness. He was going through one of the bad spells now, with Angelo in the Stockade waiting trial. He felt he should have been able to stop the little guy from going off the deep end that night, even though it was himself, he felt, who caused it. He should have foreseen it. He should not have left him alone to step to the water to jettison the trunks. He should have pitched into the fight, in spite of what the little guy had yelled. The two of them could have whipped the MPs, clubs and all, and gotten away, back to the Company and safety. He saw a thousand things he should have done, but had not done. He held himself responsible for what happened to Angelo. That was why he wanted to see Angelo so badly, maybe he could explain it to him. But he did not get to see Angelo.

In fact, he might never have gotten to see Angelo again at all, if it had not been for the queer investigation the city police started downtown.

They came for them in trucks, two of them, the big 2½ ton jobs, from the MP Company at Shafter driven by an armed MP with another armed MP beside him in the cab, and led by a high-bellied recon driven by another armed MP. A big half-white, half-Hawaiian police lieutenant in the mustard worsted poplin of the city force, and with a build like a beachboy, was in charge of the expedition. He rode in the recon with the First Lieutenant from the Shafter MP Company who carried the blanket warrant signed by the Department Provost Marshal. Riding with them were the two young FBI men, looking like bright-faced rich men's sons in their very conservative but expensive business suits, who were the liaison between the civilian police and the military.

The convoy descended upon the quadrangle and parked in front of G Company and assaulted Capt Holmes's orderly room, the two shining, scrubbed, young graduate lawyers of the FBI in the lead, looking bright and mild and innocent almost to the point of adolescence, low voiced and tactful and flowing over with discretion, but underneath this erroneous impression immitigable with that calm implacability a man gets when he knows his word is revered as law and to be feared. The CQ was dispatched out to the drillfield with a list of names immediately.

He came back marching a detail that appeared to be at least two-thirds of G Company, and drill for G Company the rest of that day was a skeletal sophism. The detail lined up before the barracks were counted off and answered another check roll call, looking sheepish and shuffling and very badly scared (the CQ had mentioned the presence of the FBI), yet wearing underneath the fear that unmistakable festive air that any holiday from the monotony of drill will bring, even if the holiday is an investigation by the FBI. They all knew the FBI, that it had jurisdiction over civil crimes committed by the Army, and they had all read the gang-buster comic books. The CQ had no idea why they were wanted, but there was only one civil crime that could have called in so many participants. It could only be a queer investigation.

Nearly all the Waikiki Tavern gang were there. Corp Knapp was there, so was Sgt Harris, so was Martuscelli. Polack Dyzbinski was there, so was Bull Nair, so was Dusty Rhodes, The Scholar, so was fat Readall Treadwell. Champ Wilson and Liddell Henderson were both there, so was Corp Miller, so was Sgt Lindsay, so were Anderson and Friday Clark, and Prewitt.

They were allowed to go upstairs to wash and change to CKCs since they were being taken down to town. Neither the CQ nor the armed MP guards were sent up with them. Nobody was worried about anybody trying to escape. The names were on the roll call.

They came downstairs to catch one fleeting glimpse of the departing recon with the city police mustard, the Shafter suntan and black brassard, and the dark conservative business suits that were more of a uniform than either of the others, and were fallen in and counted off and given another check roll call, and then were herded into the open trucks to find Pvt 1cl Bloom and one other Pvt 1cl from the NCO School sitting disconsolately waiting for them. The MP guards rode in the cabs with the drivers boredly. There was no fear of anybody trying to jump out and escape a roster of the FBI.

Having the entire backs of the trucks to themselves, conferences of strategy were called in the backs of both trucks simultaneously, as if by the same natural instinct that makes southbound geese and schools of fish rendezvous at certain predetermined places, both conferences following instinctively the same identical pattern, each truckload instinctively knowing and trusting that the other truckload was doing the same thing, so that in effect it was really one big conference of strategy, instead of two.

By checking back and utilizing each man's memory, each truckload was able to determine just who was in the other truckload, and from that to deduce just who was missing. It was discovered, then, that there were at least six queer-chasers from G Company as persevering and proficient as any queer-chaser present, who had not been called at all.

In both trucks, almost simultaneously, there were indignant cries of

"What the hell" and *"Those lucky bastards"* and *"How the hell do they get off so easy"* and *"They aint no goddam bettern we are."*

In both trucks, almost simultaneously immediately, there were answering cries, by the same men who had voiced the other cries, of *"Shut up, for god sake"* or *"Hell yes. We got enough worrying to do about us without worrying about them"* or *"Yeah, drop that. Lets decide what we going to do."*

When quiet was restored, it was also discovered there were two men from F Company and one from E in the truck Prew was in. There was one man from F in the other truck, they said, but none from E. It was decided by the board of strategy that whoever it was that had informed was pretty well acquainted with G Company, although that did not greatly narrow down the choice. Apparently there were no men from the 1st or 3rd Battalions being called in at all, although all of them had run into plenty of men from both the 1st and 3rd Battalions working the circuit at Waikiki. It was decided that this was only a little local flurry, and not a general roundup. The best thing to do was to clam up and know nothing and recognize nobody. They didnt have any proof or they would have made a general roundup, all they were doing was to try and scare some proof out of somebody, that was all, just putting on the heat to scare somebody.

In both trucks when this deduction had been reached there was, almost simultaneously, a chorus of sighs of relief. This did not lessen either the nervousness or the worried anxiety of fear. Neither did it lessen the happy holiday air of Payday that accompanies any release from drill. Both conferences were adjourned practically simultaneously and broke up into excited discussions of the prospects.

Friday Clark, his long Wop nose a waxy yellow, was scared to death. When the conference was over, he got up and moved down the swaying jouncing truck, holding to the ribs above his head, and squeezed in beside Prewitt.

"Jees, Prew. I'm scared. Why they want to call me for? I never been out with one. In my whole life."

"Neither has none of the rest of us," Bull Nair drawled.

It drew a general laugh.

"In your *whole* life?" Readall Treadwell said.

"Oh," Nair drawled. "You mean in my *whole* life."

It got another laugh.

"Christ no," Dusty Rhodes said. "You shewn me a queer, I wunt even know one of em things from a woman."

"Thats no lie," somebody said.

"Yeah, dont forget to tell the cop that, Scholar," somebody else said.

"I dint mean it like that," The Scholar protested. "What I meant is you show me a queer, I'd probly gap at him like this." He bugged his eyes and gaped his mouth until it looked like the rictal cavern of a hungry young bird.

"Hey, Nair," he said, liking the idea. "I'm gapping at you, Nair."

"I'm gappin at you," Nair drawled, and gaped back.

The Scholar laughed uproariously, and they started gaping at each other regularly.

"Look at Knapp," Nair drawled, and pointed to the long thin unruffled form of the Corporal sprawled out on the bouncing seat. "He looks worried, dont he? Lets gap old Knapp."

"Okay," Rhodes said. "Probly do him good."

They gaped at him in unison.

"We're gappin you, Knapp."

They laughed uproariously, looking at each other slyly with a countryman's secret humor, as if they had discovered the greatest comedy routine that had ever been discovered.

"Gap this," Knapp grinned, grabbing himself.

They were untouched. They started using their routine on first one and then another down the truck. It did not make much of an impression on the general anxiety.

"Its all right for them," Friday said to Prew, his fawn's eyes shy and wild with fear. "They chased queers. I aint never. What if they thrown my ass in jail? for something I aint never done?"

"I was only down there once myself," Prew grinned. "You're safe. They wont do anything to anybody anyway."

"But look at how my hands are shakin," Friday said. "I dont want to go to jail."

"Hell, if they threw all the queens and queer-chasers in Honolulu into jail, the city'd go broke tryin to feed them and half the businesses would have to close down for lack of help and the Army'd have to declare a holiday."

"Yes," Friday said. "But."

"Ahh, shut up," Bloom said, from down the seat. "Whats a matter, you yellow? What do you have to lose? Look at me, I'm liable to get kicked out of NCO School."

Bloom was sitting on the swaying seat, his elbows braced on his knees, cracking his knuckles, beside the other candidate, a man named Moore.

"You think they'll kick us out over this?" Bloom asked him.

"Christ, I hope not," Moore said.

"Sure I'm yellow," Friday blazed at Bloom. "Least I admit it I'm yellow. Who was it got old Andy started chasin queers down town, and to quit the git-tars?" he said accusingly. "It wasnt me."

Andy, sitting legs out on the floor with his back against the cab and grinning painfully trying to hide the fear that was in his eyes, looked as if he wished he had stayed with the guitars, but he made no comment.

"Are you callin me a goddam queer?" Bloom said, getting up, keeping his balance by holding a rib above his head. "Watch how you talk to me, you crummy little Wop."

"Kiss my ass," Friday said suddenly, startled by his own audacity.

"Why, goddam you." Bloom leaned forward, hanging by his left hand on the rib and grabbed him by his shirt front and jerked him up and shook him, the slender Friday's head and arms flopping loosely like a shaken rag doll.

"Leave me alone, Bloom," Friday stuttered. "Leave me alone. I didnt do nothing to you, Bloom."

"Take that back," Bloom said, shaking him. "Take it back."

"Okay," Friday gargled, flopping. "I take it back."

Prew stood up, holding another rib for balance, and grabbed Bloom's wrist and bent his thumbnail in hard on the tendon.

"Let go, you son of a bitch. He dont take nothing back. Do you, Friday?"

"Yes," Friday gargled. "No. I dont know."

Bloom's hand opened under the thumbnail pressure and Friday fell back limply on the seat, his eyes wide with his fear, and Bloom and Prew stood in the truck bed swaying, looking at each other, each trying to keep his balance by holding with one hand on a rib above him.

"Yeah, and you're another one I've got my eye on," Bloom sneered. "If you're such a hot shot fighter why dont you go out for fighting?" He looked around the truck. "If you're such a tough son of a bitch, why aint you on the boxing squad?"

"Because theres too many sons of whores like you on it, thats why."

They stood swaying, staring, neither one able to concentrate on his staring properly because he had to use all his concentration to keep his balance.

"Someday you're going to make me mad," Bloom said.

"You're kiddin," Prew said.

"Right now I got more important things to worry about," Bloom said. He sat back down.

"Any time you're ready," Prew said. "And I'll give you plenty of time to take your shirt off, too." He sat back down himself.

"Thanks, Prew," Friday said.

"Ahhh," Prew said. "Listen, Friday," he said loudly, looking at Bloom, "if that son of a bitch picks on you any more dont fool with him. Pick up a chair or a bar and crown him like Maggio did." He was boiling that Bloom should have ignored the taboo that made Friday Off Limits and a sort of Company mascot, any more than anyone would hit the village idiot boy.

389

"Okay, Prew," Friday gulped. "Anything you say."

"Yeah," Bloom snorted. "Do that. And you'll end up the same place Maggio ended up."

"Through no fault of yours," Prew amended.

Bloom hunched his shoulders contemptuously then, and turned back to Moore, the other NCO candidate who was of his own status, the great indignant rage fading off his face as suddenly as it had come, to be replaced by the astonished anxiety of outrage that had been there before, as if he had suddenly remembered he was being carried downtown against his will, to be investigated as a queer.

"Jees," he muttered tensely to the other, "I sure hope this here dont get us kicked out of the School."

"Christ," the other said nervously, "me too."

Bloom shook his head. "Guy has to watch his step, things like that."

"Thats right," the other said. "I never should of went down there in the first place."

They were almost to the branch highway to Pearl and Hickam Field by then. The two trucks roared slowly in through Honolulu, keeping to the back streets as much as possible, running around the northern outskirts on Middle Street, past the church that had the big red electric sign above it: JESUS, COMING SOON!, and then east on School Street, but still having to come down Nuuanu right through town to get to the city police station, where the recon was parked at the curb as they pulled in.

Pedestrians on Nuuanu and Queen Streets coming and going from the docks where a new tourist liner was pulling in amidst many leis and a band playing in the bright morning sunshine, stopped to stare at them, probably thinking there must be another sabotage problem in the Army's new security program coming off today, and musing momentarily solemnly upon the seriousness of life in this year of Our Lord 1941 before getting back to business, watching curiously the trucks pulling into the alley and the men dismounting and trooping up the steps into the station.

Angelo Maggio, flanked by two MP guards with riot guns and sidearms, was sitting in the anteroom to the police lieutenant's office, as the mob trooped in.

"My god," Maggio cheered. "This here looks like a regular G Compny roll call, or else convention. Who's got the beer?"

One of the big MPs jerked his head. "Shut up," he said.

"Okay, Brownie," Maggio grinned cheerfully. "Whatever you say. I wouldnt want you should shoot me with that buckshot cannon."

The MP looked discomfited and his eyes narrowed at Maggio, and Maggio's eyes narrowed back, above his grin.

"Hey, Angelo. Hello, Angelo. Hi, Angelo. Theres Angelo. Look at

Angelo. Hows it goin, Angelo." Men who had liked him in the Company, men who had not liked him in the Company, men who had hardly known he was in the Company, even Bloom who would have liked him out of the Company, they all crowded around to say hello to Angelo.

"I aint allowed to talk," grinned the celebrity. "I'm under orders. I'm a prisoner, I mean internee. And prisoners aint allowed to talk. They allowed to breathe though, if they good that is."

He seemed to be the same old Angelo. He wanted to know how the Dodgers were making out with their first games.

"I aint had time to keep up on the sports sections lately," he grinned.

And at first glance, a month in hock did not appear to have changed him any. But a closer look saw that he had lost a lot of weight, and the hollows under his scrawny cheekbones were even deeper, the narrow bony shoulders if that were possible were more narrow and more bony, there were deep crescents of purple doeskin underneath his eyes. He looked harder, both physically and mentally, and when he laughed there was a metallic glitter in it now.

Prew got himself a seat next to him when the detail was told to sit and wait. They talked, low and fast. The two Schofield MPs were obviously at a disadvantage here in public to control their charge.

"They cant do nothing to me here," Angelo grinned complacently. "They on their good behavior. They got to make a good impression on this gook lieutenant. Orders from headquarters."

"Wait'll you get home," the MP called Brownie said emphatically. "You'll find yourself wishin you could learn to keep your big mouth shut, when you get home."

"You're telling me," Angelo grinned. "He's telling me," he said to Prew. "Thats only been to me the biggest trouble all my life, and he's tellin me."

"You think its been trouble?" the MP called Brownie said, "you just think its been trouble, Wop."

Angelo grinned narrowly. "What can you do to me? thats worse than what I'm doin? Throw me in the Hole maybe for a couple days, is all. You can kill me, but you cant eat me, Brownie."

He went on talking, leaving the MP looking discomfited again at the unfair advantage that was being taken of him.

"Maybe you better take it easy," Prew suggested.

"Hell," Angelo grinned, "I dont get to do this very often. I'm in bad anyway now. I might as well get the good out of it."

"How is it up there?" Prew said.

"Not so bad. Look at the muscles I'm gettin. And," he added, "I'm gettin so I like Duke's Mixture bettern tailormades now. Save me a lot of money when I get out."

"They treat you all right then," Prew said. "No rough stuff."

"Well, it aint exactly a school for young ladies. But at least you know they got your best interests at heart. Aint that right, Brownie?" he grinned.

The MP called Brownie did not answer. He was still discomfited. He stared straight ahead of him.

"He aint use to bein treated like that," Angelo explained to Prew. "Come to think of it, I aint use to treatin him that way neither."

"I came up to visit you with a couple cartons of tailormades," Prew said apologetically. "But they wouldnt let me in."

"Yeah, I heard about it," Angelo said expansively. "Like to got me on the shitlist. Ony I was already on it. Thought I was a sissy, to be smokin tailormades. Had a hard time convincin anybody I wasnt."

"Whats going to happen?" Prew asked. "You found out what the deal is?"

"Hell no. They tell me nothin. But my trial ought to come up soon, and I've already served a month already. So even if I get a Special and they give me the limit, I'll still only have five months more rehabilitation. I come out, I ought to be a thirdy year man myself.

"Listen," Angelo said. "Dont worry about it. It'll work out okay. I already done one month, see? They'll take that off. It wont be so long. Have you still got that forty dollars?" He swung his eyes narrowly without moving his head, toward the MP behind him and back to Prew.

"Part of it," Prew said. "I spent part."

"Well, I wanted to tell you. That forty's yours, see? You earned it. You spend it. Dont worry about what you owe me, see?" Again he swung his eyes narrowly without moving his head, toward the MP standing behind him and back to Prew.

"Okay," Prew said.

"They check all your dough in the guard room anyway," Angelo said. "So you just spend it."

"I'm using it to work on Lorene," Prew said.

"She give you a hard time Payday, dint she?" Angelo said.

Prew nodded.

"Well, you use it. And more power to you, buddy."

"Okay," Prew said.

"Looks like they gettin ready to get this show on the road," Angelo said.

A police clerk had come out of the inner office with a long list in his hand. He called off a name. One of the men rose and followed him inside. The door remained closed for quite a while, then it opened and the clerk with the list called Maggio's name.

"Thats me," Angelo said, and got up. "I think I'm the decoy, or would you call it guinie pig?" He went in through the door, one MP with riot gun going in ahead of him, then him, then the other MP with riot gun following him. The door closed. In a few minutes Maggio came back out, one MP with riot gun coming out first, then Maggio, then the other MP with riot gun.

"Regular Dillinger, aint I?" Angelo grinned at the crowd. It got a general laugh, even in the nervousness.

"Shut up, Maggio," the MP called Brownie warned. "Come on." They took him on through and out another door in the opposite wall, not the corridor door which was on the left wall, but a door into another room. The fourth wall opposite the corridor door was all windows. There were no bars on them.

Pretty soon the man whose name had been called first came back out too and the clerk escorted him through the door where Maggio had gone and shut it. One of the Shafter MPs who had ridden in the trucks came and stood by it, when the clerk motioned for him. Then he called another name. The second man followed him through the door into the police lieutenant's office.

"Looks like the old single shot routine," somebody said nervously.

In a few minutes the clerk came back and went to the opposite door and called Maggio again.

"Told you I was the decoy, dint I?" Angelo grinned at the crowd. It got another nervous laugh and the tension relaxed a little, because everybody was comparing himself instinctively to the bony little Wop and deciding he was not so bad off after all.

"Shut up, Maggio," the MP called Brownie said. "Come on."

They went in. Pretty soon they came out and went back into the other room. Then the clerk led the man out and into the other room and called another name. That was the procedure that was followed down through the whole list.

When Prew's name was called he got up and followed the clerk, his knees feeling loose. In the inner office the half-Hawaiian police lieutenant was behind his desk in his mustard uniform. In a big deep wooden arm chair beside the desk sat Tommy, a look of petulant sullen resignation on his face. The Shafter MP First Lieutenant sat against the wall. The two young-faced FBI stood unobtrusively across the room, seeming a dead part of the furnishings.

"You know this man?" the police lieutenant asked Tommy.

"No," Tommy said wearily. "I've never seen him before."

The police lieutenant consulted a list. "Prewitt," he said. "Prewitt, have you ever seen this man before?"

"No, Sir," Prew said.

"Havent you ever been out to the Waikiki Tavern?" the lieutenant asked patiently.

"Yes, Sir."

"And you mean you've never seen this man out there?"

"Not that I remember, Sir."

"He hangs out there all the time, I'm told."

"I may have seen him then, Sir. But if I did I dont remember."

"Have you ever seen any queers out there?"

"I've seen some men that looked like queers. Looked womanish. I dont know if they were."

"Dont you know a queer when you see one?" the lieutenant asked patiently.

"I dont know, Sir. Theres only one sure way to tell a queer, isnt there?"

The lieutenant did not smile. He looked tired. "Have you ever been out with a queer, Prewitt?"

"No, Sir."

"Not once? In your whole life?"

Prew wanted to grin, remembering Nair's: *Oh. You mean in my WHOLE life*, but he did not. "No, Sir," he said.

"You dont have to lie to me," the lieutenant said patiently. "The psychological textbooks say that almost every man, at one time or another in his life, has been out with a queer. This is all in the strictest of confidence. We're not trying to put the finger on any of you men. We're trying to protect you from these people."

Tommy sat in his chair staring out the window, his face set. He made a very poor monster. Prew felt suddenly sorry for him.

"To do that," the lieutenant said tiredly, "we have to have legal evidence, to put these people where the law says they belong. We're not after you men."

"I thought the law said both parties are held equally responsible," Prew said. "At least," he said, "thats what I've always heard."

"Thats true," the lieutenant said tiredly, "legally. However, as I said, nobody wants to bring charges against you men. We only want you to help us clean up this nest of vice out around Waikiki. The Waikiki Tavern is a respectable place. They dont want to be used as an esoteric trysting place any more than we want them to. But they can hardly handle a thing of this magnitude. Its a job for the law."

"Yes, Sir," Prew said. The police lieutenant looked very tired, and there were still ten more men after him to be run through. He felt suddenly sorry for the lieutenant.

"All right, I'll ask you again, Prewitt: Have you ever been out with a queer."

"I rolled one once," Prew said, "when I was on the bum before I got in the army."

The lieutenant's tired mouth tightened a trifle. "Okay," he said. He nodded to the clerk standing by the door. "Bring him in."

The clerk went out and came back with Maggio and the two big MPs, one MP with riot gun coming through the door first and turning around, then Maggio, then the other MP with riot gun following Maggio. The clerk started to cross the room. His line of march would have passed between the MP called Brownie and Maggio. The MP called Brownie stepped in front of the clerk, standing at port arms wooden faced.

"You cant pass between the prisoner and his guard, Corporal," Brownie said woodenly.

"Oh! I'm sorry," the clerk said. He was terribly embarrassed. "I forgot," he explained lamely, and went around.

"Prewitt, do you know this man?" the lieutenant said wearily.

"Yes, Sir."

"Is he a friend of yours?"

"Not exactly a friend, Sir," Prew said. "He's in my Compny."

"Werent you talking to him outside a while ago?" the lieutenant said.

"Yes, Sir," Prew said. "So were a lot of other people."

"You were sitting beside him though, werent you?"

"Yes, Sir."

"You ever go on pass with this man?"

"Yes, Sir. Several times."

"You ever go to Waikiki with him?"

"No, Sir," Prew said. "I've run into him out there once or twice, but I never went out there with him."

"You say you have run into him out there?"

"Yes, Sir. I've run into lots of men from the Compny out in Waikiki. We all go out there from time to time."

"We're concerned with this man now," the lieutenant said. "Who was he with when you saw him out there?"

"I dont remember, Sir."

"Was it someone from the Company?"

"I dont remember, Sir. I dont think he was with anybody."

"You mean anybody you knew? Or with nobody?"

"With nobody, Sir."

"You didnt see him with any of these men you say you've seen out there that looked like they might be queers?"

"No, Sir."

"Okay," the lieutenant said wearily to the clerk. "Take him out."

They took Maggio out, the same way they had brought him in, first one MP with riot gun, then Maggio, then the other MP with riot gun.

"They aint takin no chances on him gettin away, are they," Prew said to nobody in particular, unable to resist it.

"Soldier," the Shafter MP First Lieutenant said sharply, "you've been in the Army long enough to know the procedure of guarding a prisoner."

"Yes, Sir," Prew said, and shut up.

"Lets have no more of that then," the Shafter MP First Lieutenant said sharply.

"Yes, Sir," Prew said, and shut up.

The police lieutenant was playing with a pencil, tiredly. "You have nothing to say, then, about this man here?" He nodded at Tommy who was still staring set-faced out the window, trying hard to be above such disgusting implications and besmirchments. "Nothing at all?"

"No, Sir," Prew said. "I dont know him at all, Sir."

"We're trying to help you men get out of this mess you've gotten into," the lieutenant said patiently. "You're all of you treading on dangerous ground out in Waikiki. All of you men ought to already know that." He paused.

"Yes, Sir," Prew said. "I mean, no, Sir."

"Any time a man breaks any law," the lieutenant recited wearily, "he's treading on dangerous ground. Eventually, the law always catches up with him. We're trying to help you men before you get in that deep, Prewitt. But we cant help you if you dont help us to help you." He paused.

"No, Sir," Prew said. "I mean, yes, Sir."

"You still have nothing to say?"

"I dont know anything to say, Sir."

"Okay, thats all," the lieutenant said wearily. "Bring in the next one."

"Yes, Sir," Prew said. Before he could stop himself, he saluted the civilian police lieutenant instinctively. The lieutenant smiled, and the Shafter MP First Lieutenant laughed sharply. The two bright-faced young FBI men did not do anything, except to lean on against the wall, seeming a part of the furnishings.

"Okay, Prewitt," the half-Hawaiian police lieutenant smiled. "Show him out. Who's the next one?"

The clerk escorted him across the anteroom and through the door which the Shafter MP stood beside. He shut the door behind him. There was nobody in the long room except the two Schofield MPs guarding Maggio down at the other end, and the men from Schofield who had already been through the mill, sitting on the wooden benches along the walls. Their faces still looked strained. Prew stood looking at them, feeling the sweat from his armpits still trickling coolly down his ribs, then he walked down toward Maggio and the MPs.

The MP called Brownie jerked his head. "Stay back there, Mack," he said. "This man is a prisoner."

Prew stared hard at him, then moved his eyes to Maggio and winked and grinned. Angelo winked and grinned back, but his heart did not appear to be in it any more. Prew turned back toward the others. Somebody had gotten out a pack of cards and some of them were sitting in a circle on the hardwood floor playing stud for matches. He sat down on the bench and watched.

Something had been touching lightly at his mind ever since he had first gone in there and seen that it was Tommy. It did not make sense that they were using Angelo for bait, when it was Tommy. Angelo had never been out with Tommy, Bloom had been out with Tommy. So had Andy. So had Readall Treadwell. So had Prewitt, one time. But the only connection Angelo had with Tommy was last Payday, when he had picked him up for Prewitt, which was the only time Prewitt had been out with any of them, yet Prewitt gets called in on the investigation, too. Where did they get Prewitt's name? and where was Hal the French tutor? If they really had enough on Angelo to use him as the bait, Hal the French tutor ought to be there too. It began to look like whoever had informed had used last Payday for his informing material, but if that was so where was Hal the French tutor?

Somebody else had gotten out their packs of the always present, large size, poker cards and now there were three or four stud games for matches going on the floor. They all played concentratedly, not talking, and as they played the strain began to fade off of their faces.

Prew gave it up in disgust and sat in on one of the games. Hell, it was all just his imagination probably. He was getting jumpy. He always had an inclination to want to play the leading role. I yam ze great EEtalian actore, I play ze leading role, everybody die.

The players moved over silently to let him in. Nobody contested his presence. This common adversity took precedence over The Treatment. The Treatment would start in again as soon as they got safely home. But for now it was suspended before this narrow escape from the law.

Pvt 1cl Bloom was the second man after Prewitt to be run through the mill. He came into the room and stared blankly at the stud players and then at Maggio and then he went over to the bench along the other wall and sat down by himself. He did not sit in on any of the games. He sat by himself cracking his knuckles and cursing in a low monotone of astonished outrage and affront, the sound going on and on never changing tone as if it were a pure reflex arising from a great misunderstanding. When Moore, the other NCO candidate, came over to sit beside him he got up and moved away by himself again, looking at Moore indignantly for having interrupted his monotone of cursing.

The rest of them played stud for matches concentratedly until the last man had been run through. Then they were herded back out to the trucks by the Shafter MPs wearing only sidearms. Prew turned back for one last look at Angelo at the other end of the room, still sitting between the two big riot-gunned Schofield MPs and also looking outraged, now that this windfall of a vacation he would have to pay for when he got back was over so soon.

The trucks pulled out under the same scrutiny of the pedestrians, different pedestrians probably, but as far as the soldiers in the trucks could see, the same identical pedestrians, still coming from the same docks where the same brass band still played the same song for the same new boatload of tourists. As if by a common command, the men in the trucks all stared back conjointly with such a weary ferocity that the pedestrians got uncomfortable and looked away at something else and tried to appear occupied, thinking that if it did come to a war at least we could put as tough and bloodthirsty an Army in the field as anybody. Then the trucks were out on the open highway, riding over the steep gulches of crumbling crimson rock, past the cane fields, some of them burning in the crisp summer air with great black clouds of smoke, past the mathematical fields of pineapple, back toward Schofield. It was after three o'clock, and under the vast bowl of the cerulean sky everything looked very small and far away and very quiet, as far as the eye could see to the blue smoke of the mountains on both sides.

At the monthly Sex Hygiene Lecture and short arm inspection, a week later, Capt Holmes made a short embarrassed speech about perversion and degeneracy, after the movies showing what syphilis and clap can do to you had been run off. The Chaplain, in his address on the importance of love in the sexual act and the necessity of sexual faithfulness and continence on the part of the male before marriage, did not mention either.

Lorene, Prew thought, listening to both of them. It was such a perfect whore's name; Lorene. It fitted her so well. It had all the right sounds, the right connotations. It was a much better name than Billy, or Sandra, or Maurene. He was glad she was named Lorene, instead of Agnes or Gladys or Thelma or some other name like that. Lorene was better.

Chapter 29

He had not even used up his three trips at $15 ea. before he found out her real name was not Lorene at all, it was Alma.

Apparently, along with all the rest of it, he was to be denied even this meager satisfaction. It was almost unnerving. The only thing that kept it from reducing him to absolute defeat was that it was so much in keeping with everything else that had happened to him in the past three months, since he had quit the Bugle Corps.

It seemed that Lorene was only a house name Mrs Kipfer had picked for her out of a perfume advertisement. Mrs Kipfer did not think Alma was either French enough or intellectual enough for the star performer of her establishment. But her real name was Alma Schmidt, of all names. And she lived in Maunalani Heights, of all places. If he had tried, he could not have picked a more un-whorelike name out of the phone directory. And if he had guessed, he could not have picked out of a real estate classified section a more un-whorelike place for her to live.

Maunalani Heights was the donjon and inner keep of the upper middle class of Honolulu, as distinguished from the rich men. The rich men, like Doris Duke, owned beach estates along Black Point and Kahala Beach and Kaalawai between the foot of Diamond Head and the sea. The rich men, like Doris Duke, owned these estates but did not live in them. The upper middle class of Honolulu owned Maunalani Heights and lived on it—rising up and up above Kaimuki, high up, where they could look out across the eroded ancient crater of Diamond Head which was a US Military Reservation, on out past that far out to sea along the world's curve where sometimes they could watch far out the rain coming in from Molokai on the south wind like a curtain to cover Diamond Head, then Kaimuki, then finally themselves. It was a fine place for the upper middle class to live but it was a long ways from the beach.

Kaimuki was the saddle between the Heights and Diamond Head; it was also a densely settled community of the more well-off Japanese, except for the big square of it between 13th and 18th Avenues against the flank of Diamond Head which was the government's cut of Kaimuki that was called Fort Ruger. It was almost symbolic, the way Maunalani Heights dominated the well-off Japanese of Kaimuki.

And up here, Alma Schmidt and a girl friend from the Service Rooms had a house, on Maunalani Heights. He was even more astounded when he saw the house they rented.

More accurately, Alma Schmidt and girl friend from Service Rooms lived on Wilhelmina Rise, not Maunalani Heights. Wilhelmina Rise was the steep sloped ridge running up from Kaimuki to the Heights at the very top of Kalepeamoa, elev. 1116 ft. Wilhelmina Rise was sort of the outer keep to the donjon of the Heights which, strictly, included only Maunalani Circle at the tip top and Lurline Drive a little lower down and Matsonia Drive a little lower still and Lower Lurline Drive still lower and then Lanipili Drive which was so short it hardly counted and, possibly but doubtfully, Mariposa Drive; all of these like regressive stairsteps below the Circle but still well up at the top, on Maunalani Heights. Still, it was legitimate for Alma to tell him Maunalani Heights, because all the other inhabitants of Wilhelmina Rise told people they lived on Maunalani Heights. And anyway, he did not know the difference. He had even thought that it was all rich men, like Doris Duke, who lived on Wilhelmina Rise. He never admitted this to her, however, after she explained it to him.

The house itself was on Sierra Drive which runs tortuously up the ridge twisting back and forth between houses on so many different levels that it reminds you of an illustration from a fairy tale, just off Wilhelmina Rise Street which runs straight up crossing and recrossing Sierra so steeply that even in coming down you have to take the drop in second, running down and out under trees that a moment ago you were looking down at the tops of through the windshield and thinking of those steep streets in the Casbah movies or in fairy tales. It was a small one-storey house of something, probably concrete block, but plastered over so smoothly it looked all of a piece with its low pitched roof that hung far out over the walls like in a Spanish hacienda in a fairy tale, and it was set right out on the edge of the steep western drop to Palolo Valley, like a castle in a fairy tale.

In fact all of it, when he thought about it, seemed to have a great deal of the fairy tale about it. That same thinness and unreality of great gentleness and leisurely beauty that he could believe as long as he was still reading the story but that when he put the book down afterwards, reluctantly, he no longer could believe, to his unassuageable disgust. It was, he felt, a very fitting place for The Princess to live; Alma thought so too; and he wondered if all rich men's lives were always as beautiful as this.

The house had a little roofless side porch on the very lip of the drop that fell straight down at least a hundred feet where you could stand and look far down into the streets of Palolo Valley as if you were God, and further west the buildings of St Louis College off by themselves and still further west, a little hazy across the valley, and still below you, St Louis Heights, elev. 483 ft. It was a beautiful little porch and behind it were two solid plate glass doors you could look out of from the big sunken living room three steps down, if you were not inclined to go outside. It was on this porch in the late afternoon of a Saturday, when the sun was just beginning to light everything a crimson gold preparatory to dropping in the sea, the first time that he was ever up there, that Alma Schmidt first told him she was in love with him. He made his first mistake immediately.

Remembering the little permanent-party post under the ancient elms and maples, and fatuously attempting in his mind to favorably compare that way of life with this, he told Alma he was in love with her too and asked her to marry him.

It was his first mistake in judgment since the inauguration of the $60 planned economy. If he had brought a musette bag full of live grenades he could maybe have done as good a job of blowing up his own investment, but he doubted it.

It might have been the sunset, sunsets always stupefied him. Or it might have been the nearness of her body, the head of which just topped his shoulder. He had noted in the past that the nearness of women's bodies had a tendency to upset his mental processes, and he could not control it, sometimes they even stupefied him more than sunsets, a reaction which he had found over a period of years was usually not reciprocal, giving them a certain initial advantage over men. Or, it might have been just the overwhelming newness of all this that he had not had time to get adjusted to. Even so, whatever it was, there was no excuse for such dangerous stupidity.

For a while there it was touch-and-go, and he could see the reflections of decisive action passing and repassing across her face, whether to kick him out now or to make it a slow gradual withdrawal of interest. It was only this doubt as to which way to get rid of him that saved him. It gave him time to salvage what he could by looking slyly at her and laughing out loud, and then lighting a cigarette to show her that his hands were not shaking. The lighting of the cigarette was unadulterated brilliance. But even so, he knew it was only luck he thought of it, the catching at straws of a man paralyzed by his own chuckleheadedness.

She watched his hand not shaking, and finally began to look relieved. Then she even joined in the laughter. She led him back inside and mixed them both Martinis, before she put the New England boiled dinner that she had had ready, on the stove. Then while it cooked and filled the place with the homey smell of the cooking she mixed them both more Martinis. They were good Martinis. One of the things he had found out when the planned economy first began to work was that Alma did like to drink some after all, it was just that she did not like to drink when she was working. She would even drink straight whiskey, now and then, if the occasion were propitious. Drinking made Alma much more likeable. It loosened her up. Or maybe it was just that drinking made him more prone to like Alma. Whichever it was, he still had sufficient presence of mind in his paralysis to utilize it now and suggest still more Martinis. The New England boiled dinner was as good as the Martinis, and after they had eaten they went very marriedly to bed, as if nothing untoward had happened.

But he did not let himself forget that it had still been a very near thing. He could not understand what in hell had ever possessed him to say such a dim-witted thing. He could not afford to be making mistakes like that often. The $60 planned economy had barely lasted long enough to get him up here. If it had required the expenditure of $5 more he would not have made it, and he could not go around like that making serious mistakes in judgment and trusting to chance that they would be overlooked.

He was very careful after that. There were plenty of chances to make mistakes in judgment. Once they drove Alma's roommate's Chrysler convertible out to Kaneohe Valley to go swimming; Alma did not have a convertible because she was saving her money. That time was an excellent time for a mistake in judgment, with the precipitous eastern slopes of the Koolau Range rising horse-shoe-shaped behind the beach with the sugarloaf of the Pali in the foreground and the black cliffs of Makapuu Point where the lighthouse was, peeking over Rabbit Island, but he was wise now and he took great care. After handling that time so well, he got his confidence back, and it all went along smooth as the imported rum that Alma's roommate from the Service Rooms bought by the case and was very liberal with.

Because he was broke, Alma kept him supplied with car fare money to get down from Schofield. She gave him a key and after that he took to coming down regular every weekend. If he did not have duty, he would take off Saturday morning right after inspection and cut noon chow and make a beeline for there.

It was a long trip. He got to know it well. He would always be pushing hard to get there, and he would always be pooped out when he did get there. Then, he would let himself in with his key and suddenly it would all drop away and leave him and there wasnt any Army. The enormous living room that was floored with square red tiles was three steps down from the door, the two bedroom doors three steps up on the left wall as you came in, and the glass doors and the porch three steps up on the right. In the far corner near the porch doors three steps up to the kitchen on the south and its tiny glassed-in dinette. Next to it east, three steps up to a bathroom and shower. There was another bath and shower connecting between the bedrooms. The whole place paneled from floor to ceiling in a plywood stained a honey color, except the kitchen which was very Americanly efficient and had cupboards for walls.

If she had had to work and was not there, which was usually the case on Saturday, he would get icecubes from the refrigerator in the kitchen and mix himself a stiff drink from the radio-bar in the living room, maybe some of Georgette's the girl friend's rum, maybe gin and gingerale, maybe scotch or maybe bourbon with soda, anything he wanted, and get into his trunks in the bedroom and get a book out of the open bookcase on the living room wall between the bedroom doors and go out on the porch. He liked to lie around barefooted in his trunks on the chaise longue on the porch and drink. He would not read much. He liked to look out at that view and get slowly savoringly mellow drunk. He would get up in his bare feet and walk across the heavy Japanese matting that covered the porch floor and felt good on his feet, and go inside to the bar and mix himself another drink and then go back out on the porch. All the things he had taken all week in the Company would finally go clear away so that by the time Alma got home from work around two o'clock he would be all right again.

Maybe once in a while she would be there waiting for him when he came in on Saturday. But he liked it better when she was gone and he came in alone, used his own key, and moved familiarly through the silence of nobody there. Doing that made the place belong to him. It was his. Nothing could take it away from him, as long as he could do that. He had never had a key before. Just having the key in his pocket all week long was worth not mentioning getting married. Even half of what all of this was would have been more than worth the not mentioning getting married.

There were never any soldiers up in around here. It was almost supernatural, how as soon as you got above Waialae Avenue and onto the Rise in the bus there were no soldiers. There were always hordes of them downtown weekends. There were always lots of them in Kaimuki, on Waialae in the business section, mostly men from Ruger. But above Waialae it was like another country. The rich (he could not get over calling the upper middle class of Wilhelmina Rise and Maunalani Hts the rich, no matter how often Alma explained it to him) the rich did not take to soldiers well up here. That was one of the reasons he liked it so well up here.

It never failed to surprise him, how Alma could have gotten in up here at all. Of course nobody knew where she worked. One of their near neighbors was Clare Inter, the famous Hilo Hattie. The three of them, Alma, Georgette, and himself (Georgette, if she had boyfriends, never brought them home) would sit around and laugh relishingly over it often, over being up here, in this house, up here.

It must have cost the two girls plenty, in rent. Alma never told him just how much, but he knew it would be high. Alma admitted it was high, but it was the one luxury she was not going to let her savings deprive her of. Well, Alma could afford it. Alma had gotten onto the place through Mrs Kipfer. Mrs Kipfer had friends, she had connections in Honolulu. Nobody knew just who or what they were, but Mrs Kipfer had them. And Alma, Lorene that is, was her favorite. Alma could get a day or two off from her any time, just for the asking, because Mrs Kipfer did not want her premier danseuse coming to work looking worn out and run down. Whenever Alma got a night off like that she would call him up at the Company and he would catch a cab down town and then take a metered cab clear out to the house. If he did not have the money, he would go in the house like any married commuter and bring it back out to the guy. And she would always wake him up early, in plenty of time to make Reveille, and cook his breakfast for him. She liked to get up like that and cook his breakfast for him, before he went back. Sometimes even Georgette would get up and eat with them, bitching goodnaturedly at being waked so early, but all of it as if it were in the family. He had told them about the boxing squad and Dynamite and about The Treatment. It was almost religious, the way Alma would always set the alarm, no matter how drunk any of them were. It was almost wifely, the way she would not let him overtalk at breakfast and miss the early bus.

But he still liked the Saturdays best, when he came in alone and used his key and made himself at home. He would usually be asleep in the big double bed in her room, on Saturdays, when she got home from work. And she would pummel him until he was awake, and make him come out to the living room and she would mix drinks for them both, before they went to bed. Or maybe she would just crawl in beside him and wake him up to have a party as she always called it. It was those times she would tell him how much she loved him, how much she needed him, how dreadfully she needed him, he didnt know.

Well, he needed her too, and she didnt know.

Yes, but the need was not as great with him. It was easy for him, take it or leave it. He didnt really need her, not like she needed him, after that place.

Ha, that was just what she thought. His need for her was greater than hers would ever be. Without this sanctuary they would have cracked him with The Treatment long ago.

Yes, but if he only knew.

Well, if she only knew.

It did not develop into an argument often, but sometimes it did. Apparently neither one of them would ever know, and all this time he would be having to be very careful about making a mistake in judgment. There were plenty of other opportunities for it too. Almost every day he spent there, there were at least two opportunities to make a mistake in judgment. He did not mind though, and none of the opportunities quite hooked him, until the first time they went out together in public.

He did not care if they ever went out anyplace. He had developed a great domesticity. It was her idea to go out. She wanted to show him off, she said. Before they left the house she handed him two twenties and they went to Lau Yee Chai's. He had never been to Lau Yee Chai's. It took the whole forty dollars. It was worth it though. They had a fine time. She was an excellent dancer, too good for him. She said she would teach him at home.

It was not until on the way home in the cab, after spending her forty dollars, that he realized with a small shock that he was now a kept man, and had been for some time. He might even be called a pimp, by using the term elastically, although he did not solicit business. At first he felt degraded with a sinking in his stomach, but when he analyzed it he realized that he did not feel any different, that he was still the same man. So this is what being a kept man is like? he asked himself. It scared him a little and shamed him, because he did not feel any different. He felt he should have felt different.

It was not until after they got home and went out on the porch in the freshness of the night air, still in their party clothes (his that she had taken his measurements for and picked and bought for him), and stood looking down at the strings of white lights in Palolo Valley and across on St Louis Heights more strings of white lights and way off to the left the searchlights on the Royal and the red and blue and green and yellow neon flowers among the white strings that indicated Waikiki, where they had just come from; it was not until then that he asked her again to marry him. Maybe he felt it would make him not quite so kept.

It seemed it was always on the porch that he asked her. The porch and the view from it seemed to affect him that way. As he asked her, he was aware of a great delicious feeling of throwing all consequences to the winds and to hell with it; at the same time at the back of his mind a small voice told him he could get by with it without risking anything since he had been coming here so long now, if he did not do it too often.

This time he explained to her all about the little permanent-party post and the community of married noncoms, it seemed great to him as he explained it; he even included the year of waiting before he could ship Stateside and how that fitted with her plans, too. They could use some of her money to live well until he worked up into the first three graders bracket which would not be long, if he really felt like trying, and he did not give a damn about being supported by her or that the money was earned in whoring. He was, he pointed out with eloquence, doing all that right now anyway. As he talked, he was very proud of his broad mindedness.

She listened to it all intently, not once looking at him. She did not say anything for quite a while.

"You say you love me," he summed up for the defense, "and how much you need me. Okay. I believe you. And I love you and need you just as much. Then its the only logical thing for us to do, isnt it?" he said logically.

"You're just feeling lonely because you're taking such a beating in the Company," Alma said. "Lets go in and have a drink."

"No," he said. "Answer me."

"You need me now," Alma said. "But will you need me a year from now? after you've gotten out of this bad situation and are back in the States?"

"Of course I will. If I love you."

"But people dont love somebody unless they need them badly. If you didnt fill a definite need in my life now, I wouldnt love you."

"I'll always love you," he said. He said it because it was the logical answer to fulfill his argument, before he thought.

Alma looked at him in the dim light and smiled. He had not realized how ridiculous it would sound, or that it would be so patently obvious a lie, when he had said it. He had only said it because the trend of the conversation seemed to require it.

"You trapped me," he said.

"You trapped yourself," she said.

"But I do love you now," he said.

"Well, I love you now too," she said. "And why? Because you fill a definite need in the pattern that my life is now. I like to be able to come home to you, after there. But that doesnt mean I'll still love you a year from now, when the pattern of my life changes. How could anybody promise that and keep it?"

"You could, if you wanted to."

"Of course. But suppose that after the need was gone we neither one of us wanted to?"

He did not say anything.

"You see? Of course, I could always kid myself. Just like you could kid yourself—when you told yourself you didnt really care if your wife was a whore; or when you told yourself you didnt really doubt your wife; or when you told yourself you were not really afraid to let your wife out of your sight; or when you told yourself you wouldnt really be ashamed if other people found out your wife was a whore; or when——"

"Okay," he said. "Okay, okay." It sounded as if she were going to go on into infinity with an unlimited number of *Or when you told yourself you didnt reallys*, and he found he was wanting to shake his head like a fish that has got a hook it cannot comprehend stuck through its jaw, simply because it bit at an ordinary fly like any other fly.

She stopped and there was a large silence.

"But that aint the real reason," he said, feeling he had to say something. "Whats the real reason you wont marry me?"

"Maybe I just dont want to be the wife of a non-commissioned officer in the US Army."

"All right. But I could become an officer, if I wanted, under the new advancement program that came in with the draft. If I worked for that."

"Maybe I dont want to be the wife of a commissioned officer of the US Army either."

"All right, all right," he said. "Thats the top that I could ever do for you."

"You want to know the real reason?" Alma said. "I'll tell you the real reason," she smiled, "why I cant marry you. Income has nothing to do with it. I cant marry you simply because you're not respectable enough.

"Now lets go have that drink," she said.

"Okay," he said. "A drink would be fine."

He was convinced. He would not bring it up any more. They made a kind of celebration of his convincement. They got very drunk and cried in each other's arms because they could not get married. When Georgette came home from work she found them that way and when she wanted to know why they told her and Georgette got drunk too and they all cried together.

"She has to marry a man," Georgette, who knew Alma's plans, explained to Prew, "who is above suspicion and has so much position and prestige that it would be impossible for his wife to have ever been a whore. Its a shame, isnt it? You can see why she cant marry a soldier, even a general. Isnt it a shame?" Georgette started to cry again and mixed herself another drink.

It was a very fine celebration and it lasted almost all night. He told them all about Harlan Kentucky. Alma told them all about her little town in Oregon. Georgette, who was born and raised in Springfield Illinois, told them all about the State House and the Governor's Mansion and Lincoln's Mausoleum that some people still suspected had been mysteriously robbed of its glorious remains.

It was also a very apt celebration because he did not see either of them again for quite some time, although none of the three of them suspected that at the time.

When he got back to the Company, still hung over, in time for Reveille, he found field orders had been posted on the bulletin board. They were going into the field on one of the new sabotage problems for two weeks. They were going to Hickam Field to guard the plane revetments. There had been rumors in the Regiment that a sabotage problem was coming up but nobody had known just when it would come. He did not mind two weeks so much. He liked living in the field better than in garrison. Two weeks in the field would have been fine, if it was not that he could not get away to go to Maunalani Hts.

He managed to get away in the confusion of the packing and slip over to Choy's to the pay phone and call her reversing the charges. Alma was not there, but Georgette took the call and said she would give her the message and wished him luck in the field. He told her two weeks was not so long. He did not know then of course that it would be longer than two weeks, much longer than two weeks, three months in the Stockade longer than two weeks. If he had he would probably have sent Alma a different message, but he thought he had all that taken care of. He thought he could get along with The Treatment almost indefinitely, now that he had this sanctuary down town. And he could have. As it happened, The Treatment had nothing at all to do with it. As The Warden would have said, it was just about his speed, what happened. Irony pursued him, or he pursued it.

The long string of big two and a half ton trucks from the motor pool pulled lumberingly rumblingly into the quad and parked in front of the 2nd Battalion, and there was a final great bustle of crablike confusion on the floor as everybody unmade full field packs to stick in a Handy oiler or a bore brush they had forgotten and then rolled full field packs again. Wall lockers banged tinnily as they got into the field uniform of OD wool shirt open at the neck and CKC slacks stuffed into leggins, and the little go-to-hell caps with the robin's-egg-blue piping of the Infantry that you could stuff in your pocket when you had to wear the soup plate helmet. They swarmed downstairs and fell in and were counted off and assigned to trucks and then clambered up onto the tailgates and the tailgates were shut and latched behind them and the big trucks moved out belching exhaustively. That was the kind of soldiering Prewitt liked.

Chapter 30

It was while they were at Hickam Field on this problem that they wrote the Re-enlistment Blues.

It was to be the original, the real, the one and only, Army blues; when they got it written. They had talked about it a long time. They had never done it. Probably they never would have. But with Bloom gone to NCO School and Maggio in the Stockade and no chance for Prew to go to Maunalani Heights, he and Anderson and Friday Clark suddenly found themselves thrown back together for a little while with nothing else to do. The Re-enlistment Blues came out of that.

They had moved in and made their bivouac at the foot of an old abandoned railroad embankment that jutted up nudely out of the scrubby liana and keawe jungle a couple of hundred yards inside the fence. It was on the Field side, hidden from the Pearl Harbor-Hickam

Highway, in a low grove in the tangle where the ground was open and thick-dusty smooth as if once occupied by feeding cattle, under the gnarled closefitting branches that had kept the undergrowth from growing back and provided cover. Then they had strung three hundred yards of double apron wire and laid out a chain of staggered interlocking posts founded on the Hickam Main Gate to the north, and they were home. It was a fine place except for the mosquitoes. They settled into the regulated ebb and flow of two hours on and four hours off around the clock.

Only two-thirds of the Company was here. The other third was over on Kamehameha Highway five miles east, guarding an electric substation from sabotage as the two-thirds here were guarding planes from sabotage. It was strictly a sabotage problem. Over there they were even using ready-rolled accordion wire instead of double apron. The boxing squad had stayed in Schofield, to train for Company Smokers.

Capt Holmes had set up his CP over there, where the mosquitoes were not so bad. Stark set up his kitchen here, where the most men were. Stark had been willing to let Capt Holmes have two cooks and one of his field stoves, if he would furnish his own KPs, but that had been as far as Stark would budge. It worked out fine, for the men on post at Hickam. They did not mind having the mosquitoes. Stark always had one cook or KP up all night with hot coffee and hot sandwiches for them. Andy, who as company bugler had to go with the CP, would ride over every night with his guitar from the CP in the light truck that brought the lieutenant to inspect the posts. The lieutenant always made a beeline for the kitchen. Andy did most of his eating then. The cooks would always feed him if he was with the lieutenant. Stark would always feed anybody anytime. Then while Lt Culpepper was off on foot with Old Ike and the corporal on duty, checking the posts, they would climb to the top of the embankment with the guitars where they could catch the breeze off Pearl Channel that helped keep the mosquitoes down, for an hour, just the three of them, and the guitars, or maybe just two of them, if either Prew or Friday happened to be on post.

Prew's post was along the top of the embankment, two hundred yards down the other way, toward the Main Gate. He would roll up out of three or four hours sleep and back into the wadded blankets to the accompaniment of a hand shaking his foot through the mosquito bar, his mind rising slowly-dreamlike like a rubber ball under the water and then popping up out of the surface, into full alerted wakefulness to find Old Ike or The Chief cursing him monotonously in tempo to the shaking foot.

"Wake up. Wake up goddam it Prewitt. Wake up. Come on wake up. Your relief is on wake up."

"Okay, I'm awake," huskily sleepily. "Let go my goddam foot I'm awake."

"You sure you're awake?" still shaking. "Come on get up."

"Let go my foot. I'm awake, I tell you," sitting up to prove it and bumping his head mellowly against the canted drumhead of the pup-tent wall, trying to rub the novocaine of sleep out of his paralyzed face muscles. Then fighting his way out of the blankets and mosquito bar carrying the shoes rolled up in his pants that had been his pillow and crawling out bare-assed so he could stand up to put them on, squeezing past the tent pole trying not to wake Friday who was on the third re-lief, but always unable to keep from half-waking him, as Friday was al-ways unable to keep from half-waking him when he went on post. Then standing barefooted in the thick dust of the clearing, the mosqui-toes shrilling triumphantly over this new bonanza of bare rump while he hurried struggling into the pants and socks and shoes to save himself as many stabbings as he could, and reaching back inside the clutter for the wool OD shirt that felt thick prickly warm in the chilliness of night, putting it on gratefully over the T shirt he would not take off but maybe once during the whole two weeks. Protected now, he could take more time with the hook-and-lace intricacies of the leggins in the darkness. Then the web rifle belt to coil turgid pythonlike around the waist, and working the rifle out under the mosquito bar from among the blankets where it was protected from the dust and dew, somewhat protected anyway, then the helmet lying on the ground outside and damp-rusty with the dew, and stumbling heavy-footed under full equip-ment, irritably half-sleepily across the root-webbed moondappled clear-ing under the always faintly sighing branches toward the light of the Coleman lantern in the cook tent showing dimly dull brown through the canvas.

And in the cook tent, the relief huddling silently gratefully around the gasoline field stove that was always warm for them by Stark's order, drinking the scalding coffee with its coconut flavor of canned milk as if gulping spiritual inspiration, and munching between gulps on the Stark Specials of hot fried Spam and toasted cheese that the accusing cook (who held them, not Stark, responsible for his loss of sleep) fixed grudgingly for them, and that were as different to the belly from the cold Spam and cheese on untoasted bread of normal mess sergeants, as hot coffee was from cold.

The can of milk with its top sliced open by a cleaver butt. The thick white, dripping out past the congealed yellow of past pourings that had almost sealed the gash, into his canteen cup. A dipper of the rainbow-oil-spotted coffee out of the kettle black-waterfalling in on top of it. And then cupping the whole steamheat of it in his hands like a private hearth, sucking the coffee out gratefully without touching his lips to the blistering cup edge, and then one of the good greasy hot fried meat-cheese toasted sandwiches and standing huddled dumbly like about-to-be-slaughtered sheep with the others around the stove, while The Chief looked at them blandly sympathetically.

"Lets hurry it up now. Them men on post is waitin to come in. Two hours from now you guys be waitin to come in, and bitchin like hell if you relief's a minute late, so get a move on now and lets get it over with."

And then filling the cup one more time to carry with him and an extra sandwich, wrapping it in the waxed paper Stark insisted the cooks leave out for them (which normal mess sergeants also never furnished), buttoning it down in the pocket of the OD shirt warm against the chest, to leave the disgusted sleepy cook who believed fervently that they were being coddled, The Chief staying sensibly in the kitchen with the coffee, to climb the steep path behind the cook tent to the top of the embankment.

Maybe a little of the Re-enlistment Blues also came out of that.

And he would stand, after the relief was made, and from the suspended animation that is guard duty in the field at night he would watch the headlights passing on the highway beyond the fence to turn in at the brightly lighted Main Gate to the north, slow for the Air Corps' guards inspection, and then move off toward the concentration of cloud-reflected light that was Hickam Field, a mile to the west inside. And he would watch them then, feeling the sleepiness run down out of him like water, with the rapt absorption of a cougar or a deer or bear standing on a mountainside at night studying with wonder the brilliant moving trains that brought the hunters for the opening of the season without realizing their significance, him watching, not as a man, but as an unseparated part of nature and the intuitive night itself, as if two hours alone in the silence of it had finally driven him, forced him, back, out of himself and into the great awareness he had convinced himself he did not believe in any more.

And he could see then, at those times momentarily, how the deer and other game might also love the hunters who would kill them, just as he could see then that the hunters loved the game they tried so hard to kill, far more than any SPCA humane society would ever love it. And he would not, if he could, have had it any other way. Because he was a soldier, and because he could see it all then, in the easily shattered crystal clarity of the thin glass goblet of the silence that is guard duty in the field at night the last half hour before you are relieved.

Maybe the Re-enlistment Blues also came out of that.

He heard his relief, before he saw him, coming down the top of the embankment. Then Readall Treadwell hove into view, following his own footfalls into life, looking like a walking Woolworth's under full equipment and slapping at mosquitoes.

"Friday said to tell you he be down along the bob wire to the south," Readall Treadwell said.

"What the hells he doin way down there?"

"How the hell should I know? I'm just tellin you what he tole me."

"Okay," he grinned. He cleared his throat. He always cleared his throat. After two hours on post he always felt his vocal cords might not work. "I must of woke him up when I came on," he said.

"Yeah? Too goddam bad. Has the goddam lieutenant been around yet?"

"Nope, not yet." He would get Friday and they would get the guitar and come up and wait for Andy.

"Then I'll catch him sure," Readall Treadwell said bitterly. "That son of a bitch never comes around after eleven. No sleep again tonight."

"Yeah? Too goddam bad," Prew grinned. "You can always go down and talk to one of the other posts and sneak a cigarette."

"Piss on that noise," Readall Treadwell said. "Sleep is what I need. And sleep is what I never get. You tell Big Chief to send a man around when he sees the truck," Reedy called after him, "if he wants this post to be awake."

Chief Choate was lying placidly on his back in his puptent among the messy blankets, his bulk seeming to bulge the sides, reading a comic book inside his mosquito bar by the light of a candle stuck to his helmet. The Chief bunked by himself, there was hardly room for Choate, let alone a partner, in a regulation shelter tent; and when he went in the field, which was seldom, he packed two shelterhalves instead of one, ever since the time when Leva the supply clerk had had to bunk with him once.

"Reedy said to tell you to send a man around if the lootenant comes."

"This aint my relief," the Chief protested. "I aint on duty."

"I'm only tellin you what I was told to tell you."

"That lazy son of a bitch," the Chief said mildly, letting the book fall open like a postage stamp upon his chest. He stretched. "Build a fahr under him and he would holler for somebody to come put it out. Okay," he said, "I'll fix it," and went back absorbedly into the adventures of Dick Tracy.

Friday was a full hundred and fifty yards down along the big loose curve of the double apron, through the stumbling root-tripping darkness. He was talking across the wire to the Air Corps night sentry from the Field junk yard across the road. Down here, where the wire cut back sharply from the gravel road to the flank that rested on one of the brackish ponds that became the swamp below where the mosquitoes bred, they were worse than fierce. They were fierce back at the bivouac.

"What the hell are you doing way off down here?" Prew said as he came up, slapping at the whirling spinning cutting knives that hovered thirstily around his ears.

"Me and this guy arguing the Army," Friday grinned.

"Well you dont have to stand in this goddamned swamp to do it, do you? God damn these mosquitoes!" They hung in kaleidoscope-shifting phantom clouds, frenzied buzzsaws never quite in his ears, wheeling and darting and as untouchable as fighting Indians on horseback.

"He got to stay close. His post is right over there," Friday nodded at the road. He grinned. "He says the Air Corps is the worst and I claim the Infantry's the worst. What do you think?"

"They none of them worth a damn," Prew said, slapping at mosquitoes. "You ask me."

"You dont mean that!" the Air Corps man said in a shocked, startled voice.

"I dont?" Prew said, startled himself. "Why dont I?"

"I was ony kidding," Friday explained.

"Because—" the Air Corps man began.

"This is my buddy Prewitt," Friday grinned at him, "that I was telling you about."

"Oh," the Air Corps man said. "Thats different. I didnt know."

"You dont want to pay any attention to what he says," Friday grinned. "He's a thirdy year man in the Infantry. He loves it. He can tell you all you want to know about it."

"Swell," the Air Corps man said eagerly; he stepped up and put his hand formally across the fence. "Sure glad to know you, Prewitt. My name is Slade."

"All he wants to know about what?" Prew said, taking the hand.

"He wants to transfer to the Infantry," Friday said.

"To the Infantry!"

"Yeah. To the Compny. Our Compny."

"Not our Compny! What the hell for?"

"What for!" the Air Corps man Slade said excitedly. "Because I joined the Army to be a soldier, not a goddam gardener, thats why."

Prew looked at him closer. "Most the guys I know are trying to get into the Air Corps."

"Well, if they do they'll sure regret it," Slade said, waving indifferently at the swooping hordes around his head. "Unless they like being gardeners, that is."

"Gardeners?" Prew said. "I thought everybody in the Air Corps went to a School."

413

"Ha," Slade said. "Sure. Join the Air Corps and learn a trade. Thats what my dad thought."

"Your dad," Prew said.

"Yes, when he got me to enlist in the Air Corps."

"Oh," Prew said.

"If I'd had any sense I'd have enlisted in the Infantry right then, like I wanted to do in the first place."

"I told him you'd know how," Friday said.

"How what?"

"How to go about transferring to the Compny."

"Oh," Prew said. "Sure. All you have to do is go up to Schofield and see the Compny Commander after we get back in garrison and——"

"In garrison," Slade said enthusiastically. "Thats a good phrase, you know it? That sounds like soldiering."

"Yeah?" Prew said. "It does? Well, you see the CC and get his permission to put in for transfer to his compny and then you see your First Sergeant and give him the letter from the CC and put in for it. Thats all."

"Is that all there is to it?" Slade said. "I thought it would be hard. You know what I mean, complicated."

"Me too," Friday said.

"Hell," Slade said. "If I had known it was that easy, I'd have done it before now."

"What'd they do?" Prew said, "screw you out of your rating?"

"Ahh," Slade said disgustedly. "They're nothing but a bunch of goddam civilians in uniforms. Why, hell, when I got out of recruit drill and they gave me my classification interview I——"

"Your what?" Prew said.

"My classification interview," Slade said, "I put in for armament school so I could be a gunner. So what do *they* do? They send me to clerical school at Wheeler Field and as soon as I graduate they put me in a regular goddam office. Desks, filing cabinets, and all." He looked at them indignantly.

"Oh," Prew said. "I see. And they cut you out of the rating that went with it, is that it?"

"Rating hell," Slade said with outrage. "I didnt stay long enough to get any rating. I quit and went on the guard. Hell, I could have stayed at home in Illinois and worked in a goddam office, or mowed yards. Without having to enlist in the Army and come to Wahoo to do it."

"But how come you to pick the Infantry?" Prew said. "From what I hear, most guys in the Air Corps dont think so much of us Infantry."

"I've always liked the Infantry," Slade said eagerly. "In the Infantry they're soldiers, not goddam civilians in uniform. They have to soldier in the Infantry."

"The Infantry's all right," Prew said quickly. "If you like it."

"Thats what I mean," Slade said enthusiastically. "The Infantry's the backbone of the Army. The Air Corps, the Artillery, the Engineers —all they are for is to assist the Infantry. Because, in the final analysis, its the Infantry that has to take the ground and hold it."

"Thats right," Prew said.

"They have to be soldiers in the Infantry," Slade told them. "The Infantry hikes and fights all day, and then goes out and drinks and dances with the women all night, and then hikes and fights all day the next day."

"Sure," Friday said happily. "Thats a man's life."

Prew moved his head. "Where'd you learn all this anyway?" A mosquito trapped itself inside his ear and he smashed it and dug it out.

"I dont know," Slade said. "Read it somewhere I guess. I use to read a lot when I was younger, in high school. But what the hell good does reading do you?" he demanded angrily. "The thing is to live, act, do. You read all your life and what have you got?"

"I dont know," Prew said. "What?"

"Nothing," Slade said. "Thats what. Not a damn thing. I envy you fellows. I've been watching you ever since you first moved in here and started putting up this barbed wire. You guys are experts at it." He took hold of one of the long pickets and shook it vigorously. He kicked one of the short pickets. "I wish I could handle barbed wire as expertly as you fellows do."

"There is an art to it," Prew said.

"Sure there is. I watched you putting it up. I wish I could do it."

"It takes practice," Prew said.

"Sure it does. You know, I've been wanting to come over and talk to you fellows ever since you first moved in. You have a swell camp over here, and you all have such a good time together. Always laughing and singing. You work hard and you play hard, thats the kind of an outfit for a man to be in. I didnt know it was you two," he nodded at Friday, "until he told me, that play those guitars. It sounds really fine from over here at night on the road. Do you always take them out in the field with you like that?"

"Sure," Prew said. "When we can."

"Guy never hears anything like that at Hickam," Slade said.

"We're going to play some tonight," Prew said, "as it happens. When our buddy gets here from the CP. How would you like to come over and listen?"

"Hey, you really mean it?" Slade said eagerly. "I wasnt hinting or anything like that. I didnt even expect I'd get to come over."

"We'd be glad to have you," Prew said.

"Hey, I'd love it," Slade said. "But I'm on post now. Wont be off for a half hour yet."

"Well, I guess we could wait on you," Prew said. "If you really want to come over, that is."

"Hey, that would be fine," Slade said. "Would you really do that?"

Prew moved his head. "Sure. Dont see why not. If you really like that kind of music. It wouldnt discommode us none to have you. We're not very good," he said, "but if you want——"

"I think you're terrific," Slade said.

"Hey, Slade!" Friday interrupted. "Theres a car coming down your road over there!"

Slade whirled. "That will be Sergeant Follette," he said. "This makes the third time he's been around since I came on."

"Maybe its our truck," Prew said.

"No it aint," Friday said. "Already passed our turnoff."

"Its Follette all right," Slade said. "He has been trying to hang something on me for a couple months now and get me kicked off the guard and back to mowing grass."

"He got it in for you?" Prew said.

"Yeah," Slade said. "He dont like me because I told him he was a pompous ass once and he had to look it up in the dictionary."

"You better get back over there then," Prew said.

"Yeah," Slade said. "Dont I know it. I'll see you fellows in a half an hour, okay?"

"Yeah."

"You wont forget it now?"

"No."

"You better get back over there," Friday said nervously, watching the steadily advancing headlights.

"Yeah," Slade grinned. He turned and started to run across to the road where the headlights were steadily creeping up past his margin of safety. Then he stopped and turned back.

"You know, you guys dont know what it means to have gotten to talk to you fellows. I dont get to talk to fellows like you guys often that understand how a fellow feels. They dont have real comradeship in the Air Corps, not like you fellows in the Infantry, not the old all-for-one and one-for-all. They're not comrades-in-arms.—You'll really be here in half an hour, wont you?" he said embarrassedly.

"Hell yes," Prew said. "We said we would. For Christ's sake get the hell back over there."

"Thanks," Slade said. "Gee, thanks. Thanks a lot, Prewitt." He turned and sprinted for the road, holding down his flapping holster and the bouncing club.

Prew took hold of a rusty spiral picket and watched him go, fading into invisibility in the darkness, and both of them waited tensely. Then they heard the shouted challenge and saw him again in the light of the headlights that had stopped moving now.

"Whew," Friday said. "I dint think he was goin to make it."

"Neither did I." He let go of the picket and looked at the rust marks on his hand, then wiped them on his pants. "Son of a bitch is a goddam fool taking chances like that."

"He dint much seem to care," Friday said. "He's a pretty smart fella, you know it. He sure thinks a lot of the Infantry."

"Well? the Infantry's a pretty goddamned good outfit, aint it? Compared to the others."

"Sure it is," Friday said. "The Infantry hikes all day, and drinks and lays up with the snatch all night, and then hikes all day the next day. I'm glad I'm in the Infantry and not in no goddam Air Corps." He slapped at a mosquito.

"Come on," Prew said irritably. "Lets get out of here. These goddam things will eat us up alive."

"Aint we going to wait for him?"

"Wait in the goddam kitchen tent, and come back for him. I aint going to stand out here no goddam half hour, thats sure."

"Okay," Friday said, "okay."

The Coleman lantern was still burning in the kitchen tent, but the tent was empty except for the cook and the corporal who had relieved The Chief. The cook was asleep on the table. The corporal was half asleep in the one camp chair. His head jerked up when they came in.

"What is it?" he said. "Is the lootenant— Oh," he said. "Its you guys. What the hell are you doing up? Oh," he said, seeing the guitar. "Might know," he said. His head dropped back down, in slow stages. His eyes shut.

The cook on the table sat up irritably. "What the hell do you guys want? This aint no goddam all night restaurant. You suppose to eat when you go on post or when you come off. And thats all."

"We dont want to eat," Prew said.

"You woke me up," the cook said.

"But we'll take a cup of coffee?" Prew said.

"Like hell," the cook said indignantly. "How you expect me to get any sleep, guys comin in all hours. You aint got no business in here unless you getting ready to go on post."

"A cup of coffee aint going to bother you any," Prew said.

"Like hell," the cook said angrily. "Its already bothered me. Its woke me up. I aint no goddam——"

The corporal's head came up again, and his eyes opened on nothing. Then he looked at the cook. "Shut up, will you?" he said, "for god sake? Its you thats makin all the noise. Leave them have a cup of coffee, long as they be quiet."

"A lot you know," the cook said indignantly. "Oh, balls," he said, and stretched back out.

"Go ahead and get your coffee," the corporal said. "But be quiet." His head dropped in slow stages and his eyes shut, on nothing. He settled himself blissfully.

The coffee was still hot and they stood against the warm stove while they drank it.

"We better get there early," Friday whispered nervously. "He come back and we aint there he liable to think we ditched him."

"Okay," Prew whispered luxuriously, "pretty soon," not wanting to think about the stumbling back down along the wire through the dark without a flash and the slapping at the clouds of mosquitoes that would be rising from the grass at every step.

They sipped at the coffee in the breathing silence.

"We better go soon," Friday whispered nervously.

Prew set his cup down. "Goddam it, come on then," he whispered. "Lets get it over with."

"Man," Friday said happily when they were outside, "we'll show him some real git-tar playin, man, when ole Andy comes over with the truck. We'll show him Infantry."

"Yeah," Prew said, stumbling along. "God damn this hole."

Slade was already waiting for them at the wire.

"I thought you werent going to come back. I was about ready to give it up and go home."

"Listen," Prew said, "when we tell a guy we'll do a thing, by god we do it. And he can count on it. We dont welch."

Slade turned his flashlight on at their feet. "Sure," he grinned. "I knew that too. Its just that I've been around these pricks in the Air Corps too long, is all."

"You better turn your light off," Friday said. "We're supposed to stay blacked out on this problem."

"Oh," Slade said quickly. "Sure." He shut it off. "You fellows must think I'm awful green. How do I get across this fence?"

"Have to go back up," Prew said, "and come through the gap we left for our trucks."

"Okay," Slade grinned. "I'll walk it up and come back down by myself. Theres no need for you fellows to have to walk clear up there just for me. You're doing enough for me the way it is."

"We got to go back ourselves anyway," Friday said quickly, waving his hand uselessly around his ears again.

"The kitchen's back up that way," Prew explained, as they started back up toward the bivouac, them on one side, Slade on the other, stumbling over roots and bumping into branches.

"Dont these mosquitoes bother you none?" Friday said.

"Naw," Slade said. He hesitated. "I almost kind of like them, in a way."

"Like them!" Friday said.

"Yes," Slade said embarrassedly. "Not exactly like them, you know, but they make me feel like I'm really doing something. They make this horseshit more like real soldiering. You can stand out here and imagine you're really soldiering. Of course they're not anything, not really, not compared to what you guys have to put up with, I bet."

"I dont see that," Friday said. He thought a moment. "You dont mean you really like to get bit up like this? You dint volunteer for this post, did you?"

"Oh, for Christ's sake, Friday," Prew said irritably.

"I guess it does sound kind of crazy," Slade said embarrassedly. "No, I didnt volunteer for it. I was on the Main Gate, but Follette got me kicked off and put down here."

"These here is worse than anything I ever seen in the Infantry," Friday said, slapping.

"Oh, I dont know," Prew said, slapping. "I've had to soldier in spots a hell of a lot worse than this. You take winter maneuvers at Myer now. Say," he said, "how'd you like to have a cup of coffee, Slade? Before we go up the embankment?"

"Swell," Slade said eagerly. "You guys even have coffee at nights, hunh? out in the field. We dont even have coffee at night, and we got a permanent guardhouse."

"No coffee!" Friday said. "Why, man, thats awful. Night guards got to have coffee."

"Sure they do," Slade said. "Oh, we got a Silex coffee-pot in the dayroom, and we could make it ourselves. But half the time they run us off at night and wont let us use it. Thats the Air Corps for you."

"Would you like to have a sandwich, too?" Prew said.

"A sandwich?" Friday said. "Say, listen, Prew."

"You dont mean you have sandwiches too, whenever you want them?" Slade said. "Christ, you guys live like kings."

"Hell," Prew said. "What good is coffee without hot sandwiches?"

"You mean they're hot, too?" Slade said.

"But, listen, Prew," Friday said.

"Sure," Prew said. "We got a real mess sergeant in this outfit."

"You must have," Slade said.

"He knows how to take care of his men," Prew said, "when they got to pull guard at night. You dont mind it being rugged, you got a guy like that to look after you."

419

"But, Prew," Friday said. "Listen, Prew."

"Come on," Prew said. "We almost there."

At the truck gap through the wire Slade came inside, and they cut back straight for the kitchen tent, Prew leading. It was exactly the same inside as when they had left it. The cook sat up as they came in.

"Now what?" he cried. "Jesus Christ. This aint no pleasure resort. Who the hell is that guy?"

"A friend of ours from the Air Corps," Prew said, coming on inside. "He'd like to have a cup of coffee."

Friday stopped just inside the flap and backed against the tautness of the wall, trying to be as inconspicuous as possible.

"A cup of coffee, hunh?" the cook said. "What does he think this is, the Red Cross?" he said.

"How about a sandwich, cookie?" Prew said doggedly.

"A *sand*wich!" the cook said. "A SANDwich!"

"Sure," Prew said doggedly. "To go with our coffee."

"Mother of God," the cook said. "A sandwich."

"You got the meat and stuff already all laid out there," Prew said. "We fix it ourself and save you work."

"Oh, no," the cook said. "No, sir. Not on your goddam life. To hell with that noise. Them rations is for the Third Relief."

"Friday's on the Third Relief," Prew said.

The corporal sat up in his chair and looked at all of them disgustedly. "What the hell is this? Grand Central Station? I aint going to get no goddam rest in here. I might as well go inspect my goddam posts." He elbowed his way out bitterly past Friday and went out through the flap.

"I aint running no mess hall for the whole of Hickam Field, Prewitt," the cook said. "My god."

"You got plenty," Prew said doggedly.

"Like hell," the cook said. "And I give you guys a sandwich and every son of a bitch and his brother will be wandering in here all hours of the goddam night for sandwiches. I wont never get no sleep."

"You're off all day tomorrow," Prew said doggedly. "You can sleep then. All day. We'll be on post."

"I'm goin to town tomorrow."

"What the hell has got into you all of a sudden, cookie?" Prew said. "You never act like this before."

"I didnt?" the cook said blankly.

"Why hell no. What kind of a impression you think you making on the Air Corps? acting like this all of a sudden. And here I been telling what a fine kitchen force we got."

"Like hell," the cook said, recovering. "I say no sandwiches. And thats all. You got nerve, coming in here like a goddamned officer and demanding sandwiches. And just for the record, no coffee neither, see? You just had coffee."

"What you want to get temperamental for all of a sudden?" Prew said puzzledly. "You never turned us down before."

Friday gasped, then coughed.

"Yeah?" the cook jeered, not taken in this time. "No sandwiches."

"If they want sandwiches," a voice like the clap of doom said thickly from the flap behind them, *"give them sandwiches."*

As one man the three of them turned, even Friday turned, to see what the cook was already staring at so unbelievingly.

Maylon Stark stood just inside the flap like the hero of the melodrama come on stage at the last possible second of the last scene of the last act, to save the situation. The deepest purple crescents under his eyes were puffy with sleep, and his face was fat with puffiness. His voice was thick with it and his uniform looked very slept in. Dangling from his right hand was a bottle.

"Why hello, Maylon," the cook smiled apprehensively. "What are you doing up at this hour?"

"As long as I run this goddam Mess," Stark said thickly to no one, "there will be sandwiches and coffee for night guahds, any time they want it."

"And I agree with you, Maylon," the cook said stoutly. "One hundred percent. But these guys aint goin on post nor comin off, they just wanderin around, when they ought to be in bed asleep. One of them aint even from the Compny, he's from Hickam Field. Howm I ever gonna get any sleep, I got to feed the whole of Hickam Field."

"You aint supposed to sleep," Stark said thickly. He looked around solemnly and then marched stolidly sedately as a row of fenceposts to the vacant camp chair and sat down heavily, staring at nothing. A strong smell of raw whiskey wafted through the tent.

"You aint supposed to sleep, and you aint going to sleep. You get all day off tomorrow to sleep, because you stayin up all night tonight. You want to work tomorrow, you can sleep now."

He turned his head and stared grimly at the cook. The cook did not say anything.

"Well?" Stark said solemnly. "What do you say, cookie? You want to sleep. Go on. Turn in. I'll stay up with this the rest of the night. And you can go on shift tomorrow."

"I dint say that, Maylon," the cook explained. "All I said was——"

"Then shut up," Stark said.

"Okay, Maylon. I was ony——"

"I said SHUT UP."

He turned and looked at Prew without seeing him. He appeared to be looking through him at the wall behind him. "You men want sandwiches, you get sandwiches. Men got to eat," he said. "They kin kill each other off all day long, but the ones that left still got to eat. Thats one thing a man can always count on," he said. "As long as they is one man left, he got to eat," he said thickly.

Nobody said anything.

"Fix these men some sandwiches, you son of a bitch," Stark said to the wall behind Prewitt.

"Okay, Maylon," the cook said. "Whatever you say."

"Then move, you son of a bitch," Stark said thickly.

"We can fix them, Maylon," Prew said soothingly. "He dont need to do it."

"He's a greaseball," Stark said to nobody. "He gets paid to fix sandwiches. You want him to fix you sandwiches, he'll fix you sandwiches."

"Sure," the cook said. "I dont mind fixing them."

"Shut up, you son of a bitch," Stark said.

"I just as soon do it myself," Prew said uneasily. "We get us a sandwich and cup a hot coffee and take them up on the embankment with us where we wont bother nobody. Then he can get some sleep."

"Fuck his sleep," Stark said. "This is the mess tent. You want to eat in the mess tent, you eat in the mess tent. He say anything I kill the son of a bitch. Need some good cooks for change anyways."

"We really rather take them up there," Prew said uneasily.

"Okay," Stark said. "Going to play the git-tar, hunh?" he said woodenly.

"Yeah," Prew said, from the stove, putting the meat on.

"Okay," Stark said thickly. "Go on back to sleep, you worthless basrad."

"I aint sleepy, Maylon," the cook said.

"I *said go back to sleep*," the doom crack voice said.

"Okay," the cook said. He lay back down on his table as silently and unobtrusively as possible. Stark did not look at him. He did not look at any of them. He raised his right hand with the bottle in it and unscrewed the cap with his left hand and took a long drink and screwed the cap back and let his arm fall back down dangling outside the chair arm. He did not say another word.

When Prew had them done he handed them around and they poured their coffee nervously in the screaming unbreakable silence that rose like mist from Stark. Then they tiptoed out gladly, like evacuees leaving the ominous stillness before a hurricane that is more frightening than any storm. Prew turned back at the flap to thank him. Stark did not move or look around.

"Men got to eat," he said gravely, heavily, like an unbeliever trying to convince himself by taking an oath in church.

From the top of the embankment Hickam Field made a glow on the night sky. They were having night flying training every night and the hangars were lit up like empty theaters. Red and blue and green lights winked high overhead from the flying planes, and from around the hive that was the tower. Now and then a searchlight fingered the bellies of the clouds.

A hundred yards inside the road, the B 18s, ultimate and ungrateful purpose of all this regulated life that had been rolled out to give the problem realisticness, squatted like sullen birds in the nest of their revetments, looking like they resented being used as decoys for reality. Far down to the left they could just barely pick out Slade's relief moving on the road.

"What do you think of our mess sergeant?" Prew said, chewing and swallowing ravenously in the clear sharp still air. "I told you he was a good man."

"He wasnt quite what I expected," Slade said, cautiously.

"He runs that kitchen like a dictator," Prew said.

"I could see that," Slade said.

"Course, he had a couple drinks tonight," Prew said.

"He didnt seem very happy," Slade said charily.

"Happy?" Prew said. "He's the happiest man I know."

"How about *Thousand Mile Blues*?" Friday said, tuning the guitar. "While we wait for Andy."

"I'll buy that," Slade said eagerly and relievedly. "I'm a blues man."

"Then Andy's your boy," Friday said. "He'll be here soon."

The truck turned off its lights as soon as it turned in off the road, and then they could hear the low gear grinding in through the gap. A little cluster of lights formed around a central blackness, and all moved off bobbing toward the kitchen.

"I thought you said it was a blackout," Slade said.

"Thats the lieutenant," Prew said.

"Oh," Slade said.

One of the lights came away from the tent, looking tiny and alone now by itself, and started up the path. It became Andy, carrying the other guitar.

"Was Stark in the kitchen?" Prew said.

"Yeah," Andy said.

"Did he have a bottle?"

"Hell no. At least it wasnt showing. He was sound asleep. At least his eyes was shut."

"He aint so drunk," Prew said.

"Neither am I," Andy said. "But look what I got." He opened his shirt and pulled a bottle out of it.

"Hey," Friday said. "Where'd you get it?"

"Oh, I got angles," Andy said.

423

"Come on," Prew said. "Where'd you get it?"

"I dint get it," Andy grinned. "The Warden got hold of it someplace. I bought it off of him. That sumbitch could find whiskey on a desert island. He came over with them in the truck, drunkern hell."

"Dint the lieutenant say anything?"

"Hell, you know the lootenant never says nothing to The Warden. About nothing."

"Who's The Warden," Slade said.

"The first sergeant," Prew said. "Name's Warden." He introduced Slade to Andy and appropriated the bottle for the Air Corps man.

"Thats them now," Andy said, pointing to the lights coming from the tent and starting off to make the rounds of the posts. "Theres only three. I guess The Warden aint with them."

"Well, we got at least an hour yet," Prew said.

"Gimme the pitch," Andy said to Friday.

"Gimme the bottle," Prew said to Andy. "Here, Slade. You want a nuther drink?"

"Christ," Slade said happily. "Christ. You fellers really have the life."

"You think so?" Prew said. "It aint so bad, is it?

"I wonder what The Warden come over for," he said.

Chapter 31

Milt Warden did not exactly know just what he was doing over here himself. He had left the CP on drunken impulse with the first outgoing vehicle, because he did not like the CP and because he was tired of looking at Capt Holmes's increasingly less aristocratic and more moonlike face. And he had found himself in this godforsaken mosquito infested hole with young Lt Culpepper. Looking at Lt Culpepper, Milt Warden could not make up his mind which was worse.

Back at the CP he had felt for some time that Capt Holmes had been secretly laughing at him, as if Holmes knew some terribly amusing private joke on him. Milt Warden had not wanted to fall in love with Capt Holmes's wife, all he had meant to do was to get even with Capt Holmes for being a goddamned officer. The other part had slipped up on him, and recently he had acquired a ridiculous but increasingly insistent tendency to hold Capt Holmes personally responsible. If the son of a bitch had only taken care of his own wife like any decent man ought to, none of this would ever happened. And Milt

Warden, instead of being deeply in love, would still be able to enjoy life.

Milt Warden had seen Karen Holmes twice more since Payday. The first time they spent the night in the Moana again. The second time they had spent the night in the Alexander Young downtown, on the theory that it was best to keep moving around. Both times had ended in a big argument over what they were going to decide to do about it. Both of them agreed they could not go on like this. Both of them agreed they could not stop being in love. Finally, Karen advanced the solution that Milt should take one of the extension courses that had come into prominence with the peacetime draft and become an officer.

If he was an officer, she said, he would automatically be shipped back to the States to a new command where none of the EM knew him, and she could follow. If he was an officer, she could divorce Holmes and marry him and let Holmes have his heir. But it was a cinch she could not do that as long as he was an EM, especially an EM in her husband's company. Milt would, Karen thought, make a truly fine and remarkable officer.

Milt Warden was not only deeply shocked, he was humiliated. It was not that he was not willing to do anything within reason, but he felt that this was asking too much. And so, for the seventh time, he had made up his mind not to see her any more. That was one of the reasons he was drunk.

"Lets eat," Lt Culpepper commanded, as Pfc Russell turned off the ignition, and switched on his flash. This was the signal for the others to switch on their flashes. "What a miserable fucking place to have to inspect posts in," Lt Culpepper said bitterly. "You'd think it was about time we got in some junior officers, what with this expansion."

Warden climbed out, grinning at him savagely. Lt Culpepper looked the other way and started toward the kitchen tent. He did not know what the hell the 1st/Sgt wanted to come over here for anyway. He did not like to be around 1st/Sgt Warden, it made him uncomfortable. Sometimes he had an awkward suspicion that Milton Anthony Warden was mad. He did not seem to give a damn for anything.

Warden waited until Lt Culpepper and Anderson had gone on, and grabbed Pfc Weary Russell by the arm and pulled him back.

"Listen, you son of a bitch," he whispered fiercely. "If I dont show up to go back on the truck with you bastards, you are to come back here and pick me up at two o'clock, see?"

"But Jesus Christ, Top!" protested Weary Russell, picturing a night of wakefulness sitting in his tent with his watch.

"No back talk," Warden said. "You heard me."

"What the hell're you going to do over here?" Weary Russell said.

Warden grinned at him slyly with his eyebrows.

"Theres no women nor nothing," Weary said.

Warden merely grinned at him.

"Well, at least gimme a drink then," Weary conceded.

Warden got the bottle out from under the seat where he had hidden it.

"I may be right here to ride back with you," he said as Weary drank. "This is just in case I aint, see? But if I aint, and you dont come back for me, I'll cut your fucking heart out, see?" He clamped a big hand down on Russell's arm for punctuation.

"Ouch! Okay," said Weary Russell wearily. "I said okay, dint I? Heres your bottle."

"Okay," Warden grinned. "Dont forget, hear? Now take off," he said, and slapped him hard on the rump to start him. He waited till Russell was out of sight, before he hid the bottle between the roots of a keawe tree and followed.

Stark was sitting in the camp chair when he and Russell came in through the flap. The cook was at the stove with the lieutenant fixing sandwiches for them. Stark did not get up and offer the seat to the lieutenant.

"Hello," Warden grinned at him ferociously.

"Hello," Stark said dully. He did not say another word all the time they were there. He did not look at anybody and he did not move his arms from where they dangled over the wood arms of the chair.

Andy left first, carrying his guitar in one hand and a second sandwich in the other. Then the lieutenant left with Russell and the corporal to inspect the posts. Warden stayed in the tent. The cook lay back down on the table.

"Hey, you," Stark said.

"Who, me?" the cook said, sitting up.

"Yas, you," Stark said. "Who the hell you think I mean?"

"Now what?" the cook said. "What now?"

Stark jerked his head. "Get out," he said. "Take off. You make me sick lookin at you."

"Well, where'll I go?" the cook said.

"Go to bed and sleep," Stark said. "You look half dead. I cant stand to look at you. I'll run the rest of this shift. I'd ruther do that than have to look at you."

"But what about my day off tomorrow?" the cook said.

"You'll get your goddam day off," Stark said. "You lazy bastard. Get the fuck out."

"Okay," the cook said, trying to sound unhappy. "If you say so, Maylon." He was out and gone before anybody could say another word.

"Whats the matter with you?" Warden said.

"Nothing," Stark said ominously. "Whats the matter with you?"

"You're one hell of a glutton for punishment," Warden said. "To stay up all night when you dont have to."

"Maybe I like it," Stark said. "Whats it to you?"

"You're drunk," Warden said.

"So're you," Stark said.

"Sure," Warden grinned savagely. "And about to get drunker. Wheres your goddam bottle?"

"Maybe I had a reason for gettin rid of him," Stark hinted darkly. He leaned back in the chair and pulled the bottle out from between a utensil chest and the tent wall, and tossed it up to Warden. "Wheres your bottle?" he said.

"Back at the CP," Warden lied. "Empty."

"Yeah?" Stark said broodingly. "Well have a drink of mine then."

"Thanks," Warden said. "I will."

"You're going to need it," Stark said. "I want to talk to you."

"Save it," Warden said, around the bottle. "I'm on vacation. And not in no mood to listen to greaseball complaints. You and your goddam kitchen like a couple dry hole old maids. I dont feel like talking official." He handed back the bottle.

"This aint official," Stark said ominously. "This is private. I hear you got yourself a new girl friend," he said.

Warden was on his way to the meatblock to sit down. He did not stop. He did not even pause. He went on and sat down casually, thinking it was just as if somebody had flipped on the dial of a radio. He could feel the old wide angle range tuning in his mind come on and begin to warm up and give off signals, but it was having a hard fight with the static of the red mist of outrage that had been in his brain all evening. He lit himself a cigarette, wondering abstractedly which would win. After he sat down and got himself all comfortably fixed and crossed his legs, he said, "Yeah? Where'd you hear that?"

Stark was still staring at him broodingly. "Oh," he said mellowly, "I got ways of findin things out."

"Yeah?" Warden said. "Well suppose you utilize them same ways to find out how to mind your own fucking business."

"Suppose I dont want to," Stark said. Without getting up he moved his right arm and tossed the bottle. Warden caught it.

"Suppose you have to," Warden said. He looked at the long brown bottle dubiously, then upended it and drank. Then he screwed the cap back on and tossed it distastefully. "How'd you find all this out," he said.

Without moving in the chair Stark raised his right arm languidly and caught the bottle. He let his arm fall dangling over the chair arm and let the bottle sit on the ground.

427

"Nem-mine how I found it out," Stark said. "Nem-mine that. The thing is I know it. The thing is its a wonner the whole damn post dont know it. I tole you once to watch out for that stuff or you would get burnt. I tole you all about it. I know all about that stuff, I had some of it at Bliss."

"Was it good?" Warden asked him thoughtfully.

"No," Stark said. "Yes. I dont know. Fack is, I dint know enough then to be able to judge. But that aint the point. The point is—" He stopped and shook his head. "I thought you was a smart man," he said.

Warden got up from the meatblock that was beside the chair and stepped around the chair and bent to get the bottle. There was a way to handle this. There was a way to handle everything. All you had to do was be careful. But then, you got so tired of always going around always being careful.

"I want to know how you found it out," he roared suddenly, with unexpected violence, almost in Stark's ear.

"I seen you down to the Alexander Young Hotel," Stark said placidly. "Lessn a week ago. Probly ten thousand other dog soljers from Schofield seen you too. You must be nuts."

"Probly," Warden grinned at him savagely. He stepped back with the bottle hanging from his hand, his left hand. "And just what the fuck do you propose to do about it? Or have you decided yet?"

"So!" Stark said. "You dont deny it, do you?"

"Why the hell should I? You seen me, dint you?"

Stark drew himself up drunkenly formally in the camp chair and stared at the other woodenly. "I done already got my mind made up. What to do about it. Nothing you can say will change me. Its useless to try."

"I aint tryin yet," Warden said.

"Wont do you any good," Stark said. "You might as well give up. If you cant take care of yourself, Firs Sarnt, somebody got to take care of it for you. And it looks like I'm elected.

"You aint leavin this heah tent tonight, Firs Sarnt," Stark said solemnly, folding his arms to pronounce the sentence, "until you promise me on your word of honor as a soljer you wont have nothin more to do with that slut."

"Haw!" Warden snorted. "My word of honor as a soljer, 'ey? Wont leave this tent, 'ey?"

"Aint you got no self respeck lef a tall?" Stark said. "Dont you respeck the organization yore servin in? Dont you respeck the un'form of yore country you wornd for so many yeahs? You ought to be ashamed. Yore a dis-grace to the chevrons on yore arm, Firs Sarnt."

"Piss on that," Warden snarled.

Stark shook his head. "Ats my last word. I got my mind made up. You aint leavin this tent till you promise. Ats my last word, Firs Sarnt."

Warden snorted. "Last word, 'ey? Threatening me, 'ey?"

"Don't you *know* what she *is?*" Stark hollered violently. He waved his arms. "Cant you *see* what she's *doin* to you? She's *terrible!*" he hollered, "she's *aw*ful. Oh, you dont know her like I do, Firs Sarnt. She's a rotten goddam whoor, she's worse than a whoor, she is— She's a goddam rich man's daughter of a degenerate, thats what she is. Why, she would—" He clamped his mouth shut and folded his arms. "But I wont let her," he said. "You'll promise like I said, Firs Sarnt, or else."

"Or else what?" Warden said.

"Take care," Stark said. "Dont trifle with me, Firs Sarnt. I know you backwards and forewards. Preem warned me about you, Firs Sarnt, before he left. But I know how to handle you. Theres only one way to handle men like you. And I know how to do it." He settled his folded arms into an even more final finality. "I'm waiting for you to promise," he said.

Warden was still looking at him thoughtfully. Stark was drunk, and tomorrow he would forget all about it. And tomorrow Milt Warden would also still be seeing the same triumphant face he had seen hanging on the stairway wall the time he hurt his hand.

"Promise!" he roared suddenly. "I'll give you promise, you son of a bitch. You cant talk about the woman I love like that!"

He stepped in happily, putting all of his weight behind it joyously, and hit Stark sitting with folded arms in the camp chair as hard as he could hit him.

The folded arms flailed out sideways as the chair went over backward, shooting Stark out onto the back of his neck on the ground between the meatblock and the utensil chest, already scrambling and kicking to get back up, almost before he hit the ground. He bounced back up like a rubber ball, hoisting himself with his hands on the meatblock and the chest and trying to disentangle his feet from the canvas of the chair, his mouth open roaring inarticulately.

He wrenched the cleaver out of the meatblock and advanced on Warden like a slow thunder storm, his mouth hanging wide open bellowing. Furious, senseless, outraged, his roars filled the tent like gas fills an airtight balloon.

Warden stepped back happily and threw the bottle still hanging from his left hand. Stark ducked without even batting his bulging eyes or closing his mouth, and came on. The bottle crashed and exploded into fragments against the side of the meatblock.

Warden skipped out through the flap and hit running, hearing the cleaver hit the tent wall behind him and tear through it with a sound like a zipper being yanked open. He ran on down the path, a full dead run in the darkness, until he hit a tree branch the height of his fore-head and felt his legs go right on running out from under him. Then he was flat on his back on the ground, trying to pull air into the empty paralyzed lungs. He could hear Stark bellowing and cursing and fumbling on the dark ground for his cleaver.

Warden crawled, like a rifleman working in under fire, back in under the bushes behind him off the path. Now you've done it, he told himself as soon as he could breathe again, now you've cooked it, the only man in the outfit who would even make a cook let alone a good mess sergeant. But he could not stop himself from laughing. He had looked so stupidly surprised, standing there, with the cleaver in his hand and bellowing like a castrated bull.

He lay in the bushes, trying to stifle his laughing, listening to Stark wandering vaguely up and down the paths looking for him, bellowing and cursing and smashing at the branches of trees with his cleaver. He sounded like Old Pete with his teeth out.

"No godam good," Stark bellowed to the darkness. "Worshn fuggin whoor. Shno fuggin good. Ruinm whole fuggin life. L show im. No godam good for nothin no more. Whersh ee at? Cant even get a hard on thout bein drung. Whert ee go? L kill im. L show im. Sombishes. Whersh ee?"

Warden listened to it fade away, silently shaking with the bottled laughter. What would the drunken bastard do if he had told him the truth? how it was Holmes in the first place who had given her the dose? Probly take his cleaver and go ramming over to the CP hunting for the Company Commander. Warden lay still and waited, shaking silently and uncontrollably with laughter, and trying to fight off the clouds of mosquitoes that were like packs of baying bloodhounds trying to get at his throat. In the Roman Army they required each dogface to perform his drill bearing a burden twice as heavy as in actual combat. They conquered the world. We ought to win at least that much.

Pretty soon Stark came back to the tent. But he had figured that. He could hear the tinkling of glass fragments as the mess sergeant cleaned up the mess, then the bang and rattle as the still cursing Stark threw it all meticulously into the GI trash can and came back out and started to look for him again, this time cunningly quiet.

From up on the top of the embankment he could hear them still beating on the guitars ringingly. They were playing blues, old ones one right after another. Saint Louis, Birmingham, Memphis, Truckdriver's, Sharecropper's, Hodcarrier's, 219, Route 66, L & N, Thousandmile. Friday Clark carrying the rhythm base and singing, Anderson roving and ranging up and down and around behind him like a tethered falcon.

The dam fools, he giggled fighting the mosquitoes, sit up there and let themselves be eaten up by mosquitoes when they could be in bed asleep. He started in to laugh again. Stark was still crashing around in the undergrowth.

No son of a bitching Texas gut robber was going to tell Milton Anthony Warden what woman he could go out with and what one he couldnt. If he wanted to go out with Karen Holmes, he was by Christ going to go out with her.

He lay happily, laughing, listening to Stark crashing and cursing, and hearing the beating guitars.

Chapter 32

"Listen to this one," Andy said.

"Hit it," Friday said, palming his strings dead.

They all stopped talking and casually, in this attentive silence that it was his right as an accomplished craftsman to demand, Andy ran through a chord progression in diminished minors that was the latest addition to the series he had been making up all evening.

It rose out of the box like a delicately intricate filigree, then ended falling off on a diminished ninth that seemed to hang, leaving the whole thing suspended weirdly melancholy, a single unit fading off into the upper air like a rising hydrogen balloon.

From under it, Andy stared at them indifferently, very boredly wooden-faced, sitting on his legs tucked under him in that way he had when he was playing. In the silence he ran through it again.

"Hey, man!" Friday said worshipfully, like the student manager talking to the football captain. "Where'd you drag that one up from?"

"Ahh," Andy said lazily. He pulled his mouth down. "Just stumbled onto it."

"Play it again," Prew said.

Andy played it again, the same way, looking at them bright-eyed but boredly wooden-faced, the same way. And they stopped talking again, as they had learned to always stop whatever they were doing and listen when Andy had been fiddling around and stumbled onto something, listening to this one now fading off the same way as before, seemingly still up in the air unfinished, so that they wanted to say *Is that all?* yet knowing that was all because this was more finished and complete and said all there was to say, than if it had been ended. He had been doing it all evening, cutting out to experiment and fiddle with something he had stumbled on to, then calling a halt while he played it to them if it satisfied him, or else if he was not satisfied cutting back in and picking it up from Friday, until now finally he had come up with this that was better than any of the others, which were all good, but could still not touch this now with its haunting tragedy that was so obviously tragedy that it became the mocking ironic moreheart-breaking travesty of its own heartbreak, so that now he could relax a little on his triumph.

"Who's got a cigarette?" Andy said boredly, laying the guitar aside. Friday made haste to hand the great man one.

"Man," Slade, the Air Corps boy, said. "Man, thats reet. You talk about blues, man, thats really blues."

Andy shrugged. "Gimme a drink." Prew handed him the bottle.

"Thats blues," Friday said. "You cant beat blues."

"Thats right," Prew said. "We got an idea for our own blues," he told Slade. "An Army blues called *The Re-enlistment Blues*. Theres *Truckdriver's Blues, Sharecropper's Blues, Bricklayer's Blues*. We'll make ours a soljer's blues."

"Hey," Slade said excitedly. "That sounds fine. Thats a swell idea. You ought to call it *Infantry Blues*. Christ, I envy you guys."

"Well, we aint done it yet," Prew said.

"But we're going to," Friday said.

"Hey, listen," Slade said eagerly. "Why dont you use what Andy just played for your blues? Thats what you ought to do. That would make a great theme for a blues."

"I dont know," Prew said. "We aint quite worked it all out yet."

"No, but listen," Slade said enthusiastically. "Could you do that?" he asked Andy eagerly. "You could make a blues out of that, couldnt you?"

"Oh, I reckon," Andy said. "I reckon I could do it."

"Here," Slade said excitedly, "have a drink." He handed him the bottle. "Make a blues out of it. Finish it up. Repeat the first line with a little variation and then bring it all down to a third line major ending. You know, regular twelve bar blues."

"Okay," Andy yawned. He wiped his mouth off with the back of his hand and handed the bottle back and picked up the guitar and went back into the private sealed communion with the strings.

They listened while he fiddled with it. Then he played it for them. It was the same mock-haunting minors, only this time set into the twelve bar blues framework.

"You mean like that?" Andy said modestly. He laid the box down again.

"Thats it," Slade said excitedly. "Thats a terrific blues. I bet I got five hundred records back home, and over half of them are blues. But there aint a blues I ever heard could touch that blues. And that includes *Saint Louis*."

"Oh, now," Andy said demurely. "It aint that good."

"No, I mean it," Slade said. "Hell, man, I'm a blues collector."

"You are?" Andy said. "Say, listen," he said, forgetting to be bored, "have you ever heard of a guy named Dajango? Dajango Something."

"Sure," Slade said expansively. "Django Reinhardt. The French guitarman. You pronounce it Jango. The D is silent. He's the best."

"There!" Andy said to Prew. "You see? You thought I was lyin. You thought I was makin it up." He turned back to Slade excitedly. "You got any of this Django's records?"

"No," Slade said. "They're hard to get. All made in France. And very expensive. I've heard a lot of them though. Well what do you know," he said. "So you know old Django?"

"Not personally," Andy said. "I know his music. Theres nothing like it in the world." He turned to Prew. "Thought I was kiddin you, dint you?" he said accusingly. "Thought I was ony makin it all up. What do you think now?"

Prew had another drink and shrugged defeat. Andy did not even see it. He had already turned back to Slade and launched into his story.

Andy only had one story. It was as if it was the only thing in his whole life that had ever happened to him, the only experience that had impressed him strongly enough to provide a story. Prew and Friday had both heard it a thousand times but they listened now as intently as Slade while Andy told it, because it was a good story and they never got tired of hearing it.

It was a story of 'Frisco and low hanging drifts of fog, the kind of fog a Middle-Westerner or Southerner half expected a Chinese hatchet man to step out in front of you as you walked up and down the steep rain-water running rough-brick-cobbled streets. It was a story of Angel Island, big sister of Alcatraz, the Casual Station in 'Frisco Bay where you waited for the transport that would ship you over.

Andy's story brought Angel Island back to all of them: The *President Pierce*, the little launch that would take you over and deposit you at the foot of Market Street to go on pass; it brought back the Rock with the East Garrison of concrete barracks built in tiers up from the dock, and West Garrison of tar paper and wood where they put the Casuals and that you took the road that wound up through the officers' quarters and then ran fairly level off across the flanks of the hills to get to, the West Garrison, a two mile walk you had to make three times a day for chow, two miles over and two miles back, getting up chilled by the fog at dawn and hungry for coffee with that two mile walk ahead of you before you could eat; it brought back the high steep hills that you were free to climb up through the sparse trees to the timber line of light second- and third-growth woods at the top because the Casual had no duty beyond policing up in the morning and an occasional KP, the Casual was only waiting on a boat and the permanent-party-men at

Angel were superior and contemptuous and worked them like niggers on KP, and from the light timber you could look down across to the gray man-factory the steep-walled soul-assembly-line and shudderingly at the callous grayness decide you werent so bad off after all, here where you would walk the gravel road clear around the Island every day, past the Immigration Quarantine Station on the other side where they had the six Germans who had given up off of an injured merchant vessel interned and you could talk to them and give them cigarettes and they seemed human just like you but you never knew how they would have been if the situation was reversed.

It was a story of Telegraph Hill, Andy's story. Or was it Knob Hill, in Andy's one and only story. It was a story of steep-streeted Chinatown and the Chinese tonks and tourist nightclubs, and of a green recruit from the Mississippi Valley who looked in awe and wonder. It was a story of the fabulous Eddie Lang, and of the mythical Django the Frenchman the "Greatest Guitarman In The World" whose last name, something German, Andy never could remember.

A rich queer had picked Andy up in one of the Chinese nightclubs, a slightly effeminate, very sad, quite rich queer. And learning that Andy was a guitarman, had taken him up to the very expensive and exclusive apartment house that he derided, but still lived in, to hear the "Greatest Guitarman In The World." It was a lovely bachelor apartment, so lovely Andy had felt transported to some unreal other earth, because surely Andy had never seen an earth like *this* earth before, a place so rich and beautiful and harmonious and clean. It even had a den, and the den even had a bar, and the bar even had pyramids of glasses under colored lights, and the dark wood panelled walls lined from floor to ceiling with books and record albums. Oh, he remembered all of it, every last detail.

But when it came to describing for them who had never heard it the poignant fleeting exquisitely delicate melody of that guitar, memory always faltered. There was no way to describe them that. You had to hear that, the steady, swinging, never wavering beat with the two- or three-chord haunting minor riffs at the ends of phrases, each containing the whole feel and pattern of the joyously unhappy tragedy of this earth (and of that other earth). And always over it all the one picked single string of the melody following infallibly the beat, weaving in and out around it with the hard-driven swiftly-run arpeggios, always moving, never hesitating, never getting lost and having to pause to get back on, shifting suddenly from the set light-accent of the melancholy jazz beat to the sharp erratic-explosive gypsy rhythm that cried over life while laughing at it, too fast for the ear to follow, too original for the mind to anticipate, too intricate for the memory to remember. Andy was not a jazzman, but Andy knew guitars. The American Eddy Lang was good, but Django the Frenchman was untouchable, like God.

They were all foreign recordings, those of this Django, all made in France or Switzerland. Andy had never heard of him before, and never heard of him again, until Slade. He tried, but the record clerks had never heard of Django, they did not handle foreign recordings, and Andy could not tell them his last name. Just that one night remained, a half-dream half remembered, that he was not even sure any more was real. He had told and retold it so often, elaborating this or that, that he no longer knew where memory stopped and imagination started. He was glad to prove by Slade that it really had existed.

The queer said he was a real gypsy, a French gypsy, and he only had three fingers on his left hand, his string hand. Incredible. They had sat almost all night, Andy and the queer, playing them and replaying them, and the queer expanded and began to talk, how he had seen him once in the flesh in a Paris bistro, how Django had quit without giving notice, leaving a thousand francs a week to go off with a third-rate gypsy band that was touring in the South, the Meedee, he called it. The queer thought that was wonderful. The queer did not offer to proposition Andy. Either he forgot all about it in the excitement of the music, or else he wanted to keep his real love and his business separate. It was as if this queer only propositioned men who were too dull and insensitive to appreciate guitar, so he could degrade them for their lack, and himself for associating with them. He had driven Andy down through the fog to the dock to catch the last launch, and in the fog Andy could not even remember where he had been. He tried to find the house again, once later on, when he found he could not buy the records anyplace. But he never could find it. He could not even recognize the street. He was not even sure which hill it was. It was as if street and house had vanished from the earth, and he was pursuing the fading ghost of a long dead dream. He shipped out without ever seeing the man again.

That was the end of Andy's story.

Nobody said anything for quite a while.

"Thats the kind of a story I like," Slade said finally. "That poor lonely queer. All that money and nobody he could talk to."

"Queers never have anybody they can talk to," Prew said bitterly, remembering Maggio. "They like it like that. Poor little rich boy," he said bitterly. But still, it was the kind of story Prew liked too, weird and unreasonable and senseless, almost occult, yet with a thread of hope still running always through it that maybe his theory that all men were basically alike, all hunting the same phantasmal mirror, was true.

"You dont know where I could fine some of them records, do you?" Andy asked.

"I wish I did," Slade said. "I wish I could help you. All I know about him is his name," he told them guiltily. "I didnt know it meant so much to you. I lied to you a while ago, I've never even heard any of the records." He looked at them anxiously. Nobody said anything.

"Gimme a drink," Andy said finally.

"I'm sorry," Slade said. "Listen," he said, "play that blues again, will you?"

Andy wiped his mouth and played it.

"Jesus," Slade said. "Hey, listen," he said embarrassedly. "Now that you've got the melody for them, why dont you write your blues right now?"

"Oh, he'll remember that all right," Prew said. "We can always do it some other time, when we get back in garrison. He wont forget the tune, will you, Andy?"

"Oh, I dont know," Andy shrugged disconsolately. "It aint much good anyway, is it?"

"No!" Slade said. "No, listen. If you put it off, it'll end up just like your story about Django. A half forgotten memory," he said, "of something you were going to do once, when you were young."

They all of them looked at him.

"Never put things off," Slade said, almost frantically. "You'll wake up and find them gone."

"We aint got no paper nor pencil," Prew said.

"I got a notebook and a pencil," Slade said eagerly, getting them out. "Always carry them. To write down thoughts, you know. Come on, lets write it now."

"Well, hell," Prew said embarrassedly. "I dont know how to start."

"Figure it out," Slade said eagerly. "You can figure anything out. Its about the Army, aint it? Its about re-enlisting. Look," he said. "Start it with the guy getting discharged, paid off."

Andy picked up the guitar and began to play through the minor melody slowly thoughtfully. Slade's almost frantic enthusiasm was catching. He was high and pouring out the energy on them, like Angelo Maggio used to work himself up to when he wanted to win at poker, Prew thought.

"Here," he said, "give us your flash so we can see."

"You think its all right to have a light?" Slade said.

"Sure," Prew said. "Hell. The lootenant and them all had their lights on, dint they?" He trained the light down on the notebook.

"How's this for a start?" Prew said. "*Got paid out on Monday*. Write that down. Then we can start with Monday when the guy gets paid off, and then work right on through each day of the week, until the next Monday when he re-enlists."

436

"Thats fine!" Slade said excitedly. He wrote it down. *"Got paid out on Monday*. What next?"

"Not a dog soljer no more," Andy said softly, still playing.

"Swell!" Slade said. He wrote it down. "What next?"

"They gimme all that money," Friday grinned, *"so much my pockets is sore."*

"More dough than I can use. Re-enlistment Blues," Prew said.

"Fine!" Slade cried. "Swell! Wait'll I get it down. You're going too fast for me."

Andy went on playing softly, the same haunting three lines, over and over, as if his mind had gone a way off into them.

"How about *Went to town on Tuesday?*" Slade said.

"Say: *Took my ghelt,*" Prew suggested. *"Took my ghelt to town on Tuesday*. Sounds more like Army," he said, thinking of Angelo Maggio.

"It doesnt rhyme," Slade said. "I mean rhythm. You know."

"Thats all right," Andy said softly. "You can run the first three words together."

"Okay then," Slade said. He wrote that down.

"Got a room and a big double bed," Friday said excitedly, suddenly high.

They were all high now, pulled up by Slade's excitement. It was like they were four statues standing wide-legged in an electric storm with spatulate spread fingers emitting sparks that jumped from one of them to another, then back again.

"Find a job tomorrow," Prew said.

"Tonight you may be dead," Andy said softly, playing.

"Aint no time to lose. Re-enlistment Blues," Slade laughed delightedly, scribbling faster.

"Hit the bars on Wednesday," Prew said. *"My friends put me up on a throne."*

"Found a hapa-Chinee baby," Friday grinned. *"Swore she never would leave me alone."*

"Did I give her a bruise?" Andy said softly, almost sadly. *"Re-enlistment Blues!"*

"Wait. Wait," Slade cried delightedly. "Let me get this down. God damn. Its coming *too* fast now."

They waited while he scribbled frantically. Then they went on, holding themselves up high by the bootstraps of their own creativeness that they had not believed they had, looking at each other a little astonishedly that it could be so easy.

They finished two more verses, in rapid fire, before Slade called another halt, his round face and the barrel of his pencil gleaming ecstatically in the light from the flash.

"Let me get it now," he pleaded. "Wait'll I get it down. There," he said, "now. Let me read it to you. Before we go ahead. See just what we've got."

"Okay, read it," Prew said. He was snapping the fingers of both hands nervously. Andy was still chording the melody softly, as if to himself. Friday had got up and was moving around.

"Okay," Slade said. "Here goes. *The Re-enlistment Blues——*"

"Hey, wait a minute," Friday said, looking down toward the bivouac. "Aint that somebody comin up here?"

They all turned to look down the hill, watching like balcony spectators of a drama. The little cluster of lights had appeared again around the deeper blackness of the truck. One of them had detached itself from the cluster and was rocking and bouncing toward them, up the path.

"That'll be old Weary Russell," Andy said. "Come to get me to go back to the goddamned CP."

"Oh, hell," Friday said anxiously. "Aint we goin to get to finish it?"

"You guys can finish it," Andy said. "After I'm gone," he said bitterly. "You can show it to me tomorrow."

"Oh, no," Prew said. "We all started it. We'll all finish it. Old Weary wont mind waitin a little."

Andy looked at him sourly. "No, Weary wont. But the lootenant sure as hell will."

"Thats all right," Prew frowned nervously. "You know how they are. They always hang around for half an hour or so before they take off. Come on," he said nervously to Slade. "Come on, read it."

"Okay," Slade said. "Here goes. *The Re-enlistment Blues—*" He held the notebook and the flash up to his face. Then he dropped the notebook and slapped savagely at his neck.

"Mosquito," he said guiltily. "I'm sorry."

"Here," Prew said urgently. "Let me hold the flash. Now read it, goddam it. We aint got much time to get it finished."

"Okay," Slade said. "Here goes. *The Re-enlistment Blues—*" He looked around at all of them. "*The Re-enlistment Blues.*"

"*The Re-enlistment Blues,*" he said again.
"*Got paid out on Monday*
Not a dog soljer no more
They gimme all that money
So much my pockets is sore
More dough than I can use. Re-enlistment Blues.

"*Took my ghelt to town on Tuesday*
Got a room and a big double bed
Find a job tomorrow

> *Tonight you may be dead*
> *Aint no time to lose. Re-enlistment Blues.*

> "*Hit the bars on Wednesday*
> *My friends put me up on a throne*
> *Found a hapa-Chinee baby*
> *Swore she never would leave me alone*
> *Did I give her a bruise? Re-enlistment Blues!*

> "*Woke up sick on Thursday*
> *Feelin like my head took a dare*
> *Looked down at my trousers*
> *All my pockets was bare*
> *That gal had blowed my fuse. Re-enlistment Blues.*

> "*Went back around on Friday*
> *Asked for a free glass of beer*
> *My friends had disappeared*
> *Barman said, 'Take off, you queer!'*
> *What I done then aint news. Re-enlistment Blues.*"

"There!" Slade said triumphantly. "I dont give a flying fuck what anybody says," he said proudly, "I say thats pretty damn good. What next now?"

Prew was still snapping his fingers. "*That jail was cold all Sa'day,*" he said, "*standin on a bench lookin down.* Make it like that, see? Sa'day. Two syllables."

"Okay," Slade said, writing.

"Hey!" Friday interrupted. "Thats not Weary!"

They stopped, and all of them looked at the figure coming toward them on the path. It was not Weary Russell. Andy kicked the almost empty bottle down over the embankment quickly. Slade brought his flash to bear on the coming figure. The beam reflected back at them from two gold bars on the shoulders. Slade turned questioningly to Prew, not knowing what to do.

"Attennsh-Hut!" Prew yelled. It was automatic.

"What the hell are you men doing up here at this hour of the night?" asked Lt Culpepper's voice sharply, sharp as his Culpepper nose or his ramrod Culpepper back.

"Playing the git-tars, Sir," Prew said.

"I surmised that," Lt Culpepper said in a dry droll tone. He came up to them. "What in hell do you mean by turning a flashlight on up here?"

"We were using it to copy out some notes, Sir," Prew said. The other three were looking at him as the spokesman. He went on, trying to keep the rage of frustration out of his voice. There would be no more blues writing this night. "There were flashlights on all over the bivouac area, Sir," he said. "We dint think having one on here for a few minutes would hurt anything."

"Now you know better than that, Prewitt," Lt Culpepper said in a dry droll tone. "You men are supposed to be on a field problem approximating actual war conditions. That includes a full blackout."

"Yes, Sir," Prew said.

"Those lights below were inspection lights," Lt Culpepper said. "The only time they are ever used is to inspect the posts."

"Yes, Sir," Prew said.

"Would they use lights to inspect posts under actual war conditions?" Slade said. His voice was trembling.

Lt Culpepper turned his head without moving his straight Culpepper shoulders or stiff Culpepper back, in the traditional Culpepper military style, developed over many Culpepper generations. "When you address an officer, soldier," Lt Culpepper said crisply, "it is customary to either precede or conclude your question with the title *Sir*."

"Yes, Sir," Slade said.

"Who is this man?" Lt Culpepper said, in a dry droll tone. "I thought I knew everybody in the Company."

"Private Slade, Sir," Slade said. "17th Air Base Squadron, Hickam Field, Sir."

"What are you doing here?"

"I came over to listen to the music, Sir."

Lt Culpepper turned his light from Prew to Slade. "Are you supposed to be on post, soldier?"

"No, Sir."

"Why havent you reported in?"

"When I'm off post my time's my own, Sir," Slade said in a kind of abortive outrage. "I broke no rules by coming over here when I got off post."

"Perhaps not," Lt Culpepper said in a dry droll tone. "But in the Infantry, soldier, we do not allow men from other outfits to hang around our bivouac area. Particularly in the middle of the night. *Got it?*" he popped.

Nobody said anything.

"Prewitt," Lt Culpepper popped.

"Yes, Sir."

"You are the senior man here. I hold you responsible for all this. There are men down in camp trying to sleep. Some of them have to go on post—" he peered at his chronometer, "in thirty-seven minutes."

"Thats why we came up here, Sir," Prew said. "Nobody has complained about it that I know of."

"Perhaps not," Lt Culpepper said in a dry droll tone. "But that does not alter the fact that it is against regulations generally, and against my orders specifically, as of right now. It also does not change the fact that you were up here on the skyline with a lighted flash during a total security blackout." Lt Culpepper turned his light from Slade back to Prewitt.

Nobody said anything. They were all thinking of the unfinished blues that were still in Slade's hand, and that might not ever be finished now, that you could not just run off like a mimeograph, that you had to get the mood right for, and that the right mood for might not come again soon. They all felt Lt Culpepper was to blame for this. Still, they did not feel like saying anything.

"Now if there are no more arguments or discussions," Lt Culpepper said in a dry droll tone, "I suggest we end this interview. You may use your light going down the path, if you wish," he said.

"Yes, Sir," Prew said, and saluted. Lt Culpepper returned it formally. Andy, Slade and Friday saluted too then, if as suddenly remembering. Lt Culpepper returned them formally and collectively. He waited until they had gone on ahead and followed them down the path at a distance with his light. They did not turn their light on.

"God damn," Slade muttered thickly. "God damn. They always make you feel like a schoolboy who has had his hands slapped with the ruler."

"Forget it," Prew said loudly. "How do you like the Infantry now?" He said it bitterly. His little farce was over.

Nobody else said anything.

Weary Russell met them at the truck.

"I dint have a chance," he whispered. "He started right up as soon as he seen the light. I couldnt even give you a yell. I couldnt do a thing."

"Yeah?" Prew said dully. "Ats all right. Forget it. What the hell are you whispering for?" he said angrily.

Lt Culpepper came up behind them to the truck. "And Prewitt," he said in a dry droll tone. "I thought I'd tell you it wont do you any good to plan to go back up after we are gone. I've already given the corporal on duty orders to keep an eye out up that way."

"Yes, Sir," Prew said, and saluted. "I think we're all through anyway, Sir," he said. It sounded very pompous. He cursed himself. Lt Culpepper grinned. Lt Culpepper climbed in the truck.

"Wheres the First Sergeant, Russell?" he said.

"Dont know, Sir," Weary said. "I guess he aims to stay over here."

"How'll he get back?"

"I dont know, Sir," Weary said.

"Well," Lt Culpepper grinned happily, "thats his tough luck, isnt it? He has to be back for Reveille. I guess he'll have to walk. Come on,

Anderson, lets go. Lets get the hell out of this sinkhole," he said to Russell.

"Yes, Sir," Weary said.

The truck backed and turned and pulled out, leaving a large empty hollow behind it. They stood by the opening through the wire and watched the truck pull out grindingly over the rough ground. In the light from the headlights they could see Andy sitting in the back holding his guitar.

Friday laughed, trying to fill the hollow. "Some fun, hey? A good time was had by all."

"Here," Slade said. He handed Prew the sheets of paper from his notebook. "These are yours. You'll want them."

"Dont you want a copy?"

Slade moved his head. "I'll get one from you some other time. I guess I better get going. I've got to walk back to the Field."

"Okay," Prew said. "Take it easy."

"You better watch it," Friday said, "after this. Not let him catch you over here no more."

"I know it," Slade said. "You dont have to tell me. I'll see you all, sometime." He started off across the truck tracks to the road.

"You think he'll transfer in?" Friday said.

"No; I dont," Prew said. "What do you think? Would you? Here," he said, and thrust the papers at him. "These are Andy's. Its his tune."

"We'll finish it sometime," Friday said, taking them and buttoning them down in his pocket carefully. "We'll finish it later. When we get back in garrison."

"Yeah," Prew said. "Sure."

"We could finish it now," Friday said eagerly. "You and me. Do it in the kitchen tent. We wont need no music now."

"Do it yourself," Prew said. "I think I'll take myself a little walk."

He went out through the gap in the wire and across the truck tracks toward the road.

"But dont you want to do it now?" Friday called eagerly after him, "finish it now?"

Chapter 33

When he reached the gravel, Prew stopped. He could hear Friday still talking to himself eagerly, behind him. Slade had already disappeared out of both sight and sound. Pretty soon Friday would disappear too, if he walked far enough.

He turned north toward the Main Gate on the gravel. The other way south, led past the junk yard where Slade's relief would be on post. Slade's relief would challenge him. Then finding it was an EM Slade's relief would want to pass the time of day. He did not want to talk to anybody. He did not want to make any more new friendships tonight either. He turned north. One new friendship a day was about all any one strong man could take. He walked very slow, so he would not catch up to Slade.

He walked along the road in the darkness. The deep gravel grated under his field shoes. The unreleased energy of the whiskey was fuming up through him like whiffs of laughing gas. He wished he had more whiskey. He would get stinking, rotten, blind. It seemed you could not only not bugle but you could not even write a stinking lousy blues, about the Army.

He had already had the whole next verse in his head, when the Culpepper family had arrived. The next verse was Saturday, and he had had it.

> *That jail was cold all Sa'day*
> *Standin up on a bench lookin down*

He thought as he walked along the road in the darkness.

> *Through them bars I watched the people*
> *All happy and out on the town*
> *Look like time for me to choose, them Re-enlistment Blues.*

—They had stood on the benches of the bull pen on the second floor of the city jail in Richmond Indiana and watched the Saturday night crowds. They had had to stand on the benches because the windows were so high. There were four of them. That time. All booked as vags. They kept them a week, then turned them loose. There had been too many vags for the jail space. That had been in '35—

It was like with the bugle, you had to do the things yourself before you could put the ring of truth in them, and he had had it all in his head, ready for Slade to write down. None of the rest of them could write that verse because they had never been in jail. Now maybe it would never be written down. He did not have a pencil and paper to write it down now, and if he did have he would not write it down anyway. He would tear the paper up and throw the pencil away. He felt bitterly happy at having denied the world something.

What was the world anyway? but a lot of Culpepper families? They had you by the balls from the minute you were bornd.

He walked along the deserted gravel road in the darkness, filled with a great rending pity for all the Prewitts of this world, thinking about the blues they had not finished and would not even have begun if it had not been for Slade's asinine enthusiasm for the Infantry. There was a good one for you. And even then, if Slade had not felt guilty over lying about Django's records and wanted to do something to square it, he would not probably have bludgeoned them into starting it. There was a better one for you. It was laughable.

The voices of Friday arguing with Friday had disappeared too now, and he was alone in a private world whose radius was ten feet of gravel. That was what he had wanted. Now he did not want it. This world kept pace with him with all the inexorableness of a spotlight following a dancer.

He ran a little ways. He could not outrun it. He could not outrun this world any more than he could outrun the world of Culpepper families.

He slowed down and walked on, wondering if the blues would ever be finished now. Probably not, unless Slade transferred to Schofield to inspire them. Slade could appreciate the Infantry because he was in the Air Corps. He laughed out loud, bitterly happily.

"Halt!"

Prew stopped, and stopped dead. There was not supposed to be a sentry along here. Still, you did not argue with a challenge. Not when it might contain a guard with a loaded pistol.

"Who goes there?" the voice demanded.

Something moved just outside the ten foot gravel world, and he caught a glint of light on what looked like a pistol.

"A friend," Prew said, in the prescribed manner.

"Advance, friend, and be recognized," the voice boomed.

Prew walked forward slowly, in the prescribed manner.

"Halt!" the disembodied voice boomed instantly.

Prew stopped dead. This was not in the prescribed manner.

"Who goes there?" the voice boomed again.

"A friend, goddam it."

"Advance, friend goddam it, and be recognized."

Prew started forward.

"Halt!" the voice boomed instantly, waving the oily glint.

Prew halted. "Say, what the hell is this?"

"Quiet!" the figure roared, shaking the glint at him. "At ease! Rest! Fall Out! About Face! Right Dress! Who goes there?"

"Private Prewitt, Company G, —th Infantry," Prew said, a suspicion growing in his mind.

"Advance, Private Prewitt, Company G, —th Infantry, and be executed," the figure bellowed.

"Up yours, Warden," Prew said, advancing.

"Boom!" the figure yelled, backing off. It shook the glinting object. "Boom! Boom! Gotcha, gotcha! You're dead! Boom!"

"Cut the comedy, Warden," Prew said disgustedly. He could make out the glinting object now. It was a bottle.

"Well, well," Warden giggled drunkenly. His face lit up mischievously. "Fooled you, dint I? Hello, kid. What ever are you doin out all by yourself? Dont you know you're liable to get shot wanderin around in the dark like that?"

"I'm takin a walk," Prew said belligerently.

"Well, well," Warden said hollowly. "A walk. The lootenant kind of broke up your little party, din ee?"

"The son of a bitch," Prew said.

"Ah-ah," Warden said, raising a finger. "Is that any way to talk about a Culpepper? Dont you know theres been a Culpepper serving his country in every war since Zachary Taylor took California away from Mexico? How would *you* like it if this country didnt have no California? What would you do for movies then, I guess? Where you think this world would be? without the Culpeppers?"

"To hell with the Culpeppers," Prew said.

"Tsk-tsk," Warden said owlishly. "No education. No feeling for world good. Not even no refinement, even. You're better off executed. Boom!" he said. "Boom! Boom! You're dead. Gotcha. What do you think of my new gun, kid?" He held out the bottle. Prew reached to take it. Warden drew it back. "Ah-ah," he said. "Watch out. Its loaded."

"So are you," Prew said.

"Have a drink," Warden said.

"I can get liquor," Prew said. "I dont need yours."

Warden was studying his bottle-gun. "Its loaded," he said. "Loaded for bear. Boom!" he said. "Have a bear?" He flipped the bottle up and caught it. "I'm a shooter, kid. How would you like to shoot with me sometime, kid?" he grinned.

"What're you doin, braggin?" Prew said. Warden, along with Pete Karelsen, was only just the best shot in the Regiment, was all. Both of them had star gauge '03s that they worshipped. Along with Regimental Personnel Sergeant Major O'Bannon and Capt Stevens of B Company, they were the Regimental rifle team. No matter what any poor son of a bitch seemed to be able to do, Warden always seemed to be able to do it better. It wasnt even fair.

"Naw," Warden grinned, "I aint braggin. I hear you're a hotshot shooter. I hear you showed the boys some tricks with a rifle on the combat range last month. So I figure you like a little match with some real competition."

445

"Okay," Prew said. "Any goddam time you say, Warden."

"Reglar match competition," Warden said. "Make a little side bet. Say about a hundred bucks?"

"Even money?" Prew said.

"I ought to give you a little odds."

"I thought maybe you'd want me to give you odds."

"Naw," Warden grinned slyly. "I wouldnt cheat you."

"Where'll we shoot?" Prew said. "Shoot now?"

"Shoot on the range," Warden grinned. "Reglar match competition. Range season comin up in a month or so."

"Hell," Prew said. "I thought you meant tonight."

"Aint got no gun. Except my baby here. Have to do it range season."

"Even money?" Prew said, "and we both use your BC scope?"

"Sure."

"I may not be here during range season," Prew said.

"By god, thats right." Warden ducked and snapped his fingers. "I clean forgot. You'll be in the Stockade by then, wont you? Aw hell," he said unhappily.

"What're you doin?" Prew said. "Backin down?"

"Sure," Warden grinned at him slyly. "Always back down." He sat down in the middle of the gravel road and crossed his legs. "Here, old buddy. Have a lil drink."

"Okay." Prew took the bottle. "I dont mind drinkin your liquor any morn I'd mind drinkin Culpepper's."

"Ats fine," Warden said. "I dont mind havin you drink it any morn I would havin Culpepper drink it."

The liquor mingled hotly with the fumes already boiling in his belly. Prew sat down beside him and handed back the bottle and wiped his mouth. "This is a helluva fuckin life, you know it?"

"Miserble," Warden nodded loosely. He drank. "Perfeckly miserble."

"Guy cant have any fun."

"Ats right," Warden nodded. "No fun a tall. Now you've got yourself on Culpepper's shitlist too."

"I'm on everybody else's. I might as well be on his too."

"Ats right," Warden said. "Make it a royal flush. Make it a full house."

"Make it five of a kind," Prew said. "Joker kicker."

"You're the joker," Warden said. He handed him the bottle. "Right?"

"Right."

"I went and got myself on Stark's list too. Probly have to buy all my meals out now. Who am I to talk to you?"

"How'd that happen?" Prew said conversationally. He drank and gave the bottle back. In front of them and in back of them, the light yellow of the road stretched away to dimness that became invisibility, running like a trail of moonlight across a blackened sea.

"Never mind," Warden said slyly, "never mind."

"Oh," Prew said. "You dont trust me. I trust you."

"We're talkin about you," Warden countered. "Not me. What for do you want to go and fuck up for all the time, Prewitt? What do you want to be a bolshevik for?"

"I dunno," Prew said disconsolately. "I been tryin to figger that out fer years. I guess I was just bornd that way."

"Horshit," Warden said. He took another drink and peered at him owlishly. "I say horshit. Pure plain unadulterated horshit. You disagree with me? Come on, disagree with me."

"I dont know," Prew said disconsolately.

"Horshit, I say," Warden said rhetorically. "Nobody's bornd that way. Look at me. Here," he said. "Have a drink."

He peered at Prewitt slyly as he drank. "Aint this a fuck of a world?" he said. "Here you are going right straight to the Stockade and here I am goin right straight to gettin busted someday. And here we both are sittin in the middle of this crummy road. What if a truck was to come along and run over us?"

"That'd be awful," Prew said. "We'd be dead, wouldnt we?" He could feel the raw whiskey mingling in him smokily explosively with the other, Andy's whiskey, that was already there. Dead, he thought, dead dead dead.

"And nobody to give a damn," Warden said. "Nobody to even mourn. Hell of a note. You better not sit there any more. You better get up and move over to the side of the road."

"What about you?" Prew said, handing back the bottle and looking off down the yellow road for the truck. "You got more to live for than I have. You got to take care of your goddam compny."

"I'm old," Warden said, taking a drink. "Dont matter if I die. My life's behind me," he said, "all behind me. But you're young. Your life's ahead of you."

"But theres nothing in it to look forward to," Prew said stubbornly. "While your life's important. Hitler said if it wasnt for our noncoms we wouldnt have no Army, dint he? We got to have a Army, dont we? What would all the Culpeppers do? if we dint have a Army? No, sir," he said stubbornly. "Its you should get up."

"No, by god!" Warden bellowed. "My life is over. I'm an old man. Nuther five years I be like ole Pete. You cant talk me out of it. You get up."

"No," Prew insisted. "You get up."

"I wont do it!" Warden hollered.

"Well neither will I. I'll sit here as long as you do, by god. I wont let you kill yourself."

Warden handed him the bottle. "You're crazy, kid," he said kindly. "You're insane. You cant save an old man like me. And a young man like you has so much to live for. It'd be a shame, thats what it'd be. A crying shame. Please, kid, please get up. Do it for my sake, if you wont think of yourself."

"No sir," Prew said bravely. "Not Prewitt. Prewitt never deserted a friend in need. I'll stay to the bitter end."

"Oh, what have I done?" Warden hollered, "what have I done?"

"Nobody cares," Prew said. "Nobody gives a damn. To hell with it all. I'm better off dead." Tears rose up in his eyes and made the big crosslegged Buddha that was Warden shimmer.

"So am I," Warden choked. He sat up straight and squared his shoulders. "Then we'll both die. Its better that way anyway, its more tragic. Its more like life."

"I dont think I could stand up anyway," Prew said sleepily.

"Me neither," Warden said. "It is too late. Good by, Prewitt."

"Good by, Warden."

They shook hands solemnly. Bravely they choked back the unmanly tears of parting and sat straight as soldiers, staring proudly down the yellow ribbon from which the doom would come.

"I just want you to know," Warden said, "that I never had a better friend."

"That goes for me too," Prew said.

"No blindfold," Warden said contemptuously, tossing back his head. "Do you think we're boys? Save it to wipe your ass on, you son of a bitch."

"Amen," Prew said.

They shook hands solemnly again, for the last time, split the last drink in Warden's bottle between them, threw the bottle in the weeds, squared their shoulders, and quietly passed out and went peacefully to sleep.

They were still there at two o'clock, stretched out in the middle of the gravel, when Weary Russell came ramming his weapons carrier down the road to take The Warden home.

Weary slammed on his brakes hard, fighting the topheavy little truck hard in the loose deep gravel, skidding sideways back and forth across the road fighting the wheel with all his skill to keep it out of the ditch. He got it stopped about three yards from Warden's oblivious feet. He climbed out and looked at them.

"Jesus Christ!" he whispered awfully. "Jesus Christ."

Warden was clear out, sleeping peacefully happily, but he managed to shake some life back into Prewitt.

"Come on. Wake up, goddam it. You crazy bastard. Come on, you cant snow me, I know you aint dead. You got to help me load him in the back so I can get him back to the CP. If Dynamite ever found out about this he'd bust him sure."

"Dynamite cou'nt bust him," Prew said vaguely.

"He couldnt, 'ey?"

"Hell no," Prew scoffed. "Who'd he get to be First Sarnt?"

"I dont know," Weary said thoughtfully. "Maybe he could— Aw, to hell with that," he snarled. "Help me to get him loaded. What would you crazy dumb screwballs of done if it was someone else who come along? Why, I might of run over you and killed you both," he raged. "Come on, will you?" he pleaded disgustedly, "help me get him loaded."

"Ats right," Prew said stoutly. "Done want nothing happen to my friend Warden."

"Your what?" Weary asked with outraged astonishment. "Your what did you say?"

"You heard me," Prew said indignantly. "I said my buddy Warden. Whad you think I said? My good friend Warden that I done want nothing to happen to is what I said. You heard me."

He struggled up, with Weary's arm around him. "Wheresee? Oh, theree is. Leggo me. I'm awright. Mon," he said, "talk later. Mon, help me get my buddy Warden in a fuggin truck. Got to take care of him, see? Got to look out for Warden. Best fuggin soljer ina Compny." He paused thoughtfully. "Ony fuggin soljer ina Compny," he amended.

Weary let him go and watched disgustedly as he wavered over to the sleeping Warden and leaned over to take hold of him and fell on him.

"Ohh," Prew said. "A'm drunk."

"No stuff," Weary said disgustedly.

He helped him back to his feet. Between them they managed to half-carry half-drag the big man's lax body that was slippery as an eel around to the back of the truck. Twice they dropped him; Warden fell like a stone. They heaved and pushed and shoved and finally got him in the truckbed. As soon as he was in Warden opened his eyes and grinned at them slyly. "Is that Russell?" he mumbled vaguely.

"Yeahr," Weary said disgustedly. "Russell the nursemaid. Russell the goat."

"En listen to me, Russell," Warden said. "I want you da zu sompin. I mean za du sompin. See?"

"Yeah?" said Weary learily. "What?"

Warden reared half up and looked around. Prewitt was already lolling in the rider's seat, asleep again. "I tell you," Warden whispered with all the quiet of a hissing locomotive. "I want you to drive ziz man home tiz bivouac."

"Okay," said Weary wearily. "But quit talkin in z's and playin drunk. You fooled me once, actin passed out so I'd put you in the truck. You aint drunk. You aint as drunk as he is."

Warden laughed. "I sure did, dint I?" he giggled. "But that aint all: when you get him home, I want you to tell his corprl of the guard the Firs Sarnt says he is relieve from duty the rest of the night. For halping the Firs Sarnt on a private reconnaissance."

"But you cant do that, Top," Weary said wonderingly.

"I cant, 'ey?" Warden said. "I already done it. You heard what I said, dint you?"

"Yeah," Weary said, "but——"

"No buts," said Warden savagely. "Do like I said. Am I the Firs Sarnt or not the Firs Sarnt?"

"You're the First Sarnt."

"Maybe you dont know which side that Pfc of yours is buttered on. But me on buts. Just do like I said."

"Okay, Top. But you sure demand a hell of a lot for a lousy goddam Pfc."

"Cmere," Warden said and grabbed him by his arm. "Dont you know we got to look out for this man, Weary?" he whispered. "He's the best fuckin soljer in the Compny." He paused thoughtfully. "The *ony* fuckin soljer in the Compny," he amended.

"What is this?" Weary said. "A mutual backslapping society I stumbled into?"

"We got to take caref him while we can, see?" The Warden told him urgently. "This man may not be with us for long, and we got to take caref this man."

"Okay, okay, Top," Weary said. "Go back to sleep."

"Its important," Warden said. "You dont know. Very important."

"All right," Weary said. "For god sake, go to sleep."

"You promise?" Warden said.

"Yeahr," said Weary Russell wearily. "I promise. Now go back to sleep."

"Okay then," Warden said contentedly. "But dont forget. Zvery important." He rolled over comfortably complacently in the dirty ribbed wood floor of the truckbed. "Because it may happen any day," he said.

Weary looked at him and shook his head and put the tailgate up and drove off down the gravel toward the bivouac, carrying two drunks, who both fatuously drunkenly imagined, that once in a dream somewhere, sometime, somespace, they had managed for a moment to touch another human soul and understand it.

Chapter 34

It happened the day after they got back from Hickam. It had been coming a long time so that everybody was spoiling for it, and they had all been anticipating it, but it turned out to be very involved and when it happened it was so complex that almost no one could get any satisfaction out of it, especially Prew. Prew had planned to go to Maunalani Heights that night.

They had pulled in and unloaded the trucks late the afternoon before and worked late that night cleaning personal equipment, scrubbing the web, saddlesoaping the leather, working with the toothbrushes on the gummy rifles. Nobody liked that kind of work, and the whole next day was given to cleaning the company equipment, the stoves, flies, pyramidal tents, the officers' sleeping tent, and generally policing up for the full field inspection.

To everyone's surprise, Pfc Bloom was standing on the porch with the rest of the boxing squad which had turned out to watch, when they rolled in. It turned out that Bloom had been relieved from NCO School a week before. The story was that Bloom had been called out of ranks to give calisthenics. His first exercise had begun with the command: "Hips on shoulders, Place!" The platoon of Candidates had immediately degenerated into a disorganized and howling pandemonium. Bloom had been excused and sent back to the ranks. That afternoon he had been relieved.

It was great news to the grimy Company, just back from the wilds of field duty. The non-jockstrap faction lost no time in being very pleased to point out this result of Dynamite's policy of promoting punchdrunk fighters. The jockstrap faction countered by pointing to Candidate Malleaux, the new featherweight, who was not only still in NCO School but was leading his half of the class. Bloom, they said, was not the whole story, and anyway a man did not need to graduate from NCO School in order to become a good noncom.

Bloom himself insisted to everyone who would listen that the queer investigation downtown had been the real reason. Very few would listen. The allusion to the queer investigation puzzled all of them, and the other story made much better telling. The non-jockstrap faction had never liked him anyway, and now the jockstraps felt he had compromised their reputation and were not sympathetic either.

All the first afternoon while they were unloading, and most of the next morning during the fatigues, Bloom wandered around from one detail to another belligerently explaining his position. Bloom had not been out in the field, so he was not on any of the details. He did not have to train that day either because tonight they were running off the first card of the Company Smoker season and he was on the card and today was his day off to rest. So he had all of his time free all day to work on this other and protest his innocence.

It was Bloom's first bout as a middleweight. He was only eligible for Company Smokers again this year because he had fought as a light-heavy in the Bowl. He had had to dry out for three days to make the weight and eat nothing but Horlick's Malted Milk Tablets and do his roadwork in a sweatsuit, two sweaters, and a GI slicker. He was drawn very fine. It was bad for him to be so upset.

But he worked hard to prove his innocence, just the same. It did not do much good. He might as well have rested. Wherever he went the other story had already preceded him, moving on the swift wings of gossip that were faster than the legs of any man. He offered all of them to rest his case with Capt Holmes. Dynamite was too big a man to be influenced by malicious gossip. Bloom had faith in Capt Holmes. He offered them to bet anybody even money Capt Holmes would still give him his corporalcy. Nevertheless, any time his big bulk would heave up on the horizon someone would look up from work and holler: "Yaaaaa, Hips on shoulders, PLACE!"

Finally, early in the afternoon, he had to give it up. He went off to the matinee at Theater # 1. He was terribly upset and very nervous, and they were showing Clark Gable in *The Prizefighter and the Lady*, and he needed badly to rest up and relax, for tonight.

Prew was on the detail that was scrubbing out the kitchen trailer. When Bloom had come around to them he had kept out of it. He would not be sorry if Bloom lost the rating, but he did not care much any more one way or the other. All he wanted was to get down to Alma's. It had been two weeks now. He did not want to see the fights and it would be more tactful for him not to be there anyway.

The kitchen trailer was sitting in the company street and they had the floorboards out of the refrigerator part and leaning against the side while they scrubbed down the bilge. One of them was hosing down the floorboards. All they had left to do after that was scrub out the bread box in the other end and then hose it all down and wipe it off outside and they were done. That was where they were with it when Bloom left for the show. They watched Bloom leave amid hoots of "Yaaaaa, Hips on shoulders, PLACE!" They knew where he was going. If you were in fifty yards of Bloom, you always knew where Bloom was going. They went on working.

They were still working when Champ Wilson and Liddell Henderson came back from the Regimental gym with a bunch of other fighters who had all been working out. Sgt Wilson and the other fighters had not been in the field either, and were not on any of the details. Sgt Henderson was not a fighter but he had not been in the field either, he had stayed up at the Packtrain to take care of Capt Holmes's horses. He had only gone along with Wilson over to the gym to watch his sidekick train. It was Sgt Henderson who cornered Bloom's dog that was trotting inoffensively among the work details, and suggested that they have a little fun and help the big police dog from F Company to mount her.

"At ole po-lice dawg's been nosin aroun for a couple weeks now. Bout time he got a break," Sgt Henderson grinned in his high thin lazy Texas drawl. "That goddam Bloom, will he be susprised when ole Lady drops a littah of po-lice dawgs on his pillah."

"I never did like that son of a bitch Bloom anyways," Sgt Wilson said grimly, as he knelt to hold her forelegs. Sgt Champ Wilson always said everything grimly, inside the ring or out. Sgt Champ Wilson was a grim guy. He had to be. He was the champion lightweight of the Hawaiian Department. You did not carry an honor like that lightly. He held Lady's forelegs grimly.

There were men scattered all over the company yard, working and loafing. There were details on the porch repacking the barrels of the watercooled machineguns that Leva had decided he might as well have done today, since they were working. There were details in the street and at the garbage racks and across the street in the quad where they were working on the tents. Before long Henderson and Wilson had quite a crowd around them, offering advice and encouragement.

Bloom's dog was a little part-terrier mongrel. There were always plenty of stray dogs drifting around any Army post, because everybody always fed them to get to pet them, but Bloom wanted his own dog. He had found this one over by the Post Beergarden and brought her home and named her Lady and religiously begged scraps from the cooks who would have fed her anyway to get to pet her, so that he could feed her three times a day himself and win all her affection. Just as religiously, but with an even greater vigor that almost amounted to affronted outrage, he drove off all the male dogs that ventured into the company area. The big police dog from F Company next door was his especial enemy.

It became one of the biggest jokes in the Company. And Lady herself, who was a meek frightened-faced little bundle of nerves that carried her tail perpetually between her legs, did not help it any. She was completely devoid of any military sense, and it was a delight to the formation to watch Bloom bellow and curse and threaten Lady as she meekly with her tail tucked between her legs tried to follow him out to drill morning after morning.

Lady was no virgin, it was obvious her morals were no better than the average, and she did not mind the big police dog half as much as Bloom did, but now they had frightened her. The police dog was willing but he was too tall for her, without Lady's cooperation. And Lady was not cooperating. Lady could have stood up at full height under his belly without touching him, but she was hunkering down as low as Sgt Henderson would let her. Sgt Wilson held her front legs grimly while Sgt Henderson tried to elevate her stern. The police dog jumped around barking excitedly and pawing the air vainly. The circle of onlookers cheered and offered more advice. Everybody thought it would be a big joke on Bloom.

Lady was beginning to whine and yelp and lunge until it was all the two sergeants could do to hold her. The novelty was wearing thin. It was not so much fun any more. The crowd began to wander away, a little vague-eyed and shame-faced, back to the jobs. But Sgt Henderson would not give up. The few who stayed on began to get half ashamed looks on their faces mingling with the eagerness. Sgt Henderson still would not admit defeat.

Prew did not say anything for quite a while. It was none of his business and it was not his dog. Bloom should take care of his own damned dog. But it had all been building up in him, coming on to the saturation point where you were just looking for an excuse, a sorehead asking for an excuse, and he looked at them, the ones who had shamefacedly walked away just as much as the ones who had guiltfacedly eagerly stayed, just as much as the Champ Wilsons and Dogrobber Hendersons of this world who never never went out in the field, and he hated all of them, as savagely and implacably as he hated Bloom and Bloom's goddam sniveling little dog.

He walked over from the trailer and elbowed in through the half-eager half-reluctant faces and bumped Henderson hard on the shoulder with the heel of his open palm. Henderson was on his knees battling with Lady's squirming hindquarters, and he went over backwards releasing his hold to catch himself as he fell back.

Lady, her traction free, dug in. Wilson could not hold her. She scuttled off across the quad with the police dog hot on her heels. She turned once and snarled and nipped him in the shoulder and after that he followed at a distance.

"Now what the hell'd you want to do that for?" Sgt Henderson demanded.

"Because I dont like to see a man be any more of a son of a bitch than he just naturally is," Prew said. "Go on back to the stables with your goddam horses."

Sgt Henderson grinned and leaned back on his elbow indolently and put his right hand in his pocket. "Whats a mattah, Prewitt? You got a weak stommick or something? Quite a nice girl all of a sudden, aint you?"

Prew was looking at the hand lovingly fingering something in the pocket. "Dont ever pull that knife on me, you son of a bitch," he said, "or I'll kill you with it."

The grin went off of Sgt Henderson's face, but Champ Wilson, the always cool, was already at his sidekick's elbow helping him up. "Come on, Liddell," he said soothingly. He held Henderson by his right arm and pulled him toward the barracks.

"You'll go too far someday, Prewitt," Henderson screamed suddenly, "and I'll cut your fucking heart out."

"When," Prew said.

"Shut up, Liddell," commanded Wilson grimly. "You better learn to use your head, Prewitt," he said coolly. "Someday you'll get yourself into a trouble you cant get out of. They aint many people around this outfit like you the way it is."

"There aint many of them around this outfit I'd care much to have them like me, Wilson," Prew said.

Wilson did not answer. He led the raging, but unresisting, Henderson inside to the dayroom, patting him tenderly on the shoulder. Prew went back to the trailer. The crowd broke up and went back to work, a little disappointed at having been denied what might have turned out to be a decent fight. Prew was not sure whether he was disappointed or not. Nobody at the trailer mentioned it to him. Apparently, he thought grimly, the word had already gone out some time before now, that Prewitt was just about at the edge.

Nobody else said anything about it either, the rest of the afternoon. It was already forgotten, another one of those thousand little incidents that almost start a fight. Nothing should have come of it. It would have ended there. Of course it would have to have been Pfc Isaac Bloom who brought it back to life again that night at chow.

They were having franks fried whole and Stark's hashbrowns that were as good as any Toddlehouse hashbrowns, and utilized the left-over spuds from dinner. There were green limas on the side, and those large half peaches canned in syrup for dessert. It was a good meal, and it was not until the platters and dishes were beginning to stay emptied that there was conversation. Prew inspected his last frank butt, crisp skinned and dark, and put it in his mouth and watched Stark come in from the kitchen and go to the sergeants' table for his post-meal coffee and a butt and conversation, his undershirt soaked with sweat, sweat glistening from his chunky arms and shoulders, sweat dripping from the hair of his armpits. He liked Stark, warmly, he liked him a lot,

Stark was about the only man in this outfit he would give a decent fart for. Maybe The Warden. No, not that sly son of a bitch. Andy and Friday maybe. And Maggio. He swallowed the last of the meat and lit a cigarette, smoky on the tongue over the saltiness. Now to add the taste of coffee to the others.

That was when Bloom moved his dishes over to the table where Prew was and sat down across from him. There was a hopeful lull of conversation around the room.

"I want to thank you for takin care of my dawg when I wasnt here to look out for her, Prewitt," Bloom hollered.

"You're welcome," Prew said. He reached for his coffee mug.

"Here," Bloom hollered. He seized the metal coffee pitcher and refilled Prew's cup. "A man can always tell who his friends is," he hollered. "I always say," he hollered, "that you can tell what kind of man a man is by the way he treats your pets. I owe you a lot."

Prew let the coffee sit. "You dont owe me nothin, Bloom."

"Oh yes I do," Bloom hollered.

"Oh no you dont."

"And I'm a man who pays his debts."

"I would of done the same for any dawg. I just dont like to see some son of a bitch torment a goddam dawg. Any goddam dawg. I dont give a goddam whose goddam dawg," he said. "In fack, I dint even know it was your goddam dawg," he lied, and watched Bloom through the exhaled smoke.

"Why, everybody knows it is my dawg," Bloom protested.

"No they dont. I dint know it. If I had I wount of stopped it," he said. "So you dont owe me nothin. All I ask from you is you stay away from me." He stood up and picked up his dishes. "See you later, Bloom," he said.

The conversation that had billowed up again disappointedly across the coffee mugs and cigarettes faded attentively again, like a turned down radio.

"Well, Jesus Christ," Bloom said. "Is that any way to treat a goddam man when he tries to thank you?" He stood up himself and emphatically collected his own dishes. "I only come over here to show you my appreciation, Prewitt. Certainly not because I wanted to."

"Well, I dont want your fucking appreciation, Bloom," Prew said. "How do you like that?"

"Ha," Bloom said. "If that aint a laugh. Who the hell are you? the King of England? Its awys the poor white trash that runs down the Jews."

"What're you tryin to do?" Prew said. "Insult me?"

"Did me and my dawg ask you for any help?" Bloom hollered. "No. We dint. Well, wait till you're asked next time. Me and my dawg dont need your goddam help, you son of a bitch. In the future please leave me and my dawg alone."

Prew had set his plate down, but the cup was still in his hand and he threw it. The heavy handleless mug hit Bloom in the center of the forehead. Bloom blinked his eyes and frowned. The cup bounced onto the concrete floor and rolled off unbroken; unconcerned, indifferent, impervious.

Stark was between them before they met, the cigarette still hanging from his crooked about to laugh, about to sneer, about to cry, impassive mouth. He blocked Prew off with his hip and pushed Bloom back in the chest.

"Not in my messhall," he grunted. "You want to play rough take it outside on the green. Nobody fights in this messhall. This messhall is to eat in," he said proudly, "and thats all, by god. And its a good thing for you, Prewitt," he added, "that you dint break that cup, or it would of cost you one thin dime next Payday."

Bloom looked around the room. There was a little red spot on his forehead. "You want to go outside?" he said.

"Sure," Prew said. "Why not? Lets go."

"Well," Bloom said. "What're you waitin for? You scared or something?" He started for the door, unbuttoning his shirt as he went, and Prew followed him out the door and across the street into the quad where the tents were still pitched from the afternoon. The rest of them crowded happily out the messhall door behind him. From other messhalls and porches around the quad other men were already running, as if they had already known about it before it even happened and had only been passing the time until they could start running. They made a big circle around the two of them where Bloom was still taking off his shirt to expose the enormous milkwhite barrel of his bare chest. Prew took his own shirt off.

They fought for an hour and a half. It was five-thirty and not dark yet when they started. The first bout on the smoker card was to start at eight o'clock, but Bloom was not on till the main event which would not be till ten or ten-thirty, and they were still fighting when the detail from the gym began to set up the corners in the ring in the bandstand on the quad.

The only way to fight Bloom was to box him. Bloom had been more or less in training ever since last December and his belly was as hard as a rock. His head had always been as hard as a rock. If Bloom had not been so gunshy of being hit he could have finished it up quick. As it was, Prew would not have had a ghost of a chance anyway if it had not been for the natural speed he had always had and had developed into a personal style even more so, later at Myer. Even so, it took everything Prew had to keep away from him at all after the first ten minutes, he was so out of shape.

He could hit Bloom almost at will, but even with his punch which had always been remarkable for so light a man he could not even faze Bloom. He hooked Bloom tentatively in the belly several times with his left and gave that up. He decided to work on Bloom's nose with his left. The first really good left he landed on Bloom's nose broke it. He could feel it go under his hand, he knew it was broken, but it did not bleed much, just a tiny trickle that stopped soon, and that was all the effect it had. Bloom's eyes watered badly for about five seconds and his face looked stunned for a moment, but his upper lip did not swell at all. It was like trying to knock out a bull moose with your fists.

Prew kept shooting at the nose but Bloom developed a trick of crouching way down like Arturo Godoy so that the left went way over his head, and then swinging up a whistling roundhouse right. The first two or three times Bloom did it he could have torn Prew apart with a left hook to the belly, but he did not do it, he kept swinging up the roundhouse right. After the first times Prew noticed Bloom moved his left way over to the right side of his face when he ducked, leaving a big hole in to the left side of his face. Prew started feinting the left then and stepping in and throwing a straight right, straight down, at the place where the hole should be by then. The first few times he tried it he missed, but the next time he landed under Bloom's left eye and knew Bloom would have a shiner out of that one but it was a small consolation because this punch did not faze Bloom any either. It was like one man trying to push a car over on its side.

Also, the next time Bloom ducked and he snapped down the right, Bloom bent his head and Prew hit him full force on top of the head and felt one of his knuckles go. It was not broken, only jammed back, but that was enough. Bloom came up out of his crouch grinning broadly. Prew gave up the right then and went back to jabbing his left for the nose and keeping his hurt right hand back for a shot at Bloom's adam's apple. That was about all there was left for him to do. It was like walking around a house and trying all the doors and finding them locked and then picking up a rock to break a window and then finding all the windows barred. By this time Prew was getting very tired.

The crowd around them, that was still growing, was having a fine time though. Several self-appointed custodians were going around making them keep back and give them room, and it was a lot like watching an exhibition in the ring. There was not much blood but the crowd did not mind in this case because they were all professionally interested in studying Prew's problem. They were able to enjoy a vicarious part in Prew's intellectual efforts without having to take the chance of being hit by Bloom, and every time Prew tried something they were very interested in seeing how it would work out and he could hear them discussing its prospects of success behind him as if they were watching the trying of a new gambit in a chess game.

Prew's legs were very tired and his forearms, elbows and shoulders were getting sore from the punches he had caught with them. His right hand was swollen some and Bloom had seen it and gotten less gunshy and taken to rushing him. He still had not had a chance to land the right on Bloom's adam's apple. He was beginning to wonder if there would ever be a chance to. He did not want to try it unless he was sure because his hand would not stand many more misses that ended on Bloom's head.

Anyway, Bloom was rushing him, swinging both hands, and he had all he could do to keep out of the way especially when Bloom got him back against the crowd. Once, like that, Bloom managed to land a straight right that way, a straight punch not a roundhouse, when he was back against the crowd and it exploded on his temple and then he was on his knees in the crowd lying across some spectator who had fallen under him, feeling very sleepy and very tired and everything sounding funny and far off and he had a very hard time getting himself back up because his legs did not want to work any more.

Another time, considerably later he felt, he tripped over somebody's feet when Bloom rushed him back into the crowd, and fell without being hit. He saw the kick coming and rolled away from it feeling very angry, which he had not felt all day until now. Somebody had stepped in and pushed Bloom back and was admonishing with him about not fighting fair. He saw that it was Stark in the gathering darkness. The crowd was loudly agreeing with Stark. The crowd did not want their boxing exhibition ruined now after it was so fine by having them start fighting on the ground. Bloom was disagreeing.

When he stepped back in Bloom had his right drawn way back and cocked, to hit him, standing as close as they would let him get to him, and Prew came down with the heel of his field shoe smashing it down on Bloom's instep. Bloom opened his mouth wide to yell, his right still drawn back and cocked but forgotten, and Prew jabbed hard with his left landing flush on the bad nose and Bloom yelled and put both hands up and he hooked with his left to the belly as low as he could get without actually hitting Bloom in the balls and Bloom did not grunt but he put both hands down, probably because the jab on the nose and the hurt instep had stunned him a little, and he was wide open for the right to the adam's apple, and Prew threw it. It hurt his hand like hell but it was worth it. Bloom choked and grabbed his neck with both hands and fell down off his feet for the first time.

On his knees his head hanging Bloom choked and hawked and gasped and felt of his neck gingerly and his face turned red, then purple, then almost black and he lay down. He vomited his supper and then got back up choking and rushed at Prew with his head down like a ram.

Prew had stepped back to give him room and it was lucky he had because if he had been any closer he would not have had time to bring his knee up in Bloom's down-turned face if he had been any closer. As it was, the bone of his knee hit Bloom's chest and only the thick pad of thigh muscle hit Bloom's face and nose. Bloom went over backward and landed in the vomit, his nose that was broken but not bleeding or swollen, his eye that was blacked but not closed or swollen, his belly that was punched repeatedly but not bruised, his adam's apple that should be mashed but could still swallow, all showing nothing, no worthwhile damage, and lay on his elbow breathing desperately and looked at Prew. Then he got up and started to come again, this time with his hands up cautiously, and Prew wondered Jesus Christ I've hit him with everything but the ringpost waterbucket and referee what do you have to do to him, and that was when the Battalion Chaplain, Second Lieutenant Anjer C Dick, stepped in from the back of the circle.

They were both very glad to see him.

"Boys," Lt Dick said, "dont you think its gone far enough now? I hate to see you boys fight like this. Its only a waste of energy and nothing is ever decided by it. If you boys would put half as much energy into helping each other," Lt Dick said in his mild religious voice, "that you do into hurting each other we would all be a lot better off and I would probably lose my job."

The crowd laughed and Lt Dick looked around at them and smiled broadly.

Neither of them said anything.

"Besides," Lt Dick said, "Bloom here is supposed to fight tonight, isnt he? If you boys fight much longer he wont have time to change clothes before he gets in the ring."

The crowd laughed and Lt Dick looked around at them and smiled broadly. Then he put his arm around Prew and the other arm around Bloom and said, "Shake hands, boys. A little friendly fight like this is always all right, it cleans up a boy's blood, but you dont want to carry it too far, do you? I want you to stop now," he said. "Now shake hands," he said.

They shook hands grudgingly and Lt Dick took his arms from around them and Prew staggered off to the barracks and Bloom staggered off to the gym to get ready to fight. Lt Dick stayed and talked with the crowd.

Prew sat on his bunk in the empty squadroom a long time. He decided he would not go to town. He went in the empty latrine and vomited up his supper but he did not feel any better. His head hurt and was very sore on the temple where Bloom had connected and that ear burned like fire. His hand was still swelling. His arms felt like he could not lift them and were beginning to show dark bruises of the punches he had caught on them. His legs quivered every time he stood up. He did not feel he had accomplished a whole hell of a lot. The thought of going to bed with Alma, or anybody else, made him feel utterly hollow. After a while, when he heard the first cheers from the quad of the first bout of the smoker, he showered and put on a clean uniform and went down shakily and out through the empty dayroom over to the Post Beergarden.

Chief Choate was sitting at one of the tables out on the grass under the trees. The Chief had moved over from Choy's on account of the crowd at the smoker, but the forest of empty bottles and cans on the table might have been the same forest transplanted from his old corner table every evening at Choy's. He looked up at Prew ponderously contentedly from out of his forest.

"Sit down," he said. "You got a nice ear there."

Prew pulled out a chair. He could feel his face grinning. "Its sore. But it dint catch enough the punch to get thick on me."

"Here," Chief said happily, "have a beer." He inspected his forest with weighty deliberation and uprooted one of the trees. He pushed it over to Prew with all the formality of bestowing a medal. "What I hear," he said in his slow careful way, "I'd say you done pretty fair. Considerin you wasnt in trainin."

Prew looked at him, suspecting sarcasm. Then he saw that it wasnt. He accepted with dignity. He was beginning suddenly to feel a lot better. Chief Choate did not hand out beers and seats at his table promiscuously.

"I'm gettin too old for that kind of stuff," he said modestly, and tiredly. "Jesus!" he said. "I dont see how he can even climb in a ring. Let alone fight. You really reckon he'll still be able to fight?"

"He'll fight," Chief said. "That boy's a horse. And he wants that rating."

"I hope you're right. I wouldnt want to of thrown him out of bein able to fight. I wouldnt want to do that."

"What I hear you sure dint ack like it," Chief grinned gently.

Prew grinned back and leaned back in his chair and picked up the beer. It was salty sharp in the long draught that cut through the thick spit in his throat clearing it, icily clearing his head. "Ahhh," he said gratefully. "Well, he's had it coming to him for a long time. He's been askin for it ever since I got in this compny."

"He sure has," Chief said happily.

"But I wount want to cut him out of bein able to fight."

"He'll fight," Chief said. "He's a reglar horse. If he had the kind of mind to go with the rest of him there wouldnt be a heavyweight, even, in the Department could touch him."

"He's gunshy," Prew said.

"Thats what I mean," Chief said. "He'll fight. And probly win. They got him matched with a green hand from I Compny. He'll fight, but I bet he wont talk much for a couple days."

"By god, I bet he wont," Prew said happily.

"And he'll always believe you done it on purpose to screw him."

"So will Dynamite."

Chief nodded his great head ponderously, as if it took considerable effort. "You'll be on the shitlist for fair now. But you was already on it before. And I dont see how even Dynamite can court-martial you over a fair fight on the green when thats his own policy."

"Hell no," Prew said happily. "I dont see how they can do that."

"Bloom wount be so bad," Chief said thoughtfully philosophically, "if he just forgit for a while he was a Jew."

Prew felt something come up into his mind again. "Hell," he protested. "I dont give a damn he's a Jew."

"Me neither," Chief said. "The guys call Sussman Jewboy all the time. He dont care. They call Bloom Jewboy and he wants to beat up on everybody. Hell, they call me Indian, dont they? Well, I am a Indian, aint I? Well, Bloom's a Jew, aint he?"

"Thats right," Prew said. He felt the something go back down again in his mind. "Hell, man, I'm French and Irish and German. So what? They call me Frenchy or Mick or Squarehead I wount be mad, would I?"

"Thats right," Chief said ponderously.

"Thats right," Prew agreed happily.

"Course," Chief said, "I know some dumb fucks treat a Jew mean, but not in our Compny."

"Sure," Prew said. "Well, look how they treated the Indians."

"Thats right," Chief said. "And a man's got to learn who to hit and who not to hit."

"Thats right," Prew said. He leaned back expansively, the beer had hit him quicker than usual, and looked around the yelling lattice-fenced triangular plot with its roofed U-shaped bar in the center of the three meeting streets that for the last twenty years had been hallowed ground. Over in one corner a grizzled knot of old master sergeants huddled over their beers excluding the young punks of forty by reminiscing about Villa in Mexico and the Philippine Insurrection when they had taught the Goddam Moros and spiks what was what. Men hollered three deep at the bar. A group of recruits in shiny unfaded suntans were standing with their arms around each other's shoulders singing *We're Captain Billy's troopers, We are riders of the night, We*

462

are dirty sons of bitches and we'd rather fuck than fight. Over the hubbub now and then came the faint sound of a roar from the quad that told of a knockdown. It was all very permanent, and he knew that he was part of it. He had a place in all of it.

"Dont look like the other regmints takin much intrest in our compny smokers," he grinned maliciously.

"Why the hell should they?" the Chief said gently. "We aint got a chance of a fart in a whirlwind of takin that trophy back next December, and everybody knows it."

Prew looked at the great solid bulk of him, utterly unshakeable, and grinned, loving him for his unshakeability in what in the last month had become an unfounded maelstrom of the whole universe. "Old Chief," he said happily. "Old Chief. The jockstraps," he said. "The fucking jockstraps."

"Watch that, Mack," Chief grinned. "I jockstrap a little bit myself."

Prew laughed wildly.

"Have nuther beer," the Chief said.

"Naw sir, my turn to buy one."

"Plenty here. Help yourself. You earned it."

"No sir," Prew said stoutly. "I'm buying this one. I got money. I always got money, now."

"Yeah," the Chief grinned somberly. "I noticed that. You must of really line yourself up quite a deal with that snatch down town."

"I aint doin so bad," Prew grinned expansively. "Not bad atall.— Ony trouble is," he heard his voice saying, "is the goddam rip wants to marry me."

"Well hell," the Chief rumbled philosophically, "she got that much money you be smart to go ahead and marry her, and let her support you in the style to which you would like to be accustomed."

Prew laughed. "Not me, Chief. You know I aint the marrying kind."

He walked over to the bar at the north end happily. You liar, he told himself happily, you and your big deals. Well, it was a good deal, a damned good deal, wasnt it? looked at one way. What the hell? A goddam man ought to have the goddam right to goddam dream. "Hey, Jimmy!" he hollered belligerently.

"Hey there boy!" big Jimmy hollered at him from down at the other end of the bar. His broad Kanaka face was grinning through the sweat and his hands opening and passing out cans and bottles as fast as he could pull them out of the cooler. At the other end of the cooler stood the Beergarden guard, always a Regimental fighter from first one outfit then another hired to keep order by the manager in compliance with Post orders, wearing his garrison belt and billy, badges of temporary office, and helping himself to can after can from the depths of the cooler while the helpless Jap manager watched him with frustrated pain on his smooth flat face.

"Gimme four, Jim," Prew hollered over the rippling field of heads.

"Right," Jimmy hollered, a grin flashing dazzlingly out of the dark face. "Four beer for four queer." He brought them down. "Compny smokers you outfit tonight, boy. You no fight?"

"Not me, Jim," he grinned happily. "I'm scared I'll git a caulyflower ear."

"Boy, you a hot one," Jimmy laughed, wiping his face with a hand like a deep-smoke-cured ham. "You no kid me, boy. I hear you just take at big Jewboy white hope over, eh?"

"Is that the story?" he grinned. "Way I heard it, he took me over." He could feel through the back of his neck several men pausing to look. Somebody whispered something. It must have spread fast. He did not look around.

"Hah," Jimmy grinned. "Listen, boy, I see you fight em last year in a Bowl. You good boy. At Jewboy big an he hit hard but he no got the heart. Jewboys never got the heart. You got the heart, eh?"

"Is that the way it is?" he grinned modestly. "How about my four beers."

"Right here, boy. Sure, way it is," Jimmy said. "Those Jewboy they better learn who to pick on, eh? I fight again next mont downtown myself, kid."

The other men were still watching.

"Where at?" Prew said happily, feeling very esoteric. "The Civic?"

"Ats it. Six round semi-windup. Win at one, get a main go. Win a main go, take big trip Stateside to fight. What you think of him, eh? Quit this goddam job."

"Another regular Dado Marino, eh?" Prew grinned.

Jimmy exploded in laughter and swelled his big chest that almost filled up the bar. "Ats me. Make good flyweight-bantamweight, eh?" he laughed. "No," he said seriously. "Go Stateside, like grandfather. Last name Kaliponi, you know? Jimmy Kaliponi. Name for grandfather take big trip Stateside in old days. Hawaiian language, no f, no r. Cant say California, say Kaliponi. Got to win fight, go Kaliponi like grandfather, live up to name, see it over there, no mo hila-hila, eh?" he grinned. "I like at Stateside, boy, what I hear about em."

"I'll come down and see you lay him out," Prew grinned.

"Good old Civic," Jimmy said. "Lots of fight. Old Dixie use to fight Civic all a time. Remember old Dixie? My good frien, Dixie. Plenty good boy, eh?"

Prew felt a big hollow open up suddenly under the happiness and suck it down out of him. He reached for the beers.

"Yeah," he said, "plenty good boy."

Jimmy was shaking his head, the big laughing face suddenly sad. "Too plenty bad about Dixie go blind like that." It was the first time he had ever mentioned it to Prew. "You have tough time, boy, tough luck. You good frien like that. Too plenty dam bad, boy."

"Yeah, yeah, too bad," Prew said. "Gimme my beers."

"Here you go." Jimmy shoved them to him. "No pay. On me this time." The big sad face was just as suddenly laughing again. "I sure glad to see you take at white hope Jewboy over, eh? Godam Jews bad as godam Germans. Just the same Try to own whole world. But us America no take at stuff, eh? We got the heart. Jewboys and Germans no got the heart."

"Yeah, yeah," Prew said, backing out of the press with the beers. "Jewboys and Germans no got the heart," he said, repeating it in a low voice, as if to himself. Jewboys and Germans, and Wops, and Spiks, and Boston Irishes, and Hunkies, and Guinies, and Niggers, no got the heart. He turned back toward the table feeling a little sick now in the hollowness in his stomach. He didnt fight Bloom because Bloom was a Jew. Why did they always have to make a racial issue of it all the time?

Behind him he heard Jimmy holler, "Right! Two beer for two queer." It was Jimmy Kaliponi's favorite joke. Wait till Jimmy Kaliponi got to go Stateside, if he won his main go, and found that niggers no got the heart either, Stateside. Would that surprise him, Jimmy Kaliponi. Maybe he would even try to explain the difference between niggers and Hawaiians to them, eh? You explain, eh? You tell them, eh? Or maybe he would come back home quick, Jimmy Kaliponi, where only Jewboys and Germans no got the heart.

Walking to the table across the carpet of rich grass, he knew he would have to look Bloom up and explain to Bloom he did not fight Bloom because Bloom was a Jew. He would do it tonight, right now, except Bloom would be waiting in the gym to go on for his fight. After the fights, then. Only Bloom would be pooped and in the yelling gym right up until he went to bed, or else out celebrating with some of the punchies, if Bloom won. Tomorrow, then. He would do it tomorrow. He would explain it to Bloom.

He had fought Bloom because he had had to fight somebody, or else bite himself and go mad, the same reason Bloom had fought him, two men who were on edge and ridden raw, and they got in a fight for the amusement of all concerned, except themselves, and fought each other, and that was all, him and Bloom who probably had more in common than any other two men in the Company, except maybe Angelo Maggio, fighting each other, because it was so much easier than trying to find the real enemy to fight, because the real enemy the common enemy was so hard to find since you did not know what it was to look for it and could not see it to get your hands on it, so you fought each

465

other, which was easier, and also made it easier to put up with the real enemy the common enemy, whatever it was, that you could not find, but not because Bloom was a Jew or you a something else.

He had not thought about Dixie Wells for a long time now. He had almost forgotten Dixie Wells. Who would ever have thought he could have ever forgotten Dixie Wells! He would have to explain to Bloom.

Then he knew, hollowly, that he could not explain to Bloom. Because Bloom himself would always firmly believe it was because he was a Jew. And nothing he could ever say or do would ever convince Bloom it was not because he was a Jew, and because Prewitt hated Jews. And it was pointless to try to explain to Bloom, tonight, or tomorrow, or the next day, or any other time.

He looked down at the Chief who was peering up at him out of the forest of bottles and cans like a platoon scout peeking out of the woods, the big mild moonface that was rocklike in unshakeability and that was redblack with layer after layer of tropic burn from every foreign Department of the US Army, laid over the dark Choctaw blood that was there from the beginning, the same face that all over the world where US soldiers congregated to discuss sports was always mentioned with reverent awe, that held alike indifferently the former heavyweight championship of Panama and the current still unbroken Philippine record for the 100 yard dash and that was running down into beerfat now, but still was well known and idolized by Islands sport fans as Lou Gehrig was back in the States, and who was now steadily and efficiently drinking himself into his regular nightly stupor. What would his ecstatic worshippers at the YMCA say if they could see him now?

He sat down at the table with the beers, looking at the great ponderous frame, so cumbersome in the frail chair but that could be so swift and accurate on the ball diamond or basketball floor or track field or football gridiron. How many times had he watched with the thrill of seeing a Pacific sunset as the big figure leaned lithely into a throw from shortstop to beat the runner at first by a fraction?

"Chief," he said urgently. "Chief, whats the story?"

"Hunh?" Chief Choate grunted blandly. "What story? Story on what?"

"I dont know," Prew shrugged. He was embarrassed. He hunted frantically in his mind. "The story on Warden," he said lamely, as if that were the only thing that could explain it. "Whats the deal with The Warden, Chief? I cant figure him. What makes him like he is, anyway?"

"Warden?" Chief Choate said. He looked out at the dark street through the white screen of latticework, as if fumbling in his mind clumsily for what the other wanted. "Warden? I dont know. Nothing especial I know of, why?"

"Oh, I dont know," Prew said, lamely, beginning already now to curse himself for a fool. "I cant figure him, thats all," he said. "He was our Staff in A when I was in the Corps, before he got his First. I seen him around a lot then. He can be the meanest man I ever seen, and next minute he sticks his neck clear out to get you out of a jam he helped to get you into."

"Yeah?" said Chief Choate awkwardly, "he does, dont he?" He was still staring out. "He's a hard one to figure, all right, I guess. All I know, he's the best kicker in the Regmint. I wouldnt be surprised he's the best one on the Post. You dont see many Firsts like him no more." Chief Choate grinned bitterly. "They are a vanishing race," he said.

Prew nodded eagerly lamely. "Thats what I mean," he persisted, now that he was into it. "Sometimes I feel like I could understand a lot of things if I could understand The Warden. Sometimes I— If he was a plain out and out son of a bitch like Haskins in E, you could figure him. I know a rotten top like that when I was in Myer; meanest bastard livin; liked to hurt people; liked to see them squirm. I clerked for him a while and finally quit and transferred out."

"Yeah?" Chief Choate said with easy interest. "I dint know you ever pushed a pen, Prew."

"Not many people do," Prew said shortly. "I got it kept off my Service Record and Form 20 with the clerk in that outfit, so nobody'd know and draft me back into it ever." He paused. "I learnt myself typin out a book in the Post Liberry, I guess I was huntin, lookin around for somethin," he said. Then doggedly he came back. "But you see what I mean. This guy I'm tellin you about was just mean through and through. He couldnt handle men and he hated them because he cou'nt, see? You can figure him. He got his rating ass-kissing, and he was always scared there was a browner nose than his around someplace. Easy to figure."

"Yeah," Chief Choate said. He nodded his great head slowly, listening respectfully, trying hard. "I know guys like that when I come here. I know them here."

"But that aint the story with The Warden, though," Prew said. "I dont feel he's bein mean. I got a kind of funny feelin about him. A kind of—weird feelin, you know?"

Chief nodded. "Some guys is just bornd unlucky," he said slowly. "I personally figure Warden is one of them guys."

"How do you mean, unlucky?"

"Well, its hard to explain," Chief Choate said restlessly.

Prew waited.

"You take me," Chief said, "for instance. I was a kid on the reservation. Bornd and raised there. And I wanted to be a jockstrap. The worst way I wanted to be one. Jim Thorpe was my idol. I use to read every-thing about him I could find. And I listened to the stories they all told about him. He was a hero to the people. And I thought Jim Thorpe was wonderful, and I wanted to be just like him, see?"

Prew nodded. These were things he had never heard before, nor any-body else he knew of. Maybe there was something here, maybe here was—something. Important.

Chief emptied off a can with a long swallow and set it back on the table carefully with sausage fingers among the forest. "Well, they kicked him out of the Olympic Game," he said slowly. "After he'd won damn near every medal they had. They kicked him out on a techni-cality. They wouldnt even let him keep his medals. Then I seen him playin them wild Indians in them western movies. You see what I mean?"

Prew nodded, watching the big calm face look off across the yard.

"I got bigger," Chief said, "I wanted to go to college and jockstrap. But I dint even have no highschool. And besides, my old man dint have enough dough to keep the fambly in levis. And I couldnt get no scholarship. How could I get a scholarship?

"And there was Jim Thorpe, playin Indians in western movies for a livin." He shrugged his great shoulders and it was like a small earth-quake in the forest on the table. "He was probly the greatest jockstrap this country ever had," he hazarded shyly. "Well, thats just the way it is. Thats the way things go, see? Thats life. Well, could you see me wearin buckskin pants and warpaint and a big old feather bonnet? run-nin around yellin with a tommyhawk? Well, neither could I. I'd feel like a goddam ass. The ony gadgets like that I ever even seen was all shipped down from a factory in Wisconsin to the Trading Post to sell to tourists. I'd feel like it was a . . . I'd feel ashamed.

"So I shipped into the army, where jockstrappin would do me some good and live easy. It dont bother me none. You see what I mean?"

"Yeah," Prew said, his grin bitter as the edge of a razor.

"Well, with me, thats okay. I got no complaints." Chief looked good-humoredly around the smokedrifting talkhumming lawn.

"You know where the words Dogface and Dog Soldier come from?" he said suddenly. "They come from the old Cheyenne War Society in the Plains Wars, they called themselves Dog Soldiers. The Cavalry took it from them."

"No," Prew said. "I didnt know that."

"Well," Chief said, "thats where we got them." He looked around the place again. "And I bet not ten men ever know where they come from.

"I like to take things pretty much like they come," he said. "Thats the way it is, then thats the way I am, see? I do what I can, and what I cant, I dont worry about. I live easy and I figure I got nothin much to bitch about.

"But Warden's differnt. They's something eatin him up inside. Its like he's got a fire in him that burns him up, and ever now and then it'll pop up into his eyes. If you ever watched him, you see it. Warden dont belong in the Army."

"Well, why the hell dont he get out then?" Prew said. "Nobody's ast him to get in the Army and stay in it. If he dont like it, whynt he get out and get where he does belong."

Chief Choate looked at him levelly. "You know where he belongs?" Prew dropped his eyes. "Okay," he said.

"A man knows where he belongs is lucky, way I see it," Chief Choate said. "Warden's a good man, but he just dont belong in the Army. Pete Karelsen's a good man, too, but he dont belong in the Army neither. I dont neither. Dynamite belongs in the Army."

"Okay," Prew said again, "okay. But why does he want to ride *me* so much for. If he was mean, and really had it in for me, I could figure it. But somehow I always feel like he dont have nothing against me really."

"Maybe he's tryin to teach you somethin," Chief said.

"What?" Prew said.

"What!" Chief said. "I dont know. How would I know what Warden's tryin to teach you?" he said angrily embarrassedly. His perpetually placid face was still good-natured, but behind his eyes suddenly was the cold flat look of the Reservation Indian toward the white tourists who have come to watch his dances during their two week vacation. "Why the hell dont you ask The Warden, if you want to know so bad? Maybe he'll tell you."

Prew grinned, his starched campaign hat pushed back to show his lank black hair that might have come from some forgotten Cherokee among his own Kentucky ancestors.

"Snow me," he grinned. "Snow me some more. Bury me deep."

Chief grinned. "I dont know," he said, mollified. "I dont know what he's tryin to teach you. And I dont think anybody'll ever know, except maybe Warden, and maybe not him. Thats what I think. He's just a wild son of a bitch. He aint got nothing against you personal, he's the same way with everybody. Old Pete swears onct a week he's gonna move out on him if he has to sleep in the squadroom even—but he never does."

"But if I could ony just understand why," Prew persisted. He was beginning to feel disgusted with it now, foolish with it. He wished now he had kept his stupid mouth shut. For a minute he had thought he

469

was going to learn something, something important. But it all sifted through your fingers like sand and left you holding nothing.

Chief Choate was looking vaguely out through the lattice toward the dim light of the PX lunchcounter lights across the street. "Warden's one of them men who cant get killed," he said with bearlike gentleness. "He was in the 15th when they seen their action in the Settlement in Shanghai. I heard about it down in PI even. He was just . . . He got himself a Purple Heart and a DSC out of it, but you never knew it, did you? Aint many does. He's just a wild man, thats all, cant find nothin to pin onto. When this next war comes, Warden will be right in there, standin up on the skyline, trying to get himself killed, but nothin will ever touch him. He'll come right through in spite a hell nor high water, maddern, wildern, craziern ever. Thats just the way he is. Thats all I know. All I know is he's the best soljer I ever saw."

Prew did not contradict him. He sat looking at him, feeling something, trying to feel something else.

"What do you say we drink some beer?" Chief said. "I like beer."

"Thats the best idea yet," Prew said, and hunched himself down over the beer cans Black Jimmy had insisted on setting him up to. It didnt make sense. He knew he would have to see Bloom tomorrow anyway, even if it wouldnt do any good. Something in what Chief Choate'd said, something unspoken in the garbled mess of the conversation, had made him know it. He had to try to explain it to Bloom. Maybe it wouldnt do any good, but he knew he had to try it.

The fights got over early. The crowds from the smoker began to swell in through the lattice gates of the Beer Garden before it was even ten o'clock. There had been an unusual number of knockouts. All three of the G Company men had won their bouts, but everybody talked excitedly about Bloom. Bloom had won his main go with a TKO in the first round. Everybody had great hopes of Bloom. He had climbed in the ring with a broken nose, black eye, and unable to talk and scored a knockdown in the first half minute. Doc Dahl, the Regimental surgeon, had not wanted him to go on at all.

"That boy knows which side his corporalcy is buttered on," Chief Choate said without enthusiasm.

"I'm glad he got to go on, though," Prew said. "And I'm even gladder he won."

"He's a horse," the Chief said blandly. "A regular horse. Use to be one myself. He could do the same thing over again right now and not even feel it."

"It took a lot of guts though."

"Not for a horse," the Chief said.

Prew sighed. The beer was spinning brightly in him. "I think I'll take off and go home to bed. I'm sore as a boil, and I feel about as popular as a dildoe in a virgins' convent right now."

Chief grinned. "I guess it would make you feel a little self-conscious maybe."

Prew managed to laugh, and threaded his way out through the crowd. At the gate he looked back. Chief Choate sat at table as before. The empty cans had grown visibly since Prew came. Chief's eyes were getting a little swimmy now as he raised his hand ponderously slowly to return a greeting. Prew went on out. It was very quiet outside as he crossed the street. The lights were off in all the quadrangles and they were mopping out the Main PX lunchcounter for closing. He walked slow, so as to give the quad plenty of time to be cleared out. He did not want to meet anybody.

It looked deserted as he turned in through the truck entrance and the lights were off in the bandstand-ring, but as he walked up the Company walk to the porch a shadow came out from under it moving to meet him. Even in the dark he could recognize the long-armed apeshape. It was Ike Galovitch, drunk and weaving.

"Py Gott," Ike bawled. "Ham telling you dis tonight a great night are. Der own into dis night G Gomny and da Gaptn Holmes have gome," he hollered happily. "Did we taking them toonight or not taking dem. I ask you? Are proud dis gomny to be of or not? 'Ey?"

"Hello, Ike," he said.

"Who that is?" Ike Galovitch stopped grinning and the long lippy jaw came out as he leaned forward drunkenly to peer. "That not is Prewitt? What that is?"

"Prewitt that is, all right," he grinned back tightly.

"Gott am," Ike exploded. "A lot of guts you got your face around here heven showing, Prewitt. In dese barricks it is no right heven have a traitor like you to be sleeping."

"Thats right, but till transfer me out they do sleep here I got to notwithstanding." He stepped out to go around but Ike stepped across in front of him.

"Transfer you to da Stockade," Ike growled. "Dat bites de hand dat feeds it dey shoot dogs for. Heven a Commonist is batter. Dan to stabbing in da back da best frien any man ever having hafter da breaks da Gaptn Holmes having giving you. Infortunately, ony dogs dey are allowed to shoot not men."

"And you'd sure like to see them change the laws, wouldnt you I bet, Ike, hunh?" Prew grinned. He stood passively, he had tried once, he would not try to go around again.

"For you, hyes," Ike raged. "For mad dogs shooting is too good. Dis Harmy only strong has weakest links. It is da rebel ones like you mak-

471

ing da Fascisti over der I leave for come dis country. Bolsheviki like you har should not heven be allow dis country. Should be run out dis country."

"If you've had your say now, old man," he said, "get out of my way and I'll go to bed."

"Had my say!" Old Ike raged on. "Not heven an Hamurican you are. Not heven enough be grateful for tings good men like da Gaptn Holmes are willing do for you. What you need is lesson teach you to respeck your betters when they nice enough are to do tings for you."

"And theres nothin you'd like better than to have the job," he grinned, "right? Listen, I stepped around you once. I aint going to step around you again. See me tomorrow during duty hours, when I cant talk back. But right now get the fuck out of my way so I can go to bed."

"Yeahr?" Ike said. "And maybe I just take da job, laws or laws not. Has done everting for you can one man do, da Gaptn Holmes. You are grateful?" he hollered furiously. "Like shit. Fine man offer you chance do someting, do you do? No. Not you. Maybe I give to you da lesson by myself, since da Gaptn Holmes too nice to do him. How you like den?"

"Fine," he grinned. "When do we start? Tomorrow at drill?"

"Drill hell. Py Gott am you, I show you dont need drill or sargint ratting."

Cursing drunkenly, Ike Galovitch, American, pulled his knife out of his pocket. It was not the professional knifer's snap blade job like Sgt Henderson's, but Ike opened it almost as quickly, thumbnailing the slot to raise the point out of the cradle far enough to catch it on his pantsleg as he ripped it up one handed, all in one movement too fast to see, and the blade was out and bare throwing oily glints of light.

Prew watched him almost happily. Here, at last, was the enemy. The real enemy. The common enemy.

When Ike Galovitch, American, lunged drunkenly with his knife, he stepped to meet him, parrying the wrist and arm outside him with his left hand, and stepped in again turning on the balls of his feet deftly. Ike went off balance sideways and was already falling when he swung with his right hand, putting his whole weight and everything he had behind it viciously. It was a Sunday shot and he timed it perfectly and the pain shot up his swollen hand into his wrist.

Ike Galovitch, American, moved backward off the walk still holding out the knife, his feet going backward very fast across the grass. His heels hit the kitchen sidewalk on the other side and he skidded the last three feet on his rump and came up against the concrete garbage rack platform, his head lolling back in the drippings.

472

Prew stood on the walk and watched him, rubbing his hand. Ike did not move, and he walked over and put his ear to the old man's mouth. Ike Galovitch, American, was sleeping peacefully and breathing regularly and stinkingly, an ugly, seamed-faced, beat-up and battered, tired old man who had come all the long way from Yugoslavia to Hawaii to find an idol he could worship. This was no common enemy, this was only a foul-breathed, rotting-toothed, repulsively ugly old Slav of a peasant whom nobody on this earth, not even Dynamite Holmes least of all his mother, had ever given a damn for if he lived or died. How would you like to look at that face in the mirror every morning and know yourself as so repulsive? Only just wait till he wakes up, he thought, and the mind begins to work again, what then? He might easily have killed you, he would have if he could. He stood looking down at the incredibly innocently sleeping patheticness, then he took the knife and snapped the well honed blade off in a deep crack in the concrete of the platform and put the bladeless handle back in the open palm and went upstairs to bed.

He did not see the two figures of Sergeant Henderson and Sergeant Wilson that weaved out from under the shadow of the porch to where Ike lay, after he was gone, and he would not have cared much then if he had.

It was a flashlight in his face that woke him. His watch said midnight. He was still a little drunk. All he could think of was it was another sabotage alert.

"Here he is," a voice whispered, and an arm with corporal's stripes reached inside the cone of light that he could not see beyond and shook him by the shoulder. "Come on, Prewitt, lets rise and shine. Drop your cocks and grab your socks," the voice chanted automatically. "Get up out of there."

"What's the matter?" he said out loud. "How about gettin that goddam light out of my eyes."

"Goddam it, be quiet," the voice whispered. "You want to wake up the whole goddam Compny? Come on. Get up." It was Cpl Miller's, the CQ's, voice.

He knew what it was. In the last month he had pictured the whole thing many times. Now, he wanted suddenly to laugh, at the cautious solicitude for the Compny's rest. He had not pictured that.

"What is it?" he said.

"Get up," the CQ whispered. "You're under arrest."

"What for?"

"I dont know. This is him, Sergeant," the CQ said. "This is the man you want."

"Okay, Corporal," said the second voice. "You can go on back to bed.

I can handle it from here." The voice paused and changed its angle of direction. "This is the man, Sir," it said. "Private Prewitt. I think the man's still drunk."

"Very well then," the third voice said boredly. "Rout him out and get some clothes on him. I havent got all night. The OD must inspect the posts, you know. Lets rout him out."

"Yes, Sir," the guard sergeant said.

The same arm with the corporal's stripes came inside the cone at him again. He's surely working hard, he grinned to himself.

"Come on, lets go," the CQ said. "Get up. Get some clothes on. You heard what the OD said." The arm gripped his naked shoulder.

He moved his shoulder out from under it. "Keep your goddam hands off of me, Miller. I can get up by myself. Just take it easy."

The leather of the sergeant's billy thong squeaked.

"Lets have no trouble, Private," the OD's bored voice said. "The more trouble you make the harder it will go with you. We are quite able to take you in by force, if necessary."

"I dont want no trouble, only just keep your hands off me. I wont run. Whats the charges against me?"

"Say Sir, when you speak to an officer, buddy," the sergeant said. "Whats the matter with you?"

"Never mind," the OD said. "Just get him dressed. I havent got all night. The OD must inspect the posts, you know."

He slid himself up from between the sheets by force of habit, leaving the bunk needing only to be tightened, before he remembered. The flashlight followed him as he climbed out nakedly.

"Would you mind takin that goddam light out of my eyes? So I can see my clothes? What am I being taken in for?"

"Never mind," the OD said. "Just do as you're told. You'll have plenty of time to find that out. Move the light, Sergeant."

"My wallet's in my footlocker," Prew said, when he was dressed. Around them in the squadroom men were sitting up watching, their eyes very big reflecting the light of the flash.

"Never mind the wallet," the OD said impatiently. "You wont need it. Your equipment will be taken care of. You men there," he said. "Go back to bed and go to sleep. This is none of your affair."

As one man the lights reflecting from the eyes went out. The bunks squeaked as they lay down and rolled over in silence, away from the light.

"Theres money in it, Sir," Prew said. "If I dont take it with me, it wont be here when I get back."

"All right then," the OD said impatiently. "Get it then. But hurry up."

He was already shaking the footlocker key out from the bottom of his pillowslip. The Sgt led him down the stairs with the OD behind him and the CQ bringing up the rear.

"I aint going to take off on you," Prew grinned.

"Dont I know it," the Sgt said.

"Never mind," the OD said.

"And shut up," the Sgt said.

Downstairs in the corridor the CQ's light was on, the mosquito netting still hastily thrown back from his bunk beside the little desk, and in the light Prew could see them. The OD was 1st Lt Van Voorhees of Battalion Headquarters, tall and big-nosed and flat-headed, three years out of the Point. The sergeant was a man he didnt know by name but he recognized his face. Cpl Miller he had soldiered with for months. They were strangers.

"Hold it up, you," the Sgt said and turned to Miller. "You got this on your report yet?"

"No," Miller said. "I was just going to ask you."

They stood by the desk talking in low secret voices. Prew listened to them reciting the names and numbers that went on the report. He felt peculiar. Lt Van Voorhees stood by himself at the door tapping his fingernails in succession on the jamb.

"Lets hurry it up, Sergeant," Lt Van Voorhees said.

"Yes, Sir," the Sgt said. "Well, thanks a lot, Corporal," he said. "Sorry we had to wake you up. You can go back to bed now."

"You're very welcome," Miller said. "Any time I can be of help. You sure theres nothing more I can do?"

"Nope," the Sgt said. "Its all done now."

"Okay," Miller said. "Just ask me though."

"No," the Sgt said. "Thanks though. We appreciate your help."

"Any time," Miller said.

Prew turned to Lt Van Voorhees. "Whats the charges, Sir," he said, "on me."

"Never mind," the Lt said impatiently. "You'll have plenty of time to find that out tomorrow." He looked at his watch impatiently.

"But I've got a right to know the charges against me," Prew said. "Who preferred charges?"

Van Voorhees peered at him. "You dont have to inform me of your rights, soldier. I know what they are. Capt Holmes preferred the charges. And I dont like guardhouse lawyers. Are you finished, Sergeant?"

The Sgt nodded busily.

Prew whistled. "They sure worked fast," he grinned, "whoever it was. Must of got him up out of bed." As a joke, it did not come off very well.

"Well, lets get gone then," Van Voorhees said to the Sgt, as if nobody else had spoken. "I've got work to do."

"Shut up, Mack," the Sgt said to Prew. "The more you pop off, the harder you make it on yourself. Come on, lets go. You heard what the OD said."

In the long low corrugated-iron Regimental guardhouse across the street they gave him a blanket and sent him back through the row of bars that separated the lockup from the office. They did not shut the door of bars hinged onto the wall of bars.

"We dont lock the door," the OD said from behind the desk, "on account of the members of the guard are back there. And you'd better not wake them up, by god. But there will be someone here all night awake and armed. Okay, thats all. You can go on back there and go to sleep."

"Yes, Sir," he said. "Thank you, Sir." He took the blanket down through the double row of cots and huddled sleeping figures of the guard until he found an empty one. He sat down on it and took his shoes off.

(*he was not new to this feeling of having crossed the line of bars into another heavier world of heavy air and heavy water he was not new to jails he knew that you would get used to breathing the heavy air eventually and then your lungs would no longer threaten to collapse on you because the heavy air did not want to go into them you just had to get acclimated that was all he knew all about jails jails were just as intimate to his life and heritage as being on the bum or soldiering he had learned to breathe the heavy air and drink the heavy water they were the same in every jail whether in Florida or Texas or Georgia or in Richmond Indiana he had learned jails even before he learned the Army in fact they kind of seemed to go together one way it just took a little time was all*)

He lay down on the cot and pulled the blanket over him.

Under the panic, that was fading, he thought: It must be because of Galovitch, it had to be that.

If Wilson and Henderson, he thought, had not tried to help the police dog to mount Bloom's dog Bloom would not have tried to thank me. If I, he thought, had not fought Bloom Old Ike would not have tried to knife me.

It was very complex and that tended to make it confusing, somewhat. But then, he knew the real thing did not lie in these circumstantial co-incidences. The real thing lay underneath that. He knew that. It was hard to remember, though.

As he dropped off to sleep he could hear the OD and the Sgt still sitting at the lighted desk talking in low voices.

Chapter 35

Lt Culpepper was appointed his defense counsel. The second or third or was it the fourth day (they were all the same, they were identical, every day they took him out under guard three times and fed him under guard at the E Company Mess where the guard was rationed, every day they took him out under guard two times and worked him under guard for the P&P pulling weeds under guard from the flowerbeds of the Officers' childrens' playground back of the married officers' quarters where he pulled the weeds on his knees in the fatigues under guard the guard standing over him guarding him and the children laughing yelling playing on the teetertotters swings and in the sandbox, it was not especially unpleasant) the second or third or was it the fourth day, Lt Culpepper came bustling in through the line of bars with the open door of bars from the other world like a whirlwind bringing the smell of the sea inland to the heavy drought-stricken prairies, and carrying the brand new briefcase with the zipper on three sides he had bought to carry the papers of the trial in, when he was appointed his defense counsel.

It was the first time Lt Culpepper had been appointed a defense counsel and he was enthusiastic over the case. The case had good prospects, if not of making a winning fight for an acquittal, at least a Pyrrhic victory he said, and they did not take him out under guard to pull weeds under guard in the afternoons any more, only in the mornings, after Lt Culpepper started coming in to talk about the case.

"Its a big responsibility," Lt Culpepper said enthusiastically. "Its my first chance to put in practice the semester of law and courts martial procedure they gave us at the Point, and they will all be watching to see how well I handle it. Naturally I want to do the very level best with it I can. I want to see you get the squarest deal I can possibly wangle for you and I mean to see you get it too."

Prew, unable to stop remembering the night at Hickam and the unfinishing of the Re-enlistment Blues, felt unaccountably embarrassed. He did not say much. He did not mention anything about the knife, which was not mentioned in the witnesses' signed statements Lt Culpepper showed him. He did not want to disappoint Lt Culpepper on his first case, but he absolutely refused to plead guilty. The whole of Lt Culpepper's campaign for the defense hung on pleading guilty.

"Well, of course," Lt Culpepper said enthusiastically, "that is your right. But I'm sure you will change your mind when I lay out our strategy for you."

"No I wont," Prew said.

"When you understand it is absolutely legally impossible to get you an acquittal," Lt Culpepper went on enthusiastically. "They've got Wilson and Henderson as witnesses, and Sgt Galovitch's own sworn statement, swearing under oath you were drunk and that you struck Sgt Galovitch when he remonstrated with you for causing a disturbance after lights out. We cant beat that."

He showed Prew the charges. Prew was charged with Drunk & Disorderly, with Insubordination, with Disobeying A Direct Order, and with Striking A Non-Commissioned Officer In The Performance of His Duty. He was also charged with Conduct Unbecoming To a Soldier. They were recommending a Special Court.

"As you see, its practically the same lineup they had on Maggio," Lt Culpepper beamed, "except for the Resisting Arrest."

"Dont you reckon they could work that one in too some way?" Prew said.

"However this is all within the Regiment," Lt Culpepper said. "Whereas with Maggio it happened downtown and the Department Provost Marshal's office came into it. In your case though, its only Capt Holmes your Company Commander who preferred the charges against you. So even with this Special Court, you cant possibly get more than three months and two-thirds."

"Thats good," Prew said.

"And if we work it right," Lt Culpepper said, "we can make it even less. But they've got the goods on you right, and theres no doubt you are guilty. Also, you have gotten yourself on just about everybody's shitlist in the Regiment. They've all more or less got it in for you and you've got a bad reputation as a bolshevik and a fuckup since you came to G Company. And of course that makes a tremendous difference, since its all politics anyway, you see. They've really got you."

"I can see that," Prew said.

"Well, thats why I want you to plead guilty," Lt Culpepper said triumphantly. "We have to fight it the same way. Politically. Not with this legal crap. I've made a study of these things, Prewitt. I wrote a very radical term paper for that course in courts martial procedure that created a hell of a hullabaloo at the Point. Got me all sorts of recognition. I pointed out how legal procedure has always tacitly been concerned with human relations, rather than abstract justice, and that consequently in spite of legal codes it is really the human relations underneath that determine the verdicts in the courts. And that, of course, means politics. You see? You understand that?"

"It sounds reasonable," Prew said.

"Reasonable hell!" Lt Culpepper exploded. "It was a veritable bomb. I proved conclusively that there just aint no such thing as abstract justice, simply because all legal decisions are influenced by the temporary inconstant of public feeling. For my best example I used the imprisonment of Debs and the 101 IWW Wobblies during the last war, which could never have happened without the high public feeling because of the war hysteria, not only because it was legally unsound but because Landis would never have dared do it in ordinary times. Then I brought in the political angle by showing how Darrow, who had defended the Wobblies before out west, had suddenly developed business that prevented him from defending them this time. You see how it all tics in together?" Lt Culpepper said enthusiastically.

"Oh, it was a beauty of a paper, Prewitt. Why, I even prophesied the time would come—after this next war, and the resulting civilian army—when EM would be allowed to serve on courts with officers! But, I pointed out also, that it would actually still be the same thing as now because any EM who got on a court would naturally be a M/Sgt or Tech or 1st/Sgt, or even if he was a Private, whose human relations would be naturally on the same side as the officers.

"You can imagine what *that* did to them. It got me more publicity than the fencing championship did. None of them, not even the profs, could break the logic of it. You can see that yourself. The way to get recognition in this world is to startle people. Somebody once said that bad publicity was better than no publicity. But I say, bad publicity is better than good publicity. Shock people and they remember you. Any dumb son of a bitch can get *good* publicity."

"I bet you felt good about it," Prew said.

"Good!" Lt Culpepper said. "Why Prewitt, it was the thing that made me at the Point, thats all. After that paper, I was a made man. But thats what we're working with here, you see? The same damn thing."

Lt Culpepper took a deep breath. "And thats why I want you to plead guilty. Why, its a thing that I dont think has ever been done in the history of courts martial. Nobody ever pleads guilty at a court martial because the court never makes concessions for clemency."

"Then it wont do much good, will it?" Prew said. "I——"

"You wait a minute. Let me lay it out for you before you go off half cocked. You dont see the implications yet."

"In the first place," Prew said, "I wasnt drunk. Not drunk enough that I dint know what I was doing."

"Thats my whole point," Lt Culpepper grinned triumphantly. "Whether you were really drunk or not doesnt matter. What matters is the witnesses say you were drunk. And by pleading guilty and admit-

479

ting that you were, you merely turn around and use their own testimonies against them."

"In other words," Prew said, "you mean I can prove they were lying by admitting what they say is true."

"Well," the lieutenant said, "you can put it that way, yes. But I didnt say they *were* lying. Maybe they're telling the truth."

"How can they be telling the truth if I'm telling the truth when I say I wasnt drunk?"

"Well in one sense they are lying, if you werent drunk. But in another sense they may be telling the truth, in that they really believe you were drunk. So actually, you both may be telling the truth, as you see it, and still disagree. See?"

"Yeah," Prew said. "Its deep, aint it?"

Lt Culpepper nodded. "And a lawyer has to take all those things into account for you. Thats why they appoint one. But all that is beside the point. The point is what is in the testimonies. The court wont believe you if you say you werent drunk. They may not come right out and say it, but in their minds they will. Because every criminal always protests he is innocent. Thats SOP. That only helps convict you, you see? What you'll really be doing is only trading a worthless fiction for three or four months in jail. The truth has nothing to do with the legal code a court martial runs by, or with the human relations that run the legal code. You see?"

"I guess so," Prew said. "But I——"

"Now wait a minute. I had this typed out, saying you were drunk and didnt know what you were doing."

Lt Culpepper opened the new yellow leather briefcase with the zipper on three sides and hunted in it and pulled out a paper and handed it to him. Then he closed the zipper lovingly.

"You read it over, to see its not putting you in a hole. I wouldnt want you to sign anything without reading it. Never sign anything without reading it, Prewitt. It'll get you in trouble someday, if you do. And then after you've read it and signed it, we'll turn it in out of the blue at the trial and I'll ask for clemency with the court. Then they cant honorably give you more than a month and two-thirds, maybe only the two-thirds fine with no jail time."

"I was always told military courts never accepted appeals for clemency," Prew said.

"Thats it," Lt Culpepper said enthusiastically. "Now you're getting it. I bet its never been done before in the history of courts martial. If it has, I never heard of it. We'll floor them."

"But I dont——"

"Now wait," Lt Culpepper admonished. "You havent heard the tipoff yet. Nobody;" he paused; "in the Army;" he paused; "considers drunkenness a misdemeanor or a sin, now do they? You know thats true. Its illegal but everybody does it. I get teed up myself up at the Club all the time, they all do it. In fact, although they never publish it in a Special Order of course or anything like that, most commanding officers like their wild and woolly boys by far the best because they know that kind of devil-may-care attitude is what makes the best soldiers. Actually, most officers feel that a soldier who doesnt get drunked up and go on a rampage now and then isnt worth his salt and is a suspicious character. Right?"

"I dont see how that has anything to do with me pleading guilty," Prew said.

"Well my God, man, dont you see? If you admit you were drunk and were just feeling your oats was all, then we turn the tables right back on them, because the getting drunk itself is tacitly considered more of a virtue than a sin, to a real soldier. The court, who understand and believe that, couldnt honestly give you three months, let alone the limit, just for being a hell-for-leather wild-and-woolly soldier. Of course, legally you would be guilty; but we dont care about that. What we're aiming for is to influence the human relations of the court that underlie the legal code and in reality are what determine their decisions."

Lt Culpepper looked at Prew triumphantly brilliantly and got out his Parker 51 pen for him to sign with, but Prew would not take the pen.

"That sounds like a swell idea, Lootenant," he said grudgingly. "And I hate to disappoint you after you figured it all out and worked on it so hard. But I just cant plead guilty for you, Lootenant."

"But why the hell not, man!" Lt Culpepper exploded. "And besides, you're not doing it for *me*. I explained it all to you, didnt I? The whole key of my case lies in your pleading guilty. I cant do a thing for you if you dont. It'll be just another run-of-the-mill court martial, no different from ten thousand others. Neither one of us will get any recognition out of it."

"I cant help it," Prew said. "I aint guilty. And I aint going to plead guilty. Not even if it would mean a full acquittal. I'm sorry, but thats the way it is."

"My god, man!" Lt Culpepper cried exasperatedly. "What has that got to do with it? Nobody gives a damn whether you're guilty or not. The court doesnt care. Its all governed by the legal code, and the human relations beneath it that run it. No court could possibly give a soldier the maximum just for feeling his oats and getting drunk and in trouble, not if he admits it. Why, getting drunk and running wild is not only a soldier's nature, its almost his sacred duty; just like the way Ernest Hemingway said that syph was the occupational disease of bullfighters and soldiers. Its the same damn thing."

"Did you ever have it, Lootenant?"

"Have what?"

"The syph."

"Who? Me? Hell, no. Whats that got to do with it?"

"Well, I've never had it either," Prew said grimly. "But I've had the clap. And if syph and clap are the occupational diseases of soldiers, then I'll get out and be a garage mechanic.

"Besides," he said, "I aint begging none of them for nothing. If they want to railroad this case like that, they can do it. I wont brownnose with none of them, even if they are proud of their men getting drunk. I aint never asked nobody for nothing, and I aint starting now, Lootenant."

Lt Culpepper scratched his head with his Parker 51 pen and then put it back in his pocket. He took out his Parker 51 pencil and got a piece of blank paper out of the briefcase and began to draw doodles on it with the pencil.

"Okay, but you think it over. I'm sure you'll come around when you see how important it is. Why, Prewitt, do you realize we might establish a whole new legal procedure for military courts? Think what it might mean to whole future generations of soldiers."

"I've thought about it all I need to," Prew said. "I'm sorry to disappoint you, after you've worked so hard on it, Lootenant. But I aint pleading guilty," he said, with finality.

"You hit the man, didnt you?" Lt Culpepper cried. "My god, man!"

"Sure I hit him. And do it again, too."

"If you hit him, you are guilty. Thats open and shut. Why try to hide the truth?"

"I wont plead guilty, Lootenant," Prew said.

"Jesus Christ!" Lt Culpepper said. "I never saw such a stubborn bastard. You'll deserve all you get. You got no more gratitude than a fish. If you dont give a damn for yourself, you might at least think of me. I didnt ask to be appointed your defense counsel."

"I know it," Prew said. "And I'm sorry about it." He did not look up from his shoes, but his face was still set just as stolidly as ever.

Lt Culpepper sighed. He put his Parker 51 pencil back in his pocket with his Parker 51 pen and put the confession paper and the doodle paper back in the briefcase and closed the zipper and stood up. "All right," he said. "Just the same, you think it over. I'll be back tomorrow."

Prew got up from the bunk with him. Lt Culpepper shook his hand. "Chin up," he said.

Prew watched him hustle back out through the line of bars with the open door of bars, past the guard corporal who saluted, back into the other world with his new yellow briefcase with the zipper on three of its sides. Then Prew got the old deck of cards out from under the pillow.

He had played five games and come within an ace of running one of them out when The Warden came into the office on the other side of the line of bars with the open door of bars. The Warden was carrying the clean suit of fatigues the OD had requested from the Company to replace the dirty ones he said were beginning to stink so bad it was hurting the morale of the guard, although this was an exaggeration.

"I have to have a goddam permit to give this monstrous criminal his goddam clean clothes?" The Warden said to the guard corporal, "or can I do it informal like this?"

"What?" the corporal said guiltily, trying to cover the comic book with his arm. "Oh," he said. "Thats all right. Go right on back, Sergeant. You didnt need to bring them yourself, Sergeant."

"Who the fuck would bring them," The Warden snorted, "if I dint bring them myself."

"I dont know," the corporal said defensively. "I just said——"

"What're you reading?" The Warden snorted viciously. "The story of J Edgar and Mel Purvis and the Stool Pigeon In Red? Dont tell me you want to grow up to be a G Man too? If the whole next generation becomes G Men who they going to find to arrest?"

"What?" the corporal said. He took his arm off the comic book. It was *The Batman.* "Oh," he laughed, "I see. Thats pretty good, Sarge." He closed the comic book and put it in the desk drawer guiltily. "Just passin the time was all," he said defensively.

"Aint you going to search this bindle?" The Warden said. "Maybe I got a couple files in there."

The corporal looked at him dumbly. Then he laughed, and shook his head.

"You're sure you trust me now," The Warden said. "How you know I aint a cop-killer in disguise?"

"Thats pretty good," the corporal laughed. "I *dont* know," he laughed. "Maybe you are. Go right on back, Sarge, if you want."

Milt Warden snorted disgustedly and walked down between the two rows of cots that were empty now in the afternoon and the corporal wiped his face off with his hand.

"I dont know what I want to waste my wit on dumb jerks like that for," Warden grunted disgustedly as he threw the fatigues on the cot. He looked at the hand spread out on the blanket. "You beating him?" he said.

"Not yet," Prew said.

"Well, dont worry, kid. You'll have plenty time yet to practice."

"Aint they got a date fixed for the trial yet?" Prew said collecting the cards. "Jesus Christ."

"No," Warden said, "I mean after you leave here."

"Oh," Prew said. "But maybe they wont let me play sol in the Stockade." He got up and began to strip off the musty stale fatigues. By god, they did smell bad at that.

"Probly not," Warden said, watching him. "They'll make you wear your GI underwear though. The trial's for next Monday," he said, "just come through while ago. Thats four days yet. Maybe you can run it out once by then."

"I might," Prew said. He put on the clean fatigues and sat down again. "Culpepper said he dint think I'd get more than three months and two-thirds. Since, like he said, this one's all in the family."

"Thats about right," Warden said. "Unless you say something to make them mad at you at the trial."

"I'm keepin my mouth shut."

"I'll believe that when I see it," Warden snorted. "Oh," he said, "here." He pulled a carton of tailormades out of his hip pocket. "Heres some butts."

"Well thanks," Prew said.

"Dont thank me, kid. Them's from Andy and Friday. I wouldnt buy you no cigarettes. You've made me about a week's extra paper work as it is."

Prew felt himself grinning. "Well I'm sure sorry," he said. "I sure feel for you, Warden. But," he said, "I cant quite seem to reach you."

The Warden stood staring down at him angrily indignantly, then suddenly he grinned. "You're sure usin up the fatigues in a hurry. What're they doin, workin you for a change?" He sat down on the bunk and ripped open the carton viciously, opened one of the packs and lit one of Prew's new tailormades.

"Not much," Prew said. "Pull a few weeds up to the playground. I dont mind it."

"That aint so bad."

"You reckon," Prew said, "all them cute little kids will all grow up to be officers."

"Probly," Warden said. "A shame, aint it?

"I got the forms out and sent in yesterday," he said. "That was the best I could do. I had to light on Mazzioli all spraddled out to get the typescript witnesses' statements done in time to go in that early. That son of a bitch is so lazy I even thought for a while I'd have to do them myself too."

"I dont suppose," Prew said slowly, "any of them mentioned the knife this time either, did they?"

Warden did not say anything. He studied him narrowly. "What knife?" he said.

"Old Ike's knife he pulled on me," Prew grinned.

Warden did not say anything for quite a while this time. "You told anybody else about this?" he said finally.

"Nope," Prew said. "I aint."

"Could you prove he pulled a knife on you?"

"I reckon they could take a couple sledgehammers and bust open the garbage rack and find the blade down in the crack where I broke it off for him."

Warden rubbed his chin thoughtfully. "Culpepper might just do it," he said. "Nobody else would. But Culpepper wants to make a big splash since this is his first case. He might just do it. Its worth a try. Are you going to tell him about it?"

"No," Prew said. "I dont think I am."

"Why the hell not? Its worth a try."

"Well," Prew said. "I kind of hate to break up their little party. They couldnt try me for Bloom, and The Treatment dint work, and they've got this one pretty well fixed up now. I busted it, they'd have to start all over again."

Warden laughed suddenly. "I bet Old Ike is sweatin blood about now."

"No he aint. I wish he was, but he aint. He already believes his own story by now. Maybe Wilson and Henderson dont believe it yet, but Old Ike does, I bet."

"I guess thats so," Warden said. "And Wilson and Henderson never sweated blood over nothing, have they?" He rubbed his unshaven chin with his hand. "I got to shave," he said abstractedly. "I aint had time the past day or so. You know," he said, "maybe you ought to tell Culpepper about it. Maybe it would be a good thing if you did. Hell, I might even be able to get a couple of them busted out of it."

"No," Prew said. "Not with Holmes in there pitching. He'd get them out of it some way. They'd just twist it around and use it themselves, someway. They've got the high ball up and the switches all open. If they goin to railroad me, they aint goin to get the satisfaction of seeing me squirm for them and put on a show. I can take everything they can all of them hand out, and come back for more, Top. Fuck them."

Warden did not say anything then for a long time. When he got up from the bunk there was an oddly strange squint in his light blue eyes in the deeply tanned face. "Maybe you're right," he said. "Anyway, its your show and you got a right to run it however you want."

Prew felt he could see a respect in Warden's eyes as they looked at each other and neither one said anything, neither one needed to say anything, an understanding on the big man's face that made him feel proud, because for some obscure reason he valued that respect more than he valued anybody else's respect, although he could not explain why, and that was what he had wanted and why he had told him, and now he was proud that he had had it.

"They can kill you," he said, "but they cant eat you, Top."

Warden slapped him stingingly on the shoulder. It was the first frank gesture of friendship he had ever seen The Warden make toward him, or toward anybody else. It warmed all through him like a drink. It was worth three months in any Black Hole in any Stockade. His face stayed stolidly impassive.

"See you later, kid," Warden said, and started out toward the line of bars with the open door of bars, down at the other end of the one long single room that was the lockup. Prew laid the cards back down and watched him.

"Warden?" he called. "Would you do a favor for me?"

The big man turned around. "Any time," he said. "If I can."

"Will you go down to Maunalani Heights for me and tell—Lorene for me why I cant make it down?" He could not, he found, call her Alma even to Warden. He gave him the address.

"Why dont you write her a letter?" Warden said. "I dont want to go down there. Every time I go around women they all fall for me and folly me around like a friggin sheep. I'm gettin kind of tired of it," he said, his eyebrows quivering. "And besides, I like you too well to risk it. I dont want your woman."

"Well," Prew said tightly, "call her up on the phone for me then." He gave him the number.

"If I did," Warden said, "as soon as she heard my voice she'd probly try to make a date with me. And I'm scared I wount have the will power to refuse."

"All right," Prew said doggedly. "Then go down to the New Congress and tell her and take her to bed while you're there."

Warden was grinning at him impishly.

"Oh by the way," Prew said stolidly, "last time I was down there your dear friend Mrs Kipfer ask to be remember to you and said why aint you been in to see her. I forgot to tell you before."

Warden's face exploded suddenly into laughter. "Old Gert?" he said. "Well what do you know. Old Dirty Gerty," he said. "Gert missed her calling in life. Gert should of been a fraternity mother."

"Well," Prew said again, "will you call Lorene for me then?"

"Okay," said The Warden shortly. "I'll call her. But I aint makin no promises not to go out if she asks me."

"I aint askin you any, am I?" Prew said.

"All right, on them grounds I'll chance it. See you later," he said over his shoulder. "Oh," he said, and stopped and turned around again, "I almost forgot. I got some other news for you. Pfc Bloom is makin corporal. We got two short time corporals goin home next boat, Bloom gets one of them. I made the Company Order out today. As soon as the boat leaves Saturday it'll be posted on the board. I thought you'd be happy to know."

"Bloom ought to feel good now," Prew said.

"Oh no," The Warden said. "Not yet. We got two sergeants leavin on the boat next month," he said. "Well," he said. "Only four more shopping days till Monday, kid. Then you can start in marking them off."

Prew watched the big shouldered narrow hipped swinging out through the door of bars in the line of bars into the other world. He picked up the cards.

During the next four days he played a lot of solitaire. During the next four days he also suddenly began to have other visitors besides Culpepper in the afternoons. Warden did not come back any more, just that one time, but Andy and Friday came, and Readall Treadwell, and Bull Nair, and Dusty The Scholar Rhodes, and the rest of them. They came and talked a little. The Scholar did not even try to sell him a diamond ring, or a genuine gold watch chain. And Chief Choate came. Most all of the non-jockstrap faction came over at least once. Even a few of the jockstraps came over. He did not know he had so many friends. He found that like Angelo he had suddenly become a Company celebrity.

Chapter 36

He was not a celebrity in the Stockade. Of course, in the Stockade, they could not know about the sensational trial. He fervently hoped they never did know about it. The trial went off all right with all the precision of a well drilled cast doing a well rehearsed play, the trial looked fine, up to the very last minute. The three witnesses told their stories clearly and simply, as if quoting their typescript statements from memory; their stories all jibed. The prosecutor explained with incontestable lucidity the infractions of the AWs that had been committed and the penalty required by the AWs for such infractions. The accused, who had remained silent, was offered his chance to testify and refused. Everything looked rosy, everything was according to Hoyle. Then, at the last moment, with a sort of abortive outrage against destiny, Lt Culpepper suddenly entered a furious plea of guilty and appeal for clemency on the grounds that all good soldiers were drunkards. There was a startled hush in the court room. The accused could gladly have shot him. But the court rose to the occasion nobly. With all due decorum they had the unorthodox plea written into the record just as if it were proper, then they went right on into the usual 30-second huddle and pronounced the sentence of Three-months-at-hard-labor-plus-Two-thirds-forfeiture-of-pay-for-like-period as if nothing had happened. The accused could have kissed them.

He was greatly relieved when he was conducted back to the guardhouse where he did not have to look at Lt Culpepper, to wait for transportation to the Stockade.

They came for him Monday afternoon after the trial that morning and signed for him and his two suits of clean fatigues at the desk of the guardhouse and deposited him carefully in the front seat of the recon which one of them drove while the other one sat in the back behind him. He felt like a tackily dressed midget between the well-bucked gleaming six-foot-four-inch splendor of the two of them. They did not say anything to him. He did not say anything to them. They delivered him inside the chainmesh fence of the greenroofed, chainmesh windowed country school house and he listened to the riotgunned guard at the chainmesh gates close and lock them. The sound had a certain finality, but nobody seemed to think it was anything very unusual or exceptional. The two gleaming giants escorted him inside the country school house as if they did things like this every day. He was still wearing the suntans with tie he had worn at the trial.

The first thing the two giants did, inside the door, was to exchange their billies and pistols for unpainted grub hoe handles with the armed sentry who stayed locked inside the weapons room.

Then they escorted him to the supplyroom. They still did not say anything to him. The supplyroom was down a long corridor past some doors and turn left past the bulletin board on the left and the barred doors of the three barracks wings on the right, to a cubbyhole on the left. The man in fatigues behind the countertop half door, obviously a trustee, grinned at him unpleasantly.

"Welcome to our city," he said happily, as if it overjoyed him to see somebody at least as bad off as himself.

"Fix him up," one of the giants snapped, as though it hurt him to expose his own talkativeness.

"Yes, sir," beamed the man in fatigues, "yes, sir." He rubbed his hands together in a passable imitation of a hotel manager welcoming a convention. "We have a nice corner room on the tenth floor overlooking the park with a tile bath and plenty of closet space, I'm sure you'll be comfortable there," he said.

"I said fix him up," the first giant said. "Cut the comedy. You can bullshit later. Dont get me irritated."

The grin on the face of the man in fatigues turned into a snarl that was three quarters whine. "Okay, Hanson, okay, just havin a little fun was all."

"Well dont," the first giant said.

The second giant did not say anything.

The two of them leaned against the wall with their grub hoe handles under their arms like overgrown swagger sticks and smoked silently while the trustee issued Prew toilet articles. The first giant, Hanson, stepped up and silently possessed himself of Prew's wallet, counted the money in it and wrote it down on a slip of paper, put the paper in the wallet and the money in his pocket with a lewd grin at Prew. The second giant came and looked over his shoulder and silently moved his lips, counting the money. The trustee took Prew's two fatigue jackets and exchanged them for two others which had large white capital Ps stenciled across the back.

"These heres so you can start right in to work today," the trustee explained happily, "without havin to wait till we paint yours. Then we'll issue yours out to somebody else later, see?" he explained.

Spitefully he grinned wider, as if it warmed the cockles of his heart, when Prew stripped off his suntans and turned them in and put on the fatigues. His own had fitted him, as well at least as the sacklike GI denim jackets ever fitted anybody; these, the shirt hit him almost to the knees, the sleeves dangled down over his fingertips, the shoulder seams hung almost to his elbows.

"Jeez, thats too bad," the supply trustee grinned happily. "And thats the nearest thing to your size I got on hand. Maybe someday later on we can change them for you, hunh?"

"Thats all right," Prew said.

"Well," the trustee consoled, "aint no women goin to see you anyways for a while, less they officers' wives ride up past the rockpile. And you couldnt never get into them anyway. So dont let it worry you."

"Thanks for the tip," Prew said. "I wont."

The two giants were grinning above their cigarettes.

"May worry you for a little while," the trustee advised. "You may have a little trouble at first. Specially if you're use to gettin yours wet every night. You'll get over it though," he said confidently. "It wont kill you. You'll just think it will."

One of the giants snorted. Prew thought of Alma and felt a wave of sickness go down through his belly into his thighs, at the picture of her on the bed in the room three steps up from the tiled living room in the house on the edge of the hill over Palolo Valley. He had not seen her for over two weeks now. Three months was six times two weeks. Fourteen weeks, of not seeing her or knowing where she was or what she was doing with whom.

"Also," said the trustee from the height of his superior experience, "you get to wondering what they're doin all this time."

"Yeah?" Prew said. The picture of the man lying beside Alma on the bed was a blank (he looked at it closely) a silhouette. It was not Warden. It was not Prewitt, either. As he watched, the blank of the man moved over her. No, he told himself, no, you know she doesnt like sex for sex sake she's told you that herself hasnt she? Sex for sex sake bores her doesnt it? This is only your own mind tricking you with your own like of sex for sex sake. What she likes is to have you near her, the personality interest, the warmth of the companionship and understanding, the being loved, the not being lonely. He went on naming them. It wasnt working. Three months was too long. Maybe she'd stumble onto somebody else interesting, just for the interest maybe, just to keep herself occupied you know, not to be lonely. Lots of interesting guys around. Lots of them more interesting than you.

He hoped Warden would not forget to call her up. At the same time he dreaded the thought of Warden calling her up. A man was only human. And Warden was an attractive man. Big, and husky, and masculine, and—interesting.

Memories of what he would lose ran through his mind. Sharp, clear, personal pictures of Alma like candid camera snaps. The pictures ran through his mind like negatives flashed on a screen, ten times life size in magnification, all the most intimate details (every pore, every hair, every wrinkle, of her body that he knew as well as his own, he could suddenly visualize them all perfectly) he stood and watched the pictures. And in each picture moved the same tin blank, the same two-dimensional black silhouette, the same black seducer, standing where Prewitt had stood and sitting where Prewitt had sat and lying where Prewitt had lain, taking all of Prewitt's most cherished secrets unto himself. The son of a bitch was using his mind and memories to seduce the woman he loved and he could not stop the black bastard. It was agony. He stood and watched the woman he loved being callously outwitted and seduced by himself. He could feel the panic he had put down that first night in the guardhouse coming back on him.

The thing was, she was too easy fooled (he felt) too generous for her own good, just let any lonely unhappy guy come along with a good snow job and she'd let him have it just to make him feel better, maybe. Take him right in. He remembered how easily she had sucked in his loneliness spiel. The fact that his had been true did not make any difference. They all were true. Nobody ever lied about being lonely. But they were all lies too, he knew from himself, because as soon as you started to talk to a woman about your loneliness you werent alone any more, you were like the playwright believing in the hero of his own play, the novelist trying to live his own novels. As soon as you saw

490

the audience was affected you knew you had something to gain and you started to act, to make the truth more convincing. And then the truth wasnt there any more, it had got lost in the shuffle. He felt if he could only talk to her a minute, and warn her. He was terribly afraid suddenly she would not be able to see that the guys who spieled her were lying. After all, she had not seen it with him, had she? *Or had she?* maybe she had and that was why she kept refusing to marry him? Because she didnt trust him. But, she had to trust him! The panic was getting into him; he could hardly restrain himself from turning to stare at the chainmesh grills locked on the windows. He felt that any second he would fall down on the floor and start screaming and beating his fists on the floor. In front of these three watching him, watching so closely.

This had never happened to him before. He had gone without any for longer than three months without hurting any, plenty times. It had never bothered him in the old days on the bum and at Myer. But then he had not had any idea of what it really could be like with a woman, then. It wasnt like this with Violet either. Suddenly, he wondered if Violet had ever felt this way about him. Maybe it was because he loved Alma? But he had thought he loved Violet. Or maybe it was because he was so sure Alma didnt love him. You're crazy, you must stop it, he tried to convince himself desperately, as he went right on straining his eyes to try and recognize the black silhouette, I'll kill him, I'll kill the evil black son of a bitch.

"Whats the matter?" the trustee grinned solicitously. "Did I say something?"

Prew felt his face grinning somewhere. Thank God! he thought. He looked around behind him at the two giants. "What?" his voice said. "You mean to me? Not to me," his voice said, "why?" I made it, I made it, he thought, I have made it. But how will it be at night in the bunk in the dark when they're all asleep and theres nobody around to make your pride work, he thought sickly.

The two giants were still grinning appreciatively and he knew he was not fooling any of them. He was not covering it up. He was only just barely saving his pride. They could all see what a goddam lovesick fool he was. Everybody could always see what a goddam lovesick fool he was. Why couldnt he stop being a goddam lovesick fool sometime? other people werent.

"Heres your hats, bud," the trustee said. "Dont forget your hats." He passed him two of the GI fatigue hats, brand new with the brims stiff as a board and the thin denim crowns mashed flat in millions of wrinkles, that always looked like rags on your head no matter how sporty you fixed them and that were the main reason every man on the Post owned two campaign hats, one for good and one for fatigue.

491

"Sorry, bud," the trustee grinned relishingly, as if reading his mind again. "But we dont issue no campaign hats here. Guess the QM forgot us on the campaign hats."

The two giants laughed out loud. The second giant, the silent one, spoke for the first time.

"Campaign hats is for soljers," he said, "not prisoners."

Nobody argued with him. Prew tried on one of the hats, farcically. If you can only laugh, if you can only turn it into a joke. Then you'll be all right. For a while. The hat came clear down onto his ears and the brim stood out sharp all around and the crown was tight to his head, a pot, but still wrinkled.

"Look just like Clark Gable, bud," the trustee grinned. "Specially you keep it down on the ears."

"How can I help but keep it down on the ears," Prew kidded.

"Hell, you ought to see some of them, bud," the trustee told him spitefully, as if putting him back in his place for trying to hog into the humor—he thinks I'm playing for their benefit, Prew thought wanting to laugh, he thinks its them, he dont know I'm doing it for my own self, and just barely that— "You aint nothing special, you ought to see the ones that *dont* fit," the trustee told him.

The two giants laughed again.

"Howm I doin?" the trustee grinned at them.

"Pretty good," the first giant, Hanson, the talkative one, said. "Pretty good, Terry. Lets go, you," he said to Prew.

Terry the trustee stuck his head out the halfdoor cautiously and looked up and down the long hall. "Well how about givus a fuckin tailormade then, Hanson," he pleaded anxiously. "Give you joes some laughs, dint I?"

The giant Hanson looked cautiously up and down the hall himself. There was nobody in sight. He reached quickly in his shirt pocket and pulled a single tube out of the pack in the pocket and tossed it into the supplyroom door. Terry the trustee scrambled for it on the floor hungrily. Hanson jabbed Prew in the buttocks with the butt of his grub hoe handle.

"Okay, Mack," the talkative Hanson said.

They all went down the hall toward the barracks wings.

"You'll get your ass in trouble someday, Hanson," the silent one said, "doin damfool things like that."

"Yeah?" Hanson said. "You wount be the son of a bitch to turn me in, would you, Turniphead?"

"Not me," the silent one said. They walked on.

"His name's Turnipseed," Hanson explained to Prew.

"I wount turn my own *mother* in," Turnipseed said proudly, after long thought, "much as I hate *her* guts."

"You turned a prisoner in last week," Hanson said, unimpressed. "For *smokin* tailormades."

"Thats business," Turnipseed said. "And he was a fuckup anyway." Apparently the unanswerable had been said. The longwinded conversation died abruptly.

The barred double doors to the three barracks wings were wide open. They took him into the first one they came to, the west one. There was nobody in it. It was very long with windows on both sides. The windows were nailed shut. They had chainmesh grids on them. The barrack was just wide enough for two rows of double deck bunks down the sides and a six foot aisle in the middle. There were no footlockers or wall lockers, each bunk both upper and lower had a small shelf nailed to the wall at the head. Each shelf was stacked in identically the same way with identically the same items: one suit of fatigues, pants on the bottom; one fatigue hat on top of the jacket; one suit of GI underwear on top of the hat, pants on the bottom; one khaki GI handkerchief on top of the underwear; one pair of rolled socks sitting on top of all of that like an apple on top of a layer cake. On the left side of the shelf the toilet articles: one GI Gillette razor to the front, box open toward the aisle; behind it one GI shaving brush and one GI shaving stick, side by side even with the ends of the razor box; behind them one GI khaki plastic soapbox with bar of soap inside and one GI washcloth folded in fours under it and squared with the soapbox corners.

The two giants lounged smoking, leaning their arms at the armpit on a top bunk like an ordinary man standing up at a bar, while Prew made up his bunk and studied the shelf next to his and arranged his equipment. After he got it arranged he stepped back and looked at it, the not quite double handful of possessions that for three months now would be all he owned in the world. Hanson came over and looked at it too.

"The beds all right," Hanson said.

"Whats wrong with the shelf?"

"Lousy," Hanson said. "Get a demerit first thing."

"Whats a demerit? I mean, in this place?"

Hanson grinned.

"I mean, what does it get you?"

Hanson grinned. "Shelf's lousy," he said. "You're new so I'll give you a chance to fix it. Tomorrow you wont get a second chance."

"It looks all right to me," Prew argued.

"It does," Hanson grinned. "Look at the others."

"Dont look any different to me," Prew insisted.

"How long you been in the Army?"

"Five years."

"Suit yourself," Hanson said. "You ready to go?" He started away for the door, and Prew felt something dangerous touch at his mind delicately and then go clear away again.

"Wait," he said. "I want it to be right," he said lamely.

The silent one, Turnipseed, still lounging smoking, suddenly laughed snortingly.

Grinning, Hanson came back and screwed up his eyes at the shelf. "Major Thompson inspects ever morning; he carries a plumb bob in his pocket," he said.

Prew looked at his shelf. He went over and took the stack of clothes down off it. He started putting them back one at a time, and Hanson came over and peered over his shoulder professionally.

"The lines from the ends of the razorbox dont biseck the handles of the shaving brush and shaving stick," Hanson said. "The soapbox aint in the center of the washcloth."

Prew fixed them and went back to the clothes stacking.

"You know what a plumb bob is?" Hanson asked.

"Yeah."

"I never heard of it till I come here," Hanson said. "Its somethin carpenters use, aint it?"

"Yeah," Prew said. "And bricklayers."

"What they use it for?"

"I dont know. Get their corners straight. Make sure a board is straight up and down. Stuff like that." He was beginning to feel better now. He had it choked back down. But he could feel it still lying there, just under his swallowing mechanism, still waiting. It was not gone. Even as he thought about how he felt better the association caused it to start to rise up again, sickeningly, dizzily, ponderously, like a fairgrounds balloon. With something like astonished disbelief he realized again that he was *here*, locked in behind chainmesh grids, while she was *there*, still in Maunalani Heights that he knew so well in his mind, and he could not leave *here* and go *there* when he wanted to. He swallowed and set his jaw tight and kept his tongue pressed against the roof of his mouth. It pressed up against them a moment tentatively and then sank back patiently waiting, as elemental a force as that which kept the planets in their courses and as unfeeling. Fooled you that time, he told it, seen you coming. If you couldnt swallow it, you were licked, you were through. Alma, he thought, Alma. No, he told himself, no, you dumb bastard, no.

He had been in other jails, hadnt he? He had been in some tough ones, back in the days on the bum. And none of them had ever gotten into him, none of them had ever broken him down. A couple of them, a county outfit in Georgia and a city lockup in Mississippi, had been as tough as they come. Even the Nazis had nothing on them. He still wore their scars. And they had not cracked him.

But he had not been in love then, had he? Being in love made you especially vulnerable. You wanted something. He must immediately fall out of love temporarily, he informed himself, it was the only way. He tried to think of all the things he disliked about Alma. He couldnt remember any. He couldnt remember a one. It was strange how he had not realized how much in love he was until he heard the chainmesh gates close and lock after him.

"There," Hanson was saying to Turnipseed, "I told you, you dumb fuck. This dumb fuck Turniphead," he grinned at Prew, "he tried to tell me Major Thompson invented it."

"Invented what?" Prew said dazedly.

"Plumb bob," Hanson said. "Just to use in inspections."

"Well, I never heard of the goddam thing before," Turnipseed said angrily. "An he's the kind of guy would do it. I still think he did."

"Aa, shut up," Hanson said disgustedly. "Dint you hear what the guy just said?"

"Sure," Turnipseed said stubbornly. "But does that prove it?"

"Oh for Christ's sake," Hanson said.

Prew stepped back from his shelf. "Hows that?" he said.

"Pretty good," Hanson said grudgingly.

"It looks perfect to me."

"Me too," Hanson said. Then he grinned that grin. "But I aint personally guaranteeing it for you, bud."

"Lets move, men," Turnipseed suggested. "Somebody liable come around."

They took him out through into the hall again. They went back past the other barracks doors, back the way they had first come. Prew noticed each barrack was a completely separate wing. Between the outside barracks and the middle one there were yard spaces of about ten feet.

"Yeah," Hanson grinned, watching him, "the middle wing's for recalcitrants."

"Bolsheviks," Turnipseed grinned.

"Fuckups," Prew grinned.

"Ats right," Hanson grinned. "Got two searchlights trained on them yard spaces where they come out in the open, see? Like a defile, see? Never turned off at night."

"Be pretty hard to get out of there," Prew said conversationally.

"Pretty hard," Hanson grinned.

"How many machineguns?" Prew asked sociably.

"One on each," Hanson grinned. "But theres plenty more around if they needed."

"Efficient," Prew said.

Turnipseed snorted. "Efficient," he said. "I guess."

"Shut up you dumb fuck Turniphead you," Hanson grinned affectionately. He touched Prew on the arm with his grub hoe handle delicately. "Stop here, bud," he said.

Prew stopped, feeling he had come off pretty well in that exchange, they werent bad joes at all, feeling again the old, good toughness in him that made him think maybe he would come out of this without a smudged reputation after all.

They were standing in front of the bulletin board.

In the center of the bulletin board, holding the place of honor among the mimeographed memorandums and sheets of detailed instructions about inspections, was a Robert Ripley "Believe It Or Not" that had been clipped from a newspaper. The clipping was brittle and yellow with age. It had been mounted on cardboard to preserve it, and there was a black border of cardboard around it. On the bulletin board it caught the eye instantly.

Hanson and Turnipseed were grinning down at him proudly, like the old nigger guides conducting a party around the sacred environs of Mount Vernon Virginia as if they personally owned it. Prew stepped up to the board.

The chief subject of the clipping was a bust drawing in the familiar style of Mr Ripley, of John Dillinger grinning behind his dark moustache he had grown shortly before he died. Prew remembered having seen the newsfoto it was drawn from. Under it was the legend, in Mr Ripley's familiar block printing and equally familiar Gabriel Heatterish style.

THE FIRST PLACE WHERE FORMER PUBLIC ENEMY #1 JOHN DILLINGER EVER SERVED TIME IN PRISON WAS IN THE POST STOCKADE AT SCHOFIELD BARRACKS IN THE TERRITORY OF HAWAII, WHERE THE SCHOFIELD BARRACKS MILITARY POLICE COMPANY RUNS WHAT IS SAID TO BE THE TOUGHEST JAIL IN THE U S ARMY. IT WAS SO TOUGH THAT JOHN DILLINGER UPON BEING RELEASED FROM IT SWORE TO HAVE VENGEANCE UPON THE WHOLE UNITED STATES SOMEDAY, EVEN IF IT KILLED HIM.

Under this, neatly printed in small letters with a pencil, were the words

WHICH IT DID

Prew looked again at the pencilled words *which it did* and the black border of one inch cardboard. A flaming rage burned up fiercely through him like fire sucked up a flue, burning out the soot and cleansing it so it will draw well. There was a cool calm solace of protection in the unreasoning rage. But his mind was functioning enough to recognize it was a false protection.

496

The two giants still grinned down at him, waiting. He felt he must not say something debasing.

"Great stuff," he said. "Why show it to me?"

"Show it to every new man," Hanson grinned. "Major Thompson's orders."

"You'd be surprised," Turnipseed grinned, "all the differnt reactions we get from this clipping."

"Very illuminatin," Hanson grinned. "Some guys fly into a reglar fit and cuss and fart and snort like a stud bull in the pasture."

"On the other hand," Turnipseed grinned, "other guys actually get the shakes."

"Major Thompson must be quite a guy," Prew said. "To put that up there. I wonder where he got hold of it."

"Hell, he dint put it there," Turnipseed said indignantly. "I been here longer than he has, and it was there when I come here."

"I been here longer than you have," Hanson said. "And it was here when I first come here."

"Well," Prew said, "you've showed it to me. Where to now?"

"Take you in for your visit with the Major," Hanson grinned, "then we'll take you out to work."

Prew studied him. There was no malice in that odd grin, only a humor of amusement, like when you watch a child mispronounce a word too big for it. It seemed to be a stiff grin.

"Well, lets go," he said. "What're we waitin for?"

"Major Thompson's very proud of that clipping," Turnipseed said. "You'd almost think it was his. He claims you can tell just what kind of prisoner a guy will make just by the way he reacts to it."

"Well, lets shove," Hanson grinned friendlily. "From now on you're marching at attention, bud," he added.

As they rounded the corner back down the long gleaming corridor to the outside door they had first entered by, Hanson made the old familiar quick shuffle movement with his feet, like a sliding boxer, to pick up the step. Their footsteps in unison reverberated crashingly ahead of them down the long hall.

"Prisoner, column right, harch!" Hanson said, when they reached the first door on the right, and both giants marked time while Prew cut the pivot and then followed him in one pace behind him, half a step on his right and left.

"Prisoner, halt!" Hanson said from his left. It was a beautiful movement, beautifully executed with professional precision. Prew was standing two paces from the mission oak desk of Major Thompson and bracketed exactly between the two statues of the gleaming giant MPs.

Major Thompson looked at them approvingly. Then he picked up the sheaf of papers on his desk and looked at them through his gold rimmed spectacles.

Major Thompson was a short barrelchested man whose OD blouse and summer pinks fitted like a glove. On his chest was a World War Victory ribbon with three stars and a Legion of Merit ribbon, joined on the same steel band. He peered myopically from his gold rimmed spectacles. He had the ruddy complexion and close cropped gray hair common to Regular Army officers of long service. He had evidently been an officer ever since 1918.

"I see you are from Harlan Kentucky," Major Thompson said. "We get quite a few boys from Kentucky and West Virginia here. I could almost say they are our chief stock in trade. Most of them is coal miners," he said, "but you dont look big enough to be a coal miner."

"I'm not a coal miner," Prew said. "I never was a—"

The butt of a grub hoe handle thudded into the small of his back above the kidney on the left side and he was afraid for a second he would vomit.

"—Sir," he said quickly.

Major Thompson nodded at him from behind his gold rimmed spectacles. "Much better," he said. "Our purpose here is to re-educate men to both the manual skills and right mental thinking of soldiers, and to reinstill in them (or teach them, if they never have learned) the desire to soldier. You dont want to get off on the wrong foot, do you?"

Prew did not answer. His back ached and he thought the question was purely rhetorical. The butt of the grub hoe handle whacked into the small of his back in the same spot making his testicles ache, informing him differently.

"Do you?" Major Thompson said.

"No, Sir," Prew said quickly. He was catching on.

"We feel here," Major Thompson said, "that if you men had not mislaid either your manual skills of soldiering, or your mental conditioning, or your desire to soldier, you would not be here. Whatever the legal reason for your restriction. So our every effort is bent toward reaching the objective of re-education with the minimum of wasted time and the maximum of efficiency. Both to the men personally and to the government. We all owe that much to the American taxpayers who support our Army, dont we?"

"Yes, Sir," Prew said quickly, and was rewarded by hearing a rustle subside behind his left. That would be Hanson, he thought, my old pal Pfc Hanson.

"I think you will make a model prisoner," Major Thompson said, and paused.

"Sir, I hope so," Prew said quickly into the breach.

498

"We may appear to be unduly harsh in our methods," Major Thompson said. "But the quickest, efficientest, least expensive way to educate a man is to make it painful for him when he is wrong, the same as with any other animal. Then he will learn to be right. Its the same way you train yourself a birddog. Our country is at present building a rather reluctant civilian army with which to defend itself in the greatest war in history. The only way to do that is to make the men want to soldier. To be a good soldier a man has to want to soldier more than he wants not to soldier.

"Chaplains' talks on patriotism and indoctrination films are not enough. Perhaps if there was less egotistical selfishness and more willing sacrifice in the world it would work. But it dont. This policy works. We wont talk to you about patriotism here. We will make not wanting to soldier so painful you will prefer to soldier. We mean to see when a man gets out of this Stockade he will be willing to do anything not to get back into it again, even die. Are you following me?"

"Yes, Sir," Prew said quickly. The nausea in his stomach was beginning to subside a little.

"There is always some men," Major Thompson said, "who because of psychological shortcomings and poor home training who will never be good soldiers. If there are men like that here we want to find out about it. If its more painful for them to soldier than to stay in this Stockade then they are useless, and we want to get rid of them before they taint the men around them. They will be discharged as unfit for service. We are not concerned with individual soldiers, we're concerned with the Army. But we want to be quite sure they really dont want to soldier, and are not just goldbricking. You see what I mean?"

"Yes, Sir," Prew said quickly.

"We have the perfect system to carry out this policy," Major Thompson said. "You cant beat it. We'll find out if you really dont want to soldier or not." He turned in his chair toward the other desk. "Wont we, Sgt Judson?"

"Yes, Sir," rumbled the man behind the other desk. Prew turned his head to look at him and the butt of the omniscient grub hoe handle immediately thudded into his back in the same place that had grown very sensitive now, nauseating him sickly. He snapped his head back to the front, but not before he had seen an enormous head and hogshead chest with deep concentric layers of fat over the even deeper layers of muscle that made S/Sgt Judson somewhat resemble Porky Pig in the Walt Disney cartoons. S/Sgt Judson was staring at him with the deadest eyes he had ever seen in a human being. They looked like two beads of caviar spaced far apart on a great white plate.

"Theres a few rules," Major Thompson said. "All of them is designed toward the single objective of seeing how bad a man wants not to soldier. For instance," he said, "when in the presence of superiors, prisoners move only on command. Especially in this office," he said.

"Yes, sir," Prew said quickly. "I'm sorry, Sir." The nausea had come back full force, worse than before, and he wanted to take his hands and knead and massage the place on his back that had become so sensitive now that it seemed to have a mind of its own with which to anticipate the grub hoe handle.

When Major Thompson did not acknowledge his apology but went right on naming off rules, the spot on his back seemed to leap quiveringly in its own private panic for fear he had made another mistake in talking when not asked, but the omniscient grub hoe handle did not fall. He waited for it eternally, while trying to listen to the rules Major Thompson was naming.

"Prisoners are not allowed to have visitors, and they are not allowed to have tailormade cigarettes," Major Thompson said. "Prisoners are issued one bag of Duke's Mixture a day and any other tobacco, either tailormade plug or pipe, found in the possession of a prisoner earns him an immediate demerit."

Prew felt he was beginning to learn what a demerit was finally. It seemed to be a very elastic medium that covered a multitude of sins.

"We have barracks inspection daily," Major Thompson said, "instead of just on Saturday, and any discrepancy of personal equipment earns a prisoner an immediate demerit. Repeated infractions of any rule gets solitary confinement.

"While here," Major Thompson said, "every internee is called by the title of 'Prisoner.' Men serving time in this Stockade have lost their rights to the title of rank, and to the complimentary title of 'Soldier.'

"S/Sgt Judson here is the second in command. In the event of my absence his decision will be final. Is that understood?"

"Yes, Sir," Prew said quickly.

"Then I think thats all," Major Thompson said. "Any questions, Prisoner?"

"No, Sir," Prew said quickly.

"Then thats all. Pfc Hanson will take you out to work."

"Yes, Sir," Prew said, and snapped out a salute. The butt of the grub hoe handle slammed into the small of his back above the kidney in the same spot with the precision of a clock, the Godlike reprimand of a schoolteacher's ruler.

"Prisoners do not salute," Major Thompson said. "Only soldiers have got the right to the mutual compliment of the salute."

"Yes, Sir," Prew said thickly through the sickness in his belly.

"Thats all," Major Thompson said. "Prisoner, about face! Prisoner, forward march!"

At the door Hanson took over and gave him a column right and they were headed for the outside door they had first come in by. Prew's back hurt sickly all the way down to his knees and his mind was in a delirium of rage. He did not notice where Turnipseed went, or when. Hanson halted him at the tool room, next to the locked weapons room. Another trustee handed him out a 16 pound sledgehammer. Then Hanson stopped him at the weapons room and exchanged his grub hoe handle for a riot gun with the armed sentry who stayed locked inside, before he took him on outside to the 2½ ton waiting just inside the gate.

"You done pretty fair," Hanson grinned, as they climbed in the thick-dusty back and he signaled the driver. "What was it, only four wasn't it?"

"Just four," Prew said.

"Hell, thats good," Hanson grinned. "I've seen them get as many as ten or twelve, during their first session. I've even seen a couple of them that clean lost their head and had to actually be carried out finally they got so fuckedup. I think the least I ever seen is two, and that was Jack Malloy who's a three time loser. You really done exceptional."

"Thats good," Prew said grimly, "I was beginning to think for a minute there I'd failed my first examination."

"Naw," Hanson grinned. "I was real proud of you. Four is fine. The saluting always gets one, so it was really only three. Even Jack Malloy got one on the salute, a guy just does it by instinct."

"That makes me feel better," Prew said, as he watched the gates close behind them and felt the air and saw the Waianae Range up there at Kolekole where they were going.

"You'll be all right," Hanson grinned.

The truck had to pass back down toward the Post and around the golf course to hit the Kolekole black top.

"Look at them sons of bitches," Hanson said bitterly, sitting on the tailgate. "Did you ever play golf?"

"No," Prew said.

"Me neither," Hanson said. "The sons of bitches."

The truck delivered them to the rockpile a hundred yards below the crest of the pass, where Paluso had hiked him up that time and the prisoners had hooted at him. He found himself hoping some other poor jerk got hiked up there so he could hoot at him back. Hanson turned him over to the guard on the road.

"See you later, bud," he grinned as he climbed up in the cab with the driver.

Prew watched the truck roar away back down the grade. Schofield Barracks was spread out like a map down on the plain below him.

"Over there," the guard said, "anywhere." He waved his riot gun. "Just keep that hammer going."

The rockpile was a halfmoon surface quarry that had been worked back maybe forty yards into the hillside. There were two other guards besides the one on the road, one up on top looking down into the arena below, the other off to the right where the cleft petered out into the thin woods that led back toward the wilderness of Mount Kaala, elev 4030 ft and the highest peak on Oahu. At least over there he would be that near to the free wilderness of the mountain.

Prew moved over toward that side, carrying the sledge. A gray rock-dust-grimed gnome rested its hammer, looking like one of the Mountain People out of Rip Van Winkle, or one of Richard Wagner's smithy-dwarfs grimy from deep caves in the hidden mountain fastnesses. It put a hand against its back and straightened itself and grinned at him feverishly, teeth and eyes wolfish white in the grey seams of the face.

"Hello, you son of a bitch," Angelo Maggio said. "How are you?"

"My back hurts," Prew grinned.

"Ha. You should of seen mine, buddy," Angelo grinned wolfishly. "Blacknblue for two weeks. Every time I took a piss I thought I had the clap for sure."

Prew laughed and set down his hammer and they shook hands.

"You son of a bitch," Angelo said. "You no good bastard you. I been wonderin when the hell you'd turn up. Goddam you," he said, "goddam you."

"You're lookin good yourself," Prew said. "What I can see of you under that dust."

"Hey you!" the guard yelled up from the road. "What're you guys passin back and forth up there?"

"Shakin hands," Maggio yelled back wolfishly. "Ever hear of it? A gesture, done between two civilized men of Christian society, used to denote friendship and long time no see. Or did you?"

"Can that lip, you Maggio!" the guard yelled, "you're buckin for the Hole. You better watch your step, with me goddam you, I wont take your crap. Swing the hammer and shake the hand later. You know you aint supposed to talk up here."

"Okay, chickenshit," Maggio yelled. Some of the hammerswingers around him looked up and laughed wolfishly, but he did not see them.

"Goddam," he said; "goddam but you look good, goddam. I never seen a uglier face."

"I love you to," Prew grinned.

"Come on," Angelo said, "make like you're workin." He picked up his hammer and bent his back and let the hammer fall once of its own weight on the rock. "Come on," he invited, "plenty room on this rock for two." He looked up at the recently blasted slab, measuring it with his eyes as if estimating an enemy. "I aint greedy," he said, "you can have half." He raised the hammer and let it fall once more of its own weight on the rock.

"Thanks," Prew said, getting into position. "Dont do me no favors."

Angelo leaned forward to peer where he had hit. "This here seems to be an unusual hard rock," he said.

"Get to work," the guard yelled from the road, "up there, you two."

"Yes, Sir," Maggio yelled. "Thank you, Sir."

"I dont suppose they'll let you take your shirt off up here?" Prew asked him.

"Ha," Maggio said. "No. Nor your hat neither. The shirt has the P on the back which is the mark of the prisoner and also a very good target. The hat they throw in extra for free. Well," he said, "well goddam. What'd they finally get you for?"

Prew told him the story.

"Well, well," Angelo said happily. "Joy, joy. So you whipped old Bloom's ass."

"It was about even," Prew said. "Maybe I had a little edge."

"But he couldnt fight could he. That night, in the Smoker. He wasnt able to fight was he."

"Yeah, he fought. The main go. And won TKO in the first."

"The son of a bitch," Angelo said bitterly. "Well, hell," he said philosophically, "a man cant have everything, can he? A man had everything he wount have nothing to hope for, would he? And so then you busted Old Ike when he draw his knife?"

"Yeah."

"And all that for ony Three Months and Two-thirds," Angelo said incredulously. "Why, its worth double that. For double that I'd do it myself, right now, and do that extra time standin on my head holdin my breath with my dick in one hand," he said.

"In Macy's window at high noon on Sataday," Prew said. "Old Angelo."

"Did you meet Father Thompson yet?" Angelo said. "Yeah, you must of," he answered himself, "you said your back was sore. But did you meet old Fatso yet?"

"You mean S/Sgt Judson."

"Thats him. In person. The man, the right hand man, who carries out the orders to the best of his ability—and then even volunteers a few ideas of his own. How'd you like him?"

"He dint seem to be too much inclined toward friendliness," Prew said. "But maybe he's just bashful."

"Friendliness," Maggio grinned at him wolfishly. "Fatso is the orignl man who burned the orignl book that had that word in it. Whatever you do, stay away from Fatso. If Fatso tells you to eat a plate of shit, you eat it, and whats more, you like it, hear?"

"I may eat it," Prew said, "but I wont like it."

"If its Fatso," Angelo grinned wolfishly, "you'll like it. He'll even have you back for seconds just to prove it."

"What barracks you in?" Prew said. "I'm in the west one."

"I'm in the middle one," Angelo grinned.

"Oh," Prew grinned, "a fuckup."

"Thats me," Angelo grinned happily. "I guess I talk too much. They got on me right after that queer investigation down town, remember? Remember Brownie? Brownie turned me in on that. That started it. They rode me and I talked some more and got three days in the Hole. Man," he said, "wait till you see the Hole."

"I aint anxious."

"Listen," Angelo said eagerly, and his eyes lit up feverishly. "I got a plan, see? I—"

He stopped and looked around nervously, at where the other prisoners toiled endlessly in the blue fatigues with the great white Ps on the back. Automatically he placed the position of all three of the guards. The working prisoners were carrying on, out of the corners of their mouths, grinning wolfishly, the conversations that could never be entirely stamped out. The guards were trying to keep all of them working, and at the same time stay far enough back out of the dust to keep their uniforms and riotguns clean. None of them were paying any attention to Angelo Maggio, but Angelo glared at them wildly and still shook his head warily nervously.

"Too many stools," he said cautiously. "I'll tell you later on. But I got it all planned out, see? I figured it out myself, and Jack Malloy says its a lead pipe cinch for me. Nobody knows anything about it but me and him. I'll tell *you*, but I aint taking no chances, see?" he said with a sly cunning. "They got stools spotted all over the joint, but they aint pulling that on Angelo Maggio."

Watching him, Prew seemed to see him change subtly into a totally different man, as if he had drunk the magic potion and was pulling a Jekyll and Hyde. He was like a man gloating secretly over a jewel that he knew everybody was trying to steal and he even stared at Prew calculatingly suspiciously, as if he had learned the hard way that even friendship was suspect before so great a temptation. Then slowly he changed back, becoming the old Angelo that Prew knew again.

"Anyway," he said, "when I come out of the Hole they thrown me in Number Two, right along with all the tough boys. I was scared at first, but hell, we got the best bunch of guys in the joint. More fun than a barrel of monkeys. Jack Malloy's in Number Two. You got to get yourself in with us as soon as you can."

"How do I do it?" Prew said.

"Best ways to complain about the food. That always works. Thats how Jack Malloy got back in, first thing he did was bitch over the food to get back in Number Two. They may let you off the first time because you're new maybe. But the second time they'll sock it to you, give you a couple days in the Hole, then throw you in Number Two.

"Jack Malloy's in Number Two," Angelo said. "He's my buddy. Wait'll you meet him. He's a three time loser and the smartest joe in this hockshop. You wait, you'll like him. Jack Malloy's your kind of a guy."

"Who the hell is this Jack Malloy anyway?" Prew said testily. "All I hear since I came here is this Jack Malloy. He seems to be the number one topic of conversation. That guard Hanson who brought me out here talked about him all the time, too."

"Sure. They all talk about him," Angelo grinned wolfishly. "Because he's too tough for them and too smart for them both. He makes them eat it and like it."

"You sure he aint Superman in disguise now," Prew said irately.

"I know he's the squarest, straightest, fairest joe I ever met in my life," Angelo said glowingly.

"He is, hunh?" Prew said irritably. He could sense his own jealousy. You dont want Angelo to have another hero, do you, Prewitt? You sure did him a lot of good when you were his hero, didnt you? "Well, he's beginning to get in my hair," he said.

Angelo looked a little shocked. "And I know he's the smartest operator I ever met, too," he said coolly, "if that means anything to you."

"It dont mean nothing to me," Prew said. "Why aint he out here with the rest of the fuckups, if he's so tough?"

"He was a mechanic by trade," Angelo said, "and he works in the Stockade motorpool. When he aint in the Hole. Thats why he aint out here: He says they got so now they always keep his old job back for him because he's the ony guy they can get to fix up their trucks."

"He must be quite a guy," Prew said. "Has he got a halo?"

"If I was the Pope," Angelo said without hesitation, "he would have."

"But you aint the Pope," Prew told him, "and so Jack Malloy aint no saint. Okay, then what the hell is he then?"

Angelo laughed feverishly between swings of his hammer. "He says he's the Rockpile."

"The what?" Prew said, stopped momentarily. "The rockpile?"

"Yeah." Angelo laughed again harshly. "This heres the rockpile for the prisoners, see? Well, Jack Malloy says he's the Rockpile where Father Thompson and Fatso and all the rest of them are condemned to for hard labor the rest of their natural lives," he said, looking at Prew to make sure he got it. When he saw he had, he laughed again. "He had to explain it to me, too," Angelo said.

"Thats pretty good," Prew admitted reluctantly, unable to escape a twinge of interested curiosity about any man who could conceive of a thought like that one.

"You wait till you meet him," Angelo promised triumphantly.

"I will," Prew said.

"And you'll meet him," Angelo went on. "You wouldnt be able to stay in Number Three with the punks and the ass kissers if you wanted to. And you wont want to, not after you find out what our bunch of guys in Number Two is like."

"It sure sounds like I got some complainin to do," Prew grinned at him.

Angelo nodded. Then he shook his head and grinned wolfishly. "It wont be pleasant," he warned. "You never know just what they'll do, especially if Fatso's in on it. They play rough. Whatever it is, you can bet it wont be pleasant. But it'll be worth it to you after."

"And it sounds like Number Two's the place to be," Prew said.

Angelo grinned back at him with that feverish wildness, his white eyes narrowing in the gray dust of his face. "I knew you wount give a damn," he said proudly. "I knew you'd know the score." He dropped the head of his hammer down to the ground and leaned on the shaft. "Goddam," he said. "Goddam. You old son of a bitch you. So you took Old Ike and Bloom both."

"Old Angelo," Prew said. "Old Fuckup Angelo. Get to work, you social parasite you."

"How'd you leave your girl?" Angelo said. "How's Lorene?"

"Okay," Prew said. "She's fine." He swung with all his strength with his hammer. Alma, he thought sickly, Alma, Alma; and swung it again. No, he told himself furiously, no. He swallowed and set his jaw tight and kept his tongue pressed up against the roof of his mouth and it went away a little bit.

"We'll have you all moved in tomorrow," Angelo said. "We'll pull it tomorrow at noon and when you come out of the Hole your stuff will already be moved for you."

"Whats wrong with today?" Prew asked him wildly.

"I want to take it home with me first and talk it over with Jack Malloy," Angelo said. "I aint takin no extra risks, not on you. I want to get Jack Malloy's seal of approval on the whole thing before we make a move."

"Jesus Christ," Prew exploded. "I dont need Jack Malloy's permission to complain about the goddam food, do I?"

"Take it easy, buddy," Angelo said. "Jack Malloy knows the ropes a hell of a lot bettern me. You aint in no hurry. You got three whole months yet."

Prew felt a murderous rage crack and burst in him like an orgasm.

506

Three months! Ninety days!! Fourteen weeks, it would be! Oh, Alma, he thought. Oh, Jesus! Alma. He wanted to beat Maggio over the head with his hammer and beat him down into a bloody bonejagged mess on the ground, for reminding him.

"Jack Malloy knows the little things that help make pulling a job like this easy on you," Angelo said, "things I either forgotten or dint even ever know. And in this place, thats important."

"Okay," Prew said. "Okay okay. You're the boss. You run it. If you want to make it next week, make it next week."

"We'll do it tomorrow," Angelo said. "A day or two dont make no difference to you, and theres a right way to do things like this and thats plan everything out that you can figure." He took off his wrinkled denim hat and wiped his face with it. It came away gray black but there was no noticeable difference in the color of his face. "These hats," he said. "These goddam hats. Nobody knows how I hate these goddam hats. I wouldnt wipe my ass on these goddam hats," he said, wiping his face, and put it back on and grinned.

The grin, Prew thought, there was something about the grin. Then he remembered. It was like the grin that was in Hanson's face and Turnipseed's. He could even feel it some now on his own face already, as he looked at Angelo Maggio, the grin, the same special grin, that was in Maggio's and Hanson's and now in his face, a stiffness that pulled the lips up stiffly, tightly, you started out to smile and it turned itself into this grin, stiff, wolfish, feverish, wild. Probably after a while you did not even notice it?

"Old Angelo," he grinned. "The Gimbel's Basement Terror. Take up thy sledge and work."

"You men!" the guard yelled from the road. "You Maggio! and you that new man! You're suppose to break them rock. If we was afraid you'd hurt them we'd of give you rubber hammers. You've had time to say hello, now cut out that goddam talk and get your ass back to work!"

"See what I mean?" Prew grinned at him.

"Up him," Angelo said. "Up em all."

Chapter 37

They talked over the plan the rest of the afternoon, working on the rockpile. It made a good thing to talk about, working on the rockpile. It was exciting and since the excitement was intrinsic it could not go bad and leave them working on the rockpile.

Bad things, Prew thought, were never quite so bad, if you could force somebody you knew and liked to suffer them with you. Usually you couldnt; they were too busy suffering something themselves and trying to force you to suffer it with them. But if you could, it helped thin that sense of seeing the whole damned world move past you on the corner without knowing you were standing there. Of course, it was hard on the friends. You hated to see them suffer.

One thing about the Stockade, it made the bad things general so that your sufferings were equivalent. You did not have to get into a fight and accuse each other of your lack of sympathy.

Angelo Maggio's face had changed during the past two months. There was no longer any trace of the naively-cynical, city-bred, lovable young Italian boy. This face had discarded cynicism as being as useless a pose as optimism, and it was a face without nationality, now that the long Wop nose was broken. Then there were the scars, all new and still red yet with youth, not faded brown yet by memory, a gradual accumulation the beginnings of which Prew had only noticed vaguely at the queer investigation down town that time, but which had grown considerably since then. His left ear was cauliflowered now, not badly, but enough to give him that wild lopsided ribald look of a punchy. He had lost three upper teeth on one side that satirized his grin and his lips were thicker, like an old prizefighter's. There was one scar that ran up over the point of his chin almost to his lower lip, and another lower-case-v-shaped one on his forehead. He looked competent.

He was still the same personality, just changed. Except for that wild wary miserly look that he got whenever he inadvertently mentioned his secret plan which he could not keep from doing every five minutes; that was new. Then, when he was like that, it was as if Prew did not know him and he did not know Prew.

But when they knocked off for the day and split up to go to their separate trucks for the separate barracks, his little black eyes were clear and he gave Prew a quick deliberate wink to remind him of tomorrow.

The next day he did not show up for work on the rockpile.

Prew had to content himself with wondering in silence. He was a new man and a stranger, to everybody but Angelo. It would have been useless to try to get any of the men around him to talk to him.

Under the steadily heavier morning sun the rockpile was like some dim, dust haunted, fear crazed fantasy out of a madman's imagination. The half moon quarry caught all the available sun and reflected it back on them blazingly. Prew worked on doggedly, wondering crazily after a while if he had only conjured a vision of Angelo yesterday maybe. The heat threatened to sizzle his brains in their pan. That anyone could actually take a man of his talents and sensibilities and unconcernedly hold his nose against this grindstone nine hours a day seven days a week for three months was not only inconceivable, it was patently impossible. He refused to believe it. There had been a mistake somewhere. He knew there had been a mistake somewhere, in a minute an MP giant would come up and touch him on the arm and inform him obsequiously that there had been a mistake, that he was not like these other craven wild-glaring wolfish-grinning animals and had no business here, please to come with me, back into civilization, where men are men, he thought bitterly, and women hate them for it, and they hate the women for not loving it.

My God! he thought horrifiedly, I'm getting to talk just like The Warden!

He hated to think Angelo would actually ditch him deliberately. If he wasnt back in the Black Hole or something like that, then it must have been this Jack Malloy character. This latter day Robin Hood who ruled Major Thompson's Stockade with an iron hand. This 20th Century Jesse James who was iron enemy to the railroads, symbol of hated authority, and protected widows and orphans. We have become a nation of cop haters, he thought sadly, we have taken for our hero a Robin Hood myth that never existed except in the history books, and only then 500 years after, when it was safe to print it. It must be hard on a man, being a cop. I'm glad I'm not a cop. I'd rather be a Robin Hood iron man, like Jack Malloy. The iron man has probably turned thumbs down on Prewitt, cold, he thought, hating both of them wildly, as if all this were their fault. Angelo had to choose, and it was easy to see which way he had.

He went on swinging his hammer wildly, in a kind of rhythmical frenzy, feeling the new blisters squash wetly and burst on the already grittily sweatslick handle, and relishing it—until finally a long, thin, ferret-headed, gimlet-eyed old man of twenty named Berry who said he was from Number Two barrack managed to convey to him guardedly, with the secrecy of a conspirator helping to lay a vast Global Plot, that Maggio was back in the Hole.

"I figured that," Prew whispered back, wanting to yell with relief. "I knew something like that had happened. What'd he do?"

The guard on the road had turned him in last night for talking yesterday. They had come and got him after bedcheck, their favorite time, and worked him over and given him 48 hours. The Wop, Berry whispered lovingly grinning wolfishly, sent Prewitt his love and his deepest regrets that their business arrangement would have to be postponed temporarily, but that he had every assurance of its early success, as soon as this other little matter that had come up had been attended to.

"Thats the message," Berry chuckled. "Word for word. He's a hot one, The Wop is. Aint he a hot one?" Scrupulously, Berry did not inquire of Prew into the nature of the business arrangement.

509

"He sure is," Prew whispered. "Thanks." He was beginning to feel conspiratorial, too. He was careful to keep on swinging his hammer and not look around, as Berry was doing beside him. Poor old Angelo, he thought feeling better than he had felt for some time. "I mean that:" he said, "thanks a lot."

"Dont thank me," Berry whispered. "Thank The Malloy."

"For what?"

"It was him give me the message."

"All right, I'll thank him," Prew conceded. "When I see him."

"He'll appreciate it," Berry whispered. "He's the roughest drill in this factory—but he's got a heart just like a great big baby," Berry said with great sentiment.

The Wop, Berry whispered, had slipped the message to The Malloy before Mister Brown and Handsome Hanson and Hayseed Turniphead had taken him out. Berry had been up at the other end talking to Billyclub Burke. The Malloy had told Berry, later, to tell Prewitt.

"An whats your nickname?" Prew whispered foolishly.

"My what?" Berry whispered.

"*Your* moniker. What they call *you?*"

"Oh," Berry whispered. "Why? Call me Blues Berry some time. Razz Berry, Jazz Berry, Fuckle Berry, Goosy Berry—all them like that. Why?"

"Just curious," Prew whispered happily.

"Use to call me Beer Belly," Berry grinned wolfishly, "but not any more."

"But will again," Prew whispered.

"Sure," Berry grinned. "I should live so long. This time's The Wop's fifth trip since he been here," Berry whispered proudly. "You know that?"

"He dint tell me. I seen he was pretty scarred up though."

"Hell," Berry snorted, "you think he's scarred? The Wop aint scarred. Look at that." He showed a long line down his jaw. "Look at *my* nose. Someday I show you my back and chest, where Fatso work me over, one time."

"You mean he used a whip!"

"Hell no!" Berry exploded indignantly. "Dont you know whips is unlegal in this country? He jst use a plain grub hoe handle but he's good with one. Someday I'm going to kill him for it," Berry chuckled, as if that would be a joke on Fatso.

Prew felt something cold. "Does he know it?"

"Sure," Berry grinned. "I told him."

Prew felt something colder, as if he were standing out in a raw wind in a thin shirt and with no jacket to put on. He remembered Fatso's eyes. "What'd he say?"

"Dint say nothing," Berry chuckled. "Just hit me again."

"I wonder why they didnt come get me too, last night?" Prew asked him.

"They got it in for The Wop," Berry whispered. "Because he wont take none of their shit. They wear themselves out on him and they still cant get a peep out of him. He's a tough little baby, pal."

"He sure is. He's from my Compny, you know."

"They bang him around like a tackling dummy," Berry chuckled. "Till their old ass is draggin the ground. And they cant make a dent in that boy. They've made plenty them *on* him," he laughed merrily, "but they sure cant make them *in* him. He's got them stumped. The Wop's got that old college try, pal, I mean. Next to The Malloy he's just about the hardest artery in this hospital."

"He's a good boy," Prew whispered proudly.

"You just bet your sweet life he is, pal," Berry chuckled. "Well, I see you later. I got to shove before that guard sweats me. They all fartin fire today." He slouched off thinly, through the gray cloud of rockdust that Prew swore made as much resistance to a hammerswing as water, a long thin phantomshape straight out of a good citizen's nightmare, moving unrepentantly through the hell to which they and himself had consigned him.

Prew remembered to let him go a few seconds, before he risked turning to get a better look at him. Angelo was really getting up there, when he had earned the unreserved admiration of an old hand like this Berry. He must have used his time well and worked very hard, to amass such an enviable reputation in only two months. And now Prewitt was getting to ride in on the skirts of the garment he had once helped to fit, in a way.

He felt a twinge of envy, like the schoolteacher watching her star pupil get the medal for winning the county spelling bee. But he also felt suddenly warm and protected, as if the invisible cloak of the long-termers' secret brotherhood that was as hard to get into as the Elks or the Country Club, was being wrapped slowly around him.

He was picking it up again fast. It was like a different universe, and when you were out of it for a while you forgot it was there and almost had to learn it all all over again. It was so easy to forget it, on the Outside. Then when you first came back it shocked you a moment.

That Berry would get Fatso some day, or literally die trying. Remembering Fatso's eyes again, Prew felt cold again. He hoped he would never get himself into the position where he would have to make up his mind like Berry had had to. He hoped that was one test he would not be put to. Because he did not know if he could cut her.

He remembered suddenly, with a strange sense of disbelief, that there were people living on the Outside who did not even know this other world really did exist, except in the movies. But there was always a Skid Row, somewhere, in every town, where the great dividing line between the Guilty and the Innocent melted away before the one real immediate need, Mutual Defense. In France we called it the Underground, which was a heroic term. Here we called it the Underworld, and gave it a different connotation. But it was the same world, and the same kind of people, and with the same purpose. He had almost forgotten all of it, in the last five years, but he was beginning to get the feel of it again.

He had already had his first taste of the daily inspections.

In one way, to an old jailbird like him who had lived on the bum so long, it was almost like coming home.

First Call was at 0430 hours in the Stockade. Breakfast was at 0530 hours. The inspection started at 0600 hours and usually lasted till seven.

They inspected unarmed, Major Thompson and S/Sgt Judson, carrying their grub hoe handles loosely in their right hands just after of the balance as they moved down the line, S/Sgt Judson always just two paces in the rear. Major Thompson also carried his plumb bob and the white cloth dressglove he used for dust. It was the first dressglove Prew had seen since Myer, in the Old Army. S/Sgt Judson carried the demerit notebook and a pencil. That was all they carried, but there were two giants armed with riotguns at port arms and also wearing pistols standing just inside the locked double doors of bars that a third riotgun-and-pistoled giant standing outside held the key to.

That first day there were only three men in the west barrack to get demerits. The almost weird versatility, speed, and accuracy of a grub hoe handle administering a demerit in the hands of these experts made Pfc Hanson look like a rank amateur. Berry had been right: Fatso was good with one. So was Major Thompson. And you had to admire their skill.

The first of the three men had his right foot an inch or so out of line. Major Thompson pointed to it with his grub hoe handle in passing and went on around the bunk to inspect the man's equipment without looking back. The man tried frantically, during an infinite second, to retrieve the offender but S/Sgt Judson, two paces in the Major's rear, had already raised his grub hoe handle and reversed his grip in midair without breaking stride or stopping and said *Dress it up* and brought the square-sawed headend down sharply on the foot like a man driving down the piston of a churn, and went on around the bunk behind the Major without looking back before he stopped and entered the demerit in his notebook. The man's face went white with a grimace of outraged affront at both himself and his goddamned stupid foot, and Prew had to smother the same tickling impulse to laugh out loud that you get when you have just watched the look of surprise on the face of a man who has slipped on a banana peel and broken his hip. The man's equipment passed the inspection perfectly and the Major and S/Sgt Judson went on down the line without looking back.

The second man had a belly which was out of line. He was a fat man from the 8th Field, a former cook, and he really had an unusual belly. Major Thompson, as he passed him going back up the other side some fifteen minutes later, raised his arm and drove the butt of his grub hoe handle backhand into the belly and said "Suck it in" without stopping to look back. Instead of sucking it in as he was told, the fat man, still staring straight ahead as if he had not had time yet to be surprised, grunted protestingly and raised both hands to his belly tenderly, and S/Sgt Judson, moving two paces in the Major's rear, raised his own grub hoe handle and rapped the fat man across the shins as he came up abreast and said "You're at attention, Prisoner. Suck it in" and went on around the bunk to the Major before he stopped and entered the demerit in his notebook. The fat man, like a runner caught off base flatfooted, still without time yet to think of moving his head, dropped his hands as if he was trying to throw them away. Still staring straight ahead, his fat lips began to quiver and two single trickles of tears began to run down out of his eyes into the corners of his mouth so that, watching him, Prew felt so painfully embarrassed he had to look away. By this time the Major and S/Sgt Judson were already three beds away.

The third man, a thin young Indiana farmboy, tried to watch the Major from the corner of his eye as the Major looked over his equipment. He would have been better off if he had not worried. His equipment was excellent. S/Sgt Judson said "You're at attention, Prisoner. That means eyes, too" without turning or even lowering his notebook and swung his grub hoe handle backhand by one end like a man warming up with a bat, across his chest loosely, all in one movement lightly, from where it hung at his side grasped loosely just aft of the balance. The flat of the headend caught the farmboy accurately with just the right force in the side of the head without touching the vulnerable temple and the farmboy began to walk sideways, tacking off across the barrack as if he had decided to go away from this place, but his knees went out from under him almost immediately and he hit the floor on his face tiredly without getting far. S/Sgt Judson said "Pick him up" without looking up from his notebook that he was entering the demerit in, and the two men on either side jumped out and stood him up and started him back but his knees sagged as soon as they let go and he started down again so they just stood and held him up by his armpits helplessly and looked guiltily, as if it was their fault he would not stand up, at S/Sgt Judson. S/Sgt Judson said "Slap his face" as he and the

Major moved on to the next bunk, and one of them slapped him and he came back enough to control his legs although he looked like he resented it. His head was bleeding some and some of the blood was on the floor where he had fallen and S/Sgt Judson said "*Get a rag and wipe that blood up, Murdock, before it dries and you have to scrub it*" as he and the Major came out into the aisle again to move on to the next bunk. The boy turned to his shelf, where there was no rag, and stopped. Then he had an inspiration. He got his GI khaki handkerchief out of his pocket and wiped the blood up carefully dreamily and then as an afterthought wiped off his head too, still looking as if he was listening to a faroff musical concert of infinite beauty, and put the khaki GI handkerchief back into his hip pocket meticulously. By this time the Major and S/Sgt Judson were already finished with the last bunk which was only four up from the boy's, and on their way to the door where the two riotgunned giants stepped aside for them while the third giant outside unlocked the doors.

S/Sgt Judson stopped in the door, without looking to see if the blood was wiped up, and said "*At ease. Rest*" and was gone. The guard outside locked the doors after him and followed. A sort of collective silent sigh seemed to go up from the barrack.

Cautiously at first like accident victims who dont know yet if they're hurt, then with increasing confidence, the men inside began to move around stiffly, vague-eyed and self-conscious like bus passengers stretching after a long ride. They cleared their throats and began to talk loudly against a great silence which they could not dent and rolled themselves cigarettes out of their Duke's Mixture thirstily, avoiding the three casualties guiltily in the same way combat soldiers avoid their own wounded.

Prew stood by himself, without smoking. He wanted one, bad, but he would not let himself smoke one. He watched the others coldly, feeling himself begin to fill up slowly like a large bucket under a hard-pouring tap with the greatest disgust he had ever felt in his life. He did not know whether the greatest part of this disgust was directed at them or at the Major and S/Sgt Judson. Or at himself, for being a member of the human race. But he did know, with a kind of first-dawning understanding, why Angelo and Jack Malloy and Beer Belly Berry not only preferred to be in Number Two barrack, but were proud of it. He would be proud of it, too, when he got in Number Two, and he wanted to get there now, in a hurry.

Stonily he sat by himself on the floor at the end of his bunk until the whistles blew Work Call, and the men seemed to sense his distaste because they left him alone and none of them tried to talk to him. Only when the rest of them had eased off from that first hungry smoke, did he compromise and let himself roll a cigarette.

The men did not try to talk to the three casualties either. They were like the neighbors who feel guilty because omniscient disaster has struck and burned down the home of a friend and left their own standing. The casualties themselves did not seem to care whether they were talked to or not; it was as if they understood they had moved into a class by themselves where the consolations of the lucky would not help them anyway.

The fat man, still standing at attention staring straight ahead crying silently long after Fatso had gone, suddenly collapsed himself down onto his carefully-made drumtight bunk that he would have to tighten again now, and put his head in his hands and began to sob rackingly.

The first man, the one with the foot, had sat down on the floor in his tracks immediately, as soon as Fatso was gone, and taken off his shoe tenderly. Then he just sat, momentarily happy with the relief, like a fat woman just out of her corset, massaging his foot concentratedly, his lips moving silently cursing disgustedly.

The Indiana farmboy didnt do anything, but just stood in the same spot, still staring dreamily at his shelf, as if wondering why no rag had been there, or perhaps still hearing his music.

Prew watched all three of them through the cold hard crystal of his general disgust, wondering with a kind of dispassionate scientific interest just how this would affect them overall, and making a mental note to watch and see.

Within a week the fat man had wangled an angle and got himself assigned to the kitchen as an apprentice cook. Two days later he was a trustee, and moved over to Number One, the east barrack, where the trustees bunked together, and Prew did not see him any more.

The man with the foot limped around for two days before he got his nerve up to go on Sick Call. He was pleased to find, when he finally did, that he was suffering from a broken metatarsal for which the Stockade doc sent him up to the prison ward at the Station Hospital with a report on how a rock had fallen on his foot while at work on the rockpile. He rode off in a recon happily, expecting to spend four or five weeks of vacation in a cast. He was back in four days, very bitterly, in working splints and eventually he ended up in Number Two where he and Prew became quite friendly.

The Indiana farmboy, who had looked the worst, had less trouble than any of them. He stayed in his daze all that day and had to be led out to work and led in to chow. At the rockpile they put his hammer in his hands and he stood in the same spot all day swinging it dreamily while the rest of them, including Prew, more or less tried to keep an eye on him. The next morning he came out of it in a fighting rage and knocked three men down, cursing and yelling, before the ones working nearest him could swarm over him, leaving an arm waving and a leg kicking here and there out of the press, and hold him down and quiet him. After that, he was his same old mild placid uncomplaining self again as if nothing had happened.

That was all there was to it. By that time there were other no less interesting casualties to observe, and by that time Prew had lost that first overwhelming disgust. Perhaps that was what horrified him the most: that he had lost it. He was afraid if he was not very careful he might even get so he did not mind any more. Because try as he would, he could not find anybody to fix the blame on. He felt it would help a lot if he could only find somebody to blame. He hated Major Thompson and Fatso, but that was not the same thing as being able to blame them. He also hated the casualties who let themselves be beaten around like somebody's burro, and he certainly could not blame them. He hated the Major and Fatso, he analyzed shrewdly, because he feared them; and the casualties because he feared being like them. Both hates were personal. He felt morally obligated to refrain from basing the blame on personal hatreds. He could not even blame the Army. Angelo could blame the Army; Angelo hated the Army. But he didnt hate the Army, not even now. He remembered what Maureen had told him once; that it was the system that was at fault, blame the system. But he could not even blame the system, because the system was not anything, it was only a kind of accumulation, of everybody, and you could not blame everybody, not unless you wanted the blame to become diluted into a meaningless term, a just nothing. Besides, this system here in this country was the best system the world had ever produced, wasnt it? This system was by far and above the best system anywhere else in the world today. He felt if he did not find somebody to blame pretty soon he would hate everybody.

He talked on the rockpile about it to Angelo, when the little guy came back from the Black Hole the morning of the third day, and especially Prew mentioned that swift lessening of the disgust; that was what bothered him most. Even worse than fixing the blame.

"I know," Angelo Maggio smiled at him grimly out of the flinty battered new face that never failed to surprise Prew each new time he saw it. "I know, the same thing happen to me. I even got scared I might even turn into a trusty."

"So did I!" Prew confessed.

"But you wont feel that way when you're the one getting hit," Angelo advised, "when its you that its happening to."

"It hasnt any of it happened to me yet though, except that interview the first day."

"Thats one of the reasons I'm glad I'm in Number Two," Angelo grinned at him wolfishly. "Least they know where I stand. And," he said, "when you're in Number Two you dont have to worry about if you will try to keep it from happening to you. You aint got no choice."

Angelo grinned again, savagely, from behind the new scar he had brought back from the Black Hole. His left eyebrow had been split and the dark line of the new scab ran down through it diagonally like a meticulous part in a balding man's hair. It made the one eyebrow look derisively lifted.

"Thats why you need to get into Number Two yourself, Prew, soon as you can. Bein in Number Two gives a guy's conscience a rest."

Angelo had talked the plan over with Jack Malloy, both before he went into the Hole and last night after coming out. The Malloy was all for it. It was the best plan available to get yourself disciplined just enough to get yourself in, but it was still a minor offense like making mistakes at inspection which only got you demerits and a trip to the Hole (if you got enough demerits) but did not ever get you thrown into Number Two. Also, this plan never failed because they were strict about food complaints, so that you did not have to worry about having to go through with it two or three times before it finally clicked. The Malloy absolutely swore by it.

"I'm sold," Prew said. "You dont have to sell me. I was sold before you took this last trip. The only reason I waited at all was because you made me promise I would."

"An a damn good thing for you, too, buddy," Angelo said fervently. "The Malloy passed along a couple of tips that will help you plenty. An I wount of thought to tell you any one of them.

"The first thing," he warned, "is to not ever let them know you want into Number Two. You want to make them think that compared to getting thrown into Number Two, the being worked over and the time in the Hole are heaven-sent pleasures."

"Okay," Prew said.

But the main thing, Jack Malloy said, the secret, was to not fight back with the guards when they worked him over; take it and keep his mouth shut. That was the really important thing. The other thing was how to handle himself after they locked him up in the Hole.

"Why the hell not fight them back?" Prew said quickly.

"Because it will only get you a worse working over and not accomplish a damn thing."

"I dont aim for none of them to get the idea I'm yellow."

"Yellow my big fat ass," Angelo said. "Yellow my balls. You go into it thinkin like that, you sure to fight them back."

"Well, I notice you and Berry both fight back."

Angelo grinned bitterly. "Sure, an we aint the ony ones. But its a mistake on our part, not somethin to copy. Thats one of the things The Malloy is awys givin all us guys hell over.

"I know he's right," Angelo said, "but when I get in there I just cant help it. Berry, he dont know no better; but I do. But I get in there with them I awys forget. I fly off the handle and then I dont care if they kill me or not."

"Maybe I cant help it, either," Prew grinned, wishing they could stop talking about it and get on with it. Three days ago the excitement had been a pleasantly thrilling escape from the rockpile. Now it was so strong it had become distinctly unpleasant.

"Its not for to joke with," Angelo bored on inexorably. "A guy is a sap to get himself messed up when he dont have to. And you can get under their skin worse that way than you can by fighting them. The Malloy calls it the Principle of Passive Resistance. Says Ghandi invented it. And it works, too, because I've seen Jack Malloy make it work. If I dont do it, its because I just aint that good of a man yet, not because I dont want to."

"Okay!" Prew said irritably, "I'll do what I can. How do I know I can do it or not? What makes you so sure I can do it? when you cant even do it yourself?"

"Because I know how you work," Angelo said defiantly. "I aint never seen you fight in the ring, but I have heard about that also. You're a good soljer," he admitted grudgingly unwillingly, "just like The Malloy's a good soljer," he said. "Ordinarily, I aint got no use for good soljers; but it takes a crack soljer with plenty control, to beat another good soljer like Fatso who's holding the reins and got all the cards," he said angrily, "and you mights well admit it."

"Balls!" Prew said, embarrassedly because Angelo had touched him on his soft spot, derisively because he felt a sunburst of pride, pride that he knew he had no right to in front of any man who had earned this face from behind which Angelo Maggio of Atlantic Avenue looked out at him so devotedly.

"You ask me!" Angelo said argumentively. "I tole you!"

"Awright, awright," Prew growled. "Now what else?"

"Theres just one other thing," Angelo said. "And thats the Hole. You got to know how to act, in the Hole."

"The Hole? I thought you were all by yourself in the Hole."

"Thats just it, you are. Thats what makes it bad. The Malloy says you can beat that too, if you just go at it the right way, but I never been able to do it. And neither has nobody else I know of, except The Malloy.

"The main thing," Angelo said, "is to remember to make yourself relax. You got two, maybe three days, maybe more, to do in there. Theres no way to get out of it, and no way to cut it short. You mights well accept it and get use to it, and relax."

"Thats logical," Prew said. "Whats hard about that?"

"Well," Angelo said, "you aint never been in there."

"Course I aint never been in there. Thats why you're briefing me, aint it?"

"Well, I dont want to scare you off nor nothing."

"You wont scare me off," Prew said quickly. "Lets have it. Lay it out."

"I've been in there five times myself you know. I dont look no differnt, do I?"

"Well," Prew said, "not much differnt. Come on, lay it out."

"Okay, I'll see can I explain it to you. But it aint really near as hard as it sound, when you tell it. You got to remember," he said sheepishly, "that it aint near so hard as it sound."

He went on swinging his hammer, carefully, punctuating his sentences with the hammerblows, carefully, so the guard would not notice and interrupt, as he talked.

"The first half hour," Angelo Maggio said, "after they throw you in, that aint so bad. They've probly work you over a little bit and the relief of gettin free from that carries you a while. You just lay there and relax for a while."

"Yes," Prew said.

"Ony, that begins to wear off after a half hour or so," Angelo Maggio said. "Thats when your mind starts to workin again. The Malloy says thats what causes it: Theres nothin to do but sit, and of course there aint no light, and you aint got no outlet for your thinkin, see?"

"Yes," Prew said.

"Well," Angelo said. "I dont know what causes it myself," he said apologetically, "but after the first hour or so you awys get to imaginin, somehow or other, that the walls is on wheels like, see?"

"Yes," Prew said.

"Well, you think they're closin in on you, like, on them wheels," Angelo Maggio said, "and thats when you first get so you cant breathe. Now I know it sounds silly as hell," he said.

"Yes," Prew said.

"You see, there aint enough room to stand up in there without bending over, and if there was you'd ony be able to take three steps from front to back. Course, theres no room to walk sideways at all. So you cant walk it off, you have to just sit, or lay, on the bunk, and do all your relaxin in your mind. I know it sounds stupid," he said.

"Yes," Prew said. "Come on," he said.

Angelo took a deep breath like a man about to dive from a board too high for his ability but that he cant back down from now that he is up there in front of everybody.

He let part of the breath out. "The first time I was in I thought I was goin to suffocate to death. It was all I could do to keep from startin to yell. If you once start to yell you're gone. Dont start to yell. You'll still be yellin when they come to take you out. Or until you get hoarse and lose your voice. And then you'll still be yellin inside. Even then." He stopped.

"Yes," Prew said. "What else?"

"If you can sleep a lot, that helps, but some guys its hard to sleep because you see the bunk aint really a bunk. Or a cot. Its ten or twelve iron pipes hung lengthwise from the wall on two chains and course theres no mattress nor blankets on it."

"Yes," Prew said. "Is that all?"

"The Malloy says you can beat all that if you can control your mind. I never can," Angelo Maggio said. "The Malloy can control his mind to stop thinkin. I cant do that. I've pick up a few little tricks that help some, but I cant do that other. One way I learn myself was count your breaths off: pull in eight, hold four, let out eight, hold four; that way helps that feeling how you are suffocating."

"All that happens to you every time you're in there?" Prew said.

"Another thing, I get hungry. They give you one slice of bread and a tincup of water three times a day.

"(The Malloy,)" Angelo Maggio said parenthetically, "(says he never eats a thing when he goes in there. He drinks the water but he dont eat nothing. He says if he dont eat nothing he dont get hungry after the first day; also, he says, that helps you to control your mind.)

"I never been able to do it," he grinned sheepishly, "I awys get hungry and eat the bread, and that makes me hungrier. The worse thing I got to keep my mind from thinkin about is chickens and turkeys—you know how they hang them up roasted in the delicatessens?—and steaks and frenchfries, and bread and gravy."

Angelo Maggio grinned apologetically. "I'm ony tryin to lay it out for you. You got to remember it aint near as hard as it sound."

"Yes," Prew said.

"I get to seein all kinds of food, big meals all laid out on a big table-cloth with silverware and glasses and candles and all that like in the magazine advertisements. I'silly, aint it?"

"Yeh," Prew said. "I like to eat too."

"Another thing is sex," Angelo said delicately. "You want to stay away from thinkin about women too. You see they strip you and put you in there naked and you get to thinkin about women you come all apart at the seams and be floggin your meat all a time which ony makes it worse instead of relievin it and makes you get wilder. Berry does that sometimes. It happen to me onct." Under the coat of the gray rock dust he blushed deeply.

"What the hell *do* you think about?" Prew said tightly, "for Christ's sake?"

"Well," Angelo Maggio said, "thats the catch. According to The Malloy you dont think about nothing. The Malloy says he can lay in there for three or four or five days, or however long he's in, without thinkin a single thing. He says he read it in some Yogi books when he was a lumberjack up in Oregon one time, how to do it. Some old guy workin up there had them who use to be a Wobbly. Malloy says he tried it but he never could do it until he got in the Black Hole. You concentrate on a black spot inside your head in front of your eyes and whenever a thought starts to come in your mind, you kind of push it away from you, sort of, and dont think it. After a while, you do it long enough, they stop coming and all you see is just light, kind of."

"Jesus Christ!" Prew said tightly. "I cant do stuff like that. You mean he goes into traces like them mediums and talks to dead people and all that kind of stuff?"

"Nah," Angelo said sheepishly, "nothin like that, nothin supernatural. Its just mind control. A way to control your mind."

"Can you do stuff like that?" Prew asked incredulously.

"Nah," Angelo said. "He tried to teach me, but I couldnt cut it. Maybe you could, though."

"Not me; not that kind of stuff."

"You never know till you tried it. I tried it."

"What do *you* do?"

"Me? I got two ways. I alternate them. One way is I make it to myself a game, see?"

"A game!" Prew said.

"Between me and them. They're tryin to crack me up and I aint going to crack. They can see me, but they'll never see me saw. I play the game with them and lay there and take everything they got to give."

"You make it a game!" Prew said.

"Thats one way. The other way is to remember things out of your life. You remember nice things, pleasant things."

"I might be able to do that one," Prew said tightly.

"But they got to be things with no *people* in them," Angelo warned him quickly. "And they got to be about things that you dont *want*."

"How?" Prew said. "Why is that? I dont get that."

"Because thats the way the mind works," Angelo Maggio said. "Dont ask me why it works that way. I dont know. All I know, it does. When you start thinkin about *people,* then that reminds you of things you done with them or because of them, things you wish you could do again. That brings *you* and where you *are* back into it."

"Yes," Prew said, remembering Violet Ogure and Alma Schmidt. "I can see that."

521

"And when you think about things *you want, you* already are in it, see? You want those things *now*, right *then*. And you cant have them. The main thing is to keep *you* out of it."

"Yeh," Prew said. "But how?"

"I think about scenes of Nature," Angelo Maggio said. "Woods I been in. Trees is awys good. Lakes and mountains you've seen. How it is in the fall, with all the colors. The way it is in winter with snow all over everything. I saw an ice storm onct—" he said eagerly and then stopped. "Anyway," he said sheepishly, "you see what I mean."

"I see," Prew said.

"Then," Angelo said, "when the people begin to come into it, like they awys do, sooner or later, I switch to the game a while, until I can go back where there aint no people in it."

"What was the longest time you ever did in the Hole?" Prew asked him tightly.

"Six days," Angelo Maggio grinned proudly out of the bent dented face. "But it was easy. It was like nothin. I could do twenty days, or fifty days, just as easy," he said, "I know I could. Why hell, if they—"

He stopped suddenly, guiltily startled, as if he had almost been trapped into making an admission. As Prew watched, the old wild wary miserly look that Prew had learned to recognize now, came onto his face.

"Never mind," said Angelo Maggio slyly. "You'll find out: I'll tell you all about that later. Right now, the thing is to get you in with us."

"Whatever you say, buddy. This is your show. And you're running it," Prew told him tightly. Six days, he thought. "When do we start? You name it."

"Today," Angelo said without hesitation. "Any time is okay, but its better to do it quick and then you dont have so much time to stew over it. Do it at chow this noon."

"Check," Prew said, and stood looking at him, at the tiny narrow-chested bonyshouldered undernourished frame of him with the thin legs and pipestem arms in the sacklike fatigue suit under the ridiculous looking fatigue hat that shaded the black burning eyes that were looking at him intensely. Six days, he thought, thats 144 hours.

"I got to tell you something," Angelo told him painfully. He paused. "It was The Malloy made me tell you all that about how it is in the Hole," he confessed. "I wasnt going to tell you. I was just going to let you find it out. Like I did. I guess I was scared you'd back out if you knew ahead of time."

"What made you think I'd back out?"

"Because," Angelo Maggio said violently, "I know damn well I'd of back down if I'd of knew what I was getting into the first time I got in there."

Prew laughed. To himself it sounded very nervous. "I feel like a collegekid must feel goin in to take his first big exam," he explained.

"Probly. Me, I wount know."

"Me neither. Remind me to ask one some time and see."

"Theres the whistle," Angelo said. "Its quittin time."

"Yeah," Prew said, "it is, aint it?"

"I see you in three days, old buddy," Angelo grinned at him, as they moved down, carrying their hammers, toward where the trucks had come up.

"I wonder how our dear friend Corporal Bloom is doing along about now?" Angelo tried to joke him.

"Probly made sergeant by now," Prew joked back automatically, but his mind was not with it. His mind was sealed up in gum.

"Maybe only two days," Angelo said, "and," he said, "in Number Two Barricks, is where I'll see you. Not on no rockpile." He turned and went to his truck.

"Okay," Prew said vaguely after him; "see you."

Then he was alone, in the truck with the rest of the men from Number Three barrack, who could not understand this, and would probably not do it if they could, he thought proudly, trying to bolster himself a little.

But he would do it. And he knew he would do it. He had to do it. Because he wanted Angelo Maggio and Jack Malloy, and even Berry, to admire him, he wanted to be liked by them, he wanted them to accept him. And because if he wanted to keep on calling himself a Man, by his definition, there was no way out but to do it.

His mouth was dry and he wished he had a drink of water.

It was very lonely there in the close crowded truck.

Chapter 38

It was always very lonely, Cpl Isaac Nathan Bloom thought as he left the messhall that same noon. For a noncom it was always lonely.

He went on upstairs to his bunk.

As usual, the squadroom was deserted. Bloom did not know why he had expected it to be not deserted. For over two weeks now he had been the first one out, every meal, and the squadroom was always deserted, but he always hoped it would be not deserted. Today, in this heat, he had thought maybe there would be somebody who had passed up chow. Bloom did not see how any man could stuff his gut with hot food on a scorcher of a day like this. Himself, he had spent fifteen minutes of agony toying with the steaming food, making himself swallow bites his stomach did not want. He did it for two reasons: because, as a fighter, he had to maintain his health; and because he did not want to look conspicuous among all the hungry tables; and now what he had eaten lay sourly heavy in his belly like a ten course dinner. Bloom was worried about his appetite.

He pulled off his fatigue blouse, shoes and socks, and lay down on his bunk, digging his hot feet into the shaded air that gave a false hope of coolness to the squadroom when you first came in. Funny—tonight it would be cold enough for the extra blanket.

Its this heat, Bloom told himself. This heat would ruin anybody's appetite. As long as a man had his appetite he could figure he was all right. But when he lost it it was a cinch that there was something wrong. What they ought to do was serve the big meal in the evening, like the rich did. Leave it to the rich to know how to live. You never saw an officer eat his dinner in the middle of the day.

Bloom lay on his back and stared at the grayness of the concrete-beamed ceiling, trying to understand it. This had never happened to him before. He had no appetite at breakfast or supper, either, so it couldnt all be the heat. This had never happened to him before. If he didnt do something he was going to waste clear away to a shadow. If a man wanted to keep up his strength, especially a fighter, he had to eat. This had never happened to him before. It had been going on for over two weeks now, ever since around the time his corporalcy had been posted. It was an awful responsibility, being corporal; maybe that was what had done it, partly. Anyway, it had never happened to him before. Then there was the Smoker season, which still had two weeks to run yet. Fighting always bothered him; actually, he was too high strung a type for fighting; he knew it was too nerve-racking for him; that might have something to do with it, too. Because nothing like this had ever even happened to him before. If it wasnt for letting the Regiment down in the clutch, he would have quit the racket a long time ago.

Bloom gave up intellectual analysis and let his mind drift off into a pointless but happy contemplation of the end of the Smoker season.

Two more weeks, Bloom thought. Just two more weeks. Then no more fights nor training until December when the Bowl season opened. It was almost too wonderful to believe. He was basically at heart a peaceful man, and the prospect of five whole months of peace stretched away like a bonanza. The silly damn thing was, he already had the Regimental middleweight championship cinched already. Whether he even fought these last two fights or not. It seemed silly to have to go ahead and fight these last two bouts when he already had it cinched on points and longed so much for peace. But what could you say, you couldnt say anything? He wasnt yellow; he'd had more fights on the green than any man in this Compny; it was just that it made him uneasy; he was of too peaceful a nature; he didnt *like* it and it put him under a strain. Now you take Prewitt—Prewitt was different, Prewitt loved it. Bloom would be glad when it would finally be over, maybe then he could eat again.

Still lying on his bunk, Bloom heard the first few of the light eaters beginning to come out through the kitchen now and disgustedly listened to them come upstairs, expecting some of them to come squat on his bunk and start brownnosing him now he had made corporal. Instead, they scattered to their bunks. Bloom felt relieved. Thank God for small favors.

Three of them sat down together, pulled out dice and started shooting craps for tailormades. They each had two or three open packs filled with the various mixed brands from former games which they had gotten from their footlockers and which they did not smoke. When they wanted a smoke they rolled one. Bloom half sat up and made as if to go over and sit in, then decided not to. Anyway, he had no tailormades.

Bloom lay back down hoping they had not seen him look just as Cpl Miller passed by his bunk on his way in from the latrine and Bloom watched him waiting to see if he would maybe speak or offer to sit down but Miller went on to his bunk.

For a second Bloom was hurt but he reminded himself that Miller had done right. It was always bad policy for noncoms to get together in front of the privates and let them see you letting down and being human. That was SOP, but you had to get use to it when you were new. It was no soft cinch, being a noncommissioned officer, like you thought it was when you were a private.

Bloom fingered himself through the thinness of his fatigue pants pocket wishing he had enough dough to make a trip over to Big Sue's in Wahiawa tonight. Then he remembered how Sue had called him Jewboy, to his face in front of all her girls, last time he was over there and his face darkened angrily. He had made himself a sworn resolution not to give that whorehouse any more of this Jew's money, but he reminded himself that he had not been wearing those two stripes then. They wouldnt be so goddam wise when they saw those two stripes and that money—

—and dont forget that third stripe, kid, he told himself secretly, after that short-timer boat leaves next month, with the middleweight division in your pocket you've got that cinched, kid; old Dynamite practically told you in so many words himself, after that last knockout.

With that one, it really would be different then. Big Sue's could whistle; it would be the New Congress downtown whenever Sgt Bloom wanted to get his differential overhauled; it would be nothing but

Marlboros then, the ivory tips, nothing but the Ivory Tips, he said it over to himself slowly with relish, trying to work up some enthusiasm but the heavy heat would not let him, this goddam heat, Bloom thought, Marlboro Ivory Tips, the kind that goddam queer bastard Flora smokes all a time so highhat, let her stink in her own sweat, then, stew in her own juice, then, he thought metaphorically.

Bloom rolled over again savagely happily, to let his chest up for air again (at least he didnt have to fall out for Fatty-gyou this afternoon, he didnt even have to train if he dint feel like it, he could lay here on this bunk all afternoon), just in time to see Friday Clark come in past him from the PX eating a chocolate icecream cone. Bloom snorted disgustedly, feeling outraged that a dimwit Wop of a buckass private should have money for icecream while the corporals went broke. If he had money for icecream, maybe he could get back his appetite. A fighter needed an appetite. Especially a fighter. He suddenly felt panicky and hated his stomach savagely for having betrayed him in this crisis.

Friday Clark had gone to the PX for a much needed bottle of shoepolish with fifty cents borrowed from Niccolo Leva. He was surprised to see so many up from chow already and their presence enhanced his loneliness, it was funny about loneliness, he never was so lonely when he was alone as when he was in the midst of people. That was one of the reasons he had deliberately missed chow. With Andy on guard again, and Prew in the Stockade, Friday couldnt eat in the messhall. When he thought of Prew in the Stockade, Friday had the same awful, empty feeling he use to have when his mother would tell him he would turn black like a nigger if he didnt stop playing with himself. It was days like these that made Friday almost wish he wasnt a Special Duty man sometimes. Besides that, he had not gotten the shoepolish he had gone for. He had spent 15¢ for an icecream sundae—chocolate which he dearly loved—and another 15¢ for a new comic book to read while he ate the sundae. That was allright, that still left 20¢ for the shoepolish, and he wasnt going to eat in the messhall anyway, and reading the comic book kept him from feeling embarrassed like he always did in the PX restaurant, and he still had the 20¢ for shoepolish. Then he had had to go and buy another sundae for 15¢! just to finish up the comic book with! just because he felt funny about sitting and reading in the PX restaurant when he wasnt eating anything. He did not even remember the shoepolish. He did not see how he could of possibly of forgotten it. He ate the second sundae slow and careful and made it come out even with the end of the comic book, but that still did not get him any shoepolish. By then there was only a nickel left. So he had gone ahead and brought this chocolate icecream cone, like for dessert sort of, since he might as well, and now he finished the icecream and dropped the rest of the cone in the can under his bunk feeling a sudden panic about what to do for shoepolish. He tossed the comic book on his bunk wishing he hadnt spent 15¢ for it. He could have bought a pack of tailormades, and maybe run it up to a carton in a game. He sat on his bunk and rolled a cigarette, looking at the gaily colored cover against the olive drab. The covers always made them look like they had so much inside, but they never did. He smoked cautiously, trying to keep the flaky Bull Durham from getting on the back of his tongue and gagging him. He sure wished he had the will power not to have bought a goddam comic book. Old Prew had the will power not to buy a goddam comic book. Andy did sometimes. He bet old Prew would loan him shoepolish, if he was here, instead of in the Stockade. Old Prew always had shoepolish.

Finally, when the heaviness of his own weakness bore down on him too hard, he squashed the butt out in the can under his bunk and got out his guitar, the old one. He followed his mood, striking blue minors. When he joined the Army he had visions of coming home bronzed by southern seas like Errol Flynn, a world traveler like Ronald Colman, an adventurer like Douglas Fairbanks Jr, a man to be reckoned with like Gary Cooper, a man of the world like Warner Baxter, a man people would listen to respectfully like President Roosevelt—not as much as President Roosevelt, but that same idea. And in a year and a half now he could not see how he had changed a bit. It was discouraging. Friday leaped full force, like a standing broadjumper, into practicing the *Steel Git-tar Rag* with a sudden savage energy. Someday he would have to get onto old Prew and old Andy to finish up *The Re-enlistment Blues*, or they probly never would do it. Someday he would go back to Scranton a civilian, and he would play *The Re-enlistment Blues* on his new git-tar he would have by then for his old man and the neighbors on the block, and his old man would say: "Well, boy, where hell you larn a play a git-tar like at?" and he would say: "In the *Hawaiian Islands,* Pop, across the *Pacific Ocean,* where I helped to write this song myself." He had it all figured out, what he would say. And his old man would say: "Look a my boy play at git-tar, pizon, look a him! he wrote that song himself he's playin!" And the dames on the block would go for him; they would fight for a chance to take him to the bushes in the park then. Maybe he would go on the stage. Like Andy was always talking about Eddy Lang and Da-jango. Eddie Lang was a Wop, too. In this country a Wop could go on the stage like anybody else. He bet a Wop couldnt go on the stage in Germany. He practiced furiously, going back and back, and over and over a phrase until he knew he had it perfect, the notes of the fast gay piece disturbing the hot heavy drowse of the noon air insistently.

Cpl Bloom, on his bunk, wanting to relax into the dry summer hum that this music was overpowering so he could escape his appetite, waited for someone to shut the dimwit up. Bloom felt indignant. Didnt the halfwit know guys were trying to sleep in here? Even a dimbrain ought to have that much consideration. Bloom did not care for himself, he had all afternoon, but these men were going out on Fatigue, they only had an hour off.

"For the love of God," he bellowed humorously at the ceiling finally, "stop that goddam racket. These men tryin to get a little sacktime. Aint you got no consideration?"

Friday did not hear. He was entranced by his own ability to make such beautiful sounds. He had gone into his private world where nobody laughed at anybody else.

When he did not stop, Bloom sat up incredulously. Maybe the dummy didnt know who it was had yelled? Or, he thought, maybe having Prewitt around to baby him all the time has made him too big for his britches, maybe?

He didnt have anything against the halfwit, if anything he liked him, he was all right for a dimbrain, but you couldnt let the men see somebody get by with a thing like that, not if you expected them to treat you like a noncom.

Bloom jumped up from his bunk and assumed the necessary indignant rage and charged across the room, remembering to thrust his head forward savagely, and his chin savagely ahead of that, and grabbed the guitar out of Friday's hands.

"I told you to cut the racket, Wop," he raged in his close order voice. "That was an order. From a noncom. It applies to Wops, just like other people. If I *have* to bust this noisebox over your head to back it up, I'm the guy can do it."

"What?" Friday said, looking up startled from his suddenly empty hands he had been staring at, the sweat of concentration still shining on his forehead. "Whats the matter?"

"I'll show you whats the matter," Bloom read him off, remembering to wave the guitar behind him at the room. "These men are trying to rest. They gettin ready to go out to work and they'll work all afternoon while you and me layin here on our ass. They want rest, I mean to see they get it, see? When a noncom tells you to stop a thing, you're suppose to stop it, even if you are a Wop."

"I dint hear you, Bloom," Friday said. "Dont hurt my git-tar, Bloom. Please be careful of my git-tar."

"You heard me all right," Bloom, the defender, roared. "Dont try to tell me you dint hear me, Wop. Everybody heard me."

"No, I dint, Bloom," Friday pleaded. "Honest, Bloom. Oh, please dont hurt my git-tar, Bloom."

"I'll hurt your git-tarbloom," Bloom, the crusader, bellowed, joyously feeling the just cause that was beginning to carry him away. "I'll wrap it around your goddam neck. As long as I'm a noncom its my job to see my men get their sacktime they got coming to them, and I mean to do it, see?" He was warming up good. There was still no room for Nazis and Wop Fascisti in this country with their roughshod overriding of the wishes of the majority, at least not yet.

He was just coming to that when a third voice cut in on him from behind, crackling with command.

"Oh, for Christ's sake, Bloom," it said disgustedly. "Shut up. You makin more racket than the kid was with the git-tar."

Still holding Friday by his shirtfront for further emphasis, Bloom swung around to find himself looking down deep into the flat black Indian eyes of Cpl Choate, old, wise, indifferent, bored. He felt his righteous indignation run down out of him and evaporate into a puny feeble protest that he could not articulate.

The Chief had reared his bulk up to a half sitting position despite the protest of the springs. "Leave go of him and go on back to your fartsack and relax," he drawled in that tone old noncoms acquire after being bored for years by giving orders that are not argued with.

"Okay, Chief," Bloom said. He released Friday's shirtfront and at the same time gave a little push to sit him back down on the bunk. He dropped the guitar down beside him.

"I'm going to let you off this time, Clark," he said. "But watch your step. You just happen to be lucky I was feeling especially good today, see?"

He turned and went back to his bunk, hearing Chief Choate's bulk squeak back down sighingly appreciatively. He lay down himself, and put his arms over his eyes and pretended to go to sleep, and the squadroom settled back into its interrupted noontime drowse while Bloom's arms and legs twitched wild signals to him to let them get up and carry him away.

He could not quiet them or ignore them, but he could refuse their request. He lay, arguing with them but not convincing them, while he listened to Friday Clark steal off quietly out the door past him and downstairs. He belched sourly again.

He heard Fatigue Call gratefully, and half an hour after that, his arm still across his eyes as if in sleep, he listened to the baseball and boxing jockstraps dwindle away in twos and threes to training periods, and then finally at last he was alone. Alone in the squadroom, Bloom lay on his bunk and faced it.

He was Isaac Nathan Bloom. And Isaac Nathan Bloom was a Jew. It did not make any difference that he had made corporal and become a noncom. It did not make any difference that he had won the Regimental middleweight division and become a Schofield Class I fighter. He was still Isaac Nathan Bloom. And Isaac Nathan Bloom was still a Jew. It did not matter that he was up next in line for sergeant, that Holmes himself had practically promised it to him. It did not matter that he was the Regimental white hope for the Schofield Division's middleweight crown, that he had even been picked for it in Big Red's Hoomalimali *Schofield Red Dirt* column in the *Advertizer*. Because after all that, he would still be Isaac Nathan Bloom. And Isaac Nathan Bloom would still be a Jew.

He had done it all, a lot of it things he did not like, because he thought he could change it and prove it did not matter. When he had seen how fighters were respected in the Compny, he had become a fighter. Did they think he liked being a fighter? When he had seen how noncoms were looked up to and liked, he had become a noncom. Did they think he wanted to be a noncom? He had worked hard at it. When he saw that Regimental and Division champions were admired even more than the ordinary fighters, he had set his sight on that—and in less than a year achieved half of it and was well on his way to achieving the other half. When he saw that the higher the noncom the more he was venerated, he determined to gain that too. He was not going to leave them one single loophole they could turn to for escape. It wasnt easy; what he had done was not handed to anybody on a silver platter. But he had stuck to it; because he meant to make them like him, meant to prove beyond any shadow of a doubt to them that there were no such things as Jews.

But in the end it hadnt any of it made any difference. And he knew it never would make any difference. Instead of liking him, the more honors he gained the more they hated him. Facts didnt have anything to do with the stubbornness of those minds; they twisted the facts to suit whatever they already believed in the first place. How could you fight a thing like that?

He had thought it was going to be different, for once, when he enlisted in the Army. But it wasnt ever going to be any different, any place.

Bloom went ahead, a little deeper, and faced the rest of it.

He didnt have what it took. He had never had what it took. Prewitt had whipped him, hands down. He had been kicked out of NCO School point blank, cold turkey. He had been called in and questioned about being a homosexual, to his face: He was suspected as a queer.

It did not matter that the Chaplain had stopped the fight. It did not make any difference that he had still gone in the ring afterward, either. Or that he had won. Prewitt still had whipped him, and they all knew how Prewitt still had whipped him. And they would never let themselves forget it either. A little guy half his size, a natural welter, had whipped him, a natural light-heavy.

It did not matter that it was the queer investigation that had partly caused the NCO School to get down on him. It did not make any difference that he had still made corporal anyway, either. Or that he would make sergeant. He had still been kicked out of NCO School as unfit noncom material, and all of them knew he had still been kicked out of NCO School as unfit noncom material. And that was the thing they would pick out of all of it to remember. One of the three men out of one-hundred-and-seven candidates who had received that singular distinction.

Almost half the company had been called in on that queer investigation. Why was it none of them had been suspected of being queer? Of course that bitch Tommy had spread it all around how Bloom had let him talk him into it that one time. That was Tommy's meat, that; he loved those. But what about all the others that had tried it, too? What about them? They all tried it sooner or later, if they hung around with them long enough. Familiarity bred laxity, like that Hal guy was always saying. But they found it inconvenient to remember that, the rest of them, when they got together to snicker about Bloom.

How could he know it would backfire like that when he telephoned in the anonymous tip on Prewitt and Tommy after he saw them in the Tavern payday night? He had called from a public booth in a drugstore clear downtown. He had not mentioned it to anybody else. He had been careful not to mention Hal and Maggio to the cops. Because he knew Tommy wouldnt talk. But how could he be expected to know the goddam gook coppers had their rotten stoolpigeons scattered all over? That wasnt his fault, was it?

He had wanted to prove to them a Jew was no different than anybody else. He had meant to *make* them admit it, for once. But he had failed. Because he had not had what it took.

If he had whipped Prewitt—

If he had graduated high up from NCO School—

If he had not been called in for that queer investigation—

But what was the use?

You could only whistle in the dark about it just so long. You could only kid yourself about it just so long. You could only hope they would forget about it just so long. Eventually it caught up with you, and you had to come back to it again, that you were Isaac Nathan Bloom, and that Isaac Nathan Bloom was a Jew, and that everybody else knew it too. It poured over him like clear cold water, or like molten iron poured from one of the giant crucibles onto the standing men below like he had seen happen once in the steel mills in Gary where he had worked that year—this fact that everybody else knew it too, and he got up off his bunk in the empty squadroom and went to the rifle racks in the center of the big still room. God, what he wouldnt give for a bandolier

531

of clips and run amok and shoot all of the sons of bitches he could get until they finally got him. That was the only way a man got anything in this world.

His should be third from the right on this side. He ran down the serial numbers on the breeches. It was fourth from the right. Just like with every other goddam thing, always just one place off from first, thats Isaac Nathan Bloom. He took it out.

It would be a good one on them all right, if he did do it. The CQs would start locking the racks right after drill then, like they were supposed to, instead of waiting until Tattoo.

Memorial to Isaac Nathan Bloom, Yid: *They Locked the Rifle Racks at Noon.*

He took it back to the bunk with him and sat down with it on his lap. They would be getting the new M1 gas-operated semi-automatics sometime soon. They had been talking about getting them for months now. Like with everything else the Army would be about six months late with it. But they would never find anything to beat the old Springfield, he thought affectionately, looking at it, at the long sleek streamline, very slim but with the potent bulges all in the just exactly right places to give it that pugnaciously forward-leaning eager look that marked the Springfield. Beside it, the M1 looked like a fat old man puffing with lack of training. He rubbed his hand pleasurably along the stock. Who was it had told him how they had read someplace that the two most beautiful things ever made in America were the Axhandle and the Clippership? and then said they should have added one more thing: the Springfield '03 rifle? It was Prewitt! Prewitt, one day when he had first got in the Compny! Even here and now, you couldnt get away from that goddam son of a bitching Prewitt, who was not a Jew, and who shamed you with that big put-on act of his of being perfect. Bloom laid the pregnant heaviness down on the bunk and went to his footlocker.

There were three rounds of live .30 caliber hidden in the tray that he had swiped last range season because he loved to handle the sleek brassy potencies and clink them in his hand. He took one of them out and relocked the lid and held the cartridge up alongside the breech of the rifle on the bunk. So powerful! so beautiful! in its inert foreboding of destruction.

Bloom pushed the cutoff up and opened the bolt and slid the long deadly torpedoshape into the chamber sensuously and locked the bolt and pushed the safety on carefully and sat and looked at the rifle lying innocently silent on his lap.

There were two kinds of Jews. There were the Jews like Sussman, him and his goddam motorcycle, who would rather be Gentiles and therefore smiled queasily and sucked the ass of every Gentile who

532

would drop his pants. And there were the Jews like his old man and his mother, them and their goddam unsalted butter and Kosher meat the Rabbi had to bless before they could eat it, who would rather be Jews than anything else in the world and who never let anybody forget they would rather be Jews than anything else in the world because Jews were God's Chosen People and always between God's Chosen People and the Infidel was the Wall that no Gentile ever could climb over. Those were the only two kinds of Jews there were. Take it or leave it. It was a fine choice to present to a man who wanted only to be accepted as a man, according to his individual virtues and vices, but who could never be that, as long as this open advertizement of a nose hung dangling out from his face.

Bloom felt it gingerly with his fingers, still looking at the rifle, wincing a little because it was still a little sore where Prewitt the Aryan had broken it and made it maybe not quite as much a Jewish nose as before, but still leaving it plainly a Jewish nose.

You cant get away from the Bloom nose, Isaac Nathan. You are the locomotive and here is your cowcatcher which precedes you down the dwindling rails of life. You want to be accepted? you want to be respected? you want to be admired? you want to be just plain liked?—tell it to the Bloom nose, Isaac Nathan.

In all the world Bloom could not think of a single person who liked him for himself, for his own personality.

Checking to make sure the safety was still on, he put the muzzle of the rifle in his mouth. He had to put the muzzle far back at the roof of his mouth for the sight cover to get in behind his teeth. It tasted very oily. He reached for the trigger with his thumb, knowing the safety was still on. His thumb would not reach even to the trigger guard. He tried with his index finger, but the tip of it barely reached inside the guard. He strained with his shoulder and arm trying to reach it, just curious was all, but all he could do was just touch the tip of his finger to the concave surface of the trigger.

Thats what I thought, Bloom thought.

He took the muzzle out of his mouth and laid the rifle across his lap and sat and looked at the long sleek deadly thing lying innocently across his knees with the safety catch still on. It was almost unbelievable it could do that.

Bloom leaned down and unlaced his right shoe deliberately, feeling tough and positive. Then he stuck the muzzle against the roof of his mouth again and put his big toe inside the guard. There was no give in the trigger under the pressure of his toe.

He laid the piece across his knees again. The barracks was suddenly tomblike in its emptiness. Bloom wished somebody would come in.

If they did come in, they would only laugh him out of the barracks for a showoff. All his life it seemed he had been laughed out of someplace or other for a showoff who didnt have the guts to back it up. All his life he had tried to act, to do, to be strong and forceful enough to be able to point to something just once and say I did this, to just once commit one irrevocable act through his own willful motivation. And always, in the end, it was outside influences that governed him and he was blown by chance, by pure happenstance, coincidence, one way or the other, without having anything to say about it.

He still wished somebody would come in, and break up this silence. He pictured in his mind how they would look if they were to come in too late. He stood off to one side and watched them as they felt a great pity and sorrow that was too late now to help the poor dead thing there. We could have done so much, their tragic faces said, we could have made it so much easier. They would be sorry for the Jewboy, when it was too late. They would not think he was yellow then. Or a queer.

A war was coming, it was already here in Europe. Fighting and death and blood and hate. It was taught to children with their mother's milk, Bloom thought tragically, and called Christianity and Judaism. Christians were taught to hate Jews; Jews were taught to hate Christians. And in all of it, not anywhere in any part of it, Bloom thought in a perfect ecstasy of sadness, was there one living soul who liked Isaac Nathan Bloom for his own self, for his personality, for his own individual character.

"A man might as well be dead," Bloom said tentatively out loud.

In the empty squadroom no one contradicted him.

He picked the rifle up again and placed the muzzle in his mouth again, uncomfortably, because it was very awkward. He held the rifle up with his extended left arm, the muzzle with his right. As an afterthought he set the butt on the concrete floor. These '03s had a hell of a kick. His hand would not reach the safety and he had to take the muzzle out of his mouth again. His hand did not want to release the safety.

You're a queer, Bloom thought bitterly, a monster. Lets face it all, while we're facing. You did it, and you liked it, and that makes you a queer. And everybody knows you are a queer. You dont deserve to live.

His hand released the safety. He put the muzzle back in his mouth and placed his bare big toe inside the guard against the trigger. A man's bare foot was an ugly, sickening, repulsive thing. He pulled the trigger.

In the prolonged sustained roar during the split second left him, Bloom felt as if somebody had stepped up behind him and grasped his chin and the base of his skull and lifted with both hands like a weightlifter doing a snatch lift. They kept lifting and lifting, his head was going higher and higher.

I dint mean it! he tried to yell. I take it back! I was ony kiddin! I was just showin off!

Then, as his head continued on up through the ceiling, he knew it wasnt any good. He had always wanted to commit an irrevocable act, and he had finally done it, only to find it was the wrong one. He knew a great many things that he wished he had time to say. He could explain so much. There were so many steaks to be eaten, so many whores to be laid, so much beer to be drunk. Dont forget the steaks and whores and beer, boys, he wanted to yell, dont ever forget that.

What a silly thing to do, he thought. What a goddam silly thing to do. You wont even be there to watch their faces.

Bloom died.

It was Friday Clark who found him, technically. Friday was standing on the ground floor porch doing nothing when the shot shattered out through the screens and across the quad, and he had a straight path to the stairs. He beat Niccolo Leva, who had to turn the corner of the supplyroom, to them by almost a second and that made him the first man. The Warden, coming on a dead run from the orderly room, was right behind them. Behind The Warden streamed the rest of them, the kitchen force, the KPs, the fatigue details working in the Company yard, everybody from the Company who was within running distance, all charging up the stairs together, before the buildings around the quad had quit playing catch with the echo of the shot as it died away.

Bloom was lying back across his bunk in that peculiarly lifeless position dead people get into, with the top of his head gone and the rifle on the floor and the one pastywhite bare foot dangling down ridiculously. There was a large blot of blood and phlegmy matter on the ceiling around the hole where the bullet had gone on through. It was still Bloom's face, but it looked as if all the bones had been taken out from behind it, like one of those cured headhunter's heads you could see in the curio shop windows downtown on Hotel Street.

"Jesus Christ!" Niccolo Leva protested, and headed right on out the other door for the latrine, without stopping.

Nobody else said anything. Several men pushed through the still growing crowd in the doorway and on the porch and followed Leva. The rest of them just stood, as it slowly dawned on them, looking like embarrassed plumbers who had blundered into the wrong bathroom.

Friday Clark, watching the remains of the man who had so recently had him by the collar, wondered why he did not get sick himself. It surprised him. He would of thought if anybody would get sick it would be him. He felt a little proud that he did not get sick.

"All right," The Warden said finally in a kind of frustrated choke.

"Outside, you men. Theres nothing you can do here. Get back to work."

When nobody moved or answered, he swung on them blazing, almost gratefully. "Hear what I goddam said?" he roared. "Outside! You've all seen it now. Everybody's had a good look now. Now get the goddam hell outside! And dont anybody touch anything till we've got the OD over here from the guardhouse."

The crowd responded with a reluctant milling movement that took nobody noplace. There was a look of indignant protest and impotent outrage on all their faces. Not at The Warden, but at Bloom. They looked as if they had just offered their last glass of cold beer to a man on a hot day, only to have it turned down and thrown in their face.

"He dint have no goddam right to do a goddam thing like that," somebody said inarticulately vaguely.

"Not in the goddam squadroom," somebody else said.

They all looked like if The Warden had not been there holding them at bay they would have swarmed on Bloom, dead or not, and beaten him with their fists for having reminded them of this thing they spent the best years of their lives trying to forget.

"But it took a lot of guts though," Friday Clark said, feeling vaguely that he must tell them something. "It took a lot of guts though, to do it. I wouldnt—"

The Warden cut in on him. "Okay," he said, his voice crackling with suppression, "you men want to hang around you might as well make yourselves useful. Couple of you get some buckets and mops and a stepladder from the supplyroom. Somebody else go up on the roof and see if the bullet went on through, and if it did get some paper and tar from Leva and patch the goddam thing."

There was a chorus of indignant protests from the crowd and it began to break up suddenly and move toward the stairs.

"I aint goin to clean up after no son of a bitch that shoots hisself," somebody said.

"Yeah, let him clean it up himself, the son of a bitch, he done it," somebody else said.

There was a general half-wild laugh.

"Come back here," The Warden ordered briskly. "Lets go. The holiday is over."

The crowd evaporated swiftly and was gone, just as Niccolo Leva came back in from the latrine, looking pale. "Christ, what a mess. I got to sleep in here tonight." He looked at the ceiling. "Just a couple hours ago I was issuin him a brand new pair of field shoes," he said helplessly.

"What do you suppose he wanted to do it for?" Friday asked, feeling vaguely ashamed like he used to feel when the littler kids at home messed their pants.

"Christ, how the hell do I know?" The Warden bellowed. "Sometimes I feel like doin it myself, in this fucking outfit. Niccolo," he said, "after the OD's been here, you get some men and have them clean this up."

"I'll do it," Friday Clark said. "I dont mind doin it."

"It'll need more than one man," The Warden said grimly. "You go with Leva."

"Okay, Top," Friday said admiringly.

"I wonder what he wanted to do it for," he said wonderingly, on the stairs. "He had everything to live for. He was middleweight champion and a corporal and due to make sergeant, he had everything. I wonder what would make a guy like that want to do a thing like that."

"For Christ's sake, shut up!" said Niccolo Leva savagely.

"It took a lot of guts," Friday Clark said, feeling he had to explain it to him, sensing vaguely there was something about Bloom he ought to say. "I wouldnt have that much guts."

Wait'll old Prew hears about this, he thought.

Chapter 39

Prew did not hear about it until he came out of the Black Hole three days later. That was the day they were burying Bloom. It is very hard to communicate with anyone in the Black Hole, which is called Solitary Confinement officially. "Black Hole" is only a descriptive slang term created by prisoners. College professors call it an "Americanism," a descriptive slang term created by college professors.

He came out at 1840 hours, right after evening chow, shaky from loss of food and blinded by the dazzling brilliance of the bare 40-watt bulbs, just seven and one half hours more than three days from the moment he had sat down at the mess table and taken the first bite of food for appearances' sake and banged on his plate with his fork in one hand and his heart squeezed up into his ears. He was a different man than when he had gone in, and he was very surprised to find the world basically unchanged.

It had not turned out to be nearly as bad as he had thought it would be. He came out of it feeling he had been tested and not found wanting, he was almost as proud of it as he was of the Taps he had once played at Arlington; but it was not any of it nearly as bad as he had thought it would be. That was one of the virtues of being a pessimist: nothing was ever as bad as you thought it would be.

They served dinner chow, just like breakfast chow, and supper chow, to one barrack at a time in the Stockade. This was because the messhall was small. Because the daily schedule in the Stockade was large, it only allowed half an hour per meal (plenty of time plenty of time, a half hour, Maj Thompson said, for any man to eat in). There being three barracks, each barrack had to eat in ten minutes. Actually, in practice, it did not quite amount to ten minutes. It amounted to five minutes. After you subtracted the time spent forming, and coming and going, and getting seated and served. Many prisoners felt this was not enough time. But then nobody had ever tried to accuse the Stockade of being a pleasure resort. They ran things on a hard, fast schedule in the Stockade.

Prew, according to The Malloy's instructions via Angelo Maggio, had had two choices: He could either eat real fast and ask for seconds, in which case he would be forced to eat two more platefuls and then dosed with castor oil; or, he could eat just a little and then gripe about the poor food, in which case he would be forced to eat two more platefuls and then dosed with castor oil. He had, beforehand, objectively, chosen the second alternative on the theory that it would mean one less plateful of food in his stomach for the castor oil to work on.

He was still working on the second plateful when Barrack Number Two filed in (they always served Barrack #1, the trustees, first and Barrack #2, the recalcitrants, last in the Stockade) and sat down to eat ignoring him and he picked out Angelo Maggio and Blues Berry and the big man with the soft vague eyes of an unabashed dreamer whom he had never seen before but who could only be Jack Malloy, but he clamped down on the feeling of happiness and relief and did not look at them because he had been warned of that, too.

S/Sgt Judson administered the castor oil to him personally, after he had seen to it that he ate the two platefuls. Fatso's method of administering castor oil was to grab the seated man by the hair and pull his head back and put the bottle between his lips against the clenched teeth while two other guards held him and then have a third guard hold his nose. With Prew, they did not have to hold the nose; he kept The Malloy's instructions firmly in the front of his mind all the time and swallowed dutifully all the castor oil Fatso offered him, which was all the castor oil in the pint bottle. Even later, when they took him down to the "gym," he kept The Malloy's instructions firmly in the front of his mind. While all this was going on, Barrack Number Two ate on indifferently stolidly.

In the "gym," a small bare room down at the other end of the T corridor from the barrack wings, where the guards took the boys to give them their workouts, Fatso asked him how his gut felt. He answered truthfully that he felt a little sick to the stomach, whereupon Fatso hit him in the sick stomach with his fist, and Prew gratefully vomited a large part of the commingled castor oil and food onto the floor. While he was cleaning it up with the bucket and mop rags provided for this purpose, he was kicked down into it face first several times but this did not really hurt any. Then they stood him up against one of the bare walls and Fatso, assisted by Turnipseed and Pfc Hanson both of whom had been on shift in the messhall, gave him his workout, relieving each other whenever they got tired. The only time they actually used a grub hoe handle on him was the last time Fatso told him to get up off the floor and he couldnt and Fatso gave him the grub hoe handle across the shins, splitting open one of those old footlocker scars, and he got up. But outside of that, the only other battlewound he got was a small cut from Fatso's GI signet ring of the Army's spread Eagle, under his right eye which was closed by the time they took him out of the gymnasium and led him down to the Black Hole. In general, they refrained from hitting him in the face and he could see that The Malloy's instructions were valid when he remembered Angelo's face.

There were moments when it was difficult to keep from getting angry and saying something nasty or doing something regrettable, as The Malloy via Angelo Maggio had warned him it would be, but he kept reminding himself over and over how it was him who had asked for this in the first place not them, to get into Number Two, and that in the second place they were not enjoying it in the third place, as Fatso told him, any more than he was, and that worked.

"This is hurtin us worse than it is you," Fatso told him.

The Black Hole was beyond the gym at the end of the right arm of the T. You went down a short flight of steps. There were four cells in a row on one side. They were all empty. They threw him into the first one. There was a small barred hole at the very top of the door that he could reach with his hand but not see out of, and at the back end of the bunk of iron pipes was a #10 can for a latrine. When they brought the bread and water three times a day they shoved it in through a sliding steel panel in the bottom of the door. The cup was heavy cast iron so he could not break it. He thought it was all very professional.

It was the Black Hole he had been scared of more than anything else because he knew he could not do The Malloy's system any more than Angelo could, and when he had first heard the footsteps receding and then the closing of the trapdoor to the stairs he had had a bad moment. With the door shut it was very quiet. All he could hear was the measured dispassionate blows of his own coldblooded heart that did not seem to give a damn what was happening to him. That, and the more or less regular sigh of his breathing. He had not realized how much noise a human body made in just staying alive and it scared him because it seemed such an unstable way to preserve something as important as life. He began to be afraid that the noise, which irritated him and kept him awake, would suddenly, for no reason, stop.

He remembered what Angelo had said about utilizing that first sense of relief, but he did not feel any relief, and he was afraid to let himself doze off for fear the noises would stop if he quit listening to them.

By evening, when they brought his first meal, he had changed his mind and decided he might as well give The Malloy's system a trial after all. He had thought the guard bringing the meal was Fatso coming to take him out because the three days were over. When he found it was only the guard bringing the first meal, he knew definitely he must try The Malloy's system. He remembered not to eat the bread but he drank the water.

The funny thing was it did not seem hard at all, when he tried it. The only way he could ever explain it to himself afterwards was that he had been very worn out and had not had a very tight hold on his mind. His mind had kept slipping away from him. At first he had a little trouble concentrating on the black spot and pushing the thoughts aside, but they seemed to be very weak thoughts, and finally they just stopped altogether and the black spot got very large and his mind went off somewhere into it. He could feel it going away, clear off out of him, but he was not scared at all, he was very objective. He remembered pushing away the thought that he *ought* to be scared. Then the last thought he pushed away was the thought that he was surprised how easy it was and that he could not see why Angelo had thought it so hard. Then he was gone.

He did not see any light, like The Malloy. It was more as if there were two of him, and one of him went out of and away from the other of him. He could look back down and see the other of him there on the bunk, and he did not know any more which of him was him. There was a kind of cord that looked like it was made out of jism connecting the two of him and he knew from somewhere, but unconcernedly this time, that if that cord ever got broken he was dead. Then he went further on into the still growing black spot and could not see the other of him down there on the bunk any more.

But wherever he went there was always his end of the jism cord stretching away in the ballooning black distance back to the other of him back there, it was not weird at all, it was all very natural, he went many places, and he could understand many things that had always upset him and bothered him, it was as if for the first time he had gone off the world like a spaceship and could really see all of it, and grasp the reason for all of it, and realize how all of it each had its own private point and that nothing was ever ever wasted, which surprised him, and that more than anything else it was like a small boy going to school every day, maybe he did not want to go but he had to go anyway, and if he does not learn one lesson one day it still isnt wasted because the wasted day helps him learn it that much quicker the next day and while certain of the upperclassmen may believe the lessons taught in the lower grades are not only stupid and wasteful but actively harmful and would even pass resolutions against them, still they would never have been upperclassmen themselves if they had not first gone through the grade school, which was just one more lesson to learn, and anyway the principal didnt pay any attention to their resolutions, even though they were his valedictorians, and this reassured him and he felt the sense of peace and contentment he had always felt he was about to feel, but never quite had, when he was having one of his drunken moments of almost-but-not-quite-reaching-it, because now he could see clearly that each one received only just what he wanted and secretly asked to receive, no more no less, and the secret to the combination on the lock of the understanding was all in the different qualities of the wanting, which depended on how long you had been going to school, which required time, much much time, time that could not even be measured as time, not at least as he measured time, so it was useless to worry and hurry for time, and that if all men killed the things they loved it was only because they loved them so hard, while if all the Beloveds killed the things that loved them that was only because they wanted so bad to be loved so much more, and it was so terribly much harder to reach what you loved, especially if you really truly loved whatever it was, the harder you loved the harder to reach, he could see it all clearly.

Then a few minutes later somebody opened the door and shook him and he came back reluctantly, because he felt if he had only had a minute more just a few seconds more he could have gotten it absolutely clear in words of one syllable to bring back with him and lay it all out in black and white, and then he opened his eyes and saw it was S/Sgt Judson.

"Hello, Fatso," he grinned sillily, noticing that his voice hardly had enough wind to bring it up out of his chest, and wondering why they had come back so soon for. Behind Fatso, he heard somebody gasp.

S/Sgt Judson without any change of expression slapped him hard across the face experiencedly with a grub-hoe-handle-calloused palm, the way a mother deftly but bored by long practice slaps her small boy, but he did not even feel it.

"Tough guy," Fatso said expressionlessly, "another tough guy. How would you like about three more days of it, hunh, tough guy?"

Prew giggled weakly. "You cant snow me, Sergeant. What do you mean three more days. You think I dont know I've ony pulled one day yet? Yes, I think I'd like three more days of it, I was having a wonderful dream. Lets make it six more days," he giggled: "then we add up the whole nine days to make the full 72 hours. Hows that?"

"Hard sister," Fatso said without any change of expressionlessness, and slapped him again. "Rough monkey. Come on, wake up, rough monkey."

Then they were hoisting him up and taking him out and he realized the three days truly were over after all. On the way out his foot kicked itself against the nine slices of bread on the floor that proved it. Man, was that a good one on him.

"Yuh," Fatso said unheatedly, "I seen em, rough monkey. But if you think you can get yourself out the Hole any quicker by goin out on a hunger strike, we know that one too. We let you go hungry. You notice you done your full three days you notice," Fatso said proudly. "Plus four hours because I was too busy at the moment to get to you—and you'll do the same every time. I had my way, you'd go right back in now for three more. Hunger strikes dont scare nobody here, rough monkey."

From Fatso, a speech that long amounted to an oration. Must of impressed him, Prew thought happily as they propped him up against the wall and threw his clothes at him.

"You dont need to pull at stuff neither," Fatso said. "You can stand up."

He leaned against the wall grinning sillily while he put his clothes on, noticing for the first time that it was Pfc Hanson again with Fatso this time, Pfc Hanson alone, and realizing dimly that it must therefore have been Pfc Hanson who had gasped. I made Pfc Hanson gasp, he thought proudly. Hanson was grinning at him proudly, fully as proudly as Angelo Maggio grinned at him a few minutes later when they shoved him in through the door of Number Two Barrack. They both grinned at him as though he had at last fulfilled all the promise they had seen in him.

His stuff had already been moved into Number Two for him and the men in Number Two had gotten together and fixed it all up for him. Even his bunk was made up for him. They were proud men in Number Two. They were the toughest of the tough. They were the cream. They wore their barracks number like a medal of honor and guarded its bestowal as jealously as any Masonic Lodge or midwestern Country Club ever guarded theirs. They could not fight back and win, so they were very strict with their great pride in losing, and they were so meticulous that when they did take a man in it was an occasion and they went all the way. All Prew had to do tomorrow to be ready for inspection was to remake his bunk in the morning.

Angelo sat on the side of the bunk and proudly did all the honors. Blues Berry came over a while, and then the others came over too, one or two at a time, to listen to Prew tell the story. The last man to come over, after the others had settled back down and gone back to sitting around on the chairless floor smoking and talking, was the big man with the soft, penetrating, unabashed-dreamer's eyes, who had been sitting three bunks away taking all of it in.

Prew lay on top his new bunk, deliciously wrapped in a blanket, and acknowledged all the introductions and compliments, deliciously savoring his great sense of accomplishment. There was a satisfaction that came from having borne pain that nothing else could ever quite equal, even though the pain was philosophically pointless and never affected anything but the nervous system. Physical pain made its own justification. That must be your Indian forebearers talking, he thought. Except, he thought, that Angelo Maggio from Atlantic Avenue Brooklyn sure dont have no Indian blood, thats for sure. But he felt he could understand Angelo much better now.

In between all the introductions and coming and goings Angelo told him about Bloom, complete with all the gory details. Angelo had the whole entire story. The Stockade grapevine had had it the evening of the day it happened, just six hours after Prew had gone in the Hole. Apparently the Stockade grapevine had everything the evening of the day it happened, although nobody could say exactly just how this was accomplished. The Stockade grapevine more often than not had things before the guards themselves had them; one of Blues Berry's greatest delights was to pass on to the guards tidbits of Post gossip they had not had yet.

The reaction in the Stockade had been pretty much the same as it had in the Company. There were several other men from the Regiment in the Stockade besides Prew and Angelo, and all of them knew Bloom. The rest, if they did not know him personally, had all seen him fight last year in the Bowl. They went around with the same indignant look on their faces and the same outraged tone in their voices; if anything, this open slap in the face to everything that good soldiers stood for was even more of an affront to them than it was to G Company. Just because they were in the Stockade, their faces and voices implied, did not mean they had turned up their nose with contempt and sneered at all Bloom's advantages; if they had had Bloom's advantages, their faces and voices implied, they would not have been in the Stockade in the first place and they certainly would not be dead by their own gun in the second place. They had all been very angry about it, in the Stockade.

To Prew, hearing Angelo tell it, it was like something that had happened in another country. He had a hard time making himself visualize it.

543

"You say he put the muzzle in his mouth and pulled the trigger with his big toe?"

"Thats right," Angelo said indignantly.

"And it took off the whole top of his head and plastered it up on the ceiling."

"Yep," Angelo said complacently. "Made a hole three inches across. Ony I dont guess he figure on that probly."

"And they going to bury him here you say."

"Thats right. In the old sojer's graveyard. Nobody can find out where his folks is."

"Thats a hell of a place to be buried."

"Man, you aint just kidding," Angelo said fervidly.

"You ever been up there? Its up back of the Packtrain. I've played Taps there."

"I never been there, and whats more I dont never mean to go there. Neither feetfirst nor even dickfirst," Angelo said perfervidly.

"Theres some big pine trees. One row. Along the far side. I wonder who'll play Bloom's Taps?"

"Some punk, probly," Angelo said. "I wonder what makes pine trees like that so lonesome?"

"Every dogface deserved to have at least one good Taps. At his funeral."

"Well, maybe he'll be lucky. Maybe he'll draw a good one."

Bloom was already buried, had been buried ever since two-thirty that afternoon; they both knew that. But it was as if they had agreed tacitly not to speak of it in the past tense.

"I'd play him a Taps," Prew said, angrily because he had promised himself he would not mention that and it had slipped itself out anyway, "I'd play him a real Taps. Every dogsoljer deserves that," he said lamely, trying to explain it away.

"Aww, hell," Angelo said embarrassedly, with far too much understanding. "Hell, he's dead, aint he? What difference does it make?"

"You dont understand," Prew said furiously. What it was, he told himself, was he still could not visualize it. He felt he should be able to visualize it. But the last picture he had of Bloom was of a tremendous undammable vitality heading off across the quad for the gym to get ready to go into the ring while he himself stared after it incredulously and exhaustedly.

"I wonder what the hell made him *do* it?" he said wonderingly, conscious of so overpowering a will to live in himself.

"My personal opinion," Angelo said sagaciously, "is that he was afraid he had gone queer."

"Hell, Bloom was no queer."

"I know it."

"If I ever saw a not-queer, it was Bloom."

"I know it," Angelo said.

"Well then, what the hell?"

"Theres a difference," Angelo said, "between being queer and thinking you're queer."

"I wanted to go over and see him after that fight," Prew confessed. "Tell him I dint fight him because he was Jewish or anything like that personal. I was going to tell him the next day," he said. "But they picked me up that night," he said.

"Hell, he dint shoot hisself over you whippin him, if thats what you thinkin."

"I didnt whip him."

"All right. Over you fightin him then. A long time ago old Hal said Bloom would kill hisself someday, remember?"

"I just barely broke even with him. If anything, he whipped me."

"Hal said he was *dropping down the ladder rung by rung.*' I guess ats a quotation from some poem. He was a pretty smart boy, old Hal," Angelo said grudgingly. "The son of a bitch."

"Not so smart," Prew said, remembering the forty dollars he had finally spent on the seduction of Alma. "I'd hate to think I had anything to do with it."

"Oh, balls," Angelo said disgustedly.

"Well," Prew said, "I would."

They sat silent, looking at each other, neither one of them able to put their finger on just exactly what it was Bloom's death made them feel.

"Its funny," Angelo said, trying reluctantly. "How a guy dies and then he's gone and isnt there any more. Even if you dont like him. All the things he's done in his life, and been, all just gone like that."

"Yeah," Prew said. "But I cant see what the hell made him *do* it."

That was when the last man, the big man with the odd dreaming eyes, came over and sat down on the bunk with them. Without seeming to try to, he drew to himself all the available attention and interest in the same way a magnet collects iron filings, and for this they both looked up at him gratefully.

"Every man has the right to kill himself," the big man said gently, appropriating the subject as if there was no question to his right to it. "Its the only absolute inviolable right a man does have, the only act he can commit which nobody else has a sayso in, the one irrevocable deed he can execute without outside influence. The old Anglo-Saxon term of 'freedom' came from that: 'free' and 'doom,' with the idea that every man always had that last final resort that nobody could take away from him, if he wanted to avail himself of it.

"But like with everything else," the big man said gently, "it has its price, too: its price is its own absoluteness and irrevocableness and inviolableness. 'Doom' is the only thing thats ever 'free,' citizens," the big man said, as if speaking out of some very sure personal source not open to them.

"I'd hate to believe that," Prew said distastefully.

"I dont see why," the big man said tranquilly. "If its the truth. And anyway, maybe you're right: Maybe even that isnt free."

"I didnt mean that," Prew said.

"I know what you meant," the big man said. He stopped and smiled at them. The subject he had appropriated seemed to have been pretty well covered.

"Except for one thing," Angelo said worriedly. "Even for us guys, here, dont you think its wrong?"

"You're a Catholic," the big man grinned gently.

"Not a good one."

"But still a Catholic."

"Okay, so I'm a Catholic," Angelo said belligerently. "Somebody else is a Methodist. So what does that prove?"

"Nothing. But I wasnt talking about the moral right. I was talking about the physical right, the fact, the opportunity. No laws or preachments or physical restraints can take away the concrete physical right, if a man wants to do it. But you, being a Catholic, or a follower of any other religion, immediately transposed the physical right into a moral right."

"But *is* it right?" Angelo insisted. "Or is it wrong?"

"Its all how you look at it. Would you say the early Christian martyrs committed suicide?"

"No."

"Of course not. You're a Catholic. But they didnt have to go into the arena, did they?"

Angelo frowned. "No, they didnt have to. But they did have to. Besides, somebody else killed them."

"But they knew what they were getting into. They were accepting death of their own free will, werent they?"

"Yes, but—"

"Isnt that suicide?"

"Well, in a way, yes," Angelo frowned. "But they had a reason."

"Sure. They had a reason. Either they were too proud to back down; or else they figured they'd get a free ticket to Heaven. Do you think Bloom shot himself just to see how it'd feel? And what difference does it make who pulled the trigger?"

Angelo frowned again. "None, I guess. When you put it that way."

"Well, would you say the Christian martyrs were wrong?"

"Of course not."

"Then it must all depend on the circumstances, whether suicide's right or wrong."

"But the Christian martyrs were different than Bloom. Or me."

"Only in the fact that they did it in mass formation for an impersonal ideal, whereas Bloom did it for a purely personal reason that nobody will ever know. And you cant say it was wrong until you know that personal reason.

"Now what you should of asked," the big man grinned gently, "was is it immoral?"

"Yeah, thats it," Angelo said, "thats what I meant. Well, is it?"

"Of course," the big man grinned. "Everybody knows its immoral. To the Romans it was very immoral, what the Christian martyrs did, it was cowardly, and a running away, and immoral. Theres no doubt that suicide, especially mass suicide, is immoral. Because every human society teaches that its immoral. Even in Japan and Russia suicide is only moral when you're in disgrace with the government; but any other brand is just as immoral as here. How long would a society's framework hold up if every time there was a Depression all the ones without jobs marched on Washington or London or Moscow and committed suicide on the Capitol lawn? A couple deals like that and there wouldnt be any labor market left. The Russians and Japs, who have utilized it, know that better than anybody."

"But hell," Angelo said, "that would be crazy."

"Sure," the big man grinned, "but thats just what your Christian martyrs did, citizen."

"Yeah," Angelo said thoughtfully, "thats right. But times was differnt then," he said.

"You mean the people then didnt want to live as bad as the people do now."

"Yeah. I guess thats it. Sure thats it. We got more to live for now."

"Movies," the big man said without smiling, gently, almost lovingly. "Automobiles. Trains, buses, airplanes, niteclubs, bars; sports, educations, businesses. Radios," the big man said gently.

"Yeah," Angelo said. "All that. It wont be long till we got television. They dint have none of that stuff."

"Would you say a man in a Nazi concentration camp had the right to commit suicide?"

"Hell yes."

"Then why not a man in an American corporation?"

"But thas differnt. He aint bein tortured."

"You think not? And why not a man in the American Army? Why not a man in the Stockade? Why not any man anywhere, anytime, if he is being tortured?

"Everybody talks about freedom, citizens," the big man said gently, seeming to draw upon that very sure source of personal knowledge again, "but they dont really want it. Half of them wants it but the other half dont. What they really want is to maintain an illusion of freedom in front of their wives and business associates. Its a satisfactory compromise, and as long as they can have that they can get along without the other which is more expensive. The only trouble is, every man who declares himself free to his friends has to make a slave out of his wife and employees to keep up the illusion and prove it; the wife to be free in front of her bridgeclub has to command her Help, Husband, and Heirs. It resolves itself into a battle; whoever wins, the other one loses. For every general in this world there have to be 6,000 privates.

"Thats why," he smiled at them, "I wouldnt stop any man from committing suicide. If he came up and asked to borrow my gun, I'd give it to him. Because he is either serious or else he's trying to maintain that illusion of freedom. If he was serious I'd want him to have it; if he was play-acting I'd want to call him."

"Thats one way to look at it," Prew said, somehow carried along into agreement in spite of himself, carried by those long-range-vision eyes and that absolute-tender voice.

"In our world, citizens," the big man said gently, "theres only one way a man can have freedom, and that is to die for it, and after he's died for it it dont do him any good. Thats the whole problem, citizens. In a nutshell."

"This is Jack Malloy," Angelo said proudly, as if introducing his personal friend the Nizam of Hyderabad, the richest man in the world. "Wait'll you hear some of the real conversations we have in here."

"I've heard a lot about you," Prew said, feeling tongue-tied and shy. Looking at those soft vague unabashed-dreamer's eyes he could see why an arch-cynic like Blues Berry could make such a fatuous remark about The Malloy's big-baby heart.

"I've heard a lot about you, too," Jack Malloy said warmly, sticking out a paw like a ham. "I want to shake your hand, citizen. Out of all the drafthorses in this stable, you're the only one who ever listened to what I told them to do and did it, exactly," he said, raising his voice.

Without turning either his trunk or his head, he seemed suddenly to be staring behind him at the rest of Number Two sprawled out talking on the chairless floor. He was not looking at them but they all lowered their eyes and inspected their cigarettes, the conversations seeming to stop dead in the air.

Jack Malloy ruthlessly let the silence ring on for almost a full minute. Then he turned back, or seemed to turn back, because he was still looking at Prew, and winked down at Prew, a quick deliberate but absolutely impersonal wink that was as if he did not even see Prew at all but was only fulfilling a social ritual like a host who gives a big dinner party for a prospective customer so he can sell him.

"If I had twelve men;" he said loudly, "an even dozen, citizen; who would do like you did, I could have Father Thompson and Fatso both in the nut ward in three months as permanent boobyhatch material.

"Of course," he said, "there would be two more just like them the next day and we would have to start over again, but the Toughest Jail in the US Army would soon become also the Toughest Assignment in the US Army. And if we sent enough of them along after Father Thompson and Fatso, eventually they would have to close up this shop in despair and let us all go home."

The ever-present thirty-year-man that was always there in Prewitt wondered if he meant home to their outfits or home to civilian life, but somehow he did not feel like asking.

Jack Malloy let the silence ring on for another minute. He had said it all loudly, and nobody said anything this time either. There seemed to be a general feeling that he could do just exactly what he said.

There was another feeling, too, Prew noted, here in Number Two. It was a feeling that had not been in Number Three. The only way he could describe it was that it was a feeling that you could say anything loudly, absolutely anything, loudly. It was a good feeling.

"Have a smoke, citizen," Jack Malloy said, lowering his voice back to normal, and offering him from a full pack of tailormades. It was like a signal and the men on the floor who had been chastened began to smoke and talk again.

"Hey," Prew said, embarrassedly, "tailormades. Thanks."

"I got plenty more," Jack Malloy said. "Any time you want one. If this little son of a bitch," he nodded at Angelo, "with all the pure unadulterated guts he's got, would follow my advice half as well as you did, he could have pulled off his plot and been out of here a month ago."

"Thats all right," Angelo countered, taking the offered cigarette, "you just wait. I can do it anyway. I know I can."

Prew watched his eyes go a little crazy again, hungrily, like they always did at the mention of his great secret plan, but this time his eyes did not get that murderous suspicion in them that they always got out on the rockpile.

"I'm just biding my time," he said craftily. "I can do it all right. Dont worry about that."

"Sure you can," Jack Malloy said gently. "Sure you can, citizen. But you could do it a whole lot easier, and save yourself a whole lot of nasty bumps, if you'd listen to me."

549

"I listen to you," Angelo said violently. "More than once've I listen to you. And I've tried it. Not ony Passive Resistance, but the other in the Hole. I just cant do it, Jack. Either one."

"The citizen here did it," Jack Malloy nodded at Prew, "he did both of them."

"I still dont know how though," Prew put in.

"That doesnt matter," Jack Malloy said. "I dont know either. You still did them."

"Okay, so maybe he can do them," Angelo said hotly. "For him thats fine. For me thats from nothing. What a use for me keep on trying I cant do them?"

"None," Jack Malloy said, in the same gently tender tone that his voice never seemed to get out of, even when he spoke loudly. "Thats why I told you to stop. But you could do it—if you only believed you could strong enough, so that you didnt knock yourself out trying so hard."

"That tells me a lot," Angelo said. "That tells me a hell of a lot. Maybe Prew can do it. Well, I told you he was your kind of a guy. But nobody else around here has ever been able to do them."

"That doesnt mean they cant do them," Jack Malloy said. "The same thing is in every man's mind. My mind's no different than your mind, citizen."

It was a habit of his, Prew found out later, he never called anybody anything but citizen. Once, the story went, he had even called Major Thompson citizen a couple times. It had earned him four extra days in the Hole. Prew wondered why he did things like that, and then all the time told everybody else not to?

"Like hell it aint differnt," Angelo grinned. "I had your mind, I wount never of been in this fucking place in the first place."

"You had my mind," Jack Malloy grinned ruefully, one of those rare flashing grins of his, always rueful, that were different from his smile which never quite reached clear up into the vague unlistening eyes, "you had my mind, citizen, you'd been in here a hell of lot sooner than you were."

"I guess thats no lie," Angelo grinned with a great pride in the big man.

"How about this big secret plot?" Prew asked them. "What the hell is this great plan anyway? I've been killing myself with curiosity for a week now, wondering about it."

"Let him tell you," Jack Malloy deferred gently.

Apparently Prew had addressed the question to Malloy instinctively, although he did not know why because it was Angelo's idea.

"Its his plan," Jack Malloy said. "It was his idea, he thought of it, and he deserves the telling of it."

And Prew thought suddenly that he had never seen such tenderness, in man or woman, as was in Jack Malloy's eyes looking at Angelo Maggio. It was worth it, he thought exultantly, it was more than worth it, it was worth ten days in the Hole, to be here with these men.

"Come on down here then," Angelo said, his eyes gone cunning and miserly again. He got up and started down toward the other end where the two commodes were.

"You can tell it here, citizen," Jack Malloy tried to dissuade him gently.

"Nosir," Angelo grinned at them crafty-eyed. "Nosiree."

"Maybe Prew dont feel like getting up," Jack Malloy suggested gently.

"Then he'll have to wait," Angelo said emphatically, and started to come back. "I tell it at all, I tell it down there, where nobody is."

"I feel okay," Prew said, and got up and the two of them followed the little guy down. And it was sitting on the closed commodes, with Jack Malloy leaning against the iron sink, that Angelo Maggio unfolded his big secret plan, his great dream.

The rest of the barrack, led by Blues Berry, drifted unobtrusively down toward the far end with their conversations, like healthy people tactfully humoring an invalid. Prew looked at Malloy, then swung his eyes back to Maggio quickly.

"I've ony told it to Berry and The Malloy," Angelo explained insistently. "Nobody else knows about it, not a single soul."

Prew looked at Malloy; Malloy's face was closed.

"Aint that right, Jack?" Angelo said anxiously.

"Thats right, citizen," Jack Malloy said gently.

"If they did," Angelo said fiercely, "I'd kill them, see? Even in here, see? Some of these guys find out about it, they liable as not to try it first. And half the chances of success depends on it bein the first guy who tries it. After the first time it wouldnt work. Father Thompson aint no fool. Neither's Fatso. And I'm the guy who thought of it so I got the right to be the first guy to try it.

"Aint that right, Jack?" he said anxiously.

"Thats right," Jack Malloy said, his face still closed.

"Well," Angelo said, "here it is." He interrupted himself. "You see I'm right," he said, "Jack says I'm right; you want to try it later, after me, thats okay, although I wouldnt guarantee it, but I got the right to have the first shot."

"The truth is," Jack Malloy said, "nobody else has got the guts to try it."

"Dont kid yourself," Angelo snarled.

"I'm not," Jack Malloy said. "They havent the guts because nobody wants out as bad as you do."

"Dont you believe it," Angelo said. "I aint takin no chances." He turned to Prew. "But you see how it is, dont you, Prew?"

"I see," Prew said.

"Okay. Well, heres the deal. Any man who goes in the Hole and stays there 21 days is automatically sent up to the nutward in the Station Hospital and given a Section 8. I never heard of it happening yet, but thats the rule."

"I've heard of it happening," Jack Malloy interrupted gently. "It happened twice during my first trip. Thats why I like the plan. The idea is, you see, that any man who gets violent in the Stockade—I mean homicidally violent—is too far gone to salvage. I mean, really off his nut. They put him in the Hole to cool him off, but if he doesnt cool off in 21 days (some say 30 days), then they figure its the McCoy and he's not acting and they Section 8 him. Thats happened twice I know of, during my first trip. But those two guys were really off their nut. The citizen here," he nodded at Angelo, "proposes to fool them."

"Thats it," Angelo said eagerly. "I'm going to flip my lid out on the rockpile and go for the guard with a hammer, see?"

"Aint he liable to shoot you?" Prew said.

"Yeah, but I got to chance that. Thats the ony really dangerous part to it. What I figure is, if I go *for* him, instead of *away* from him, toward the woods, he wont shoot; he'll ony bean me with his riot gun. I figure to fix it as easy as I can for him to bean me. I aint going to really ever hit him, see? just make him think I am."

"They'll work you over pretty good, wont they?" Prew said.

"Sure," Angelo said earnestly, "but what the hell? They wont be getting any cherry. They cant make it any worse than they have already. All they can do is make it last longer, way I figure. And after so long a time you kind of blank out on them anyway, see?"

"Yeah," Prew said, "I see."

"I got everything to gain, and all I got to lose is a little more scalp. And the Black Hole part is the least of my worries. I can do that standin on my head, see? 21 days?" he snapped them away with his fingers.

Prew watched him blow it away like milkweed, and thought about it hollowly; 21 days of it, maybe 30 Malloy said, 21 days of bread and water, 21 days of silence, 21 days of blindness; three weeks maybe a month, in the Black Hole.

"A man couldnt pull that trick of yours for that long, could he?" he asked Jack Malloy, "even if he knew how."

"I dont know," Jack Malloy said. "I've read where its been done for longer. But I wouldnt want to try it."

"I can cut it," Angelo said. "With a butterknife. And I dont need The Malloy's trick to do it."

"It'll mean a DD, wont it?" Prew said.

"I dont know," Angelo said. "And frankly, I dont give a good goddam. I aint never going to work in Gimbel's Basement no more anyway. What I need with an Honorable? Besides, Jack says they give blue ones with Sections 8s sometimes."

"Not if the man comes from the Stockade, do they?" Prew said. "Way I understood, any man Section 8ed out of the Stockade automatically gets a yellow discharge."

"Not always," Jack Malloy said gently, his face still closed. "I think it all depends on the circumstances and how much of a convincing act the man can put on for them."

"Thats not how I heard it," Prew said.

"Well, its a cinch he aint going to get a white discharge," Angelo grinned tautly, "so what the hell's the difference? Yellow or blue? Who wants to be a goddam citizen of this goddam country anyway? I'll go to Mexico. Dont even have to do that. All you lose is the right to vote and pay taxes. Who the hell wants to vote anyway? You cant vote in the Army, can you? Anyway, whoever the hell a man does vote for anyway, its always all the same: They all of them get together ahead of time and figure it out and make their trades and put in the men they want anyway."

"You cant get a job," Prew said.

"Who the hell wants a job? They all the same goddam thing. Gimbel's Basement. You work for some big outfit that takes all the money and gives you just barely enough to live on and punch a timeclock all your life and kiss the boss's ass for a job you never liked. Who wants that? Not Maggio. I'll go to Mexico," he said. "I'll go to Mexico and be a cowboy or something," he said wildly.

"I dont know why I'm arguing with you," Prew said. "Its your deal, and if you've figured all that into it, what the hell? I'm for you, Angelo."

"You think I'm crazy, dont you?" Angelo grinned at him.

"Hell no. Its just that I hate to think of losing my citizenship. I guess I just like this country."

"I like it too," Angelo said. "I love this country. Much as you or anybody, and you know it."

"I know it," Prew said.

"But I still hate this country. You love the Army. But I dont love the Army. This country's Army is why I hate this country. What did this country ever do for me? Gimme a right to vote for men I cant elect? You can have it. Gimme a right to work at a job I hate? You can have that too. Then tell me I'm a Citizen of the greatest richest country on earth, if I dont believe it look at Park Avenue. Carnival prizes. All carnival prizes. Pay fifty cents a throw and get a plasterparis bust of

Washington—if you win. A man can just stand so much from anything, no matter how much he loves the thing."

"I'll buy that," Prew said.

"Well, I've stood all I can stand—if I can get myself *out* of standing any more of it. They aint going to drive this soldier to any goddam suicide. And they aint going to drive this soldier into growing a brown nose. They shouldnt teach their immigrants' kids all about democracy unless they mean to let them have a little of it, it ony makes for trouble. Me and the United States is disassociating our alliance as of right now, until the United States can find time to read its own textbooks a little."

Prew thought, a little sickly, of the little book *The Man Without a Country* that his mother used to read to him so often, and how the stern patriotic judge condemned the man to live on a warship where no one could ever mention home to him the rest of his whole life, and how he had always felt that pinpoint of pleased righteous anger at seeing the traitor get what he deserved.

"And thats the story," Angelo said, "and thats the way she is."

"I'm for it then," Prew said.

"Are you?" Angelo asked him anxiously. "You really are? Thats one reason I wanted to tell you, because I knew if you heard me out and you were still for it, then I know it was all right, it wasnt wrong."

"I'm for it," Prew said.

"Okay," Angelo said. "Then thats all. Lets go on back."

Prew watched him go. Thin, narrowshouldered, bowlegged, the toothpick arms moving with the swagger, one of the newer race of cliff dwellers he thought again, who had no use for muscles: for legs to walk take the subway; for arms to climb use the elevator; for back to lift hire a stiffleg derrick. A minor casualty of his 20th Century culture and civilization. Go to Mexico and be a cowboy! Even his country's history screwed him.

Maybe if his father had been a watchmaker, or an auto mechanic, or a pipefitter, so that he might have inherited a trade he could love, then he would not have had to love democracy so much. If he had only found some undangerous channel that would have let him utilize the talent for honesty and belief in democracy that the unwise foolish virgins who taught Social Science in the public schools had fostered in him.

If he had only been born a millionaire's son. Then he would have been all right.

The trouble with Angelo Maggio, the serious trouble, the dangerous trouble, the inconsiderate unreasonable insoluble frightening trouble, was Angelo Maggio had not been born a Culpepper.

"They all know it, dont they?" Prew said.

"You cant have a secret in a place like this."

"Wont they talk?"

"No. They wont."

"You didnt try to talk him out of it," he asked Jack Malloy.

"No," Jack Malloy said, his face still closed, "I didnt."

"Neither did I," Prew said.

"There are some things," Jack Malloy said, his face still closed, "it doesnt do any good to try to talk a man out of."

"Lets go on back," Prew said.

"Okay," Jack Malloy said, his face still closed.

Angelo was sitting on Prew's bunk and Prew crawled in under the deliciousness of the blanket again. Then, and only then, Blues Berry and the others began to drift back down again. They were tough men in Number Two, they were the toughest of the tough, they were the cream.

During the rest of the time before Lights Out they sat around on the chairless floor smoking Duke's Mixture and now and then a hoarded filched tailormade, or leaned standing back against the bed ends, or maybe half-lying on a shaded bottom bunk, and they talked. There were no cards or checkers, no Monopoly boards, no Mah-Jong sets. But they never ran out of plenty to talk about. Most of them had bummed across the country at least once, before they finally enlisted. Most of the younger ones had grown up in the CCCs during the Depression, and graduated into the Army from there. Without exception they had all spent time on the bum. They had worked in North Carolina paper mills, cut timber up in Washington, maybe tried a shrift of raising cukes in southern Florida, worked in the Indiana mines, poured steel in Pennsylvania, followed the wheat harvest in Kansas and the fruit harvest in California, loaded cargoes on the docks in Frisco and Dago and Seattle and N.O.LA, helped spud in wells in Texas. They were men who knew their country, and in spite of that still loved it. A generation before them men just like them had tried to change it and been defeated. These now did not have the others' organization. These now did not go for organization. These now were members of a still newer race jerked loose from ties by the Depression and set to a drifting that had ended finally in the Army as the last port of call where they went through one more sifting process and came here, to the Stockade, to be sifted down once again into Number Two.

At eight the lights were turned off. Each man crawled in his bunk until the flashlight bedcheck had been made. Then they got back up and sat down on the floor again and went on smoking Duke's Mixture with deep drags that lit up faces redly, and still they went on talking. Smoking Duke's Mixture was no hardship to them who had grown up on rolled cigarettes, and they had no trouble passing the time talking because they did not talk to pass the time but because they just loved to talk. Each man always had more stories with himself as hero than he could tell, and if he told the same story with himself as hero again a week later it was still almost new again by then, and anyway he had always developed it and elaborated it in the same way a writer rewrites a story with himself as hero, so that usually it was not even recognizable. Talking had always been their chief recreation, who could only afford the more expensive amusements like women and whiskey once a month on Payday, and they were experts in their field. When they could have slept, always the best method of time passing as any man who has spent time in the Black Hole knows, they still preferred to sit up and talk and tell stories with themself as hero.

It was almost like the days back on the bum, Prew thought sleepily. No women, no whiskey, no tailormades, no money. If you shut your eyes, you could believe you were back in a jungle on the outskirts of some little jerkwater town, smooth dusty under the trees on the leeward side of a grade that passed the watertank and cut off the wind, sitting around the small fire with a belly full of a good mulligan that you had been assigned the bumming of the carrots for, or maybe the onions, or the spuds. The faces were the same faces, and the voices were the same voices, and the flavor of the talk was the same American flavor.

American faces, he thought sleepily happily with that ecstasy of the martyr that had always been his goal and his destiny, American faces and American voices, weak with all the lustful-hungry greedy-lying American weaknesses, but strong now with the strength bred of necessity which is the only real strength ever, leathery lean hardbitten faces and voices in the old American tradition of the woodsmen and the ground-clearing farmers who also fought bitterly to stay alive. Here is your Army, America, he sleepily wanted to tell Them, here is your strength, that You have made strong by trying to break, and that You will have to depend on in the times that are coming, whether You like it or not, or want to or not, and no matter how much it may hurt Your pride. And here in Number Two was its cream, sifted and resifted and then sifted again, until all the dry rot had been winnowed out, all the soft spots squeezed out, all the rotting gangrene that all the social columnists were so afraid of excised out, so that only the firm hardy remainder of the most absolute of toughness, that would not only hold its own but would triumph, in a whole world of toughness, was all that was left now.

Thank your various Gods for your prisons, You America. Pray to Them hard, to not teach you how to get along without them,—until They has first taught you how to get along without your wars.

And he, Robert E. Lee Prewitt, Harlan Kentucky, was one of them, one of these here, in the old hungry tradition, here where there was not one single fat-layered insurance salesman's face in the new American tradition to be found.

You could not be one of them unless you shared it all with them, and for the first time in a long time he felt sleepily he was back with his own kind again, that he did not have to explain to, because each one of them had the same hard unbroachable sense of ridiculous personal honor that he had never been able to free himself from either.

And it had all been more than worth it, from the moment he had sat down at the mess table and taken that first single bite he had been too scared to taste, and he would start gladly right in on a second round again right now, if it was required to clinch it.

Poor Bloom, he thought sleepily, poor Bloom.

It was only later on, after the others had all finally gone off to sleep, that he was not sleepy any more and began to think of Alma Schmidt whom he had almost believed he had forgotten and, trying The Malloy's black dot system again here in the bunk and failing miserably, lay for a long time wide awake, and thinking of her.

Everything you swear you will not do you always end by doing, he thought sleepy again now finally. I remember distinctly you swore once you would never lay in your bunk and do this and so now you can add this one to the still growing list. At least this is one degradation Bloom didnt have to suffer.

Or maybe Bloom was in love with someone, too. Maybe that was why he killed himself.

The more he thought about it, sleepily again, the more he was quite positive that that was it, that Bloom had killed himself for love.

Chapter 40

Milton Anthony Warden, on the other hand, having been out with Karen Holmes every afternoon since he had closed out Prewitt's trial, did not speculate on why Bloom killed himself. It was enough for Warden, more than enough, that he had done it. It put the quietus on Milt Warden's private life as effectively as if the Third Reich had invaded New York City, or the Japanese tried to attack Pearl Harbor in broad daylight, or the Martians captured California.

He had started seeing her in the afternoons after the Hickam problem. They had decided on that as being the best time for her to get away with the least amount of risk. They both felt the need of a plan that would give their deception dailyness and regularity and at the same time still be foolproof. This was, and under it they both had blossomed. The days had arranged themselves into a comfortable pattern that seemed to have been like this always and promised to go on like this forever. If there was work in the afternoons he let Mazzioli do it and to hell with it. It was all routine stuff and he could always straighten it out later and the kid was supposed to be in there to learn. Leva could handle the supplyroom, and he did not have to worry about Stark's kitchen. He would meet her in town along the bright hot tourist-crowded streets and they would drive her husband's battered old Buick club coupé around and around the Island, him in trunks and barefooted, her in a legless briefbra-ed swimsuit that was as sensual as her bare painted toenails, taking every new back road they had not driven, stopping to swim whenever they felt like swimming. They stopped to love whenever he felt like loving, although Karen felt he was inclined to stop too often and insisted that while sometimes she liked it it had no place in her love and she could have done as well, or better, without any of that which was such a vulgar way of proving your love; but still she did not try to dissuade him from stopping, and those afternoons, like all the rest of the time he spent with Karen Holmes, seemed to elongate themselves into infinity like a backward telescope until nothing else existed. If there was anything lacking that kept them from being absolute perfection, it was that her husband's Buick was not a convertible.

There were no stormy sessions, not a single argument, because they had already settled it between them (the day they came back together hungrily after the two weeks at Hickam Field) that Milt would put in for officer's extension course. They settled it in the following manner:

Karen made it plain that she would never ask it of him. He then volunteered it. Karen said no, understanding and sympathizing with the way he felt about Officers, she could not ask or expect it of him, that he was not to do it on her account, ever, even if it meant her losing him. Whereupon Milt insisted he would too do it, and do it on her account, and only on her account, and nothing she could say would deter him. She cried, and he almost cried, and that was how they left it. He did not do anything about putting in the application.

When she asked him about it later on, he told her it was already in the mail (he would have told her a lot worse things than that, to keep those afternoons) and made a mental note to make it out and have Holmes sign it and get it in the mail tomorrow, but he did not get around to it. It would have been easy, because after they decided it she had started working on Holmes some at home and Holmes had started urging him to put in for it, but he could not get around to it. He did not intend to undertake a course of stupid lessons that might interfere with those afternoons, those hot bright swim-cool afternoons, that seemed to be more dream than reality and that he wanted to go on like that forever. The future was too vague of an investment to risk all the capital he had. Let the future look out for itself, like everybody else. It was of age, wasnt it? To hell with the future, as long as these afternoons go on like this forever.

And for a while, after he had cleared up Prewitt's trial, it almost looked as if they would. He could even believe it, that they would.

There were things that were beginning increasingly to come up—like next week every rifle in the Company less ten had to be turned in for the new M1 Garands that had finally come in and were sitting over at S/4 waiting to be issued, and that Leva would need help with. There was the crisp new War Department Circular that had just come out authorizing for the first of next month the much-rumored new TO which would make S/Sgts out of mess and supply and raise all field NCOs one grade; that would necessitate a whole flock of Company Orders and Service Records entries, not counting the wholesale salvage of old chevrons that he would also be expected to take care of for O'Hayer.

Did they think that exchange of chrome bayonets for black ones back in March had just been somebody's whim? He had warned Holmes. He had prophesied to O'Hayer. Now it was coming true. Barely four months later. You could hear the grinding of the Government changing gears. And as usual, G Company's pants were down.

But if these things were threats, so had Prewitt's trial been a threat, and he had handled that. Without missing one single afternoon.

If the Government was getting ready for a war in July of 1941, that was not the same as being in one. That it was bound to come eventually did not mean it would be here tomorrow. It would take something pretty big, before the country would be willing to get in; and all the rifles in the world did not make a war-Army until you had talked the people into shooting them.

And that part, Milt Warden figured carefully, would come slow. And therefore the other changes, geared to that main wheel, would also be slow. The actual work required in the orderly room of G Company —th Infantry would not be so much. He could handle that part easy. If there was going to be any trouble at all, the heart of it would be O'Hayer and the supplyroom.

Well, Leva would just have to handle the supplyroom. Leva had handled it before, in as bad or worse than this, and while it might be years off yet it did something to a man to see the future run up to, and stop at, the blank wall of a war. It made him aware that he had better get all he was going to get out of his life now, and it made him want his afternoons.

Figuring it all like that, carefully foreseeing and apportioning every-thing, even the war whose inevitability he had already accepted three years ago, Milt Warden was not going to be caught off balance. He could still go on juggling his two lives, even if now he did have to do it on a tightrope. If Milt Warden had his back to the wall, at least Milt Warden knew it. And if there was one thing in the world that had never let Milt Warden down, it was Milt Warden.

What he could not foresee, of course, was that some stupid ass in his outfit would kill himself. And even if he could have foreseen it, it would not have helped. Court-martials he could handle, from memory blindfolded, court-martials he had done by the bushel. But a suicide was something else again, he had never had a suicide before, and the Army disliked suicides, especially now, at this time. It disliked them even worse than murders, and it required that an almost infinite num-ber of reports be made out to prove the fault was not the Army's.

In addition, there was all the usual death work: the personal effects that would have to be sorted and according to policy carefully screened for all pornography before they could be packaged up for shipment home, the letters to the parents he would have to write for Holmes, the equipment of the Deceased to be turned in and itemized so the short-ages could be checked and subtracted from the Final Payroll that would be paid to the parents of the Deceased, the closing out of person-nel files and the Service Record, the arranging of the details of the mili-tary funeral.

The very least the son of a bitch might have done, Milt Warden felt, was make it look like an accident by jumping off the Pali. At least then he would have been remembered with affection.

That afternoon, after the OD had been called in to make the corpse official, he managed to get away long enough to call her. He caught a Post cab over to the Kemoo Liquor Store that perched like a mushroom on the edge of the Wahiawa Reservoir across the highway from the gate, and, knowing its Chinee proprietor from his bachelor days, used his private phone in the back. He got her just as she was leaving for town to meet him.

Her first reaction was one of anger. Male operators were no less prone to gossip than the female ones, especially if they were EM and the subject was an Officer. The Signal Corps operators on the Post knew every number in the Officers' Quarters by heart. They had al-ways avoided using the phone as much as possible, and when they did they resorted to a sort of secret language in which everything stood for something else.

She was less angry when she learned that he had called from Kemoo, which had to go back through the Wahiawa civilian circuit before it could reach the Post, but even so she made him hang up and wait until she could go out somewhere and call him back. It was just one more of the little things about being in love with a married woman that you had not envisioned when you started it.

He waited, of course—having a couple of quick nervous drinks with Al Chomu who wondered unnervously where he had been for so long—until she called him back from a booth in the main PX.

It was hard trying to explain what had happened because the secret language had never made allowances for suicides or for Isaac Nathan Bloom. When he finally got it across, he could hear her become suddenly cool and fully collected, almost in mid-word in that wholly admirable but almost frightening way she had, as she realized it was really an emergency. The anger disappeared, replaced by an absolutely cold-bloodedly calculating calmness that never failed to put his much-prided realism to utter shame.

"Well, what are we going to do?" the muffled unreal phone voice that never sounded human asked him coolly. "Have you thought about what to do?"

"Yes. This new job will take almost a full month of my time. I'm afraid I'll have to postpone the party. Will your brother have to be going to the Mainland on business again soon?" he said carefully.

Translated, that meant would Dana Holmes be going to a stag.

"You know how his business is," the cool voice answered. "He never knows just when he'll have to go. He hasnt had to go for some time now, so they're liable to be calling him. But of course," the cool voice said carefully, "you know it all depends on just when his superiors get in a new shipment, and have enough material on hand to need him."

He had to stop a second to translate this, and it made him mad; all this childish conspiracy; it was damn near as bad as being in the Elks or the Masons. What she meant was that while Holmes had not been to a stag recently, and so would probably go to one soon, still she could not say with accuracy when he would go. She was refusing to use that as a time for meeting him.

"I do not want to postpone the party," Warden said savagely.

"Neither do I. But of course," the cool voice reminded him, sounding incredibly unbelievably indifferent, "my brother's daily work here never amounts to enough to keep him from making it."

That would mean his usual evenings at the Club for poker and barflying, or wherever the hell it was he went, could not be counted on to give her a chance to get away.

"Then maybe we could make it some night, some evening maybe, before he has to leave. You know how much I'd hate to have him miss it," he grinned into the blind funnel furiously, unable to resist the opportunity. Her coolness that he admired so much was making him madder than the conspiracy business.

"If you could have it some afternoon," the cool voice said, "while he's still here."

"I told you," he said, trying to rein in the exasperation, "I told you I wouldnt be able to make it in the afternoon. You dont understand. This work just has to be done."

"Then I think," the cool voice said very logically, "that the best thing is just to postpone it, until you get your work done, dont you?"

"But its liable to take a whole month," he told the blind unfeeling funnel. It was easy for her, she wouldnt care if they carried on their love affair entirely by correspondence. She would probably prefer it.

"I think the best thing is to plan to have it sometime soon," he insisted, "even if it is the next time your brother's on a trip." That meant have it the next time there was a stag. He felt it was obscure. "You understand?" he said carefully. "Even if he is off on a trip?"

"I understand," the voice said, coolly, "but the trouble with that is I have no idea of when he will be going. And of course, theres no way I can get in touch with you."

That meant she was refusing to call him.

"Well, maybe I could find out from him and get in touch with you," he said desperately.

"But how will you know where to reach me?" the cool voice said.

And that, of course, meant she did not want him to call her. Even if it meant she would not see him for a month, she still did not want him to call her. That anybody could be that cold-bloodedly calculating about love made him want to shudder. Who the hell ever said it was the men who were tough.

"God damn it!" Warden said angrily, finally giving way. "You dont understand about this party. I owe this party. Its an important party. I owe it to a lot of people."

"And do you think I'm not disappointed too?" the voice said angrily.

If there is an operator listening, he thought bitterly, he sure as hell will think he's listening to a couple crazy people when he hears this gibberish. Warden found it absolutely impossible to believe that any operator listening in on them could gossip enough to cause the kind of scandal Karen was afraid of, even if he spoke to her in nothing but four-letter words.

"If you try to give your party," the again calm collected voice was saying irreconcilably, "when you are up to your ears in work like this, you will only spoil it anyway, you know that. You dont want to spoil your party, do you? Isnt there any possible way you could hurry the job through? so that it wouldnt take a whole month? There are other people," the cool voice said, "looking forward to your party just as much as you are. I've talked to some of them. But I'm sure they wouldnt want

562

you to rush your party out against all these handicaps, and then spoil it."

The muffled faroff inflection was so intensely familiar he could look into the black much-perforated funnel and almost see her. She would be sitting there in the hot booth with the door tight shut for secrecy, her face flushed hotly as she brushed back the damp hair from her forehead but still icily cool and logical in the mind while the beads of sweat welled under her drawnup knees which seemed to be the only place she ever sweated and trickled down the long skislide of her calves as she thought on detachedly, with that calm objectivity that infuriated him with his own outraged admiration. She would be wearing one of those square wide-necked prints that were so absolutely female without ever being fluttery or fluffy.

Didnt she know what she did to him? She always said she didnt, but he always disbelieved it. She must know.

Warden wanted to tear Al Chomu's phone out of the wall and smash it. At that moment he would have gladly emasculated Alexander Graham Bell for inventing this instrument of torture that was emasculating him.

"All right," he said, "all right. I'll see if I cant step it up and get it done in a week. Will that satisfy you? Will that be better?"

"It would be wonderful, if you could. But, darling," the cool voice said, carefully using the word darling only as a sophisticated form of address, "it isnt me. Its your party. Dont be angry."

"Angry!" he snarled. "Who's angry? I'll have it done in a week," he promised, knowing it was impossible, "and then give the party one week from today, at the same old place. You're invited," he snapped, wanting to hang up on that triumph of abbreviated sarcasm.

But he didnt.

"Have you got that?" he asked anxiously. "One week. At the same place. The same place, see?"

"I have it," the cool calm voice that was still way ahead of him said in the same indifferent tone that had so surely manipulated everything, including him, so logically and objectively that it was coming out exactly as she wanted, and had known it would. "I have it, darling."

That same impersonally toned address, which was as near as she would ever let herself come to affection on the phone. On that note he hung up, reluctantly, feeling it was unfinished but knowing it was all he'd get, and went back out to Al Chomu's bar.

And they called them the weaker sex! That was prone to crack up and cry at every crisis! Like hell. The women ran this world; and nobody knew it better than a man in love. Sometimes he thought they did it deliberately, all this conspiracy stuff, just to satisfy some ancient racial love of intrigue inherited from the generations of conspiring to play the role of being dominated.

The cab driver was still waiting for him outside in that hot bright drowsing summer ecstasy of existence, that Warden had not noticed when he came in but he was now aware of intensely, and he honked his horn irritably. But Warden did not go on out until he had had another big drink with Al so as to make sure that when he got back to the Company they would smell it on his breath and not think anything unusual about his having disappeared, which they surely would have if he had come back sober.

He stood in the cool cave of the bar against whose big plate window the sun beat vainly and he drank, feeling mad as hell and tough as nails, and wildly ecstatically enjoying the fact that he was Milt Warden and alive, savoring pugnaciously that combative joy that he had lost and had not felt since the battle to get Stark in the kitchen but that now had suddenly come back, while Al Chomu talked on to him about his eldest niece whose picture in white cap and gown was sitting on the backbar and who was staying on at Stanford for her Master's on the money of all the dogfaces who bought their whiskey at the Kemoo Liquor Store just because it was old Al, Warden wondering half-mindedly if her haole girlfriends at Stanford had ever heard of fat old Al Chomu (or his money) and answering himself that they undoubtedly had not.

Clicking fast and sharp and thinking powerfully: What if it was a full month's work? What the hell if it was impossible? If there was one man in the Army who could close out a suicide in a week, that man was Milt Warden.

Knowing he would surely have to marry that woman, who could make him feel like this.

Then he went out into the summer ecstasy of being alive and radiating powerfully, to the cab whose driver obviously was too blunt to feel it, but who still made him for five bucks, and whom he was careful to have let him off in front of the Post Library from which he walked back into the quad and plunged roaring into the heaving upset that was G Company with a suicide.

From then on it was chaos. Nobody knew anything. In crisis, the Old Army maxim ran, seek refuge in anonymity. Automatically, everyone brought everything to The Warden, who was getting paid to do the work and the deciding. He had to handle every tiniest detail personally, without benefit of clergy, working with the big looseleaf volumes of the ARs at his elbow because he had never done a suicide before either.

He drove Mazzioli almost as crazily as he drove himself, expanding explosively, until the clerk who had thought he had suffered everything began to realize he had never even understood the surface meaning of that term and as a defense against such enervating energy languidly started seriously contemplating straight duty with longing for the first time in his career.

It was he who talked Holmes into sending, with money from the Company Fund, the cablegram by which they learned that Bloom's parents were not available, instead of the customary letter.

"Dint the Capn want to get the corpse home quickly? Think about the poor mother. Was it her fault her son was a disgrace? Would that make a mother love her son any the less? Surely the mother deserved some consideration. After all, she was a mother. Dint the Capn want to do the right thing by the mother?"

Holmes, being known publicly as a father, had no choice but to succumb; the cablegram came back marked undelivered for the following reasons: ADDRESS UNKNOWN PARTY SAID TO HAVE MOVED FROM CITY; they could not find any letters in Bloom's footlocker; the case was turned over to the Office of the AG in Washington.

Warden slapped himself on the back. A lucky break.

That saved him at least two weeks, not counting drawnout weary months of correspondence, and he was able to get Bloom in the ground in three days. It was almost a record, except of course for the really old timers who had never laid claim to a family. And if Holmes pestered him with worried recriminations about an AGO inspection for the wasteful misappropriation of company funds which were to be used only for the good of the Company as a whole, well, Holmes had pestered him before, and he had learned to ignore it.

It was those nights, during that wildly oscillating week, when he always went to bed close to midnight with the mind always still bucking like a frightened horse, that in order not to think about how he could be meeting her right now someplace downtown if she wasnt so goddamned conservative and getting raging mad at her, he started toying with the idea of taking the 30-day re-enlistment furlough that he had been postponing ever since he had taken this outfit, over a year. He would lay in bed and plan it all out, how they could swing it, a 30-day idyll, just the two of them.

They would have to get off the Island. He only knew of one place on Oahu where they could possibly swing it, and that one was dubious. But there were plenty other places they could go.

They could go to Kona on the big island; fly Inter-Island to Hilo and hire a U-Drive in Hilo for a month and drive around to Kona by way of Kilauea Crater and the National Park; they could stay at Honaunau (that meant City of Refuge, didnt it? that would be a good place for them to stay: The City of Refuge). They could charter a guide fisherman; off the Kona Coast was one of the best fishing grounds in the Islands. He could see them in his mind, sitting in the cockpit with the rods out in the sockets and the lines drifting deep on the swell, getting burned blacker even than now, with a couple cases of beer in the cooler under the canopy and the Chink handling the boat and cutting the bait so that there was absolutely nothing to do if they didnt want to.

Or—

If she didnt like that outdoor stuff, they could fly to Maui. He had never been there but he had heard them talk about Wailuku as a good place to take a woman, with good hotel-inns that served good food and if there were no U-Drives the organized sight-seeing trips for the tourists if they wanted to get out. But maybe they wouldnt even want to get out. Maybe they would want more to stay in.

Or—

They could do any of them, it didnt matter. He still had $600 gambling money in a savings account downtown that he had been hanging on to. They could splurge and spend it all. Christ, he thought happily, Christ. I'm sure glad I thought to start putting half of it away every time I made a killing.

Milt Warden had it bad.

He would lie in the bunk on those nights with his arms under his head and Pete Karelsen snoring nervously across from him, and think about them over and over, planning them, envisioning them down to the small detail relishingly, each with its different facet of this same jewel, until finally it became as if they were things he had done and was remembering instead of something he wanted to do and was imagining, so that he would look back on them and think how fine they had been and that they were something nothing could ever take away from you, because once you had had them.

"Ahh, yes, I have memories," his daemon popped up and prodded devilishly. "Whatever happens, I still have my memories."

But he already knew it was only a dream, and that he was dreaming himself away from and out of reality, but what did it matter as long as you knew what you were doing? He did not expect any of them to come true; he was only dreaming them; they helped put him to sleep. And he had to sleep. If he was going to lick this suicide. And he was licking it. . . .

Then, less than three days after Bloom was in the ground, just when he was finally making the output of reports match the decreasing intake, a new complication exploded into his orderly room like a grenade fragmentation.

Niccolo Leva finally made good his threat and transferred into M Company as supply sergeant.

Warden was working on a sworn statement to be signed by both Holmes and himself to the effect that the Deceased had suffered no abuses in his organization, when Niccolo came into the orderly room that morning, his moldy-leather face sheepish under a too-thin coat of the old cynicism, his wry dry jerked-beef frame trying valiantly to retain the old insolence, and told him.

"They've got the papers all made out and signed except for my signature. Capt Gilbert stop me yestday on the quad and shown me. Col Davidson has promise him he's got a absolute face-to-face promise of a green light from old Delbert soon as he puts it through. I never thought old Jake would okay it, Milt, so I never cared.

"But its now or never, Milt. Gilbert put it up to me straight take it or leave it. I cant stall him any more. He's got another man lined up down in the 21st who'll take it if I dont."

Warden, who had to have this report along with three others done and signed and in by noon tomorrow to be finished, looked at it and put it down. "You sure picked a fine time for it."

"I know it," Leva said disconsolately.

"The new M1 rifles are in over at S-4. They'll be out now in a couple days."

"I know it."

"The new WD Circular on the new TO goes into effect in less than a week. The QM's got two boxcars of new chevrons sitting on the siding at the Depot."

"I know it," Leva said. "I know all that. Lay off, will you?"

"Lay off!" Warden said. "Jesus Christ, Niccolo!"

"Okay," Leva said. "All right."

"I dont suppose it would do any good to ask you to wait three weeks or a month?"

"What do you think?"

"Thats what I thought."

"You know thats why Gilbert wants me now, Milt," Leva said unhappily, but stubbornly. "Somebody got to do that work for M Compny too, Milt."

"I wish Bloom could of picked a slack month to kill himself," Warden said.

"Goddam it," Leva cried indignantly, "if I dont take it, that guy in the 21st will. Thats how Gilbert put it up to me. I either got to shit or get off the pot. And you know when I'll get another chance like that."

"A hell of a fine officer, Capt Gilbert," Warden said, gauging it carefully. To make him too mad was just as bad as not making him mad enough. "A hell of a fine officer and gentleman. I wonder did they teach him how to stick it up his brother officers' ass and break it off like that so politely at the Point? or did he just pick it up all by himself?"

"Gilbert's got to have a supply man," Niccolo defended.

"So has G Compny got to have a supply man."

"Yas," Leva said, "but Gilbert's willing to pay his."

"So will G Compny be, before long."

"Sure," Niccolo grinned at him evilly. "And I know you mean it, Milt. From the bottom of your heart. But I retire in eighteen more years."

He was trying hard, trying heroically, but it was obvious his heart wasnt in it.

"Well," Warden said, "you know me. I wount be the man to try to hold you back from bettering yourself, Niccolo."

"No," Leva said. "No, you sure wouldnt." But the scorn wasnt genuine.

"I promised you you'd get the rating, if you'd only stick around long enough. Things like that take a little time. But did you ever know me to go back on a promise, Niccolo?"

"No," Leva said reluctantly, "I havent." He made a great effort and marshalled his forces to try and turn the flank. "But times has changed," he said angrily. "Things aint like they was. Time's more important now. We're getting ready to get in this war, Milt. You know that yourself. A thirty-year-man's got to take advantage of his wars; he's ony liable to get one or two. If he gets two he's damn lucky. How many men in the Compny was in the last war? Just one: Pete Karelsen. Wars dont come as easy any more as they did back in the Indian days when ever little skirmish counted as a fullgrown war. And I'm almost forty. I wont get a chance at another one. To end up with a permanent retirement of Master I'll have to be at least a Staff when it starts," he summed up feebly.

He was going now. He was ripe. He'd shot his wad and the anger was gone and he was ready for it. It was like the chess game played over and over out of the textbook, move and countermove, that you both know the winner of beforehand and do not play to win but only for the enjoyment of the style. He was all set up for the kill and Warden had only to pick up the piece and move it on in, to the same square where he had always moved it, and it was Mate.

Warden opened his mouth and then closed it. He sat that way almost a minute. "Well," he said finally, as surprised as Niccolo, and ran his fingernails tearingly through his hair. Then he remembered Karen had told him that was what was making his hair so thin, and stopped it. He looked at Niccolo blankly, old leatherfaced Niccolo, 40 years old, who was staring at him astonishedly. "Well?" he said again, vaguely.

"Ever other old soljer in the Regmint'll be a goddam temporary Warrant Officer or Captain," Leva argued him hopefully, as if there was still some chance the old Warden might yet appear and prove to him how wrong his irrefutable logic was, "when this war's over. You'll probly be a full fucking temporary Major. And old plughorse Leva'll still be the same old First and Fourth."

"In a pig's asshole I'll be a Major!" Warden roared. "You're the son of a bitch'll be the goddam Major, Niccolo, you'll make a goddam good Major." It stopped as suddenly as it had begun, and they stared at each other startled.

The old Warden roar had come, but it was in the wrong place. And it was not the same old roar. This was more like the roar of a bad-wounded animal, and Leva did not know how to react to it. He felt embarrassed.

"I cant make up your mind for you, Niccolo," Warden said. "You'll have to make up your own goddam mind."

"I already got it made up," Leva protested. "I had it made up when I come in here."

"Then stop coming in here expecting me to change it for you. I aint stopping you. You're right when you say you'll never get another chance like it again. Go ahead over and sign the son of a bitch."

"It'll probly take a couple days to go through."

"Okay, so what? Maybe it'll take ten days. Maybe it'll take a full goddam year. So what?"

"It wont take ten days," Leva said; "it wont take a week. It wont take over two."

"Well, fuck it," Warden said. "And how long it takes."

"I'll try and get the supplyroom straightened up pretty good for you by then," Leva said. He sounded hurt, as if somehow The Warden had let him down.

"Okay," Warden said indifferently. "Thanks."

"Say, what the hell's wrong with you?" Leva said.

"Nothing," Warden said. "Not a damn thing. Whats wrong with you?"

"Nothings wrong with me," Leva said. "Well," he said, "well, I'll see you, Milt," and paused one last time in the doorway, all vestiges of the old wry cynicism and insolence, even the attempt at them, gone. Niccolo Leva looked suddenly worried and old like an aging man who has been named executor of a will that carries too many responsibilities.

"No," Warden said, "you wont see me, Niccolo. The only place you would see me would be at Choy's."

"Well, whats to keep you from being at Choy's?"

"I'll be too busy," Warden said.

"Oh," Leva said, seizing it happily. "Too busy workin. Well, what do you want? You want me to stay and work for you on a lousy First and Fourth the rest of my life? Is that what you're tryin to say?"

Warden stared at him reflectively without answering.

"All right then, goddam you," Leva raged, "if thats what you want."

"Its no go, Niccolo," Warden said.

"I'll tell Gilbert to take his rating," Leva raged, "and paint it green and—"

"No," Warden roared. "Goddam you, I said you'd have to make up your own goddam mind. I'm tired of making up everybody's goddam mind for them. They all come to me and want me to make up their goddam mind for them. From now on they can make up their own goddam mind. I'm sick and tired of it. I'm a first sergeant, not a goddam priest of God, and I'm tired of being drafted in as everybody's conscience. How would you like to be drafted in as everybody's conscience?"

"Well Jesus Christ!" Leva said stiffly. "Of all the goddam gall! I dont need nobody's help for my conscience."

"Then go," Warden said. "Or stay. But for Christ's sake make up your mind."

"Would you turn down a rating like that?"

"There," Warden said, "see? Thats what I mean. How the hell do I know?"

"Well," Leva said, "well, I'll see you then, Milt," but this time he said it as a formality.

"Sure," Warden said, just as formally. "I'll see you, Niccolo. Good luck with it."

He watched him cross the quad through the window. It would be Sgt Niccolo Leva now, finally, after twelve years. S/Sgt Leva; after the new TO came out. When the times changed they were thorough. Niccolo Leva, as he went up the walk to M Company under Warden's eyes, was carrying on his back the burden of an older order that was dwindling fast, carrying it inside for salvage, and Warden felt a rage bloom and balloon in him. If a lying two-faced bastard wants to run out on his friends like that and leave them holding the sack, thats his right, aint it? I dont begrudge him the goddam rating. But I never thought *he'd* do that, not Niccolo.

Milt Warden felt raped. But it was of something that had not been virginity for a long time now.

That afternoon, without even trying to work on the remaining Bloom papers that had to be done by tomorrow so he could meet Karen, he took off. He went over to Al Chomu's Kemoo Bar and got drunk with Al and they talked about the old days before Schofield Barracks had become an Induction Center when life had been simple. There did not seem to be many of the old bunch left any more. They got so drunk Al's wife had to angrily take over the bar for Al; Al wanted to close it up altogether. Al's wife did not like Warden, and Warden did not find there the summery ecstasy of being alive he had left there with a week ago. Secretly, he felt quite sure Al's wife had done something to it.

It did not take two days for Leva's papers to go through. Capt Gilbert put them through that afternoon and they were back the next morning. Apparently old Jake Delbert was not only willing, but more than happy, to do a favor for the 3rd Battalion's Lt Col Jim Davidson.

It made a fine cataclysm for such a fine summery morning, that was without the summery ecstasy of being alive. Capt Holmes flopped like a chicken without head and appealed to Warden. Warden, still a little hungover, grinned at him foolishly and remained as silent as a stone. While Leva was packing, Jim O'Hayer came in and made formal request to be returned to straight duty. Holmes relieved him without argument. After half an hour sweating over a roster he finally created Champ Wilson supply sergeant and sent the CQ out to the drillfield to corral him. Before noon The Champ was back in the orderly room and flatly quit, and if it meant his rating they could have it. Holmes relieved him without busting him either and put Ike Galovitch in his place. Ike was overjoyed at being chosen for such a responsible position. He would, he said, do his level best for the Captain Holmes; Captain Holmes thanked him gratefully; Ike disappeared into his new castle with proud tears standing in his eyes; Milt Warden watched in stony silence.

He knew he was watching the destruction of the Milt Warden legend. He watched it with the same painful sense of fitting rightness and sweet satisfaction as a boy who has spent weeks building a model airplane watches it crash in flames from the match he has applied to its wings with his own hand just before it took off. When the holocaust was over, he took off for town.

She was very lovely when she picked him up from the shaded bench on the King Street side of Aala Park and he felt no more sexual attraction for her than a man does for his wife on a hot day and it frightened him. He climbed in the car out of the shrill yammering of the Asiatic-crowded grass from across the shrill yammering Asiatic-flowing sidewalk and flopped back in the seat and lit another cigarette, impressed overwhelmingly with that sense of the end of something which he had had earlier but which had not hit him fully until now when he saw her. He did not even say hello.

Chapter 41

Karen Holmes had been saving up for this moment for almost a full week. The evening of the same day Milt had called her she had learned, by carefully probing her husband about the new catastrophe of Bloom's death in his Company, a thing she already had suspected but did not intend to ask about pointblank: that 1st/Sgt Warden had not, as yet, been induced to put in his application for the Infantry Officer extension course. In discussing Bloom with her, her husband had been especially bitter on this point since Warden's mere application, let alone his acceptance for a commission which was a foregone conclusion, would have been a feather in his cap that would more than have offset this new stroke of ill fortune. (A selling point presented to him by his wife some weeks before in connection with the trial of Prewitt, which he had since made his own.) Times certainly had changed, was his bitter comment, when an Officer had to beg an Enlisted Man to become an Officer, and then he refused. All of which philosophizing went impatiently in one of Karen's ears and out the other, now that she had learned what she wanted; her suspicions were confirmed; she had been taken for a fool; she barely refrained from pouring out the whole story to her husband for his sympathy. All she could think of was that during those two weeks of a greater happiness than she had ever known, while she was deliberately refraining from testing her suspicions in order to prove her faith in him, he had been just as deliberately deceiving her.

Feeling a great singing happiness at the prospect of being near him once more, she had laid out carefully, with an excess of both love and vengeance, the penalty she would inflict down to the smallest lash of the tongue, knowing in the love what would cut him deepest, and determined in the vengeance to cruelly make him drink every last bitter drop before allowing herself to be mollified, and when he climbed in the car with that brilliant-eyed wild look of precariously contained agony and did not even notice her, she knew immediately something was drastically wrong and forgot all about the vengeance, while the love began to fill up with a maternal anxiety for him and a wild unhinged murderous anger at whatever had hurt him, as she shifted the gears coolly and drove on around the Park calmly and out Beretania without saying a word.

They went through the slow-cooking business district and past the dry-baking Punchbowl in silence, Karen driving expertly and Warden smoking bitterly, and on past the Masonic Temple into the tree-leafy shade of the residence section across Punahou where Round Top and Tantalus, unseen but invisibly felt, dominated everything. They were almost out to the University Avenue before he flipped his cigarette away viciously and began to tell her the whole story. He told it clear across Kaimuki, Waialae, and Wailupe. By then they were almost out of town and across the causeway to Koko Head and instead of going on out into the country Karen turned off at Koko Head and drove down in under the grove of kiawe trees and out onto the bluff where the big gravelled parking lot for Hanauma Bay was.

There was a bunch of haole highschool kids, thin-limbed in swimsuits, out there on a picnic and running yelling up and down the zigzag path down the bluff to the beach where somebody had once blasted out a hundred yards of coral reef to make a swimming place, the boys chasing the girls, and the girls being chased by the boys.

While they watched the kids (who suddenly seemed more alien to both of them than any foreigners could ever have been) he went through it one more time, this time with her asking the questions.

"So o o," he wound it up shruggingly, "the son of a bitch took off and transferred."

"Wasnt there anything you could do?"

"Sure. I could have talked him out of it again."

"No you couldnt," Karen said positively. "Not if you're the kind of man I've always thought you were."

Warden looked at her disgustedly. "You think not. I've done it plenty times before."

"Then why didnt you do it this time then?" she said triumphantly.

"Why?" he hollered violently. "Because I just wanted to see if the son of a bitch would turn it down on his own, thats why. And of course he didnt."

"Did you expect him to?"

"Hell no," he lied. "Do you think I would?"

She did not answer. It had taken a little while for the enormity of it to penetrate in to her.

"Then that means our seeing each other afternoons will have to be postponed almost indefinitely," she said finally.

Warden grinned at her stiffly, as if that was something he had failed to think of, and yet somehow was expecting.

"Thats about the size of it, yes."

"And just when we thought we had it all worked out. Oh, Milt! And after you working so hard! Isnt there a thing we can do?"

"I dont know what. Unless you can get away sometimes at night."

"You know I cant do that."

"You're going to do it when I'm an officer, aint you?"

"Yes, but thats different; that will be for good. Who would I get to stay with the boy? that I could trust?"

"Okay, maybe you got some suggestions."

"If you worked hard, couldnt you do most of the work in the mornings?"

Warden looked bitterly at a panorama of the unbelievable work he had been doing for the past week, wanting to laugh wildly.

"I might, yes. Ony this time it aint the work. This time its the mere fact of not being present during duty hours. With a situation like this nobody supposes you'll get the work done, not even your loving hus-

573

band can expect that. It'll take months before it even begins to be straightened out; thats why its so important for everybody to be on hand and put on a big act of trying to help with the emergency. And every man who has to stay will make it his job to check up on the others."

"Then you couldnt just go ahead and take off anyway. That would ruin all your chances of becoming an officer. And we certainly dont want that."

"No," Warden said, "we dont want that. Any more suggestions?"

Karen, watching his face, felt the vengeful cruelty (that she had carried for him as carefully as eggs for seven full days and then lost completely in as many seconds) suddenly blossom again in her, this time aimed at her husband, who had been such a stupid fool as to let things get into this state. With the indignation of an experienced wife who is sure of her control she promised herself firmly that he'd wish he'd never seen the day.

"I dont know the intricacies of your work the way you do," she said, "but it would seem to me that the best thing and the first would be to get Sgt Galovitch out of that supplyroom as quickly as possible."

"Apparently you dont know your husband either. The ony way he'll ever consent to relieving Ike Galovitch now will be after a month, or maybe two, but certainly no less than one, and probly a lot more than two; after he has saved his face, and after Ike has fouled him up enough times personally to make him mad."

"Not when I get hold of him," said Karen crisply. "Who do you want in the supplyroom in Sgt Galovitch's place?"

For a moment, with a certified heart-skip, Warden found himself staring fullface at a new 100%-unbeatable method of rejuvenating and running his whole outfit; wanting to kick himself in the ass for not having thought of it before. With a deal like that there would be no limit to what a man could accomplish.

Then he remembered that it was already too late, that Leva had already flown the coop, that he couldnt be touched in M Company even with this wand, and the bottom fell out of it.

"Pete Karelsen," he said without hesitation, bitterly viewing the fading wings of all the splendid opportunities he had let get past him. "He's the only one who's had supply work. And what he's had was too damn little and too damn many years ago."

"He certainly will be better than Sgt Galovitch," Karen told him calmly. "And if he's all there is he's what you want. You're in no position to pick and choose."

"Sure, he'll be better. But not enough better."

"Then thats settled. Sgt Karelsen's the man. You give me a week," she said crisply. "Just one week. And Sgt Karelsen will replace Sgt

Galovitch in the supplyroom. It mightnt," she said firmly happily, "even take a week."

"Either way it will take months."

"But, darling, thats the best I can do for you. Certainly Sgt Karelsen will be better than Sgt Galovitch in the long view. And thats what we're looking at, the long view. I thought we were working for something stable and permanent.

"If we have to be separated for a while, for the sake of our future," she said firmly, "then we'll just have to, thats all."

"You've got it all figured out. Okay, say we only have to be separated for four months. For the sake of the future. Just four months. And thats conservative. Have you forgotten that by a year from now we will be in the war?"

"Well, theres nothing I can do about that," Karen said, calmly cancelling it.

"Mark it on your calendar. On July the 23rd 1941 Milt Warden told you we'd be in the war in a little over a year. We're liable to be in it in less than a year," he said, enjoying making it even worse.

"Very well," Karen said calmly. "Suppose we are in it in less than a year. Does that mean everything thats been between us is just to be marked off the slate? Does that mean we should just say to hell with the future and to hell with the plans? And what'll we do then, after the war?"

"I didnt say that!" Warden said, beginning to be angry at her lack of understanding. "What I said is its stupid to live all your life in the future when there may not be any. I say plan for the future, sure. But dont let the plans for the future that there may not be any of, displace what little life you can live now."

"And I say," Karen said, beginning to be angry at his lack of understanding, "that we shouldnt take chances now and do things that in themselves arent even happy and may cost us any chance at a future. I say if anything has to suffer, let the present suffer for the sake of the future."

"And I say if we cant have the goddam afternoons," Warden said, coming to the point they both knew he was approaching, "like we've planned, then we can at least have some nights, even if it is a little more dangerous. We may never get a chance at them, after a year from now."

"You know how I feel about that," Karen said.

"Sure I know how you feel about it. Now you know how I feel about it."

"Do you think I give a damn, you fool?" Karen said, openly angry finally. "And I've got a whole hell of a lot to lose if we get caught, havent I? I'm only thinking of you, you damned fool. Where will you be? if we should happen to get caught in a scandal? You, an Enlisted Man involved in an affair with an Officer's wife,—and not only just any Officer's wife, *but your own Company Commander's wife!*"

"And I say *piss* on that," Warden snarled. "They cant shoot me any farther off my cross than the war will shoot me off it. When you got a war staring you in the face, you believe in living today. If you'd ever been in China, like I have, you'd believe it too."

"Perhaps," Karen said icily. "But let me ask you something: Is that the philosophical tenet that kept you from putting in your application for Officer's extension course as you told me you had?"

He had been going good, and getting well warmed up, and even almost coming on to proving it. But that stopped him.

There was a considerable silence.

Karen fixed on him now the same steely-eyed look he had enjoyed so much seeing her get for Holmes, but that he did not enjoy now, as she waited for his answer.

"Yes," he said in a strangled voice. "Thats why."

"Then I fail to see," she said crisply, "how I can be expected to take risks and jeopardize myself for the sake of your purely animal desires for a few nights in the bed.

"And let me tell you something else, my friend," she said in the precise enunciations of a trained nurse talking to a worried patient. "It is all very easy for a man to talk about living in the present. Much more so than for a woman, who is liable to get knocked up higher than a kite every time the man enjoys himself in the present. Thats one thing I dont have to worry about, thank God. But there are a lot of others: such as what I am going to do when my husband kicks me out and then my lover throws me over when he has to support me, and me not being trained for anything but to be somebody's wife and having to do all my politicing and achieving and gain what little success I can by getting behind some stupid man and pushing him.

"Perhaps that is what you meant by living in the present? That we will just do it when you want to, which apparently is all the time, and let the Officer part and the marriage part, which depends on it, take care of themselves? Or better yet, take themselves off somewhere and conveniently die? Perhaps that is what you meant?"

"I did it, I mean I dint do it, because I dint want anything to come in and disrupt those afternoons, which doing extension course lessons surely would have," Warden said strangledly and subduedly. "Thats why I did it."

"And why was it you didnt tell me, instead of lying to me?"

"Because I knew goddam well you would've reacted just like you did. Thats why."

"But if you had been honest, maybe I wouldnt have. Did you ever think of that?"

"You would have," Warden said.

"And so now," Karen, who had had him coming and going either way he answered, said triumphantly, "so now you have already reached the place of the husband who only tells the lit-tle wo-man whatever percentage of the truth he feels she ought to know. And without even having the virtue of being the husband yet. Dont you think that is a lit-tle previous? not to say presumptuous?"

"No more presumptuous than you reading me off like the heavy-handed better half," Warden exploded violently into flame under the lash, like a piece of paper under a very accurately focused magnifying glass.

"Well, you may not have to put up with it very much longer," Karen threatened crisply.

"And you wont have to put up with the masculine foibles."

"And so they got married and lived unhappily ever after," Karen smiled.

"Thats it," Warden said. He grinned back crookedly, feeling the woman-generated guilt spreading all through him like the slow groping tentacles of a fungus.

"Dont look so goddamned guilty," Karen said distastefully.

"Who the hell looks guilty?"

"Well, at least you wont have the excuse of our lovely afternoons anymore," she said cruelly, "to keep you from putting in your application."

"And I'll put the son of a bitch in, too, dont think I wont," he said, stung again. How they could do it, on and on, one after the other, each a new climax of sharpness, it was unbelievable, even for a superior race.

"I dont know whats happened to you," Karen said, less classically, going down under the crust a little. "You were honest once. That was the thing that first caught me about you. You were honest, and if you thought it by god you said it, and to hell with the consequences. I admired that. You were harsh and strong and unwavering like—" she halted, searching for an adequate comparison, "—like a GI blanket on a cold night. But you've lost it. I was looking for something when you came along, something proud, and I thought I'd found it. I thought you were it.

"Well, it appears I'm still looking for it. It seems you have developed into being only a reasonable facsimile. Perhaps I'm a perfectionist, but I dont seem to care much for reasonable facsimiles.

"I've made a pompous ass out of Dana, and now it seems I'm making a pompous ass out of you. You werent like that when I met you. Apparently thats what I always do to men. I touch them and they all start to crumble."

"I've been thinking the same thing myself," Warden said. "And I dont like the way it feels either. You were tough and solid as a rock, at first, and as proud as a lion. And now you've developed into a goddam whining crybaby that I *cant* tell the truth to, because you cant take it. That first day there at the house—" he said.

"And so they got married and lived unhappily ever after," Karen said bitterly.

"Amen," he said.

"You think its easy," Karen said, "you think theres nothing to it. Your mistake was that you ever let me trust you. How many times I've seen you mentally undress every young flip we pass on the street—even if we shoot past her at fifty in the car, while I sit there knowing as well as I know my name you've forgotten me entirely and are mentally taking her to bed."

"But Jesus Christ!" Warden protested horrifiedly, "I dont do that!"

Karen smiled.

"What I mean, its not the same thing at all. Honest. The two things have nothing to do with each other. With them its like going to a whorehouse, like a—"

"It makes me want to tear your eyes out," Karen said.

"Oh," Warden said. "And how many times do you think I've watched you drive off home knowing you were going to sleep in the same room with that son of a bitch, maybe in the same bed for all I know? While I go home to my bunk and imagine every last little physical detail and picture? I dont guess you got to worry much about being privately owned."

"Why, you silly damned fool," Karen raged, "how could you of all people ever think I'd have anything to do with Dana again? I dont feel that way about him. I dont know if either of us ever did. I could be friends with him, close friends, if he'd let me; but as for that—why its just out. I never go back to a man once he's let me down. If I'm not chaste, at least I have that much pride. The thought of another man makes me physically sick."

"And that makes it a lot easier on me, dont it?"

"I dont think your lot with me is too very much harder on you than my lot with you is on me," Karen said precisely.

"And so they got married and lived unhappily ever after," Warden grinned at her viciously.

"Yes," Karen said. "That seems to be the traditional procedure."

They sat looking at each other absolutely inarticulately furiously, every argument that could have been offered already postulated, every protest that could be framed already charted, overwhelmingly aware that they had reached the absolute end of sane verbal conversation without having explained a single damned thing to the other, overwhelmed by the eternal semantics of the sexes.

They must have sat that way for almost half an hour, each wanting sympathy but refusing to give sympathy and boiling indignantly at the other's lack of sympathy, as if there were at least one room between them and they were lying each in his own bed in the darkness tensely, until finally the indignation of not being understood boils over into another emotion which is the tragic sorrow of not being understood. And all around them the yelling haole highschool boys ran on chasing the shrilling haole highschool girls who also ran on.

"You know what?" Warden said stifledly, "we're just exactly alike. We're absolute opposites; and yet we're just alike."

"We both imagine the other one's trying to throw us over," Karen said, "and neither one of us thinks the other appreciates us as much as we appreciate him."

"We curse and storm at each other for doing the same identical things," Warden said, "and we're both of us so goddam jealous we cant hardly stand it."

"We imagine all sorts of horrible things," Karen said, "and we know the other one isnt near good enough for us."

"I've never been so miserable in my life as I have since I met you," Warden said.

"Neither have I," Karen said.

"I wouldnt trade a minute of it," Warden said.

"Neither would I," Karen said.

"You'd think we were old enough to know better," Warden said.

"We ought to," Karen said.

"I still wouldnt change it," Warden said.

"Loves like ours have always suffered," Karen said bright-eyedly ardently. "We both knew that when we went into it. Loves like ours have always been hated," she said, looking at him with the half-parted mouth and warm-shining eyes of a Joan of Arc that made him suddenly want terribly to take her to bed. "Society does everything it can to prevent love like ours and what it cant prevent it destroys. Securely married American men dont like to think their wives have the right to leave them—not for love, which has never bought anything yet. And securely married American women who have been talked into believing it, know they've been duped, thats why they hate that kind of love worst of all because they have all had to sacrifice it for security and hate themselves for doing it so much they dont want anybody else to have a chance at it. Because if they ever once admit its true, then both their lives and their men's have all been for nothing. Two or three years of foolish adolescent love in their youth—that they gave up and convinced themselves they had outgrown.

"Thats why its so important we dont lose ours; thats why we have to fight so hard to keep it; fight all of them, and fight ourselves too."

"Yes," Warden said.

"And theres only one way, Milt. The only way we can defeat them is to make our love conform to their conventions—outwardly. We can keep the core of it private and clean, but if we dont conform it outwardly they'll end up by not only killing our love but us too."

"Yes," Warden said. "And the only way we can conform it is for me to accept the customary hogwash of success so we can give it the security. Its easy for you, whose job is to handle the core. But I'm the one who has to do the outside conforming. I have to make the living, that the security depends on. I'm the one who'll have to agree with them and do things their way.

"All my life, from the time my goddam brother became a priest, I've fought their beef-eating middleclass assurance. I fought everything it stood for. I've made myself stand for everything they were against.

"Who do you think it was put Hitler up? The workers? No, it was that same middleclass. Who do you think gave the Communists Russia? The peasants? No, the Commissars. That same goddam middleclass. In every country everywhere that same middleclass holds every rein. Call it Fascism or call it Individual Initiative or call it Communism, and you still dont change it any. Each country calls it by a different name so they can fight all the other countries that look liable to get too powerful. I've stood up against all of that, I've stood up for me Milt Warden as a man, and I've made a place for myself in it, by myself, where I can be myself, without brownnosing any man, and I've made them like it.

"And now I'm supposed to go on and become an Officer, the symbol of every goddam thing I've always stood up against, and not feel anything about it. I'm supposed to do that for you.

"You're the bait in the trap. They know how to work it, dont think they dont. What does dear mother do when sonny comes home from college all full of revolt and dissatisfaction with the way the world has always been run?

"They find him a sweet young thing thats around handy to relieve himself on and they finagle and finagle till they got him married to her, and then sonny quiets down to his duty and lets his revolt run off and accepts the status quo."

"I'm not the bait," Karen said. "I dont want to be the bait. I hate it as bad as you do. You must know that."

"Do you think the pig tied in the trap for the tiger wants to be bait? And how much good does it do him?"

"Is that really the way you feel about it, Milt?"

"Thats the way I feel. All my life I've had to fight for one thing, the one thing nobody wants a man to be, to be honest. And now, to become an Officer— Did you ever see an honest Officer? that stayed an Officer?"

"Then you cant do it."

Warden grinned at her combatively. "Yes, I can. And I will." If she had told him he could do it, instead of letting him tell it to her, he would have been indignant and angry. But now, with her looking at him brimmingly admiringly, he felt a great sense of power that comes with accomplishment. "I'll shove it up all their asses," he told her, "and steal the bait out of the trap without springing it and to hell with them," and he believed every word of it with her watching him proudly and he felt Milt Warden swell up stronger in Milt Warden than he had ever felt Milt Warden.

"We are just alike," Karen said. "We're just alike."

"And I wouldnt trade a minute of it," he said.

"Oh, Milt," Karen said. "I dont want to be bait, Milt. I love you, Milt. I want to help you, not hurt you."

"Listen," Warden said enthusiastically, "I've got a 30-day re-up furlough coming to me that I've been putting off ever since I got in this Company. And I've got $600 downtown in the bank. You and me are going to take that furlough, to anyplace in the Islands you want to go, and we're going to have us a time none of them will ever be able to take away from us, war or no war, hell or high water."

"Oh, Milt," she said softly, and in the saying of it made him feel finer than he could remember ever having felt in his life, "that would be wonderful. Imagine it, just the two of us, with no hiding and no acts to put on. Wouldnt it be wonderful."

"It will be wonderful," he corrected.

"Oh, if we only could."

"We not only can; we will. Whats to stop us?"

"Nothing," she said. "Nothing except ourselves."

"Okay then."

"Oh, dont you see, Milt? I couldnt leave for that long. Its a wonderful dream, and I love you for it, but we couldnt do it. I couldnt leave Junior for that long."

"Why not? You're going to leave him for good someday," he said doggedly. "Aint you?"

"Of course I am," Karen said helplessly, "but thats different. Until I make the break I have a responsibility to him that I cant just shrug off. The poor little devil will have a hard enough time of it as it is, with the life he's had all picked out for him. I owe him at least that much.

"Oh, Milt, dont you see? Its a dream. We couldnt get by with it. How would I explain my being gone for a whole month? Dana suspects something now, and if—"

"Let him suspect, the son of a bitch. He's been true to you, hasnt he?"

"But we cant do that. We have to keep it a secret until you've gotten a commission and are out of his Company, the whole thing depends on that. Dont you see?"

"I've never liked hiding from him," Warden said stubbornly, "who the hell is he I should hide from him?"

"Its not *who* he is, its *what* he is. You know that, Milt. And if I were to be gone for a month just at the same time you took your furlough . . ."

"I know it," Warden said sullenly. "Its just that sometimes it gets my goat and I get sick of it."

"We couldnt get by with it, Milt. Dont you see? Not for thirty days. Maybe for ten. I could probably get away for ten days. But not thirty. You could take your furlough and then a week later I could leave and meet you somewhere for ten days and then come home early, before you did."

Warden was trying to divide his dream down by three. It was a hard job. You couldnt even spend $600 in *ten* days. He did not answer.

"Oh, Milt," she said, "dont you see how it is? I'd love it. I'd do anything to have the chance. But not for thirty days, Milt, dont you see? I just cant."

"I guess thats right," he said. "I guess it was only a pipedream anyway."

"Oh when?" she said. "Oh, Milt, when? Are we going to have to go on like this forever? Wont we ever be able to do things without being afraid? without having to calculate and scheme and hide out like criminals? When, Milt, when?"

"There now," Warden said. "There, baby, there now. Ten days is all right. Ten days is fine. It'll work out, you'll see," he said, stroking the back of the small fragile head that always made him feel loutish and clumsily dangerous as if he were handling eggs. "Ten days? Hell," he said, "ten days is a lifetime. You'll see."

"I cant take it like this much longer, Milt," Karen said muffledly into the big CKC shirt with its male smell, allowing herself the luxury of letting the bars all the way down for once, enjoying for just this moment the eternal degradation of being a woman.

"I cant take it much longer," she whimpered, tasting it, the eternally caught and held hard in the grasp of some man, the forever humiliated under his improper liberties, the eternally imprisoned under his lead-heavy weight it was impossible to squirm out from under, the forever helpless except for the mercy of him who always takes what he wants without any, and that all women learn instinctively not to expect. "I cant even walk over to the Commissary without feeling all their eyes on the back of my neck. I've never been so openly degraded in my whole life," she said, savoring it. That was all they wanted. That was all any of them wanted. You give them the greatest thing you possess, the most intimate secret, and they—just take it. Well, let them have it. Let them all have some of it. Let them root and rut and rowel, if it was no more important than that why were they all so anxious to keep it away from each other? "I cant take it much longer, Milt," she whispered.

"There," Warden said, feeling the blood come up chargingly into his eyes and turn everything red like a mountain twilight, and not knowing why, "there, there. You wont have to, baby. You wont have to take it. Come on," he said, "lets go down to the beach and have a good hard swim and then go someplace and have a party." The second it was out he knew he shouldnt have said it.

Karen sat up and stared at him piercingly with eyes like a cat's, the tears still dribbling out of them.

"It isnt just sex, is it, Milt?" she asked, with the ringing tension of a rockcrystal that too heavy a touch will crack all apart. "It isnt just animal sex, is it? You want more than that, dont you? Theres more to it than that, isnt there, Milt? I know theres more to love than that. Isnt there, Milt?"

Warden held his love up by one corner and inspected it under the magnifying glass of animal sex.

"Isnt it, Milt?"

"Of course it is. Its a lot more than that." There was no use trying to argue it, or explain it again. He had wanted her badly, there for a moment; now he didnt care much. You had to work so hard to get it that finally, when you did get it, it was a letdown. The peak, like that first day there at the house, was already passed and the starch was all gone out of you for it.

"Come on," he said, feeling the steam pressure which the fire had generated but not provided with a safety valve, "lets go swim."

"But dont you have to get back to the Post?" Karen said apprehensively.

"To hell with it."

"No," Karen said, quite calmly positive now. "I wont let you do it. No matter how much I would like to. I'm going to drive you back to town, and you're going to catch a cab right back to the Post."

"Okay," Warden said. "Okay. I didnt want to swim anyway." It wouldnt have been any good now anyway, neither the good hard swim nor the party he had wanted to have, it was just too much work. He sat back in the seat and let her drive back to town proudly as if she were making a great sacrifice as happily as a Boy Scout doing his good deed for the day. And he sat beside her, smoking almost as viciously, and staring out the windshield almost as moodily, as he had on the way out, but for a different reason.

"You can write me when you find out about the furlough," she said. "Write it in a plain envelope with no return address and mail it from downtown. Instead of calling me up. Thats not too much to ask, is it?"

"No," he said. "Thats not too much to ask."

She insisted on parking on Richards Street down at the corner of the block from the Y until she had seen him in his Schofield Cab. He did not even have a chance to sneak across to the Black Cat for a drink.

Warden sat in the back seat of the cab, between two drunken swabbies just in from Dago who were going sightseeing at Schofield, and watched her drive past him and off down Hotel Street, while the cabbie completed his full load he had been waiting for.

For a long time now Milt Warden had felt that Dana had been secretly laughing at him. Dana could (he almost always called him Dana now in his mind; sleeping with a man's wife apparently bred intimacy; maybe that was why the Army policy was against it so much, for the EM)—Dana could afford to laugh. Because lately, more and more, Warden had begun to divine out the reason:

She was Dana's *wife*. Meaning she was married to him by the Law, had borne him his child, and depended on him for the security and freedom and money she had to have to be able to carry on a love affair with Milt Warden. Money that came in regular every month year after year, not just now and then haphazardly like poker money. Security that Milt Warden could not provide her with for years. Freedom that Milt Warden could never provide her with, as long as Milt Warden loved her.

No wonder Dana could afford to laugh. She might love Milt Warden, but Dana Holmes was the base that she worked out of. If she went out with Milt Warden every afternoon, she was still always religiously home to Dana before nine. It was as if they had a business contract that he could not break.

Dana held all the cards. And with that sanguine beef-eating middle-class assurance, that Warden who had never had it suddenly hated more implacably than ever, Dana knew he held all the cards. All Dana had to do was sit tight and wait, give her her head like you always give a nervous high-spirited mare her head. (You never snaffle a high-spirited mare, gentlemen; and you never set your foot down with a high-spirited wife.)

You just wait, gentlemen. And employ patience, that greatest of all virtues.

Eventually she will get tired of love again, and come creeping back to the warm hearth again.

Dana had Society, Respectability, Tradition, Moraljudgment, Time, Security (especially Security), and the generations of cuckolded husbands who had provided him with lessons in how to win by employing patience.

Dana Holmes could afford to laugh at Milt Warden.

And Milt Warden felt this every time he watched her drive her husband's battered Buick club coupé back home again.

Probably, Milt Warden thought the many times he watched her drive off down King Street through the traffic, she had come creeping back home often enough in the past that Dana knew the procedure ahead of time in advance.

Probably, Milt Warden thought the many times he watched her taillight disappear into a myriad of other taillights from the corners she had let him out on, she lets him have enough in between times to keep him hanging fire from going all the way and divorcing her.

Maybe, he thought the many times he carried the argument on out to its logical end, she even lets him have some now and then during the big love affairs, if she gauges the wind and finds it going against her. Maybe she's going home to do it right now.

Certainly Dana would not let her get away with all she's getting by, not unless he was getting *some*thing. Because Milt Warden knew positively that he wouldnt.

Probably, Milt Warden thought the many times he watched her leave him and go on back home, she doesnt really mind it. A woman couldnt live with a man for twelve or fifteen years without at least getting used to it, without its becoming at least less than uncomfortable.

Because Milt Warden thought all of these things, every time he watched her drive the Buick home.

His trouble was when he had admitted to her and to himself that he loved her. That was always the greatest single blunder in this game. That put him in her power as Dana had never been in her power. She could make him do anything now, even become an officer, now that she was sure he did love her. He was no longer a free agent, and as a result the old wild terrible strength that had been the power and pride of Milt Warden was gone.

But he only thought these things when he watched her driving back home. He never seemed to think them when he was with her. When he was with her, he only thought about how fine it was to be in love.

He got home early enough to make out his application for Infantry Officer's extension course before chow. The remaining Bloom papers were still on his desk and he shoved them out of the way to make out the application. Then he signed it and put it on Holmes's desk and went back to the Bloom papers and finished them up and sat back in his chair to await chow, and further developments.

Within a week the developments came, and Ike Galovitch was unceremoniously relieved from the supplyroom in favor of now-S/Sgt Pete Karelsen, to whom Dana (—oops; Capt Holmes—) bequeathed the by now more unintelligible snarl and coerced him into taking it by threatening his rating and the solemn promise that as soon as he trained the new featherweight NCO School Graduate Malleaux to take over he could go back to his beloved weapons platoon. Pete refused to speak to Warden for two weeks.

But before that, Capt Holmes had come in in the morning to find the signed application there on his desk and been so overjoyed that he offered his 1st/Sgt a three-day-pass on the spot, in spite of the state of the Company Administration, and when Warden refused it because (as he said) he did not feel he could take off at a time like this when the Company was in such a bad hole, was not only more overjoyed but could barely speak his appreciation and began for the first time in months to carry his topkicker around on a chip. Warden waited until the day after Pete was installed in the supplyroom to ask for his thirty days re-enlistment furlough.

Before such a request even Holmes's ardent goodwill blanched visibly.

"But my god, Sergeant! Thirty days!" he said, without even clapping his hand to his head. "Its impossible! You know that. I'll gladly give you a three-day-pass; I told you so; even two consecutive three-day's. Then you would be able to save up your furlough time without having anything put on the books. But thirty days! my god!" he protested. "At a time like this?"

"Sir, I've had it coming to me for over a year," Warden bored on implacably. "And I've kept on postponing it. If I dont take it now, I'll never get it. With Sgt Karelsen in the supplyroom we're as near as we'll be to an even keel for at least another six months. And if I wait that long I'll never get it."

"By the books," Holmes said flatly, his goodwill receding still further, "you're not even entitled to it at all, now. You know that yourself, Sergeant. If you let a re-up furlough lapse for over three months its cancelled. You should have taken it then, at the time."

"By the books, I should have let this outfit go on down the shutes," Warden said. "The reason I didnt take it was to get this Compny back on its feet, and you know it. Sir."

"Even so," Holmes said waveringly. "Thirty days! At a time like this! Its just simply impossible."

"I postponed it for the good of the Compny," Warden said doggedly. He knew better than to make it anything as crude as an open threat, that would only have made Holmes refuse out of pride. But the implication was there; and the memory of Leva's week-old transfer was still fresh. Capt Dynamite Holmes was no longer Jake Delbert's fair-haired boy.

Dynamite pushed his hat back on his head and sat down at his desk. "I'll tell you something, Sergeant," he said confidentially. "You're going to be an Officer yourself soon, and it might help you a little about how to get on.

"Sit down," Dynamite said, "sit down, Sergeant. Hells fire, you'll be beating me at poker up at the Club within two or three months. Theres no need for us to go on maintaining the formality of Officer and EM."

Warden sat down gingerly.

"I dont expect to be in the Regiment very much longer," Dynamite said expansively, but still confidentially. "Of course, you understand, this mustnt go any further. But I'm expecting to be reassigned to Brigade Headquarters as a Major at the personal order of General Slater, within the next month or two."

"Thats fine," Warden heard himself say.

"You may have thought, as so many others have, that I've been cutting my own throat around here by getting on the Great White Father's shitlist," Dynamite grinned. "Well, theres been a method in my madness. Thats what they dont know. I expect to be taken on as General Slater's personal aide," he said extravagantly, and paused.

"Well I'll be damned!" Warden said, as if surprised.

"The first thing an Officer has to learn is to be able to switch horses often and in midstream without getting his feet wet," Dynamite smiled. "Of all the things an Officer has to know, that one's the most important. Its different with Enlisted Men, they can get along without politics. It can help them of course, but its not the prime requisite; they can make good without it. But an Officer cant. Thats the first thing you'll have to learn."

"Yes, Sir," Warden heard himself say. "Thanks."

"Now it wont be for a couple of months," Dynamite said. "But its as sure as God made little green apples. If you werent becoming an Officer yourself and I hadnt thought it might help you, I wouldnt have told you at all. But when I leave this outfit for Brigade, I'll put you through for a fourteen day furlough. Hows that?"

"I'd rather have it now," Warden said. "And I want the full thirty days. If I didnt have them coming, it'd be different."

Dynamite shook his head. "I'm making you a fair proposition, Sergeant," he said kindly. "More as a brother-in-arms than as a Commanding Officer. If you werent going to become what you're going to become, I probably wouldnt even do that. Because of that, I'm treating you as an equal.

"But," he said friendlily, "thats absolutely the best I can do. I dont give a damn what happens to this outfit any more than you do, but if I put you in for a full thirty-day furlough, with the Company in the state its in, and especially at a time like this, it would only be turned down anyway and be a black mark against both of us. Thats politics. Theres more going on at the present time than meets the eye, Sergeant," he said slyly with the air of a man who was on the inside.

Warden watched him narrowly, still feeling uncomfortable to be formally sitting down.

"Well, what do you say?" Dynamite said kindly. "Fourteen days," he said. "Two months from today. Its the best *any*body could do for you, under the circumstances."

"Then I'll take it," Warden said. You could only push any man just so far. If you squeezed an orange past that certain point you not only got no more juice, but you tore the orange all apart.

"Fine!" Holmes said. "Its a bargain then. Under the stipulation, of course, that both your furlough and my reassignment go no further than right here and now."

"Thats fair enough," Warden said.

"Its protection," Holmes corrected. "Believe me, Sergeant, theres nothing for an Officer like protection."

"I believe you," Warden said sourly.

"Well," Holmes said cheerily, "I'll see you later. I've got a little business over at Headquarters."

Warden watched him through the window go off across the quad, wondering how many times in how many different circumstances he had watched how many people go off across that quad. If it had not of happened to him he could not have believed it. So that was what it was like, being an Officer? It was like all the big corporation men who sent presents to each other every Christmas and paid for it all out of the Company advertising funds; many wonderful expensive presents for themselves and their wives to stack up under their trees; and it didn't hurt anybody; and still nobody had to pay for it. Of course, the presents were always restricted to each other and each other's wives.

What surprised him the most was that it was so easy. One minute you were one thing, then the next minute you were something entirely different and opposite. Just like that. By signing a large sheet of paper.

Two months, he thought. Two whole months. It looked like Gert Kipfer was going to get some more of his money after all, whether he wanted to spend it or no. That poor bastard Prewitt, up there in the hole. Prewitt and Maggio, two ordinary normal commonplace fuckups, up there in the hole without any. Not heroes, or Robin Hoods, or legendary paladins, but just two common ordinary verynormal fuckups, paying the common ordinary verynormal price of not getting any. Tough luck.

If you couldnt have thirty days, you would settle for ten. If you couldnt have Karen when and how you needed her, you would settle for her when and where you could get her. If you couldnt have a thirty day furlough now, you would settle for a fourteen day one two months from now. Even The Prophet went to the mountain when the mountain refused to come over to him. That was the commonplace ordinary normal way of doing it, even for Prophets, and you were no Carolingian douzeper, you were no Robert of Locksley, you were just a commonplace ordinary verynormal—whatever it was that they called them.

Chapter 42

They played a game in the Stockade. In the evening after chow the mattress from an empty bunk would be hung on the chainmesh grid across the center window in the back wall with strings of knotted shoelaces. Then one man, usually the smallest unless there was a volunteer, would stand with his back against the mattress and the rest would line up at the far end of the aisle according to size with the smallest first and, one at a time, run at the man against the mattress and hit him in the belly with their shoulders like a fullback throwing a checkblock at the end on an offtackle shoot, except that in this case with the mattress behind him there was no place to fall back to and it was up to the belly muscles to protect themselves.

Since cards dice roulettewheels and coins were not allowed in the Stockade, this game provided the chief recreation of Barrack Number Two in the evenings. It was not played at all in either of the other barracks, but in Number Two no man was allowed the privilege of not participating.

It was a rough game. But then they were hard men in Number Two, they were the toughest of the tough, they were the cream. If the man at the mattress could stay up there clear through the entire line, he had won the game. As the prize, he got a free run at every man in the line. Not very many got to enjoy the prize. At the time Prew came into Number Two only two men had ever succeeded in staying up. They were Jack Malloy and Blues Berry, the two biggest; bigness helped, in the Stockade; and they were the only two, although Angelo The Wop Maggio had been knocked senseless several times trying it. The first time Prew played he made it up to the last man, which was Jack Malloy, the biggest. Then his belly and knees betrayed him, even though Malloy was the last man and all he had to do was stay on his feet to win, and after Malloy's run he collapsed weakly and Malloy had to help him back to the commode to vomit, Prew cursing furiously and bubblingly weakly. His feat was considered quite an accomplishment for a little man, but he was not satisfied with it, and before he had been there a week he had managed to stay up past Malloy and win, although he had to drop out and let them go on playing for a while before he recuperated enough to claim his prize and take his free runs at the line.

Next to The Game, which had no other name, pitching matchbooks at a crack for tomorrow's ration of Duke's Mixture was the favorite sport in Number Two. There were other games, such as the one called Can-you-take-it where one man blocks his solar-plexis with his left arm and his genitals with his right and allows his opponent to hit him as hard as he can in the belly, each taking turns at hitting until one man has to quit. Also, the old Indian-wrassles had been stolen from the Boy Scouts and given extra teeth to make them interesting. Indian-wrassle-on-the-table, where the two men place their elbows together and lock hands and try to put each other's arm down, was played by putting lighted cigarette butts behind each man's hand as added inducement. Indian-wrassle-on-the-floor, where the two men lie on their backs and lock legs and try to throw each other over, was played with pieces of ⅜ths slatting with ½-inch wire brads driven through them placed behind each man, and in spite of all the efforts to roll sideways when thrown more than one man wore blue-rimmed punctures in his knees out to work in the mornings. But of all the games, The Game itself, always took first precedence in popularity.

Jack Malloy had invented it during his first stretch and since then it had become an institution in Number Two. He had gone back to duty and forgotten it, and come back for his second stretch to find it still being played in its original form without embellishments (which was a compliment in itself), and stayed to take it over again. He played with a live combative sense and indomitable will that, coupled with his physique, was almost impossible to down. When Malloy played, the contest, instead of being a fight for Malloy to stay up, was a fight for all the others to try and put him down. Prew made him go down once, and only once, and felt as if he had accomplished something that was magnificent. If there was anything that Jack Malloy of the gentle smile and dreamer's eyes was vain of, it was his physique and his prowess with it. He was a big man in the sense in which Chief Choate was big, rather than in the sense that Warden was big, and he was without Chief Choate's fat-degeneration. And, compared to his intellectual attainments which (to them) were almost mystical, he was proud of his physical prowess in the same way a high school football captain is vain of his swimming and diving. But this was no more strange to them than everything else about him.

To Number Two, Jack Malloy was an enigma in the same way that all living symbols are enigmas to the men who symbolize them. Prew came to know him pretty well during the time Angelo was in the Hole making his fight, better than any of the others ever got to know him. He came to know him well enough to realize that the sole reason The Malloy let him get behind the curtain shrouding his past was not because Malloy saw him as an equal who would understand, but because to Malloy he was an inferior who openly needed help. The need for help seemed to be the only key that could unlock Jack Malloy.

It was a bad time for Prew, when Angelo was doing his "30 Days" in the Hole. He had pictured it ahead of time how it would be, with Angelo deciding definitely one night that tomorrow was The Day, and the resulting handclasps and last final conversations and farewells. He had expected to have a chance to say good-by. But when it came, it did not happen that way.

He had been there a full month with Angelo trying every day to make up his mind to do it, to lay it out and then push it through, and every time something happened to make the little guy postpone again. In spite of his fantastic courage, even Angelo did not quite have the nerve to start it off. It was going to be a bad ordeal, the worst yet, and Angelo knew it, and he could never quite bring himself to make a beginning. When it happened, it came as a surprise to all of them including Angelo, as a result of something clear outside Maggio's control, and there were no farewells at all.

The guard Turniphead Turnipseed had taken quite a dislike to Angelo for some obscure private reason, and this dislike had grown until it was an open flagrant heckling every time Turnipseed got near him. This one morning on the rockpile, when Turnipseed was on detail "in the pit" as the guards called the post down in the quarry, which because of the heat and dust was considered the worst detail on the place, Turnipseed, probably through irritation, had ridden Maggio even worse than usual, calling The Wop down every time he stopped his hammer long enough to breathe, reading him off particularly insultingly every time he spoke a word, obviously trying to goad him into something Turnipseed could turn him in for; until finally Turnipseed came clear over to him where a group of them were working, carrying his riotgun cradled in his left arm and slapped him in the face for not stopping talking. Prew was in the group and close enough to Angelo so that he could see the snapping bright black eyes. For the first time since he had known him there was none of that pinpoint-concentrated fury that liberties against his person always brought to the little Italian's eyes. Maggio's eyes were cold and calculating, as if he was also realizing at the same moment Prew's heart skipped with it, that this was it, this was his chance, the situation he had been waiting for and trying to create, and that if he did not take advantage of it now he never would. There was the reluctant look on Angelo's face of a man faced with a proposition of either doing a thing he would rather have avoided or else admitting to himself once and for all he was a coward.

As Turnipseed stepped back to observe the effect of his action with a careful eye toward finding something that would merit turning in, Angelo dropped his hammer and went for Turniphead's throat with his bare hands and an excellent imitation of a gibbering insane scream. It was a greater offense than Turniphead had bargained for. He was caught flat-footed and Angelo had him on the ground choking him before he could move. The group of prisoners, including Prew, all of whom except for two were from Number Two, just stood, still holding their hammers, and watched. Turnipseed managed to beat him loose with the butt of the riotgun and get up, before Maggio came at him again, still screaming insanely, but closer this time, too close for Turniphead to even attempt to use the buckshot, and Turniphead flattened him with the gunbarrel using both hands, thus fulfilling Angelo's plan and hope to the letter.

With Maggio unconscious at his feet in the sudden overwhelming silence, Turniphead stood dazed, breathing heavily and rubbing his neck with one hand, and staring at the group of other prisoners who had not moved, and were careful not to move now.

"Yeah," he gasped finally. "Go ahead and try something. Just try it."

Nobody answered.

"I wish you would," Turniphead said hopefully, still rubbing his neck and breathing heavily. "I'd love to shoot one of you fuckers. You'd stand right there and let that crazy man choke me to death and not do a goddam thing. A hell of a lot of mercy a guy can expect from a bunch of blood-thirsty wolves like you," he said accusingly.

Nobody answered.

"Couple of you carry him down to the road," he said, jerking his head behind him without moving his eyes. "The rest of you get the hell back to work. And I mean now."

Nobody from Number Two moved, and the two men from Number Three stepped forward quickly reluctantly, as if they had been pushed.

"Go on, pick him up," Turniphead said. "He aint dead, worse luck. Hey!" he called up the manmade cliff to the two guards with rifles who had come over and were watching. "Keep an eye out on the rest of this bunch here," he hollered. "I like to had a goddam mutiny. Go on, you two, pick him up."

When they picked him up, Prew saw vaguely the knot beginning to rise from his forehead at the hairline where it had been split and a trickle of blood started down toward his eye. One more medal for Angelo. But his mind had already gone ranging ahead, reviewing the prospect of the thirty days to come, and nothing else could touch him.

Turniphead followed the temporary stretcherbearers on down and had them leave him by the road and go on back up, before he put in the call from the box on the phonepole. The two guards with rifles up on the cliff were still watching closely and the group went on back to work. The last time Prew saw Angelo Maggio in his life was when the two MPs who had responded to the hurry-up phonecall tossed him, still unconscious, in the back of the 2½-ton truck and started with him back down the grade.

It had been a very long time in Robert E Lee Prewitt's life since any individual had impressed himself upon it as much as Angelo Maggio, if you did not count Jack Malloy and The Warden. But while both of these, each in his totally different way, were superior beings of another grade that moved on another orbit, Angelo Maggio—first American-born generation of Brooklyn immigrant Italian stock, absolute hater of the Army; the total opposite of a mountain boy and thirty-year-man soldier whose white ancestors had come from Scotland and England before the Revolution, and still hated foreigners—Angelo Maggio was more nearly his own kind and caliber and closer to him than the big guns like Malloy and Warden. He left a very large hole.

That he would never see or hear from him again, once he was discharged, he accepted without question; that was the way it was, in the Army, where alliances are formed out of the stock in hand today. And that he would be discharged, he accepted as unquestionably as the fact that he would not get to see him either before he went in the Black Hole or after, when he was transferred to the Station Hospital nut ward. There were only two alternatives: either Angelo would die in the Black Hole, or else he would be discharged. Knowing Angelo, Prew did not believe he would die in the Hole. But neither the knowledge of what was to come, nor the acceptance of it, helped to fill up the hole.

Prew followed the fortunes of the engagement from the sidelines of Barrack Number Two with an openly frank anxiety that would have embarrassed him at any other time, and it was during those weeks that Jack Malloy without being asked came up and stood behind him.

Actually, Maggio was not in the Black Hole for thirty days. But outside of that, the plan of battle he had laid out was correct. He had only been in the Hole a few hours over twenty-four days, when they pulled him out and sent him up to the prison ward in the Station Hospital for mental observation. It was the guard Pfc Hanson who kept them informed of the progress of the contest. Hanson was usually the lockup man for Number Two after evening chow, and almost every evening he would pass on what had taken place during the day and the night before. Outside of that, they knew nothing, and Angelo Maggio might as well have passed clear out of existence for all they knew. No word from Maggio himself ever reached them out of the dark depths of the Black Hole.

Hanson did not know or even guess at the calculated plan behind the action. Hanson really believed Maggio had gone crazy. It did not decrease his admiration for The Wop.

"You ought to see him," he would tell them, as he locked the barred doors on the crowd gathered to hear the news. "He's terrific. You'd have to see it to believe it. Boy, if thats crazy, its a pity there aint more madmen in this world.

"He's the first one they've had since I've been here," he explained. "I've heard them talk about the old ones, but this is the first one I've ever really seen. You were here when one of the old ones was in the mill, werent you, Jack?"

"Two," Malloy said. "Both of them during my first stretch."

"Well, this is my first one," Hanson said, shaking his head again in admiration, "and boy, its really an experience. Its unbelievable, thats all. You cant tell me any man gets guts like that just from going crazy, any more than he can get it from a bottle. Guts like that is born in a guy, he's either got them or he aint, and thats all."

"I think I'd agree with you," Malloy said.

"Its a shame the Army has to part with guts like that," Hanson said. "Guts like that is what Armies needs the most."

"I think I'd agree with you on that one too," Malloy said.

"You goddam right," Hanson said. "You cant tell me. This is Fatso's first one, too, you know. Fatso wasnt here when them last ones blew."

"Thats right," Malloy said through the doors. "We had an old Master/Sgt then. Fatso didnt come in till after he was retired."

"Fatso thinks he can beat it," Hanson said. "He claims he can bring him out of it. He says he's never seen a man yet, crazy or not, that he couldnt make walk the chalkline if they give him a free hand."

"Maybe he'll do it," Malloy suggested.

"I dont think so," Hanson said. "Somebody else maybe, but not The Wop. You guys aint seen it like I have. Its out of this world, thats all."

"He was a good man, all right," Malloy said.

"He still is," Hanson said. "Crazy or not."

"Whats Father Thompson got to say about it?"

"Nothing," Hanson said. "He's letting Fatso handle it; except for killing. He's laid it out flat to Fatso there cant be no killing, or he'll have Fatso on the inside lookin out. He's dead set there cant be no killings. But outside of that its up to Fatso. But Fatso'll never make it. Take it from me."

They would always have to ply him for the latest details. He wanted to go on telling his amazement and his admiration, and it would take two or three of them interrupting constantly before they could bring him back to the facts of the latest news. Gradually, it evolved itself into a recognizable plan.

When they had brought him in that first day Fatso had revived him personally. He had taken the phonecall from Turniphead and already had the story, and he was eager to get to work to prove his theory. He had taken three guards led by Brownie, Hanson among them, and taken Maggio down to the "gym." They had given him what Hanson had described as the worst working over he had ever seen a prisoner get. It was the first time since he had been there that they had ever carried a man to the Hole unconscious. Fatso had tried to make The Wop admit he was only acting; Maggio had laughed and babbled and gone right on talking gibberish. The fourth time he went out, after they had already brought him to three times, Fatso gave it up and let them carry him on down.

"He's crazy, all right," Hanson told them. "If he wasnt crazy, even The Wop couldnt take it."

Fatso's whole plan was based on making him admit he had been acting. He developed a schedule where he came for him at regular intervals to work him over, first every eight hours, then every four, on the theory that the anticipation would break him down. When that failed, he took to coming for him at odd unspecified intervals both day and night, with the idea that that way the anticipation instead of having regular periods of rise and fall would be constant all the time. He was liable to appear for him at midnight, and then come right back fifteen minutes later, or let him go a full twenty-four hours sweating it out. Fatso was a diligent and conscientious workman. He offered him everything from a trusteeship to the reinstatement of his time-off-for-good-behavior that Maggio had lost the first week he was there to an even possible commutation of his sentence, if he would only admit he had been acting. Maggio only laughed or babbled or made faces or talked gibberish. Once he pissed on the floor at Fatso's feet. Fatso rubbed his face in it. Fatso was convinced The Wop was acting, that all the Section 8s discharged from the Stockade were just good actors. He stopped at nothing short of the application of actual torture devices, to make Maggio admit that he was acting. Every night Hanson came to lock up and tell them that The Wop had not broken. It had developed into a tougher situation than even The Malloy had anticipated, and it was then that Prew first began to develop the hatred for S/Sgt Judson that occupied all his leisure time with plans for murder. If to think murder was as great a crime as committing it, Prewitt would have to have been electrocuted fifty times to make him pay.

595

Then one night Hanson finally brought them the news that Maggio had been taken out that noon and cleaned up and patched and transferred to the Station Hospital prison ward. Along with this was the news that S/Sgt Judson's pending T/Sgt rating, which had been an accepted fact for almost two months, had been dropped temporarily. Prew wondered to Malloy if Angelo would ever know it; he hoped he would; but, to be honest, he had to admit he doubted if he ever would.

They got the story of what happened in the prison ward from another prisoner. This prisoner, "Stonewall" Jackson, had gone to the prison ward with a broken leg from a bona-fide fall on the rockpile, long before either Prew or Maggio had come in. He came back to Number Two a month after Maggio had been sent up to the hospital and gave them the first word they had of how Angelo had made out there. They had put him in a private cell, padded for violent cases—all their private cells were padded for violent cases—and when the ward attendants first came near him Maggio had crawled back in the corner and begged them babblingly not to hit him any more. The rest of the time he was there, whenever anyone, psychiatrist, medical doctor, nurse, or ward attendant, approached him, he would cringe away and try to hide in the corner and beg not to be beaten any more. This sudden change of tactics amused everybody, even Prew and Malloy. Jackson had gotten to talk to him just once, after he had been before The Board and his discharge was already certain. He had been very suspicious, but when Jackson proved to him conclusively that he really was from Number Two, he opened up with a grin and asked Jackson to pass on to the boys that he was okay—and that he was on his way out. He was very badly scarred, Jackson said, he looked like a punch-drunk fighter. But he did not, Jackson said, act like one. They had kept him in the prison ward two weeks after he went before The Board. Then they sent him back to the States. The Board recommended a yellow Dishonorable Discharge, Jackson said, on the grounds that soldier was a mental incompetent inherently unable to adjust, this disability being neither service-connected nor service-aggravated, and therefore was mentally unfit for service.

During the weeks Angelo had been in the Hole, and the month of silence before Jackson came back from the hosp to give them word, Jack Malloy had stood at Prewitt's back like a big brick wall. When it was bad he was always there to talk to, or to listen to. Mostly, he talked to Prew. Malloy would spin him yarns for hours, about his own life and past. In those weeks, without realizing it, Prew learned more about him than any of the rest of them had ever learned.

There was a singular quality about Jack Malloy. When he looked at you with his unembarrassed-dreamer's eyes and talked to you with that soft powerful voice, you began to labor under the delusion that you were the most important person on this, or on any other, planet; and you believed you could do many things you never would have thought you could.

He had been almost everywhere and done almost everything in his 36 years. Among other things, he still walked with a little bit of a seaman's roll. It set off his physique to perfection and gave him a kingly swagger that in the Stockade was no less than awesome. And there is nothing as romantic to professional soldiers as a civilian sailor. Also, there is a great respect for the printed word in the Army. Jack Malloy had read a tremendous lot. He seemed to have thumbnail biographies on his fingertips of everyone from old John D Rockefeller clear on down to the obscure Philippine Department General, Douglas MacArthur. And he could not talk without quoting books they had never heard of. But he did not even need these accomplishments to cinch his reputation. Jack Malloy was the kind of man who did not have to *earn* his reputation; it was tendered to him free-gratis by the imagination of every man in the Stockade.

Born the son of a county sheriff in Montana in 1905, he had been 13 in 1917 when his father started jailing the IWWs in earnest. That was what started him off: The Wobblies had taught him to read. He started his reading in his father's jail with their books they always carried with them. In his gratitude he offered to help them escape from his dad's jail. When the Wobblies turned down his offer, he learned the first lesson in what was to become his passion for passive resistance.

"They utilized it," he would tell Prew, "but they didnt use enough of it. They didnt understand the principle. That was their greatest fault, and damn near their only one. But it was enough to make them fail. They believed in militant force. It was written into their covenant. They never fought or killed one-tenth as much as they were accused of, and not one-twentieth as much as their enemies fought and killed them; but the point is they believed in it abstractly, and thats what defeated them: a mistake in abstract logic.

"But they were all great guys just the same. With their courage and intelligence, nothing on earth could have stopped them if they had understood the principle of passive resistance.

"You dont remember the Wobblies. You were too young. Or else not even born yet. There has never been anything like them, before or since. They called themselves materialist-economists, but what they really were was a religion. They were workstiffs and bindlebums like you and me, but they were welded together by a vision we dont possess. It was their vision that made them great. And it was their belief in it that made them powerful. And sing! you never heard anybody sing the way those guys sang! Nobody sings like they did unless its for a religion."

The sharpest memory of his youth was of bunches of them, ten or twenty at a time, in out of the harvest fields in the fall for one of their free speech fights, sitting in the barred windows of the second floor of the jail singing their songs Joe Hill had written for them, or Ralph Chaplin's *Solidarity Forever*, a singing that swelled through the town until nobody could escape it.

"The townspeople would have been better off if they'd have let them go ahead and read the Constitution on the street corners unmolested. Then they would have drifted on."

When he made up his mind to run away from home, in protest, his father's prisoners had realistically advised him to arm himself with a certified birth certificate.

"'Its almost funny, kid,' one of them told me, 'how many people will try to accuse you of being an unnaturalized foreigner.' His name was Bradbury," Malloy grinned, "the guy who told me that, and his people had fought the French and Indians before the Revolution."

One of them gave him a copy of Veblen's *Theory of the Leisure Class* and *The Little Red Songbook* with Joe Hill's songs, to take with him, and since then he had always carried his quota of new unread books in his pack or bindle or suitcase or seabag, even in the Army. The first book he had bought for himself, with the first money from the first job, was Walt Whitman's *Leaves of Grass*, to add to Veblen and Joe Hill, and since that first copy he had worn out ten others. The second thing he bought was his Red Card and his membership dues in the IWW. The rest went for his first real drunk and his first piece of ass. He had not been back home since.

"It was only an excuse," he said. "I was just waiting for an excuse. My father was too lawful a sheriff, and my mother was too religious a Christian. No kid could beat that combination from the inside. I had already learned, long before I met the Wobblies, how much everybody hated conscientious cops and religious ladies. And above everything else I wanted not to be hated."

After that, it was the harvest fields and timber camps as a bona-fide IWW with his dues paid up. He was too young for the war and they couldnt get him for that, and he always carried his birth certificate although as often as not they ignored it. He learned to know jails from the prisoners' side. When they jailed the hundred-and-one on September 28, 1918, he joined the protest and the attempts to raise funds for them. During the two years the principals were in and out of Leavenworth most of his money went for that. He even cut down on the whorehouses. He had never seen or met any of the General Executive Board, but he had learned to worship Bill Haywood, Ralph Chaplin, George Andreytchine, Red Doran, Grover Perry, Charley Ashleigh, Harrison George and the rest—perhaps even more than the old timers who knew them. He worked hard for them, and went on reading. He felt he was being trained for something.

But already the old solidarity was shifting and beginning to break up. The wartime trial and the Leavenworth sentences had broken the back of the IWW. The Communist Revolution that scared the world had succeeded in Russia, and in the Wobblies disagreement over the Communists grew into a dissension and then into open factions. He went on reading; he wanted to be ready. He become a veteran of Centralia Washington, where they castrated first, and then lynched, Wesley Everest and afterwards sentenced seven other Wobblies for 2nd degree murder for having fought back but he was one of the young ones that Old Mike Sheehan helped to get away. He escaped both castration-lynching and trial. He beat his way down into California and joined the longshoremen's union and went on reading.

Then Haywood and Andreytchine jumped their bail and went to Russia to throw in with the Communists, and that finished it. Chaplin and the others out on bond went back to Leavenworth.

"The funny thing is," he smiled, "was that we were the first to adopt the color Red. The Communists stole it from us. That wasnt all they stole from us either."

Prew, who had sung *Casey Jones* all his life without ever hearing of Joe Hill and the Wobblies, had already learned enough to know he meant the driving force that was Big Bill Haywood.

"They stole it and threw it away," he said. "Like kids robbing a candy store of more than they can eat and throwing it away. They killed Bill Haywood."

After that there were three more years of formality, up and down California from one isolated unit that still made pretense of paying dues to another, always trying to help get the rest of the old by-now-almost-forgotten hundred-and-one out of Leavenworth. In California he studied, and came to love, the memory of Jack London and the old group of Socialists in Frisco, George Sterling, Upton Sinclair, and the rest, whose outfit also had shrivelled down to death; London himself almost as much as he loved Joseph Hillstrom. He went on reading. Then the bottom that had been sliding and sliding finally fell clear out. Some gave up and went to Russia like Haywood; others, like Chaplin, embarked on the philosophy that would eventually lead them to chauvinism. Jack Malloy went on reading, wondering what he was training for, and finally decided to take to the sea. He was nineteen. An era had ended.

He served several years as an AB on South American freighters out of Frisco. He was still looking. He went on reading. It was during that time that he had, for lack of something better, become a disciple of Upton Sinclair's leftover brand of Socialism that he later rejected. The Sage of Monrovia who lived with posterity eternally in his thoughts was just about the only contestant left in the field, and the 19-year-old disciple-in-search-of-a-Messiah helped distribute the pamphlets on all the ships he worked on at a time when, while it was not against the law, you were through working for that line if the officers ever caught you.

"It taught me two things," Malloy grinned. "One; you never could succeed with what I wanted to succeed with by using propaganda; logically, in the end, the end will not only not justify the means, it will not even be achieved by them; you cant divide the mass by a common factor that will give you a norm to work by, because while it may be mathematically correct it is false when applied to the individual member. The masses are one thing, the amalgam of individuals is another. And you cannot escape that paradox by leveling them off to a fourth-grade-mind common to all. We were going to have to do better than that; I didnt know what, or how; and I dont know now. But we'll have to.

"The second thing it taught me was that you cant live for posterity, especially if you are a prude, because posterity's morals are always different from your morals. Sinclair is as big a prude about sex as Ralph Chaplin: they're both married. It hurt them terribly to see us common rank and file patronize whorehouses. When they couldnt convince us, they decided to ignore it. I suspect that both of their revolutionary activities were brought on by a parentally-installed horror of the grossness of the penis and the vulva and a hunger for the Ideal Love. But you cant escape life by rebelling any more than you can escape it by playing blind. You cant take one subject, like economics, and with it escape the problems of all the rest of the subjects, like sex. Eventually, unless you become a liar, you always come back to the one thing you're running from. And you cant force the individual who makes up your non-existent masses into anything unless he wants it (the Communists will have to learn that too, someday, or die like Sinclair's Socialism), and if the men like to get their guns off you'll have to accept that foundation fact along with all the other foundation facts, one way or another."

Harry Bridges was just a punk then, in those days. But he kept growing. He grew enough, finally, to drive Jack Malloy along with a lot of others away from their Frisco-South America home-run to trans-oceanic and trans-global berths, and after that Jack Malloy had sailed for ports everywhere from Hamburg to Manila and Shanghai to London. He had worked at every kind of job from bartender to tourist-guide between berths. And he had loved every kind of woman from bony Jap geisha to featherbed German barmaid.

"I've never laid a woman that I didnt love. Maybe she made me dislike her afterwards, for some other reason. But at the moment of screwing her, I was in love with her. I offer that as an observed fact, without attempts at explanation or justification. It is a thing that I have found is true of most men, if you can get them to talk and admit it."

Prew, mulling this one over and applying it to himself, was a little shocked to find he had to admit it was true of him too.

"I offer no plans by which to coordinate it into future social structures," Malloy grinned, "but before Millennium comes somebody is going to have to take it into account some way or other—in spite of the economist-idealists like Sinclair and Chaplin. It is one of the reasons I've never got married."

As a deepsea sailor Jack Malloy had had the clap six times—

"The syph never, knock on wood."

—and it still did not cure him, yet there was still something in him, deep in the unabashed-dreamer's eyes, that none of it had ever really touched. He had always kept on reading. And of it all, all the places, all the jobs, all the experiences, all the women, he still wanted the USA. That was where he belonged, that was where his faith lay, and that was where he needed to be.

It was in 1937 when Harry Bridges who was no longer a punk, but still was still growing, finally reached the level of the trans-oceanic and trans-global sailors and pushed Jack Malloy clear off the sea for good.

"And he isnt through yet," Malloy said. "Before this war is over three years, he'll have all Hawaii in his pocket along with the rest."

Jack Malloy, with eleven years experience as a deepsea man behind him, at the age of 32, came back home. He enlisted as a green hand into the Regular Army. He wanted to be there for the war. He still kept on reading.

"Of them all," he said, "I think the Wobblies came the closest. Nobody ever really understood them. They had the courage, and whats more important, they had the soft heart to go with it. Their defeat was due to faulty technique of execution, rather than to concept. But also, I dont think the time was right for them yet. I'm a fatalist. If you believe in the logic of evolution you have no choice but to be a fatalist.

"I've thought about it a lot. Christ had to have his Isaiah; even Martin Luther had his Erasmus. I think the Wobblies were the prophets and forerunners of a new religion. Christ knows, we need one. And if you had ever studied the evolution of religions as natural facts instead of supernatural mysticisms, like I have, you wouldnt look so startled.

"You think religions are constant things? inflexible and solid and born full-grown? Religions evolve. They grow out of a need, just like any other natural phenomenon, and they follow the same natural laws. They are born, grow, have sons, and illegitimate sons, and die.

"Every true religion follows the same logical path. First come the prophets, growing new faith out of the deathrot of the old. Every Christ has to have his Isaiah and John the Baptist to prepare the way for him. Read up on religions sometime and see. You can see how they all follow the same logical principles:

"Every religion starts at the bottom level, with the whores, publicans, and sinners. Logically, it has to start there, with the dissatisfied. You cant get the satisfied to accept new ideas.

"And every religion brings martyrdom to its innovators. That part is a test of natural selection. If the new faith is strong enough, it conquers persecution and goes on to glory.

"And then—and only then—in every religion, the satisfied ones (who through fear did the persecuting) do an about-face and climb on the bandwagon, through the same fear that made them once persecute it.

"And, also, every religion begins to die then, at that moment. When the Emperor Constantine accepted Christianity because it won a battle for him and made it the Roman State religion, he also at the same moment decreed the inevitable decline and death of Christianity.

"The stronger the religion, the longer it takes to triumph, and the longer it takes to die, and the more illegitimate offspring it has. But they all follow the same step-by-step logical process.

"They are prophesied, they come up, they triumph, they are accepted, they degenerate, and they decline. A religion that has done its work and made its point and taught its lesson has no other place to go but down. It must crack up and begin its degeneration to make room for its successor, that will take the old one's lesson and elaborate it and evolve it—just as Christianity once did for Judaism.

"Look," he said excitedly, "what was Judaism? Judaism taught that God was fixed as the earth around which the universe revolved, unchangeable, a God of perpetual punishment and vengeance; Judaism taught the Ten Commandments.

"Okay.

"What did Christianity do? Christianity took Judaism and changed it a little. It still taught that God was fixed, unchangeable, but fixed as the sun around which the earth and universe revolved, further away but still unchangeable, a less personal Center. It changed the God of perpetual punishment and vengeance to a God of perpetual love and forgiveness that only punished evil when He absolutely had to. Christianity replaced the Ten Commandments with the Sermon on the Mount.

"Okay, what would be the next step, the next logical evolvement? Mightnt it be a religion that would teach that God was not fixed at all? A religion that would teach that God was nothing at all if He was not eternally Changeable? That neither the earth nor the sun is the fixed unchangeable center, but that instead there is no center, as Einstein says the universe is a circle in time where both the earth and sun are small minor parts and everything is in constant flux and forever changing. Mightnt the new religion teach that instead of being permanently fixed God is growth and evolution, a God which is never the same twice?"

When he had gone that far with it, he was no longer talking to Prew to take Prew's mind off of Angelo. He was caught up and expounding

602

the theory that had grown to obsess his whole life. The unabashed-dreamer's eyes did not recognize Prew as Prew or remember a person named Angelo. And, curiously, it was at those times and only those times when Prew was able to lose himself in listening sufficiently to forget there was a Maggio, as the dreamer's eyes dominated him and the soft gentle voice spun on and on.

"You see what that implies? If God is Instability rather than Fixity, if God is Growth and Evolution, then there is no need for the concept of forgiveness. The mere concept of forgiveness implies the doing of something wrong, Original Sin. But if evolution is growth by trial and error, how can errors be wrong? since they contribute to growth? Does a mother feel called upon to forgive her child for eating green apples or putting his hand on the stove? Did you ever truly love some body, or some thing? A woman; did you ever love a woman? If you ever really truly loved a thing, you never even considered forgiving it something, did you? Anything it did was all right with you, wasnt it? No matter how much it hurt you. You dont have to forgive something you love. You forgive the ones you dont love.

"If you love someone," Jack Malloy said, "you never even think of forgiving them. You may fight them like hell over something, and use every pressure to change them. But when the brawl is all over and you havent changed them one bit, you go right on accepting them. You're never so smug, or so righteous, or so superior, to tell yourself—or tell them—you forgive them."

And with that Jack Malloy's philosophy was expounded, his religion preached, his credo stated. All the years of the Wobblies, the fights with the Communists, Haywood and Chaplin, Upton Sinclair, Harry Bridges, the years at sea, the women he had loved to sleep with, and the Army; all rolled into one superhuman distillation of experience in an attempt to account for everything. He came back to it again and again, later on. He couldnt stay away from it. It meant too much to him. But always it amounted to this same thing: that over the old God of Vengeance, over the new God of Forgiveness, was the still newer God of Acceptance, the God of Love-That-Surpasseth-Forgiveness, the God who saw heard and spoke no Evil simply because there was none.

And with it came out the secret that Prew had puzzled over, the secret of his power over the men in the Stockade, the secret of the bigheartedness that an archcynic like Blues Berry could worship unreservedly:

Jack Malloy was able to love the human race because he expected ahead-of-time to be let down by his friends and hurt by his enemies and betrayed by his leaders. He saw these things as natural reactions to be anticipated, instead of perfidies to be decried.

If there was one single regret in Jack Malloy's life, it was that he had been born in the wrong time. He had been born with the prophets, instead of with the Messiah.

"Because it will come," he said. "It hasnt come yet, but eventually it will have to come. Logic and evolution demand that it will come. And it will come here in America, because it is here in America, the home of the most hated race, where the hope of the world will lie. The greatest religions always come up out of the most hated races. Maybe I wont live to see it. Maybe you wont. But it has to come."

He did not expect to live to see it. He had had his fling, with the Wobblies, and they had turned out to be only one of the forerunners. He attributed his bad luck to something terrible he had done once ages past, some bad mistake, that he was still working out and paying for. Jack Malloy believed in reincarnation, because to his logical mind it was the only logical explanation. And it was for this same reason that he worshipped the memory of Joseph Hillstrom so.

"He was a saint. He had to be one, to have been given the life he was allowed to have."

Joe Hill, who had written *Casey Jones* and *Hallelujah, I'm A Bum* without ever even getting the credit of authorship, who had died back in 1915 before Jack Malloy ever heard of the Wobblies, who had been shot to death by a Utah firing squad for a murder he did not commit after asking that his body be transported to the Montana State Line because he "didnt want to be found dead in Utah," who had not lived to see the degeneration, destruction and death of his beloved IWW.

Joe Hill, whom Jack Malloy envied more than any other man.

"Thats the way to go out. That shows what can be done. But you have to have what it takes. And then on top of that you have to have the luck. Someday they will rank Joe Hill right up alongside old John the Baptist. He must have done something great, back a long time ago before he was ever Joe Hill, to have earned a chance at a ticket like that one."

When Prew asked what he meant, he said, "In one of his previous lives."

Chapter 43

It was during the month after Angelo had gone to the hosp and before Stonewall Jackson came back with news of him, that the young Indiana farmboy Prew had seen beaned in Number Three was transferred into Number Two. Of all the men that had been in Number Three with Prew he was the one Prew would have picked as least likely to succeed, but he came in with them after his three day jaunt in the Hole as mildly affable as ever.

They had been expecting him since before Angelo had gone in the Hole. Apparently, after that first spell of lapse that resulted from the beaning itself and had lasted only one day, the Indiana farmboy had started having them more and more often and for longer and longer periods. When he was normal, he was the same old mild uncomplaining self; when he was in one of the lapses, he was the same docile dreamy idiot Prew had seen. But every time he came out of a period of lapse he went crazy fighting mad and attacked whatever happened to be closest to him. Twice he had attacked guards on the rockpile. Once in the messhall he had emptied his plate of catsup and beans over the head of the man eating next to him and started sawing on him with the dull edge of his table knife; the only thing that saved the man was the fact that the GI cutlery would hardly cut butter. He got three days in the Hole for that one, served them uncomplainingly affably, and the day after he got out tried to brain the man next to him on the rockpile with a medium-sized boulder. A number of times at night in the barracks some man in Number Three would wake to find a crazy-faced demon wildly choking his neck and grapple with him until three or four others, roused by the scuffle, would come to his aid and sit on the Indiana farmboy until he was all right again. The boys in Number Three loyally covered these up for him and finally set up a system of guard duty in which there was always one man awake at night to keep an eye on him. But finally he went after Fatso himself one day in the messhall. He was beaned with a grub hoe handle again for his trouble, and it was decided he was worthy Number Two Material.

The truth was, he was not. He was as out of place in Number Two as a white chicken amongst a black flock. But he accepted this with the same equanimity that he accepted everything else. He remembered Prew and eagerly made friends with him, and he quickly arrived at a worship of Jack Malloy that surpassed even that of Blues Berry and came very close to the point of embarrassment the way he followed Jack around like a puppy. When they came to playing games in the evenings he tried as hard with that as he tried with everything else, when he was normal, and suffered the knee-punctures and burned hands of Indian-wrassle and the sore ribs of The Game as uncomplainingly as he suffered everything else. Once, he even managed to stay up at The Game through the five smallest men and was cheered roundly. He achieved the distinction of being the first man in the history of Number Two who was ever offered exemption from playing games, but he refused to sit on the sidelines and not play, although he was never known to have won any game from anybody, up to the time they all started taking it easy on him.

They took him under their wing and looked after him and adopted him as a sort of a mascot. His crazy spells when he was coming out of one of his lapses did not bother them and they did not need to set up a guard system because without exception they were all adepts at rough and tumble fighting and had been since childhood. If one of them woke up to find him choking on him he would wrassle loose from him, knock him out, and then put him back to bed where he would wake up in the morning his old mild affable self again. None of them in Number Two, in fact nobody in the Stockade, considered him even remotely dangerous. Even a mind like Jack Malloy could not have seen danger in such an ineffectually murderous Indiana farmboy. That he would ever be the match that would touch off the fuse that would blow apart the tautly balanced status quo of the Stockade as a whole and Number Two in particular, and alter the whole lives of several of them, even unto the Outside, was frankly laughable.

It happened without warning or expectation, out on the rockpile one afternoon. Since he had come into Number Two, the Indiana farmboy had gradually grown more and more bitter about life in an affable sort of a way. It was not like him, and nobody ever knew afterwards if it was because he was trying to emulate his new heroes, or if it was because his spells had cost him his time-off-for-good-behavior and, with his final removal to Number Two, lengthened his one-month sentence into a two-month one.

That afternoon he was in one of his dreamy lapses. Prew was working between Blues Berry and Stonewall Jackson when he came out of it. They had been watching for the signs, and no sooner had the Indiana farmboy dropped his hammer and looked up wildly than the three of them fell on him and held him down until he was all right again. Then they all four went on back to work without thinking anything much about it since they were all used to the procedure by now.

But a little while later the Indiana farmboy stepped over to them with an unusually affably resolute look and asked if one of them would break his arm for him.

"What the hell for, Francis?" Prew wanted to know.

"Because I want to go to the hospital," the Indiana farmboy explained.

"What do you want to go to the hospital for?"

"Because I'm sick and tired of this goddam hole," the Indiana farmboy said affably. "I've pulled my whole month's sentence and I've still got twenty-six days to do. Twenty-six more days."

"How would you like to have six months to do, like me?" Jackson said.

"I wouldnt like it," the Indiana farmboy said.

"Breaking your arm wont help you to get out any quicker," Prew said reasonably.

"It'll get me two or three weeks in the hospital though."

"Anyway, how the hell could we break your arm? Take it over our knee like a stick and break it?" Prew said. "An arm's hard to break, Francis."

"I've already thought of that," the Indiana farmboy said triumphantly. "I can lay my arm down between two rocks and one of you can hit it with a sledgehammer. That would break it quick and easy and give me at least two weeks vacation in the hospital."

"I dont want to do it, Francis," Prew said, suddenly feeling a little bit queasy.

"Will you do it for me, Stonewall?" the Indiana farmboy said.

"What the hell do you want to go to the hospital for?" Jackson evaded. "It aint no better than here. I've been there, and I'm telling you true. It aint a dam bit bettern here."

"Well, at least there wont be no Fatso there, and you wont have to work in this goddam sun breaking rocks with a hammer."

"No," Jackson said, "but you'll sit around on your dead ass looking out through them goddam chainmesh grids till you'll wish to hell you was breaking rocks with a hammer."

"At least the food will be better."

"Its better," Jackson admitted. "But you'll get just as sick of it anyway."

"Then you wont do it for me? Even as a favor?" the Indiana farmboy said reproachfully.

"Oh, I guess I'd do it for you," Jackson said reluctantly squeamishly, "but I'd a hell of a lot rather not, Francis."

"I'll do it," Blues Berry grinned. "Any old time you want it done, Francis. If you really want to do it, that is."

"I want to do it," the Indiana farmboy said affably firmly.

"Well, wheres some rocks?" Berry said.

"Theres a couple over here where I'm working that'll do just fine."

"Okay," Berry said. "Lets go." Then he paused and turned back to the others. "You guys dont care if I do it for him, do you? I mean, what the hell? If he's that sick of it. I can see how I might want somebody to do it for me sometime maybe."

"No," Prew said reluctantly. "I dont care. Its none of my affair. I just dont want to do it, thats all."

"Thats the way I feel," Jackson said queasily.

"Okay, I'll be right back," Berry said. "Keep an eye out for them guards."

The guard down in the pit was clear out of sight, but the two guards up on the cliff were both in position to see them.

"You better watch them up there," Prew said.

"Hell, if I waited till they got out of sight, I'd wait till the earth looked level."

"They probly move off a piece in a little bit," Prew suggested.

"Ahh, hell with them," Berry said disgustedly. "They too blind to see anything anyway."

He took his hammer and followed the Indiana farmboy off about five yards where Francis pointed out two rocks he had selected, two smooth flat-topped ones about six or eight inches apart and three or four inches off the ground. The Indiana farmboy knelt down and laid his left arm out across the rocks with his elbow and upper forearm on one and his wrist out onto the other.

"This way, you see, it wont break any joints," he explained affably. "I figured my left arm because I'm righthanded. It'll be easier to eat with and I can still write letters home to the famly. Okay," he said. "Hit it."

"All right, here goes," Berry said. He stepped up and measured the swing with the head of his hammer and then swung, back over his head, a full double-armed swing, and hit the arm between the two rocks with all the force and accuracy of an expert axman notching a tree.

Francis the Indiana farmboy screamed with just as much surprise as if he had not been expecting it, like a man who had been shot by a sniper he didnt see. If there was any sound of bone breaking, the scream smothered it. He stayed on his knees a few seconds, looking white-faced and faint, then he got up and came over to show it to them. In the middle of his forearm where the line should have run straight there was a kind of square-cornered offset. In the few seconds it took him to cross the five yards it had already started to swell. As they watched it, it swelled until the recessed part of the offset was filled out level again and there was only a big bulge on the bottom.

"I think its broke in two places," Francis said happily. "Hell, that ought to get me at least three whole weeks. Maybe more." He broke off strangledly and got down on his knees, holding his left arm gingerly with his right, and vomited.

"Boy, it sure hurts," he said proudly, getting back up. "I sure didnt think it would hurt that much," he said, with the same astounded surprise that had been in his scream. "Thanks a hell of a lot, Berry."

"Think nothing of it," Berry grinned. "Glad to help out."

"Well, I think I'll go on down and show this to the guard," Francis said happily. "See you guys later." He went off down the hill still holding his left arm gingerly with his right.

"Jesus!" Prew said, feeling an unusually cool trickle of sweat down his back.

"Man, he can have it," Jackson said. "I dont want any of that. Not even if it would get me clear out of the Stockade."

"What the hell?" Berry grinned. "You hear about criminals operatin on themself all a time to get bullets out. Thats lots worse than this."

"I never heard about it anywheres outside of the movies," Prew said.

"Me neither," Jackson said. "I never seen it."

"Hell, it was easy," Berry grinned at them. "There wasnt nothing to it."

Between hammerswings they watched the guard on the road make a call in from the box while the Indiana farmboy stood beside him happily, holding his left arm gingerly in his right. Then pretty soon the truck came up for him and he climbed in the back, still holding his left arm gingerly in his right.

"See?" Berry said. "Easy as pie. Hell, I got a goddam good notion to do it myself."

"If two guys showed up with broken arms, they'd sure as hell suspect something then," Prew said.

"I know it," Berry grinned wolfishly. "Thats why I aint. But thats about the ony goddam reason."

That evening when they came in from work they learned that Francis Murdock the Indiana farmboy was already in the prison ward with a certified broken arm from a fall on the rockpile. It was, however, only broken in one place, instead of two as he had hoped.

Nothing was said about it and no questions were asked and it appeared as if it had all gone off like clockwork. Evening chow went off just as usual.

But after chow, shortly before lights out, Fatso and Major Thompson himself came into Number Two with the grub hoe handles and looking madder than hell.

It was almost like an inspection. They lined them up at attention by their bunks and the two riot-gunned guards stood just inside with the third guard standing outside holding the key to the locked door. Major Thompson looked as if he had just caught his wife in bed with a private.

"Young Murdock broke his arm out on the rockpile this afternoon," the Major said crisply. "He claimed it was broke by a fall. He went to the hospital with that disposition because we like to keep our fights in the family here. But just between us, somebody broke that arm for him. Murdock and the man who broke it for him are both guilty of malingering. We do not tolerate malingering in this Stockade. Murdock's sentence is going to be lengthened, and when he comes back from the hospital he's going to find it pretty tough around here. Now I want the man who broke Murdock's arm to step forward."

Nobody moved. Nobody answered.

"All right," the Major said crisply. "We can play hard too. You men are in Number Two because you are recalcitrants. I dont have no sympathy for any of you. You've been getting away with murder lately and its about time all of you learned who runs this Stockade. I'll give the man one last chance to step forward."

Nobody moved.

"All right, Sergeant," the Major said crisply and nodded at Fatso.

S/Sgt Judson stepped up to the first man and said, "Who broke Murdock's arm?" The man was a skinny little old-timer from the 8th Field with a craggy lined face that portrayed absolute cynicism and eyes that stared straight ahead as immovably as two stones. He had been clear over at the other side of the quarry but he already knew the whole story. He said, "I dont know, Sergeant" and Fatso rapped him across the shins with the grub hoe handle and asked him again. The craggy face never moved and the solid stone eyes neither wavered nor flickered. He said, "I dont know, Sergeant" again and Fatso slammed him with the head in the belly and asked him again. He got exactly the same results.

It was the same way all up and down the line. Fatso started methodically at one end and worked his way diligently down and back up to the other. He asked each man the same question "Who broke Murdock's arm?" five times. Not a figure moved and not an eye flickered or wavered and nothing but infinite contempt for Fatso's hard methods and Fatso himself showed on any face. This was not Number Three; this was Number Two. And Number Two was as solidly together as a morticed stone wall.

Neither the contempt nor the unbreakability bothered Fatso. His business was to ask each man the question and hit him if he gave the wrong answer, not to worry about the results, and he did his job thoroughly and methodically. When he had worked his way through the line, he came back to the Major and they both went down the line and stopped in front of Blues Berry.

"Who broke Murdock's arm for him?" Major Thompson said.

Everybody knew they knew, then.

Berry stared straight ahead without answering.

Fatso hit him.

"Did you break Murdock's arm for him?" Major Thompson said.

Berry stared straight ahead, at attention, without answering.

Fatso hit him.

"It just happens," the Major smiled, "that we already know you was the man who broke Murdock's arm for him."

Berry grinned.

Fatso hit him.

"Step forward," Major Thompson said.

Berry took two paces forward, still grinning.

Fatso hit him across the bridge of the nose with the head of the grub hoe handle. Berry went down to his knees. He stayed there several seconds, nobody helping him, before he got back up shakily. Blood was pouring out of his nose, but he did not raise his hands or move his eyes from the wall. He licked his lips with the tip of his tongue and grinned at the Major.

"I'm going to make an example out of you, Berry," Major Thompson said crisply. "You're too big for your pants. I'm going to cut you down till you fit them. You think you're too tough. I'm going to show these men what happens to a man who gets too big for his pants and thinks he's too tough. Did you break Murdock's arm?"

"Fuck you," Berry said huskily.

This time Fatso hit him in the mouth with the head of the grub hoe handle. Berry's knees went loose but he did not quite go down. His eyes came unfocused but he did not move them from the wall. When he straightened up, he worked his mouth a little and spat two teeth out at Fatso's feet contemptuously and grinned at him.

"And I'm going to kill you, Fatso," he grinned. "If I ever get out of here, I'm going to hunt you down and kill you. So you better get me first. Because if I ever get out, I'll kill you."

Fatso was as unmoved by this as he had been by the general contempt and uncooperativeness. He raised his grub hoe handle again, methodically, diligently, impassively, but Major Thompson stopped him.

"Take him down to the gym," the Major said. "I dont want to dirty the barracks up any more than necessary. Some of you men clean this mess up."

Fatso took Berry by the arm and started to lead him to the door but Berry jerked his arm loose and said, "Keep your fat paws off of me. I can still walk," and walked to the door by himself. The guard outside unlocked the door. Berry walked through it. Fatso and the Major and then the two guards followed him.

"The crazy son of a bitch," Jack Malloy said contortedly. "Thats not the way to handle them. I told him thats not the way to handle them."

"Maybe he's tired of handling them," Prew said narrowly.

"He'll be tireder," Malloy said unforgivingly. "They're serious."

It was the first time any of them had ever heard a man scream when he was in the gym getting a workout. The fact that it was Blues Berry whom they heard screaming proved they were serious, that this time the Major and Fatso were out to make it or break it, showdown or else. In Number Two they cleaned up the floor and settled down to wait. It was already after nine-thirty, and the fact that the lights were still on showed this was really going to be an occasion. They managed to find out from Pfc Hanson who passed by the door under arms hurriedly, that it was one of the guards up on the cliff who had seen him.

It was eleven-thirty when Major Thompson, wearing his sidearms, came for them with the guards. There were ten guards, each wearing sidearms and carrying a riotgun.

They were lined up in a column of twos and marched down to the gym. The guards were spaced along the walls with their riotguns at port arms. More guards lined the walls of the gym. Apparently, every guard on the place had been called out tonight. The column from Number Two was marched into the gym and distributed around three of the walls with the guards in back of them.

Blues Berry stood against one of the side walls in his GI shorts under the lights, still trying to grin with a mouth that was too swollen to do more than twist. He was barely recognizable. His broken nose had swollen and was still running blood in a stream. Blood was also flowing out of his mouth, whenever he coughed. His eyes were practically closed. Blows from the grub hoe handles had torn the upper half of both ears loose from his head. Blood from his nose and mouth, and the ears which were not bleeding much, had spotted his chest and the white drawers.

"He's dead," somebody whispered behind Prew with finality.

Fatso and two other guards, Turnipseed and Angelo Maggio's old friend Brownie, all looking exhausted, stood near him. Major Thompson, wearing his sidearms, stood off by himself near the corner.

"We want to show you men what happens to men who think they can run the Army," he said crisply. "Sergeant," he nodded.

"Turn around," S/Sgt Judson said. "Put your nose and toes against the wall."

"You better kill me, Fatso," Berry whispered. "You better do a good job. If you dont, I'll kill you. If I ever get out of here, I'll kill you."

S/Sgt Judson stepped up and drove his knee up into Berry's testicles. Berry screamed.

"Turn around," S/Sgt Judson said. "Put your nose and toes against the wall."

Berry turned around and put his nose and toes to the wall. "You son of a bitch," he whispered, "you fathog son of a bitch. You better kill me. If you dont, I'll kill you. You better kill me." It was as if it was the one solitary idea he had left and he had fixed his mind on it to keep something with him. He said it over and over.

"Did you break Murdock's arm for him, Berry?" S/Sgt Judson said.

Berry went on whispering his passion to himself.

"Berry, can you hear me?" S/Sgt Judson said. "Did you break Murdock's arm?"

"I can hear you," Berry whispered. "You better kill me, Fatso, thats all. If you dont, I'll kill you. You better kill me."

"Brown," Fatso said. He nodded at Berry. "Take him."

Cpl Brown stepped into position like a man stepping into the batter's box at the plate and swung his grub hoe handle with both hands into the small of Berry's back. Berry screamed. Then he coughed, and some more blood splashed down from his mouth.

There are two kinds of grub hoe handles, curved ones and straight ones. The straight ones are longer and heavier than the curved ones. A pick handle is longer and heavier than any ax handle, and a grub hoe handle is longer and heavier than a pick handle. A straight grub hoe handle is about four inches longer than a pick handle and around a pound heavier in weight and can be recognized by the double hump at the head end. The steel head of a grub hoe, which is like the mattock half of a pick-mattock with the pick half left off the other end, fits between these two humps on the handle and makes the grub hoe a fine tool for clearing brushy root-matted ground.

"Did you break Murdock's arm?" Fatso said.

"Fuck you," Berry whispered. "You better kill me. If you dont, I'll kill you. You better kill me."

They kept them there fifteen minutes. Then they marched them back between the lines of guards to the barrack and turned off the lights. The occasional screams from the gym did not stop however, and there was not much sleep. But in the morning they were got up at 4:45 just the same.

At chow they learned that at one-thirty Blues Berry, unable to urinate and with his ears knocked half loose from his head, had been taken up to the prison ward of the Station Hospital for treatment of a fall from the back of a truck.

He died the next day about noon, "from massive cerebral hemorrhage and internal injuries," the report was quoted as stating, "probably caused by a fall from a truck traveling at high speed."

Prew did not tell Jack Malloy what he intended to do until after Berry had died. He knew what he was going to do before Berry died, but he waited till then to tell Malloy.

"I'm going to kill him," Prew said. "I'm going to wait till I get out of here and then I'm going to hunt him up and kill him. But I'm not going to be stupid like Berry was and go around advertising it. I'll keep my mouth shut and wait till I get my chance."

"He needs to be killed," Malloy said. "He ought to be killed. But it wont do a damned bit of good to kill him."

"It'll do me some good," Prew said. "It'll do me a lot of good. It may even make me into a man again."

"You couldnt kill a man in cold blood," Malloy said. "Even if you wanted to."

"I dont aim to kill Fatso in cold blood," Prew said. "He'll get an even break. Theres a bar he hangs out at downtown all the time; I've heard some of the guys talk about it, and about how he always carries a knife. I'll kill him with a knife. He'll have as good a chance at me with his knife as I'll have at him with mine. Only—he wont kill me; I'll kill him. And nobody'll ever know who did it and I'll go on back home to the Compny and forget it just like you forget other carrion."

"It wont do any good to kill him," Malloy said.

"It would have done Berry some good."

"No it wouldnt. Berry would have got what he got eventually anyway. Berry was slated for it from the day he was born in a shack down on the wrong side of the tracks in Wichita Kansas."

"Fatso was born on the wrong side of the tracks, too."

"Sure he was," Malloy said. "And he might have been Berry, and Berry him, just as easy. You dont understand him. If you want to kill something, kill the things that made Fatso what he is. He doesnt do what he does because it is right or wrong. He doesnt think about right or wrong. He just does what is there to be done."

"So do I. I've always done what is there to be done. But I've never done anything like Fatso's done."

"Yes, but you have a strong sense of right and wrong. Thats why you got in the Stockade in the first place, same as me. But if you asked Fatso if he thought what he did was right, he would probably look surprised as hell. Then, if you gave him time to think, he would say yes it was right; but he would be saying it simply because he had always been taught that he ought to do what is right. Therefore, in his mind, everything he does must be right. Because he did it. And because he knows he had been taught it is wrong to do what is wrong."

"You're only talking now," Prew said. "You're not saying anything. Fatso's wrong. Too wrong. And there will be plenty of guys go through this Stockade after you and me are out."

"Did you know Fatso was a Life Scout once?"

"I dont give a damn if he was President."

"If it would do any good to kill him, I'd say go ahead, kill him. But all that will happen will be they will get somebody else just like him to take his place. Why dont you kill Major Thompson?"

"They'd just get somebody like him to take his place, too."

"Of course," Malloy said. "But he gave Fatso the orders."

"I dont know," Prew said. "I've never felt about him like I've felt about Fatso. Major Thompson's an officer; you expect that from officers;

they're on the other side of the fence. But Fatso, Fatso's an enlisted man. And that makes him a traitor against his own kind."

"I can see what you mean," Malloy said. "And you're right. But you are wrong to kill him—just simply because it wont do any good."

"I got to do what I got to do," Prew said impassibly.

"Yes," Malloy said. "So have we all. So has Fatso."

"Then thats whats the matter," Prew said, falling back on the old phrase of finality.

"You love the Army, dont you?" Malloy said.

"I dont know," Prew said. "Yes. Yes, I do. I'm a thirty-year-man. I've always been one. Ever since I first signed up."

"Well, Fatso is as much a part of the Army you love as your 1st/Sgt, Warden, that you're always talking about. One as much as the other. Without the Fatsos you couldnt have the Wardens."

"Someday we will."

"No. You never will. Because when that day comes you wont have any Armies, and there will be no more Wardens. You cant have the Wardens without the Fatsos, either."

"You dont mind if I go on thinking we will?"

"No. You ought to think that. But what you want cant be achieved by killing off all the Fatsos. When you kill your enemy Fatso, you are also killing your friend Warden."

"Maybe so. I still cant help what I got to do."

"Okay," Malloy said, and grinned. "And is this the end-product of all I've tried to teach you about passive resistance? You didnt understand it any more than Berry or Angelo did."

"Passive resistance did them a lot of good, didnt it?" Prew said. "They both used it, and look where they are now."

"Neither one of them used it," Malloy said. "Their resistance was always active, not passive."

"They didnt fight back."

"They didnt have to. In their minds they fought back. They just didnt have access to clubs, that was all."

"You can only expect so much of a man," Prew said.

"Thats right," Malloy said. "But listen. A guy named Spinoza wrote a sentence once. He said: *Because a man loves God he must not expect God to love him in return.* Theres a lot in that, in lots of ways. I dont use passive resistance for what I expect it will get me. I dont expect it to pay me back any more than it ever has. That isnt the point. If that was the point, I'd of given it up years ago as a flop."

"I understand that," Prew said, "and I was wrong. But I'm going to kill Fatso, just as sure as God made little green apples. I aint got no choice. Thats the ony thing a fathog prick like him understands. Thats the only way."

615

"Okay," Malloy said. He shrugged and looked away, down the barrack. The lights had been out quite a while, and the others were already in their bunks. The two of them sat on their bunks facing each other talking, their expressions lit only by the glow of their cigarette ends. Prew had, by a common tacit consent, moved into Angelo's bunk next to Malloy after the little guy went up to the hospital. Malloy kept on looking down the darkened aisle, as if debating something.

"All right," he said finally, turning back. "Now I'll tell you something. I hadnt meant to tell you. But maybe it'll do me good; just like your telling me about Fatso done you good. Sometimes it helps to talk about something you're going to do that you dont want to do. I'm going to bust out of here," he said.

Prew felt a stillness that was not of the quiet night creep over him slowly. "What for?"

"I dont know if I can explain it," Jack Malloy said. "You see, theres something wrong with me."

"You mean you're sick?"

"No, I'm not sick. This is something else. Something that has to do with what I told you about being born in the wrong time. Theres something lacking in me that keeps me from doing what I want to do. You see, I'm responsible for what happened to both Angelo and Berry, just as surely as if I had signed the Discharge and swung the club. Just as surely as I'm responsible for you killing Fatso."

"Aw now, thats a lot of stuff, Jack."

"No, it isnt, its the truth."

"I dont see why the hell you should feel that."

"Because they were trying to follow what I had been trying to teach them," Malloy said. "Whether you see it or not or believe it or not. The same thing has happened to me all my life. I've tried to teach people things I saw but they always take them wrong and use them wrong. Its because theres something lacking in me. I preach passive resistance and a new kind of God with a new kind of love that understands, but I dont practice it. At least not enough. Sometimes, I dont think I've ever loved anything in my life.

"If it hadnt been for me and my talk, neither Angelo nor Berry would have done what they did. Or got what they got. And if I stay here (I've got seven more months to do, this stretch) the same thing is going to happen to other guys. Its already happened to you. I say resist passively, but you all fight, because I *feel* fight, even if I say *dont* fight. I dont want it to happen to anybody else."

"I dont think thats true at all," Prew said helplessly, inadequate before the mental task of arguing back.

"Well, its true," Malloy said. "And thats why I'm busting out."

In the glow of his cigarette Prew saw him grin bitterly gently.

"Its a thing," Malloy said, "that apparently happens to guys when they try to do what I've tried to do all my life and lack what it takes. Probably, after I bust out, they'll misunderstand that too and start making a goddam hero out of me for escaping."

"How do you figure to do it?"

"Thats the easy part," Malloy said. "I could bring enough tools in from the motorpool to cut through these walls easy."

"What about the searchlights?"

"They'd never even see me."

"But what about the electric fence? And the alarm?"

"Rubber-handled Klein pliers from the motorpool," Malloy said. "And a long piece of baling wire for each strand, back of where I cut it on both sides, to keep the circuit closed.

"But it'll be easier just to go out from the motorpool; theres not a man there that would turn me in or want to stop me. A pair of grease-monkey coveralls to get me down into the Post to my outfit to borrow civilian clothes, and I'm gone."

"What about money?"

"I dont need money. I've got half a dozen different friends in town who would hide me out long enough to get me out on a Matson liner for the States."

"Theres a war coming up soon," Prew said.

"I know it. Probably, I'll enlist again Stateside under an assumed name, when it comes up. Thats what I've figured. But I'm finished here, and theres no point in staying. And until the war does come theres some things I want to do—without having it all taken the wrong way so that it hurts the guys that I like."

"Take me with you," Prew said.

In the glow of the cigarettes Jack Malloy looked up, startled. Then he grinned what Prew always remembered afterwards as the saddest, gentlest, bitterest, warmest grin he had ever seen on a human face.

"You dont want to go with me, Prew."

"Sure I do."

"No you dont. What about Fatso?"

"Beside going with you, to hell with Fatso."

"You dont know what you'd be getting in to. I've been on the run from the Law before."

"So have I."

"Yes, but not from town to town and sheriff to sheriff. And this time theres about a fifty-fifty chance I'll never get off the Island and back to the States. Theres nothing romantic about it. And it isnt easy."

"You said yourself it would be almost as easy to go out of here as it would be to go out through the motorpool," Prew argued.

"It would. I dont mean that. I mean afterwards, after we were out.

With two men it would be five hundred per cent harder. We'd have to head for the hills and go down that way in prison clothes, instead of back through the Post. And thats where they'd be looking for us. It would take a week to get down to town safely, we'd have to skirt every house and settlement, then go clear across Honolulu to my friends."

"I'd like to go," Prew said.

"I know how to travel," Malloy said. "I've done all this before. I know how to go on shipboard like a rich man above suspicion. I know how to dress and act—like ordering dinners, the way to treat stewards and servants, and especially other passengers—a million little things it takes years to learn. You'd give it away the first day."

"But I learn fast," Prew said. "Listen, I know I'd be lots of trouble, at first. But I'd more than pay it back later on, in the things you plan to do."

Malloy smiled. "You dont know what I'm planning to do."

"I got a pretty good idea."

"I dont even know myself, Prew."

"Okay," Prew said stiffly. "I wont force you. But I would've liked to of gone."

"You dont belong with me," Malloy said. "You belong in the Army. What do you want to go with me for?"

"I dont know. Because I want to help, I guess."

"Help what?"

"I dont know. Just help."

"Help change the world?"

"Maybe. Yeah, I guess thats it."

"The little bit you and me might change the world," Malloy smiled, "it wouldnt show up until a hundred years after we were dead. We'd never see it."

"But it'd be there."

"Maybe not," Malloy said. "Thats why I say you dont belong with me. You got a romantic picture. It would mean years of living too close together, always on the jump. I'm not good at living close to people; I'm better when they're always a little way off. And you'd soon get disillusioned with it. I'm doing what I'm doing for my own self only, not for what it might or might not produce. You know what I told you a while ago was wrong with me? You remember what I told you?"

Prew did not answer. It would have sounded stupid and inane to say he did not think there was anything wrong with Malloy.

"You dont know me at all," Jack Malloy said. His voice had suddenly taken on the contorted abortive tone of a confessional. "You got a romantic picture of me too, just like all the rest. I've never loved anything enough in my life. Thats whats wrong."

"What about the Wobblies? What about America?"

"The Wobblies are gone. Have been for a long time. But I dont think I even loved the Wobblies enough because if I had, I'd of been able to do something.

"And America isnt a thing. America is an idea. An idea that everybody has a different definition of. I can love ideas, as long as they're my own, but ideas arent *things*. I'm the kind of a guy who dont like to get too close to any individual, to see his faults; if I do, it shuts off the love I feel; then I get angry and hate myself for it afterwards; and if I have to stay close to the guy, or the thing, I eventually get to hate him, or it, too. You see, the same things wrong with me thats wrong with everybody else. I preach against it with them, but its true of me, too. Even though I can prove logically that its not."

"I dont believe that," Prew said. "Thats not true. You're just tearing yourself down."

"Dont like to discover the feet of clay, do you?" Jack Malloy smiled painfully. "If you went with me, you'd discover it soon enough. Because its true. Believe me, its true. But you're different. You love the Army. Really love it. Are a part of it, and belong in it. I've never loved anything enough to belong in it. The things I've loved have always been too phantasmal, too immaterial, too idealistic. I suffer from the same disease I try to diagnose, the same disease thats destroying the world.

"Thats the thing that has always dogged my steps haunting me," he said abortively, for all the world like a good Irish Catholic confessing his customary Saturday night infidelity. "The thing thats always followed and tripped me up, the thing I've always been looking for, still am looking for, and never will find, and know I never will find. I'd give whatever place in heaven I've got coming to have been able to love something as much as you love the Army.

"Dont leave it," he said. "Dont ever leave it. When a man has found something he really loves, he must always hang onto it, no matter what happens, whether it loves him or not. And," he said with an almost religious fervor, "if it finally kills him, he should be grateful to it, for having just had the chance. Because thats the whole secret."

Prew did not say anything. He still did not believe him. But how could he argue against a brain like Malloy.

"'Because a man loves God,'" Jack Malloy said, his voice coming back up to normal again, "'he must not expect God to love him in return.' At least, not according to his limited definition of love."

Prew still did not say anything. He did not know what there was for him to say.

"I wont say good-by to you," Malloy said, his voice entirely normal now, "because I wont know just when I'm going out. I'll have to wait till the time comes up right. Then I'll recognize it. Thats the only way to work a thing like that. So just forget all about it, and expect to see me till you dont."

"It seems like," Prew said contortedly, "it seems like life is made up of saying hello to people we dont like and good-by to people we do."

"Thats horse shit," Jack Malloy said. "Sentimental horse shit. Dont ever let me hear you say a thing like that again. You just happen to be going through a period of the good-bys. Every man has them to go through at different times. Now shut up with that crap. And lets hit the sack."

"Okay," Prew said contritely. He squashed out his cigarette in the can and slipped under the blankets. He lay in the bunk in the silence, feeling suddenly a vague presentiment that somehow Jack Malloy with his slick brain had tricked him but he could not put his finger on just how.

It was a week before Malloy's opportunity presented itself. Prew saw him every day when they came in from work, and every day he expected not to see him. In spite of all Malloy had told him about forgetting it, every evening he expected not to see him. Then the evening came when he did not see him, and Hanson when he locked up for them told the story of how Jack Malloy had just walked out of the motorpool in a pair of stolen greasemonkey overalls and nobody in the motorpool knew a damn thing about it. Pfc Hanson, whose worship of The Malloy was perhaps exceeded only by that of the late Pvt Blues Berry, was tickled to death. MP patrols were sent out through the pineapple fields and along the Honouliuli Trail; the gate guards down in the Post were alerted; the Wahiawa Patrol and the Shafter MPs downtown were furnished with full particulars and instructions. It was the first time anybody had ever escaped from the Schofield Barracks Post Stockade, except for three men ten years ago who had been brought back in less than twelve hours. But no trace of Jack Malloy was found anywhere. In Number Two, as Malloy had prophesied, they were as proud as party members whose candidate had just been elected as President.

Prew sat by himself and wondered wildly if he had not already met the new Messiah of the new faith Malloy had also prophesied. A Messiah who refused a following and preferred to work alone. Met him, and lived alongside of him, and failed to recognize him.

After two weeks of a fruitless search, accompanied by as intense an interest inside the Stockade as the outcome of the World Series, Jack Malloy's escape tapered off into old stuff and, like everything else, before the constant pressure of the work like a stone against a steel blade, eroded away into boredom and nothingness.

In the Stockade, whatever else happened, you worked. You swung your 16 lb hammer to crush this rock, or you swooped a scoopshovel to load this rock you had already crushed, into the trucks that came. Work without purpose, work without end, work without pride. Your hands blistered, broke, bled, calloused. They corned up like a mailman's feet. By their blisters, you thought wildly, shall ye know them, Lord, when the day of judgment came. And as soon as you had busted all of this rock available, the Engineers came in and accommodatingly blasted more slabs of it out of the mountain for you. It was an unlimited mountain. And your muscles ached and toughened. And your mind ached and toughened. And your asshole ached and tightened, when you thought about a woman. You would be a tough, good, dangerous soldier, when you got out of this.

Chapter 44

In all, counting the extra time for the trip to the Black Hole and the transfer into Number Two, he served 4 months and 18 days, and G Company was changed.

The Warden was gone; on a 14 day furlough. Leva was gone; transferred to M Co and a S/Sgt Maylon Stark was a S/Sgt, and Lt Culpepper was the Company Commander now. Dynamite Holmes had been reassigned to Brigade HQ with a majority. Holmes had taken S/Sgt Jim O'Hayer with him and O'Hayer was a M/Sgt. They were expecting a new Company Commander, a Captain, to be shipped in any day. It was a different company.

He pulled in from the Stockade wearing the same CKC uniform he had worn at the trial. It felt strange and new after 4 months and 18 days of nothing but the outsize Stockade fatigues. The suntans were neither dirtier and more wrinkled, nor cleaner and more pressed. They had hung on a hanger in the Stockade supplyroom for 4 months and 18 days and except for the faint crease across the knees were just exactly like they had been when he took them off. He could not overcome a feeling of surprise at this. It was the same with everything.

He drew his bedding and equipment and his same old footlocker with all the old familiar personal possessions in it just like he had left them but looking strangely new and unused. They were the same blankets, and the same riflebelt and pack and canteen, but Leva did not issue them to him. They were issued to him by the welcome-grinning S/Sgt Malleaux, the new supply sergeant. From behind Malleaux Pete Karelsen, a S/Sgt too now, and still on SD in the supplyroom, came up grinning to shake hands also. Apparently, he was still a celebrity. They asked him about Maggio. He had promised himself he would wait nine days.

In the orderly room Acting First Sergeant Baldy Dhom, sweating grimly to bend his sausage fingers to a fountain pen, gladly dropped his work and shook hands happily. The new clerk, a Jewboy named Rosenberry, did not offer to shake hands and stared at him with frightened awe.

Rosenberry, he found out somewhere, was a peacetime draftee. He had taken Mazzioli's place when the new reorganization of Personnel Section had moved Mazzioli and the other Company Clerks to desks in Regiment. Rosenberry was a Pfc. They called him the "forward echelon clerk." Mazzioli was still Company Clerk but Company Clerks stayed with Regimental HQ in the "rear echelon" now. Mazzioli was a buck sergeant now.

There were new faces besides Rosenberry's. At chow that night there were more new faces than familiar ones. The company strength had been filling up steadily, but the short timers were still going home. The new faces all stared at him with the same frightened awe as Rosenberry.

After chow he sat on his bunk and worked on his rifle, a brand new Garand M1 with its barrel still full of cosmolene. He worked on it in silence, studying the awkward unwieldy lines that would never become comfortable. In the dim lights the new faces watched him covertly with the same unchanged frightened awe. Chief Choate and all the other new buck/sgt squad-leaders and s/sgt platoon-leaders, with the exception of platoon-guide S/Sgt Ike Galovitch, came over and shook hands and slapped him on the back. Apparently The Treatment was off. He was a celebrity. Everybody wanted to know about Maggio. He had promised himself that he would wait nine days.

With Capt Holmes gone and G Co no longer a jockstrap outfit, all the old forces that had caused the trouble were gone now, obsolete, rescinded. They were expecting the new CC any day now. He felt somewhat like a man on a mountainside to whom someone has thrown a rope too late and who watches the now useless rope receding uselessly up into the heights as he falls.

But they did not any of them really seem to matter much anyway, any more. The Stockade was still real. They were not real. Gradually, an intense pinpoint focus of will-effort, like a magnifying glass bending the sun's rays to the burning of a paper, had built up in him concentratedly. They could not break through the only reality, which was the Stockade, and that he had nine days to wait.

The only time anything came near to breaking through was when Andy and Friday came in from somewhere and saw him and came right over, very glad to see him, and highly conscious of the new faces

622

still watching with frightened awe. They got out the guitars and came back to his bunk familiarly and the new faces began to watch them with frightened awe, too.

Then they brought out their surprise. They had bought an electric guitar on time two months ago, complete with a jackplug attachment and the speaker to plug it in to. It had cost $260, of which there was still $200 yet to pay. They enjoyed showing him the new guitar, and the awed attention they were getting from the frightened draftee faces. He was a celebrity and they were his buddies.

He made himself wait the full nine days. He did not go anywhere. He sat home on his bunk in the squadroom and made no trouble and was silent. He did not even go down to Maunalani Heights to see Miss Alma Schmidt. He did not want anything to disturb the crystal clarity of concentration that kept getting steadily stronger.

The new Company Commander, a 1st/Lt instead of a Captain, arrived and took over. That was on the fifth day. He made them a speech. He was a Jewish lawyer from Chicago with a Reserve Commission earned by four years of ROTC in college. His name was Ross and he had only recently been called to duty. Lt Culpepper, whose father and grandfather had both started out in G Co —th Infantry as shavetails and risen to command the Company and then the Battalion and then the Regiment, was not happy. He had expected a Captain, which would not have been so bad. Lt Culpepper did not think much of Lt Ross as a soldier, but Pvt Robert E Lee Prewitt could not see that it made much difference.

He did not intend to suffer martyrdom if he could help it. He wanted to do more than stay alive, he wanted to spend that life in the Army. He had checked up before he left and six other men would be discharged from the Stockade in the first nine days after he got out. That would, he felt, at least spread the suspicion out a little, even if they neglected to count the hundreds of men who had passed through the Stockade before him. Nine days was a nice round uneven figure that would not appear to be a predetermined period, like say ten days, or one week. And Fatso Judson went down town to the Log Cabin Bar and Grill every night that there was not something special on, such as the midnight training of Blues Berry. So there was no need for hurry on that score.

He bought the knife in an Army-Navy Service Store, the night he went to town. He had figured that out ahead of time deliberately. It was one of those dingy little Jew stores on Hotel Street, exactly like a thousand other dingy little Jew stores that always spring up wherever soldiers live, except that in Hawaii all the Jew stores were run by Chinamen. It sold the same CKCs and did the same tailoring of pants and cutting down of shirts. And it offered the same fare of chevrons, shooter's medals, garrison caps with patent leather bills and solid brass insignia, brilliantly colored shoulder patches, solid brass whistles, campaign ribbons, solid brass waistbelt buckles, souvenir scarves and pillows, and knives. Even the enforced anonymity of the Army had its compensations.

The knife he picked was one of a row of an identical dozen, lying in the glass case in a jumbled mass of whistles, insignia rings and shoulder patches, brass bound clasp knives with five-inch snap-button blades and walnut handles that terminated in little handguards that the blades passed between in closing. They were SOP equipment. He had owned perhaps a dozen in his life at different times. The Chink probably sold half a dozen every day. He paid for it in small change and took it outside and tried the snap a few times and put it in his pocket and went to look for a drink.

The Log Cabin Bar and Grill was one of those downtown serviceman hangouts with indirect fluorescent lighting where it was safe for tourists to go slumming to see the Army in its natural habitat, very clean and very modern and a shade lower class than Wu Fat's Chinese Bar and Restaurant. It was set back off Beretania Street, in a business block of stinking grocery markets and sweet-smelling whorehouses, on a small paved alley. A hundred feet inside the Log Cabin the alley, instead of running straight on through the block, made a right angle turn and came out on the side street to the east. Prew, stone cold sober after a dozen drinks, was waiting at the corner of the alley when the Log Cabin closed at one o'clock.

There was no mistaking Fatso when he came out, even in the dimness of the alley. He came out walking with two sailors. Bar acquaintances. No complications there. One of the sailors was telling a joke and Fatso and the other sailor laughed. It was the first time Prew had ever heard S/Sgt Judson laugh.

They were walking away from him toward Beretania, and he stepped out from the corner feeling a crystal clarity of focused attention such as he had known only a few times in his life when he was bugling.

"Hello, Fatso," he said. The old Stockade nickname would catch him as surely as a rope.

S/Sgt Judson stopped and turned, the sailors stopping with him. He peered back into the dim uneven light that seeped through the closed venetian blinds of the Log Cabin and lighted the immobile figure of Prewitt dimly.

"Well, look who's here," Fatso grinned. "You guys go on," he told the sailors. "I'll see you next week. Old buddy a mine back here I use to soljer with."

"Okay, Jud," one of the sailors said unevenly. "See you."

"Thanks," Prew said, as Fatso came up unhesitantly, unreluctantly, and the sailors moved on down the brick toward Beretania.

"For what?" Fatso grinned. "I dont need no sailors. Now," he said. "You want to see me about something, Prewitt?"

"Yes," Prew said. "Lets step around the corner here where we can talk."

"Okay," Fatso grinned. "Anything you say."

He followed around the corner, carrying his arms out a little and just barely bent the way an old fighter moves when he's expecting anything.

"How's it feel to be on the Outside again?" he grinned.

"Bout like I figured it would," Prew said. Behind them around the corner of the alley he heard the Log Cabin door open and close again, and some more late drinkers moved talking down the brick toward Beretania.

"Well?" Fatso grinned. "What was it you wanted to see me about? I aint got all night."

"This," Prew said. He pulled the knife out of his pocket and snapped it open, the snick of the sprung blade sounding loudly in the alley. "I cant whip you with my fists, Fatso. I wouldnt want to if I could. I hear you carry a knife. Use it."

"Maybe I aint got one," Fatso grinned.

"I hear you awys carry one."

"Okay. But supposin I dont want to use it?"

"You better use it."

"Supposin I run?" Fatso grinned.

"I'll catch you."

"People might see you. Or, supposin I holler po-lice?"

"They might catch me. But they wount get here quick enough to do you any good."

"You got it figured all out, aint you?" Fatso grinned.

"I tried to."

"Well, if thats the way you want it," Fatso grinned. "Okay." He put his hand in his pocket, drew the knife and snapped it open, and began to move forward, all in one movement, incredibly fast for a fat man. Behind him the Log Cabin door opened again admitting more late drinkers to the alley. Their voices faded off toward Beretania.

"But I hate to take candy away from babies," Fatso grinned.

His knife, that was almost identical to Prew's, was waving back and forth slowly like a snake head, as he came on in in the classic stance of the practiced knife fighter, crouched a little, right arm out a little, blade projecting from across the upturned palm between the thumb and index-finger, left arm up a little palm open as a guard.

Prew moved to meet him silently, saving his breath, wishing momentarily he had been born a different person, wishing something, maybe if Warden had been home, he had meant to talk it over with Warden, wishing he had remembered to buy himself some chewing gum. Then it was gone and he was seeing everything in the finally-climaxed focus of the crystal clarity that was like slow motion as if he had been smoking gauge and was nothing like the hectic swiftness of the ring.

It did not last long. It is only in the movies that knife fighters stab and miss and slash and miss and tussle over several city blocks. Figure one offensive thrust and miss, maybe two if you are very lucky. Most knife fighters are counter-punchers.

Behind them as they circled cautiously just beyond arm reach, the Log Cabin disgorged the last of its most insistent customers. Just a few feet around the corner they moved leisurely down the brick toward Beretania.

Fatso slid in a little like a boxer and raised his left hand toward Prew's face and feinted with his knife outside Prew's left arm as if he were going to go in over it and in the same movement, as Prew automatically raised his left hand to block, flicked back down and went in under it. The knife burned like dry ice along Prew's ribs and cut itself into the wide muscle of his back under the armpit. Prew brought his left hand down sharply but it was already too late and the knife streaked off down his side in a comet tail.

If he had not stepped in at the same moment Fatso cut, if he had been gunshy or muscularly reluctant, if he had flinched, the fight would have been all over and it would have been up to Fatso, to go ahead and kill him or not kill him. But the years of boxing carried with them an instinct that no longer required either thought or courage. His knife went into Fatso at the diaphragm, just under the ribs, an automatic counterpunch right-cross to the solar plexis.

They stood that way perhaps a second or two, perhaps five seconds, thigh to thigh, Prew with his lower lip between his teeth pushing and twisting the knifeblade probing in the fat until the haft was buried in it gouging searchingly in the opening, two statues, the only visible movement Fatso's right arm that was still trailing off down to its full length. When the arm reached full extension and pulled up snap-short, the knife went on, out of it, and clattered tinnily on the brick. Then Fatso started down.

As he felt him going, Prew with his left arm clamped tight against the burn of his side clenched the handle and turned his wrist to bring the blade-edge up, letting the body tear itself off by its own weight bending his wrist slowly like too big a fish straightening out the hook, cutting deep, down across the left side with the ribcase as a guide-edge. He had come down here to kill him. And he did not want to have to stab him on the ground, or cut his throat.

S/Sgt Judson lit on his right shouldertip and rolled on over on his back, his head propped just a little on the brick wall of the building, his eyes already glazing. His right arm was still stretched out as if trying by sheer will to draw the knife back up into it, as if that might change things. He wheezed and managed to put his left hand over his cut belly.

"You've killed me. Why'd you want to kill me," he said, and died. The expression of hurt surprise and wounded reproach and sheer inability to understand stayed on his face like a forgotten suitcase left at the station, and gradually hardened there.

Prew stood looking down at him, still shocked by the reproving question. Around the corner of the alley the two bartenders of the 'Log Cabin came out together and clinkily locked the door and moved off talking quietly down the brick toward Beretania.

Prew moved then. He closed the knife and wrapped it in his handkerchief and snapped the rubber band around the handkerchief and put the package in his pocket.

His side was bleeding steadily and he took the other handkerchief, the clean one, and wadded it and stuck it inside his shirt and clamped his arm down on it, working hurriedly to catch it before it soaked down through his pants; it had already come through his shirt in spots and the gook shirt had been ripped open where the knife had gone in. But his arm would partly cover that.

Then he moved on out the east end of the alley, walking north away from town. After he had walked two blocks he stepped into another alley and sat down and leaned back against the wall to think it over now. It felt very cozily safe in the alley.

He ought to be somewhere up around Vineyard Street now. This was gook quarters up here above Beretania, tenements, and he didnt know this part very well. But Vineyard Street, he remembered, ran east quite a ways. It was east that he would have to go.

It was useless to think about going back to Schofield now, cut up like this; they'd have him the first thing in the morning as soon as they found Fatso even if he did manage to get in through the gate. The only thing left to do now was to make it across town to Alma's. If he could get to Alma's he would be all right.

His mind was working very clearly, with the same crystal intensity of focus as in the fight, and he grinned at it ruefully. Lock the barn after the horse is stolen. If the son of a bitch could only think as clearly all the time as it did when it had to, we wouldnt never get into these positions where it had to.

He had not even considered the possibility of getting cut up so bad he could not go back to the Post. Any fool ought to of thought of that.

He had not thought to bring extra handkerchieves either; dry handkerchieves would have helped to coagulate it faster.

The steady bleeding, slow, but still as inexorably logical and indifferent to plans and wishes as one of Jack Malloy's Natural Laws, was beginning to soak through the handkerchief in spots and drip down his side again. He shifted the handkerchief again and clamped his arm back down on it and that stopped the dripping, but he still would not be able to climb on a bus or streetcar looking like this with a ripped-open shirt showing spots of blood. It might soak through on the bus where he could not shift it again and his mind coldly flashed him a picture of the consternation he would cause getting up to walk off a brightly lighted city bus. There was nothing in this world as red as blood. Not even Jack Malloy's archenemies the Communists were as red as blood. Especially your own blood.

It was probably four miles to Kaimuki from here, then almost another mile up Wilhelmina Rise to Alma's. And that was as the crow flies. You could add another mile for detours to keep on the side streets that were not lighted bright enough to show like the buses would. That made it about six miles to do, figuring liberally. And he would have to walk it. But if he could get to Alma's he would be all right.

We want to figure this out right, he told himself, we want to be damn sure, we want all the percentages we can cluster. He might risk a taxi, provided he could find one on the side streets, if he thought he couldnt make it. We'll keep that for the old ace in the hole. Some of them write to the old folks for coin, thats their old ace in the hole. Others have girls on the old tenderloin, thats their old ace in the hole. They tell you of trips they are going to make, from Frisco down to the South Pole; but their names would be mud, like a chump playing stud, if they lost their old ace in the hole. You're already getting nuttier than a peach orchard boar, Prewitt. Pretty soon you wont know whether Christ was crucified or died with the screen door flux.

Sitting with his back against the wall of the alley he allowed himself time for one cigarette before starting, thinking it would clot up some if he held quite still. It was the best cigarette he had ever tasted. He smoked it slowly feeling cozily safe in the alley. Then he grinned again. Funny how the little things like a smoke seemed so wonderful and good when you were bad off and you thought if I ever get out of this one I'll take more time to enjoy the little things. And then you never hardly noticed them when everything was going good in your favor again.

Well, he told himself, I guess we might as well go on and get started. The sooner we get started, you know, the sooner we get there.

It was hard to make himself leave the false security of the alley. He had to remind himself he would have to get moving before it started to stiffen up on him, now while it had not started to hurt bad yet. Already it was beginning to have the nightmarish quality of a dream where you know you will wake up pretty soon, and that was dangerous. You take it easy in dreams because you always know you will always wake up. But this wasnt a dream. This isnt a dream, Prewitt, he reminded himself, this you wont wake up from. And whatever else happened he did not intend to ever go back to the Stockade.

At the next corner he was very careful to check the street sign and make sure it was Vineyard, before he turned east. You're really over the hill for good, this time, Prewitt. Your days as a thirty-year-man are over. When you dont show up tomorrow, and then they find old Fatso and start checkin, they wont be no doubt who it was done it. This time there wont be no gettin back to the Post before you're picked up, so as to get off with company punishment. This time its desertion. He did not know how far east Vineyard went, but it was the only street around here that went more than a block or two and he turned down it.

Below Beretania and King Streets toward the beach he knew the town like the back of his hand, but he did not know it up here. He knew enough to know that when you got out as far as the University all the east-west side streets stopped and then you had to either use Beretania or King to keep going east, or else cross over both of them to the beach side. That was going to be the hard part, crossing Beretania and King. The only chance was to find a straight street that ran down through both of them, so you would not have to walk along either one of them under the lights. They were not as populous out near the University as they were back in town, but they were still the main streets.

He followed Vineyard down to Punchbowl Street, then up Miller to Capt Cook, and back down Capt Cook to Lunalilo. There was a straight stretch on Lunalilo of over half a mile, but then it deadended at Makiki. From the corner he could see the Masonic Temple, so he knew there were no through cross streets here, because this was just a block from Kalakaua Ave that cut off toward Waikiki. Beyond Kalakaua there were side streets on the beach side, but here there were only a few dead end lanes and then nothing, clear down to the KGHB radio station on Kapiolani Boulevard. He had to go up Makiki till he hit a street east and go clear across Punahou and then cut back down.

Complicated. Very complicated. Why was it everything was always so goddam complicated? Even the simplest things was so goddam complicated when you come to doing them.

It was over a quarter of a mile up Makiki before he hit Wilder Ave east. He followed Wilder half a mile before he found Alexander Street that cut clear down to Beretania, but when he got down there he found Alexander did not cross it. It was beginning to get into him by then, and he was having to keep a very tight hold on his mind. He scouted up and down above Beretania half an hour, looking for a street that went clear through. But by then it had become all nightmare and wasnt so bad. From Alexander Street on he was laughing all the time.

He crossed Beretania and King on McCully Street that ran clear down to Kalakaua. There was Fern Street and Lime Street and Citron Street and Date Street and he remembered from somewhere that Date Street crossed Kapiolani Boulevard and the Territorial Golf Course clear into Kaimuki. It was over a mile across the golf course to Kaimuki and after that he did not remember the streets he used to angle up through Kaimuki to Waialae where he hit Wilhelmina. All he remembered was that after he got to Alma's he would be all right.

When he crossed the drainage canal in the middle of the golf course on Date Street, he dropped the package containing the knife into the water and watched the string of bubbles come up.

He was going to have a nice scar there, he thought with a giggle. The scars on a man's body were like a written history of his life. Each one had its own story and memory, like a chapter in a book. And when a man died they buried them all with him and then nobody could ever read his histories and his stories and his memories that had been written down on the book of his body. Poor man, he thought whose written history is buried with him. Poor Fatso. He bet Fatso had lots of scar-histories. He had guts too, Fatso did. And Prewitt killed him. Poor Prewitt.

You're getting silly, he warned himself, you better straighten up and fly right. You aint even to Kaimuki yet. You got a good piece to go yet, lets you and me go over our scars and see can we remember the stories. We've got a good many histories, too.

There was the one on the index finger of his left hand he had got that time in Richmond Indiana on the bum when the nigger saved him from the guy with the knife, but that was only a little one, he'd been a kid then. Wonder where the nigger is now? Wonder where the guy is?

Then there was the one on his left wrist. That was a bigger one. He had fell off the roof of the house in Harlan and gashed it on a nail and cut the artery. His mother run and got Uncle John and Uncle John stopped the bleeding or he would of died probly. When his father came home he laughed about it. His father was dead now. Uncle John was dead too. His mother was dead too. And it had all seem so important to all of them at the time, except his father, who wasnt there. And where was it now? It was on his left wrist, thats where.

And when you die?

Then its gone.

He come awful close to dyin lots of times. He had the scars to prove it. And he wasnt dead yet.

But you'll have to die sometime.

Thats right. Thats true. And then they're all gone. If they cremate you, it'll be a regular book burning, wont it?

There was the scar under his left eyebrow on his eyelid, just a thin pencil line now, that he got at Myer in the ring. They wanted to stop the fight but he talked them out of it and won by a knockout. The doc was going to sew it up, but the trainer raised such hell and insisted so loud for an adhesive bridge that that was what they finally did and hardly left any scar at all. It would have been a hell of a scar if they'd sewed it or clamped it. Wonder where the doc is now? Wonder where the trainer is? Both still at Myer? At the time he'd wish they would ot sewed it because he wanted a good scar then.

What a kid, Prewitt. What a wise punk. Well, you've got it now. You've got a lot of them now.

There was the scars he got in the Stockade, still new and red. And there was all the scars he'd got in all the barracks, coming in drunk and falling over the footlockers. He had lots of scars. He had a real history. *Robert E Lee Prewitt*, a history of the United States in one volume, from the year 1919 to the year 1941, uncompleted, compiled and edited by We The People. There were the scars he had got on the county road gang in Georgia, and the scars he had got in Mississippi in the city lockup. There were the scars he had got from the police, and the scars he had got from the enemies of the police.

He knew when it was Wilhelmina Rise Street because it was so goddam steep. It really winded him. Really getting out of shape any more. Ought to do a little roadwork. Getting old.

There was the two scars he had got the last year at Myer on the fatigue detail when he was working in the attic and fell through the skylight of the Officers' Gymnasium. The glass cut a line from his left sideburn down to his mouth-corner, and a big gash in his right hip. It was the ony time he ever got to see the inside of the Officers' Gymnasium. And now you couldnt even see the line on his face except right after he'd shaved.

So many years. So many scars. Where the hell they all go to anyway?

There was the scar he got in the fist fight in Washington, from an uppercut right on the point of the chin, and he went all fuzzy and then he was on the ground, and the other guy was gone, and the scar turned coal black afterwards and he never could understand why unless it was because of his beard but he had another scar in his beard where Koleman'd knocked two teeth through his lower lip when Koleman beat him for the Class I Championship and that one never turned coal black. Maybe when he fell he got dirt in it maybe, the one on his chin.

The lights were on in the house. That was good. That meant he wouldnt have to use his key and he couldnt remember if he'd brought his key or not. You see, he hadnt meant to go over the hill and come up here tonight. He had meant to go right back to the Post. That was what he had meant to do.

He knocked with the brass knocker and Alma opened the door in person, Georgette right behind her.

"Oh my God!" Alma said.

"Jesus Christ!" Georgette said.

"Hello, Baby," he said; "Hi, Georgette. Long time no see;" and fell in through the door.

Book Five

THE RE-ENLISTMENT BLUES

Chapter 45

The pain did not really start until the next morning. The next morning, of course, it was worse. The stiffness had come by then, and with it the soreness and dull pain of healing that was always worse than the sharp clear pain of getting it. He was a pretty sick boy for a couple of days.

But then pain was a thing he knew about. Pain was like an old friend he had not seen for a long time. He knew how to handle pain. You had to lie down with pain, not draw back away from it. You let yourself sort of move around the outside edge of pain like with cold water until you finally got up your nerve enough to take yourself in hand. Then you took a deep breath and dove in and let yourself sink down in it clear to the bottom. And after you had been down inside pain a while you found that like with cold water it was not nearly as cold as you had thought it was when your muscles were cringing themselves away from the outside edge of it as you moved around it trying to get up your nerve. He knew pain. Pain was like ring-fighting; if you kept going back in there long enough you finally got an instinct for it; you never knew just when it came, or where it came from, but suddenly you discovered you had it and had had it a long time without knowing it. That was the way it was with pain.

Pain was like with a village at the foot of a mountain that had a cathedral built on its shoulder high up over the town and the bells in the cathedral never stopped playing "The Old Rugged Cross."

He had come to on the divan about five-thirty, rising fighting up out of exhausted sleep with the impression that they had him back in the Stockade and Major Thompson was branding him under the left arm with a large capital P for the killing of Fatso, thinking it was the same as the stencil they used on the fatigue jackets except they were brand-

635

ing him for life with it but every time he tried to jerk away from it the brand only burned that much deeper.

Then he had seen Georgette sitting in the big armchair watching him unwinkingly and Alma lying back in the wicker chaise-longue with her eyes closed above the dark circles. They had undressed him and cleaned him up and put a compress over the cut and bandaged it on with gauze around his chest.

"What time is it?" he said.

"About five-thirty," Georgette had said, and got up.

Alma jerked upright wide awake, her closed eyes coming wide open staring at nothing without sleepiness, and then followed Georgette over to him on the divan.

"How do you feel?" Georgette said.

"Pretty sore. This bandage pretty tight."

"We made it extra tight on purpose," Alma said. "You lost quite a bit of blood. Tomorrow we'll take it off and put on one not so tight."

"How does it look?"

"Not so bad," Georgette said. "It could have been a lot worse. The muscles isnt severed. You owe a great debt of thanks to your ribs though, my boy."

"You'll have a nice scar," Alma said. "But it'll heal up all right in a month or so."

"You gals should of been nurses."

"Every good whore should have a course in practical nursing," Georgette grinned. "It comes in handy."

He noticed there was a new look on both their faces that he had never seen there before.

"What did the other guy look like?" Alma had smiled.

"He's dead," Prew said. Then he added, rather unnecessarily he had thought later, "I killed him."

Both their smiles had gradually faded off. They had not said anything.

"Who was he?" Georgette said.

"Just a dogface," he said, and paused. "He was the Chief Guard in the Post Stockade."

"Well," Georgette said. "Well, I'll go make you a cup of hot beef bouillon. You need to build up your strength."

Alma watched her until she had gone up the three little steps into the kitchen.

"Did you kill him on purpose?"

Prew nodded. "Yes."

"Thats what I thought. That was why you came here, wasnt it?"

"I meant to go back to the Post so they wouldnt suspect me. Then I was going to come down later, after this'd blown over."

636

"And how long have you been out of the Stockade?"

"Nine days," he said. He said it automatically, without having to count.

"Over a week," she said, "and you didnt even call me up. You might at least have called me up."

"I didnt want to take any chances of fouling up." Then he grinned. "And I didnt want to risk getting you into trouble. Course, I forgot all about the possibility of getting cut up so bad I couldnt go back."

Alma didnt seem to think it was humorous.

"Didnt Warden get in touch with you?" he said. "I ask him to."

"Yes," Alma said, "he got in touch with me. He came down to the New Congress. That was how I found out you were in jail. Otherwise, I wouldnt even have known. I think you might at least have written a letter."

"I cant write letters," Prew said. He paused and looked at her.

"Well," Alma said, "of course if you cant write them . . ."

"Did Warden—" he said, and stopped.

She looked at him, waiting for him to finish it, a look of almost contempt coming onto her face. When he didnt go on, she said, "Did Warden what? He was a perfect gentleman, if thats what you mean."

Prew moved his head vaguely, looking up at her.

"He was kind," she said, enumerating them, "and considerate, and thoughtful, and gentle, and a perfect gentleman."

Prew tried to imagine Warden being like that.

"Much moreso than a lot of other men I have met," Alma told him.

"He's a good joe, all right."

"He certainly is. He's a fine man."

Prew clamped his jaws shut on what he wanted to say.

"You dont know what its like up there," he said, instead. "Its not a big help to a guy's imagination. Four months and eighteen days, and every night there is all that time you lay in your bunk with the lights out, before you finally go to sleep."

The contempt faded off of her face and she smiled at him brimmingly apologetically. It was the same smile of a while ago that he had never seen on her face before—maternal, solicitous, tender, almost happy, and infinitely more gentle than he had ever seen her look.

"You've had a hard time," she smiled self-castigatingly. "And here I am being mean and nasty, when you're sick and in pain and need rest more than anything. I guess," she said, "I'm afraid I'm in love with you."

Prew looked at her proudly, even with his side prodding him angrily, thinking she was a professional whore which instead of making him less made him even more proud, because a professional whore who knows the score is even harder to make fall in love with you than a respectable woman. Not many men are ever loved by professional whores, he thought proudly.

"Hows for a kiss?" he grinned. "I've been here this long and you aint even kissed me."

"Yes I have," Alma said. "But you were asleep."

But she kissed him again anyway.

"You've had a hard time," she said softly.

"Not as hard as some guys," he said woodenly, seeing again the by now familiar, every-detail-sharply-remembered, picture of Blues Berry standing nose and toes against the gym wall and by inference seeing Angelo Maggio in the same spot.

"I guess I'm over the hump for good now," he said. "Even after I'm well I still cant go back. When I dont show today they'll know I did it. They'll be looking for me."

"What do you plan to do?"

"I dont know."

"Well, at least you'll be safe here. Nobody here knows who we are. So you can stay here if you want," she said, looking up with a question at Georgette coming in with the hot soup.

"You can stay as long as you want, kiddo," Georgette grinned, "as far as I'm concerned. If thats what you two are wondering."

"We hadnt mentioned it," Alma said. "But thats a point that would have to be considered: how you felt."

"I've always had a soft spot for crazy sons of bitches," Georgette grinned. "And I aint got nothing to thank the Law for except my free medical examination every Friday."

"I'm glad you feel that way, Georgia," Alma said.

"I'll be a fugitive from Leavenworth," Prew reminded her. "A murderer, to the Law."

"To coin a phrase," Georgette said, "up the Law's."

The coined phrase obviously did not appeal much to Alma, but she did not say anything.

"Can you sit up by yourself for this?" Georgette said, moving the cup.

"Sure," Prew said, and swung his legs down over the side of the divan, pulling his trunk up. Bright hot spots danced on a warm moist film in front of his eyes.

"You crazy dam fool!" Alma cried angrily. "You want to start it bleeding again? Lay back down and let me help you."

"I'm up now," Prew said weakly. "But I'll let you help me back down after I drink the soup."

"You're going to get lots of this," Georgette said, holding the cup to his lips. "You'll probly get so much of it you'll probly be damned sick of it."

"It tastes good now though," he said between swallows.

"Wait till tomorrow."

"Tomorrow," Alma smiled, "we'll feed you a good big thick steak, rare and bloody."

"And liver and onions," Georgette grinned.

"A T-bone?" Prew said.

"Or a porterhouse," Alma said.

"Man, man," he said, "stop it, you're killing me."

There was that same loving look on both their faces again, more pronounced now, of an almost unbelievable happy tenderness.

"You gals sure treat your invalids right," he grinned at them. "How about a cigarette now?"

Alma lit it for him. It tasted wonderful, better than the one in the alley, because now he could relax with it. He dragged the smoke deep into his lungs and it seemed to ease the stiff sore fire of indignant protest from his side, even though it hurt to breathe that deep.

It hurt also, considerably, when they had helped him back down; and that, he reminded himself, is only today. Wait till tomorrow. And then wait till the second day which will be even worse. But it didnt hurt nearly so much as the big gesture of sitting up by himself. Well, okay, to hell with the gestures, he thought, letting himself sink back down into the luxurious willess irresponsibility that is the nicest thing about being bad sick.

"Okay," he said. "I'm all right now. You gals might as well go on back to bed."

"We've stayed up this long," Alma smiled happily. "We might as well stay up the rest of the night."

"You dont get any more chances to doctor invalids than I get chances to be sick, do you?" he grinned.

"Now you just go back to sleep," she said bossily. "Try not to talk. Try to rest."

"But dont you want to hear all about the big fight?"

"We'll read about it in the paper tomorrow," Georgette said.

"Okay, doc," he grinned.

"Do you think you can sleep all right?" Alma said.

"Sure," he said. "Sleep like a top."

"I'll give you a sedative if you want."

"Wont even need it." And he had lain and watched them as they turned off all the lights but the night light on the endtable and then go back to their chairs in the gloom, Alma to the armchair this time and Georgette to the chaise-longue.

The radio-bar was still in the corner of the sunken tile floor by the steps to the kitchen and the record-player was still on the little table by the record-cabinet and the three steps still went up to the glass doors

639

that opened out onto the fairy-tale porch over Palolo Valley. He could hear their breathings there in the dark room, positive, comforting, reassuring, as he tried to get comfortable with the soreness. In a way, it was a good bit like coming home from someplace. And he did not care much if he couldnt sleep. He was more than content to just lie and look at all of it. Hell, it was almost like being a regular civilian. And he had lain like that for a long time without disturbing either one of them.

But he did not feel nearly so chipper next morning, when he awoke to the stiffness and soreness that is always worse the next day. Alma and Georgette were already up and had gone out for the steak and studied the paper. There was nothing in the paper. He did not have any appetite but they fed him the steak anyway, Georgette holding him up while Alma cut it and forked it into his mouth like a farmer forking hay into a mow, and every hour or so they made him drink a cup of the beef bouillon that, as Georgette had prophesied, he was already sick at the thought of.

Alma phoned in to Mrs Kipfer and asked for, and got, three days off. Mrs Kipfer did not believe she was menstruating, and Alma knew she did not believe it. But it was the time-honored excuse of her business, that the favorites could get by with, just like the dead-grandmother-furlough in the Army, that the favorites could always get away with; nobody was expected to believe it.

They settled down to taking care of the invalid. They made him stay on the divan until almost evening, before they moved him in on Alma's bed, and they absolutely refused to change the tight bandage until at least the second day. He did not turn down the sedatives this time.

It was in the paper the second day. They had searched for and found it before he woke up. After they fed him his breakfast of liver and onions, they showed it to him. Right then, he would not have cared enough to have looked for it. He hardly bothered himself to read it when they held it up in front of him.

He had expected to see it in 60-point banner headlines spread over the whole front page, with his name as the hunted killer just below it in 20-point; instead, it was on page 4 almost down at the bottom with a bannerhead of 12-point and not quite two inches of type that was a marvel of brevity and said, in effect, that another soldier had been found dead in another alley of a knife wound, that his name was S/Sgt James R Judson, that he had been in the Army 10 years and came from Breathitt County Kentucky, that he had been Chief Guard at the Schofield Barracks Post Stockade and because of this it was believed that he had been murdered by some vengeance-crazed ex-prisoner for some fancied wrong, possibly by a recently escaped convict whose apprehension was expected by the Army at any moment named Pvt John J Malloy. The deceased, it said, had been unarmed and was apparently not expecting to be attacked as there was a look of complete surprise still on his face. No witnesses could be found. The employees of the Log Cabin Bar and Grill near which the body was found remembered the deceased who had patronized them that evening but could not say when he had left or with whom.

He had a hard time coming back up out of the pain of his sorely stiffening side that almost had him giggling again now, to concentrate his mind on it. But he was able to glean two or three things. Apparently nobody, neither the two sailors who had not come forward nor the bartenders who had been called forward, wanted any part in it, for one. And apparently someone had found the body before the Law did and acquired themselves a good knife, for another. And, after figuring quite a while, he came up with the startling discovery that the recently escaped convict named Pvt John J Malloy must be Jack Malloy and that, for lack of anything better, they were going to pin it on him for a while, for the public at least.

And this brought him to the thing he had been searching his mind for all the time he was reading it but had not been able to quite catch up with: that this was only a newspaper article for the public in general. And newspapers had a notorious reputation, even amongst us illiterates in the Regular Army, he thought gigglingly, of writing only what was thought to be the best for the public at the moment without hampering or hamstringing their more important purpose too terribly much with the truth. It might not any of it be true at all since it was in a newspaper, and maybe they ony wrote it in hopes that Prewitt the murderer would tip his hand and give himself up with the expectation of getting off with no more than a charge of AWOL. It might be, he thought laughingly craftily, they were ony laying for him and waiting.

And as for them ever catching up with Pvt John J Malloy—he had to laugh outright, even though it hurt his sore side. Nobody but a goddam stupid fool would ever believe a newspaper article anyway.

"It dont look too awful bad," Georgette offered, finally.

"Yeah," he grinned at them slyly, "but how I know this aint just a spiel to make me feel safe enough to show my hand?"

"Thats just it," Georgette said. "You dont."

"Did anyone see you at all?" Alma asked.

"He came out of the Log Cabin with two sailors. I know they saw me, but I dont know if they saw me well enough to recognize me because it was dark and they were 30 or 40 yards away."

"Well anyway," Alma said hopefully, "they havent shown up yet. It looks like they dont want to get mixed up in it either way."

"Yeah," he said, "—if you can believe this newspaper article. The cops may have them down to headquarters right now, for all I know."

"Amen," Georgette said fervently.

641

"Even if I was to go back after I was all healed up," he said, "they'd still get me for an AWOL. And with my record, that'd mean at least six months. I aint going to put no more time in no more Stockades, even for an AWOL."

"After hearing you talk about Stockades," Georgette grinned, "I cant say I blame you a whole hell of a lot."

"Well," Alma said, "we better get out of here and let him rest, whatever happens. How does it feel now?"

"Okay," he said, "a little sore." He could feel himself grinning sillily like he always did when he was in pain and he had to choke back a hunger to laugh.

"I'll give you another sedative, if you want," Alma said.

"I dont much like them things," he grinned sillily.

"They cant hurt you any."

"I couldnt sleep anyway," he grinned sillily. "Whynt you save them for tonight."

"That would be the best idea," Georgette said.

"I hate to see you in such pain," Alma said nervously.

"Hell, this aint nothin," he grinned sillily. "Lemme tell you about the time I broke my arm on the bum and dint have no dough to go to a doctor."

"Come on," Georgette said. "Lets get out of here and leave him alone."

He watched them go out and then lay back with it, wanting to laugh again. He moved his slitted eyelids a little and watched the kaleidoscope play of distorted light fragments against his eyeballs for a while, they were unending variations that were never quite the same twice and he could watch their shiftings for hours. Then after a while the pictures started coming up in his brain and he shut his eyes all the way and lay, letting the half-formed images rise, watching the stories they acted out, curious to see what would happen in the end, like with a mystery movie. It was the way it is just before sleep, and while you knew you could not sleep now, you could stay like this for hours at a time, if you knew how, watching the stories that were just as good— were even better than—movies, because these stories were not subjected to any Hays Office, and if you wanted a movie with naked women you could have it, all you had to do was think it. There was one he played with a long time that had as its jumping off place the last time they had fed him when Georgette held him up and he wondered, as he went on absorbedly watching the movie, why he had never noticed Georgette at the Ritz Rooms, he had been to the Ritz Rooms quite a few times before he got in the Company.

Alma gave him three sedatives that night, but in the morning he knew it had made the top of the grade and was starting down hill finally. He could tell because he wanted to get out of bed. It took all his will power to get himself up stiffly onto his feet, and the sore stiffness in his side protested indignantly, but the thing was, not so much that he could, but that in spite of the hurt he still wanted to do it. He knew it was on the downgrade then.

He navigated the three steps down to the living room shakily, and found that Alma had moved a sheet and pillow onto the divan and was sleeping there where she could hear him if he called. He had assumed she was sleeping with Georgette in the other bedroom, and it hit him hard. So hard that tears came up into his eyes and he remembered, again, suddenly, how much he loved her, and went over and sat down and kissed her and put his hand on her breast solid-soft under the silk pajamas.

She woke immediately, and was as immediately angrily horrified to find him out of the bed. She not only insisted he go back to bed but insisted on helping him.

"Come on," he grinned from the bed, "lie down here for a while. Its a lot more comfortable than out there."

"No," she said irrefragably, more shocked than angry. "Absolutely not. You know what'll happen if I do, and you're in no condition for any parties."

"What the hell," he said, "sure I am. Its my side thats sore," he grinned.

"No," she said angrily, she was always angry at him afterwards, whether it reached the plane of action or not, as if he had deliberately degraded her. "You need to save your strength."

He could have argued that one, but it was useless to argue once it was gone, argument only drove it further away, he knew from experience you could not arouse whatever it was by argument and the best he would get would only be the ice statue again all locked up inside, and the ice statue wasnt worth even the argument let alone the energy, so he did not argue; instead he lay in the bed while she went out to fix breakfast, feeling a hot fever all over that had absolutely nothing to do with the sore side and that greatly colored the mental movies until they had nothing to do with love at all, this fever that burned up all the meat (called Love) and left only the bare bones (called whatever it was the Hays Office called it, Rut maybe, Lust probably, raw hot bloody Lust) that were the skeleton under the meat of every man's love no matter how much they denied it, and that could be satisfied anywhere anyway anyhow anywho (although the women always stoutly refused to believe this and were therefore the Board Founders and Charter Designers of the whorehouses male and female that they decried), but that he could not get up and go satisfy now, so he just lay in the bed with the burning hot fever that had nothing to do with his sore side, and listened to her fix breakfast.

That afternoon they finally changed the tight bandage and put on a looser. The compress was incorporated into the scab by the coagulation so they left it on. They took *it* off two days later, amid much cursing and sweating, and exposed the lumpy corrugated wet pink new scar tissue beginning to fill in at the edges and bottom, before they put on a new one. But that time the ice statue, because of his increasing insistence which he had sworn he would not voice but still had voiced anyway, had suffered him once.

They kept him in the bed for a week. They even changed the sheets with him in it, pushing the slack of the clean sheet up against him on one side and having him roll over onto it while they pulled the slack out the other side and tucked it in in the accepted hospitalnurse manner. And on the faces of both, the brilliant crystal-hard Georgette, and the opaque thoughtful absolute-realist Alma, was the same beaming lambency like on some painter's *St Anne and Madonna cuddling St John and Jesus,* the same smile of the first day that he had never seen on either of them before then: maternal, solicitous, very happy, infinitely protective, such a bottomless flood of maternal tenderness that it threatened to engulf him forever and drown him in the soft bosoms of matriarchy. He was surprised at them, two such self-avowed realists, they were not even ashamed of it enough to try to hide it. Their motives were openly obvious. Two whores who finally found something to mother. A guy could write a book about it, he thought bitterly, call it *From Hair to Maternity.* It would probly be a very long book. Whores did not produce as fast as rabbits. At first he had abandoned himself to this joyous nursing gratefully, but now he forgot all about enjoying being sick and struggled against it, suddenly afraid it was so powerful they would end up making an invalid for life out of him.

He did not, of course, stay in bed all afternoon and evening while they were both gone to work. As soon as they were out of the house he got up and dressed himself in the civie slacks they had washed the blood out of for him and put on one of the new T-shirts they had bought for him to take the place of the ruined shirt they had burned for him, and practiced walking up and down and around the house they had made into a hideout for him, so as to keep them from making a goddam permanent cripple out of him. He knew enough to know that when it had reached this stage of mending it was better to use it than to lie there in the bed and let it atrophy like they wanted him to. He did not intend to let himself be turned into an invalid for life just because their frustrated maternal instincts needed something to baby.

It was nice there in the house by himself. At first he had trouble getting into the clothes, but every day he made himself do it and it made it noticeably that much easier the next day, and by the second week (when they allowed him to get out of bed—after being openly surprised at how well he managed—and helped him into the dressing gown they had bought him after much discussion of styles and colors) he could get out of the dressing gown and into the clothes almost as easily as if he had never been cut at all, after they left for work.

He would mix himself a good stiff drink (they did not let him have any liquor, when they were home) and go out and sit on the porch in the afternoon sun (they did not allow him outside on account of catching a cold, when they were home) and maybe read a little in one of their books (Georgette belonged to the Book of the Month Club, "just for the hell of it," she grinned, "after all, I do live on Maunalani Heights, and the books look good in the livingroom even if I dont read them") and get himself pleasantly three-fourths tight and watch the sunset. He was always in bed asleep when they got home from work, so they did not find out about it until the end of the second week when Alma came home half-tight from work one night and came in and fell on his bed maulingly, forgetting all about his sore side, and smelled the liquor on his breath and came to herself and gave him all kinds of hell for drinking.

That let the secret out of the bag, so he got up and showed them both how well he got around and how easily he dressed himself. They did not like it, but they both accepted the inevitable, Alma a little more reluctantly than Georgette. They watched him go through his act with a kind of hurt look on their faces, like a mother whose son has come home so drunk and with such an easily readable address of the local whorehouse sticking out of his pocket that she finally has to admit, even to herself, that he is, at last, grown up. They did not say much; and congratulated him, half-heartedly; and after that the restrictions were off and it was all right.

But even then he still liked it better when he was there by himself. He would look around at everything and think how there was all the time in the world, no Reveille to be back for tomorrow, no weekend pass that would have to end again Monday morning, no place to go and no specified time to go there in. He lived perpetually in the old on-pass feeling of life did not begin again till Monday morning except now there was no Monday morning to worry about. He would play through all the records, and run through all the books, and go around feeling the furnishings, and feel the tile floor and the Jap mats on the porch with his bare feet, and in the evening he would make his own evening meal himself in the shining white kitchen where he knew just exactly where everything was. All the books with their brightly colored jackets (Georgette had been in the Book of the Month Club three years and she always took every book, plus all the dividends) were very pretty in the recessed bookcase over the divan. The record albums were fine clean parallel lines of gold print on black in the mahogany cabinet. And there was all the time in the world. And there was the bar, the lovely big well-stocked bar, where you can make yourself a drink whenever you want, he would think happily, mixing himself a scotch-and-soda that he was finally beginning to like the taste of now. And all the time in the world. It was, all of it, as near to being a full-fledged 24-carat civilian as any thirty-year-man ever could get.

Then he would remember he was not a thirty-year-man any more.

Chapter 46

Prewitt had been gone two days when the 1st/Sgt of G Company came back from furlough.

It is an aged proverb in the Regular Army that guys come back from furlough in order to rest up, or otherwise they would have gone right on over the hill. And Milt Warden was no exception. He came in shakily after two days of earnest drunkenness, his prize $120 Brooks Bros. powder-blue tropical suit crumpled and dirty. Acting 1st/Sgt Baldy Dhom met him in the orderly room with the hoary joke that he was four hours late and already marked AWOL on the Morning Report.

Warden did not even bother to laugh. He had been falling-down slobbering drunk for two days, but it was not enough, and he would have preferred more. The two days' drunk had come out of the admission that his ten-day idyll with his future wife had developed into a profound and absolute bust, and for an admission like that a man needed at least a week of it. Two days was not nearly enough. But then neither was it a pleasant thought to know your Company Administration was being strangled by the sausage fingers of a stupid ox like Baldy Dhom for fourteen days.

He had hardly collapsed himself into his swivel chair, still in his prize $120 Brooks Bros. powder-blue tropical suit, before Baldy was briefing him on the peculiarities of the new Company Commander. Baldy had not wanted the Company Administration any more than Warden had wanted him to have it.

Warden listened in bitter silence. Dynamite had put through the furlough the day before he left for Brigade, just like he promised, so that Warden had not even met 1st/Lt William L Ross. He had not, in fact, known anything about him except that he was coming. Neither his rank nor his name nor that he was going to be Jewish. Typical, he told himself sourly, typical. The well known Warden luck. No sooner do I get rid of one screwball Jewboy who at least was decent enough to commit suicide than I get another one. Only this time its an officer. The Company Commander, no less. And now I'll have my tempermental Jewish race complexes right with me in my own orderly room, instead of in the rear rank. Jesus Christ.

Then, while he was still trying to digest that one, Baldy informed him of the next new development. Prewitt had been absent for two days.

"What!"

"Thats right," Baldy said guiltily.

"Why, the son of a bitch wasnt even out of the Stockade yet when I left!"

"I know it. He come out three days after you took off. Acted meek as a lamb. He was ony back nine days, all told."

"Well, Jesus Christ."

Warden felt something stronger than the Jewish Problem come over him and displace the contemplation of Lt William L Ross. It was somewhat the same feeling you get watching a line squall moving across the sky and covering the face of the sun on a hot day with a wind-chill sense of rain.

"A hell of a fine mess you made of my orderly room, Baldy. Its pretty goddam bad when a man cant even go on a goddam furlough without having it all fall down on his head."

"It wasnt my fault," Baldy said lamely.

"No," Warden said. Why in the name of Christ wasnt he informed Prewitt was coming out of the Stockade in three days? Did he have to do everything by himself in this outfit? "Well, have you dropped him for rations and picked it up on the Morning Report?"

"Well, no," Baldy said uncomfortably, "not yet. You see—"

"*What!*"

"Well, you see—"

"What do you mean, not *yet?* My god how long do you need? He's been gone two whole days, aint he?"

"Well now wait a minute," Baldy said. "I'm tryin to esplain. You see, Ross dont know a single soul in the Compny by name yet, except for a few noncoms."

"What the hell has that got to do with this?"

"Well," Baldy said, "you see Chief Choate turn him in present for duty at Reveille the first morning. I dint know nothing about it till the next day."

"All right, so what? Jesus Christ, Dhom," he said painfully, "this is an Infantry Compny, not a goddam YMCA."

"Well," Baldy said uncomfortably, but stubbornly, "you was due in the next day. So I figure one day already whats one day more? The harms already done to the Morning Report."

"Well of all the goddam ways to run an outfit."

"Well," Baldy said impassibly, "what the hell? This is your orderly room. I ony ride shotgun on it. And," he said, "I figure he might even come back in of him own self before you got back."

"Oh," Warden said. "You figured he'd just come back."

"Thats right."

"Say, what the hells eating you?"

"Nothing, why?"

"Since when is Prewitt such a goddam good friend of yours?"

"He aint."

"Then why the hell try to cover up for him?"

"I didnt. I just figured he'd probly come back."

"But he didnt though, did he?"

"Nope," Baldy admitted. "Not yet."

"And you're left holding the sack."

Baldy shrugged massively and looked at him with the open innocence of a guilty man who knows he is safe just the same.

"Hell, First. I thought you'd be glad I waited for you to handle it."

"Horse shit!" Warden hollered. "Now I'll have to pick him up retroactive to the 16th—what month is this? October—retroactive to the 16th of October. How the hell you think thats going to look on the Morning Report?"

"I was ony trying to do you a favor," Baldy said.

"Do me a favor hell!" Warden bellowed.

"Okay," Warden said, he ran his fingers tearingly through his hair, "all right. Just tell me one thing. How'd you manage to keep it a secret from the rest of the Compny?"

"What do you mean the rest of the Compny?" Baldy asked blandly.

"Now dont tell me they didnt even notice he was gone now?"

"I never thought about it," Baldy said. "But I reckon they did. But you see, like I said, Ross dont know none of them. They dont owe Ross nothing, either. And you know featherhead Culpepper, he never pays no tension to nothing. I mean—"

"I see what you mean," Warden cut in. "Just one other thing. How did Choate manage to get it past Ike Galovitch? Dont tell me Ike's in on it too?"

"Well, thats another thing," Baldy said. "I hant got to that yet. You see, Galovitch aint the platoon guide of the 2nd Platoon any more. Galovitch is been busted."

"Busted," Warden said.

Baldy nodded.

"Who busted him?"

"Ross."

"What for?"

"Inefficiency."

"Whatd he do?"

"Didnt do nothing."

"You mean Ross just up and busted him? For nothing? Under a blanket charge of inefficiency?"

"Thats right," Baldy said.

It was like pulling teeth out of an elephant, if an elephant had teeth. "But he must of done something, Baldy."

Baldy shrugged. "Ross seen him give close order one day."

"Well I'm a dirty bastard," Warden said happily. "All right, who'd he make in his place?"

"Chief Choate."

"Well now I am a dirty bastard," Warden said happily.

Baldy seized the opening. "So you can see how I wunt know nothing about it. Who'd ever of thought Choate would turn him in Present? Would you, First?"

"Oh, no," Warden said. "Oh, no. Of course not."

"And you know how Champ Wilson is with his platoon. He never pays any mind to whats going on. Especially during training season. You can see how it wasnt my fault."

"Oh, sure," Warden said. "All right," he said, "what else has happened."

"Thats all, I guess," Baldy said blandly and got up from his chair. He always looked uncomfortable when he had to sit in a chair. "You care if I take the rest of the morning off?"

"Take the rest of the morning off," Warden bawled. "What the hell for? What the hell did you do to rate a morning off?"

"Well," Baldy said immovably, "its practicly noon already. Time I change uniforms and get out to the drillfield they be practicly ready to come in." He paused in the doorway and looked back at Warden with a closed face. "Oh," he said, as if just remembering. "Theres one other thing. You see the papers this morning?"

"You know I never read the goddam newspapers, Dhom."

"Well," Baldy said, looking at him, "Fatso Judson—you know? the Chief Guard of the Stock-ade?—he was killed the night before last down to the Log Cabin Bar and Grill. Somebody knife him in the alley."

"Is that right," Warden said. "And so what?"

"I thought you knew him," Baldy said.

"I wouldnt know Fatso Judson from Buster Keaton. If I saw him in the middle of the street."

"I thought sure you knew him," Baldy said.

"Well I dont."

"Then I guess thats my mistake," Baldy said.

"It sure is."

"Then I guess thats everything. I tole you Galovitch was busted, dint I?"

"You told me."

"Then thats all," Baldy said. "Do you care if I take the rest of the morning off?" he said. "I got to fix a bad faucet over to the house."

"Listen, Dhom," Warden said in his official voice, taking a deep breath. He was conscious of the new clerk Rosenberry still sitting quietly at the filing table in the closet. "I dont know what kind of screwy ideas you got in your goddam head, but I know you're old enough and got enough service to know you cant get by with carrying a goddam man present for duty when he's over the goddam hill. Even in the goddam Air Corps they cant do that. It always comes out. I've had a lot of orderly rooms in my time, and I've seen some bad ones. But I never seen an orderly room get so completely 100% fuckedup in such a short goddam time. You may be worth a four stripe rating as a straight duty man. But as an acting first sergeant you stink. You wouldnt make a good Pfc. You're miserable. It'll take me two months to straighten out my goddam orderly room and get it over your two weeks as first sergeant."

He paused, for breath, and looked up at Baldy who was still standing impassively in the doorway. Warden tried to think up something else to say, something that would make it sound a little bit better, a little more stronger.

"I just want you to know I never seen such a lousy acting top kicker since I been in the goddam Army," he said in summation. It still sounded thin.

Dhom did not say anything.

"Okay," Warden said, "go ahead, take off. And you might as well take the rest of the morning off since you wouldnt do no goddam work anyway."

"Thanks, First," Baldy said.

"Go to hell," Warden said. Angrily he watched the big man go out, the massive shoulders brushing the door jamb on both sides, the huge head almost touching the top of the frame. Baldy Dhom, husband to a fat Filipino lardmama sow of a shrew, father to innumerable runny-nosed half-nigger brats, trainer to one of the worst boxing squads in the history of the Regiment, duty sergeant to one of the miserblest Companies. An old soldier with 18 yrs serv under his belt in his paunch along with 18 yrs beer, and condemned by his nigger family to foreign service for the rest of his natural life. The man who had loyally and sanguinarily led the pack in executing The Treatment that Dynamite had prescribed for Prewitt; and who now, just as loyally, led the attempt to cover up for him when he went over the hill and killed a man because of it. Probly he explained it to himself by some sentimental crap about us old-timers got to stick together, with so many draftees about to take over the Compny. And as he watched him go out, he watched with him, beyond and around him, the whole tacit network of the whole tacit conspiracy, nothing open, nothing said or admitted, just a sudden common movement toward a blindness of not seeing, a sudden tacit ignorance, all over the whole Company, and that you could no more fight than you could fight a solid mountain.

If you wanted to, he told himself. Which you do not. You dont like the Stockade any better than they do. Nobody likes the Stockade—unless they work for it.

Well, he thought, he finally did it. He finally went and did it. Just like you have always known he would do it.

"Rosenberry!" he bellowed.

"Yes, Sir?" Rosenberry said quietly. He was still sitting quietly at the closet table, still quietly filing things.

A quiet boy, Rosenberry, altogether a quiet boy. That was one of the reasons he'd picked him to replace Mazzioli. He had spent the whole last week before his furlough, after Mazzioli had been shifted to Regiment, in picking him.

"Rosenberry, I want you to get the hell over to Regiment and pick up today's batch of useless memorandums and worthless circulars, while I straighten this goddam mess out, and come back and worthlessly file them."

"I already have, Sergeant," Rosenberry said quietly. "I'm filing them now."

"Then get your ass over to personnel and tell Mazzioli I want Ike Galovitch's Service Record. I cant stand to look at your goddam face."

"Yes, Sir," Rosenberry said quietly.

"And while you're there, get the Service Record of every other man who's changed status while I been gone."

"Do you want Prewitt's Service Record, too, Sergeant?" Rosenberry asked quietly.

"No-goddam-it-I-dont-want-Prewitt's-Service-Record-too-Sergeant," Warden bawled. "If I want Prewitt's-Service-Record-too-Sergeant, I'd of told you, you stupid son of a bitch. Remember? you're a soljer now, Rosenberry; not a goddam civilian."

"Yes, Sir," Rosenberry said quietly.

"A draftee maybe," Warden temporized craftily.

"Yes, Sir," Rosenberry said quietly.

"—But neverteless still a soljer," Warden roared triumphantly. "Just a plain goddam stinking mucky out-at-the-ass soljer. Who's suppose to do what he's told, when he's told, without askin goddam civilian foolish questions. *Get me?*" he roared.

"Yes, Sir," Rosenberry said quietly.

"All right then, move it. And dont call me Sir; only officers is called Sir. I'll get Prewitt's Service Record later on. When I need it. *And when I'm goddamned good and ready.*"

"Yes, Sir," Rosenberry said quietly.

"I got to get the rest of this crap straightened out first, before I can even use Prewitt's Service Record," he explained in a somewhere near almost normal voice.

"Yes, Sir," Rosenberry said quietly, already on his way out the door.

Warden watched him cross the quad, still moving quietly. You didnt fool him a goddam bit either. He was a quiet boy all right. A Jewish secret, quietly contained, and open to members only. Maybe not even open to members, he amended. He probly dont miss much, but you wont have to worry about him talking too much.

If only, he exploded suddenly, the goddamned ass wouldnt look at a man like he thought he was the Prophet Isaiah returned to earth from someplace. Rosenberry looked at him like he thought he was a frigging four-star General.

You couldnt blame him for that. That was the goddam draftee influence, that and the Officer's Extension Course. Rosenberry must have heard about the Officer's Extension Course. He must have. The whole Compny had heard about it. Only, with Rosenberry, instead of needling him about it to relieve their own baffled surprised disappointment, like the rest of the Company, Rosenberry kept it inside that quietly contained Jewish secret along with everything else he heard saw or felt.

Hell, he thought, maybe he even admires you for it. He's a draftee, aint he?

He would never find out, though, not from that sealed vacuum of quietly contained Jewish secret. It was a secret he would like to unravel someday, just for the exercise, just to see what was inside.

You never will though, he told himself, not as long as he knows you're going to be an officer. He leaned back in his chair and lit a vile-tasting hangover cigarette, wondering suddenly what Prewitt had thought. When Prewitt found out Milt Warden was going to become an officer.

As he came out of it and his eyes refocused themselves, he found himself staring at the Morning Report Book that Dhom had fouled up for him. Pass the buck, pass the buck, he told himself angrily. Let somebody else do it.

Well, Warden, what are you going to do? You got to do something. That Dhom, if he'd only learned himself to speak good grammar he would probly be a Major today, he had all the other qualifications. The no good stupid son of a bitch, he raged furiously as he locked the Book up in his private desk drawer, theres nothing stupider than a stupid German.

He ought to be able to give him ten days or two weeks. Unless something special or unusual came up, like maneuvers. Annual maneuvers would be coming due pretty soon now. But even five days would be that much extra protection, on the records, later on, when he did come back. Because there was not any doubt in his mind that he would come back. Thirty-year-men went over the hill, sure. Often. Thirty-year-men did not desert.

Not because they didnt want to, he thought, because they couldnt. Where the hell was a thirty-year-man going to desert to?

It was possible they might send somebody around from the Provost Marshal's office, but he doubted it. Fatso Judson was not worth that much to the Army, or to the Stockade. Fatso Judsons were dime a dozen in any outfit. There was at least one of them in every company, and usually there were more. The Commandant of the Stockade—

—lets see, he thought going over them in his mind, who was it? He watched an almost endless parade of officers' faces, then his mind stopped the film and backed up to one of them. Thompson, the mental dossier informed him, Major Gerald W Thompson, formerly of the Umteenth Infantry, commanded I Co as a Captain, moved to Battalion Adjutant, on to Regimental Aide-de-Camp, made Major in charge of S-3 Plans & Training, graduated to Post Headquarters and promoted to Commandant of the Stockade; the one whose wife both Holmes and Culpepper use to take up on the Honouliuli trail riding—

—anyway, he thought, still proud the old automatic filing system functioned so perfect, Thompson would already have another Fatso Judson already in stock. And plenty more on the waiting list. We got at least two of them in this outfit: Liddell Henderson and Champ Wilson would both make good Fatso Judsons with a very slight proper training.

No, he did not think anybody would be around. But if they did he would still be covered. The day they came around was the day he would have just discovered Prewitt was gone. And, if they did prove anything, he was still covered. The furlough would cover him. Let Choate and Dhom take the blame, the sons of bitches, they started it. But when a whole compny went stone-deaf and blind on a thing like this you did not have to worry much. Nobody would rat; Dhom and Choate sure wouldnt; the only one who would be likely to rat would be Ike Galovitch, and who the hell would listen to an old nut like Ike who was busted for Inefficiency? But even Ike wouldnt have the guts to squeak in the face of all this opposition.

Having figured it out to his own satisfaction, he crushed out the foul-tasting cigarette that he had not wanted anyway and, on second thought, got up and went to the filing cabinet and got out his bottle that he had been careful to mark with indelible pencil before he left on furlough, and took a big drink for his hangover.

It tasted very thin.

Has that sly quiet son of a bitch Rosenberry been watering my whiskey?

No, it wouldnt be Rosenberry. Not Rosenberry. It was probly more likely that son of a bitch Dhom!

He took another big drink, because it was thin, and then sat back down at his desk, still in the dirty crumpled but prize $120 Brooks Bros. powder-blue tropical-worsted that he had given so much thought to before he picked it to wear on his idyll. He was thinking that that was what a man got for trying to take a little time off. They not only fouled up his Morning Report for him but they watered his goddam whiskey. It was getting so you couldnt trust no son of a bitch any more.

Not even yourself.

The hotel—inn, they called it—had been out in Kaneohe Valley, perched up high on the shoulder of the Koolau Range above the valley where the mountains made their inside-curve to the west to include the Nuuanu Pali. He had selected it very carefully, both for esthetic reasons and because it was the only place on the Island where they could go safely without being seen by somebody, like that sharp-eyed son of a bitch Stark. They had driven over the Pali in the U-Drive to get there, after he had taken her off the boat for Kauai to visit a sister that Holmes had brought her down to and seen her off on. Just like the goddamned iceman who comes in the backdoor as hubby goes out the front to the office. He just barely got her off the son of a bitch before they cast off the gangplank, Holmes hung around for so long.

Karen always loved to drive over the Pali. This time he stopped and pointed the hotel—inn, they called it—out to her in the blue distance haze across the steep drop. It was strictly a tourist hotel—inn, they called it—but in a class with the Halekulani, so that nobody but the most e-lite tourists even knew about it. He had happened to go there once before on a weekend back when he had been working on the Molokai moonlight cruises. That was how he happened to know about it. This time, he had already called up ahead of time and chartered a two-room corner suite on the third (and top) floor with the big windows looking off down across the valley to the sea on one side and right back into the mountains on the other. This time he was going to make sure it was perfect ahead of time. This time there werent going to be any loopholes. It was a beautiful view. It was also very secluded and very exclusive. It was really a very beautiful hotel—inn, they called it. The Haleiolani Inn. That meant Truly Heavenly House Inn, in Ka Beretania. There was always wind in Kaneohe Valley, but it had big trees around it so that you could utilize even the wind. It had a park-garden, too. And stables. This time it couldnt help but be perfect. This time it couldnt possibly have any loopholes. This time he meant to seal every chink by which the world could seep through ahead of time.

One of the first things she wanted to know was how he had ever come to know about such a lovely place that was so exclusive and expensive. He gave her some answer, he couldnt remember what, but it didnt make much difference. The motif for the next ten days was already set.

They had two luxurious rooms with eight luxurious walls and the world was not anywhere in evidence. Even during the meals they ate in the dining room to break the monotony of having them all sent up to the suite the world was still not anywhere in evidence, neither in the soft-spoken maître nor the softer-footed waiters and busboys. He even had the hotel—inn, they called it—on his side. They made their living holding the world back out of evidence.

They went riding a number of times back in on the mountain trails. She loved to ride.

They went driving in the U-Drive almost every evening.

Twice they went swimming in the afternoon at Kalama Beach.

And at no time, no where, no how, was there ever any relief from the two rooms and the eight walls. The eight luxurious walls of the two luxurious rooms that he had very carefully sealed so the world could not get in. He had sealed it all right. He had sealed it so tight it would have made a wonderful tomb. In fact, that was just what it resembled, an airtight worldtight wonderful tomb. What he had overlooked was that after he sealed it they had to open the door to get into it. They brought the world inside with them. By the time the ten days was up he could not remember ever having hated any one place so much in his life.

Perhaps if they had had more money now . . .

But no. It wasnt the money. He still had over $300, over half of the original $600 left. And it had been hard work, it had been labor, to be able to spend that much, with her giving him holy hell for being so extravagant, just like a wife.

Perhaps if they had had more time then . . .

But no, it wasnt the time either. If anything they had had too much time. Before the third day was over it was all both of them could manage to do just to keep from suggesting that it was time to go home. It had been hard work, it had been labor, for him to keep from paying the bill and packing them up and going home early from what had turned into the debacle of the annual vacation, just like a husband.

What had happened, ironically, was that the fact that they had had to stay hidden for fear of meeting somebody who knew them, had, without their realizing it, approximated on this honeymoon the situation that would exist when the honeymoons were all over, just like a husband and wife.

They were always making each other pay for something. You hurt my pride and I hurt your pride. It use to be you build me up and I build you up, but once the masterpiece had been made it was you tear me down and I tear you down.

She made him pay for having made her love him so much that she had gone off and left her son in the care of a gook maid.

He made her pay for having made him love her so much that he had run out and left his Company in the sausage fingers of Dhom.

She made him pay for having made her a whore.

He made her pay for having made him an officer.

The eight luxurious walls of the two luxurious rooms were still eight walls and two rooms. And sixteen walls and four rooms, or thirty-two walls and eight rooms, even with a furnace, even with an American Kitchen, garbage disposal unit, automatic dish washer, fully equipped bar, glassed in breakfast nook, even with a Bendix washing machine and a rumpus room, it would not in the end really make a whole hell of a lot of difference.

No matter how often you changed that part, the rest would always still be the same forever and ever amen if there be any man present who can show just cause why this man and this woman should not be united in holy matrimony let him speak now or forever hold his peace.

So this is what married life is like, hunh? his mind said.

The masterpiece was made, created. When you go on creating on a masterpiece that is already created you dont make it more of a masterpiece, you unmake it. You go on spending the rest of your life changing semi-colons to commas and commas to semi-colons.

So this is what you are condemning us both to? his mind said. Me, your best friend?

They both knew it. It was just that neither wanted to be the first to admit it because they both felt too guilty about always making each other pay for something. Besides, they didnt have any other blueprint to go by. They told you love was the end. But love wasnt the end. But they didnt tell you where to go next. If only they could stop and not go on creating. But who ever saw a human being who could stop and not go on creating?

Married life, his mind told him indignantly, appears to be vastly similar to the bracketing in of a battery of 155's. First a long that goes over, then a short that goes under, then a long and a short and a long and a short, a see and a saw and an up and a down, each a little bit closer to target, until finally we are in and we lay down our barrage and we're married. A constant roaring, marriage, in which the individual explosions are no longer even distinguishable so that it itself even finally tapers off into monotony and boredom, leaving only a charred churned-up countryside in which there is nothing alive anymore. Not even the parakeets that once rose up in white clouds screeching out of the jungle, every time a bracket shell dropped. The bracketing-in always use to be fun, remember? But laying a barrage, that begins to wear after a while. Whether you're the Artilleryman on the guncrew, or the Infantryman lying out under it. Even the excitement of almost dying loses its appeal after a while and subsides into just gloom.

The only real relief either one of them had got from the other in the whole 10 days was the night they went in town to the luau.

That was, of course, if you did not count the whiskey, the case of I. W. Harper he had bought the first day in town while waiting for her, and that she had given him hell for buying, but which later on she had drunk at least half of, sitting in the two luxurious rooms with the eight luxurious walls.

During the past three or four months, his mind grinned sardonically, in which you have been so busy, having had nothing else better to do, I have occupied myself with making a searching and profound study of the institution of married life as practiced in these United States, somewhat in the manner of the psychiatrists who write those articles for the *Ladies' Home Journal*. Oh, yes; dont look surprised; didnt you know; sex is an open topic in the United States now. Would you care to hear my conclusions?

He, Warden, had never seen her drink so much. Usually she drank very little if any. She did not even like for him to drink much. This time she ended up by getting as drunk or drunker as often or oftener than he did, and he resented it. Not only had he needed that whiskey himself, but it frightened him. He did not want a wife who was going to turn into an alcoholic anonymous. He did not want to have to add that guilt onto all of the other guilts. He must have overlooked something. He must have made some mistake.

My conclusions, his mind went on anyway, are that marriage in the United States is based upon the principle of romantic love. Not wholly, of course, but in the majority; you will agree that the majority in the United States accept the principle of romantic love. They accept it so strongly, in fact, that even the minority who marry for other reasons such as money or social position or business or just plain security still strive to give the impression of having married for romantic love. This is, incidentally, perhaps the only country in the world where that is true, even among the most ignorant lower classes of peasantry, if you discount England. Myself, I always discount England. Well, by personal observation and careful experimentation, during these three or four months I had nothing to do, I have finally isolated the virus of the illusion of romantic love. My conclusion, in this paper, is that the epidemic of romantic love which is threatening to decimate the United States is the direct result of a viscid vicious virulent virus, or infection, which, for lack of a better name, I shall call Ego-stimulation; or, naming it after its discoverer, Warden's Bacillus.

By way of proof, his mind said, let us take a case in point. Let us take a hypothetical young female aged 18 and a hypothetical young male aged 19, both you understand of the acceptedly superior type considered most likely to succeed (both in life and in love), such as, say, a-football-hero-recipient-of-the-DAR-medal and a straight-A-girls'-college-prep-major-who-also-doubles-as-cheer-leader.

If we take, his mind said, this hypothetical young couple, at the beginning of their—

"Oh, go fuck yourself!" Warden hollered.

He got the bottle out of the filing cabinet again and drank, this time not because it was thin, but in pure self-defense. If a man could just hang onto one illusion he could still love. The main trouble with being an honest man was that it lost you all your illusions.

Penetrated by a sudden cunning idea, he set the bottle up in plain sight on the corner of his desk, instead of putting it back in its hiding place. Then he leaned back in his chair still in the dirty, crumpled, prize $120 Brooks Bros. tropical suit and cocked his feet on the desk and grinned at the innocent bottle slyly. He locked his arms behind his head and settled back hopefully to wait for that Chicago stupid Jew lawyer son of a bitch Ross to come in. Maybe that was the ambulance chasing bastard that had been watering his whiskey.

The very least he can do is transfer me. Maybe he'll even bust me, he thought hopefully, he busted Ole Ike, dint he?

Chapter 47

If it could only all be like the luau had been, all the time, Warden thought with his feet cocked on the desk and his head cradled in his locked fingers. That was what it ought to be like. The luau had been on the eighth night. He had been desperate, even to suggest it. And she had been even more desperate to accept. Because this was a tourist luau in Waikiki and like as not they would run into somebody one or both of them knew. But they hadnt run into anyone. They had gone into town to the luau and each taken a new lover, and gotten the only real relief either one of them got from the other during the whole 10 days.

The fact that the new lover she took was named Warden, and the new lover he took was named Karen Holmes, that did not matter.

It was a tourist luau, not a real one, but after a few drinks it was practically just as good and you did not mind the fat white vacuum-cleaner faces watching, or the neatly pressed jackets and pants catching the light from the fire whitely. The tourists had all read Somerset Maugham, as preparation for their trip to the tropics, and went in for white linen suits and dresses. But you did not mind, not after a few drinks. Because everything else was there, just like in a real luau.

The long ditch with the fire dying down on the hot rocks and the black Kanaka kuke with skin catching red glints from the bonfire putting his layers of banana leaves in the kapuahi ditch to lay the food on, and then the music and hula dancing while the smells began to fan out from under the scorched banana leaves' smell in the still breeze bringing a flood of water into the mouth—the pipi oma roastbeef, and the roasting puaa with a big ohia in his mouth and the pink scrubbed skin beginning to crisp brown (*pig-skin and poi, pig-skin and poi*), the heikaukau rock crab and welakaukau Hawaiian hot stew in the calabashes cooking. And in front of you the poi and kukui nuts and the i-a paakai salt fish, i-a uahi smoked fish, i-a maloo dried fish, i-a hou raw fish, fish fish fish (*pig-skin and poi, pig-skin and poi*), and the fruits, papaya, pineapple, malala, peels of raw cane—all this just to chew on while you waited for the real dinner (*pig-skin and poi, pig-skin and poi*) to get itself cooked. And all the time firelight flickering on naked bronze bodies as the greased muscles rippled under the koa trees in the hula.

The only luaus she had ever seen were the put-up jobs at Schofield for the officers. She had never seen the kane hula dancers whose masculine grace and swift agile angularity, savage and powerful, outshown and dimmed the hip-swinging wahine dancers as much as the ballet's *Spectre de la Rose* outshone and dimmed a walkathon. She had never seen the pi-le noseflute either, or the little-tom-tom that they played with the knees and elbows sitting crosslegged. She had never eaten pig-skin and poi. And this place in Waikiki with its stone wall hiding the glade just across the street from where Kuhio Park narrows in to the highway seawall, she had never even heard about.

The real dishes, the others, the old ones that smelled like feces until you had ignored your nose and gotten them into your mouth and then forever after never smelled that way again, and that were not on this menu, she did not miss because she did not know about them. And if the songs they played and danced here were mostly songs that the tourists would already know—*Song of the Islands, Sweet Leilani, Lovely Hula Hands, Hilo March* and *Kahala March, Hanakai Tomboy,* and the *War Chant*—still, she did not know because she had never heard the old ones, the ancient ones, like we use to play at Tony Paea's family luaus, old Tony, who ran a battery shop on Nuuana, and whose father Ioane Paea had once been sole owner and proprietor of the Island of Paea, before the missionaries. Old Tony was somewhere Stateside now.

She had really taken it all in, eaten it up. And by the time the roast whole hog and pipi oma roastbeef had been finished off everyone was drunk, even some of the tourists were drunk, and he had stripped off his gook shirt and kicked off his sandals and rolled his slacks up to his knees and jumped out into the firelight and danced *Meliani Oe* for them with a gardenia snatched from the hair of the youngest wahine stuck over his ear, and that had really gotten her. With the grinning dancers who could not keep from forgetting they were paid entertainers egging him on solo, the seated ones beating time on the ground with their hands, the standing ones stamping it with the feet.

It made quite a sensation. Not many white men could dance the hula at all, let alone dance it well. But he had learned well, what old Tony had taught him better. And he had the figure for it, if I do say so as shouldnt.

And then when he came back grinning and put the gardenia in her hair, just as a gesture, just to carry it on out. And the fat-faced tourists whispering to each other about the crazy haole wondering who he was must be from old Island family who appeared to be more savagely Hawaiian than the Kanaka natives. Natives, he grinned, who would go back tomorrow morning to their jobs as waitresses at Walgreen's and mechanics in some auto paint-and-body shop on Nuuanu with very unnative haole hangovers and the tourists if they went into Walgreen's for a coke or stopped to get their carburetor fixed would not even recognize them.

"You're always full of surprises," she had smiled. "You're always coming up with something. You just love to shock people, dont you? Where on earth did you ever learn to dance like that?"

And when they got back to the hotel—inn, they called it—that night, it was again like it had once used to be, hot biting wiggling sweating savage, her playing the White Goddess again and him the savage. Like he liked it. But like it had not been very often lately now for a long time, and like it was not to be again, after that one time, during the rest of the last two days.

"*My* savage," she had whispered biting gently. "My primitive crazy savage."

The next night, the last but one, he made the mistake of trying to get it back again. He called her His Chippy, *My* Chippy, as he had done before; but this time she not only pushed him off but flounced out of the bed crying and after a seeming endless period of name-calling in which the worries about the kid came out again ("What if he should get sick? How would I find out? Here, shacked up with another man in a hotel like a common whore? What if he *died*? Would you care? Yes, a lot you'd care!") ended up by sleeping in the other bed. Just like bundling in the old days, he had thought wanting to beat his fist into the wall, bite blood from his knuckles with the frustration of being unable to say one word that did not sound guilty and apologetic, except that now instead of a board inbetween we have this rocklike silence.

It was during those last two days, when he had been very angry about his slacked Morning Report, that he had told her the full story of Prewitt including Fatso Judson and the whore Lorene from Mrs Kipfer's with whom he was in love, to let her know for once how the other half lived. And even he was surprised at how greatly concerned she had been, concerned enough to cry, which only made him love her, goddam it, that much more.

My point, his mind said, the apex of *my* conclusions, is that the illusion of romantic love, being an illusion grounded on the principle of you build me up and I build you up, cannot last through the years of you tear me down and I tear you down. Thats why the men step out and the women take to religion.

But as long as you can *keep* the illusion, he argued grimly, you can *love*. And if you've *got* the illusion, then by god you *do* love. Reality or no reality.

True, his mind said, coolly. And marriage is the great illusion breaker. You dont believe me, try it.

I intend to, he told it.

You see, it said, the foundation principle behind the illusive principle of Romantic Love—the Reality, in other words, behind the Fantasy —is Love of Self; which, up to the time of this paper, has remained undiscovered.

Probably, Warden said, thats because the illusion has received such general recognition and acceptance through the medium of commercial advertizing?

Yes, it said indifferently. Now, to get back. What you really love, then, is Milt Warden. As long as she builds you up and makes you love Milt Warden more, because he is such a fine outstanding man, you love her too, naturally. Because she *makes* you a finer better man. *But,* when she begins to tear you down and make you love Milt Warden less, because he's such an obvious no good son of a bitch, you naturally dont love her near so much any more. Because you *arent* such a nice person any more. And eventually, when it keeps on long enough, you dont love her any more at all. Its really very simple, once you understand it.

All right, Warden said impatiently. But whats to keep two people from just building each other up indefinitely.

Well, his mind frowned, its a little hard to explain to a layman. Theoretically, there is nothing. But in practice it gets rather repetitious. It gets rather hard to keep on inventing new compliments. Eventually, you reach a saturation point beyond which you can do no more than repeat. Naturally, the other party gets suspicious, if not actually bored.

A pretty picture, he said. You leave me a very pretty picture. Okay, you've diagnosed the ailment, how about the cure?

You misunderstood, his mind said. The subject of this paper is the isolation of the virus. We are not attempting to lay out a course of treatment.

Well, thats fine, Warden said. Thats just fine. You prove to me I'm dying from a disease, and then tell me its incurable.

Well, his mind said, the isolation of the virus opens several avenues of approach. We have a few ideas we're working on—

Better, he said, to have let me died in blissful ignorance.

I thought you were a man who liked to know the facts? his mind said stiffly.

Facts, hell! How do you think I'm going to tell her the facts?

Thats your problem. Of course, it said, there is always the possibility that she already knows the facts.

Yes, he said, thats just what I'm afraid of.

To date, his mind said, the only known path of recovery from the disease of love is to get married.

You mean, just let it wear itself out.

Thats it.

And walk on crutches the rest of your life.

Well, his mind said, at least you wont be dead.

Give me polio any time, he said.

Well, his mind said, I guess I'll sign off now. If I find anything new I'll let you know.

Well, thanks, he said. Well, thanks a lot.

Think nothing of it. Glad to help out. Well, pau for now, it said.

He sat on in the chair alone, wondering if this was how a man felt whose doctor has just told him he has cancer, and waiting for mortageforecloser Ross to come in.

He wondered if the man with cancer also would worry most of all about how to tell his wife?

Even whiskey had no medicinal value for this disease. Hadnt he just tried two days of it?—because he was afraid to go down to Mrs Kipfer's for another shock treatment? That showed how far gone he was.

You're nothing but a husk, Milt, he told himself, and took another drink. A dried up eaten out empty husk. Not so long ago he had at least been able to get temporary relief in a whorehouse. Now he could not even do that, because he was afraid of ruining his reputation with a fiasco.

Back in the old days, before the moral United States got a throttle-hold on the literary world, they used to write quite a bit about fiascoes. It was quite a subject, then. Now, they did not write about them any more; either because fiascoes were less frequent, which he doubted; or else because they were considered more shameful, which he suspected. After all, you could not propagate the race with fiascoes; and today propagating the race was of the utmost importance, in Germany and in Russia and in the USA, because where the hell are we going to get the manpower for the *next* war, after this one's done, unless we propagate the race?

Why dont you write a paper on that one? he told it. A lot of people would like the answer to that one.

But there wasnt any answer from the gallery.

In fact, when you thought about it, just about the only consolation for this disease was the fact that it was not a rare one. That you were not the only one who suffered from it.

Well, lets wait and see what litigationprolonger Ross has got to say. He's about the only hope thats left.

Lt Ross, when he came in, did not say anything. He ignored the bottle sitting in plain sight on the desk. He moved around the orderly room, shaking hands with his new 1st/Sgt, talking to get acquainted, and taking no notice whatever of either the whiskey or the crummy $120 Brooks Bros. suit or the three days stubble of beard on his 1st/Sgt's jaw.

The dirty kosher schmuck a mingia, Warden thought. He knows goddam good and well he cant run this fucking Compny without me. For two cents I'd offer the schlemiel a drink; then he'd have to notice it. Kotz, Warden said to himself throatily, letting it lie on the back of his tongue like butter. Kotz; kotz. The shithead.

"I've got something for you, Sergeant," Lt Ross said, apparently feeling he was sufficiently acquainted. He pulled a paper out of his pocket. "Instead of taking the full correspondence course for Reserve Officer's Training, they are going to let you just take this examination. Because of your service, and experience, and rank; and because Col Delbert wrote a letter asking that in your case they waive it." He paused, smiling expectantly.

Warden did not say anything. What did they expect him to do? scream with joy?

"Here is a copy of the examination you will take next Monday," Lt Ross went on, laying the paper out on the desk. "Col Delbert sent it over for you to glance over and told me to give it to you with his compliments."

"Thanks," Warden said lazily, without looking at it. "But I wont need it. Hows about a drink, Lieutenant?"

"Why, thanks," Lt Ross said. "I dont mind if I do. Col Delbert said you'd probably say that. He said you probably wouldnt want it or need it, but he thought it would be a good idea to bring it over anyway, just to let you know we're all back of you."

Furiously, indignantly, outraged, Warden watched him calmly take the bottle off the desk and uncork it.

"It tastes a little thin," Lt Ross said.

"Some son of a bitch is been watering it while I was on furlough," Warden said, staring hard at him.

"Thats too bad," Lt Ross said.

Warden grinned at him. "You know," he said lazily, "I'm surprised at the Great White Father Delbert. I thought old Jake would be doin everything he could to screw me out. Instead of tryin to help me. Especial what with this feud him and Holmes been having the past three or four months."

"From what I can gather," said Lt Ross, "the Colonel thinks very highly of you as a soldier. Much too highly to let a thing like a personal disagreement stop him from pushing your application, when he thinks you deserve it."

"And," Warden grinned, "when it'll be a feather in his bonnet if I make it."

"Yes," Lt Ross grinned. "And in mine, too."

Warden did not say anything. There was not anything else left to say. He stopped grinning and stared at Ross, but that didnt do any good either. Apparently it was going to be just like with Sgt Wellman back in A Co, who put in for the OEC last January; every officer in the battalion helped him with his correspondence lessons. Wellman who didnt know a squad column from a skirmish line; now he was a hotshot 2nd Lt down in the 19th.

"Thats too bad about your whiskey, Sergeant," Lt Ross said, looking at his watch. "Well, I guess I better be getting on up to the Club for lunch. I'll see you later on this afternoon. If you have any questions about that exam paper, you just ask me. I'll try to answer them for you."

Warden sat up after he was gone and picked up the copy of the exam. No wonder they had such stupid shitheads for officers, if they give them such childish examinations as this. He knew the answers to these questions before he even finished reading them. If you have any questions, he minced, you just ask me. Shit. He stuffed the exam in his pocket and turned to watch Lt Ross through the window, crossing the quad in his bent-kneed back-bobbing shambling walk, his uniform hanging from him dismally. Picture of a soljer. The son of a bitch walks like a goddam ragman. Or a plow jockey. Looks like a ragman, too.

A gentleman, he sneered, a gentleman. Manners, no less. Politeness he's got. His old man is probly a pork packer on Millionaire's Row or something. He took the bottle off the desk and put it back in the filing cabinet. Them and their goddam examination papers.

But that night, while Pete was off visiting some sidekick in the 27th, he looked over the copy of the exam again in his room. And Monday morning, when he went over to Regiment to take it, he sat right down and wrote them off contemptuously. Then he tossed the paper contemptuously on the desk of the 2nd Lt who was acting as timer and walked out, with over half of the two hour time limit still to go, feeling the Lt staring after him incredulously.

It was when he got back to the Orderly Room that morning that Rosenberry handed him the Department Special Order decreeing that the annual fall maneuvers would start on the 20th, two days hence.

He carried Prewitt present on the Morning Report until the morning they left, before he finally picked him up as absent. He had been able to give him an extra week. If there was ever any investigation about Fatso Judson, that ought to cover him. Anyway, it was the best he could do.

The evening before they pulled out, on the strength of a hunch, he went down to the Blue Anchor Cafe on King Street two doors from Mrs Kipfer's New Congress which had been the Company hangout ever since he got in the outfit, both because it was cheap and because it was two doors from Mrs Kipfer's—The Blue Chancre, they called it in the Company. There was nobody there tonight; they were all home getting ready to move in the morning. He waited four hours, swilling straight shots with beer chasers, and talking to Rose the Chinese waitress.

Prewitt did not show. Rose said she could not remember that he had been there, not for long time now. But then, Rose wouldnt have told him if he had. She and Charlie Chan the bartender-proprietor knew fully as much about the personal affairs of G Company as its Company Administration ever did. At one time or another Rose had been shacked up with almost every noncom in the Company. Sort of a community wife.

Somehow, he had had a hunch Prewitt might show up down there. He might never come back to the Post, but he wouldnt be able to stay away from news of the Company for ever. So, logically, the Blue Chancre would be the place he would head for. It was only a hunch.

He knew it was a wild last-gasp shot in the dark. In the morning they moved out for the beaches and he dropped him for rations and picked him up AWOL on the Morning Report.

Lt Ross, who was having a nervous time with his first maneuvers and did not know Prewitt from his name on the roster, was very angry about it at first. He wanted to court martial him. Warden had to explain to him that Prewitt was probably drunked up lying in somewhere with a wahine and would probably show up at the Hanauma Bay CP in a day or two, before he would accept Warden's idea of Company Punishment. Lt Ross was trying hard to learn the ways of the Regular Army. He laughed, and relented.

Warden could teach him a lot, he said, if he wanted to, during these next two months before his commission came through.

That was true, Warden agreed, aware that this was only a holding action. If Prewitt didnt come back, it wouldnt mean anything. What he was hoping was that the maneuvers would bring him in. Prewitt would know about the maneuvers; everybody in Hawaii always knew about maneuvers. On an island the size of Wahoo the annual maneuvers were almost as much of a territorial holiday as the Army Field Day in April. Truck convoys moved through town stopping traffic, and details set up machineguns at all the important civic installations, and other details laid road blocks on all the highways, and the bars in town always did a land office business. An old soldier snorts over maneuvers like an old firehorse snorts over a dry-run fire.

Warden went about setting up his CP at Hanauma Bay and waited, wondering why it was he was bothering so much about a common fuckup. Maybe he was losing his touch. He was getting as sentimental as Dynamite Holmes. He must be, to go out of his way to try and save the neck of a man he had called clean for a fuckup the first day he came in the Company.

Yet somehow there was something else. Prewitt seemed to hold the key to something. He felt if he could save Prewitt he would be saving something else. A something that if it was saved would provide the justification for still something else. Prewitt had become a symbol to him of something. When he did not show as the days passed and Lt Ross's good-humored leniency got thinner and thinner, Warden found himself taking it almost as hard as if it really meant something to him personally.

Probly its because you feel guilty about becoming an officer, he told himself. Probly thats all it is.

He decided he was staying away because he still thought they were looking for him for Fatso. That must be the reason. But how to get word to him that that was blown over? You couldnt, unless you knew

666

where he was. And you couldnt look for him, not with the maneuvers on and you out in the field.

The maneuvers started out to be pretty much the same as last year, and the year before that. It was the same old stuff. They moved out in the trucks to the beach and set up the MGs according to the Defense Plan and settled down to wait till they were called into action. G Company's sector of beach ran from Sand Island in Honolulu Harbor east clear to Makapuu Point and included Waikiki Beach and the estates along Black Point and Maunalua Bay. It was one of the choicest sectors on the rock; Waikiki had the best bars on the rock and the Black Point estates had the most wahine maids, and most of the maids had their living quarters right there on the estates. But since the whole Company knew they would be pulled off and relieved by the Coast Artillery as soon as the reds landed they did not get very excited.

This year the master plan was built around the landing of an enemy assault force at Kawela Bay on the north end of the island. The 27th and 35th with the 8th Field were the red attacking forces; the 19th and 21st, together with the rest of the Field Artillery and all the Coast Artillery, were the white defensive forces. The reds landed the third day. At the very least it took two days to lay the groundwork with even the most amenable wahine maids. G Company, instead of laying groundwork, made a 35-mile forced march up Kamehameha Highway through Wahiawa to Waialua where it made rendezvous with the Regiment and took up defense positions. They dug slit trenches all the next day and the day after were picked up by trucks and carried around by back roads in the dust to the other side of the island while another outfit took over their slit trenches. At Hauula, five miles below Kahuku where the main white line rested, they went into reserve. In an open field with no shade they dug more slit trenches and set up a bivouac that could have passed, and did pass, a regular full field inspection. They stayed there the rest of the two weeks and did nothing. It was the same old stuff. A typical maneuvers. They played cards and talked about how they wished they were back on the beach positions and compared notes on wahine maids and waited till word came that the battle was all over and the enemy all repulsed or captured and then they broke camp and piled into the trucks to go home where, if there was not a plethora of wahine maids, there were at least showers.

Then it changed, and was not a typical maneuvers any more. The trucks, instead of taking them back to Schofield, took them back down to their beach positions from which the Coast Artillery had already gone home to Fort Ruger. Other trucks, from Schofield, arrived simultaneously and unloaded piles of picks and shovels and axes, sacks of cement and mortar hoes. One truck even unloaded thirty Barco gasoline-driven jackhammers.

667

Nobody knew what the hell for.

As if in answer, orders came down through channels that they were to construct pillboxes on all their positions. At the time they were still sleeping in the shelter tents used on maneuvers, but before they could bitch about it still other trucks arrived from Schofield with both pyramidal tents and the cots to put in them. They already had their mosquito bars; in the field on Oahu you always had your mosquito bars. And instead of temporary bivouacs the beach positions suddenly became permanent encampments.

Warden went about setting up his CP at Hanauma Bay for the second time, still with no Prewitt, but forgetting that now. Even in the memory of the old Island men like Pete Karelsen and Turp Thornhill, nothing like this had ever happened before.

Up to then they had always moved onto the beach, set the MGs up in the open, and slept on the sand in their blankets—or, if they were lucky like Position #16 on Doris Duke's estate, in a beach cabana with the compliments of the estate's manager (Nobody ever even saw Doris). That was the way it had always been, and that was the way they had assumed it would always be. That an enemy naval force could blow them to hell sitting out there in the open like that, long before it started to send barges in, they fully realized; and, knowing the Army like draftees will never know it, that was just what they expected to happen if the Island was ever attacked. But as long as there were bars to sneak off to and so many Americanized gook girls around to invite onto the position to inspect the awesomely lethal machineguns, they didnt give a damn one way or the other. Anyway, who the hell was ever going to attack this island anyway? The Japanese?

Showing them the MGs was an inspiration. It was practically irresistible. In addition to the awesomeness of the potential death in them there was the intriguing mechanical mystery of an unknown machine function that no American black brown or white can ever resist tinkering with to find out how it works. And with the hard cases you could even let them sit down behind the gun and swing it on the pintle and pull the dead trigger. Not even a virgin wahine could resist that. A haole girl, yes. But not a wahine, because in spite of the absolute triumph of American mechanics, plus all the efforts of the self-chosen-missionaries, American morals had come no nearer to winning a victory in the Islands than had American standards of comfort, so that they did not even mind being screwed in a shelter tent on the sand.

Rumor had it that the rest of the Infantry outfits were doing the same thing and building pillboxes on their positions, but G Company was getting more ass than it had ever gotten before in its history, in spite of the work. Not to mention all the pints and fifths they gave the wahines the money to buy for them, or that if they were broke the wahines bought and brought by themselves—(the good thing about wahines, Mack, that is different from white women, is that wahines like whiskey with their panipani almost as much as us soljers).

If there was anyone in the Company who wondered at all, it was Milt Warden who was unable to take advantage of the bonanza because of his newly acquired fear of fiascoes. Warden, perhaps alone, wondered if maybe this was finally the beginning? if perhaps somebody in Washington or somewhere had gotten ahold of some information or something that had finally worked its way down through channels. He had always wondered just how they began to begin; nobody that ever wrote about them ever seemed to mention just exactly how they began. But since nobody else said anything about it, he did not bring it up either. Maybe he was just being foolish. Besides, it would be a shame to spoil all the fun that everybody but him seemed to be having.

The job lasted a month. It was a wonderful time, even though there was a strict order against giving passes. In a situation like this who the hell wanted passes? Engineer Companies delivered them ready-cut beams and planking of koa wood that they had cut on the slopes of Barber's Point. All they had to do was dig holes in sand and set beams in them and line them with planking and then put beams over them and line them with planking, and then cover it all up with sand, after they had made sure the MG apertures pointed the right direction. Their nights were their own. The officers hardly ever came around from the CP in the daytime, let alone during the night. The Company took care not to strain themselves with overwork in the daytime, so as not to detract from the nights. In fact, they were usually so hungover and worn-down from the nights that they could not have strained themselves if they had wanted. That was one of the reasons the job took a month. It was a wonderful time.

Another reason the job took a month was Position #28 at Makapuu Head. It was not a wonderful time at Makapuu Head. The thirty gasoline driven Barco drills had been for Makapuu Head. Makapuu Head, a foot under the surface, was one solid rock. Also, the Waimanalo Girls School was eight or ten miles away down in Kaneohe Valley. And, because Makapuu Head was manned by more than a full platoon, instead of just three or four men, there was always an officer there; he even slept there. There were no estates, bars, dwellings, or places of recreation at Makapuu Head—unless you wanted to count the two public outhouses down below on the Kaupo Park beach just opposite Rabbit Island, from which a number of men caught the crabs. All there was at Makapuu Head was the lighthouse out on the Point and the one solid rock, and the Engineers across the highway with the pneumatic drills, digging and blasting into the cliff wall where the highway demolition would be.

Makapuu Head was the most crucial spot in the Company sector. If an enemy landed at Kaneohe, there were only two roads he could take into Honolulu without going clear around the whole island, the Pali road that came down Nuuanu Avenue into town, and Kalanianaole Highway at Makapuu Head. The majority of Pete Karelsen's weapons platoon, under Pete, formed the nucleus of the Makapuu Head complement because they were the best machinegunners in the Company, and there was another whole platoon of riflemen to protect them because they were precious. But now both machinegunners and riflemen worked together side by side with the Barco drills and shovels like a nigger labor battalion. At Makapuu it was definitely not a wonderful time.

Gradually, as the work on one position after another was completed, and Makapuu still made no headway into the one solid rock, more and more men were shifted out there to help cut with Barco drills the one solid rock. Until finally the whole Company was out there, working in eight-hour shifts, around the clock 24 hours a day. A kind of frenzied ecstasy for work got into everybody, particularly the night shifts for some reason, and especially after The Warden made it his headquarters and took to operating a Barco while lashing sarcastically at everybody in a voice that drowned even the stuttering one-cylinder engines. The cooks stayed up all night in shifts voluntarily, to keep them supplied with hot sandwiches and coffee. Even the clerks and cooks took their turns at working the Barcos; Mazzioli, when he came down from Schofield for a couple of days to look around, put on his unfaded fatigues he had hardly worn in a year and displayed his surprisingly good physique naked to the waist on a Barco and it turned out much to everybody's surprise that his old man had been a sandhog on the Holland Tunnel job in New York. It was inexplicable, the whole thing. The men who had been out there from the start wrapped handkerchieves proudly around bleeding blisters and laughed uproariously as the blisters on the hands of the new men began to break.

Maybe somebody would even sing the old soldier's parody of Chow Call.

> We've built a million kitchens,
> For the cooks to burn our beans;
> We've walked a hundred million miles,
> We've cleaned out camp latrines.
> If we ever get to heaven, the angels all will yell:
> Take a front seat, Men of Schofield,
> You've done your hitch in hell.

It turned out to be even more fun than wahines and whiskey, which was fun. Even The Warden's wild driving leadership could not account for it. It was the thing that makes Infantry Companies Infantry Companies, and gives old men who were once soldiers the sentimentality with which to tell stories that bore their grandchildren.

A Barco drill has no trigger like an air hammer and it is twice as heavy because its one-cylinder gasoline engine is built right onto the barrel. When they picked it up to move it to a new spot, they had to pick up the whole vibrating bucking mass, bracing it against a thigh to even hold it, because if you turn it off it takes five minutes to start it again with the spring plunger and you have to move it every minute or so. And the only place on a Barco that you can touch without getting burned, except for the grips, is the gas tank under the handles, and after half an hour of bracing the gas tank against your thigh your fatigue pants leg is scorched rusty brown and all the hair is worn off and burned off your leg. Compared to an air hammer a Barco is an antiquated monstrosity, and if you had asked any of the men who complained because they didnt have air hammers (and all of them did) to trade the Barcos in for them, they would have snorted and said they didnt need air hammers like the goddam Engineers. It was as if they liked burning the hair off their legs, and shaking their back teeth loose when they moved them, and wearing the skin on their hands down to raw meat. It was as if they used them and hated them and loved them and would not have had anything else. It was as if they had never had so much fun in their lives.

And across the road the Engineers with their pneumatic drills digging the demolition listened to them sing and watched them enviously, and they knew the Engineers watched them and laughed and sang even more loudly. Until finally even some of the Engineers, after they got off their own shifts, came over to help.

And in a month it was done, and they laid the brace-steel and poured the concrete themselves for the roofs, and went back to Schofield and garrison soldiering, some of them with a new disease that made it feel like the veins in the shoulders and elbows and wrists were swollen and aching while their fingers and hands and finally their whole arms got tingly numb, a disease that every time they did any work with their hands they would wake up with in the middle of the night and get up and shake their arms back awake while the veins in their joints kept aching a long time afterwards so that they had to go out to the latrine for a Piss Call and smoke a cigarette while they let the aching subside so they could go back to bed, but a disease that they never went on sick call with because they had never even heard of it and did not know it was a disease.

The date was November 28th, 1941.

671

Chapter 48

It was during the same six weeks of grace, from the 16th of October to the 28th of November, while the Company was out in the field sweating their butts off and would have sacrificed a left arm to trade places with him, that Robert E Lee Prewitt began to realize just how necessary being a thirty-year-man was. If you wanted to enjoy being on pass.

It kept coming into Prewitt's mind more and more frequently how he was not a thirty-year-man any more.

He was still pretty sick when the maneuvers started. At least, his side was still sore enough for him to get up in the middle of the night and sit and smoke in the wooden-armed occasional chair by the bed, when the irritated tossing for sleep in the bed got too frustrating. He had learned that trick at Myer the first time his nose had been broken; the sitting up and not *trying* to sleep always relaxed you enough so you could doze in the chair.

But by the time the red forces had made their landing, he was much better. Enough better to discover that the secret of at least 50% of the enjoyment of a pass seemed to be the disagreeable knowledge that soon it would end and you would have to go back.

He knew about the maneuvers, all right. Both girls brought the news home with them from work two full days before the maneuvers even got started. Then there were the newspaper articles that mentioned them and used them, just like last year and every year since the European war started, as a springboard for editorials about the world situation and the possibility of being drawn into war. He read them all. He had taken to reading both newspapers thoroughly, by then.

He did not particularly believe what the newspapers said (excluding the sports page and the comics). What they said did not even interest him; it consumed two hours every morning. It put off his enjoyment of the radio-bar and the record-player and the porch over Palolo Valley for as long as he could make the newspapers last.

The enjoyment of the radio-bar and the record-player and the rest of the furnishings had thinned with the knowledge that he was not going to leave them. He did not enjoy having his own key any more because he never left the house so he could use it. Except at sunset, the porch over Palolo Valley showed exactly the same view all day long, every day, including Sundays, even when he was drunk. All he had left was the newspapers.

Both girls would always still be asleep when he got up, and he would make his own coffee and breakfast and then go into a huddle with the papers on the breakfast-nook table in the midst of the crumbs. Usually, he could make them last until the girls got up at noon, if he worked the crossword. Then he would have coffee with them again. With the Sunday papers, which lasted until three or four in the afternoon, he felt like a veritable rich man.

The newspapers did not say anything at all about the construction of the beach position emplacements after maneuvers ended. So he did not know about that until he finally went down to see Rose and Charlie Chan at the Blue Chancre. But the newspapers did give him an idea.

He went on a reading jag. It was the second real reading jag in his life. The first had been when he was laid up in the hospital at Myer getting over the clap that the rich girl had given him. They had had a good, though small, library at the Myer hospital and he had read his way through almost all of it with a dictionary at his elbow mainly because there hadnt been anything else in the GU ward to do. Reading, he had found, was like with pain, or a delicate appetite; you minced your way around the outside tasting this dish and that and getting more and more irritable. And nothing suited you, until you had made up your mind to promise yourself you would read every word on every page. Once you got yourself started and into it you werent irritable any more and it was kind of fun, in a way.

He did that with every book in Georgette's Book of the Month Club collection, even the bad ones that did not sound true to life, at least not as he had become acquainted with life. But he was willing to give them the benefit of the doubt since obviously he had not known every kind of life (like, the life of the rich, say) and anyway, if you just shut off part of your mind from asking acerbic questions about this and that and limited yourself to just the words you read in through your eyes, you could almost believe all of them, even the worst ones. Besides, it was a good way to pass the time. Much better than newspapers. And it did not give you a hangover.

He read night and day like that for over two weeks. If the girls got up at noon, or came home from work at 2 AM, they would find him curled up in a book with the dictionary and a drink at his elbow. He had found that three or four drinks made many of them much more believable. He would be so engrossed that the girls never got more than a grunt for an answer.

Alma didnt like it. She would try to talk to him and when he would only grunt and go on reading she would usually end up by going off and sitting in silence on the other side of the room. Sometimes she would play records loudly. Alma very rarely played records.

He ran through Georgette's collection midway in the second week and proceeded to get stinking drunk. There was not another book in the house. He had averaged two, and even three, books a day; without giving any thought to the fact that his stockpile was beginning to run low. He got very drunk. It was while he was very drunk that it suddenly hit him how much Georgette looked like most of the heroines in her Book of the Month Club collection.

When Alma came home from work and found him passed out on the throwrug in front of the divan, she blew her top that had been accumulating since he first went on this reading jag. They had quite a scene and ended up with a compromise. If she would get him books at the library, he would lay off the liquor—at least to the point of getting wall-eyed. Neither she nor Georgette had a card, but she took one out and started bringing them home to him. Most of the ones she brought were mystery stories. Being a murderer himself, he was interested in finding out more about it as far as it concerned murderers themselves, and he read a lot of them but nowhere in none of them—not even in Raymond Chandler, whom he liked best of all—could he find anything that even remotely resembled his own feelings as a murderer, and finally he got tired of looking.

But there was another thing that took him off the mysteries, too. He remembered one day for no good reason how Jack Malloy had always talked about Jack London all the time, and how he had worshipped him almost as much as Joe Hill. The only book of Jack London's he had ever read was *The Call of the Wild*. So he started Alma to bringing home London and went into him really in earnest.

Although he had to use the dictionary more often with London, he could still seem to read him faster. His writing seemed simpler. One day, when he was along toward the last of them, like *John Barleycorn* and *The Cruise of the Elsinore,* he read five in one day. Of them all, he liked *Before Adam* and *The Star Rover* the best because for the first time they gave him a clear picture of what Malloy had meant by reincarnation of souls. He thought he could see now, how there could just as easily be an evolution of souls in different bodies, just like there had been an evolution of bodies in different souls from the prehistoric times like Redeye and those, in *Before Adam*. It seemed to be logical. At least, it did when he was drunk.

It was while he was reading *Martin Eden* that he got the idea to start writing down titles of other books to read, like Martin had done. There were lots of them in London. Most of them he had never heard of. A few he had heard Malloy mention. He wrote down all of them, with the author's name, in the little notebook he had had Alma buy for him. He would look at the growing list as proudly as if it was a Presidential Citation. Before he was done, he would read them all. The next time he ran into Jack Malloy he would be able to talk back instead of just listen.

He did the same thing with a Thomas Wolfe book that Alma brought home on a hunch, writing them down in his notebook as he came on them. But when he had finished that one he found he had so many titles of books he wanted to read that it would take him at least a year of doing absolutely nothing but reading just to get through them.

It was partly that, the hopelessness of ever reading all of them, that brought the reading jag to its end.

The other thing that helped to end it and break it off short was Alma.

She got up early one morning and cornered him in the kitchen before Georgette was up. He was reading another Thomas Wolfe book, the one where the kid went to New York to become a great writer. He never did get to finish it to find out what happened to him. He was sitting behind the table of the glassed-in breakfast nook and could not get out.

"I want to know what you plan to do?" Alma said after she had got a cup of his coffee that was still heating on the stove.

"Plan to do when?" he said.

"Anytime," Alma said crisply. "Now. Tomorrow. Next week. Shut that book and listen to me. What are you going to do?"

"Do about what?" he said.

"About the way things are," she said. "Shut that book and listen to me! I'm getting tired of talking to the front covers of books!"

"Whats wrong with the way things are?"

"Just about everything," Alma said. "I hardly talk to you from one day to another. You look at me as though you were half asleep—like now. As if you hardly knew who I was. I'm Alma, remember? Maybe you've forgotten? It was almost five months since I'd seen you, and then you were hurt."

"Maybe being hurt got to my brain and made me remember," he said, trying to be humorous. It did not come off very well.

"You dont expect to go on living here like this indefinitely, do you?" Alma said brittlely. "I think its time you figured out what you plan to do, dont you? Do you plan to go back to the Army? Do you plan to try to live here and get a job? Do you plan to try to get back to the States? Just what do you plan to do?"

Prew tore off a strip of newspaper to mark his place and pushed the book down the table out of reach. "Frankly, I aint planned anything. Does it make any difference?"

"Ugh," Alma said. "This coffee is horrible."

"Tastes all right to me," he said defensively; her complaint of the coffee, like everything else, seemed to be directed at him personally.

675

"Its been simmering on the stove so long its as muddy and thick as sorghum molasses," Alma said. She got up and threw her cup out and emptied the rest and put a new filter paper in the Silex hourglass and put on water for a new pot.

Prew watched her. Her long black hair was still matted from sleeping and the thin print dressing gown had smudges of powder on it. His hand wanted to reach out and pick up the book again, but it was out of reach and he would have had to get up. He did not feel like getting up. That was why he had pushed it out of reach down the table.

She came back and sat down across from him again.

"Well? What *do* you plan to do?"

"Nothing," he said, wishing now he had got up for the book. "Why worry about it? I'm doing all right."

"Yes," Alma said. "Yes, you are. But in less than a year I'm going back home to the Mainland and home. You're going to *have* to figure out something before then."

"All right," he said. "I'll work on it. A year is a long time off yet. Now why the hell dont you lay off of me?"

"You certainly cant go home with me to Oregon," Alma said coolly, too coolly, "if thats what you're thinking."

He *had* thought about it, sketchily. But he had given it up, even sketchily.

"Did I ask you to go home with you?"

"No," she said, "but I wouldnt be surprised to find you with your bag already—"

"Then why dont you wait till you're ask? Before you start tossing refusals around?"

"Because I dont intend to wake up on the boat and find you in the bed."

"Okay; you wont. Believe me, you wont. Now why dont you relax and wait till that time comes, to worry about me? I said I was doing all right."

"You sure are," Alma snorted. "You've done nothing for the past three weeks but sit around here in a trance and read books and get drunk and make a big play for Georgette. I'd say you were doing fine."

"Is that whats been eating you?"

"Maybe you'd like to live on here and just switch over to Georgette, after I leave, and shack up with her?"

He had already thought of that, too. He had, in fact, thought of a lot of things. But it made him mad to hear her say it out loud.

"Maybe thats not such a bad idea at that," he said.

"Perhaps not," Alma said coolly, "at first glance. But in the first place, Georgette might not be able to keep this place and support you

676

in the style to which you are getting accustomed. It takes both of us to pay for it. And you're already beginning to run me in over my budget."

"We could probly figure something out," he said.

"And in the second place," Alma said, "if thats what you've got in mind, you can get the hell out now and wait till I'm gone before you come back. Because I dont want to live in the same house with such a bad smell. And—if it comes down to it—I think Georgette would prefer me to living with you."

"She probly would," Prew said. "She's known you longer."

"I'm quite sure she would," Alma said. "Completely apart from the fact that I help pay for the house."

"Okay," he said, and crawled out from behind the table and got up. "You want me to leave now?"

Alma's eyes widened perceptibly, and she had to make a big effort to keep from catching her breath. She did not say anything.

Prew watching her in silence, feeling quite proud.

"Where would you go?" Alma said.

"What difference does it make?"

"Oh, be sensible," Alma said, irately.

Prew grinned, knowing that somehow he had suddenly finally gained the advantage. It was getting to be more and more every day like a tight tennis game: your ad; my ad; your ad; my ad.

"Theres lots of places I could go," he said, not wanting to lose it again now that he had it. "I could go on the beach. I might even find another whore in the market for a pimp. I might even turn back in to the Army; they probly dont know I killed Fatso anyway," he lied.

The whore part, of course, did not touch her. It never did. "You'd be putting your head in a noose," she said irritably, "and you know it."

"I might even ship out on a tramp," he said, remembering Angelo Maggio, "and go to Mexico and be a cowboy."

"I didnt mean you had to leave until you'd found someplace to go," she said irritably. "What do you think I am? You know me better than that. You dont have to leave at all, unless you want to. *I* want you to stay."

"You sure as hell act like it."

"Well," she said angrily, "its just that it gets under my skin, seeing you sitting around ogling Georgette all the time, knowing you're figuring your chances of getting in on the inside with her as soon as I'm gone. How do you think that makes me feel?"

"What the hell do you want me to do? Sit around here and be your true love for as long as you feel like staying, and then see you off on the boat when you go home to marry a rich man? You think I like layin around on my ass livin off you so you can throw it up to me every time you get mad at me? What am I suppose to do when you marry the rich guy? go blow my brains out with a broken heart? It seems to me you ask a whole hell of a lot of a man."

"I dont think its too much to ask you to prefer me to other women," Alma said earnestly. "At least as long as I'm here. I know how men are; I ought to. I'm no dewy-eyed virgin Cinderella. I dont expect miracles. But I dont think thats too much to ask."

"Its pretty hard to prefer a woman when she plainly dont want to sleep with you any more."

"Its pretty hard to want to sleep with a man who prefers other women," Alma said. "Especially if he looks at you all the time from a trance as if you're not even there."

"Well?" he said. "Do you want me to leave or dont you?"

She was beginning to gain ground again, and he could always get back the ad there. Because she knew he would do it. He might never win the game with it, but it would take a lot of ad points.

"Oh, sit down and be sensible," Alma said. "No, I dont want you to leave. I already told you that. Do you want me to get down on my knees and beg you?

"But Georgette is my friend," she said, "and if it came down to sleeping with you or keeping my friendship, I think she'd prefer to keep the friendship. You might remember that, for future reference."

He sat down. "But she'll never see you again after you're gone," he said, just to let her know he was not giving ground, "and she knows it."

"After I'm gone," Alma said, "you can do what you want."

"Son of a bitch if you dont demand a whole hell of a lot from a man. I'd rather earn my living soljering, its easier. Only I cant," he said. "You coffee water's boiling."

Alma got up and went to the stove to turn the heat off under the Silex hourglass. Then she stood without saying anything and watched the coffee begin to run back down the spout.

"Oh, Prew, Prew." She turned around. "Why did you have to do it? Why did you have to kill him? We were getting along so fine. Until you had to do something like that. Why did you have to spoil it?"

He was sitting with his elbows on the table and his fists clasped, looking at them. Not staring. Just looking. As if he were examining a tool to see if it was adequate for the job.

"I've always done it," he said simply, neither gladly nor guiltily, but just simply stating it. "I've always spoiled everything I've ever touched all my life. Maybe all men do it," he said, remembering Jack Malloy. "I dont know about that. I know I have. I dont know why, though."

"Sometimes I dont think I even know you," Alma said. "Sometimes you're almost like a complete stranger. When your First Sergeant Warden came down to see me, he said you wouldnt even have had to go to the Stockade. He said you could have gotten off scot free if you'd wanted to."

Prew looked up quickly. "Has he been down there to see you again? Has he? Answer me, goddam you?"

"No," Alma said; "that was the first time, when he told me you were in hock. He's only been there once. Why?"

"I dont know," Prew said, relaxing back on his elbows to look at his hands again. "I just wondered."

"You dont think he'd turn you in, do you?" Alma said. "You cant think that!"

I dont know," he said, looking at the tools his hands. "I honestly dont know. I never been able to figure out if he would or he wouldnt."

"Thats a terrible thing to admit," Alma said.

"You dont understand," he said. "Sometimes," he said simply, "I wish I *was* back in the Stockade."

—Angelo Maggio. Jack Malloy. Blues Berry. Francis Murdock. Stonewall Jackson. The long dark evenings of cigarette-lighted conversations. Between them all they had covered every part of the country. Damn near the whole world.—

"In the Stockade it was easy, it was simple. You had somebody over you that you hated and plenty of time to hate them, and plenty of help hating them, and you did what they told you and just hated them, without having to worry about hurting them any because you couldnt have hurt them anyway."

"After you got out, you didnt even call me up," Alma said. "You were out nine whole days, without coming up to see me or even calling me up."

"I was trying to protect you, goddam it!"

She did not laugh. She felt more like you feel with a child. Since he had got well from the knife wound he did not give her the chance to feel like you feel with a child any more.

"Prew, Prew, Prew," she said and came over to him and pulled his head against her. "Come on," she said. "Come with me."

Prew got up and followed her.

She went into the bedroom.

But it was like too many other times, when they had fought, and made up, and then gone warmly to bed. Your ad and my ad, and every day a Millennium. He could not keep himself from remembering how he was not a thirty-year-man any more. Then, after he had remembered it, he re-remembered it. About the only time he was not remembering it any more was when he was reading a book with three or four drinks in him for convincingness.

Alma knew it. They both knew it. The transparent wall of the trance was back down, and apparently the only way to get under it was to get so mad that the anger cut through it. It was a hell of a way to get close together. They heard Georgette moving around getting up and, afterwards, went back out to the kitchen. Neither one of them cared much about lying in bed, afterwards, any more. They sat in the kitchen and drank the coffee and in the loss of the desire and the superimposed silence they could not break through suddenly felt very old and, in feeling very old, suddenly were much closer and warmer to the other, who was also very old, than they had either one ever felt before in the desire that neither one had any more.

Then Georgette came in friendlily like a big overgrown puppy, but with the big body like most of the heroines in her Book of the Month Club collection and that was covered with only the thin print wrapper whose powder smudges, strangely, instead of being distasteful were rut-and-crotch-sexily enticing.

Alma looked at Prew and then looked away coolly.

Prew tried not to look at Georgette. Even when he talked to her he looked at Alma, or at the stove, or at the tools his hands.

After half an hour of this Georgette got up, looking puzzled and hurt, and went to her room to get dressed. She went out early. She had some shopping to do, she said, and would not be back before two o'clock so she would just go on down to work.

Alma went out early too and ate lunch downtown.

He tried to read after they were gone, but the morning had exploded the myth that was already getting threadbare anyway, and he could not get back inside the book. He could only read it. Even after five or six drinks, he could still only read it. He could not forget to remember how he was not a thirty-year-man any more.

Well, what *do* you plan to do?

Alma had a .38 Police Special Smith & Wesson which one of the local cops had given her for a present that she kept loaded in a drawer of the desk along with a box of cartridges, and he took it.

Whatever else, he did not intend to ever go back to no Stockade no more. Go back to the *old* Stockade, with Angelo and The Malloy and Blues and the rest of them all there like they had been before—yes. But he was not going back to any new Stockade, where they were all gone and there was doubtless a new Fatso Judson, and everything else was changed, except perhaps Major Thompson.

He removed the old cartridges that had probably been in it for years and reloaded it with new ones from the box and put some more of them in his pocket. Then he helped himself to the money that Alma also kept in the desk, and walked down the hill to Kaimuki and caught a Beretania streetcar to town to pay a visit to Rose and Charlie Chan at the Blue Chancre.

It was wonderful to be outdoors again in sunlight and air. His side was still a little stiff but it did not hurt him to walk. He had to wear a jacket because of the .38 Special stuck in his belt, but it was light tropical worsted (Alma and Georgette had bought it along with the slacks and dressing gown) and it had saddle-stitched lapels and he did not mind it even in the sun because he felt very ritzy in it.

He got off the bus a couple blocks up and sauntered down past the alleyway that ran back to the Log Cabin Bar & Grill. It looked just the same as it always had.

There was nobody in the Blue Chancre when he went in. A few sailors drinking beer and trying to make time with Rose who was strictly an Army girl. But nobody from the Company. He sat at the bar and drank whiskey-sodas, so he would not get drunk enough to get noticed and get picked up, and talked to Charlie.

G Company was all out at Makapuu Head building pillboxes, Charlie told him, that was why there was nobody there. Hadnt been nobody here since before the maneuvers started. Place velly dead.

Rose came over and sat down by him after a while and asked grinningly how he liked being a civilian now? It scared him at first, or rather startled him, but he told himself he should of known they would know it, and they both laughed and seemed to think it was big joke and wanted to know how long he planned stay vacation? Nobody mentioned Fatso Judson. He sat and talked to them about the free life of a civilian quite a while.

He did not know just exactly what he had expected. He had expected to find some of the Company there, for one thing. He did not know about the beach positions. He knew it was reckless to show up down there, but he did not expect anyone from the Company would turn him in, unless it would be Ike Galovitch. And Old Ike never went to the Blue Chancre.

He found out from Rose that Old Ike had been busted. It must have happened the day after he left, he figured. And Rose told him about how Warden was up for a commission which, if he had heard it during the nine days he waited for Fatso, had failed to register. The new Company Commander, Rose said, maybe turning out not be such bad joe after all, look like.

The more they talked the more homesick he got. He had to watch himself carefully not to get drunk. He bet they were having a rough time out at Makapuu, building pillboxes in that rock. But the roughness, strangely, instead of making him glad he was out of it, excited him and made him want to get in on it.

He stayed until 9:30 or 10:00 o'clock, eating Charlie's hamburgers cooked out back that were at least one-third cereal, with plenty of onion and mustard, to keep the liquor from getting into him, and telling himself it was the best food he had had in weeks.

681

There were plenty sailors at the six booths and four tables, but almost no soldiers. Hardly any soldier coming town now any more, Charlie said. Rose's latest shackjob, a S/Sgt of Field Artillery, came in; and Rose, with her Chinese eyes and Portagoose nose and mouth and the startling eye-arrestingly beautiful waggling waggling take-a-hold-of-me bottom that seemed to be distinctively peculiar to Portagoose-Chinese girls also, left Prew at the counter and spent her time between beer calls in a booth with the S/Sgt.

Charlie could not talk about anything but how this pillbox job luin the blisness, not like old maneuvels use to be, be plenty glad when him oveh.

It was just before he left that Rose happened to remember how The Warden had been in asking for him, just before maneuvers, the very night before, in fact. She thought it was big joke.

What he want them tell The Warden? if he come back? They both wanted to know.

"Tell him I been here," he said immediately. "Tell him I miss him, I cant hardly stay away from his beautiful face. Tell him I'm lookin for him, too," he added, "and if he wants to see me, this is the best place to look."

They both nodded. They did not look surprised. They were used to screwball soldiers. Him Army. Awys think screwy, Army guys.

He got home around twelve. He had ridden the streetcar again, going home, instead of a taxi. Maybe it was because he felt more like a free man, sitting in the streetcar with all those people, people who could come and go when they pleased without feeling funny every time they passed a cop on a corner. He put the pistol away in the desk drawer, and put the rest of the shells back in the box. He was already in bed asleep when Georgette and Alma got home at two-thirty.

Chapter 49

It was what Rose told him about The Warden that made him go back. He knew it was reckless. Once, just for gossip, that was all right. But any more than once was pushing your luck. He went back anyway.

In all, he went back five times, before he finally ran into Warden. Each time he took the pistol and extra cartridges out of the drawer to take with him, and each time he put them back when he got home. Georgette and Alma did not even know he had been out of the house at all. They noticed he seemed to be in a much better humor lately; but they did not know why.

He was careful to spread the trips out over a period. Somehow, he had a hunch Warden could fix it. If Warden was anything, he was a fixer. So he kept going back doggedly, but to go back two days in a row was pushing your luck too much for even his doggedness.

The first three times he drew a blank because the Company was still out at Makapuu building pillboxes. Charlie was adamant. Charlie was beginning to think this job never get done. Even Rose, when she was not sitting with her S/Sgt of Field Artillery, was worried.

The fourth time he went back was the night of November 28th, the day they got back in from the field, and he ran into a whole bunch of them—tanned, horny handed, cracked nailed, freshly shaved, tough—Chief Choate (a S/Sgt now), Andy and Friday, Sgt Lindsay, Corp Miller, Pete Karelsen, Malleaux the supply sergeant, Scholar Rhodes, Bull Nair, and a bunch of the new draftees. It was funny how quick the draftees in the Company had fallen into the scheme of things and picked up the Blue Chancre as their hangout. They all looked good, even the draftees. The old bunch were all glad to see him. They slapped him on the back as if he had just won the inter-Company track meet single-handed like a decathlon. Stark was not there. He had wanted to see Stark. He had a hard time to keep them from getting him drunk. Warden did not show, and he did not mention him.

But he took a chance and went right back the next night, in spite of the risk. He did not think any of them would turn him in. And somehow he had a hunch; he had more than a hunch, even though none of them had mentioned The Warden either. The same ones were not all there, but the ones who werent there when he arrived were either coming in or going out the rest of the evening, either on their way to or on their way from Mrs Kipfer's or the Service Rooms or the Ritz Rooms or some of the others, because this was an occasion, this was the feast after the six weeks of fasting out in the desert. The Warden was not mentioned this time either.

While he drank beer and watched the door, Prew tried not to think how some of them were either going to or coming from the Ritz where they might have just been in the bed with Georgette. But his hands got sweaty anyway.

He saw Warden, it seemed, almost before he came in sight around the pushed-back latticework of the open front. Warden did not come in. He did not even look in. He sauntered on past and disappeared beyond the other side of the open front. Apparently nobody else in the place saw him at all. Prew waited a couple of minutes and finished his beer, before he went out.

Warden was leaning against the wall at the corner of the alley smoking.

"Well, I'll be damned!" he said. "Look who's turned up."

"Bad pennies," Prew said.

"I thought you'd be back in the States by now," Warden said.

"Did you see Rose?"

"This afternoon. I figured you couldnt stay away forever."

"Listen," Prew said. "Whats the deal?"

"Lets go across the street," Warden grinned. "This is no place to talk unless everybody's got a pass in their pocket."

"I've got my SP Card."

"They've been revoked since the day maneuvers started," Warden said. "And I dont want my draftee chicks to see the 1st/Sgt consorting with awols. They dont understand the Army yet."

He led the way across the street to another identical bar that was identically crowded with other men from another identical company except that this company was from the 8th Field. They ordered whiskey and Warden paid for it.

"Why the hell didnt you come back after maneuvers started?" Warden said disgustedly. "I had it fixed then."

"I couldnt. I was gettin over a cut in my side. Whats the deal about Fatso? Have they got me down for Fatso or havent they?"

"Who's Fatso?" Warden said.

"Fatso Judson," Prew said. "You know who I mean. Fatso Judson. Come on, quit stalling."

"Never heard of him," Warden said.

"You've heard of him," Prew said. "Do you mean *they've* never heard of him? What *do* you mean? Quit playing secret service agent. This is serious, to me."

They were talking in low voices across the low table in the general hubbub of Artillerymen. Warden looked around him once before he spoke.

"I'll lay it all out for you," he said. "Then you can do what you want. But first, you better push that gun down in your belt or else lean over farther. That pistol butt shows through your coat plain as day."

Prew leaned over quickly and looked around before he reached down to push it down.

"Its not a good place to carry it," he explained.

"Hell," Warden said. "It stuck out so plain I could even name it for you. Its a .38 Colts Police Special."

"Smith & Wesson."

"Well," Warden said, "I couldnt see the hump on the handle."

"Well, come on," Prew said. "Whats the deal?"

"You're loaded for bear, aint you?" Warden said.

"I aint going back to no Stockade, if thats what you mean. Come on, goddam it," he said, "quit stalling. Whats the deal?"

"So you finally decided you want to come back after all," Warden said.

"I aint going back to no Stockade."

"You said that before."

"And I'll say it again."

Warden signaled to the waitress for another round for them. "There dont nobody know anything about Fatso Judson. At least they dont connect you with it."

"How do you know?"

"I dont know for sure," Warden admitted. "But there hasnt been anybody around asking about you from the Provost Marshal's office. If they connected you with it, they'd have been around. I'll stake my reputation on that."

"What reputation?" Prew said sarcastically, but already feeling a tenseness begin to relax inside of him.

"My reputation as a lover, you jerk," Warden sneered.

"Then I can come back," Prew said. "Boy. I'll tell you something. I'll never go coon hunting or possum hunting again in my life."

"Theres more to it than that," Warden said. "If you'd of come back the first two or three days after maneuvers started, I could of got you off with a couple weeks extra duty. But you've been gone six weeks since then. Even with a shithead like this Ross, I cant explain that away. You cant get off without at least a Summary Court."

"I aint going back to the Stockade," Prew said quickly. "Not even if I have to hide out on this Rock the rest of my life."

"I'll lay it out for you straight," Warden said narrowly. "I could tell you you get off with a Summary Sentence of two weeks in the Regimental guardhouse, but I wont. If you get a Summary at all, you're lucky. You've been gone six weeks on the records. If you get a Summary at all, you're sure to get the limit."

"One month in the Stockade," Prew said.

"And two-thirds pay," Warden nodded. "And you may even get a Special Court. You already got one offense against you. But if you get a Special, I think I can guarantee you wont get more than two months and two-thirds."

"But I might get the full six."

"No," Warden said. "I can promise you wont get over two. I think I can get you off with a Summary."

"Then I aint going back."

"I dont know what you expected. My Christ, you've been gone six weeks."

685

"I dont know what I expected either. But I know I aint going back to that Stockade. Even for one month. And thats all she wrote."

Warden straightened up in his chair. "Suit yourself. But thats the best I can get for you. Ross is mad because he thinks you took off on him just to get out of maneuvers."

Prew was puzzled. "But what about all the time before that? I was gone a week before maneuvers started."

"He dont know about that."

"But how . . . ?"

"God damn it!" Warden said. "Baldy Dhom carried you present. I was on furlough and he was Acting First and he carried you present. He was still carrying you present when I got back. He had me by the balls and I either had to go back and pick you up retroactive, or else carry it."

"But your furlough was up three days after I left."

"Dont kid yourself," Warden said viciously. "I wouldnt of done it for you. I wouldnt of carried you one single day. You were a fuckup when you got in this compny and you're still one and you'll always be one. I dont know why the fuck I'm down here bothering to talk to you right now."

"Because you're ashamed of being an officer," Prew grinned.

"I've never been ashamed of anything I ever did in my life," Warden snorted. "Includin that. Shame aint a spontaneous emotion; shame is an induced emotion. A man who knows his own mind dont know what shame is."

"What book did you read that in?"

"If I had any brains I never would have fucked off and come down here in the first place."

Prew did not say anything. He did not try to uncover any more of the unexplained four days grace, and he did not try to bore any deeper into what was such an obvious lie. He would have felt ashamed if he did.

"I guess you think I'm ungrateful," he said finally.

"Everybody's ungrateful," Warden snorted. "I'm even ungrateful to myself, for all the favors I do me."

"A man's got to decide for himself what he has to do," Prew said.

"Everybody decides for themselves," Warden said. "And always wrong."

"You aint been in that Stockade. I saw them kill a man in that Stockade. They beat him to death."

"He probly ask for it."

"Whether he ask for it or not aint the point. Nobody's got the right to do that to another human being."

"Maybe not, but they do it," Warden grinned. "All the time."

686

"Matter of fact, the guy did ask for it," Prew said. "But that still dont give them the right to do it to him. He happened to be a friend of mine. Fatso Judson was the man who was responsible for it."

"Dont tell me your worries," Warden said. "I got worries enough of my own. I told you what I could do for you, and thats the best I can do."

"Can you see why I cant go back there any more?"

"I cant see anything," Warden said. "Can you see why I'd be an officer?"

"Sure," Prew said. "I can see it. I'd like to be one myself sometimes. You'd make a good officer."

"Then you can see more than I can," Warden said viciously. "Lets get out of this firetrap."

They pushed out through the surging mass and stopped outside to light cigarettes. Across the street the Blue Chancre was lighted and yelling. The sidewalks were crowded with Men of Schofield. Letting down, letting way down, after six weeks to two months in the field.

They had to stand back against the building to keep from being carried along in the press. From the dark of River Street down at the end of the block to as far up the other way as they could see Beretania was blazing at them with neon and lighted display windows interspersed with the dark stairways of the whorehouses.

"Its pretty," Prew said. "I've always liked neon signs. I like to stand at one end of a street and look at them all strung out down along it. Theres fifty towns in this country that got prettier streets than Broadway. Memphis, Albuquerque, Miami, Colorado Springs, Cincinnati. I like the crowds, too—except when I get in them."

Warden didnt say anything.

"I wish I *could* go back," Prew said. "I *want* to go back. But I cant do any more time, even to go back."

"The only way you'll ever go back without having to do time," Warden said viciously, "is if the Japs or somebody bombs this fucking island and they let all the prisoners out to go fight."

"You're a big help," Prew said.

"You can see what I think of your chances."

"Yeah."

"You'd better stay away from the Blue Chancre," Warden said. "Or anywhere down in here. They've pulled in all the SP cards and Class As. And since maneuvers, they've been checking passes."

"Thanks for the tip."

"Keep the change."

"Well," Prew said, "so long."

"So long," said Warden.

The big man crossed the street to the Blue Chancre and Prewitt turned up Beretania toward town away from the river. Neither one of them tried to look back.

The thing that stayed in Prew's mind as he pushed in and out up the street was what Warden had said about his chances. Fat chances! If they bombed the rock and let the prisoners out! It burned all over him like a fire of gall. Some chances!

As he crossed Maunakea he saw Scholar Rhodes and Bull Nair weaving down toward him arm in arm. They insisted on buying a drink.

"We just come from the Ritz," Nair said happily drunkenly as they stood up to the bar. "Aint as ritzy as Mrs Kipfer's, but thats why I like it better. Them ritzy places gives me the willies."

"I use to go to the Ritz all the time before I got in the Compny," Prew said. "Its good."

"Christ!" Rhodes said dreamily. "It was jest like losin my cherry all over again."

"It was wonderful," Bull Nair said.

"When you coming back?" Nair said, as they came out into the street again.

"I don't know," Prew said. "I aint tired of being a civilian yet."

"Christ!" Rhodes said, still dreamily. "Wisht I had the guts to go over the hill. If I had the money."

"Boy, we really gapped them up to the Ritz," Nair grinned foolishly, "dint we, Dusty?"

Rhodes guffawed. "Yeah, we sure gapped them."

"Lets gap old Prew," Nair suggested.

"Naw," Rhodes said. "My jaws is tard."

"Well," Nair said, "we see you when you git back. Too tard to gap you."

"See you," Rhodes said, still dreamily.

Prew watched them weave away arm in arm, the bitterness of gall burning him fiercer than ever until he wanted to twitch, itching him, where he could not scratch, until he wanted to drive his fist into the face of the first man who came within reach.

When they were out of sight, he turned right and crossed Beretania and instead of going on up to the car stop he went on down the side street. The Ritz Rooms was just down the block.

The Ritz was crowded, and he had to wait quite a while before he even saw Georgette anywhere. His hands were sweating freely and his face was flushed and his throat thick, and the savage wildfire scourged him harder. To hell with it, to hell with all of it, burn it all down, tear it all up, smash all of it.

688

He caught her in the hall, finally, and stopped her. When she saw it was him, she pulled him into an empty room to see what he wanted and find out what was wrong. At first she was embarrassed. Then the embarrassment stopped.

Afterwards, when he held out the money, she laughed and refused it. But when he continued to hold it out to her stubbornly she looked at him and then at the money and that look came back in her eyes and she took it.

When he got home to the house, after the long taxi ride sitting alone in the dark savoring it, he sat up to wait for them, drinking one scotch and soda after another. Have it out right now, get it over with. But he passed out on the living room floor before they got home.

When he got up in the morning and went out to the kitchen to get water for his head, Alma was already sitting at the table over coffee. He could tell by the cool way she looked that Georgette had already told her, either last night when they got home, or else early this morning. He might have known she would; he had expected her to. But he had meant to tell her first himself. Only, he had passed out.

Alma did not say anything to him, either then or later. She did not blow up, or get mad, or anything else. She was very polite. She was warm, and friendly, and she smiled, and talked to him, and she was very polite. She was so polite he could never get his nerve up enough to tell her. She never gave him an opening, and she never referred to it.

So, instead, he moved out onto the divan in the living room.

She never questioned or referred to that, either. She had never treated him so nice since he had known her. They got along fine. Once, during the next week, she came out to the divan and slept with him and then got up and went back to bed and that was very nice too, very polite.

Georgette did not treat him nicer, nor worse. She neither stayed home more often nor went out more often. They all sat around the breakfast nook table in the morning for coffee and talked to each other nicely, and Georgette did not go out early to shop any more like that one time. They were just one big happy family.

It was during that week that he copied down from memory the first verses, and then went on to finish, *The Re-enlistment Blues.*

Rummaging in the desk for paper, one afternoon, he noticed Alma had taken out all the money that she kept there. She had not touched the gun. She did not lock up the radio-bar either. He was drunk most of the time.

He did not care about the money because he had no place to go and no impetus to go there, but he was glad she did not lock up the radio-bar on him. She did not say a word to him about being drunk. She did not ask him to leave either, because he would obviously have no place to go; they had been over that before.

That was the way it went that week.

Somewhere, either out of her silence and politeness, or else out of his own imagination, he got the idea that she had been planning to marry him all along until this happened. He felt like a man who had got his ring back.

Once or twice they got into heavy arguments over nothing, absolutely nothing, like whether St Louis Heights was 483 feet elevation or 362 feet elevation. They would start with something like that, but before they were finished everything would be dragged in. Your ad; my ad; your ad; my ad. He held his own, in these; it was the silence that got him. And he took a lot of ad points with his old threat of just walking out. It still seemed to work just as good as ever.

Even, he thought, if he didnt have the guts to actually do it.

Chapter 50

Milt Warden did not really get up early the morning of the big day. He just had not been to bed.

He had gone around to the Blue Chancre, after Karen had gone home at 9:30, on a vague hunch that Prewitt might be there. Karen had asked him about him again and they had discussed him a long time. Prewitt hadnt been there, but he ran into Old Pete and the Chief; Pete was helping the Chief to celebrate his last night in town before going back into his garrison headquarters at Choy's. They had already made their bomb run on the whorehouses and dropped their load on Mrs Kipfer's New Congress. After Charlie Chan closed up the Blue Chancre, the four of them had sat out in the back room and played stud poker for a penny a chip while drinking Charlie's bar whiskey.

It was always a dull game; Charlie could not play poker for peanuts; but he always let them have the whiskey at regular wholesale prices and if they complained loud enough he would even go in on it and pay a full share, although he drank very little. So they were always willing to suffer his poker playing. They would always overplay a hand to him now and then to keep him from finding out how lousy he was.

When they had drunk as much as they could hold without passing out, it was so late the Schofield cabs had stopped running. They had hired a city cab to take them back because there was nowhere else to go at 6:30 on Sunday morning.

Besides, Stark always had hotcakes-and-eggs and fresh milk on Sundays. There is nothing as good for a hangover as a big meal of hotcakes-and-eggs and fresh milk just before going to bed.

They were too late to eat early chow in the kitchen, and the chow line was already moving slowly past the two griddles. Happily drunkenly undismayed, the three of them bucked the line amid the ripple of curses from the privates, and carried their plates in to eat at the First-Three-Graders' table at the head of the room.

It was almost like a family party. All the platoon sergeants were there, and Stark was there in his sweated undershirt after getting the cooks started, and Malleaux the supply sergeant. Even Baldy Dhom was there, having been run out by his wife for getting drunk last night at the NCO Club. All of this in itself did not happen often, and today being Sunday, nobody was less than half tight and since there had been a big shindig dance at the Officers' Club last night none of the officers had shown up, so that they did not have to be polite.

The conversation was mostly about Mrs Kipfer's. That was where Pete and the Chief had wound up last night, and most of the others had gone there. Mrs Kipfer had just got in a shipment of four new beaves, to help take care of the influx of draftees that was raising Company strengths all over Schofield. One was a shy dark-haired little thing who was apparently appearing professionally for the first time, and who showed promise of someday stepping into Lorene's shoes when Lorene went back home. Her name was Jeanette and she was variously recommended back and forth across the table.

At least one officer was always required to eat the men's food in the messhall, either Lt Ross, or Chicken Culpepper, or else one of the three new ROTC boys the Company had been issued during the last week; the five of them passed the detail around among them; but whichever one got it, it was still always the same and put a damper over the noncoms' table. But today it was just like a big family party. Minus the mother-in-law.

Stark was the only one, outside of Warden and Baldy, who had not been around to Mrs Kipfer's last night. But he was drunk, too. Stark had picked himself off a shackjob down at the Wailupe Naval Radio Station while they had had the CP out at Hanauma Bay. Some of them had seen her, and she was a hot-looking, wild, I'll-go-as-far-as-you-will wahine, but Stark would not talk about her. So he did not enter the conversation much at the table; but he listened. He had not spoken to Warden since the night at Hickam Field except in the line of duty, and at the table he ignored Warden and Warden ignored him.

It was a typical Sunday morning breakfast, for the first weekend after payday. At least a third of the Company was not home. Another third was still in bed asleep. But the last third more than made up for the absences in the loudness of their drunken laughter and horseplay and the clashing of cutlery and halfpint milk bottles.

Warden was just going back for seconds on both hotcakes and eggs, with that voracious appetite he always had when he was drunk, when this blast shuddered by under the floor and rattled the cups on the tables and then rolled on off across the quad like a high wave at sea in a storm.

He stopped in the doorway of the KP room and looked back at the messhall. He remembered the picture the rest of his life. It had become very quiet and everybody had stopped eating and looked up at each other.

"Must be doin some dynamitin down to Wheeler Field," somebody said tentatively.

"I heard they was clearin some ground for a new fighter strip," somebody else agreed.

That seemed to satisfy everybody. They went back to their eating. Warden heard a laugh ring out above the hungry gnashings of cutlery on china, as he turned back into the KP room. The tail of the chow line was still moving past the two griddles, and he made a mental note to go behind the cooks' serving table when he bucked the line this time, so as not to make it so obvious.

That was when the second blast came. He could hear it a long way off coming toward them under the ground; then it was there before he could move, rattling the cups and plates in the KP sinks and the rinsing racks; then it was gone and he could hear it going away northeast toward the 21st Infantry's football field. Both the KPs were looking at him.

He reached out to put his plate on the nearest flat surface, holding it carefully in both hands so it would not get broken while he congratulated himself on his presence of mind, and then turned back to the messhall, the KPs still watching him.

As there was nothing under the plate, it fell on the floor and crashed in the silence, but nobody heard it because the third groundswell of blast had already reached the PX and was just about to them. It passed under, rattling everything, just as he got back to the NCOs' table.

"This is it," somebody said quite simply.

Warden found that his eyes and Stark's eyes were looking into each other. There was nothing on Stark's face, except the slack relaxed peaceful look of drunkenness, and Warden felt there must not be anything on his either. He pulled his mouth up and showed his teeth in a grin, and Stark's face pulled up his mouth in an identical grin. Their eyes were still looking into each other.

692

Warden grabbed his coffee cup in one hand and his halfpint of milk in the other and ran out through the messhall screendoor onto the porch. The far door, into the dayroom, was already so crowded he could not have pushed through. He ran down the porch and turned into the corridor that ran through to the street and beat them all outside but for one or two. When he stopped and looked back he saw Pete Karelsen and Chief Choate and Stark were all right behind him. Chief Choate had his plate of hotcakes-and-eggs in his left hand and his fork in the other. He took a big bite. Warden turned back and swallowed some coffee.

Down the street over the trees a big column of black smoke was mushrooming up into the sky. The men behind were crowding out the door and pushing those in front out into the street. Almost everybody had brought his bottle of milk to keep from getting it stolen, and a few had brought their coffee too. From the middle of the street Warden could not see any more than he had seen from the edge, just the same big column of black smoke mushrooming up into the sky from down around Wheeler Field. He took a drink of his coffee and pulled the cap off his milk bottle.

"Gimme some of that coffee," Stark said in a dead voice behind him, and held up his own cup. "Mine was empty."

He turned around to hand him the cup and when he turned back a big tall thin red-headed boy who had not been there before was running down the street toward them, his red hair flapping in his self-induced breeze, and his knees coming up to his chin with every step. He looked like he was about to fall over backwards.

"Whats up, Red?" Warden hollered at him. "Whats happening? Wait a minute! Whats going on?"

The red-headed boy went on running down the street concentratedly, his eyes glaring whitely wildly at them.

"The Japs is bombing Wheeler Field!" he hollered over his shoulder. "The Japs is bombing Wheeler Field! I seen the red circles on the wings!"

He went on running down the middle of the street, and quite suddenly right behind him came a big roaring, getting bigger and bigger; behind the roaring came an airplane, leaping out suddenly over the trees.

Warden, along with the rest of them, watched it coming with his milk bottle still at his lips and the twin red flashes winking out from the nose. It came over and down and up and away and was gone, and the stones in the asphalt pavement at his feet popped up in a long curving line that led up the curb and puffs of dust came up from the grass and a line of cement popped out of the wall to the roof, then back down the wall to the grass and off out across the street again in a big S-shaped curve.

With a belated reflex, the crowd of men swept back in a wave toward the door, after the plane was already gone, and then swept right back out again pushing the ones in front into the street again.

Above the street between the trees Warden could see other planes down near the smoke column. They flashed silver like mirrors. Some of them began suddenly to grow larger. His shin hurt from where a stone out of the pavement had popped him.

"All right, you stupid fucks!" he bellowed. "Get back inside! You want to get your ass shot off?"

Down the street the red-haired boy lay sprawled out floppy-haired, wild-eyed, and silent, in the middle of the pavement. The etched line on the asphalt ran up to him and continued on on the other side of him and then stopped.

"See that?" Warden bawled. "This aint jawbone, this is for record. Thems real bullets that guy was usin."

The crowd moved reluctantly back toward the dayroom door. But one man ran to the wall and started probing with his pocketknife in one of the holes and came out with a bullet. It was a .50 caliber. Then another man ran out in the street and picked up something which turned out to be three open-end metal links. The middle one still had a .50 caliber casing in it. The general movement toward the dayroom stopped.

"Say! Thats pretty clever," somebody said. "Our planes is still usin web machinegun belts that they got to carry back home!" The two men started showing their finds to the men around them. A couple of other men ran out into the street hurriedly.

"This'll make me a good souvenir," the man with the bullet said contentedly. "A bullet from a Jap plane on the day the war started."

"Give me back my goddam coffee!" Warden hollered at Stark. "And help me shoo these dumb bastards back inside!"

"What you want me to do?" Chief Choate asked. He was still holding his plate and fork and chewing excitedly on a big bite.

"Help me get em inside," Warden hollered.

Another plane, on which they could clearly see the red discs, came skidding over the trees firing and saved him the trouble. The two men hunting for metal links in the street sprinted breathlessly. The crowd moved back in a wave to the door, and stayed there. The plane flashed past, the helmeted head with the square goggles over the slant eyes and the long scarf rippling out behind it and the grin on the face as he waved, all clearly visible for the space of a wink, like a traveltalk slide flashed on and then off of a screen.

Warden, Stark, Pete and the Chief descended on them as the crowd started to wave outward again, blocking them off and forcing the whole bunch back inside the dayroom.

The crowd milled indignantly in the small dayroom, everybody talking excitedly. Stark posted himself huskily in the doorway with Pete and the Chief flanking him. Warden gulped off the rest of his coffee and set the cup on the magazine rack and pushed his way down to the other end and climbed up on the pingpong table.

"All right, all right, you men. Quiet down. Quiet down. Its only a war. Aint you ever been in a war before?"

The word war had the proper effect. They began to yell at each other to shut up and listen.

"I want every man to go upstairs to his bunk and stay there," Warden said. "Each man report to his squad leader. Squad leaders keep your men together at their bunks until you get orders what to do."

The earth shudders rolling up from Wheeler Field were already a commonplace now. Above it, they heard another plane go roaring machinegun-rattling over.

"The CQ will unlock the rifle racks and every man get his rifle and hang onto it. *But stay inside at your bunks*. This aint no maneuvers. You go runnin around outside you'll get your ass shot off. And you cant do no good anyway. You want to be heroes, you'll get plenty chances later; from now on. You'll probly have Japs right in your laps, by time we get down to beach positions.

"Stay off the porches. Stay *inside*. I'm making each squad leader responsible to keep his men *inside*. If you have to use a rifle butt to do it, thats okay too."

There was a mutter of indignant protest.

"You heard me!" Warden hollered. "You men want souvenirs, buy them off the widows of the men who went out after them. If I catch anybody runnin around outside, I'll personally beat his head in, and then see he gets a goddam general court martial."

There was another indignant mutter of protest.

"What if the fuckers bomb us?" somebody hollered.

"If you hear a bomb coming, you're free to take off for the brush," Warden said. "But not unless you do. I dont think they will. If they was going to bomb us, they would of started with it already. They probly concentratin all their bombs on the Air Corps and Pearl Harbor."

There was another indignant chorus.

"Yeah," somebody hollered, "but what if they aint?"

"Then you're shit out of luck," Warden said. "If they *do* start to bomb, get everybody outside—on the side *away* from the quad—not *into* the quad—and disperse; *away* from the big buildings."

"That wont do us no good if they've already laid one on the roof," somebody yelled.

"All right," Warden hollcrcd, "can the chatter. Lets move. We're wasting time. Squad leaders get these men upstairs. BAR men, platoon leaders and first-three-graders report to me here."

With the corporals and buck sergeants haranguing them, the troops gradually began to sift out through the corridor to the porch stairs. Outside another plane went over. Then another, and another. Then what sounded like three planes together. The platoon leaders and guides and BAR men pushed their way down to the pingpong table that Warden jumped down off of.

"What you want me to do, First?" Stark said; his face still had the same expression of blank, flat refusal—like a stomach flatly refusing food—that he had had in the messhall; "what about the kitchen force? I'm pretty drunk, but I can still shoot a BAR."

"I want you to get your ass in the kitchen with every man you got and start packing up," Warden said, looking at him. He rubbed his hand hard over his own face. "We'll be movin out for the beach as soon as this tapers off a little, and I want that kitchen all packed and ready to roll. Full field. Stoves and all. While you're doin that, make a big pot of coffee on the big stove. Use the biggest #18 pot you got."

"Right," Stark said, and took off for the door into the messhall.

"Wait!" Warden hollered. "On second thought, make two pots. The two biggest you got. We're going to need it."

"Right," Stark said, and went on. His voice was not blank, his voice was crisp. It was just his face, that was blank.

"The rest of you guys," Warden said.

Seeing their faces, he broke off and rubbed his own face again. It didnt do any good. As soon as he stopped rubbing it settled right back into it, like a campaign hat that had been blocked a certain way.

"I want the BAR men to report to the supplyroom right now and get their weapons and all the loaded clips they can find and go up on the roof. When you see a Jap plane, shoot at it. Dont worry about wasting ammo. Remember to take a big lead. Thats all. Get moving."

"The rest of you guys," Warden said, as the BAR men moved away at a run. "The rest of you guys. The first thing. The main thing. Every platoon leader is responsible to me personally to see that all of his men stay inside, except the BAR men up on the roof. A rifleman's about as much good against a low flying pursuit ship as a boy scout with a slingshot. And we're going to need every man we can muster when we get down to beach positions. I dont want none of them wasted here, by runnin outside to shoot rifles at airplanes. Or by goin souvenir huntin. The men stay inside. Got it?"

There was a chorus of hurried vacant nods. Most of the heads were on one side, listening to the planes going over and over in ones twos and threes. It looked peculiar to see them all nodding on one side like that. Warden found himself wanting to laugh excitedly.

"The BARs will be up on the roof," he said. "They can do all the shooting that we can supply ammo for. Anybody else will just be getting in the way."

"What about my MGs, Milt?" Pete Karelsen asked him.

The easy coolness in old Pete's voice shocked Warden to a full stop. Drunk or not, Pete seemed to be the only one who sounded relaxed, and Warden remembered his two years in France.

"Whatever you think, Pete," he said.

"I'll take one. They couldnt load belts fast enough to handle more than one. I'll take Mikeovitch and Grenelli up with me to handle it."

"Can you get the muzzle up high enough on those ground tripods?"

"We'll put the tripod over a chimney," Pete said. "And then hold her down by the legs."

"Whatever you think, Pete," Warden said, thinking momentarily how wonderful it was to be able to say that.

"Come on, you two," Pete said, almost boredly, to his two section leaders. "We'll take Grenelli's because we worked on it last."

"Remember," Warden said to the rest of them as Pete left with his two machinegunners. "The men stay inside. I dont care how you handle it. Thats up to you. I'm going to be up on the roof with a BAR. If you want to get in on the fun, go yourself. Thats where I'm going to be. But make damn sure your men are going to stay *inside*, off the porches, before you go up."

"Like hell!" Liddell Henderson said. "You aint goin to catch this Texan up on no roof. Ah'll stay down with ma men."

"Okay," Warden said, jabbing a finger at him. "Then you are hereby placed in charge of the loading detail. Get ten or twelve men, as many as you can get in the supplyroom, and put them to loading BAR clips and MG belts. We're going to need all the ammo we can get. Anybody else dont want to go up?"

"I'll stay down with Liddell," Champ Wilson said.

"Then you're second-in-command of the loading detail," Warden said. "All right, lets go. If anybody's got a bottle laying around, bring it up with you. I'm bringing mine."

When they got out to the porch, they found a knot of men arguing violently with S/Sgt Malleaux in front of the supplyroom.

"I dont give a damn," Malleaux said. "Thats my orders. I cant issue any live ammo without a signed order from an officer."

"But there aint no goddamned officers, you jerk!" somebody protested angrily.

"Then there aint no live ammo," Malleaux said.

"The officers may not get here till noon!"

"I'm sorry, fellows," Malleaux said. "Thats my orders. Lt Ross give them to me himself. No signed order, no ammo."

"What the fuckin hell is all this?" Warden said.

"He wont let us have any ammo, Top," a man said.

"He's got it locked up and the keys in his pocket," another one said.

"Gimme them keys," Warden said.

"Thats my orders, Sergeant," Malleaux said, shaking his head. "I got to have a signed order from an officer before I can issue any live ammo to an enlisted man."

Pete Karelsen came out of the kitchen and across the porch wiping his mouth off with the back of his hand. From the screendoor Stark disappeared inside putting a pint bottle back into his hip pocket under his apron.

"What the hells the matter?" Pete asked his two machinegunners happily.

"He wont give us no ammo, Pete," Grenelli said indignantly.

"Well for— Jesus Christ!" Pete said disgustedly.

"Thats my orders, Sergeant," Malleaux said irrefragably.

From the southeast corner of the quad a plane came over firing, the tracers leading irrevocably in under the porch and up the wall as he flashed over, and the knot of men dived for the stairway.

"Fuck your orders!" Warden bawled. "Gimme them goddam keys!"

Malleaux put his hand in his pocket protectively. "I cant do that, Sergeant. I got my orders, from Lt Ross himself."

"Okay," Warden said happily. "Chief, bust the door down." To Malleaux he said, "Get the hell out of the way."

Choate, and Mikeovitch and Grenelli the two machinegunners, got back for a run at the door, the Chief's big bulk towering over the two lightly built machinegunners.

Malleaux stepped in front of the door. "You cant get by with this, Sergeant," he told Warden.

"Go ahead," Warden grinned happily at the Chief. "Bust it down. He'll get out of the way." Across the quad, there were already two men up on top of the Headquarters Building.

Chief Choate and the two machinegunners launched themselves at the supply room door like three blocking backs bearing down on an end. Malleaux stepped out of the way. The door rattled ponderously.

"This is your responsibility, Sergeant," Malleaux said to Warden. "I did my best."

"Okay," Warden said. "I'll see you get a medal."

"Remember I warned you, Sergeant," Malleaux said.

"Get the fuck out of my way," Warden said.

It took three tries to break the wood screws loose enough to let the

Yale night lock come open. Warden was the first one in. The two machinegunners were right behind him, Mikeovitch burrowing into a stack of empty belt boxes looking for full ones while Grenelli got his gun lovingly out of the MG rack. There were men up on both the 3rd and 1st Battalion roofs by now, to meet the planes as they came winging back, on first one then the other of the cross legs of their long figure 8.

Warden grabbed a BAR from the rack and passed it out with a full bag of clips. Somebody grabbed it and took off for the roof, and somebody else stepped up to receive one. Warden passed out three of them from the rack, each with a full bag of clips, before he realized what he was doing.

"To hell with this noise," he said to Grenelli who was unstrapping his tripod on his way out the door. "I could stand here and hand these out all day and never get up on the roof."

He grabbed a BAR and clip bag for himself and pushed out the door, making a mental note to eat Malleaux's ass out. There were a dozen bags of full clips in there, left over from the BAR practice firing in August. They should have been unloaded and greased months ago.

Outside, he stopped beside Henderson. Pete, Grenelli and Mikeovitch were already rounding the stair landing out of sight with the MG and eight belt boxes.

"Get your ass in there and start passing them out," Warden told Henderson, "and start loading clips. And belts. Have Wilson go up and get a detail of men. Soons you get a batch loaded send a couple men up with them. Put three men on belts, the rest on BAR clips."

"Yes, Sir," Henderson said nervously.

Warden took off for the stairs. On the way up he stopped off at his room to get the full bottle that he kept in his footlocker for emergencies.

In the squadroom men were sitting on their bunks with their helmets on holding their empty rifles in black despair. They looked up hopefully and called to him as he passed.

"What gives, Sarge?" "Whats the deal, First?" "Are we going up on the roofs now?" "Where the hells the ammunition, Top?" "These guns aint worth nothing without no ammunition." "Hell of a note to sit on your bunk with an empty rifle and no ammunition while they blow your guts out." "Are we soljers? or boy-scouts?"

Other men, the ones who had slept through breakfast and were now getting up tousle-headed and wide-eyed, stopped dressing and looked up hopefully to see what he'd say.

"Get into field uniforms," Warden said, realizing he had to say something. "Start rolling full field packs," he told them ruthlessly in an iron voice. "We're moving out in fifteen minutes. Full field equipment."

Several men threw their rifles on their beds disgustedly.

"Then what the hell're you doin with a BAR?" somebody hollered.

"Field uniforms," Warden said pitilessly, and went on across the squadroom. "Full field equipment. Squad leaders, get them moving."

Disgustedly, the squad leaders began to harangue them to work.

In the far doorway onto the outside porch Warden stopped. In the corner under an empty bunk that had three extra mattresses piled on it, S/Sgt Turp Thornhill from Mississippi lay on the cement floor in his underwear with his helmet on hugging his empty rifle.

"You'll catch a cold, Turp," Warden said.

"Dont go out there, First Sergeant!" Turp pleaded. "You'll be killed! They shootin it up! You'll be dead! You'll not be alive any more! Dont go out there!"

"You better put your pants on," Warden said.

In his room on the porch splinters of broken glass lay all over Warden's floor, and a line of bullet holes was stitched across the top of his foot-locker and up the side of Pete's locker and across its top. Under Pete's locker was a puddle and the smell of whiskey fumes was strong in the air. Cursing savagely, Warden unlocked his footlocker and flung back the lid. A book in the tray had a slanting hole drilled right through its center. His plastic razor box was smashed and the steel safety razor bent almost double. Savagely he jerked the tray out and threw it on the floor. In the bottom of the locker two .30 caliber bullets were nestled in the padding of rolled socks and stacked underwear, one on either side of the brown quart bottle.

The bottle was safe.

Warden dropped the two bullets into his pocket and got the unbroken bottle out tenderly and looked in his wall locker to make sure his recordplayer and records were safe. Then he hit the floor in the broken glass, holding the bottle carefully and under him, as another plane went over going east over the quad.

As he beat it back out through the squadroom the men were beginning bitterly to roll full field packs. All except Turp Thornhill, who was still under the bunk and four mattresses in his helmet and underwear; and Private Ike Galovitch, who was lying on top his bunk with his rifle along his side and his head under his pillow.

On the empty second floor, from which men were hurriedly carrying their full field equipment downstairs to roll into packs, at the south end of the porch by the latrine Readall Treadwell was going up the ladder in the latrine-supplies closet to the roof hatch carrying a BAR and grinning from ear to ear.

"First time in my goddam life," he yelled down; "I'm really goin to git to shoot a BAR, by god. I wount never of believe it."

He disappeared through the hatch and Warden followed him on up, and out into the open. Across G Company's section of roof most of G Company's first-three-graders were waiting to meet the enemy from behind one of the four chimneys, or else down on their knees in one of the corners, the BAR forearms propped on the crotch-high wall, or a chimney top, their muzzles looking eagerly into the sky, and their bottles of whiskey sitting beside them close up against the wall. Reedy Treadwell, who did not have a bottle, was just dropping down happily beside Chief Choate, who did. Two of the first-three-graders had hopped across the wall onto F Company's roof and were standing behind two of their chimneys. A knot of first-three-graders from F Co were just coming up through their own hatch. They crossed the roof and began to argue violently with the two first-three-graders from G Co, demanding their chimneys. All down the 2nd Battalion roof, and on the 1st and 3rd Battalion roofs, first-three-graders were coming up through the hatches eagerly with BARs, rifles, pistols, and here and there a single MG. There were a few buck sergeants visible among them, but the only privates visible anywhere were Readall Treadwell and the two other BAR men from G Co.

"Throw your empty clips down into the Compny Yard," Warden hollered as he moved down the roof. "Pass it along. Throw your empty clips down in the Compny Yard. The loading detail will pick em up. Throw your empty—"

A V of three planes came winging over from the southeast firing full blast, and the waiting shooters cheered happily like a mob of hobos about to sit down to their first big meal in years. All the artillery on all the roofs cut loose in a deafening roar and the earth stopped. The argument on F Co's roof also stopped, while both sides all dived behind the same chimney. Warden turned without thinking, standing in his tracks, and fired from the shoulder without a rest, the bottle clutched tightly between his knees.

The big BAR punched his shoulder in a series of lightning left jabs. On his right Pete Karelsen was happily firing the little air-cooled .30 caliber from behind the chimney while Mikeovitch and Grenelli hung grimly onto the bucking legs of the tripod laid over the chimney, bouncing like two balls on two strings.

The planes sliced on over, unscathed, winging on down to come back up the other leg of the big figure 8. Everybody cheered again anyway, as the firing stopped.

"Holymarymotherofgod," Chief Choate boomed in his star basso that always took the break-line of the Regimental song uncontested. "I aint had so much fun since granmaw got her tit caught in the wringer."

"Shit!" old Pete said disgustedly in a low voice behind Warden. "He was on too much of an angle. Led him too far."

Warden lowered his BAR, his belly and throat tightening with a desire to let loose a high hoarse senseless yell of pure glee. This is *my* outfit. These are *my* boys. He got his bottle from between his knees and took a drink that was not a drink but an expression of feeling. The whiskey burned his throat savagely joyously.

"Hey, Milt!" Pete called him. "You can come over here with us if you want. We got enough room for you and the bottle."

"Be right with you!" Warden roared. Gradually his ears had become aware of a bugle blowing somewhere insistently, the same call over and over. He stepped to the inside edge of the roof and looked down over the wall.

In the corner of the quad at the megaphone, among all the men running back and forth, the guard bugler was blowing The Charge.

"What the fuck are *you* doing," Warden bellowed.

The bugler stopped and looked up and shrugged sheepishly. "You got me," he yelled back. "Colonel's orders." He went on blowing.

"Here they come, Pete!" Grenelli hollered. "Here comes one!" His voice went off up into falsetto excitedly.

It was a single, coming in from the northeast on the down leg of the 8. The voice of every gun on the roofs rose to challenge his passage, blending together in one deafening roar like the call of a lynch mob. Down below, the running men melted away and the bugler stopped blowing and ran back under the E Company porch. Warden screwed the cap back on his bottle and ran crouching over to Pete's chimney and swung around to fire, again with no rest. His burst curved off in tracer smoke lines well behind the swift-sliding ship that was up, over, and then gone. Got to take more lead.

"Wouldnt you know it?" Pete said tragically. "Shot clear behind that one.

"Here, Mike," he said. "Move back a little and make room for the 1st/Sgt so he can fire off the corner for a rest. You can set the bottle down right here, Milt. Here," he said, "I'll take it for you."

"Have a drink first," Warden said happily.

"Okay." Pete wiped his soot-rimmed mouth with the back of his sleeve. There were soot flecks on his teeth when he grinned. "Did you see what they done to our room?"

"I seen what they done to your locker," Warden said.

From down below came the voice of the bugle blowing The Charge again.

"Listen to that stupid bastard," Warden said. "Colonel Delbert's orders."

"I dint think the Colonel'd be up this early," Pete said.

"Old Jake must of served his first hitch in the Cavalry," Warden said.

"Say, listen," Grenelli said, "listen, Pete. When you going to let me take it a while?"

"Pretty soon," Pete said, "pretty soon."

"Throw your empty clips down in the Compny Yard, you guys!" Warden yelled around the roof. "Throw your empty clips down in the Compny Yard. Pass it along, you guys."

Down along the roof men yelled at each other to throw the empties down into the yard and went right on piling them up beside them.

"God damn it!" Warden roared, and moved out from behind the chimney. He walked down along behind them like a quarterback bolstering up his linemen. "Throw them clips down, goddam you Frank. Throw your clips down, Teddy."

"Come on, Pete," Grenelli said behind him. "Let me take it a while now, will you?"

"I got firsts on it," Mikeovitch said.

"Like hell!" Grenelli said. "Its my gun, aint it?"

"Shut up," Pete said. "Both of you. You'll both get your chance. Pretty soon."

Warden was behind the Chief and Reedy Treadwell on the inside edge when the next ones came in, a double flying in in echelon from the northeast like the single, and he dropped down beside them. Down below the bugler stopped blowing and ran back in under the E Company porch again.

Straight across from Warden on the roof of the Headquarters Building there were only two men up. One of them he recognized as M/Sgt Big John Deterling, the enlisted football coach. Big John had a .30 caliber water-cooled with no tripod, holding it cradled in his left arm and firing it with his right. When he fired a burst, the recoil staggered him all over the roof.

The winking noseguns of the incoming planes cut two foot-wide swathes raising dust across the quad and up the wall and over the D Co roof like a wagon road through a pasture. Warden couldnt fire at them from laughing at Big John Deterling on the Headquarters roof. This time Big John came very near to falling down and spraying the roof. The other man up over there had wisely put the chimney between him and Big John, instead of between him and the planes.

"Look at that son of a bitch," Warden said, when he could stop laughing.

Down below the loading detail dived out to pick up the clips in the lull, and the bugler ran back to the megaphone.

"I been watching him," Chief grinned. "The son of a bitch is drunk as a coot. He was down to Mrs Kipfer's last night when me and Pete was there."

"I hope his wife dont find out," Warden said.

"He ought to have a medal," Chief said still laughing.

"He probly will," Warden grinned.

As it turned out, later, he did. M/Sgt John L Deterling; the Silver Star; for unexampled heroism in action.

Another V of three flashed sliding in from the southeast and Warden turned and ran back to Pete's chimney as everybody opened up with a joyous roar. Firing with the BAR forearm resting on his hand on the chimney corner, he watched his tracers get lost in the cloud of tracers around the lead plane spraying the nose, spraying the cockpit, and on back into the tail assembly. The plane shivered like a man trying to get out from under a cold shower and the pilot jumped in his seat twice like a man tied to a hot stove. They saw him throw up his arms helplessly in a useless try to ward it off, to stop it pouring in on him. There was a prolonged cheer. A hundred yards beyond the quad, with all of them watching it now in anticipatory silence, the little Zero began to fall off on one wing and slid down a long hill of air onto one of the goalposts of the 19th Infantry football field. It crashed into flames. A vast happy college-yell cheer went up from the quad and helmets were thrown into the air and backs were slapped as if our side had just made a touchdown against Notre Dame.

Then, as another V of three came in from the northeast, there was a wild scramble for helmets.

"You got him, Pete!" Grenelli yelled, bobbing around on the bucking tripod leg, "you got him!"

"Got him hell," Pete said without stopping firing. "Nobody'll ever know who got that guy."

"Hey, Milt!"

In the lull, Chief Choate was yelling at him from the roof edge.

"Hey, Milt! Somebody's yellin for you down below."

"Comin up!" Warden bawled. Behind him as he ran, Grenelli was pleading:

"Come on, Pete. Let me take it for a while now. You got one already."

"In a minute," Pete said. "In a minute. I just want to try one more."

Looking down over the wall, Warden saw Lt Ross standing in the yard looking up angrily, large bags under his eyes, a field cap on his uncombed head, his pants still unbuttoned, and his shoes untied and his belt unbuckled. He started buttoning his pants without looking down.

"What the hell are you doing up there, Sergeant?" he yelled. "Why arent you down here taking care of the Company? We're going to move out for the beach in less than an hour. Its probably alive with Japs already."

"Its all taken care of," Warden yelled down. "The men are rolling full field packs right now in the squadroom."

"But we've got to get the kitchen and supply ready to move, too, goddam it," Lt Ross yelled up.

"The kitchen is bein pack," Warden yelled down. "I gave Stark the orders and he's doing it now. Should be all ready in fifteen minutes."

"But the supply—" Lt Ross started to yell up.

"They're loading clips and belts for us," Warden yelled down. "All they got to do is carry the water-cooled MGs for the beach out to the trucks and throw in Leva's old field repair kit and they ready to go.

"And," he yelled, "they makin coffee and sandwidges in the kitchen. Everything's all taken care of. Whynt you get a BAR and come on up?"

"There arent any left," Lt Ross yelled up angrily.

"Then get the hell under cover," Warden yelled down as he looked up. "Here they come."

Lt Ross dived under the porch for the supplyroom as another single came blasting in from the southeast and the roaring umbrella of fire rose from the roofs to engulf it. It seemed impossible that he could fly right through it and come out untouched. But he did.

Right behind him, but flying due north along Waianae Avenue and the Hq Building, came another plane; and the umbrella swung that way without even letting go of its triggers.

The plane's gastank exploded immediately into flames that engulfed the whole cockpit and the plane veered off down on the right wing, still going at top speed. As the belly and left under-wing came up into view, the blue circle with the white star in it showed plainly in the bright sunlight. Then it was gone, off down through some trees that sheered off the wings, and the fuselage, still going at top speed, exploded into some unlucky married officer's house quarters with everyone watching it.

"That was one of ours!" Reedy Treadwell said in a small still voice. "That was an American plane!"

"Tough," Warden said, without stopping firing at the new double coming in from the northeast. "The son of a bitch dint have no business there."

After the Jap double had flashed past, unscathed, Warden turned back and made another circuit up and down the roof, his eyes screwed up into that strained look of having been slapped in the face that he sometimes got, and that made a man not want to look at him.

"Be careful, you guys," he said. Up the roof. Down the roof. "That last one was one of ours. Try and be careful. Try and get a look at them before you shoot. Them stupid bastards from Wheeler liable to fly right over here. So try and be careful after this." Up the roof. Down the roof. The same strained squint was in his voice as was in his eyes.

"Sergeant Warden!" Lt Ross roared up from down below. "God damn it! Sergeant *Warden!*"

He ran back to the roof edge. "What now?"

"I want you down here, god damn it!" Lt Ross yelled up. He had his belt buckled and his shoes tied now and was smoothing back his hair with his fingers under his cap. "I want you to help me get this orderly room ready to move out! You have no business up there! Come down!"

"Goddam it, I'm busy!" Warden yelled. "Get Rosenberry. Theres a goddam war on, Lieutenant."

"I've just come from Col Delbert," Lt Ross yelled up. "And he has given orders we're to move out as soon as this aerial attack is over."

"G Compny's ready to move now," Warden yelled down. "And I'm busy. Tell that goddam Henderson to send up some clips and belts."

Lt Ross ran back under the porch and then ran back out again. This time he had a helmet on.

"I told him," he yelled up.

"And tell Stark to send us up some coffee."

"*God damn it!*" Lt Ross raged up at him. "What is this? a Company picnic? Come down here, Sergeant! I want you! Thats an order! Come down here immediately! You hear me? thats an order! All Company Commanders have orders from Col Delbert personally to get ready to move out within the hour!"

"Whats that?" Warden yelled. "I cant hear you."

"I said, we're moving out within the hour."

"What?" Warden yelled. "What? Look out," he yelled; "here they come again!"

Lt Ross dove for the supplyroom and the two ammo carriers ducked their heads back down through the hatch.

Warden ran crouching back to Pete's chimney and rested his BAR on the corner and fired a burst at the V of three that flashed past.

"Get that goddam ammo up here!" he roared at them in the hatchway.

"Milt!" Chief Choate yelled. "Milt Warden! They want you downstairs."

"You cant find me," Warden yelled. "I've gone someplace else."

Chief nodded and relayed it down over the edge. "I cant find him, Lootenant. He's gone off someplace else." He listened dutifully down over the edge and then turned back to Warden. "Lt Ross says tell you we're moving out within the hour," he yelled.

"You cant find me," Warden yelled.

"Here they come!" Grenelli yelled from the tripod.

They did not move out within the hour. It was almost another hour before the attack was all over. And they did not move out until early afternoon three and a half hours after the attack was over. G Company was ready, but it was the only company in the Regiment that was.

Warden stayed up on the roof, by one subterfuge or another, until the attack was over. Lt Ross, it turned out, stayed down in the supplyroom and helped load ammunition. The Regimental fire umbrella claimed one more positive, and two possibles that might have been hit by the 27th and already going down when they passed over the quad. Stark himself, personally, with two of the KPs, brought them up coffee once, and then still later brought up coffee and sandwiches. In gratitude for which, Pete Karelsen let him take the MG for a while.

After it was all over, and the dead silence which no sound seemed able to penetrate reigned, they all smoked a last cigarette up on the roof and then, dirty-faced, red-eyed, tired happy and let-down, they trooped down reluctantly into the new pandemonium that was just beginning below and went to roll their full field packs. Nobody had even been scratched. But they could not seem to get outside of the ear-ringing dead silence. Even the pandemonium of moving out could not penetrate it.

Warden, instead of rolling his pack, went straight to the orderly room. In the three and a half hours before they finally left he was in the orderly room all the time, getting it packed up. Lt Ross, whose Company was the only one that was ready ahead of time, had already forgotten to be angry and came in and helped him. So did Rosenberry. Warden had plenty of time and to spare, to pack the orderly room. But he did not have any time left to roll his full field pack or change into a field uniform. Or, if he did, he forgot it.

The result of this was that he had to sleep in the popcorn vender's wagon at Hanauma Bay without blankets for five days before he could get back up to Schofield to get his stuff, and he would have welcomed even a woolen OD field-uniform shirt. He did not see how the hell he could have possibly have forgotten that.

One by one, each company's consignment of trucks lined up before its barracks in a double file and settled down to wait. One by one, the platoons of troops filed out into their company yards and sat down on their packs holding their rifles and looked at the waiting trucks. The Regiment moved as a unit.

No two companies were going to the same place. And when they got there each company would be a separate unit on its own. But one company, that was ready, did not leave out by itself for its beach positions ahead of the other companies, that were not ready. The Regiment moved as a unit.

Everywhere trucks. Everywhere troops sitting on their packs. The quad filled up with trucks until even the Colonel's jeep could not worm through between them. The yards filled up with troops until even the Colonel's adjutants and messengers could not work through them. There was much swearing and sweaty disgust. The Regiment moved as a unit.

And in the G Co orderly room, Warden chortled to himself smugly, as he worked.

Once, when Lt Ross had gone to the supply room, Maylon Stark stuck his head in at the door. "The kitchen truck's loaded and ready to roll."

"Right," Warden said, without looking up.

"I want you to know I think you done a hell of a swell job," Stark said reluctantly strangledly. "It'll be two hours, anyway, before any other kitchen in this outfit is ready; and some of them probly have to stay behind to get loaded and come down later."

"You done a good job yourself," Warden said, still not looking up.

"It wasnt me," Stark said. "It was you. And I just want you to know I think you done a hell of a job."

"Okay," Warden said, "thanks," and went on working without looking up.

He rode down in the jeep at the head of the Company's convoy with Lt Ross, Weary Russell driving. There was terrific traffic. The roads were alive with trucks and taxis as far as the eye could see, bumper to bumper. The trucks were taking them down, to beach positions; the taxis were taking them up, to Schofield, where their outfits would already be gone. Recons and jeeps slithered in and out among the long lines of trucks, but the big two-and-a-halfs could only lumber on, a few feet at a time, stopping when the truck in front of them stopped in back of the truck in front of him, waiting to move on until the truck in front of them moved on a little in back of the truck in front of him.

The trucks had been stripped of their tarps and one man with his BAR or machinegun mounted over the cab rode standing on the truckbed wall. Helmeted heads were poked above the naked ribs watching the sky like visitors inspecting the dinosaur's skeleton in the Smithsonian Institute.

In the jeep, riding up and down haranguing on the road shoulder alongside the Company's column, Warden saw them all, a lot of times. Their faces were changed and they did not look the same any more. It was somewhat the same look as Stark had had in the messhall, only the drunkenness was evaporating out of it leaving only the hard set of the dry plaster. Out here on the highway, lost among hundreds of other outfits, the idea was not only clearer but bigger, much bigger, than back at your home barracks in your own quad. Chief Choate, riding with a BAR up, looked down at him from above his truck cab and Warden looked back.

They had all left everything behind, civilian clothes, garrison shoes and uniforms, campaign hat collections, insignia collections, photograph albums, private papers. To hell with all that. This was war. We wont need that. They brought nothing but the skeletal field living equipment, and the only man who packed in anything comfortable to bring with him was Pete Karelsen. Pete had been in France.

Gradually, foot by foot, the trucks moved on down toward Honolulu and whatever waited on the beaches. Up till now it had been a day off, it had been fun.

Pearl Harbor, when they passed it, was a shambles. Wheeler Field had been bad, but Pearl Harbor numbed the brain. Pearl Harbor made a queasiness in the testicles. Wheeler Field was set back quite a ways from the road, but parts of Pearl Harbor were right on the highway. Up till then it had been a big lark, a picnic; they had fired from the roofs and been fired at from the planes and the cooks had served them coffee and sandwiches and the supply detail had brought them up ammo and they had got two or three planes and only one man in the whole Regiment had been hit (with a .50 caliber in the fleshy part of his calf, didnt even hit a bone, he walked up to the dispensary by himself), and he was getting himself a big Purple Heart. Almost everybody had had a bottle and they all had been half-drunk anyway when it started and it had all been a sort of super-range-season with live targets to shoot at. The most exciting kind: Men. But now the bottles were fast wearing off and there was no immediate prospect of getting any more and there were no live targets to shoot at. Now they were thinking. Why, it might be months—even years—before they could get hold of a bottle again! This was a big war.

As the trucks passed through the new, Married NCO Quarters that had been added onto Pearl Harbor recently, women and children and an occasional old man standing in the yards cheered them. The troops rode on through in silence, staring at them dully.

Going through the back streets of town, all along the route, men, women and children stood on porches fences cartops and roofs and cheered them roundly. They waved Winnie Churchill's V-for-Victory sign at them, and held their thumbs up in the air. Young girls threw them kisses. Mothers of young girls, with tears in their eyes, urged their daughters to throw them more kisses.

The troops, looking wistfully at all this ripe young stuff running around loose that they could not get into, and remembering the old days when civilian girls were not allowed—and did not desire—to speak to soldiers on the street in broad daylight let alone at night in a bar, gave them back the old one-finger salute of the clenched fist jabbing the stiff middle finger into the air. They returned Winnie Churchill's V-for-Victory sign with an even older one of their own, in which the fist is clenched and the middle finger and thumb are extended and pinched repeatedly together.

The ecstatic civilians, who did not know that this last was the Old Army sign for the female, or that the first meant "Fuck you!" cheered them even more roundly and the troops, for the first time since they'd left Schofield, grinned a little bit at each other, slyly, and redoubled with their saluting.

From Waikiki on east, the trucks in the Company's convoy began to peel off to deliver the various three- and four-man details each with its noncom to their various beach positions. By the time they reached the rise up over the Koko Head saddle where the road turned off down to the CP at Hanauma Bay, there were only four trucks left. The two for Position 28 at Makapuu Head, one for the CP personnel and Position 27, and the kitchen truck. The first two, the CP truck and the kitchen truck, pulled off onto the side road and stopped and the last two bound for Makapuu went on, then, past them. They had all had their big day with the civilians, which most of them had waited from two to five years for, and now they were preparing to pay for it.

Among the troops in the trucks there was a certain high fervor of defense and patriotism that exploded into a weak feeble cheer in the heavy perpetual wind, as they passed Lt Ross and The Warden who had climbed out of the jeep on the road-shoulder to watch them go past. A few fists were shaken in the air up between the bare truck ribs and Friday Clark, current-rifleman and ex-apprentice-Company-bugler, shook a wildly promising two-finger V-for-Victory sign at Lt Ross from over the tailgate of the last truck as they pulled on away.

This general patriotic enthusiasm lasted about three days.

Lt Ross, standing beside his jeep to watch his men go off to possible maiming and death, certainly off to a war that would last a long time, looked at Friday sadly and without acknowledgment from across a great gulf of years pity and superior knowledge, his eyes set in a powerful emotion, a look of great age and fearful responsibility on his face.

1st/Sgt Warden, standing beside his Company Commander and watching his face, wanted to boot his Company Commander hard in the ass.

It was perhaps the stringing of the barbed wire, more than anything else, that ate into the patriotism of the troops in the next few days. The men who had acquired the new unknown disease of aching veins in their arm joints from the building of these positions now found it coming back on them doubly powerfully from putting up barbed wire to protect these positions. So that even when they were not pulling guard at night, they couldnt sleep anyway. The stringing of the barbed wire, after the first day, was an even more powerful astringent to the patriotism than their getting crummy with no prospect of a shower, or their getting itchy with beard and no prospect of a shave, or their having to sleep on the rocks with nothing but a single shelterhalf and two blankets over them when it rained.

Actually, this war that had started out so well Sunday morning and given them such high hopes of the future, was turning out to be nothing more than an extended maneuvers. With the single difference that this showed no prospects of ending.

It was five days before things were organized enough to allow the sending of a detail back to Schofield for the rest of their stuff, that they had not thought they'd need, and the Company's quota of pyramidal tents. But even these didnt do the men at Makapuu any good since out there there werent any trees to set them up under.

Warden, armed with the request list of each man which altogether covered an entire pad of legal-size scratch paper, led the detail of three trucks. Pete Karelsen, who was the only man in the Company who had been anywhere near comfortable in the five days, was his second-in-command. They pulled into the quad with their three trucks to find another outfit already moved into the barracks and the footlockers and wall lockers of G Company thoroughly rifled. Their lists were useless. Pete Karelsen, again, had been practically the only man in the Company who had bothered to lock either his footlocker or wall locker that Sunday morning. But even Pete's extra set of false teeth, which had been out on the table, were gone.

And, of course, none of the new tenants they talked to knew a damn thing about it.

Warden's records and player were gone, also his $120 Brooks Bros. suit, saddle-stitched Forstmann jacket, and the white dinner jacket and tux pants he had bought but never worn yet, together with all of his uniforms. Also, the brand new $260 electric guitar, still less than half paid for, that Andy and Friday had bought while Prew was in the Stockade, was gone too, speaker jackplug and all.

If it had not been for 1st/Sgt Dedrick of A Company, who was about his size and had remembered to lock his wall locker, he would not have even been able to scare up two whole field uniforms. Just about the only thing that had been left untouched were the folded pyramidal tents in the supply room.

By the end of the seventh day, when they had got the tents back downtown and distributed out to the positions and set up ready to occupy, every man on the Company roster—including the two men serving time in the Stockade who had been released with the rest of the prisoners—had shown up and reported for duty. With the single exception of Prewitt.

Chapter 51

Prewitt slept through the entire attack. He had gotten even drunker than usual the night before while the girls were at work because Saturday night is always supposed to be holiday. He did not even find out there had been an attack, until the insistently dynamic voice from the radio talking on and on tensely finally beat a hole through the thick, very dry, dehydrated hangover in his mouth that, even while still asleep, he knew was there and did not want to wake up to.

He sat up on the divan in his shorts, (since he had moved out on the divan he had taken to sleeping in shorts for the sake of modesty,) and saw them both crouching before the radio in their dressing gowns tensely.

"I was just going to call you!" Alma said excitedly.

"Call me for what?" The strongest thought in the dry eye-ache that was his mind was to head immediately to the kitchen for water.

". . . but the damage inflicted upon Pearl Harbor itself was by far the most serious," the radio said. "Hardly a building appears to be left standing undamaged. At least one of the battleships that were resting in harbor is sunk to the shallow bottom with its superstructure awash in the stillflaming oil-covered waters. Most of the high altitude bombers were concentrated there and upon Hickam Field right across the channel. Next to Pearl Harbor itself, Hickam Field appears to have suffered the worst damage."

"Its Webley Edwards," Georgette said.

"He's broadcasting back to the Mainland," Alma said.

"Either a very large bomb, or else a torpedo," the radio said, "was dropped into the main messhall of the new Hickam Field barracks where four hundred of our unsuspecting airmen were seated at breakfast."

Prew knew what it was by this time, but he was having a very hard time getting it through the mud of his head. He could not get it out of his head that it was the Germans; even later on after he had learned it was the Japs, he still could not get it out of his head that it had been the Germans. They must have developed some totally new kind of bomber, that would be able to fly that far nonstop, even with a base on the east coast of Asia. Because they never could have gotten a carrier task force out into the Pacific past the British navy. What a hell of a time to be caught short with a hangover! Water would never help a hangover like this; the only thing would help a hangover like this was a couple of stiff drinks, and even that wouldnt be quick enough.

"Wheres my pants?" he said, getting up in his shorts. A violent throb passed through his head like a concussion, and he headed across the room toward them and the bar in the top of the radio.

"They're right there on the chair," Alma said. "What do you think you're doing?"

"No, not those. My uniform pants," he said, opening the bar over their heads and pouring a stiff shot of scotch into one of the long-stemmed cocktail glasses. "I've got a uniform around here someplace. Where is it?"

He downed the shot, shuddering; but he could tell it was going to help.

"What are you going to do!" Alma demanded, inarticulately wildly. "What are you doing!"

"Going to put enough liquor in me so I can see past this hangover and then get the hell back to the Post. What the hell do you think?" he said, pouring another one and downing it.

"There is no denying that our Navy has suffered a great defeat," the radio said. *"Perhaps the greatest defeat in its history. It would . . ."*

"But you cant do that!" Alma said frantically. "You cant go back!"

"Why the hell cant I? You nuts?"

". . . but through it all," the radio said, *"through the hours of darkness and ignoble defeat, there remains a great shining light that shall forever be an example to all Americans: . . ."*

"Because they're still looking for you!" Alma said hysterically. "For a murder rap! You dont think they'll dismiss a murder rap against you! Even on account of *two* wars."

He had already poured the third drink, and his head was clearing some. The warm electric glow of the nerve-ends was beginning to dry out the sodden cells. He went on and downed the drink anyway.

"I forgotten all about that," he said.

". . . and that is the courage and heroism of our fighting men," the radio said, *"who, in the face of death and overwhelming odds, caught by surprise and without adequate equipage, stuck to their guns and fought back valiantly with all the greatness of spirit that has always been the hallmark of the United States Army and Navy."*

"Is he talking about the US Army and Navy?" Georgette grinned to nobody in particular.

"Well, you better remember it," Alma said, a little more calmly. "If you go back now, they'll only throw you in the Stockade, and then try you for murder. War or no war. That wont be helping to win the war any."

Still holding the bottle in one hand and the glass in the other, he sat down on the footstool between them in front of the radio, looking like he had been rabbit-punched by a judo man.

"I forgotten all about that," he said dully. "Clean forgotten all about it."

"Well, you better think about it," Alma said.

"*By their quiet heroism under fire,*" the radio said, "*their devotion to duty no matter how trivial, and their silent uncomplaining bravery as they lie wounded and dying—even now, as I speak these words to you—in the hospitals and dressing stations, they are setting an example of faith and service and stoic heroism that we civilians here in Hawaii who have witnessed it will remember for a long long time. They are creating a legend, these men, these boys—and most of them are just that: boys—a legend of Democracy that will for long and long remain unequalled and unsurpassed, and that will strike fear into the hearts of the enemies of freedom.*"

"By God!" Georgette exclaimed suddenly and excitedly, "the yellow little bastards'll learn they cant do that to us and get by with it!"

"I was asleep," Prew said dully. "I dint even wake up."

"Neither did we," Georgette said excitedly. "We didnt even know about it. I just happened to turn the radio on."

"And I was asleep," Prew said. "Sound asleep." He poured another drink from the bottle in his left hand into the glass in his right hand and swallowed it off. His head was completely clear now; his head was clear as a bell.

"Those goddam fuckin Germans!" he said.

"What Germans?" Georgette said.

"Them," he said, pointing with the glass to the radio.

"*I have stood in the wards of Tripler General, the Army's new modern hospital here,*" the radio said, "*and watched them bringing them in, some in full uniform, some in their underwear, some in nothing at all, all of them horribly wounded, horribly burned.*"

"What about Schofield?" Prew demanded rigidly. "What did he say about Schofield?"

"Nothing," Georgette said. "Aint even mentioned it. Wheeler Field was bombed, and Bellows Field, and the Kaneohe Naval Air Base, and the Marine Base at Ewa. And Hickam and Pearl Harbor; they got the worst."

"But what about Schofield?" Prew said. "What about *Scho*field, goddam it?"

"He hasnt even mentioned it, Prew," Alma said soothingly.

"Not a tall?"

"She told you no," Alma said.

"Then they must not of bombed it," he said relievedly. "He would of mentioned it. They probly only strafed it a little. Thats what they would do," he said. "They would be after the airfields. Thats what they'd be after. Of course they wouldnt bomb Schofield."

"*Tripler General is a large hospital,*" the radio said, "*equipped with every convenience and every modern device of medical science, but it was not designed to handle such an inconceivable catastrophe as this. There is not room for even a small percentage of the casualties I saw brought in, some of them already dead and dying on their improvised stretchers in the halls and corridors simply because there was neither the room nor the trained personnel to take care of their numbers. Yet nowhere in the whole hospital was there so much as a single whimper of pain, a single complaint. Here and there some terribly mangled lad of nineteen or twenty, his hair and eyebrows and lashes burned completely off, would say to the doctors when they got to him: 'Take care of my buddy here first, Doc; he's hurt lots worse than I am.' But all else was silence. An accusative silence. An angry silence.*"

"The dirty bastards," Prew said dully. He was weeping. "Oh, the dirty bastards. Those babyraping dirty German bastards." He reached up with the hand holding the bottle and wiped off his nose with the back of his hand and poured another drink from the bottle into the glass.

"It was the Japs," Georgette said. "The *Japs*. The dirty yellow-bellied little Japs. They sneaked in without warning and made a cowardly attack while their decoys was still in Washington crying peace."

"*It has been,*" the radio said, "*a tremendously uplifting spiritual experience to me, to see the manliness with which these boys are enduring their sufferings, it has richened and deepened my faith in a form of government that can produce heroes like these, not in tens and twenties, but in hundreds and thousands, and I only wish I could have taken every American citizen into the wards of Tripler General with me, to see what I have seen.*"

"Is that Webley Edwards?" Prew said, weeping.

"We think so," Alma said.

"It must be," Georgette said. "It sounds like him."

"Well, he's a great guy," Prew said. He gulped down his drink and refilled the glass. "A *great* guy, thats all."

"You'd better lay off that liquor a little," Alma said uneasily. "Its still early yet."

"Early?" Prew said. "Early! Oh, those dirty bastardly Germans. What the hell differnce," he hollered, and paused, "does it make? If I get drunk. I cant go back, can I? What the hell differnce, I'd like to know? Lets all get drunk.

"Oh," he said. "Oh, goddam them, goddam them."

"*The total extent of the damage,*" the radio said, "*is of course entirely unknown at the present time, and will probably be unknown for some time. Because an emergency exists, and to facilitate coordination and cooperation of all agencies, General Short has declared the Territory to be under Martial Law."*

"I'll tell you something," Prew wept, pouring another drink, "there aint no murder rap against me."

"There isnt?" Alma said.

"There aint no murder rap against anybody. Warden told me, and he wouldnt lie."

"Then you can go back," Alma said. "But," she said, "if you went back wouldnt they still put you in the Stockade for being AWOL?"

"Thats just it!" he said. "Now I cant go back anyway. Because I wont go back to no Stockade, see? If I went back, I'd get at least a Summary, and maybe a Special. But they'll never send me back to that Stockade. Never! see?"

"If only you could go back without going to the Stockade," Alma said. "But you cant. And you wouldnt help the war any in the Stockade."

She put her hand on his arm.

"Please lay off the liquor, Prew. Let me have the bottle."

"Git away from me!" he said, jerking his arm loose. "I'll knock you on your goddam ass. Git away! and stay away! from me. Lee me alone." He poured himself another cocktail glass full of whiskey and looked at her belligerently.

After that, neither one of them said anything to him or tried to stop him. It was not an exaggeration to say that there was murder staring at them out of his red-rimmed eyes.

"And as long as they put me in their fuckin hogpen of a Stockade, I'll *never* go back," he said ferociously. "You nor nobody else."

They did not contest this either. So the three of them sat that way, in silence, listening to the reports come in over the radio, until hunger for the breakfast nobody had had drove them out to the kitchen, and Prew finished off the bottle he was working on and started another. He would not leave the radio to eat. When they brought him food he refused it. He stayed in front of the radio on the footstool, drinking cocktail glasses of whiskey and weeping and nothing could budge him.

"Our young men have paid dearly," the radio said, *"for the lesson the nation has learned this day. But they have paid fairly, and squarely, without fear and without complaint and without bitterness at the high cost. Hired to be ready to fight and die for us, our Regular Army and Regular Navy have this day upheld the faith and confidence we have always placed in them, have proved their right to the esteem we have always had for them."*

"I was asleep," Prew said dully, "sound asleep. I dint even wake up."

716

They had hoped he would drink himself into a stupor and pass out, so they could put him to bed. The wildness in him made them uneasy to even be in the same room with him. But he did not pass out, and he did not drink himself into a stupor. He was apparently in one of those moods when a man can just go on drinking indefinitely, after he reaches a certain point, without ever getting any drunker but only getting wilder and wilder. He stayed there in front of the radio on the footstool, first weeping and then glaring blackly.

Early in the afternoon the radio gave a repeat call of Dr. Pinkerton's request for volunteer blood donors to report immediately to Queen's Hospital. More to get out of the heavy-bellying atmosphere of the house than anything else, away from the ominous electricity with which the wild dynamo in front of the radio was charging the air, both Georgette and Alma decided to go down and give blood.

"I'm going too!" the dynamo hollered, and lurched up from the footstool.

"You cant go, Prew," Alma said uneasily. "Be sensible. You're so drunk right now you cant even stand up. Besides, everyone'll probably have to show some kind of identification. And you know what that would mean for you."

"Cane even give any blood," he said dismally, and lurched back down onto the footstool.

"You stay here and listen to the radio," Alma said soothingly. "We'll be back in a little bit. Then you can tell us all thats happened."

Prew did not say anything. He did not even look up again from the radio as they went to get dressed.

"I've got to get out of here!" Alma said. "I cant breathe."

"Do you think he'll be all right?" Georgette whispered. "I didnt realize!"

"Of course he'll be all right," Alma said firmly. "He just feels guilty and he's upset and a little drunk. He'll get over it by tomorrow."

"Maybe he ought to go back anyway?" Georgette suggested.

"If he went back, they'd only put him in the Stockade again, wouldnt they?" Alma said.

"Thats true," Georgette said.

"Well, dont talk silly," Alma said.

He was still sitting there when they came back out. The radio was droning on with staccato tenseness. Something else about Wheeler Field. He did not look up or say anything, and Alma shook her head warningly at Georgette and they went on out and left him sitting there.

He was still sitting there two hours later when they came home, looking as if he hadnt moved a muscle since they had left, except that the bottle in his left hand was well down toward being empty. The radio was still going.

If anything, he seemed soberer, with that intent crystal sobriety that comes to a heavy drinker after a long, intense, concentrated consumption of liquor. But the heavy crackling tension in the air of the house, like low-hanging clouds roiling and rubbing together before an electrical storm, seemed—after the excitement of all the traffic and the bright indifferent Sunday sunlight outdoors—to be even more oppressive than when they had left.

"Well, we had quite a foray," Alma said brightly into the bleakness.

"We sure did," Georgette said.

"If we hadnt had Georgette's car we'd never have even got down there," Alma said. "Let alone got back home. The whole town's a madhouse. Trucks, buses, laundry trucks, private cars, every vehicle that can move."

"We met a guy at the hospital who's going to write a book about it," Georgette said.

"Yes," Alma said, taking it up. "He's an assistant Professor of English at the University—"

"I thought he was a newspaper reporter?" Georgette said.

"—No," Alma said, "an English Professor.— And he was helping to evacuate women and children from the bombed areas; and now he's helping drive people in to the hospital to give blood."

"He's going to talk to everybody who had anything to do with any of it," Georgette explained. "Then he's going to put all their stories together in their own words in a book."

"He's going to call it *Praise the Lord and Pass the Ammunition*," Alma said. "Thats what one of the Chaplains at Pearl Harbor said."

"Or else, *Remember Pearl Harbor*," Georgette said. "He dont know which yet. You know, like Remember the Alamo."

"Or Remember the Maine," Alma said. "He's very intelligent."

"And polite, too," Georgette said. "He treated us just like anybody else. He said all his life he had wanted to live history, and now he had his wish."

"A house on Kuhio Street was bombed out," Alma said.

"And the drugstore on the corner of McCully and King is smashed flat," Georgette said. "And the man and his wife and two daughters were all killed."

"Well," Alma said, "I guess we'd better fix something to eat. I feel a little bit weak."

"Me too," Georgette said.

"Do you want some food?" Alma said.

"No," Prew said.

"You really ought to eat something, Prew," Georgette said. "You need food, after all that liquor."

Prew reached out and switched off the radio and then looked at them blackly. "Listen, all I want is for you to lee me alone. You want to eat, go eat. Just lee me alone."

"Did anything new happen on the radio?" Alma said.

"No," he said violently. "Its the same old crap over and over."

"Well, you dont care if we listen to it?" Alma said, "do you? While we fix supper?"

"Its your radio," Prew said, and got up with his bottle and cocktail glass and went out onto the porch over Palolo Valley and shut the glass doors behind him.

"What are we going to do with him?" Georgette said. "He's driving me nuts."

"Oh, he'll be all right," Alma said. "Give him a couple of days to get over it. Just ignore him."

She turned on the radio and went out to the kitchen, and Georgette followed her restlessly.

"Well I just hope you're right," she said uneasily, looking out through the glass doors at the black silhouette against the reddening sky. "He gives me the willies."

"I said he'd be all right," Alma said sharply. "Just leave him alone. Ignore him. Come on and help me fix supper; we'll have to put up the blackout curtains in a little bit."

They fixed coldcut sandwiches with Durkee's Dressing, of which Alma was very fond, and one of those cellophane bags of chopped salad that were just beginning to come out in the stores with French dressing. They poured glasses of milk and put the Silex hourglass on for a pot of coffee, and then they went to draw the blackout curtains that Alma had fixed to hang open like black drapes in the daytime, back when they had had the practice blackout alerts.

"You'd better come inside," Alma told him crisply, when she got to the glass doors onto the porch. "We're putting up the blackout curtains."

He came in, without saying anything, and went on across the living room and sat down on the divan still holding the nearly empty bottle in his left hand and the cocktail glass in his right.

"Dont you want to eat something?" Alma said. "I fixed some sandwiches for you."

"I'm not hungry," he said.

"I've made some for you anyway," Alma said. "In case you want them later."

"I'm not hungry," he said.

"I'll wrap them in waxed paper so they'll stay fresh," Alma said.

Prew poured himself another drink and did not say anything, so she went on back out into the kitchen, after she had drawn and fastened the blackout curtains over the glass doors.

719

When they came back out with their coffee after they had eaten, he was still on the divan. He had opened a new bottle. In all, he drank over two full fifths of Georgette's scotch whiskey in that one day. The first bottle had been a little over half full, and he had finished that one, and the whole second bottle, and half of the third.

They sat for a while and tried to listen to the radio, but the reports were repetitious now, and the obdurate presence sitting silently on the divan finally drove them to bed and they left him sitting there, not drunk and not sober, not happy and not unhappy, not conscious and not unconscious.

He stayed that way for eight days, never what you could really call drunk, but certainly never anywhere near sober, and always with a bottle of Georgette's expensive scotch in one hand and a glass in the other. He did not talk at all except to say "Yes" or "No", mostly "No", when confronted with a direct question, and he never ate anything when they were there. It was like living in the same house with a dead person.

When they got up Monday morning, he was asleep on the divan in his clothes. The bottle and glass were sitting on the floor beside him. The two sandwiches Alma had wrapped in waxed paper and left in the kitchen were gone. Neither one of them went to work that day.

Honolulu tapered off quickly from the first great rush of emotion in the next several days. The radio began to have musical programs and commercials again, and outside of the soldiers putting up barbed wire on Waikiki Beach and the helmeted sentries outside the vital installations such as the radio stations and the governor's mansion, and the few wrecked buildings such as the Kuhio Street house and the drugstore at McCully and King, the city did not seem to be greatly changed by the metamorphosis of having passed through the crucible.

Apparently businessmen were keeping a stiff upper lip and the Provost Marshal's office was advising business as usual, because Mrs Kipfer phoned the house on the third day and told Alma to report for work at ten in the morning next day, rather than the old time of three in the afternoon. Georgette's boss at the Ritz Rooms phoned her later with identical instructions. Because of the sundown curfew instituted by the Martial Law, after which no person without an authorized pass was allowed abroad, all business had to be transacted during the hours of daylight.

Business, it turned out, had fallen off drastically at both Mrs Kipfer's and the Ritz. And apparently this was true all over. The Army and Navy were not yet issuing passes to their personnel, and the girls ended up by playing rummy and casino for most of their working hours. A number of them were already securing themselves passage home on one of the ships being used to evacuate Officers' and Enlisted Men's wives and children back to the Mainland.

Mrs Kipfer had, however, received information that passes—on a strict rotation plan—would be issued to both Army and Navy personnel within a short time. But at the present time about the only business the New Congress Hotel had was when the small parties of brass came down, in the afternoons now, instead of at night as they used to.

There was another thing too, about which Mrs Kipfer worried to Alma considerably, and that was that she had received reliable information to the effect that both Stateside and in the Islands pressure was being brought to bear upon the Armed Services to close down the whorehouses. The pressure was coming from Washington, Mrs Kipfer was told, where a number of female constituents who had sons in the Services were creating quite a rumpus and threatening not to re-elect their representatives to the Congress unless something was done.

But in spite of these handicaps Mrs Kipfer, with a tremendous burst of patriotism and a singular devotion to duty, swore she would stick to her post just as long as she by god could and would do her bit toward the Total Victory, just as long as she had a single girl left to command. (And she seldom cursed.)

Alma, because Prew had sometime or other Sunday night eaten the two sandwiches she had left out, took to making them regularly both before she left for work and before she went to bed. They were always eaten. But when she forgot to make them, which she did several times, nothing in the refrigerator or the cupboards was even so much as touched. He just was not acting even human. He did not shave, and he did not bathe, and he did not even take off his clothes but just flopped down in them on the divan when he slept. He looked like the wrath of God. His hair had not been touched with a comb since she could remember, and his face had gotten puffy and fat-looking with big pouches under the eyes while the rest of him, which had never been heavy, got thinner and thinner. He would wander, bottle in one hand and glass in the other, from the kitchen to the living room to the bedrooms to the porch and sit down blankly in one place for a while only to get up and go someplace else. The thing that had first attracted her to him—a kind of intensity in the face, if she could have expressed it, a sort of deep tragic fire in the eyes—was not there any more; and you could smell him from clear across on the other side of the room.

And he did not seem to be getting any better. Instead, it looked as if he would go on that way indefinitely—until he either wasted away to a shadow and died, or else went completely crazy and went for somebody with a knife.

She could not help remembering what he had done to that guard from the Stockade.

And Georgette was frankly and openly afraid of him, and said so.

Yet, in spite of Georgette, she could not make up her mind to give up hope and let go of him.

"In the first place," as she expressed it to Georgette, "theres nowhere for him to go, except here. We all know that if he went back to the Army they'd only throw him in the Stockade again, and maybe kill him. And the whole Island is alive with people checking passes and things. This is the only place where he is safe. We couldnt possibly book passage for him back to the States, like we could have before Pearl Harbor, every bit of space is taken for evacuating non-combatants; and the Army controls all the ships because of having to convoy them.

"And besides all that, I just cant give up hope for him somehow."

"You mean, you dont *want* him to leave," Georgette said.

"Of course I dont want him to leave!"

"What'll become of him when we go back to the Mainland?" Georgette said.

"Well," Alma said, "maybe I wont go back to the Mainland."

"You've already booked yourself up," Georgette said, "just like me."

"Well, I can always turn it down, cant I?" Alma said crossly.

This conversation took place on the evening of the fifth day, in Georgette's bedroom which Alma had entered through the connecting bath.

Prewitt did not know anything about it. He did not know anything about anything else, either. He was sitting on the divan in the living-room, with the bottle and glass within easy reach. He got frantic if they werent always where he could see them.

The only thing he knew anything about, or cared anything about, was liquor. There was something supernatural and occult about liquor, the way it warmed through the blood and brightened every thing up. There was something wonderful and holy about it. If you know how to use it.

It was just like with any other religion. You got yourself just so high on it, and then you coasted along on that for a while, and only added another drink when you began to feel it start to taper off and begin rolling downhill toward the hangover. Otherwise, you would bring on the reaction.

It was a delicate balance, with liquor. If you got too high, you passed clear out, or else ended up getting sick; either way you got sobered into the hangover. And if you let it taper off too far, of course, your mind began to thaw out like frozen mud with the sun on it. He had seen a lot of frozen mud in his time: back at Myer; and the winter maneuvers that the whole regiment had gone down into Georgia to the Benning Reservation for; and all the times on the bum, he had seen mud frozen so hard in Montana and the Dakotas that it cut the soles of your shoes like a lava flow. But mud, when the sun hit it and it began to soften, that was the worst mud of all. It would mire you down then. That was the mud we must never get into.

It was a very delicate balance. Almost a mathematical problem. It took a great deal of concentration, and a whole hell of a lot of energy, just to stay up on the tightrope. Because when you got just high enough, you always wanted to go higher because it was so wonderful. That was what took the will power: not to go higher. It required concentration, and study, and energy, and will power, and a great deal of thought; to really be a really successful drunkard. Anybody could be a half-assed drunkard. But to be a real drunkard . . .

And they all talked about drunkards and spinelessness, all the books you read, that *John Barleycorn* now of London's, that was all pure crap and the truth was not in it. It seemed like any of them, all of them, that ever write about drunkards, they always use the words drunkard and spinelessness as synonymous. They just didnt know, that was all. They were ony showin up their own ignorance. They've never really worked hard at drunkenness—or else they have tried and failed and therefore feel a great need to run drunkenness down and prove to the world that drunkenness is really nothing, that any half-assed fool can do it.

But a half-assed fool couldnt do it, any more than a half-assed fool could do anything, and do it well. Of course, if you had all the qualities of greatness already anyway, then you could be a great drunkard— but then you would have been great at anything else you did, too. To be a great drunkard required a great deal of concentration, and energy, and study, and will p—— . . . .

The hardest thing, outside of not letting yourself go off too high when you get up there, was the first twenty minutes or so in the morning after you wake up. Before the first drink really takes hold. But you could outsmart that one by sleeping twice a day for four hours, instead of once a day for eight hours. By doing it that way you could still get the necessary sleep to maintain your health, and at the same time a couple extra drinks just before you hit the sack would last over till you woke up. Theres tricks to all trades.

But the hardest thing, he re-decided, the text of the sermon I have chosen today, was when you got up there just high enough, and the liquid magic began to warm through you and the low pressure area suddenly dissolved into fair weather and the sun suddenly got brighter and everything took on that new look, bright and clean-looking and sharply outlined in color, like after the world just been washed by a rain.

That was the hardest: to refrain and hold yourself back from going on any higher, no matter how much you want to. That was where they separated the sheep-drunkards from the goat-drunkards. That was where they told the men from the boys.

Prewitt reached for the bottle and glass on the floor happily, proud of his accomplishment and at peace with the whole world. It was time for another dose of your medicine. It was time for another Revival.

What day was this?

Ha! What the hell difference did it make? You got all the time in the world. You got years. He had seen members of the Canned Heat Brigade stay on a kick like this for years. But then they were really experts. One old guy, up in Seattle that time, and then he had met him in Indiana sixteen months later—just the same. And they didnt even have whiskey; all they had had was canned heat from Woolworth's that they had to strain the alcohol out of the paraffin through a handkerchief and then strain the alky through a piece of stale bread.

With a sudden great optimism he suddenly believed that he might even actually break the world's record. That same record that had remained in America ever since the Gay 90's and the days of Diamond Jim Brady. There was a lot of history behind that record. They would put his name up on a bronze plaque on all the distilleries in Louisville, a mark for the world to see, that would remain forever a shining target to young hopefuls to shoot at. TO THE MEMORY OF ROBT E LEE PREWITT, HOLDER OF THE WORLD'S RECORD. The same identical championship record, that had been held in unbroken succession in American hands, for the last five or six generations. It was a great country, America; any guy could hold the world's record, if he was good enough; that was why they always got all the records in America; there wasnt no getting around it it was a great country; and Jesse Owens beat Hitler in the Olympic Games; and they got the biggest oranges and grapefruits in the world. YOU ARE ENTERING MADISONVILLE KENTUCKY, the sign said, THE FINEST TOWN ON EARTH. It was the ony country on the face of the earth that used the shooting gunsling, as distinguished from the carrying gunsling; they had *always* had the best riflemen; they dint have to take nothing off nobody.

Oh, those goddam bastardly Germans.

He got up quickly and then walked vaguely across to go out on the porch but the blackout curtains were drawn so instead he went into the kitchen, and sat down there.

In the bedroom, behind the carefully locked door that Georgette always locked now every night, Georgette was saying:

"Well, I dont care what you say! Sooner or later something is going to crack. I'm a nervous wreck. He just cant go on like this indefinitely, Alma."

They both of them knew it, but they did not either one know what to do about it. Because they had both already done everything they could either one think of. And in the end it was Prewitt himself who precipitated the transmogrification.

He found the article in the afternoon paper, on the afternoon of the eighth day. He had been reading the papers regularly again, if you could call running your eyes over the black marks on the white paper "reading," but this item when he saw it was not black marks but words. It was a small item on a back page that told how on the morning of December 7th the guards at the Schofield Barracks Post Stockade had flung open the gates and turned the prisoners out to go back to their outfits.

The Warden's remark about his chances—if the Japs or somebody bombed this Rock and they turned all the prisoners loose to go fight— had stuck in his mind like a dart thrown into a whirling board, and now it pulled everything else into a vortex of juxtaposition around it. The Warden had strained to think up the least likely possibility he could think of—and that was just exactly what happened!

It all quite suddenly became very reasonable. He could feel his mind crawling up out of the frozen mud and standing forth to look on the sun. All he had to do was get back to the Company without getting picked up. After he had hunted out the uniform, he got Alma's .38 Special out of the desk and checked the cartridges in the cylinder and put some extras from the box in his pocket.

The last paragraph of the article had gone on to say that, since they had opened the gates on the 7th, there had been fewer new prisoners committed than during any other eight day period in the Stockade's history. That was fine; he was all for it; but he was not going to be one of them. Not when all he had to do was get back to the Company. The MPs were not going to pick him up now.

After he had tucked the gun in his belt, he looked around for anything else of his valuable enough to take with him, because if he never saw this place again it would be too soon. But outside of the civilian clothes they had bought for him, there wasnt anything; except the one finished copy of *The Re-enlistment Blues* which he folded carefully and stuck in his notebook of book titles and buttoned down carefully into his breast pocket. Then he sat down to wait for them to come home.

And so it was that, when they came home from work on the evening of the eighth day, he was waiting for them eagerly in the living room, holding the afternoon paper impatiently. His eyes, though not what you could strictly call sober, were reasonably clear; and he had shaved, and bathed, and changed his clothes; he had even combed out his hair, which was getting quite long by this time.

They were both so surprised that they were inside the door and already sitting down, before they either one even noticed that the clean clothes he had put on happened to be his uniform. In the starched uniform, his face startlingly clean and shining, he looked boyishly hopeful and eager, beneath the puffiness under his eyes.

"If I'd had an ounce of goddamned sense," he said happily, as he held out the paper, "I'd of gone back Sunday morning like I had a hunch to. Hell, if I'd gone right on out to the CP at Hanauma Bay I'd of probly got there before they did."

Alma took the paper, and read it, and handed it on to Georgette.

"If I'd of left then," he said, "I wouldnt of had any trouble at all getting back. Everything was so confused and so many guys were trying to get back that nobody would have noticed me. Now its going to be harder, but once I get back to the Compny under my own power and report in, I'm all right."

"I see you've got my gun," Alma said.

Georgette, who had finished reading the article, laid the paper down on the chair and got up without saying anything and went to draw the blackout curtains against the twilight outside.

"I dont think I'll need it," Prew said. "Its just a precaution. I'll bring it back first time I get a pass. Well," he said, on his way to the door, "I'll see you all. You better turn out the lights when I go out."

"But arent you going to wait until morning?" Alma said. "Its almost dark now."

"Wait, hell," Prewitt said. "The ony reason I waited this long was to let you know where I went so you wouldnt wonder what happened to me."

"Well, that was certainly considerate of you," Alma said tightly.

"I figured I owed you that much," he said.

"Yes," Alma said, "I guess you owe me that much."

With his hand on the knob he turned back from the door. "Hey, whats the matter? You sound like you think I'm going away for ever. I may get compny punishment for a couple weeks, but soon as they let me have a pass I'll be back up."

"No you wont," Alma said. "Because I wont be here. And neither will Georgette," she added.

"Why not?"

"Because we're going back to the States, thats why!" she said wildly.

"When?"

"We're scheduled for a boat leaving January 6th."

"Well," he said, and took his hand off the knob. "How come?"

"Because we're being evacuated!" Alma said recklessly.

"Well," he said slowly, "then I'll try and get back up before then."

" 'I'll try and get back up before then,' " she mimicked. "Is that all it means to you? You know god damned well you wont be able to get back up before then."

726

"I might," he said. "What the hell do you want me to do? stay here till you're ready to leave? I've already stayed out over a week now. I stay much longer I wont be able to go back at all."

"You could at least stay until morning. They'll have patrols out all night," she said, her voice beginning to crumble. "And theres a curfew at sundown."

"They'll have patrols out all day, too. As far as that goes, it'll be easier to make it at night."

"Maybe if you stayed till morning you'd change your mind," she wept at him, openly and suddenly weeping, nakedly and without preparation, in the same way a bullet is suddenly nakedly and without preparation in flight from a gun barrel.

Georgette, who had silently drawn all the blackout curtains, just as silently came down the steps from the glass doors and went up the steps into the kitchen.

"I dont think thats too much to ask," Alma wept.

"Change my mind about what?" Prew said uncomfortably. "About going back? And what'll I do when you ship out for the States? Jesus Christ!"

"Maybe I wouldnt go back," Alma offered weepingly.

"Well, Jesus Christ!" he said fuddledly. His distaste and impatience were both frank in his voice. "I thought you *had* to go back."

"No, I dont have to go back!" Alma yelled potently between weepings like an angry face thrust out between bars. "But if you walk out that door I sure as hell will go back!

"What do you want to go back to the Army for?" she cried, getting her breath. "What did the Army ever do for you? besides beat you up, and treat you like scum, and throw you in jail like a criminal? What do you want to go back to that for?"

"What do I want to go back for?" Prewitt said wonderingly. "I'm a soldier."

"A soldier," Alma said inarticulately. "A soldier!" Through the fast-drying tears on her face she began to laugh at him wildly. "A soldier," she said helplessly. "A Regular. From the Regular Army. A thirty-year-man."

"Sure," he said, grinning uncertainly like a man who does not get the joke, "a thirty-year-man." Then he grinned genuinely. "With only twenty-four years to go."

"Jesus!" Alma said. "Jesus! Jesus Christ!"

"Will you turn off the lights while I go out?" he said.

"I will," Georgette said firmly, but gladly, from the steps to the kitchen. She came down then and went over to the switch by the blackout-curtained glass doors, and in the darkness he slipped the night lock and went out and closed the door after him.

Chapter 52

From outside the house looked full dark as if there was not a soul home. He stood a minute happily and looked back at it, still feeling a little drunk although he had not had a drink since around three o'clock, feeling free.

She would get over it in a couple days. He knew that. When he got a pass and came back up she would be as glad to see him as ever. He was not worried about her going back to the States.

One good thing about the Army. It kept you separated from your women so much they never had the chance to get sick of you. And vice versa.

After he had gone a block he stopped and took the pistol out of his belt and put it in his pants pocket. Then he went on. The pistol, and the shells in the other pocket, dragged at his thighs as he walked. The pistol especially was very bulky.

But if he put his hands in his pockets if they stopped him.

There was always the chance he could talk them out of it.

But no bunch of lousy MPs were going to take him in and keep him from getting back to the Company. He had made up his mind.

It would be best to follow Sierra down into Kaimuki. Wilhelmina was shorter. But most of the houses were close to the street on Sierra. So were their garages. And the yards were all terraced with brick or stone walls. There were more dark nooks and niches among the fairy tale houses of Sierra. He was not worried about after he got out of Kaimuki.

When he got out of Kaimuki he would cross Waialae Avenue and go over into the Waialae Golf Course.

The Waialae Golf Course was a strip of dull barren but slightly higher ground between the Highway and the beach, treeless and all sand hills and scrubgrass, which had never been good for anything else but a golf course. Where Waialae Avenue that ran through Kaimuki met Kealaolu Avenue it changed its name and became the Kalanianaole Highway to Makapuu Head, and the resulting triangle between the two avenues and the beach was the Waialae Golf Course. He knew the Waialae Golf Course like the back of his hand. They had used to meet a couple of gook maids on the 5th Tee every night, last year during maneuvers. Going through the golf course meant he would have to cross the Highway twice because at its eastern end the Highway narrowed in almost to the beach. But going through the golf course, which he knew, was worth the risk of crossing the Highway twice.

After that, the only hard thing was the causeway over the salt marsh clear out just this side of Koko Head. The causeway was about half a mile long and he would probly have to sprint it. But after that, it was made.

All the beach positions along here belonged to G Company and he could have turned in at any one of them. But he did not want to turn in to one of the beach positions. He wanted to turn in at the CP at Hanauma Bay. Under his own power.

The trip through the golf course was something like the wild loud nightmare of the long walk to Alma's after Fatso had cut him. And it was something like the dreamy stillness of the stalk through Waikiki the night he had hunted Angelo Maggio drunkenly down Kalakaua. There was no sound except his breathing and the scuff of his shoes in the sand. Not a living soul moved anywhere in the blackness. He was completely alone in a world as soundproofed and as black as the inside of a coal mine. There was not a single light to be seen anywhere. No windows. No streetlights. No neon on the juke joints. Not even car headlights. Hawaii had gone to war. He was glad to be getting back.

Once, over on the Highway as he moved east he saw one patrol car with blue headlights rolling slowly west in the opposite direction. It excited him strangely. He stopped for a minute to watch it. He had been very careful when he crossed Waialae the first time. He had waited a long time and made very sure there was nothing on the Highway. Those blue headlights were supposed to be invisible from the air and maybe they were. But on the ground you could see them a mile away.

He was just as careful when he came up to the second crossing, near the end of the golf course. He was coming down from higher ground with no obstructions and he could see almost half a mile each way and there was not a blue light anywhere. So he did not stop. He just started on across. If there had been a patrol car with its light on anywhere within a mile he could have seen it easily.

What he could not have seen easily, if at all, was a patrol car with its lights off. But he was not expecting to see any patrol cars with their lights off. So he did not look for any.

It was sitting about thirty yards to the west of him in the middle of the Highway.

As he came up onto the shoulder and stepped out on to the asphalt it turned its lights on, the two blue headlights and one spot that was a much lighter blue, almost white. He saw it then. He was caught square in the center of the beam. If he had crossed a hundred yards back or fifty yards further on, it might not have heard him, even though he was not trying to move quietly.

His first instinct was to run but he choked it off. It wouldnt have done any good anyway. He was almost in the middle of the Highway, with flat open ground on both sides of it. Besides, there was still always the chance he might talk them out of it, before he had to make the break.

"Halt!" a voice erupted at him nervously.

But he was already halted. It made him think of the night Warden had halted him, that time at Hickam Field, and he wanted to laugh wildly. Oh, the bastards, the bastards, the smart smug bastards. Sitting there with their lights off. Just when it was all going so good. They would have to pull a smart one like that.

The patrol car, it was a jeep, pulled up slowly and cautiously to within ten yards of him. There were four scared MPs in it; he could see their blue faces and the blue light reflecting from the white letters of their brassards. They all had helmets on. The one beside the driver was standing up staring at him over a Thompson gun above the windshield; he could see the bulge of the Cutts Comp on the muzzle.

"Who goes there?"

"A friend," he said.

The two in the back, who doubtless considered the answer to be a stock reply to a stock question, were climbing out over the side reluctantly slowly. They were covering him with pistols.

"Advance, friend, and be recognized," said the bigger one squeakily. Then he cleared his throat.

And he, Prewitt that is, the unrecognized friend, came toward them slowly. Thinking how now, for a split minute out of the time run, by a happenstance of smartness on their part and dumbness on his, they held it all in their hands. A thing that had started almost a year ago, with Chief Bugler Houston, and led up through Dynamite Holmes and the boxing into The Treatment and Ike Galovitch and from there to the Stockade and Jack Malloy and the late Fatso Judson, and a lot of other things both before and after, to finally here, where, for this split minute that was the current point of time in the line of time which was not a line but an infinite series of points, four strangers held it all in their hands without even knowing it.

"Halt!" the bigger one said again. With four eyes and two pistol holes the two of them looked him over cautiously.

"Its all right, Harry," said the bigger one, a little more confidently. "He's a GI."

Well, at least there was that, anyway.

The man standing up staring at him over the Thompson gun sat back down, and there was an unheard sound of a great relaxing, like a vast sigh of relief.

"Douse that spot," called the bigger one. In the dimmer light the two of them came up to him.

"What the hell you doin out here, Mack?" said the bigger one indignantly. He was a S/Sgt. The other was a Cpl. "You like to scared the livin shit out of us. We get a call from Position Sixteen somebody movin aroun out on the golf course and we think we got a whole battalion of parachutists in our lap."

He understood it then. Somebody had seen his silhouette against the blue headlights of the patrol car he had stood in the golf course and watched. Somebody from C Company. But you'd think a goddam man who claimed to be such a hotshot Infantry soldier would have remembered that.

"I'm going back to my position," he said.

"Yeah. What position."

"Number Eighteen. Down the road."

"Eighteen, hunh. What outfit."

"G Company, —th Infantry."

The S/Sgt relaxed a little bit more. "Dont G Company —th Infantry know theres a goddam curfew on?"

"Yes."

"Then what the hell you doin off your position?"

"I'm just goin home from seein my wahine. She lives right over there," he nodded across the golf course.

"You got a pass?"

"No."

"No pass," said the other one with finality. "Come on, lets take him in and get it over with." He was being tough. He had relaxed some too now. He had been bad scared and now he was being tough. He had put his pistol back in the holster.

"Just hold your horses, Corprl Oliver," said the S/Sgt.

"Its immaterial to me," said the Cpl.

"Who's in charge of Position Eighteen, friend?" said the S/Sgt.

"S/Sgt Choate."

The two MPs looked at each other.

"You know who's in charge of Eighteen, Harry?" the S/Sgt called back to the jeep.

In the jeep there was a consultation. "No," Harry said. "But we can sures hell find out in a minute."

"Okay," said the S/Sgt. "Lets run him down there."

"Its immaterial to me," said the Cpl. "But I say take him down to the Station. I dont like his looks, Fred. Look at that uniform. Its garrison, and starched neat as a pin. Whats he doin in a garrison uniform? There aint no barricksbag press on that uniform. That uniform aint seen the inside of a barricksbag since it was last to the cleaners."

"It wont hurt to run him down there," said the S/Sgt.

"Its immaterial to me," the Cpl said. "But it might hurt a lot. If he taken off on us."

"How the hell is he goin to taken off on four of us, for Chrisake?"

"What if he just happen to of stole that nice clean uniform?" said the Cpl. "He might be a sabatoor. And his buddies waitin down the road to cut us down. Its immaterial to me. But how do we know he aint a spy or something?"

"How about that, friend?" said the S/Sgt. "You got buddies waitin down the road to cut us down?"

"I aint no spy, for Christ's sake. Do I look like a spy?" That was one he had not anticipated. To be taken in for a possible spy. That would really be good.

"But how the hell *we* know you aint a spy?" said the Cpl. "Its immaterial to me."

"Thats right," said the S/Sgt. "You might be Tojo for all we know."

"Maybe he's gettin ready to blow up the Governor's Mansion," said the Cpl. "Or something. Its immaterial to me. But I say take him down to the Station. Then it aint our responsibility."

"Ah, he aint no spy," said S/Sgt disgustedly. He had not put his pistol away, but it was hanging down at arm's length by his side. "You got any identification on you, Mack? So we could tell who you are?"

"No."

"Aint you got nothing?"

"No."

"Then I'm afraid we'll have to taken you in, friend," the S/Sgt said. "You ought to have some kind of identification. I hate to do it. But then we just cant let every son of a bitch and his brother go runnin around all over at night without no identification like they was generals, either."

Well, it was what he had expected. It had only been a shot in the dark anyway. But the S/Sgt was a pretty good joe and had come so near there for a minute. He made a try.

"Wait a minute. Listen you guys. You guys know I aint no spy. I been in this man's Army six years. And plan to stay in twenty-four more. But you know what the Provost will do if you taken me in. He have me in the Stockade sure as you're born. Theres a goddam war on and the whole Army needs ever man it can lay hands on. It wont do the war no good to send me to the Stockade. And I been waitin six years for this war. Please, give me a break."

"You shoulda thoughta all that before you taken off," said the Cpl.

"If there was any chance of me bein a spy, it would be differnt. But you guys know I aint no spy or nothing like that."

"You knew what the orders was," said the Cpl. "You knew there was a curfew. So you taken off to see your shackjob. Okay. You knew what you'd get if you got caught.

"Besides, how we suppose to know who you are. Its immaterial to me. But you could say you're anything. Everybody knows G Company of the —th is all down along here."

"Shut up, Oliver," said the S/Sgt. "Who's in charge of this detail, me or you? That what you said about the Stockade," he said. "Thats true as Christ's cross. There aint no sense in throwin a man in there where he's useless when theres a war on for some little thing like this here. Its a waste of valuble manpower. Its stupid."

"Of course its stupid!"

"But at the same time, I got to be *sure*. Aint you got *no* kind of identification on you, Mack? If you just had *some* kind of identification on you. So we could be sure. Any old thing, that would identify you."

"No," he lied, "not a thing," fingering with his left hand in his pocket among the cartridges the old, green, frayed, SP Card. The used-to-be passport. The once-was visa. Back into the promised land, that everybody always acted like was the desert and made like they wanted to get out of. The last year's membership card. That would not get you into the Clubroom this year why the hell dint you remember to keep up your dues this card and five cents will get you a good nickel cigar. And that, because everybody who was not over the hill had had to turn their's in a month ago, was now not only useless, but actively dangerous, to show. There was a good one for you. There was the best one yet. The Warden would *really* love that one.

"Then we'll just *have* to take you in," the S/Sgt said.

He tried once more time.

"You could take me down to Position Eighteen? and let them identify me?"

"Yeh, I could do that," the S/Sgt said.

"I swear to you they know me there," he swore to them. Because he would settle for that. He hadnt wanted to. But he would. Gladly. He wasnt proud. What difference did it make? if Chief Choate sent him on down to the CP after he'd lied the MPs off? or if he went there under his own power? What did he care?

"You aint got the right to take the chance, Fred," said the Cpl. "Its immaterial to me. But this guy."

"He's right there," Fred said. "My job is to not take no chances whatever. If you aint got no identification, I'm afraid we'll have to take you down."

"Well for Christ's sake do something," Harry called indifferently from the jeep. "Time's a wastin."

"You shut up," Fred the S/Sgt hollered. "Its my job, I got to answer for it. Not you.

733

"I'm afraid we'll have to take you down, Mack," he said reluctantly. He raised his pistol that was still hanging at arm length and made a half-hearted shooing motion toward the jeep.

"Dont *you* know I aint a spy?"

"Sure. I know it. But."

"And take your goddam hands out of your pockets," said the Cpl disgustedly. "Its immaterial to me. But how the hell long you been in the Army, friend? to keep your hands in your pockets?"

"Lets go Mack," said the S/Sgt.

Well, then that was the way it was then. Okay. Then so be it. He could still work back up and around them. There was only four. And sneak past across the Highway. They wouldnt look for him on the other side of the Highway. And work on east from there. So thats whats the matter. They werent going to take this one back. They'd never take this one back.

"Come on, Mack," the S/Sgt said, still shooing half-heartedly. "Lets go."

He let the mind, which at a great cost in Kentucky pride had been kept loose and open with the mineral oil of belief, constipate itself and close down into the old, narrow, clear, hard, crystal something which was the trademark of Harlan Kentucky and which was the only gift his father had ever given him in his whole life, and even that unwittingly, or he would probly tried to take it back.

"I said take your goddam hands out of your pockets," the Cpl said disgustedly.

He jerked his hands out of his pockets, Alma's Police .38 in the right one, and with the left one snatched the S/Sgt's still shooing pistol and threw it sailing heavily across the other side of the road, and with the right one bent the barrel of the .38 over the jaw of the helmeted Cpl.

And Prewitt, feeling airishly free in the arms and legs, without ropes, without handcuffs, without shackles, free to breathe too, without a strait jacket, feeling so free all over he was almost able to believe he was free, was running freely and without restriction into the night, into the levelness, into the darkness, of the Territory of Hawaii's Waialae Golf Course. Treelessness, sand hills, scrubgrass, and all. There was a big sandtrap right around here someplace.

Running hard, sprinting, he flashed a look back over his shoulder and saw the two of them still there in the blue light of the headlights. They never should have done that, his mind registered automatically, they should have headed for the darkness first thing, he could shoot them both, even with this gun he did not know.

Then, in the middle of the split flash of the glance, he realized they did not know yet he had a gun, and were therefore not technically guilty of a mistake. At least not a reckless mistake. That made his sense of propriety feel a little less offended. Mistakes in knowledge were at least excusable. But a good soldier should never make a *reckless* mistake.

Fred the S/Sgt was yelling. "Back down to the corner. Theres a field phone station there." The Cpl, his left hand holding his jaw, was just coming up shakily off his knees and there was the big red merry wink of his .45, before he was even clear up yet.

Prewitt quit looking and stopped sprinting and started the skirmicher's zigzag, wanting to grin. They would measure up all right. Except for that one mistake of not getting out of the light, they were doing fine. And doing it fast. Where the hell was that sandtrap?

"All the men they got available," Fred the S/Sgt was still yelling. "And alert all the beach positions. This guy wasnt no soldier." The motor of the jeep roared. "No, not now, you fool!" Fred the S/Sgt yelled. "The light, first! The spot. Turn on the spot."

Off to his left not far Prew saw the sandtrap.

Then the spotlight went on.

He stopped and turned around facing them.

Almost simultaneously, from the rider's seat of the jeep, Harry's Thompson gun batted its one big eye in a series of winks that had all the false coy merriness of a bloodshot one-eyed bar pickup.

Prewitt was standing facing them, almost on the lip of his sandtrap.

Maybe it was what Fred the S/Sgt yelled about alerting the beach positions. He had the Infantryman's abhorrence of being shot at by his own outfit. Or maybe it was that about getting out every man available. There was still yet the causeway over the salt marsh and he saw in his mind the blue-lighted jeeps crowding on it waiting, till it looked like a rich man's Christmas Tree in the front yard and he had been running from them a long time now he was out of breath now. Or perhaps it might have been because he felt such a strong affection for them suddenly the way they were handling it, almost proud of them, a confidence in them, they were really handling it well, it was a sound competent piece of work. He could not have done better himself. They were competent. Or, maybe it was just, simply, that last thing the S/Sgt had yelled: *"This guy wasnt no soldier."*

Perhaps it was only a mechanical thing caused by the going on of the spotlight, the instinctive move of the Kentuckian who, unlike the Infantryman, is used to being shot at by friends, but has an almost religious abhorrence of being shot in the back.

Anyway, he knew Harry's Thompson gun was winking at him, as he turned around.

Standing there, in that couple of seconds, he could have fired twice with the .38 and killed two of them, Fred and the Cpl, standing there in the light of the headlights, they were perfect targets, but he did not shoot. He did not even want to shoot. He hardly even thought about shooting. They were the Army, too. And how could a man kill a soldier for just simply doing a sound competent job? It was still the rottenest word in the language. He had killed once. It did not do any good. Even though it was justified, and he did not regret it, it still did not do any good. Maybe it never did any good. The other still went right on. And if he could not kill the other, he would kill nothing. You could kill and kill and kill. He would not become a Disciple of the Word. And these were the Army, too. It was not true that all men killed the things they loved. What was true was that all things killed the men who loved them. Which, after all, was as it should be.

Three somethings rent their way agonizingly through his chest in echelon and he fell over backwards into the sandtrap and Harry's Thompson gun ceased its short burst that had been going on for what seemed such a long time.

Well, I learned it, Jack. I learned it. The sandtrap was deep and the slope was steep and he had fallen on a downhill lie and had bounced over onto his face in the sand of the bottom. His chest hurt numbly, but it was not especially uncomfortable. But he could hear them coming up, and he did not want them to see him like this. Not facedown in the sand. His legs would not work, but using his elbows a little he managed to roll himself over downhillwards onto his back and to pull himself on down out onto the sand where it was level. Then he was done. Well, Jack, I learned it.

He would look better this way. And he could look up at them. I bet you never thought I'd learn it, did you, Jack?

"He just stopped," Harry's voice was saying, still shocked, as they came on up. "He just stopped. I wasnt firing at nothing special. I was just firing. Then the light went on. And he just stopped."

He was glad he had been able to roll himself over and get down level onto the sand. And so this was it, this was the one. He remembered his mother lying on the cot. Well, you got something to shoot at there, kid. You always wondered just how it would come. You always thought it would somehow be special. What you couldnt imagine was how it would have this just everyday quality. Like taking a crap. Or getting your rocks off. Or rolling a smoke. Just common, ordinary, every day. You sweated and sweated it out, and waited and waited on it, all your life you waited on it, and then finally it came, and all the time you had hoped you would be able to do it well, and then it came, and there it was, and now you would see if you would do it well. You did not guess it would be everyday, though. It would have been a lot easier to do well if it had been special. He felt glad when he saw their heads come over the rim of the sandtrap and watched them sliding down the slope. It would be a lot easier to do it well when you had an audience.

"Jesus," the Cpl said. "Those Thompsons sure mess them up."

"You know I didnt mean to shoot him," Harry said. "He just stopped. It makes you feel pretty shitty."

Thats what they call passive resistance, soldier. Aint that right, Jack? He was sliding down a long skislide of long snow, like. And he could feel himself beginning to go clear out of himself. And the cord he had seen that time in the Stockade that looked like it was made of come kept stretching and stretching as he coasted. Then he slowed and stopped coasting, delicately like, as if something hadnt quite made up its mind yet, and then began to come back in a little. So this was the way it was, hunh. Who would of guessed it was like this. He was glad he had been able to get off his face in the sand.

"Is he dead yet?" the Cpl said.

"Not yet," Fred said.

"Look," the Cpl said. "He had a gun. In the sand there. He didnt fire it?"

"He just stopped," Harry said.

"You want me to take a look now?" the Cpl said.

"Wait a while," Fred said.

That Fred. He was a good boy. He understood. It was like the having them find you with your face in the sand. He wanted to say something, to do something, something good, a joke maybe, that would show them how well he was going to do it. But when he tried to speak he found he couldnt. Cant even speak. Cant move now either. Can just lay and look at them. No audience after all. Well, it wont be so long. It'll just be for a little while.

He wished he'd got a chance to read the rest of those books. And he hated to see the ones he had read be wasted. Somehow he had felt they would be used. The worst was to think how it would all go right on afterwards. Alma. And Warden. Maggio, somewhere. All go right on. He was selfish. He did not want it all to go right on.

You wouldnt think it would take so long. Even all tore up, it took so long. My body's all tore up. My body. He did not want his body to be all tore up.

You can let go if you want to. They'd never know. You cant speak. You cant move. And its taking too long. And my body's all tore up. Tore to pieces. Tore all up. Its a shame. And they'd never know.

But you'd know. You got to do it right. It wont take very long. Just a minute more now. And you want to do it good. Even if nobody will know it. Just another minute. Then it will end. Then it will be over.

He lay, feeling sweaty, and made himself look at it. At its being over. Looked it in the face, feeling sweaty.

I'm scared.

If you could just say something. Just a word. If you could just even move a little. If you could just do anything, besides just lay and look at them, and look at it. Christ, but the world was a lonesome place.

But then, as if in a way he was seeing double, he realized that it wasnt really going to end after all, that it would never end. There wasnt even that consolation, he thought sweatily. What he had thought once a long time ago, he thought, that day in Choy's with old Red. How that there was always an endless chain of new decidings. It was right after all. That made him feel good, the being right.

"Man, those Thompsons sure do make a mess of them," Cpl Oliver said. "Aint he dead yet?"

"I cant understand why he stopped," Harry said complainingly. "Or why he didnt shoot. It makes you feel like an awful son of a bitch. Hell, I didnt know. I was just firing. Honest, I didnt know a tall. Fred, listen?" Harry Temple was crying nervously. "Fred; Fred; listen?"

"Shut up," Fred Dixon said.

"Honest, Fred? Fred, listen?"

"I said shut up," Dixon said. He slapped him. "Take it easy, now."

"I might as well look him over," Tom Oliver said.

"Go over there and sit down, Harry," Dixon said. "Oliver, what'd you find?"

"Nothing yet," Tom Oliver said. "I knew he's no soljer. Hey, wait a minute. Look at this. Heres an old SP Card. Dint I tell you that uniform looked funny? He's over the hill, thats what he is."

"Yeah," Fred Dixon said. "What outfit does it say?"

"Pvt Robt E L Prewitt, G Compny, —th Infantry," Oliver said. "Well. So he is a soljer, after all."

"Yeah," Dixon said. "Tryin to get back to his outfit. Well, we better get in touch with them and have somebody come out and identify this body. Come on, Harry. Tom, you stay here. We'll drive up the field phone station."

Warden was in the orderly tent when the call came in over the field phone. He sent Rosenberry over to get Weary Russell and went himself. Lt Ross was gone to Schofield with Pete Karelsen for the day to see the Colonel to try and get Pete re-instated, and they were not back yet. Warden was glad they were not back yet.

"You're in charge, Rosenberry, till we get back," he said. "Make a note of any calls not emergency. Emergency calls relay right on in to Battalion."

"Yes, Sir," Rosenberry said quietly.

"Come on, Weary. You got the jeep?"

"So old Prewitt's dead," Weary said when they were on the road. "You really think its Prewitt, First?"

"I dont know. We'll know pretty soon. Its right this end of the golf course," he told him.

He did not say anything else during the rest of the ride, till they got there.

"There it is," he said.

There was quite a cluster of blue headlights and flashlights alongside the road. They couldnt have missed it. It was about forty yards back in off the road.

"Pull right on in there with them," Warden said.

"Right," Weary said, and put her in low range.

There was the patrol jeep, two other jeeps, two captains, one major, and one lieutenant colonel. All of them clustered around the sandtrap.

"You are the Company Commander of G Company, —th Infantry?" the Lt Col asked him as he and Weary climbed out.

"No, Sir. I'm the first sergeant."

"First sergeant!" the Lt Col said. He looked at his chevrons. "Wheres your Company Commander?"

"He's out on a mission, Sir."

"Well, where are your other officers?"

"They're all out on missions, Sir."

"Thats incredible!" the Lt Col exclaimed. "They cant all be out on missions!"

"Sir, we have a ten or fifteen mile stretch of beach positions that have to be inspected."

"Of course," the Lt Col said. "But what we need here is an officer. This is a serious matter."

"Sir, I am authorized to act in any contingency if the Company officers are absent."

"You have written orders to that effect?"

"Yes, Sir," Warden said. "But not with me."

"Well," the Lt Col said. Then he said, "Did you know this man personally, Sergeant?"

"Yes, Sir." Weary Russell was down in the sandtrap, squatting on his hams talking to two of the patrol detail.

"Well," the Lt Col said. "Go ahead and identify him then."

Warden stepped down into the sandtrap and looked at him. One of the patrol detail turned on a blue flashlight.

"Thats Prewitt, Sir. He has been absent without leave since the 20th of October."

"Then you identify him," the Lt Col said. "Officially."

"Yes, Sir." He came back up out of the trap.

"I wish we could have had an officer," the Lt Col said. "A thing like

739

this is serious. Very well," he said, and moved with a paper into the blue lights of one of the jeeps. He was a tall spare man. "Sign here, Sergeant.

"Thank you. Now here are the man's effects. I had them itemized. You'll have to sign for those too, please."

"These are all, Sir?" Warden said.

"You realize, of course," the Lt Col said, "that my men are in no way responsible for what has happened. They were acting in the line of duty. That will all come out at the inquest."

"Yes, Sir," Warden said.

"The man is obviously a deserter," the Lt Col said. "When my men tried to bring him in he broke and ran. Then when they fired, the man stopped and turned and turned back directly into the line of their fire. I wish we could have had an officer out here. You tell your Company Commander to stop in the Provost's office and see me tomorrow. Lt Col Hobbs. All right, sign here, Sergeant. For those effects. I do not know, of course, what verdict the inquest board will bring in. You will be informed."

"For the sake of the man's relatives, Sir," Warden said, "it might be better if they could just simply make it Killed in Line of Duty. The names of your men could be left out, and that way there would be less of an incident all the way round."

The Lt Col looked at him a little curiously. "Thats an excellent idea. I was just going to mention it myself, as a matter of fact."

"Yes, Sir," Warden said.

"Still, of course," the Lt Col said carefully, "you realize I have absolutely no sayso with the board's verdict."

"Oh, no, Sir," Warden said.

"Well, I guess that about covers it, Sergeant. We will take the body down to the mortuary, of course."

"Which mortuary, Sir?"

"The customary one," the Lt Col said. "I forget the name. You know the one I mean. The same one that used to do all the Army's business before the war."

"Yes, Sir."

"He will be interred here, of course. Probably the Red Hill cemetery. That will all be taken care of later."

"Sir," Warden said formally, "I would like to make formal request that this body be buried in the Army's permanent cemetery at Schofield Barracks."

The Lt Col looked at him again. "Upon what authority, Sergeant?"

"None, Sir," Warden said. "Expect that I'm sure my Company Commander would prefer it. Our Company has other men buried there."

"The Schofield cemetery is a permanent cemetery," the Lt Col said. "I thought you said this man had relatives. Since the Pearl Harbor attack all temporary interments have been made in the new Red Hill Cemetery."

"Yes, Sir," Warden said. "But it will be some time before any bodies can be shipped home, Sir. Probably until after the end of the war. And this man was a Regular Army soldier. He had at least eight years service," he lied.

"Oh," the Lt Col said. "Well," he said finally, "I believe I can attend to that for you. I'm an Old Army man myself, Sergeant."

"Yes, Sir," Warden said.

The Lt Col made a note in his pocket notebook. "Now. If you will just sign for these effects, please. There is nothing but this wallet, a small pocketknife, this obsolete SP Card, and a keychain with one key. Sign here, please."

"These are all, Sir?" Warden said.

"Except the pistol. I shall have to confiscate that, of course. And the cartridges." He extended his pen. "Now sign here, please."

Warden did not take it. "I want to be sure its everything, Sir."

"Sergeant, I told you it was." The Lt Col looked around frowningly. "Now if you will just—"

"Begging the Colonel's pardon, Sir." The S/Sgt in charge of the patrol detail stepped up to them and saluted.

"Yes, Sgt Dixon," the Lt Col said impatiently. "What is it?"

"Sir, I believe there was another item that is not on the list."

"There was?" the Lt Col said. "And why wasnt I told of this before, Sergeant?" he said sternly.

"I guess it just slipped past in the confusion, Sir."

"What was the item, Sergeant?"

"A small black pocket notebook, Sir," the S/Sgt said. "The last time I saw it it was lying on the seat of our jeep there."

"Then I am forced to beg your pardon, First Sergeant," the Lt Col said.

"Thats quite all right, Sir," Warden said.

"I'll get it for you, Sergeant," the S/Sgt said.

"I'll go with you," Warden said.

At the jeep they had to turn on the flashlight to look for it. It had fallen off the seat down into the floor well of the rider's seat.

"Here you are, Sergeant," the S/Sgt said. As he picked it up a paper fell out of it onto the jeep floor.

"Just a minute, Sergeant," Warden said. He borrowed the flash and got the paper.

"I didnt see it," the S/Sgt apologized.

"Its all right." Warden opened the paper and held the flash on it. It looked like short lines of rhymed verse, a poem. At the top was the title printed in capitals. THE RE-ENLISTMENT BLUES. He did not try to read it. He folded the paper and buttoned it down in his shirt pocket carefully and looked at the notebook. There was nothing in it but a long list of books under the printed caption: TO READ. Somehow, even in the midst of all this, he felt an apart aloof moment of vague surprise, to find a list of books like that in Prewitt's effects. Most of them, he had read himself, at one time or another. But he did not expect Prewitt to have wanted to read them.

"You know," the S/Sgt said as Warden buttoned the notebook into his other shirt pocket, "we feel pretty bad about this, Sergeant." He looked around him, and then went on in a low voice. "Harry Temple, he's a Pfc, the one who did the shooting, is all busted up over it. Its not like a Jap or something like that. I guess you think we're lying. But that was what he actually did. He turned right back into our fire."

"What *did* he do?" Warden said.

"Nothing," the S/Sgt said. "He was running. Cpl Oliver, he's my second in command, he fired two or three times. But he kept running. Then Harry Temple opened up with the Thompson. Just firing. Then the light went on. And your man just suddenly stopped and turned around right into the fire. He had that .38 in his hand, but I dont think he even raised it. We found it in the sand later. You know how those Thompsons are. They spray all over. He was right on the edge of that sandtrap. He could have jumped down in it. I guess you think I'm lying?"

"No," Warden said.

"Was he a friend of yours?"

"No," Warden said. "Not a friend."

"Well, I wanted you to know we were all awfully sorry."

"Everybody's always very sorry," Warden said. "Afterwards."

"Thats right," the S/Sgt said. "He was tryin to get back to his Compny. I could have let him gone. But I didnt. I didnt know. I wasnt sure. This sand," he said vaguely; then he said it again, viciously, "this sand. This goddam sand. Its like a goddam fuckin desert."

"Its all in the game," Warden said. "The whole thing was all in the cards. It wasnt your fault. Forget it."

"I'm going to put in for relief," the S/Sgt said, "from this place. And request another beat on the other side of town. I dont like this goddam sand."

"You cant get away from sand in Hawaii."

"Well, I just wanted you to know, Sergeant," the S/Sgt said.

"Okay," Warden said. He put his hand on the boy's shoulder. "Thanks a lot, Sergeant."

He went on back over to the jeep by the trap, where Weary was still talking earnestly to the two men from the patrol, and signed the receipt for the effects that was still lying on the hood. Then he found the Lt Col and saluted.

"Is that everything now, Sir?"

"Have you signed for the effects?"

"Yes, Sir."

"Then I think that is all. You found the notebook?"

"Yes, Sir."

"I must apologize again for the oversight, Sergeant," the Lt Col said formally.

"Thats quite all right, Sir," Warden said formally.

"I do not like things like that to happen," the Lt Col said. "Well, you're free to leave any time, Sergeant."

"Thank you, Sir." He saluted, and went over to the trap. "Weary! Come on, lets go."

After they had got back on the Highway and Weary had put the jeep back into high range, Warden turned in the seat and looked back at the dwindling cluster of lights. All he seemed able to think about was how there wasnt even going to be any boxing season this year at all now, anyway.

"It gives me the creeps," Weary said. "You'd think he would of at least jump down in the trap."

Warden swung back around in the seat. At least he had been able to do those two things for him, anyway. That of the Service Record, and the getting of him buried in the permanent cemetery at Schofield. Which was where he would have been buried anyway, if the Provost's Lt Col had known he didnt have relatives. Once they had him in the ground they would never bother to move him.

"Remember that time at Hickam?" Weary said. "When you and him got all drunked up and passed out in the middle of the road and I nearly ran over both of you?"

Warden did not answer. There was still the third thing. He knew he ought to go down and see Lorene. She would want the key to her house back, if nothing else. But then, he could mail the key with the letter if he took the keychain off it.

"Boy, you were both of you sure drunk that time," Weary said.

"Yeah," Warden said. He would rather take a beating, than to have to go down and see her. But he knew he would go.

"What the hell do you suppose made him do it?" Weary said.

Warden did not answer because he was wondering why did it always all seem to come in bunches?

Chapter 53

Milt Warden had, that morning, received the confirmation of his appointment as a Second Lieutenant (Infantry) in the Officers' Reserve Corps.

In the same batch of dispatches was another letter, from Regiment, informing G Company of the impending removal of its Weapons Platoon Sergeant, Peter J Karelsen.

But they did not know about Pete until later. Lt Ross opened Warden's appointment first.

It was a War Department letter, addressed to the CO of G Company for approval, and it had a long string of endorsements on it. It must have been kicking around channels on the Island since clear before Pearl Harbor. The effect upon Warden, when Lt Ross (with studied indifference) tossed it over onto his desk, was that of a man surprised red-handed in a guilty act. His first, instinctive, reaction was to tear it up quickly and stuff it down in the bottom of the waste basket before anybody saw it. Then he thought about Karen Holmes.

Anyway, Lt Ross had already opened it and seen it first.

At Hanauma Bay, during the first five days after the bombing, they had set up the CP in the popcorn vender's wagon under the grove of kiawe trees. Then when they got the tents from Schofield they still left it in there anyway, ostensibly for camouflage, but in reality because it had a wood floor and was up off the ground.

It was not very big in there and there were four of them, plus the field phone switchboard to the Positions, crowded into it when the Message Center truck delivered the G Company dispatch bag that morning. Him and Rosenberry and Ross, and Culpepper; since Pearl Harbor Culpepper had been promoted to 1st/Lt and been made the Company Exec. And when Warden looked up, they were all three grinning at him.

It was, he had thought sourly looking at them, the same half-assed foolish grin that everybody always got knowingly when some jerk passed out cigars because his stupid wife had a goddam baby. *We know how you did it,* the grins always implied slyly, *we know what was required.* Then the stupid jerk blushes; and if his wife is anywheres around she blushes; and if the goddam baby wasnt red as a beet it would probly blush too. I baptize thee in the name of the Grin, the

744

Blush, and the Holy Twitchett; thou art born of woman; let us kneel, brothers, and all blush together before God; somebody had a baby.

"There'll be some papers to sign yet," Lt Ross grinned at him happily, when he handed it back. "And the oath to take. But to all intents and purposes you are now an Officer in the US Army, Sergeant. My congratulations."

"Army of the US, Ross," Culpepper corrected grinning. "How do you feel, Sergeant?"

"How the hell I supposed to feel?"

"Different," Culpepper grinned. "Consecrated. Like a nun."

"Will I sprout little gold wings, too? To go with the bars?"

They all insisted on shaking his hand. Even Rosenberry insisted on shaking his hand. And 2nd Lt Cribbage, one of the new ROTC boys, who came in along about then from his new command at Makapuu, insisted on shaking his hand.

"When are you going to pass out those cigars?" Cribbage grinned. He was a Purdue man.

"Sgt Warden would never pass out cigars," Culpepper grinned, "not for a little old thing like a commission. You dont know your man, Cribbage."

"Just the same," Cribbage grinned, "I mean to get a cigar out of this promotion."

"Of course, you understand, Sergeant," Lt Ross grinned, "that this is only in the Reserve Corps. So dont get any big ideas. You're still my 1st/Sgt until they send you to Active Duty back Stateside someplace."

"You lucky bastard," Culpepper amended, grinning.

"Amen," Cribbage grinned.

"Oh, Christ," Lt Ross said. Lt Ross had just opened the other letter.

"Whats the matter, Ross?" Culpepper said.

"Look at this, Culpepper," Lt Ross said. He handed him the letter.

Watching them, Warden thought again how much it was all like some kind of a club, a young gentlemen's club, warm, friendly, completely secure, with its own comforting set of rules for parliamentary procedure. The letter went down the chain of command from Ross to Culpepper to Cribbage. Warden was fourth on the list. Rosenberry was last.

When it got to Warden and he saw what it was, he felt a little bit sick in his thighs. In the envelope was a WD policy circular to the effect that all EM of a certain age who were below the Grade of M/Sgt and were engaged in any form of active combat duty, as distinguished from administrative duty, were to be relieved from the active duty list immediately and their names submitted for the evacuation shipping list along with a request for replacements. And that was the end of Pete.

Just to clinch it, stapled to the circular was a mimeograph cut of a Regimental Special Order with the names of thirty or forty EM from the Regiment who would be affected, and two of the names

S/Sgt Peter J Karelsen, G Co
Pvt   Ike (NMI) Galovitch, G Co

were underlined in red pencil.

"Christ, I wont have any platoon left," Cribbage said, "if I lose Sgt Karelsen."

"It'll sure put a hole in the dyke," Culpepper said.

Neither mentioned Ike (NMI) Galovitch.

"I think I'll run down and take a look around Position 16," Lt Culpepper said suddenly. "Then I wont have to go out that way tonight."

"I might as well be getting back out to Makapuu," 2nd Lt Cribbage said, "since theres no mail for me."

"They sure got out from under that one quick," Lt Ross said when they had gone. "Do you suppose if I wrote a letter?"

Rosenberry was finally reading the order.

"A letter wouldnt do any good," Warden said.

"I suppose not," Lt Ross said unhappily. "Goddam it, Sergeant!" he exploded. "They cant do this to me! I cant afford to lose Sgt Karelsen! I just cant, thats all!"

Lt Ross did not mention Ike (NMI) Galovitch either. Lt Ross had been trying to find a way to get Ike transferred ever since he had busted him. Warden had even worked on it some himself. To no avail, because no other outfit on the Post would have him. At any price.

"God *damn* the sons of bitches!" Lt Ross said. "They sit on their ass in Washington and cut their orders according to statistics. What do they know about the real situation? What the hell do they care what its going to do to my Company? They dont have to run it. Well? Come on, Sergeant? Think of something."

Warden had been thinking of something. He had been thinking of Retirement Row down along Kahala Avenue at the foot of Diamond Head. That was where Snuffy Cartwright had gone, when they retired him out of G Co to make room for Warden. Warden suddenly felt an astonishingly, almost unreasonably, powerful twinge of fear and refusal, for Pete, go all over him. And he did not have any illusions of Pete's love for G Company, once the sentimentalities of parting were over.

"Pete's been in this Compny six years," Warden suggested. "You might use that."

"Sure," Lt Ross nodded. "Why, it'll probably break his goddamned old heart. An old man like him."

Rosenberry silently laid the order back on the desk without comment.

"Rosenberry!" Lt Ross cried fretfully. "You dont look so good. You look peakéd. Like you needed some air. Go take yourself a walk someplace, Rosenberry."

"Yes, Sir," Rosenberry said quietly.

"That boy gets on my nerves," Lt Ross sighed when he had gone. "He's too damn quiet. Well, what're we going to do?"

They said old soldiers never died. No, they went to live in cottages on Kahala Avenue at the foot of Diamond Head. And bought surf-casting rods and bait-casting rods. To fish with. And used their old Army rifles to hunt some. At least the ones who had money did, like Snuffy Cartwright. Pete had not made the money gambling Snuffy Cartwright had made; or at least not saved it. Snuffy's wife had saved his for him. Pete did not have a wife. Pete did not even have enough money to buy a middle-aged housekeeper to sleep with, let alone a young wife. Again the astonishingly strong spasm of fear and refusal, for Pete, rolled down over him. Unmarried, sterile from the syph, no gambling savings. No wife no kids no Cadillac. And no prospect of any. Just a lonely old retired ex-soldier. Warden felt, for some obscure reason, he *must* get Pete out of *that*.

"You'll have to take Pete up to Schofield with you," he told Lt Ross, "and see Col Delbert personally."

Lt Ross, who had been leaning forward eagerly, drew back a little. "Oh, I rather hesitate to do anything that drastic."

"You want to keep him, dont you?"

They would put him to teaching draftees about machineguns in the States someplace, for a year, maybe two years, maybe even till the end of the war. It would be a nice soft easy job for an old man. The johns would buy an old timer like Pete all the free beer his gut would hold. He could get drunk every night. And know he was helping the War Effort.

"Well, why dont you go up, Sergeant?" Lt Ross said finally. "You've been in the Regiment a lot longer than I have."

"Hell, I cant go, Lieutenant. You're the Company Commander."

"Thats right. I am," Lt Ross said without joy. "You understand, dont you? I want to do whats right, Sergeant. But then how do we know it would do any good?"

"Its the only chance."

"You really think it would work?"

"It has to."

"But if it doesnt work I'm the one that'll get on the Regimental shitlist," Lt Ross said. "Not you."

747

"Well, what're you tryin to do? Run your Compny?" Warden said. "Or make Captain."

"Ha," Lt Ross cried angrily. "For you its easy. You'll be shipping out of here in a month or so. Ah, piss on it!" he said violently. "Goddam you, Sergeant. You sure talk a great war, anyway."

He went to the door and hollered, a look of outrage against fate dark on his swart Jewish face. "Rosenberry! What the fuck are you doing! Why arent you in here? Go find Sgt Karelsen and tell him I want to see him. And get the lead out of your ass!"

"He's out at Makapuu, Sir," Rosenberry, who had been quietly waiting outside, said quietly.

"Then get a jeep and go the hell after him!" Lt Ross cried. "Dont you think I know where he is? What the hells the matter with you today, Rosenberry?"

"Yes, Sir," Rosenberry's fading voice said quietly.

"God damn that boy," Lt Ross said, coming back. He sat down at his desk and scratched his head. "I think I'll drive the jeep up by myself and leave Russell here. That way there'll just be the two of us, and I can break it to him gently, on the way up. Dont you think that would be best?"

"Yes."

Lt Ross got out his notebook and began making notes on what to say to the Colonel. After he made a few, he muttered "Shit!" and began crossing them out.

"You and your goddam bright ideas," he said angrily. "I dont know why the hell I let you talk me into these things."

"Because you want to do the right thing," Warden said.

"Hunh," Lt Ross said. "Sometimes I wonder who the hell is in command of this outfit. You or me."

He was still making notes concentratedly and, between nervous chewings on his pencil, concentratedly crossing them out, when Rosenberry brought Pete in from Makapuu.

"Come on, Sergeant," Lt Ross said blackly, putting his notebook away. "You and I got to make a business trip to Schofield."

"Yes, Sir," Pete said formally, and saluted. He was too old a hand not to know an ax was about to fall someplace. He had put his teeth in, the first time he'd had them in since Pearl Harbor, except for meals.

The two of them, Ross gloomily, Pete inscrutably formal, took off in silence, complete with gas masks, rifle belts, helmets, and their carbines, and Warden went back to work and settled down to wait for the outcome. He was still waiting for them to come back when the call had come in about Prewitt.

And when he and Weary got back from the identification of Prewitt's body, the other jeep still was not in the motor pool. Which meant that Ross and Pete still were not back yet.

Weary delivered him to the popcorn wagon and then hurried off to bed down the jeep so he could start circulating with the story. Inside the blacked out wagon Rosenberry was sitting in a fog of cigarette smoke at the single panel switchboard working methodically at his latest crossword book.

"Any calls, kid?"

"Not a thing, Sir."

"Good," Warden said. *"And God damn you, Rosenberry, you son of a bitch, quit calling me sir!"* he said murderously. *"I am not a goddam Officer! I am a goddam enlisted 1st/Sgt!"*

"Yes, Sir!" Rosenberry said pop-eyedly. "I mean, okay, Sarge! I'm sorry, Sarge!"

"If you dont quit calling me sir, Rosenberry, I'll tear your fucking heart out by the roots with my bare hands and feed it to you," Warden said in a low vibrant voice that sounded as if he actually hungered to do just exactly that.

"Okay, Sarge," Rosenberry said soothingly. "I'm sorry, Sarge. I dont mean nothing. Its just a habit. Was it really Prewitt, Sarge?"

"Yas, it was Prewitt. Deadern a goddam mackerel. In a sandtrap. And his chest scattered all over the goddam fairway. By a Thompson gun. Now get the fuck out and le me a *lone*."

When the kid was gone, he spread the stuff out on his desk. It was a hell of a lot to show for one man's life.

He got the ten-cent notebook and the folded paper out of the other pocket and added them to the pile.

Then he picked the paper up and opened it again and smoothed it out on the desk. He read the printed title at the top, THE RE-ENLISTMENT BLUES, and then he read the nine hand-written verses. Then he looked at the whole thing again, and then he smoothed the paper out on the desk again, and then he read the whole thing through again.

It was another hour, almost eleven, before they got back from Schofield. When he heard the jeep grind up outside, he refolded the paper, carefully, along its already worn creases, and together with the ten-cent notebook locked it up in his little Art-Metal lockbox.

He could see by their faces, when they came in, that it had not worked with Col Delbert at Schofield.

"Well," Lt Ross said. He threw his helmet viciously at the bare cot in the corner. A puff-cloud of dust rose from the cot. "All I can say is its a great fucking war," Lt Ross said bitterly, and leaned his carbine carefully against the desk. Then he sat down and rubbed a grimy hand over his dusty face.

"The traffic's still terrific, even this late at night. I bet it took us four hours to get down here."

Pete Karelsen, his carbine slung on his shoulder, stepped forward and came to attention in that big-butted-like-a-round-bottomed-doll way of his and made his wide-swinging, sweeping old timer's salute.

"Sir, Sgt Karelsen wishes to thank the Company Commander for what he has done."

"I didnt do anything," Lt Ross said. "All I did was to get my ass on the Great White Father's list."

"Sir, the Company Commander tried. Thats what counts."

"No, its not what counts either!" Lt Ross cried violently. "The only thing that counts"— He managed to bring his voice back down to normal. "—in this world is results. I failed," he said, "utterly and miserably."

"Sir, the Company Commander did everything he could," Pete said.

"For Christ's sake, Sgt Karelsen!" Lt Ross said, "quit talking to me in the third person like I was somebody else! At ease. Rest. Relax. You dont have to be formal with me."

Pete moved his foot twelve inches to the left and clasped his hands behind his back. "Sir, I wish the Company Commander to know that I appreciate everything he did," Pete said emotionlessly, his face still rock-hard like a soldier at attention. "I will never forget it, Sir."

Lt Ross looked at him a moment, and then rubbed his hand over his face again. "You might as well sleep here the next couple of days, Sgt Karelsen," he said. "Till they call you in. You might as well be comfortable. Tell Sgt Malleaux I said give you a cot, and set it up in the Headquarters tent. The Weapons Platoon may as well start getting along without you right now."

"Yes, Sir," Pete said. "Thank you, Sir." He came back to attention slowly and with style, bending forward a little bit from the waist, and made that slow wide-sweeping snap of a salute again. It was a beautiful salute.

"Sir, if the Company Commander will excuse the Sergeant, the Sergeant will retire," Pete said.

"Go ahead," Lt Ross said.

Pete did a slow, precise, perfect aboutface and started off for the door at a solid 120 per.

"Whats that stuff?" Lt Ross said, pointing at the little pile of effects.

"Wait a minute, Pete," Warden said from his chair. "You'll want to hear this, too." He separated the effects and spread them out and told them about Prewitt.

"Well," Lt Ross said. "Thats fine. Thats wonderful. That makes it a grand slam. We're batting a thousand."

"When did it happen, Milt?" Pete said from the door, his voice genuinely human for the first time. There was a kind of a heartsick note in it that made a dull anger flare up in Warden.

"About eight o'clock," he said impassively.

He told them the story just as the MP Sgt had related it to him. Then, for Lt Ross's benefit, he went back and sketched in the rest of it from the beginning when Prewitt quit the Bugle Corps.

He left out a few things. For instance, he did not say anything about the late S/Sgt Fatso Judson. And he did not mention how with Baldy Dhom's initial shove he had covered up for him on the Morning Report for a week or so. Also, he did not mention Lorene of the New Congress.

"Well," Lt Ross said when he finished. "That boy had a pretty good batting average himself. He managed to violate just about every AW in the book. He managed to just about ruin the reputation of my organization; and I dont even remember ever having seen the man, to recognize him."

"Sir," Pete said from the door, "if the Company Commander will excuse me now, I will leave. I can be of no further use to the Company Commander and 1st/Sgt in this matter."

"Sure. Go ahead, Sergeant," Lt Ross said. "Get some sleep. We both need it."

"Yes, Sir," Pete said. "Thank you, Sir." He came back to his slow precision of attention, making that same beautiful salute as he did so, and aboutfaced slowly and perfectly.

As he went out through the blackout flap, he whispered to Warden.

"I got a couple bottles up at Schofield, today, Milt. They're extra. Come down to the tent after."

"What the hells the matter with him," Lt Ross said when he had gone. "He dont have to be formal with me. Hell, I did the best I could for him."

"You dont understand him," Warden said.

"I sure as hell dont."

"He's being a soldier," Warden said. "He's proving he's still a soldier. Its got nothing to do with you, Lieutenant."

"Sometimes I wonder if I'll ever understand any of you guys," Lt Ross said. "Or the Army."

"Dont push it," Warden said. "You try to push it too hard. You got plenty time yet."

He leaned back deep in his chair and began to brief him about Lt Col Hobbs of the Provost's office, and how he had fixed it so all Ross had to do was keep his mouth shut and look agreeable.

"But I thought Prewitt didnt have any relatives?" Lt Ross said.

"He dont. But it will make it easier all the way round, this way. And in addition," Warden said pointedly, "you will not have any mention of a dead deserter on your Company's records, Lieutenant."

"I see," Lt Ross said. "You can count on me." He rubbed his hand over his face again. "This is sure going to make a swell report to send in to Col Delbert; after today. I think its just about as well we're finally rid of this man Prewitt."

"Just about," Warden said.

"I guess you think thats calloused?" Lt Ross said quickly.

"No."

"My first responsibility is to this Company as a whole," Lt Ross said. "Not to the individuals in it. And any individual who threatens the security of the whole threatens my responsibility. I still say, I think its just as well we're finally rid of him."

"You dont have to justify yourself to me, Lieutenant," Warden said.

"No, but I have to justify myself to myself," Lt Ross said.

"Well, then just dont use me as your punching bag then, will you?"

"You thought a lot of this Prewitt, didnt you, Sergeant?"

"No. I thought he was a good soldier."

"Yes, he sure as hell sounds like it," Lt Ross said bitterly.

"I think he was nuts. He loved the Army. Anybody who loves the Army is nuts. I think he was crazy enough to have made a good paratrooper, if he wasnt so small, or commando. He loved the Army the way most men love their wives. Anybody who loves the Army that much is nuts."

"They sure are," Lt Ross said.

"In a war a country needs every good soldier it can lay hands on. It cant have too many."

"One soldier more, or less, dont matter much," Lt Ross said tiredly.

"You think not?"

"Production is what wins wars," Lt Ross said.

"Thats why a man who loves the Army is nuts," Warden said.

"I guess thats right," Lt Ross said. "Well, *you'll* be out of it, before long, anyway. Out of this, anyway." He rubbed the same grimy hand over the same face, that was smeared now, and then got up and collected his carbine and his helmet.

"I have to go out and take a look at Makapuu yet before I turn in, Sergeant. Its going to be rough on Cribbage with Sgt Karelsen out. They're going to have a hard time for a while. If anything comes up, you'll know where to find me."

"Send Anderson or Clark up to relieve me on this switchboard when you go down, will you?"

"Which one's on first?"

"I dont know. Let them decide. But I want Rosenberry to get the last shift; he was up with this all the time I was gone."

"Okay," Lt Ross said. He went out.

In a few minutes Company Bugler Anderson, sleepy-eyed and tousle-headed, came in looking sullen like a man who bet on red when the black had come up.

"Lost, hunh?" Warden said.

"I should of made him cut the cards," Andy said. "I never can beat Friday matching."

"Its midnight. There's only eight hours left. Take three, give Friday three, and let Rosenberry have the last two," Warden said. "He was up with it all evening while you guys were hanging ear." He got his rifle out of the corner.

"Okay, Top," Andy said. He did not look happy, but then you did not argue with The Warden any more than you would have argued with Jesus Christ. Especially when he was in this mood.

"Hey, Top?"

"Yeah?"

"Is that really true about Prewitt?"

"Yeah, its true."

"Gee. Thats tough," Andy said. He got his comic book out of his hip pocket and sat down by the switchboard. "Thats really tough."

"Yeah," Warden said. "Sure is."

Outside, in the fresh sea air under the kiawe grove, the late-rising moon was just coming above the mountains back of Koko Head, its silver light making one dark cave of the whole grove. From the wagon, and below him, the ground sloped down sharply through the patchy darkness under the trees of the grove to the bright levelness of the parking lot at the top of the cliff, where he and Karen had parked that time and watched the highschool kids having their picnic.

Feeling very remote, and aware of the weight of the rifle, he picked at random one of the new paths in the sandy soil that were becoming more packed and smooth every day now since Pearl Harbor, and that formed a many-choiced web through the grove amongst the newly placed tents and the old popcorn wagon and two WPA septic-tank outhouses that had been there before. The air felt very good in his lungs and on the outside of his head.

He walked on in the shade-dappled moonlight, feeling something ugly and hard flare up inside his chest. He went up another path toward the scattered tents of the camp.

The Headquarters tent was dark and Friday and Rosenberry were asleep on their cots, and he took still another path toward the supply tent over by the blacktop.

In the supply tent Pete and Maylon Stark were sitting up with Pete's Schofield bottles, by the light of a blanket-shaded Coleman lantern. On the improvised table of sawhorses and one-by-six planks against the back wall Pete's portable radio, that he had carefully packed and brought along on The Seventh, was playing dance music.

"It aint hahdly even the same outfit any more," Stark said gloomily drunkenly.

"Come on in, Milt," Pete said sympathetically from the cot. He moved over. "We just been talking about how fast the Compny's changed the last couple of months."

Warden noted the open bottle was less than half empty. Stark must have started in earlier with one of his own.

"Balls!" he sneered at them. "It aint changin any fastern it ever was." He unslung his rifle and sat down beside Pete and accepted a canteen cup half full of straight whiskey. He drank it off quick and handed it back for a refill. "Wheres Russell? I thought he'd be in here tellin his story."

"He's already been," Stark said darkly.

"He's over across the road to the kitchen tent," Pete said, "tellin the cooks."

"What'll he do when he runs out of people to tell?" Stark said.

"Bust, probly," Pete said.

Behind them the music on the radio stopped and an announcer came on.

"*Lucky Strike green has gone to war,*" the announcer said. "*Yes, Lucky Strike green has gone to war.*"

"I aint never seen no outfit change so much in so short a time," Stark said funereally.

"Say, what the hell is this?" Warden jeered. "I thought this was a party. Its more like a wake."

"It could be a wake," Stark said belligerently.

"Then lets liven it up a little. A wake's supposed to be lively. Lets dial out that crap and get some good gutty hot jazz."

"Leave it be," Pete said. "Its the hit parade."

"What. On Monday night?"

"Prewitt happened to be a good friend of mine," Stark said testily.

"Its a re-broadcast from the States for Servicemen," Pete explained.

"No stuff?" Warden derided. "A re-broadcast? For servicemen? Boy, they really treatin us right any more, aint they? Pretty soon they be wipin our ass for us maybe, hunh?"

"He may not of been a good friend of yours," Stark said. "But he was a good friend of mine."

"He was no goddam friend of mine," Warden sneered. "All he caused me was headaches and troubles."

"You're a hard hearted son of a bitch," Stark said pugnaciously, "you know it?"

"Thats no way to talk about a man from your own Compny, Milt,"

Pete said, "after he's been killed. Even if he was over the hill. Even if you are kidding."

"Kidding," Warden said. "Who the hells kidding?"

"I just cant get over it," Stark said. He started naming them. "Leva; transferred to M Co as Supply Sgt. Bloom; a suicide. Maggio; discharged a Section Eight. Holmes and Big Jim O'Hayer gone to Brigade Hq. And then all these heah ROTC jokers comin in. And now Prewitt."

"Balls," Warden scoffed, "sometimes we lose that many men in a single month, as short timers."

"You dont think dyin is any differnt from goin home as a short timer?" Stark said.

"They didnt all die," Warden said.

"You try it sometime," Stark said, "and see."

"The effect on the Compny Roster's no differnt," Warden said. "Pour us another drink, Pete."

"And now old Pete will be leavin in a couple days," Stark said gloomily.

"Dont forget Old Ike," Warden grinned.

"Well, I for one will be damn glad to get out of this outfit," Pete said. "Six years in an outfit is long enough."

"And I, for one, dont blame you," Stark said.

"You guys think I like layin on my ass in them holes in the rock out at Makapuu like a lizard?" Pete said.

"Because it aint even the same outfit no more," Stark said.

"You guys sound like a couple kids," Warden snorted. "No outfit ever stays the same. What do you want? Everybody all grow old together and all retire on the same day and go live somewheres in a body?"

Behind them the music stopped again and the announcer came back on.

"*Dont look for your Luckies in their familiar green package on the tobacco counters,*" the announcer said. "*No, your Luckies are wearing a different color now.*"

"Mark my words," Pete said with accurate prophecy. "The golden days on this rock are over. When they do start givin passes, there'll be men lined up for blocks at every bar and every whorehouse. And they'll run them through like an assembly line."

"Like to get out of it myself," Stark said. "Ony I aint got no place to go."

"But old Pete," Pete said, "is going to be sitting on a rosy cloud of plenty. Back Stateside."

"If I did have a place to go," Stark said, "I couldnt get a transfer now."

755

"And then I'll think about you boys still sitting on the rocks at Makapuu," Pete said.

"If I could transfer," Stark said, "it would still be the same. Draftees everywhcrc. ROTC jokers everywhere."

"You're both of you nuttiern fruitcakes," Warden jeered. "No outfits ever any different than another; peace or war. And it'll be closed down just as tight back Stateside as it will here."

"Oh, no!" Pete said. "Oh, no!"

"So it wunt do me any good to transfer if I could," Stark said.

"Oh, no!" Pete said. "There'll be women everywhere. All of them out on the loose. With the sky the limit."

Warden looked at him carefully. "For Christ's sake, shut up," he said boredly, "both of you."

"I envy you," Stark said gloomily.

"Goddam right you do," Pete said. "They'll put me to training draftees. I'll have a nice soft easy job. Just like a business man in an office. I'll do my eight hours and then I'm through for the day. Why the hell should I want to stay in this goddam outfit?"

"I envy you," Stark said dismally. "Oh, god, how I envy you."

"Shut up!" Warden said to him.

"Bars!" Pete said. "Cocktail lounges! Nice hotels to take them to! Good restaurants! I know what its like. I was in the last war."

"You'll be gettin out just as the old Compny folds," Stark said. "You wont be here to see the end."

"I said shut up, Stark!" Warden said.

"And you'll be sleepin on rocks!" Pete hollered. "Eatin cold chow off a messkit! Workin your ass and arms off puttin up bob wire!" He got up off the cot.

"You'll be living on the beaches!" he yelled, throwing it at them. "Standin in line for a drink or a piece of ass! You'll be the first Infantry outfit under the gun! The first ones to be shipped down south when we start into them crummy islands!"

He was leaning forward at them stiffly, shooting it down at them, his arms straight down at his sides against the round-bottomed-doll fat hips. His face was very red. Some tears ran down off his face and, leaning forward as he was, dripped onto the blunt round toes of his issue shoes.

"Livin on a goddam powder keg!" Pete hollered. "Thats all primed to blow, the minute this country starts to fight!"

Warden jumped up off the cot and grabbed him, still leaning like a defiance of the law of gravity, with both arms around him. "All right, all right, Pete, all right. Sit down. Have another drink. Lets listen to the music for a while."

"I'm allright," Pete said strangledly. "I guess my enthusiasm just got the best of me for a minute. Let go of me." Warden let him go and he sat back down. "Wheres my drink?"

"Here," Warden said, holding him out a canteen cup of whiskey.

"Guess who I ran into up to Schofield today, Milt," Pete said painfully, in an almost rupturing effort to be casually conversational.

"I dont know," Warden said. "Who." He held out his cup.

"I'll have to get the other bottle," Pete said, getting up. "This one's done." He went back to the table.

Behind them the music stopped and the announcer came on.

"*Lucky Strike green has gone to war,*" the announcer said. "*Yes, Lucky Strike green has gone to war.*"

"Who did you run into up at Schofield, Pete?" Warden prompted as Pete came back.

"*Your Lucky Strikes have put on khaki and enlisted,*" the announcer said.

"Capt Holmes's wife," Pete said. He poured whiskey into Warden's cup. "Imagine that? Aint seen her for months. She was in the Evacuation Office at Regiment when I went in to get my chit. She's going back to the States on the same boat I am."

"Haw!" Stark guffawed drunkenly.

"Who?" Warden said.

"Capt Holmes's wife," Pete said. "Hell, you remember Capt Holmes's—Major Holmes's—wife, dont you?"

"Sure," Warden said, "I remember her."

"Haw!" Stark hooted drunkenly.

"Well," Pete said, "seems they're still living in their old quarters in the Regiment's MOQ, so she had to report to Regiment instead of Brigade for her evacuation number and shipping list chit for her and her kid. Christ, there was a whole bunch of them in there; Major Thompson's wife; Col Delbert's wife; I dont know who all. And Holmes's wife is booked for the same boat they got me booked for. Leaves on January 6th."

"Haw!" Stark guffawed explosively again.

"Whats the matter with you?" Pete said.

"Nothin," Stark grinned. "I just happen to think of something."

"Of course," Pete went on, "she'll be goin back First Class, and I'll be down in the hole, but still she's goin on the same damn boat I am. Its sure a damn small world, you know it?"

"Haw!" Stark giggled. "It sure is."

"You want another drink, Stark?"

"Naw," Stark grinned. "I'm doin fine. Just fine."

"Well?" Warden said casually. "What'd she seem like? What'd she have to say?"

"Haw!" Stark guffawed drunkenly.

"Ask about the Compny," Pete said. "Wanted to know how the Compny Administration was makin out. And how the supplyroom was makin out with the new supply sergeant. And ask how you were getting along with the new Compny Commander."

"Me?" Warden said.

"Haw!" Stark guffawed.

"Yes," Pete said. "Say, whats the matter with you?" he said to Stark.

"Nothin," Stark giggled happily.

"You know," Pete said to Warden, "she knows a hell of a lot more about this Compny than I ever thought she did."

"She ought to," Stark said.

"She even ask me if Prewitt was back yet."

"Him too?" Stark grinned. "She loves this Compny," Stark grinned. "All of it. Aint that right, Milt?"

"You know I believe she does," Pete said. "It surprised me. How much she knew about it. I liked her a lot."

"You did, hunh?" Stark grinned. "Well then you ought to look her up on board ship. Dont you think, Milt?"

"She'll be upstairs," Pete said. "Officer Class. I'll be down the hole. I wont even see her."

"Dont let that bother you," Stark grinned. "Just look her up and ask her to invite you up to her stateroom. She'll do it. Aint that right, Milt? . . . And then while you're there ask her for a piece of ass. She'll give you that, too. She loves this Compny."

Pete was a little slow on the uptake. But a shocked look began to spread over his face, as it dawned on him what Stark had said.

"Shut up, you son of a bitch," Warden said.

"You think I'm lyin, Pete?" Stark guffawed. "I aint, though. Ask Warden; she give him some. She had him fooled. Ask me; she give me some, too. Only she never fooled me any.

"But you want to watch out though," Stark said confidentially, "and take a good pro afterwards, or you're liable to come out with a good dose of the clap."

Warden, watching the thin mask of ribald laughter on Stark's face that just barely hid something else, felt a pause coming. He'd have to run down in a minute, and Warden was content to wait. A tremendous gratification filled him. This was what he had been looking for all day and couldnt find.

"All right, you son of a bitch," he said when the pause came full. He enunciated it carefully and clearly. "Now I'll tell you something. You want to know how she got the clap at Bliss? You want to know who give it to her? I'll tell you. It was her beloved husband, Capt Dana E Holmes, who give it to her."

Under the flush of the whiskey, Maylon Stark's face went white as a sheet. Warden watched him with a completely inexpressible, absolutely luxurious, positively exquisite satisfaction.

758

"I dont believe it," Stark said.

"Its true, though," Warden said, feeling himself grinning supremely happily.

"I dont believe it," Stark said. "They said it was a Lieutenant who was Adjutant at the Officers' Club. He got relieved for having it. I talked to a couple of the guys who said they seen them. Besides, it happened six months before I ever met her. But I talked to them."

"The story wasnt true, though," Warden said.

"I dont believe it," Stark said. "It has to be true."

"Its not, though," Warden said gently.

"It has to be," Stark said.

"Its not, though."

Pete was watching both of them, a first faint glimmer of dawning beginning to push up into his face through the bewilderment.

Behind them the music went off the radio and the announcer came on.

"Lucky Strike green has gone to war," the announcer said. "Yes, Lucky Strike green has gone to war."

"I'll kill him," Stark said, working his whole face to get the words out of his throat. "I'll kill the son of a bitch. I'll kill him."

"You wont kill anybody," Warden said sympathetically tenderly. "Any more than I killed anybody."

"I was going to marry that woman," Stark said. "She was eight years oldern me, but I was going to marry her. I was going to get out of the Army, so I could marry her. I would have married her, too."

"And done what?" Warden said gently. "Taken her, a rich man's daughter, to live on a Texas cropper's farm?"

Stark's face was chalk white. "She was in love with me, too. I know she was. A guy can tell when a woman's in love with him. We went together on the sly in Bliss for over six whole months. I was going to marry her, too."

"But you didnt," Warden said kindly. "Instead, you thrown her over."

"I would have," Stark said.

"Without even givin her a chance to say her side of it," Warden chided tenderly, aware of Pete still watching them, first one then the other. Well, it ought to take his mind off his troubles. You didnt come by a juicy tidbit like this every day.

"She didnt tell me," Stark said desperately.

"But you didnt ask her," Warden said tenderly, determined to leave no loopholes.

"Shut up," Stark said. "Shut up, shut up."

"You Southern men," Warden censured kindly. "You're all alike. With your drinking and whoring. You're the worst moralists there are."

Stark stood up and threw the canteen cup of whiskey at Warden's

759

gently solicitous face, in the same unthinking reflexive way that a cat that has been pinched will unsheath its claws and strike.

"You think *I* wont kill him?" Stark screamed at him. "*I'll* kill him. I'll *kill* him. I'll chop his fucking head off."

Warden, who was watching, ducked the cup but Pete, who was a little older, a little drunker, and a little more preoccupied, caught both cup and whiskey in the chest, drenching his shirt.

Stark was gone, out through the flap of the tent.

Warden slumped back on the cot, feeling as completely empty and relaxed as if he had just had orgasm. Except for one thing, one tiny fly in the ointment, it was perfect. He suspected all along they had gone together longer than she said, but all along he had hoped it wasnt true.

"Jesus!" Pete said. "I smell like a goddam brewery." He daubed at the dripping shirt. "You better go after him, Milt. He's pretty drunk. He might hurt himself."

"Okay," Warden said. He got his rifle from the corner.

Behind him as he went out the music went off and the announcer came back on.

"*Lucky Strike green has gone to war,*" the announcer said. "*Yes, Lucky Strike green has gone to war.*"

Outside, the moon had risen further and the grove, the parking space, the whole earth, was a colorless painting done in black and white. He took the path that crossed the blacktop to the kitchen tent.

So they had gone together six whole months at Bliss. That was almost as long as he had gone with her himself. He wondered what it had been like with them. She was much younger then, for one thing. He wondered what she had been like when she was younger. What things had they done? What places had they gone? What things had they laughed at? He wished, suddenly, he could have been present, as an unseen third party, so he could have shared it. He felt that way about everything about her. Not envy so much, nor jealousy, as just a tremendous hunger to have shared. Poor old Stark.

In the kitchen tent he found a small cluster of frightened cooks, huddled together like sheep as far away from the meat block as they could get.

"Where'd he go?"

"I dont rightly know," one of them said. "I didnt really feel like asting him. All I know, he come chargin in talking and cussin and got his cleaver and took off."

He started back toward the supplyroom, thinking he might have gone down on the beach to sleep it off and if he had the best thing was to let him go. He stopped in the middle of the blacktop and looked up it up the hill where it curved up to the highway in the moonlight, but nobody was on it. Stark was not drunk enough to start off to walk to Schofield with his cleaver after Major Holmes.

As he came back up to the supply tent, a figure came flying out of the dark and collided with him.

"Top!" Company Bugler Anderson's scared voice said huskily. "Is that you, Top?"

"What the hell're you doin out here. Why aint you in the wagon with the switchboard?"

"Top, Stark's up there! He's got his cleaver and he's tearin it up! He's bustin everything! He's ruinin it!"

"Come on!" Warden said. He unslung his rifle and took off up the path

"He come in cussin and yellin and sayin he'd kill him," Andy yelled breathlessly behind him. "He kept yellin he'd kill him, he'd kill the son of a bitch. I thought he meant you. Then he says Capt Holmes, he'll kill Capt Holmes. Capt Holmes aint been around here for months, Top. And he's a Major. I think he's went off his nut."

"Save your breath," Warden said.

Stark was already gone. But the little popcorn wagon was a shambles. Both spindly homemade tables that served him and Ross for desks had been chopped down into kindling and smashed flat. Of the four chairs not one was left in a suitable condition for sitting. Warden's field desk, that was still locked, lay on the floor with a great gash in the top. His Art-Metal lockbox had a foot-long dent in it. Papers, and pieces of chopped papers, were scattered everywhere. There were long tear-shaped gashes in the thin plywood walls. Only the panel switchboard, luckily, appeared to be untouched.

And in the middle of all this holocaust, lying on the floor, pure white, virgin, unmarked, untouched, like a baby sitting unharmed and indifferent in the middle of a fallen house, was a War Department letter with a sheaf of endorsements stapled on it, Warden's confirmation of appointment as Second Lieutenant (Infantry) in the Army of the United States.

Warden stood a moment in the doorway and surveyed the wreckage. Then he threw his rifle viciously into the corner and the little wagon rocked on its wheels as the stock of the Star Gauge '03 burst across the grip.

Andy, who had been raised in the Regular Army where to drop your rifle on the ground at drill was a major sin punishable with no less than two weeks' extra duty, gasped audibly and looked at him with open horror.

"Get on that thing," Warden said thinly, indicating the switchboard, and grinned at him wildly slyly. "Start at the bottom and call every position for a check call to see if they're all coming through. Then check Battalion and the Message Center. Check every tab."

"Okay, Top," Andy said, and got on it.

Warden picked up the two pieces of the rifle contritely, the stock butt dangling limply from the sling. He had had that rifle four years; he had brought it into A Co with him, and taken it out of A Co with him into G. He had nosed out Sgt/Maj O'Bannon for Regimental high score with that rifle. He checked the action lovingly. It was all right. He could get a new stock, but the action could not have been replaced. He laid the two pieces down tenderly by the door, feeling a little better. Then he picked up the offensively unharmed, still virgin, War Department letter with its endorsements and tore it across, then across again, then across a third time, and scattered it over the floor. With the rest of the wreckage.

"They all check in okay, Top," Andy said from the switchboard.

"Okay. Good. You still got two and a half hours of your shift to do yet. I'm going to bed."

"Well, what about the Orderly Room? What about the wagon? Aint you going to clean it up any?"

"Let Ross do it," he said, and got the pieces of his rifle and went out.

Outside, everything was still as death. After a while, after so long a time, there wasnt anything left but to go to bed. You went so long, and did so much, and were done so much, until finally there came a time when there was absolutely nothing anywhere left on earth to do but to go to bed.

Warden put the pieces of the rifle at the foot of his cot and went gratefully to bed.

In the morning they found Stark down on the beach sleeping peacefully in the sand with his tear-stained cheek resting on his trusty cleaver.

Warden, who was up fresh and early, had already taken it up with Lt Ross, who was furious (furious was no word to describe it), before they had even found Stark.

"You cant bust him, Lieutenant. He's the only man we've got who can come anywhere near running the mess at all, with the men scattered all over hell's half acre like they are."

"The hell I cant bust him!" Lt Ross said furiously. "I'll bust him if every manjack in this Company starves to death!"

"Who'll you get to run the mess for you?"

"I dont give a damn who runs the mess for me!" Lt Ross said furiously. "Look at this place! My god, Sergeant, I cant let a man get away with a thing like that! We'll never have any discipline! We've got to have discipline!"

"Sure, but we got to have food, too."

"He can run the mess as a private!" Lt Ross said furiously.

"He wouldnt do it."

"Then he can be court-martialed for malingering!" Lt Ross hollered furiously.

"You couldnt make that stick. You're a lawyer, Lieutenant. You know you couldnt make it stick, to court-martial him for refusing to run the mess without the rating."

"I cant let him get by with this!" Lt Ross said furiously.

"You just dont understand him, Lieutenant. He's a funny guy. He goes on rampages like this every now and then. He did it once at Hickam Field before you got in the Company. He dont really mean any harm. And he never hurts anybody. He's just a cook, thats all. Cooks and mess sergeants are just temperamental, thats all. You never saw a good mess sergeant that wasnt half crazy."

"All right," Lt Ross said furiously.

"You know you cant run the mess without him, Lieutenant."

"All right!" Lt Ross said furiously.

"I'm only being realistic, Lieutenant. If we had a man could run the mess, I'd be the first to want him busted. But we havent got a man that can do it."

"All *right!*" Lt Ross said furiously.

"Its for the good of the Compny, Lieutenant."

"I know, I know," Lt Ross said furiously. "For the good of the Compny!"

"Your responsibility is to the Compny as a whole."

"Okay," Lt Ross said furiously. "Okay, okay. I know what my responsibility is."

"Yes, Sir," Warden said.

With that settled, he informed him of his decision not to accept a commission.

"What!" Lt Ross cried furiously. "But, Jesus Christ!"

"My mind's made up," Warden said.

"I wish to hell I'd got my commission in the Coast Guard!" Lt Ross said furiously. "I'll *never* understand the fucking Army."

Chapter 54

He saw her once more before she left. It was a very strange experience.

In the first place, it was a hard thing to arrange. It was not like before the war, when you could put on civvies and go anywhere you wanted simply because you wanted to go there. You could not go anywhere without an official reason now. And you had to have an officially documented explanation. Soldiers were not allowed in civilian clothes. Even to have them was a court-martial offense. And a soldier in uniform running around town in the daytime would be stopped immediately.

The ban on liquor by the Military Government was still in effect then, and the bars were closed down tight. The movies did not run at all. The big hotels had suddenly become very inquisitively careful about their registrations. All the tourists had either gone home, or else were sitting tight in their hotel rooms waiting for the Army to evacuate them. There were no new tourists. Even a car stopped along a road in the daytime was liable to investigation and inspection.

There was not anywhere they could meet. There was nowhere they could go. Even in the daytime.

And at night there was the curfew. At sundown Honolulu crawled quickly into its various holes and died until morning. After dark, nothing moved anywhere, except for the blue headlights of the patrols.

She was at Schofield. She would have to drive down. She could only drive in the daytime. She would have to drive back in the daytime, too. But it was an impossibility for him to get away from the CP in the daytime without being discovered. Even for an hour. And an hour was not long enough.

He could sneak away at night, after the switchboard relief went on. Stark had been sneaking off every night to see his wahine at the Wailupe Naval Radio Station, which was not far away. But Karen, she could not make the trip at night, not without being stopped. She could not even come down before dark and park and wait for him.

The only possible answer was a place, some place, where she could go in the afternoon and wait for him without being noticed, and then stay all night and drive back the next day. The hotels at Waikiki were out. Besides, he was ten or twelve miles from Waikiki out here on the highway, and there were no Motels or Tourist Courts on the highways of Hawaii.

He did not know any people out this way to whom she could go. All the people he knew lived either in Waikiki, or else in downtown Honolulu, which was further. Besides, he was not even sure she would be willing to go that far. To come down and stay all night. Even if he could find a place.

He sweated with it for over a week from the night that he had made the identification of Prewitt's body. He told himself he meant to have that much, if he never had any of the rest of it.

And finally he went to Stark.

Stark's wahine was a very beautiful Chinese-Hawaiian girl, the most beautiful blood-mixture type that comes out of Hawaii. She and her husband, a Japanese-Filipino, had one of the little houses in Kuliouou

Valley less than two miles from Hanauma Bay. Her husband, who had started out as a mess-attendant in the Navy, was now one of the operators at the Wailupe Station. A very considerable advance in the Navy, for a Filipino.

Rather awkwardly, and not without embarrassment, he asked Stark if he could fix it up with them to let Karen have a room there for one night, so he could see her before she left.

"Sure," Stark said immediately and without hesitation. "They'll be glad to."

"Hadnt you better ask them first?"

"No need to. They'll do damn near anything I ask them to. I'm helping them to pay off their FHA loan."

"Okay," Warden said.

"You let me know what day she'll be there, and I'll tell them next time I go over. I'll show you the way over myself, so you wont get lost."

"Okay," Warden said.

He could not call her over the field phone, which made its connection into the public system through the Battalion Message Center, but that part was easy. The next time he had an excuse to go down to Position 17 he made the call from the home of the old couple upon whose small estate the pillboxes had been built, and who had practically adopted all the men on the position.

The call went through perfect. Karen said immediately and without hesitation that she would come.

It was a very strange experience, in more ways than one.

As Stark brought him up the little side street that ran inland off the highway in the absolute blackness, the stocky Texan stopped and pointed out the house.

"Thats it there," Stark said. "The beach type bungalow with the corner windows."

Warden, looking, saw also the intensely familiar old Buick with the well-remembered, long-ago-committed-to-memory license plate.

"You can find your way back all right, cant you?" Stark said.

"Sure."

"Then I'll leave you here and go on back."

"But, aint you comin in?"

"Naw," Stark said. "I was over last night. And probly will come over again tomorrow night."

"But she'll want to thank you."

"She dont need to thank me."

"But hell, we're running you out of your own home, practicly."

"I'm afraid seein me would embarrass her," Stark said. "Anyway," he said, "I dont want to see her. I aint seen her since at least two months before Holmes left the Compny. Why should I see her now?"

"Okay," Warden said.

"You might—" Stark said, and stopped.

"Might what?"

"Nothing," Stark said. "I'll see you," he said. He walked away into the lightless blackness and became invisible. Warden listened to his quiet footsteps fade away before he went up to the door.

It was a strange experience, in a great many more ways than one.

The beautiful, almost-unearthly-lovely, Chinese-Hawaiian girl opened the door for him with brightly luminous eyes. Then the eyes clouded.

"Didnt May-lon come?"

"He had some work to do. He said tell you he'd see you tomorrow."

"Ahhh," she said reproachfully, from behind the cloudy eyes. Then she smiled. "Come on in, Sergeant."

She shut the door behind him and turned back on the lights. Her husband, in his dazzling white shirtsleeves and blue Navy pants beneath the deep mahogany face, was sitting in the dinette with the Japanese-language newspaper.

"Your friend is in there," the beautiful, almost-unearthly-lovely, Chinese-Hawaiian girl said broodingly, and moved her eyes toward the closed door across the room. "She is very lovely, your friend," she said.

"Thank you," Warden said. "And also I want to thank you for what you've done for us."

"It is nothing, Sergeant. Do not speak of it. Everyone has troubles, now."

"John," the beautiful, almost-unearthly-lovely, Chinese-Hawaiian girl said softly, "come and meet May-lon's First Sergeant, Mr Warden."

The husband, in his dazzling white shirtsleeves and blue Navy pants beneath the dark mahogany face, left his Japanese-language daily paper and came and smiled and shook hands warmly.

"But you will want to see your friend," the beautiful, almost-unearthly-lovely, Chinese-Hawaiian girl said sadly. "Not to stand and talk with us. I will show you."

It was all strange, and the sense of strangeness colored everything.

Karen was sitting in a big chair by the bed under the floor lamp reading a book, as the girl closed the door behind him softly. She had her legs drawn up against the chair arm in the green skirt tucked tight under her knees. Her small bag that he remembered was sitting on the floor by the dresser. She looked completely secure and at home. She looked at peace.

"Hello, darling," she smiled.

"Hello," Warden said. "Hello." He went to meet her, and she left the book on the chair arm and rose to meet him, in that same funny odd reserved way she had that he had almost forgotten.

He put his arms around her and it was not like touching a foreign object but rather, like touching your own body, the way a man will clasp his own two hands together, in the cold perhaps, to keep them warm, as he has every right to do, without asking anyone's permission, since they are his hands.

He could not tell her yet. Not just yet.

He kissed her, and she kissed him back. Then she drew away with that funny odd reserve of hers, and he let her go watching her smile that deeper smile.

"You'll get yourself all excited," she smiled. "Lets talk a while. Lets sit down."

She sat back down in the chair and drew her legs up tight against her with her arms, and smiled at him over her knees.

Warden sat down on the bed edge.

"You dont look a bit different," she smiled.

"I feel different," Warden said.

"It was nice of them to let us come here."

She said it sincerely, yet there was no gratitude in her, and no surprise, at the free use of a stranger's house. It was like her smile, that same smile he had never seen in any other woman, at once so warmly loving and so very very far away.

"It was Stark who arranged it," Warden said.

"I know," she smiled. "The girl told me. She's a very lovely girl."

"Yes."

"And she's very much in love with Stark."

"Yes."

"Is he in love with her?"

"I dont know. I think so. Some. But not as much, and not in the same way, as she loves him."

"I know," she said quickly. "I've hurt him very much."

"No. He hurt himself."

He did not mention the six months at Bliss. He looked at it in his mind, and watched it fade away, so that he had no need to say it.

"Oh, I do hope he can fall in love with her," Karen burst out suddenly, "the same way she loves him."

"Maybe he will," Warden lied.

"Oh, I hope so. He deserves it. He's a fine person. I'd like a chance to thank him for this, before he leaves."

"He didnt come. He had some work to do and had to go back."

"That isnt true," Karen said.

"No, it isnt true. He was afraid it would embarrass you."

Moisture welled up in her eyes, as he had seen it do before, over Prewitt, and then sank back down quietly, without ever overflowing.

"He's a fine person," she said, "a very fine person."

"Yes," Warden said.

"He deserves much more than he's had."

"Everyone does."

"Maybe he'll find it with her."

"Maybe he will," Warden lied again. He felt a very great tenderness, such as one feels with a beautiful child, and with it the same selfish unreasonable urge to protect it from all the things it does not know yet, not because of saving it hurt, but to keep it beautiful.

"Did you have any trouble getting away?" he asked.

"No."

"Didnt Holmes say anything at all?"

"He forbade me to come," she said simply.

"And you came anyway?"

"Of course, darling," she smiled. "I love you."

For a moment Warden thought he could not stand it, not mental agony, but purely physically, physiologically, could not stand it.

"I've got something I have to tell you," he said.

"Yes?"

"Its about my appointment in the Reserve Corps."

"I already know," Karen smiled. "Its all they have been talking about back at Schofield for the past week."

"And you mean you've known it all along? When I first came in the room?"

"Yes."

"Even when I called you?"

"Yes."

"And still you came anyway?"

"Yes."

"Even when Holmes forbade you?"

"Yes."

"Why?"

"Because you wanted me to come. Because I wanted to come."

"I'm not worth it," he said. "I'm not worth it. I'm a long way from worth it."

She put her feet down to the floor with a startling suddenness, and leaned over and put her fingers over his mouth.

"Hush," she said. "Dont say that. I wont have you say that."

Warden moved her hand with an urgency that was almost savage. "I couldnt help it. I couldnt do anything else. I tried, but I couldnt."

"I know you couldnt," she said soothingly.

"And you knew all the time," he said inexpressively, "even when I called you."

"I've known a lot longer than that. I think I've known for a long time. Only I just wouldnt let myself admit it. I think thats maybe why I love you, because I knew all along you couldnt.

"Maybe we only love the things we cannot have. Maybe thats all love is. Maybe its supposed to be that way.

"I've hated you," she said. "I've hated you bitterly, at times. All love has hate in it. Because you are tied to anyone you love, and it takes away part of your freedom and you resent it, you cant help it. And while you are resenting the loss of your own freedom, you are trying to force the other to give up to you every last little bit of his own. Love cant help but make hate. As long as we're living on this earth, love will always have hate in it. Maybe thats the reason we're on this earth, to learn to love without hating."

She was still leaning forward toward him, her arms on the fatless so-lovely knees, her eyes shining, her hand that Warden had moved from his mouth still in his hand.

"I tried," he said contortedly. "Nobody'll ever know how I tried."

"I'll know."

"No you wont. But I looked at them, Ross and Culpepper and Crib-bage and the rest of them, and I saw what they were—I couldnt do it."

"Of course you couldnt. If you could have you wouldnt really be Milt Warden. And I wouldnt love you."

"But the plans. The rest of it. All the rest of it. I've ruined all that."

"It isnt important."

"It is important."

"I've owned a thousand houses that I've never built," she said. "Never had the money to build. Couldnt have used if I had had the money. Never really wanted to build, maybe. But I still own the houses."

"Live in your memories," Warden said bitterly.

"No. Not at all," she said clearly. "Not that at all. But I still have my houses."

"Why does the world have to be like it is?" Warden said, letting himself go completely. "I dont know why the world has to be like it is."

"I dont know either," she said. "And I used to be very bitter about it. But now I know it has to be that way. Theres no other way for it to be. Whenever a menace is conquered, a new more subtle menace arises. There is no other way it could be."

"I've never done anything but take from you," Warden said contort-edly. "You've given and given. I've never given. I've only taken."

"No," Karen said. "Thats not true. You've given me my freedom. Dana can never touch me any more. Never hurt me any more. You've made me know I'm attractive. You've made me loved."

"Stark gave you the same thing. At Bliss."

"What Stark gave me, he took away and nullified in the end. He made sure he destroyed all of it, before he left it."

"Like I am doing now."

"No. You're not. And, really, the truth, I dont think I would have it any other way. I dont think, now, I would want to marry you. We've both been slowly throttling our love to death. We've been losing it slowly. You know we have."

"Yes," Warden said. "Thats true."

"But this way we will never lose it. Love either starves to death and becomes a shadow, or else it dies young and remains a dream. The only way we could have kept love was to have never had each other. If we could have gone on here as we were, always hungering, never having, we could have kept love. But neither one of us could do that; we both were fighting that very thing, with every force we knew. To have gotten married would have been the coup de grace to a starving man. But the war has stopped that. Wars have their good sides, too."

"Karen," Warden said, "how did you learn the things you know?"

"By living as long as I have, and seeing what I could see."

She leaned back in the chair, her eyes still shining with that lovely light that was never in them except when she was talking about love in theory, the fragile fine-boned hands lying lax along her hips on the chair.

And then he, Milt Warden, 1st/Sgt Milt Warden, was on his knees. Beside the chair.

"I cant lose you," he, Milt Warden, whispered. "I need you."

He put his hands up, touching her on her bare thighs.

"Dont," Karen said restlessly. "Please dont do that. Please dont spoil it."

"I dont want to do it," he, Milt Warden, lied. "I just want to touch you."

"You'll get all excited," she said, almost irritably. "You know you will."

"No I wont."

"You always do. And I dont want that. I dont want sex. I want love."

"I just want to touch you," he lied. "Thats all." He put his face down onto the solid three-dimension firmness of the long thighs under the green skirt.

"Its been so lovely, Milt. Please dont spoil it now."

"I wont," he promised. "I wont spoil it for you. I promise. But cant you feel me love you? Cant you feel it through my hands?"

It was a very strange experience, in a very great many more ways than one.

She submitted gradually reluctantly to his caresses, as a suspicious tame doe only submits by gradual easy stages to the petting, until finally her hands were on his hair, his face, his neck, his shoulders, down his back, and he raised himself up to the chair arm sitting half beside her half on the arm so that he might kiss her, and they were engaged in an ecstasy of sexual love that was sexless.

"I love to touch you," Karen whispered, "to cuddle you, be fondled by you, love you. But it always leads to sex. You'll never know the times I've wanted to touch you, but not done it, because it always leads to sex."

"No it wont," he whispered. "It wont this time." And went on loving her.

And then finally, she whispered lovingly, "Let me turn the covers back. I dont care. Really I dont. I know you want to do it. We dont want to mess up their bed after they've been so nice, though."

Up to that point, it had all happened before, many times.

But this time, when she offered, Warden refused. Maybe it was partly out of his humility and gratitude that, even knowing, she still had come down anyway. Maybe it was partly something else.

"I wont care, really," she offered lovingly givingly. "Its different now. It wont spoil it now. And I know you want to."

But he refused again. Apparently there were unsuspected depths of something in him that even he did not know. But the thought of doing it to her now actually offended him. Apparently he had not exorcised his Catholic moralism after all. Apparently he had not outgrown his virgin mother any more than any of the rest of the great race of American males.

"If you want to, its all right," Karen smiled. "I wont care. I want you to know I wont care."

"I'd rather not," he said, at least fifty percent truthfully.

"Oh, my darling!" Karen cried, throwing her arms around him. "My darling darling!"

It was a very strange thing.

She relaxed back into the chair, her hands on his hair, his face on her breasts, and they went on making potent love to each other, touching each other, talking without hearing, saying the stupid inane words that were not even meant to be a conveying of thought but only a self-expression of emotion expressed to the self only, as a man who has been punched in the belly will grunt "Oh!" or a man hit with a bullet will cry out, "I'm hit!"

It was a love-making of a caliber and muzzle velocity he had never experienced, and a greater intensity and a higher peak than he had believed in. It was tremendously satisfying to something.

At the moment of the highest intensity, as if feeling it instinctively, he got up and left her and lay on the bed and lit a cigarette, while Karen smiled at him from the chair brimmingly. He felt exactly as if he had had an orgasm physically, except that he hadnt. He was not frustrated, nor thwarted, nor did he feel unaccomplished. He lay on the bed smoking the cigarette, relaxed, peaceful, and ready to sleep; and feeling obscurely proud of himself and triumphant, under his hunger, as if he had conquered something.

It was the most wonderful feeling he had ever had in his life, but he decided it was a little too intense for every day use.

"Now you know what love can be like," Karen said from the chair.

They lay in the bed together the rest of the night, without sleeping, and without sexual intercourse, and they talked over many things. They talked over almost everything. He told her the last chapter and finis of Prewitt's story. She cried over it. They were very happy. They talked until the alarm on her little clock that she always carried in her bag for him went off at four-thirty, and then Warden got up and dressed.

"It isnt good-by, darling," Karen said from the bed.

"Of course it isnt," Warden said.

"Two people who have meant as much to each other as we have dont fade out of each other's lives," Karen said.

"Of course they dont," Warden said. "They cant."

"It looks dark now," Karen said. "The time will be longer, and the plans are changed. And there will be the war. But we'll see each other again."

"Sure we will," Warden said. "I know that we will."

"We'll meet again someday. People who have been as close to each other as we have, always meet again," Karen said. "You have my home address in Maryland?"

"Yes," Warden said. "I've got it. And you can always write me to the Company. Wherever we go, the APO will stay the same."

"Of course I can write you," Karen said.

"You can get home all right," he asked.

"I'm all right," she said. "Perfectly all right."

"You wont have any trouble with Holmes," he asked.

"He wont bother me."

"I love you," Warden said.

"I love you," she said.

"Well," Warden said. "I'll see you," he said.

"Kiss me once more, Milt," she said from the bed.

After he had kissed her, he went to the door. Before he closed it, he looked back and waved once.

772

Karen smiled at him from the bed and waved.

Then, as the door closed, she lay back and relaxed the hard knot. With the relaxing of it everything else seemed to all come apart, too. Her mind drifted. She listened for the closing of the outer door that would mean that he was gone and when she heard it she turned over and lay on her belly with her cheek on the pillow, exhausted. It had taken everything out of her. But she was glad and happy she had been able to protect him. He needed protecting so very badly. It was hard on him. He looked so completely lost. She could not stand it, to see him look so lost. Men were so much softer than women were. She was glad she could make it easier for him. And it wasnt a lie. Maybe they *would* meet again someday. It didnt hurt anything to believe it. She went to sleep.

Warden, picking his way back down the side street to the highway, was thinking of the White Russian girl during his hitch in China. There had been her, and then before that the old Chinese merchant's young wife in Manila, and before that the college girl from Chicago U when he was at Sheridan (He was younger then.), and still working backward the Protestant girl back home in Connecticut that was the reason he first enlisted.

Four.

Five, counting Karen Holmes.

Five real ones. Five that counted. Out of how many years? Out of sixteen years.

Maybe if he was lucky, if he was very lucky, there would be time enough left him for two more, three more perhaps, before he got too old. Men got old much quicker in the Army. Pete Karelsen wasn't fifty yet.

He had that much to look forward to. Maybe.

And he had that much to look back on. For sure.

Three more, to look forward to, if he was very lucky.

But he suspected, somehow, none of them would ever measure up to this one, that had come in his early 30s. He suspected; he was afraid; that this one was going to turn out to have been the top of the hill.

Warden, working his way back toward the CP along the highway, did not think she had seen through his lie. There was no use making a thing harder on someone than it already was. Besides, someday maybe they really would meet again. So it didnt hurt anything, if it made it easier for her, to believe it. And he was sure she hadnt seen through it.

Then, still thinking about it, he realized with a shock why she hadnt seen through it. She had been too busy concentrating on making her own convincing to him, to notice his.

He hoped she didnt have any trouble with Holmes.

773

Chapter 55

Major Holmes was waiting for his wife when she got home the next morning.

Karen did not get there till almost eleven. The beautiful almost-unearthly-lovely Chinese-Hawaiian girl had thoughtfully been very quiet for her in the house, and she had slept till after nine. Then, when she did get up, the lovely girl cooked breakfast for them, and the two of them sat for another hour in the little dinette, over their eggs and canned ham and coffee, with the sun streaming summer-bright through the windows, two happily adulterous wives, discussing with each other in a warm friendly intimacy the fine traits of character in their lovers. The sun, the air, the whole day had the feel of a summer holiday. It was an experience Karen had never had, and would not have missed if Holmes had had to wait till four o'clock. The feeling of holiday stayed with her all the way home.

Holmes was sitting stubbornly doggedly at the kitchen table with a cup of his own coffee.

Being a Major had not changed Capt Holmes greatly. He had put off the breeches and boots and Cavalryman's hat, in exchange for the staff officer's slacks and low-quarters and regular Infantry hat. And now, like the rest of the staff officers in Brigade, he wore the regulation wartime uniform of OD woolen shirt and CKC slacks stuffed into leggins over field shoes. But basically, it had not changed him much. Of course, it had only been a few months.

"I want to know where you've been," he said, as she came in.

"Hello," Karen said gaily. "How come you're not at the office?"

"I called them and got the morning off."

"Wheres Bella?"

"I gave her the day off."

Karen poured herself a cup of his coffee and sat down at the table with him.

"I bet that made her happy," she said happily. "And so now, everything's all prepared for the show."

"I said, I want to know where you've been," Holmes said. "And with whom."

"But I told you all that yesterday, darling," Karen said merrily. "I was saying good-by to a very dear friend."

"Dont call me darling."

774

"All right," Karen said cheerfully. "It was figurative."

"You didnt tell me anything yesterday." Holmes's eyes were like two frantically brilliant diamonds in the dried, cracked plaster of his face. "You didnt tell me where you were meeting him, and you didnt tell me who he was."

"I didnt say it was a him," Karen said.

"But it was. You think I havent known about it. But I've known about it all along. I even tried to ignore it, as long as I could. Until it got too flagrantly open. Now I want to know where you met him and just who he is."

"I dont think thats any of your business," Karen said.

"I'm your husband," Holmes said. "It is my business."

"No it isnt. Its my business," Karen said. "And no one else's. You sound like a page right out of Hemingway."

"Maybe I'll make it my business."

"No," Karen said, "I dont think you will."

"I suppose now you want a divorce."

"I hadnt really thought about it. One way or the other."

"Well, I wont give you one."

Karen sipped her coffee. She could not remember having felt so happy, so zestful, so full of just plain healthy animal spirits, since before she was married.

"You hear me? I wont give you one."

"All right," Karen said agreeably.

Holmes looked at her, the frantic diamonds of his eyes sparkling at her desperately out of his plaster-paris face. Even in his acute distress, he could see she was not acting.

"Maybe I'll get the divorce," he said, trying a frontal attack.

"All right," Karen said agreeably.

"We might as well settle it right now," Holmes said. "I want to get this thing settled once and for all."

"As far as I can see, its already settled. You're going to get the divorce."

"Ha," Holmes said. "Yes, you'd love that, wouldnt you? Well, I'm not. I'm not giving you any divorce. And if you try to get one, I'll fight you through every court in the land."

"All right," Karen said cheerfully. "Then I guess thats settled. No divorce."

"How does it feel to know you'll have to live with a horror like me the rest of your life?" Holmes said contortedly.

"Not very nice," Karen said cheerfully. "But then, on the other hand, there is the compensation of knowing you'll have to live with me the rest of your life, too."

775

"God!" Holmes said agonizingly, "how can you be so cruel? How can you sit there and smile? After what you've done. Didnt your responsibilities mean anything to you? Didnt the years of your marriage mean anything? Didnt your own son, our son, mean a damn thing to you? Dont you feel any shame?"

"I dont seem to," Karen said. "Not a bit. Its odd, isnt it?"

"Well, you ought to!"

"I know," Karen said. "But I dont. Its terrible, isnt it."

"Terrible?" Holmes exclaimed frenziedly. "A woman of your background? and upbringing? and breeding? A happily married woman with an eight year old son? And you call it terrible?"

"I cant understand it myself," Karen said cheerfully.

Gradually, one by one, the inviolable spears of right-mindedness were breaking themselves against this undentable armor of cheerfulness.

"Dont you know what you've done to me?"

"What have I done to you?"

"You've ruined my marriage, is all. You've knocked the bottom out from under my whole life. You were my wife. I trusted you."

"Well, I'm sorry," Karen said. "I'm truly, genuinely, sorry. To have done that to you. But I guess it couldnt be helped."

"Why do you think I've done all I have? All this," Holmes said contortedly. He spread his arms.

"Done all what?"

"Why, worked my ass off with this goddamned miserable boxing squad that I've hated. Brownnosed with Col Delbert and Gen Slater. Degraded myself. Had my nose rubbed in it."

"I dont know. Why?"

"Why; for you, thats why. Because you're my wife, and I love you. For you and our son and our home, thats why."

"I always thought you did it because you wanted to get ahead," Karen said.

"But why does a man want to get ahead? Do you think its just because he wants money? and power?"

"I had thought so."

"What good will money and power do a man? If he's alone. A man tries to get ahead because of his wife and his sons. So he can give them the things he's never had. So he can make life nice for them. So he can have a home. And a family."

"I guess I just have no gratitude," Karen said.

"Gratitude!" Holmes said desperately. "For God's sake, Karen!"

"Perhaps I'm amoral," Karen said cheerfully. "You know, like criminals?"

Somehow or other, without quite knowing how, the last spear gone, broken against the unbreachable armor, Holmes found himself on the defensive. He was pleading.

"Where would this country be? If all the wives felt like that?"

"I have absolutely no idea," Karen said. "In fact, I've never even considered the possibility."

"A man hears about other men's wives," Holmes said. "But his own . . ."

"But you didnt think it could happen in your own home?"

"Happen!" Holmes said. "If anyone had told me it would happen in my home, I'd have killed them! I tried not to believe it. I told myself it wasnt true. As long as I possibly could."

"But it has happened in your own home. Right?"

Holmes nodded dumbly. "I convinced myself it was all my imagination."

"So it has to be dealt with. Right?"

"You dont know how a man feels," Holmes said.

"No," Karen said. "I suppose not."

"Men dont feel like women do. About a thing like that. Women know it doesnt mean anything to a man. But it breaks a man all up, inside. It destroys his manhood."

"I wonder why men feel so different from women?" Karen said.

"I dont know," Holmes said miserably. "All I know is, they do."

"I'll tell you what," Karen said cheerfully. "Its a lovely day out. I think I'll go for a walk, and then walk up to the Club and lunch by myself. I'm good and hungry. And then you'll have time to decide before I get back."

"Decide what?"

"What you're going to do."

"I'd rather you didnt go yet," Holmes asked. "I'd like to get this whole thing settled up first."

"I thought it was already settled."

"Well, its not. You havent hardly said anything."

"What is there for me to say?"

"I'm willing to forgive you," Holmes said. "Tell me where you were, and who you were with. Make a clean breast of it. I'll forgive you."

"I'm sorry," Karen said. "I'm afraid thats something you'll never know."

"You'll have to tell me someday."

"Why?"

"Well, you just will. After all, I'm your husband. You cant hide things from me forever."

"My God," Karen said, grinning, "if you surely dont sound like a page out of Hemingway. I'm not going to hide anything from you. I'm just not going to tell you.

"I will tell you something else, though. I've deceived you before. Once. You never knew about it. And it is very likely I'll deceive you again someday. One never knows. But I think you ought to know that before you decide anything. We're going to have to change the terms of our agreement, you see.

"Now you just sit right there," she said maternally, "and take it easy, and decide what you want to do. If you want to divorce me, all right. And if you dont, thats all right, too. Whatever you decide is just fine.

"But Junior will be coming home from school for lunch in a few minutes now, and we dont want him to see us having a big scene, do we?"

"I'm hungry," Holmes said dismally.

"Theres plenty of cold meat and stuff in the refrigerator," Karen said. "And I'll be back before dinner."

"But what about Junior's lunch?"

"Bella always fixes it right after breakfast and puts it in the refrigerator, remember?" she explained patiently. "Its all right in there on the plate. He knows where it is."

"Well, do you care if I go up to the Club with you?" Holmes asked humbly.

"I'd rather go by myself. Its a lovely day out, and I want to enjoy it. Without having to talk over problems."

"But we cant both go up to the Club and eat at separate tables," Holmes protested.

"Then you can go over to the PX," Karen said gently, but firmly. "If you dont want to fix yourself something here. I'll tell you something," she said from the door. "If you wont let the coffee boil in the pot, but just let it barely start to come to a boil, it wont be so bitter."

"I'll use the Silex," Holmes said.

"All right," Karen said solicitously. "I'll see you later on then."

She went on out the back door and down and out from under the big old trees into the summer-bright sunlight on Waianae Avenue. It was really a remarkably lovely day, and its lazy summery loveliness tingled all through her. She walked on along Waianae Avenue. Schofield Barracks was really a very lovely Post. There were anti-aircraft guns set up on the ball diamonds in sandbagged emplacements, and there was a lot of raw dirt around from the bomb shelters they were digging. But even all that was lovely. Everything was lovely. Everything was so lovely, in fact, that Karen felt with the right amount of balance and proportion and the proper timing of everything from now on, the proper savoring of every morsel, and no greediness, she actually believed she might keep it that way almost indefinitely.

Last night, when Milt came, she had been reading about Stendhal's philosophy of happiness. It was not a moral philosophy; it was a very materialistic philosophy. Many people probably would not approve of it. Its only purpose was to deduce and plan ahead of time rationally, how to make life completely interesting and fully happy. The good thing about that Stendhal, he understood the very important place that misery and tragedy played in the making of a full happiness. She had never thought of that, any more than she had never thought of a philosophy constructed for the sole purpose of making life happy.

She felt she would never love another man. But if love was over, life need not be.

Suddenly, walking along Waianae Avenue, she began to cry, over the lovely anti-aircraft guns and the beautiful piles of raw dirt.

Major Holmes, staff G-3 of the —rd Brigade, sat on heavily at his kitchen table after his wife had gone out through his back door. Then he got up heavily and went to his refrigerator and got out the cold meat and fixed himself two sandwiches with mustard. He drank milk, instead of coffee.

He stacked up the dishes, and put the stuff away in the refrigerator, and brushed off the table. He washed and dried the dishes in the sink, and put them away. He emptied the overfull ashtray and washed and dried it. Then, when there was nothing left to do, he sat down at the table and smoked a cigarette.

The cigarette did not taste any better than the sandwiches and cold milk. Major Holmes detested cold milk; and he could not cook. He wished he had not given the maid the day off. As soon as Karen and the boy left for home, he could start eating at the Bachelor Officers' Mess. That was only a couple of weeks off, only until January 6th.

He mashed the cigarette out in the clean ashtray before it was half finished and got up from his table and bolted out through his back door, away from his house. He was back to the safety of his office long before his son came home for his lunch.

Chapter 56

On January 6th Milt Warden was in town on pass. Maylon Stark went with him.

It was the first day that passes were issued to the troops of the Hawaiian Department since the Saturday night before Pearl Harbor, and at ten o'clock in the morning a well-primed yowling horde of wild men from all around the 90-mile perimeter descended upon Honolulu like spokes descending upon a wheel hub and began to line up outside the bars and whorehouses until even the lines got entangled and men heading for the New Congress Hotel suddenly found themselves inside Wu Fat's Restaurant four doors up the street ordering drinks. It stayed just about like that all day long until the curfew. It, and the two days following, were a sort of red letter day. Not a bartender in town will forget them. Neither will many of the madams who were there then. Even a few of the respectable people still remember it.

The pass order stated explicitly that no more than one-third of the complement of any installation might be absent at one time. For G Company on the beach it was a problem in distribution. G Company had fourteen beach positions. The commander of each position (more often a noncom than an officer) was ordered by Lt Ross to turn in the names of one-third of his men to go on pass. Warden was given charge of the passes for the CP personnel. Stark had charge of the passes for the kitchen force.

There was an unwritten law that a commander did not go on pass until his men were served, and since they could not go themselves, the noncom-commanders (who unlike officers were not above conniving with enlisted men) gleaned what they could and there was a great exchanging of handclasps, currency, souvenirs, and not a few of the almost-priceless too-swiftly-dwindling whiskey bottles changed hands on the eve of January 6th.

Honor forbade Warden and Stark to put their own names down on their pass lists, but Warden saw to it that they both got their passes anyway. He simply filled out two extra pass forms beyond the quota and had Lt Ross sign them. Nobody in the Company disputed his breach of etiquette, least of all Lt Ross. Lt Ross knew a good thing, once it had been pointed out to him. From the day he turned down his commission Warden had had G Company wrapped and tied and stamped with the Indian sign the way he used to kid himself he had it under Holmes, but hadnt.

Stark had a pint bottle he had milked out of the pass situation. They finished that off on the way in to town. They made their first stop at Charlie Chan's Blue Chancre. The Blue Chancre was not as crowded as the better bars. There was no line outside on the sidewalk. At the Blue Chancre people only stood three deep at the bar. They had to drink six drinks standing in the press before they could get stools at the bar and start drinking in earnest.

"Ahhh," Stark sighed, as they slid onto the stools. "My feet was made for hikin, not for standin up in no bars. Even a Fort Bliss payday night in Juarez aint this bad."

"Herro, Walden! Herro, Stalk!" Charlie beamed. "Long time no see. Him wondelful day, eh?"

"Yeah," Warden said. "Fine day."

"Such a fine day," Stark said serenely, "that I feel like getting good and lousy drunk and beatin some loudmouth clean to death."

"Stark, you're a Texan," Warden said. "Texans love their buddies, the State of Texas, and their mother. And they hate niggers, and Jews, and strangers, and immoral women—unless they happen to be screwing them."

"Looks like we're early," Stark said. "Or else G Compny has dissolved its alliance with the Blue Chancre Bar & Grille."

"I can see through you like glass," Warden said. "Hey, Rose!"

As a matter of fact, they were early; they had left the CP at five minutes after nine, instead of ten o'clock with the rest of them. The only familiar face in the place was Rose's boy friend the S/Sgt of Artillery, sitting in the same back booth as if he'd never left it, this time with three buddies.

"Get dlunk," Charlie beamed. "Evelybody get dlunk. Fine day. This one on me, boys." He nodded at them beaming sweatily and moved away down the bar he was trying to handle alone.

"Fine fella," Stark said.

"Yeah. Great guy," Warden said.

"You suppose he can afford to give away a drink?"

"No. I doubt it."

"He needs more help behind the bar," Stark said.

"He needs more help out in front, too," Warden said, watching Rose, who although she had another girl to help her, still was not doing much better than Charlie because she was trying to handle her orders and sit with her S/Sgt at the same time.

"I said, hey, *Rose!*" Warden bellowed.

She was sitting in the Artillery booth, but she came over. Her swarthy wanton little face, which was Portagee but was betrayed as a racial misalliance by the faintly slanted eyes, was a little irritated though.

"What you want, Warden?"

"Whats your boy friend's name?"

She eyed him sullenly. "What you want to know for? Is none of your business."

Warden ogled her lush breasts openly. Rose followed his gaze down and then raised her eyes angrily to stare into his light blue eyes defiantly.

"What outfit is he in?" Warden asked conversationally.

"Say! What you care? I thought you want something. You drunk, eh? Lissen, Charlie wait on you. I no wait on bar." She turned with a flounce, and marched back to the Artillery booth.

As one man, Warden and Stark both swung on their stools to watch her go. Her round bare legs slithered together prophetically under the swirling skirt. The small of her back made a concave surface that rounded out breathtakingly into the firm curved cheeks of her little bottom that waggled at them impishly.

"Christ!" Stark said reverently. "What an ass!"

"Amen," Warden said tranquilly. He pursed his lips and ran his tongue over his mustache mellowly. He could feel the old cloudy belligerence of drunkenness rising up through his chest into his head soothingly, like a deep breath of camphor. Everything had that startling clarity of forgotten things being seen again.

"Are you happy?" Stark said.

"Sure I'm happy."

"Man this is the life," Stark said pointedly. "I wouldnt trade this life for nothing. Would you?"

"No," Warden said. "Stark," he said, "you know whats wrong with you? You're a Texan, and you aint got no sense of humor."

"I got a sense of humor."

"Sure you have. Everybody has. But yours aint the right kind. Its too thick. Like blackstrap. You cant distinguish pride from a sense of humor. A proud man without the right kind of sense of humor beats himself to death before he's thirty. Now take me. I got a real sense of humor. Thats why I can make a guy like you do anything I want him to."

"You cant make me do nothing I dont want to," Stark declared.

"I cant, hunh?" Warden said slyly. "You want to bet?"

"Sure, I'll bet."

Warden turned back to his drink, grinning slyly. Then he straightened up. "Hey, *Rose!*"

Rose came back up to the bar frowning. "Goddam Warden, what you want now?"

"Another shot of rye, Rose baby. Thats what I want. Fill my glass."

"The man will fill your glass. Charlie fill it."

"To hell with him. I want you to fill it, Rose."

"Hokay. But you costing me. You want another beer too?"

Warden looked at his bottle. "Yeah. Throw that out. Gimme cold one."

"You more trouble than I'm worth," Rose smiled.

"You think so? Whats your boy friend's name, Rose?"

"You go to hell."

"What outfit's he in?"

"I said you go to hell."

"You know why I like for you to fill my glass, Rose? Its because I like to watch you walk away afterwards. You got a lovely bottom, Rose."

"I'm married," Rose said with dignity, meaning she was shacked up. But she was flattered.

"Whats your boy friend's name?"

"Goddam it," Rose exploded. "You shut up and go to hell."

"My name is Berny," the Artillery S/Sgt said, coming over from the booth. He was almost as big a man as Warden. "Sgt Ira Berny. 8th Field Artillery. Anything else you want to know, Sergeant?"

"Well," Warden said thoughtfully. "How old are you?"

"Twenty-four next June," the S/Sgt said. "Anything else?"

"You got a very lovely shackjob for so young a man."

"And I aim to keep her," the S/Sgt said. "Anything else?"

"Yes. Would you be so kind as to have a drink with me and my friend here?" Warden said.

"Sure."

"Rose honey," Warden said, "pour him one."

"Whiskey," the S/Sgt said.

Rose poured it. Warden paid her. The S/Sgt tossed it off. "Well, be seein you," Warden said in dismissal, and turned back to Stark, his back toward them. "Have a good time." He began to talk to Stark.

They stood a moment, caught up short. Then they both went back to the booth. In the booth they began to talk to each other violently, and the three buddies listening.

"What the hell you doin?" Stark said. "Tryin to start a fight?"

"I never start fights."

"But I suppose you finish them," Stark said.

"No I dont even finish them."

"Shall we take him now?"

"Take who where?" Warden said.

"Yore buddy, the S/Sgt."

"What are you talking about?" Warden demanded. "Oh, I forgot. You're a Texan. Hey, Texan," he said. "I hear you're a hotshot rifle shooter. Is that right?"

"I know the front end from the back," Stark said.

"How'd you like to shoot with me, Texan? Make a little sidebet. Say about a hundred bucks."

Stark reached in his pocket. "Even money?"

Warden grinned.

"Any time you say," Stark said. He extracted a ten and three ones from the fold of bills and tossed the rest of it on the bar. "One hundred bucks. Any old time you say."

The roll was mostly fives and ones and it looked very big lying loose on the bar folded once.

Warden bent to look at it. "Well, well, if the Texan aint gone and collected himself a great big pile of dough. Hows it feel to be rich, Texan?"

"Theres a shootin gallery right up the street," Stark said. "Or we can go over to Mom's gallery on Hotel Street. Get there in five minutes."

"You'd have a better chance there than you would out on the Range."

"Do you want to bet? or dont you?" Stark demanded. "Put up or shut up."

"You're a sucker, Texan; dint I tell you I could make you do anything I want? Why, I could even make you go over there and fight that whole bunch of Artillerymen, if I wanted to. Dont you know I can outshoot you hands down? Put your money in your pocket like a good little boy. There aint three men on this Rock can outshoot me, and you know it."

"You cant make me do nothin I dont already want to do," Stark insisted.

Warden tapped his temple with his second finger. "Brains, Texan. Brains and a sense of humor. Why you could be an Officer in three months, with me guidin you."

"Who the hell wants to be an Officer?" Stark exclaimed indignantly. "You dont have to insult me. I can take care of myself, Firs Sarnt. I get along."

"Now thats just where you're wrong, Texan. Thats what I'm tryin to teach you. Its results that count. You dont have to lose your pride if you dont want to. You could be an Officer easy as not."

"Dont do me no favors."

"You still want to shoot with me, Texan?"

"Anytime you say."

"Okay," Warden grinned slyly. "We'll go over to Mom's and shoot ten rounds at a card, a hundred bucks even money. Let Mom hold the stakes. Here." He tossed the dampened fold of bills in front of Stark contemptuously. "Put this in your pocket, or you wont have it long around here."

Stark folded it back in with his ten and three ones and stuffed the loose sheaf back into his pants pocket. While he was occupied with this, Rose walked past the corner of the bar again where they sat, to fill another order, her beautiful bottom trembling enticingly with each step.

Warden swung suddenly on his stool as she passed and reached out and pinched one of the soft cheeks lightly. Rose stopped in midstride and turned, swinging her open palm. Warden caught her wrist easily, in his left hand, without even moving. She swung her right at his face, arched into a claw, the long bloodred nails like talons. Warden, grinning, caught it just as easily, in his right hand, and held her, his hands crossed in front of him, just holding her and grinning seditiously.

Unable to jerk loose, Rose delivered a vicious kick at his privates on the edge of the stool. Warden turned his right knee in gracefully, with such ease that it seemed effortless, and caught her shin on his knee. Then he rose from the stool on his left leg, pushing it between her legs, and the struggling cursing girl was off balance and powerless. Warden held her easily, letting her struggle.

"Take it easy, baby," he grinned contentedly. "I wont hurt you. You're a woman after my own heart, but dont get me all excited. I'm liable to lay you right here on the floor."

Rose's lips writhed back in a snarl and she spat at him explosively. Warden weaved to the left like a boxer, and except for a fine spray, the gob of spittle missed him and hit Stark square in the center of the shirt.

The whole thing had happened so swiftly that Stark had hardly looked up from putting away his roll.

"Goddam bastard son of a whore goddam," Rose hissed fervently.

Rose's boy friend and his buddies were already on their feet.

"Hey, thats no way to treat a lady," the boy friend said.

"Yeah," one of the buddies said. "Leave go of the lady."

Warden looked at them, his eyes wide in mock amazement. "What? So she can hit me? Dont be silly, friend."

"Easy, baby. Take it easy," he said to the struggling Rose. "You'll have a stroke."

The four Artillerymen moved toward him simultaneously, like a row of cars leaving a stoplight.

Warden shook his head disapprovingly. "Now-now, fellas," he said.

"Son of a bitching son of a goddam," Rose was hissing passionately.

Warden gave her a little shove that plumped her against the back wall out of his way, as if she were something that had served its purpose, and moved to meet the four advancing Artillerymen with a sanguinariness so blindlingly sudden that it caught them all off balance. His big fist flashed out viciously with the full weight of his moving body behind it and landed on the S/Sgt's nose with a crunching sound. Ira slid back against the booth in a sitting position, his broken nose bleeding profusely. Warden met the three buddies chest on with a hungry bellow.

Rose, who had bounced off the wall like a fighter off the ropes, was climbing his back, her talons in his neck, her sharp little teeth searching for his ear.

The S/Sgt got up from the floor, shook his head a couple of times, and started back into it again. Stark, who had been watching astonishedly, met him with a measured punch, his thick Mess/Sgt's arm moving in a blur of speed like the tail-lash of a whip. Ira fell back, feet working fast. His rump hit the booth table and he slid back across it and came to rest with his head propped up by the wall.

Rose, on Warden's back, unable to find an ear, settled for the back and sank her teeth into his shoulder through shirt, T-shirt, and all. By this time the five of them, the three buddies, Warden, and Rose, were all down on the floor in a churning mass of arms and legs. Warden twitched his back irritably, and Rose was flung off and against the wall, in spite of her three holds.

She came right back, screaming in a high shrill senseless falsetto, and jumped for Warden's back again with both feet off the floor. A fist belonging to one of the S/Sgt's friends, flashing out of the writhing mass, met her directly in the forehead and she was knocked back, down, out, and out of the fight.

Charlie Chan, chattering frantically in Chinese, stopped wringing his hands long enough to drag her slack lax body back behind the bar. Then he went back to wringing his hands and chattering in Chinese, stooped down behind the bar ready to duck. The large crowd, over which he had been so happy, had melted away. Most of them were standing just outside the open front watching the show.

It was a good show.

Stark was wading into the four scrambling bodies. He pulled out a foreign leg until a back emerged and began beating shattering blows into the kidneys of the unknown back.

From down in the mass a muffled voice raised itself, calling plaintively, "Hey, Ira. Where ya? Comen'n give us a hand." Warden's malevolently joyous laugh was a bellow, also strangely muffled. "You'll need more than just four, friend."

Ira the S/Sgt, still lying numbly on his table with his head propped against the wall, heard the call and slid down off the table shaking his head and holding his streaming nose. He paused long enough to mumble, "This is getting rough," to nobody, and then dived back in.

The churning mass on the floor broke up, and Warden rose up like a colossus out of it, grinning silently murderously, blood trickling down out of his mouth onto his CKC shirt and tie. He worked his lips around and spat out two teeth dramatically. The uniform was ruined, both shoulders ripped out of the shirt, one pants leg torn almost off revealing the hairy hard slim column of muscle. Between his feet lay one of the S/Sgt's buddies, in the same lax condition and as out of action as Miss Rose. Warden stood over him solidly, grinning happily silently, and punching with abandon at every face and belly he could reach.

His punches spun two of them back and away like pebbles flung off a spinning wheel.

Stark grasped the third one, who happened to be Ira the S/Sgt, and swung him sharply and drove a pulverizing punch into his adam's apple with surgical precision as he turned. Ira staggered back wildly into a booth and sat down, choking in terrible pain, and gave up.

Of the other two, whom Warden had spun back out of range, one sat down apathetically in the booth with Ira. The second one, who had come up against the bar, grabbed a beer bottle and smashed it on the rail and ran past Stark at Warden with it, like a dagger, cursing sobbingly under his breathing. The smashing of the bottle brought a reproving murmur from the audience, but none of them moved to stop him.

Warden, still grinning sanguinarily, waited for him, his hands out before him like a wrestler, ready to grab if he got the chance.

But as the man ran past Stark at the bar, Stark stuck his foot out delicately and blasély. The running knifer crashed to the floor, still trying to reach Warden with his bottle.

Warden stepped back and let him hit the floor and then stepped up again and kicked him carefully in the head.

It had lasted perhaps six minutes.

But already, from down the street, shrilled the urgent and ever-alert whistles of the MPs getting nearer.

Charlie Chan, who was still wringing his hands, began to cry. Tears streamed down his face. "Now blingee goddam MP. Was so fine day. Now luin blisniss. Closem up tight."

"Here they come, Texan," Warden said, laughing witlessly. "Come on. I know a place."

He jerked loose the rest of the hanging pants leg and stepped out of it, and then they were shoving and elbowing out through the still-gathering crowd. They ran down the block toward River Street, Warden still laughing riotously, away from the approaching urgent whistles.

"That Rose," Stark laughed breathlessly. "She really fell for you, buddy. Next time you go back there you better wear your groin cup or she wont even let you wait till she gets you home, before she rapes you."

"Thats why I aint figuring on ever going back," Warden laughed. "Come on, this way."

He turned left into the alley in the middle of the block, still laughing brainlessly happily. It was the same alley where he had stood and talked to Prewitt that night before they went across the street for a drink, the last time he had seen him. He thought of it momentarily, running, and ran on.

"This'll be the first place they'll look for us," Stark said.

"Never you mind. Come on. I know where I'm going."

Halfway through the alley Warden called, "This way!" and turned left again up the middle of the block, back the way they had come. They passed the back door of the Blue Chancre. Then he ran left over the cinders to the back of the next building whcre there was a fire escape and began to mount. Stark followed him up and crouching, hearing the urgent whistles down below in the babble, they ran lightly over three or four roofs before Warden stopped.

"Lets see," he said. "I think this is the one. Yes, its this one here."

He leaned across the three foot chasm of shadows and rapped sharply on a window of the next building. He waited impatiently, then rapped again.

From up here, on the third story roof, they could see the roofs of the whole town below Beretania down the hill, sloping away toward the harbor at the foot of Nuuanu. In the bright sunshine glinting on the deep blue of the water down there, out beyond the upright finger of the Aloha Tower and in the Sand Island channel, a ship was pulling out. One of the Matson liners; the *Lurline,* it looked like.

Involuntarily surprised, both of them stood and watched it. The big ship slid on, silently and pitilessly, as resistless and impossible to stop as a birthday or a moving clock. The bow was already out of sight behind one of the big bank buildings. They watched it until the whole ship, foot by foot silently, had slid behind it and on out of sight.

"Well," Stark said raspingly, "are we goin in this goddam place, or aint we?"

Warden swung around and looked at him, his eyes wide and violent, as if he had not known he was there. As if Stark had slipped up on him and he had not known he was there. He looked at him that way a moment, widely, violently, silently. Then he turned to the window and rapped again.

"Who is it?" a woman's voice said this time.

"Let us in, Gert," Warden laughed. "The MPs is after us."

The woman opened the window. "Who *is* that?"

"Its Milt. Why dont you wash your windows? Come on, get out of the way."

He stepped from the parapet down across to the window sill and squeezed through. Stark took one more look down at the empty blue bay and then followed him.

They were in a long empty hallway, ending in a big barred metal door. The woman was tall and narrow-faced, of about forty-five or fifty. She wore a beautiful evening gown with a corsage of gardenias at her throat.

"Mrs Kipfer!" Stark said disbelievingly. "Well, shoot me for a Jap."

"Why, Maylon Stark!" Mrs Kipfer said. "I know this one," she frowned at Warden. "But I never thought I'd see *you* coming in the back door."

Warden laughed uproariously. "Why, Sgt Stark is the hero and savior of the evening, Gert. If it hadnt been for Sgt Stark here and his quick thinking, yours truly might have even got hurt. Who knows? maybe left for dead in one of these rotting Honolulu alleys through which we so elusively eluded the strong arm of the Law and claimed sanctuary in your Church of All Souls."

"It appears to me you're hurt anyway." She stepped closer and inspected his mouth primly, with the efficient reproving air of a trained nurse.

"Oh, Milt! You've lost two of your teeth! What a shame. And for what. All for some silly brawl with no purpose but entertainment. When *are* you going to grow up?"

"I'll have you know I was defending the cause of chivalry," Warden grinned at her charmingly. "I was protecting that fairest of all the sexes, the female." He bowed to her. Warm golden glints in his eyes shone down at her laughingly. "Besides, the Army'll buy me new ones."

Mrs Kipfer shook her head hopelessly to Stark. "What are you going to do with one like that?"

"He's a character, aint he?" Stark said.

"Are you hurt, too, Maylon?"

"No, Maam," Stark said. "Nothing but this." He touched a sizeable lump on his cheekbone that was gradually spreading a purple sunset up into the hollow of his eye.

Mrs Kipfer examined the eye and clucked her tongue.

"Hows your First Aid, Gert?" Warden said. His eyes sparkled at her devilishly. "You think you need a refresher course?"

"I wish you would stop calling me Gert," Mrs Kipfer said irately. "Its vulgar. To me the name Gertrude always has the connotation of a whore."

Warden laughed out loud.

"And you know it, Milt Warden. If I didnt know you were being playful, I'd really resent it."

"I'm sorry, Gert," Warden grinned at her. "You know quite well I never mean to be vulgar."

"I know," Mrs Kipfer said. "And thats the only reason I dont have you thrown out."

"Noww, Gert," Warden grinned at her.

"Well, come on," she said irritably. "You two cant go out front looking like this. You'll have to wash up, and I have some stray uniforms lying around you can both change into."

She led them down the hall like a hostess conducting her guests, Warden keeping up a laughing patter all the way.

"I've always said you missed your calling, Gert. You should of been a fraternity mother."

Stark followed them, looking around curiously. It was the first time he had ever been out in back, in the "living quarters." The bathroom was scented with feminine powders and ointments and bathsalts, and a soap that smelled like gardenias. He was going to enjoy washing up, voluptuously.

"Hey!" he said suddenly. He had his hand in his pocket. "Hey, my money's gone!"

Warden began to laugh. "Whats the matter. You didnt lose that precious hundred bucks?"

"I cant find it," Stark said dully.

Warden leaned back against the wall and began to laugh uproariously. Stark was still trying pockets. He tried them all, numbly, even the watch pocket. The folded sheaf of bills was gone.

"Maybe," Warden said between peals of laughter, "maybe Gert's got a flashlight so you can hunt all up and down the alley. No, I forgot. Its still daylight, aint it?" He began to laugh again, his head leaned back weakly on the wall, his big hands hanging at his sides.

"Whats this about the alley?" Mrs Kipfer said. She was coming down the hall with an armload of CKCs.

"Oh," Warden gasped, rolling his head back and forth on the wall and leaving a grease spot, "oh. Oh. This damn fool lost his roll in the fight. He is without doubt the biggest sucker I ever seen in my life. What'd you flash it for? Thats probly why they started the fight in the first place."

"It was you started the fight," Stark said dumbly, his hands still working at the pockets.

"Oh, thats right, I did, dint I? Oh," Warden gasped. "Oh, Christ. Oh."

"I think its unkind of you to laugh, Milt," Mrs Kipfer said.

"It is," Warden said. He began to laugh uproariously again.

"How much did you have in your roll, Maylon?" Mrs Kipfer said.

"Hunderd and thirteen bucks," Stark said dully.

"Oh, that is too bad," she said. "Is there anything I can do?"

"You can loan him a hunderd and thirteen bucks," Warden said, still laughing.

"Naw," Stark said. "I couldnt find it anyway."

"Flashing a roll like that in that joint," Warden gasped. He burst out laughing uproariously again. "No wonder somebody rolled you. I'll bet it was Rose! What'll you bet; I'll bet it was Rose."

"Naw," Stark said. "She was never near me."

"Oh, Brother!" Warden gasped. He shoved himself away from the wall weakly. "You better re-enlist, Texan."

"Well, I guess that cooks me," Stark said. "I'm done. I might as well go home."

"You could sit out in the waiting room and wait for Milt, I suppose," Mrs Kipfer said sympathetically. "Of course, its terribly crowded," she added. "I doubt if you could find a seat."

"Well, I guess I better get into this uniform," Stark said dully.

"Wait a minute," Warden said. "Dont go yet.

"I tell you what," he said. "Its crowded as hell out front. They're lined up outside all the way down to the corner. Its worse than Payday when the fleet's in."

"Well?" Mrs Kipfer said cautiously.

"I got two hundred and six bucks here, Gert," Warden said effervescently, getting out his wallet. "I'll give you a hundred and fifty of it, if you'll go out front and get me and my pal two of your lovely, young ladies and bring them back here to us and let us have this place the rest of the day."

Stark turned around and looked at him disbelievingly, the CKCs still hanging from his hand.

"But they can make more money than that out front," Mrs Kipfer said carefully, "on a day like this."

"I doubt it," Warden said irrepressibly. "I sincerely doubt it. But I tell you what I'll do. I'll go up to two hundred bucks, if you'll provide us with a bunch of steaks and half a dozen bottles."

"Steaks!" Mrs Kipfer exclaimed. "Where on earth would I get steaks."

"Dont kid me," Warden grinned. "Dont try to snow an old bull like me, Gert. I know you keep steaks around here for when the big brass comes down from Shafter for a party. Now what do you say? Two hundred bucks, and you throw in the steaks and whiskey."

"Well—" Mrs Kipfer said dubiously.

"We'll cook them ourselves," Warden said. "I love to cook steaks. The Texan here is the best Mess/Sgt in the Army. If you furnish your own steak, I'll have him cook you one, too."

"Heavens, no!" Mrs Kipfer said. "If I ate a steak today, the nervous strain I'm under, it would kill me. I dont know," she said doubtfully.

"Yes, you do," Warden grinned. "You know you'll never get a better deal. And if you think you can get any more, you're crazy. Two hundred bucks is all I got. What do you say? Its nearly noon."

"Its ten-thirty," Mrs Kipfer corrected.

"Its nearly noon and we'll have to leave at five-thirty to make it home before the curfew. How about it? Take it or leave it. Is it a deal?"

"Well," Mrs Kipfer said.

"Its a deal!" Warden said irresistibly. "Its a deal. If you love me,

Gert. You always said you did." He grabbed Mrs Kipfer and danced her, capering, around the hallway.

"For goodness sake!" Mrs Kipfer said breathlessly. "Let go of me!" She stepped back, blushing, and smoothed her hair. "I'll go out and get them. You know where the icebox is. And the stove."

"I want that new gal," Warden said, wiggling his eyebrows. "That Jeanette."

"All right. Who do you want, Maylon?"

Stark, who liked to spend money himself, but who had been too flabbergasted to say anything at all, scratched his head. "I dont know. Lorene?"

"Lorene left on the *Lurline* today," Mrs Kipfer said. "But Sandra's still here. She's not leaving till next month."

"Well," Stark said.

"Thats all right," Warden put in irrepressibly. "Thats all right. We'll suffer that inconvenience. This time."

"Sure, thats all right," Stark said.

"All right," she said. "I'll go get them."

"Come on," Warden said, as she left. "Lets fry a steak. Right now. I'm hungry as hell. Come on, lets fry all four of us a steak."

"We got to get into these uniforms first," Stark said.

"I'll put the steaks on," Warden said. "You go ahead. I'll be right with you."

"You know something?" Stark said excitedly. "Something's happened to me. I'm not drunk at all. I used to have to be drunk as hell. I'm changed."

"You used to be an American male," Warden said. "Now you're a man of the world, like me. Its the same thing as going to Europe and seeing the uncensored movies before they cut them in this country. You're never the same again."

"Its *some*thing," Stark said.

"Would you like your steak rare, medium or well?" Warden said. "We serve them all ways."

"Rare," Stark said.

When the two girls came in and locked the big metal door against the hubbub behind them, the smell of the frying porterhouses was already floating through the place.

"Oh!" the little dark girl Jeanette, the new one, squealed. "This is going to be a lovely party. I love lovely parties."

"Thank the man there," Stark said.

Warden, standing at the stove, laid down the spatula and bowed. "Come here, little thing," he said. He sat down and picked her up and set her on his knee like a doll. "Tell me, are you French?"

"Wheres the liquor?" Stark said.

"My momma and pappa are," Jeanette said. "Oh, this is going to be a lovely party!"

"I'll get some," Sandra said. "What did you show the old bitch? to make her loosen up like this?"

"Then you and I have much in common," Warden said. "I got French ancestors myself."

"Money," Stark said. "Get the liquor."

"Tell me, little thing," Warden said. "Do you love me?"

"Yes, I love you," Jeanette squealed happily. "I'd love anybody who'd get me out of *there*, on a day like today."

"Well, I love you, too," Warden said.

"Oh, honey," Sandra said, setting two bottles on the table. "Do I love you. I've been hungry for the past hour and a half. Do I love you."

"I love you, too," Stark said.

"Me and my dollbaby are going down the hall," Warden said, "and play some pattycake. You watch the steaks."

Stark, sitting half on the chair beside Sandra with his arm around her, turned his head over his shoulder toward the door as Warden went out through it.

"You hurry back," he said.

"Dont you burn those steaks," Warden said.

Chapter 57

Karen Holmes, standing at the promenade deck railing of the ship and looking back, thought it was too beautiful a place to leave.

She had stood there while the confetti had been thrown and the Navy band had played *Aloha Oe* and the bunting streamers had come down with the gangplank and the yoohooing passengers had crowded the rail to wave good-by. And now, while they slid out past Fort Armstrong through the channel past Sand Island and on out through the reef and the restlessly excited passengers began to thin out and go below, she still stood there.

They said there was an old Hawaiian legend that if you threw your lei overboard as you passed Diamond Head it would tell you whether you would ever come back again. Don Blanding had squeezed a few poems and a great many tears out of it. Karen did not think she would ever be back but she decided to try the legend anyway, as they passed Diamond Head, and see.

She was wearing, altogether, a total of seven leis. The bottom one was a red and black paper lei the Regiment gave to all its short-timers and there were, progressively more expensive, a carnation lei from the Officers' Club, another one from Major Thompson's wife, one from Holmes's old Battalion Commander's wife, a ginger lei from Col Delbert's wife, a pikaki lei from General Slater, and on top the pure white gardenia lei Holmes had bought her when he saw her off. The seven leis made a collar of flowers that came clear up above her ears, as she stood on at the rail.

Dana Junior, freed from the necessity of standing at the rail to wave good-by to his father, was already back toward the rear of the ship in the middle of the deck at the shuffleboard courts with two other lovable small boys screaming at each other that they were shuffleboards and pushing each other up and down the slick wood courts to prove it. He was out of harm's way there, and she would let the stewards worry about the damage to their shuffleboard courts. That was one of the fine things about being on shipboard, and she might as well avail herself of it.

Behind them, seeming to wheel as the big ship swung out of the channel east down along the reef, the city clustered around Fort Street and Nuuanu Avenue with that antheap look all downtown cities have. Behind it climbing the shoulders of the mountains sat the profuse multi-colored houses of the suburbs, their windows every now and then catching the sunshine gaily. And above it all the solid unchanging mountains stood in their tropic greenness that seemed to drip down in patches and threaten to engulf the carefully man-constructed streets and houses. And between them, ship and shore, nothing but air. Air reaching clear down to the water and clear up into the sky, with that expansive far-vista look that you got nowhere else except on the sea or the tops of high mountains. There was no more true a picture of Honolulu anywhere, than from out here.

On shore straight in front of them she picked out Kewalo Basin the harbor for the fishing fleet. Next would come Moana Park, and then the Yacht Basin. Then pretty soon Fort De Russey, and then Waikiki.

"Its very beautiful, isnt it?" a man's voice said beside her.

She turned to find the young Air Corps Lt/Col, who had been standing beside her in the press when they left the pier, leaning on his elbows on the rail a few steps off and grinning ruefully. After they had lost sight of the pier and the crowd had begun to thin he had moved away up the rail, and then he had gone off somewhere, probably to take a turn around the deck, and she had forgotten all about him.

"Yes it is," she smiled. "Very beautiful."

"I think its the most beautiful place I've ever seen in my life," the young Lt/Col said. "Let alone had a chance to live in." He flipped his cigarette overboard and crossed his ankles, and the effect was the same as if he had made a fatalistic shrug.

"I feel the same way about it," Karen smiled. She could not get over a feeling of astonishment at how young he was, for a Lt/Col, but then they were all like that in the Air Corps.

"And now they're shipping me back home to Washington," he said.

"How come they are sending a pilot like you back on a ship?" Karen smiled. "I should think you'd fly."

He touched his left breast, where there were some ribbons but no wings, deprecatingly.

"I'm no pilot," he said guiltily. "I'm in the administrative corps."

Karen felt a twinge but hid it. "Still, I'd think they'd fly you back?"

"Priority. Priority, my dear lady. Nobody knows what it is. Nobody understands it. But its priority. Anyway, I'd just as soon go by boat. I get air sick, but I dont get sea sick. Aint that a riot?"

They both laughed.

"Thats the God's truth," he said earnestly. "Thats what washed me out. They say its something in my ears." He sounded as if it was the greatest tragedy of his life.

"Thats too bad," Karen said.

"Ce la guerre," the young Lt/Col said. "So, now I am going back to Washington where I know absolutely no one. To help the War Effort. After I've been here two and a half years and know every place and damn near every body."

"I know quite a few people in Washington," Karen offered. "Maybe I can give you some addresses before we leave ship."

"Would you really?"

"Surely. Of course, they're not any of them Senators or presidents of anything, and none of them know Evelyn Walsh McLean."

"Never look a gift horse in the mouth," the young Lt/Col said.

They both laughed again.

"But I can promise they're all nice people," Karen smiled. "You see, my home is in Baltimore."

"Not really!" the young Lt/Col said. "Is that where you're going?"

"Yes," Karen said. "My son and I are. For the duration."

"—and six months," the young Lt/Col said. "Your son?"

"Thats him over there. The biggest one."

"He looks like a lot of boy."

"He is. And all of it already betrothed to the Point."

The young Lt/Col looked at her then, and Karen wondered if she had not sounded bitter.

"I'm originally an ROTC man, myself," he said.

He looked at her again, carefully, out of the boyish eyes and face, and then he stood up. Karen felt subtly complimented. "Well, I'll be seein you. Dont forget about those addresses. And dont wear your eyes out on that shoreline."

Then he put his hands back on the rail. "Theres the Royal Hawaiian," he said ruefully. "They've got the most beautiful cocktail lounge in that place I ever saw. I wish I had back a dime for every dollar I've spent in there. I wouldnt be rich but I'd have a lot of poker money."

Karen turned to look and saw the familiar pink gleam from among the green, way off there on shore in the distance. It was the first thing everybody pointed out to her, when they had first come in. That was almost two years ago. And right next to the Royal was the dead white gleam of the Moana. As she remembered, she did not think anyone had pointed out the Moana to her, coming in.

When she looked back the young Air Corps Lt/Col was gone. She was alone at the rail except for a small slight girl dressed all in black.

Karen Holmes, for whom love was over, felt a little relieved. She also felt even more complimented. Still looking up forward toward the bow, she watched Diamond Head slowly coming towards them.

If the lei floated in toward shore, you would come back. If it floated out to sea, you wouldnt. She would throw them all over, all seven of them; it would be better than keeping them and seeing them dry up sourly and wither. Then she amended it. She would keep the red and black paper lei from the Regiment. That would do for a souvenir. Probably every Enlisted Man who had ever served in the Regiment and gone back Stateside had one in his footlocker. Karen had acquired a new understanding, and a very powerful affinity, for the ways of Enlisted Men in the past ten months.

"Its all very lovely, isnt it?" the girl in black said from down the rail.

"Yes. It is," Karen smiled. "Very."

The girl took a couple of polite steps nearer her along the rail, and then stopped. She was not wearing any leis.

"One rather hates to leave it," she said softly.

"Yes," Karen smiled, her communion broken. She had noticed the girl before. She wondered momentarily, now, from her poise and carriage, if the girl was not perhaps a movie star caught over here on vacation by the blitz and unable to get home any sooner. Dressed all in such very simple, almost severe, but quite expensive black like that. She looked remarkably like Hedy Lamarr.

"No one would know there was a war, from out here," the girl said.

"It looks very peaceful," Karen smiled; out of the corner of her eye she looked at her jewels, the single ring on her right hand and the necklace, both pearls, that unobtrusively carried out the exquisite perfection of the simplicity. The pearls did not look like cultured pearls, either. And such flawless simplicity as that did not come simply. Karen had spent that time once herself, but not anymore. It required either the services of a couple of maids, or else painstaking hours of hard work. Before the evidence of it now, enviously, she felt almost frowsy. A woman with a small child could not compete in the league this girl played in.

"I can almost see where I worked from here," the girl said.

"Where is that?" Karen smiled.

"I could point it out to you, but you couldnt see it unless you already knew the building."

"Where did you work?" Karen smiled encouragingly.

"American Factors," the girl said. "I was a private secretary." She turned and smiled at Karen slowly out of the lovely childlike face, pale white, hardly touched by the sun, and framed starkly by the shoulder-length raven-black hair parted in the middle.

She has a face like a Madonna, Karen thought exquisitely. Watching her was like being in an art gallery.

"I should think that would have been a position to have hung on to," she said.

"I—" the girl said and stopped and the Madonnaface clouded somberly. "It was," she said simply. "But I couldnt stay."

"I'm sorry," Karen said. "I didnt mean to intrude myself."

"It isnt that," the exquisite girl smiled at her. "You see; my fiancé was killed on December 7th."

"Oh, I am sorry," Karen said, shocked.

The girl smiled at her. "Thats why I couldnt stay any more. We were planning to be married next month." She turned and looked back out across the water at the shore, the lovely Madonnaface sad and pensive. "I love the Islands, but you can see why I couldnt stay."

"Yes," Karen said, not knowing what to say. Talking helped, sometimes. Especially if it was with another woman. The best thing was to just let her talk.

"He was shipped over here a year ago," the girl said. "I came over afterwards and took a job, so I could be near him. We were both saving our money. We were going to buy a little place up above Kaimuki. We wanted to buy the place before we married. He was going to ship over for another tour of duty, maybe several. You can see why I wouldnt want to stay, cant you?"

"Oh, my dear," Karen said, helplessly.

"Excuse me," the girl smiled brightly. "I didnt mean to use you as a wailing wall."

"If you feel like talking," Karen smiled, "you talk." It was these young people, like this couple, and their courage and their levelheadedness, unsung unknown unheroized, that were making this country the great thing it was, that made the winning of the war a foregone conclusion. Before this bravery Karen felt worthless and a slacker. "You go right on and talk," she said.

The girl smiled at her gratefully and looked back at the shore. They had passed Diamond Head now, and the bluntness of Koko Head was looming up in the distance.

"He was a bomber pilot," the girl said out across the water, "stationed at Hickam Field. He tried to taxi his plane off the apron and down to the revetments. They made a direct hit on it. Maybe you read about it in the papers."

"No," Karen said, impotently. "I didnt."

"They awarded him a Silver Star," the girl said out across the water. "They sent it to his mother. She wrote me she wanted me to have it."

"I think thats very fine of her," Karen said.

"They're very fine people," the girl smiled tremulously. "He comes from an old Virginia family. The Prewitts. They've lived there since before the Revolution. His great-grandfather was a General under Lee in the Civil War. Thats who he was named after: Robert E Lee Prewitt."

"Who?" Karen said numbly.

"Robert E Lee Prewitt," the girl said tremulously on the verge of tears. "Isnt that a silly old name?"

"No," Karen said. "I think its a fine name."

"Oh, Bob," the girl said quiveringly out across the water. "Bob, Bob, Bob."

"Now: now," Karen said, feeling all the grief that had been in her boiling over into a wild desire to laugh out loud. She put her arm around the girl. "Try to get hold of yourself."

"I'm all right," the girl said, drawing a quivering breath. "Truly I am." She touched her handkerchief to her eyes.

"I'll walk down with you to your stateroom," Karen offered.

"No," the girl said. "Thank you. I'm perfectly all right now. I owe you a tremendous apology. And I do thank you. Excuse me, please."

She walked away, the poise and the carriage both exquisitely perfect, in the exquisitely simple expensive black outfit, with the real-looking pearl ring and necklace, all looking as if she had walked right out of a page in *Vogue*.

Karen watched her go, thinking so this was Lorene of the New Congress, and that this was the first time she had ever really met a professional whore, at least to know who she was.

"Who's your friend?" the young Air Corps Lt/Col said from the other side of her. He had just come up. "She certainly is a beauty."

"Isnt she lovely?" Karen said, still wanting to laugh wildly. "I dont know her name, but perhaps I can arrange an introduction for you."

"No; thanks," the young Lt/Col said, looking after her. "She's so beautiful she makes me feel uncomfortable. What is she, a movie star?"

"No, but I think she's connected with show business. I dont honestly think an introduction would do you much good anyway. Her fiancé was killed December 7th. He was a bomber pilot at Hickam."

"Oh," the young Lt/Col said subduedly. "Thats rough."

"She's taking it pretty hard," Karen said.

"I was at Hickam on The Seventh," the young Lt/Col said in the same funereal voice. "What was his name. Maybe I knew him."

"Prewitt," Karen said. "Robert E Lee Prewitt. She said he came from an old Virginia family."

"No," the young Lt/Col said thoughtfully funereally. "I dont guess I knew him. There were an awful lot of bomber pilots at Hickam," he apologized. "And an awful lot of them got it."

"He was awarded a Silver Star," Karen said, some bitterness in her making her unable to resist saying it.

"Then I ought to know him," the young Lt/Col said funereally. "But, truthfully, just between you and me, they handed out such a lot of Silver Stars, both posthumously and otherwise, at Hickam, that it alone isnt much to go on," he apologized.

"I suppose thats true," Karen said.

"I got one myself," he said.

Karen looked at his shirt then and saw it there, right next to the Purple Heart ribbon.

"Oh, I didnt do anything," he said hastily, "except get blown up by a bomb concussion that I couldnt have avoided anyway. But I took it anyway," he added. "I suppose I shouldnt have." He looked at her boyishly searchingly.

"I dont see why not," Karen said.

"Well, there were so many guys who should have got one but didnt," he said.

"Your refusing yours wouldnt have helped them."

"Thats true," he said, relievedly. "Thats what I told myself." He leaned his elbows on the rail and crossed his ankles. "And so you're from Baltimore," he said pleasedly. "I cant get over it. Its sure a small world."

"It certainly is," Karen smiled, "and getting smaller." Now it will come, she thought, now he will ask me if he can drop out and see me sometime when he gets lonesome in Washington.

But he didnt.

"What table are you at, at dinner?" he said, instead.

"Table Eleven," Karen said. "What one are you?"

"Table Eleven," the young Lt/Col grinned. "Isnt that coincidence for you?" He took his elbows off the railing. "Well, see you at dinner, hey? I have things to do."

"All right," Karen smiled. "I ought to do some unpacking myself."

She watched him walk off. But after he had gone a few steps, he turned and came back.

"I'm not really at Table Eleven," he said. "I'm at Table Nine. I lied to you. But I'm going to be at Table Eleven by dinner time. Thats one of the things I have to do."

"You mustnt wear yourself out," Karen smiled, "doing it."

"No." He grinned engagingly. "You wont mind?"

"Why should I mind?" Karen smiled. "I appreciate your telling me, though."

"Well," he said, "I thought I ought to." He looked at her, carefully but politely, and then he smiled. "Well, see you at dinner then."

"We'll be there," Karen smiled, and looked over to see how Junior was making out at the shuffleboards. They were still playing the game, and there were five of them now.

The young Air Corps Lt/Col looked over at them, too, and then nodded at her and grinned, and Karen turned back to the rail.

They had passed Diamond Head quite a while ago. They were almost past Koko Head now. To the east of the big hump that always made her think of a whale's head she could see the drop and depression that was the parking lot at the top of the cliff above Hanauma Bay. From this far out, if you did not already know it was there you couldnt have seen it.

Behind her, the five boys had swelled to seven and had given up being shuffleboards and taken to shooting at each other with cocked thumbs and explosive "Bohww!"s from behind corners and stanchions.

She took the six flower leis off over her head and dropped them over the side. This was as good a place to drop them over as any. Diamond Head, Koko Head, Makapuu Head. Perhaps Koko Head was the best place, really. The six leis fell together and the wind blew them back against the side of the ship and out of sight and she did not see them light on the water.

"Mother," her son said from behind her. "I'm hungry. When do we eat on this old boat?"

"Pretty soon now," she said.

"Mother, do you think the war will last long enough so I can graduate from the Point and be in it? Jerry Wilcox said it wouldnt."

"No," she said, "I dont think it'll last that long."

"Well, gee whiz, mother," her son said, "I want to be in it."

"Well, cheer up," Karen said, "and dont let it worry you. You may miss this one, but you'll be just the right age for the next one."

"You really think so, mother?" her son said anxiously.

THE RE-ENLISTMENT BLUES

Got paid out on Monday
Not a dog soljer no more
They gimme all that money
So much my pockets is sore
More dough than I can use. Re-enlistment Blues.

Took my ghelt to town on Tuesday
Got a room and a big double hed
Find a job tomorrow
Tonight you may be dead
Aint no time to lose. Re-enlistment Blues.

Hit the bars on Wednesday
My friends put me up on a throne
Found a hapa-Chinee baby
Swore she never would leave me alone
Did I give her a bruise? Re-enlistment Blues!

Woke up sick on Thursday
Feelin like my head took a dare
Looked down at my trousers
All my pockets was bare
That gal had blown my fuse. Re-enlistment Blues.

Went back around on Friday
Asked for a free glass of beer
My friends had disappeared
Barman say, "Take off, you queer!"
What I done then aint news. Re-enlistment Blues.

That jail was cold all Sa'day
Standin up on a bench lookin down
Through them bars I watched the people
All happy and out on the town
Looked like time for me to choose, them Re-enlistment Blues.

Slep in the park that Sunday
Seen all the folks goin to church
Your belly feels so empty
When you're left in the lurch
Dog soljers dont own pews. Re-enlistment Blues.

So I re-uped on Monday
A little sad and sick at my heart
All my fine plans was with my money
In the poke of a scheming tart
Guy always seems to lose. Re-enlistment Blues.

So you short-timers, let me tell you
Dont get yourself throwed in the can
You might as well be dead
Or a Thirty-Year-Man
Recruitin crews give me the blues,
Old Re-enlistment Blues.

ACKNOWLEDGMENT

Looking back, it seems to me now that the writing of this book was a collective enterprise. This is a rather startling development. If someone had suggested such a thought to me a couple of years ago when it was somewhat less than half completed, he would have been met with such a vehement attack of denial that he would have been forced to retire in embarrassment. Nevertheless, it is true.

Grateful acknowledgment is here tendered to the late Mr. Maxwell E. Perkins, for his help in even getting it started and his aid in keeping it going up to the time of his death; to Mr. John Hall Wheelock, for his periodic injections of encouragement and his help in editing it; to Mr. Burroughs Mitchell, for his sweating of it out over a period of almost three years without the slightest whimper and his fine work of editing; and to Mr. & Mrs. Harry E. Handy of Robinson, Illinois, without whose initial impetus I would never have started out to be a writer at all, and whose material and spiritual expenses over a period of seven years provided me with necessary nourishment.

Without all of these people this book would never have been written.

R38